SIMENON SIMENON SIMENON SIMENON SIMENON SIMENON SIMENON SIMENON SIMENON SIMENON SIMENON SIMENON SIMENON SIMENON

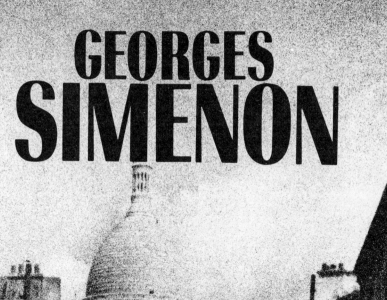

GEORGES SIMENON

GEORGES SIMENON

Maigret's Memoirs

Maigret Takes a Room

The Brothers Rico

Maigret and the Burglar's Wife

The Little Man from Archangel

Maigret and the Minister

Striptease

The Premier

Maigret in Society

Maigret Loses his Temper

Heinemann/Octopus

Maigret's Memoirs (*Les Mémoires de Maigret*) first published in France in 1950
and in Great Britain in 1963 by Hamish Hamilton Ltd

Maigret Takes a Room (*Maigret en Meublé*) first published in France in 1951
and in Great Britain in 1960 by Hamish Hamilton Ltd

The Brothers Rico (*Les Frères Rico*) first published in France in 1952
and in Great Britain in 1954 by Hamish Hamilton Ltd

Maigret and the Burglar's Wife (*Maigret et la Grande Perche*) first published in France in 1953
and in Great Britain in 1955 by Hamish Hamilton Ltd

The Little Man from Archangel (*Le Petit Homme d'Arkhangelsk*) first published in
France in 1957 and in Great Britain in 1957 by Hamish Hamilton Ltd

Maigret and the Minister (*Maigret chez le Ministre*) first published in France in 1954
and in Great Britain in 1969 by Hamish Hamilton Ltd

Striptease (*Striptease*) first published in France in 1958 and in Great Britain in 1959
by Hamish Hamilton Ltd

The Premier (*Le Président*) first published in France in 1958 and in Great Britain in 1961
by Hamish Hamilton Ltd

Maigret in Society (*Maigret et les Vieillards*) first published in France in 1960
and in Great Britain in 1962 by Hamish Hamilton Ltd

Maigret Loses his Temper (*La Colère de Maigret*) first published in France in 1963
and in Great Britain in 1965 by Hamish Hamilton Ltd

This edition first published in 1978
jointly by

William Heinemann Limited
15–16 Queen Street
London W1

Secker & Warburg Limited
14 Carlisle Street
London W1

and

Octopus Books Limited
59 Grosvenor Street
London W1

ISBN 0 905712 23 4

Maigret Takes a Room © 1951 by Georges Simenon
Translation copyright © 1960 by Hamish Hamilton Ltd
Maigret and the Minister © 1954 by Georges Simenon
Translation copyright © 1969 by Hamish Hamilton Ltd
The Premier © 1958 by Georges Simenon
Translation copyright © 1961 by Hamish Hamilton Ltd
Maigret in Society © 1960 by Georges Simenon
Translation copyright © 1962 by Hamish Hamilton Ltd
Maigret Loses his Temper © 1963 by Georges Simenon
Translation copyright © 1965 by Hamish Hamilton Ltd

Inside photographs reproduced by kind permission of
the Popperfoto Photographic Agency, Spectrum Colour Library
and Barnabys Picture Library
Jacket – Spectrum Colour Library

Printed in Great Britain by
Jarrold and Sons Limited, Norwich

CONTENTS

Maigret's Memoirs

Maigret's Memoirs

Translated from the French by Jean Stewart

Chapter One

Which affords me a welcome opportunity of
explaining my relations with Monsieur Şimenon

It was in 1927.or 1928. I have no memory for dates and I am not one of those who keep a careful record of their doings, a habit which is not uncommon in our profession and which has proved of considerable use and even profit to some people. And it was only quite recently that I remembered the notebooks in which my wife, for a long time without my knowledge and indeed behind my back, had stuck any newspaper articles that referred to me.

Because of a certain case that gave us some trouble that year–I could probably discover the exact date, but I haven't the courage to go and look through those notebooks.

It doesn't matter. At any rate I remember quite clearly what the weather was like. It was a nondescript day at the beginning of winter, one of those colourless grey and white days that I am tempted to call an administrative day, because one has the impression that nothing interesting can happen in so drab an atmosphere, while in the office, out of sheer boredom, one feels an urge to bring one's files up to date, to deal with reports that have been lying about a long time, to tackle current business ferociously but without zest.

If I stress the unrelieved greyness of the day it is not from any desire to be picturesque, but in order to show how commonplace the incident itself was, swamped in the trivial happenings of a commonplace day.

It was about ten o'clock in the morning. We had finished making our reports about half an hour ago, for the conference had been short.

Nowadays even the least well-informed members of the public know more or less what's involved in the conferences at Police Headquarters, but in those days most Parisians would have found it hard to say even which Government Service was housed in the Quai des Orfèvres.

At nine o'clock sharp a bell summons the various heads of departments to the Chief's big office, whose windows overlook the Seine. There is no glamour about these gatherings. You go there smoking your pipe or your cigarette, usually with a file tucked under your arm. The day hasn't got going yet, and is still vaguely redolent, for most people, of café au lait and croissants. You shake hands. You gossip, leisurely, waiting for everybody to turn up.

Then each in turn informs the Chief about what has been happening in his sector. A few remain standing, sometimes looking out of the window to watch the buses and taxis crossing the Pont Saint-Michel.

Contrary to general belief, we don't talk exclusively about crime.

'How's your daughter, Priollet? her measles?'

I remember hearing cookery recipes being knowledgeably set forth.

More serious problems are also discussed, of course; for instance, that of some deputy's or minister's son who has been behaving foolishly, who wilfully persists in his folly, and whom it is imperative to bring back to his senses without causing a scandal. Or that of a rich foreigner who has recently taken up residence in some Grand Hotel in the Champs-Elysées, and about whom the Government has begun to worry. Or of a little girl picked up in the street a few days previously, whom no relative has claimed, although her photograph has appeared in all the newspapers.

This is a gathering of professional people, and events are considered from a strictly professional point of view, without useless talk, so that everything becomes very simple. It's all in the day's work, so to speak.

'Well then, Maigret, haven't you arrested your Pole in the Rue de Birague yet?'

Let me hasten to say that I've nothing against Poles as such. If I happen to speak of them fairly often, it's not that I consider them a particularly aggressive or delinquent set of people. The fact is merely that at that time France, being short of labour-power, imported Poles by the thousand and settled them in the mines in the North. They were collected haphazardly in their own country, whole villages at a time, men, women and children, and piled into trains rather as negro labour was once recruited.

The majority of them have proved to be first-class workers, and many of them have become respected citizens. Nevertheless there was a certain proportion of riffraff, as was only to be expected, and for some time this riffraff gave us a good deal of trouble.

I am trying to convey the atmosphere to the reader by talking thus, somewhat disconnectedly, about the things that were preoccupying me at that time.

'I should like to keep him on the run for two or three days longer, Chief. So far he's led us nowhere. He's sure to end up by meeting some accomplices.'

'The Minister's getting impatient because of the Press . . .'

Always the Press! And always, among the powers that be, that dread of the Press, of public opinion. No sooner has a crime been committed than we are urged to find a culprit immediately, at all costs.

We are practically told, after a few days: 'Put somebody or other in jail in the meantime, just to satisfy public opinion.'

I shall probably revert to this point. In any case it was not the Pole that we were discussing that morning, but a burglary that had recently been committed according to a new technique, which is an uncommon thing.

Three days earlier, on the Boulevard Saint-Denis, in the middle of the day, just as most of the shops had closed for the lunch-hour, a van had stopped in front of a small jeweller's. Some men had unloaded an enormous packing-case, which they had put down close to the door, and had gone off again with the van.

Hundreds of people had passed in front of that case without thinking twice about it. As for the jeweller, when he came back from the restaurant where he had been lunching, he knit puzzled brows.

And when he had shifted the case, which had now become very light, he discovered that a hole had been cut in the side that touched the door, and another hole in the door itself, and that of course all his shelves had been ransacked and his safe as well.

This was the sort of unsensational enquiry that is liable to take months and requires the largest number of men. The burglars had not left a single fingerprint, nor any compromising object.

The fact that the method was a new one made it impossible for us to hunt in any known category of thieves.

We had nothing but the packing-case, an ordinary case although a very large one, and for the past three days a round dozen of detectives had been visiting all manufacturers of packing-cases, and all firms making use of the largest size of packing-case.

I had just returned to my office, where I had begun to draw up a report, when the house telephone rang.

'Is that you, Maigret? Will you come to my room for a moment?'

Nothing surprising about that either. Every day, or almost every day, the Big Chief used to send for me at least once to his office, apart from the conference; I had known him since my childhood, he had often spent his holidays close to our home in the Allier, and he had been a friend of my father's.

And this particular Chief was, in my eyes, the real Chief in the fullest sense of the word, the chief under whom I had served my first term at Police Headquarters, who, without actually protecting me, had kept a discreet eye on me from above, and whom I had watched, in his black coat and bowler hat, walking alone under fire towards the door of the house in which Bonnot and his gang had for two days been resisting police and gendarmes.

I am referring to Xavier Guichard, with his mischievous eyes and his white hair, as long as a poet's.

'Come in, Maigret.'

The daylight was so dull that morning that the lamp in its green shade was alight on his desk. Close by, in an armchair, I saw a young man who rose to offer me his hand when we were introduced to one another.

'Chief-Inspector Maigret. Monsieur Georges Sim, who's a journalist. . . .'

'Not a journalist, a novelist,' the young man protested smilingly.

Xavier Guichard smiled too. And he had a whole range of smiles which could express all the various shades of what he was thinking. He also had at his disposal a sort of irony, perceptible only to those who knew him well and which, to others, sometimes made him appear a simpleton.

He spoke to me with the utmost seriousness, as if we were concerned with an important affair, a prominent personality.

'For his novel-writing, Monsieur Sim needs to know how Headquarters functions. As he has just explained to me, a good many dramatic stories wind up in this house. He has also made it clear that it's not so much the workings of the police machine that he wants to study in detail, for he has been able to get information about these elsewhere, but rather the atmosphere in which these operations take place.'

I merely glanced at the young man, who must have been about twenty-four and who was thin, with hair almost as long as the Chief's, and of whom the least I can say is that he seemed to have no lack of confidence about anything, least of all about himself.

'Will you show him round, Maigret?'

And just as I was moving towards the door I heard the fellow Sim remark:

'Excuse me, Monsieur Guichard, but you've forgotten to mention to the Chief-Inspector . . .'

'Oh yes, you're quite right. Monsieur Sim, as he has reminded us, is not a journalist. So there's no danger of his reporting to the newspapers things that ought to remain unpublished. He has promised me, without being asked, to use only in his novels whatever he may see or hear amongst us, and that in a form sufficiently altered to create no difficulties for us.'

I can still hear the Chief adding gravely, as he bent forward to look at his mail:

'You needn't worry, Maigret. He has given me his word.'

All the same, Xavier Guichard had let himself be led astray, I felt that already and my feeling was subsequently confirmed. Not only by the youthful audacity of his visitor, but on account of something that I only discovered later. The Chief, apart from his profession, had one passion: archaeology. He belonged to several learned societies and had written a fat book (which I have never read) about the remote origins of Paris and its surroundings.

Now young Sim had discovered this, whether or not by chance, and had made a point of talking to him about it.

Was it on this account that I had been sent for personally? Almost every day somebody at Headquarters gets the job of showing round visitors. Generally these are distinguished foreigners, or those connected in some way with the police force of their country, or sometimes merely influential voters, come up from the provinces and proudly exhibiting a card from their Deputy. It has become a routine. There is practically a little lecture that everybody has more or less learnt by heart, like guides to historical monuments.

But usually a sergeant serves the purpose, and the visitor has to be somebody very important for the head of a department to be disturbed.

'If you like,' I proposed, 'we'll go first to the anthropometrical department.'

'If it isn't too much bother, I'd rather begin with the waiting-room.'

This was my first surprise. He said it quite nicely, too, with a disarming glance, explaining:

'You understand, I should like to follow the route that your clients usually follow.'

'In that case you ought to start at the Police Station, for most of them spend the night there before being brought to us.'

He replied, calmly:

'I visited the Police Station last night.'

He took no notes. He had neither notebook nor fountain pen. He stayed for several minutes in the waiting-room with its tall windows, where are displayed, in black frames, the photographs of members of the Force killed on duty.

'How many casualties each year, on an average?'

Then he asked to see my office. Now it so happened that at that period the workmen were busy refitting it. I was provisionally installed on the mezzanine, in a disused office in the oldest administrative style, thick with dust, with black wooden furniture and a coal-burning stove of the sort you can still see in certain provincial railway stations.

This was the office in which I had started my professional life, in which I had worked as Detective-Sergeant for some fifteen years, and I must admit that I harboured a certain fondness for that huge stove, whose iron bars I loved to see glowing red in winter, and which I used to stoke up to the brim. This was not so much an inveterate habit as a trick to keep myself in countenance. In the middle of a difficult interrogation I would get up and poke the fire lengthily, then throw in noisy shovelfuls of coal, looking quite bland, while my client stared at me in bewilderment.

And the fact is that when at last I had a modern office at my disposal, equipped with central heating, I missed my old stove, but I was never allowed, nor ever even made the request—which would not have been granted—to take it with me into my new premises.

I must apologize for lingering over these details, but I know more or less what I'm getting at.

My guest looked at my pipes, my ashtrays, the black marble clock on the chimney-piece, the little enamel basin behind the door, and the towel that always smells like a wet dog.

He asked me no technical questions. The files did not seem to interest him in the slightest.

'This staircase takes us to the laboratory.'

There, too, he stared at the ceiling, which was partly glazed, at the walls, at the floor, and at the dummy which is used for certain reconstructions, but he paid no attention either to the laboratory itself with its complicated apparatus or to the work which was going on there.

Out of habit, I tried to explain:

'By magnifying several hundred times any written text, and comparing it . . .'

'I know. I know.'

And then he asked me, casually:

'Have you read Hans Gross?'

I had never heard the name mentioned. I have since learnt that it was that of an Austrian magistrate who, in the 1880s, held the first chair of scientific criminology at the University of Vienna.

My visitor, however, had read Hans Gross' two fat volumes. He had read everything, quantities of books of whose very existence I was ignorant and whose titles he quoted at me in an offhand manner.

'Follow me along this passage, and I'll show you the Records Office, where we keep the files of . . .'

'I know. I know.'

I was beginning to find him irritating. It looked as if he had put me to all this bother solely in order to stare at walls and ceilings and floors, to stare at us all, as if he were drawing up an inventory.

'We shall find a crowd in the anthropometric department just now. They'll have finished with the women by now. It'll be the men's turn . . .'

There were some twenty of these, stark naked, who had been rounded up during the night, and were waiting their turn to be measured and photographed.

'In short,' the young man said to me, 'all I've still got to see is the Special Infirmary of the Police Station.'

I frowned.

'Visitors are not admitted.'

It is one of the least-known places, where criminals and suspects are put through a number of mental tests by police doctors.

'Paul Bourget used to watch the proceedings,' my visitor calmly replied. 'I shall ask for permission.'

The fact is that I retained a wholly uninteresting memory of him, as uninteresting as the weather itself that day. If I made no effort to cut short his visit, it was primarily on account of the Chief's recommendation, and also because I had nothing important to do, and that it was, after all, a way of killing time.

He happened to pass through my office again, sat down and held out his tobacco pouch to me.

'I see you're a pipe smoker too. I like pipe smokers.'

There were, as usual, a good half dozen pipes lying about, and he examined them with a connoisseur's eye.

'What case are you on at the moment?'

In my most professional tone I told him about the robbery where the packing-case had been left at the door of the jeweller's shop, pointing out that this was the first time this technique had been used.

'No,' he said to me. 'It was used eight years ago in New York, at a shop in Eighth Avenue.'

He must have been pleased with himself, but I must admit that he did not seem to be boasting. He was smoking his pipe gravely, as if to add ten years to his age and put himself on an equal footing with the mature man that I already was.

'You see, Chief-Inspector, I'm not interested in professionals. Their psychology offers no problems. They are just men doing their own job, and that's all.'

'What are you interested in?'

'The others. Those who are made like you and me, and who end up one fine day by killing somebody without being prepared to do so.'

'There are very few of those.'

'I know.'

'Apart from crimes of passion . . .'

'There's nothing interesting about them either.'

That's all I remember of that encounter. I must have spoken to him incidentally of a case on which I had been busy a few months earlier, just because professionals were not involved in it, a case concerning a young girl and a pearl necklace.

'Thank you, Chief-Inspector. I hope I shall have the pleasure of meeting you again.'

Privately, I said to myself: 'I sincerely hope not.'

Weeks passed, then months. Once in the middle of winter I thought I recognized the fellow Sim in the main corridor of Police Headquarters, pacing up and down.

One morning I found on my desk, beside my mail, a little book in a revolting illustrated cover, such as are displayed on newspaper stalls and read by shop girls. It was called: *The Girl with the Pearl Necklace*, and the author was called Georges Sim.

I hadn't even the curiosity to read it. I read few books, and no popular novels. I don't even know where I put the book, a paperback printed on cheap paper, probably in the wastepaper basket, and I thought no more about it for several days.

Then one morning I found an identical book in the same place on my desk, and thenceforward each morning a fresh copy appeared beside my mail.

It was some time before I noticed that my Inspectors, particularly Lucas, were glancing at me with amusement. At last Lucas said to me, after beating about the bush for a long time, as we made our way to the Brasserie Dauphine one day for a drink before lunch:

'So you're a character in a novel now, Chief.'

He pulled the book out of his pocket.

'Have you read it?'

He confessed that it was Janvier, the youngest member of the squad at that time, who had been putting a copy of the book on my desk each morning.

'It's quite like you in some ways, you'll see.'

He was right. It was like me to the extent that a sketch scribbled on the marble top of a café table by an amateur caricaturist is like a flesh-and-blood human being.

It made me bigger and clumsier than life, peculiarly ponderous, so to speak.

As for the story, it was unrecognizable, and I was made to use some quite unexpected methods, to say the least.

That same evening I found my wife with the book in her hands.

'The woman in the dairy gave it me. Apparently it's about you. I haven't had time to read it yet.'

What could I do? As the man Sim had promised, no newspaper was involved. The book concerned was not a serious work, but a cheap publication to which it would have been absurd to attach any importance.

He had used my real name. But he might have replied that there are quite a number of Maigrets in the world. I merely promised myself to receive him somewhat coldly if I happened to meet him again, convinced meanwhile that he would avoid setting foot in Police Headquarters.

In which I was mistaken. One day when I knocked at the Chief's door without having been sent for, to ask his advice on some point, he said:

'Come in, Maigret. I was just going to call you. Our friend Sim is here.'

No signs of embarrassment about our friend Sim. On the contrary, complete self-confidence and a bigger pipe than ever in his mouth.

'How are you, Chief-Inspector?'

And Guichard explained:

'He's just been reading me a few passages from something he has written about our place.'

'I know about it.'

Xavier Guichard's eyes were full of laughter, but this time it was of me that he seemed to be making fun.

'Then he told me some rather relevant things which may interest you. He'll repeat them to you.'

'It's quite simple. Hitherto, in France, in books, with very few exceptions, the sympathetic character has always been the offender, while the police have been exposed to ridicule, if not worse.'

Guichard was nodding approvingly.

'Quite true, isn't it?'

And it was, in fact, quite true. Not only in books but in daily life. I was reminded of a rather painful episode in my early days, when I was serving in the Public Highways Squad. I was on the point of arresting a pickpocket

outside a Métro station when the fellow began yelling something–possibly
'Stop thief!'

Instantly a score of people fell upon me. I explained to them that I was a
policeman, that the man now making his escape was a habitual criminal. I am
convinced that they all believed me. They none-the-less managed to delay
me by every possible means, thus allowing my pickpocket time to get away.

'Well,' Guichard went on, 'our friend Sim is proposing to write a series of
novels in which the police will be shown in their true light.'

I pulled a face, which the Chief did not fail to notice.

'More or less in their true light,' he corrected himself. 'You follow me?
His book is only a rough draft of what he plans to do.'

'He has made use of my name.'

I thought the young man would be covered with confusion and would
apologize. Not a bit of it.

'I hope you weren't offended, Chief-Inspector. I couldn't help it. When I
have imagined a character under a particular name I find it quite impossible
to change it. I tried out all possible combinations of syllables to replace those
of the name Maigret, but in vain. In the end I gave it up. It wouldn't have
been *my* character any longer.'

He said *my* character, quite calmly, and the amazing thing was that I never
turned a hair, possibly on account of Xavier Guichard and the mischievously twinkling eyes he kept fixed on me.

'He is thinking this time not of a popular series but of what he calls . . .
What did you call it, Monsieur Sim?'

'Semi-literature.'

'And you're counting on me to . . .'

'I should like to know you better.'

I told you at the beginning: his self-assurance was complete. I really
believe that was the secret of his strength. It was partly through this that he
had already succeeded in winning over the Chief, who was interested in
every type of human being and who announced to me, without a smile:

'He is only twenty-four.'

'I find it hard to construct a character unless I know how he behaves at
every moment of the day. For instance, I shan't be able to talk about
millionaires until I have seen one in his dressing-gown eating his boiled egg
for breakfast.'

This happened a long time ago and I wonder now for what mysterious
reason we listened to all this without bursting out laughing.

'In short you'd like . . .'

'To know you better, to watch you living and working.'

Of course, the Chief gave me no orders. I should no doubt have rebelled.
For quite a time I felt uncertain whether he wasn't playing a practical joke on
me, for he had retained a certain Latin Quarter streak in his character, from
the days when the Latin Quarter still went in for hoaxes.

It was probably in order not to seem to be taking the whole affair too
seriously that I said, shrugging my shoulders:

'Whenever you like.'

Then young Sim jumped up delightedly.

'Right away.'

Once more, in retrospect, it may seem ridiculous. The dollar was worth I
don't know what fantastic sums. Americans used to light their cigars with

thousand-franc notes. Montmartre was teeming with negro musicians, and rich, middle-aged ladies let themselves be robbed of their jewellery by Argentinian gigolos at *thés dansants*.

The sale of *La Garçonne* was reaching astronomical figures, and the Vice Squad was overwhelmed by orgiastic parties in the Bois de Boulogne, which they scarcely dared interrupt for fear of disturbing Consular personalities having their fun.

Women had short hair and short skirts, and men wore pointed shoes and trousers tight round the ankles.

This explains nothing, I know. But everything is interconnected. And I can still see young Sim coming into my office next morning, as if he were one of my Inspectors, remarking kindly: 'Don't let me disturb you . . .' and going to sit down in a corner.

He still took no notes. He asked few questions. He tended rather to make assertions. He explained to me subsequently—and it doesn't follow that I believed him—that a man's reactions to an assertion are more revealing than his replies to a specific question.

One day at noon when we went for a drink to the Brasserie Dauphine, Lucas, Janvier and I, as was our frequent custom, he followed us.

And one morning, at the conference, I found him installed in a corner of the Chief's office.

This went on for several months. When I asked him if he was writing, he answered:

'Popular novels, still, to earn my living. From four to eight in the morning. By eight o'clock I've finished my day's work. I shall only start on semi-literary novels when I feel ready for it.'

I don't know what he meant by that, but, after I had invited him to lunch one Sunday in the Boulevard Richard-Lenoir and had introduced him to my wife, he suddenly stopped coming to the Quai des Orfèvres.

It seemed odd not to see him in his corner, getting up when I got up, following me when I went out and accompanying me step by step through the offices.

During that spring I received an invitation that was, to say the least, unexpected.

> Georges Sim has the honour of inviting you to the christening of his boat, the *Ostrogoth*, which will be performed by the Curé of Notre-Dame on Tuesday next, at the Square du Vert-Galant.

I did not go. I learnt from the police of the district that for three days and three nights a rowdy gang kept up a tremendous din on board a boat moored right in the middle of Paris and flying all its flags.

Once, as I crossed the Pont-Neuf, I saw the aforesaid boat and, at the foot of the mast, somebody sitting at a typewriter, wearing a master-mariner's cap.

The following week the boat had gone, and the Square du Vert-Galant had resumed its usual appearance.

More than a year later I received another invitation, written this time on one of our fingerprint cards.

> Georges Simenon has the honour of inviting you to the Anthropometrical Ball which will be held at the *Boule Blanche* to celebrate the launching of his detective stories.

Sim had turned into Simenon.

More precisely, feeling himself now fully adult, perhaps, he had resumed his real name.

I did not bother about it. I did not go to the ball in question and I learned next day that the Prefect of Police had been present.

Through the newspapers. The same newspapers that informed me, on the front page, that Chief-Inspector Maigret had just made his sensational entry into detective fiction.

That morning, when I arrived at Headquarters and climbed the great staircase, I was met with sly smiles and amused averted faces.

My inspectors did their utmost to keep straight faces. My colleagues, at the conference, pretended to treat me with unwonted respect.

Only the Big Chief behaved as if nothing had happened and asked me with an absent-minded air:

'And what about you, Maigret? How are things going?'

In the shops of the Richard-Lenoir district, there was not a tradesman who failed to show my wife the paper with my name in large letters, and ask her, full of wonderment:

'It *is* your husband, isn't it?'

It was myself, alas!

Chapter Two

*In which it is argued that the naked truth is often
unconvincing and that dressed-up truths may
seem more real than life*

When the news got round that I was writing this book, and then that Simenon's publisher, without having read it, before I had even finished the first chapter, had offered to publish it, I was conscious of the somewhat dubious approval of my friends. They were saying, I'm convinced of it: 'So Maigret's having a go too!'

The fact is that during the last few years, at least three of my former colleagues, men of my own generation, have written and published their memoirs.

Let me hasten to point out in so doing they were following an old tradition of the Paris police, to which we owe, among others, the memoirs of Macé and those of the great Goron, each in his time chief of what was then called the Sûreté. As for the most illustrious of them all, Vidocq, he unfortunately left no recollections written by himself which we might compare with the portraits drawn of him by novelists, often under his real name, or else, as in the case of Balzac, under that of Vautrin.

It is not my business to defend my colleagues, but nevertheless I take this opportunity of replying to an objection which I have frequently heard raised.

'According to their writings,' I have been told, 'at least three of them consider themselves responsible for the solution of every famous case.'

And people would quote, in particular, the Mestorino case, which made a great sensation in its time.

Now I might make a similar claim myself, for a case of that scope demands the collaboration of every branch of the Force. As for the final interrogation, that famous twenty-eight-hour-long interrogation that is cited as an example nowadays, there were not four but at least six of us taking it in shifts, going over the same questions one by one in every conceivable fashion, gaining a little bit of ground each time.

Under these conditions, it would have been hard to say which of us at a given moment had pulled the trigger that provoked a confession.

I wish to assert, moreover, that the title of *Memoirs* was not chosen by myself and was finally tacked on because we couldn't think of a better word.

The same is true (I make this point as I correct the proofs) of the subtitles, of what it seems are called chapter-headings, which the publisher asked me to let him add as an after-thought, for typographical reasons, he told me kindly; in actual fact, I suppose, to give a touch of lightness to my text.

Of all the tasks I fulfilled at Headquarters, the only one I ever shirked was the writing up of reports. Was this due to an atavistic desire for accuracy, to scruples with which I have seen my father wrestling before me?

The joke has been made so often that it is almost a classic:

'Maigret's reports consist largely of parentheses.'

Probably because I try to explain too much, to explain everything, and because nothing seems to me clear or definite.

If *memoirs* implies the story of events in which I have been involved in the course of my career, I'm afraid the public will be disappointed.

In the space of almost half a century I don't think there have been more than a score of really sensational cases, including those to which I have already referred: the Bonnot case, the Mestorino case, plus the Landru case, the Sarrat case and a few others.

Now my colleagues, my former Chiefs in some cases, have spoken about these at length.

As for the other investigations, those which were interesting in themselves but hit no headlines in the newspapers, Simenon has dealt with them.

This brings me to what I wanted to say, what I've been trying to say ever since I started this manuscript, namely the real justification for these memoirs which are not proper memoirs, and now I know less than ever how I am to express myself.

I once read in the papers that Anatole France, who must at any rate have been an intelligent man and who was fond of indulging in irony, having sat for the painter Van Dongen for his portrait, not only refused to accept the picture once it was finished but forbade it to be shown in public.

It was at about the same period that a famous actress brought a sensational lawsuit against a caricaturist whose portrait of her she thought insulting and injurious to her career.

I am neither an Academician nor a stage star. I don't consider myself unduly susceptible. Never, during the course of my professional life, have I sent any single correction to the newspapers, although these have never been slow to criticize my activities and my methods.

Nowadays everyone cannot have his portrait painted, but at least we have all had the experience of being photographed. And I suppose everyone is familiar with that discomfort we feel when confronted with a picture of ourselves which is not quite a true likeness.

Is my meaning quite clear? I am rather ashamed of insisting on this. I know I am dealing with a vital, ultra-sensitive point, and I feel suddenly afraid of appearing ridiculous, a thing which rarely affects me.

I think I should scarcely mind if I were depicted under an appearance completely different from my own, even libellously so.

But let me revert to the comparison with photography. The lens does not permit of complete inaccuracy. The image is different without being different. Faced with the print, you are frequently incapable of putting your finger on the detail that offends you, of saying exactly *what* isn't you, *what* you don't recognize as belonging to yourself.

Well, for years this was my position when faced with Simenon's Maigret, whom I watched growing day by day beside me, so that some people ended by asking me quite seriously whether I had copied his mannerisms, and others whether my name was really my father's name or whether I had borrowed it from the novelist.

I have tried to explain more or less how the thing began, quite innocently on the whole and seemingly without importance.

The very youthfulness of the fellow whom worthy Xavier Guichard had introduced to me one day in his office inclined me rather to shrug my shoulders than to harbour suspicions.

And then, a few months later, I was properly caught up in a mesh from which I never managed to escape and from which the pages I am now scribbling will not completely rescue me.

'What are you grumbling about? You're famous!'

I know! I know! It's easy to say that when you've not experienced it. I even admit that at certain moments, in certain circumstances, it's not disagreeable. Not merely because it flatters one's vanity. Often for practical reasons. For instance, merely to secure a good seat in a crowded train or restaurant, or to avoid having to queue.

For so many years I never protested, any more than I corrected misstatements in the newspapers.

And I'm not suddenly going to claim that I was boiling inwardly, or chafing at the bit. That would be exaggerating, and I detest exaggeration.

None the less I promised myself that one day I would say what I've got to say, quite quietly, without rancour or ill-feeling, and once for all put things in their true perspective.

And that day has come.

Why is this book called *Memoirs*? I'm not responsible for that, as I said before, and the word is not of my choosing.

I'm not really concerned here with Mestorino or Landru or with that lawyer in the Massif Central who exterminated his victims by plunging them into a bath full of quicklime.

I'm concerned, more simply, with setting one character against another, one truth against another truth.

You shall soon see what some people understand by truth.

It was at the beginning, at the time of that anthropometrical ball which, together with certain other somewhat spectacular affairs in questionable taste, served to launch what people were already beginning to call 'the first Maigrets', two volumes entitled: *The Hanged Man of Saint-Pholien* and *The Late Monsieur Gallet*.

Those two, I frankly admit, I read immediately. And I can still picture Simenon appearing in my office the next morning, pleased at being himself, even more self-assured than before if that were possible, but none the less with a trace of anxiety in his eyes.

'I know what you're going to say to me!' he flung at me as soon as I opened my mouth.

Pacing up and down, he began to explain:

'I'm quite aware that these books are crammed with technical in-accuracies. There's no need to count them up. Let me tell you they're deliberate and this is why.'

I didn't take note of the whole of his speech, but I remember the essential point in it, which he often repeated to me subsequently with an almost sadistic pleasure:

'Truth never seems true. I don't mean only in literature or in painting. I won't remind you either of those Doric columns whose lines seem to us strictly perpendicular and which only give that impression because they are slightly curved. If they were straight, they'd look as if they were swelling, don't you see?'

In those days he was still fond of displaying his erudition.

'Tell someone a story, any story. If you don't dress it up, it'll seem incredible, artificial. Dress it up, and it'll seem more real than life.'

He trumpeted out those last words as if they implied some sensational discovery.

'The whole problem is to make something more real than life. Well, I've done that! I've made you more real than life.'

I remained speechless. For a moment I could find nothing to say, poor unreal policeman that I was.

And he proceeded to demonstrate, with an abundance of gestures and the hint of a Belgian accent, that my investigations as told by him were more convincing–he may even had said more accurate–than as experienced by myself.

At the time of our first encounters, in the autumn, he had not been lacking in self-confidence. Thanks to success, he was brimming over with it now, he had enough to spare for all the timid folk on earth.

'Follow me carefully, Inspector. . .'

For he had decided to drop the *monsieur le commissaire*.

'In a real investigation there are fifty of you, if not more, busy hunting for the criminal. You and your detectives aren't alone on the trail. The police and gendarmerie of the whole country are on the alert. They are busy in railway stations and ports and at frontiers. Not to mention the informers, let alone all the amateurs who take a hand.

'Just try, in the two hundred or two hundred and fifty pages of a novel to give a tolerably faithful picture of that swarming activity! A three-decker novel wouldn't be long enough, and the reader would lose heart after a few chapters, muddling everything, confusing everything.

'Now who is it that in real life prevents this confusion from taking place, who is there every morning putting everyone in his right place and following the guiding thread?'

He looked me up and down triumphantly.

'It's you yourself, as you know very well. It's the man in charge of the investigation. I'm quite aware that a Chief-Inspector from Central Police Headquarters, the head of a special squad, doesn't roam the streets in person to interview concierges and wine merchants.

'I'm quite aware, too, that, apart from exceptional cases, you don't spend your nights tramping about in the rain in empty streets waiting for some window to light up or some door to open.

'None the less things happen exactly as if you were there yourself, isn't that so?'

What could I reply to this? From a certain point of view it was a logical conclusion.

'So then, let's simplify! The first quality, the essential quality of truth is to be simple. And I have simplified. I have reduced to their simplest form the wheels within wheels that surround you, without altering the result in the slightest.

'Where fifty more or less anonymous detectives were swarming in confusion, I have retained only three or four, each with his own personality.'

I tried to object:

'The rest won't like it.'

'I don't write for a few dozen police officials. When you write a book about schoolmasters you're bound to offend tens of thousands of schoolmasters. The same would happen if you wrote about station-masters or typists. What were we talking about?'

'The different sorts of truth.'

'I was trying to prove to you that my sort is the only valid one. Would you like another example? One doesn't need to have spent as long as I have in this building to know that Central Police Headquarters, which belongs to the Prefecture of Police, can only operate within the perimeter of Paris and, by extension, in certain cases, within the Department of the Seine.

'Now in *The Late Monsieur Gallet* I described an investigation which took place in the centre of France.

'Did you go there, yes or no?'

It was yes, of course.

'I went there, it's true, but at a period when . . .'

'At a period when, for a certain length of time, you were working not for the Quai des Orfèvres but for the Rue des Saussaies. Why bother the reader's head with these administrative subtleties?

'Must one begin the account of every case by explaining: This took place in such and such a year. So Maigret was seconded to such and such a department.

'Let me finish . . .'

He had his idea and knew that he was about to touch a weak point.

'Are you, in your habits, your attitude, your character, a Quai des Orfèvres man or a Rue des Saussaies man?'

I apologize to my colleagues of the Sûreté Nationale, who include many of my good friends, but I am divulging no secret when I admit that there is, to say the least, a certain rivalry between the two establishments.

Let us admit, too, as Simenon had understood from the beginning, that particularly in those days, there existed two rather different types of policeman.

Those of the Rue des Saussaies, who are directly answerable to the Ministry of the Interior, are led more or less inevitably to deal with political jobs.

I don't blame them for it. I simply confess that for my own part I'd rather not be responsible for these.

Our field of action at the Quai des Orfèvres is perhaps more restricted, more down to earth. Our job, in fact, is to cope with malefactors of every sort and, in general, with everything that comes under the heading 'police' with the specific limitation 'judiciary'.

'You'll grant me that you're a Quai des Orfèvres man. You're proud of it. Well, that's what I've made of you; I've tried to make you the incarnation of a Quai des Orfèvres man. And now, for the sake of minutiae, because of your mania for accuracy, have I got to spoil the clarity of the picture by explaining that in such and such a year, for certain complex reasons, you provisionally changed your department, which enabled you to work in any part of France?'

'But . . .'

'One moment. The first day I met you, I told you I was not a journalist but a novelist, and I remember promising Monsieur Guichard that my stories would never involve indiscretions that might prove awkward for the police.'

'I know, but . . .'

'Wait a minute, Maigret, for God's sake!'

It was the first time he had called me that. It was the first time, too, that this youngster had told me to shut up.

'I've changed the names, except for yours and those of two or three of your colleagues. I've been careful to change the place-names too. Often, for an extra precaution, I've changed the family relationship between the characters.

'I have simplified things, and sometimes I've described only one cross-examination where there were really four or five, and only two or three trails to be followed where, to begin with, you had ten in front of you.

'I maintain that I am in the right, that my truth is the right one.

'I've brought you a proof of it.'

He pointed to a pile of books which he had laid on my desk when he arrived and to which I had paid no attention.

'These are the books written by specialists on matters concerning the police during the last twenty years, true stories, of that sort of truth that you like.

'Read them. For the most part you're familiar with the investigations which these books describe in detail.

'Well! I'm willing to bet that you won't recognize them, precisely because the quest for objectivity falsifies that truth which always is and which always *must* be simple.

'And now . . .'

Well! I'd rather admit it right away. That was the moment when I realized where the shoe pinched.

He was quite right, dammit, on all the heads he had mentioned. I didn't worry in the least, either, because he'd reduced the number of detectives or made me spend nights in the rain in their stead, or because he had, deliberately or not confused the Sûreté Nationale with Central Police Headquarters.

What shocked me, actually, although I scarcely liked to admit it to myself, was . . .

Good Lord, how hard this is! Remember what I said about a man and his photograph.

To take merely the detail of the bowler hat. I may appear quite ridiculous, but I must confess that this silly detail hurt me more than all the rest.

When young Sim came to Headquarters for the first time, I still had a bowler hat in my cupboard, but I only wore it on rare occasions, for funerals or official ceremonies.

Now it happened that in my office there hung a photograph taken some years earlier on the occasion of some congress or other, in which I appeared wearing that cursed hat.

The result is that even today, when I am introduced to people who've never seen me before, I hear them say:

'Why, you're wearing a different hat.'

As for the famous overcoat with the velvet collar, it was with my wife that Simenon had to have it out one day, rather than with myself.

I did have such a coat, I admit. I even had several, like all men of my generation. It may even have happened that, round about 1927, on a day of extreme cold or driving rain, I took down one of those old overcoats.

I'm not a dressy man. I care very little about being smart. But perhaps for that very reason I've a horror of looking odd. And my little Jewish tailor in the Rue de Turenne is no more anxious than I am to have me stared at in the street.

'Is it my fault if that's how I see you?' Simenon might have answered, like the painter who gives his model a crooked nose or a squint.

Only in that case the model doesn't have to spend his whole life in front of his portrait, and thousands of people aren't going to believe ever after that he has a crooked nose or a squint.

I didn't tell him all this that morning. I merely averted my eyes and said modestly:

'Was it absolutely necessary to simplify *me?*'

'To begin with, it certainly was. The public has to get used to you, to your figure, your bearing. I've probably hit on the right expression. For the moment you're still only a silhouette, a back, a pipe, a way of talking, of muttering.'

'Thanks!'

'The details will appear gradually, you'll see. I don't know how long it will take. Little by little you'll begin to live with a more subtle, more complex life.'

'That's reassuring.'

'For instance, up till now, you've had no family life, whereas the Boulevard Richard-Lenoir and Madame Maigret actually take up a good half of your existence. You've still only rung up your home, but you're going to be seen there.'

'In my dressing-gown and slippers?'

'And even in bed.'

'I wear nightshirts,' I said ironically.

'I know. That completes the picture. Even if you were used to pyjamas I'd have made you wear a nightshirt.'

I wonder how this conversation would have ended—probably with a regular quarrel – if I hadn't been told that a young informer from the Rue Pigalle wanted to speak to me.

'On the whole,' I said to Simenon, as he held out his hand, 'you're pleased with yourself.'

'Not yet, but it'll come.'

Could I really have announced to him that henceforward I forbade him to use my name? I was legally entitled to do so. And this would have given rise to a typically Parisian lawsuit which would have covered me with ridicule.

The character would have acquired a different name. But he would still have been myself, or rather that simplified myself who, according to the author, was going to grow progressively more complex.

The worst of it was that the rascal was quite right and that every month, for years, I was going to find, in a book with a photograph on its cover, a Maigret who imitated me more and more.

And if it had only been in books! The cinema was shortly to take it up, and the radio, and later television.

It's a strange sensation to watch on the screen, coming and going, speaking and blowing his nose, a fellow who pretends to be yourself, who borrows certain of your habits, utters sentences that you have uttered, in circumstances that you have known, through which you have lived, in settings which have sometimes been reconstructed with meticulous care.

Actually the first screen Maigret, Pierre Renoir, was tolerably true to life. I had become a little taller, a little slimmer. The face was different, of course, but certain attitudes were so striking that I suspect the actor of having observed me unawares.

A few months later I grew some six inches shorter, and what I lost in height I gained in stoutness, becoming, in the shape of Abel Tarride, obese and bland, so flabby that I looked like an inflated rubber animal about to float up to the ceiling. Not to mention the knowing winks with which I underlined my own discoveries and my cunning tricks!

I couldn't sit the film out, and my tribulations were not yet over.

Harry Baur was no doubt a great actor, but he was a full twenty years older than myself then, with a cast of features that was flabby and tragic at the same time.

Let's pass over that!

After growing twenty years older, I suddenly grew almost that much younger again, a good deal later, with a certain Préjean, about whom I have no complaint to make – any more than about the rest of them – but who looks far more like certain young detectives of the present generation than those of my own.

And finally, quite lately, I have been made to grow stout again, almost to bursting point, while I have begun, in the shape of Charles Laughton, to use English as my native tongue.

Well! of all those, there was one at least who had the good taste to cheat Simenon and to consider my truth more valid than his.

It was Pierre Renoir, who did not clap a bowler hat on to his head but wore a perfectly ordinary felt hat, and the sort of clothes worn by any civil servant, whether or not attached to the police.

I see that I have spoken only of trivial details, a hat, an overcoat, a stove, probably because those details were what first shocked me.

You don't feel any surprise at growing up first, then at growing old. But let a man so much as cut off the tips of his moustaches and he won't recognize himself.

The truth is that I'd like to have finished with what I consider as trivial defects before confronting the two characters on essential points.

If Simenon is right, which is quite possible, my own character will appear odd and involved by the side of that famous simplified–or dressed-up–truth of his, and I shall look like some peevish fellow trying to touch up his own portrait.

Now that I've made a beginning, with the subject of dress, I shall have to go on, if only for my own peace of mind.

Simenon asked me the other day–actually, he has changed too, from the young fellow I met in Xavier Guichard's office–Simenon asked me, with a touch of mockery:

'Well, what about the new Maigret?'

I tried to answer him in his former words.

'He's taking shape! He's still nothing but a silhouette. A hat, an overcoat. But it's his real hat. His real overcoat! Little by little, perhaps the rest will come, perhaps he'll have arms and legs and even a face, who knows? Perhaps he'll even begin to think by himself, without the aid of a novelist.'

Actually, Simenon is now just about the age I was when we met for the first time. In those days he tended to think of me as a middle-aged man and even, in his heart of hearts, as an elderly one.

I did not ask him what he thought about that today, but I couldn't help remarking:

'D'you know that with the course of time you've begun to walk and smoke your pipe and even to speak like *your* Maigret?'

Which is quite true and which, you'll agree, provided me with a rather piquant revenge.

It was rather as if, after all these years, he had begun to take *himself* for *me*!

Chapter Three

In which I shall try to talk about a certain bearded doctor who had some influence on the life of my family and perhaps, all things considered, on my choice of a career

I don't know if I am going to be able to hit the right tone this time, for I've already filled my wastepaper basket this morning with the pages I've torn up one after the other.

And last night I almost gave the whole thing up.

While my wife was reading what I had written during the day, I watched her, pretending to read my paper as usual, and at a certain point I had the impression that she was surprised, and from then on to the end she kept glancing up at me in astonishment and almost in distress.

Instead of speaking to me immediately, she went to put the manuscript back in the drawer in silence, and it was some time before she said, trying to keep her remark as light as possible:

'Anyone would think you didn't like him.'

I did not need to ask of whom she was speaking, and it was my turn to be perplexed, to stare at her in wide-eyed surprise.

'What are you talking about?' I exclaimed. 'Since when has Simenon ceased to be a friend of ours?'

'Yes, of course . . .'

I wondered what could be at the back of her mind, and tried to recollect what I had written.

'I may be mistaken,' she added. 'Of course I must be mistaken, since you say so. But I had the impression, while reading certain passages, that you felt really resentful about something, and were having your revenge. I don't mean a big, open resentment. Something more secretive, more . . .'

She did not add the word—but I did so for her—'. . . more shameful . . .'

Now Heaven knows how far that was from my mind while I wrote. Not only have I always been on the most cordial terms with Simenon, but he quickly became a family friend of ours, and on the few occasions when we have travelled in the summer holidays it has almost always been to visit him in his various homes, while he was still living in France: in Alsace, at Porquerolles, in the Charente, the Vendée and so forth. More recently, when I agreed to go on a semi-official tour of the U.S.A. it was mainly because I knew I should meet him in Arizona, where he was then living.

'I give you my word . . .' I began gravely.

'I believe you. But perhaps your readers won't.'

It's my own fault, I'm convinced of it. I am not accustomed to using irony and I realize that I'm probably heavy-handed about it. Whereas on the contrary I had tried, out of diffidence, to treat this difficult subject with a light touch, since it caused me a certain personal embarrassment.

What I am trying to do, in short, is nothing more or less than to size up one image against another image, one character against its double, rather than against its shadow. And Simenon was the first to encourage me in this undertaking.

I add, to pacify my wife, who is fiercely loyal in her friendships, that Simenon, as I said yesterday in other terms, jokingly, is quite different now from the young man whose aggressive self-confidence occasionally made me wince; that on the contrary he himself is inclined to be taciturn nowadays, and speaks with a certain hesitancy, particularly about any subject on which he feels strongly, reluctant to make assertions and, I'd take my oath, seeking my approval.

Having said that much, am I to go on teasing him? Just a little, after all. This'll be the last time, no doubt. It's too good an opportunity, and I cannot resist it.

In the forty-odd volumes he has devoted to my investigations, there are perhaps a score of allusions to my origins, to my family, a few words about my father and his profession as estate-manager, one mention of the Collège de Nantes where I was partly educated, and other brief allusions to my two years as medical student.

And this was the same man who took over four hundred pages to tell the story of his own childhood up to the age of sixteen. It makes no difference that he did so in fictional form, and that his characters may or may not have been true to life, the fact remains that he did not consider his hero complete without the company of his parents and grandparents, his uncles and aunts, whom he describes with all their failings and complaints, their petty vices and their ulcers, while even the neighbour's dog is allotted half a page.

I am not objecting to this, and if I comment on it, it's an indirect way of forestalling any accusation that could be levelled at me of being too longwinded about my own family.

To my mind, a man without a past isn't a whole man. In the course of certain investigations, I have sometimes spent more time over the family background of a suspect than over the suspect himself, and this has often provided the key to what might otherwise have remained a mystery.

It has been said, quite correctly, that I was born in Central France, not far from Moulins, but I don't think it has ever been specified that the estate of which my father was manager was one of seven and a half thousand acres and included no less than twenty-six small farms.

Not only was my grandfather, whom I remember, one of these tenant farmers, but he followed at least three generations of Maigrets who had tilled the same soil.

An epidemic of typhus, while my father was still young, had decimated his family, which included seven or eight children, and left only two survivors, my father and a sister who was later to marry a baker and settle at Nantes.

Why did my father go to the lycée at Moulins, thus breaking with such old traditions? I have reason to believe that the village priest took an interest in him. But it did not mean a break with the land, for after two years at an agricultural school he came back to the village and joined the staff at the château as assistant estate-manager.

I always feel a certain embarrassment when speaking about him. I have the impression, indeed, that people think: 'He has retained a child's picture of his parents.'

And for a long time I wondered whether possibly I was mistaken, whether my critical sense were not failing me.

But I have had occasion to meet other men of the same type, particularly among those of his generation, mostly from the same social class, which might be described as an intermediary one.

For my grandfather, the family at the château, their rights, their privileges, their behaviour were not subjects for discussion. What he thought of them in his heart of hearts I never discovered. I was quite a youngster when he died. I'm convinced none the less, when I remember certain looks of his, certain silences particularly, that his approval was not always passive, was not even always approval, nor yet resignation, but that it proceeded, on the contrary, from a certain pride and above all from a highly developed sense of duty.

This was the feeling that persisted in men like my father, mingled with a reserve, a sense of propriety which may have looked like resignation.

I can picture him very well. I have kept some photographs of him. He was very tall, very thin, his thinness emphasized by narrow trousers, bound in by leather gaiters to just below the knee. I always saw my father in leather gaiters. They were a sort of uniform for him. He wore no beard, but a long sandy moustache in which, when he came home in winter, I used to feel tiny ice-crystals when I kissed him.

Our house stood in the courtyard of the château, a pretty house of rose-coloured brick, one storey high, overlooking the low buildings in which lived several families of farm-hands, grooms and gamekeepers, whose wives for the most part worked at the château as laundresses, needle women or kitchen helps.

Within that courtyard my father was a kind of ruler to whom men spoke respectfully, cap in hand.

About once a week he used to drive off at nightfall, sometimes at dusk, with one or more farmers, to go and buy or sell livestock at some distant fair from which he only returned at the end of the following day.

His office was in a separate building, and on its walls hung photographs of prize oxen or horses, calendars of fairs and, almost invariably, the finest sheaf of wheat harvested on the estate, shrivelling up as the months went by.

About ten o'clock he used to cross the courtyard and go into a private part of the grounds. He would walk round the buildings until he came to the big flight of steps up which the peasants never went, and remained closeted for a time behind the thick walls of the château.

It was for him, in a word, what our morning conferences are for us at Headquarters, and as a child I felt proud to see him, very upright, without a trace of servility, as he climbed that awe-inspiring flight of steps.

He spoke little, and he seldom laughed, but when this did happen it was a surprise to discover how young, almost childish, his laugh was, and to see how much simple pleasantries amused him.

He never drank, unlike most of the people I knew. At each meal a small decanter was set aside for him, half filled with a light white wine harvested on the estate, and I never saw him drink anything else, even at weddings or funerals. And at fairs, where he was obliged to stay at inns, he had a cup of his favourite coffee sent up from the kitchen.

I thought of him as a grown man, and even as a middle-aged one. I was five when my grandfather died. As for my mother's parents, they lived over fifty miles away, and we only visited them twice a year, so that I never knew them well. They were not farming folk. They kept a grocer's shop in a largish village, with a café attached to it, as is often the case in country places.

I am not sure, in retrospect, that this was not the reason why our relations with our in-laws were not closer.

I was not quite eight years old when I finally realized that my mother was pregnant. By remarks overheard by chance, by whispers, I more or less grasped that the thing was unexpected, that after my birth the doctors had declared that she was unlikely to have any more children.

I reconstructed all this later, bit by bit, and I suppose this is always the case with childhood memories.

There was at this time in the neighbouring village, which was bigger than ours, a doctor with a pointed red beard whose name was Gadelle – Victor Gadelle if I am not mistaken – about whom people talked a great deal, almost always with an air of mystery, and, probably on account of his beard, and also on account of all that was said about him, I was almost inclined to take him for a kind of devil.

There was a drama in his life, a real drama, the first I ever came across and one which impressed me deeply, particularly as it was to have a profound influence on our family, and thereby on my whole existence.

Gadelle drank. He drank more heavily than any peasant in the neighbourhood, not only from time to time but every day, beginning in the morning and only stopping at night. He drank so much that, in a warm room, the atmosphere would be pervaded by a smell of alcohol which I always sniffed with disgust.

Moreover he was careless of his person. In fact you might have called him dirty.

How, under these conditions, could he have been my father's friend? That remained a mystery to me. The fact remains that he often came to see him and chat with him at our home and that there was even a ritual, which consisted of taking out of the glass-fronted sideboard, as soon as he arrived, a small decanter of brandy that was kept for his exclusive use.

About the original drama I knew almost nothing at the time. Doctor Gadelle's wife was pregnant, and this must have been for the sixth or seventh time. I thought of her as an old woman already, whereas she was probably about forty.

What had happened on the day of her confinement? Apparently Gadelle came home more drunk than usual, and, while waiting for his wife's delivery, went on drinking at her bedside.

As it happened, the first stages of her labour were unusually prolonged. The children had been taken to some neighbour's. Towards morning, as nothing seemed to be happening, the sister-in-law who had spent the night at the house went off to see to things at her own home.

Then, apparently, a great noise was heard in the doctor's house, with cries, and footsteps coming and going.

When people got there, they found Gadelle weeping in a corner. His wife was dead. So was the child.

And for a long time after I would overhear the village gossips whispering in each other's ears, with expressions of indignation or horror:

'A real shambles!'

For months the case of Doctor Gadelle was the main topic of conversation, and, as was to be expected, the neighbourhood was split into two factions.

Some people—and there was a good number of them—went into town, which was quite a journey in those days, to consult a different doctor, while others, through indifference or because they still trusted him, went on sending for the bearded doctor.

My father never took me into his confidence on this subject. I am therefore reduced to conjecture.

Gadelle, at any rate, never stopped coming to see us. He called on us as he had always done, in the course of his rounds, and the familiar gilt-edged decanter was put before him as usual.

He was drinking less, however. People said they never saw him tipsy now. One night he was sent for to the remotest of the farms for a confinement, and he acquitted himself with honour. On his way home he called at our house, and I remember he was very pale; I can still see my father clasping his hand with unwonted persistence as though to encourage him, as though to tell him: 'You see, things weren't so hopeless after all.'

For my father never gave up hope of people. I never heard him utter an irrevocable judgment, even when the black sheep of the estate, a foul-mouthed farmer of whose malpractices he had had to complain to the landlord, had accused him of some dishonest trick or other.

It's quite certain that if, after the death of Gadelle's wife and child, there had been nobody to stretch out a helping hand to the doctor, he would have been a lost man.

My father did so. And when my mother was pregnant, a certain feeling which I find hard to explain, but which I understand, obliged him to see the thing through.

He took precautions, none the less. Twice, during the last stage of her pregnancy, he took my mother into Moulins to consult a specialist.

When her time came, a stable lad went on horseback to fetch the doctor in the middle of the night. I wasn't sent away from home, but stayed there shut up in my own room, in a great state of agitation, although like all country lads I had acquired a certain knowledge of these things at an early age.

My mother died at seven in the morning, as day was breaking, and when I went downstairs the first thing that caught my eye, in spite of my emotion, was the decanter on the dining-room table.

I was left an only child. A local girl was brought in to look after the house and take care of me. I never saw Doctor Gadelle cross our threshold since that day, but neither did I ever hear my father say one word about him.

A blurred and colourless period followed this drama. I went to the village school. My father spoke less and less. He was thirty-two, and only now do I realize how young he was.

I did not protest when, on completing my twelfth year, I was sent as a boarder to the lycée at Moulins, since it was impossible to take me there every day.

I only stayed there a few months. I was unhappy there, an utter stranger in a new world that felt hostile to me. I said nothing about it to my father, who fetched me home every Saturday evening. I never complained.

He must have understood, for during the Easter holidays his sister, whose husband had opened a bakery at Nantes, suddenly came to see us, and I realized that they were discussing a plan already sketched out by letter.

My aunt, who had a very high colour, had begun to put on weight. She was childless and this grieved her.

For several days she hovered round me anxiously, telling me about the house at Nantes with its good smell of new bread.

She seemed very cheerful. I had guessed. I was resigned. Or, more precisely, since that's a word I don't care for, I had accepted.

My father and I had a long talk together as we walked through the countryside one Sunday morning after Mass. It was the first time he had talked to me as if I were a man. He was considering my future, the impossibility of studying if I stayed in the village, and if I remained at Moulins as a boarder the absence of normal family life.

I know now what he was thinking. He had realized that the company of a man like himself, who had withdrawn into himself and lived mainly with his own thoughts, was not desirable for a young boy who still had everything to hope for from life.

I went off with my aunt, a big trunk jolting behind us, in the cart that took us to the station.

My father did not shed a tear. Neither did I.

That's more or less all I knew about him. For years, at Nantes, I was the nephew of the baker and the baker's wife, and I almost got used to the man whom I saw every day with his shaggy chest glowing in the red light of his oven.

I used to spend all my holidays with my father. I won't go so far as to say we were strangers to one another. But I had my own private life, my ambitions, my problems.

He was my father, whom I loved and respected, but whom I'd given up trying to understand. And it went on like that for years. Is this always the case? I'm inclined to think so.

When my curiosity reawakened, it was too late to ask the questions which I so longed to ask then, and which I reproached myself for not asking when he was still there to answer me.

My father had died of pleurisy at the age of forty-four.

I was a young man, I had begun my medical studies. On my last visits to the château I had been struck by the flush on my father's cheekbones and the hectic glitter of his eyes at night.

'Has there ever been any tuberculosis in our family?' I asked my aunt one day.

She said, as though I had spoken of some shameful taint:

'Good heavens, no! All of them were as tough as oak-trees! Don't you remember your grandfather?'

I did remember him, precisely. I remembered a certain dry cough which he put down to smoking. And as far back as I could remember I always pictured my father with the same cheekbones under which a fire seemed to be glowing.

My aunt had the same pink flush too.

'It's from always living in the heat of a bakery,' she would retort.

She died, none the less, from the same illness as her brother, ten years later.

As for myself, when I got back to Nantes to collect my belongings before starting on a new life, I hesitated for a long while before calling on one of my professors at his private house and asking him to examine me.

'No danger of anything like that,' he reassured me.

Two days later I took the train to Paris.

My wife will forgive me this time if I hark back to Simenon and his picture of me, for I want to discuss a point raised by him in one of his latest books, which concerns me very closely.

It is indeed one of the points that vexed me most—and I'm not referring to such petty questions as dress, which I raised as a joke.

I should not be my father's son if I were not somewhat touchy about all that concerns my job, my career, and that's precisely the question.

I have sometimes had an uneasy feeling that Simenon was somehow trying to apologize for me to the public for entering the Police Force. And I am sure that in some people's eyes I only took up this profession as a last resort.

Now it is certainly a fact that I had begun my medical studies and that I chose that profession of my own free will, without being pushed into it by somewhat ambitious parents, as often happens.

I had not thought about the matter for years, and it had never occurred to me to ask myself any questions about it, when, precisely on account of something that had been written about my vocation, the problem gradually forced itself upon me.

I spoke to nobody about it, not even to my wife. Today I have to overcome certain feelings of diffidence to put things in their true light, or try to do so.

In one of his books, then, Simenon has spoken of 'a man who mends destinies', and he did not invent the phrase, which was one of my own, which I must have uttered one day when we were chatting together.

Now I wonder if it didn't all spring from Gadelle, whose tragic story, as I subsequently realized, must have struck me far more than I supposed.

Because he was a doctor, because he had failed, the medical profession had acquired in my eyes an extraordinary prestige, it seemed almost a sort of priesthood.

For years, without realizing it, I tried to understand the drama of this man at grips with a destiny that was too great for him.

And I remembered my father's attitude towards him. I wondered whether my father had understood the same thing that I had, whether that was why, at whatever cost to himself, he had let the man try his luck.

From Gadelle I went on instinctively to consider the majority of the people I had known, almost all of them simple folk with apparently straightforward lives, who none the less had had at one time or another to measure themselves against destiny.

Don't forget that I am trying to set down here not the reflections of a mature man but the workings of a boy's mind, then of a youth's.

My mother's death seemed to me so stupid a drama, so unnecessary.

And all the other dramas that I knew, all these failures plunged me into a sort of furious despair.

Could nobody do anything about them? Might there not be, somewhere, some man wiser or more experienced than the rest—whom I pictured more or less in the shape of a family doctor, of a Gadelle who was not a failure—capable of telling them gently, firmly:

'You're taking a wrong turn. By acting thus you're heading for disaster. Your right place is here rather than there.'

I think that was it; I felt dimly that too many people were not in their right places, that they were striving to play parts that were beyond their capacities, so that the game was lost for them before they started.

Above all, please don't imagine that I ever dreamed of becoming that sort of God-the-Father-figure myself.

After trying to understand Gadelle, and then to understand my father's attitude towards him, I went on looking around me asking the same questions.

One example may raise a smile. There were fifty-eight of us in my class one year, fifty-eight pupils with different social backgrounds, different qualities, ambitions and failings. Now I had amused myself working out the ideal destiny of all my fellow-pupils and, in my mind, I called them: 'the lawyer . . . the tax collector . . .'

For quite a while, too, I exercised my wits in guessing what the people I came across would eventually die of.

Is it clearer now why I wanted to become a doctor? The word police, for me, suggested at that time merely the constable at the street corner. And if I had heard speak of the secret police, I had not the least conception what it could be.

And then suddenly I had to earn my living. I arrived in Paris without even the vaguest notion of what career I was to choose. In view of my unfinished studies I could at best hope for some office job, and it was with this in mind that, without enthusiasm, I started reading the 'small ads' in the newspapers. My uncle had in vain offered to teach me his trade and keep me at the bakery.

In the little hotel where I was staying, on the Left Bank, there lived on the same landing as myself a man who aroused my curiosity, a man of about forty who, Heaven knows why, reminded me somewhat of my father.

Physically, indeed, he was as different as possible from the fair, lean, slope-shouldered man whom I had always seen wearing leather gaiters. He was rather short and squat, dark-haired, with a prematurely bald patch which he concealed by carefully combing his hair forward, and black moustaches with curled tips.

He was always neatly dressed in black, wore an overcoat with a velvet collar, which accounts for a certain other overcoat and carried a stick with a solid silver knob.

I think the likeness to my father lay in his bearing, in a certain way of walking without ever hurrying, of listening, of watching, and then, somehow, of withdrawing within himself.

I met him by chance in a homely restaurant in the neighbourhood; I discovered that he took his evening meal there almost every day and I began, for no definite reason, to want to get to know him.

In vain did I try to guess what his occupation in life might be. He must be unmarried, since he lived alone at the hotel. I used to hear him get up in the morning and come back at night at irregular hours.

He never had any visitors and, the only time I met him with a companion, he was standing at the corner of the Boulevard Saint-Michel talking to an individual of such unprepossessing appearance that one might unhesitatingly have described him, at that period, as an *apache*.

I was on the point of taking a job in a firm that made *passementerie*, in the Rue des Victoires. I was to call there next day with references for which I had written to my former teachers.

That evening at the restaurant, moved by some instinct or other, I decided to rise from table just as my hotel neighbour was replacing his napkin in his pigeonhole, so that I happened to be there to hold the door open for him.

He must have noticed me. Perhaps he had guessed that I wanted to speak to him, for he gave me a long look.

'Thank you,' he said.

Then, as I was standing still on the pavement:

'Are you going back to the hotel?'

'I think so . . . I don't know . . .'

It was a fine late-autumn night. The river bank was not far off, and the moon was visible rising behind the trees.

'Alone in Paris?'

'I'm alone, yes.'

Without asking for my company, he accepted it, he took it for granted as a *fait accompli*.

'You're looking for work?'

'How do you know?'

He did not even trouble to answer and slipped a cachou between his lips. I was soon to understand why. He was afflicted with bad breath and knew it.

'You're from the provinces?'

'From Nantes, but I come from the country originally.'

I spoke freely to him. It was practically the first time since I had come to Paris that I had found a companion, and his silence did not embarrass me at all, no doubt because I was used to my father's friendly silences.

I had told him almost the whole of my story when we reached the Quai des Orfèvres, on the other side of the Pont Saint-Michel.

He stopped in front of a great door that was standing ajar, and said to me:

'Will you wait a moment for me? I shall only be a few minutes.'

A policeman in uniform was on duty at the door. After pacing up and down for a moment I asked him:

'Isn't this the Palais de Justice?'

'This is the entry to Police Headquarters.'

My hotel neighbour was called Jacquemain. He was, in fact, unmarried, as I learned that evening while we were walking up and down the Seine, crossing the same bridges over and over again, with the massive Palais de Justice almost continuously towering over us.

He was a Detective-Inspector and he told me about his profession, as briefly as my father would have done of his, with the same underlying pride.

He was killed three years later, before I had myself acquired access to those offices in the Quai des Orfèvres which had come to hold such glamour for me. It happened in the neighbourhood of the Porte d'Italie, during a street fight. A bullet which was not even intended for him hit him right in the chest.

His photograph still hangs among the rest in one of those black frames surmounted by the inscription: 'Died in the performance of his duty.'

He didn't talk to me much. He chiefly listened to me. This did not restrain me from asking him, towards eleven o'clock that night, in a voice quivering with impatience:

'Do you really think it's possible?'

'I'll give you an answer tomorrow evening.'

Of course there was no question of my going straight into the Sûreté. The age of diplomas had not yet arrived, and everyone had to start in the ranks. My only ambition was to be accepted, in any capacity, in one of the Paris police stations, and to be allowed to discover for myself an aspect of the world of which Inspector Jacquemain had merely given me a glimpse.

Just as we were parting on the landing of our hotel, which has since been pulled down, he asked:

'Would you very much dislike wearing uniform?'

I felt a slight shock, I must admit, a brief hesitation which did not escape his notice and which can scarcely have pleased him.

'No . . .' I replied in a low voice.

And I wore it, not for long, for seven or eight months. As I had long legs and was very lean, very swift, strange as that may seem today, they gave me a bicycle and, in order that I might get to know Paris, where I was always losing my way, I was given the job of delivering notes to the various police stations.

Has Simenon talked about all this? I don't remember. For months, perched on my bicycle, I threaded my way between cabs and double-decker buses, still horse-drawn, of which I was horribly frightened, particularly when they were tearing down from Montmartre.

Officials still wore frock-coats and top-hats and, above a certain rank, they sported morning-coats.

Policemen were mostly middle-aged men with reddish noses who were to be seen drinking at bar-counters with coachmen and of whom song-writers made relentless fun.

I was unmarried. I felt shy of going courting in uniform, and I decided that my real life would only begin on the day when I should enter the house in the Quai des Orfèvres as a detective, using the main staircase, and not merely as a messenger carrying official notes.

When I mentioned this ambition to my hotel neighbour, he did not smile, but looked at me reflectively and murmured:

'Why not?'

I did not know that I was so soon to attend his funeral. My forecasts about human destiny were still not entirely adequate.

Chapter Four

How I ate petits fours *at Anselme and Géraldine's, thereby shocking the Highways and Bridges*

Did my father or my grandfather ever wonder whether they might have become something other than what they were? Had they ever had other ambitions? Did they envy a different lot from their own?

It's strange to have lived with people for so long and yet to know nothing of what nowadays would seem essential. I have often asked myself the question, with the feeling that I was straddling two worlds, totally foreign to one another.

We talked about it not long ago, Simenon and I, in my flat in the Boulevard Richard-Lenoir. I think it may have been on the eve of his departure for the United States. He had paused to stare at the enlarged photograph of my father, although he had seen it for years hanging on the dining-room wall.

While he studied it with particular attention, he kept casting searching glances at me, as if he were trying to make comparisons, and this set him pondering.

'The fact is,' he finally remarked, 'you were born in an ideal milieu, Maigret, at the ideal moment in a family's evolution, to become a top-rank official.'

I was struck by this comment because I had already thought about it, in a less precise and above all a less personal fashion; I had noticed how many of my colleagues came from peasant families having quite recently lost direct contact with the land.

Simenon went on, almost regretfully and as though he envied me:

'I'm a whole generation ahead of you. I have to go back to my grandfather to find the equivalent of your father. My own father had already reached the civil servant stage.'

My wife was gazing at him attentively, trying to understand, and he added in a lighter tone:

'In the normal course of events I'd have had to make my way up from the bottom in some profession, and work hard to become a G.P. or a lawyer or an engineer. Or else . . .'

'Or else what?'

'To become an embittered rebel. Of course that's what usually happens. Otherwise there'd be a plethora of doctors and lawyers. I think I come from the stock that has provided the greatest number of misfits.'

I don't know why this conversation has suddenly recurred to me. Probably because I'm recollecting my early years and trying to analyse my frame of mind at that period.

I was all alone in the world. I had just landed in an unfamiliar city in which wealth was flaunted more blatantly than today.

Two things struck one: that wealth on the one hand, and that poverty on the other; and I belonged to the second group.

A whole social set, in full view of the masses, lived a life of sophisticated leisure, and the newspapers reported all the doings of these people who had no other preoccupation than their own pleasures and vanities.

Now not for one moment did I feel tempted to rebel. I did not envy them. I did not hope to be like them one day. I did not contrast my lot with theirs.

For me they belonged to a world as different from mine as if it had been another planet.

I remember that in those days I had an insatiable appetite, which had already been legendary when I was a child. At Nantes my aunt used often to tell how she had seen me eat a four-pound loaf when I got back from school, which did not prevent me from having dinner a couple of hours later.

I earned very little money, and my great concern was to satisfy that hunger of mine; I looked for luxury not on the terraces of the famous boulevard cafés, nor in the shop-windows of the Rue de la Paix, but more prosaically on pork-butchers' counters.

In the streets through which I usually passed I had discovered a number of pork-butchers' shops, which fascinated me, and in the days when I still travelled about Paris in uniform, perched on a bicycle, I used to calculate my time so as to save the few minutes necessary to buy a piece of sausage or a slice of pâté, and devour it, with a roll from the nearby bakery, while standing on the pavement outside.

When my stomach was appeased I felt happy and full of self-confidence. I did my job conscientiously. I attached importance to the slightest tasks entrusted to me. And there was no question of overtime. I considered that all of my time belonged to the police, and it seemed to be quite natural that I should be kept at work for fourteen or fifteen hours at a stretch.

If I mention this it is not that I want to take any credit for it, but rather, on the contrary, because as far as I can remember it was a common attitude at that time.

Very few police constables had more than a primary education. On account of Inspector Jacquemain, the authorities knew–although I myself didn't then know who knew, or even that anyone knew–that I had begun advanced studies. After a few months I was greatly surprised to find myself appointed to a post which I had never dared to hope for: that of secretary to the Station Officer of the Saint-Georges district.

And yet the job had an unglamorous name at the time. It was called 'being the Station Officer's dog'.

My bicycle, my cap and my uniform were taken away from me. So was my chance of stopping at pork butchers' on my way through the Paris streets.

I was particularly grateful for the fact of being in plain clothes when one day, walking along the pavement of the Boulevard Saint-Michel, I heard a voice hailing me.

A tall fellow in a white overall was running after me.

'Jubert!' I cried.

'Maigret!'

'What are you doing here?'

'And you?'

'Listen. I daren't stop out just now. Come and pick me up at seven o'clock at the door of the chemist's shop.'

Jubert, Felix Jubert, was one of my fellow students from the medical school at Nantes. I knew he had broken off his studies at the same time as myself, but, I believe, for different reasons. Without actually being a dunce, he was slow-witted, and I remember they used to say about him:

'He works so hard he comes out in spots, but he's no wiser next day.'

He was very tall and bony, with a big nose, coarse features, red hair, and as long as I'd known him his face had always been covered, not with those small acne pimples that are the bane of young men's lives, but with big red or purple spots which he spent hours smothering in medicated ointments and powders.

I went along to wait for him that same evening at the chemist's shop where he had been working for some weeks. He had no relatives in Paris. He was living in the Cherche-Midi district with people who took in two or three lodgers.

'And what are you doing yourself?'

'I'm in the Police Force.'

I can still picture his violet eyes, clear as a girl's, trying to conceal their incredulity. His voice sounded quite odd as he repeated:

'The Police Force?'

He was staring at my suit, instinctively looking for the constable on duty at the corner of the boulevard as though to make a comparison.

'I'm secretary to the Station Officer.'

'Oh, good, I understand.'

Whether from conventional pride, or, more likely, because of my own inability to explain myself and his inability to understand, I did not confess that three weeks earlier I had still been wearing uniform, and that my ambition was to join the detective force.

In his opinion and in that of a great many people, a secretary's was a good, respectable job; I sat at a desk, nice and clean, with books in front of me and a pen in my hand.

'Have you many friends in Paris?'

Apart from Inspector Jacquemain I really knew nobody, for at the police station I was still a novice and people had to watch me before they would make friends with me.

'No girl friend either? What do you do with all your spare time?'

In the first place I hadn't much of that. And in the second, I spent it studying, for in order to reach my aim faster I had resolved to pass the examinations which had just been instituted.

We dined together that evening. Towards the end of the meal he told me, as if promising me a treat:

'I shall have to introduce you.'

'To whom?'

'To some very nice people. Friends of mine. You'll see.'

He gave no further explanation that first day. And I don't know why, it was several weeks before we saw each other again. I might quite well never have seen him again. I had not given him my address. I had not got his. It never occurred to me to go and wait for him outside the chemist's shop.

Chance, once again, brought us face to face at the door of the Théâtre Français, where we were both queuing.

'Isn't it silly,' he said. 'I thought I'd lost you. I don't even know at which police station you're working. I mentioned you to my friends.'

He had a way of talking about these friends which suggested that they were a very special set of people, almost a mysterious sect.

'You've got a dress suit, I hope?'

'I've got one.'

It was pointless to add that it had been my father's dress suit, which was somewhat old-fashioned, since he had worn it at his wedding, and which I'd had cut to fit me.

'I'll take you there on Friday. You must manage to be free without fail on Friday evening at eight o'clock. Can you dance?'

'No.'

'It doesn't matter. But it would be better if you took a few lessons. I know a good school that's not expensive. I've been to it myself.'

This time he had made a note of my address and even of the little restaurant where I used to have dinner when I was not on duty, and on Friday evening he was in my room sitting on my bed, while I dressed.

'I must explain to you, so that you don't drop any bricks. We shall be the only people there, you and I, who aren't connected with the Highways and Bridges Department. A distant cousin of mine, whom I happened to run into, introduced me. Monsieur and Madame Léonard are charming people. Their niece is the loveliest girl in the world.'

I gathered at once that he was in love with her and that it was in order to show me the object of his passion that he was dragging me off with him.

'There'll be others, you needn't worry,' he promised me. 'Very nice girls.'

As it was raining and we didn't want to arrive covered with mud, we took a cab, the first cab I had ever taken in Paris except on duty. I can still picture our white shirt-fronts as we passed under the gas lamps. And I can picture Felix Jubert stopping the cab in front of a florist's shop so that we might decorate our buttonholes.

'Old Monsieur Léonard,' he explained. 'Anselme they call him, retired about ten years ago. Before that he was one of the top officials in the Highways and Bridges Department, and even now his successors still come to consult him sometimes. His niece's father is in Highways and Bridges too, on the administrative side. And so is all their family, so to speak.'

To hear him talk of this Government service you realized that for Jubert it was Paradise Lost, that he would have given anything not to have wasted those precious years studying medicine, so that he too could have made a start on such a career.

'You'll see!'

And I saw. It was in the Boulevard Beaumarchais, not far from the Place de la Bastille, in an oldish but comfortable and fairly well-to-do block. All the windows were lit up on the third floor, and Jubert's upward glance as we got out of the cab showed me clearly that the party in question was being held there.

I felt rather ill at ease. I began to wish I hadn't come. My stiff collar hurt me; I was convinced that my tie was getting twisted and that one of the tails of my coat tended to curl up like a cock's crest.

The stair was dimly lit, the steps covered with a crimson carpet that seemed to me sumptuous. And the landing windows were filled with stained glass which for a long time I considered the last word in refinement.

Jubert had smeared his spotty face with a thicker coat of ointment, which for some reason gave it a purplish sheen. He reverently pulled a big tassel which hung in front of a door. Within, we could hear the buzz of conversation, with that touch of shrillness in voices and laughter which suggests the excitement of a social gathering.

A maid in a white apron opened the door to us, and Felix, as he held out his overcoat, was delighted to show himself a regular frequenter of the house by remarking:

'Good evening, Clémence.'

'Good evening, Monsieur Felix.'

The drawing-room was fairly big, rather dimly lighted, with a great deal of dark upholstery, and in the next room, visible through a wide glass partition, the furniture had been pushed against the wall so as to leave the floor free for dancing.

With a protective air Jubert led me up to an old white-haired lady sitting by the fireside.

'May I introduce my friend Maigret, about whom I had the honour of telling you, and who was most anxious to pay you his respects in person.'

No doubt he had been rehearsing his sentence all the way there, and was watching to see if I was making a proper bow, did not seem too ill at ease, and in short was doing him credit.

The old lady was charming, tiny, with delicate features and a lively expression, but I was disconcerted when she said to me with a smile:

'Why don't you belong to the Highways and Bridges? I'm sure Anselme will be sorry.'

Her name was Géraldine. Anselme, her husband, was sitting in another armchair, so still that you'd have thought he had been carried in bodily and set down there to be displayed like a waxwork figure. He was very old. I learned later that he was well over eighty and Géraldine just that age.

Somebody was playing the piano softly, a podgy youth in a tight coat, while a girl in a pale blue dress turned the pages for him. I could only see her from the back. When I was introduced to her I dared not look her in the face, so embarrassed did I feel at being there, not knowing what to say or where to stand.

Dancing had not yet begun. On a small table there stood a tray of *petits fours*, and a little later, as Jubert had left me to my fate, I went up to it. I still don't know why, certainly not out of greed, for I wasn't hungry and I have never liked *petits fours*, probably to keep myself in countenance.

I took one mechanically. Then a second. Somebody said:

'Hush!'

And a second girl, this time one in a pink dress, with a slight squint, began to sing, standing beside the piano, on which she leaned with one hand, while waving a fan with the other.

I kept on eating. I was not conscious of it. I was still less conscious that the old lady was watching me with stupefaction, than that others, noticing my performance, couldn't take their eyes off me.

One of the young men made some remark to his neighbour and once again somebody said: 'Hush!'

You could count the girls by the light-coloured patches they made against the men's black coats. There were four of them. Jubert apparently was trying to attract my attention without success, in great distress at seeing me pick up *petits fours* one by one and eat them conscientiously. He later admitted that he had felt sorry for me, being convinced I had had no dinner.

Others must have thought the same thing. The song ended. The girl in pink bowed, and everybody clapped; and then I noticed that I was the centre of all attention as I stood there beside the little table, my mouth full and a biscuit in my hand.

I was about to disappear without apologies, to beat a retreat, to run away, literally, from the room and the lively crowd that was so utterly foreign to me.

Just then, in a shadowy corner, I caught sight of a face, the face of the girl in blue, and on that face a gentle, reassuring, almost friendly expression. It looked as if she had understood me and was encouraging me.

The maid came in with refreshments, and after having eaten so much at the wrong time I dared not take a glass when it was offered me.

'Louise, won't you pass round the *petits fours?*'

That was how I learned that the girl in blue was called Louise and that she was the niece of M. and Mme Léonard.

She waited on everybody before coming up to me, and then, pointing to some cake or other on which there was a small preserved fruit, she said to me with an air of complicity:

'They've left the nicest. Just taste those.'

The only answer I could find was:

'Really?'

Those were the first words that passed between Madame Maigret and myself.

Presently, when she reads what I've been writing, I know she'll shrug her shoulders, murmuring:

'What's the good of telling all that?'

Actually, she's delighted with Simenon's picture of her, the picture of a good housewife, always busy cooking and polishing, always fussing over her great baby of a husband. It was even on account of that picture, I suspect, that she was the first to become his staunch friend, to the extent of considering him as one of the family and of defending him when I haven't dreamed of attacking him.

Now this portrait, like all portraits, is far from being strictly accurate. When I met her on that memorable evening she was a rather plump young girl with a very fresh face and a sparkle in her eyes that was lacking in her friends'.

What would have happened if I hadn't eaten those cakes? It's quite possible that she would never have noticed me among the dozen or so young men there who all, except my friend Jubert, belonged to Highways and Bridges.

Those three words, Highways and Bridges, have retained an almost comic significance for us, and if either of us utters them it sets us both smiling; if we hear the words spoken somewhere we cannot, even now, help casting a knowing glance at one another.

To do things properly I ought here to insert the whole genealogy of the Schöllers, Kurts and Léonards, which I found most confusing for a long time, and which represents my wife's side of the family.

If you go anywhere in Alsace between Strasburg and Mulhouse you'll probably hear speak of them. I think it was a Kurt from Scharrachbergheim who first, under Napoleon, founded the almost dynastic tradition of Highways and Bridges. Apparently he was quite famous in his day, and he married into the Schöller family, who were in the same Government service.

The Léonards in their turn entered the family, and since then, from father to son, from brother to brother-in-law or cousin, practically everybody has belonged to the same organization, to such an extent that it was considered a comedown for a Kurt to become one of the biggest brewers in Colmar.

I only guessed at all this that first evening, thanks to the few hints that Jubert had given me.

And when we went out into the driving rain, not bothering this time to take a cab, which, in any case, we'd have had difficulty in finding in that district, I had almost begun to feel regretfully that I'd chosen the wrong career myself.

'What d'you think of that?'

'Of what?'

'Of what Louise did! I'm not going to scold you. But it was a very awkward situation. Did you see how tactfully she put you at your ease, without showing it? She's an amazing girl. Alice Perret may be more brilliant, but . . .'

I didn't know who Alice Perret was. The only person who had made any impression on me that whole evening was the girl in pale blue, who, between dances, had come to chat with me.

'Alice is the one who sang. I think she's going to get engaged to the boy who came with her, Louis, whose parents are very rich.'

We parted very late that night. At every fresh downpour we went into some bistro that was still open, to take shelter and drink a cup of coffee. Felix would not let me go, talking unceasingly about Louise, trying to make me admit that she was the ideal girl.

'I know I don't stand much chance. It's because her parents want to find her a husband in Highways and Bridges that they've sent her to stay with her uncle Léonard. You see, there are no more available at Colmar or at Mulhouse, or else they're in the family already. She's been here two months now. She's to spend the whole winter in Paris.'

'Does she know?'

'What?'

'That she's supposed to marry into Highways and Bridges.'

'Of course. But she doesn't care. She's a most independent girl, far more so than you might think. You didn't have time to appreciate her. Next

Friday you must try and talk to her more. If you could dance, it would make things easier. Why don't you take two or three lessons in the meantime?'

I took no dancing lessons. Which was just as well. For Louise, contrary to the worthy Jubert's belief, disliked nothing so much as gliding round in the arms of a dancing partner.

A fortnight later there occurred a trivial incident which, at the time, seemed of great moment to me—and which perhaps was so, but in a different way.

The young engineers who used to visit the Léonards were an exclusive clique and affected the use of words which had no meaning for anyone outside their own set.

Did I detest them? Most likely. And I objected to their insistent habit of calling me 'the Police Inspector'. It had become a wearisome game.

'Hi, Inspector . . .' they would call to me from one end of the drawing-room to the other.

Now, that particular evening, while Jubert and Louise were chatting in one corner, close to a green plant which I can still picture, a young fellow in glasses went up and whispered something to them, with a laughing glance in my direction.

A few minutes later I asked my friend:

'What was he saying?'

Visibly embarrassed, he said evasively:

'Nothing.'

'Something spiteful?'

'I'll tell you when we're outside.'

The spectacled boy repeated his performance with other groups, and everybody seemed to be having a good laugh at my expense.

Everybody except Louise, who refused a good many dances that evening and spent the time talking to me.

Once outside, I questioned Felix.

'What did he say?'

'Tell me frankly first. What did you do before you became the Station Officer's secretary?'

'Well . . . I was in the police . . .'

'In uniform?'

So that was the great sensation. The spectacled fellow must have recognized me from having seen me in my policeman's outfit.

Just imagine a policeman among the gentlemen from Highways and Bridges!

'What did she say?' I asked, with a lump in my throat.

'She was wonderful. She's always wonderful. You won't believe me, but you'll see . . .'

Poor old Jubert!

'She told him that you must certainly have looked better in uniform than he would.'

Nevertheless, I kept away from the Boulevard Beaumarchais the following Friday. I avoided meeting Jubert. A fortnight later, he came himself to hunt me out.

'Well, they were asking after you on Friday.'

'Who was?'

'Madame Léonard. She asked me if you were unwell.'

'I've been very busy.'

I felt sure that if Madame Léonard had spoken of me it was because of her niece . . .

Now. then! I don't think there's any point in going into all these details. It's going to be hard enough to make sure that what I've written already doesn't get thrown into the wastepaper basket.

For nearly three months Jubert played his part without suspecting anything, and indeed without our making any effort to deceive him. It was he who used to come and fetch me at my hotel and tie my bow-tie for me on the pretext that I didn't know how to dress. It was he, again, who used to tell me when he saw me sitting by myself:

'You ought to pay some attention to Louise. You're not being polite.'

And when we left, it was always he who insisted:

'You're quite wrong to suppose that she's not interested in you. On the contrary, she's very fond of you. She's always asking me about you.'

Towards Christmas, the girl friend with the squint got engaged to the pianist, and they stopped coming to the Boulevard Beaumarchais.

I don't know if Louise's attitude was beginning to discourage the rest, if we were perhaps less discreet than we imagined. The fact remains that there were gradually fewer guests every Friday at Anselme and Géraldine's.

Jubert finally had it out with me in February, in my room. That Friday, he was not wearing evening dress, as I noticed immediately. He had that look of resigned bitterness that the Comédie Française actors wear in certain famous roles.

'I've come to tie your bow-tie, in spite of everything!' he said with a forced smile.

'You're not free tonight?'

'I'm utterly free, on the contrary, free as the air, freer than I've ever been.'

And standing before me with my white tie in his hands, and his eyes boring into mine:

'Louise has told me all.'

I was dumbfounded. For so far she'd told *me* nothing. And I had told her nothing either.

'What are you talking about?'

'About you and her.'

'But . . .'

'I put the question to her. I went to see her on purpose yesterday.'

'But what question?'

'I asked her if she would marry me.'

'And she said no?'

'She said no, that she was very fond of me, that I should always be her best friend, but that . . .'

'Did she mention me?'

'Not exactly.'

'Well then?'

'I've understood! I ought to have understood that first evening, when you ate those *petits fours* and she looked at you indulgently. When a woman looks so indulgently at a man who's behaving as you were . . .'

Poor Jubert! We lost sight of him almost immediately, just as we lost sight of all the Highways and Bridges gentlemen, apart from Uncle Léonard.

For years we never knew what had become of him. And I was getting on for fifty when one day, on the Canebière at Marseilles, I went into a chemist's shop to buy some aspirin. I hadn't read the name on the shop front. I heard an exclamation:

'Maigret!'

'Jubert!'

'What's been happening to you? Silly of me to ask, since I've known all about you from the newspapers for a long time. How is Louise?'

Then he told me about his eldest son who, by a nice irony of fate, was preparing for the Highways and Bridges examination.

With Jubert missing from the Boulevard Beaumarchais, the Friday soirées became even more sparsely attended, and often, now, there was nobody to play the piano. On such occasions Louise would play and I would turn over for her, while one or two couples danced in the dining-room, which had now grown too big.

I don't think I asked Louise if she was willing to marry me. Most of the time we talked about my career, about the police, about a detective's job.

I told her how much I should earn when I was at last appointed to Headquarters, adding that this would take at least three years and that until then my salary would scarcely be adequate to set up house with properly.

I told her, too, about the two or three interviews I had had with Xavier Guichard, who was already our Big Chief, who had not forgotten my father and had more or less taken me under his wing.

'I don't know if you like Paris. For, you see, I shall have to spend all my life in Paris.'

'You can live there as quietly as in the provinces, can't you?'

Finally, one Friday, I found no guests there, only Géraldine who came to open the door to me herself, in her black silk dress, and who said to me in a rather solemn voice:

'Come in!'

Louise was not in the drawing-room. There were no trays of cakes and no refreshments. Spring had come, and there was no fire burning in the hearth. I felt I had nothing to cling on to, and I kept my hat in my hand, ill at ease in my dress suit and patent leather pumps.

'Tell me, young man, what are your intentions?'

That was probably one of the most painful moments in my life. The voice sounded to me hard and accusing. I dared not raise my eyes, and I could see nothing but the edge of a black dress against the flower-patterned carpet, with the tip of a very pointed shoe showing. My ears turned scarlet.

'I swear . . .' I stammered.

'I'm not asking you to swear, I'm asking you if you intend to marry her.'

I looked at her at last and I don't think I have ever seen an old woman's face expressing so much affectionate mischief.

'But of course!'

Apparently—I've been told so often enough since—I jumped up like a jack-in-the-box and repeated, still louder:

'Of course!'

And I almost shouted a third time:

'Why, of course!'

She did not even raise her voice to call:

'Louise!'

And Louise, who was standing behind a half-open door, came in awkwardly, blushing as much as myself.

'What did I tell you?' said her aunt.

'Why?' I broke in. 'Didn't she believe it?'

'I wasn't sure. It was auntie . . .'

Let's skip the next scene, for I'm sure my wife would censor it.

Old Léonard, for his part showed much less enthusiasm, I must admit, and he never forgave me for not belonging to Highways and Bridges. He was very old, almost a centenarian, and riveted to his armchair by his infirmities; he would look at me and shake his head, as if something had gone badly wrong with the way of the world.

'You'll have to take leave to visit Colmar. What about the Easter holidays?'

Old Géraldine wrote herself to Louise's parents, a series of letters—to prepare them for the shock, as she said—breaking the news to them.

At Easter I was allowed barely forty-eight hours' leave. I spent most of it in trains, which were less rapid then than today.

I was given a perfectly proper reception, without rapture.

'The best way to find out if both of you are serious is to keep apart from one another for some time. Louise will spend the summer here. In the autumn you can come back to see us.'

'May I write to her?'

'Within reason. Once a week, for instance.'

It seems funny today. It was not at all funny at the time.

I had promised myself, without a trace of secret spite, to choose Jubert as best man. When I went to try and find him at the chemist's in the Boulevard Saint-Michel he had left, and nobody knew what had become of him.

I spent part of the summer hunting for a flat and I found the one in the Boulevard Richard-Lenoir.

'Until we find something better, you understand? When I'm promoted Inspector . . .'

Chapter Five

Dealing somewhat haphazardly with hobnailed socks,
apaches, *prostitutes, radiators, pavements and*
railway stations

A few years ago some of us talked of founding a sort of club, more likely a monthly dinner, which was to be called 'The Hobnailed Socks Club'. We got together for a drink, in any case, at the Brasserie Dauphine. We argued about who should and who shouldn't be admitted. And we wondered quite seriously whether the chaps from the other branch, I mean from the Rue des Saussaies, should be considered eligible.

Then, as was only to be expected, things got no further. At that time there were still at least four of us, among the Inspectors in the Detective Force, who were rather proud of the nickname 'hobnailed socks' formerly given us by satirical song-writers, and which certain young detectives fresh from college sometimes used amongst themselves when referring to those of their seniors who had risen from the ranks.

In the old days, indeed, it took a good many years to win one's stripes, and exams were not enough. A sergeant, before hoping for promotion, had to have worn out his shoe-soles in practically every branch of the Force.

It is not easy to convey the meaning of this with any sort of precision to the younger generation.

'Hobnailed shoes' and 'big moustaches' were the terms that sprang naturally to people's lips when they spoke of the police.

And in fact, for years, I wore hobnailed shoes myself. Not from preference. Not, as caricaturists seemed to imply, because we thought such footwear was the height of elegance and comfort, but for more down-to-earth reasons.

Two reasons, to be exact. The first, that our salary barely enabled us to make ends meet. I often hear people talk of the gay, carefree life at the beginning of this century. Young people refer enviously to the prices current at that time, cigars at two sous, dinner with wine and coffee for twenty sous.

What people forget is that at the outset of his career a public servant earned somewhat under a hundred francs a month.

When I was serving in the Public Highways Squad I would cover during my day, which was often a thirteen or fourteen hour day, miles and miles of pavement in all weathers.

So that one of the first problems of our married life was the problem of getting my shoes soled. At the end of each month, when I brought back my pay-packet to my wife, she would divide its contents into a number of small piles.

'For the butcher . . . For rent . . . For gas . . .'

There was hardly anything left to put in the late pile of small silver.

'For your shoes.'

Our dream was always to buy new ones, but for a long time it was only a dream. Often I went for weeks without confessing to her that my soles, between the hobnails, absorbed the gutter water greedily.

If I mention this here it is not out of bitterness but, on the contrary, quite lightheartedly, and I think it is necessary to give an idea of a police officer's life.

There were no such things as taxis, and even if the streets had been crowded with them they'd have been beyond our reach, as were the cabs which we used only in very special circumstances.

In any case, in the Public Highways Squad, our duty was to keep walking along the pavements, mingling with the crowd from morning till night and from night until morning.

Why, when I think of those days, do I chiefly remember the rain? As if it had rained unceasingly for years, as if the seasons had been different then. Of course, it is because the rain added a number of additional ordeals to one's task. Not only did your socks become soaked. The shoulders of your coat gradually turned into cold compresses, your hat became a waterspout, and your hands, thrust into your coat pockets, grew blue with cold.

The roads were less well lighted than they are today. A certain number of them in the outskirts were unpaved. At night the windows showed as yellowish squares against the blackness, for most of the houses were still lighted with oil lamps or even, more wretchedly still, with candles.

And then there were the *apaches*.

All round the fortifications, in those days, their knives would come into play, and not always for gain, for the sake of the rich man's wallet or watch.

What they wanted chiefly was to prove to themselves that they were men, tough guys, and to win the admiration of the little tarts in black pleated skirts and huge chignons who paced the pavements under the gas jets.

We were unarmed. Contrary to the general belief, a policeman in plain clothes has not the right to carry a revolver in his pocket and if, in certain cases, a man takes one, it's against the regulations and entirely on his own responsibility.

Junior officers could not consider themselves entitled to do so. There were a certain number of streets, in the neighbourhood of La Villette, Ménilmontant and the Porte d'Italie, where one ventured reluctantly and sometimes trembled at the sound of one's own footsteps.

For a long time the telephone remained a legendary luxury beyond the scope of our budgets. When I was delayed several hours there was no question of ringing up my wife to warn her, so that she used to spend lonely evenings in our gas-lit dining-room, listening for noises on the stairway and warming up the same dish four or five times over.

As for the moustaches with which we were caricatured, we really wore them. A man without a moustache looked like a flunkey.

Mine was longish, reddish brown, somewhat darker than my father's, with pointed ends. Later it dwindled to a toothbrush and then disappeared completely.

It is a fact, moreover, that most police inspectors wore huge jet-black moustaches like those in their caricatures. This is because, for some mysterious reason, for quite a long time, the profession attracted chiefly natives of the Massif Central.

There are few streets in Paris along which I have not trudged, watchful-eyed, and I learned to know all the rank and file of the pavements, from beggars, barrel-organ players and flower-girls to card-sharpers and pickpockets, including prostitutes and the drunken old women who spend most of their nights at the police station.

I 'covered' the Halles at night, the Place Maubert, the quays and the reaches beneath the quays.

I covered crowded gatherings too, the biggest job of all, at the Foire du Trône and the Foire de Neuilly, at Longchamps races and patriotic demonstrations, at military parades, visits from foreign royalties, carriage processions, travelling circuses and second-hand markets.

After a few months, a few years at this job one's head is full of a varied array of figures and faces that remain indelibly engraved on one's memory.

I should like to try—and it's not easy—to give a more or less accurate idea of our relations with these people, including those whom we periodically had to take off to the lock-up.

Needless to say, the picturesque aspect soon ceases to exist for us. Inevitably, we come to scan the streets of Paris with a professional eye, which fastens on certain familiar details or notices some unusual circumstances and draws the necessary conclusion from it.

When I consider this subject, the thing that strikes me most is the bond that is formed between the policeman and the quarry he has to track down. Above all, except in a few exceptional cases, the policeman is entirely devoid of hatred or even ill-will.

Devoid of pity, too, in the usual sense of the word.

Our relations, so to speak, are strictly professional.

We have seen too much, as you can well imagine, to be shocked any longer by certain forms of wretchedness or depravity. So that the latter does not arouse our indignation, nor does the former cause us that distress felt by the inexperienced spectator.

There is something between us, which Simenon has tried to convey without success, and that is, paradoxical as it may seem, a kind of family feeling.

Don't misunderstand me. We are on different sides of the barricade, of course. But we also, to some extent, share the same hardships.

The prostitute on the Boulevard de Clichy and the policeman who is watching her both have bad shoes and both have aching feet from trudging along miles of asphalt. They have to endure the same rain, the same icy wind. Evening and night wear the same hue for both of them, and they see with almost identical eyes the seamy side of the crowd that streams past them.

The same is true of a fair where a pickpocket is threading his way through a similar crowd. For him a fair, or indeed any gathering of some few hundreds of people, means not fun, roundabouts, Big Tops or gingerbread, but merely a certain number of purses in unwary pockets.

For the policeman too. And each of them can recognize at a glance the self-satisfied country visitor who will be the ideal victim.

How many times have I spent hours following a certain pickpocket of my acquaintance, such as the one we called the Artful Dodger! He knew that I was on his heels, watching his slightest movements. He knew that I knew. While I knew that he knew that I was there.

His job was to get hold of a wallet or a watch in spite of it all, and my job was to stop him or catch him in the act.

Well, it sometimes happened that the Dodger would turn round and smile at me. I would smile back. He even spoke to me sometimes, with a sigh:

'It's going to be hard!'

I was well aware that he was on his beam-ends and that he wouldn't eat that night unless he was successful.

He was equally well aware that I earned a hundred francs a month, that I had holes in my shoes and that my wife was waiting impatiently for me at home.

Ten times at least I picked him up, quite kindly, telling him:

'You've had it!'

And he was almost as relieved as I was. It meant that he'd get something to eat at the Police Station and somewhere to sleep. Some of them know the lock-up so well that they ask:

'Who's on duty tonight?'

Because some of us let them smoke and others don't.

Then, for a year and a half, the pavements seemed to me an ideal beat, for my next job was in the big stores.

Instead of rain and cold, sunshine and dust, I spent my days in an overheated atmosphere reeking of tweed and unbleached calico, linoleum and mercerized cotton.

In those days there were radiators at intervals in the gangways between counters, which sent up puffs of dry, scorching air. This was fine when you arrived soaking wet. You took up your position above a radiator, and immediately you gave out a cloud of steam.

After a few hours, you chose rather to hang about near the doors which, each time they opened, let in a little oxygen.

The important thing was to look natural. To look like a customer! Which is so easy, isn't it, when the whole floor is full of nothing but corsets, lingerie or reels of silk?

'May I ask you to come along with me quietly?'

Some women used to understand immediately and followed us without a word to the manager's office. Others got on their high horse, protested shrilly or had hysterics.

And yet here, too, we had to deal with a regular clientèle. Whether at the Bon Marché, the Louvre or the Printemps, certain familiar figures were always to be found, usually middle-aged women, who stowed away incredible quantities of various goods in a pocket concealed between their dress and their petticoat.

A year and a half, in retrospect, seems very little, but at the time each hour was as long drawn out as an hour spent in the dentist's waiting-room.

'Shall you be at the Galeries this afternoon?' my wife would ask me sometimes. 'I've got a few little things to buy there.'

We never spoke to one another. We pretended not to recognize each other. It was delightful. I was happy to watch her moving proudly from one counter to the next, giving me a discreet wink from time to time.

I don't believe that she ever asked herself either whether she might have married anyone other than a police inspector. She knew the names of all my colleagues, spoke familiarly about those whom she had never seen, of their fads, of their success or their failures.

It took me years to bring myself, one Sunday morning when I was on duty, to take her into the famous house in the Quai des Orfèvres, and she showed no sign of amazement. She walked about as if she were at home, looking for all the details which she knew so well from hearsay.

Her only reaction was:

'It's less dirty than I'd expected.'

'Why should it be dirty?'

'Places where men live by themselves are never quite so clean. And they have a certain smell.'

I did not ask her to the Police Station, where she'd have got her fill of smells.

'Who sits here on the left?'

'Torrence.'

'The big fat one? I might have guessed it. He's like a child. He still plays at carving his initials on his desk.

'And what about old Lagrume, the man who walks so much?'

Since I've talked about shoes I may as well tell the story that distressed my wife.

Lagrume, Old Lagrume as we called him, was senior to all of us, although he had never risen above the rank of sergeant. He was a tall, melancholy fellow. In summer he suffered from hay-fever and, as soon as the weather turned cold, his chronic bronchitis gave him a hollow cough that sounded from one end of Headquarters to the other.

Fortunately he was not often there. He had been rash enough to say one day, referring to his cough:

'The doctor recommends me to keep in the open-air.'

After that, he got his fill of open-air. He had long legs and huge feet, and he was put in charge of the most unlikely investigations through the length and breadth of Paris, the sort that force you to travel through the town in all directions day after day, without even the hope of getting any results.

'Just leave it to Lagrume!'

Everybody knew what was involved, except the old fellow himself, who gravely made a few notes on his pad, tucked his rolled umbrella under his arm and went off, with a brief nod to all present.

I wonder now whether he was not perfectly well aware of the part he was playing. He was one of the meek. For years and years he had had a sick wife waiting for him to do the housework in their suburban home. And when his daughter married, I believe it was he who got up at night to look after the baby:

'Lagrume, you still smell of dirty nappies!'

An old woman had been murdered in the Rue Caulaincourt. It was a commonplace crime that made no sensation in the Press, for the victim was an unimportant small *rentière* with no connections.

Such cases are always the most difficult. I myself, being confined to the big stores—and particularly busy as Christmas drew near—was not involved in it, but, like everybody else at our place, I knew the details of the investigation.

The crime had been committed with a kitchen knife, which had been left on the spot. This knife provided the only evidence. It was quite an ordinary knife, such as are sold in ironmongers' shops, chain stores or the smallest local shops, and the manufacturer, who had been contacted, claimed to have sold tens of thousands within the area of Paris.

The knife was a new one. It had obviously been bought on purpose. It still bore the price written on the handle in indelible pencil.

This was the detail which offered a vague hope of discovering the tradesman who had sold it.

'Lagrume! You deal with that knife.'

He wrapped it up in a bit of newspaper, put it in his pocket and set off.

He set off for a journey through Paris which was to last for nine weeks.

Every morning he appeared punctually at the office, to which he would return in the evening to shut away the knife in a drawer. Every morning he was to be seen putting the weapon in his pocket, seizing his umbrella and setting out with the same nod to all present.

I learned the number of shops—the story has become a legend—which might possibly have sold a knife of this sort. Without going beyond the fortifications, and confining oneself to the twenty-arrondissements of Paris, the number makes your head reel.

There was no question of using any means of transport. It meant going from street to street, almost from door to door. Lagrume had in his pocket a map of Paris on which, hour after hour, he crossed out a certain number of streets.

I believe that in the end his chiefs had even forgotten what task he had been set.

'Is Lagrume available?'

Somebody would reply that he was out on a job, and then nobody bothered any more about him. It was shortly before Christmas, as I have said. It was a wet, cold winter, the pavements were slimy, and yet Lagrume went to and fro from morning till night, with his bronchitis and his hollow cough, unwearying, never asking what was the point of it all.

During the ninth week, well into the New Year, when it was freezing hard, he turned up at three o'clock in the afternoon, as calm and mournful as ever, without the slightest gleam of joy or relief in his eyes.

'Is the Chief there?'

'You've found it?'

'I've found it.'

Not in an ironmonger's, nor a cheap store, nor a household goods shop. He had gone through all those unavailingly.

The knife had been sold by a stationer in the Boulevard Rochechouart. The shopkeeper had recognized his handwriting, and remembered a young man in a green scarf buying the weapon from him more than two months previously.

He gave a fairly detailed description of him, and the young man was arrested and executed the following year.

As for Lagrume, he died in the street, not from his bronchitis but from a heart attack.

Before discussing stations, and in particular that Gare du Nord with which I always feel I have an old score to settle, I must deal briefly with a subject of which I am not very fond.

I have often been asked, with reference to my early days and my various jobs:

'Have you been in the Vice Squad too?'

It isn't known by that name today. It is modestly called the 'Social Squad'.

Well, I've belonged to that, like most of my colleagues. For a very short period. Barely a few months.

And if I realize now that it was necessary, my recollections of that period are nevertheless confused and somewhat uneasy.

I mentioned the familiarity that grows up naturally between policemen and those on whom it is their job to keep watch.

By force of circumstances, it exists in that branch as much as in the others. Even more so. Indeed, the clientèle of each detective, so to speak, consists of a relatively restricted number of women who are almost always found at the same spots, at the door of the same hotel or under the same street lamp, or, for the grade above, at the terrace of the same brasseries.

I was not then as stalwart as I have grown with the passing years, and apparently I looked younger than my age.

Remember the *petits fours* incident at the Boulevard Beaumarchais and you will understand that in certain respects I was somewhat timid.

Most of the officers in the Vice Squad were on familiar terms with the women, whose names or nicknames they knew, and it was a tradition when, during the course of a raid, they packed them into the Black Maria, to vie with one another in coarseness of speech, to fling the filthiest abuse at one another with a laugh.

Another habit these ladies had acquired was to pick up their skirts and show their behinds in a gesture which they considered, no doubt, the last word in insults, and which they accompanied with a torrent of defiance.

I must have blushed to begin with, for I still blushed easily. My embarrassment did not pass unnoticed, for the least one can say of these women is that they have a certain knowledge of men.

I promptly became, not exactly their *bête noire*, but their butt.

At the Quai des Orfèvres nobody ever called me by my first name, and I'm convinced that many of my colleagues did not know it . . . I shouldn't have chosen it if I'd been asked my opinion. I'm not ashamed of it either.

Could it have been some sly revenge on the part of some detective who was in the know?

I was specially in charge of the Sébastopol district which, particularly in the Halles area, was frequented at that time by the lowest class of women, particularly by a number of very old prostitutes who had taken refuge there.

It was here, too, that young servant girls newly arrived from Brittany or elsewhere served their apprenticeship, so that one had the two extremes: kids of sixteen, over whom the pimps quarrelled, and ancient harpies who were very well able to defend themselves.

One day the catchphrase started—for it quickly became a catchphrase. I was walking past one of these old women, stationed at the door of a filthy hotel, when I heard her call out to me, showing all her rotten teeth in a smile:

'Good evening, Jules!'

I thought she'd used the name at random, but a little further on I was greeted by the same words.

'Hullo, Jules!'

After which, when there was a group of them together, they would burst out laughing, with a flood of unrepeatable comments.

I know what some officers would have done in my place. They'd have needed no further inducement to pick up a few of these women and lock them up at Saint-Lazare to think things over.

The example would have served its purpose, and I should probably have been treated with a certain respect.

I didn't do it. Not necessarily from any sense of justice. Nor out of pity.

Probably because this was a game I didn't want to play. I chose rather to pretend I hadn't heard. I hoped they would tire of it. But such women are like children who have never had enough of any joke.

They made up a song about Jules which they began to sing or yell as soon as I appeared. Others would say to me, as I checked their cards:

'Don't be mean, Jules! You're so sweet!'

Poor Louise! Her great dread, during this period, was not that I might yield to some temptation, but that I might bring home an unpleasant disease. Once I caught fleas. When I got home she would make me undress and take a bath, while she went to brush my clothes on the landing or at the open window.

'You must have touched plenty today! Brush your nails well!'

Wasn't there some story that you could catch syphilis merely by drinking out of a glass?

It was not a pleasant experience, but I learned what I had to learn. After all, I had chosen my own career.

For nothing on earth would I have asked to be transferred. My chiefs did what was necessary of their own accord, more for the sake of results, I imagine, than out of consideration for myself.

I was put on stations. More precisely, I was posted to that gloomy, sinister building known as the Gare du Nord.

It had the advantage, like the big stores, that one was sheltered from the rain. Not from the cold nor from the wind, for nowhere in the world, probably, are there so many draughts as in the hall of a station, the hall of the Gare du Nord, and for months I had as many colds as old Lagrume.

Please don't imagine that I'm grumbling, or deliberately dwelling on the seamy side so as to get my own back.

I was perfectly happy. I was happy trudging along the streets and I was equally happy keeping an eye on so-called kleptomaniacs in the big stores. I felt that I was getting on a little each time, learning a job whose complexity was more apparent to me every day.

When I see the Gare de l'Est, for instance, I can never help feeling depressed, because it reminds me of mobilization. The Gare de Lyon, on the other hand, like the Gare Montparnasse, suggests holidays.

But the Gare du Nord, the coldest, the busiest of them all, brings to my mind a harsh and bitter struggle for one's daily bread. Is it because it leads towards mining and industrial regions?

In the morning, the first night trains, coming from Belgium and Germany, generally contain a certain number of smugglers, of illicit traders with faces as hard as the daylight seen through the glazed windows of the station.

It's not always a matter of small-scale fraud. There are the professionals in various international rackets, with their agents, their decoys, their right-hand men, people who play for high stakes and are ready to defend themselves by any method.

No sooner has this crowd dispersed than it's the turn of the suburban trains which come not from pleasant villages like those in the West or South, but from black, unhealthy built-up areas.

In the opposite direction, it's towards Belgium, the nearest frontier, that fugitives for the most varied reasons try to escape.

Hundreds of people are waiting there in the grey atmosphere redolent of smoke and sweat, moving restlessly, hurrying from the booking office to the waiting-rooms, examining the boards that announce arrivals and departures, eating or drinking, surrounded by children, dogs and suitcases, and almost always they are people who have not slept enough, whose nerves are on edge from their dread of being late, sometimes merely from their dread of the morrow which they are going elsewhere to seek.

I have spent hours, every day, watching them, looking amongst all those faces for some more inscrutable face with a more fixed stare, the face of a man or woman staking their last chance.

The train is there, about to leave in a few minutes. He's only got to go another hundred yards and hold out the ticket he's clutching. The minute hand jerks forward on the enormous yellowish face of the clock.

Double or quits! It means freedom or jail. Or worse.

I am there, with a photograph or a description in my wallet, sometimes merely the technical description of an ear.

It may happen that we catch sight of one another simultaneously, that our eyes meet. Almost invariably the man understands at once.

What follows will depend on his character, on the risk he's running, on his nerves, even on some tiny material detail, a door that's open or shut, a trunk that may happen to be lying between us.

Sometimes they try to run away, and then there's a desperate race through groups of people who protest or try to get out of the way, a race among stationary coaches, over railway lines and points.

I have come across two men, one of them quite young, who, at three months' distance, behaved in exactly the same way.

Each of them thrust his hand into his pocket as if to take out a cigarette. And next minute, in the thick of the crowd, with his eyes fixed on me, each of them shot himself through the head.

These men bore me no ill-will, nor did I bear them any.

We were each of us doing his job.

They had lost the game, and there was an end to it, so they were quitting.

I had lost it too, for my duty was to bring them into the courts alive.

I have watched thousands of trains leaving. I have watched thousands arriving too, each time with the same dense crowd, the long string of people hurrying towards something or other.

It's become a habit with me, as with my colleagues. Even if I'm not on duty, if by some miracle I'm going on holiday with my wife, my glance slips from one face to the next, and seldom fails to fall on somebody who's afraid, however he may try to conceal it.

'Aren't you coming? What's the matter?'

Until we're settled in our carriage, or rather until the train has left, my wife is never sure that we're really going to get our holiday.

'What are you bothering about? You're not on duty!'

There have been times when I've followed her with a sigh, turning round for a last look at some mysterious face vanishing in the crowd. Always reluctantly.

And I don't think it's only from professional conscientiousness, nor from love of justice.

I repeat, it's a game that's being played, a game that has no end. Once you've begun it, it's difficult, if not impossible, to give it up.

The proof is that those of us who eventually retire, often against their will, almost always end by setting up a private detective agency.

Moreover that's only a last resort, and I don't know one detective who, after grumbling for thirty years about the miseries of a policeman's life, isn't ready to take up work again, even unpaid.

I have sinister memories of the Gare du Nord. I don't know why, I always picture it full of thick, damp early-morning fog, with its drowsy crowd flocking towards the lines or towards the Rue Maubeuge.

The specimens of humanity I have met there have been some of the most desperate, and certain arrests that I have made there left me with a feeling of remorse rather than of any professional satisfaction.

If I had the choice, none the less, I would rather go on duty again tomorrow at the platform barrier than set off from some more sumptuous station for a sunny corner of the Côte d'Azur.

Chapter Six

One staircase after another!

From time to time, almost always on the occasion of some political upheaval, troubles break out in the streets which are no longer merely the manifestation of popular discontent. It would seem that at a certain moment a breach is formed, invisible sluices are opened, and there suddenly appear in the wealthier districts creatures whose very existence is generally unknown there, who seem to have emerged from some haunt of beggars and whom the inhabitants watch from their windows as they might watch ruffians and cutthroats suddenly appearing from the depths of the Middle Ages.

What surprised me most, when this phenomenon occurred with notable violence after the riots on February 6th, was the astonishment expressed next day by most of the newspapers.

This invasion of the heart of Paris, for a few hours, not by demonstrators but by haggard individuals who spread as much terror around them as a pack of wolves, suddenly alarmed people who, by their profession, are almost as closely acquainted as ourselves with the underworld of a metropolis.

Paris was really frightened that time. Then, the very next day, once order was restored, Paris forgot that this rabble had not been destroyed, that it had simply gone to earth.

Of course, it's up to the police to keep it there.

Is it generally known that there is one squad solely concerned with the two to three hundred thousand North Africans, Portuguese and Algerians who live in the outskirts of the 20th arrondissement, who camp out there, one might rather say, scarcely knowing our language or not knowing it at all, obeying other laws, other reflexes than our own?

We have, at Headquarters, maps on which are marked little islands, as it were, in coloured pencil, the Jews of the Rue des Rosiers, the Italians of the Hôtel de Ville district, the Russians of Les Ternes and Denfert-Rochereau . . .

Many of them ask nothing better than to be assimilated, and our difficulties don't come from them, but there are some who, whether as a group or as individuals, keep deliberately on the fringe and lead their mysterious lives, unnoticed by the crowd around them.

Highly respectable people, whose petty frauds and meannesses are carefully camouflaged, are almost always the ones who ask me, with that slight quiver of the lips that I know so well:

'Aren't you sometimes disgusted?'

They aren't referring to any particular thing, but to the whole set of people we have to deal with. What they would like is to have us disclose really nasty secrets to them, unheard-of vices, a lot of filth at which they could express their horror while secretly relishing it.

Such people often use the term 'the dregs of society'.

'What dreadful things you must see among the dregs of society!'

I prefer not to answer them. I look at them in a certain way, without any expression on my face, and they must understand my meaning, for they generally look uncomfortable and don't ask any more.

I learned a great deal on the public highway. I learned much, too, on fairgrounds and in big stores, wherever crowds were gathered.

I have spoken of my experiences at the Gare du Nord.

But it was while I was in the Hotels Squad that I learned most about men, particularly those men who frighten the inhabitants of wealthy districts when the sluices happen to open.

Hobnailed shoes were no longer needed here, for one's job was not to cover miles of pavement but to trudge in a vertical direction, so to speak.

Every day I collected the index cards of some tens of hundreds of hotels, usually furnished apartment houses, where there was seldom a lift and one had to climb six or seven floors up a stifling staircase, amid a sickeningly acrid smell of poverty-stricken humanity.

Big hotels with revolving doors flanked by liveried servants have their own dramas too, their secrets into which the police pry daily.

But it's chiefly in thousands of hotels with unfamiliar names, inconspicuous from outside, that a certain floating population goes to earth, a population which is difficult to get hold of elsewhere and seldom law-abiding. We went in couples. Sometimes, in dangerous districts, we went in larger groups. We would choose the time at which most people were in bed, shortly after midnight.

Then a sort of nightmare would begin, with certain details always recurring, the night watchman, the landlord or his wife lying in bed behind the wicket and waking up unwillingly to try and forestall my accusation.

'You know quite well we've never had any trouble here . . .'

In the old days the names used to be written in registers. Later, when identity cards became compulsory, there were forms to be filled in.

One of us would stay below. The other went upstairs. Sometimes we were spotted in spite of all our precautions, and from the ground floor we would hear the house beginning to stir like a beehive, busy comings and goings in the rooms, furtive footsteps on the stairs.

Occasionally we would find a room empty, the bed still warm, and at the top of the house the skylight that gave on to the roofs would be open.

Usually we managed to reach the first floor without rousing the lodgers, and we would knock at the first door and be answered by grunts, by questions almost invariably in a foreign language.

'Police!'

That's a word they all understand. And then, in their underclothes or stark naked, men, women and children scurry about in the dim light, in the stench, unfastening unbelievable cases to hunt for a passport hidden under their belongings.

There's no describing the anxious look in those eyes, those sleep-walker's movements, and that particular brand of humility which is found only in the uprooted. A proud humility, shall I call it?

They did not hate us. We were the masters. We had—or they believed we had—the most terrible of all powers: that of sending them back across the frontier.

For some of them the fact of being here represented years of scheming or waiting. They had reached the promised land. They owned papers, real or forged.

And while they held them out to us, fearful lest we should thrust them in our pockets, they tried instinctively to win us with a smile, found a few words of French to stammer:

'Please, Mister Officer . . .'

The women rarely bothered about decency, and sometimes you would see a hesitant look in their eyes, and they would make a vague gesture towards the tumbled bed. Weren't we tempted? wouldn't we like to?

And yet all these people had their pride, a special pride that I cannot describe. The pride of wild animals?

Indeed, it was rather like caged beasts that they watched us pass, without knowing whether we were going to strike them or stroke them.

Sometimes you'd see one of them brandishing his papers, panic-stricken, and he'd start talking volubly in his own language, gesticulating, calling the rest to his aid, striving to make us believe that he was an honest man, that appearances were misleading, that . . .

Some would start weeping and others crouched sullenly in their corner as if they were about to spring, though actually resigned.

Identity check-up. That's what the operation is called in administrative language. Those whose papers are indisputably in order are allowed to stay in their rooms, where you hear them lock the door with a sigh of relief.

The others . . .

'Come downstairs!'

When they don't understand, you have to add a gesture. And they get dressed, talking to themselves. They don't know what they ought to take, or are allowed to take with them. Occasionally, as soon as our backs are turned, they slip back to get some hidden treasure and thrust it into their pockets or under their shirts.

They all stand about on the ground floor in a small silent group, each thinking only of his own case and how he's going to defend himself.

In the Saint-Antoine district there are certain hotels where I have found up to seven or eight Poles in a single room, most of them sleeping on the floor.

Only one was inscribed on the register. Did the landlord know? Did he exact payment for the additional sleepers? It's more than likely, but it's useless to try and prove such things.

The others' papers, needless to say, were not in order. What did they do when they had to leave the shelter of the room at daybreak?

For lack of work-cards, they could not earn a regular living. But they had not died of starvation. So they must have been eating somehow.

And there were, and still are, thousands, tens of thousands in the same case.

You may find money in their pockets, or hidden on top of some cupboard, or more frequently in their shoes. Then you have to discover how they procured it, and that's the most exhausting kind of cross-examination.

Even if they understand French they pretend not to understand it. Looking you in the eyes with an expression of good will, indefatigably reasserting their innocence.

It's useless to ask the others about them. They never betray one another.

They will all tell the same story.

Now, on an average, sixty-five per cent of the crimes committed in the Paris area are due to foreigners.

Stairs, stairs and yet more stairs. Not only by night but by day, and tarts everywhere, professionals and others, some of them young and fine-looking, come, God knows why, from the depths of their own country.

I knew one of these, a Polish woman, who shared a hotel room in the Rue Saint-Antoine with five men, whom she used to send out on robberies, rewarding those who were successful in her own fashion, while the others fretted impatiently in the same room and afterwards usually fell savagely upon the exhausted winner.

Two of them were enormous powerful brutes, and she was not afraid of them, she could hold them in awe with a smile or a frown; while I was questioning them, in my own office, after some remark or other made in their own language I saw her calmly slap one of these giants in the face.

'You must see a queer lot of things!'

Well, we see men and women, all sorts of men and women in the most unbelievable situations, at every social level. We see them, we take note and we try to understand.

I don't mean understand some deep human mystery or other. That romantic idea is possibly the thing against which I protest the most earnestly, almost angrily. This is one of the reasons for this book, for these attempted corrections. Simenon has endeavoured to explain this, I admit. Nevertheless I have felt a certain embarrassment on seeing attributed to myself in his books certain smiles, certain attitudes which I have never assumed and which would have made my colleagues shrug their shoulders.

The person who has understood things best is my wife. And yet when I get back from work she never questions me with any curiosity, whatever the case with which I am concerned.

For my part, I don't deliberately take her into my confidence.

I sit down at table like any other official coming home from work. In a few words, as though for my own benefit, I may describe an encounter, an interview, or talk of the man or woman about whom I am making investigations.

If she puts a question, it's almost always a technical one.

'In which district?'

Or else:

'How old?'

Or again:

'How long has she been in France?'

For she has come to consider such details as revealing as we have ourselves.

She does not question me about sordid or pathetic side-issues.

And Heaven knows it's not for lack of feeling!

'Has his wife been to see him at the Police Station?'

'This morning.'

'Did she take the child with her?'

She takes a particular interest, for reasons on which I need not enlarge, in those who had children, and it would be a mistake to fancy that law-breakers, malefactors and criminals have none.

We had one of these in our own home, a little girl whose mother I had sent to prison for life, but we knew that the father would take her back as soon as he was restored to normal life.

She still comes to see us. She is a grown girl now, and my wife takes pride in going round the shops with her in the afternoon.

What I want to stress is that our behaviour towards those with whom we have to deal involved neither sentimentality nor hardness, neither hatred nor pity in the usual sense of the word.

Our job is to study men. We watch their behaviour. We take note of some of the facts. We try to establish others.

When, as a young man, I had to visit a disreputable lodging house from cellar to attic, exploring rooms like cells in a honeycomb, surprising people in their sleep, in their most elementary privacy, examining their papers through a magnifying glass, I could almost have foretold what would become of each of them.

For one thing, certain faces were already familiar to me, for Paris is not so big that one doesn't constantly come across the same individuals, in a given environment.

Certain cases, too recur almost identically, the same causes producing the same results.

The wretched Central European who had saved for months, if not years, to buy himself false passports from a clandestine agency in his own country, and who thought his troubles were over once he had safely crossed the frontier, will inevitably fall into our hands before six months, or twelve at most, are out.

Indeed, we could even follow him in our mind's eye from the frontier, and foretell in what district, in what restaurant, in what lodging house he will end up.

We know through whom he will try to procure the indispensable labour permit, genuine or forged; we shall merely have to go and pick him up in the queue that stretches out every morning in front of the big factories at Javel.

Why should we feel anger or resentment, when he lands up where he was bound to land up?

The same thing happens with the fresh-faced servant girl whom we see paying her first visit to a certain dance hall. Can we tell her to go back to her employers and keep away from that flashy companion of hers?

It would do no good. She'll come back. We shall meet her at other dance halls, then, one fine evening, outside the door of some hotel in the Halles or Bastille district.

Ten thousand go that way on an average, every year, ten thousand who leave their village and start off in domestic service in Paris, and who before a few months or a few weeks are out will have taken the plunge.

Is it so very different when a boy of eighteen or twenty, who has been working in a factory, begins to dress in a certain way, to adopt certain poses, to lean on the zinc counters of certain bars?

We shall see him presently in a new suit, wearing artificial silk socks and tie.

He'll end up in our hands too, looking shifty or crestfallen, after an attempted burglary or smash and grab raid, unless he has joined the car thieves' brigade.

There are certain signs you cannot mistake, and it was really these signs which we were learning to recognize when we were sent to serve in every squad in turn, to cover miles of pavement on foot, climb up stair after stair and make our way into every sort of hovel and amidst every type of crowd.

That was why the nickname 'hobnailed socks' never annoyed us, quite the reverse.

There are few of us at Headquarters who, by the time they are forty, aren't well acquainted, for instance, with all the pickpockets. We even know where to find them on such and such a day, on the occasion of such and such a ceremony or festivity.

In the same way we know, for instance, that there will shortly be a jewel robbery, because a certain specialist who has seldom been caught redhanded has begun to run short of cash. He has left his hotel in the Boulevard Haussmann for a humbler one in the République district. He hasn't paid his bill for a fortnight. The woman with whom he's living has begun to have rows with him, and has bought no new hats for a long time.

We cannot follow him step by step; there would never be enough detectives to shadow every suspect. But we have him on the end of a string. The Public Highways Squad have been warned to keep a special eye on jewellers' shops. We know his way of working. We know he'll never work any other way.

It doesn't always come off. That would be too much to hope for. But it sometimes happens that he's caught in the act. It sometimes happens after a discreet interview with his girl friend, who's been given the hint that her future would be less problematic if she provided us with information.

The papers talk a great deal about gangs settling accounts with one another in Montmartre or the area round the Rue Fontaine, because there's always something exciting for the public about revolver shots by night.

But those are just the cases that worry us least at Headquarters.

We know the rival gangs, their interests and the points at issue between them. We also know their personal hatreds and resentments.

One crime calls forth another, by repercussion. If someone shoots down Luciano in a bar in the Rue de Douai, the Corsicans will inevitably take their revenge before very long. And almost always there's one amongst them who will give us the hint.

'Something's being plotted against Flatfooted Dédé. He knows it and he won't go out without a couple of killers as bodyguard.'

The day when Dédé gets his, it's ninety per cent certain that a more or less mysterious telephone call will put us in the picture about every detail of the story.

'There's one the less!'

We do arrest the guilty men, but it really makes little difference, for those people only exterminate one another, for reasons of their own, according to a certain code which they apply strictly.

It was to this that Simenon was alluding when, during our first interview, he declared so categorically:

'Professional crimes don't interest me.'

What he did not know then, but has learnt since, is that there are very few other sorts of crime.

I'm not including crimes of passion, which are straightforward for the most part, being merely the logical issue of an acute crisis between two or more individuals.

I'm not including those brawls where a couple of drunks knife one another one Saturday or Sunday night in the slums.

Apart from such accidents, the most frequent crimes are of two sorts:

The murder of some lonely old woman by one of more hooligans, and the murder of a prostitute in some piece of waste ground.

In the first case the culprit rarely escapes. Almost always he is one of those youngsters I mentioned before, who quit factory work a few months back, and is dying to show off his toughness.

He's had his eye on some tobacconist's or haberdasher's, some small shop in a quiet back-street.

Sometimes he's bought a revolver. At other times he makes do with a hammer or spanner.

Almost invariably he knows his victim and, in at least one case out of ten, she has done him a kindness at some time or another.

He has not planned to kill. He's put a scarf over his face so as not to be recognized.

The scarf slips, or else the old woman begins to scream.

He fires. He strikes. If he fires he empties the whole barrel, which is a sign of panic. If he strikes he strikes ten or twenty blows, savagely so it seems, but really because he's crazy with terror.

Does it surprise you that when we've got him in front of us, in a state of collapse and yet still trying to swagger, we merely say to him:

'You fool!'

They almost always pay with their lives. The least they can get away with is twenty years, when they're lucky enough to interest some first-rate counsel.

As for the murderers of prostitutes, it's only by a miracle that we lay hands on them. These investigations are the longest, the most discouraging, the most sickening I know.

They usually begin with a sack being fished up by some waterman on the end of his boathook, somewhere along the Seine, and containing, almost always, a mutilated body. The head is missing, or an arm, or both legs.

Weeks go by before identification is possible. Generally the victim is one of these elderly whores who don't even take their customers to a hotel or to their room, but make do with some doorway or the shelter of a railing.

She hadn't been seen lately in her neighbourhood, one of those districts which, as soon as night falls, becomes full of mystery and silent shadows.

The women who knew her are not anxious to get into contact with us. When we question them they give only the vaguest answers.

Eventually, by dint of patience, we manage, after a fashion, to discover some of her usual clients, lonely individuals themselves, solitary men of indefinite age who are remembered merely as shadowy figures.

Was she killed for her money? It's hardly likely. She had so little! Had one of these old fellows suddenly gone crazy, or did someone come from elsewhere, from another district, one of those maniacs who at regular intervals feel a fit coming on, know exactly what they will do and with incredible lucidity take precautions of which other criminals are incapable?

No one knows how many there are of these. There are some in every capital city, and, once the deed is done, they disappear once more, for a greater or less length of time, into anonymity.

They may be respectable people, fathers of families, model employees.

Nobody knows exactly what they're like, and when by chance we catch one of them it has almost always been impossible to establish a satisfactory conviction.

We possess more or less exact statistics for crimes of every sort.

Except one.

Poisoning.

And any rough guess would inevitably err in one direction or the other.

Every three months, or six months, in Paris or in the provinces, particularly in the provinces, in some very small town or in the country, a doctor may happen by chance to examine a dead body more closely than usual and be puzzled by certain symptoms.

I say chance, for the dead man is usually one of his patients, somebody he has known to be ill for a long time. The man has died suddenly, in his bed, in the bosom of his family, who display all the traditional signs of grief.

The relations dislike the suggestion of an autopsy. The doctor only insists on one if his suspicions are strong enough.

Or else, weeks after the funeral, an anonymous letter reaches the police, providing details which at first sight seem incredible.

I stress this to show all the circumstances that must be combined before such an investigation can be held. The administrative formalities are complicated.

The commonest case is that of a farmer's wife who has been waiting for years for her husband to die in order to set up house with the farm hand, and who has lost patience.

She has come to the help of Nature, as some people crudely put it.

Sometimes, though more rarely, a man will use the same method to get rid of an ailing wife who has become a dead weight in his home.

They are found out by chance. But how many other cases are there where chance does not play its part? We don't know. We can only risk hypotheses. There are some of us at Headquarters, as there are in the Rue des Saussaies, who believe that of all crimes, particularly of those that go unpunished, this particular sort is the most frequent.

The others, those that interest novelists and so-called psychologists, are so unusual that they absorb only an insignificant part of our activities.

But that is the part with which the public is most familiar. These are the cases about which Simenon has written most and will, I suppose, go on writing.

I refer to those crimes which are committed suddenly in the most unlikely settings, and which are, as it were, the final outcome of something that has been brewing for a long time in secret.

Some well-kept, prosperous street in Paris or elsewhere. People who have a comfortable house, a family life, an honourable profession.

We have never had occasion to cross their threshold. Often the *milieu* is one to which we should normally not have access, where our presence would jar, where we should feel awkward, to say the least.

Now somebody has died a violent death, and so we come and ring at the door, and find ourselves confronted by inscrutable faces, by a family of which each member seems to have his own secret.

Here the experience acquired through years in streets, in stations, in lodging houses is no longer involved. Nor is that sort of instinctive respect felt by small fry towards authority, towards the police.

Nobody here is afraid of being sent back over the frontier. Nobody is going to be taken off to an office at Headquarters to be subjected for hours to a painstaking examination, gone over again and again.

The people we have before us are those highly respectable folk who in other circumstances would have asked us:

'Don't you sometimes feel disgusted?'

We do, in these very homes. Not immediately. Not invariably. For the task is a long and chancy one.

Even when a telephone call from some minister, some deputy, some important public figure doesn't try to divert us from our path.

There is a whole varnish of respectability to be peeled off little by little; there are family secrets, more or less repulsive, which they all combine to conceal from us and which have to be brought to light, regardless of protests and threats.

Sometimes five or six of them, or more, may have conspired to lie on certain points, while surreptitiously endeavouring to get the rest into trouble.

Simenon is apt to describe me as awkward and gruff, feeling ill at ease, with a furtive glance and a cantankerous way of barking out my questions.

It's in such cases as these that he has seen me thus, faced with what one might call amateur crimes, which one *invariably* discovers, in the end, to have been committed for motives of self-interest.

Not for money. I mean not crimes committed from an urgent need for money, as in the case of those petty ruffians who murder old women.

The interests involved behind these façades are more complicated, they are long-term interests, coupled with a concern for respectability. Often the thing goes back many years, concealing a whole lifetime of intrigue and dishonesty.

When these people, brought to bay, finally confess, the whole revolting story comes out, almost always with a panic fear of consequences.

'Surely it's impossible for our family to be dragged in the mud? There must be some way out.'

That does happen, I'm sorry to say. Some people who should only have left my office for a cell at the Santé prison have disappeared from circulation, because there are certain influences against which a detective, even a chief-inspector, is powerless.

'Don't you sometimes feel disgusted?'

I have never done so when, as detective in the Hotels Squad, I spent my days or my nights climbing the stairs of squalid, overcrowded apartment houses, where every door disclosed some distressing or dramatic scene.

Nor does the word disgust convey my reaction to the thousands of professionals of every sort who have passed through my hands.

They have played their game and lost it. Almost all of them prided themselves on being good losers and some of them, after they had been sentenced, asked me to go and see them in prison, where we chatted like old friends.

I could mention several who have begged me to be present at their execution and saved their last dying look for me.

'I shall do all right, you'll see!'

They did their best. They were not always successful. I used to take away their last letters in my pocket, promising to send them off with a covering note of my own.

When I got home, my wife had only to look at me without asking questions to know how things had gone off.

As for the other cases, on which I prefer not to dwell, she was well acquainted with the meaning of certain angry moods of mine, a certain way of sitting down when I got home at night, and of filling my plate, and she never pressed me.

Which is ample proof that she was not destined for the Highways and Bridges!

Chapter Seven

Describes a morning as triumphant as a cavalry trumpet and a young fellow who was no longer thin, but who had not yet grown really stout

I can still recall the taste and the colour of the sunlight that morning. It was in March. Spring had come early. I had already formed the habit of going on foot, whenever I could, from the Boulevard Richard-Lenoir to the Quai des Orfèvres.

I had no outside work that day, only files to classify in the Hotels section, in which were probably the gloomiest offices in the whole Palais de Justice, on the ground floor, with a little door leading into the courtyard, which I had left open.

I kept as near to it as my work allowed. I remember the sun cutting the courtyard exactly in two, and also cutting across a waiting police van. From time to time its two horses stamped on the paving-stones, and behind them there was a fine heap of gleaming dung, smoking in the keen morning air.

I don't know why the courtyard reminded me of certain break-times at school, at the same season of the year, when the air suddenly begins to have a special fragrance and, when you've been running, your skin smells of spring.

I was alone in the office. The telephone bell rang.

'Will you tell Maigret the Chief wants him?'

The voice of the old office clerk up there, who had been nearly fifty years in his job.

'Maigret speaking.'

'Come up then.'

Even the great staircase, which was always full of dust, seemed gay, with rays of sunlight slanting down as in churches. The morning conference had just ended. Two Inspectors still stood talking, with their files under their arms, by the Chief's door, on which I went to knock.

And inside the office I could still smell the pipes and cigarettes of those who had just gone out. A window was open behind Xavier Guichard, who had plumes of sunlight in his silky white hair.

He did not hold out his hand to me. He seldom did so in the office. And yet we had become friends, or, more precisely, he had been good enough to honour my wife and me with his friendship. On one occasion, the first, he had invited me alone to his flat in the Boulevard Saint-Germain. Not the wealthy, fashionable part of the Boulevard. He lived, on the contrary, right opposite the Place Maubert, in a big new block that rose amidst rickety houses and squalid hotels.

I had gone back there with my wife. They had immediately got on very well together.

He was undoubtedly fond of her and of myself, and yet he has often hurt us without meaning to.

In the beginning, as soon as he saw Louise, he would stare insistently at her figure and, if we seemed not to understand, he would say with a little cough:

'Don't forget that I want to be godfather.'

He was a confirmed bachelor. Apart from his brother, who was Chief of the Municipal Police, he had no relatives in Paris.

'Come now, don't keep me waiting too long . . .'

Years had gone by. He must have misunderstood. I remember that when he told me of my first rise he had added:

'Perhaps that'll enable you to give me a godson.'

He never understood why we blushed, why my wife lowered her eyes, while I tried to touch her hand to comfort her.

He was looking very serious that morning, seen against the light. He left me standing, and I felt embarrassed by the insistent way in which he examined me from head to foot, as a sergeant-major looks over a recruit.

'D'you know, Maigret, you're putting on weight?'

I was thirty. Little by little I had stopped being thin, my shoulders had broadened, my chest had expanded, but I had not yet become really stout.

It was obvious. I must have seemed flabby in those days, with a somewhat boyish look. It struck me myself when I passed in front of a shop window and cast an anxious glance at my own silhouette.

It was too much or too little, and no clothes fitted me.

'I think I'm getting fatter, yes.'

I almost wanted to apologize and I had not yet realized that he was joking as he loved to do:

'I think I'd better transfer you to another department.'

There were two squads in which I had not yet served, the Sports Squad and the Finance Squad, and the latter was my nightmare, just as the trigonometry exam had long been the terror of my summer terms at school.

'How old are you?'

'Thirty.'

'The right age! That's fine. Young Lesueur will take your place in the Hotels Squad, from now on, and you shall put yourself at Inspector Guillaume's disposal.'

He deliberately said this in an unemphatic tone, as if it were something quite trivial, knowing that my heart was going to leap in my breast and that, as I stood before him there, I could hear triumphant clarion calls ringing in my ears.

Suddenly, on a morning that seemed to have been chosen on purpose—and I'm not sure that Guichard hadn't done so—the dream of my life was being realized.

At last I was to enter the Special Squad.

A quarter of an hour later I moved upstairs with my old office jacket, my soap and towel, my pencils and a few papers.

There were five or six men in the big room reserved for Detectives in the Homicide Squad, and before calling me, Inspector Guillaume let me settle down, like a new pupil.

'Stand us a drink on it?'

I wasn't going to say no. At midday I proudly took my new colleagues to the Brasserie Dauphine.

I had often seen them there, at a different table from the one I shared with my former pals, and we used to watch them with the envious respect felt by schoolboys for sixth formers who are as tall as their masters and treated by these almost on an equal footing.

The comparison was an apt one, for Guillaume was with us, and the Superintendent from the General Information Department came to join us.

'What'll you have?' I asked.

In our old corner we used to drink half-pints of beer, seldom an apéritif. Obviously that wouldn't do for this table.

Somebody said:

'A mandarin-curaçao.'

'Mandarins all round?'

As nobody objected, I ordered I don't know how many mandarins. It was the first time I had tasted one. In the intoxication of my triumph, it seemed to me barely alcoholic.

'Let's have another round.'

Wasn't this the moment, if ever, to show myself generous? We had three each, we had four. My new Chief insisted on paying his round too.

The town was full of sunlight. The streets were streaming with it. The women in their bright dresses were a delight. I threaded my way between pedestrians. I looked at myself in shop windows and thought I wasn't so fat after all.

I ran. I flew. I was exultant. As soon as I reached the foot of the stairs I began the speech I had prepared for my wife.

Going up the last flight, I came a cropper. I hadn't had time to get up again when our door opened, for Louise must have been getting anxious at my delay.

'Have you hurt yourself?'

It was a funny thing. At the precise moment when I stood up again I felt completely drunk and was amazed at it. The staircase was whirling round me. My wife's silhouette was blurred. She seemed to have at least two mouths and three or four eyes.

Believe it or not, it was the first time in my life that this had happened to me, and I felt so humiliated that I dared not look at her; I slunk into the flat like a guilty thing without remembering the triumphant phrases I had so carefully prepared.

'I think . . . I think I'm a bit drunk.'

I was painfully sniffling. The table was laid, with our two places opposite one another in front of the open window. I had promised myself to take her out to lunch at a restaurant, but I dared not propose it now.

So that it was in an almost gloomy tone that I announced:

'It's happened!'

'What's happened?'

Perhaps she was expecting me to tell her that I'd been flung out of the Force!

'I've been appointed.'

'Appointed what?'

Apparently I had great tears in my eyes, tears of vexation but also, no doubt, of joy, as I let fall the words:

'To the Special Squad.'

'Sit down. I'm going to make you a cup of strong black coffee.'

She tried to get me to lie down, but I was not going to desert my new post on the first day. I drank I don't know how many cups of strong coffee. In spite of Louise's insistence. I couldn't swallow any solid food. I took a shower.

At two o'clock, when I went along to the Quai des Orfèvres, my cheeks had a peculiar rosy glow, my eyes were glittering. I felt limp and light-headed.

I went to sit down in my corner and spoke as little as possible, for I knew that my voice was unsteady and that I might get my syllables confused.

Next day, as though to put me to the test, they entrusted me with my first arrest. It was in the Rue du Roi de Sicile, in an apartment house. The man had been shadowed for five days already. He was responsible for several murders. He was a foreigner, a Czech if I remember rightly, a strongly-built fellow, invariably armed, invariably on the alert.

The problem was to immobilize him before he had time to defend himself, for he was the sort of man who would fire into the crowd, kill as many people as possible before letting himself be brought down.

He knew that he was at the end of his tether, that the police were on his heels but were still hesitating.

Out of doors he always managed to stay in the middle of a crowd, well aware that we could take no risks.

I was sent as assistant to Inspector Dufour, who had been following the man for several days and knew all his movements.

This was the first time, too, that I disguised myself. To have appeared in that sordid hotel dressed as we usually were would have provoked a panic under cover of which our man might have escaped.

Dufour and I put on old clothes and, to make things more convincing, went forty-eight hours without shaving.

A young detective, a skilled locksmith, had got into the hotel and had made us an excellent key of the man's bedroom.

We took a room on the same landing ourselves, before the Czech came back to bed. It was just after eleven when a signal from outside warned us that he was coming up the stairs.

The tactics we followed were not suggested by myself but by Dufour, an old hand at the game.

The man, not far away from us, had shut his door and was lying fully clothed on his bed, and he probably had a loaded revolver at least within reach.

We did not sleep. We waited for dawn. If you ask me why, I shall give the answer that my colleague, to whom I put the same question, gave me.

The murderer's first reflex, on hearing us, would undoubtedly have been to smash the gas burner in his room. We should thus have been in darkness, and he would have had an advantage over us.

'A man's resistance is always lower in the early morning,' Dufour told me, and I've confirmed this subsequently.

We crept into the passage. Everybody was asleep around us. Taking infinite care, Dufour turned the key in the lock.

As I was the tallest and the heaviest, it was my job to rush forward first, and I did so at one bound, and found myself on top of the man as he lay stretched out in bed, grabbing him by whatever I could get hold of.

I don't know how long the struggle went on, but it seemed to me interminable. I felt myself rolling on the ground with him. I could see a fierce face close to my own. I remember particularly a set of huge dazzling teeth. A hand, clutching my ear, was trying to wrench it off.

I was not conscious of what my colleague was doing, but I saw an expression of pain and rage on my opponent's face. I felt him gradually loosen his hold. When I was able to turn round, Inspector Dufour, sitting cross-legged on the floor, was holding one of the man's feet in his hand, and it looked as if he'd been giving it at least a double twist.

'Handcuffs,' he ordered.

I had already handcuffed less dangerous prisoners, such as refractory prostitutes. This was the first time I had carried out a forcible arrest, and the sound of handcuffs put an end for me to a fight which might have ended badly.

When people talk about a detective's flair, or his methods, his intuition, I always want to retort:

'What about your cobbler's flair, or your pastrycook's?'

Both of these have gone through years of apprenticeship. Each of them knows his job and everything concerned with it.

The same is true of a man from Police Headquarters. And that's why all the stories I have read, including those of my friend Simenon, are more or less inaccurate.

We sit in our office, drawing up reports. For this is also part of the job, a fact too frequently forgotten. I might even say that we spend far more time over administrative papers than on actual investigations.

We are told that a middle-aged gentleman is in the waiting-room, looking very nervous and asking to speak to the Chief immediately. Needless to say, the Chief hasn't time to receive all the people that turn up and want a personal interview because their little problem, to them, is the only important one.

There is one word which recurs so often that it has become like a refrain, and the office boy recites it like a litany: 'A matter of life and death.'

'Are you seeing him, Maigret?'

There is a little room next to the Inspectors' office for such interviews as these.

'Sit down. Cigarette?'

More often than not, before the visitor has had time to tell us his profession and his social status we have guessed them.

'It's a very delicate matter, quite personal.'

A bank cashier, or an insurance agent, a man with a quiet regular way of life.

'Your daughter?'

It's either his son or his daughter or his wife. And we can foretell almost word for word the speech he's going to pour forth to us. No. His son hasn't taken money out of the boss's cash box. Nor has his wife gone off with a young man.

It's his daughter, a very well-brought-up young girl about whom there has never been a word of criticism. She saw nobody, lived at home and helped her mother with the housework.

Her girl friends were as serious-minded as herself. She practically never went out alone.

And yet she's vanished, taking some of her belongings with her.

What can you tell him? That six hundred people disappear every month in Paris and that about two-thirds of them are found?

'Is your daughter very pretty?'

He has brought several photographs, convinced that they'll be useful for our search. If she's pretty, so much the worse, for the number of chances is lessened. If she's ugly, on the contrary, she'll probably come back in a few days or a few weeks.

'You can rely on us. We'll do what's necessary.'

'When?'

'Right away.'

He's going to ring us up every day, twice a day, and there is nothing to tell him, except that we haven't had time to look for the young lady.

Almost always a brief enquiry reveals that a young man living in the same block of flats, or the grocer's assistant, or the brother of one of her girl friends has disappeared on the same day as herself.

You cannot go through Paris and France with a fine tooth-comb for a runaway girl, and her photograph will merely go next week to join the collection of prints sent to police stations, to the various branches of the Force and to frontier posts.

Eleven o'clock at night. A telephone call from the Emergency Office, over the way, in the building of the Municipal Police, where all calls are centralized and inscribed on a luminous board that takes up the whole breadth of a wall.

The Pont de Flandre station has just heard that there's been trouble in a bar in the Rue de Crimée.

It's right the other side of Paris. Nowadays Headquarters has a few cars at its disposal, but formerly, you had to take a cab, or later a taxi, for which you couldn't be sure you'd be refunded.

The bar, at a street corner, is still open, with a broken window, figures standing prudently at some distance, for in that district people prefer not to attract the attention of the police.

Uniformed constables are there already, an ambulance, sometimes the Station Officer or his secretary.

On the ground, amidst the sawdust and spittle, a man lies crumpled up, one hand on his breast, from which a trickle of blood is flowing to form a pool.

'Dead!'

Beside him, on the floor, a small suitcase, which he was holding when he fell, has burst open, letting drop some pornographic postcards.

The anxious barkeeper tries to put himself in the right.

'Everything was quiet, as usual. This is a respectable house.'

'Had you seen him before?'

'Never.'

The answer was inevitable. He probably knows him very well, but he'll go on asserting to the end that it was the first time the man had set foot in his bar.

'What happened?'

The dead man is a drab figure, middle-aged or rather of indeterminate age. His clothes are old, of doubtful cleanliness, his shirt collar is black with grime.

Useless to hunt for relatives or a home. He must have been staying in the lowest type of furnished lodgings, on a weekly rate, and set off thence to hawk his wares in the neighbourhood of the Tuileries and the Palais-Royal.

'There were three or four customers . . .'

No point in asking where they are. They've flown away, and will not come back to give evidence.

'Did you know them?'

'Vaguely. By sight only.'

Of course! We could give his answers for him.

'A stranger came in and sat down at the other side of the bar, just opposite this chap.'

The bar is horseshoe-shaped, with overturned glasses on it and a strong smell of cheap spirits.

'They didn't speak to one another. This chap looked frightened. He put his hand into his pocket to pay . . .'

That is so, for he had no weapon on him.

'The other chap never said a word, but pulled out his gun and fired three times. He'd have gone on probably if his revolver hadn't jammed. Then he calmly pulled his hat down over his eyes and went out.'

That's clear enough. No need of flair. The *milieu* in which we had to hunt is a particularly restricted one.

There aren't so many of them who peddle dirty pictures. We know nearly all of them. Periodically they pass through our hands, serve a short sentence in gaol and then begin again.

The dead man's shoes—his feet are dirty and there are holes in his socks—bear the mark of a Berlin firm.

He is a newcomer. He must have been given the hint that there was no room for him in the district. Or else he was a subordinate to whom the goods were entrusted and who had kept the money for himself.

It'll take three days, four perhaps. Hardly longer. The Hotels Squad will promptly be called upon to help and, before the next night, will know where the victim was staying.

The Vice Squad, armed with his photograph, will pursue their separate enquiry.

This afternoon, in the neighbourhood of the Tuileries, they'll arrest some of those individuals who all offer passers-by the same trash with an air of mystery.

They won't be very nice to them. In the old days they were even less so than they are today.

'Have you ever seen that fellow?'

'No.'

'Are you sure you've never seen him?'

There's a certain little cell, very dark, very narrow, a sort of cupboard rather, on the mezzanine floor, where people like that are helped to remember, and it seldom happens that after a few hours they don't start banging on the door.

'I think I've caught sight of him . . .'

'His name?'

'I only know his first name: Otto.'

The skein will unwind slowly, but it will unwind to the end, like a tapeworm.

'He's a queer!'

Good! The fact that a homosexual is involved restricts the field of enquiry still further.

'Didn't he often go to the Rue de Bondy?'

It was almost inevitable. There's a certain little bar there frequented by practically all homosexuals of a certain social level–the lowest. There's another in the Rue de Lappe, which has become an attraction for sightseers.

'Whom have you seen him with?'

That's about all. It only remains, when we get the man between four walls, to make him confess and sign his confession.

All cases aren't as simple as that. Some investigations take months. And certain criminals are eventually arrested only after long years, and then sometimes by pure chance.

In practically every case, the process is the same.

You have to *know*.

To know the *milieu* in which a crime has been committed, to know the way of life, the habits, morals, reactions of the people involved in it, whether victims, criminals or merely witnesses.

To enter into their world without surprise, easily, and to speak its language naturally.

This is as true whether we are concerned with a bistro in La Villette or the Porte d'Italie, or with the Arabs in the Zone, with Poles or Italians, with the streetwalkers of Pigalle or the young delinquents of Les Ternes.

It's still true if we are concerned with the racing world or the gambling world, with safe-breaking specialists or jewel thieves.

That is why we aren't wasting our time when we spend years pacing the pavements, climbing stairs or spying on pilferers in big stores.

Like the cobbler, like the pastrycook, we are serving our apprenticeship, with this difference, that it goes on for practically the whole of our lives, because the number of different circles is almost infinite.

Prostitutes, pickpockets, cardsharpers, confidence tricksters or specialists in cheque forgery recognize one another.

One might say the same of policemen after a certain number of years on the job. And it's not a matter of hobnailed shoes or moustaches.

I think it's the look in our eyes that gives us away, a certain reaction – or rather lack of reaction–when confronted with certain creatures, certain states of destitution, certain abnormalities.

With all due deference to novelists, a detective is, above all, a professional. He is an *official*.

He's not engaged in a guessing game, nor getting worked up over a relatively thrilling chase.

When he spends a night in the rain, watching a door that doesn't open or a lighted window, when he patiently scans the pavement cafés on the boulevards for a familiar face, or prepares to spend hours questioning a pale, terrified individual, he is doing his daily job.

He is earning his living, trying to earn as honestly as possible the money that the Government gives him at the end of every month in remuneration for his services.

I know that my wife, when she reads these lines presently, will shake her head and look at me reproachfully, murmuring maybe:

'You always exaggerate!'

She will probably add:

'You're going to give a wrong idea of yourself and your colleagues.'

She's quite right. I may possibly be exaggerating somewhat in the contrary direction. It's by way of reaction against the ready-made ideas which have so often irritated me.

How many times, after the publication of one of Simenon's books, have my colleagues looked at me mockingly as I went into my office!

I could read in their eyes what they were thinking: 'Well, here comes God the Father!'

That is why I insist on the term official, which others consider derogatory.

I have been an official almost all my life. Thanks to Inspector Jacquemain, I became one on the threshold of manhood.

Just as my father, in his day, became estate-manager at the château. With the same pride. With the same concern to know everything about my job and to carry out my task conscientiously.

The difference between other officials and those of the Quai des Orfèvres is that the latter are, as it were, balanced between two worlds.

By their dress, by their education, by their homes and their ways of life, they are indistinguishable from other middle-class people and share their dream of a little house in the country.

Most of their time is spent none the less in contact with the underworld, the riffraff, the dregs, often with the enemies of organized society.

This has often struck me. It's a strange situation about which I have sometimes felt uneasy.

I live in a bourgeois apartment where the savoury smells of my carefully-prepared dinner await me, where everything is simple and neat, clean and comfortable. Through my windows I see only homes like my own, mothers walking with their children along the Boulevard, housewives going to do their shopping.

I belong to that social group, of course, to what are known as respectable people.

But I know the others too, I know them well enough for a certain contact to exist between myself and them. The tarts at the Brasserie in the Place de la République, when I go by, know that I understand their language and the meaning of their attitudes. So does the street-arab threading his way through the crowd.

And all the others whom I have met and still meet every day, under the most intimate conditions.

Isn't this enough to make some sort of bond?

It's not my business to make excuses for them, to justify or absolve them. It's not my business, either, to adorn them with some sort of halo, as was the fashion at one time.

It's my business simply to consider them as a fact, to look at them with the eye of one who knows them.

Without curiosity, because curiosity is quickly dulled.

Without hatred, of course.

To look at them, in short, as creatures who exist and who, for the well-being of society, for the sake of the established order, have got to be kept, willy nilly, within certain bounds and punished when they overstep them.

They are well aware of this themselves! They bear us no grudge for it. They often say:

'You're doing your job.'

As for what they think of that particular job, I'd rather not try to find out.

Is it surprising that after twenty-five or thirty years in the Force we walk with a rather heavy step, and have in our eyes an even heavier look, sometimes a blank look?

'Don't you sometimes feel disgusted?'

No, I don't! And it's probably through my job that I have acquired a fairly unshakeable optimism.

Paraphrasing a saying of my first religious instructor, I should like to say: a little knowledge turns one away from man, a great deal of knowledge brings one back to man.

It's because I have witnessed depravities of every sort that I have come to realize that they were compensated by a great deal of simple courage, good will or resignation.

Utterly rotten individuals are rare, and most of those I have come across, unfortunately, functioned out of my reach, out of our sphere of action.

As for the rest, I tried to prevent them from doing too much harm and to see to it that they paid for the harm they had already done.

After which, surely, we've settled our accounts.

That chapter is closed.

Chapter Eight

The Place des Vosges, a young lady's engagement and some little notes from Madame Maigret

'On the whole,' Louise said, 'I don't see all that much difference.'

I always look rather anxiously at her when she's reading what I have just been writing, trying to forestall her criticisms.

'Difference between what?'

'Between what you say about yourself and what Simenon says about you.'

'Oh!'

'Perhaps I'm wrong to give my opinion.'

'No, no, of course not!'

All the same, if she is right, I've given myself needless trouble. And it's quite possible that she is right, that I haven't known how to go about it, how to set things out as I had promised myself.

Or else the famous tirade about made-up truths being truer than naked truths is not a mere paradox.

I have done my best. Only there are heaps of things that struck me as essential at the beginning, points I had determined to develop and which I have abandoned on the way.

For instance, one shelf of the bookcase is full of Simenon's books, which I have patiently stuffed with blue pencil marks, and I was looking forward to correcting all the mistakes he's made, either because he didn't know, or else for the sake of picturesqueness, often because he hadn't the courage to ring me up to verify some detail.

What's the use? I should look like a fussy fellow, and I'm beginning to believe myself that these things are not so very important.

One of his habits that irritated me most sometimes was that of mixing up dates, of setting at the beginning of my career investigations that took place much later on, and vice versa, so that sometimes my detectives are described as being quite young, whereas they were really staid fathers of families at the period in question, or the other way round.

I had even thought seriously, I confess it now that I've given up the idea, of establishing, thanks to the files of newspaper cuttings which my wife has kept up to date, a chronology of the principal cases in which I've been involved.

'Why not?' Simenon replied. 'Excellent idea. They'll be able to correct my books for the next edition.'

He added, without irony:

'Only, Maigret old fellow, you'll have to be kind enough to do the job yourself, for I've never had the courage to re-read my own books.'

I have said what I had to say, on the whole, and it cannot be helped if I've said it badly. My colleagues will understand, and everyone who's more or less connected with the Force, and it's chiefly for them that I was anxious to put things right, to speak not so much of myself as of our profession.

It looks as if some important question had escaped me. I hear my wife carefully opening the door of the dining-room where I am working, and tiptoeing forward.

She has just put a scrap of paper on the table before withdrawing in the same fashion. I read these pencilled words:

'Place des Vosges.'

And I can't resist smiling with private satisfaction, for this proves that she too has details to put right, one at least, and, actually, for the same reason as myself, out of loyalty.

In her case it's out of loyalty to our flat in the Boulevard Richard-Lenoir, which we have never deserted, which still belongs to us today, although we only use it a few days a year, now that we're living in the country.

In several of his books Simenon described us as living in the Place des Vosges without offering the slightest explanation.

I'm giving my wife's message then. It's quite true that for a number of months we lived in the Place des Vosges. But we were not in our own home.

That year our landlord had at last decided to get the building refaced, which it had been needing for some time. In front of the house, workmen had set up scaffolding which surrounded our windows. Others, inside, began making holes in the walls and floor to install central heating. We had been promised that it would take three weeks at most. After a fortnight they had got nowhere, and just at that time a strike was declared in the building trade and nobody knew how long it might last.

Simenon was just off for Africa, where he was to spend nearly a year.

'Why don't you move into my flat in the Place des Vosges until the job's finished?'

And so it happened that we went to live there, at No. 21 to be exact, without incurring the reproach of disloyalty to our dear old Boulevard.

There was one period, too, in which, without warning me, he made me retire when I still had several years' service to run.

We had just bought our house at Meung-sur-Loire and we used to spend all my free Sundays getting it ready. He came to visit us there. The place delighted him so much that in the next book he quite shamelessly anticipated events, made me several years older and settled me there for good.

'It makes a change of atmosphere,' he told me when I spoke to him about it. '*I was getting bored with the Quai des Orfèvres.*'

Allow me to underline that sentence, which seems to me outrageous. It's he, you notice, who was getting bored with the Quai, with my office, with the daily duties at Headquarters!

Which did not prevent him subsequently, and will probably not prevent him in future from relating earlier investigations, still giving no dates, making me sometimes sixty years old and sometimes forty-five.

Here's my wife again. I have no study at home. I don't need one. When I have to work I settle down at the dining-table, and Louise retires into the kitchen, which she's quite glad to do. I look at her, thinking she wants to tell me something. But it's another scrap of paper which she's got in her hand and has come to lay timidly in front of me.

This time it's a list, just like when I'm going to town and she writes down on a scrap torn out of her notebook what I've got to bring her back.

My nephew heads the list, and I understand why. He's her sister's son. I got him into the Police Force a long time ago, at an age when he was fired with enthusiasm about it.

Simenon mentioned him, then the boy suddenly disappeared from his books, and I can guess Louise's scruples. She's been thinking that for some readers this may have appeared suspicious, as though her nephew had committed some folly.

The truth is quite simple. He hadn't done as brilliantly as he had hoped. And he did not put up much resistance to his father-in-law's pressing offers of a place in his soap factory at Marseilles.

The name of Torrence comes next on the list, big noisy Torrence (I believe that somewhere or other Simenon makes him die in place of another detective who was in fact killed by my side in a Champs-Elysées hotel).

Torrence had no father-in-law in soap. But he had a terrific appetite for life, together with a business sense that was hardly compatible with the existence of an official.

He left us to found a private detective agency, a highly respectable agency, I hasten to add, for that is not always the case. And for a long time he kept on coming to the Quai to ask for our help, or for information, or merely to breathe the atmosphere of the place again.

He has a big American car which stops from time to time in front of our door, and each time he is accompanied by a pretty woman, always a different one, whom he introduces with unvarying sincerity as his fiancée.

I read the third name, little Janvier as we have always called him. He is still at the Quai. Probably they still call him little Janvier?

In his last letter he informs me, not without a certain melancholy, that his daughter is engaged to a young man from the École Polytechnique.

Finally Lucas who, at the present moment, is probably sitting as usual in my office, at my desk, smoking one of my pipes which he begged me, with tears in his eyes, to leave him as a souvenir.

There's one word at the bottom of the list. I thought at first it was a name, but I couldn't decipher it.

I have just gone into the kitchen, where I was quite surprised to see bright sunlight, for I had closed the shutters in order to work in a half-light which I find helpful.

'Finished?'

'No. There's one word I can't read.'

She was quite embarrassed.

'It doesn't matter at all.'

'What is it?'

'Nothing. Don't pay any attention to it.'

Of course I insisted.

'Sloe gin!' she admitted at last, averting her head.

She knew I should burst out laughing, as in fact I did.

When it was a question of my famous bowler hat, my velvet-collared overcoat, my coal stove and my poker, I was well aware that she thought I was being childish when I insisted on making corrections.

Nevertheless she has herself scribbled the words *sloe gin* at the bottom of the list, making them illegible on purpose, I'm convinced, out of a sort of shame, rather like when she adds to the list of errands to be done in town some very feminine article which she rather shamefacedly asks me to buy for her.

Simenon has mentioned a certain bottle which we always had in our sideboard in the Boulevard Richard-Lenoir—we still have it there—and of which my sister-in-law, according to a hallowed tradition, brings us a supply from Alsace on her annual visit there.

He has thoughtlessly described it as sloe gin.

Actually it is raspberry brandy. And for an Alsatian, apparently, this makes a tremendous difference.

'I've made the correction, Louise. Your sister will be satisfied.'

This time I left the kitchen door open.

'Nothing else?'

'Tell the Simenons I'm knitting socks for . . .'

'But I'm not writing them a letter, you know!'

'Of course. Make a note of it for when you do write. They're not to forget the photo they promised us.'

She added:

'Can I lay the table?'

That's all.

Meung-sur-Loire
27 September 1950

Maigret Takes a Room

Maigret Takes a Room

Translated from the French by Robert Brain

Chapter One

'Why not come back and take pot-luck with us?'

And kindly Lucas may well have added:

'I promise you my wife would be delighted.'

Poor old Lucas! This was not the truth, since his wife was the sort to panic over trifles, for whom an extra dinner guest was a nightmare; she would certainly have taken him severely to task.

They had left the Quai des Orfèvres together about seven o'clock, while the sun was still shining brightly, made for the Brasserie Dauphine and sat down in their usual corner. They had drunk their first apéritif staring into space as people do when they have just finished their day's work. Then, hardly aware of his action, Maigret had rapped on his saucer with a coin, to call the waiter, and asked for another drink.

Unimportant things, it is true. Things which are exaggerated in being told, since, in fact, they are infinitely more subtle. Maigret, nonetheless, was convinced that Lucas had thought:

'It's because his wife's away that the chief is having another drink which he doesn't need.'

Two days before, Madame Maigret had been called away to Alsace, to the bedside of her sister who was going to have an operation.

Did Lucas suppose he was feeling a little lost? or miserable? Whatever the case, he was asking him to dinner, pressing him, despite himself, a little too affectionately. He was also looking at him in a certain fashion, as if pitying him. Or did all this only exist in the chief inspector's imagination?

It was slightly ironical that for the past two days no urgent case had kept him at the office after seven o'clock. He might even have left at six, whereas it was usually a miracle if he arrived home in time for the evening meal.

'No. I'm going to take advantage of the situation and go to the cinema,' he had answered.

And he had said 'take advantage of the situation' without intending it, without the phrase reflecting his thoughts.

They had parted at the Châtelet, he and Lucas, Lucas bounding down the steps to the underground, Maigret standing hesitantly in the middle of the pavement. The sky was pink. The streets had a pink look. It was one of the first evenings with a feeling of spring, and there were people on all the terraces.

What did he feel like eating? Since he was alone and could go where he chose, he pondered the question seriously, thought of the different restaurants which might tempt him, as if he were planning a tête-à-tête meal. He took a few steps at first towards the Place de la Concorde, and it gave him a pang of conscience because he was walking unnecessarily away from home. In the window of a delicatessen he noticed some ready-cooked snails, smothered in parsley butter which gave them a glazed look.

His wife did not care for snails. He ate them only rarely. He decided to treat himself to some this evening and thus 'take advantage of the situation', so he did a right-about turn and walked in the direction of a restaurant near the Bastille, where they specialised in them.

They knew him there.

'For one, Monsieur Maigret?'

The waiter looked at him with a hint of surprise, a hint of reproach. Alone, he could not expect a good table, and he was installed in a sort of passageway, with his back to a pillar.

He had not in fact promised himself anything extraordinary. It was not even true that he wanted to go to the cinema. He didn't know what to do with his massive self. Nevertheless he felt vaguely cheated.

'And the wine?'

He did not dare choose a specially fine wine, in case he seemed to be taking advantage of the situation.

And three-quarters of an hour later, when the street-lamps were alight in the blue of the evening, he found himself standing, still alone, in the Place de la Bastille.

It was too early to go home to bed. He had found time to read the evening paper at the office. He didn't feel like starting a book which would keep him awake half the night.

He began to walk along the Grands Boulevards, determined to go to the cinema. Twice he stopped to look at the posters but they failed to excite him. A woman kept looking at him insistently and he nearly blushed, because she appeared to have guessed that he was a temporary bachelor.

Did she, like everyone else, expect him to take advantage of the situation? She passed him, turned around, and the more embarrassed he became, the more she was convinced that he was a shy customer. She actually murmured a few words as she crossed in front of him and he only got rid of her by going over to the other pavement.

There was even something reprehensible about entering a cinema alone. Ridiculous, anyway. He went into a bar and drank a calvados. A woman there, too, gave him a come-hither smile.

Thousands of times he had stood drinking at bars and he had never felt like this before.

Finally, for the sake of his peace of mind, he chose a little basement news-cinema.

At half past ten he was hanging around outside again. He stopped at the same bar, drank another calvados, as if he were already making an established habit of it, then, filling his pipe, made his way slowly in the direction of the Boulevard Richard-Lenoir.

The whole evening, in fact, he had had the same sensation of being out of place, and though he had done nothing blameworthy, there was a kind of twinge of remorse in some corner of his conscience.

He took his key from his pocket as he went upstairs, and there was no light showing under the door, no smell of cooking to greet him. He had to switch the lamps on himself. As he passed the sideboard, he decided to pour himself a drink, something he could do today without exchanging a glance with his wife.

He began to get undressed without having closed the curtains, went over to the window, and was just slipping off his braces when the telephone rang out.

In the same instant, he felt sure that some untoward event was the explanation for his feeling of discomfort all evening.

'Hello! . . .'

His sister-in-law had not died, for it wasn't his wife speaking, and the call came from Paris.

'That you, chief?'

Police Headquarters, then. He recognised Torrence's deep voice, as loud as a bugle-call over the telephone.

'I'm glad you're back. It's the fourth time I've rung you. I called Lucas, who told me you'd gone to the cinema. But I didn't know which . . .'

Torrence, in his excitement, didn't seem to know where to start.

'It's to do with Janvier . . .'

Reflex action? Maigret, unconsciously, put on his gruff voice to ask:

'Well, what does Janvier want?'

'They've just taken him to Cochin. He's been shot in the chest.'

'No!'

'By now he must be on the operating slab.'

'Where are you speaking from?'

'The Quai. Someone's got to stay here. I've seen to everything in the Rue Lhomond. Lucas grabbed a taxi to take him to Cochin. Likewise I've notified Madame Janvier, who must have got there by now too.'

'I'll be off then.'

He was about to hang up, already hitching on his braces with one hand, when it occurred to him to ask:

'Was it Paulus?'

'We don't know. Janvier was alone in the street. He had gone on duty there at seven. Young Lapointe was due to relieve him at seven in the morning.'

'Did you send some men into the house?'

'They're still there. They're keeping in touch by telephone. They haven't found anything.'

Maigret had to walk right to the Boulevard Voltaire before he got a taxi. The Rue Saint-Jacques was almost deserted, with lights on only in a few bars. He hurried through the main entrance into Cochin, and it hit him like a blast from all the hospitals he had known in his life.

Why surround the sick, the wounded, the people they are trying to keep alive as well as those who are going to die, with so mournful, so dreary an atmosphere? Why this light, at once dim and cruel, which only occurs here and in certain administrative buildings? And why, at the very door, is one met by sour faces?

He was almost obliged to prove his identity. The house surgeon on duty looked a mere youngster and wore his cap askew, to show off.

'Block C. You'll be shown the way . . .'

He was boiling with impatience. Furious with all the world, he now resented the fact that the nurse, leading him, wore lipstick and had wavy hair.

Badly lit courtyards, staircases, a long corridor, and, at the end of this corridor, three figures. The stretch between him and these figures seemed interminable, the flooring more slippery than anywhere else.

Little Lucas came a few paces to meet him, walking sidelong like a dog that's taken a beating.

'They think he'll pull through,' he said straight away in a low voice. 'He's been in the operating-theatre three-quarters of an hour already.'

Madame Janvier, red-eyed, her hat not on straight, was looking at him as if to beseech him, as if he had some power, and suddenly she burst into tears behind her handkerchief.

He didn't know the third person present, a man with long moustaches, who kept discreetly to one side.

'He's a neighbour,' Lucas explained. 'Madame Janvier couldn't leave the children on their own; she called up a woman neighbour, whose husband offered to accompany her here.'

The man, who had heard this, said good evening, smiled his gratitude to Lucas.

'What does the surgeon say?'

They were outside the door of the operating-theatre and spoke quietly. At the other end of the corridor, nurses, always with something in their hands, were incessantly coming and going, like ants.

'The bullet missed his heart, but has lodged in his right lung.'

'Has Janvier said anything?'

'No. When the police ambulance arrived at the Rue Lhomond, Janvier was unconscious.'

'Do you think they'll save him, Chief Inspector?' asked Madame Janvier, who was visibly pregnant and had reddish patches under her eyes.

'There's no reason to think he won't come through all right.'

'You can see now why I've been worried every time he's spent the night out!'

They lived in the suburbs, a small house Janvier had had built three years earlier when it became too difficult to bring up the children in a Paris flat. He was very proud of his garden.

They exchanged another phrase or two, without much conviction, looking anxiously at the door which still had not been opened. Maigret had taken his pipe out of his pocket, then replaced it, remembering that smoking was not permitted. He missed it badly. He almost went downstairs into the yard for a few puffs.

He did not want to ask Lucas what had happened, in front of Madame Janvier. Nor could he leave them. Apart from Lucas—his right hand—Janvier had always been his favourite inspector. He had been with him as a youngster, like Lapointe now, and sometimes he still called him 'young' Janvier.

The door was opened at last. But it was only a red-haired nurse who dashed across to another door without giving them a glance, retraced her steps again, shielding something in her hand which they could not identify. They weren't able to stop her and ask how the operation was going, but all four of them watched her face, all four of them were disappointed when they could make out only a look of professional preoccupation.

'I think that if anything happed to him I should die as well,' said Madame Janvier, who, in spite of a vacant chair, remained standing with them, nervously, as though she feared to lose a second by having to get up when the time came for the door to be opened properly.

There were noises. The folding doors opened. They saw a trolley.

Maigret seized Madame Janvier's arm to stop her rushing forward. He had a moment's fear because, from his angle, he had the impression that Janvier's face was covered with a sheet.

But when the trolley was wheeled past them he saw he was mistaken.

'Albert . . .' cried his wife, with a strangled sob.

'Ssssh . . .' said the surgeon, who came up to them pulling off his rubber gloves.

Janvier's eyes were open and he must have recognised them, because he had a vague smile on his lips.

They were taking him towards one of the wards and his wife followed with Lucas and the neighbour, while the chief inspector, in a window embrasure, talked to the doctor.

'Will he live?'

'There's no reason why he shouldn't. The convalescence period will be long, as is always the case with lung injuries, and precautions will have to be taken, but he is in practically no danger.'

'Have you extracted the bullet?'

The surgeon went back into the operating-theatre for a moment and returned with a piece of cotton-wool spotted with blood, which contained a piece of lead.

'I'll take it with me,' Maigret said. 'I'll send you a receipt for it later. He's said nothing?'

'No. Under the anaesthetic he muttered a few words, but it was vague, and I was too busy to pay any attention.'

'When could I question him?'

'When he's got over the shock, tomorrow, probably about mid-day. Is that his wife? Tell her not to worry. She shouldn't try to see him until tomorrow. According to the instructions, he's been given a private room and a nurse. Excuse me now, but I'm operating at seven o'clock tomorrow morning.'

Madame Janvier insisted on seeing her husband in his bed and they were kept waiting in the corridor until he was installed, and then they were allowed just to glance inside.

In a low voice, Madame Janvier gave some advice to the night-nurse, who seemed to be about fifty and looked like a man in travesty.

Outside, they didn't know what to do. There was not a taxi in sight.

'I promise you,' Maigret affirmed, 'that everything is going well, and that the doctor is not at all concerned. Come along tomorrow about mid-day, not before. I'll have all the news regularly and I'll telephone you. Think of the children . . .'

They had to walk as far as the Rue Gay-Lussac before they found a cab, and the man with the moustache carefully took Maigret to one side.

'There's no need to worry about her. You can rely on my wife and me.'

It was only when he was alone with Lucas on the pavement that Maigret wondered whether Madame Janvier would have any ready money. It was the end of the month. He didn't want to find her making the journey every day by train and underground. Taxis cost a lot. He would see to it tomorrow.

Turning at last to Lucas, he lit the pipe he had been holding in his hand for some time and asked him:

'What do you think?'

They were a few yards from the Rue Lhomond and they made their way to Mademoiselle Clément's boarding-house.

The street, deserted at that hour, was at its most provincial, with two- and three-storied houses sandwiched between blocks of flats. Mademoiselle Clément's house was one of these, with a small flight of three steps and a notice announcing:

'*Rooms let by the month.*'

Two constables of the fifth arrondissement, chatting by the doorway, saluted the chief inspector.

There was a light above the door, as well as in the windows to the right and on the second floor. Maigret did not have to ring the bell. They must have been watching out for them, because the door opened and Inspector Vacher looked at Maigret interrogatively.

'He'll be all right,' announced the latter.

And a woman's voice, from the room on the right, called out:

'What did I tell you?'

It was a curious voice, childish and jolly at the same time. A very tall, very fat woman who was framed in the door, held out her hand cordially, declaring:

'Delighted to make your acquaintance, Monsieur Maigret.'

She was like an enormous baby, with pink skin, indecisive shape, with great blue eyes, very blonde hair, a dress the colour of a lolly. Seeing her, one would suppose that nothing tragic had happened, that all was for the best in the best of worlds.

The room in which she received them was a cosy living-room, with three liqueur glasses on the table.

'I am Mademoiselle Clément,' she said. 'I have succeeded in sending my lodgers to bed. But of course I can call them back if you wish. So, your inspector is not dead?'

'The bullet pierced his right lung.'

'Nowadays the doctors can repair things like that in a twinkling.'

Maigret was a little stupefied. For once, he had imagined everything quite differently, the house and the landlady. The two inspectors, Vauquelin and Vacher, who had been sent to the spot by Torrence as soon as the news of the attempted murder had come through, seemed to be enjoying his surprise; Vauquelin, more familiar with him than Vacher, even winked and nodded at the fat girl.

She must have been about forty or forty-five, but in appearance she was ageless. It was as if, despite her impressive bulk, she weighed less than nothing. And she was so full of exuberance that they expected to see her, regardless of the circumstances, burst into vivacious laughter.

It was a case in which Maigret had hardly been concerned personally. He had not been to the scene of the crime. He had worked on the documents, in his office, leaving all responsibility for its conduct to Janvier, who had been delighted about it.

Nobody, at the Quai, would have thought for a moment that this case, which they called the 'Stork' case, had any element of danger in it.

Five days earlier, at about half past two in the morning, two men had gone to a small nightclub, 'The Stork', in the Rue Campagne-Première, in Montparnasse, just as it was closing.

Their faces were covered with black masks, and one of them had a revolver in his hand.

At that time the only people left in the place had been the owner, a boy called Angelo and the cloakroom woman, who was busy putting her hat on in front of a mirror.

'The cash-box!' one of the masked individuals had demanded.

The club-owner had put up no resistance. He had pushed the night's takings across the bar, and a few moments later the thieves had gone off in a black car.

It was Maigret who, the next morning, received the cloakroom attendant, a plump, once-beautiful woman.

'You're sure you recognised him?'

'I didn't see his face, if that's what you mean. But I certainly saw the thread on his trousers and I recognized the material.'

A crazy detail, in reality. Two hours before the robbery, one of the customers seated at the bar had gone off to the cloakroom to wash his hands and do his hair.

'You know how it is. You happen to fix your eyes on one particular spot, without paying any attention to it. Just as I handed him the towel, I was staring at a piece of white cotton on his trousers, near the knee, on the left-hand side. The piece of thread was about four inches long and made a sort of pattern. I remember thinking to myself that it looked like someone's face.'

She had been on the point of removing it, but had been prevented because the young man had gone out at that moment.

For it was a young man. A young lad, she said. She had seen him often at the bar, recently. One evening he had taken up with a girl who was a constant visitor to 'The Stork' and had gone off with her.

'Would you like to take care of this one, Janvier?'

Within three hours, no more, one of the thieves had been identified. Janvier had only had to find the girl, a certain Lucette, who lived in a hotel in the neighbourhood.

'He spent the night with me.'

'At his place?'

'No. Here. He was surprised when he heard I was from Limoges, because he was born there and his parents still live there. His name's Paulus. I'd reckoned he was no more than eighteen at most, but he's nineteen and a half.'

It might have taken a good deal longer, but from the Hotels Section Janvier had found the name 'Emile Paulus', from Limoges, registered for the past four months in a boarding-house in the Rue Lhomond.

At Mademoiselle Clément's.

'Do you want to give me a warrant, chief?'

Janvier had taken someone along with him. It was about eleven o'clock in the morning, Maigret remembered, and the sun was shining. He had come back two hours later and had placed on the chief inspector's desk an envelope containing bank notes, together with a child's revolver and a piece of black cloth.

'It's certainly Paulus.'

'The amount corresponds?'

'No. There's only half of it. The beauties must have divided it up. But there are three one-dollar bills included. I went along to question the owner of "The Stork" and he confirmed that an American had been there that evening who paid in dollars.'

'What about Paulus?'

'His bed was unmade, but he wasn't in his room. Mademoiselle Clément, the landlady, didn't see him go out and says she thinks he left the house about ten o'clock in the morning as usual.'

'You've left someone there?'

'Yes. We are going to set a trap for him.'

They kept watch for four days, without any result. Maigret did not concern himself with it, noticed in the report the name of the inspector on duty and, regularly, the phrase 'nothing of interest'.

The Press had said nothing of the police discovery. Paulus had taken no luggage away with him and it seemed likely that he would return to collect the little fortune he had left locked in his case.

'Did you keep watch too, Vacher?'

'Twice.'

'How did it go?'

'The first day I think Janvier stayed inside the house, upstairs, waiting for Paulus in his room.'

He glanced across at fat Mademoiselle Clément.

'He must have thought better of it. The boy could have been warned before he went up the stairs.'

'So what next?'

'We took it in turns outside. I didn't get the chance of having a go at night. During the day it was easy and pleasant. There's a small bistro a little farther along, on the other side, with two tables on the terrace. They serve meals there, and the food wasn't so bad either, I can tell you.'

'Was the house searched the first day?'

It was Mademoiselle Clément who answered, excitedly, as if it were all some pleasant adventure:

'From the cellar to the attic, Monsieur Maigret. I might add that Monsieur Janvier came in to see me at least a dozen times. Something was riling him, I don't know what. He spent hours upstairs, pacing up and down the room. At other times he came down here and sat chatting with me. By now he knows the life-history of all my lodgers.'

'What exactly happened this evening? You knew he was outside?'

'I didn't know it was him, but I knew there was a policeman on watch out there.'

'Could you see him?'

'I glanced out about half past nine, before I went to bed. I saw somebody was on his beat on the pavement, but the street light is too far away for me to have been able to recognise the silhouette. I went back to my room.'

'Is it upstairs?'

'No. On the ground floor. It looks on to the yard. I started to undress and I was about to take off my stockings when I heard Mademoiselle Blanche come running down the stairs, shouting heaven knows what. She opened my door without knocking.'

'Was she dressed?'

'In a dressing-gown. Why? If she's not going out she spends her evenings reading in bed. She's a nice girl. Her room, on the first floor, next to the Lotards', looks on to the street. She heard a gunshot, jumped out of bed and went to look out of the window. At first she noticed nothing. However, she seemed to think there was somebody running, but she's not sure.'

'We questioned her,' Vauquelin said. 'She isn't even at all sure.'

'Windows were opened apparently. A woman opposite pointed to something on the pavement, on our pavement, and Mademoiselle Blanche saw a body lying there.'

'What did you do?'

'I put on my dress, rushed into the passage where there is a wall-telephone, and I rang the police. Monsieur Valentin came out of his room and I wanted to stop him opening the door. All the same he did so, and I think he was the first person to go right up to the body. He is a charming man, a real man of the world, you'll see.'

Mademoiselle Blanche was a nice girl. Monsieur Valentin was charming. The Lotards were doubtless perfect angels. Mademoiselle Clément smiled on life, men and women, and Maigret.

'You'll have a small glass of liqueur, I hope?'

It was chartreuse in the glasses, and she poured one for him with a greedy gesture.

'How do your lodgers get into the house during the night? Do they have keys?'

'No. They ring. I have a door-pull at the head of my bed, the same as concierges have, as well as an electric switch which turns on the light in the passage and on the stairs.'

'They call out their name?'

'It's not necessary. Before opening the door, I turn on the passage light. My bedroom is at the end. It's an old house, oddly built. It's amusing. I only have to lean out of bed and, through a small window, I can see who comes in or goes out.'

'They also have to wake you up to go out?'

'Of course.'

'And during the day?'

'The door stays open. But there is another spy-window in the kitchen and nobody can go past without my knowing it. I'll show you.'

She promised him this as if she were promising him a little treat.

'You have many lodgers?'

'Nine. I mean to say I have nine rooms to let. Actually, with Monsieur Paulus, that makes eleven people, because I've got two couples, one on the first and the other on the second floor.'

'Everybody had come in when the shot was fired?'

'No. Monsieur Lotard had gone out and returned a quarter of an hour later, when the police were already here. Mademoiselle Isabelle was not in her room either. She came back a little before midnight. These gentlemen questioned her as well as the others. Everybody realised that they must take it all in good part. They are all very nice people, you'll see . . .'

It was almost two o'clock in the morning.

'May I use your telephone?'

'I'll show you where it is.'

It was in the passage, under the stairs. Maigret observed the two windows Mademoiselle Clément had alluded to, which allowed her to keep watch on her lodgers, either from the kitchen or from the bedroom.

He dialled the hospital's number, and his eyes fell on a sort of money-box nailed to the wall. Above the money-box there was a handwritten notice, in beautiful round letters, which said:

'*Tenants are requested to leave a franc here for every local call.*

'*For trunk calls and toll calls apply to Mademoiselle Clément. Thank you.*'

'Don't some of them cheat?' he asked with a smile.

'Sometimes. I watch them through my spy-hole. They're not always the ones one would expect. Monsieur Paulus, for example, has never failed to put the money in the box.'

'Hallo! Cochin Hospital?'

They transferred him to at least four different departments, the voices everywhere half-asleep or harassed, until they finally told him that Janvier had fallen into a deep sleep and that his temperature was satisfactory.

Then he called Juvisy to pass on the news to Madame Janvier, who spoke softly, because she was afraid of waking the children.

'Your inspector has confided in me that he is hoping for a girl this time,' said Mademoiselle Clément, when he had hung up. 'We've had lovely long chats together. He is a very engaging man!'

Chapter Two

There was a larger space at the entrance to the immense corridor, near the staircase, and two benches had been placed there, which looked like school forms.

It was here at mid-day, just as bells started ringing in various parts of the hospital–with a convent bell somewhere in the courtyards–that Maigret found Madame Janvier, who had arrived nearly half an hour earlier.

She was weary. Yet she gave him a smile to show that she intended to be strong. On all the floors they could hear a commotion as if in a barracks; it was probably the nurses, both male and female, changing duty. Some of them passed them, laughing and jostling each other.

The sunlight glittered and an occasional breath of air was almost warm. Maigret had no overcoat on: he wasn't used to not wearing it yet.

'They say they're coming to fetch us in a few minutes,' Madame Janvier remarked.

She added with a touch of irony, of bitterness:

'They're making him look smart for us.'

For here she was not allowed to do anything for her husband. Madame Janvier had periodically come to fetch her husband from the Quai des Orfèvres. Maigret met her from time to time. Nevertheless, for the first time he realised that she was looking almost faded. It was hardly ten years, nine actually, since Janvier had introduced him to his chubby-faced fiancée, whose cheeks dimpled when she laughed, and now already she had that sexless look, that too serious expression, like those women you see in the suburbs, obsessed by their housekeeping, with their aching backs.

'Give me a frank answer, Chief Inspector: do you think they had it in for him personally?'

He knew what was on her mind, and reflected before replying, although he had already considered the idea that morning.

Naturally, since Janvier had been attacked in the Rue Lhomond, everybody immediately thought of Paulus. But, as Maigret had said to the Commissioner at Police Headquarters at the time of the conference, this hypothesis was becoming more improbable the more they reflected on it.

'The boy's not a killer, chief. I've been able to find out a few things about him. When he arrived in Paris, eighteen months ago, he was employed by a property dealer in the Boulevard Saint-Denis.'

He had been there. The offices were on the entresol, they were dirty and cheap, as was the proprietor who looked like a pimp.

Round the walls, drawing-pins held up little hand-written notices advertising the different business properties for sale, mainly cafés and bars. It had been Paulus's job to write out the notices in his own hand, and also to send out hundreds of circulars.

Another half-starved adolescent, with his hair too long, was now working in the waiting-room, where the electric light had to be kept on all day.

'Paulus?' said the proprietor, in a strong peasant accent. 'I gave him the sack.'

'Why?'

'Because he kept sneaking francs every day from the petty cash.'

This was a drawer where there was always some money, not much, for small running expenses, stamps, registered letters, telegrams.

'Six months ago, chief,' Maigret had continued, 'Paulus left that place. His parents sent him a little money, but not enough to live on, since they're not rich people. Finally he started selling encyclopaedias from door to door. I found his brief-case with a sample copy in it, as well as some forms to sign for the people who bought the twenty-two or twenty-four volumes on the hire-purchase.'

They were going on with the investigation, of course. Paris smelt of spring. The buds on the chestnuts burst and spurted minute leaves of soft green. Thousands of young people like Paulus and his successor were wandering round the streets of Paris, their eyes wild, looking for a place, a future.

'He must have met an older youth, somebody with more know-how too, probably. Mademoiselle Clément says that he occasionally had a friend there and that this friend had at least twice slept in Paulus's room. He's dark, about twenty-five. We'll catch up with him. What strikes me as odd, is that to raid "The Stork" they used a toy pistol.'

To frighten a night-club owner with a toy and to shoot a detective in the street, in cold blood, are two very different things.

'You don't think, Maigret, that his friend could have done the job?'

'With what motive? There could only just have been two reasons to attack Janvier: to get into the house to collect the loot, which would have been risky, or to make the way clear for somebody to get out. Well, Mademoiselle Clément was definite. Nobody came in or went out.'

'Unless Janvier had unearthed a vital clue and . . .'

Maigret had been thinking this over all the morning while Vauquelin remained on guard at the house in the Rue Lhomond, where Mademoiselle Clément had installed him in the living-room, near the open window.

The chief inspector had even searched Janvier's private desk, drawn up a list of all the cases the detective had been working on over the last few months.

He had found out nothing.

'We'll soon see whether he has any idea!' he had sighed.

Madame Janvier was drumming nervously on her handbag, and, probably because she thought she looked too pale, she had put twice as much rouge on her cheeks as was necessary, clumsily, so that it made her seem to be feverish.

Somebody came to fetch them. The nurse, before letting them into the room, gave them some advice.

'You can stay not more than a few minutes. You're not to tire him. Don't talk about anything that might upset him.'

It was the first time Maigret had seen the detective in bed and he seemed to him even more changed, since Janvier, whose baby-face was normally closely shaven, the skin pink and tight, already had the traces of a beard.

The nurse also had something to say to him.

'Don't forget what the doctor told you. He has strictly forbidden you to speak. If the chief inspector has questions to ask you, reply by saying yes or no with your eyelids. Don't try and move. Don't get excited.'

She added, as she walked towards a small table where there was a newspaper:

'I shall stay here in any case.'

And she settled herself into a chair.

Maigret was standing near the door, so that Janvier could not yet see him. Madame Janvier, who had approached the foot of the bed, her hands clutching her bag, looked at her husband with a timid smile and murmured:

'Don't worry, Albert. Everything's all right. Everybody has been very nice to me and the children are well. You haven't been feeling too awful, have you?'

It was rather moving to see two large tears suddenly flood the eyes of the wounded man, who was staring hard at his wife as if he had not hoped to see her again.

'Above all, you mustn't worry about us. The chief inspector is here . . .'

Had she noticed that, after the first feeling of emotion, Janvier had been looking for somebody with his eyes? It was almost embarrassing. Janvier belonged to his family, of course, adored his wife and children. Nevertheless Maigret had the feeling that he was putting his duties as a policeman first.

He came forward a couple of paces, and when he saw him, the detective's face brightened, he wanted to speak in spite of the interdiction; Maigret had to prevent him with a sign.

'Quietly, young Janvier. Let me tell you first how pleased we all are you've pulled through. The Chief asked me to give you his compliments and best wishes. He'll be along himself when visitors no longer tire you.'

Discreetly, Madame Janvier had drawn back a little.

'The doctor has only allowed us a few minutes. I'm looking after the case now. Are you feeling strong enough for me to ask a few questions? You heard what the nurse said: answer by closing your eyelids. Don't try and speak.'

A broad beam of sunlight crossed the room, vibrant with fine particles of dust, as if the air had suddenly disclosed its intimate life.

'Did you see the person who shot you?'

Janvier, without hesitating, made a negative sign.

'They picked you up from the right-hand pavement, that's to say, Mademoiselle Clément's pavement, just outside her house. It doesn't appear that you had had time to drag yourself anywhere before they found you. The street was deserted, wasn't it?'

His eyelids blinked.

'You were walking up and down?'

They blinked once again.

'You didn't hear anybody coming?'

Negative sign.

'And during the previous hours, you didn't notice anybody spying on you?'

It was another no.

'Did you light a cigarette?'

There was a mark of astonishment in Janvier's eyes, then he smiled slightly. He had understood what Maigret was driving at.

'Yes,' said the eyelids.

According to the doctor, indeed, the shot had been fired from a distance of about ten yards. Now there was no street-lamp near Mademoiselle Clément's house. Janvier had been a mere silhouette in the night.

At the instant he had lit his cigarette, he had obviously offered a more distinct target.

'You didn't at any moment hear a window open?'

The wounded man took time to ponder, said no with his head, only with a certain hesitation.

'You mean that at that moment you did not hear the noise of a window?'

That was it.

'I suppose during the evening lots of windows were opened or closed?'

The evening had been such a mild one it was only to be expected. Janvier confirmed this.

'In Mademoiselle Clément's house as well?'

Yes again.

'But not about the time the shot was fired?'

No.

'You did not see or hear anybody?'

No.

'Can you remember which direction you were facing when you were hit?'

There was nothing really to be deduced from the position of the body when it had been found, since a man, when he is hit, may half-turn or turn completely as he falls.

The effort Janvier made to remember gave his face a painful expression. Madame Janvier was no longer listening to them. She was not just being discreet. She had gone over to the nurse and was speaking to her in a low voice, presumably asking questions, risking a few timid pieces of advice.

No, Janvier could not remember. This was to be expected, too. He had walked up and down so often, that evening, on the same stretch of pavement . . .

'Had you unearthed a clue, about Paulus or his accomplice, a clue which isn't mentioned in your reports?'

It was almost the only plausible explanation, but, once more, Janvier replied negatively.

'You hadn't found out anything new on another case you were working on, even an old case?'

Janvier smiled again, following Maigret's reasoning.

It was no. All the explanations were being proved false, one after the other.

'In short, you lit a cigarette and the shot rang out. You didn't hear any steps. You didn't hear any other sound. You fell and lost consciousness.'

'Chief Inspector,' broke in the nurse, 'I'm sorry to have to interrupt you; but the doctor's orders are strict.'

'Don't worry, young Janvier. Above all, don't think any more about this business.'

He saw a question on the detective's lips and he too knew him well enough to guess what it was.

'From today I'm moving into the Rue Lhomond, into Mademoiselle Clément's house, and I'm bound to find out the truth sooner or later, aren't I?'

Poor Janvier! It was obvious that he was imagining the chief inspector in the fat girl's boarding-house and wanted badly to be able to go along with him!

'I'll have to go now, Albert. Madame Dambois has been kind enough to mind the children while I'm out. I'll come every day. They tell me I'll be able to stay a little longer tomorrow.'

She was trying to be brave, but when she was outside in the corridor with Maigret, she couldn't stop herself from crying as she walked along, and he kindly took her arm, without saying anything, without trying to comfort her.

He preferred to telephone from his flat, which now seemed almost strange to him. It was not just that he was alone, without anybody to speak to, but he was not accustomed to being there at this time of day, except on Sundays.

He had opened all the windows wide, poured himself a small glass of sloe-gin, and while he waited for his call to come through, he was stuffing some clothes and his toilet articles into his old leather bag.

It was in a hospital too that he finally contacted Madame Maigret, as she had managed to obtain permission to stay there with her sister who was just starting her convalescence.

Probably because she felt far away and was afraid he would not hear her, she put on a strident voice which he did not recognise and which made the telephone vibrate.

'Of course not, nothing has happened to me. I just telephoned to tell you not to call me here this evening. And to explain why you didn't reach me last night.'

They had arranged that she should ring him every evening about eleven o'clock.

'Janvier has been hurt. Yes, Janvier . . . No. He's out of danger . . . Hallo! But because I've got to carry on with his investigation, I have to move into the Rue Lhomond . . . It's a boarding-house . . . I'll be quite all right there . . . Of course I will! . . . I promise you . . . The landlady is charming . . .'

He had not meant to use this word, and it made him smile.

'Have you a pencil and paper? Take down the number . . . From now on, call me a little earlier, between nine and ten, so we won't wake up the whole household, because the telephone is in the passage on the ground floor . . . No, I haven't forgotten anything . . . It's almost hot . . . I swear there's no need for an overcoat . . .'

He made another visit to the sideboard, replaced the small bottle with its golden rim, and finally left home, his heavy case in his hand, locked the door, with the slight feeling that he was committing some sort of treason.

Was it only because of the investigation that he was moving into the Rue Lhomond, or was it because he hated going back to an empty flat?

Mademoiselle Clément rushed out to meet him, quite excited, her great breasts shaking inside her dress at every movement like jelly.

'I haven't touched a thing in the room, since you told me not to; I've just changed the sheets and put out clean covers.'

Vauquelin had got up from his armchair near the window in the front room, where he had a cup of coffee within reach, and insisted on carrying the chief inspector's suitcase upstairs.

It was an odd house, which didn't fit exactly into any particular class of boarding-house. Though old, it was astonishingly clean, and more than anything it had an air of gaiety. The coloured wallpapers, everywhere, including the staircase, were bright, pale yellow for the most part, with little flower-designs, not a bit old-fashioned or hackneyed. The woodwork, polished with age, gleamed with flickering reflections and the uncarpeted stairs smelt pleasantly of wax.

The rooms were larger than in most boarding-houses. They were more like those in good country inns, and almost all the furniture was old, the wardrobes tall and deep, the chests-of-drawers bow-fronted.

Mademoiselle Clément had taken the unexpected trouble to put a few flowers in a vase on the middle of the round table, plain straightforward flowers which she must have bought off a little barrow while doing her shopping.

She had come upstairs with the men.

'Wouldn't you like me to unpack for you? I've got the feeling you're probably not very used to it.'

She added, laughing with a curious laugh in her throat which made her bosom quiver:

'Unless you've got things in your suitcase I mustn't see?'

He guessed she behaved just the same with all her boarders, not out of servility, nor through professional pride, but just because she liked to. He wondered even if there wasn't something of Madame Maigret in her, a Madame Maigret with no husband to care for, who made up for it by pampering her boarders.

'Have you kept this boarding-house long, Mademoiselle Clément?'

'For ten years, Monsieur Maigret.'

'Are you a native of Paris?'

'Of Lille. Strictly speaking, of Roubaix. Do you know the Brasserie Flamande, at Roubaix? My father was a waiter there for nearly forty years and everyone knew him. I was under twenty when I started there as a cashier.'

To hear the way she spoke, one might have thought that she had played at being a cashier, as she played with her dolls as a child, and now seemed to play at being a boarding-house landlady.

'It was my ambition to set up in Paris on my own, and when my father died and left me a spot of capital, I took this house. I could never live alone. I need to feel life going on around me.'

'Have you never thought of getting married?'

'I wouldn't be my own mistress any longer. Now, if you don't mind, you can go downstairs for a while. I'd be embarrassed to do your unpacking in front of you. I'd sooner you left me on my own.'

Maigret signed to Vauquelin to follow him. On the stairs, they heard a piano trilling, a woman practising singing. It was coming from the ground floor.

'Who's that?'

And Vauquelin, who knew the house already, explained:

'Monsieur Valentin. His real name is Valentin Desquerre. He was fairly well known as a light opera singer, thirty years ago, under the name of Valentin.'

'That's the room on the left, if I remember rightly?'

'Yes. Not just a room, but a flat. He has a little drawing-room in front, where he gives his singing lessons, then a bedroom, a bathroom and even a kitchen. He does his own cooking. His pupils are mostly young girls . . .'

Vauquelin added, taking some papers out of his pocket, when they reached the ground floor:

'I've drawn up a plan of the building for you, with the names of the lodgers and a brief history of each of them. Not that you'll really need it, for Mademoiselle Clément will tell you the whole lot without your having to ask. It's a funny house, as you'll see. People come in and out as if they were at home, use the kitchen, heat themselves some coffee, and, with the telephone in the corridor, everyone knows all the goings-on of everyone else. Mademoiselle Clément will want to get meals for you. She tried with me. I preferred to go to the little bistro a few doors down the street.'

They repaired there together. The awning was stretched out above the two little tables on the terrace and, inside, a builder was drinking a glass of white wine. The *patron* was an Auvergnat with a blue-grey moustache, his hair plastered low on his forehead.

It was hard to imagine that the Boulevard Saint-Michel, and all its bustle, was only round the corner. There were children playing in the middle of the street, as in a small country town. The sound of hammering could be heard from a nearby workshop.

'I think I'll be taking all my meals here for the next few days,' Maigret told the *patron*.

'So long as you're not too fussy, the missis'll do her best . . .'

As early as eleven o'clock that morning, Gastine-Renette, the small-arms expert, had submitted his report, which had slightly shaken Maigret. The bullet that had wounded Janvier, it appeared, was fired by a large-bore revolver, probably a Colt.

So it was a heavy gun, a cumbrous one, the sort they used in the army; it would have been difficult to hide in the pocket of a suit.

'Nobody's been wandering around the house this morning?' the chief inspector asked Vauquelin while they were drinking.

'A few journalists. Some press photographers.'

'You didn't have any interesting phone calls?'

'No. A man rang up for the girl called Blanche, and she came downstairs in her pyjamas and a dressing-gown. A pretty girl.'

'When was this?'

'Eleven o'clock.'

'Did she go out?'

'No. She went back to bed.'

'What does she do for a living?'

'Nothing. She calls herself a dramatic artiste, because she sometimes gets small parts at the Châtelet and places like that. An uncle comes to see her two or three times a week.'

'An uncle?'

'I'm talking like Mademoiselle Clément. Incidentally, I wonder if that woman pretends to be a fool or whether she is really so naïve. If it's the latter, she'd swallow anything she was told.'

'"Mademoiselle Blanche is learning her parts, you know," she said to me. "That's why she's almost always in bed. Her uncle takes a lot of trouble over her. He wants to make her a great actress. She's very young; only just twenty-two . . ."'

'Have you seen the uncle?'

'Not yet. It's his day tomorrow. All I know is that he "comes from a very good family" and is "always perfectly correct" . . .'

'And the others?'

'All equally charming, of course. Everybody is "charming" in that house. Above Monsieur Valentin, on the first floor, live the Lotards, who've got a baby of twelve months.'

'Why do they live in a boarding-house?'

'They haven't been long in Paris and they say they haven't been able to find a flat. They cook on a petrol stove, in the lavatory. I went into their room; there are lines stretched from one wall to the other with washing hanging up to dry.'

'What does Lotard do?'

'In insurance. About thirty years old; tall and sad; his wife's a little duck-arsed woman who comes downstairs now and then to have a chat with Mademoiselle Clément, leaving her door open so she can hear if the baby wakes up. She hates Monsieur Valentin because of his piano. Monsieur Valentin must hate her, because the baby cries every night.'

'Do they have a whole flat, too?'

'Only one room and a lavatory. Behind them, in the room which looks on to the yard, there is a student, Oscar Fachin, who makes a living by copying out music and looks as though he doesn't get a square meal every day. Now and then Mademoiselle Clément takes him up a cup of tea. She says he always refuses at first, because he's very proud. When he's away, she goes and hunts out his socks and mends them for him. He hides them, but she always succeeds in putting her hands on them.'

What could Paulus be doing as they chatted there at the bar-counter, drinking white wine, the air warm from the sun wafted in through the open door?

The police had his description. He must know by now that the house in the Rue Lhomond was being watched. He probably knew it from the time the place had first been searched, since he had not returned.

Maigret had given Lucas the job of finding him, as well as his accomplice, the dark man who was about twenty-five.

'Shall I go on looking after the house?' asked Vauquelin; he was becoming a bit bored with Mademoiselle Clément and this quiet little street.

'No. Anyway, not the house exactly. Later on, about supper-time, when everyone will be home, I would like you to go and ask all the neighbours some questions. It's possible that somebody saw or heard something.'

Maigret dined alone at the Auvergnat's, reading the evening paper, occasionally glancing across at the boarding-house.

When he went back there, at about half past seven, there was a pretty girl in the second room, which was used as a kitchen and dining-room. She was wearing a bright-red little hat. She was fresh-faced, with curly blonde hair.

'Mademoiselle Isabelle!' introduced Mademoiselle Clément. 'She lives on the second floor. She is a typist in an office in the Rue Montmartre.'

'Chief Inspector Maigret.'

He gave her a salute.

'Mademoiselle Isabelle has just been telling me that Paulus was courting her. I knew nothing about it.'

'Oh, it was so vague . . . I don't think you could call it courting . . . I only mentioned it to show what type of boy he was . . .'

'And what type was he?'

'In the mornings I usually eat a croissant in a bar in the Rue Gay-Lussac before catching the métro. One day I noticed a young man drinking his coffee at the same counter, and he stared hard at me. Or more exactly, he stared at me in the mirror. We had never had occasion to talk before, but I recognised him. He must have recognised me too. When I left, he followed me. Then I heard his steps become quicker, I saw his shadow passing me, he came up to me and asked if he might accompany me.'

'Isn't that lovely!' exclaimed Mademoiselle Clément.

'I was probably in a bad mood that morning. I'm never in a very good mood in the morning. I told him I was big enough now to find my own way.'

'And then?'

'Nothing. Before I could look round, he had turned back, muttering some excuse. That's why I was telling Mademoiselle Clément about it. It's not very often young men are quite so shy. They usually insist, if only so as not to lose face.'

'So you find it strange that such a shy young man should attack the owner of a night-club, and then, later, shoot a police inspector?'

'Doesn't it seem odd to you?'

They had not been able to hide from the Press for long the identity of the 'gangster of the Rue Campagne-Première', as the papers called him. They had even published, on the front page, a photograph found amongst his things upstairs.

'Just think, if you had listened to him, nothing might have happened,' Mademoiselle Clément said dreamily to the girl.

'What do you mean?'

'He might have become your boy-friend. He would have had other things to think about than raiding a bar . . .'

'I must be off now. I'm going to the cinema with a friend. Good-night, Chief Inspector . . .'

When she had left, Mademoiselle Clément murmured:

'Isn't she delightful? Every evening it's the same. She comes and tells me that she's not going out, that she has some sewing she's behind with, because she makes her own clothes. Then, half an hour later, I hear her coming down the stairs, with her hat on. She's suddenly remembered she had to meet a girl-friend and go to the cinema. These young things, they hate to feel shut in . . .'

'Has she got a boy-friend?'

'Only a cousin.'

'And he comes to see her sometimes?'

'He goes up for a moment when they are going out together, all fair and above board. It doesn't happen often, because I think he works in the evenings. Except, on Sundays . . .'

'On Sundays?'

'They go into the country. When it rains, they stay upstairs.'

She looked at him with a disarming smile.

'Altogether your boarders seem a very decent lot.'

'There are so many more decent folk in the world than one thinks! I just don't understand why people try to see evil everywhere. Look! Here's Monsieur Kridelka home,' she added after a glance through her spy-window.

He was a man of about forty, his hair blacker than the Auvergnat's in the bistro, with a pale skin, who was automatically wiping his feet on the mat before climbing the stairs.

'He lives on the second floor, too, in the room next to Mademoiselle Isabelle.'

Maigret consulted the notes Vauquelin had handed over to him.

'He's a Yugoslav,' he said.

'He's been living in Paris for a long time.'

'What does he do?'

'You'd never guess. He's a nurse in a lunatic asylum. That's probably why he doesn't ever talk much. They say it's a very arduous job. He deserves to be admired, since in his own country he was a lawyer. Wouldn't you like to come and sit down in the drawing-room?'

She took a seat, some pale blue knitting on her knees, and began juggling with the needles.

'It's for the Lotards' baby. Some landladies refuse to have children in their houses. As far as I'm concerned, as I said, I like the lot, pianos, babies and all. Madame Saft's expecting a baby, as well.'

'Who's she?'

'Second floor, on the right of the passage. She's French, but he's Polish. If you'd arrived a few minutes earlier you'd have seen him come in. He does the shopping on his way home from the office. They mostly eat cold food. I don't think she likes cooking. She was a student. He has finished his studies.'

'What studies?'

'Chemistry. He couldn't find a job as an industrial chemist, so he's working as a pharmacist's assistant near the Rue de Rennes. Some people have got courage, don't you find? They haven't been able to find a flat either. When a couple come to see me, I know in advance what they're going to say, that it's only temporary, that they will soon be finding a flat. The Lotards have been waiting for one for three years. The Safts hope to move before the baby comes.'

That made her laugh, her strange throaty laugh. It did not need much to make her delighted. She reminded one of those good Sisters who brighten the life of a convent by the amusement they find in the most innocent jokes.

'Did you know Paulus well, Mademoiselle Clément?'

'I knew him as well as the others. He was only here five months.'

'What sort of a boy was he?'

'You heard what Mademoiselle Isabelle told you. That's him to a tee. He was so shy that he would turn his face the other way when he passed my window.'

'Did he receive much mail?'

'Only letters from Limoges. They came from his family. I could recognise the writing of his father and his mother. His mother wrote twice a week and his father once a month. He was always a little alarmed when I gave him the ones from his father.'

'He never had any women in his room?'

'He wouldn't have dared.'

'When his friend came to see him, did you know he would be sleeping here?'

'No. And I was even worried about it, the first time. I was waiting for him to leave before I went to sleep, because I hate to be woken up after I've just dozed off. In the morning he crept down on tiptoe, just before it was really daylight, and that amused me. I had a brother like that. He's married now and lives in Indo-China. When we were at home and he was seventeen or eighteen, he used to bring friends to his room on the sly, boys who were frightened to go home because it was too late!'

'Paulus never confided in you?'

'We became quite friendly, towards the end. He sometimes came in to say good evening, tell me how difficult it was to sell those encyclopaedias. His brief-case was so heavy, with that big book inside it, that his arm became stiff. He didn't always eat enough, I'm sure of that.'

'How do you know?'

'Now and then he came in as I was about to eat. I only had to see the look he gave my plate, the way he sniffed at the smell of cooking, to understand. I said to him kindly: "At least you'll share a bowl of soup with me, Monsieur Paulus!" He refused at first, pretending that he'd just had a meal. Then he finally sat down opposite me.'

She looked at him with her clear eyes.

'Did he pay the rent regularly?'

'It's obvious you've never run a boarding-house, Monsieur Maigret. They *never* pay regularly, *nobody* does, you understand. If they had enough to pay me regularly, they would probably not be here. I don't want to be indiscreet or I would show you my notebook, where I write down all the amounts they owe me.

'But they're honest, all the same. They always give me the money in the end, if it's often in tiny sums.'

'Even Monsieur Valentin?'

'He's more broke than anybody else. The little girls who come for singing-lessons pay even less regularly and some of them don't pay him at all.'

'But he gives them lessons all the same?'

'Probably because he thinks they've got some talent. He is so kind!'

Just at that moment Maigret turned towards her, for no precise reason, and he felt he caught a look on the fat girl's face that was different from usual. Unfortunately it was only for a flash, and the next moment her eyes were lowered over her pale blue knitting.

He thought he had noticed, in place of the joyful candour which she usually showed, a look of irony, no less gay, no less childlike, but it was a look that troubled him.

To start with, he had told himself that she was a phenomenon one came across from time to time.

Now he was wondering whether her gaiety did not arise from the fact that she was acting a part, not only to deceive him, not only to hide something from him, but for the fun of play-acting.

'Do you enjoy yourself, Mademoiselle Clément?'

'I always enjoy life, Monsieur Maigret.'

This time she looked at him with all her old candour. In girls' schools it is not unusual to find a t least one little girl who outgrows the others by a head and has this same distended mass of flesh. At thirteen or fourteen they look like enormous rag dolls, with bright eyes which see nothing of real life, and smiles turned inward on their dreams.

Until now Maigret had never known one of forty.

The smoke from his pipe was making the air in the room bluer every moment and it formed a moving sheet around the salmon-pink lampshade.

It was an odd sensation, to be there in an armchair, almost as if he were at home, except that, at home, he would have taken off his jacket. But then again, he was convinced that in a day or two she would be inviting him to do just that.

He jumped when he heard the telephone ring, looked at his watch.

'That will probably be for me . . .' he said, hastening out.

And, as on the previous evening in the streets, he was a little embarrassed, felt almost guilty.

'It's me, yes . . . You didn't have too much trouble getting through? . . . I'm fine . . . Fine . . . I assure you I'm very well . . . Of course not, everything's quiet . . . They're looking after me, yes . . . How's your sister? . . .'

When he had hung up and returned to the sitting-room, Mademoiselle Clément's eyes were lowered over her work and she waited till he was seated and had lit his pipe again before asking in a light-hearted voice:

'Your wife?'

Chapter Three

Maigret spent a good part of the night swearing, grunting, occasionally moaning; a dozen times he cursed himself for having had the idea of moving into the boarding-house in the Rue Lhomond and there were moments when he felt ashamed, as if he were accusing himself of falling for some shameful temptation, in any case for some inadmissible weakness; then, all things considered, in the morning, he was very happy to be there.

Was it the fault of the chartreuse? He had always hated liqueurs. Mademoiselle Clément, on the contrary seemed to delight in them.

As had already happened the previous night, she had before long gone to fetch the bottle from the sideboard, and the mere sight of the syrupy green liquid transformed her expression into one of child-like greed, her eyes gleamed, her lips moistened.

He had not had the strength of mind to refuse. The evening had consequently been one of green and blue, the green of the liqueur and the pale blue of the knitting which was lengthening imperceptibly in the landlady's lap.

They had not drunk much, for the glasses were minute. When he had gone upstairs to his room, Maigret was not the slightest bit tight, and Mademoiselle Clément, when he said good night to her downstairs, had only let out a laugh a little louder than usual.

He had not turned on the lights at once. After removing his tie and opening his collar, he had walked over to the window and leant his elbows on the sill, as thousands of other Parisians must have done that night.

The air was soft like velvet, almost palpable. Not a movement, not a sound disturbed the peace of the Rue Lhomond which slopes gently down towards the lights of the Rue Mouffetard. Somewhere, behind the houses, could be heard a dull roar, the deadened noise of cars driving along the Boulevard Saint-Michel, of brakes and horns, but that was in another world and, between the roofs of the houses, between the chimneys, one could enjoy a glimpse of infinity inhabited only by stars.

Monsieur Kridelka must have been asleep in the next room, for there was not a sound and no light in his window.

By craning his head, Maigret could see, or rather guess in the darkness, the spot on the pavement where Janvier had fallen.

The street-lamp was farther along, brilliant, solitary.

After a moment of stillness, the pulse-beat of the house could be felt or imagined.

On the first floor, the Lotards were in bed, too. But one of them, the wife probably, was getting out again before long, because the baby was whimpering. She didn't put on the light, only a night-light, since there just came a very faint glow from their window. In her nightdress, bare-footed, she must have been preparing something for the child, probably a bottle; he thought he heard the clink of a glass, and at the same time she hummed a tune in an automatic voice.

About this time, around half past eleven, Mademoiselle Blanche put out her light. She had finished her book and, shortly afterwards, there came the rush of the lavatory cistern.

The little bistro, farther along, where Maigret had dined, had been shut for a long time, and it was about this very time, too, that Maigret, for some reason, began to think of a glass of ice-cold beer. Perhaps because a bus had just braked near the Boulevard Saint-Michel, conjuring up the brasseries there?

It quickly became an obsession. The chartreuse left him with a nasty taste in his mouth, and he felt his throat was still fatty from the mutton stew he had eaten at the Auvergnat's and had found so savoury.

For a second, he hesitated whether to put on his tie again, go down the stairs without making a sound, dash for the nearest brasserie.

Mademoiselle Clément was in bed. He would have to wake her when he went out, then again when he came in.

He lit his pipe, still leaning against the window-sill, breathing in the night air, but the idea of the beer would not leave him.

Here and there, in the blackness of the houses opposite, were etched rectangles, more or less luminous, not many, five or six, and every so often one of them disappeared; every so often, behind the curtains or the blinds, shadows could be seen moving in silence.

It must have been exactly the same the night before, when poor Janvier was walking up and down on the pavement.

He heard a noise, from the bottom of the street. Then voices resounding oddly between the houses, a man's voice and a woman's voice. You could almost make out what they were saying. They were walking arm in arm. They stopped two houses farther down. A hand pulled the bell and a little later the couple disappeared, a door closed again loudly.

Opposite him, on the first floor, behind a faintly illuminated blind, a man was continually going to and fro, then became invisible, only to reappear again.

A taxi stopped outside the door. Several minutes passed and nobody got out, and Maigret thought a couple must be kissing inside. It was Mademoiselle Isabelle who finally emerged, friskily, and walked towards the threshold, turning round several times to the person in the cab.

He heard the muffled bell, thought of Mademoiselle Clément, asleep, who would press her face to the spy-window after turning on the light. Steps on the stairs. Then, very near him, a key in a lock and, almost immediately afterwards, the creaking of a mattress, a pair of shoes falling on the floor. He could have sworn that the girl had given a sigh of relief as she took her shoes off and that she was now stroking her sore feet.

She undressed and ran the tap.

This noise made him even thirstier and he too walked over to the basin, filled his tooth-mug. The liquid was tasteless.

Then he undressed, in a bad mood, the window still open, brushed his teeth and went to bed.

He imagined he was going to sleep immediately. He felt drowsy. His breathing was becoming regular. The images of the day began to become confused as he dozed.

But, five or ten minutes later, he was wide awake, eyes open, thinking more insistently than ever of a glass of beer. This time he felt burning in his stomach and he knew for sure that it was the mutton stew. At the Boulevard Richard-Lenoir, he would have got up and taken a little bicarbonate of soda. He had brought none with him, and he did not dare wake Mademoiselle Clément to ask her for some.

He shut his eyes again, burrowed down into the bed as far as possible, and then he began to feel little eddies of cold air creeping about his head and the nape of his neck.

He got up to close the window. The man opposite had still not gone to bed. He was pacing up and down the room behind the blind, and Maigret wondered what he could be doing, going around in circles like that. Perhaps he was an actor learning his part? Or was he talking to somebody sitting down, whose silhouette could not be seen?

There was another light, high up, in an attic window of the same building, and he was to see that same light in the early hours of the morning.

He slept, he must have slept. An uncomfortable, disturbed sleep, without quite losing consciousness of his environment, nor of his problems, which, on the contrary, took on an exaggerated importance.

It was becoming almost an affair of state, even worse, a matter of life and death. The smallest details grew swollen as though seen through a drunken stupor. He became responsible not only for Janvier, but for Janvier's wife, who was expecting a baby and was so brave and so tired.

Had she not looked at him as though to say she was putting her own fate, and that of the baby which would soon be born, into his hands? And Madame Maigret was not there. And for this too, God knows for what reason, he felt guilty.

He was thirsty. From time to time, the burning in his chest became sharper and he found himself groaning; he must be careful not to wake the other tenants, especially not the Lotards' baby, which had gone back to sleep.

As for himself, he had no right to be asleep. He was here to keep a watch on the place. His job was to listen for noises, to keep an eye on all comings and goings.

A taxi passing in the street made such a din that it seemed to insult the silence. It stopped. A door banged. But it was farther up the street, ten houses farther on, at least.

Everybody was asleep. He thought of Mademoiselle Isabelle turning over in bed and the blonde girl's body, already damp with sweat. The Safts, in the other room, were sleeping in the same bed. He had visited their room. The bed was so narrow he wondered how the two of them managed.

He sat up in bed. Or, more correctly, he found himself sitting up in bed without being aware of having moved, and then, suddenly, he pricked up his ears. He was sure he had heard an odd noise, probably the clinking of china or crockery.

He waited, motionless, not breathing, and there came a second noise, on the ground floor, the noise, this time, of a cupboard door shutting.

He struck a match to see his watch. It was half past two in the morning.

He walked in bare feet to the door, half opened it with care, then, certain that someone was out of bed, he pulled on his trousers, crept down the stairs.

He hadn't reached the first floor when a step creaked. It probably creaked like that always. In every house there is at least one creaking step. He could have sworn that the instant before there had been a dim gleam from the passage, as if it had filtered below the door of a lighted room.

So it had been swiftly extinguished. He stopped. And the more he listened the more he was sure somebody else was listening, someone who, like himself, was holding his breath in the dark.

He went down more quickly, felt around for the handle of the kitchen door.

A cup fell to the ground and broke.

He switched on the light.

Before him stood Mademoiselle Clément, in her nightdress, her hair held up in a sort of net. For a moment her face revealed nothing more than an expression of confusion, but then, just when he was least expecting it, she let out that great throaty laugh which made her big bosom shake.

'You gave me a fright,' she cried. 'My God, you frightened me!'

The gas was burning on the stove. The kitchen smelt of freshly made coffee. On the oilcloth spread over the table, there was an enormous ham sandwich.

'I was so frightened when I heard your footsteps that I put the light out. As the steps came closer I dropped my cup . . .'

In spite of her fatness, her body beneath the nightdress was still young and attractive.

'Were you hungry too?'

He asked, not knowing where to look:

'You got up to have something to eat?'

She laughed again, more shortly, blushed a little.

'This happens almost every night. I know I shouldn't eat so much, but I can't help it. I'm like the King of France who always had a cold chicken on his bedside table.'

She took another cup from the cupboard.

'Would you like some coffee?'

He didn't dare ask if she had some beer by any chance. She poured him out a cup, allowing no refusal.

'I think I'd better go and put on a dressing-gown. If someone came in . . .'

It was really very funny. Maigret had no jacket on. His braces hung down his legs and his hair was standing on end.

'Will you excuse me a moment?'

She went into her bedroom, came back almost immediately, and he noticed that her lipstick was on crooked, giving her a very different mouth.

'Will you have a little to eat?'

He wasn't hungry. Only thirsty.

'Sit down . . .'

She had turned off the gas. The coffee was steaming in the cups. The sandwich on the plate was golden-brown, crusty.

'Was it me who woke you, Monsieur Maigret?'

'I wasn't asleep.'

'I'm not usually frightened. I never even think of locking my door. But after what happened yesterday, I feel a little less confident . . .'

She bit into the bread. He swallowed a mouthful of coffee. Then, automatically, he began to fill his pipe. But he had left his matches in his jacket and he got up to fetch the box which was on top of the stove, on the baking-tray.

At first she ate large mouthfuls, like a starving creature, then little by little she began to chew more slowly, occasionally giving Maigret a puzzled glance.

'Is everybody home?' he asked.

'Everybody except Monsieur Fachin, the student, who's working at a friend's place. They go shares in the books they have to buy. Each in turn goes to lectures, and then they meet and study together. This gives them time to earn a living. I had one who was a night-watchman in a bank and only slept about three or four hours a day.'

'Do you sleep a lot?'

'That depends. I am more of an eater than a sleeper. What about you?'

The last mouthfuls were becoming more difficult.

'I feel better. Now I shall go and really get some sleep. You don't need anything?'

'Nothing, thank you.'

'Good night, Monsieur Maigret.'

He climbed back up the stairs. On the first floor, he heard the murmuring of a baby, half asleep, and a regular, measured sound, probably that of the cradle which the mother was rocking from her bed, in the dark, to stop the baby waking up altogether.

This time, in spite of the coffee, he went to sleep straight away, a dreamless sleep which seemed very short. The light wakened him, since he had not closed the curtains, and it was half past five when he went to lean out of the window once again.

The street was even emptier than last night, in the light of morning, and, because of the chill, Maigret had to put on his jacket.

The sky, between the roofs, was a very bright blue, cloudless, and most of the houses looked golden. A police constable on his way to the station walked by, taking long, regular steps, towards the foot of the street.

On the first floor, opposite, the blind had been raised, and Maigret's gaze rested on an untidy bedroom, with a box open near the window. It was an old-fashioned kind of box, practical, well worn, the sort owned by business representatives who travel a lot and take their samples with them.

A middle-aged man was moving about, and, when he bent down, Maigret could see, from above, that his head was balding. He could not see much of the face.

He gave him about fifty-five years, perhaps a little more. Yes, probably a little more. He was fully dressed, in a dark suit. He was finishing putting some white shirts in the top compartment of the case, then lowered the lid, sat on it to shut the lock.

Half the bed was visible, a pillow which still had a hollow in it from the head that had rested there.

For a while the chief inspector wondered if there might not be someone else in the bed, and the answer was immediately provided by a woman's arm.

The man dragged his trunk away, probably out on to the landing, came back, leant over the bed to kiss the woman. Then he returned again and, this time, took a little box from the drawer in the bedside table, removed two tablets, filled a glass with water and held it out to the invisible person.

He must have made a telephone call, because a taxi came up the street and stopped outside the house. Before leaving, the man closed the curtain, and Maigret saw nothing more until the street door was in due course opened.

The box was heavy, and the taxi-driver got out to help his passenger.

Then came the voices.

'Gare Montparnasse. Quickly.'

The door slammed.

A window opened on the opposite side of the street, above Maigret's head, on the third floor, and a woman, her hair in curlers, holding her mauve wrap in place over her chest with one hand, leant out over the narrow cleft of the street.

She noticed the chief inspector. It was a new face to her, and she showed a certain surprise, took her time to examine him before disappearing into the room.

The only other thing he saw was her hand shaking a duster in the air.

There were movements in the Lotards' flat. A tall, red-haired young man entered the house, and after listening to the sound of his steps Maigret knew that it was Oscar Fachin, the student, who went straight off to bed.

Would Mademoiselle Clément go back to sleep after being woken up by the student's return?

At half past six it was the Safts' turn to get up, and there came a vague smell of coffee from their door.

Mademoiselle Isabelle did not leave her bed until a quarter past seven, and she immediately started running water.

Monsieur Kridelka was still asleep. Monsieur Valentin as well. As for Mademoiselle Blanche, she didn't make a sound and, much later, when the house was empty, she would still be wrapped in her sleep.

Maigret had smoked his third or fourth pipe when he decided to get washed and dressed. Monsieur Lotard left, then Monsieur Saft, whom he saw on the pavement, a worn brief-case under his arm.

He did not want any coffee, but a glass of white wine, and it aroused his thirst to see the Auvergnat take down his shutters, bring out the tables and chairs.

He went downstairs, looked in the direction of the spy-windows, the one in the bedroom and the other in the kitchen-dining room, but failed to see Mademoiselle Clément. It was true that the window in the bedroom was screened by a dark curtain. She too was probably at her toilet.

The front door was open, and as he walked through, he met a thin woman, short, dressed entirely in black, who walked in a determined way and entered the living-room as if it belonged to her. She turned round to look at him. As he turned round too, their eyes met, but she did not lower hers, he even imagined that she shrugged her shoulders and muttered something between her teeth. He noticed, without undue surprise, that she was wearing men's shoes.

'A nip of white wine,' he ordered from the Auvergnat, whose shirt was the same washed blue as the sky.

'Well. How was it last night? Anybody murdered?'

He saw Mademoiselle Isabelle go by, looking very fresh in a navy suit. He did not take his eyes off the house, and anyone who was used to working with him, like Lucas, or like the unfortunate Janvier, would have realised that an idea was running through his head.

'Do you know where Mademoiselle Clément does her shopping?'

'In the Rue Mouffetard, like everyone else round here. There are shops in the Rue Gay-Lussac, but they're dearer. And the butcher's not too good in the Rue Saint-Jacques.'

Maigret drank three glasses of the white wine, which had greenish reflections in it, and then, hands in the pockets of his jacket, he walked slowly down the street as if he already lived in the district. A little old man in front of him was taking his dog for a walk and greeted him as one greets people in the country one doesn't know. Was it perhaps because he looked so much at home here? He returned the greeting, smiling, and a few minutes later he arrived in the narrow Rue Mouffetard, cluttered with small barrows which gave off strong smells of vegetables and fruit.

Pearls of dew still trembled on the cauliflowers and lettuces–or maybe the stall-women had sprinkled them to freshen them up.

He was looking for the delicatessen and found it at once; behind the white marble counter stood a woman with rosy cheeks, her bodice laced high, who still retained a trace of village manners.

He waited to be alone with her, letting two women customers, who had come in on his heels, go in front of him.

'What would you like?'

'Some information. Mademoiselle Clément, in the Rue Lhomond, gets her things from you, doesn't she?'

'Has done for the last ten years.'

'Is she a good customer?'

'Of course it's not the same as if she got her lodgers' meals, as they do in some boarding-houses. But she comes in regularly.'

'She has a large appetite? . . .' he said, jokingly.

'She likes her food, that's true enough. Are you living at her house?'

'From yesterday.'

'Is she getting your meals?'

'Now and then.'

She hadn't bothered to worry about what was behind these questions. Suddenly a thought seemed to strike her.

'From yesterday? Is that all?'

'Yesterday evening . . .'

'I'd have thought you'd been there a number of days . . .'

He was opening his mouth to say something more when an old lady came in and he preferred to keep quiet. When he was out again in the Rue Mouffetard, he was feeling gay. He nearly went into a bar to make a telephone call. Then a kind of feeling of loyalty to his Auvergnat made him decide to wait until he was back in the Rue Lhomond; perhaps he also remembered the white wine which left an after-taste that recalled some country inn.

'Have you a telephone?'

'Behind the door at the back.'

It was nine o'clock in the morning. Time for the conference, at the Quai des Orfèvres. The heads of departments, carrying files under their arms, would be entering the Commissioner's big office, with its broad windows open on to a stretch of the Seine.

'Hallo! . . . Give me Lucas, please . . .'

The man on the switchboard had recognised his voice.

'I'll put you through right away, Chief Inspector.'

Then Lucas:

'Is that you, chief?'

'Nothing new?'

'Vauquelin is just writing out his report on the job you gave him. I don't think he found out much.'

'Have you any news of Janvier?'

'I just telephoned Cochin. He had a restless night, but the doctor said that was inevitable. His temperature is fine. Are you still at Mademoiselle Clément's? Did you sleep all right?'

There was no mockery in Lucas's voice, but the chief inspector winced all the same.

'Are you doing anything? Will you get the car and come round to the Rue Lhomond? Stop just a bit down from the house and wait there. There's no hurry. Don't trouble to get here for half an hour.'

Lucas didn't dare ask any questions, and Maigret was sniffing at the smell of cooking in the kitchen where the telephone was situated, pulled a face when he realised it would be mutton again and went to have a last drink at the counter.

When he got back to Mademoiselle Clément's, the woman in men's shoes he had passed as he left was barring his way, head down, her behind in the air, busily swabbing over the tiles in the passage.

There was nobody in the living-room, where everything was now clean and tidy. Mademoiselle Clément was in the kitchen, wearing a light-coloured dress, her face fresh, her expression cheerful.

'You've been out for breakfast?' she enquired. 'If you'd only asked me, I would have got it for you.'

'Do you often get your lodger's meals?'

'Not their meals, really. Sometimes I make them some coffee in the mornings. Or they come down with their little coffee burners and make it themselves.'

'Did you sleep all right, after your snack during the night?'

'Quite well. And you?'

There was something a little aggressive in her good-humour, perhaps a little irritated. Nevertheless Maigret was sure he was behaving in exactly the same manner as on the day before. But she probably had antennae. She was busy peeling potatoes.

'Is that your charlady working in the passage?'

'It's obviously not somebody who comes along to do that just for fun or just for the exercise.'

'I didn't see her yesterday.'

'Because she only comes four days a week. She's got five children and has her own housework to do. Did you speak to her?'

'No. Is she the one who cleans all the rooms?'

'Not all of them. Only on Fridays and Saturdays when she does them out properly.'

'Your room as well?'

'I'm still capable of looking after my own room, wouldn't you think?'

She was still gay, certainly, but her gaiety was forced, and there was an electric atmosphere.

'I should like to have a look at your room, Mademoiselle Clément.'

'Your detectives looked in it the first day.'

'The time they could not find Paulus in the house?'

'Yes.'

'Would it be too much trouble to show it again to me?'

She shrugged her shoulders, stood up, brushed the peelings from her apron.

'The room hasn't been cleaned. But since you saw me in my nightdress last night . . .'

Her throaty laugh.

'Come on . . .'

She opened the door and went in first. The room was dark, because it looked on to the narrow yard of the building next door. While the sun bathed the front of the house and enlivened everything it touched, here there was a feeling of stillness, of emptiness.

Nevertheless it was a feminine room. The bed was unmade. A pretty dressing-case lay open on the dressing-table, and there were still a few blonde hairs in the comb. A curtain of flowered cretonne hid the basin from view and a strong smell of soap floated in the air.

'Have you seen it?'

Maigret had so far seen that there was no wall cupboard. Disregarding the impropriety of doing so, he pulled aside the toilet curtain, while Mademoiselle Clément heaved a sigh behind his back:

'Now you know what an old spinster's bedroom looks like . . .'

On the bedside table there was a cup with coffee dregs in it and, in the saucer, the crumbs from a croissant.

'You bring yourself breakfast in bed?'

Maigret's eyes were laughing now, as he watched the enormous baby, whose face was beginning to show alarm.

'You are charming, Mademoiselle Clément. It would really upset me to cause you any embarrassment, but I feel obliged to look under your bed.'

He didn't have time to bend down. From underneath the bed appeared a pair of men's shoes, trousers, arms, and then an extremely pale face with the pupils glowing with terror.

'Get up, Paulus. Don't be scared. I shan't hurt you.'

The young man was trembling. When he opened his mouth, it was to mutter, with his throat constricted:

'She didn't know.'

'What didn't she know?'

'That I was hiding under the bed.'

Maigret laughed. He was in as playful a mood as suited this spring morning.

'You shave when she's out then?' he asked, because the youth's face showed no sign of a four-day beard.

'I swear . . .'

'Listen, Monsieur Maigret . . .' Mademoiselle Clément began.

She was laughing now. She managed to laugh and she probably didn't take the adventure so very tragically, if the truth were known.

'I deceived you, I know. But it didn't come about as you might think. He wasn't the one who shot the inspector.'

'Were you with him at the time?'

'Yes.'

'In the bed?'

'I might have guessed you'd say that. Everybody simply must see the worst in everything. If he did sometimes sleep in my bed, I promise you it wasn't when I was in it.'

'That's right . . .' interrupted Paulus.

'It was not my idea, whatever you may think, to get him into this room. I was frightened enough, that evening, when I heard a slight sound coming from under my bed.'

Maigret now began to treat Paulus in a more familiar manner; in a way he did this to show the boy that he was under arrest.

'So you were upstairs when the detectives arrived, were you, my lad?'

'Yes. I was expecting something of the sort. I was scared stiff. I saw them from the window. As the house has only one exit, I climbed up to the attic.'

'Didn't they search the attic?'

'Yes, they did. I'd had time to get out on to the roof. I stayed there most of the day, pressed against a chimney.'

'Did you get dizzy?'

'Yes. When I thought there was no longer any danger, I went back inside the house through the skylight and came downstairs without making a sound.'

'You didn't think of getting away?'

'Of course. But I guessed there'd be some policemen left outside in the street.'

He was not an ugly boy, a little thin, a little too nervous, and he had an abrupt way of speaking. Sometimes the words came out so jerkily that one would have thought his jaw was shaking.

Nevertheless he was much less frightened than one might have supposed. He even seemed to be relaxing. It was probably a relief for him, after all, to have been caught.

'So you went off and hid in Mademoiselle Clément's room?'

'I had no idea it would be for so long as this. I imagined that I'd soon have the chance to escape.'

'And she caught you?'

'I must have moved without knowing it. I was asleep. I swore to myself that I wouldn't go off to sleep, but I did all the same.'

It was curious to look at them both together; he long-legged like a young deer, she fat and placid like a provincial aunt.

It would have been even funnier to have witnessed the scene which must have taken place that night. Had Mademoiselle Clément been quite as surprised as she tried to make out?

He had probably wept and she no doubt had comforted him. She had gone and found him something to eat and drink. Almost certainly, she would have given him a small glass of chartreuse.

They had been living, since then, that's to say for five days, in the same room, with one bed, where they must have taken it in turns to sleep. For Maigret believed them on that score.

From morning till evening young Paulus had gazed at the springs in the mattress, jumping at the slightest sound. He had heard the detectives coming and going, Maigret, the questions and answers.

Because of the continuous watch being kept, Mademoiselle Clément had been obliged to get up during the night to give him something to eat.

Maigret smiled as he thought of the enormous sandwich he had forced her to consume at half past two in the morning, when she was not at all hungry.

A car drew up not far from the house, one of the Headquarters cars, in which Lucas, following his instructions, was waiting patiently beside the driver.

'What are you going to do?' asked Mademoiselle Clément, who had also heard the car. 'Are you going to arrest me?'

She gazed around, woebegone, at her walls, at her furniture, her house from which she thought she would now be parted.

'Not right away,' he said. 'It all depends. Come with me, young man. You can bring your toothbrush and comb with you.'

'My parents will find out, I suppose?'

'They're bound to have heard yesterday from the newspapers.'

'What did my father say?'

'I haven't seen him yet. More than likely, he caught the Paris train last night.'

'I'd sooner not have to meet him.'

'I can see that! Come on.'

The boy hesitated, pointed at Mademoiselle Clément.

'Honestly it's not her fault, you know. She's been . . .'

He hunted for the word, couldn't find it.

'She's been . . .'

'Charming, I know. You can tell me all about it at the Quai des Orfèvres.'

They went out through the kitchen, through the living-room where

Maigret had spent the evening tête-à-tête with the fat girl. From the stone threshold, he made a sign to Lucas.

And he, seeing the young man, let out a little whistle of admiration. He obviously thought the case was over.

It was only beginning.

Chapter Four

In the small Headquarters car, Maigret had not once ceased to watch young Paulus out of the corner of his eye, and Lucas, who was studying his chief, noticed he wore a curious expression.

They had not put handcuffs on the boy. He was looking eagerly out of the window and was no longer scared, he no longer trembled as he had when he emerged from under Mademoiselle Clément's bed. At one point he made the most unexpected remark Lucas had ever heard from somebody who had just been arrested. The car had turned into the Boulevard Saint-Michel and was passing a municipal fountain.

A little farther on, between a glove shop and a cinema, they saw a tobacconist's red sign gleaming in the sunlight.

Behaving just like a schoolboy raising his hand to ask to be excused, Paulus said:

'Couldn't we stop a moment so I could buy some cigarettes?'

It was not a trick whereby to get away from them. That would have been too naïve. Without sign of alarm, without taking his big dreamy eyes off him, Maigret had replied:

'I've got some in my office.'

The chief inspector had settled down there with obvious pleasure, the same kind of pleasure the boy had shown at life going on in the sunlit streets.

'Sit down.'

He had taken time to read the mail which was waiting for him, to give some instructions on current cases. He had opened the window, filled his pipe, handed a packet of cigarettes to his young companion.

'Now, start talking.'

'You know it wasn't me who shot the inspector. I promise you. In any case I haven't got a revolver. The one I used at "The Stork" was a toy gun.'

'I know.'

'You do believe me, don't you? I never left Mademoiselle Clément's room. Why should I have tried to kill a policeman?'

'Didn't you want to get out of the house?'

'Not in the slightest.'

He said this so quickly, with such earnestness, that it was almost comic.

'Where would I have gone to? Since the police had come to the Rue Lhomond, they knew who I was. So they were on the hunt for me. So, once outside, they would have got me in the end.'

'Was it your idea or Mademoiselle Clément's?'

'Mine. I begged her to keep me there, promising I'd be good and not look at her as she got undressed.'

'Didn't you look at her?'

'A bit.'

'Did you reckon on staying long in that room?'

'Until the police had given up worrying about me.'

'Where would you have gone?'

'Maybe to look for . . .'

He bit his lip, blushed.

'Go on . . .'

'I don't want to.'

'Why not?'

'Because I mustn't give the game away.'

'You don't want to reveal your accomplice's name? That was who you thought you'd go and join?'

'Yes. But I'm no squealer.'

'You'd rather take all the blame, even though you are the less guilty of the two?'

'I'm not the less guilty.'

Maigret had had dozens of youngsters of this age in his office, who had all done more or less the same thing, for the same reasons; boys who had, almost always foolishly, got on the wrong side of the law in order to obtain money.

It was the first time he had come across one like Paulus. Some of them, almost from the moment of their arrest, would break down, beg, weep, talk of their parents, sometimes sincerely, at other times with sidelong glances to see what effect they were making.

The majority were nervous, on edge, cocky. A lot of them poured out their resentment and attacked society in general.

Paulus, on the other hand, sat still like a good boy. He was puffing gently at his cigarette, self-contained, only giving a start whenever someone knocked on the door, thinking each time that it was his father, of whom he seemed more scared than of prison.

'Who thought up the raid in the Rue Campagne-Première?'

'We both did.'

'But you were the one who knew "The Stork"?'

'Yes. I went there by chance for the first time a few weeks ago.'

'Did you often go to night-clubs?'

'When I had the money.'

'Was it you who also thought of the toy gun?'

'Jef . . .'

He'd been caught out. He blushed again, then smiled.

'I know you'll make me say something I don't mean to in the end.'

'Then you may as well spill the beans right away.'

'Can you be extradited from Belgium?'

'That depends on the crime.'

'But we haven't committed any crime!'

'In law, it would be called a crime.'

'Why, if I didn't fire a shot, and couldn't have done, even if I'd wanted to?'

'Go on, Paulus. If your pal were here, I'm pretty certain he'd soon land you in the soup.'

'You're right there.'

'What's his name?'

'Jef Van Damme; he's a Belgian. Now you know. He's been a waiter in a café.'

'How old?'

'Twenty-five. He's married. He got married almost the moment he arrived in Paris, three years ago, after he'd done his national service. In those days he worked in a restaurant in the Boulevard de Strasbourg and he married a model. They've got a child, a little boy.'

He was relaxed now. He'd come to the end of his cigarette, so he asked for another.

'Where did you meet him?'

'In a bar, near Les Halles.'

'A long time ago?'

'Nearly a year.'

'Was he a waiter then?'

'He had no regular job. Every now and then he filled in for someone. He was very poor.'

'Have you his address?'

'I suppose you haven't got anything on his wife? I can tell you now that she's in the dark about all this. I'll explain it all and you'll see. Her name's Juliette. She's not well, always got something wrong with her. Jef often said he didn't know why he married her, that he wasn't going to spend the rest of his life with her, and that he wasn't sure the child was really his.'

'Their address?'

'Rue Saint-Louis-en-l'Ile, 27a, at the back of a yard, on the third floor.'

Maigret, who had jotted down the address on a scrap of paper, went through into the next office to give Lucas some instructions.

'Everything all right, chief?'

He shrugged his shoulders. It was almost too easy.

'Right! Let's get back to Jef and Juliette. You were saying?'

'Have you sent a detective to see her?'

Maigret nodded.

'You'll soon confirm that I've not been lying, that he's not there and his wife knows nothing. Only, if you pass on to her what I've told you, it will upset her, and she's a decent girl.'

'Have you been to bed with her?'

'It just happened.'

'Did Jef know?'

'Maybe. It's always hard to tell with him. He's a lot older than me, you see. He's travelled a lot. When he was seventeen, he was a steward on a liner and he's been round the world.'

'Was he intending to leave Juliette?'

'Yes. And he'd had enough of Paris. His ambition was to go to America. That's why he wanted the money. I needed money too.'

'To do what?'

'I couldn't go on starving.'

He pronounced these words with a disarming simplicity. He was thin, underfed, with irregular features, but there was something attractive about his eyes.

'Have you committed other thefts between the two of you?'

'Once.'

'How long ago?'

'It was when I lived with them.'

'You lived with the Van Dammes?'

'For two months. At first, when I arrived in Paris and was working in the Boulevard Saint-Denis, I had a room in a hotel in the Rue Rambuteau. Then I got the sack.'

'Because you pinched money from the petty cash?'

'How did you know that?'

'What did you do next?'

'I looked around for a job. Wherever I went they asked me if I'd done my national service. Nobody wanted to hire a boy just for a few months. At nights, I lugged vegetables around Les Halles. I've been a sandwich-board man. My parents used to send me a little money, not enough, and I didn't dare admit to them that I was out of work, or they would have made me go back to Limoges.'

'Why didn't you go back to Limoges?'

'Because it's no sort of life there.'

'While the life you led here was?'

'I could always hope for something to happen. I owed two months' rent and they were just about to throw me out, when I met Jef. He let me sleep at his place, on a divan.'

'Tell me about the first theft. Whose idea was it?'

'It was his. I didn't know such things happened. We were both in a café together. A middle-aged man started staring at me hard, I didn't understand why. He looked like some businessman or the owner of a big shop in the provinces.

'Jef told me that the man would be sure to make a pass at me as soon as I was left alone, and that I only had to let him talk. See what I'm getting at?'

'I see only too well.'

'Once in his room, I should threaten to call for help, and he would offer me money to keep my mouth shut.'

'Is that what did happen?'

'Yes.'

'You didn't try it on again?'

'No.'

'Why not?'

'I don't know. Maybe because I was too scared. And anyway it all seemed a bit dirty.'

'No other reasons?'

'A few days later, I saw the man with a middle-aged woman, probably his wife, and he gave me a pathetic look.'

'You and Jef shared the proceeds?'

'Naturally. He was the one who put me up to it.'

'And Juliette?'

'I don't know. I think he would have liked to send her out on the streets. She didn't want to. They quarrel all the time. He often left me alone with her. She used to undress in front of me, even when he was there. They didn't find my presence at all embarrassing.'

'And that's how it happened?'

'Yes. Almost without my knowing it. I didn't have many other opportunities, for lack of money.'

'What was Van Damme living on?'

'He never let on to me what he was up to. He hung around the low bars near the Porte Saint-Denis. He often went to the races. Sometimes he had money to spend, other times not.'

'Did he trust you?'

'He thought I was too innocent.'

'Why did you leave their place?'

'Because I couldn't stay there for ever, especially after what happened with Juliette. I tried all the jobs I saw advertised. I began selling encyclopaedias. I did fairly well at it to start with and took a room at Mademoiselle Clément's.'

'Who gave you her address?'

'It was just by chance, when I was going from door to door with my books; I saw her notice up. I went in and she seemed to take to me from the start.'

'Did she buy an encyclopaedia?'

'No. She showed me the vacant room and that very evening I moved in. She's always been kind to me. She's a nice person. She's kind to everybody. I owe her three months' rent and she hasn't turned me out. Just the opposite; you know what she did for me.'

'There's been nothing going on between you?'

'Never, on my word of honour.'

'Didn't you try?'

Paulus looked at him, sincerely astonished.

'She's over forty!'

'We know that! You've told her everything you've just been saying to me?'

'Not everything.'

'Van Damme and Juliette?'

'Yes. But not the business with the man up from the provinces. Van Damme sometimes came to see me and he occasionally slept in my room, days when he'd been quarrelling with his wife. We were both trying to think up some way of making a lot of money at one swipe.'

'Why?'

'I've already told you. Jef wanted to go back to Belgium and get his papers to go to the States from there.'

'Leaving his wife and child?'

'Yes. As for me, I reckoned that I'd soon find some clever racket if only I had a bit of ready money.'

'Didn't you also rather want to have money to spend on women?'

'That'd be all right, naturally.'

'Did you know that it was through a girl you met one evening at "The Stork" that we tracked you down?'

'I'm not surprised. She wasn't much fun. She was in too much of a hurry to get me outside and, afterwards, she rushed off to another bar which was still open, in the hope of finding a better customer.'

He said all this without rancour, but there was perhaps a touch of bitterness. He went on, of his own accord:

'Jef and I had read in the papers about a hold-up which they said had raked in three million francs. Some young masked men had attacked a bank messenger. The paper explained how it was there was practically no chance of catching them.'

'Did you think of trying a bank messenger?'

'Not seriously, since they're almost always armed. But I remembered

"The Stork"; the cashier's desk there is near the door, and after two o'clock in the morning, the place is nearly empty.'

'Who got hold of the car?'

'Jef. I can't drive.'

'He stole it?'

'He pinched it from the corner of the road, and afterwards we abandoned it a few streets away.'

'Did Jef possess a revolver?'

Paulus did not hesitate.

'Yes.'

'Do you know its make?'

'I've often seen it at his home. It's a small automatic, made in Belgium, at the Herstal state armaments factory.'

'He didn't have another one?'

'I'm sure he didn't.'

'You never considered using it for the raid on "The Stork"?'

'I was against it.'

'For what reason?'

'So that it wouldn't be so serious if we got nabbed.'

Maigret picked up the internal telephone, which had just rung. It was Lucas, to say that he was back from the Ile Saint-Louis, and Maigret, looking Paulus in the eyes, asked the latter:

'You're not likely to try and run away?'

'What would be the use?'

He left him alone in his office while he went in to see Lucas.

'Van Damme?' he asked.

'He disappeared five days ago. His wife doesn't know what's become of him. She's been expecting him to leave her for some time now. Things weren't going too well between them. They've got a baby.'

'What's she like?'

'A perky little thing, the kind you see everywhere. She looked tubercular to me.'

'Has she any money?'

'Not a penny.'

'How is she living then?'

Maigret comprehended Lucas's look and sigh.

'Nothing found in the flat?'

Lucas laid a Belgian automatic on the desk. Paulus had not lied. It was plainly not the weapon with which Janvier had been shot. If Van Damme had not taken it with him, it was because he was counting on crossing the frontier, where he would run the risk of being searched.

'She hasn't the least idea where he might be?'

'She thinks he's gone back to Belgium. He talked about it quite a lot. He felt a bit lost in Paris, where people made fun of his accent.'

Lucas produced a passport photograph, showing a fair-haired man, with an almost rectangular face and jutting jaw, who gazed fixedly in front of him like a soldier on duty. He looked more like a gangster from La Villette than a waiter.

'Send a copy of it to the Belgian police. They'll probably find him hanging around the American consulate.'

'What did the lad say?'

'The lot.'

'Was it him?'

'He didn't shoot Janvier.'

'His father's just arrived and is waiting outside.'

'What sort of a man?'

'Clerk, or cashier. What shall I do with him?'

'Let him wait.'

Maigret went back in his office, where he found Paulus leaning out of the window.

'Can I take another cigarette? You wouldn't have a glass of water?'

'Sit down. Your father's here.'

'Are you going to make me see him?'

And, for all that he had been so calm until then, there was a look of panic in his eyes.

'You're scared of him? Is he strict?'

'No. It's not that.'

'What then?'

'He won't understand. It's not his fault. He's bound to be upset and . . . Please, Chief Inspector! . . . Don't bring him in now . . .'

'You know what's waiting for you?'

'I'll be put in prison.'

'For how long?'

'I don't know. I haven't killed anyone. It was a toy revolver. I haven't even spent my share of the money. You must have found it by now.'

He had said it quite naturally: 'my share'.

'You'll be lucky if you get away with less than five years. And, after that, you'll be sent off to the regiments in Africa.'

This did not dishearten him. He was only thinking of the unpleasantness of the meeting with his father.

He was not out to win pity. He did not understand why Maigret, who was childless, who had always so much wanted a son, was looking at him in some distress.

What sort of a man would he be, with what hopes for the future, when they released him from serving in Africa—if he ever got out?

'What an idiot you are, Paulus!' sighed the chief inspector. 'If I thought your father would give you a thorough thrashing, I'd fetch him in this minute.'

'He's never hit me in my life.'

'Pity.'

'He starts crying. That's worse!'

'I'm going to send you to the Depot. Do you know any lawyers?'

'No.'

'I expect your father will appoint one for you. Come this way . . .'

'We shan't meet him?'

'No. Put your cigarette out.'

And Maigret handed him over to Lucas, who dealt with the formalities.

The half-hour with the father was still more disagreeable. As Paulus had foreseen, he wept. And Maigret, also, could not bear to see a man weeping.

'We've done everything for him, Chief Inspector . . .'

But of course! Maigret was not blaming anyone. Everybody did his best. Unfortunately, people could not do very much. Otherwise Police

Headquarters would probably not have come into being.

The fact remained that Janvier had been shabbily shot on the pavement in the Rue Lhomond, and that it was up to the chief inspector to find his assailant.

To take his mind off everything, he went with Lucas to lunch at the Brasserie Dauphine, where they sat on the terrace, at a table covered with a red check cloth. It was the first time this year that he had eaten out of doors. He was distracted, preoccupied. Lucas sensed this and hardly spoke, hesitated before asking a question.

'You're sure those two have nothing to do with the Janvier case, chief?'

'Positive. You'll see, they'll pick up Van Damme in Brussels; he'll have run off there the moment he had the money in his pocket. Whereas Paulus, after the robbery, went to earth in the Rue Lhomond house, and nothing in the world would have brought him out. He felt safe with Mademoiselle Clément. He'd have stayed there for months if he'd been allowed to. He could only have had one reason for shooting Janvier: to make the way clear for his escape. But he didn't escape. And I believe Mademoiselle Clément when she asserts that he was under the bed at the time the shot was fired and that she was in the room.'

'What now?'

'Nothing. I've just been through Janvier's desk once again. I examined the smallest scraps of paper, reread the dossiers of all the cases he's been engaged on recently. It could have been someone taking his revenge.'

But still! It's very seldom that a criminal revenges himself on a policeman, even the one who got him arrested. Yet the chief inspector was anxious not to neglect any possibility.

'I also got hold of the list of all those who have recently been released from prison. There isn't a single one who was arrested by Janvier or through his agency.'

'Are you thinking of going back over there?'

'Over there' plainly meant Mademoiselle Clément's house.

Maigret did not reply straight away. He ate in silence, watching the shadows of people passing by on the pavement.

'Who knew Janvier would be on duty that night, in the Rue Lhomond?'

He put the question to himself. But it was Lucas who replied.

'I didn't even know myself,' he said. 'He worked it out to suit himself with Vauquelin and the other inspectors.'

'It's hard to believe that someone could have gone up the Rue Lhomond by chance, recognised Janvier and, for some reason or other, shot him down. Whoever it was could not have approached so silently that Janvier didn't even hear him coming.'

'I'm beginning to see what you're driving at.'

'It wasn't Janvier in person they were after, that's the point. *It was the inspector who was on pavement duty, that evening, in the Rue Lhomond.* Vauquelin, or any of the others, might just as well have been shot.'

'Unless they took Janvier for someone else?'

Maigret shrugged his shoulders. He debated whether to have a liqueur with his coffee, eventually ordered a calvados, as a protest against the chartreuse he had drunk the night before.

'I'm going round to see Janvier. Possibly the doctor will let him talk now.'

'Can I come with you? I'd like to say hello to him.'

They went there together. Madame Janvier had not yet arrived. They hadn't long to wait. This time the inspector had grown almost a proper beard, and his eyes were brighter.

'Don't over-excite him. The doctor says he can talk for a bit, quietly, but he must keep calm.'

Maigret sat down astride a chair, his pipe unlit in his mouth, while Lucas leant against the window-sill.

'We've arrested Paulus. Don't you say anything. I'll tell you what it was in one sentence. He was hiding under Mademoiselle Clément's bed.'

And, as Janvier's face seemed to take on a crest-fallen look, Maigret added:

'Don't get worried. I'd never have dreamt of looking under that woman's bed either. Paulus is just a novice. It was neither he nor his accomplice, a Belgian who has skedaddled, who fired at you. Don't move. Don't say anything. Just let me ask you a few questions and take time to think about the answers.'

Janvier signified that he understood.

'I've thought of one possibility, though I don't set much store by it. Supposing that you'd got hold of a clue, either in this or some other case, which might have led suspicion to fall on somebody, that somebody might have decided to get rid of you.'

Janvier lay motionless for some time.

'I can't think of anything,' he said finally.

'You had done several spells outside the house. Did you notice anything unusual?'

'Nothing that's not in my report.'

Madame Janvier's visit was announced. This time, she was certainly entitled to spend a few minutes alone with her husband. She saw Maigret and was embarrassed by the bunch of violets she held in her hand.

'Don't you worry, my lad. We'll be sure to find him in the end.'

Once outside with Lucas, he seemed less optimistic.

'Someone shot at Janvier. That's a fact. The bullet didn't fire itself and the bastard who pressed the trigger must be somewhere.'

'Do you think he's still in the Rue Lhomond?'

Maigret did not think anything at all. He no longer knew. He was in a bad temper, and the spring weather no longer gave him any feeling of pleasure.

'You may as well go back to the Quai. If there's any news, telephone me.'

'At Mademoiselle Clément's?'

At moments like this the chief inspector was understandably a little more touchy than usual. He gave Lucas a nasty look, as if he suspected him of mockery.

'Yes, at Mademoiselle Clément's!'

And, filling his pipe, he went off heavily towards the Rue Lhomond.

'I was wondering if you were going to come back.'

'Well! I'm back.'

'Have you put him in prison?'

'Certainly.'

'Are you cross?'

'Who with?'

'With me.'

She did not yet fully understand either. There she stood, more like a doll than ever, smiling at him timidly, but that was the limit of her apprehension.

'You realise what you've done?'

'I don't think he's a bad boy. He's all right at heart.'

'Nonetheless I ought to charge you with harbouring a criminal.'

'Is that what you're going to do?'

One might think she found it amusing, that she rather looked forward to going to prison, too, as others look forward to going to Nice.

'I can't say yet.'

'Why don't you sit down?'

Indeed he had no good reason to remain standing in the living-room. It was silly. But he was annoyed with the big fat girl, without exactly knowing why. He was sulking.

'Are you still hiding something from me?'

'I can assure you that there's nobody under my bed now, if that's what you mean. Nor in the cupboards. You can search the house.'

'Are you making fun of me, Mademoiselle Clément?'

'I would never allow myself to do that, Monsieur Maigret.'

'Then why are you smiling?'

'Because I find life amusing.'

'And what if my inspector had been killed, would that have been amusing too? He has a wife, two children, and a third on the way.'

'I hadn't thought of that.'

'What were you thinking of?'

'Of you.'

He could find nothing to answer. She was quite as frank, in her way, as that little scamp Paulus.

'Are you going upstairs?'

'Yes.'

'Wouldn't you like a cup of coffee?'

'No, thanks.'

But he did not go up straight away, and, remembering his thirst the night before, he went across to the bistro opposite, where he drank three glasses of beer, one after the other, with the feeling that he was getting his own back.

'Have you found him yet?' asked the Auvergnat.

Maigret shot straight back at him:

'Who?'

And the man preferred to drop the subject.

It was just an ordinary stretch of street, with almost no passers-by, a pair of pavements, some houses, a few hundred people living in the houses, men who set out in the morning and came back in the evening, women who did their housekeeping, children squealing, old people enjoying the fresh air at their windows or on their doorsteps.

There were a fat girl with a babyish expression who played at running a boarding-house, a pathetic old duffer who gave singing-lessons to opera-mad girls, a starving student who fought grimly against sleep in the hope of one day putting up a doctor's or dentist's plate on his door; there were a lazy little whore who spent the whole day reading novels in bed, where she entertained an elderly gentleman three times a week, and a young typist who was brought home every night in a taxi; there were the Lotards and their baby, the Safts who were expecting one; Monsieur Kridelka, who looked like a screen villain, but who was probably the gentlest person in the world. There were . . .

Charming people, as Mademoiselle Clément would say. The sort of people you meet all over the place, who had to find enough money every day to eat, and enough money every month to pay their rent.

There were the neighbours: a man who had left home that morning with a commercial traveller's box, a woman who shook her duster out of the window, and someone, right at the top, under the roof, who kept the light on late into the night.

What would they have found, if the street had been gone through with a fine-tooth comb? A majority of what are called decent people, probably. No rich ones. A few poor ones. A few semi-scoundrels too, no doubt.

But the murderer?

The Auvergnat narrowed his bushy eyebrows as he heard Maigret, still holding his glass of beer in his hand, order casually:

'A glass of white wine.'

Perhaps he was forgetting he had just drunk three glasses of beer? Perhaps he considered that they did not count, that they just made up for last night? Perhaps, after all, he was just thinking of something else?

The *patron* chose to say nothing, hastily seized hold of the bottle and filled a long-stemmed glass.

When the chief inspector crossed the street a little later, he watched him going, shook his head and muttered:

'That's a strange one!'

For each of us is strange to somebody or other.

Chapter Five

She must have done it deliberately. It was her own way of waging a curious little warfare. Despite her surprising lightness for her size, there was still no need for her to climb up two flights, when she might just as well have called him from the bottom of the staircase.

Was it to rub in the fact that he was a heavy sleeper? Perhaps he was, in the mornings. Madame Maigret, too, teased him about it. But it was not true when he dozed off during the day. Anyway, after knocking on the door, she opened it at once, to find him fully dressed on his bed.

'Please forgive me. I thought you were busy working. You're wanted on the telephone.'

She bore no ill-feeling. Far from it. She looked at him, her eyes sparkling with good-will, and even affection.

It was something that only concerned the two of them; others would not have understood. Maigret was cross with her. That was a fact. It had been going on for more than two days. A dozen times a day, at least, he would leave the house and then come back again. Each time she would contrive to be there, with an odd little look, as if to say:

'Are we friends again?'

Either he pretended not to see her, or he replied to her advances with a grunt.

For the past two days also, it had been raining, with an occasional gleam of sunshine piercing the clouds.

'Hallo. Yes it's me . . .'

'Do you remember someone called Meyer, chief?'

He was sure she was listening, from the living-room or the kitchen, and it was probably for her benefit that he answered, grumpily:

'There must be ten pages of Meyers in the telephone directory.'

'He's the cashier from the Boulevard des Italiens; he's cleared off. We've just had news of him. The Dutch police have picked him up in Amsterdam, with a red-haired girl. What do we do now?'

It was as if, too, he were deliberately keeping away from the Quai des Orfèvres. The house in the Rue Lhomond had become a kind of annexe of Police Headquarters, and it even came to the point that the Commissioner of Police himself had to call the chief inspector there.

'Is that you, Maigret? The examining magistrate has given me a ring about the Piercot case . . .'

And hardly had he hung up before Maigret seemed to sink back again voluptuously into the atmosphere of his little back-street.

The charwoman in men's shoes was scared of him, heaven knows why, and hastily withdrew out of his way when she heard him coming. The others also regarded him with some embarrassment, one might say even some anxiety, as if they felt that for two pins suspicion might fall on them.

In fact it was only Mademoiselle Clément who refused to take him seriously, but smiled at him as if she were sure that sooner or later he would drop his mask.

Without making a show of it, she paid him numerous little attentions. In the morning, she took it upon herself to place a cup of coffee outside his door · as soon as she heard him getting up. In the evening, there was always a bottle of beer on the table in the little living-room, where he would eventually look in on some pretext or other.

If he had been asked what he was doing there he would probably have replied that he had no idea, that he was floundering, and that he had almost had enough of it; while Madame Maigret, on the telephone–for she was still in Alsace–adopted an attitude similar to Mademoiselle Clément's.

One unusual thing was that he had made lots of notes. Whenever he interrogated someone, he drew his big black notebook from his pocket, a notebook fastened with an elastic band, and he wrote down what he was told.

Later, in his room, when he was tired of looking out of his window, he would sit down at his table and copy out his notes. He realised it would probably serve no purpose. It was a kind of discipline, or perhaps a way of punishing himself, for some Godforsaken reason.

Whenever a curtain moved in one of the houses opposite, he would get up and go to stand at the window, which he had to keep closed, for the rain had so lowered the temperature that it was almost cold enough for a fire.

EUGÈNE LOTARD—32, born at Saint-Etienne. Son of a railwayman. Insurance agent with the National. Married three years ago Mlle Rosalie Méchin, born at Bénouville, near Etretat (Seine-Inférieure).

BLANCHE DUBUT—22, born at La Châtaigneraie (Vendée). Stage artiste. Single.

It was all boringly pointless. These people had come to Paris from all over

France, and even from all over Europe, and had settled in Mademoiselle Clément's house.

Kridelka was waiting for his naturalisation papers, although he spoke atrocious French. Saft had his already.

He had interrogated them all, some of them several times over. He had been in their rooms, had seen their beds, their toothbrushes above the basins, and the little spirit or petrol cookers on which they made most of their meals.

He had come to know the most intimate details of their lives, as he watched them with his big eyes, which at such moments took on a look of gloom.

And what besides? Nowhere, of course, not in the cupboards, not on top of the furniture, nor under the mattresses, had he found the Colt revolver which someone had used to shoot Janvier.

Poor Janvier! Maigret had even given up going to the hospital to see him, merely telephoned twice a day to the nurse, and sometimes he was put through to the wounded man, who would say a few words in a voice he did not recognise. How much longer would he speak with that awful whistling sound?

Faces he had never seen three days before had become so familiar to him that, later on, he would probably nod to them in the street, mistaking them for friends.

The woman with the duster, for instance, watched his window almost as often as he watched hers, with a look of reproach as if to convey to him that a big, strong-looking man like himself ought to be engaged on some more worthwhile occupation.

She was a widow, Madame Boulard, whose husband had been employed by the Ministry of Transport, and she had a small pension.

In a block of six houses, he had already come across five widows. He saw them go out each morning, carrying their shopping-baskets on their arms, to the market in the Rue Mouffetard. He saw them return, their bags overflowing with leeks or lettuces.

He would almost have been able to tell what everybody round here ate and at what times, when and how they went to bed, at what times, too, their alarm-clocks began ringing beside their beds.

On the first floor opposite, the bed had been slightly moved, so as to bring it nearer the window. It was the room from which a man had left one morning with a large suitcase to take a taxi to the Gare Montparnasse.

Often, at odd hours of the night, the light would be switched on, but he could see no other shadow against the blind.

The woman was ill. She stayed in bed all day. The concierge would go up about ten o'clock each morning, open the window and start cleaning.

Behind the attic window lived the maid of a well-to-do old woman— another widow; she lived in, and men visited her there every night.

He had taken up Vauquelin's work where it had been left off, had been to interrogate everyone, all the neighbours, all those who might have seen or heard something. To do this, he was obliged to knock at their doors at meal-times, or in the evening after dinner. Some of them he had interviewed twice over.

'I've told the inspector all I know already,' they would say to him.

Nonetheless he would sit down, invited or not. It was an old trick. When people see you sitting down, they give up hope of getting rid of you in a few minutes and try to help you.

'What were you doing at ten o'clock last Monday evening?'

He would add:

'The evening a shot was fired in the street.'

They would be impressed by his big notebook. Most of them searched their memories.

'I was getting ready for bed.'

'Were your windows shut?'

'I think so . . . Wait a minute . . .'

'It was quite warm.'

'If I remember rightly, one of the windows was half open.'

His work certainly required patience. He took Vauquelin's notes with him. Sometimes they agreed, sometimes not.

Three times, he had started to draw up a kind of timetable, which he had to amend continually.

Or else he would go and drink a glass of white wine or have a snack at the Auvergnat's bar, where he came to know all the regulars. They treated him now as an old customer. Each morning he was informed what the meals would be, and the wife, who wore her hair in a tight bun on the top of her head, would add:

'Unless there's something special you fancy . . .'

More often than not, he didn't bother to put on his overcoat. He would turn up the collar of his jacket, lower the brim of his hat and bunch his shoulders as he crossed the street. At the homes of some of the women he went to question like this, they would look at his shoes meaningfully, as if to remind him to wipe his feet.

'You're sure you didn't hear any footsteps?'

His final résumé, drawn up at four o'clock on Friday afternoon, when he got back from having a drink at the Auvergnat's, was roughly as follows. He had read it through so often, his pencil in his hand, that there were doodlings all over it, as in the margin of a schoolboy's exercise book.

> Mlle Clément's house. Twenty past ten (a few seconds before the shot).
>
> Mlle Clément is in her room, getting ready for bed, and Paulus is under her bed.
>
> On the ground floor, on the left, M. Valentin is making himself a hot drink in his kitchen, as he does almost every evening.
>
> On the first floor, the Lotards are in bed. Mme Lotard has not yet gone to sleep, since the baby has just begun whimpering, and she is waiting to see if she will have to get up.
>
> Blanche Dubut is reading in bed.
>
> Fachin out (studying at a friend's place; won't be back till morning).
>
> M. Mège, clerk, whose window, like Fachin's, looks on to the yard, sitting on his bed cutting his toenails.
>
> Second floor. No one in Paulus's room. Kridelka out. Will be in a quarter of an hour later. Has gone to a public meeting. (Checked by Inspector Vacher.)
>
> Mlle Isabelle out. (Cinema, impossible to check. Repeats quite confidently the story of the film she is supposed to have been to see.)
>
> M. and Mme Saft. She in bed. He busy reading a newspaper in an armchair.

Similar pages summarised the activities of the inhabitants of the neighbouring houses.

Then, finally, on a separate sheet, there was as precise a reconstruction as possible of everybody's movements at the time of the shot and immediately afterwards.

This one, especially, differed noticeably from Vauquelin's report, probably because the people concerned had had time to remember.

One fact seemed certain: nobody had heard footsteps before the firing of the shot.

'You didn't hear the inspector's footsteps?'

'No. I saw him a little earlier on, as I was closing my window. I didn't realise he was a detective, and, as he looked quite young, I thought he was waiting for his girl-friend.'

That was the woman with the duster.

Monsieur Valentin too had noticed Janvier, as he closed his window, before going into his kitchen, but that was about ten o'clock. He didn't wonder what he was doing there.

Then the shot rang out in the silence of the deserted street.

Blanche Dubut, it seemed, was the first to rush to her window, which was half open, but the curtains were closed. She had pulled them apart.

'Did you see lights on in any of the other windows?'

'I have a feeling there was one on in the window opposite. It nearly always is at that time; but I looked down at the street first.'

The window opposite belonged to the flat from which a man had left with his travelling-case, and where there lived a woman who was ill or crippled.

'Were there any other windows open?'

'Yes. Almost all of them.'

'Were they open before you opened yours?'

'I don't think so. I'm pretty sure I was the first to see the body on the pavement and call the alarm.'

That was true. Four people at least had heard her scream, including Monsieur Saft, who had rushed out on to the landing, thinking she was calling for help.

'Who went out into the street first?'

In all probability, it was Monsieur Valentin, wearing his black velvet smoking-jacket. The concierge of the next-door house had emerged from her lodge at almost the same moment.

Maigret had asked the same question a hundred times:

'In which windows were there lights on then?'

But thereupon everything became muddled. Most of the windows were in fact opened one after the other. Mademoiselle Clément did not even leave her threshold. She had asked:

'Is he wounded?'

And, not losing a moment, she had rushed off to telephone the police.

'How long elapsed between the shot and the moment when Monsieur Valentin came out of the house?'

'Less than half a minute. A few seconds.'

He had simply to walk through his bedroom, which was next to his kitchen. He had even forgotten to turn off the gas and had gone back a few minutes later to do so.

Yet neither Valentin nor any of the others had heard footsteps. The gunman scarcely had time to get out of sight. He would have had to pass under at least one street-lamp, yet no one had seen a thing.

It might not amount to very much, but these few established facts were the outcome of a considerable number of interrogations.

The concierge of the house opposite, Madame Keller, did her best to help the chief inspector, but she was the kind of eager little woman who talks all of a rush and, in an effort to get things straight, mixes everything up.

'Did you leave the house?'

'I went out on the doorstep, but I didn't cross the street. I thought he was dead and I don't like seeing dead bodies.'

'Did any of your tenants go out?'

'Monsieur Piedboeuf, from the second floor, the man with a beard who works at the Bon Marché, came downstairs, in his dressing-gown, and went to take a look over on the other pavement. I even told him he'd be catching cold.'

'Did you see the police ambulance arrive?'

'Yes . . . No . . . I mean that just as it turned into the street I was in my room, where I'd gone to get my coat . . .'

Maigret had telephoned four or five times to the fifth arrondissement police station to ask questions of the policemen who had arrived on the spot.

According to them, there were about twenty people on the pavement, standing in a circle around Janvier, when they drove up. They had only taken a few random names. Monsieur Valentin had given his without being asked. They had all noticed fat Mademoiselle Clément.

'You don't remember which windows had lights on?'

Nobody had any idea.

'You didn't notice whether anybody moved off towards either end of the street?'

It was confusing. Some of the neighbours had approached the initial group, mingled with them, given an occasional piece of advice, while others had gone back inside their houses. There were also two or three passers-by who had stopped.

It didn't seem to be leading anywhere. It was dismal, like the rain, which still hadn't stopped falling and which was making the whole house seem damp. There was only one fire, in the living-room, and Maigret went in there from time to time to sit down, replying with grunts to Mademoiselle Clément's approaches.

Van Damme had been easily located in Brussels, since, as Paulus had said, the first thing he did was to go to the American consulate, to the enquiries office.

He began by denying his part in the raid on 'The Stork', but when he was forced to face the facts he had thrown all the responsibility on to Paulus. One point was established, that he was in Brussels on the night that Janvier had been shot at in the Rue Lhomond. They had picked up the woman he had taken to the cinema that evening. And he had been seen in her company in a well-frequented restaurant in the Rue des Bouchers.

'You're wanted on the telephone, Monsieur Maigret.'

It had become a game. Each time, she climbed the two flights of stairs as if she enjoyed it, giving an amused glance at the pages he was scribbling on.

It was Police Headquarters again, asking his advice about a case in hand. Lucas was looking after things down there in his absence. Once or twice a day, he came to the Rue Lhomond to get documents signed.

He asked no questions, was careful not to look inquisitively at Maigret.

The chief inspector crossed the road once more, went first of all to have a glass of white wine before going into the house opposite.

'Tell me, Madame Keller . . .'

'Yes . . .?'

The concierge's room was very clean, but gloomy. An enormous stove snored away, and Maigret automatically went and stood with his back to it.

'The tenant on the first floor . . .'

'Yes, Monsieur Boursicault . . . We always call him Monsieur Désiré . . . That's his first name . . .'

'You told me he worked for the United Steamship Company . . .'

'For more than twenty years. He's purser on one of their boats.'

'You know which one?'

'He changes about. For the last year it's been the *Asie.*'

'When I saw him going off with his case, that morning, I suppose he was rejoining his ship?'

'At this very moment he's on his way to Pointe Noire, in Equatorial Africa. He's hardly ever in France. It takes almost a month to get there and a month to get back.'

'So I suppose he comes home just about every two months.'

'Yes.'

'For long?'

'That depends. It's rather complicated. He has often explained to me their rota system, but I've never understood it.'

'But I suppose that, when he's in Paris, he's here for several weeks?'

'No. That's just it. Every other visit, that's all. Then he has almost a whole month free. The other trips he only has time to give his wife a kiss, collect his things and set off again.'

'Was his last stay for a month?'

'No. He was here only two nights.'

Maigret's spirits were sinking. A dozen times, while questioning somebody, he had thought that he was on to something at last, then a very simple answer would put a damper on all his hopes.

'Two nights you say? Wait a moment. He must have arrived home the night the inspector was wounded?'

'That's right, yes. I forgot to mention that.'

'Just before the shot was fired?'

'No. He wasn't in the house when the gun went off.'

'A little afterwards?'

'A long time afterwards. His train arrived at the Gare Montparnasse about midnight. When I opened the door for him, it was almost one o'clock in the morning.'

'I suppose he came home in a taxi?'

'He couldn't have carried his box.'

'Was his wife expecting him?'

'Of course. She always knows his movements. Boats are like trains. There's a time-table. She sends him airmail letters to all the ports of call. I know that better than anybody, since I'm the one who takes them for the post.'

'So she was expecting him?'

'Anxiously.'

'Are they a happy couple?'

'The happiest couple I have ever seen, even though they're not often together, owing to Monsieur Désiré's job.'

'What sort of a man is he?'

'A good man, very kind. He's very patient. He'll be retiring in a year's time, and they are going to live in the country.'

'Is his wife ill?'

'She's hardly left her bed for five years now. She's not supposed ever to get up, but, when I'm not there, she sometimes struggles around the flat.'

'What's wrong with her?'

'I don't know properly. Something to do with her legs. She's half paralysed. Sometimes you'd think she was completely, and she can't move at all.'

'Do you know if she has any relations in Paris?'

'Not a soul.'

'Nobody comes to see her?'

'Only me. I clean the flat for her, as I've told you. I go up several times during the day to take her meals and make sure there's nothing she wants.'

'Why doesn't her husband find a house in the country, or at Bordeaux, since his ships all sail from Bordeaux?'

'He suggested that to her. I think she's got used to me. There was also some talk of putting her into a nursing-home, but she refused.'

'You say she has no relations?'

'Désiré's mother, who's very old and frail herself, comes to see her once a month and brings her a box of chocolates every time. The poor woman doesn't dare tell her that she doesn't like chocolates, and she gives them to me for my daughter.'

'You don't think there's anything you haven't told me?'

'What else could there be? They are good people, in very difficult circumstances. It's no picnic for a man to have a sick wife, and it's no fun for a woman either . . .'

'Tell me, Madame Keller, the evening of the shot, you didn't go upstairs to their flat?'

'It's true, I did. It escaped me for the minute.'

'At what time?'

'Oh, a long time afterwards. They had already taken the young man away in the ambulance. I crossed the road, to see the spot where he had fallen and to hear what everybody was saying. There was blood on the pavement. I noticed the light on in Madame Boursicault's flat, and I thought all of a sudden that the poor thing must be in a fit.'

'How long was that after the inspector had been attacked?'

'At least half an hour. I don't quite remember exactly. I went up. She wasn't asleep. I think she was waiting for me. She knew I'd come and tell her if everything was all right.'

'What did she say to you?'

'Nothing. It was I who told her what had been going on.'

'She hadn't got up?'

'I think she'd gone and had a look at the window. The doctor has forbidden her to walk, but as I have already told you, she doesn't always obey.'

'Was she nervous?'

'No. She had dark rings under her eyes, as usual, since she hardly ever sleeps, in spite of the drugs. I try to make her read, I take her books, but they don't interest her. She spends hour after hour alone, just thinking.'

A quarter of an hour later, Maigret, the telephone receiver in his hand, his eyes glued to the little notice above the money-box, was in touch with the United Steamship Company.

Everything the concierge had told him about Boursicault was substantiated. He was an excellent man, highly esteemed by the company. The *Asie* had docked at Bordeaux just in time for him to catch the train which reached the Gare Montparnasse a few minutes after midnight.

He could not possibly have shot Janvier.

Maigret had hardly replaced the receiver before a voice above his head called:

'Would you mind coming up for a moment, Chief Inspector?'

It was Mademoiselle Blanche, who was in the habit of leaving her door open and must have overheard the conversation.

There was quite an amusing development concerning Mademoiselle Blanche. Since Maigret had been living in the house, her celebrated uncle had not dared to come and see her, so that he was probably the most anxious of all concerned that the case should be solved.

'I don't know whether it's important, but I did just hear what you were saying on the phone and it gave me an idea.'

The room was full of cigarette smoke. There was a plate of cakes near the bed, in which could be seen the hollow left by the young girl's body. She was in her dressing-gown, as usual, and it was obvious that she wore nothing underneath.

Her lack of modesty was quiet, unconscious.

'Sit down. I'm sorry to have made you climb the stairs. It's about those people opposite.'

Sitting cross-legged on the edge of the bed, she held out the plate of cakes.

'No thank you.'

'Please remember that I don't know them at all; I've never even spoken to them. But I'm almost always here in the house. From my bed I can see out of the window. I'm not madly inquisitive.'

This was true. She only seemed interested in herself–and in the characters in the novels she devoured.

'Still there was one thing I did notice. I don't know why. Some days, their blind is up the whole day and I can see the woman in her bed through the lace curtains.'

'And on other days?'

'On other days, the blind is kept down from morning till night and even the window isn't opened to air the room.'

'Does that happen often?'

'Often enough for it to have made an impression on me. The first time, I wondered whether the woman was dead. As I was accustomed to seeing her in bed . . . I spoke about it to Mademoiselle Clément . . .'

'This was a long time ago? . . .'

'Oh, yes . . .'

'Months?'

'More than that. Almost two years. It was a few weeks after I moved in here. I was all the more surprised because it was summer, and the few days before, the windows had been wide open all day.'

'You don't know whether this happens at regular intervals?'

'I haven't noticed. But it sometimes lasts three days.'

'You've never seen anybody else in the room?'

'Only the concierge, every day, several times a day, occasionally an old lady, and her husband, at rare intervals.'

'Does the doctor call frequently?'

'That depends on what you mean by frequently. Possibly once a month. I'm not always looking out of the window. If I hadn't heard you on the telephone, it wouldn't have entered my head. Do you think it will help you at all? Remember that I mean them no harm at all. I've never said a word to them.'

'Would you mind thinking again? When you went to your window, after the shot was fired . . .'

'I know what you are thinking. I'm almost certain now that there were no lights on opposite.'

'The blind was down?'

'I don't think so. When it's down, it makes a pale square, because it's a light-coloured blind. Now I feel, on the other hand, it was a black square, like a window open into an unlighted room.'

Was Mademoiselle Clément going to pay him back by sulking too? When Maigret came downstairs, she did not show herself as she usually did. Perhaps she was jealous of Mademoiselle Blanche?

'It's me again,' Maigret announced as he went into Madame Keller's lodge.

'I was just about to take up Madame Boursicault's dinner.'

She was busy getting it ready on a tray.

'Does your tenant ever spend the whole day with the blind down?'

'The whole day! You mean three or four days! I'm always going on at her about it . . .'

'What reason does she give for living in the half-dark like that?'

'Well, Chief Inspector, it's no good trying to understand invalids. Sometimes, I almost get angry with her. Then I try and put myself in her place and I say to myself that I would probably be worse than she is. I think she sometimes gets a little neurotic. I've spoken to the doctor about it.'

'What did he reply?'

'Not to worry myself over it. It comes and goes with her. At times like that you'd think she hated me. If she could lock herself in, she'd probably do it. She not only has me pull the blind down, or pulls it down herself, but she forbids me to tidy up. She says she has a migraine, that the slightest noise, the slightest movement in the room will drive her mad.'

'Does this happen often?'

'Unfortunately, yes.'

'But she still eats.'

'As usual. I just manage to get the bed made and the bedroom dusted.'

'How many rooms are there in the flat?'

'Four, plus a box-room and the toilet. There are two bedrooms, one of which is never used, a dining-room, and a drawing-room which is never used either. They don't have to pay much, because Monsieur Boursicault has lived in the house for more than twenty years. He was here before me even.'

'She as well?'

'They got married fifteen years ago; neither of them was young then.'

'How old is she?'

'Forty-eight.'

'And her husband?'

'He'll be sixty next year. He admitted that, when he let me know he would be retiring and that the flat would be empty.'

'You told me that it was you who took Madame Boursicault's mail to the post office?'

'Not the post office. The postman collects it from the lodge when he comes on his rounds.'

'Who does she write to?'

'To her husband. Sometimes to her mother-in-law.'

'Is that all?'

'I've never seen any other letters.'

'Does she receive many?'

'From her husband, yes. The old lady never writes.'

'Nothing else?'

'Very rarely. Sometimes I've taken her up an envelope which has a typewritten address.'

'How often?'

'Four or five times. The rest are just gas or electricity bills, or prospectuses.'

'Do they have a telephone?'

'He had one put in, five years ago, when she fell ill, so that she could get in touch with the doctor more easily if she needed to.'

'Would you mind not telling her that I've been asking you questions about her?'

'I already have mentioned it. Was that wrong? I'm always looking for something which will interest her. I told her about the questions you were asking everybody in the street. I joked about it, saying that if her husband had arrived home a few hours earlier, he would have been a suspect. I'm very sorry.'

'What was her reaction?'

'She showed no reaction. She seemed very tired. I shouldn't be surprised if she started another migraine tomorrow or the day after.'

'You'd better take up her dinner. Tell her that I should like to have a word with her. Say that I've been interrogating all the tenants and that I should like to ask her one or two questions.'

'Straight away?'

'I'll be back in a few minutes.'

He suddenly felt a need to breathe in some fresh air and, above all, to drink a glass of the Auvergnat's white wine.

Behind the living-room curtains, opposite, Mademoiselle Clément followed him with her eyes, and he almost stuck his tongue out at her.

Chapter Six

What he really needed was courage. Already, during the preceding days, while he was disturbing peaceful households over their supper by asking them questions, staring at them with his great eyes, he had been more ill at ease than he would have liked to seem.

Still, he knew Madame Boursicault by sight; he had seen her through the window, only one naked arm that first day, when her husband had left, then, the next day, her face and the shape of her thin body beneath the sheet.

She was a creature of indeterminate age; her face was emaciated, without colour or life, rather like those of certain saints in religious paintings, and he thought with embarrassment of the two or three occasions when their eyes had met as they stared across the street. Did she know who he was? Or did she merely take him to be one of Mademoiselle Clément's new lodgers? Had the concierge talked about him as she cleaned the flat?

He had the feeling, all the same, that he had made some personal contact. She had tiny, dark pupils, and her entire vitality seemed to be concentrated in them.

'There you are, a big strong man, in good health, able to move freely about the streets, yet you stick there, leaning out of a window, gazing at a poor sick woman as if it were a fascinating sight! . . .'

Perhaps that was not what she was thinking at all. Probably it only existed in Maigret's imagination.

Nonetheless it was unpleasant, and he shrank from the moment of going up to see her, allowing her time to finish the meal the concierge had brought her. Madame Keller would have tactfully told her of his visit as a matter of little importance, a mere routine visit.

More than likely she would have tidied up the room, changed the sheets and the pillow-cases.

'I'll have another,' he ordered.

He had three drinks in all, and only left the bistro when he began to feel a kind of warmth in his throat and head. On the other pavement, he saw Mademoiselle Isabelle returning, and she gave him a happy smile. There was a woman in good health, full of vitality and . . .

What was it that led his thoughts so far away? He filled his pipe. Then he stuffed it in his pocket, remembering that he was going to call on an invalid, and scowled as he realised that he might perhaps have to do without a smoke for some little while.

He climbed the stairs, knocked at the door, beneath which there was a gleam of electric light, although it was still day outside.

'Come in!'

It was the concierge. She opened the door to him. The tray was laid down on the red velvet seat of a chair. Only half the broth had been drunk and some sort of puree had been no more than picked at with a fork.

'I do regret having to disturb you, Madame Boursicault . . .'

He had not been mistaken. There were clean sheets on the bed and the invalid's nightdress had been changed. Madame Keller had even done her hair. Her dark curls, with streaks of grey, had plainly been just combed.

She was sitting up in bed and she beckoned him, with a bony hand, to an armchair by the bedside.

'I must go down now, Madame Françoise. I'll come and say goodnight when the inspector's finished with you. Whatever you do, as I've told you before, you're not to worry.'

She spoke to her in that light-hearted tone people put on when addressing the dying, and Maigret found himself copying it too.

He improved on it: 'Now there's nothing whatever for you to worry about. You realise a crime has been committed in this street, just opposite you. I've interrogated all the neighbours, some of them several times over, because it's important to reconstruct the facts as exactly as possible.'

She had not yet opened her mouth. She was looking at him seriously, in the way that some children who are called too old for their age look at grown-ups.

'Madame Keller has assured me that it would not upset you if I called . . .'

Then she spoke for the first time.

'You may smoke your pipe.'

She must have seen him at his window, smoking a pipe all day long.

'My husband's a smoker too. It doesn't bother me.'

And, since he still hesitated:

'Please do . . .'

Perhaps on account of this, he felt obliged to give her some lengthy explanations.

'In an investigation of this type, the hardest thing is to establish for certain everybody's movements. Not because people tell lies, but because their recollections are almost always imprecise. It occurred to me that someone who can only watch the outside world from their bedside would be likely to register certain details more precisely than other people. I presume, Madame Boursicault, you were in bed at the time the shot was fired?'

'Yes, Chief Inspector. I'm so seldom up! If I did what I was told, I would never get up. I practically only do so on the sly.'

She spoke slowly, in a level voice which gave a dreary tone to her words.

'You were expecting your husband that night, weren't you?'

'I knew he'd be coming in about one in the morning.'

'Yet you had gone to sleep?'

'I wasn't asleep. I had merely put out the light. The light makes me tired after a bit.'

'Your window was closed?'

'I think it was half open. Probably just a few inches.'

'The blind was down?'

'Most likely. I don't remember.'

'You heard the shot fired?'

'How could I help it?'

'Did you know straight away that it was a shot?'

'There was no sound of a car in the street. So it couldn't have been a burst tyre.'

'You heard no footsteps just beforehand?'

'No.'

'Nor the noise of a door or window being opened or closed?'

'Not before, but afterwards. A good many of them. The neighbours looked out of their windows. Someone came out of the house opposite.'

'Just a moment. Immediately after the explosion, were there no hurried footsteps?'

'Yes, I think there were.'

'You can't say for certain?'

'No.'

'You didn't get up?'

'Not at once.'

'But you did get out of bed?'

'When I heard a babble of voices on the pavement opposite.'

'Did you switch on the light?'

She appeared to be considering.

'No. I definitely did not. I was in my nightclothes and there were lighted windows opposite. I wouldn't have liked to be seen.'

'What did you see?'

'A lot of people were gathered round the body. Others were coming to join them.'

'Did you stay long at the window?'

'Until a police ambulance drew up.'

'That means you didn't see or hear anything which could help me in my enquiries?'

'I'm afraid so, Chief Inspector. Madame Keller came upstairs a little later on to tell me what had happened. I didn't let on to her that I'd been at the window, or she would have scolded me.'

It was warm in the musty-smelling room. Maigret felt uncomfortable sitting in the too low armchair and, from a sort of modesty, only smoked in very tiny puffs.

'May I ask you your age, madame?'

'I'm forty-eight. It's exactly fifteen years since I got married. So you see that I was already what they call an old maid.'

She looked across at an enlarged photograph, opposite her bed, above the fireplace; it showed herself in her wedding dress on the arm of a man, taller than her, older, who looked serious, a little bit solemn.

'That's your husband?'

'Yes. He was a widower. His first wife died of pneumonia after they had been married seven years.'

She added in a rather lower voice:

'She died in this room, in this bed. They had no children.'

From then on, without Maigret having to ask any questions, she launched into a long monologue; she seemed to be doing it for her own sake, with the monotonous delivery of a running tap.

She no longer looked at him, but stared vacantly ahead, and there were pauses while she regained her breath.

'You see, Boursicault is the best person in the world. Everybody will tell you that, particularly in the United, where they adore him. He joined them when he was sixteen, as a messenger boy, and he made good all by himself, studying and neglecting everything else. His parents were very poor and lived at Bordeaux. His father was a drunkard, and each Saturday his mother had to look for him in every police station in town.

'That's why he's always had such a horror of drink. I'm sorry I've nothing here to offer you. There is never a drop of alcohol, not even wine, in the house.

'At first, I think he was frightened of the hereditary factor, and he kept the strictest rules . . .'

Maigret opened his mouth, but she didn't give him time to speak, so he resigned himself to listening to the rest of it.

'Some people laughed at him, particularly on board ship, where everybody drinks so much. He doesn't gamble, doesn't run after women. At sea, he spends his evenings in his cabin, reading or working. He has learnt, all on his own, five or six languages, and he speaks several native dialects.'

The furniture was old-fashioned, as was every object adorning the room.

The electric light seemed drab, because of the daylight outside, and made the whole place look dull, covered with dust.

He had come in order to ask precise questions, and now he had to submit to these interminable confidences.

'I met him while he was on leave in Paris, between ships, since, even when he was a widower, he used to come back to Paris, where he had kept on his flat.'

'Doesn't his mother live in Paris?'

She was not surprised that he knew all this.

'Yes. He brought her here a long time ago, when his first wife was alive. It's he who has always had to support her, because he's an only child. He settled her in a room in the Rue des Tournelles. He adores his mother. She's very old now. She still comes to see me occasionally, and that's practically the only time she does go out.'

'Why didn't she come and live with you?'

'She was the one who was against it. She says that that always turns out badly in the end, that a married couple should be independent.'

'Do you get on well with her?'

'I love her as if she were my own mother. When I met Boursicault, I was an assistant in a men's shop in the Boulevard Saint-Michel. He came in to buy some socks and black ties. He didn't flirt with me, but I could see that he kept looking at me closely, as if something about me had intrigued him. I learnt later what had so affected him. He didn't try to hide it from me. It seems that I resemble his first wife, feature for feature. Go over to the fireplace. There's a little photo of her on the left, in the mahogany frame.'

Maigret got up, sighing, and looked conscientiously at a bad photograph of a rather commonplace young woman, who smiled sadly, as if she sensed in advance that she would die young.

He was sorry he had come. All this dismal greyness was submerging him, made him want to be outside to breathe the quickening air, and when he sat down again in his armchair, he felt his eyelids growing heavy.

'I didn't see him again for almost three months. I had no idea what sort of a job he had. He was on one of his voyages to Equatorial Africa. When he returned, he invited me to go out with him. I didn't even hesitate.'

She was thirty-three then and he was forty-six; they were obviously old enough to do without a chaperon.

'That was the evening, after we had dined at the Rotisserie Périgourdine, that he spoke about his first wife and asked me if I would agree to marry him. I was alone, without any family, very poor. I answered yes. It was only later that I came to realise what sort of a man he was, and how lucky I had been to meet him. Just think what might have happened had I fallen ill before meeting him. I would be in a hospital now, living off public charity.

'It's no fun for him, when he comes back, to find a wife in my condition, and yet he has never uttered a word of complaint. On the contrary, he's always comforting me, trying to appear as cheerful as possible . . .'

Why did it pass through Maigret's head that there must be something lugubrious about this man's gaiety? He pitied them both, of course. But, for some reason or other, their misfortune did not succeed in touching him.

Her words seemed to reach him through a veil. The atmosphere in this room where he sat suggested the dreary boredom of some family album which strangers insist on showing you without leaving out a single aunt or tiny cousin.

He was, in actual fact, almost asleep, and had to make a continual effort to keep his eyes open. He had been going round in circles for much too long in this little street; he was suddenly sick of it all and felt a strong desire to see the lights and brush elbows with the crowds in the Grands Boulevards.

'I fell ill about five years ago, and he found me the best specialists. To start with, he took six months' leave to look after me, although that naturally meant his retiring six months later. I don't know why I'm telling you all this.' (Nor did he!) 'Perhaps it's because I noticed you a number of times at your window and saw that you were looking at me with interest? . . . Apart from Madame Keller and my mother-in-law's visits, I am always alone . . . So I think . . .'

He had nearly dozed off. He must have closed his eyes, because she was looking at him with a saddened expression.

'I'm boring you, aren't I?'

'Not at all, madame. I was merely closing my eyes because I, too, was thinking.'

'What were you thinking about?'

'About you . . . Your life . . . Were you born in Paris?'

Perhaps he would at last be able to ask her some questions.

'I was born in Le Havre.'

'Would it be prying to ask you your maiden name?'

'Binet . . . Françoise Binet . . .'

And that was enough to set her off again.

'My father was a seaman. That's a curious coincidence, isn't it? He only rose to be leading seaman. There were nine of us children. Now there can hardly be more than three or four left.'

'You don't keep in touch with your family any longer?'

'Not for ages. As the girls grew old enough, we were sent out to work as maids, and the boys found their own level for themselves. My mother and father are dead.'

'Were you a housemaid?'

'I was a children's nanny, at first, when I was fourteen, with a family who spent their summers at Etretat. I came with this family to Paris, where they lived in the Avenue Hoche. They were very rich people. I wanted to become a lady's maid. I went to a dressmaking school, in the Avenue de Wagram.'

'And then? What did you do?'

It seemed to him, all of a sudden, that there was a hesitation in her voice.

'I had a boy-friend and my employers threw me out.'

'How old were you?'

'Sixteen.'

'Why did they throw you out?'

'Because I didn't come home one night.'

'You stayed out all night?'

'Yes. I have not always been so well-behaved, Chief Inspector. I was young. I wanted to enjoy myself.'

'And you did enjoy yourself?'

'One thinks so, at that age.'

'So you stopped working—?'

'Yes, for a time. Then I became a waitress in a restaurant which catered mainly for regular customers.'

'Your husband knows all this?'

'I told him that I was not worthy of him.'

'Did you give him any details?'

'He refused to listen to them.'

'Did you sink really low?' he asked, watching her carefully.

'Not the lowest, no.'

'You had lovers?'

'Yes.'

She added with a little laugh:

'It's difficult to believe, seeing me as I am now, isn't it?'

'Did they give you money?'

'Sometimes. But if that's what you're getting at, it was never my profession.'

'Were you still having adventures when you met Boursicault?'

'I'd finished with that a long time before.'

'Why?'

'I don't know. Because I no longer wanted to. It didn't last very long, taken all in all. I don't think I was the type. I must have been made to be a respectable housewife.'

'Where were you living when you worked in the men's clothes shop?'

'I had a room in the Rue Monsieur-le-Prince, just around the corner.'

'Furnished?'

'No. I had bought a few pieces of furniture. I thought I would end up an old maid. I was already becoming a little queer.'

Why did he suddenly stand up and begin to pace the room, as he would have done had he been in his own office? He appeared to have forgotten the invalid in her bed, narrowed his eyebrows, looking puzzled.

He mechanically hunted for an ashtray so he could empty his pipe, could not find one, and she guessed.

'There's one on the dining-room table. You only have to open that door . . .'

He did so, turning on the light-switch, and found, as she said, on the Henri II table, a copper ashtray with a large curved pipe on it. It was almost as if he had met Boursicault; he imagined him in his slippers and his shirt-sleeves, smoking this pipe in the flat.

The bleak voice was going on, behind him, as if a rosary was being mumbled:

'On board ship, my husband smokes cigarettes, except in his cabin, but here he prefers his pipe and . . .'

He went back hurriedly and looked into her eyes.

'Up to now you have seemed very frank, Madame Boursicault.'

She appeared surprised by this attack, waited, and he noticed that one of her hands was clenching on the sheet.

'I was convinced that you had been telling the truth.'

She murmured:

'I have been telling you the truth.'

'Then I hope you will go on doing so.'

He hesitated a little longer before going into the attack, since he was not quite sure that he had not made a mistake, and, in that case, he would seem an unfeeling brute.

'*How did he get into the house?*'

He stood a yard away from the bed and must have looked enormous to the invalid, at whom he stared down from his full height, his empty pipe in his mouth. They were suddenly enveloped in a different quality of silence, as if both of them were holding their breath.

He was sure she had grown paler, if it were possible to become paler than she usually was. Her nostrils were pinched, like the nostrils of a corpse. She was very thin under the sheet. He felt like turning his head away, perhaps even taking his hat and leaving.

'Of whom are you speaking?'

'I don't know who he is. I'm speaking of the man who comes to see you when your husband is away at sea, and whom your concierge seems never to have met.'

'I don't understand.'

'Listen to me, Madame Boursicault. I wish you no harm. I am a policeman and I'm doing my duty. One of my inspectors was shot opposite your windows.'

'You think it was I who shot him?'

'I haven't said that and I'm pretty convinced that you didn't. But, you see, I'm equally convinced that your reason for talking about your husband and one period of your life was to hide other episodes. Presently I shall order my men to trace your life backwards from the time you were married. The police at Le Havre will be on the job there too. It will doubtless mean a long time. There will probably be some gaps. But, with patience, we will be able to reconstruct almost your entire existence and find anybody who's had any contact with you.'

This time he really did turn away his head, because she had closed her eyes and he saw a tear spurt from her eyelid. She didn't move. For nearly a minute he remained silent.

He continued, filling his pipe to give himself something to do:

'I'm sorry if I do not believe in your migraines. Presently I shall also telephone the doctor who looks after you, and I know already what he will say.'

She gave a light sigh, still kept her eyes shut.

'At this point, one of my English colleagues would be obliged to warn you, by reminding you that anything you say may be used in evidence against you. French Law does not require me to tell you this, but I don't want to trick you into anything. It's up to you to decide whether you want to confide in me or not.'

Slowly, she shook her head. He had expected something worse, a fainting fit or the pretence of one, a nervous attack, a burst of indignation. Yet it was almost as embarrassing to see her lying there motionless, prostrate.

'I am convinced, I shan't conceal it from you, that you receive visits unknown to anybody else, and that when your blinds are down, sometimes for three days, it's because you have someone with you. This person, presumably, knows the habits of the household. Every morning, the concierge is away for more than half an hour, doing her shopping. It would be easy, then, to slip into your flat. You have nothing to say?'

She took quite a while before she opened her mouth and her lips were as pale as her cheeks.

'I've nothing to say.'

'You claim that it isn't true?'

The eyelids parted at last, and a cold look rested on the chief inspector. 'You're entitled, I suppose, to imagine whatever you like.'

Suddenly he felt in her voice an energy which he would have found it impossible to suspect a few minutes earlier.

'Was there a man in your room when the shot was fired?'

She was staring at him without replying.

'A woman?' he hesitated.

The lips did not move.

'You really are ill, and I do not wish to tire you. You know that I am opposite, at Mademoiselle Clément's. The telephone is at the head of your bed. If, at any time, you feel like getting in touch with me, give me a ring.'

He hesitated, embarrassed.

'Please understand, Madame Boursicault, that, in spite of all appearances, I am not your enemy. It's my duty to find out the truth and I will find it out. I sincerely hope, and this is what I want you to realise, that it will entail as little trouble as possible.'

She still said nothing. She was looking at him steadily, as if thinking hard. He waited a little, hoping all the time that she would speak.

He had picked up his hat. He still did not make a move towards the door. One last time, he opened his mouth to speak, but he closed it again without saying anything.

He would get nothing more from her, he was sure of that. Perhaps she would telephone him later?

He was not depending on it too much. He nodded to her gravely.

'You must excuse me now. I shall send Madame Keller to you.'

Her lips still tightly closed, she watched him leave, and he shut the door behind him, sighed deeply when he was on the landing.

The concierge was waiting for him in the passage and seemed surprised to see him so serious. He himself did not realise the way he was looking.

'She's unwell?'

'You had better go up to her. If anything happens, no matter what, let me know at Mademoiselle Clément's.'

He had not dined yet. He went to the Auvergnat's, intending to eat, but he stopped at the bar and drank two glasses of wine, one after the other. There was a mirror behind the bottles and he was disconcerted to see his face looking so lined.

A few minutes later, without even waiting to eat, he was in contact with Torrence.

'Is Lucas not there?'

'He's just left for the Place d'Italie, where those Arabs have been playing with knives.'

'Will you please, as quickly as possible, ask the listening-post to tap the number of Madame Boursicault, in the Rue Lhomond? And send me over an inspector.'

'Vacher is here.'

'Good. He already knows the house. I'll probably be in the little restaurant opposite.'

As he hung up the receiver, he saw Mademoiselle Clément's face, through the little window, and he noticed that she wore an unaccustomed expression. He did not understand at once. She no longer seemed to be playing a game. She was watching him, if not with fear, at least with a trace of anxiety.

It was because he himself had suddenly changed. She did not know him in this guise. The moment had come, and he had finished with floundering and smelling around in corners.

He found her standing at the door of her living-room.

'Are you going out?'

'I'm going to eat.'

'What shall I do if someone rings you up?'

'You can come and let me know over at the Auvergnat's.'

She did not dare ask him if something new had turned up. Perhaps she had overheard his conversation with Torrence? She knew, at any rate, that it was no time to play the innocent little girl.

'Is that you, Torrence?'

This time, he was telephoning from the bar.

'She hasn't tried to get a number yet, chief.'

'In that case she probably won't try at all. They must keep a tag on her all the same. Have you many men available?'

'There are four or five free tonight.'

Maigret spelled out the name of Boursicault, then that of Binet.

'Take this down. She's forty-eight and was born at Le Havre. Her father was a sailor. She has brothers and sisters. That's for the Le Havre flying squad. Tell them to look up all the town-hall registers and wherever else they can. They probably won't find much.'

'And in Paris?'

'Get round the town-halls as well. She once lived in the Roule district. It would be just as well to have a quick look at the old Vice Squad files of around twenty years ago, twenty-five even.'

Fat Torrence, at the other end of the line, was scribbling feverishly.

'Is that the lot?'

'No. Go up to Records and see that they've got nothing under Binet. Tomorrow morning, I want someone to go along to the shirt shop in the Boulevard Saint-Michel, not far from the Rue Monsieur-le-Prince. The place may have changed hands after fifteen years, but there's a chance they'll still be there.'

All this might as easily take several weeks or a few hours. It depended on luck.

'Lastly, find out what you can about this same Françoise Binet at 48, Rue Monsieur-le-Prince. She lived in the house fifteen years ago.'

'You're staying down there?'

'Yes. I'll keep Vacher with me. Is he on night duty?'

'He came on an hour ago.'

'How's Janvier getting on?'

'He can be taken home in two or three days. He's impatient. So's his wife. The doctor would actually like to keep him a little longer.'

When he came back into the bar, Inspector Vacher was already there, drinking a cup of coffee laced with brandy.

'Have you eaten?'

'Yes. Anything new?'

'Is it still raining?'

Vacher pointed to his wet raincoat hanging on the hat-stand.

'Bad luck for you, my poor lad. I'm afraid I'm going to ask you to spend the night in the open . . .'

He changed his mind.

'On second thoughts, if you stay at the living-room window, it will do just as well. There's only one house to watch.'

He ate without enjoyment. He forgot to telephone the doctor as he had threatened Madame Boursicault he would. Besides, he hadn't even asked her her doctor's name. He could have found it out from the concierge.

It was not for this reason that he went over to Madame Keller's lodge to see her when he had finished his meal. At once, as if she were expecting him, she gave him a reproachful look.

'How is she?'

'What have you been saying to her? I found her stretched on her bed like a corpse and she took no notice of me whatsoever. Her eyes were shut. She was crying. Great tears running down her poor cheeks.'

'She didn't say anything to you?'

'She only shook her head when I asked her if she needed anything. She didn't care if the light were on or off. I shut the window and switched it off.'

Maigret almost went upstairs. But what would he say?

He was fully aware of the responsibility he had taken on himself.

'Does she have medicines in her room?'

'There are all sorts: bottles, pills, powders. The doctors have tried everything. Do you think she might . . .?'

The concierge looked frightened. He remained cool.

'I don't imagine that she's the sort of woman to do that,' he said, 'but you'd better stay near her until I send you a nurse.'

'She won't let me.'

'Tell her that it was on my orders.'

'She'll be angry with me . . .'

He shrugged his shoulders, crossed the road, rejoined Vacher on Mademoiselle Clément's doorstep and sent him off to find a nurse whose services Headquarters often called upon.

At ten o'clock in the evening, the Rue Lhomond was calm, with only the gentle sound of the rain. There was a light on opposite. The blind was not down. From his window, Maigret could see the nurse reading a novel, in the armchair he had sat in a while ago. Madame Boursicault seemed to be sleeping.

Mademoiselle Clément had just retired to her bedroom. Mademoiselle Isabelle had not gone out. The Lotards' baby was not crying. Fachin was studying, and the Safts, in their room, were chatting quietly.

On the ground floor, Vacher had opened the living-room curtains so that he could see what was happening outside and he sat there in the dark, a pot of coffee within reach, smoking cigarette after cigarette.

Maigret was waiting for his wife's telephone call before going to bed; he went down in his slippers.

'. . . But, of course. I'm feeling very well,' he assured her.

'I hope you're not going to stay in that house for ever? Listen. Hortense is much better and I might possibly get home in two days, if not tomorrow evening . . . Are you sure you'll be pleased to see me? . . .'

He repeated, his mind not on his words:

'But of course! Of course!'

Then, before going upstairs, he went in to have a few words with Vacher, in the darkness of the living-room. He could hear Mademoiselle Clément moving about in her bedroom; soon afterwards the mattress creaked under her weight.

It was a long time before he went to sleep. He was still aware of that lighted window, on the other side of the street. He also thought about that little idiot Paulus, and began to get angry with him, as if he held him responsible for everything that had happened and everything that was going to happen.

At all events, it was working out! And he had got quite a long way!

Chapter Seven

The first time he woke, a little before one o'clock, there were still two lights on in the block of houses, and he was now in a position to be able to put a name to each window and tell almost without fail what the people were doing.

Following his instructions, the nurse had not pulled down the blind, and the lace curtains were open, so that he was able to glimpse the white blob of the bed, the motionless face of Françoise Boursicault.

She was lying on her back, her eyes shut. Seen from above, her nose seemed thinner and longer.

The nurse was still reading her book, a cup of coffee at hand on the little table which she had drawn up near her armchair.

Maigret, that night, was burdened with what almost amounted to a guilty conscience. He had just had some confused dreams which he could barely remember, but they left a disagreeable impression.

He went downstairs, without putting on any lights, entered the living-room where nothing could be seen but the reddish tip of Vacher's cigarette.

'Is that you, chief?'

'Everything all right?'

'Yes, thanks. The fat lady's left me everything I need. She got up a while ago to make me some coffee. She was in her nightdress. If I hadn't been on duty, I'd willingly have made a move in that direction.'

'You haven't noticed anything outside?'

'Only a drunk who zigzagged past, half an hour ago. I followed your instructions and went out, and a bit farther on asked him for his papers. It was a tramp I know by sight; he was going to sleep in the Place Maubert.'

The telephone people at the listening-post had nothing to tell. It was true that Madame Boursicault could only have telephoned before the arrival of the nurse, that's to say during an hour at most.

'Keep watching then!' Maigret sighed.

He stopped. He knew where Mademoiselle Clément kept the beer, behind the door of the cellar. He went to find a bottle quietly, carried it with him to his room, leaving Vacher at the window.

In the Ternes district, several bistros were still open and men from Headquarters were asking questions about a certain Françoise Binet.

Was it possible to hope, after all this time, for any results? Happily there are more Parisians than one might think, for whom the greater part of the city is just foreign territory and who keep to their neighbourhood as if it were a village. Some people's universe consists of only a few streets, and for twenty years or more they frequent the same restaurants or the same little bar.

Maigret was convinced that Françoise Boursicault was not asleep, that she would not be sleeping at all that night, and that her brain was working actively.

Did she suspect that her telephone would be tapped by the listening-post? Probably. She must be thinking everything out, with the patience, the attention to tiny detail, of a person who for many years has known only the solitude of her bed.

Nevertheless, he would have bet that she would be up to something: *she would be forced to do something.*

He fell asleep once more, heavily, dreamt again, woke up for the second time a little before sunrise and saw the nurse leaning out of the window, smoking a cigarette. He did not go downstairs, but went back to bed, and when he opened his eyes, the sky was grey, the cornices were dripping, but the rain had stopped.

The night had passed uneventfully. Vacher had watched in vain, and the chief inspector went to set him free.

'You'd better go home and get some sleep. You may have to come back on the job tonight. Call in at the Quai and tell Torrence to send me somebody over. If there's anything new, he's to come and put me in the picture.'

Only once in his life, when he was twelve years old, had he tried to cut a chicken's neck, because his father was away and his mother had asked him. He could still remember it. He was pale, his nostrils pinched. The feathers trembled in his hand. The bird beat with one wing. He could not succeed in keeping its head on the block they used for chopping wood, and his other hand awkwardly brandished the axe.

His first blow had been so clumsy that he had only managed to wound the fowl and, to deal the rest of the blows, he had kept his eyes shut.

He had eaten none of it. He had never killed another chicken in his life.

Madame Boursicault also had a long thin neck. And she might be lying motionless in her bed, but he still imagined he felt her fluttering in his grasp.

Yet he had made a mistake when he thought she might put an end to herself. If she had been going to do that, she would probably have done it immediately after his departure, before the arrival of the nurse.

He telephoned the latter.

'She spent a quiet night,' she told him. 'She didn't sleep a lot, two or three hours perhaps, in small doses, but she's not distressed.'

'Did she say anything?'

'She hasn't said a word to me, not even to ask for a glass of water.'

'I think you can leave her now.'

He saw her going a little later, a raincoat over her white uniform, an umbrella in her hand. Then Madame Keller dragged the dustbins out to the edge of the pavement, looked over at the chief inspector's windows, noticed him and only gave him a black look of reproach.

He had guessed that, once the nurse had gone, Madame Boursicault would get up to close the curtains and perhaps pull down the blind.

He had underestimated her. She left the window as it was, and he felt he could understand that she did it out of bravado or spite. So he was able to continue watching her, she was not trying to hide. The concierge carried up her breakfast. He saw the lips of the two women moving, but only the concierge occasionally glanced in his direction. Would Madame Boursicault dare send her out with a message?

It was Lucas who arrived a little later in a taxi and who came upstairs to the chief inspector's room as the latter was shaving.

'Torrence has gone home to sleep. He's caught 'flu and had a filthy headache. He gave me some information for you.'

'Did they find someone who knew her?'

'At the "Diabolo", a seedy night-club in the Rue de l'Etoile. There's a drunken old woman who hangs around there most nights. You've probably come across her over in the Ternes district. She always wears the sort of clothes which were fashionable twenty-five years ago, dresses too short and too tight-fitting, which give her the odd look of a little girl; she often ends her nights at the station. They call her Thérèse.'

'What did she have to say?'

'She'd had a lot to drink when young Lapointe dug her out and he didn't get much from her. I asked the police over there to bring her to the Quai as soon as she's sweated the liquor out of her.'

'Did she know Françoise Binet?'

'She says she did.'

'"A lovely little thing," she said, "as plump as a pigeon, laughing all the time and showing the prettiest teeth in the world. She hung around with Dédé. It didn't last, though, because Dédé wanted her out on the streets."'

'Who's Dédé?'

'They think he's a bloke who now runs a bar in Nantes.'

'She didn't mention any others?'

'Always by their Christian names and nicknames. She keeps saying: "A lovely little thing . . . I'd just like to know what's become of her . . ."'

'Listen, Lucas. In a moment the concierge will probably come out to go and do her shopping. Be ready. Watch her closely. She may take a letter to the post office, or send a telegram, or even meet someone. I don't count on it too much, but if it does happen, it's important that we get hold of the message.'

'Right, chief.'

Maigret went downstairs and, on the off-chance, rang the flying squad at Nantes. Mademoiselle Clément, who was getting dressed, opened the curtain across the little window to see who was using the telephone.

'This is Maigret here, of Police Headquarters. Who am I speaking to?'

'Grollin. It's nice to hear your voice, chief.'

'Would you pay a little visit to a bar run by someone called Dédé? Know him?'

'Over at the harbour, yes.'

'Ask him questions about a certain Françoise Binet whom he knew twenty years ago or more.'

'You think he'll remember her? He seems to me the type to have known quite a few chicks in his life.'

'Try anyway. See if you can find out who took the girl over after him. Get all you can out of him. Ring me back here, not at the Quai.'

He gave him Mademoiselle Clément's number.

'It's coming down in buckets!' sighed Grollin. 'Never mind. I've got an umbrella. Dédé'll be in his bed. It's going to put the wind up him being woken by the police.'

Mademoiselle Clément came out of the living-room, her face freshly powdered, the tiny hairs around her ears and neck still moist.

'Would you like some coffee?'

'For me and Lucas, yes, if it's no trouble.'

The lodgers now greeted him as if he were one of themselves, with always a kind of query in their eyes.

'Take a good look at her window, Lucas. Note the position of the curtains. If, later on, it doesn't matter what time of day, you notice any change, don't fail to let me know.'

'Are you expecting her to try and signal to somebody?'

'I would be prepared to swear there's a signal.'

'But the telephone? Hasn't she got one within reach?'

'That's not enough.'

'Are you sure someone comes to see her when her husband is away?'

'I'm convinced of it. There's no other possible explanation. Actually it's likely that he'll ring her before coming into the street.'

'So there'd be no need for a signal.'

'Suppose that the concierge came in at the last moment, or the doctor had arrived. He doesn't come on fixed days. He calls to see her from time to time as it fits in with his visits.'

'I see.'

'They would have had to arrange some means of warning him when there was danger. It could be the position of the curtains, or the blind, or anything. I've looked at that window such a lot during the last few days that I wonder if I would see any difference. When were you last here?'

'The day before yesterday.'

Lucas, his face raised towards the window opposite, wrinkled his brows.

'Are you struck by something?'

'I'm not sure. I'd like to go and have a look from upstairs.'

They went up to Maigret's room, the one that had been Emile Paulus's. Lucas walked straight across to the window.

'When I was last here, two days ago, I remember that the window over there was open.'

'That's right. It was not raining then. It was much warmer than today. Go on.'

'Perhaps I'm wrong, but I don't think that copper pot was there.'

In the middle of the window-sill, it was true, they could now see a copper pot holding a green plant.

Maigret was certain that, the evening before, this pot was not in the same place. He had seen it in a corner of the room, on a narrow little table; he had even stared at it for quite some time as he talked to Madame Boursicault.

'Stay here. Watch the street.'

He crossed the road, went into Madame Keller's lodge and was received with deliberate coldness. She was getting ready to go and do her shopping. The postman had passed, and there were letters in the pigeon-holes, but not in Madame Boursicault's.

'Could you tell me, Madame Keller, if, when you went up to her this morning, your tenant asked you to move the green plant from its place?'

She said 'No', dryly.

'Do you ever put it outside the window?'

'No.'

'I'm sorry to go on about it. The matter is much more important than you may think. You are the one who does the housework. If I'm not mistaken, that plant usually stands in the left-hand corner, near the dining-room door.'

'That's its place.'

'You've *never* been asked to put it outside the window?'

She stared at him suddenly, and he saw that he had stirred a memory. But she did not feel like talking, because she now considered him a cruel man, who made her tenant suffer.

'She did ask you to, didn't she? When was it?'

'A long time ago.'

'Why?'

'I don't know. It's not my business.'

Pretending not to notice her obvious unwillingness, he persisted.

'Several months ago?'

'Six, at least.'

He was on to it at last and he felt a little flutter in his chest. His only fear was to see this woman in front of him withdraw into silence. He smiled at her gently.

'Six months ago, that was in the autumn. The window was probably open then?'

'I don't remember.'

'I feel sure you had already been up to do the housework, that you had come down again, that you were getting ready to go out shopping, like today . . .'

She followed him carefully, and he could tell that, as he went along, her memories were beginning to take shape. She was surprised that he had guessed so correctly. She said:

'I went up again, yes . . .'

'You went up again, when you weren't expected . . .'

'I had forgotten to ask her what she felt like to eat. I also wanted to know if she had to have a prescription made up again. She then asked me to put the copper pot on the window-sill.'

'Without saying why?'

'Because it would be good for the plant. The sun was shining.'

'What happened during the next few days?'

Defeated, she gave the chief inspector an amazed glance.

'I wonder how you could have guessed. The next day, the sun was shining again and I wanted to put the plant back on the window-sill.'

'She told you not to do it?'

'Yes.'

'Thank you very much, Madame Keller.'

He almost asked her if her tenant had wanted her to deliver a message, but he preferred to let Lucas see to this.

'Will you be worrying her any more?'

He preferred not to answer and, a few minutes later, he was knocking on the door. He wasn't asked to come in. He turned the handle, opened the door and found Françoise Boursicault's eyes fixed on him. With a sigh of resignation, she let herself fall back on to the pillow.

'I'm sorry to have to disturb you again.'

She didn't say a word, kept her lips tightly closed, her whole life concentrated in the pupils of her eyes.

'I wanted to make sure that the presence of the nurse did not prevent your sleeping . . .'

The silence continued.

'And I thought that, perhaps, you might have something to say to me this morning?'

She still did not waver. He walked up and down the room, and he stopped as if by chance in front of the green plant, and began to stroke its leaves.

Then, in the way that certain people, when they are paying a visit, cannot help straightening the pictures on the walls, he picked up the copper vase and went to replace it on the table.

'That's its right place, isn't it? The concierge must have made a mistake.'

He purposely refrained from looking at her. He lingered a little longer, then turned round, and as he had expected, he found her much paler, a look of panic in her eyes.

'Does my taking the pot from the window annoy you?'

He was afraid that she would start crying again and he remembered the chicken in his childhood. He hesitated a few seconds, seized hold of the back of a chair covered with crimson velvet, sat astride it, facing the bed, and began to light his pipe.

It was too bad if she wasn't ready for it. He had just decided to attempt the operation.

'You were expecting *him* to come to see you this morning, weren't you?'

He had probably never been given a look full of such hate, dull hate, without violence, a mixture of scorn and perhaps a kind of bitter resignation.

They were suddenly both on foreign ground, performing in an unreal atmosphere, and they understood each other before words were fully spoken; each look, each tiny movement became heavy with meaning.

'He is still in Paris, isn't he?'

After each phrase, he gave her time to reflect, listening all the while for sounds on the staircase.

'If he wasn't still in Paris, you would not be nervous and you wouldn't have put that vase at the window. Because you did get up to move it. It wasn't the concierge who did it. Nor was it the nurse.'

She stretched her bony hand towards a glass of water standing on the bedside table and swallowed a mouthful, with such an effort that her neck was stretched taut.

'The Nantes police, at this very moment, are engaged in interrogating a man you once knew well, a certain Dédé; Dédé will give us other names. And those people, in turn, will point out others.'

This was almost making him nervous.

'It's possible that he won't come, that he is suspicious. He must have been expecting a call from you, yesterday evening or during the night, but you were not able to telephone him.'

A pause.

'He knows, through you, that the police have set a trap in the street. During the last few days, he has probably been wandering around the neighbourhood, without coming too close. I'm wondering why he didn't rent a room or a flat in the house. That would have been so much easier!'

Was he mistaken? Was there perhaps a vague hint of a smile on her strained lips?

He recalled the words of the drunken old woman:

'A lovely little thing, as plump as a pigeon . . .'

'Do you realise, Françoise, what is going to happen?'

She had frowned when she heard herself being called by her Christian name.

'He will come along the street. He has probably already come and seen the copper vase warning him of danger.

'It's possible that he will follow the concierge and try to speak to her, because he is even more worried than you are.

'He thinks that we are going to arrest you.

'At any cost, he will want to prevent that happening.'

At last he obtained his first reaction. The invalid drew herself up and she said to him furiously:

'I won't let it!'

'You see he does exist, I wasn't mistaken.'

'Have you no pity?'

'Did he have any pity on my inspector, who had done him no harm whatsoever? He only thought of his own personal safety.'

'That's not true.'

'Let's say he only thought of you . . .'

She still did not suspect that in a few odd phrases she had told him more than he had dared hope for.

'Yes! Supposing that it was for your sake that he fired the shot, to prevent your husband, when he came back from Bordeaux . . .'

'Stop it, for God's sake! Can't you understand how horrible all this is?'

She was no longer cool and collected. Unable to bear it, incapable of remaining motionless in her bed any longer, she got up, in her nightdress, revealing her bare feet, her thin legs. She stood on the carpet, her eyes angry.

'Arrest me then, since you have discovered so much. It was I who fired the gun. It was I who wounded your inspector. Put me in prison and let's be done with it . . .'

She attempted to walk towards a wardrobe, probably in order to find some clothes and get dressed, but she had forgotten about her illness and she fell, ridiculously, at Maigret's feet, found herself on all fours on the floor, making futile efforts to get up.

He was more than ever reminded of the episode of the chicken.

He had to pick her up bodily, but she fought back and, intentionally or not, she dealt him blows, gripped hold of his tie.

'Calm down, Françoise. You'll hurt yourself; you know quite well that I shall not arrest you, that you did not fire the shot, that you could never have done it.'

'I tell you it was me . . .'

It lasted more than a minute, and Maigret wondered if Mademoiselle Isabelle or Monsieur Kridelka were watching them through the window. He finally managed to lift her up, and she hardly weighed anything. He put her on the bed, kept hold of her wrists until he finally felt her muscles relaxing.

'Will you be sensible?'

She shook her head negatively, but, when he let her go, she stopped moving, and with the sheet he covered up her body, which had become half naked in the struggle.

He straightened up and was tidying his hair when he heard her burst out, like an enraged child:

'I shan't tell you a thing.'

Her face buried in the pillow, she spoke through clenched teeth, to herself, and it was quite hard to hear what she said.

'I shan't tell you a thing and you will never find out. You are a brute. I detest you. If some other terrible thing happens, it will be your fault. Oh, how I hate you . . .'

He could not restrain a smile, standing there, watching her, without any malice, only pity in his eyes.

As he did not move, it was she who half-turned her head in order to watch him with one eye.

'What arè you waiting for? For me to speak? I shan't tell you a thing. You may do what you like, I shan't tell you a thing. And, anyway, what right have you to be in my room?'

She was changing her attitude once again. She was no longer a woman almost fifty years old. She was a small girl who knew she was in the wrong, but refused to own up and fought back wildly.

'You a policeman, and you don't know you aren't allowed into people's houses without a warrant? Have you got one? Show me it! If you haven't got one, you had better get out straight away. Do you hear? I order you to get out . . .'

He almost burst out laughing, feeling relaxed now himself. The reaction was setting in.

'You're saying foolish things, Françoise . . .'

'I refuse to let you call me by that name . . . If you don't leave immediately, I'll scream, I'll rouse the neighbours, I'll tell them how you enjoy torturing a sick woman . . .'

'I'll be back,' he announced, good-naturedly, and walked towards the door.

'You needn't trouble. You'll still get nothing more from me. Get out! I hate you . . . I . . .'

He saw that she was about to leave her bed again and he preferred to move on to the landing and shut the door. He was smiling in spite of himself, as he heard her, through the door-panel, continue talking all on her own.

When he reached the street, he raised his head and noted that she had replaced the copper vase outside the window, probably just to spite him.

He was drinking a glass of white wine, the first of the day, at the Auvergnat's, when the concierge returned from her shopping. He noticed Lucas following her and called to him.

'Well?'

Lucas noticed his chief's change of humour and was surprised at his happy air.

'Did she speak?'

'No. What about you?'

'I followed the concierge as you told me to do. She went to the Rue Mouffetard, and I didn't take my eyes off her. She stopped at several barrows. I got close enough to her to hear what she was saying. She was only interested in buying her vegetables and fruit. Then she went into a butcher's.'

'Nobody came up to her?'

'I noticed nothing at all suspicious. She posted no letters. It's true she knew I was on her tail.'

'And she didn't make a phone call?'

'No. Several times, she gave me a biting look and moved her lips as if she were saying some pretty disagreeable things about me to herself.'

'She's not the only one!' Maigret sighed.

He continued to watch the street.

'You think the man's in the district?'

'It's more than likely. He didn't receive her usual telephone call yesterday evening. He's worried. But I couldn't prevent Françoise from putting her copper vase back on the window-sill.'

The passers-by were happily few and far between. If one of them lifted his head towards Madame Boursicault's window, the two men couldn't fail to notice it.

When they went back to Mademoiselle Clément's, she in turn had gone out to do her shopping. They had seen her go past, a shopping-bag in her hand. Lucas settled himself at the living-room window. Maigret telephoned the Quai des Orfèvres.

Vauquelin answered him.

'I questioned the old woman a good half-hour ago,' he said. 'I was forced to offer her drinking money. She listed a heap of names, people who hung out in the Ternes district twenty-five years ago; most of them have disappeared from circulation. It's pretty much of a muddle. I'm taking notes. I'll check everything.'

'Did someone go along to the Rue Monsieur-le-Prince?'

'Colin's just got back. The same concierges are still there. They remember the young lady. She was a quiet person, who had no visitors and never went out in the evening. According to the grapevine, she met a rich man, a widower, older than herself, and only left the house when she married him.'

'She didn't receive letters from abroad?'

'No. She had no mail whatsoever.'

Maigret put some change in the money-box and went to chat with Lucas; a few minutes later the telephone rang. It was Nantes.

'Is that you chief? I've just come in from Dédé's bar. He was in bed, as I expected, and he was pretty much on his guard at first. When I spoke to him of Françoise Binet, it took him a bit of time to remember. He called her Lulu.'

'He doesn't know what's happened to her?'

'He lost touch with her. Then, two or three years later, he came across her in the company of a young man, short and very dark.'

'Another lad from the district?'

'No. That's just it. He had never seen him before. According to Dédé, he looked like a clerk or an assistant in a big store.'

'Whereabouts did this take place?'

'Around the Place Clichy. He didn't speak to her. Lulu pretended not to recognise him.'

'What does he say about her?'

'That she was a silly fool who didn't know what she wanted, and that she had probably ended up with a husband and lots of children.'

'Is that all?'

'That's all. He seemed to me to have given all the dope he could. He didn't hide the fact that he'd tried to get her to work for him, and you know what that means. She tried; but it wasn't a success. According to him, she happened to get a customer who put her off the profession for good.'

'Thanks a lot.'

The copper vase was still outside the window. Maigret went up to his room and saw Françoise Boursicault telephoning from her bed. She was looking in his direction. Their looks met. She made no attempt to hang up.

She was speaking calmly, with a serious, thoughtful expression on her face. From time to time she nodded her head affirmatively.

When she replaced the receiver, she lay down in bed and closed her eyes.

Maigret knew they would call him, so he went downstairs, paced up and down the passage waiting for the telephone to ring.

'Hallo. Is that you, Chief Inspector?'

'Yes. Who has she been ringing up?'

'A lawyer. Maître Lechat, who lives in the Boulevard des Batignolles.'

'Did she seem to know him?'

'No. She told him she wanted to consult him on a very important matter, but she was in bed and could not leave it. She asked him to come to the Rue Lhomond as quickly as he could. He made her repeat her name three or four times. He didn't seem overpleased at the thought of going all the way across Paris without knowing why. He tried to get the secret out of her, but she refused to say anything more.'

'Did they make an appointment?'

'He finally promised to come and see her later in the morning.'

Mademoiselle Clément came back, her shopping-bag in her hand, and even before seeing her, Maigret, as he hung up, could hear her breathing, panting slightly. It seemed to the chief inspector that she was hoping to avoid him, rushing towards the kitchen with a speed unusual for her.

'What's up with her?' he asked Lucas.

'I don't know. She seems quite overcome . . .'

Maigret went into the kitchen, where she was busy putting her vegetables away in the larder.

She turned her back to him, purposely avoiding having to face him. Her ears were pink; her breathing, harder than usual, made her full bosom heave.

'What is it, Mademoiselle Clément?'

'What?'

'Do you not wish to see me any more?'

She turned round suddenly, her cheeks crimson, her eyes shining.

'What are you trying to hide from me?'

'Me?'

Maigret's eyes laughed.

'What did he ask you to do?'

'Did you follow me?'

'Tell me how he accosted you and repeat exactly what he said to you.'

'That he was a journalist . . .'

'Did he look like a journalist?'

'I don't know. I don't think so. I don't know many journalists, but . . .'

'But?'

'His hair was almost white.'

'Tall, short?'

'Short. Much shorter than me.'

'Well dressed?'

'Respectably dressed, yes. I had stopped at a barrow and was buying some radishes. He took off his hat and greeted me.'

'What sort of a hat?'

'A grey felt hat. He was entirely dressed in grey.'

'Did he ask you what I was doing?'

'Not exactly. He explained to me that he represented a newspaper and would like to know where you were carrying on your investigations.'

'What did you reply?'

'I looked around for you or your inspector.'

'Were you frightened?'

'I don't know. He looked at me in such a determined way. He is very thin, with rings round his eyes and a yellow complexion.'

'"Why don't you ask Chief Inspector Maigret yourself?" I replied.

'"Because he wouldn't answer me. Is he still at your place?"

'"Yes."

'"Has he been into the house opposite?"

'Then I mumbled to him that I didn't know. I was beginning to get frightened. I knew he couldn't very well do anything in the crowd, but, all the same, I hurried into the delicatessen. He almost came in on my heels. I saw him hesitate. He looked from one side of the street to the other, worried, then he disappeared in the direction of the Boulevard Saint-Germain.'

'Are you sure you didn't disclose the fact that I had twice been to see Madame Boursicault?'

'Quite sure.'

'And that you didn't speak to him about her?'

'I didn't even know her name until you just mentioned it.'

'Whose name?'

'The invalid, on the first floor. She's the one you mean, isn't she? And he was the man who fired the shot?'

'There's quite a chance.'

The fat girl looked at him for a moment, her eyes wide open, then, out of nervousness, began laughing and could not stop.

Chapter Eight

In after years, this became one of the cases Lucas always enjoyed telling, to such an extent in fact that at Headquarters they knew many of his sentences off by heart.

'I was still sitting at the window in the little living-room. The sky suddenly became overcast, as if it were Good Friday, and hailstones started falling, as big as walnuts, bouncing on the road. I remembered that I'd left my window open at Headquarters. I decided to ring up Joseph, the porter, and get him to shut it for me.

'The chief inspector was walking up and down the passage, his pipe in his mouth, hands behind his back, and as I went past him, I thought he hadn't seen me.

'But just as I was lifting the receiver off the hook, under the stairs, he took it from my hands, put it back in its place, still as if his mind were on something else, and said:

'"Not now, son!"'

In Lucas's account Maigret frequently called him 'son', although there was hardly ten years' difference in their ages.

'The hailstorm had lasted for almost an hour, and they spoke of it in the papers as one of the most violent ever recorded; there was damage amounting to millions of francs' worth round Argenteuil. The chief inspector had left the door open. During the whole time, he kept walking from the doorway to the end of the passage.

'Mademoiselle Clément was in the kitchen, watching him through the spy-window. She came and spoke to me in a low voice, and she was worried.

'"I wonder what's wrong with him. It frightens me!"

'And then the phone finally rang.'

At this point in his story, Lucas never failed to pause, then added in a dull voice:

'He raised his head, picked up the receiver and sighed with relief.'

It was true it had hailed that morning, that Maigret paced up and down the passage for a long time, grumbling to himself, and had then rushed to the phone as soon as it started ringing. He said:

'Hallo! Maigret here.'

And a voice at the other end, a voice that seemed far away, spoke like an echo:

'Hallo!'

Then there was a silence. Hailstones bounced from the threshold into the passage. Mademoiselle Clément, holding an oven-pan in her hands in the kitchen, stood stock-still, her movements suspended as if she were the subject of a photograph.

'Do you know who's telephoning?' the voice finally said.

'Yes.'

'Who?'

'The person who shot Inspector Janvier.'

'But you don't know my name?'

'I shall know it sooner or later.'

'How?'

'We've already got to the Place Clichy.'

There was another silence.

'What did she tell you?'

'Nothing. She's put the green plant out on the window-sill.'

Another silence. The man must have been telephoning from a bar and had left the door open, because he could hear the noise of the hailstorm at the other end of the line.

'I can get across the frontier before I'm identified.'

'That's possible. But I don't think you will.'

'Why not?'

'You know quite well why not.'

Maigret rested his unlit pipe on the telephone and kept his eyes on the money-box and its little notice.

'Are you going to arrest her?'

'I may be forced to.'

'Do the papers know you've been to see her?'

'Not yet.'

'Nobody?'

'Only the concierge.'

Maigret could hear a sigh. He did nothing to encourage the man to speak. Each of them was taking his time.

'What did you find out about me?'

'That you are short, middle-aged, grey-haired, that you wear a grey suit, a grey overcoat and a grey hat.'

'Did Mademoiselle Clément tell you this?'

'Yes.'

'I've still got time to change my clothes, go to the aerodrome, and take a plane out of the country.'

'I'm not stopping you.'

'You admit that I can get away?'

'Yes.'

'If I gave myself up, would you agree to leave this person we know out of it?'

'That's an eventuality I have already considered.'

'But you won't promise anything?'

'Not before I have the details.'

'What details?'

'Of what happened twenty years ago.'

'Only those?'

'Yes.'

'You won't bring her into the business of the inspector?'

It was Maigret's turn not to answer, and the silence seemed to last an eternity.

'No,' he said, finally.

'Would you let me go and see her before you take me prisoner?'

Mademoiselle Clément was still motionless in her kitchen, pan in hand, and Lucas, in his armchair, seemed to be holding his breath.

'On one condition.'

'What?'

'That you do not attempt to put an end either to yourself or to her. Even if she asks you to.'

There was silence at the other end this time. The longest so far.

'You insist on this?'

'Yes.'

'So be it.'

'In that case, you may come along here. I presume you aren't far from the Rue Lhomond.'

'A few yards.'

'I shall stay at my window during your visit. You will not close the curtains or pull down the blind.'

'I promise.'

'When you leave the house, there will be a small black car a little farther along the street. You can just join me there.'

A silence. At last the sound of the receiver being replaced on its hook.

Maigret delayed long enough to relight his pipe, walked to the living-room door and looked vaguely in Lucas's direction.

'Will you telephone the Quai and ask for a car. Have them stop just a little way down the street.'

'Shall I wait for you there?'

'It's not worth it.'

'You don't need me any longer?'

'No.'

'May I stay all the same?'

Had Maigret really said: 'If you like'?

He was never positive about it, but Lucas took the permission as granted, and it was thanks to this that he was able to tell his story from then on almost to the end.

While Lucas went off to telephone, Maigret took a bottle of beer from behind the cellar door, not glancing at Mademoiselle Clément, who he didn't seem to realise was there. Then he set off up the stairs, climbed slowly, glanced into Mademoiselle Blanche's room and saw her stretched out on her bed, in her dressing-gown, reading the paper.

A few moments later he was leaning on the window-sill; the window was open and it had stopped hailing, as if by magic. Madame Boursicault was in her bed, hands behind her head, staring at the ceiling, motionless like someone who is aware he is being watched.

The sky was brighter, but the sun had not yet come out, the light had the hardness of certain electric-light bulbs with frosted glass. There were hailstones scattered all along the pavement.

The man was coming now from the foot of the street, quite simply, quite naturally, like any passer-by. He was small and thin, dressed in grey; even his face had a greyish look. He might be either old and well preserved, or a young man, prematurely aged.

His clothes were well cut, and altogether he looked rather elegant.

When he was only two or three houses away, he looked up towards the window and saw the chief inspector watching him. He made no sign. His features did not alter. Without stopping, he went into the house opposite, and it was only on the stairs, or on the landing, that he must have waited, because two or three minutes passed before Maigret saw the woman turn towards the door.

She opened her mouth and must have called:

'Come in.'

She saw him before Maigret did, sat up in her bed, turned almost immediately towards the window and was on the point of rushing over to it.

The man was talking to her as he moved towards her, put his hat on a chair, and he remained calm, in control of himself, with the air of reassuring a frightened child.

Without once turning in Maigret's direction, he sat down on the edge of the bed, and Françoise Boursicault pressed herself against him, her head in the hollow of his shoulder, while he stroked her forehead with one hand.

In that position she was able to see the chief inspector, and he, in embarrassment, drew back, opened the beer which he drank from the bottle, because he had forgotten to bring up a glass and the tooth-mug was of a not very appetising colour.

He went out on to the landing. Mademoiselle Blanche was surprised to see him come into her room–she thought, actually, that he was not displeased to see her in her dishabille–and particularly to find him talking to her at length, of everything and nothing, of the book she was reading, and the recent hailstorm.

He heard the telephone ring; below, Lucas's voice answered, then came his rapid steps on the stairs.

'It's for you, chief . . . They're phoning from the Quai . . . They're on to something . . .'

Lucas was equally astonished to find the chief inspector in the girl's room; he was even more so, when Maigret received the news he had brought without surprise, without pleasure.

'She lived in the Rue des Dames for some time, in a little hotel, where a man who . . .'

'Is Headquarters still holding on?'

'Yes. Lapointe is on the line, very excited. He'd like to give you the details. He's checked it all with Records. He's sure . . .'

'Tell him I'll see him in my office later.'

In Lucas's account, these details took on an almost epic quality.

'I must say I thought he was more interested in the pretty girl lying on her bed, making eyes at him, her dressing-gown more than half open . . .'

Lucas had time to go downstairs and have a talk with Mademoiselle Clément in the kitchen. She was agitated too, strangely worried.

'What's he up to? What's going on?'

Maigret did not leave Mademoiselle Blanche's room until there was nothing more to see, over the way, except a woman lying down with her face turned towards him, and on her cheeks, he could tell, the shiny trickle of tears.

He took the trouble to go in to have a few words with Mademoiselle Clément, and she noticed the suitcase he was carrying.

'Are you going for good?'

'I'll be back to see you again.'

'The case is over? You've found him?'

He didn't reply directly.

'I want to thank you for your kindness and all you've done for me.'

And, as he looked around him, at the surroundings he had come to know so well, she started to laugh, her throaty laugh which shook her big bosom.

'How funny! It's really quite a moment. I was so used to having you around I was beginning to look on you as one of my lodgers.'

Perhaps to give her pleasure, he murmured:

'So was I . . .'

Then, to Lucas:

'I'll meet you at the Quai in a short while.'

Mademoiselle Clément accompanied him to the threshold and waited there while he crossed the road. The small black car from the Prefecture was waiting a little farther down, two houses beyond the Auvergnat's bistro.

Maigret hesitated, went up to the counter.

'Are you leaving?'

'One last white wine, yes.'

He drank it, and after that it was the *patron*'s round. The *patron*'s wife rushed from the kitchen and wanted to drink his health too. Like Mademoiselle Clément, she said:

'I had grown used to your coming here . . .'

And, as he had done over the road, he replied gravely:

'So had I.'

They watched him go off; the fat girl was still on her doorstep. He opened the car door, pushed his case inside first, murmuring:

'May I?'

Well ensconced in the seat, he said at last to the Headquarters driver:

'To the Quai!'

The little grey man was sitting beside him; politely, he took off his hat and held it on his knees during the journey.

The two men did not exchange a single word.

Chapter Nine

The two men slowly climbed the dusty staircase, and Maigret sniffed with pleasure the familiar smell. As always, there were people waiting in the glassed-in waiting-room. Joseph, the elderly porter, called happily:

'Good day, Chief Inspector.'

'Good day, Joseph.'

'The chief wants you to go in and see him.'

'I will in a minute.'

'Monsieur Lapointe also asked me to let him know when you got back.'

'I know.'

'Monsieur Torrence telephoned.'

'Thank you, Joseph.'

He was gently settling back into the daily routine, opened the door into his office, which seemed to reproach him for his desertion.

'Come in!'

He opened the window, took off his hat, his overcoat.

'Make yourself comfortable. Sit down.'

At once, the internal telephone began ringing. It was Lapointe.

'I've got his name and his entire history, chief. Do you want me to come along with the dossier?'

'In a minute. I'll give you a ring.'

Poor Lapointe! He sighed, offended:

'All right!'

In front of him, the man sat down in a chair, having pulled up his trousers to avoid spoiling the creases. He was obviously fussy about his personal appearance. He was close shaven. His nails were well cared for. He had a look of extreme weariness.

'Have you lived abroad?'

'What makes you think that?'

It was difficult to say exactly. There was something indefinable. Something about his complexion, his look, that sort of premature ageing, for Maigret had come to the conclusion that his interlocutor was not much over forty-five.

'You're younger than her, aren't you?'

They were just two people talking in an office and they could have been calmly discussing business together; there was nothing to suggest that one of them would shortly cease to be an ordinary citizen.

'Do you smoke?'

'No, thank you. I haven't smoked for many years now.'

'And you don't drink either?'

They were getting to know one another, little by little, casting furtive glances which did not yet come to rest on each other for long.

'I don't drink any more, no.'

'You once drank a lot?'

'Once upon a time.'

'One of my inspectors is waiting to show me your case-history.'

Strangely enough, the man did not think for a moment that he might be bluffing. He said simply:

'It was inevitable sooner or later.'

'Were you expecting it to happen?'

'I knew it would.'

'So you are almost relieved? No?'

'Perhaps. As long as she is not dragged into it. It wasn't her fault. Don't forget your promise.'

It was the only moment he showed a trace of anxiety. He was calm; it even seemed that, as the interview proceeded in the quiet of the office, he relaxed more and more, as if it were something he had not been able to do for many years.

'As far as I am concerned, I am ready to pay for what I've done.'

He added with a timid smile:

'I suppose that will come to quite a lot?'

'Probably, yes.'

'My neck?'

Maigret made a vague gesture.

'It is difficult to know in advance what a jury's reaction will be. It might possibly be less if . . .'

The man said, in a dry voice, with a touch of anger:

'No!'

'It's up to you. How old were you when you met her?'

'Twenty. I had just been up before the medical board and been discharged.'

'Born in Paris?'

'In the Nièvre.'

'Parents well off?'

'Middling. Not too much money.'

'Did you study?'

'Three years at college.'

About the same age as Paulus. That one had also come to Paris with the idea of making a go of it.

'Did you work?'

'I have worked.'

'Doing what?'

'In an office . . . I was badly paid . . .'

Just like Paulus, again.

'So you started hanging around bars?'

'I was alone in Paris. I hated my room.'

'You met Françoise in a bar?'

'Yes. She was four years older than I.'

'She had a lover?'

'Yes.'

'Was it because of you that she left him?'

'Yes.'

'Did you live together?'

'I couldn't, because I had no money. I had just left my last job. I was looking for another.'

'Did you love her?'

'I thought so. But I wasn't sure then.'

He had pronounced those last words gravely, slowly, staring at the floor.

'Would you prefer me to have your file brought here?'

'It's not worth it. My name was Julien Foucrier. Françoise's previous friend had had his pockets well lined. It made me furious not to be able to buy things for her.'

'Did she complain?'

'No. She said we had all our lives ahead of us and that I'd make it in the end.'

'But you didn't have the patience?'

'That's right.'

'Whom did you kill?'

'I didn't want to kill anybody. Opposite the hotel where I was living, in the Rue des Dames, behind the Boulevard des Batignolles, there lived a man of about sixty, whom my landlady had pointed out to me.'

'Why?'

'Because I was always late with my rent. She told me that he lent money to people in my situation and that it would be better if I owed it to him rather than her. I went to see him. He lent me some twice, at a hundred per cent interest. He lived alone in a dingy flat which he looked after himself. He was called Mabille.'

Maigret did not mention that he could vaguely recall that case.

'Did you kill him?'

'Yes. I had gone to him a third time to ask for another loan, and he had opened the safe. There were two candlesticks on the chimney-piece. I grabbed hold of one of them.'

'What did you do afterwards?'

'The police wasted nearly a month's time. The thing was that, a little after my visit, somebody else went up to see Mabille, a man who had a criminal record, and it was his description the concierge gave them. He was arrested. They thought for a long time that he was guilty.'

'Have you told Françoise the truth?'

'No. I was living in a dream. When I read in the papers that the man who had been arrested instead of me had been released, I lost my head and went abroad.'

'All this without a word to Françoise?'

'I wrote to her that I had been summoned by my family and that I would soon be back.'

'Where did you go?'

'To Spain. Then to Portugal, from where I left for Panama. The French papers published my name and my description. In Portugal, I succeeded in getting hold of a fake passport in the name of Vermersch.'

'And you've lived under that name ever since?'

'Yes.'

'Did you stay long in Panama?'

'Eighteen years.'

'Without ever hearing from Françoise?'

'How could I have heard from her?'

'You didn't write to her?'

'Never. I began by working as a waiter in a French hotel. Later I started a restaurant of my own.'

'And you made a fortune?'

He replied, as if ashamed:

'I made some money. Enough to live without any worries. Then I fell ill. My liver. I had been drinking a lot. Over there you can buy absinthe easily, and the real thing, too. I acquired a taste for it. I spent three months in hospital and the doctors advised a change of climate.'

'How long have you been back in France?'

'Seven years.'

'That must have been before Françoise fell ill herself?'

'Yes. Two years before.'

'How did you find her again?'

'I didn't look for her. I would not have dared. I was convinced she would refuse to see me. It was only by chance that I met her one day, in the Métro.'

'Where were you living?'

'Where I still live now, in the Boulevard Richard-Lenoir.'

He smiled for the second time; if you could call it a smile.

'A few houses along from you, on the corner of the Rue du Chemin-Vert.'

'Françoise told you she was married?'

'That's right.'

'She didn't bear you any grudge?'

'No. She said it was on her account that it had all happened in the first place.'

'She was still in love with you?'

'I think so.'

'And you?'

'I had never stopped loving her.'

He did not raise his voice once, spoke very simply, in a neutral tone, and the sun, still young, damp, began to break through the clouds.

'You didn't ask her to leave her husband?'

'She didn't feel she could do such a thing. He's a very fine man, you see, and she respects him.'

'You saw a lot of each other, the two of you?'

'We met two or three times a week, when her husband was at sea, in a café in the Boulevard Sébastopol. Then I wanted to see the place where she lived. Not for the reason you're thinking. We never considered that. I went to her flat one day while the concierge was out shopping and I left again almost at once.'

'It became a habit?'

'It happened several times.'

'You had already worked out a signal?'

'The copper pot! Yes. I knew I would get caught sooner or later. It was inevitable.'

'You never suggested that she should go abroad with you?'

'She wouldn't have agreed.'

'Because of Boursicault?'

'Yes. You don't know what she's like.'

'She then became completely bed-ridden?'

'Almost. You've seen her. It's the worst thing in the world to happen to anybody. She was unable to go out. I began going to her place more often. One morning, when the concierge came back, I was still in the flat, so I hid. I stayed until the next morning.'

'From then on, you repeated your visits?'

'Yes. It gave us something of the feeling that we were a married couple. Don't forget we had never lived together. When I was in the Rue des Dames, she still kept on her room in the Boulevard Rochechouart. It's thanks to that that she was never involved. That was the start of this story! I began by staying two days, then three, sometimes more. Eventually we arranged quite a system, since there was the question of food. I brought mine with me.'

'Of course you ran no risk of the husband's returning unexpectedly, since boats follow a strict time-schedule.'

'The hardest part was during his month's leave.'

Everything about it was grey and melancholy, like the man himself, like the flat in the Rue Lhomond, like the woman who spent all her days lying in bed.

'Last week, I saw from the window that the street was being watched.'

'And you thought it was for you?'

'The papers hadn't mentioned Paulus. I had no reason to suspect that it was the house opposite the police were interested in. I thought automatically that they had got on to my trail. They were probably not sure, or supposed that I was outside and were waiting for me to return. For two days I imagined every possible solution. A dozen times, I was on the point of giving myself up, but then I would have to mention Françoise and she would have been questioned, possibly arrested, her husband would have found out . . .'

'In fact,' said Maigret as he filled his cold pipe, 'you shot the inspector so that you could leave the house.'

'Yes.'

'Because the husband would have come home and found you there?'

'That's it. For three days I waited in vain for a break in the watch being kept. I saw the inspectors relieving each other. When they moved into Mademoiselle Clément's, I was convinced it was to spy on the flat where I was. I waited till the last possible moment, so to speak. Boursicault was on his train. He would arrive a little after midnight.

'It was absolutely necessary for me to leave, don't you see?'

'Did you have a gun?'

'I have never carried a gun in my life, even in Panama. I knew that Boursicault's revolver was in the bedside table. I had often seen it there. It was a large Colt he had kept since the first war and left within reach of his wife because he imagined she was nervous.'

'You fired from the window?'

'I waited until the inspector lit a cigarette, which he did every few minutes, so that I could aim better.'

'Did Françoise know what you were doing?'

'No. She didn't even notice that I had a revolver in my hand, since we were in the dark.'

'You were careful not to leave straight away?'

'I waited until there were enough people moving about in the street for me to slip through unnoticed. When I left the house the concierge was on the opposite pavement, with the neighbours, facing the other way. She had left the door open.'

'Françoise knew that you had fired the shot?'

'How could she not know? I promised her I would leave the country.'

'When did you telephone her?'

The next day. She begged me again to get away.'

'Why didn't you?'

He didn't answer. Then he murmured, raising his eyes towards the chief inspector:

'What would have been the use?'

Not unlike Paulus, who had stayed hiding in Mademoiselle Clément's house. He had also left once and then returned.

'You knew you would be caught?'

He shrugged his shoulders.

'You don't care?'

'As long as she is not worried. She's got nothing to do with it. She had nothing to do with what happened in the Rue des Dames either. It's my fault, my fault alone. It was inevitable.'

That idiot Paulus, in his cell, must be thinking the same thing.

'I am sorry, now, that I shot the inspector. I was relieved to read in the papers that he hadn't died. Particularly when I saw that he had two children and that his wife was expecting a third.'

They were silent for a moment, and a sunbeam came to rest on the window, but was almost immediately effaced by a cloud.

'Don't forget your promise . . .'

Maigret frowned as he remembered the lawyer Françoise Boursicault had called, stretched his hand towards the telephone, but changed his mind.

'Did she tell you she had telephoned a lawyer?'

'Yes. She won't tell him anything.'

Nonetheless Maigret did pick up the receiver.

'Get me the Brasserie Dauphine . . . Hallo! . . . Justin? . . . Maigret here . . .' And, to his companion: 'A glass of beer?'

'A cup of coffee.'

'Bring over two beers for me and a cup of coffee.'

He got up, went and stood in front of the window. The bell rang.

'Right, chief. In a second . . .'

He turned towards the man who was quietly sitting in his chair.

'Do you have a lawyer?'

'I'll take the first one that comes. In my position . . . !'

Maigret began smoking and a few seconds later he opened the door for the waiter from the restaurant, told him to put the tray on his desk.

He drank the first glass in one gulp, wiped his mouth.

'I suppose I can leave you alone for a second?'

'You can.'

He went to see the chief.

'They tell me the case is wound up, Maigret?'

'It is. The man's in my office.'

'He admits it?'

'He admits it. He had tried to burgle the house opposite Mademoiselle Clément's, and when he came out he saw there was an inspector in the street . . .'

'Is that really true?'

'No. But, as far as I'm concerned, I shall act as if it were.'

'A woman?'

'Yes.'

'Pretty?'

'No. She's almost fifty and she's been bed-ridden for five years.'

'There'll be no snags?'

'I don't think so.'

'By the way, Maigret, I'd like you to see someone who has been hanging around the waiting-room for three days, and he's feeling a bit low.'

'Who?'

'Paulus's father. He insists on seeing you, to explain . . .'

'I'll see him,' sighed Maigret. 'How is Janvier?'

'They took him home this morning. Your wife?'

'She's coming back tonight. I'll be meeting her at the station.'

He walked through the duty room, where young Lapointe jumped up, very excited, and held out a thick file.

'It was sheer luck, chief! We've found . . .'

'I know, lad. You did well.'

He took the file and put it under his arm as if it were of no importance.

'You know he's already killed somebody?'

'Yes.'

'It's true that you've arrested him? Lucas says . . .'

Maigret stood in the doorway, his pipe between his teeth, and Lapointe was not certain that he properly understood what he mumbled as he went out.

'We had to!'

He turned towards Vacher, who was also there, busy drawing up a report.

'What did he say?'

'That he had to.'

'Had to what?'

'Arrest him, I suppose.'

And young Lapointe, staring at the door through which Maigret had disappeared, said simply:

'Ah!'

The Brothers Rico

The Brothers Rico

Translated from the French by Ernst Pawel

Chapter One

Again it was the blackbirds that first woke him up, just as they had done every morning. He no longer minded. At first it used to exasperate him, especially since he was not yet accustomed to the climate and the heat prevented him from falling asleep before two or three in the morning.

They started the moment the sun came up. And here, in Florida, the sun rose practically all at once. There was no dawn. The sky turned golden right away, the air was humid, astir with the cackle of the birds. He didn't know where they nested. He didn't even know if they really were blackbirds. He'd been just calling them that for the past ten years, always meaning to find out about them, but always forgetting to. Lois, the young coloured girl, had a name for them that he wouldn't have known how to spell. They were larger than the blackbirds up North, with three or four coloured plumes. Two of them always arrived first, settling on the lawn near the windows and starting their strident prattle.

Eddie didn't quite wake up any more; there was only a vague awareness of day breaking and he didn't find it unpleasant. Other blackbirds soon arrived from heaven knows where, probably from the neighbouring gardens. And, heaven knows why, they had picked his garden for their morning reunion.

Because of the blackbirds the world cut a little more deeply into his sleep and mingled shreds of reality with his dreams. The sea was calm. All he heard was one small wave, the one which, forming not far offshore in a barely perceptible undulation, rolled on to the sand in a sparkling curl and churned up thousands of shells.

Phil had called him the night before. He was never without misgivings whenever Phil got in touch with him. He had 'phoned from Miami. Mostly to tell him about the fellow, whose name he hadn't mentioned. He seldom mentioned names over the 'phone.

'Eddie?'

'Yes.'

'Phil.'

He never wasted words. It was a pose. Even calling from a 'phone booth in some bar, he'd put on his act.

'Everything okay over there?'

'Everything okay,' said Eddie Rico.

Why did Phil always pause between the most innocuous bits of conversation? Even face to face with him, it made him look suspicious, as if he expected people to hide something from him.

'How's the wife?'

'Fine, thanks.'

'No trouble?'

'No trouble.'

Didn't they know that there never was in Rico's territory?

'I'm sending a fellow over to-morrow morning.'

It wasn't the first time.

'He'd better not go out too much . . . Or get a yen to travel . . .'

'Okay.'

'Maybe Sid will meet me here to-morrow.'

'I see.'

'Could be he'll want to see you.'

It wasn't alarming in itself, or so very unusual. But Rico had never got used to Boston Phil's ways of talking and acting.

He did not go back to a deep sleep, just dozed off, conscious still of the blackbirds and the surging sea. A coconut came off one of the palm trees in the garden and hit the grass. Almost instantly Babe stirred in the adjoining room whose door was always left ajar.

She was the youngest of his daughters. Her real name was Lilian, but his older girls had started off calling her Babe. It annoyed him. In his home, he abhorred nicknames. But he was helpless against his daughters, and everybody had come to say the same.

Babe would soon start to hum, tossing about in her bed as if she wanted to go on sleeping some more. He knew that his wife, in the twin bed next to his, was also waking up. This was everyday routine. Babe was three years old. She still didn't talk. She could only utter a few indistinct words. And yet she was the prettiest of the three, with a real doll face.

'It'll probably take care of itself one of these days,' the doctor had said.

Did the doctor believe that? Eddie didn't trust doctors. No more than he trusted Phil.

Babe was prattling (or babbling) away. In five minutes, if she wasn't picked up, she'd start to cry.

Rico seldom had to wake his wife. His eyes closed, he'd hear her sigh, throw back the sheet, put her bare feet on the rug, and she'd sit that way for a little while on the side of the bed, rubbing her face and her body before reaching for her housecoat. Invariably, at that very moment, a whiff of her fragrance drifted his way, a fragrance he was fond of. Deep down he was a happy man.

She never made a noise, tiptoed into Babe's room, carefully shutting the door. She guessed he wasn't asleep, but it was a tradition. And besides, he usually did go back to sleep after that. He couldn't hear the other two girls, Christine and Amelia, whose room was further down the hall. He didn't hear the blackbirds any more. A fleeting thought to Boston Phil, who had called him from Miami, and he sank into the delectable morning sleep.

Downstairs Lois would be preparing breakfast for the children. The two older ones, ages twelve and nine, were quarrelling in their bathroom. They'd eat in the kitchen, then go out and wait at the corner for the school bus.

The big yellow bus passed by at ten minutes to eight. Sometimes Eddie heard the squeal of the brakes, and sometimes he didn't. At eight o'clock Alice came up, opened the door gently, and the smell of the coffee she was bringing would precede her into the room.

'It's eight o'clock, Eddie.'

He always took the first sip in bed, and then she'd put the cup on the night table, go to the windows, and draw the curtains. Even so he still could not look out. Behind the curtains were venetian blinds whose light-coloured slats would admit only narrow strips of sunlight.

'Sleep well?'

'Yes.'

She hadn't had her bath yet. Her hair was brown and heavy, her skin very white. This morning she was wearing a blue robe that looked good on her.

While he went into the bathroom, she combed her hair, and everything about the small everyday gestures was comforting. They had a nice house, brand-new, modern, dazzling white, in the most fashionable section of Santa Clara, between the lagoon and the sea, just a few steps from the Country Club and the beach. Eddie had given it a name he liked: *Sea Breeze.* If the garden was not very big, land prices in this neighbourhood being exorbitant, still the house was ringed by a dozen coconut trees, and on the lawn stood a regal palm tree, its trunk sleek and silvery.

'Will you be going to Miami?'

He was in the bathtub. The bathroom was most handsome, its walls covered with light green tiles, the tub and other appliances in the same shade of green, with chromium fittings. What he liked best, because he had seen it only in the biggest hotels, was the stall shower, its glass door framed in shining metal.

'I don't know yet.'

At dinner the night before he had said to Alice:

'Phil is in Miami. Maybe I'll have to go down and see him.'

It wasn't far. Just two hundred and some-odd miles. By car the trip was unpleasant, the road leading through deserted swampland in stifling heat. He usually took the plane.

He didn't know whether he would be going to Miami. He'd said that at random. He shaved while his wife, behind him, was filling the tub for her own bath. She was quite plump. Not fat. Just enough to require alterations on ready-made dresses. Her skin was exceptionally soft. As he shaved, he often glanced at her in the mirror and liked what he saw.

He wasn't like the others. He had always known what he wanted. Very young, he had singled her out, knowingly. It was their wives who showed the others up for what they were worth.

He, too, had soft white skin and, like Alice, very dark hair. Back in Brooklyn, some of the kids in school even called him Blackie. But he soon stopped them.

'I think we're in for a hot day.'

'Looks like it.'

'Will you be home for lunch?'

'I don't know.'

Suddenly, looking at himself in the mirror, he frowned, muttered a curse. There was some blood on his cheek. He always used a safety razor, almost never cut himself. But every once in a while he'd nick that one mole he had on his left cheek, and it always gave him a creepy kind of feeling. Just scraping the skin itself wouldn't have bothered him that way. But this mole, hardly the size of a pinhead when he was twenty, had gradually grown as big as a pea. It was brown, hairy. Most of the time Eddie managed to run the razor over it without making it bleed.

To-day, he had missed. He grabbed for the hemostick in the medicine cabinet. For several days this thing was going to bleed every time he shaved, and somehow it seemed to him as if that blood was not ordinary blood.

He had questioned his doctor. He didn't like doctors, but he went to them for the least discomfort. He mistrusted them, always suspected them of lying to him, tried to trap them in contradictions.

'If it weren't so deep, a flick of the knife would take care of it. As it is, it would leave a scar.'

Somewhere he'd read that flesh moles of this kind sometimes became cancerous. Just the thought of it made him feel weak all over.

'Are you sure it's nothing to worry about?'

'Positive.'

'It isn't cancer?'

'Of course not!'

He was only partly reassured. For the doctor had added:

'If it will ease your mind, we can scrape off a bit and have it analyzed.'

He hadn't had the guts. He coddled himself. Funny, because as a kid he had never been afraid of blows. It was only razors, things that cut, that made him feel that way.

This stupid incident worried him, not so much in itself, but as if it were an omen. However, he fastidiously finished dressing. He was very fastidious. He liked to feel clean, neat, to have well-groomed hair, and a silk shirt on his skin, and freshly pressed clothes. Twice a week he had himself a manicure and a facial massage.

He heard the car stop next door, and then in front of *Sea Breeze*, and he knew it was the mailman; he didn't need to pull up the blinds to visualize the man sticking his arm out of the car window, opening the mailbox, tossing in the mail, and shutting the box again before moving on.

The day was under way according to established ritual. He was ready on time. Alice was putting on her dress. He was downstairs ahead of her and went outside, crossing first the garden and then the sidewalk in order to pick up the mail. The old colonel next door, in his striped pyjamas, did the same, and they nodded in vague greeting though they never talked to each other.

There were newspapers, household bills, and a letter; he recognized both handwriting and paper. When he sat down at the table, Alice, who was serving his breakfast, asked simply:

'From your mother?'

'Yes.'

He read while he ate. His mother always wrote in pencil, on the kind of stationery she sold in folders. Each folder had six sheets and six envelopes in different colours—purple, greenish, bluish—and when the sheets were filled she didn't take a new one, she continued her letter on scraps of paper.

'Dear Joseph,'

It was his real name. He'd been baptized Joseph. Ever since he was ten or eleven he'd made people call him Eddie, and everybody knew him by that name, only his mother persisted in calling him Joseph. It annoyed him. He had told her so, but she just couldn't help herself.

'I haven't heard from you in quite a while so I hope you are well, and the wife and children too.'

His mother didn't like Alice. She hardly knew her, had only seen her two or three times, but she did not like her. She was an odd sort of woman, his mother. Reading her letters was not always an easy job. Though born in Brooklyn, she often mixed some Italian with the English and then her spelling could become highly personal.

'Life here goes on same as ever. Old Lanza, he used to live at the corner, died in the hospital last week. They gave him a nice funeral, because he was a good man and he lived more than eighty years in the neighbourhood. His daughter-in-law came from Oregon where she lives with her husband, but the husband couldn't make the trip on account of he's just had his leg amputated last month. Nice-looking man, too, healthy and just fifty-five years old. He hurt himself with a gardening tool and gangrene started right off.'

Looking up, Rico could see the lawn, the coconut trees, and a fairly large stretch of sea gleaming between two white walls. He could visualize just as sharply the street in Brooklyn from where his mother was writing, the candy store she owned, next door to the fruit and vegetable store where he had been born and which she had sold after his father's death. The El was close by. Close enough to be seen from their windows almost as he could see the ocean right now, and to hear, at regular intervals, the rumble of the trains which were briefly etched against the sky.

'Young Josephine got married. You remember her. I took her in when she was just a baby, after her mother died.'

He vaguely remembered not one, but two or three babies whom his mother had sheltered.

In all her letters there were a number of pages devoted only to the neighbours, to people whom he had more or less forgotten. Mostly about deaths and illnesses, sometimes accidents, or news of a neighbourhood boy picked up by the cops.

'A good kid who didn't have any luck,' she'd say.

And only at the very end came the serious matters, those which actually prompted her to write.

'Gino stopped by to see me last Friday. He looks tired.'

Gino was one of Eddie's two brothers. Eddie, the oldest, was now thirty-eight. Gino was thirty-six and they did not resemble one another. Eddie was rather stout. Not very fat, but roundish in shape and with a tendency to put on weight. Gino, on the contrary, had always been lanky, with much sharper features than either of his brothers. As a child, he looked rather sickly (or puny). Even now he never looked in really good health.

'He came to say good-bye, because he was leaving that night for California. Seems like he's going to stay out there for a while. I don't much like that. It never means any good when they send somebody like him out West. I tried to make him talk, but you know your brother.'

Gino had never married, never been interested in women. Surely he never trusted anybody in his whole life.

'I asked him if it was on account of the Grand Jury. Naturally there's been a lot of talk about it here. At first, everybody thought it was going to be like the other times, a few witnesses questioned and there the matter ends. Everybody figured it was all fixed ahead of time. But something must have happened that the D.A. and the cops are keeping under a tight lid. There's a rumour that someone's been singing.

'And Gino isn't the only one to push off. One of the big shots left New York kind of sudden, and the papers got hold of the news. You must have read about it.'

He hadn't. But he was beginning to wonder if there was a connection with

Sid Kubik, whom Phil had mentioned on the 'phone.

He sensed a restlessness in his mother's letter. There was restlessness in Brooklyn. He'd been right on his guard, the night before, when Phil had called.

The trouble is that one never knows exactly what's going on. You have to guess, to draw conclusions from little things, insignificant in themselves, but which, knit together, sometimes take on a meaning.

Why had they shipped Gino out to California, where, strictly speaking, he had no business to be?

And they had sent him somebody, too, who was supposed to get here this morning and whom he was instructed to keep from skipping away.

He had read the account of the Brooklyn Grand Jury investigation. Supposedly the Grand Jury was looking into the case of Carmine, killed in front of the El Charro right on Fulton Avenue, three hundred feet from Borough Hall.

It was six months now since Carmine had stopped those five slugs of lead. The police hadn't found one clue worth mentioning. Under normal circumstances, the case should have been filed long ago.

Eddie didn't know if his brother Gino was mixed up in it. By all the rules of the game he should not have been a part of it, because guys from the same neighbourhood are not picked for conspicuous jobs like that.

Was there some connection between all this and the 'phone call from Phil? Boston Phil never interfered personally without reason. His every move had a purpose and that's what made him dangerous. Besides, when he was sent somewhere, it generally meant that things weren't going the way they should.

There are men of that kind in big concerns like Standard Oil and widespread banking firms, trouble shooters who show up whenever and wherever the big bosses suspect some serious irregularity.

Phil was like that. And he acted the type. He played the part of one in the know and shrouded himself in mystery.

'There is something else I wanted to bring up in my last letter already. I didn't because it was still only a rumour. I figured Tony would have written you about it, or maybe he was going to, because you always rated high with him.'

Tony was the youngest of the Rico brothers, only thirty-three, and he had lived with their mother longer than the other two. He was her favourite of course. He was dark like Eddie, whom he resembled a little, but sleeker, more handsome. Eddie hadn't heard from him directly in over a year.

'I've been sure,' his mother continued, 'that something was up ever since he went to Atlantic City last summer. He took several trips without telling me where he was going, and I figured there was some woman in the picture. Well, it's been nearly three months now since anybody saw him. Some people stopped by to inquire about him, and it wasn't out of idle curiosity, either. Even Phil who dropped in to say hello, he said, but all he talked about was Tony. Then, three days ago a certain Karen—you don't know her; she's a girl from the neighbourhood that used to date with Tony a while back—she comes and says to me all of a sudden: Did you know Tony was married?

'I laughed out loud. But it seems it's true. And with the girl he met in Atlantic City, who isn't from the neighbourhood, isn't even from New York, her family living in Pennsylvania, so I hear. I don't know why–but it don't rest easy with me. You know Tony. He had girls by the dozen, and he sure didn't look the type that gets married. Why didn't he tell anybody about it? Why so many people needing his address, all of a sudden? I guess you understand when I say I'm uneasy. There are things going on that I'd like to find out about. If, by any chance, you're in on this, let me know right away and put my mind at ease. I don't like the looks of things.

'Mamma sends her regards. She's still spry, except that she doesn't get out of her chair any more. The hardest part for me is putting her to bed at night, because she is getting heavier and heavier. You can't imagine the amount of food she puts away. An hour after each meal she starts complaining about being what she calls a little hungry. The doctor told me not to give her what she asks for, but I just can't do it.'

To Eddie, his grandmother had nearly always been enormous and, as far as he could remember, an invalid.

'That's all for to-day. I'm worried. You probably know more than me, so write as soon as you can, especially about Tony.

'Has the baby started to talk? There is a case here in the neighbourhood, not a girl, but a little boy the same age who . . .'

The rest followed on a piece of paper of a different colour with, in the corner, the traditional 'love and kisses'.

Eddie didn't hand the letter over to his wife. He never asked her to read his mail, not even his mother's letters, and she would never think of requesting it.

'Everything all right?'

'Gino is in California.'

'For long?'

'My mother doesn't know.'

He preferred not to mention anything about Tony. He seldom discussed business matters with her. She came from Brooklyn, too, but not from the same people. That's the way he had wanted it; of Italian origin, like him, because he wouldn't have felt at ease otherwise; but her father held a pretty big job with an export firm, and when Eddie had met her, she was working in a store in Manhattan.

Before he left, he went in to kiss Babe who was squatting in the kitchen, under Lois's watchful eyes. He also kissed his wife, absently.

'Don't forget to 'phone if you do go to Miami.'

Outside, it was already getting warm. The sun was shining. The sun was always shining, except during the two or three months of the rainy season. And there were always flowers, around the lawns, among the bushes, and palm trees along the roads.

He walked through the garden to get his car out of the garage. Everybody who came to Siesta Beach agreed that it was paradise itself. The houses were new, each set in its own garden, between the sea and the lagoon.

He took the wooden bridge across the lagoon and, at the end of the avenue, entered the town itself.

The car purred along. It was one of the best cars on the market, always kept sparkling clean.

Everything was beautiful. Everything was bright and clean. Everything bathed in light. At times, it felt like living in the middle of a travel poster.

On the left, sailboats swayed gently in the harbour. And, along Main

Street, scattered between the business establishments, were the neon signs that at night were brightly lit–Gypsy, Rialto, Coconut Grove, Little Cottage.

Their doors were closed. Or, if one did happen to be open, it was just for the cleaning women who were working in the place.

He turned left into the St Petersburg road and, just before reaching the town limits, came to a long wooden building with a sign over the door that read:

West Coast Fruit Emporium, Inc.

The whole store front was one long counter where all the species of fruit on earth seemed on display–golden-brown pineapples, grapefruit, polished oranges, mangoes, avocados, each variety forming a pyramid close to the vegetables to which a constant spray of water gave an unusual freshness. And produce was not the only merchandise: most grocery products could be found inside, cans stacked up from floor to ceiling.

'How are you, boss?'

A place in the shade was reserved for his car. Every morning, old Angelo, in a white shirt and a white apron, came out to greet him.

'Okay, Angelo.'

Eddie rarely, if ever, smiled, and it bothered neither Angelo nor Alice. That was part of Eddie's make-up. It didn't mean he was in a bad mood. It was his way of looking at people and at things, not exactly as if he suspected a trap, but with a sort of calm deliberation. Back in Brooklyn when he was still in his teens some of the fellows had already nicknamed him The Accountant.

'Someone's here to see you.'

'I know. Where is he?'

'I made him wait in your office. I didn't know . . .'

Two grocery boys in smocks were putting fresh fruit into the stands. In a glass-partitioned office in the back Miss Van Ness was banging away on the typewriter, her blonde head turned sideways.

Eddie opened the door.

'Any calls?'

'No, Mr Rico.'

She did have a first name–Beulah – but he had never called her by it. He was not given to easy familiarity, least of all with her.

'There is someone waiting in the office.'

'I know.'

He entered, avoided looking right away at the man who, sitting in a chair, his back to the light, was smoking a cigarette, and who didn't budge. Eddie took off first his straw hat, his coat, hung them both on the clothes tree. Then he sat down, hitching up the legs of his pants so as not to ruin the creases, and lit a cigarette.

'They told me . . .'

Rico finally glanced at his visitor, a tall, husky fellow in his middle twenties, with curly reddish hair.

'Who told you?'

'You know, don't you?'

Eddie didn't repeat his question, merely stared at the redhead, who, finally embarrassed, got up and mumbled:

'Boston Phil.'

'When did you see him?'

'Saturday. Three days ago, that is.'

'What did he tell you?'

'To report to you here.'

'What else?'

'Not to leave Santa Clara.'

'That all?'

'Not under any circumstances.'

Eddie still stared, and the other added:

'And to hole up.'

'Sit down. Name?'

'Joe. Up North, they call me Curly Joe.'

'We'll give you a smock and put you to work behind the counter.'

The redhead let out a sigh.

'I was afraid of that.'

'It doesn't suit you?'

'I didn't say nothing.'

'You'll sleep at Angelo's place.'

'That's the old guy?'

'Yes. You're not to go out without his permission. Who's after you?'

Joe's expression grew sullen. 'They told me not to say nothing,' he said, looking like an obstinate kid.

'Not even to me?'

'To nobody.'

'Did they tell you expressly not to say anything to me?'

'Phil said: "To nobody," he said.'

'You know my brother?'

'Which one? Bug?'

That was Gino's nickname.

'Know where he is?'

'He cleared out just before I did.'

'Did you ever work together?'

Joe did not answer, but neither did he deny the statement.

'Do you know my other brother too?'

'I've heard about Tony.'

Why was he looking at the floor as he said that?

'You never met?'

'No. Least I don't think so.'

'What did you hear about him?'

'I forgot.'

'How long ago was that?'

'I don't know.'

It was better to let the matter drop.

'Do you have any money?'

'A little.'

'When you run short, let me know. You're not going to need much here.'

'Any girls around?'

'We'll see about that.'

Eddie rose and walked over to the door.

'Angelo is going to give you a smock and get you started.'

'Right away?'

'Right away.'

Rico didn't like that boy at all. Mostly he disliked his laconic answers and his shifty eyes.

'Take care of him, Angelo. He'll sleep at your place. Don't let him go out till I get the details from Phil.'

Cautiously he ran his finger over the mole on his cheek where a drop of blood had dried. He went into the office next door.

'Any mail?'

'Nothing special.'

'Still no call from Miami?'

'You're expecting one?'

'I don't know.'

The 'phone rang, but the call was from a citrus fruit grower. He went back into his office, did nothing but wait. He hadn't thought of asking Phil the night before what hotel he was staying at in Miami. He didn't always stay at the same place. Besides, maybe it was better not to have asked. Phil didn't like inquisitive people.

He signed the letters that Miss Van Ness brought him and caught a whiff of her perfume, which he disliked. He liked and knew good perfume. He used some himself, discreetly. Actually, he didn't like the smell of his own body. He was almost ashamed of it, always used deodorants.

'If there is a call from Miami . . .'

'Are you going out?'

'I'm going over to see McGee at the Flamingo.'

'Should I forward the call to you?'

'I'll be there in ten minutes.'

Phil hadn't said anything about a 'phone call. All he said was that Sid Kubik would probably arrive in Miami this morning. At the very most he had hinted that Kubik might want to see him.

Why, then, take it for granted that they would 'phone?

He stepped from the shade of the store into the broiling sun. The redhead, followed by Angelo, was just coming out of one of the cubicles, looking taller and bigger in his white clerk's smock.

'I'm going over to McGee's,' said Rico.

He got into his car, backed up, turned left into the highway. There was a traffic light less than a hundred feet away. It was green, and Eddie was just about to drive on when he saw a man on the sidewalk waving to him.

He almost didn't recognize the fellow, mistaking him for a hitch-hiker. Giving him another look, he frowned and slammed on the brakes.

It was his brother Gino, who should have been in California.

'Get in.'

He glanced back to make sure no one had seen them from the store.

Chapter Two

At first it was just as if Eddie had picked up some stranger on the road. He hadn't even glanced at his brother as he got in, hadn't asked a thing. And Gino, an unlit cigarette between his thin lips, had slipped in so fast the door was shut again before the light turned red.

Eddie drove on, looking straight ahead. They passed gas stations, a second-hand car lot, a motel with lemon-coloured bungalows grouped around a swimming pool.

The brothers hadn't seen each other in two years. They'd last met in New York. Gino had come to Santa Clara only once, five or six years ago, when Eddie had not yet built *Sea Breeze*; so he had never seen the youngest of the girls.

From time to time they passed a truck. They were a good mile out of town when Eddie asked at last, barely opening his mouth, still looking fixedly ahead:

'Do they know you're here?'

'No.'

'You're supposed to be in L.A.?'

'San Diego.'

Gino was thin. He was not good-looking. He was the only one in the family to have a long and somewhat crooked nose, deep-set but flashing eyes, a sallow complexion. His hands were strange, all bones and tendons, with exceptionally long and flexible fingers, the skin stretched tautly over their skeletal frame. And those fingers were never at rest, fiddling with a few bread crumbs, a piece of paper, or a little rubber ball.

'Did you come by train?'

Gino didn't ask where they were going. The town was behind them. Eddie turned left into an almost deserted road, bordered by a pine forest and some gladiola fields.

'No. Not by plane, either. I took the bus.'

Eddie frowned. He understood. It was more anonymous. His brother had come on one of those huge blue and silver buses, a greyhound painted on either side, that cross the length and breadth of the United States in the fashion of the old mail coaches, stopping in every town at bus depots that have replaced the coach stops of yesterday, swarming with motley crowds where the coloured folk predominate, especially in the South, crowds of travellers loaded down with bags and packages, mothers surrounded with children, people headed for distant places and others for the next stop, people buying sandwiches to take along or eat at the counter during a stopover, along with a cup of hot coffee, people sleeping, people worrying, people talking, spewing their life story.

'I told them I'd take the bus.'

Silence again, two or three miles of silence. A number of prisoners, thirty or more, naked to the waist, most of them young, in straw hats, were mowing the embankments, and two guards, rifle in hand, kept them under watch.

They did not look at them.

'How's Alice?'

'Fine.'

'And the kids?'

'Lilian still doesn't talk.'

They were fond of each other. The Rico brothers had always been close. It wasn't just that they were of the same blood, but they had gone to the same school, belonged, as kids, to the same street gangs, taken part in the same fights. In those days, Gino had a positive admiration for his older brother. Did he still admire him? Could be. With him, one could never tell. There was in his nature a sombre, passionate side which he never revealed.

Eddie had never understood him, never felt at ease in his presence. Certain minor details shocked him, too. Gino, for instance, still dressed in the flashy fashion of the punks they used to admire when they were adolescents. He had kept the same mannerisms, the posture, the searching yet furtive look, right down to the cigarette stuck to the lip, and the affectation of incessantly twirling some object or other in his long pale hand.

'Did you get a letter from Mom?'

'This morning.'

'I figured she'd write to you.'

They had reached water again, a lagoon larger than the one at Siesta Beach, with a very long wooden bridge from which men were fishing and which led to an island. The planks of the bridge clattered under the wheels. On the island, they went through a village, followed an unpaved road that skirted brushwood, swampland, and a tangle of palm trees and pines, until it reached the dunes. Half an hour had passed since they met, and they had said next to nothing, when Eddie headed the car into a path between the dunes and stopped, at the outermost point of the island, on a glaring beach with a roaring surf and no living creature in sight but the sea gulls and the pelicans.

He didn't open the car door, remained in his corner, ignition off, lit a cigarette. The sand underfoot was no doubt burning-hot. Rows of shells indicated the line reached by the sea at high tide. A very big wave, too white, too glaring to follow, rose at regular intervals to sink back in one slow motion, shedding a cloud of sparkling dust.

'What about Tony?' Eddie finally asked, turning towards his brother.

'What did Mamma write to you?'

'That he got married. Is it true?'

'Yes.'

'You know where he is?'

'Not exactly. They're looking for him. They tracked down his wife's parents.'

'Italians?'

'Lithuanians originally. The father farms a plot out in Pennsylvania. Seems like he doesn't know where his daughter is either.'

'Did he know she was married?'

'Tony went to tell him. The way I heard it, the girl used to work in an office in New York, but Tony met her in Atlantic City, on her vacation. They must have dated in New York after that. About two months ago they went to see her old man to break the news they'd just gotten married. They stayed about ten days at his place.'

Eddie held out a packet of cigarettes, and his brother took one without lighting it.

'I know why they're looking for him.' said Gino, barely moving his lips.

'Carmine?'

'No.'

Eddie hated talking about such things. It was all very remote now, almost in another world. Deep down, he would have preferred not knowing. It is always dangerous to know too much. Why hadn't his brothers gotten out like he had? Even Gino's nickname, Bug, shocked him, seemed a little indecent to him.

'I'm the one who bumped off Carmine,' Gino calmly announced.

Eddie did not flinch. Gino had always been a killer by instinct. That was another reason why Eddie, who hated brutality, had never felt on a level with him.

He didn't judge, didn't consider that wrong in itself. It was more of a physical uneasiness, like what he felt when Gino used certain slang terms which he himself had long outgrown.

'Tony was driving?'

He was familiar with the routine. As a kid, in Brooklyn, he had seen the technique being slowly perfected, and by now the procedure was practically hard and fast.

Everyone had his job, his speciality, from which he almost never switched. First, there was the one who furnished the car at the appointed time, a fast car, not too flashy, with a tankful of gas and, preferably, out-of-state plates, because that delayed the search. He had carried through that part of a job twice by the time he was seventeen. And that was how Tony had started too, only he had been even younger. He would deliver the car at a prearranged spot and get paid ten or twenty bucks.

Tony was so crazy about speed and motors that he did it for the fun of it, picking out a smooth job parked along the kerb, just for the kick of racing it a few hours on the highway where he'd finally abandon it. Once, when he had crashed into a tree, his buddy had been killed, and he had got away without a scratch.

At nineteen, he had been promoted to a bigger job. He was assigned to drive the killer and his assistant to the scene, and afterwards, with or without the cops on their tail, to a meeting place where another and unreported car waited for them all.

'Fatty did the driving on the Carmine job.'

Gino was talking with a kind of nostalgia. Eddie knew Fatty, the shoemaker's son, a big boy, younger than he, who used to run errands for him once in a while.

'Who was the boss?'

'Vince Vettori.'

He had been wrong to ask, especially if Vettori was involved, because then it would mean serious business, connected with a settling of accounts between the bigshots.

Carmine and Vettori, like Boston Phil, were men who worked on a level above his. They gave orders and didn't like people to pry into their affairs.

'Everything worked as planned. We knew Carmine would leave El Charro at eleven, because he had a date someplace else a little later. We were parked about fifty feet from the entrance. When he went for his hat and coat, we got the signal. Fatty started the car real slow, and we reached the place just as he was coming out of the door. All I had to do was plug him.'

The word shocked Eddie. He wasn't looking at his brother, kept watching a pelican that glided above the whitecaps ready to dive in after the fish. Envious sea gulls wheeled around the pelican, screeching at every catch.

'But there was a catch, after all. This I only heard through the grapevine.'

That's the way it always went. It was hard to know exactly what was going on. The bigshots were careful not to talk. Nothing to go on but vague rumours. And drawing one's own conclusions.

'Remember old man Rosenberg?'

'The one who runs the cigar store?'

Eddie remembered the news-stand and cigar store, directly across the street from the El Charro. In the days when Eddie was taking small bets for a bookie, he had sometimes planted himself right in front of the store. Rosenberg knew about him and used to send him customers against a small commission. He was an old man then. At least he seemed old to him.

'How old can he be?'

'In his sixties. Apparently, they'd been keeping an eye on him for a while. Claim he's been giving the cops a hand. Anyway Sergeant O'Malley went to see him a couple of times. Then, the third time, he took him along to the D.A.'s office. I don't know if Rosenberg really was a stoolie. Maybe they just didn't want to take chances. He was closing up when we took care of Carmine. He could have recognized us. So they decided to rub him out, too.'

The old routine. Time and again, when he was living in Brooklyn, he'd heard the same story. And how many times, later, had he read it in the newspapers?

'For some reason, they didn't want me to go and they picked a new guy, a redhead called Joe.'

'With Tony driving?'

'Yeah. You must have read about it in the papers. Rosenberg must have squealed, all right, because he had a bodyguard, a guy in civvies not from the neighbourhood. Rosenberg always opened up the shop at eight in the morning. There's a lot of traffic on that corner on account of the subway entrance. The car came up on them. The old man was stacking the papers when he got three slugs in the back. I don't know if Joe saw the guy standing next to Rosenberg and smelled a cop, or what. Anyway, he cut him down, too, and before the crowds caught on to what had happened, they had made their getaway.'

Eddie wouldn't have known the details, but the scene itself was familiar enough that he saw it as clearly as if he'd been watching a movie. He had once witnessed this same kind of thing – or almost–when he was four and a half years old. He was the only one of the three brothers, to have seen it. Gino, not yet two at the time, had been crawling around in Grandma's room. Tony wasn't even born. His mother was still pregnant with him, and they had put a chair up for her behind the counter in the store.

Not the same store she now ran. Their father was still alive. Eddie remembered him very well, with his thick dark hair, his large head, his calm look.

Eddie used to think of him as an old man, too, when actually he was only thirty-five.

He was born on the other side, in Sicily, near Taormina, where he used to work for a ropemaker. He came to Brooklyn when he was nineteen and must have worked at many jobs, very humble jobs, no doubt, because he was shy and timid, slow-moving, with a somewhat naive smile. His name was Cesare. Some people in the neighbourhood still remembered when he was selling ice cream in the streets.

Around thirty, he had married Julia, who was only twenty and had just lost her father.

Eddie always suspected that his father had been chosen because a man was needed to run the store. It was a neighbourhood store selling fruit, vegetables, and some groceries. Even then Julia's mother was fat.

Eddie could still picture his father opening the trap door behind the left counter to go down to the cellar for butter or cheese, or climbing up with a bag of potatoes on his shoulders.

One particular afternoon it was snowing, and Eddie was playing outdoors with another kid. They were both on the sidewalk across the street. It was still pretty bright, but the lights in the shop windows were already burning. There was some commotion over by the corner, people running, voices shouting.

Cesare, in a white apron, had come out of the shop and was standing among his baskets. Somebody, one of the men that came running, gave him a shove, and, just at that moment, two shots were fired.

Had Eddie really seen all that, remembered it all? The story had been told and retold so many times around the house that other people's impressions must have mingled with his own.

Anyway, he still saw his father lift both his hands towards his face, totter for a moment, then the drop to the sidewalk. Half his face was gone, and Eddie could have sworn that that part of it was his own memory.

'The whole left side was just one big hole,' he often used to repeat.

The man who had fired the shots must have still been pretty far away, because the fellow he was chasing had had time to slip into the store.

'He was young, wasn't he, Mom?'

'Nineteen or twenty. You couldn't remember.'

'Of course I do. He was all dressed in black.'

'It just looked like that to you on account of the dark coming down.'

A cop in uniform, then another, had rushed into the store without so much as glancing at the body of Cesare Rico. They found Julia sitting on a chair behind the counter on the left, hands folded over her protruding belly.

'Where'd he go?'

'That way . . .'

She pointed towards the back door that led into a hallway. They were living in an old block of houses, with a labyrinth of alleyways in back where people used to park their wagons; one of the storekeepers next door even had a stable there, with a horse in it.

Who had called the ambulance? No one ever found out. But the ambulance did arrive. Eddie saw it suddenly swing into their street and stop; two men in white jumped out, and only then did his mother appear at the door and rush out towards her husband.

More cops had helped search the neighbourhood. Ten times they passed through the store. The back alleys had at least two or three exits.

It was years before Eddie found out the truth. The man they were hunting for had not escaped into the alley. When he had dashed into the store, the trap door was open. Julia, recognizing him, had made him jump in, shut the door after him and put her chair right on top of it. Not one of the cops had been any wiser.

'So I couldn't rush out to your poor father . . .' she'd conclude, simply.

It seemed quite natural to them all. In their neighbourhood, everybody would have found that natural.

The man was a young Pole with a funny name who hardly knew any English at the time. For a long time, for years, nobody heard from him.

When he reappeared, he had become a man of impressive appearance who called himself Sid Kubik and, even then, was almost a bigshot. He bossed the off-track betting, not only in Brooklyn, but in Lower Manhattan and Greenwich Village, and Eddie went to work for him.

With the father dead, and it being hard for a woman to lug fruit crates and vegetable baskets, Julia had bought the candy store and soda fountain right next door.

Kubik had stopped by to see her several times. He always called her Mama Julia, with his funny accent.

The two men in the car were silent. Very far away on the beach Eddie noticed a red spot, the silhouette of a woman in a scarlet bathing suit walking slowly, stopping from time to time. Probably collecting shells. It would take quite a while before she came close.

One detail bothered him. The Carmine business was six months past. Four days after the El Charro affair the only witness had been liquidated. Under these circumstances, no district attorney in his right mind would challenge the organization.

They don't tackle a case until it's airtight, with ironclad testimony. The proof was that for weeks and months they've been soft-pedalling the investigation. The Grand Jury was looking into it, but half-heartedly, only because the citizenry demands to be reassured.

Eddie knew that his brother was thinking the same thing.

'Somebody talked?' he finally mumbled, averting his glance.

'I haven't been able to find out anything definite. There are all kinds of rumours. The last two weeks, especially, people have been speculating; the regular hangouts are full of new faces: O'Malley keeps grinning like a horse, as if he was getting ready to pull a fast one. And everybody asking me about Tony. The same damn question, casual as hell:

'"What's new with Tony?"'

'I'd also swear that certain people didn't care to be seen in my company. Some others told me:

'*So Tony's decided to settle down, I hear. Got himself a real high-class broad, huh?* And then I got orders to go to San Diego and stay there.'

'What made you come here?'

Gino gave his brother an odd look, as if he mistrusted him as much as anybody else.

'On account of Tony?'

'What do you mean?'

'If they find him, they'll kill him.'

Without real conviction, Eddie mumbled:

'Do you think so?'

'They won't take any more chances with him than with Rosenberg. In the first place they don't much like a quitter.'

This Eddie knew himself, damn it all; but he didn't like to think of it in such crude terms.

'Tony was in on that last deal, the one the D.A. is working on. They figure if the cops give him a real going-over, he might sing.'

'Do you think that too?'

Gino looked out of the window, spat into the hot sand, paused, and uttered:

'Could be.'

Then, through tight lips:

'He's in love.'

And finally:

'They say his wife is pregnant.'

It was almost as if the word disgusted him.

'You really don't know where he is?'

'If I did, I'd go to see him.'

Eddie did not dare to ask why. Brothers or no brothers, there was, between them and above them, this organization which they talked about only in veiled terms.

'Where would he be safe?'

'Canada, Mexico, South America. Anywhere. Till things calm down.'

Gino went on, in a different tone of voice, as though talking to himself:

'The way I figured it, you have more freedom of movement that I. You know a lot of people. You're not mixed up in this. Maybe you can find out where he's hiding and help him get away?'

'Has he got any money?'

'You know damned well he never has.'

The woman in red was only some three hundred feet away, and Eddie suddenly switched on the ignition, stepped on the gas. The car backed up in the sand, turned among the dunes.

'Where's your baggage?'

'All I got is one suitcase. I checked it in a locker at the bus depot.'

Gino had never owned more than one suitcase. Ever since he'd left their mother's house at eighteen, he had not had a real home. He lived in furnished rooms, one month here, two weeks there, and could be reached in person or by mail only in certain bars, although he never touched any liquor.

They drove on in silence. Gino still hadn't lit his cigarette. Eddie was wondering if he had ever really seen him smoke.

'We'd better not take the highway,' murmured the older brother, not without a slight sense of embarrassment.

'Joe is here,' he added.

They both understood. Sure, it was natural for them to get Joe out of town just as they had done with Gino. It wasn't the first time they sent somebody down to Eddie's for a few days or a few weeks.

But was this guy there only to hide out? There were at least fifty other places they could have picked, yet they had shipped him out to one of the Rico brothers.

'I don't like him,' said Eddie.

His brother shrugged his shoulders. They were driving along a road running parallel to the highway, and suddenly, as they came to a rather deserted spot, Gino said:

'You'd better drop me here.'

'What are you going to do?'

'Hitch-hike.'

Eddie preferred it that way, but was careful not to show it.

'I guess you won't be doing anything about Tony?'

'Of course I will. I'll do my best.'

Gino didn't believe it. He opened the door, then, with a curt nod, he said only:

'So long.'

Ill at ease, Eddie started the car again and, without turning, saw his brother's silhouette dwindling in the rear-view mirror.

He had told Miss Van Ness that he was going to the Club Flamingo. If Boston Phil had called from Miami, she must have told him, in which case Phil had certainly called the Flamingo. He didn't like that. Sure, he was free to come and go as he pleased. He could have been delayed, could have met somebody on the way. The car could have stalled. The fact remained that the timing was bad.

He drove very fast, got back on the highway and, a few minutes before noon, stopped his car in front of the Flamingo. 'Cocktails–Grill–Dancing,' said the sign in the window.

Three or four other cars were parked out front, so he had to leave his car half in the shade and half in the sun. It was cool, almost chilly, in the air-conditioned bar.

'Hello, Teddy.'

'Hi there, Mr Rico.'

'Pat in?'

'The boss is in his office.'

He went through the clubroom, its walls decorated with red flamingos, where a waiter was serving lunch to a few customers. Then, there was a sort of anteroom, all done up in red velvet, and at the back, a door marked, 'Private.'

Pat McGee answered at once, held out a muscular hand.

'How's things?'

'Fine.'

'You just had a call.'

'Phil?'

'Right. From Miami. Here is his number. He wants you to call him back.'

'Did he say anything?'

Why be suspicious of McGee? It didn't make sense. Phil wasn't the man to spill anything to a guy like McGee.

McGee had taken the receiver off the hook. Two minutes later he was handing it to Eddie.

'He's staying at the Excelsior,' he announced. 'I think he's not alone.'

Phil's disagreeable voice at the other end of the wire.

'Hello, Eddie?'

Eddie knew the sumptuous apartments of the Excelsior in Miami Beach. Phil always took a suite, where he liked to receive company and mix his own cocktails. He knew a surprising number of newspapermen and of people from every walk of life—actors, professional athletes, even a few oil magnates from Texas.

'I had to stop at a garage. My car—'

The other didn't give him a chance to finish.

'Sid's here,' he interrupted.

What was there to answer? Eddie waited. There were other people in the room over there; he could hear the drone of conversation, the high-pitched voice of a woman.

'There was a plane at noon. You missed it. Take the two-thirty flight.'

'You want me to come over?'

'What the hell do you think I'm talking about?'

'Sorry—I wasn't sure.'

He was talking the way a book-keeper talks to his chief or to an inspector who demands to see the books, and McGee's presence bothered him. He didn't want to be humbled in front of him.

Because after all, here, in his territory, he was the boss. He was the one from whom McGee, in another minute, was going to take orders.

'Did you see the boy yet?'

'I put him to work in the store.'

'See you later.'

Phil hung up.

'That guy's in a rut,' said Pat McGee. 'He keeps thinking he's big as the world.'

'Yeah.'

'Did you want to check the week's accounts?'

'I don't have time to-day. I'm going to Miami.'

'That's what I thought. I'm told Sid is there.'

Incredible how things got around. Even to McGee, who was a nobody, just a roadhouse manager who ran a joint with a few slot machines, an occasional crap game, and some betting.

Twice a week Rico made the rounds and collected his cut. The bets were called directly to Miami by Miss Van Ness.

All that he cashed in that way was not, of course, for him. He passed on most of the take to the higher-ups. Even so, he made enough on it to afford the kind of comfort he had always dreamed of.

He was no bigshot. He was never mentioned in the papers and only rarely talked about in the bars of New York, New Jersey, or Chicago. But in his own territory he was boss. And every single night club paid up without a fuss.

None of them ever tried to welsh any more. He knew his figures too well. He never got mad, never uttered any threats. On the contrary, he always talked quietly, used as few words as possible, and everybody understood.

Actually, he behaved towards others a little bit the way Boston Phil behaved towards him. Perhaps there were some who claimed, behind his back, that he was aping him?

'How about a martini?'

'No. I've got to drop by at the house and change.'

In hot weather he sometimes changed twice a day. Wasn't it Phil who did that too?

Unconsciously he scratched his cheek, and the mole started bleeding again. Barely a drop. Even so, he frowned as he examined his handkerchief.

'Is it true that the Samoa is offering roulette again?'

'Once in a while, when they get the right kind of customers.'

'With Garret's blessing?'

'Provided there are no complaints.'

'I'd like to—'

'No. Not here. This is too conspicuous, too close to town. There would be too much risk.'

Sheriff Garret was a friend of his. They had dinner together every so often. Garret had good reason not to refuse him anything. Still, it was delicate work. Concessionnaires like McGee didn't always realize just how delicate it was, and they tended to exaggerate.

'See you in two or three days.'

'Regards to Phil. It's damn near five years since he's been here.'

Eddie got back into his car, wondering if Pat had noticed that he was worried. He was worried, all right. He stopped by at the store and announced that he wouldn't be in for a couple of days. How much did Miss Van Ness actually know? He hadn't picked her for the job. The top brass had assigned her. Joe, in his white smock, was waiting on a customer and seemed to be having a fine time. He winked at Rico a little too familiarly for Eddie's taste.

'Keep an eye on him,' Eddie told Angelo, whom he trusted.

'You can count on me, boss.'

The older girls ate lunch at school. Alice, who was waiting for him, knew right away that something was up.

'Are you going upstairs to change?'

'Yes. Come along and pack my suitcase, will you?'

'You're going to Miami?'

'Yes.'

'For several days?'

'I don't know.'

He wondered if he should tell her about Gino. He felt sure she would not betray him. And she never indulged in idle chatter.

No, it was mostly a sort of reserve that kept him from talking over his business with her. Of course, she knew more or less what he was doing. Just the same, he preferred not to go into details. His home and his family were a thing apart, and, to his way of thinking, should remain so.

He was fond of Alice. And what he appreciated most was that she loved him unconditionally.

'Will you call me?'

'To-night.'

He phoned home every day, sometimes twice a day, whenever he was away on a trip. He'd ask about the children, about everything. He needed to feel that the home and all that went with it were always there, waiting for him.

'Are you taking your white tux?'

'Better pack it. You never know.'

'Three suits?'

She was used to this sort of thing.

'There's some blood on your cheek.'

'I know.'

Again he touched the styptic pencil to it, went in to kiss Babe, who was already taking her nap, and wondered if she would ever talk.

What would the two older girls think of him, say about him, later on? What sort of memories would they keep of their father? That thought often troubled him.

He took his wife in his arms, and her whole body was soft, she smelled good, her lips were good.

'Don't stay too long.'

He had ordered a cab so he could leave Alice the car. The driver knew him and called him boss.

Chapter Three

The passengers, coming from Tampa and other points, had taken off their ties and jackets. Eddie rarely made himself comfortable in public. He sat as straight as he would in a bus, staring vaguely ahead, with an occasional glance devoid of curiosity at the green and reddish jungle over which they were flying. The stewardess who had asked him with a smile if he wanted tea or coffee he had merely refused by a shake of his head. He did not feel bound to be gracious with women. He was not rude, either. Just mistrustful.

All his life he had mistrusted a good many things, and it had worked out rather well. Now and then, through the cabin window, he caught sight of the gleaming highway running alongside the ruler-straight line of a canal that had no boats on it. It was an irrigation canal, stagnant, black, slimy, and in its mud slithered alligators and other beasts whose presence was revealed only by the big air bubbles that continuously rose to the surface.

On one stretch of road some one hundred and fifty miles long there was not one house, not one gas station. No shade, either. And sometimes it was a whole hour before a car passed.

He was always nervous driving that route, especially when he was alone. Even the air, as if thickened by the sun, seemed to be alive with something hostile. At one end, there was Miami, with its palm-lined avenues, its big hotels etched in white on the sky; at the other end, the clean and peaceful little towns along the Gulf of Mexico.

Between the two there was literally a no man's land, a steaming jungle ruled over by nameless beasts.

What might happen if he suddenly were sick at the wheel?

On the air-conditioned plane the trip didn't take much longer than, when he was a child, to go by bus from Brooklyn to Manhattan.

Yet a certain nervousness took hold of him whenever he left his own little stronghold, just as it would long ago, when he strayed from his own neighbourhood.

In Miami he was no longer The Boss. In the streets, in the bars, no one recognized him. The people he was about to meet lived on a different level. They were more powerful than he. They were the ones he depended upon.

He had gone to Miami several times under similar circumstances. Almost all the bigshots spent a few weeks out of every year in Palm Beach or Miami.

They scorned the western shore, and if they wanted to talk to him, they made him come.

He always prepared himself for those interviews the way he did now—not by trying to plan what he was going to tell them, but by bolstering his self-confidence. That was the essential thing. He had to know he was right.

And he'd been right all his life. Even when some of his Brooklyn pals were making fun of 'The Accountant.'

How many of them were alive to-day? How many of them had lived long enough to admit that he had made the right choice?

True, they probably wouldn't admit it anyway. Even Gino didn't admit it. Eddie had a feeling that Gino not only didn't envy him, but looked down on him with a certain scorn.

Still, it was Gino, and all the others who were wrong.

Once convinced of that, he felt strong and could look forward with detachment to the approaching meeting with Phil and Sid Kubik.

Boston Phil's opinions didn't really count, for all his mighty airs. It was Kubik that mattered. And Kubik knew him.

Eddie had always followed a straight course.

At the time when he had staked his claim, a great many possibilities were open to him. The organization was far from what it had become. In fact, it hardly existed at all. The gangsters who had come up during Prohibition were still making headlines. Occasionally, they would get together on some specific job, divide a given territory between themselves or join forces now and then, but these temporary alliances generally ended in an all-around massacre.

And, outside of their orbit, gravitated hundreds of smalltime bosses. Some of them ran a neighbourhood, or a couple of streets. Some specialized in a particular racket.

That was the setup in Brooklyn and Lower Manhattan. At twenty, some of Eddie's school chums thought they were bigshots and, with two or three buddies, tried to cut out a monopoly for themselves. They not only had to liquidate those who stood in their way—they also had to kill for the sake of establishing their prestige.

True enough, they did gain some prestige, and the whole street would envy and admire them when, in their flashy clothes, they climbed out of their snazzy convertibles and strolled into the bars and poolrooms.

Was that what Gino had been dazzled by? Eddie truthfully didn't believe so. Gino was in a class by himself. He had never tried to bluff or put on airs, never bothered about women's opinion of him. He had a vocation for killing, cold-bloodedly, as if he were out for revenge or, rather, as if pulling the trigger of a gun aimed at a live target procured some secret voluptuous pleasure.

Some people held that opinion and expressed it crudely. Eddie preferred not to thrash the matter out. Gino was his brother, after all. Where was he now—on the bus, jolting along the highways, headed for Mississippi and California?

Eddie had never tried to work alone. He had never been arrested, either. He was one of the few survivors of that era who had no police record and whose fingerprints were not on file anywhere.

When he was taking small bets out in the streets, before he even needed his first shave, he was working for a local bookie who didn't pay a fixed commission but who, if the day's take had been fair, gave him two or three dollars for his trouble.

In school he had been a good student. He was the only one of the Rico brothers to go to school till he was fifteen.

One day, a big betting office was organized in the rear of a barbershop and that's where he really got his start. A blackboard, listing the horses and the current odds, took up part of the wall. There were nine or ten 'phones, at least as many clerks, and benches for the punters watching for the outcome of the races. The boss's name was Falera, but everybody knew he wasn't working on his own, that some important people were behind him.

Was he still running the place?

Because above Phil, above Sid Kubik, even above a man like Old Mossie, who owned several casinos and had built a million-dollar night club in Reno, there was yet a higher echelon about which Eddie knew next to nothing.

No more than the run-of-the-mill concessionnaires of Santa Clara and of the two counties he controlled knew who was behind him.

People talked about 'the organization'. Some speculated, tried to know, blabbered too much. Others believed themselves strong enough to do without protection, wanted to be their own masters, and they rarely got away with it. In fact, Eddie didn't know one single instance of its having worked. One after the other—like Nitti, Caracciolo (and they used to call him Lucky!), Dillon, Landis, and a dozen more—had one fine day been taken for a ride that ended in a vacant lot, or else, like Carmine more recently, got a belly full of lead at the end of a good dinner.

Eddie had always stuck to the rules. Sid Kubik, who was a friend of his mother's, knew that. The others, above him, must have come to know it too.

For years he, Eddie Rico, had been the one they sent out wherever a new setup was being opened. He had become a real expert. He'd worked in Chicago, Louisiana, put in several weeks to help straighten out business operations in St Louis, Mo.

He was calm, reliable. He had never asked for more than his share.

He could figure out, almost to the dollar, the revenue from a slot machine installed in any given place, the receipts from a roulette or crap game; and what he didn't know about lotteries wasn't worth knowing.

'He knows his figures,' they used to say about him.

For a while after his marriage he had gone on travelling. It wasn't till after his first daughter was born that he asked for a steady job in one place. Others would have made demands, for he had well earned it. Not Eddie. Instead, he submitted a precise proposition.

For a long time, it had been his ambition to get a territory of his own, and he knew the map of the United States inside out. All the good locations seemed to have been taken. Miami and the eastern coast of Florida, with their casinos, their luxury hotels, with the cream of the international set congregating there every winter, was one of the biggest ones, so big, in fact, that there were three or four who each had a slice of it, with the result that Boston Phil had to come down quite often to straighten them out and keep tabs on them.

There was nobody on the west coast of Florida. And nobody cared. The small towns rising every twenty or thirty miles along the beach and the lagoons were chiefly frequented by the quiet sort of people, retired army officers, government officials, industrialists who came from all over to escape the rigours of winter, or to retire for good.

'Okay, kid,' Sid Kubik had said to him. Sid had become a massive fellow, whose features might have been carved out of white marble.

Who else but Eddie had built the Gulf-coast territory into what it was to-day? The bosses knew it, too. They had the figures to show what they cashed in every year.

And, in almost ten years now, not one shot fired, not one campaign in the press.

For a front, Eddie had been the one to hit on the idea of buying up for a song the fruit and vegetable place which was then on its last legs.

To-day, the West Coast Fruit Emporium had branches in three different localities, and Eddie could have lived on the income it brought him.

He hadn't started building right away. He had rented a house, in a section that was nice but not too fancy. He hadn't swooped down on the sheriff, or on the chief of police, as others would have done.

He had waited until he had acquired a reputation as an honest businessman, a good family man, a quiet fellow who went to church every Sunday and contributed generously to local charities.

Then, and only then, did he approach the sheriff, having steeled himself for the interview as he was steeling himself now, on the plane, for his Miami conference. He had talked commonsense.

'There are eight gambling houses in the county, ten places where bets are taken, and at least three hundred slot machines in different spots, including the two country clubs.'

They were the exact figures. All that was in the hands of smalltime operators, working independently.

'Periodically, clubs and lodges set up an indignant roar, thunder about vice, prostitution, and what have you. So you go and arrest a few guys. They get sentenced, or maybe they don't. In any case, either they pick up again right off, or else somebody soon takes their place. You know damn well these things can never be stamped out for good.'

But just give him, Eddie, a free hand and the gambling houses will be strictly limited in number, properly supervised, orderly. There would be no more complaints from one-shot customers about having been cleaned out in a rigged game. There would be no more under-age pickups walking the streets, or hanging out in bars. In short, there would be no more scandals.

There had been no need to talk about compensation. The sheriff had understood. His jurisdiction did not extend to the city proper, but the chief of police, a few weeks later, had contacted Eddie.

With the concessionnaires his ways had been a good deal more persuasive; a good deal colder, too. He knew those fellows inside out.

'Right now, you're making so and so much per week. But you got an overhead that cuts into your income. Cops and politicians keep coming after more money, and even so you're liable to have the place raided and go up before the judge.

'With the organization, you start off by doubling your profit because there's no trouble, no sudden expenses, and you can operate practically out in the open. Everything is settled once and for all. So that you win out in the end even when you turn fifty per cent over to us.

'Now, if you don't want to co-operate, I know a few guys who can be pretty rough if they have to. They'll be around this neck of the woods and they might want to have a little talk with you.'

Those were the times he liked best. He was completely self-possessed. At most, during the very first instants, when the interview had not taken shape yet, did his upper lip quiver imperceptibly.

He was never armed. The only gun he owned was in the drawer of his night table. As for fighting, he had too much of a horror of blows and of blood for that. He had fought but once in his life, when he was sixteen, and the blood running from his nose had made him sick.

'Think it over. I'm not rushing you. I'll be in to see you to-morrow.'

A different sheriff had since been appointed; but things were working out just as well with Bill Garret, the present one, and with Craig, the chief of police.

The newspapermen had understood, had found their reward also, not in cash, for the most part, but in dinners, cocktails, and girls.

Eddie knew what Gino thought of him. But he still believed he was right. He owned one of the nicest homes on Siesta Beach. He had a wife, and he could introduce her to anybody without fear that she would make a blunder. His two older daughters went to the best private school. Most residents of Santa Clara and surroundings considered him a prosperous businessman whose word was as good as his cheque.

Three months ago he had tried a little experiment that might have been very delicate. He had applied for membership at the Siesta Beach Country Club, a very exclusive affair right near his home. For eight whole days he had been on edge, nervous to the point of biting his fingernails. When the 'phone call finally came through notifying him of his election, tears had welled up in his eyes and for a long moment he had stood there hugging Alice unable to utter a word.

He didn't like Phil, who had never lived in Brooklyn and had risen through means quite different from his own. What those means were he didn't know and didn't put much stock in what was being rumoured on the subject.

In any case there was Sid Kubik, who knew what kind of a man he was and whose life had been saved by Eddie's parents.

He got out of his seat, took his suitcase from the rack, and followed the line of passengers down the steps, descending into the hugging, humid heat. He carefully picked his cab. He hated dilapidated old taxis and liked the chauffeur to look natty.

'The Excelsior.'

He wasn't dazzled by Miami. It was big, aggressively luxurious. There was something really sumptuous about those long, palm-lined avenues where all the better Fifth Avenue firms had branch stores. Most of the white or pink mansions, with gardens overlooking the lagoon, had their yachts anchored near a private jetty, and there were countless motor-boats and hydroplanes.

Back in New York and in Brooklyn they claimed that one of the bigshots lived all year round in one of those huge structures, with an armoured bedroom and half a dozen bodyguards permanently in attendance.

Eddie wasn't interested in such things. They didn't concern him. His strength lay in not bothering about them.

He kept his distance, envied no one, didn't try to supplant anybody. That's why he was not afraid.

The Excelsior had twenty-seven floors, a huge swimming pool right by the sea, exclusive shops all along the lobby, and the uniforms worn by the personnel probably cost a fortune.

'Mr Kubik, please.'

Polite. Self-possessed. He waited. The clerk 'phoned.

Phil would have done it on purpose, to unnerve him, or to flaunt his own self-importance. Not Sid Kubik. It was natural for him to be busy, to be in conference. The scope of his business operations was more extensive than of the biggest store in New York, and possibly of any insurance company. More complicated, too, because there were no ledgers to rely upon.

After a quarter of an hour Eddie was tempted to go and have a drink. A bar opened into the far end of the lobby, its lights soft and reassuring like in most bars. Sometimes, before an important interview, he might have one glass of whisky, seldom two. If he didn't have any to-day it was to prove to himself that he wasn't afraid.

Why should he be afraid? What blame could he deserve? Kubik would most probably talk to him about Tony. Eddie was responsible neither for his younger brother's marriage, nor for his recent attitude.

One of the elevators was nearby, continually going up and down, and every time he saw people emerging he wondered if they were the ones with whom the boss had been in conference.

'Mr Rico?'

'Yes.'

He felt a kind of tightness in his chest.

'No. 1262. Mr Kubik is expecting you.'

The elevator shot up noiselessly. The corridors were bright, with thick, pale green carpeting, and brass numbers on the doors of the rooms.

The door at 1262 opened without his having to knock, and Phil silently held out his hand for an impersonal, listless hand-shake. He was tall, with thin hair, and he looked flabby in his beige silk suit.

The room probably had a view of the sea, but the blinds were let down, their slats almost closed.

'Where is Kubik?' asked Eddie, glancing around the empty drawing room.

With a movement of his chin Phil indicated a half-open door. There definitely had been a conference; glasses were still standing on the end tables; four or five half-smoked cigars had been left in the ash trays.

Kubik came out of his room, bare to the waist, a bath towel in his hand, giving off a strong odour of cologne.

'Sit down, kid.'

He had a powerful, hairy chest. His arms were as muscular as those of a boxer, and his entire body was strong and hard, especially the chin.

'Mix him a highball, Phil.'

Eddie raised no objections for, according to his code, he should not refuse.

Again Kubik disappeared, came back a few moments later tucking the shirt-tails into his linen slacks.

'Did you hear anything from your brother?'

Eddie wondered if they already knew that Gino had not gone straight to California. It was dangerous to lie.

'Tony?' he asked instead, while Phil was putting ice into a tall glass.

'He wrote you?'

'Not him. My mother. I got a letter from her this morning.'

'What does she have to say? I like your old lady. She's a brave woman. How is she?'

'Fine.'

'Has she seen Tony?'

'No. She says he's married but she doesn't know the girl.'

'He hasn't stopped in to see her lately, has he?'

'No. That's just what she is complaining about.'

Kubik had dropped into an armchair, legs stretched out. He reached for a box of cigars, and Phil held out a gold cigarette lighter engraved with his initials.

'Anything else you know about Tony?'

It was better to play it straight. Sid Kubik didn't seem to be watching him, yet Eddie was aware of the furtive looks scanning him, quick and sharp.

'My mother said that a number of people she doesn't know came to ask about Tony, and she wonders why. She seems worried.'

'Does she think they were cops?'

Eddie looked Kubik straight in the face.

'No,' he said distinctly.

'Do you know where Gino is?'

'In the same letter my mother says he's been sent to California.'

'Do you have the letter with you?'

'I burned it. I always burn them when I'm through.'

It was true. There was no need to lie. As far as possible, he always tried to manœuvre so that he would not have to lie, especially to Kubik. Phil, long and lithe, kept going back and forth with a smug kind of smile that Eddie didn't like, as if he were impatiently waiting for what was yet to come.

'We don't know where Tony is, either, and that's bad,' said Kubik, contemplating his cigar. 'I'd hoped he might have got in touch with you. We know the three of you always used to stick together.'

'It's been two years since I last saw Tony.'

'He might have written you. It's too bad he didn't.'

Phil was happy; that much was obvious. He was not of Italian origin. He was very dark, probably had Spanish blood in his veins. Rumour had it that he'd been to college. Eddie suspected him of harbouring contempt, perhaps even hatred, for all those who had got their start in the teeming streets of Brooklyn.

'The last time your brother Tony worked on a job for us was six months ago.'

Eddie didn't budge. He wasn't supposed to know.

'Nobody has seen him since. Didn't he even send you a card for Christmas or New Year's?'

'No.'

And that, too, was the truth. Eddie had to smile in spite of himself, because these were the very questions he would also have asked. He had never consciously imitated Kubik's mannerism, Phil's even less, and yet, instinctively, in his own territory, where he was boss, he acted in more or less the same fashion.

He didn't touch his glass, in which the ice was melting. The other two weren't drinking either. The 'phone rang. Phil answered.

'Hello—yes. . . . Not before a half hour. . . . He's in conference.'

He hung up. 'Bob,' he announced to Sid, in a confidential aside.
'Let him wait.'

He leaned way back into the chair, still busy with his cigar, on which the ash had turned a silvery white.

'The name of the girl your brother married is Nora Malaks. She used to work in an office on Forty-eighth Street in New York. She's twenty-two, and reported to be beautiful. Tony met her in Atlantic City last summer.'

He paused and Phil peered out through the narrow slats of the blinds.

'Three months ago, a marriage licence in Tony's and the girl's name was issued at City Hall in New York. We don't know where they got married. They could have done it anywhere, in one of the suburbs or out in the country.'

Kubik had kept a slight accent and his voice was harsh.

'There was a Malaks family I used to know, but this is a different one. The father has a small farm near a small village in Pennsylvania. In addition to Nora there is at least one son.'

Eddie had a disagreeable feeling that things had gone too smoothly up to now. Phil's calm smile was a bad omen. Phil wouldn't have smiled that way if the interview had been meant to continue in this vein.

'Now listen good, kid. The brother's name is Pieter. Pieter Malaks. He's twenty-six, and for the past five years he's been working in the New York offices of General Electric.'

Instinctively, he spoke those words with a tinge of respect. General Electric was a big outfit, bigger even than the organization.

'In spite of his age, young Malaks is already an assistant manager. He's not married, has a small apartment in the Bronx, and all he ever does at night is work.'

Eddie was convinced that this last was not a chance remark, and that Sid was looking at him earnestly.

'He's ambitious, see? He figures on getting ahead, maybe as far as the board of directors. Who knows?'

Was this to imply that Pieter Malaks was the same sort of person as Eddie? Well, it just wasn't so and Phil quit looking wise. He, Eddie, had never aimed that high. He was satisfied with his Florida setup, had never tried to make up to the bigshots. Didn't Kubik know that?

'Show him the picture, Phil.'

Phil took a photograph out of a drawer, handed it to Eddie. It was a snapshot taken in the street, probably with a Leica, and blown up. Obviously recent, since the young man in the picture was wearing a seersucker suit and a straw hat.

He was tall, rather thin, his hair looked blond, and he had a fair complexion. He walked with long, determined strides, looking straight ahead.

'Recognize that building?'

There was no more than part of a wall and a few steps.

'Police Headquarters?' Eddie asked.

'That's it. I see you still know your New York. The picture was taken on this gentleman's second visit with the big chief, exactly a month ago. He hasn't been back there since, but a lieutenant went to see him at his own house several times. Secret palavers.'

Kubik, who had stressed the last two words, guffawed heartily.

'Except that we have our own informers. Well the story young Malaks handed out, probably with an air of wounded righteousness, is that his poor little sister fell into the clutches of a gangster and went ahead and married him in spite of what her loving brother told her. Do you get it?'

Eddie nodded, embarrassed.

'But that isn't all. Remember the Carmine business?'

'I read about it in the papers.'

'Is that all you know?'

'Yes.'

This time he was forced to lie.

'Well, there was another job right after that one. A talkative guy we had to keep from blabbering to the Grand Jury.'

Both men were watching him. He didn't flinch.

'On that second job, Tony was the driver.'

The effort to manifest neither emotion nor surprise was almost physically painful.

'On the first one, the Carmine job, your brother Gino played his usual role.'

Kubik let his cigar ash drop on the carpet. Planted behind his chair, Phil was staring straight at Eddie.

'All that, young Malaks told the police. It seems that Tony is so much in love with his wife that he told her all about his past.'

'And she repeated it to her brother?'

'That's not all.'

The rest was much more serious, infinitely more serious than anything Eddie had expected, and he felt choked, he avoided looking at Phil, who went on smiling his vicious smile.

'According to Pieter Malaks, a solid citizen who wants to help the Law rid these United States of gangsters and who would be getting some nice publicity in the process, your brother Tony is supposed to have made a clean break with his past and to be racked by remorse. You know Tony better than me.'

'It doesn't sound like him.'

He would have liked to protest vigorously, to recall the past history of the Ricos, but he was so upset that he found himself speechless, drained of strength, and he could have wept.

'Maybe Malaks is bragging. Could be. Anyway, he told the cops that if Tony was questioned in a certain way, if they gave him a chance and weren't too rough on him, he, Malaks, was sure his brother-in-law would sing.'

'That's a lie!'

He had almost jumped out of his chair. Phil's look restrained him. That, and the fact that he himself didn't feel sufficiently convinced.

'I'm not saying it's true. But it's at least probable. Neither of us can tell just what Tony would do, once arrested, if he were offered a decent deal. There have been cases before. By and large, though, we haven't given people a chance to get bribed. Take Carmine, for instance; he might have fallen for it, and your brother Gino settled that. Gino wasn't alone that night. Somebody important was with him in the car.'

Vince Vettori, Eddie knew, but he wasn't supposed to. Though Vettori was not quite top brass, he counted almost as much as Kubik.

And those men were never permitted to be caught. It's too dangerous. It might expose the entire setup.

'Do you know Vince?'

'I met him once.'

'He was there too when they erased the witness.'

A pause, more impressive than the preceding ones, during which Phil lit a cigarette and fondled his lighter.

'You agree that, at all cost, Tony must not be allowed to talk. Right?'

'He won't talk.'

'To be sure, we'd have to find him.'

'It shouldn't be impossible.'

'Maybe not for you. I have an idea that old man Malaks, up there on his farm, knows a lot more than he lets on. The love-birds went to see him. If we ask questions, he'll get suspicious. But you, you're Tony's brother.'

Tiny drops of sweat had broken out on Eddie's forehead. Mechanically, he was fingering the mole on his cheek and it started to bleed again.

'Well, that's the story, kid. Your father saved my life without meaning to. So did your mother, but she knew what she was doing. She's been helpful to us for over thirty years now. Gino is straight. You've always done good work, and up to now we've had no cause to complain about Tony. He just must not talk. That's all. Since I was passing through Miami, I thought I'd have a talk with you, because, the way I figure it, you've got more of a chance than anybody else to pull us through. Was I wrong?'

Eddie looked up, said almost in spite of himself, 'No.'

'I'm sure you'll find him. They must have sicked the F.B.I. on Tony, and the U.S.A. just isn't big enough for him. I wouldn't even like to know that he was in Canada or Mexico. But if he was over in Europe, for instance, I'd feel much better. Are there any Ricos still living in Sicily?'

'Our father had eight brothers and sisters.'

'Well, now, this would be a swell chance for Tony to get to know his family, and introduce his wife if he wants to.'

'Yes.'

'The point is to help him make up his mind, to find the right kind of arguments.'

'Yes.'

'And it's got to be done fast.'

'Yes.'

'If I was you, I'd start with old man Malaks.'

He said yes once more, while Sid Kubik was rising with a sigh, crushing his cigar in an ash tray, and Phil moved towards the door.

'Everything all right in Santa Clara otherwise?'

'Everything is fine.'

'Nice place, isn't it?'

'Yes.'

'It would be a shame to leave it.'

If only Phil had not kept on smiling.

'I'll do everything I can.'

'You can never do too much.'

His head was spinning, and yet he hadn't touched his drink.

'If I was you, I'd go straight on to Pennsylvania. I wouldn't even go back to Santa Clara.'

'Yes.'

'By the way, how's Joe behaving himself?'

'He works at the counter.'

'Someone keeping an eye on him?'

'I left instructions with Angelo.'

Kubik held out his big paw and pressed Eddie's hand so hard that it showed white when he retrieved it.

'Tony mustn't get a chance to talk, under any circumstances.'

'Yes.'

He forgot to say good-bye to Phil. Two women in shorts were waiting for the elevator, but all he saw of them were two bright blurs. Out in the cool of the lobby, a sudden spell of dizziness forced him to sit down next to a pillar.

Chapter Four

The man who had rented him the car at the service station in Harrisburg had also shown him the route on a map tacked up on the wall. Despite the rumble of thunder, it still didn't rain. Take the Turnpike to Carlisle and turn right on 274, then left on 850, right after a little place called Drumgold, and be careful not to go on to Alinda. Somewhere in between, he'd come to a brick building, a former sugar mill with a high chimney. The road was right next to it.

The information had registered automatically, the way it used to in school, complete with mileages between the different points. The rain had started coming down while he was still driving along the highway between its white lines. There had been no progression. Within seconds there poured an avalanche of water against which the windscreen wipers were practically useless, the layer of rain coursing down the windscreen was so thick that it distorted the landscape.

He hadn't slept well. When, the night before, on landing in Washington, he'd found out that a plane was leaving for Harrisburg within the hour, he had decided to take it, neglecting to reserve a room by telephone. He had already been nervous throughout the trip. At the Jacksonville airport they had seen, at the far end of the field, a plane just like theirs that had crashed an hour earlier and was still smouldering.

There was no vacancy in the two or three good hotels in Harrisburg, because of some sort of festival, a fair, most likely, for streamers had been strung across the streets, an archway was erected somewhere, and bands kept marching till way past midnight.

The cab-driver had finally taken him to a rather dubious hotel where the enamel of the bathtub was streaked yellow and where, along with the Gideon Bible, there was by the bedside a radio that worked only when you dropped a quarter in the slot.

A drunken couple, who'd got a bottle of whisky off the bell-hop, raised hell all night long. Eddie knocked on the wall several times, but they didn't give a damn.

Of course, he'd known worse in his youth. When he was small there wasn't a bathroom in the whole house; you washed in the kitchen once a week, on Saturdays. Maybe it was to own a real bathroom someday that he had toiled so. To own a bathroom and change his clothes every day.

He missed the exit at Carlisle. There were signs posted all along the highway, but the cars were racing along, the tyres, on the wet pavement, made a terrific noise, you had to keep up with the traffic, and there simply was no time to read, through all that wetness, what the signs were saying.

By the time he could get off the Turnpike he was way past 274 and had to make a big detour, first through back country, and then through sullen suburbs, before he got back to it. As fate would have it, two miles further the road was blocked; a newly erected sign, with an arrow several feet long, announced: 'Detour.'

Since then, he was pushing on more or less blindly, hunched over the wheel to peer through the windscreen trying to make out something in this storm, passing from an unpaved road on to a tarred surface that gave him some hope but changed back into an ordinary road after running through some little village.

Now, he was up in the mountains, where the trees looked black, with now and then a farm, some fields, a few motionless cows, numb with fear, that watched him go by.

He must have got lost. No trace anywhere of Drumgold, which he should have reached quite a while ago, and not a single road sign anywhere in sight. Asking directions would have meant stopping in front of some farmhouse, leaving the shelter of the car, and getting drenched to go knock on a door behind which he was by no means sure of finding anybody. The whole universe seemed empty of human beings.

But in the end he did find a gas station. A huge red-haired fellow in a slicker came out after he'd honked his horn about a dozen times.

'How far is White Cloud?'

The man scratched his head and disappeared into the shanty next door to find out. And then there were more hills and forests and a lake as gloomy as the skies. Finally, in a narrow valley, after driving for hours and not eating a bite since breakfast, he saw a few wooden houses. One of them, painted yellow, boasted in black letters: 'Ezechiel Higgins Trading Post.'

That was what the service-station man had told him to watch for. He was in White Cloud, the place where old Malaks had his farm.

There was a porch all along one side of the building. On the left was a general store dating back to pioneer days, with a wide variety of goods: bags of flour, shovels, spades, harnesses, canned food, as well as candy and overalls. Above the centre door was the word 'Hotel,' above the door on the right the word 'Tavern.'

The water was streaming down off the porch roof. Under its shelter, a man sat in a rocking chair, smoking a very black cigar, and seemed vastly amused at the sight of Eddie darting out in the rain.

At first, Eddie paid no attention to him. He wondered which of the doors he should try, finally pushed open the one leading to the tavern, where two oldsters were sitting, each with a glass in front of him, staring into it without saying a word, as though mummified. They were very old, old-timers the likes of which, nowadays, one meets only in remote country. One of them, however, after a long silence, opened his mouth and called:

'Martha!'

Whereupon a woman emerged from the kitchen, wiping her hands in her apron.

'What can I do for you?'

'Is this White Cloud?'

'Where else would you be?'

'Does a Hans Malaks live here?'

'He does and he doesn't. His farm is four miles the other side of the mountain.'

'Can I get something to eat here?'

The fellow with the black cigar was now standing in the doorway and looking at him sarcastically, as if something about the whole scene tickled his sense of humour, and right then Eddie frowned.

He didn't know the man. He was certain they had never met. He was equally certain that the fellow had grown up in Brooklyn and that he wasn't here by accident.

'You can have ham and eggs.'

That was all right with him, he said. The woman disappeared, came back to ask what he wanted to drink.

'Plain water.'

He could have been at the end of the world. The prints on the walls were twenty or thirty years old, and some were the same as used to decorate his father's store. The smell, too, was nearly the same, with the odour of country and of rain added to it.

The two old-timers, fixed as if for eternity, never took their red-rimmed eyes off him, and one of them wore a little goatee.

Eddie went to sit by the window, even less at ease here than in Miami, with the unpleasant feeling of being a stranger.

The night before he'd come close to going straight on to Brooklyn to see his mother instead of coming here. He wasn't sure just what had made him change his mind at the last moment. Perhaps because he felt he was being watched? On the Miami-Washington plane already he had scrutinized each passenger in turn, wondering if one of them wasn't there to tail him.

This fellow, here, who had grinned so smugly as he saw him get out of the car, definitely belonged to the organization. Maybe he'd been here for several days. Maybe he had gone to see old Malaks and tried to worm some information out of him.

In any case, he was expecting him. They must have 'phoned him from Miami. He hovered near Rico as if hesitating to accost him.

'Nice day, ain't it?'

Eddie didn't answer.

'Some job, finding the old guy's farm.'

What was he trying to do, anyway–kid him? He wore neither tie nor jacket, for in spite of the thunderstorm it was still hot; a humid, sticky heat.

'He's a character!'

He was undoubtedly talking about Malaks. Eddie shrugged slightly. And, after two or three desultory remarks, the other turned his back on him, grumbling:

'If that's the way you want it . . .'

Eddie ate listlessly. The woman stepped out on the porch with him to point the way. Torrents of water were cascading down the hillside, and the car had to ford a stream that was flooding the road. This time he did not get lost, but he almost got stuck in the deep ruts left by some tractors.

In the next valley, right among the meadows and the cornfields, he came upon a red-painted barn, a one-storey house, and a flock of geese quite outraged at the intrusion.

As he got out of the car, he noticed that somebody was observing him from a window, and as he approached, the face disappeared, the door opened, and a man huge and powerful greeted him.

This time Eddie had no ready gambit. He couldn't have. He wasn't on home ground. The man, who was smoking a corncob pipe, watched him as he shook the rain off his hat and shoulders.

'Pretty wet,' said he, with a farmer's satisfaction.

'Pretty wet, all right.'

In the middle of the room was an old-fashioned stove with a pipe disappearing into the wall. The ceiling was low, not white-washed, supported by heavy beams. On the wall three rifles, one of them double-barrelled. A good cow smell.

'I'm Tony's brother,' he announced, right off.

The other one seemed to approve. That was fine, his being Tony's brother.

'And then what?' he appeared to be asking as he motioned him towards a rocking chair.

Whereupon he went over to a shelf to get a bottle of white liquor, probably home made, and two thick, squat glasses without stems. He filled them with a reverential gesture, pushed one over in the general direction of his guest without saying a word, and Eddie understood that he had better drink it.

Next to this old fellow, Sid Kubik, solid and powerful though he seemed, would at best have looked average.

Malaks had tanned-leather skin, furrowed by fine wrinkles, and his muscles swelled his red-checkered shirt; his hands were huge, hard as tools.

'It's been a long time [Eddie's voice was unsteady] since I've heard from Tony.'

The old man's eyes were a very limpid blue, and the expression on his face was good-natured. He appeared to be smiling at the Good Lord's world, within which he had found his own small place and where nothing that might happen could ever worry him.

'He's a good boy,' he said.

'Yes. From what I heard, he's very much in love with your daughter.'

To which Malaks replied:

'That's their age does it.'

'I was glad to hear about the marriage.'

The farmer was sitting across from him in a rocking chair, rocking back and forth in a regular rhythm, the bottle within reach.

'You got to expect that to happen between a man and a woman.'

'I don't know if he ever mentioned me to you.'

'Some. I guess you're the one that lives in Florida.'

What had Tony told him? Had he made to his father-in-law the same confession as to his wife and had he talked about his family's activities?

It could not be said that Malaks was mistrustful. The word indifferent did not fit either. Naturally a visit from this gentleman who lived down South did not perturb him. What could possibly perturb him? Nothing, undoubtedly. He had shaped his life, identified himself with the setting he had built for it. Someone knocked on his door, and he offered him a drink of his brew. It was a chance for him to take one himself, to see an unaccustomed face, to say and hear a few words.

However, he did not appear to take it very seriously.

'My mother wrote that Tony's given up his job.'

That was a trial balloon. He was watching for the reaction. If Malaks knew, wouldn't he betray it by a sarcastic smile at the word job?

He smiled all right, but without irony. It was a smile affecting neither lips nor facial muscles, a smile residing solely in the eyes.

'Since I was passing through these parts, I stopped in to see you.'

As if to thank him, Malaks poured him a second glass of his fiery brandy.

This was so much more difficult than with a sheriff, or with any of the night club concessionnaires. Specially since he didn't feel quite so self-possessed as usual. He was a little bit ashamed of himself, tried hard not to show it. He felt pale and flabby, without substance, next to this mass of hard, solid flesh rocking in the other chair.

He got no help. That was not necessarily intentional. Men who lead the kind of life that Malaks was leading aren't much given to words.

'I figured if he'd want me to, I could easily find him a job.'

'He looks to me like he could take care of himself.'

'He's a good mechanic. He's been crazy about machines ever since he was a kid.'

'Took him just three days to patch up an old truck I'd junked near the pond and make the thing run again.'

Eddie forced a smile.

'That's Tony, all right. That truck must come in handy for you.'

'I gave it to him. Least I could do. And I'd bought me a new one last year.'

'They left with the truck?'

The old man nodded.

'It'll be a big help to them. With a truck, a fellow like my brother can always start a business.'

'That's what he said.'

It was still too early to ask the question.

'And your daughter . . . Nora, isn't it?—wasn't she worried?'

'About what?'

'About quitting her job, New York, security, to strike out like that for God knows where.'

Just a hint, 'God knows where.' It might produce a reaction. But it didn't.

'Nora is old enough. When she left here three years ago she didn't know what to expect either. And when I left my village, at sixteen, I didn't know.'

'She isn't afraid of hard luck?'

'What hard luck? We were eighteen children at home, and the day I left home I didn't know the looks of a piece of white bread, didn't even know there was such a thing. We grew up on rye bread, beets, and potatoes, with maybe a little lard now and then. They'll always be able to get hold of potatoes and lard.'

'Tony's got a lot of courage.'

'He's a good boy.'

'I wonder if he had anything in mind when he fixed the truck.'

'Probably.'

'In some places there is a shortage of transportation.'

'Sure.'

'Especially now, on account of the harvest season.'

The old man nodded in agreement, sat warming his glass with his big brown paw.

'In Florida he'd find plenty of customers. It's the gladiola season.'

It didn't work. He'd have to go about it in a more direct way.

'Did you hear from them?'

'Not since they left.'

'Your daughter doesn't write you?'

'When I left my family, I didn't write for three years. First, it took money for stamps. Then, I didn't have anything to tell them. I wrote them twice all in all.'

'Your son doesn't write you, either?'

'Which one?'

Eddie didn't know there were several. Two? Three?

'The one who works for General Electric. Tony's been telling my mother about him. I hear he's got a good future.'

'Could be.'

'Looks like your children don't like country life.'

'Not those two.'

Eddie had to get up; his patience was running thin. He walked over to the window, looked out at the pouring rain which made circles in the puddles.

'I think I'll have to push off.'

'You're going to New York to-night?'

He said yes, though he still didn't know.

'I sure would have liked to write Tony a letter. I have lots of news for him.'

'He didn't leave his address, so I guess he doesn't care.'

The old man was still devoid of sarcasm. This was his way, quite simply, of thinking, of talking. Or so, at least, Eddie hoped.

'Suppose something happens to my mother . . .'

He was more than ever ashamed of his sordid role.

'She's old. She hasn't been feeling well these past few weeks.'

'Dying's the worse thing can happen to your mother. And the truth is Tony couldn't make her come back to life.'

It was true, of course. Everything was true. He was the only one to steer a sorry course, hoping to make the old man say what he didn't know or what he didn't want to say.

He gave a start. Outside, holding up a paper in place of an umbrella, a man was examining first the licence plates of the car, then, poking his head through the side window, inspecting the registration card rolled around the steering post. The man wore red rubber boots. He was young, resembled Malaks, but uglier, with irregular features.

He shook his boots against the wall, opened the door, looked at Eddie, at his father, then at the bottle and glasses.

'Who's he?' he asked, without a greeting.

'A brother of Tony's,' said the old man.

The young one turned to Eddie:

'You rented the jalopy in Harrisburg?'

It wasn't a question, but almost an accusation. He said nothing more, paid no attention to the visitor and got himself a glass of water from the kitchen pump.

'I hope they'll be happy,' said Eddie, by way of taking leave.

'They will.'

That was all. The young man had come back into the room, the glass of water in his hand, his eyes following Eddie as he turned reluctantly towards the door. Old Malaks, who had risen, also watched him leave, without making a move to see him out.

'Thanks for the drink.'

'Don't mention it.'

'Thanks just the same. Maybe I could leave you my address, just in case . . .'

One last try.

'What's the use, when I never write? I even wonder if I still know how.'

Hunched over, Eddie ran through the open stretch separating him from the car, and, as he hadn't raised the window, found the seat soaking wet. He swung into gear, suddenly furious, the more so since he thought he heard a loud burst of laughter coming from the house.

At Higgins' place, the fellow, still rocking away on his chair, watched his arrival with unconcealed sarcasm. So that, out of sheer annoyance, Eddie didn't get out of the car, but stepped on the gas, and dashed away on the return trip.

This time he didn't get lost. The storm had ended, there was no more thunder or lightning, but the sky continued to melt in increasingly dense, fine drizzle. The rain would last two days at least.

At Harrisburg, the garageman let out a groan at the sight of the car coated with mud up to the roof. Eddie stopped at the hotel to pick up his suitcase and had a cab take him to the airport without knowing when he could get a plane.

He had to wait an hour and a half. The field was drenched, the concrete of the crisscrossing runways glistened. The waiting-room stank of wetness and urinals. There were two 'phone booths in the rear, and he went over to the counter to get some change.

The night before, he had not called home. Even now, he was doing so half-heartedly, because he had promised Alice. And having already asked for his number, he still didn't know what he would say; he had not made any decision. He had a good mind to go straight on home and forget the whole thing, despite Phil and all the organizations in the world.

No one had a right to disturb his life that way. He had made it what it was, by toil and moil, like old Malaks had built his farm.

He wasn't responsible for his brother's doings. He wasn't the one driving the car from which the shots had been fired that killed the cigar-store owner on Fulton Avenue.

All that, seen from here, seemed unreal. Was that fellow at the Trading Post really there to check up on him? If so, why hadn't he followed him? Through the window of the booth Eddie could take in the whole waiting room; nobody there but two middle-aged women and a sailor, with his duffle bag next to him, on the bench.

Everything was dirty, grey, depressing, while back in Santa Clara the house gleamed immaculately white in the sun.

If it were not on his account, then what was the guy doing in White Cloud?

As he listened absently to the 'phone girls calling all down the line, a very simple explanation occurred to him. Sid Kubik was no child; he could make a monkey out of any cop. In a corner at Higgins', behind the door leading to the store, he had seen a window that said: 'U.S. Post Office.'

That's where all the village mail arrived. If anything came for Malaks, the fellow could easily check on it when the bags were being emptied.

'That you?'

'Where are you?'

'In Pennsylvania.'

'Coming home soon?'

'I don't know. How are the children?'

'Fine.'

'Anything new?'

'No. The sheriff called, but he said it wasn't important. Are you staying up there?'

'I'm at the airport. I'll be in New York to-night.'

'Are you going to see your mother?'

'I don't know. Probably.'

He would see her. It was better to. Maybe she knew something she hadn't told Kubik.

The rest of the day was just as bleak. The plane turned out to be an old crate, and they flew through two storms. When they arrived over La Guardia, night had fallen, black silhouettes moved about in front of the buildings, people embraced each other, others dragged packages much too heavy for them.

He managed to get hold of a cab and gave the driver a Brooklyn address. He suddenly felt cold, in his light suit permeated with humidity. He sneezed several times and was afraid he'd caught a cold. As a child, he often had colds. Tony, too; as a matter of fact, Tony used to have bronchitis every winter.

A picture suddenly came to his mind—Tony in bed, with picture magazines strewn over the blanket, and sheets of paper which he covered with drawings. The three brothers slept in the same room. There was hardly any space to move between the bed and the walls.

He anticipated a very painful argument. His mother was going to insist that he sleep over at her house. It had a bathroom now, the boys' room, made over.

Right behind the store came the kitchen, used both as a dining-room and living-room, where his grandmother spent her days sitting in her armchair. Then, off a dark hall, the bedroom, where the two women slept ever since Grandmother had become scared of dying during the night. The old woman's former room was the one in which Julia always wanted her boys to spend the night whenever they came to see her, and Eddie had never been able to stand the smell that had lingered on.

He knocked on the glass partition and gave the taxi driver the address of the St George, a big hotel in Brooklyn just three blocks from his home. He registered and left his suitcase. He had eaten a sandwich at the Harrisburg airport and wasn't hungry. So he just gulped down a cup of coffee, took another cab since it was still raining.

The vegetable shop, next door to his mother's place, had been completely remodelled. Vegetables and groceries were still the main items for sale, but the store front had been modernized, the walls lined with white tiles, and day and night, even when the place was closed, the neon lights shone on brilliantly inside.

It was eleven o'clock at night. Only the bars were still open, and the poolroom across the street, where the young punks hung out and tried to make like tough guys.

The lights were out in the candy store. But it was only half dark, because the back door had been left ajar. Otherwise, the two women, who were sitting in the kitchen under the light, would have had no air. Eddie could even see his mother's skirt and feet.

The counter, to the left, had not changed, with its four stools screwed to the floor, its soda fountain and the chrome lids of the ice-cream containers. Candy, chocolate bars, chewing gum of all kinds were displayed on the other half of the counter. And over against the rear wall stood three pinball machines.

He still hesitated to knock. There was no bell. Each of the brothers had a special way of rapping on the window. He thought the street, the neighbourhood were more depressing than ever, in spite of there being more lights.

His mother moved, got up, passed through his field of vision, turned for an instant towards the store. Then, not sure that she had seen him, he knocked on the door.

She never left the key in the lock. He knew which corner of the kitchen sideboard she'd take it from. She had not recognized him. He was hidden by darkness. She pressed her face against the glass, frowning, then, with an exclamation he failed to catch, opened the door:

'Why didn't you call me? I could have got your room ready.'

She didn't kiss him. The Ricos never kissed. She looked at his hands.

'Where is your suitcase?'

'I left it at La Guardia,' he lied. 'I may be leaving again to-night.'

She always looked the same. To him, she hadn't changed from the time she was carrying him around in her arms. He had always known those slightly swollen legs, the sagging belly, the big flabby breasts heaving in her bodice. Always, too, she had been dressed in grey.

'Dirt doesn't show so fast,' she used to explain.

He greeted his grandmother, who called him Gino. It was the first time this had ever happened and he shot a questioning glance at his mother, who motioned not to pay any attention to it. She pointed a finger at her forehead, indicating that the old lady was beginning to lose her memory.

'You'll have something to eat, won't you?'

She opened the refrigerator, took out some salami, potato salad, pimentos, set it all down on the wax cloth covering the table.

'Did you get my letter?'

'Yes.'

'He didn't write you either?'

He shook his head. And he couldn't help but eat to make her happy, and drink the Chianti which she served in big heavy tumblers the like of which he had never seen anywhere else.

'Is that why you're here?'

He would have preferred to make a clean breast of it, to tell her the whole truth, about what had happened with Phil and Sid Kubik and about his trip to White Cloud. It would have been easier that way, would have meant a heavy burden off his chest.

But he didn't dare. He said no. As she went on looking at him searchingly, he added:

'There's someone here I had to see.'

'They made you come up North?'

'In a way, yes. But not on account of that. Not specially on account of that.'

'What did they tell you? You've seen them already?'

'Not yet.'

She only half believed him. She never believed people more than half-way, especially her sons, especially Eddie, and this had always puzzled him because, of the three, he was the least given to lying.

'Do you think they're after him?'

'They won't harm him.'

'That's not the way I hear it.'

'I've seen his wife's father.'

'How did you find out his name? I don't even know it myself. Who told you?'

'Somebody who came to spend a few weeks in Santa Clara.'

'Joe?'

She knew more than he had thought. It was always that way with her. The slightest rumours reached her ears. She had a special gift for guessing the truth.

'Don't trust him. I know him. He used to come in here for ice cream once in a while, three or four years ago, when he was still a young punk. He's crooked.'

'I bet he is.'

'What did he tell you? How does he know?'

'Listen, Mamma, don't ask so many questions. Who do you think you are, anyway–O'Malley?'

Among themselves they always spoke a broken Italian mixed with Brooklynese. O'Malley was the police sergeant who had worked in the precinct for over twenty years and who, when the three brothers were kids, was their bogeyman.

'I'm simply telling you I saw the father. It's true about Tony and his wife visiting him two or three months ago. The guy had junked a broken-down truck near a pond on his farm. Seems like Tony spent three days putting it back in shape, and his father-in-law gave it to him for a present.'

The grandmother, who was almost stone deaf, was shaking her head as though following the conversation with keen interest. For years, this had been a favourite trick of hers, and she'd manage to fool people into lecturing her at considerable length.

What made Julia smile all of a sudden?

'It's a big truck?'

'I didn't ask. Probably. They got no use for light trucks around a farm.'

'In that case, your brother will make out all right.'

He sensed that she was holding out on him, that she relished her discovery, watching Eddie, wondering, no doubt, if she ought to let him in on it.

'You remember when he had pneumonia?'

He had often heard her tell the story, though actually he didn't remember much about it. It sort of got mixed up with Tony's many attacks of bronchitis. Besides, Eddie was fifteen at the time and hardly ever home.

'The doctor told us that, to get well, he'd need lots of fresh air. Josephina's son . . .'

It clicked. He, too, almost felt like smiling. He was convinced that his mother was right. Josephina was a neighbour woman who did housework and used to come in every now and then to give his mother a hand. She had a son—Eddie didn't remember his name—who had gone out West and settled on a farm. Josephina claimed that he had done well, that he was married, had a son, and that he wanted her to join them.

He still couldn't recall the name of the place. It was somewhere in Southern California.

And one fine day the son had actually come for his mother. The woman had insisted that Tony, whose health did not seem to improve, come along with them for a few months, because she'd always had a soft spot in her heart for the boy.

'He'll get lots of sunshine, fresh air . . .'

He had forgotten the details. Anyway, Tony had been away from home for nearly a year. His passion for mechanics dated back to that time. He was barely eleven years old. He used to boast that Josephina's son let him drive his truck in the fields.

They had often talked about that part of the country.

'They have three or four crops a year. The problem is how to transport the vegetables.'

'I bet he's somewhere around El Centro,' his mother said.

That was the name of the town he'd been trying to remember. Vaguely ashamed, he averted his head.

'Don't you want to eat any more?'

'I ate before I came.'

'You're not going right away, are you?'

'Not right away, no.'

He would have preferred to leave. Never before had he felt so much out of place in this familiar room. Never before had he felt so much like a little boy in his mother's presence.

'When are you going back to Florida?'

'To-morrow.'

'I thought you had some people to see?'

'I'll see them to-morrow morning.'

'Did you meet Sid Kubik in Miami?'

He said no, for fear of contradicting himself. He felt a little lost. He wasn't on home grounds.

'Funny about Gino being in California too.'

'I guess it is.'

'You don't look too well.'

'I must have caught cold out in the rain.'

The Chianti was lukewarm, turbid.

'I guess it's time for me to go.'

She stood on the threshold to watch him leave, and he didn't like that last look she gave him.

Chapter Five

How many times had he left this same house, at the same late hour, with his mother in the doorway, leaning out to watch him leave? Even insignificant details were unchanged, like it having stopped raining. In the old days, she used to say:

'At least wait till it stops raining.'

He had so often seen the rain drying on the sidewalks, and the puddles which he could have sworn were still in the same spots. Some of the stores hadn't changed. There was a certain street corner, the second one, where, in the old days, without any real reason, he always expected an ambush. He felt again the tightness that gripped his chest as he entered the zone of darkness.

It was all coming back to him without joy. This was his neighbourhood. He'd grown up among these houses; they ought to recognize him. And yet, it was as if he felt ashamed. Not ashamed of them. Ashamed of himself, rather. It was hard to explain. His brother Gino, for instance, still belonged here. Even Sid Kubik, who had become a bigshot, could come back without reservations.

It wasn't just to-night that Eddie felt depressed at the sight of his childhood surroundings. Other times before, on the train or on the plane bringing him back, he had sincerely rejoiced, thinking that some kind of contact would be re-established. And then, once in his street, in his mother's house, nothing happened. There was no emotion. He felt none, and neither did the others.

They would welcome him as best they could. They put food on the table. They gave him wine. But they looked at him differently than they would have looked at Gino or Tony.

He would have liked to get together with some friends. But he had never had any real friends. It wasn't his fault. They were all different from him.

And yet he was conscientious. He had abided by the rules. Not through fear, like most of them, but because he understood that it had to be so.

Ironically, he was the one his mother always looked upon with a kind of reserve, of suspicion. Like to-night. Especially to-night.

Flushing Avenue, with its bright lights, was not far. Before he got to it, a policeman, pounding his beat, turned around to look at him. A middle-aged man. Although Eddie did not recognize him, he was convinced the cop knew him.

He reached the brilliantly lit thoroughfare, with its bars, its restaurants, its movie houses, its all-night shops and aimless couples, gangs of soldiers and sailors with their girls crowding into penny arcades to have their pictures taken, eat hot dogs and shoot at clay pigeons.

He had decided to go right back to the St George and get some sleep. He couldn't leave to-night. He needed some rest. Besides, all he had left in his pocket was two hundred dollars and he'd have to cash a cheque at the bank. He had kept an account in a Brooklyn bank. He had other accounts elsewhere, four or five of them; his type of business required that.

Alice and the children were asleep by now; and suddenly he felt very far away from them, felt as though he were in danger of never seeing them again, of never going back to his house, to the life which he had so patiently, so carefully organized. It made him panicky. He had a wild longing to return at once, without giving another thought to Tony, Sid Kubik, Phil, or anybody else. He seethed with rebellion. No one had a right to upset his life that way.

The avenue had changed so little that it was uncanny. Especially the odours, every time he approached a hot-dog stand or a restaurant. And the sounds, the music pouring from the amusement places.

Once, in this very place, he had been as young as those soldiers who laughed and shoved, as those kids who, cigarettes in their mouths, hands in their pockets, slipped past the shop windows with an air of mystery.

A car was coming down the street towards him, close to the curb, and he thought he recognized the driver's face; a hand shot out of the window, the car stopped.

It was Bill, alias Bill-the-Polack, with two girls next to him on the front seat, and in back, hidden in semi-darkness, another girl and a man whom Rico did not know. Bill did not get out of the car.

'What are you doing here?'

'Passing through. So I stopped by to say hello to the old lady.'

'Tony's brother,' the Pole explained to the girls.

Then:

'Been here long? I thought you operated some place down South. Louisiana, ain't it?'

'Florida.'

'Yeah, that's it. Like it down there?'

Eddie didn't care for Bill. A bragging, brawling brute, always surrounded by women, bluffing them blind. What was he in the organization? Nothing much, surely. He worked around the docks, had something to do with labour unions. Eddie suspected him of making small loans to dockers at usury rates and acting as a fence for their stolen goods.

'Let's go have a drink.'

He wasn't being invited for the sake of friendship. It was sheer curiosity that had made Bill stop his car in the first place and he had kept the engine running.

'We're heading for Manhattan and a cellar club over on Twentieth Street where the hoofers strip to the skin.'

'Thanks. I'm going to bed.'

'Suit yourself. Hear anything from Tony?'

'No.'

That took care of Bill. The car drove off, with the Pole no doubt gossiping about him to his buddies. What would he be saying?

Eddie did not often need the company of other people. His moments of weakness were rare. To-night, however, in spite of his resolution, he could not bring himself to go to bed. He wanted to talk to someone, someone congenial and friendly.

Names came to mind, faces he could have found just by crossing the threshold of some of the bars and restaurants along the avenue. None of them qualified. None answered his need.

The smell of garlic hitting his nostrils suddenly made him think of Pep Fasoli, a big fellow, an old school chum who had opened a small luncheonette that served food around the clock. The place was small, a kind of long, narrow hallway with a counter and a few booths, serving hot dogs, hamburgers, and spaghetti.

Sometimes, in Florida, eating spaghetti with Alice in some Italian restaurant, he'd say with a touch of nostalgia:

'Not as good as Fasoli's.'

He felt a sudden yen for some and went in. Behind the counter, two cooks in soiled uniforms were working at the electric stoves. Waitresses in black dresses and white aprons were rushing back and forth.

Half the seats were taken. A juke box ground out some sentimental tune. And there, also in a cook's uniform, shorter and fatter than Eddie had remembered him, was Pep. He must have instantly recognized Eddie, who sat down on one of the stools, but he had not rushed up to greet him. Perhaps he'd had a moment's hesitation before deciding to do so?

'I knew you were in the neighbourhood, but I wasn't sure you'd drop in.'

Usually Pep was rather expansive.

'How did you find out I was in Brooklyn?'

'Somebody saw you go into your mother's place.'

That bothered him. Several times, in the street, he had looked back to make sure he wasn't being followed. He hadn't seen a soul. The street had been empty when he left the house.

'Who?'

Pep gestured vaguely.

'Search me! People keep coming and going in this place.'

It wasn't true. Pep knew who it was that had talked about Eddie. Why didn't he want to say?

'Spaghetti special?'

Just like any other customer. He almost said no, he had already eaten. But he didn't have the courage. It was the same as with his mother's Chianti. His former pal might have taken offence.

So he nodded, and Pep passed on his order to one of the cooks.

'You don't look so good.'

Was he doing it on purpose? Eddie was only too prone to worry about his health. The wall opposite him was lined with mirrors on which the day's specials were marked up in chalk. The mirror right across from him was blurred by the steam from the ranges. Probably a poor mirror anyway. Eddie saw in it a face paler than usual, red-rimmed eyes, bloodless lips. It even seemed to him that his nose was slightly off centre, like Gino's.

'Hear anything from Tony?'

Everybody knew. Everybody was up on the news. It was like a conspiracy. And, whenever the question was asked, it was with a special kind of look, as if he were suspected of dire intentions.

'He didn't write.'

'I see.'

Pep dropped the subject, went over to the cash register, and rang up a bill.

'Are you going back South?' he asked a little later, indifferent, as if the answer did not interest him.

'I don't know when.'

The spaghetti sauce was highly seasoned and its smell nauseated him. He was no longer hungry, had to force himself to eat.

'*Caffè espresso?*'

'If you want to.'

Two young fellows at the other end of the counter were watching him intently, and Eddie knew they were talking about him. To them, he was a bigshot. They were beginners, in the lowest rank of the hierarchy, fledglings who get a few dollars now and then for some small job.

Before he would have enjoyed being looked up to in that fashion. To-day it made him uncomfortable. He didn't like the way Pep hovered around him, either. Pep, actually, came closest to being a friend of his. Eddie, when they were both in their teens, had even confided in him one night that they were erring endlessly through the streets. He had revealed his deep-rooted feeling about the necessity to follow the rule, about the folly and the peril that lies in departing from it.

'Don't you like it?'

'It's very good.'

And Eddie was making himself eat the whole plateful of spaghetti that tasted greasy, with much too much garlic. He shouldn't have stopped at Fasoli's. He shouldn't have gone to see his mother.

What would have happened if he'd gone back to Santa Clara, called Sid Kubik, and told him flatly that he hadn't picked up his brother's trail? He was too scrupulous.

'What do I owe you?'

'Forget it.'

'What for? Of course not.'

Pep let him pay. It was the first time. This, too, made him feel more like a stranger.

What he couldn't decide was whether the others were forsaking him, or whether he was withdrawing from them. His hotel wasn't far, just two blocks away. He was determined to go straight back and yet he entered another bar. If the bartender were the same, he'd shot craps with him on occasion. The bartender had changed. So had the owner. The bar was dark oak and so were the panels of the walls, hung with racing prints, photographs of jockeys and of boxers. Some of these pictures were old; he recognized two or three of the fighters that Old Mossie used to manage, for Mossie had started out by running a gym.

He pointed at the beer spigot.

'One on tap.'

The fellow serving him didn't know who he was. Nor did the man who was downing whisky next to him and who was already drunk. Nor the couple sitting in the farthest booth taking as much fun as they dared in public.

He was almost ready to call Alice again.

'One of the same.'

He changed his mind.

'No, make it a rye.'

A sudden thirst for liquor, to which, he well knew, he should not give way. It seldom happened to him. With some people it agrees. But liquor made him sad and suspicious. It was two in the morning, and he was dead-tired. But he was stubbornly staying on in this place where even the drunk didn't talk to him.

'Make it another.'

He had four ryes. Here, too, there was a mirror across from him in which he was looking at himself, thinking what a sore sight it was. He needed a shave, and his cheeks and chin looked dirty. His beard grew fast. Somewhere he'd read that beards grow faster on corpses than on living people.

When he finally started back to the hotel he was walking a bit unsteadily, and each time he heard footsteps behind him he was sure it was someone Phil had sent to tail him. Sitting in a corner of the darkened lobby, and talking in low tones, were two men who looked up and watched him walk over to the elevators. Were they there because of him? He didn't know them; but then there were thousands he didn't know who knew him: he was Eddie Rico!

He felt like striding up to them and saying: 'I'm Eddie Rico. What do you want with me?'

'Watch your step, please,' said the elevator operator.

'Thanks, son.'

He slept poorly, got up twice to gulp down big glasses of water, woke up with a headache and in a foul mood. He called the airlines from his room.

'El Centro, California. Yes, as soon as possible.'

There was a plane at noon. All seats taken.

'None available for the next three days. But if you come down to the airport half an hour before flight time, there's a good chance of getting a seat. There are usually some last-minute cancellations.'

The sun was shining, a sun more pale, more subdued than in Florida, with a transparent haze in the skies.

He had breakfast sent up to his room, but ate only a few bites, and called for a second pot of coffee. Then he placed a call to Alice, who at that hour would be busy tidying up the rooms, with Lois, the little coloured girl, making the beds, and Babe following them around and getting into everything.

'Is that you? How's everything at home?'

'Everything's fine.'

'No calls?'

'No. Babe burned her fingers on the oven this morning, but it's nothing. She didn't even cry. Did you see your mother?'

'Yes.'

He couldn't find a thing to say, asked what the weather was like, if the new dining-room curtains had been delivered.

'Are you feeling all right?' asked his wife.

'Sure.'

'You sound as if you had a cold.'

'No. Maybe.'

'Are you at the hotel?'

'Yes.'

'Did you meet any friends?'

'Some,' he said. What made him say that?

'Will you be back soon?'

'I've got some business to attend to first. Somewhere else.'

He'd nearly told her he was going to El Centro. It was unwise. He had caught himself in time. So that if anything happened at home, to one of his daughters, for instance, no one would know where to reach him.

'Hang up, will you, so I can keep the line open to Santa Clara. I want to talk to Angelo.'

He got the connection without trouble.

'That you, boss?'

'Anything new at the store?'

'Nothing much. The painters started in this morning.'

'What about Joe?'

'He'll do.'

The answer was noncommittal.

'Difficult?'

'Miss Van Ness put him in his place.'

'Did he try anything?'

Joe was probably the first one ever to get fresh with Miss Van Ness.

'She slapped him so hard he still can't get over it.'

'He didn't try to go out?'

'The first night, I played cards with him till three in the morning. After that I locked his door.'

'And now?'

'Last night, he was all worked up, and I figured he was ready to jump out the window. So I called up Bepo.'

A seamy little man who ran a house on the highway half-way between Santa Clara and the next town.

'He sent over what was needed. They drained a whole bottle of whisky. This morning Joe's out cold.'

At half-past eleven Eddie was once again at La Guardia, suitcase by his side, waiting near the ticket window. He had been promised the first available seat. He scrutinized the people around him, searching for some familiar face, someone who'd look as though he might belong to the organization.

He had stopped by at the bank and withdrawn a thousand dollars. He lacked poise unless he had cold cash in his pocket. His cheque book wasn't enough. It had to be bills.

At the airport, he had not given his real name to the girl behind the window, but the first one that came to his mind: Philip Agostino. So that, when the name was paged, he didn't answer right away, forgetting that it meant him.

'One hundred sixty-two dollars, please. Your ticket will be ready in a moment. Any baggage? Please step on the scales.'

It seemed impossible that they would let him leave without trying to find out where he was going. He kept looking back, scrutinizing the faces around him. Nobody seemed to pay the slightest attention to him.

Even this, the absence of surveillance, frightened him.

The loud-speaker summoned the passengers of his flight to Gate No. 12. He and about twenty other people gathered there. And only then, just as he was handing over his ticket, did he feel two dark eyes riveted on him. For he literally felt them before seeing them, so much so that he hesitated to give a look.

A boy of sixteen or seventeen, with dark, shiny hair and pale complexion, definitely an Italian, was leaning against a wall, watching him impudently.

Eddie did not know him, could not have recognized a youngster like that who was a baby at the time he, Eddie, had left Brooklyn. But he must have known his parents, for the features, the expression seemed familiar.

He suddenly thought of turning back, of taking some other plane, whatever the destination. But what was the good of it—wherever he went, someone would be waiting for him at the airport.

Moreover he could always get off anywhere along the way. Would they bother to check every stopping place?

'What are you waiting for?'

'I'm sorry . . .'

He surged forward with the rest of the passengers. The young man remained where he was, an unlit cigarette stuck to his lower lip, just like Gino.

The plane took off. Then, half an hour out of New York and its skyscrapers, over which they had flown at low altitude, the stewardess served lunch. In Washington, he stayed aboard. He had worked there. In the crowds milling around the gates, he would have been unable to spot someone assigned to watch him.

He slept. When he awoke, the stewardess was offering tea and he drank some, which turned his stomach.

'When do we get into Nashville?'

'In about two hours.'

They were flying very high, well above the luminous mass of clouds opening now and then to allow a glimpse of green prairie and white farmhouses.

He had passed through Nashville many times, both by train and plane, stopping but for a few minutes, never leaving the station or the airport.

The organization did not operate there. It was a peaceful town, with limited possibilities, abandoned to the local racketeers.

Why not get off there? He'd find trains, and planes, bound for any given point. And then what? The bigshots, by now, knew that he had bought a ticket for El Centro. He was expected there. Whether he got in on this plane or otherwise, they wouldn't fail to track him down.

And how would he explain?

They were every bit as sly as he, infinitely more powerful than he. Never had Eddie tried to cheat them. That was his strength. That was how he'd achieved what he had. At sixteen, when most boys make believe they're tough, did he not already talk of abiding by the rule, as he strolled with Fasoli by the light of the moon?

He caught himself being resentful of Tony; because it was Tony, actually, who had got him into this fix. Eddie had always been convinced that he was fond of his brothers, of Tony even more than of Gino, because he felt he and the younger brother were more alike.

But he was also fond of his mother, and the night before he had remained quite cold in her presence. No contact had been established between them. He had almost hated her for the way she kept watching him.

He had never felt so alone. Even Alice was becoming less real. He was scarcely able to picture her in their home, to convince himself that it really was his home, that every morning he had been awakened by the blackbirds who hopped on the lawn, then by Babe's chirping.

Where did he belong? In Brooklyn he hadn't felt at home. And yet, in Florida, just hearing the name of somebody from Brooklyn was enough to make him homesick. The reason he mistrusted Boston Phil, and rather disliked him, was that the man didn't come from Brooklyn. Phil hadn't spent his childhood in the same streets, in the same way, hadn't eaten the same dishes, talked the same language.

Because that was it, in short: Boston Phil was different, came from somewhere else.

Bigshot though he was now, Sid Kubik was closer to him, and even that redhead Joe. Then why was he running away from them?

Why did he cling to the memories of Florida?

The worst part of it was that both these poles of his life were becoming equally unreal, so that he had nothing left to lean on.

He was all alone, on this plane, with the prospect of being a stranger, if not an outright enemy, no matter where he landed.

He did not get off at Nashville. He did not get off at Tulsa either, and saw only its lights in the night. He was abdicating all thought, postponing all decisions. The sky was a dark blue, dense, full of distant stars winking ironically.

He slept a little. The brightness of dawn awakened him. Fifteen or twenty people were still asleep around him. A woman who was nursing her baby at the breast looked at him defiantly. Why? Did he look like a man who would steal a shameful glance at the breasts of mothers suckling their babies?

Stretching underneath them was an immense reddish plain from which rose golden mountains slashed with brilliant white.

'Will you have tea or coffee?'

He took coffee. At Tucson he changed to a smaller plane going directly to El Centro, and set his watch, which was already three hours ahead of the airport clock. Most of the men here were wearing light-coloured cowboy hats and tight-fitting pants. Many were of the Mexican type.

'Hi there, Eddie.'

He gave a start. Someone had slapped him on the back. He searched his mind for the name of the fellow who was greeting him with such a glad smile, but drew a blank. He'd known him somewhere, not in Brooklyn, more likely in the Middle West, in St Louis, or in Kansas City. If he remembered right, the chap was then a bartender in some night club.

'Good trip?'

'Not bad.'

'Heard tell you were coming through here, so I came to say hello.'

'Thanks.'

'I live ten miles away and run a place that does pretty well. Everybody's a gambler around here.'

'Who told you . . .'

He would have liked to take back the words. What was the sense of asking?

'I don't recall. You know how you pick up those kinds of news. Last night, in the joint, somebody got to talking about you and your brother.'

'Which one?'

'The one . . .'

Now it was the other man's turn to bite his lip. What had he been about to say–'the one that got himself into trouble'?

He found a way out:

'The one that just got married.'

Suddenly the name came back: it was Bob, and the man used to work at the Liberty, in St Louis, when it belonged to Steig.

'No point taking you over to the airport bar. They serve only soft drinks and coffee. I figured you'd like this better . . .'

Slipping a flat bottle into Eddie's hand.

'Thanks.'

He would not drink it. The bottle was warm from having been carried in the man's pocket, but it was better not to refuse.

'Seems like you're doing all right down at Santa Clara.'

'Can't complain.'

'What about the cops?'

'The usual.'

'That's what I always say. The first thing is to . . .'

Eddie wasn't listening any more, just kept nodding his head approvingly. It was a relief when at last the departure of his next flight was called.

'It was good to see you. If you come through here again, let's get together.'

There were only two more stops, Phoenix and Yuma. After that the plane would land at the El Centro airport. They shook hands. Bob's was sweaty. He still wore his smile. Another few moments and he'd be rushing to the 'phone.

'Lots of luck.'

Most of the time the plane flew over the desert. Then, without transition, tracing a sharp boundary line, there were fields criss-crossed by canals, with brightly painted houses all facing the same way.

They followed, from above, a highway on which trucks were rolling along, single file, endlessly transporting crates of vegetables into town. There were some also on the other, smaller roads that joined the main artery, and they all moved like ants, the empty vehicles travelling in the opposite direction.

Eddie would have preferred the plane not to land, for it to set its course for the Pacific coast, which lay only an hour's flight beyond.

'Fasten your safety belts,' flashed the sign.

He buckled his, and, five minutes later, as the wheels touched the concrete runway, was already unfastening it. He didn't see any familiar faces. No one slapped him on the back. There were men and women expecting someone's arrival or waiting for another plane. Couples kissed. A father was striding towards the exit gate, dragging two children by the hand, while his wife trotted behind and tried in vain to talk to him.

'Porter?'

He handed over his suitcase.

'Taxi?'

It was hotter than in Florida, a different heat, brighter somehow, and the sun burned the eyes.

He took the first available cab, and all the while, he was trying to appear calm, indifferent, because he felt sure he was being watched.

'Take me to the hotel.'

'Which one?'

'The best.'

The car started off, and he shut his eyes with a sigh.

Chapter Six

That night he dreamed the most depressing dream of his life. He seldom had nightmares. Whenever he did, once in a long while, it was almost always the same: he was waking up in a totally strange place, surrounded by people he didn't know and who weren't paying any attention to him. The dream of the man lost, he called it. Secretly, that is, for he naturally never talked about it.

This dream had no connection with the others. He had suddenly felt very tired upon arriving at the hotel. It seemed as though all of the desert sun had seeped in through his pores, and without waiting for nightfall, without even bothering about supper, he had gone to bed. The El Presidio, best hotel in town according to the cabdriver, was vaguely Moorish in style. The core of the town seemed to date back to the days of the Spaniards, and the houses were covered with rough, brownish-yellow stucco baked hard by the sun.

The slightest sounds of the main street reached him from down below, and he had rarely known as noisy a street even in New York. And yet he almost immediately sank into sleep. Perhaps he had other dreams, his body continuing to feel the throbbing of the plane. He must have dreamed about planes too, but that dream vanished and he didn't remember it upon waking. But he was to remember, down to the last detail, the dream about Tony. There was a peculiarity about it, too: it was a Technicolour dream except for two of the central figures, Tony and his father, who were in black and white.

The beginning definitely took place in Santa Clara, at home, in his house, the one he himself had named *Sea Breeze*. He was in pyjamas, going out to the mailbox to get the morning mail. In reality, he rarely ever did without being fully dressed. Perhaps he had, two or three times at the most, on days when he'd overslept, but he always wore a robe.

In his dream, there was something very important in the mailbox. It was imperative that he get there at once. Alice agreed. She even whispered:

'You ought to take your gun.'

But he hadn't taken it. The important thing in the mailbox was his brother Tony.

The strange thing is that at that moment he was perfectly aware that this was an impossibility and that he must be dreaming. Even in the dream it was just an ordinary mailbox, with his name painted on it. Besides, in the beginning, it wasn't quite Tony he found in it yet, but a grey rubber doll which he recognized immediately as one he had taken, when he was four or five, from a little girl in the neighbourhood. He had definitely stolen it. He had taken it precisely because that was real theft–for he did not covet the thing–and he had kept it a long time in a drawer in his room. Maybe his mother still had it in the chest where she kept her sons' toys?

So, even in his dream he knew what it was all about. He could have given the little girl's name. He hadn't committed this theft for the fun of it, but in order to commit a theft, because he believed that to be necessary.

And now came the sudden shift. Without transition, the doll was no longer a doll, but his brother Tony, and the fact did not surprise him. He'd known it ahead of time.

Tony was of the same spongy substance as the doll, the same dull grey, and obviously dead.

'You killed me,' he said with a smile.

Not angry. Not bitter. He talked without opening his mouth. He didn't really talk. There were no sounds, as there are in real life, but Eddie still heard the words clearly.

'I'm very sorry,' he answered. 'Come on in.'

Only then did he notice that his brother was not alone. He had brought along their father as a witness. And their father also was of that same substance, and he, too, smiled a very gentle smile.

Eddie was asking him how he went, and his father kept nodding his head without answering.

'You know perfectly well he's deaf,' said Tony.

That was probably the most disturbing element of the whole dream. And he was aware of it; he could make some very lucid observations on the side.

Their mother had never mentioned that their father was hard of hearing, nor had any of the neighbours. Perhaps nobody had noticed it? And just now Eddie felt almost certain of having made a discovery. He had kept, of his father, the memory of a peaceful man who always cocked his head slightly, and who smiled a strange, secret smile. He seldom talked, went about his work, from morning till night, with untiring patience, as if this were his destiny, as if the thought had never occurred to him that he could do otherwise.

His mother would no doubt have protested that it was a childhood fantasy, that her husband had been no different from others, but he knew he was right.

Cesare Rico had lived in a world all his own, and now, after all these years, a dream gave his son the explanation: he was deaf.

'Let's go inside,' said Eddie, embarrassed at finding himself in pyjamas.

At that point, the scene changed. The three of them were entering somewhere, but it was not his own white house in Santa Clara. Once inside, it turned out to be the kitchen in Brooklyn, with Grandma sitting in her armchair and a bottle of Chianti on the table.

'I'm not mad at you,' said Tony. 'But it's too bad just the same.'

The thought came to him of offering them a drink. It was a family custom to offer a visitor a drink. He remembered in time that Tony and his father were dead and presumably had no way of drinking.

'Take a chair.'

'You know perfectly well Dad never sits down.'

He rarely ever used to sit down when he was alive, except to eat, but, in the dream, this was more important, it had to do with his rank, with the role he had assumed. He must not sit down. It was a matter of dignity.

'What are we waiting for? Let's get started,' said a new voice.

It was his mother. She was seated, and she knocked on the table with a spoon to attract their attention.

'Eddie killed his brother,' she was saying in a loud voice.

And Tony murmured:

'It's mostly that it hurt.'

He seemed younger. His hair was more wavy than it had been the last few years, with a curl hanging down his forehead the way it used to when he was ten. Perhaps was he again ten years old? He was very handsome. He had always been the handsomest of the three, Eddie realized. Even with the dull grey colour, even with the spongy substance that were now his, he was still captivating.

Eddie did not attempt to protest. He knew that what they were saying was true. He was trying to remember how it had happened, but to no avail.

And he couldn't possibly inquire. It would have been indecent to ask: 'How did I kill you?'

And yet, that was the main point. So long as he didn't know the answer, he wouldn't be able to tell them anything. He was very hot, could feel the sweat run down his forehead and ooze between his eyelids. He was reaching into his pocket for his handkerchief, came up with a pint-size whisky bottle instead.

'There's the evidence!' his mother triumphed.

'I didn't drink one drop,' he stammered.

He wanted to show her that the bottle was full as it was when the fellow in Tucson had slipped it to him, but couldn't manage to pull out the cork. His grandmother was watching him sarcastically. She, too, was deaf. Maybe it ran in the family, maybe he would also become deaf?

'It's on account of the rule!'

Tony approved. He was on his side, mostly. So was his father. But all the rest, the crowd, were against him. Because there was a crowd. The street was full of people, like the day of a riot. Pushing and shoving to see him. And saying:

'He killed his brother!'

He was trying to talk to them, to explain that Tony agreed with him, his father, too, but no sound came out of his mouth. Boston Phil was sneering. Sid Kubik grumbled:

'I did my best because your mother once saved my life, but I can do no more.'

The terrible thing was that they maintained he was a liar, that Tony wasn't there. And he himself, searching everywhere for Tony, couldn't find him.

'Tony, you tell 'em . . .'

His father was no longer there either, and the others, threatening, began to disappear, to melt away, leaving him all alone. There was no street or kitchen any more, nothing but emptiness, an immense void in the midst of which he stood raising his arms and screaming for help.

He woke up in a sweat. It was daylight. He thought that maybe he had slept only for a few minutes, but when he walked over to the window he noticed that the street was empty, that the light was the early morning light. He drank a glass of ice water and, since it was very hot, turned on the air-conditioner.

He wanted a cup of strong coffee. He 'phoned downstairs, was told that the bellboys started work at seven. It was five o'clock. He hadn't the courage to go back to sleep. He almost called his wife, to reassure her. Then he told himself that to be awakened like that would frighten her. It wasn't till later, out in the street, that he realized his stupid mistake—there was a three-hour time difference between Florida and here. Back home, the older girls must have already left for school, and Alice was having breakfast.

Nobody, in the hotel lobby, seemed to be spying on him. The clerk merely looked a bit surprised as he watched him go. Nobody followed him as he walked up Main Street with its arcades all along the sidewalk.

There were countless bars, restaurants, and cafeterias, but it took him a good half hour to find a place that was open. It turned out to be something like Fasoli's place, with the same counter, the same electric grills, the same smell.

'Black coffee, please.'

He was alone with the boss, who was still half asleep. Behind him, up against the wall, stood four slot machines.

'No trouble with the cops?'

'They pick 'em up once every six months.'

He knew the setup. A few raids to calm down the morality leagues. The machines were supposedly destroyed. A few weeks later, they turned up in a different place.

'Doing okay?'

'Doing good.'

'Any gambling?'

'Crap games in most any bar. The guys don't know what to do with their dough!'

The coffee settled him and he ordered bacon and eggs. He was calming down very gently, was getting to feel like himself again. The proprietor had guessed that he was a man one could talk to.

'El Centro is right in the middle of a boom. There's a shortage of labour. People are piling in from all over. There's no place for them to stay, so they got to buy trailers, or rent them. Some of them, mostly the new ones, work at picking vegetables up to twelve, thirteen hours a day. The whole damn family hires itself out, father, mother, and kids. It's tough work, all right, on account of the sun, but it doesn't take brains. Well, believe it or not, there's always a lot more that needs picking, so the growers sign on a lot of Mexican hands and smuggle them in. The border is only ten miles away.'

Was Eddie going to mention the name? Because now he remembered the name of Josephina's son. It had come back to him on the plane, when he wasn't even consciously trying. Perhaps he would rather not have remembered. He knew that it sounded like a woman's first name.

He had been drowsing, eyes closed, when the letters formed in his mind: Felici.

Marco Felici. There was nobody in the cafeteria but the owner and himself. A few cars were beginning to pass by. Men were working in a garage, a little further down.

'Do you know a fellow by the name of Felici? Marco Felici?'

'What's his line?'

'Truck farming.'

The man just pointed at the 'phone book lying on a stand near the wall 'phone.

'He ought to be in there.'

Eddie leafed through the book and found the name, not among the El Centro listings, but of a small neighbouring village called Aconda.

'How far is it from here?'

'About six or seven miles, up towards the big canal.'

One of the mechanics from the garage came in for breakfast, then a woman who looked as if she hadn't had any sleep, her make-up smeared. He paid, left, stood outside on the sidewalk, not knowing what to do next.

It would have baffled him less to see somebody watching him. It seemed impossible that there should be no one. Why was he allowed to come and go without their bothering about what he was up to?

Suddenly it occurred to him: they were one whole day ahead of him. Ever since he'd left New York, they knew, of course, that he was headed for El Centro. And here there was undoubtedly someone they could count on to track down Tony.

They didn't know about the Felici lead, but it wasn't an essential clue: Tony had a truck, was accompanied by a young woman, had to be staying somewhere in a motel or in a trailer park.

That wasn't certain, though. It was merely a possibility. But what had happened if they had found him?

They were probably waiting to find out what he, Eddie, was going to do. Wasn't Phil suspecting him of wanting to cheat?

He went back to the hotel to leave his jacket. Nobody wore one over here. Two or three times, he touched the 'phone. His dream pursued him, leaving an unpleasant emptiness in his whole body.

He finally did pick up the receiver and ask for the Excelsior, Miami. It took almost ten minutes during which the receiver was warming up in his hand.

'Mr Kubik, please.'

He gave the number of the suite.

'Sorry, Mr Kubik has checked out.'

He was about to hang up.

'But his friend, Mr Philip, is still here. Shall I connect you? Who is calling, please?'

He mumbled his name, heard the voice of Boston Phil.

'Did I wake you up?'

'No. Did you find him?'

'Not yet. I'm at El Centro. I'm not sure he's in these parts, but . . .'

'But what?'

'I've been thinking. The F.B.I. is after him, too. Well, suppose they're trailing me . . .'

'You went to see the girl's father?'

'Yes.'

'And to Brooklyn?'

'Yes.'

In other words, he had been to places where the cops could have spotted him and put a tail on him.

'Give me your 'phone number. Don't do anything until I call you.'

'Okay.'

He read the number off his 'phone.

'Did you notice anybody?'

'I don't think so.'

Phil was evidently going to put the question up to Kubik or some other bigshot. After Pieter Malaks' statement, the police must be more than anxious to get their hands on Tony. The movements of his brother Eddie need not necessarily have gone unnoticed.

For the moment, he could do nothing but wait. He didn't even dare go down to the lobby for fear the page boy wouldn't find him when Phil called. For the same reason, he didn't 'phone Alice. He might be talking to her when the other call came through. Phil was bound to think he was doing it on purpose. Eddie was convinced that they suspected a double-cross. He had nothing to go on, but he'd been thinking about it ever since Miami.

His brother Gino was perhaps somewhere in town. He was bound for San Diego. He was travelling by bus, not by plane. The trip took several days. Calculating roughly, Eddie came to the conclusion that his brother had either passed through El Centro the day before, or would be passing through to-day.

He would have liked to see him. But maybe it was better not to? He had no way of telling how Gino would react. The two of them were too different. He kept pacing up and down in his room, grew impatient.

'Still no call for me, miss?'

'Nothing, sir.'

And yet Sid Kubik was in Florida. At this time of year he usually stayed several weeks. Over there, it was already much later in the day. Maybe he'd gone for a drive. Maybe he was sun-bathing on the beach of whatever resort he'd selected.

Or was it that he didn't want to assume sole responsibility for the decision? In that case, he would be busy calling New York or perhaps Chicago.

The situation was serious. With Tony as a witness, provided Tony was determined to talk, the whole of the organization was in danger. Vince Vettori was so big that under no circumstances could they afford to have him incriminated.

For years now the District Attorney had been trying relentlessly to find a witness. Twice he had almost succeeded. And once, with young Charlie—another driver, incidentally—he had even been frightfully close to a triumph. Charlie was arrested. Taking no chances, they didn't put him in jail at the Tombs, where a prisoner might shut him up for good. It had been known to happen. Only five years earlier, during recess, One-Eyed-Bert had been strangled, without its attracting any of the guards' attention.

Instead, they took Charlie, in great secrecy, to one of the cop's apartment, where four or five of them mounted guard over him night and day.

But Charlie got it just the same. A bullet, fired from a roof across the street, killed Charlie right in the cop's own room.

It was natural for people to defend themselves. Eddie could see that. Even when it involved his own brother.

And he realized how complicated it was. The Brooklyn police could not act here in California. As for the F.B.I., in principle they had no right to interfere unless a federal crime had been committed.

The killing of Carmine, the murder of the cigar-store owner did not fall under federal law. They concerned only the state of New York. Unless, for instance, the car used had been stolen in another state. But the men behind those two jobs were much too smart for that.

The most that the G-men could try, if they caught Tony, was possibly to accuse him of having stolen the truck and driven it to California. Before old man Malaks was notified, they might perhaps have time to bring Tony back to New York State.

There were other solutions. His brain kept spinning too fast. He was eager for the 'phone to ring, and keep him from thinking.

He jumped at a knock on the door, tiptoed over, opened it abruptly. It was the housemaid, asking if she could do the room.

Of course, the maids sometimes have to disturb a guest who stays in his room too late. But it was possible that *they* wanted to make sure Eddie was still there.

Now, *they* applied as well to members of the organizations as to those of the police, to the F.B.I. as to the state police.

Eddie had slept for almost fourteen hours and did not feel rested. He would have needed a few hours of calm, not to think like this, in a nervous, jerky fashion, in a confusion of ideas, but to deliberate as he usually would, with cool detachment.

It was odd, his having dreamed about his father. He rarely thought of him. He had hardly known him. And yet it seemed to him that he had much more in common with Cesare Rico than his brothers had.

He could still see his father waiting on customers in the store, always peaceful, a bit solemn, almost, but it was not solemnity. It was like a zone of calm surrounding him.

Eddie, too, was calm. And, like his father, he kept his thoughts to himself all day long. Had he ever confided in his wife? Once or twice, perhaps, and trivialities at that. Never in his brothers, or in the so-called friends.

His father never laughed either, but wore, as Eddie usually did, a vague, diffident smile.

They were the kind, both of them, that went their own way, never strayed from it, stubbornly, because they had decided once and for all what life would be like.

It was a hard thing to define in the case of the father. Cesare Rico had probably made his decision when he met Julia Massera. She was the strong one. It was obvious that she gave the orders, both in the home and in the store. He had married her, and Eddie had never heard him raise his voice either in anger or complaint.

He, Eddie, had chosen to belong to the organization and to play the game, to follow the rules, leaving it to others to rebel or to try to cheat.

Why didn't Phil 'phone him? He didn't have a paper to read. He never even thought of calling for one. He needed solitude.

The noise of the street had started up again. Cars were parked all along the kerb, and a cop had his hands full trying to keep traffic moving. This wasn't anything like Florida or Brooklyn. There were cars of every make and vintage, the oldest and the newest, ancient Model-T Fords such as survive only in the country, the hood held down with strings, and flashy Cadillacs, pickup trucks also, and motor-cycles, and people of every race, many Negroes, even more Mexicans.

He grabbed the 'phone as soon as it rang.

'Hello!'

It was still ringing. He heard the voices of distant operators, then Boston Phil, at last.

'Eddie?'

'Yes.'

'It's okay.'

'What is?'

'Go ahead and talk to your brother.'

'Even if the cops . . .?'

'In any case it's better to get there first. Sid wants you to call me as soon as you find him.'

Eddie opened his mouth without knowing what he was going to say, but he didn't get a chance to say anything, because Phil had already hung up.

So he washed his hands, his face, to cool off, changed his shirt, put on his hat, and went out to the elevator. He had left the bottle of whisky on the table, untouched. He was in no mood for liquor. He wasn't thirsty. His throat felt dry, but he lit a cigarette just the same.

In the lobby, where there were quite a few people, he did not look around him. Several taxis were parked in front of the door. He did not pick, took the first in line.

'Aconda,' he said, dropping into the seat, which was burning hot from the sun.

He saw, on the outskirts of town, the motels he had heard about that morning and the trailers clustered together in vacant lots, washing drying on lines, women in shorts, thin ones and fat ones, who cooked outdoors on camping stoves.

Then came the first fields. In most of them, rows of men and women, bent close to the ground, were busy picking, while behind them came the trucks, whose loads got bigger and bigger.

Most of the houses were new. A few years back, before the canal was built, this area was only a desert in the middle of which stood the old Spanish town. They were building fast. Some were content with mere barracks.

The car turned left into a sand road, with power lines running alongside it and, now and then, a few houses nestled together.

Aconda was bigger. Some of the homes were spacious, surrounded by lawns and flowers.

'What people are you looking for?'

'People called Felici.'

'Never heard of them! They change so often around here!'

The driver stopped in front of a general store that had farm implements spread right out to the middle of the sidewalk.

'Is there a Felici living anywhere near here?'

They were given some complicated directions. The taxi left the village, drove past more fields, stopped in front of a few mailboxes set by the side of the road. The fifth one bore the name of Felici. The house rose in the middle of the fields, and, at some distance, silhouetted against the sky, there was a row of workers stooped towards the ground.

'Do you want me to wait?'

'Yes.'

A little girl in a red bathing suit was playing on the porch. She looked to be five or so.

'Is your daddy home?'

'He's down there.'

She was pointing towards the men visible on the horizon.

'What about your mother?'

The little girl didn't have to answer. A brown-haired woman, wearing nothing but a pair of linen shorts and a halter of the same material, opened the screen door.

'What is it?'

'Mrs Felici?'

'Yes.'

He didn't remember her, and she probably didn't remember him, either. All she saw was somebody of Italian origin who had evidently come from far away.

Should he talk to her or would it be better to wait for the husband? He looked back. No one was in sight. He apparently had not been followed.

'I'd like to ask you for some information.'

She hesitated. She was still holding the door open. Reluctantly, she said: 'Come in.'

The room was large, almost dark, because the blinds were shut. There was a large table in the middle, toys on the floor, an ironing board in one corner, with the iron still plugged in and a man's shirt spread out.

'Do sit down.'

'My name is Eddie Rico, and I know your mother-in-law.'

It was only then that he became aware of someone being in the next room. He heard a noise. Then the door opened. All he saw at first was the silhouette of a woman wearing a flowered print dress. As the shutters were not closed behind her the woman stood out against a bright background, and the shape of her legs and thighs were outlined under the material.

Instead of answering, Mrs Felici turned and called softly:

'Nora.'

'I'm right here.'

She entered the room. Eddie really saw her now, and she was smaller than he had expected after meeting her father and her younger brother, smaller and more delicate.

What struck him right away was her being visibly pregnant.

'You're Tony's brother?'

'Yes. You're his wife, aren't you?'

He hadn't expected it to happen that fast. He wasn't ready. He had reckoned on having a talk with Felici first, and, as he'd imagined it, the man would, in the end, have disclosed Tony's whereabouts.

What disturbed him, too, was Nora's being pregnant. He had three children of his own and he had never thought that his brothers might have any.

She sat down on one of the benches, rested one arm on the table, examining him attentively.

'How come you're here?'

'I must talk to Tony.'

'That's not what I'm asking. Who gave you his address?'

He didn't have time to make up an answer.

'Your father told me . . .'

'You went to see my father?'

'Yes.'

'Why?'

'To get Tony's address.'

'He doesn't have it. Neither do my brothers.'

'Your father told me that as Tony had fixed up an old truck he'd given it to him.'

She was intelligent and quick. She had already caught on, was examining him even more keenly.

'And you guessed he'd come here.'

'I remembered he'd spent several months down here when he was a kid and that he'd often told me about the trucks.'

'So you're Eddie.'

Her gaze made him uncomfortable. He tried to smile at her.

'Glad to meet you,' he mumbled.

'What do you want with Tony?'

She was not smiling, and she kept observing him with the same speculation, while Mrs Felici stayed as inconspicuously in the background as she could.

What had Tony told the Felicis? Did they know? Had they welcomed him just the same?

'What do you want with him?' Nora repeated, in a tone that indicated a good deal of determination.

'I have things to tell him.'

'What things?'

'I must go . . .' murmured Mrs Felici.

'There's no reason . . .'

'I've got to get lunch.'

She went to the kitchen, closing the door behind her.

'What do you want with him?'

'He's in danger.'

'Why?'

What right had she, after all, to talk to him with the tone of a district attorney? If Tony was in danger, if he himself was in trouble, if years of hard work were at stake, wasn't it all on account of this girl?

'Certain people are afraid he'll talk,' he replied more harshly.

'These people know where he is?'

'Not yet.'

'Will you tell them?'

'They'll find him.'

'And then?'

'They might want to keep him quiet at all cost.'

'Did they send you?'

He had the misfortune to hesitate. However much he was to deny it later, her mind was made up.

'What did they tell you? What instructions did they give you?'

She was very feminine, there was no harshness to her features, on the contrary, nor to the lines of her body; yet, oddly enough, she appeared to have more will power than a man. She had taken an instant dislike to Eddie. Perhaps she disliked him before they ever met? Tony must have spoken of him and Gino. Did she prefer Gino? Did she hate the whole family except Tony?

There was anger in her dark eyes, a quiver of the lips whenever she spoke to him.

'If your brother hadn't gone to the police . . .' he attacked, his own anger rising.

'What are you saying? How dare you tell me that my brother . . .'

She had risen and was facing him, her belly protruding. He thought she was going to throw herself at him, and he couldn't lay a hand on a pregnant woman.

'Yes, your brother, the one who works for General Electric. He passed on to the police everything you told him about Tony.'

'That's not true!'

'It's the truth.'

'You're lying!'

'Listen . . . Calm down . . . I swear to you . . .'

'You're lying!'

How could he have foreseen that he'd find himself in such a ridiculous situation? In the other room, Mrs Felici surely heard the quarrelling voices. The child heard them from the porch, opened the door, showed a frightened little face.

'What's the matter, Aunt Nora?'

So they considered her one of the family. And they no doubt called her husband Uncle Tony!

'Nothing, darling. We're talking.'

'About what?'

'Things you can't understand.'

'Is he the man I'm not supposed to talk to?'

So Tony and his wife had told the Felicis everything. They were afraid that someone would inquire about them. So the child had been instructed, if a man came around and asked questions . . .

He was waiting for Nora's answer, and she, as if seeking revenge, said curtly:

'Yes, he's the one.'

She was still quivering from head to foot.

Chapter Seven

They were still glowering at each other, eyes flashing, breathing hard, when a big truck coming in from the fields shuddered to a clanging stop in front of the porch. From where he stood, Eddie could not see out of the window, but the anxious expression on Nora's face told him that it was Tony.

He had probably been working over there with the men and noticed the cab. Had it left at once, Tony might not have worried, but its prolonged parking had decided him to come and investigate.

The three people in the room could hear him walk up the porch steps and they each remained frozen in the exact pose in which the sound of the truck had surprised them.

The door opened wide. Tony wore blue jeans and a white gym shirt that bared his arms and most of his shoulders. He was very muscular, deeply tanned by the sun.

At the sight of his brother, he stopped short. He frowned, knitting his very thick, very black eyebrows, and a vertical ridge divided his forehead into two uneven parts.

Before anyone could utter a sound, the little girl had rushed up to him.

'Be careful, Uncle Tony. That's him.'

Tony didn't catch on right away, patted the little girl on the head, looking to his wife for an explanation. It was a gentle, trusting look.

'Bessie asked me if he was the man she wasn't supposed to talk to, and I said yes.'

The kitchen door opened: they just caught a glimpse of Mrs Felici holding a pan of sizzling bacon.

'Bessie, come here . . .'

'But, Mummy . . .'

'I said to come . . .'

So that the three of them remained alone, and, at first, they were painfully awkward. Because of his tan, the white of Tony's eyes seemed whiter, almost luminous in the semi-darkness of the room, and it gave a strange glow to his eyes.

He explained, without looking at Eddie squarely:

'We figured all along that somebody would come around asking questions, so we told the kid . . .'

'I know.'

Lifting his head, Tony murmured, with genuine surprise:

'I didn't reckon it would be you, though!'

An idea was troubling him. He observed his wife, then his brother.

'Were you the one who remembered my visit down here?'

He evidently didn't believe so. Eddie was in no state to lie without giving himself away.

'No,' he admitted.

'You went to see Mamma?'

'Yes.'

Nora was leaning against the table, her dress taut over the bulge of her body. Tony was moving closer to her as he talked and, finally, put his hand on her shoulder, in a gesture obviously familiar to him.

'Mamma told you I was here?'

'When she found out that you'd left with a truck . . .'

'How did she find out?'

'From me.'

'You went to White Cloud, too?'

'Yes.'

'Do you understand, Tony?' his wife interposed.

He calmed her with the pressure of his hand, then gently put his arm around her shoulders.

'What exactly did Mamma tell you?'

'She reminded me that when you came back from California you were all worked up about what could be done here with a truck.'

'And so you came!' said Tony, lowering his head.

He, too, needed to straighten his thoughts. Once more Nora tried to tell him something, and again he kept her quiet by tightening his hand on her shoulder.

'I figured they'd find me sooner or later . . .'

He said it as if speaking to himself, without bitterness or revolt, and Eddie had the impression of being in the presence of a Tony he did not know.

'I didn't reckon it would be you . . .'

Once again he looked up, and with a toss of his head, threw back a lock of hair that fell over his eye.

'Did they send you?'

'Sid called me up. Or to be exact, he made Phil telephone me that I was to go and see him in Miami. It would be better if we had a quiet talk, the two of us.'

He felt the protest in Nora, who stiffened. Had Tony asked her to leave, she would undoubtedly have obeyed, but Tony shook his head.

'There's nothing she can't hear.'

Then, with a glance, he called attention to his wife's figure, and the expression on his face was one that Eddie had never seen there before.

'Did you know?'

'Yes.'

Nothing more was said about the baby she expected.

'Exactly what did they tell you to do?'

There was a touch of contempt, of bitterness in his voice. Eddie needed all his self-control. It was important.

'First of all, you've got to know what happened.'

'They need me, maybe?' Tony sneered.

'No. This is worse. It's extremely serious, in fact. Please listen to me, carefully.'

'He's going to lie . . .' Nora warned in a still voice.

And her hand gripped the man's hand resting on her shoulder, to show that they stood as one.

'Let him speak.'

'Your brother-in-law went to the police.'

Trembling, Nora again protested:

'It isn't true.'

Once more, Tony calmed her, holding her close.

'How can you be sure?'

'Sid has informers in the place, remember? Pieter Malaks told the chief everything you told him.'

'I never talked with him.'

'Everything his sister told him.'

Tony still quieted her. He had no anger for her. Eddie had never seen him so calm, so deliberate.

'Well, what about it?'

'He claims you're willing to talk. Is it true?'

Tony withdrew his arm from Nora's shoulder to light a cigarette. He was two feet away from Eddie, looking him squarely in the face.

'And you, what do you think?'

Eddie, before replying, glanced at the pregnant woman, as if to explain his answer.

'I didn't believe it. Now I don't know.'

'What about Sid and the others?'

'Sid doesn't want to take any chances.'

After a pause, Eddie asked once more:

'Is it true?'

It was Tony's turn to look at his wife. Instead of answering directly, he murmured:

'I didn't say anything to my brother-in-law.'

'He still went to see the police commissioner and, probably, the D.A.'

'He thought he was doing right. I understand. I also understand why Nora talked to him. Pieter didn't want her to marry me. He wasn't so far from wrong, either. He'd checked up on me.'

He went over to a cupboard, took out a bottle of wine.

'Want some?'

'No, thanks.'

'Suit yourself.'

He poured himself a glass and drank it down. It was Chianti, the same as their mother had. He was about to fill his glass again when Nora whispered:

'Careful, Tony.'

He hesitated, nearly helped himself just the same, looked at his brother, and smiled as he set the straw-covered bottle on the table.

'So you saw Sid, and he gave you a message for me.'

He had resumed his place, with his back towards the table and his arm around Nora's shoulders.

'I'm listening.'

'I suppose you understand that, after what they've been told, the cops are anxious to find you.'

'That's normal enough.'

'They figure they finally have the witness they've been looking for all this time.'

'I see.'

'Are they right?'

Instead of answering, Tony said flatly:

'Go on.'

'Sid and the others can't take a chance like that.'

For the first time, Tony became aggressive.

'What gets me,' he said, with a curl of the lips that Eddie recognized, 'is that they sent you instead of Gino.'

'What's so strange about that?'

'Because Gino is a killer.'

Even Nora shuddered. Eddie had turned pale.

'I'm waiting for the rest of it,' Tony went on.

'You'll notice that you didn't tell me yet whether or not you'd talk.'

'So what?'

'So, Sid's misgivings aren't as ridiculous as all that. For years they've trusted you.'

'You don't say.'

'The fate of many people, the lives of a few depend on what you might or might not say.'

Once again Nora opened her mouth to speak, and Tony made her keep silent. With that ever-tender, protective gesture.

'Let him speak.'

Eddie was beginning to get mad. He didn't like his brother's attitude. He felt in it a criticism directed against him, and he had the impression that, from the very first, Tony was looking at him with contemptuous sarcasm, as if reading his innermost thoughts.

'They have no grudge against you.'

'Really?'

'They just want you in some safe spot.'

'Six feet under, I suppose.'

'As Sid put it, America isn't big enough for you. If you went to Europe, like others have done before, you could live in peace, and so could your wife.'

'What about their peace of mind?'

'Sid promised me . . .'

'And you believed him.'

'But . . .'

'Admit it. You didn't believe him. They know as well as we both know that it's on crossing a border that I'm most likely to be picked up. If what you say is true . . .'

'It's true!'

'Granted. In that case they sent out my description everywhere.'

'You could cross into Mexico and sail from there. The border is ten miles away.'

Eddie did not remember that Tony had ever been so muscular, so virile. Though he was still very youthful, because of his curly hair and his bright eyes, he gave an impression of maturity.

'What does Gino have to say about it?'

'I didn't see Gino.'

He had said it badly.

'You're lying, Eddie.'

'They sent Gino to California.'

'And Joe?'

'Down at my place, in Santa Clara.'

'And Vettori?'

'They didn't tell me.'

'Does Mamma know you're here?'

'No.'

'Did you tell her what Sid said?'

He hesitated. It was too difficult to lie to Tony.

'No.'

'In other words, you wanted to pump her for information.'

Tony went over to open the door, which suddenly delivered a rectangle of glaring, blinding light. Shading his eyes with his hand, Tony looked out towards the road.

Coming back to the table, he murmured soberly:

'They let you come alone.'

'I wouldn't have come otherwise.'

'That means they trust you, doesn't it? They always trusted you.'

'They trusted you, too,' replied Eddie, anxious to score a point.

'It isn't the same thing. Me, I was just a handy man who does what he's told to do.'

'Nobody ever forced it on you.'

He felt compelled to be unkind, not so much because of Tony, but because of Nora, whose hatred he sensed. Here wasn't just a couple confronting him; the woman's belly made it a family already, a clan almost.

'You didn't wait for anybody to egg you on when you started stealing cars, and I can remember how . . .'

With more sadness than indignation, Tony murmured:

'Whatever you tell her she already knows. Remember the house, the street, the people that used to come to Mamma's store? Remember our games after school?'

Tony did not go on. He was following his own line of thought, and almost in a whisper he added:

'But, with you, it isn't the same at all. It never was.'

'I don't understand.'

'You do.'

And it was true. He did understand. There had always been a difference between him and his brothers, both Tony and Gino. They had never threshed this out between them. This was not the moment to do so, still less before a stranger. And, to Eddie, Nora was a stranger. Tony had been wrong, talking to Nora the way he had. During the thirteen years of their marriage, Eddie had not once told Alice anything that might have jeopardized the organization.

It was useless to argue those questions with Tony. Others had fallen in love the same way. Not many. And then they all had felt the need to defy the world itself. Nothing mattered to them any more except a woman. The rest they didn't care about.

It had always turned out badly. And Sid knew that, too.

'When do you think they'll come?'

Nora shivered from head to foot and turned towards her husband, as if she were going to throw herself into his arms.

'They're only asking you to go to Europe.'

'Stop kidding me, will you?'

'I wouldn't have come if it had been otherwise.'

Again, with the same simplicity, Tony answered:

'Yes, you would.'

Then, with a certain lassitude in his voice:

'You always did, you always will do what needs to be done. I remember a night when you explained to me your point of view, one of the few times I ever saw you half tight.'

'Where were we?'

'Walking around in Greenwich Village. It was hot. In some restaurant, you pointed out to me one of the bigshots you looked on, from a distance, with trembling admiration. "You see, Tony", you said, "some guys think they're tough because they shoot their big mouth." Would you like me to play back your whole speech? I could still quote the words, especially the part about the rule.'

'You would have been much better off following it.'

'It would have saved you the trip to Miami, to White Cloud, to Brooklyn, where Mamma must be wondering why you went, and finally here. And I'm not holding anything against you, you know. You're just built that way.'

Suddenly his voice changed, his expression, and he became very businesslike.

'Let's talk bluntly, without kidding each other.'

'I'm not kidding anybody.'

'All right. Let's be frank just the same. You know damn well why Sid and Boston Phil made you come to Miami. They've got to find out where I am. If they'd known, they wouldn't have needed you.'

'That's not sure.'

'At least have guts enough to face the facts. They called you in and talked to you the way bosses talk to a trusted employee, to some sort of floorwalker or assistant. You often reminded me of a floorwalker.'

For the first time, a smile brightened Nora's face, and she patted her husband's hand.

'Thanks for the compliment.'

'You're welcome. They informed you that your brother was a traitor about to disgrace the family.'

'That's not true.'

'That's what you were thinking, though. Not only disgrace the family, but jeopardize it, and that, well, that's much worse.'

Eddie was beginning to discover a man he had never imagined before. To him, Tony had remained the kid brother, a good guy, crazy about motors, who chased the girls and swaggered around the bars. If anyone had asked him, he'd probably have said that Tony admired him deeply.

Was Tony actually thinking on his own? Or was he just parroting the phrases that Nora had taught him?

The heat was oppressive. There was no air-conditioning in the house. From time to time, Tony poured himself a drink, with one hand, the other never leaving his wife's shoulder.

Eddie was thirsty too. Getting some water would have involved opening the door to the kitchen, where Mrs Felici had taken her little girl. So he ended up by taking a glass in the cupboard and pouring himself a mouthful of wine.

'It's about time. I bet you were worried about getting drunk. You can sit down, even if I don't have much more to say.'

It was right then that Tony reminded him of his dream. He didn't resemble the sponge-rubber man who, with their father, was waiting for him in the mailbox, and yet he had the very same smile.

It was hard to explain. In his dream, too, there was something light and young about Tony, something free and easy, with still a strange quality of sadness.

As if the dice were rolling! As if he knew the odds were too big. As if he stood apart, beyond a point where all things stand revealed, where they are contemplated with eyes reborn.

For a fraction of a second Eddie saw him dead. He sat down, crossed his legs, lit a cigarette with trembling hand.

'Where was I?' said Tony. 'Let me finish, Nora.'

For she had stirred once more.

'It's better if Eddie and I get to the bottom of this once and for all. We're brothers. We both came out of the same womb. For years we slept in the same bed. When I was five, he was put up to me as an example.

'Well, let's get back to serious business. It isn't impossible that they really told you to offer me the deal you just said.'

'I swear to you . . .'

'I believe it. When you lie, it's written all over your face. Only, you also knew that that wasn't what they wanted. You've known right from the start that they have no desire to see me get out of the country. The proof is that you didn't tell Mamma about it.'

'I didn't want to upset her.'

Tony shrugged his shoulders.

'Besides, I was afraid she'd talk.'

'Mamma never once breathed a word that she shouldn't. Not even to us. I bet you still don't know that she buys the stuff that's stolen by punks who hang out in her store.'

Eddie had always suspected she did, but never had any proof.

'I found her out by accident. You see, Eddie, you're with them one hundred per cent to-day just as yesterday, and as always. You're with them because that's what you decided, once and for all, and because you built your whole life on that decision.

'If they came right out and asked you what ought to be done about me . . .'

Eddie sketched a motion of protest.

'Never mind! If you took part in some kind of kangaroo court and the question were asked in the name of the organization, your answer would be the same as theirs.

'I don't know what they're doing right now. Probably waiting for you back at the hotel. You're staying at the Presidio?

'Thanks to you, they know where I am. They'll know even if you swear you didn't see me.'

Never had anyone looked at him with as much hatred as he read in the eyes of Nora, who clung ever more closely to her husband.

And it was perhaps in answer to his wife's thoughts that Tony added with indifference:

'Even if I killed you here and now, so you couldn't go back to them, they'd know. They know already.

'And you, already in Miami, the moment you started looking for me, you knew they'd know.

'That's what I wanted to tell you. That I'm no sucker. Don't be one either.'

'Listen, Tony . . .'

'Not yet. I don't hold it against you. I always figured you'd act this way, given the occasion.

'I'd have preferred not being the occasion, that's all.

'You'll have to square yourself with Mamma. And with your conscience.'

It was the first time Eddie ever heard him utter that word. He said it lightly, almost jokingly.

'This time, I've had my say.'

'It's my turn now!' said Nora.

She had freed herself and taken a step in Eddie's direction.

'If anybody touches one single hair on Tony's head, I'm the one who will tell everything.'

Tony smiled at her, a young and gay smile, shook his head.

'It wouldn't do any good, darling. You see, for your testimony to be of any value, you'd have to be an actual witness to . . .'

'I won't leave you for one second.'

'Then they'll shut you up too.'

'I'd rather that.'

'Not me.'

'I didn't try to interrupt,' mumbled Eddie.

'What's the use?'

'That's not what I came for.'

'No, not yet.'

'I won't tell where . . .'

'You don't have to. You came. It's enough.'

'I'll call the police,' cried Nora.

Her husband shook his head.

'No.'

'Why not?'

'It wouldn't do any good, either.'

'The police wouldn't let them . . .'

They heard a heavy tread on the wooden porch steps. A man, outside, shook the dirt off his boots, opened the door, stood motionless on the threshold.

'Come on in, Marco.'

He was in his fifties, and when he took off his wide straw hat he revealed a head of nice evenly grey hair. His eyes were blue, his skin bronze. Like Tony, he wore jeans and an undershirt.

'My brother Eddie, who came from Miami to see me.'

And, turning to Eddie:

'Remember Marco Felici?'

A sort of truce was established. Perhaps the storm had passed? Marco, still hesitant, extended a grubby hand.

'You're having lunch with us? Where is my wife?'

'In the kitchen, with Bessie. She didn't want to intrude in this little family reunion.'

'I'll join them out there.'

'You don't have to bother any more. We're through here. Right, Eddie?'

Eddie nodded reluctantly.

'A glass of wine, Marco?'

Again the strange smile played on Tony's lips. He went to get a third glass. After a brief hesitation he took out a fourth one, filled them all, his own and his brother's included.

'Maybe we could drink a toast?'

A strange sound issued from Eddie's throat. Nora looked up quickly, but didn't understand, and he was alone to know that a sob had almost escaped.

'To our reunion.'

Tony's hand did not tremble. He really looked gay, untroubled, as if life were a frivolous and pleasant affair. To keep his composure, Eddie had to look away.

Marco, who suspected something, was watching them each in turn, and lifted his glass with evident reluctance.

'You too, Nora.'

'I never drink.'

'Just this once.'

She looked up at her husband to find out if he was talking seriously and knew then that he wanted her to drink.

'To your health, Eddie.'

Eddie tried to reply with the traditional: 'Here's to yours!'

He could not, merely raised the glass to his lips. Nora, without taking her eyes off him, just wet hers with wine.

Tony, in one gulp, swallowed every last drop and he set the empty glass upside down on the table.

Eddie stammered:

'I have to go.'

'Yes. It's time.'

He didn't dare shake hands, looked around for his hat. The strange thing was that he felt he had lived through this scene before. Even Nora's misshapen body seemed familiar.

'Well . . . See you soon.'

He'd almost said, 'good-bye.' The word had scared him. And yet he realized that 'See you soon' was worse and might sound like a threat.

He had not intended to threaten. He was sincerely moved and could feel the lukewarm tears in his eyes as he walked towards the door.

No attempt was made to stop him. Not a word was said. He didn't know if he were being observed, if Tony's hand were tightening on Nora's shoulder. He did not dare look back.

He opened the door and walked out into a solid mass of heat. The driver, who had been sitting in the shade, slipped back into his seat. The door slammed. All he saw was the little girl at the kitchen window who leaned out to watch him leave and stuck out her tongue at him.

'El Centro?'

'Yes.'

'The hotel?'

He thought he heard a car starting up somewhere. He could not see out in the fields. A house hid part of the road from his view.

He almost asked the driver about it, but couldn't work up the courage. Never in his life had he felt so drained in both body and mind. The air, in the cab, was stifling, and, as they were driving in the sun, his ears started to ring. He had a metallic taste in his dried-out mouth, and, even when he closed his eyes, black spots danced in front of them.

He got scared. He had seen cases of sunstroke. The cab was just driving through the village, passing the hardware store.

'Stop here a minute . . .'

What he needed was a glass of cold water. And a few moments in the shade, so he could get hold of himself.

'Anything wrong?'

He almost wished he would faint as he crossed the sidewalk. And stay sick for a few days. Not have to think, to decide.

The clerk took one look at him and immediately brought a paper cup full of ice water.

'Don't drink too fast. I'll bring you a chair.'

This was ridiculous. Tony would certainly have accused him of putting on an act, or Nora, anyway who throughout their talk had glowered at him with stark hatred.

'More, please.'

'Take time out to catch your breath.'

The driver had followed him in and stood waiting with the look of one used to this sort of thing.

Suddenly, as he was raising the second cup to his lips, Eddie retched. He barely had time to bend over. He vomited, in one violent gush, purple from the wine, between the lawn mowers and the galvanized pails, and stammered, his eyes full of tears:

'I'm sorry . . . It's . . . it's so stupid.'

The other two winked at each other. The clerk, trying to be helpful, smacked him on the back several times to keep him from choking.

'You shouldn't have taken red wine,' the chauffeur remarked sententiously.

And he, wretchedly, between hiccups:

'They . . . they . . . made me!'

Chapter Eight

The desk clerk had handed him his key without a word, as if he didn't see him. The elevator boy, on the way up, had kept staring at the lapel of Eddie's jacket, where there was a purple stain.

Eddie was returning to his room with the sole thought of flinging himself on the bed. Even as he opened the door, he was already letting his nerves go, ceasing to control his expression. And he had no idea what he looked like. He had taken one step inside when he remembered that he hadn't taken the precaution to turn the key in the lock.

At that very instant, he saw the man, and before his brain could function, terror rooted him on the spot, with a horrifying sensation all along his spine. It had been automatic, like the fact of pressing a button turns on a light or starts a motor. He hadn't reasoned. He had simply believed that his turn had come, and the saliva had dried in his mouth.

He had known dozens of men who had ended up this way, and some of them had been his pals. In some instances, he'd been having a drink with them at, say, ten o'clock, and by eleven or midnight, when they got home they had found two men waiting for them, two men who didn't need to say anything.

He had sometimes wondered what people think about at that moment, and then, a little later, in the car headed for a vacant lot, a river, while, for yet a few more minutes, they pass by street or lights, pedestrians, and even stop for a traffic light beneath which can be glimpsed a policeman's uniform.

It had lasted only a few seconds. He was convinced that not a muscle in his face had moved. But he also knew that the man had seen everything, first the emptiness that was inside him as he opened the door, the slackening of flesh and brain, then the electric current of fear, and now, finally, his self-control returning, with his mind working very fast.

It wasn't what he had feared, because his visitor was alone, and, for this kind of ride, they are always two, plus the one who waits, outside in the car.

Furthermore, the man wasn't the type. He was somebody important. The hotel management wouldn't have let a stranger into the room. Not only had he settled himself there, but he had called down for soda and ice cubes. As for whisky, he had opened the pint bottle, which still stood on the table, next to the glass.

'Take it easy, son,' he said, without removing from his mouth the fat cigar whose smell had had time to pervade the room.

He was over sixty, perhaps close to seventy. He'd seen a great deal, and he recognized all the symptoms.

'Call me Mike.'

But there was no mistake about it. This was no licence to get chummy with him. It applied to the respectful familiarity which in certain groups, in certain small towns, surrounds those of importance.

He looked like a politician, a state senator, or a mayor, or like someone who bosses the political machine and makes judges and sheriffs alike. He could have played any one of these parts in the movies, especially in a Western, he knew, and it was obvious that it pleased him, that he kept polishing up the resemblance.

'How about a highball?' he proposed, pointing at the bottle.

'I never drink.'

Whereupon Mike's eyes fastened on to the wine spot. He didn't bother to smile, to banter. A flicker of the eyes, and that was enough.

'Sit down.'

His suit was not white linen, but shantung, and his hand-painted tie must have cost thirty or forty dollars. He'd kept his hat on, as he no doubt did anywhere he went—a wide-brimmed Stetson, light grey, almost white, immaculately clean.

The chair towards which he had motioned Eddie was near the 'phone. Languidly, he pointed at the instrument.

'You're to call Phil.'

Eddie did not argue, picked up the 'phone, asked for the Miami number. And while he waited, the receiver at his ear, Mike just kept smoking his cigar and watching him with indifference.

'Hello—Phil?'

'Who's there?'

'Eddie.'

'Yes?'

'I . . . I was told . . .'

'Hang on a minute. I want to shut the door.'

It wasn't true. Phil stayed too long for that. Either he was conferring with someone, or else he did it on purpose to unnerve Eddie.

'Hello—hello . . .'

'Okay, I can hear you.'

Another pause. Eddie didn't want to speak first.

'Is Mike there?'

'He's in the room with me.'

'Good.'

Another pause. Eddie could have sworn he heard the sea, but that was, of course, impossible.

'Did you see Gino?'

He wondered if he had heard the name right or if Phil might not be making a mistake between his brothers. He wasn't expecting to hear about that one. He didn't have time to consider. He lied, without thinking of the consequences.

'No. Why?'

'Because he didn't get to San Diego.'

'Oh . . .'

'He should have been there yesterday.'

Knowing that Mike went on watching him, he was forced to keep his face blank. His brain was working fast, mostly in images, like a moment ago when he had thought about being taken for a ride. It was somewhat the same scene, too, with a different cast. If it hadn't been Phil talking at the other end, but

Sid Kubik, for instance, the idea would never have occurred to him.

Phil was vicious. Eddie had always known that Phil didn't like him, probably didn't like any of the brothers Rico.

Why had he called San Diego, when it was Tony they were after?

Gino was a killer. San Diego was near El Centro—two hours by car, less than an hour by plane.

Phil had already managed to bring together two of the brothers.

'Hello,' said Eddie, speaking into the 'phone.

'I was wondering if Gino hadn't stopped to see you in Santa Clara?'

He was forced to go on lying.

'No.'

It could be dangerous. He had never done this. It was against all his principles. If they knew he was lying, they'd be justified from now on, not to trust him.

'He was seen in New Orleans.'

'Oh . . .'

'Getting off a bus.'

Why keep talking to him about Gino rather than Tony? There was a reason. Phil never did anything without a reason. It was essential that Eddie guess what the other had in mind.

'It seems he was next seen on board a ship sailing for South America.'

Eddie realized that this was probably true.

'What would he do that for?' he nevertheless protested.

'I don't know. You're his brother. You know him better than I do.'

'I don't know anything about it. He didn't tell me a thing.'

'You saw him?'

'I mean he didn't write me about it.'

'Did you get a letter?'

'No.'

'How's Tony?'

Now, he caught on. They had scared him by talking about Gino. They hadn't invented anything, but they had made use of the truth. It was a way of preparing him for the business with Tony.

He couldn't lie again. Besides, Mike was there, quietly smoking his cigar. And Mike knew.

'I talked to him.'

Voluble, he went on:

'I saw his wife, too. She's expecting a baby. I explained to my brother—'

Phil cut him short.

'Mike has been briefed. Did you get that? He'll tell you what to do.'

'Yes.'

'Sid gave his okay. He's here. Do you want him to tell you himself?'

Eddie repeated:

'Yes.'

And he realized afterwards that it made him look as though he didn't trust Phil.

'I'll put him on.'

A few muffled words, then Kubik's voice and accent.

'Mike La Motte will handle everything. And don't try to play smart with him. Is he there with you?'

'Yes.'

'Let me talk to him.'

'Kubik wants to talk to you.'

'Hand me the 'phone, then. What's the matter? The cord isn't long enough?'

It was.

'Hi there, old man.'

The talking was done mostly at the other end, and Eddie could hear Kubik's distant voice, but not the words. Mike was approving laconically in monosyllables or brief phrases.

Now that he knew his name, Eddie looked upon him with different eyes. He had been right in thinking that here was an important person. What the man was doing at present he didn't know, because people didn't much talk about him any more. But there had been a time when his name made headlines.

Michel La Motte, called Mike, probably of Canadian origin, had been, on the West Coast, one of the big beer barons of Prohibition.

The organization didn't exist yet. Alliances were made and unmade. Most of the time, the bosses fought among themselves over a territory, or a load of liquor, a boat, a truck.

Due to the absence of organization there was no hierarchy, no specialization. The majority of the population played along, so did the police, and a good number of politicians.

The battles were fought chiefly between gangs, between bosses.

La Motte, after getting his start in a district of San Francisco, had not only appropriated all of California, but he had extended his operations all the way to the Middle West.

When the Rico brothers were still kids roaming the streets of Brooklyn, Mike already was said to have eliminated, by his own hand, over twenty of his competitors. He had picked off a few, too, members of his own gang, who had started talking too big.

He had finally been arrested, but no homicide charge could be made to stick. It was tax evasion that had sent him up for a stretch, not to San Quentin, like an ordinary prisoner, but to Alcatraz, the fortress on the rock in San Francisco Bay.

Eddie had never heard of him since. Had he been asked just a little while ago whatever became of Mike, he would have answered that Mike was probably dead, for the man was already middle-aged when he himself was still a kid.

He now gazed upon him with respect, admiration, and he didn't think it silly any more that Mike tried to look like a judge or politician out of a Western.

He was probably very tall and straight. He had still not lost any of his build. At one point, he lifted his Stetson to scratch his head, and Eddie saw that his hair had remained thick and heavy, its silky whiteness set off by his almost brick-coloured complexion.

'Yes . . . yes . . . I thought of that, too. Don't worry . . . Everything will be taken care of. . . . I called Los Angeles . . . I couldn't reach the one chap, but by now he's been notified. . . . I expect them both before sundown . . .'

His voice was the raucous voice of those who have been drinking and smoking for ages. That, too, was very politician-like. On the street everybody no doubt greeted him, and some would come over to shake hands, proud of their intimacy with the great Mike.

At the time of the trial several millions of his money had been seized, but he had probably not lost all of it or come out of Alcatraz without a penny to his name.

'Okay, Sid . . . He seems reasonable enough . . . I don't think so . . . I'll ask him . . .'

And, turning to Eddie:

'Do you have anything to tell Sid?'

Not like that! What could he tell him, point-blank? He could see that everything was settled beyond him.

'No. It's all right. I'll call you back afterwards.'

He handed Eddie the receiver to hang up, took a sip of whisky and kept the frosted glass in his hand.

'Did you eat?'

'Not since morning.'

'You aren't hungry?'

'No.'

'You ought to have a drink.'

Maybe. Maybe the whisky really would chase away the after-taste of the red wine he had vomited. He poured himself a glass.

'Sid is a character,' sighed Mike. 'Wasn't there some story about him and your father, in the old days?'

'My father was killed by a bullet intended for Sid Kubik.'

'That's it! I understood he was fond of you. Is this weather hot enough for you?'

'Too hot.'

'Worse than in Florida?'

'It's not the same kind of heat.'

'I've never been down there.'

He drew on his cigar. He rarely spoke two consecutive sentences. Was it because his brain had slowed down or his speech become difficult? His face was soft, flabby, his lips were slack as a baby's lips, and there were pouches under his watery eyes. These, though a very light blue, had remained lively enough to make it hard to look into very long.

'I'm sixty-eight years old son. I can claim to having lived a very full life, and I don't aim to quit yet. Well, believe it or not, I've never had the curiosity to go beyond Texas and Oklahoma in the South, Utah and Idaho in the North. I don't know New York, nor Chicago, nor Saint Louis nor New Orleans.

'Speaking of New Orleans, your brother Gino was crazy to run off like that.'

He brushed some cigar ashes off his pants.

'Hand me that bottle.'

His whisky had become too weak.

'I forget how many fellows I've known who thought they were smart and who made the same mistake. What do you think is going to happen to him? Down there, in Brazil or Argentina, or else in Venezuela, he'll try to make contacts. There are things you can't do on your own. Well, they already know how he quit and they don't want to get in Dutch with the bigshots up here.'

That was true, and as Eddie knew it. He was surprised at Gino's headlong decision. It troubled him all the more that, somehow, he vaguely understood the reason.

He would have done the same. Perhaps it was to get him to follow that his brother had come to see him in Santa Clara. And there, Gino had realized that it was useless to mention it.

Eddie felt ashamed about it. He kept trying to remember Gino's last look.

'If he insists on working alone, he'll either be pinched by the cops, or else he'll run up against some other guy who's out to defend his own racket. Then what? He'll start sinking and, before six months, he'll become a down-and-out bum they'll be fishing out of the gutter.'

'Gino doesn't drink.'

'He'll drink.'

Why didn't Mike tell him about the instructions he'd received concerning Tony?

He crushed his cigar in the ash tray, took another one out of his pocket, carefully removed the cellophane wrapper, finally clipped the end off with a nice silver instrument.

He seemed all set for a long stay in this room.

'I was saying that I never left the West.'

He talked condescendingly, as if to an adolescent. Didn't he know that, along the Gulf coast, Eddie was almost as important as Mike was around here?

'Well, what's funny about it is that all along I've met all those who count in New York or anywhere else. Sooner or later, you see, everybody passes through California.'

'You aren't hungry?'

'I never eat lunch. If you're hungry . . .'

'No.'

'Then sit down and light a cigarette. We've got lots of time.'

Briefly, the thought came to Eddie that Tony could take advantage of this respite to escape with Nora. It was a ridiculous idea. Obviously, a man like Mike had taken his precautions. His men were bound to be watching the Felici house.

It was as if the other read his thoughts.

'Your brother carries a gun?'

Eddie pretended to misunderstand.

'Gino?'

'I'm talking about the kid.'

The word hurt. His mother, too, sometimes called Tony 'the kid.'

'I don't know. He probably does.'

'It doesn't matter.'

The room was cool, thanks to the air-conditioning, and yet the heat could be felt. Outside, bearing down upon the city, the fields, the desert. The light was a thick gold. Even the cars, in the street, seemed to be laboriously going through a solid mass of overheated air.

'What time is it?'

'Half-past two.'

'I'll be getting a call.'

And, sure enough, no more than two minutes later the 'phone rang. Quite naturally Eddie took the receiver off the hook and, without a word, handed it to Mike.

'Yes . . . yes . . . okay. No. No change . . . Yes, I'm staying here . . . Right . . . Call me soon as they get here.'

He sighed, leaned further back.

'Don't be surprised if I go to sleep.'

He added:

'I've got two men downstairs.'

It wasn't a threat. Just a tip. He was giving Eddie a break, to spare him any false moves.

And still Eddie didn't dare ask any questions. He felt as if he were in disgrace and deserved it. He saw Mike gradually sink into sleep and, not without respect, took the cigar from his fingers just as it was about to drop.

Then, nearly two hours went by. And all that time he didn't budge, he remained in his chair, moving only from time to time, to reach the whisky bottle. For fear of making a noise, he didn't pour water, merely wet his lips directly from the flask.

Not once did he think of Alice, of the children, of his nice home in Santa Clara, because, no doubt, they were too far, they would have seemed unreal.

If he thought of the past at all, it was of a more distant past, of hard times in Brooklyn, his first contacts with the organization when he was so anxious to do right. All his life he had been driven by the same determination.

Up to a moment ago, when he had lied about seeing Gino, his slate was clean.

When Sid Kubik had summoned him to Miami, he'd obeyed. He had gone to White Cloud, done his level best with old man Malaks. Then to Brooklyn. And when his mother unwittingly put him on to Tony's trail, he didn't hesitate to grab a plane.

Did Mike know that? What had Kubik told him about Eddie? Mike hadn't talked tough to him. On the contrary. But he hadn't treated him like a person of importance, either. Maybe he thought that, within the hierarchy, he was on the same level as Gino or Tony.

They had a plan. Everything was settled. In this plan, he, Eddie had a part to play. Otherwise a man like Mike wouldn't have bothered to wait for him in his room and stay there.

He hadn't asked him any questions, except the one about Tony's gun. Tony was certainly carrying a gun. He always did. This morning, he had hinted at it, but Eddie couldn't recall the remark. He tried to remember. The scene was recent in time, and yet there were already gaps in his memory; he could still hear certain phrases, see the expressions on certain faces, especially Nora's, but he would have been incapable of giving a coherent account of what had happened.

Certain details assumed more importance than his brother's words, like the lock of hair on Tony's forehead, the tan of his arms and shoulders accentuated by the whiteness of the undershirt. And the little girl, leaning from the kitchen window, and sticking out her tongue.

He counted the minutes, wishing that Mike would wake, watched the 'phone, hoping it would ring. In the end he forgot to count, saw the room through a haze, then nothing, any more, but the luminous yellow piercing through his eyelids, until the moment when he leapt to his feet and saw, in front of him, the man in the grey hat who was observing him pensively.

'Did I sleep?'

'Seems so.'

'Long?'

He looked at his wrist watch and found that it was half-past five.

'And you hadn't missed any sleep last night, either!'

He knew that Eddie had gone to sleep immediately after his arrival from the airport! So his men had already been watching him then. And they surely had not lost track of him for one single second since.

'Still not hungry?'

'No.'

The bottle was empty.

'We could order something to drink.'

Eddie called for the bell-hop. The boy found it quite natural to see them in the room together, in the middle of the afternoon.

'Bring us a bottle of rye.'

The boy immediately mentioned a brand name, looking not at Eddie but at Mike La Motte, as if he knew his preferences.

'That's it, son.'

He called him back just as he reached the door.

'Cigars, too.'

He had finally taken off his hat and thrown it on the bed.

'I'm surprised they didn't get here yet. Their car must have broken down in the desert.'

Eddie didn't dare ask who they were. Besides, he preferred not knowing exactly.

'This morning I sent the sheriff up into the mountains, forty miles from here, and he won't be back before to-morrow.'

Eddie didn't ask him how he had managed that, either. Mike must have good reasons for talking to him this way. Perhaps he simply wanted to make him see that the cards were down, that Tony had nothing to hope for.

Eddie had thought of it just as he dozed off, had wondered if Nora—he could better imagine Nora than Tony doing this—wouldn't call the sheriff to ask for his protection.

'One of the two deputy sheriffs is in bed with an infection and a fever of 102°. As for the other one, Hooley, I got him appointed. If he carried out my instructions, and I'm sure he did, his 'phone is out of order and will remain so until to-morrow.'

Did Eddie really approve with the ghost of a smile?

'I'll be getting another call.'

It took a little longer, this time, but the 'phone finally rang.

'They're here? Good. You know where to take them, and see that they're not out in the street too long. Did they park the car? And change the plates? Wait a minute . . .'

The boy was coming in with the whisky and the cigars. Mike waited till he was out of the room.

'Just sit tight for the time being. Give them some food and let then play cards if they feel like it. No liquor. Is that clear?'

A pause. He was listening to the answer.

'That's it. Now, tell Gonzales I want to see him. Yes, here. In the room.'

Headquarters must be close by. Eddie wondered if they weren't in the hotel itself. Who knows if Mike didn't actually own the place?

Within less than ten minutes there was a knock on the door.

'Come in.'

A Mexican in his thirties, wearing khaki pants and a white shirt.

'Eddie Rico . . .'

The Mexican gave a slight nod.

'Gonzales. He's something like my secretary.'

Gonzales smiled.

'Sit down. What's been going on down there?'

'Marco, the owner, came back from the fields and they had a palaver that lasted nearly two hours.'

'And then?'

'He left in his car and took the kid with him. He first went to the other end of the village, to the house of a guy named Keefer, a friend of his, and left the child there.'

Mike listened, nodding his head as if it had all been planned this way.

'After that, he came to town, stopped in at Chambers', the sporting-goods store, and bought two boxes of shells.'

'What calibre?'

'For a ·22 automatic rifle.'

'He didn't go to the sheriff's office?'

'No. He went right back to Aconda. The shutters are closed, and so is the door. One thing I was forgetting.'

'What?'

'He put larger bulbs in all the lamps on the outside of the house.'

Mike shrugged.

'How is Sidney Diamond?'

'Fine. He seems sober.'

'Is Paco with him?'

'No. It's a new guy. I don't know.'

Sidney Diamond was a killer. Eddie knew about him. A young chap not yet twenty-two, who had already made a name for himself. He was manifestly the man they had sent for in Los Angeles and who shouldn't be given any liquor.

All this he perceived. It was routine. Long ago this kind of operation had been perfected like the rest, and by now they were performed according to an almost inalterable ritual. It was best to have executioners who, coming from elsewhere, were unknown in the area. Before his Los Angeles assignment, Sidney Diamond had worked in Kansas City and in Illinois.

These preparations unfolded right before Eddie's eyes, and at times he felt like opening his mouth to shout: 'But he's my brother!'

He didn't. He'd been in a daze ever since entering this room. He suspected that Mike deliberately settled everything in his presence, simply, calmly, as if it were the most natural thing in the world.

Wasn't he a member of the organization?

This was just enforcing the rules.

They had fooled him. Or rather, with him too, they had been enforcing the rules. They had used him to track down Tony. He had never had any illusions, had done his best to find his brother, and played the game.

Deep down, he'd always known that Tony wouldn't accept to leave, and that, anyway, they wouldn't let him go.

Gino, too, had known. And Gino had skipped across the border. That was still what surprised Eddie most, and gave him a feeling of guilt.

'What time?' asked Gonzales.

'What time do people go to bed in that neighbourhood?'

'Very early. They get up with the sun.'

'Let's say eleven?'

'All right.'

'Drop the men off on the road, about two hundred feet from the house. Use another car, of course.'

'Check.'

'Afterwards, you follow. Did you pick the spot?'

'It's all set.'

'Eleven o'clock, then.'

'Okay.'

'Go back with them now. Don't forget that Sidney Diamond must not touch any liquor. On the way out, order us some dinner. Cold cuts for me, salad and fruit.'

He turned to Eddie questioningly.

'The same. Anything.'

By nine o'clock, Eddie still didn't know what role he'd be given and he hadn't had the courage to ask. Mike had sent for the local paper and had read it while he smoked his cigar. He drank a lot, his face getting increasingly red, his eyes blurred, but he lost none of his lucidity.

At one point he looked up from his paper.

'He loves his wife, eh?'

'Yes.'

'What's she like?'

'She seems to love him, too.'

'I wasn't asking about that. Is she pretty?'

'Yes.'

'How soon will she have the baby?'

'In three or four months. I don't know exactly.'

The street lights had been on for quite a while. The muffled sound of a juke box in a bar, of voices drifting up occasionally, could be heard through the closed windows.

'What time is it?'

'Ten o'clock.'

Then it was a quarter-past ten, half-past, and Eddie was making every effort not to start screaming.

'Let me know when it is exactly ten minutes to eleven.'

What he feared most was that they force him to go there. If Gino hadn't sailed away, would Phil have sent him?

'What time is it, son?'

'Twenty off.'

'The men have left.'

So Eddie wasn't going. He didn't understand any more. Surely they were keeping him for something important.

'You better have a drink.'

'I've already had too much.'

'Take one just the same.'

He had no more will of his own. He obeyed, wondering if he wasn't going to vomit again.

'Do you know the Felicis' 'phone number?'

'It's in the 'phone book. I found it this morning.'

'Look it up.'

He looked it up, with the impression of seeing himself come and go as in a dream. The whole universe had no substance any more. There were no Alice, no Christine, no Amelia, no Babe, nothing left but a sort of tunnel whose end he could not see and along which he groped his way.

'Time?'

'One more minute.'

'Call the number.'

'What do I say?'

'You tell Tony to go and meet the boys on the road. Alone. Unarmed. He'll see the parked car.'

His chest was so tight that he felt he'd never breathe again.

'If he won't?' he managed to say.

'You told me he loves his wife.'

'Yes.'

'Tell him so. He'll understand.'

Mike continued to sit calmly in his armchair, cigar in one hand, paper in the other, looking more than ever like a movie judge.

Eddie scarcely realized that he had picked up the receiver, stammered the Felicis' number.

A voice he didn't recognize answered, at the other end:

'This is 1662. Who is this?'

And Eddie heard himself speak, his eyes still riveted on the man in white.

'I've got something important to tell Tony. This is his brother.'

There was a pause. Marco Felici must have hesitated. From the sounds Eddie suspected that it was Tony, who, guessing what was happening, had taken the receiver away from him.

'I'm listening,' Tony said curtly.

Eddie hadn't prepared anything. His mind did not participate in what was going on.

'They're waiting for you.'

'Where?'

'Two hundred feet down the road. A parked car.'

He needed to say but very little more.

'I suppose that, if I don't go, they'll get Nora?'

Silence.

'Answer me.'

'Yes.'

'All right.'

'You're going?'

Silence again. Mike, eyes fixed upon him, sat motionless. Eddie repeated:

'You're going?'

'Don't worry.'

Another briefer pause.

'Good-bye!'

He wanted to say something too, and he didn't know what. Then he looked at his hand clutching the receiver, now become mute.

Drawing on his cigar, Mike murmured with a sigh of satisfaction:

'I knew.'

Chapter Nine

That was all there was for Eddie. They didn't ask him anything else. They never asked him anything difficult again.

That night came to an end as all nights, since the creation of the world, do end at sunrise. He didn't see the sun rise in California, but from very high up in the skies, above the Arizona desert, in the place to which he had been driven at three o'clock in the morning. And, like Bob had done in Tucson, a pint bottle was slipped into his pocket.

He didn't touch it. Sidney Diamond and his pal were probably driving through the suburbs of Los Angeles at the time his plane made its first stop.

Somewhere along the line, Eddie took the wrong plane. He ended up, around two o'clock in the afternoon, in a third-rate airport above which a thunderstorm broke and where he had to wait until evening. Only from Mississippi, the next day, did he call Santa Clara.

'It's you?'

He was listening to Alice's voice without its rousing anything in him.

'Yes. Everything all right over there?'

The words came of their own accord, the usual words, without his having to think.

'Yes. How about you?'

'The children are well?'

'I kept Amelia home to-day. The doctor thinks she's getting the measles. We'll know by to-night, and if it is, Christine won't be able to go to school either.'

'Angelo didn't call?'

'No. I drove past the store this morning. Everything seems all right. I noticed a new clerk.'

'I know.'

'There was a call from the Flamingo. I told them you'd be back soon. Was that all right?'

'Yes.'

'I can hardly hear you. As if you were far away.'

'Yes.'

Had he said yes? It wasn't the distance between Florida and Mississippi he'd been thinking of. Besides, he wasn't thinking.

'When will you be back?'

'I don't know. I think there's a plane shortly.'

'Didn't you check the timetable?'

'Not yet.'

'You're not sick, are you?'

'No.'

'Tired?'

'Yes.'

'You're not hiding anything from me?'

'I'm tired.'

'Why don't you take a good night's rest before you catch another plane?'

'Maybe I will.'

He did. He could find only a small room without air-conditioning, because there was some sort of convention in town. In the corridors people went around with badges, arm bands, and little cardboard plaques with their names on them dangling from their buttonholes.

The hotel was noisy, but, just as he had in El Centro, he sank into a troubled sleep, woke up two or three times, only to be disgusted by the odour of his own sweat, which seemed somehow unhealthy.

His liver, no doubt. He'd been drinking, back there. He wasn't used to it any more. He'd have to see Bill Spangler, his doctor, as soon as he got back to Santa Clara.

Twice, out in the sun, especially on the airfield, he had seen black spots dancing in front of his eyes. It was probably a symptom.

Awakening in an unknown room, he suddenly felt like crying. Never had he been so tired, tired to death, tired enough, if he'd been out in the street, to lie down anywhere, on the sidewalk, people walking all over him.

He would have needed a little pity, someone to speak soothing words and rest a cool hand on his forehead. There was no one to do that. There never would be. Alice, to-morrow or the next day, whenever he'd have the courage to go home, would tenderly advise him to rest.

For she was tender. But she didn't know him. He never told her anything. She thought that he was strong, that he never needed anybody.

He hadn't understood the meaning of Gino's visit. He still wasn't sure he did understand, but he dimly felt that his brother had come to him to make some sort of sign.

Why hadn't he been more explicit? Didn't he trust him?

His two brothers had never trusted him. If he'd been able to explain to them . . .

But how? Explain what?

He took a shower and noticed that he was getting fat. He was beginning to have budding little breasts, like a twelve-year-old girl.

He shaved. As on the last morning in Santa Clara, he nicked his mole. Fortunately he always brought a styptic pencil.

He had to wait over an hour for the lightweight suit he'd sent out to be pressed. He threw the unopened bottle of whisky into the waste-paper basket.

It mattered little if others did not understand. Sid Kubik knew that he had done what he must do. When Mike had called him up, at half-past twelve, to say that it was all over, Sid had personally come to the 'phone and said, word for word:

'*Tell Eddie it's all right.*'

Mike hadn't made that up.

'*Tell Eddie it's all right.*'

If Phil was in the room, he'd surely had that nasty curl to his lips.

'*Tell Eddie . . .*'

He intentionally did not tell his wife at what time he'd arrive. He took a cab and had the chauffeur drive him straight from the airport to the store.

Angelo came down two steps to greet him.

'How are you, boss?'

'Okay, Angelo.'

Things were still dull, without colour, without taste, almost without life.

Perhaps it would come back? Already the word Angelo used was doing him good:

'Boss . . .'

He had worked hard, so very hard, since the store in Brooklyn, to get there!

Shadow Rock Farm
Lakeville, Connecticut
22 July 1952

Maigret and the Burglar's Wife

Maigret and the Burglar's Wife

Translated from the French by
J. Maclaren-Ross

Chapter One

The appointment-slip, duly filled in, and handed to Maigret by the office porter, bore the following text:

> Ernestine Micou, alias 'Lofty' (now Jussiaume), who, when you arrested her seventeen years ago in the Rue de la Lune, stripped herself naked to take the mike out of you, requests the favour of an interview on a matter of most urgent and important business.

Maigret glanced quickly, out of the corner of his eye, at old Joseph, to see whether he'd read the message, but the white-haired 'boy' didn't move a muscle. He was probably the only one in the whole of Police Headquarters that morning who wasn't in shirt-sleeves, and for the first time in so many years the Chief-Inspector wondered by what official vagary this almost venerable man was compelled to wear a heavy chain with a huge seal round his neck.

It was the sort of day when one's apt to indulge in pointless speculation. The heat-wave may have been to blame. Perhaps the holiday spirit also prevented one from taking things very seriously. The windows were wide open and the muted roar of Paris throbbed in the room where, before Joseph came in, Maigret had been engaged in following the flight of a wasp that was going round in circles and bumping against the ceiling at invariably the same spot. At least half the plain-clothes section was at the seaside or in the country. Lucas went about wearing a straw hat which, on him, assumed the aspect of a native grass hat or a lampshade. The Chief himself had left the day before, as he did year after year, for the Pyrenees.

'Drunk?' Maigret asked the porter.

'Don't think so, sir.'

For a certain type of woman, having taken a drop too much, often feels impelled to make disclosures to the police.

'Jumpy?'

'She asked me if it'd take long, and I said I didn't even know if you'd see her. She sat herself down in a corner of the waiting-room and started to read the paper.'

Maigret couldn't recall the names Micou of Jussiaume, or even the nickname Lofty, but he retained a vivid memory of the Rue de la Lune, on a day as hot as this, when the asphalt feels elastic under one's tread and fills Paris with a smell of tar.

It was down by the Porte Saint-Denis, a little street of shady hotels and small sweet-shops. He wasn't a Chief-Inspector in those days. The women wore low-waisted frocks and had shingled hair. To find out about this girl, he'd had to go into two or three of the neighbouring bars, and it so happened he'd been drinking Pernod. He could almost conjure up the smell of it, just as he could conjure up the smell of armpits and feet pervading the small hotel. The room was on the third or fourth floor. Mistaking the door, he'd first of all found himself face to face with a negro who, sitting on his bed, was playing the accordion; one of the band in a *bal musette*, probably. Quite unperturbed, the negro had indicated the room next door with a jerk of his chin.

'Come in!'

A husky voice. The voice of one who drank or smoked too much. And, standing by a window that gave onto the courtyard, a tall girl in a sky-blue wrap, cooking herself a chop on a spirit lamp.

She was as tall as Maigret, maybe taller. She'd looked him up and down without emotion; she'd said straight away:

'You're a copper?'

He'd found the pocket-book and the bank-notes on top of the wardrobe, and she hadn't batted an eyelid.

'It was my girl friend who did the job.'

'What girl friend?'

'Don't know her name. Lulu, they call her.'

'Where is she?'

'Find out. That's your business.'

'Get dressed and come with me.'

It was only a case of petty theft, but Headquarters took a rather serious view of it, not so much because of the sum involved, though this was a pretty large one, as because it concerned a big cattle-dealer from the Charentes, who had already started to stir up his local Deputy.

'It'd take more than you to stop me eating my chop!'

The tiny room contained only one chair. He'd remained standing while the girl ate, taking her time; he might not have been there for all the attention she paid to him.

She must have been rising twenty at the time. She was pale, with colourless eyes, a long bony face. He could see her now, picking her teeth with a matchstick, then pouring boiling water into the coffee-pot.

'I asked you to get dressed.'

He was hot. The smell of the hotel turned his stomach. Had she sensed that he was not at his ease?

Calmly she'd taken off her wrap, her shift and pants, and, stark naked, had gone and lain down on the unmade bed, lighting a cigarette.

'I'm waiting!' he'd told her impatiently, looking away with an effort.

'So am I.'

'I've a warrant for your arrest.'

'Well, arrest me then!'

'Get dressed and come along.'

'I'm all right like this.'

The whole thing was ludicrous. She was cool, quite passive, a little glint of irony showing in her colourless eyes.

'You say I'm under arrest. *I* don't mind. But you needn't ask me to give you a hand as well. I'm in my own place. It's hot, and I've a right to take my clothes off. Now, if you insist on my coming along with you just as I am, I'm not complaining.'

At least a dozen times he'd told her:

'Get your things on!'

And, perhaps because of her pallid flesh, perhaps because of the surrounding squalor, it seemed to him that he'd never seen a woman so naked as that. To no avail he'd thrown her clothes on the bed, had threatened her, then tried persuasiveness.

In the end he'd gone down and fetched two policemen, and the scene had become farcical. They'd had to wrap the girl forcibly in a blanket and carry her, like a packing-case, down the narrow staircase, while all the doors opened as they went by.

He'd never seen her since. He'd never heard her mentioned.

'Send her in!' he sighed.

He knew her at once. She didn't seem to have changed. He recognized her long pale face, the washed-out eyes, the big over-made-up mouth that looked like a raw wound. He recognized also, in her glance, the quiet irony of those who've seen so much that nothing's any longer important in their eyes.

She was simply dressed, with a light green straw hat, and she'd put on gloves.

'Still got it in for me?'

He drew on his pipe without answering.

'Can I have a seat? I heard you'd been promoted and in fact that's why I never ran into you again. Is it all right if I smoke?'

She took a cigarette from her bag and lit up.

'I want to tell you right away, with no hard feelings, that I was telling the truth that time. I got a year inside that I didn't deserve. There was a girl called Lulu all right, whom you didn't take the trouble to find. The two of us were together when we ran across that fat steamer. He picked us both up, but when he'd taken a good look at me, he told me to buzz off because he couldn't stand 'em skinny. I was outside in the passage when Lulu slipped me the pocket-book an hour after so's I could ditch it.'

'What became of her?'

'Five years ago she'd a little restaurant down South. I just wanted to show you everyone sometimes makes mistakes.'

'Is that why you came?'

'No. I wanted to talk to you about Alfred. If he knew I was here, he'd take me for a proper mug. I could've gone to Sergeant Boissier, who knows all about him.'

'Who's Alfred?'

'My husband. Lawfully wedded, too, before the mayor *and* the vicar, because he still goes to church. Sergeant Boissier pinched him two or three times, and one of those times he got Alfred five years in Fresnes.'

Her voice was almost harsh.

'The name Jussiaume doesn't mean much to you, perhaps, but when I tell you what they call him, you'll know who he is right away. There's been a lot about him in the papers. He's Sad Freddie.'

'Safe-breaking?'

'Yes.'

'You've had a row?'

'No. It's not what you'd think I've come for. I'm not that sort. So you see who Fred is now?'

Maigret had never set eyes on him, or, rather, only in the corridors, when the cracksman was waiting to be interrogated by Boissier. He called to mind vaguely a puny little man with anxious eyes, whose clothes seemed too big for his scrawny body.

'Of course, we don't look at him the same way,' she said. 'Poor blighter. There's more to him than you think. I've lived with him close on twelve years; I'm only starting to get to know him.'

'Where is he?'

'I'm coming to that, don't worry. I don't know where he is, but he's got in a proper jam without its being any of his fault, and that's why I'm here. Only you've simply got to trust me, and I know that's asking a lot.'

He was watching her with interest, because she spoke with appealing simplicity. She wasn't putting on airs, wasn't trying to impress him. If she took some time in coming to the point, it was because what she had to tell was genuinely complicated.

There was still a barrier between them, nevertheless, and it was this barrier that she was trying hard to break down, so that he wouldn't get a wrong idea of things.

About Sad Freddie, with whom he'd never had any personal dealings, Maigret knew little more than he'd heard at Headquarters. The man was a sort of celebrity, and the newspapers had tried their best to boost him into a romantic figure.

He'd been employed for years by the firm of Planchart, the safe-makers, and had become one of their most skilled workers. He was, even at that time, a sad, retiring youth, in poor health, throwing epileptic fits periodically.

Boissier would probably be able to tell Maigret how he had come to give up his job at Planchart's.

Whatever the cause, he had turned from installing safes to cracking them.

'When you first met him, had he still got a steady job?'

'Not likely. It wasn't me that sent him off the straight and narrow, in case that's what you've got in mind. He was doing odd jobs, sometimes he'd hire himself out to a locksmith, but it wasn't long before I saw what he was really up to.'

'You don't think you'd do better to see Boissier?'

'Housebreaking's his line, isn't it? But you deal with murder.'

'Has Alfred killed anybody?'

'Look, Chief-Inspector, I think we'll get along faster if you just let me talk. Alfred may be anything you'd like to call him, but he wouldn't murder for all the money in the world. May seem soppy to say so about a bloke like him, but he's sensitive, see? Why, he'd pipe his eye for the least little thing. I ought to know. Anyone else would say he was soft. But maybe it's because he's like that, that I fell in love with him.'

And she looked at him quietly. She'd uttered the word 'love' without particular emphasis, but with a sort of pride all the same.

'If one knew what was going on in his head, one wouldn't half get a surprise. Not that it matters. Far's you're concerned, he's just a thief. He got himself pinched once and did five years inside. I never missed going to see him a single visiting-day, and all that time I'd to go back on my old beat, at the risk of getting in trouble, not having a proper card and those being the days when you still had to have one.

'He always hopes he'll pull off a big job and then we can go and live in the country. He's always dreamed of it ever since he was a nipper.'

'Where do you live?'

'On the Quai de Jemmapes, just opposite the Saint-Martin Lock. Know where I mean? We've two rooms above a café painted green, and it's very handy because of the 'phone.'

'Is Alfred there now?'

'No. I already told you I don't know where he is, and believe me I don't. He did a job, not last night, but the night before.'

'And he's cleared out?'

'Hang on, will you, Inspector! You'll see later on that everything I tell you's got its point. You know people that take tickets in the National Sweep at every draw, don't you? There are some of them that go without eating to buy them, because they reckon in a day or two they'll be in the money at last. Well, that's the way it is with Alfred. There're dozens of safes in Paris that he put in himself, and that he knows like the back of his hand. Usually, when you buy a safe, it's to put money or jewels away in.'

'He hopes to strike lucky one day?'

'You got it.'

She shrugged, as though speaking of a child's harmless craze. Then she added:

'He's just unlucky. Most times it's title -deeds it's impossible to sell or else business contracts he gets hold of. Only once there was real big dough, that he could've lived on quietly for the rest of his days, and that time Boissier pinched him.'

'Were you with him? Do you keep the look-out?'

'No. He never liked me to. At the start, he used to tell me where he was going to be on the job, and I'd fix it so I was nearby. When he spotted that, he gave up telling me anything.'

'For fear you'd get pulled in?'

'Maybe. Or it may have been because he's superstitious. See, even when we're living together, he's all alone really, and sometimes he doesn't say a word for two whole days. When I see him go out at night on his bicycle, I know what's up.'

Maigret remembered this characteristic. Some of the newspapers had dubbed Alfred Jussiaume the burglar-on-a-bike.

'That's another of his notions. He reckons that nobody, at night, is going to notice a man on a bike, specially if he's got a bag of tools slung over his shoulder. They'd take him for a bloke on his way to work. I'm talking to you like I would to a friend, see?'

Maigret wondered again why she had really come to his office and, as she took out another cigarette, he held a lighted match for her.

'We're Thursday today. On Tuesday night Alfred went out on a job.'

'Did he tell you so?'

'He'd been going out for several nights at the same time, and that's always a sign. Before breaking into a house or an office, he sometimes spends a week on the watch to get to know the people's habits.'

'And to make sure there'll be no one about?'

'No. That doesn't signify to him. I even think he'd rather work where there was somebody than in an empty house. He's a bloke that can get about without making a sound. Why, hundreds of times he's slipped into bed beside me at night and I never so much as knew he'd come home.'

'D'you know where he worked the night before last?'

'All I know, it was at Neuilly. And then I only found it out by chance. The day before, when I came in, he told me the police had asked to see his papers,

and must've taken him for a dirty old man because they stopped him in the
Bois de Boulogne, just by the place where women go and tidy up.

'"Where was it?" I asked him.

'"Behind the Zoo. I was coming back from Neuilly."

'Then, night before last, he took his bag of tools, and I knew he'd gone to
work.'

'He hadn't been drinking?'

'Never touches a drop, doesn't smoke. He'd never be able to take it. He
lives in terror of his fits, and he's that ashamed when it happens in the middle
of the street, with masses of people who crowd round and feel sorry for him.
He said to me before he set out:

'"I reckon this time we're really going down to live in the country."'

Maigret had begun to take notes which he was surrounding automatically
with arabesques.

'What time did he leave the Quai de Jemmapes?'

'About eleven, like on the other nights.'

'Then he must have got to Neuilly round about midnight.'

'Maybe. He never rode fast, but then, at that time, there'd be no traffic.'

'When did you see him again?'

'I haven't seen him again.'

'So you think something may have happened to him?'

'He rang me up.'

'When?'

'Five in the morning. I wasn't asleep. I was worried. If he's always scared
he'll have a fit in the street, I'm always scared it might happen while he's
working, you see? I heard the 'phone ringing downstairs in the café. Our
room's right up above. The owners didn't get up. I guessed it was for me,
and I went down. I knew right away from his voice there'd been a hitch. He
spoke very low.

'"That you?"

'"Yes!"

'"Are you alone?"

'"Yes. Where are you?"

'"In a little café up by the Gare du Nord. Look, Tine," (he always calls me
Tine), "I've simply got to make myself scarce for a bit."

'"Somebody see you?"

'"It's not that. I don't know. A bloke saw me, yes, but I'm not sure it was a
policeman."

'"Got any money?"

'"No. It happened before I'd finished."

'"What happened?"

'"I was busy on the lock when my torch lit up a face in the corner of the
room. I thought somebody'd come in silently and was watching me. Then I
saw the eyes were dead."'

She watched Maigret.

'I'm sure he wasn't lying. If he'd killed anyone, he'd have told me. And
I'm not going telling you any stories. I could tell he was near fainting at the
other end. He's so scared of death. . . .'

'Who was it?'

'I don't know. He didn't make it very clear. He was going to hang up the
whole time. He was scared someone'd hear him. He told me he was taking a

train in a quarter of an hour. . . .'

'To Belgium?'

'Probably, as he was near the Gare du Nord. I looked up a time-table. There's a train at five forty-five.'

'You've no more idea what café he was 'phoning from?'

'I went on a scout round the district yesterday and asked some questions, but no good. They must've taken me for a jealous wife, and they weren't giving anything away.'

'So all he really told you was that there was a dead body in the room where he was working?'

'I got him to tell me a bit more. He said it was a woman, that her chest was all covered in blood, and that she was holding a telephone receiver in her hand.'

'Is that all?'

'No. Just as he was going to do a bunk—and I can imagine the state he was in!—a car drew up in front of the gate. . . .'

'You're sure he said the gate?'

'Yes. A wrought-iron gate. I remember it struck me particularly. Somebody got out and came towards the door. As the man went into the passage, Alfred got out of the house by the window.'

'And his tools?'

'He left them behind. He'd cut out a window-pane to get in. That I'm sure of, because he always does. I believe he'd do it even if the door was open, he's sort of faddy that way, or maybe superstitious.'

'So nobody saw him?'

'Yes. As he was going through the garden. . . .'

'He mentioned a garden as well?'

'I didn't make it up. As I say, just when he was going through the garden someone looked out of the window and shone a torch on him; maybe Alfred's own, which he hadn't taken with him. He jumped on his bike, went off without looking round, rode down as far as the Seine, I don't know exactly where, and threw the bike in, for fear they'd recognize him by it. He didn't dare come back home. He got to the Gare du Nord on foot and 'phoned me, begging me not to say a word. I pleaded with him not to clear off. I tried to reason with him. He finished up promising to write me *poste restante* saying where he'd be so I could go and join him.'

'He hasn't written yet?'

'There hasn't been time for a letter to get here. I went to the post office this morning. I've had twenty-four hours to think things over. I bought all the papers, thinking they'd surely say something about a murdered woman.'

Maigret picked up the telephone and called the police-station at Neuilly.

'Hello! Headquarters here. Any murder to report during the last twenty-four hours?'

'One moment, sir. I'll put you through to the desk. I'm only the duty constable.'

Maigret persisted for some time.

'No corpse found on the roads? No night calls? No bodies fished up from the Seine?'

'Absolutely nothing, Monsieur Maigret.'

'Nobody reported a shot?'

'Nobody.'

Lofty waited patiently, like someone making a social call, both hands clasped upon her bag.

'You realize why I came to you?'

'I think so.'

'First, I reckoned the police had maybe seen Alfred, and, in that case, his bike alone would have given him away. Then there were the tools he left behind. Now he's bolted over the frontier, no one'll ever believe his story. And he's no safer in Belgium or Holland than in Paris. I'd sooner see him in jail for attempted burglary, even if it meant five years all over again, than see him had up for murder.'

'The trouble,' Maigret retorted, 'is that there's no body.'

'You think he made it up or that I'm making it up?'

He didn't answer.

'It'll be easy for you to find the house he was working in that night. Maybe I shouldn't tell you this, but I'm sure you'll think of it yourself. The safe's bound to be one of those he put in at some time. Planchart's must keep a list of their customers. There can't be that many in Neuilly who bought a safe at least seventeen years back.'

'Apart from you, did Alfred have any girl-friends?'

'Ah! I guessed that was coming. I'm not jealous and, even if I was, I wouldn't come to you with a pack of lies to get my own back, if that's what you've got in mind. He hasn't a girl-friend because he doesn't want one, poor blighter. If he wanted to I'm the one who'd fix him up with as much as he liked.'

'Why?'

'Because life's not so much cop for him, as it is.'

'Have you any money?'

'No.'

'What are you going to do?'

'I'll get by, you know that all right. I only came here because I want it proved that Freddie didn't kill anyone.'

'If he wrote to you, would you show me his letter?'

'You'll read it before I do. Now that you know he's going to write me *poste restante*, you'll have every post office in Paris watched. You forget that I know the racket.'

She had risen to her feet, very tall; she looked him over as he sat at his desk, from top to toe.

'If all the tales they tell about you are true, there's an even chance that you'll believe me.'

'Why?'

'Because otherwise you'd be a mug. And you're not one. Are you going to ring Planchart's?'

'Yes.'

'You'll keep me posted?'

He looked at her without replying, and realized that he couldn't restrain himself from smiling good-humouredly.

'Please yourself then,' she sighed. 'I could help you; you may know an awful lot, but there're things people like us understand better than you do.'

Her 'us' obviously stood for a whole world, the one that Lofty lived in, the world on the other side of the barrier.

'If Sergeant Boissier's not on holiday, I'm sure he'll bear me out in what

I told you about Alfred.'

'He's not on leave. He's going tomorrow.'

She opened her bag, took from it a bit of paper.

'I'll leave you the 'phone number of the café underneath where we live. If by some fluke you need to come and see me, don't be scared that I'll start undressing. Nowadays, if it's left to me, I keep my clothes on!'

There was a touch of bitterness in her tone, but not much. A second later she was poking fun at herself:

'Much better for all concerned!'

It wasn't until he closed the door behind her that Maigret realized he had shaken, quite as a matter of course, the hand she'd held out to him. The wasp still buzzed in circles at ceiling level, as though seeking a way out, without thinking of the wide open windows. Madame Maigret had announced in the morning that she'd be coming round to the flower market and had asked him, if he were free about noon, to go and meet her there. It was noon now. He paused irresolute, leant out of the window from which he could see the splashes of vivid colour beyond the embankment of the quay.

Then he picked up the telephone with a sigh.

'Ask Boissier to drop in and see me.'

Seventeen years had slipped by since the absurd incident in the Rue de la Lune, and Maigret was now an important official in charge of the Homicide Branch. A funny notion came into his head, an almost childish craving. He picked up the telephone once more.

'The *Brasserie Dauphine*, please.'

As the door opened to admit Boissier, he was saying:

'Send me up a Pernod, will you?'

And, looking at the Sergeant, who had large half-moons of sweat on his shirt underneath the arms, he changed it to:

'Make it two! Two Pernods, thank you.'

The blue-black moustache of Boissier, who came from Provence, twitched with pleasure, and he went over to sit on the window-sill, mopping his forehead.

Chapter Two

After swallowing a mouthful of Pernod, Maigret had to come to the point:

'Tell me, Boissier, old man, what d'you know about Alfred Jussiaume?'

'Sad Freddie?'

'Yes.'

And immediately the Sergeant's brow had darkened, he'd shot Maigret a worried glance, had asked in a voice no longer the same, forgetting to take a sip of his favourite drink:

'Has he done a job?'

It was always like this with the Sergeant, Maigret knew. He also knew why and, by using the utmost tact, had become the only Chief-Inspector to find favour in Boissier's eyes.

The latter, by rights, ought to have been one himself, and would have been a long time ago, had an absolute inability to spell and the handwriting of a first-form schoolboy not prevented his passing the simplest examinations.

For once, however, the administrative staff had not made a bloomer. They had appointed at the head of his branch Chief-Inspector Peuchet, an old has-been, always half-asleep and, save for drawing up the reports, it was Boissier who got through all the work and governed his colleagues.

That department wasn't concerned with homicide, as Maigret's was. It wasn't concerned with amateurs either, shop-assistants who run off one fine day with the till, or any tripe of that sort.

The customers Boissier and his men dealt with were professional thieves of every kind, from the jewel robbers who put up at the big hotels in the Champs-Élysées, to the bank-smashers and hustlers, who hid out mostly, like Jussiaume, in seedy neighbourhoods.

Because of this, they had an outlook quite different from that of the Special Division. In Boissier's line, they were all craftsmen, on both sides. The battle was a battle between experts. It wasn't so much a question of psychology, as of knowing, from A to Z, the little quirks and eccentricities of everyone.

It was not unusual to see the Sergeant sitting quietly outside a café with a cat-burglar, and Maigret, for one, would have found it hard to hold a conversation of this sort with a murderer:

'Here, Julot, it's a long time since you did a job of work.'

'That's right, Sergeant.'

'When was the last time I pulled you in?'

'Must be going on six months, now.'

'Funds getting low, eh? I'll bet you're cooking something up.'

The idea that Sad Freddie might have done a bust without his knowledge put Boissier's back up.

'I don't know if he's really been on the job lately, but Lofty has just left my office.'

That was enough to reassure the Sergeant.

'She doesn't know a thing.' he stated. 'Alfred's not the type to go blabbing his business to a woman, not even his own wife.'

The picture of Jussiaume that Boissier now set himself to draw was not unlike that previously outlined by Ernestine, even though he, the Sergeant, tended rather to emphasize the professional angle.

'I get browned off with pinching a bloke like that and sending him to the nick. Last time, when they dished him out five years, I damn nearly gave his lawyer a piece of my mind for not knowing how to go about his job. He's wanting, that lawyer is!'

It was hard to define precisely what Boissier meant by 'wanting,' but the point was plain enough.

'There's not another in Paris like Alfred for breaking into a house full of people without a sound and going to work there without even waking the cat. Technically, he's an artist. What's more, he doesn't need anyone to tip him off, keep a look-out and all that palaver. He works on his own, without ever getting jumpy. He doesn't drink, doesn't talk, doesn't go acting tough round the bars. With his talents he ought to have enough dough to choke himself with. He knows just where to find hundreds of safes that he put in himself, and exactly how they work, and you'd think he'd only have to go and help himself. Instead, every time he has a go, he comes a cropper or else gets a spell inside.'

Perhaps Boissier only spoke thus because he saw a parallel between Sad Freddie's career and his own, except that he himself enjoyed a constitution that could withstand any number of *apéritifs* imbibed on café terraces and nights spent standing to in all kinds of weather.

'The joke is that, if they put him away for ten years or twenty years, he'd start all over again directly he came out, even supposing he was seventy and on crutches by then. He's got it into his head that he only needs one lucky break, just one, and that he's earned it by this time.'

'He's had a nasty knock,' Maigret explained. 'It seems that he was just getting a safe open, somewhere at Neuilly, when he spotted a dead body in the room.'

'What'd I tell you? That could only happen to him. Then he cleared off? What'd he do with the bike?'

'In the Seine.'

'He's in Belgium?'

'I dare say.'

'I'll ring through to Brussels, unless you don't want him picked up?'

'I want him picked up most decidedly.'

'D'you know where this took place?'

'I know that it was at Neuilly, and that the house has a garden with a wrought-iron gate in front.'

'That'll be easy. Be back right away.'

Maigret had the grace to order, in his absence, two more Pernods from the *Brasserie Dauphine*. It brought back to him not only a whiff of the Rue de la Lune period, but a whiff of the South of France, particularly of a little dive in Cannes, where he'd once been on a case and, all of a sudden, the whole business was lifted out of the general rut, took on almost the aspect of a holiday task.

He hadn't definitely promised Madame Maigret to meet her in the flower market, and she knew that she ought never to wait for him. Boissier returned with a file, from which he produced, first of all, the official photographs of Alfred Jussiaume.

'That's what he looks like!'

An ascetic face, really, rather than that of a guttersnipe. The skin was stretched tight across the bones, the nostrils were long and pinched, and the stare had an almost mystical intensity. Even in these harshly lit photographs, full face and side view, collarless, with a protruding Adam's apple, the man's immense loneliness made itself felt, and his sadness that was still in no way aggressive.

Born to be fair game, it had been natural for him to be hunted.

'Would you like me to read you his record?'

'It's not necessary today. I'd rather go over the file with an open mind. What I'd like to have is the list.'

Bossier was pleased by this last sentence. Maigret knew that he would be, as he said it, for he intended it as a tribute to the Sergeant.

'You knew I'd have it?'

'I was certain you would.'

For, in point of fact, Boissier really did know his job. This list in question was that, drawn from the books of Messrs Planchart, of the safes installed in

Alfred Jussiaume's time.

'Wait till I look up Neuilly. You're sure it's at Neuilly?'

'I've Ernestine's word for it.'

'You know, she wasn't really so dumb to come and look you up. But why you?'

'Because I arrested her, sixteen or seventeen years ago, and because she played me quite a dirty trick.'

This didn't surprise Boissier, it was all in the game. They both knew where they stood. From the glasses, the pale-coloured Pernod could already be smelt all over the office, inciting the wasp to a kind of frenzy.

'A bank . . . it's certainly not that. . . . Freddie never took to banks, because he's windy of the burglar-alarms. . . . A petrol company that's been out of business for ten years. . . . A scent manufacturer . . . he went bankrupt a year ago.'

Boissier's finger came to a stop finally on a name, on an address.

'Guillaume Serre, dentist, 43b, Rue de la Ferme, Neuilly. You know it? It's just past the Zoo, a street parallel with the Boulevard Richard-Wallace.'

'I know.'

They looked at each other for a moment.

'Busy?' asked Maigret.

And in so doing he was again pandering deliberately to Boissier's self-esteem.

'I was classifying some files. I'm off to Brittany tomorrow.'

'Shall we go?'

'I'll get my coat and hat. Shall I 'phone Brussels first?'

'Yes. And Holland as well.'

'Right you are.'

They went there by bus, standing on the outside platform. Then, in the Rue de la Ferme, quiet and countrified, they found a little cafè-restaurant where there were four tables on the terrace between green potted plants, and sat down there for lunch.

There were only three bricklayers in white smocks inside, drinking red wine with their meal. Flies circled round Maigret and Boissier. Farther along, on the other side of the road, they could see a black wrought-iron gate that should correspond with No. 43b.

They weren't in any hurry. If there'd really been a dead body in the house, the murderer had had over twenty-four hours in which to get rid of it.

A waitress in a black dress and a white apron looked after them, but the proprietor came over to greet them.

'Nice weather, gentlemen.'

'Nice weather. Would you, by any chance, know of a dentist anywhere about here?'

A sidelong nod.

'There's one opposite, over there, but I don't know what he's like. My missus prefers to go to one in the Boulevard Sebastopol. This one'd be expensive. I'd say. He hasn't all that many patients.'

'D'you know him?'

'A wee bit.'

The proprietor paused, looking them over for a while, particularly Boissier.

'You'd be police-officers, eh?'

Maigret thought it better to say yes.

'Has he done anything?'

'We're just making a few enquiries. What does he look like?'

'Taller and bigger than you and me,' he said, looking this time at the Chief-Inspector. 'I weigh fifteen stone ten, and he must go all of sixteen.'

'How old?'

'Fifty? Round about, anyway. Not too well turned out, which is odd, him being a dentist. Seedy looking, like what old bachelors get.'

'He isn't married?'

'Wait a bit. . . . Matter of fact, if I remember rightly, he did get married, it'd be about two years ago. . . . There's an old woman living in the house, too—his mother, I suppose—who does the shopping every morning. . . .'

'No maid?'

'Only a charwoman. Mind you, I wouldn't be sure. I only know him because he comes in here now and then for a foxy drink.'

'Foxy?'

'In a manner of speaking. People like him don't come to places like this, as a rule. And when he does, he always takes a quick look round at his house, as if to make sure he can't be seen. And he looks sheepish, coming up to the counter.

'"Glass of red wine!" he'll say.

'Never takes anything else. I know right away not to put the bottle back on the shelf, because he's bound to have another. He drinks 'em at a gulp, wipes his mouth, and he's got the change all ready in his hand.'

'Does he ever get drunk?'

'Never. Just the two glasses. As he goes out, I see him slip a cachou or a clove into his mouth, so that his breath won't smell of wine.'

'What's his mother like?'

'A little old woman, very dried up, dressed in black, who never passes the time of day with anybody and doesn't look easy to get on with.'

'His wife?'

'I've scarcely seen her except when they go by in the car, but I've heard tell she's a foreigner. She's tall and stout like him, with a high colour.'

'D'you think they're away on holiday?'

'Let's see, I believe I still served him with his two glasses of red two or three days ago.'

'Two or three?'

'Wait a bit. It was the evening when the plumber came to mend the beer-pump. I'll go and ask my wife, to make sure I'm not talking through my hat.'

It was two days previously, in other words Tuesday, a few hours before Alfred Jussiaume discovered a dead woman's body in the house.

'Can you remember the time?'

'He comes, as a rule, about half-past six.'

'On foot?'

'Yes. They've got an old car, but that's the time of day he takes his constitutional. You can't tell me what this is all about?'

'It's not about anything at all. A check-up.'

The man didn't believe them, you could see it plainly in his eyes.

'You'll be back?'

And, turning to the Chief-Inspector: 'You're not Monsieur Maigret, by any chance?'

'Did someone say so?'

'One of the bricklayers thought he recognized you. If you are, my wife'd be very happy to meet you in the flesh.'

'We'll be back,' he promised.

They'd had a jolly good meal, and they'd drunk the Calvados which the proprietor, who came from Falaise, had offered them. Now they were walking together down the pavement on the shady side of the street. Maigret was taking little puffs at his pipe. Boissier had lit a cigarette, and two fingers of his right hand were stained brown with nicotine, coloured like a meerschaum pipe.

One might have been fifty miles outside Paris, in almost any small town. There were more private houses than buildings with flats, and some were big middle-class family mansions about a century or two old.

There was only the one gate in the street, a black wrought-iron gate beyond which a lawn was spread like a green carpet in the sunshine. On the brass plate was the legend:

GUILLAUME SERRE
Dental Surgeon

And, in smaller letters:

From 2 to 5 p.m.
By appointment only

The sun struck full on the façade of the house, warming its yellowish stone, and, except for two of the windows, the shutters were closed. Boissier could sense that Maigret was undecided.

'Are you going in?'

'What have we got to lose?'

Before crossing over, he cast a quick glance up and down the street and suddenly frowned. Boissier looked in the direction towards which Maigret was gazing so steadily.

'Lofty!' he exclaimed.

She'd just come from the Boulevard Richard-Wallace, and was wearing the same green hat as earlier that morning. Catching sight of Maigret and the Sergeant, she paused for a moment, then made straight for them.

'Surprised to see me?'

'You've got hold of the address?'

'I 'phoned your office about half an hour ago. I wanted to tell you that I'd found the list. I knew it must be somewhere about. I've seen Alfred looking at it, and putting in crosses here and there. When I came out of your office this morning, I thought of a place where Alfred might have hidden it.'

'Where?'

'Do I have to tell you?'

'It might be as well.'

'I'd rather not. Not right away.'

'What else did you find?'

'How d'you know I found anything else?'

'You'd no money this morning and you came here by cab.'

'You're right. There was some money.'

'A lot?'

'More than I'd have expected.'

'Where's the list?'

'I burnt it.'

'Why?'

'Because of the crosses. They might have marked the places where Alfred worked and, whatever else, I'm not going to give you evidence against him.'

She glanced at the house.

'You going in?'

Maigret nodded.

'D'you mind if I wait for you outside the café?'

She hadn't said a word to Boissier who, for his part, was staring at her rather sternly.

'Please yourself,' Maigret told her.

And, followed by the Sergeant, he crossed from the shade into the sunlight, while the tall figure of Ernestine moved off towards the café terrace.

It was ten past two. Unless the dentist had gone on holiday, he ought, according to the brass plate, to be waiting for patients in his surgery. There was an electric bell-push on the right of the gateway. Maigret pressed it and the gate swung open automatically. They crossed the small garden and found another bell-push by the front door, which was not mechanically operated. After the peal of the bell inside, there was a long silence. The two men listened, both of them aware that someone was lurking on the other side of the panel, and looked at each other. At last a chain was unhooked, the bolt withdrawn, a thin crack showed round the lintel of the door.

'Have you an appointment?'

'We'd like to speak to Monsieur Serre.'

'He only sees people by appointment.'

The crack did not widen. They could dimly make out, behind it, a silhouette, the thin face of an old woman.

'According to the brass plate . . .'

'The plate is twenty-five years old.'

'Would you tell your son that Chief-Inspector Maigret wishes to see him?'

The door remained for a moment longer without moving, then opened; it revealed a wide hallway with a black-and-white tessellated floor which resembled that of a convent corridor, and the old lady who stood back to let them enter would not have looked out of place dressed as a nun.

'You must excuse me, Chief-Inspector, but my son doesn't really care to receive casual patients.'

The woman was far from unpresentable. She'd an innate elegance and dignity which were remarkable. She was attempting to efface by her smile any bad impression that she might have created.

'Do please come in. I'm afraid that I'll have to ask you to wait a moment or two. For some years, my son has been accustomed, especially in summer, to take a siesta, and he's still lying down. If you'd care to come this way. . . .'

She opened, on the left, a pair of polished oaken doors, and Maigret was reminded more than ever of a convent or, better still, a rich parsonage. Even the soft, insidious smell reminded him of something; he didn't know what, he tried to remember. The drawing-room that she showed them into was lit only by daylight seeping through the slots of the shutters, and to enter it from outside was like stepping into a cool bath.

The noises of the town, one felt, could never penetrate this far, and it was as if the house and everything in it had remained unchanged for more than a century, that the tapestried chairs, the occasional tables, the piano and the chinaware had always stood in the same place. Even the enlarged photographs on the walls, in black wooden frames, which looked like photographs from the time of Nadar. The man strapped into a collar of the last century, above the chimney-piece, wore bushy side-whiskers and, on the opposite wall, a woman of about forty, her hair parted in the middle, looked like the Empress Eugénie.

The old lady, who might almost have stepped herself out of one of those frames, hovered at their side, motioned them to seats, folded her hands like a Sister of Mercy.

'I don't wish to seem inquisitive, Chief-Inspector. My son has no secrets from me. We've never lived apart, although he's now past his fiftieth year. I haven't the slightest idea of your business or of what brings you here, and, before going to disturb him, I would like to know . . .'

She left the sentence unfinished, glancing from one to the other with a gracious smile.

'Your son is married, I believe?'

'He's been married twice.'

'Is his second wife at home?'

A shade of melancholy clouded her eyes, and Boissier began to cross and uncross his legs; this was not the sort of place he felt at home in.

'She's no longer with us, Chief-Inspector.'

She moved softly over to close the door, and returning, sat down in the corner of a sofa, keeping her back very straight, as young girls are taught to hold themselves in convent schools.

'I hope she hasn't done anything silly?' she asked in a low voice.

Then, as Maigret remained silent, she gave a sigh, resigned herself to begin once more:

'If it's anything to do with her, I was right to question you before disturbing my son. It is about her that you've come, isn't it?'

Did Maigret make a vague sign of assent? He was not aware of doing so. He was too intrigued by the atmosphere of this house, and even more by this woman, behind whose meekness he could sense an indomitable strength of will.

Everything about her was in good taste: her clothes, her bearing and her voice. One might have expected to meet her in some château or, better still, in one of those enormous country houses that are like museums of a bygone age.

'After he became a widower, fifteen years ago, the thought of remarrying didn't enter my son's head for a long time.'

'He did remarry, two years ago, if I'm not mistaken?'

She showed no surprise at finding him so well-informed.

'He did, indeed. Two and a half years ago exactly. He married one of his patients, a woman also of a certain age. She was then forty-seven of Dutch origin, she lived alone in Paris. I won't live for ever, Chief-Inspector. As you see me now, I am seventy-eight.'

'You don't look it.'

'I know. My mother lived to the age of ninety-two, and my grandmother was killed in an accident at ninety-eight.'

'And your father?'

'He died young.'

She spoke as though this were of no importance, or rather as if men in general were doomed to die young.

'I almost encouraged Guillaume to marry again, by saying that thus he would not be left to live alone.'

'The marriage was unhappy?'

'I wouldn't say that. Not to begin with. I think that the trouble arose mainly from her being a foreigner. There are all sorts of little things that one cannot get used to. I don't quite know how to explain. Oh yes. Food, for instance! A preference for this or that dish! Perhaps, too, when she married my son she imagined him to be wealthier than he actually is.'

'She'd no income of her own?'

'A certain competence. She was not badly off, but, with the rising cost of living . . .'

'When did she die?'

The old woman's eyes opened wide.

'Die?'

'I'm sorry. I thought she was dead. You yourself speak of her in the past tense.'

She smiled.

'That's true. But not for the reason you imagine. She isn't dead; only for us it's as though she were, she's gone away.'

'After a quarrel?'

'Guillaume is not the kind of man who quarrels.'

'With you?'

'I am too old to quarrel now, Chief-Inspector. I've seen too much. I know life too well, and I let everybody . . .'

'When did she leave the house?'

'Two days ago.'

'Did she tell you she was going?'

'My son and I knew that she would go in the end.'

'She had talked to you about it?'

'Often.'

'Did she give you any reasons?'

She did not reply at once, seemed to be pondering.

'Do you want me to tell you frankly what I think? If I hesitate, it's because I fear you may laugh at me. I don't like to discuss such things in front of men, but I suppose that a police officer is rather like a doctor or a priest.'

'You are a Roman Catholic, Madame Serre?'

'Yes. My daughter-in-law was a Protestant. That made no difference. You see, she was at the awkward age for a woman. We all, more or less, have to go through a few years during which we are not our normal selves. We get upset over trifles. We are apt to see things out of perspective.'

'I understand. That's what it was?'

'That and other things, probably. In the end, she dreamed only of her native Holland, spent all day writing to friends that she had kept up with over there.'

'Did your son ever go to Holland with her?'

'Never.'

'So she left on Tuesday?'

'She went on the nine-forty from the Gare du Nord.'

'The night-train?'

'Yes. She had spent the whole day packing.'

'Your son went with her to the station?'

'No.'

'Did she take a taxi?'

'She went to fetch one from the corner of the Boulevard Richard-Wallace.'

'She hasn't got in touch with you since?'

'No. I don't suppose she feels it necessary to write to us.'

'Was there any question of a divorce?'

'I've told you that we are Catholics. Moreover, my son has no wish to get married again. I still do not understand why the police have seen fit to call upon us.'

'I would like to ask you, Madame, exactly what happened here on Tuesday night. One moment. You haven't a maid, have you?'

'No, Chief-Inspector. Eugénie, our charwoman, comes every day from nine till five.'

'Is she here today?'

'You have come on her day off. She'll come in again tomorrow.'

'She lives in the neighbourhood?'

'She lives at Puteaux, on the other side of the Seine. Above an ironmonger's shop, directly opposite the bridge.'

'I suppose she helped your daughter-in-law to pack?'

'She brought the case downstairs.'

'How many cases?'

'One trunk and two leather suit-cases precisely. Then there was a jewel-box and a dressing-case.'

'Eugénie left at five as usual?'

'She did, indeed. Please forgive me if I seem disconcerted, but this is the first time I've ever been cross-questioned like this and I must confess . . .'

'Did your son go out that evening?'

'What time of evening do you mean?'

'Let's say before dinner.'

'He went out for his usual stroll.'

'I suppose he went to have an *apéritif*?'

'He doesn't drink.'

'Never?'

'Nothing except a glass of wine and water at meal-times. Still less those horrible things called *apéritifs*.'

It seemed then that Boissier, who was sitting on his best behaviour in his arm-chair, sniffed the smell of aniseed which still clung to his moustache.

'We sat down to table as soon as he came in. He always takes the same stroll. It became a habit with him in the days when we had a dog that had to be exercised at set times and, I declare, it's become second nature to him.'

'You haven't a dog nowadays?'

'Not for four years. Not since Bibi died.'

'Or a cat?'

'My daughter-in-law loathed cats. You see! I spoke of her again in the past tense, and it's because we really do think of her as belonging to the past.'

'The three of you had dinner together?'

'Maria came down just as I was bringing in the soup.'

'There was no quarrelling?'

'None. Nobody spoke during the meal. I could tell that Guillaume, after all, was a little upset. At first sight, he seems cold, but really he's a terribly sensitive boy. When one has lived on terms of intimacy with someone for over two years. . . .'

Maigret and Boissier had not heard a thing. But she, the old lady, was sharp of hearing. She bent her head as though she were listening. It was a mistake, for Maigret understood, rose to his feet, and went and opened the door. A man, undoubtedly taller, broader and heavier than the Chief-Inspector, stood there, slightly shame-faced, for he had plainly been eavesdropping for some time.

His mother had told the truth when she claimed that he'd been taking a siesta. His sparse hair, ruffled, clung to his forehead and he'd pulled on trousers over his white shirt, with his collar still unbuttoned. He wore carpet slippers on his feet.

'Won't you come in, Monsieur Serre?' asked Maigret.

'I beg your pardon. I heard voices. I thought . . .'

He spoke deliberately, turning his heavy, brooding stare upon each of them in turn.

'These gentlemen are police officers,' his mother explained, rising to her feet.

He didn't ask for any explanation, stared at them again, buttoned up his shirt.

'Madame Serre was telling us that your wife left the day before yesterday.'

This time he turned round to face the old lady, his brows together. His big frame was flaccid, like his face, but, unlike many fat men, he did not give an impression of agility. His complexion was very pale and sallow, tufts of dark hair sprouted from his nostrils, from his ears, and he had enormously bushy eyebrows.

'What exactly do these gentlemen want?' he asked, carefully spacing out the syllables.

'I don't know.'

And even Maigret felt at a loss. Boissier wondered how the Chief-Inspector was going to get out of the situation. These weren't the sort of people who could be put through the first degree.

'Actually, Monsieur Serre, the question of your wife merely cropped up in the course of conversation. Your mother told us that you were lying down, and we had a little talk while we were waiting for you. We're here, my colleague and myself'–the term 'colleague' gave Boissier so much pleasure!–'simply because we've reason to believe that you have been the victim of an attempted burglary.'

Serre was not the sort of man who is unable to look others in the face. Far from it, he stared at Maigret as though attempting to read his innermost thoughts.

'What gave you that idea?'

'Sometimes we come into possession of confidential information.'

'You are speaking, I suppose, of police informers?'

'Let's put it like that.'

'I'm sorry, gentlemen.'

'Your house hasn't been burgled?'

'If it had been, I would have lost no time in lodging a complaint myself with the local police.'

He wasn't trying to be civil. Not once had he shown even the vestige of a smile.

'You are, however, the owner of a safe?'

'I believe that I'd be within my rights in refusing to answer you. I don't mind telling you, however, that I have got one.'

His mother was attempting to make signs to him, advising him, probably, not to be so ill-tempered.

He realized this and remained obdurate.

'If I'm not mistaken, it's a safe installed by Messrs. Planchart about eighteen years ago.'

He remained unperturbed. He continued to stand, whilst Maigret and Boissier sat in semi-darkness, and Maigret saw that he had the same heavy jowl as the man in the portrait, the same eyebrows. The Chief-Inspector wondered whimsically what he'd look like with side-whiskers.

'I don't remember when I had it put in, nor is that anybody's business but mine.'

'I noticed, as we came in, that the front door is secured by a chain and a safety-lock.'

'So are lots of front doors.'

'You sleep on the first landing, your mother and yourself?'

Serre deliberately made no reply.

'Your study and surgery are on the ground floor?'

From a gesture on the part of the old lady, Maigret understood that these rooms led out of the drawing-room.

'Would you mind if I took a look round?'

He paused, opened his mouth, and Maigret felt certain it was to say no. His mother sensed this, too, for she intervened.

'Why not comply with these gentlemen's request? They will see for themselves that there has been no burglary.'

The man shrugged his shoulders, his expression as stubborn, as sullen, as ever, and he refrained from following them into the neighbouring rooms.

Madame Serre showed them first into a study as peaceful and old-fashioned as the drawing-room. Behind a black-leather-bottomed chair, stood a big safe, painted dark green, of a rather obsolete type. Boissier went up to it, smoothed the steel with a professional touch.

'You see that everything is in order,' said the old woman. 'You mustn't mind my son being in a bad temper, but . . .'

She stopped as she saw the latter, framed in the doorway, fixing them with the same morose stare.

Then, waving a hand towards the bound volumes which filled the shelves, she went on, with a strained sprightliness:

'Don't be surprised to see mostly books on law. They're part of my husband's library, who was a solicitor.'

She opened one last door. And here the furnishings were more commonplace; it might have been any dental surgery, with a mechanical chair and the usual instruments. Up to half the height of the window, the panes were frosted.

On their way back through the study Boissier crossed to one of the windows, again felt with his fingers on it, then gave Maigret a significant nod.

'Has this window-pane been put in recently?' asked the latter in his turn.

It was the old woman who answered immediately:

'Four days ago. The window was open during the big thunder-storm which I'm sure you remember.'

'Did you call in the glazier?'

'No.'

'Who replaced the pane?'

'My son. He likes doing odd jobs. He always sees to any of our little household repairs.'

At which Guillaume Serre said with a touch of irritation:

'These gentlemen have no right to pester us, Mamma. Don't answer any more questions.'

She turned so that her back was towards him, and smiled at Maigret in a way that meant plainly:

'Don't mind him. I did warn you.'

She showed them to the front door, while her son remained standing in the centre of the drawing-room, and leaned forward to whisper:

'If you have anything to say to me, come and call when he isn't here.'

They were outside in the sunlight again, which made the clothes cling immediately to their skin. Once outside the gate—its faint creak was reminiscent of a convent gate—they caught sight, on the opposite pavement, of Ernestine's green hat as she sat at a table outside the café-restaurant.

Maigret halted. They could have turned left and avoided her. If they joined her, it would look almost as though they had to give her an account of themselves.

Perhaps out of a sense of decency, the Chief-Inspector growled: 'Shall we go and have one?'

With an enquiring expression, she watched them come towards her.

Chapter Three

'What did you do today?' asked Madame Maigret, as they sat down to eat in front of the open window.

In the houses opposite also people could be seen eating, and, on every side, the same bright splashes of shirts showed where the men had taken off their jackets. Some of them, who'd finished dinner, were leaning on their elbows out of the window. Wireless music could be heard playing, babies crying, raised voices. A few concierges had brought their chairs out in front of their doorsteps.

'Nothing out of the way,' replied Maigret. 'A Dutchwoman who may have been murdered, but who's probably still alive somewhere.'

It was too early to talk about it. On the whole, he'd behaved slackly. They'd sat about for a long time outside the little café in the Rue de la Ferme, Boissier, Ernestine and himself, and of the three it was Ernestine who'd been the most worked up.

She took umbrage:

'He made out it wasn't true?'

The proprietor had brought them pints of beer.

'Actually he didn't say anything. It was his mother who did the talking. On his own, he'd have thrown us out.'

'He says there wasn't a corpse in the study?'

She'd obviously found out from the café owner about the residents in the house with the wrought-iron gate.

'Then why didn't he tell the police that somebody'd tried to burgle the place?'

'According to him no one tried to burgle him.'

Of course she knew all about Sad Freddie's little ways.

'Wasn't there a pane missing in one of the windows?'

Boissier looked at Maigret as if advising him to say nothing, but the Chief-Inspector took no notice.

'A pane has been mended recently; it appears that it got broken four or five days ago, on the night of the storm.'

'He's lying.'

'Somebody's lying, certainly.'

'You think it's me?'

'I didn't say so. It might be Alfred.'

'Why should he have told me all that story on the 'phone?'

'Perhaps he didn't,' interposed Boissier, watching her narrowly.

'And what should I have made it up for? Is that what you think, too, Monsieur Maigret?'

'I don't think anything.'

He was smiling vaguely. He felt comfortable, almost blissful. The beer was cool, and in the shade it smelt almost like the country, perhaps because the Bois de Boulogne was close by.

A lazy afternoon. They'd drunk two pints apiece. Then, so as not to leave the girl stranded so far from the centre of Paris, they gave her a lift in their taxi and dropped her at the Châtelet.

'Ring me up directly you get a letter.'

He felt she was disappointed in him, that she'd imagined him otherwise. She must be telling herself that he'd got old, had become like the rest of them, and couldn't be much bothered with her case.

'D'you want me to put back my leave?' Boissier had suggested.

'I suppose your wife's done all the packing?'

'The bags are at the station already. We were due to go on the six o'clock train tomorrow morning.'

'With your daughter?'

'Naturally.'

'Off you go.'

'Won't you be needing me?'

'You've trusted me with the file.'

Once alone in his office, he nearly dozed off in his chair. The wasp was no longer there. The sun had moved round to the other side of the quay. Lucas had been off duty since noon. He called Janvier, who had been the first to take his leave, in June, because of a wedding in some branch of his family.

'Sit down. I've got a job for you. You've made out your report?'

'I've just this minute finished it.'

'Right! Take a note of this. First you've got to look up, at the Town Hall in Neuilly, the maiden name of a Dutchwoman who, two and a half years ago, married a man called Guillaume Serre, residing at 43b Rue de la Ferme.'

'Easy.'

'I dare say. She must have been living in Paris for some time. You must try to find out where, what she did, what relatives she had, how much money, etc. . . .'

'Right you are, Chief.'

'She's supposed to have left the house in the Rue de la Ferme on Tuesday, between eight and nine in the evening, and to have taken the night-train to Holland. She went to fetch a taxi herself from the corner of the Boulevard Richard-Wallace to take her luggage.'

Janvier was writing words in columns on a page of his note-book.

'That all?'

'No. Get some help to save time. I want the people in the neighbourhood, tradesmen and so on, questioned about the Serres.'

'How many are there?'

'Mother and son. The mother's nearly eighty and the son's a dentist. Try to locate the taxi. Also make enquiries from the staff at the station and on the train.'

'Can I have transport?'

'You can.'

And that was about all he'd done that afternoon. He'd asked to be put through to the Belgian police, who had Sad Freddie's description but had not yet found him. He also had a long conversation with the passport inspector on the frontier, at Jeumont. The latter had himself gone over the train which Alfred was thought to have taken, and didn't remember any passenger resembling the expert safe-cracker.

That meant nothing. He just had to wait. Maigret signed a few papers on behalf of the Chief, went to have a drink at the *Brasserie Dauphine* together with a colleague in the Records Office, and then back home by bus.

'What shall we do?' asked Madame Maigret, when the table had been cleared.

'Let's go for a stroll.'

Which meant that they'd amble along as far as the main boulevards to finish up sitting at a café terrace. The sun had set. The air was becoming cooler, though gusts of warm air still seemed to rise up from the paving-stones. The bay-windows of the *brasserie* were open, and a depleted orchestra played inside. Most of the customers sat there without speaking, like them, at their tables, watching the passers-by, and their faces melted more and more into the dusk. Then the electric-light made them look quite different.

Like the other couples, they turned back towards home, Madame Maigret's hand crooked in her husband's arm.

After that it was another day, as clear and sunny as the one before.

Instead of going straight to Headquarters, Maigret made a detour by the Quai de Jemmapes, identified the green-painted café, near the Saint-Martin Lock, with the sign 'Snacks served at all hours,' and went in to lean against the counter.

'A white wine.'

Then he put the question. The Auvergnat who served him answered unhesitatingly:

'I don't know at what time exactly, but someone rang up. It was already daylight. My wife and I didn't get up, because, at that time, it couldn't have been for us. Ernestine went down. I heard her talking a long time.'

That was one thing at least she had not lied about.

'What time did Alfred go out, the night before?'

'Eleven, maybe? Maybe earlier. What I do remember is that he took his bike.'

A door led straight from the café into the passageway, from which a staircase mounted to the floors above. The wall of the staircase was whitewashed, as in the country. One could hear the racket made by a crane unloading gravel from a barge a little farther on.

Maigret knocked at a door, which half-opened; Ernestine appeared in her underclothes and merely said:

'It's you!'

Then she went at once to fetch her dressing-gown from the unmade bed, and slipped it on.

Did Maigret smile in memory of the Ernestine-that-used-to-be?

'You know, it's really a kindness,' she said frankly. 'I'm not a pretty sight these days.'

The window was open. There was a blood-red geranium. The bedspread was red, too. A door stood open into a little kitchen, out of which came a good smell of coffee.

He didn't quite know what he'd come for.

'There was nothing at the *poste restante* yesterday evening?'

She answered, worried:

'Nothing.'

'You don't think it odd that he hasn't written?'

'Perhaps he's just being canny. He must be surprised to see nothing in the papers. He probably thinks I'm being watched. I was just going to the post office.'

An old trunk lay in a corner.

'Those are his belongings?'

'His and mine. Between the two of us, we don't own much.'

Then, with an understanding look:

'Like to make a search? Of course! I know. It's your duty. You'll find a few tools, because he's got a spare set, also two old suits, some dresses and a bit of linen.'

As she spoke, she was turning out the contents of the trunk onto the floor, opening the drawers of a dressing-table.

'I've been thinking it over. I've grasped what you were getting at yesterday. Of course somebody must have been lying. Either it's those people, the mother and her son, or it's Alfred, or it's me. You've no reason to believe any of us in particular.'

'Has Alfred no relatives in the country?'

'He's got no relatives anywhere now. He only knew his mother, and she's been dead twenty years.'

'You've never been anywhere together outside Paris?'

'Never farther than Corbeil.'

He couldn't be hiding out at Corbeil. It was too near. Maigret was beginning to think that he hadn't gone to Belgium either.

'There's no place he used to talk about, that he'd have liked to visit one day?'

'He always said the country, no special part. That summed it all up, to him.'

'Were you born in the country youself?'

'Near Nevers, in a village called Saint-Martin-des-Prés.'

She took from a drawer a postcard that showed the village church, standing opposite a pond which served to water cattle.

'Did you show him this?'

She understood. Girls like Ernestine soon understand.

'I'd be surprised to find him there. He really was near the Gare du Nord when he 'phoned me.'

'How d'you know?'

'I found the bar, yesterday evening. It's in the Rue de Maubeuge, near a leather-goods shop. It's called the *Bar du Levant*. The owner remembers him because he was the first customer that day. He'd just lit the percolator when Alfred got there. Wouldn't you like a cup of coffee?'

He didn't like to refuse, but he'd just drunk white wine.

'No offence.'

He had some difficulty finding a taxi in those parts, eventually was driven to the *Bar du Levant*.

'A thin little chap, sad-looking, with eyes all red as if he'd been crying,' they told him.

Unquestionably Alfred Jussiaume, who often had red-rimmed eyes.

'He talked a long time at the 'phone, drank two coffees without sugar and went off towards the station, looking round him as if he was scared of being followed. Has he done anything wrong?'

It was ten o'clock when Maigret at last climbed the staircase at Headquarters, where dust-motes still floated like a mist in the sunlight. Contrary to his usual custom, he didn't glance in through the glass partition of the waiting-room, and went past into the Duty Room, which was almost empty.

'Janvier not in yet?'

'He came about eight and went out again. He left a note on your desk.'

The note said:

> The woman is called Maria Van Aerts. She is fifty-one and comes from Sneeck, in Friesland, Holland. I'm going to Neuilly, where she lived in a boarding-house, Rue de Longchamp. Haven't found the taxi yet. Vacher's looking after the station.

Joseph, the office-boy, opened the door.

'I didn't see you come in, Monsieur Maigret. A lady's been waiting for you half an hour.'

He held out an appointment-slip, on which old Madame Serre had inscribed her name in small, sharp handwriting.

'Shall I show her in?'

Maigret put on his jacket that he'd just taken off, went to open the window, filled his pipe and sat down.

'Yes, show her in.'

He wondered what she would seem like outside the framework of her home, but, to his surprise, she didn't look out of place at all. She wasn't dressed in black, as on the day before; she wore a frock with a white ground, on which dark patterns were traced. Her hat was not ludicrous. She moved forward with assurance.

'You were more or less expecting me to call, weren't you, Chief-Inspector?'

He had not been expecting it and refrained from telling her so.

'Do sit down, Madame.'

'Thank you.'

'The smoke doesn't worry you?'

'My son smokes cigars all day long. I was so upset yesterday at the way he received you! I tried to make signs to you not to persist, because I know him.'

She showed no nervousness, chose her words carefully, aimed at Maigret now and then a sort of conspiratorial smile.

'I think it is I who brought him up badly. You see, I had but the one child and, when my husband died, he was only seventeen years old. I spoilt him. Guillaume was the only man in the house. If you have any children . . .'

Maigret looked at her to try to sum up her background and did not succeed. Something made him ask:

'Were you born in Paris?'

'In the house that you came to yesterday.'

It was a coincidence to find in one case two people born in Paris. Almost invariably, the people he dealt with were more or less directly connected with the provinces.

'And your husband?'

'His father, before him, used to be a solicitor in the Rue de Tocqueville, seventeenth *arrondissement*.'

That made three! To end up in the atmosphere, so absolutely provincial, of the house in the Rue de la Ferme!

'My son and myself have almost always lived alone together, and I suppose that is what has made him a little unsociable.'

'I understood that he'd been married before.'

'He was. His wife didn't live long.'

'How many years after their marriage did she die?'

She opened her mouth; he guessed that a sudden thought made her pause. He even had the impression of seeing a slight flush mount to her cheeks.

'Two years,' she said at last. 'That's curious, is it not? It only struck me just now. He lived for two years with Maria, as well.'

'Who was his first wife?'

'A person of very good family, Jeanne Devoisin, whom we met one summer at Dieppe, at the time when we used to go there every year.'

'Was she younger than he?'

'Let me see. He was thirty-two. She was more or less the same age. She was a widow.'

'Had she any children?'

'No. I don't think she had any relatives, except a sister living in Indo-China.'

'What did she die of?'

'A heart attack. She had a weak heart and spent most of her time under the care of doctors.'

She smiled again:

'I haven't told you yet why I am here. I nearly telephoned to you yesterday, when my son went out for his evening stroll, then I thought it would be more polite to come and call on you. I wish to apologize for Guillaume's attitude towards you and to say that his ill-humour was not directed at you personally. He has such a fierce temperament.'

'So I saw.'

'At the very idea that you could suspect him of a dishonest action. . . . He was like that even as a small boy. . . .'

'He lied to me?'

'I beg your pardon?'

The old lady's face expressed genuine surprise.

'Why should he have lied to you? I don't understand. You didn't really ask any questions. It's precisely to answer any which you should wish to put to me that I have come here. We have nothing to hide. I've no idea of the circumstances that have led you to bother about us. It must be some misunderstanding, or some neighbour's spitefulness.'

'When was the window-pane broken?'

'I told you or my son told you, I can't remember now: during the thunderstorm last week. I was on the first floor and I hadn't had time to shut all the windows when I heard a crash of glass.'

'Was it in broad daylight?'

'It must have been six o'clock in the evening.'

'Which means the charwoman, Eugénie, was no longer there?'

'She leaves us at five, I think I explained that to you also. I haven't told my son that I was coming to see you. I thought that you might like, perhaps, to visit the house, and it would be easier when he's not there.'

'You mean during his late afternoon stroll?'

'Yes. You do understand that there's nothing to hide in our home, and that, if it weren't for Guillaume's nature, everything would have been cleared up yesterday.'

'You realize, Madame Serre, that you came here of your own free will?'

'Yes, of course.'

'And that it's you who want me to question you?'

She nodded her head in confirmation.

'We'll go over your movements again, then, from the last meal that you, your son and your daughter-in-law took together. Your daughter-in-law's luggage was ready. In which part of the house was it?'

'In the corridor.'

'Who brought it down?'

'Eugénie brought down the suit-cases, and my son took charge of the trunk, too heavy for her.'

'Is it a very big trunk?'

'What they call a cabin-trunk. Before her marriage, Maria travelled a lot. She has lived in Italy and Egypt.'

'What did you have to eat?'

The question seemed both to amuse and surprise her.

'Let me see! As it's I who do the cooking, I should be able to remember. Vegetable soup, to start with. We always have vegetable soup, so good for the health. Then I did grilled mackerel and potato purée.'

'And the sweet?'

'A chocolate custard. Yes. My son has always adored chocolate custard.'

'No argument broke out at table? What time did the meal end?'

'About half-past seven. I put the dishes in the kitchen sink and went upstairs.'

'So you weren't present at the departure of your daughter-in-law.'

'I wasn't very anxious to be. Moments such as those are painful, and I prefer to avoid emotion. I said *au revoir* to her downstairs, in the drawing-room. I've nothing against her. Everybody's as they are made and . . .'

'Where was your son during that time?'

'In his study, I think.'

'You've no idea whether he had a last conversation with his wife?'

'It's unlikely. She'd gone upstairs again. I heard her in her room, getting ready.'

'Your house is very solidly built, like most old houses. I suppose that, from the first floor, it's hard to hear sounds coming from downstairs?'

'Not for me,' she answered, pursing her lips.

'What d'you mean?'

'That I have keen hearing. Not even a floorboard can creak without my hearing it.'

'Who went to fetch the taxi?'

'Maria. I told you so yesterday.'

'Did she stay out long?'

'Fairly long. There's no rank nearby, and one has to wait for a taxi to come cruising by.'

'Did you go to the window?'

She hesitated imperceptibly.

'Yes.'

'Who carried the trunk as far as the taxi?'

'The driver.'

'You don't know what company the cab belonged to?'

'How would I know that?'

'What colour was it?'

'Reddish-brown, with a coat-of-arms on the door.'

'Can you remember the driver?'

'Not very well. I think he was small and rather fat.'

'How was your daughter-in-law dressed?'

'She wore a mauve frock.'

'No coat?'

'She had it over her arm.'

'Was your son still in the study?'

'Yes.'

'What happened then? Did you go down?'

'No.'

'You didn't go to see your son?'

'It was he who came up.'

'Immediately?'

'Not long after the taxi drove away.'

'Was he upset?'

'He was as you have seen him. He's of a rather gloomy nature. I explained to you that he's really a highly sensitive man, likely to be affected by the smallest happenings.'

'Did he know that his wife was not coming back?'

'He suspected it.'

'She told him so?'

'Not exactly. She just hinted. She talked of the necessity to change her ideas, to see her own country again. Once over there, you understand. . . .'

'What did you do then?'

'I dressed my hair for the night.'

'Your son was in your room?'

'Yes.'

'He didn't leave the house?'

'No. Why?'

'Where does he garage his car?'

'A hundred yards away, where some old stables have been turned into private garages. Guillaume has hired one of them.'

'So he can take his car out and put it back in without being seen?'

'Why should he want to hide?'

'Did he go downstairs again?'

'I have no idea. I think so. I go to bed early, and he usually reads until eleven o'clock or midnight.'

'In the study?'

'Or in his room.'

'His room is near yours?'

'Next door. There's a bathroom in between us.'

'Did you hear him go to bed?'

'Certainly.'

'At what time?'

'I didn't put on the light.'

'You didn't hear any noise later?'

'None.'

'I suppose that you're the first down in the morning?'

'In summer I come down at half-past six.'

'Did you go round all the rooms?'

'I went first into the kitchen to put some water on to boil, then I opened the windows, because that's the time when the air is still cool.'

'You went into the study then?'

'Probably.'

'You don't remember doing so?'

'I almost certainly did.'

'The broken pane was already repaired?'

'I suppose so . . . yes. . . .'

'Did you notice any disorder in the room?'

'None, except for some cigar ends, as always, in the ash-trays, and perhaps a book or two lying around. I don't know what all this means, Monsieur Maigret. As you see, I answer your questions frankly. I came especially to do so.'

'Because you were worried?'

'No. Because I was ashamed of the way Guillaume treated you. And also because I sense something mysterious behind your visit. Women aren't like men. In my husband's time, for instance, if there were a noise in the house at night, he never moved from his bed, and it was I who went to look. You understand? It's probably the same with your own wife. Really, it's in a way for the same reason that I'm here. You talked about burglary. You seemed preoccupied with the question of Maria.'

'You haven't had any news of her?'

'I don't expect to receive any. You're hiding certain facts and that makes me curious. It's the same with sounds in the night. I hold that mysteries don't exist, that one only has to look at things squarely for them to become perfectly simple.'

She was watching him, sure of herself, and Maigret had a slight feeling that she looked upon him as a child, as another Guillaume. She seemed to be saying:

'Tell me everything that's worrying you. Don't be frightened. You'll see that it'll all come right.'

He, too, looked her straight in the face.

'A man broke into your house that night.'

The old woman's eyes were incredulous, with a tinge of pity, as though he'd still believed in werewolves.

'What for?'

'To burgle the safe.'

'Did he do it?'

'He got into the house by cutting out a pane of glass to open the window.'

'The pane that was already broken in the thunderstorm? No doubt he put it back afterwards.'

She still refused to take what he was saying seriously.

'What did he take away?'

'He took nothing away, because at a certain moment his electric torch lit up something that he hadn't expected to find in the room.'

She was smiling.

'What sort of thing?'

'The dead body of a middle-aged woman, which may have been that of your daughter-in-law.'

'He told you that?'

He looked at the white-gloved hands that didn't tremble.

'Why don't you ask this man to come and repeat his accusations to me?'

'He's not in Paris.'

'Can't you make him come here?'

Maigret preferred to make no reply. He wasn't too pleased with himself. He was beginning to wonder if he too was not falling under the influence of this woman who had the comforting serenity of a Mother Superior.

She didn't get up, didn't fidget, didn't show indignation either.

'I have no idea what it's all about and I won't ask you. Perhaps you have some good reason for believing in this man. He's a burglar, isn't he? Whilst I am merely an old woman of seventy-eight who never did anyone any harm.

'Allow me, now that I know where we are, to invite you cordially to come to our house. I will open every door for you, I will show you anything that you may wish to see. And my son, once he's acquainted with the facts, will not fail, in his turn, to answer your questions.

'When will you come, Monsieur Maigret?'

Now she had risen to her feet, still perfectly at ease, and there was nothing aggressive in her manner, just a slight touch of bitterness.

'Probably this afternoon. I don't know yet. Has your son used the car, these last few days?'

'You can ask him, if you like.'

'Is he at home now?'

'It's possible. He was there when I went out.'

'Eugénie as well?'

'She is certainly there.'

'Thank you.'

He showed her to the door. Just as they reached it, she turned round.

'I'd like to ask a favour,' she said gently. 'When I've gone, try for a moment to put yourself in my place, forgetting that you have spent your life in dealing with crime. Imagine that it's you who are suddenly being asked the questions you put to me, you who are being suspected of killing someone in cold blood.'

That was all. She only added:

'Until this afternoon, Monsieur Maigret.'

Once the door was closed, he stood for a full minute without moving by the doorway. Then he went to look out of the window, soon caught sight of the old lady walking with quick short steps, in full sunshine, towards the Pont Saint-Michel.

He picked up the telephone.

'Get me the police-station at Neuilly.'

He didn't ask to be put through to the Station Officer, but to a sergeant whom he knew.

'Vanneau? Maigret here. I'm well, thanks. Listen. It's a bit tricky. Jump in a car and get round to 43b, Rue de la Ferme.'

'The dentist's place? Janvier, who came here yesterday evening, spoke to me about him. Something to do with a Dutchwoman, isn't it?'

'Never mind. Time's getting on. The chap's not easy to handle, and I can't ask for a warrant just now. You've got to act quickly, before his mother gets there.'

'Is she far away?'

'At the Pont Saint-Michel. I suppose she's going to take a cab.'

'What shall I do with the man?'

'Bring him in, on some excuse. Tell him whatever you like, that you need him as a witness. . . .'

'And then?'

'I'll be there. Just the time it takes to get downstairs and jump in a car.'

'Suppose the dentist's not at home?'

'You keep watch and grab him before he gets inside.'

'Bit irregular, eh?'

'Quite.'

As Vanneau was going to ring off, he added:

'Take somebody with you and put him to watch the stables that they've turned into garages in the same street. One of the garages is hired by the dentist.'

'Right you are.'

A moment later Maigret was hurrying down the stairs and climbing into one of the police-cars parked in the courtyard. As the car turned round towards the Pont Neuf, he thought he caught sight of Ernestine's green hat. He wasn't sure of it and preferred not to lose time. To tell the truth, he'd given way to a sudden fit of resentment against Lofty.

Once they'd crossed the Pont Neuf, he felt remorseful, but it was too late.

Couldn't be helped! She'd wait for him.

Chapter Four

The police-station was on the ground floor of the Town Hall, an ugly square building that stood in the middle of a waste land, with sparse trees around and a dirty flag dangling. Maigret could have gone straight from outside into the Duty Rooms; so as not to come face to face with Guillaume Serre, he took a roundabout way through the draughty corridors, where he soon got lost.

Here too the slackness of summer held sway. Doors and windows were open, documents fluttered on tables in the empty rooms, while clerks in shirt-sleeves exchanged seaside gossip and an occasional taxpayer wandered disconsolately about in search of an endorsement or a signature.

Maigret finally managed to light upon a policeman who knew him by sight.

'Sergeant Vanneau?'

'Second on the left, third door along the passage.'

'Would you go and fetch him for me? There should be someone with him. Don't say my name out loud.'

A few moments later Vanneau joined him.

'Is he there?'

'Yes.'

'How did it go off?'

'Middling. I'd taken good care to bring along a police summons. I rang. A servant answered and I asked to see her master. I had to wait about a bit in the passage. Then the bloke came down, and I handed him the paper. He read it, looked at me without saying anything.

'"If you'd like to come with me, I've a car outside."

'He shrugged his shoulders, took a Panama hat down from the hall-stand, shoved it on his head, and followed me out

'Now he's sitting on a chair. He still hasn't uttered a word.'

A minute or two later, Maigret went into Vanneau's office, found Serre there smoking a very black cigar. The Chief-Inspector took up a seat in the Sergeant's chair.

'I'm sorry to have troubled you, Monsieur Serre, but I'd like you to answer a few questions.'

As on the day before, the huge dentist surveyed him broodingly, and he had no trace of cordiality in his gloomy stare. Maigret, all of a sudden, realized what the man reminded him of: the sort of sultan that one used to see pictures of at one time. He had the girth, the manifest weight; in all probability the strength, too. For, despite his fat, he gave the impression of being very strong. He had also the disdainful calm of those pashas that are depicted on cigarette packets.

Instead of making some sign of agreement, uttering a polite commonplace or even voicing a protest, Serre took a buff-coloured form from his pocket, cast his eye over it.

'I've been summoned here by the Police Superintendent of Neuilly,' he said. 'I look forward to hearing what this Superintendent requires from me.'

'Am I to understand you refuse to answer my questions?'

'Emphatically.'

Maigret paused. He'd seen all sorts, the mutinous, the pig-headed, the wilful, the wily, but none had ever answered him back with such unruffled determination.

'I suppose it's no good arguing?'

'Not in my opinion.'

'Or trying to point out that your attitude doesn't show you in a good light?'

This time the other merely sighed.

'Very well. Wait. The Superintendent will see you now.'

Maigret went in search of the latter, who did not at once understand what was expected of him, and only grudgingly agreed to play his part. His quarters were more comfortable, almost sumptuous in comparison with the rest of the offices, and there was a marble clock on the mantelpiece.

'Show Monsieur Serre in!' he told the man on duty.

He motioned him to a chair with a red velvet seat.

'Do sit down, Monsieur Serre. It's just a matter of a routine check-up, and I won't waste your time.'

The Superintendent consulted a form which had just been brought to him.

'You are, I believe, the owner of a motor vehicle registered under the number RS 8822 L?'

The dentist confirmed this with a nod. Maigret had gone over to sit on the window-sill and was watching him very thoughtfully.

'The vehicle in question is still in your possession?'

Another nod of assent.

'When was the last time you used it?'

'I believe I've the right to know the reason for this interrogation.'

The Superintendent shifted in his chair. He didn't at all like the task which Maigret had entrusted to him.

'Just suppose that your car had been involved in an accident. . . .'

'Has it been?'

'Suppose the number had been notifed to us as that of a car which had knocked somebody down?'

'When?'

The police officer threw Maigret a reproachful look.

'Tuesday evening.'

'Where?'

'Near the Seine.'

'My car didn't leave the garage on Tuesday evening.'

'Somebody might have used it without your knowledge.'

'I doubt it. The garage is locked up.'

'You're prepared to swear that you didn't use the car on Tuesday evening, or later during the night?'

'Where are the witnesses to the accident?'

Once again the Superintendent looked anxiously to Maigret for support. The latter, realizing that this was leading nowhere, motioned to him not to take it any further.

'I've no further questions, Monsieur Serre. Thank you.'

The dentist rose, seemed for a moment to fill the room with his bulk, put on his Panama hat and left the room, after turning to stare fixedly at Maigret.

'I did what I could. As you saw.'

'I saw.'

'Did you get any lead out of it?'

'Perhaps.'

'That's a man who'll make trouble for us. He's a stickler for his rights.'

'I know.'

It seemed almost as if Maigret was unconsciously imitating the dentist. He had the same sombre, heavy expression. He, in turn, made for the door.

'What's he supposed to have done, Maigret?'

'I don't know yet. It may be that he's killed his wife.'

He went to thank Vanneau, and found himself outside once more, where the police-car awaited him. Before climbing in, he had a drink at the bar on the corner and catching sight of himself in the mirror, wondered what he'd look like wearing a Panama hat. Then he smiled wryly at the thought that it was, in a way, a case of two heavy-weights engaged in a fight.

He said to the driver:

'Go round by the Rue de la Ferme.'

Not far from 43b, they caught sight of Serre walking along the pavement with long, rather indolent strides. As some fat men do, he straddled slightly. He was still smoking his long cigar. As he passed the garage, he couldn't have failed to notice the plain-clothes man who was keeping a look-out there and had no means of taking cover.

Maigret was reluctant to stop the car at the house with the black wrought-iron gate. What good would it do? They probably wouldn't let him in.

Ernestine was waiting for him in the glass-panelled anteroom at Headquarters. He showed her into his office.

'Any news?' she asked him.

'Not a thing.'

He was in a bad temper. She didn't know that he rather liked feeling bad-tempered at the beginning of a difficult case.

'I had a card this morning. I brought it to you.'

She handed him a coloured postcard depicting the Town Hall at Le Havre. There was no inscription, no signature, nothing save Lofty's address, c/o *poste restante*.

'Alfred?'

'It's his handwriting.'

'He didn't go over to Belgium?'

'Doesn't look like it. He must have fought shy of the frontier.'

'D'you think he might try to get away by sea?'

'It isn't likely. He's never set foot on a boat. I'm going to ask you something, Monsieur Maigret, but you've got to give me a straight answer. Suppose he was to come back to Paris, what'd happen to him?'

'You want to know if he'd be detained?'

'Yes.'

'For attempted burglary?'

'Yes.'

'Nobody could detain him, because he wasn't caught red-handed, and, for another thing, Guillaume Serre hasn't laid a complaint, even denies that anybody broke into his house.'

'So they'd let him alone?'

'Unless he was lying and something quite different happened.'

'Can I promise him that?'

'Yes.'

'In that case, I'll put a notice in the Personal Column. He always takes the same paper, because of the crossword.'

She looked at him hard for a moment.

'You don't seem too sure about things.'

'What things?'

'The case. Yourself. I don't know. Did you see the dentist again?'

'Half an hour ago.'

'What did he say?'

'Nothing.'

She'd nothing more to say either and used the telephone ringing as an excuse to take her leave.

'What is it?' Maigret growled into the mouthpiece.

'It's me, Chief. Could I see you in your room?'

A few seconds later, Janvier came into the office briskly, obviously very pleased with himself.

'I've got plenty of leads. Shall I give 'em to you right away? You got a bit of time to spare?'

His enthusiasm was a little damped by the behaviour of Maigret, who'd just taken off his coat and was loosening his tie to set his thick neck free.

'First, I went to the boarding-house I told you about. It's a bit like the hotels on the left bank, with potted palms in the hall and old ladies sitting around in cane chairs. There aren't many guests much under fifty. Most of 'em are foreigners, Englishwomen, Swiss and Americans, who go to museums and write endless letters.'

'Well?'

Maigret knew the kind of thing. It wasn't worth going on about.

'Maria Van Aerts lived there for a year. They remember her, because she made herself popular in the place. She seems to've been very gay and laughed a lot, shaking her great big bosom. She used to stuff herself with pastries, went to all the lectures at the Sorbonne.'

'That all?' said Maigret, meaning that he couldn't see what Janvier was so excited about.

'Nearly every day she used to write letters of eight to ten pages.'

The Chief-Inspector shrugged his shoulders, then examined the Sergeant with more interest in his eye. He had caught on.

'Always to the same woman, a school friend who lives in Amsterdam and whose name I got hold of. This friend came to see her once. They shared a room for three weeks. I've an idea that even when married Maria Serre kept on writing. The friend's called Gertrude Oosting, she's the wife of a brewer. It shouldn't be hard to find out her address.'

'Ring through to Amsterdam.'

'Will you be wanting the letters?'

'The recent ones, if possible.'

'That's what I thought. Brussels still hasn't any news of Sad Freddie.'

'He's in Le Havre.'

'Shall I 'phone Le Havre?'

'I'll do it myself. Who's free next door?'

'Torrence came back to duty this morning.'

'Send him to me.'

Another heavy-weight, who wouldn't pass unnoticed on the pavement of an empty street.

'You go and stick yourself down in Neuilly, Rue de la Ferme, facing 43b, a house with a garden and an iron gate in front. Don't bother to take cover. Far from it. If you see a chap come out, bigger and taller than you, follow him so that he can see you.'

'Anything else?'

'Arrange to be relieved part of the night. There's a man from Neuilly on duty a bit farther on, opposite the garage.'

'What if the bloke goes off by car?'

'Take one of ours and park it along the kerb.'

He hadn't the energy to go home for lunch. It was hotter than the day before. There was thunder in the air. Most men were walking about with their jackets over their arms, and urchins were swimming in the Seine.

He went to have a bite at the *Brasserie Dauphine*, first having drunk, as if as a challenge, a couple of Pernods. Then he went to see Moers of the Technical Branch, under the overheated roof of the Palais de Justice.

'Let's say about eleven in the evening. Bring the things you need. Take someone with you.'

'Yes, Chief.'

He'd sent out a call to the police at Le Havre. Had Sad Freddie taken a train at the Gare du Nord after all, to Lille, for instance; or, having telephoned Ernestine, had he made a dash straight away for the Gare Saint-Lazare?

He must have gone to ground in some cheap lodging, or be wandering from bar to bar, drinking baby bottles of Vichy water, unless he was trying to stow away on board some ship. Was it as hot in Le Havre as it was in Paris?

They still hadn't found the taxi that was supposed to have picked up Maria Serre and her luggage. The staff at the Gare du Nord had no recollection of her.

Opening the paper, about three o'clock, Maigret read Ernestine's message in the Personal Column:

Alfred. Return Paris. No danger. All arranged. Tine.

At half-past four he found himself still in his chair, the newspaper on his knee. He hadn't turned the page. He'd gone to sleep, and his mouth felt sticky, his back cricked.

None of the squad cars were in the courtyard and he had to take a taxi from the end of the quay.

'Rue de la Ferme, in Neuilly. I'll show you where to stop.'

He nearly dozed off again. It was five to five when he stopped the cab opposite the already familiar café. There was no one at the tables outside. Farther on the burly shape of Torrence could be seen, pacing up and down in the shade. He paid the driver, sat down with a sigh of relief.

'What can I get you, Monsieur Maigret?'

Beer, of course! He had such a thirst he could have swallowed five or six pints at a gulp.

'He hasn't been in again?'

'The dentist? No. I saw his mother, this morning, going down towards the Boulevard Richard-Wallace.'

The wrought-iron gate creaked. A wiry little woman started to walk along the opposite pavement and Maigret settled for his drink, caught her up just as she reached the edge of the Bois de Boulogne.

'Madame Eugénie?'

'What d'you want?'

The Neuilly household wasn't conspicuous for its affability.

'A little chat with you.'

'I've no time to chat. There's all the housework to do when I get home.'

'I'm a police officer.'

'That makes no odds.'

'I'd like to ask you a few questions.'

'Do I have to answer?'

'It would certainly be better to.'

'I don't like policemen.'

'You're not obliged to. D'you like your employers?'

'They stink.'

'Old Madame Serre as well?'

'She's a bitch.'

They were standing by a bus stop. Maigret raised his arm to stop a cruising taxi.

'I'm going to take you home.'

'I don't care all that much for being seen with a copper, but I suppose it's worth it.'

She climbed into the cab with dignity.

'What have you got against them?'

'What about you? Why are you sticking your nose into their business?'

'Young Madame Serre has gone away?'

'Young?' she said ironically.

'Let's say the daughter-in-law.'

'She's gone, yes. Good riddance.'

'Was she a bitch, too?'

'No.'

'You didn't like her?'

'She was always digging into the larder, and when it came to lunch-time, I couldn't find half what I'd got ready.'

'When did she go?'

'Tuesday.'

They were crossing the Pont de Puteaux. Eugénie tapped on the glass.

'Here we are,' she said. 'D'you need me any more?'

'Could I come up with you for a moment?'

They were on a crowded square, and the charwoman made towards an alleyway, to the right of a shop, began to climb a staircase that smelt of slops.

'If only you could tell them to leave my son alone.'

'Tell whom?'

'The other coppers. The ones from hereabouts. They never stop making trouble for him.'

'What does he do?'

'He works.'

'Doing what?'

'How should I know? Can't be helped if the housework isn't done for you. I can't clean up after others all day long and do my own as well.'

She went to open the window, for a strong, stuffy smell hung about, but it wasn't untidy and, except for a bed in one corner, the sort of drawing-cum-dining-room was almost dainty.

'What's all the to-do?' she asked, taking off her hat.

'Maria Serre can't be found.'

'Course not, as she's in Holland.'

'They can't find her in Holland either.'

'Why do they want to find her?'

'We've reason to believe that she's been murdered.'

A tiny spark kindled in Eugénie's brown eyes.

'Why don't you arrest them?'

'We haven't any proof yet.'

'And you're counting on me to get you some?'

She put some water to heat on the gas, came over to Maigret again.

'What happened on Tuesday?'

'She spent all day packing.'

'Wait a moment. She'd been married two and a half years, hadn't she? I suppose she had a good many things of her own.'

'She'd at least thirty dresses and as many pairs of shoes.'

'Was she smart?'

'She never threw anything out. Some of the dresses dated back ten years. She didn't wear them, but she wouldn't have given them away for all the money in the world.'

'Mean?'

'Aren't all rich people mean?'

'I was told that all she took with her was a trunk and two suitcases.'

'That's right. The rest went a week before.'

'You mean she sent other trunks away?'

'Trunks, packing-cases, cardboard boxes. A removal van came to fetch the lot, Thursday or Friday last.'

'Did you look at the labels?'

'I don't remember the exact address, but the stuff was booked for Amsterdam.'

'Did your employer know?'

'Of course he did.'

'So her departure had been decided on for some time?'

'Since her last attack. After each attack she'd talk of going back to her own country.'

'What kind of attacks?'

'Heart, so she said.'

'She'd a weak heart?'

'Seems like it.'

'Did a doctor come and see her?'

'Doctor Dubuc.'

'Did she take any medicine?'

'After each meal. They all did. The other two still do and they've each a little bottle of pills or drops beside their plate.'

'What's wrong with Guillaume Serre?'

'I don't know.'

'And his mother?'

'Rich people always have something wrong with them.'

'Did they get on well?'

'Sometimes they didn't speak to each other for weeks.'

'Maria Serre wrote a lot of letters?'

'Nearly from morning till night.'

'Did you ever happen to take them to the post?'

'Often. They were always to the same person, a woman with a funny name who lives in Amsterdam.'

'Are the Serres well off?'

'I reckon so.'

'What about Maria?'

'Sure. Otherwise he wouldn't have married her.'

'Did you work for them when they got married?'

'No.'

'You don't know who did the housework at that time?'

'They're always changing their daily help. It's my last week now. Soon as anybody begins to know the form, they pack in.'

'Why?'

'How would you like to see the lumps of sugar counted in the sugar-bowl and have a half-rotten apple picked out for your sweet?'

'Old Madame Serre?'

'Yes. Just because at her age she works all day, which is her own funeral, she's onto you like a shot if you're unlucky enough to be caught sitting down for a moment.'

'Does she tell you off?'

'She's never told me off. I'd like to see her! It's far worse. She's only too polite, she looks at you in a down-hearted sort of way as if it made her sad to see you.'

'Did anything strike you when you came to work on Wednesday morning?'

'No.'

'You didn't notice if a window had been broken during the night, or whether there was fresh putty round one of the panes?'

She nodded.

'You've got the wrong day.'

'Which day was it?'

'Two or three days before, when we had that big thunderstorm.'

'You're sure of that?'

'Certain. I even had to polish the floor of the study because the rain had come into the room.'

'Who put in the pane?'

'Monsieur Guillaume.'

'He went to buy it himself?'

'Yes. He brought back the putty. It was about ten o'clock in the morning. He had to go to the ironmonger's in the Rue de Longchamp. They never have a workman in if they can do without one, and Monsieur Guillaume unstops all the drains himself.'

'You're certain about the date?'

'Absolutely.'

'Thank you very much.'

Maigret had no further business there. There was really nothing more for him to do at the Rue de la Ferme either. Unless, of course, Eugénie was merely repeating a piece that she'd been taught to say and, in that case, she was a better liar than most.

'You don't think they've killed her?'

He didn't answer, went on towards the door.

'Because of the window-pane?'

There was a slight hesitation in her tone.

'Does the window have to be broken on the day you said?'

'Why? Do you want to see them go to jail?'

'Nothing I'd like better. But now that I've told the truth. . . .'

She regretted it. For two pins she'd have gone back on her statement.

'You could always go and ask at the ironmonger's where he bought the glass and the putty.'

'Thank you for the tip.'

He stood for a moment in front of the shop outside, which happened in fact to be an ironmonger's. But it wasn't the right one. He waited for a taxi.

'Rue de la Ferme.'

There was no point in leaving Torrence and the plain-clothes man from Neuilly to kick their heels on the pavement any longer. The recollection of Ernestine playing her little joke in the Rue de la Lune came back to him, and he didn't find it at all funny, began to think about her. For it was she who'd started him off on this business. He'd been a fool to rush into it. Only this morning, in the Police Superintendent's office, he'd made a proper ass of himself.

His pipe tasted foul. He crossed and uncrossed his legs. The partition was open between himself and the driver.

'Go round by the Rue de Longchamp. If the ironmonger's is still open, stop there for a moment.'

It was a toss-up. This would be his last throw. If the ironmonger's was closed, he wouldn't bother to come back, Ernestine and Sad Freddie notwithstanding. Anyway, what proof was there that Alfred had ever really broken into the house in the Rue de la Ferme?

He'd gone off on his bike from the Quai de Jemmapes, agreed, and at daybreak he'd telephoned his wife. But nobody knew what they'd said to each other.

'It's open!'

Of course, the ironmonger's, where the hardware department could be seen inside. A tall youth in a grey smock came to meet Maigret between the galvanized tin pails and the brooms.

'Do you sell sheet glass?'

'Yes, sir.'

'And putty?'

'Certainly. Have you brought the measurements?'

'It's not for myself. Do you know Monsieur Serre?'

'The dentist? Yes, sir.'

'Is he a customer of yours?'

'He's got an account here.'

'Have you seen him recently?'

'*I* haven't, because I only got back from my holiday day before yesterday. He might have come in while I was away. I can easily tell you by looking up the book.'

The saleman didn't ask the reason why, but dived into the semi-darkness of the shop, opened a ledger that lay on a tall, raised desk.

'He bought a sheet of window-glass last week.'

'Could you tell me which day?'

'Friday.'

The thunderstorm had occurred on Thursday night. Eugénie had been right, and old Madame Serre as well!

'He bought half a pound of putty, too.'

'Thank you.'

It hung by a thread, by an unthinking gesture on the part of the young man in the grey smock who wouldn't be long in shutting up shop. He was turning over the entries in the ledger, more or less for form's sake. He said:

'He came back again this week.'

'What!'

'Wednesday. He bought a pane of the same size, forty-two by sixty-five, and another half-pound of putty.'

'You're sure?'

'I can even tell you that he was in early, because it's the first sale made that day.'

'What time d'you open?'

An important point since, according to Eugénie, who started work at nine, all the window-panes had been in good repair on Wednesday morning.

'Well, we get in at nine, but the boss comes down at eight to open the shop.'

'Thanks, old chap. You're a bright lad.'

The bright lad must have wondered for some time afterwards why this man, who had looked so depressed when he came in, now seemed to be in such high spirits.

'I suppose there's no danger of anyone destroying the pages in this ledger?'

'Why would anybody do that?'

'Why, indeed! All the same, I advise you to keep a look out. I'll send someone round tomorrow morning to photostat them.'

He took a card from his pocket, handed it to the young man, who read with astonishment:

Chief-Divisional-Inspector Maigret
Central Police Headquarters
Paris.

'Where to now?' asked the driver.

'Pull up for a moment in the Rue de la Ferme. You'll see a little café on your left. . . .'

This deserved a pint of beer. He nearly called Torrence and the plain-clothes man to have one with him, but finally merely asked the driver in.

'What'll you have?'

'Mine's a white wine and Vichy.'

The street was gilded by the sun. They could hear the breeze rustling through the big trees in the Bois de Boulogne.

There was a black wrought-iron gate father up the road, a square of greensward, a house as serene and well-ordered as a convent.

Somewhere in this house there lived an old woman like a Mother Superior a sort of sultan with whom Maigret had a score to settle.

It was good to be alive.

Chapter Five

The rest of the day went as follows. First of all, Maigret drank two pints of beer with the taxi-driver, who had only the one white wine and Vichy water himself. By that time it was beginning to get cooler and, as he climbed back into the cab, he'd the notion of driving round to the boarding-house that Maria Van Aerts had stayed in for a year.

There was nothing in particular for him to do there. He was simply following his habit of nosing round people's homes in order to understand them better.

The walls were cream-coloured. Everything was creamy, luscious, as in a dairy, and the proprietress with her floury face looked like a cake with too much icing on it.

'What a lovely person, Monsieur Maigret! And what a wonderful companion she must have made for her husband! She wanted to get married so much.'

'You mean she was looking for a husband?'

'Don't all young girls dream of a bridegroom?'

'She was about forty-eight when she lived here, if I'm not mistaken?'

'But she was still so young at heart! Anything could make her laugh. Would you believe it, she loved to play practical jokes on her fellow-guests. Near the Madeleine, there's a shop I'd never noticed before I found out about it through her, that sells all sorts of joke-novelties, mechanical mice, spoons that melt in the coffee, gadgets that you slide under the table-cloth to lift someone's plate up all of a sudden while they're eating, glasses that you can't drink from, and I don't know what all! Well, she was one of its best customers! A very cultured woman, all the same, who'd been to every museum in Europe and used to spend whole days at the Louvre.'

'Did she introduce you to her prospective husband?'

'No. She was secretive by nature. Perhaps she didn't like to bring him here, for fear that some of the others might be envious. He was a man of very imposing presence, who looked like a diplomat, I believe.'

'Aha!'

'He's a dentist, she told me, but only sees a few patients, by appointment. He belongs to a very rich family.'

'And Mademoiselle Van Aerts herself?'

'Her father left her a good deal of money.'

'Tell me, was she mean?'

'Oh, you've heard about that? She was certainly thrifty. For instance, when she had to go into town, she'd wait until one of the other guests was going too so that they could share the taxi. Every week she'd argue over her bill.'

'Do you know how she came to meet Monsieur Serre?'

'I don't think it was through the matrimonial advertisement.'

'She put an advertisement in the papers?'

'Not in earnest. She didn't believe in it. More for fun really. I don't remember the exact wording, but she said that a distinguished lady, foreign, wealthy, wished to meet gentleman of similar circumstances, with a view to marriage. She had hundreds of replies. She used to make dates with the suitors at the Louvre, sometimes in one gallery, sometimes in another, and they had to carry a certain book in their hand, or wear a buttonhole.'

There were other women like her, from England, Sweden, or America, sitting in the wicker arm-chairs of the lounge, from which the smooth hum of the electric fans could be heard.

'I hope she hasn't come to any harm?'

It was about seven o'clock when Maigret got out of the taxi at the Quai des Orfèvres. From the shady side of the street he'd caught sight of Janvier coming along, with a preoccupied expression, a parcel under his arm, and he'd waited to climb the stairs with him.

'How's things, Janvier, my boy?'

'All right, Chief.'

'What have you got there?'

'My dinner.'

Janvier didn't grumble, but he had a martyred look.

'Why don't you go home?'

'Because of that woman Gertrude, blast her.'

The offices were almost empty, swept by draughts, for a breeze had just got up and all the windows in the building were still open.

'I managed to track down Gertrude Oosting in Amsterdam. Or rather, I got her maid on the 'phone. I had to dig up a chap waiting for an identity-card in the Aliens Section, who was willing to interpret, because the maid doesn't speak a word of French, and then call her back.

'As luck would have it, the good lady Oosting had gone out with her husband at four in the afternoon. There's some open-air concert on today, over there, with a fancy-dress parade, and after that the Oostings are having dinner with friends, the maid doesn't know where. She's no idea when they'll be back either, and she'd been told to put the children to bed.

'And, talking of children . . .'

'What?'

'Nothing, Chief.'

'Come on, out with it!'

'Doesn't matter. Only that the wife's a bit disappointed. It's our eldest boy's birthday. She'd got a special little dinner ready. Never mind.'

'Did you find out from the maid if Gertrude Oosting can speak French?'

'She can.'

'Go on home.'

'What?'

'I told you to go home. Leave me those sandwiches and I'll stay on here.'

'Madame Maigret won't like that.'

Janvier needed a bit of pressure, but finally went rushing off to catch his train to the suburbs.

Maigret had eaten alone in his office, had gone down for a chat with Moers in the laboratory afterwards. Moers had not left until after nine, when darkness had completely fallen.

'Sure you know what to do?'

'Yes, Chief.'

He took a photographer with him, and masses of equipment. It wasn't strictly legal, but, ever since Guillaume Serre had bought two window-panes and not one, that no longer mattered.

'Get me Amsterdam, please. . . .'

At the other end the maid gabbled something and he understood her to mean that Madame Oosting still hadn't come in.

Then he called up his wife.

'You wouldn't mind coming down to have a drink at the *Brasserie Dauphine*? I've probably got another hour or so to fill in here. Take a cab.'

It wasn't a bad evening. The two of them were as comfortable as outside a café on the main boulevards, except that their view was blocked by the tall pale flight of steps leading to the Palais de Justice.

They ought to have got to work by now, in the Rue de la Ferme. Maigret had given them instructions to wait until the Serres had gone to bed. Torrence was to mount guard in front of the house to prevent the others from being taken unawares while they broke into the garage, which couldn't be overlooked from the house, and gave the car a thorough overhaul. Moers and the photographer would take care of that. Everything would be gone into: fingerprints, sample of dust for analysis, the whole works.

'You look pleased with yourself.'

'I can't complain.'

He wasn't prepared to admit that, a few hours earlier, he was far from being in such a good mood, and now he began to have short drinks, while Madame Maigret stuck to barley-water.

He left her twice to go back and call Amsterdam from the office. Not until half-past eleven did he hear a voice which was not the maid's and which answered him in French:

'I can't hear you very well.'

'I said, I'm calling from Paris.'

'Oh! Paris!'

She'd a strong accent, which nevertheless was not unattractive.

'Police Headquarters.'

'Police?'

'Yes. I'm telephoning with reference to your friend Maria. You know Maria Serre, whose maiden name was Van Aerts, don't you?'

'Where is she?'

'I don't know. That's just what I'm asking you. She often wrote to you?'

'Yes, often. I was supposed to meet her at the station, Wednesday morning.'

'Did you go to meet her?'

'Yes.'

'Did she come?'

'No.'

'Had she wired or telephoned you that she couldn't keep the appointment?'

'No. I'm worried.'

'Your friend has disappeared.'

'What do you mean?'

'What did she tell you in her letters?'

'Lots of things.'

She began to speak in her own language to someone, probably her husband, who was evidently standing beside her.

'Do you suppose Maria is dead?'

'It could be. Did she ever write to you that she was unhappy?'

'She was distressed.'

'Why?'

'She didn't like the old lady.'

'Her mother-in-law?'

'Yes.'

'What about her husband?'

'It appears that he wasn't a man, but just an overgrown schoolboy who was terrified of his mother.'

'How long ago did she write you that?'

'Almost as soon as she got married. A few weeks after.'

'She already talked about leaving him?'

'Not then. After about a year or so.'

'And recently?'

'She'd made up her mind. She asked me to find her a flat in Amsterdam, near ours.'

'Did you find one for her?'

'Yes. And a maid.'

'So it was all arranged?'

'Yes. I was at the station.'

'Have you any objection to sending me copies of your friend's letters? Did you keep them?'

'I have kept all the letters, but it would be hard work to copy them, as they are very long. I can send you the ones that matter. You're sure something's happened to her?'

'I'm convinced of it.'

'Somebody's killed her?'

'Possibly.'

'Her husband?'

'I don't know. Listen, Madame Oosting, you could do me a great favour. Has your husband got a car?'

'Of course.'

'It would be kind of you to drive to Central Police Headquarters, which is open all night. Tell the Duty Officer that you were expecting your friend Maria. Show him her last letter. Then tell him you're very worried and that you'd like the matter gone into.'

'Should I mention your name?'

'It doesn't matter either way. What you must do is to insist upon an investigation.'

'I will do so.'

'Thank you. Don't forget the letters that you promised to send me.'

He rang Amsterdam again almost at once, asking this time for the number of Central Police Headquarters.

'In a few minutes, a Madame Oosting will be coming to see you about the disappearance of her friend, Madame Serre, *née* Van Aerts.'

'Did she disappear in Holland?'

'No, in Paris. In order to take action, I need an official complaint. Directly you've taken down her statement, I'd like you to send me a wire asking us to make enquiries.'

This took a bit of time. The Duty Officer at the other end couldn't understand how Maigret, in Paris, could have known that Madame Oosting was coming along.

'I'll tell you that later. All I must have is your wire. Send it priority. I should get it in less than half an hour.'

He went back to join Madame Maigret, who'd begun to get bored sitting about outside the *brasserie*.

'Have you done?'

'Not yet. I'll have one drink and then we'll be off.'

'Home?'

'To the office.'

That always impressed her. She'd only rarely been within the walls of Headquarters, and didn't know how to behave there.

'You look as if you were having fun. One'd think you were playing a joke on somebody.'

'I am in a way.'

'On whom?'

'A fellow who looks like a sultan, a diplomat, and a schoolboy.'

'I don't understand.'

'Naturally not!'

He wasn't often in such high spirits. How many Calvados had he drunk? Four? Five? This time, before going back to the office, he swallowed a pint and took his wife's arm before crossing the couple of hundred yards of the quay to reach Police Headquarters.

'I only ask one thing: don't start telling me again that everything's covered in dust and that the offices need a good clean-out!'

On the telephone:

'Any telegrams come through for me?'

'Nothing, Chief-Inspector.'

Ten minutes later the whole squad, with the exception of Torrence, was back from the Rue de la Ferme.

'Did it go off all right? No hitches?'

'No hitches. Nobody disturbed us. Torrence insisted we should wait until the lights had all gone out in the house, and Guillaume Serre hung about for a long time before going to bed.'

'The car?'

Vacher, who'd nothing more to do, asked if he could go home. Moers and the photographer stayed behind. Madame Maigret, sitting on a chair as if paying a visit, assumed the abstracted expression of one who is not listening.

'We went over every bit of the car, which doesn't seem to have been taken out for two or three days. The petrol tank's about half-full. There is no signs of a struggle inside. In the boot, I found two or three more or less recent scratches.'

'As if a large heavy piece of luggage had been stowed in it?'

'That could be.'

'A trunk, for instance?'

'A trunk or a packing-case.'

'Were there any blood-stains inside?'

'No. Nor any loose hairs either. I thought of that. We took a flashlight along, and there's a power point in the garage. Emile is going to make enlargements of the photos.'

'I'm getting onto it right now,' the photographer said. 'If you could wait just twenty minutes. . . .'

'I'll wait. Did it look to you, Moers, as if the car had been cleaned lately?'

'Not on the outside. It hadn't been washed down by a garage. But it looked as if the inside had been carefully brushed. They must have even taken up the mat to be beaten, because I'd a job to find any dust in it. All the same, I've got several specimens for laboratory tests.'

'Was there a brush in the garage?'

'No. I looked. They must have taken it away.'

'So, except for the scratches . . .'

'Nothing out of the way. Can I go now?'

They were left alone, Madame Maigret and he, in the office.

'Aren't you sleepy?'

She said no. She'd her own special way of looking at the surroundings in which her husband had spent most of his life, of which she knew so little.

'Is it always like this?'

'What?'

'A case. When you don't come home.'

She must have thought it was easy, quiet work, more like a kind of game.

'Just depends.'

'Has there been a murder?'

'More than likely.'

'D'you know who did it?'

She turned her head away as he smiled at her. Then she asked:

'Does he know that you suspect him?'

He nodded.

'D'you suppose he's asleep?'

She added after a moment, with a slight shiver:

'It must be awful.'

'I don't suppose it was fun for the poor woman either.'

'I know. But probably that was quicker, don't you think?'

'Maybe.'

The telegram from the Dutch police came through on the 'phone, with a confirmatory copy promised for the next morning.

'Now then! We can go home.'

'I thought you were waiting for the photographs.'

He smiled once more. Really, she'd have liked to find out. She didn't feel now like going back to bed.

'They won't tell us anything.'

'Don't you think so?'

'I'm sure of it. Moers' laboratory tests won't either.'

'Why not? Because the murderer was too careful?'

He did not reply, put out the light and led his wife into the passage, where the cleaners were already at work.

'That you, Monsieur Maigret?'

He looked at the alarm clock, which said half-past eight. His wife had let him sleep on. He recognized Ernestine's voice.

'Did I wake you up?'

He preferred not to admit it.

'I'm at the post office. There's another card for me.'

'From Le Havre?'

'From Rouen. He doesn't say anything, still hasn't answered my advertisement. Nothing except my address at the *poste restante*, same as yesterday.'

There was a pause. Then she asked:

'You heard anything?'

'Yes.'

'What?'

'Something to do with window-panes.'

'Good?'

'Just depends for whom.'

'For us?'

'It may do Alfred and you some good.'

'You don't still think I've been telling lies?'

'Not at the moment.'

At Headquarters he picked Janvier to go with him, and the latter took the wheel of the little black police car.

'Rue de la Ferme.'

With the telegram in his pocket, he made the car stop outside the wrought-iron gate, through which the two of them passed looking their most official. Maigret rang. A window curtain moved on the first floor, where the shutters were not yet closed. It was Eugénie, in down-at-hell slippers, who came to the door, wiping her wet hands on her apron.

'Good morning, Eugénie. Monsieur Serre is at home and I'd like a word with him.'

Somebody leant over the banisters. The old woman's voice said:

'Show the gentlemen into the drawing-room, Eugénie.'

It was the first time that Janvier had been in the house, and he was impressed. They heard footsteps coming and going overhead. Then the door opened abruptly and the huge bulk of Guillaume Serre almost filled the entrance.

He was as self-possessed as on the day before, stared at them with the same calm insolence.

'Have you a warrant?' he asked, his lip twitching slightly.

Maigret deliberately took some time taking his wallet from his pocket, opening it, finding a document which he handed over politely.

'Here you are, Monsieur Serre.'

The man wasn't prepared for this. He read through the form, took it over to the window to decipher the signature, while Maigret was saying:

'As you see, it's a search warrant. Enquiries are being instituted into the disappearance of Madame Maria Serre, *née* Van Aerts, on a complaint lodged by Madame Gertrude Oosting, of Amsterdam.'

The old lady had entered on these last words.

'What is it, Guillaume?'

'Nothing, Mamma,' he told her in a curiously gentle voice. 'These gentlemen, I believe, would like to search the house. Go up to your room.'

She wavered, looked at Maigret as if to ask his advice.

'You'll keep your temper, Guillaume?'

'Of course, Mamma. Please leave us, I beg of you.'

Things weren't going exactly as Maigret had foreseen, and the Chief-Inspector frowned.

'I expect,' he said, when the old lady had reluctantly moved away, 'you'll want to consult your lawyer? I'll probably have a few questions to ask you later on.'

'I don't need a lawyer. Now that you have a warrant, I cannot object to your presence here. That's that.'

The shutters on the ground floor were closed. Until now they'd been in semi-darkness. Serre walked towards the nearest window.

'No doubt you'd prefer more light upon the scene?'

He spoke in a flat voice and if any expression at all could be read into his tone, it was a degree of contempt.

'Do your duty, gentlemen.'

It came almost as a shock to see the drawing-room in full daylight. Serre went into his study next door, where he also opened the shutters, then into the surgery.

'When you wish to go up to the first floor, please let me know.'

Janvier was glancing in bewilderment at his Chief. The latter wasn't quite so buoyant as he'd been that morning or the night before. He seemed to be worried.

'May I use your telephone, Monsieur Serre?' he asked with the same cold courtesy the other had shown him.

'You have every right to.'

He dialled the number of Headquarters. Moers had made a verbal report that morning which, as the Chief-Inspector had expected, was more or less negative. The particles of dust had been analysed with no result. Or rather, almost none. Moers had only managed to scrape up, from the front of the car, by the driving-seat, a minute quantity of powdered brick.

'Give me the laboratory. That you, Moers? Can you come along to the Rue de la Ferme with your men and equipment?'

He was watching Serre who, engaged in lighting a long black cigar, didn't bat an eyelid.

'All the lot, eh? No, there's no body. I'll be here.'

Then turning to Janvier:

'You can get started.'

'On this room?'

'On any one you like.'

Guillaume Serre followed them up step by step and watched what they were doing without a murmur. He wore no tie and had slipped on a black alpaca jacket over his white shirt.

While Janvier was searching the drawers of the desk, Maigret himself was going through the dentist's private files and making entries in his large note-book.

Really, it had begun to border on farce. He'd have been hard put to it to say precisely what he was looking for. What it amounted to in the end was seeing whether, at any given moment, in any particular part of the house,

Serre would show any sign of uneasiness.

When they had searched the drawing-room, for instance, he'd not moved a muscle, standing rigid and full of dignity, with his back to the brown marble chimney-piece.

Now, he was watching Maigret as if wondering what the latter could be searching for in his files, but it seemed to be more out of curiosity than fear.

'You certainly have very few patients, Monsieur Serre.'

He made no reply and shrugged his shoulders.

'I notice that there are far more women patients than men.'

The other's expression seemed to say, 'So what?'

'I also see that you first met Maria Van Aerts in your professional capacity.'

He found entries for five visits, spaced over two months, with details of the treatment given.

'Were you aware that she was wealthy?'

A further shrug.

'Do you know Doctor Dubuc?'

He nodded.

'He was your wife's doctor, unless I'm mistaken. Did you recommend him to her?'

Wonders never cease! He was talking at last!

'Doctor Dubuc was treating Maria Van Aerts before she became my wife.'

'You knew, when you married her, that she had heart trouble?'

'She told me about it.'

'Was it serious?'

'Dubuc will tell you if he considers it his duty.'

'Your first wife had a weak heart, too, hadn't she?'

'You'll find her death certificate in the files.'

Janvier was more ill at ease than anyone. He greeted with relief the arrival of the technical experts, who would start a bit of life in the house. As the car drew up in front of the gate, Maigret went to open the door himself, said to Moers under his breath:

'The whole show. Go over the house with a toothcomb.'

And Moers, who'd understood and spotted the bulky form of Guillaume Serre, muttered:

'You reckon that'll shake him?'

'It might end up by shaking someone.'

A few moments later, one might have thought that auctioneers had taken over the house and were preparing to put it up for public sale. The men from the Technical Branch left no corner untouched, taking down the pictures and the photographs, pushing back the piano and the arm-chairs to look underneath the carpets, piling up cupboard drawers, spreading out documents.

Once they caught sight of the face of Madame Serre who, having taken one glance through the doorway, had withdrawn with a look of distress. Then Eugénie came in grumbling:

'You'll put everything back where it was, I hope?'

She carried on even more when her kitchen was put through it and even the cupboards where she stored her brooms.

'If only you'd tell me what it is you're looking for.'

They weren't looking for anything in particular. Perhaps, when it came to the point, even Maigret wasn't looking for anything at all. All the time he was watching the man who followed in their tracks and never lost his poise for a second.

Why had Maria written to her friend that Serre was really nothing more than an overgrown schoolboy?

While his men continued to work, Maigret unhooked the telephone and got Dr. Dubuc on the line.

'You won't be going out for a while? Can I come and see you? No, it won't take long. Thanks, I'll tell the maid.'

Dubuc had five patients in his waiting-room and promised the Chief-Inspector to let him in by the back door. It was a stone's throw away, along the wharf. Maigret went there on foot, passed the ironmonger's, where the young assistant of the day before hailed him.

'Aren't you going to photograph the ledger?'

'Presently.'

Dubuc was a man of about fifty, with a ginger beard and glasses.

'You attended Madame Serre, didn't you, Doctor?'

'Young Madame Serre. Or rather, the younger of the two.'

'You never attended anyone else in the house?'

'Let me see. Yes! A charwoman who'd cut her hand, two or three years ago.'

'Was Maria Serre really ill?'

'She needed treatment, yes.'

'Heart?'

'An enlarged heart. Moreover, she ate too much, complained of dizziness.'

'Did she often call you in?'

'About once a month. Other times she came to see me.'

'Did you prescribe any medicine for her?'

'A sedative, in tablet form. Nothing toxic.'

'You don't think she could have had a heart attack?'

'Most unlikely. In ten or fifteen years, perhaps. . . .'

'Did she do anything to get her weight down?'

'Every four or five months she'd decide to go on a diet, but her resolution never lasted for more than a few days.'

'You've met her husband?'

'Occasionally.'

'What did you think of him?'

'In what way? Professionally? One of my woman patients went to him for treatment and told me that he was very skilful and very gentle.'

'As a man?'

'I thought he seemed of a retiring disposition. What is all this about?'

'His wife has disappeared.'

'Ah!'

Dubec didn't give a damn, to tell the truth, and he merely sketched a vague gesture.

'These things happen, don't they? He was wrong to put the police on to find her, because she'll never forgive him.'

Maigret didn't argue the point. On his way back, he made a detour so as to pass the garage, which was no longer under observation. The house opposite had been divided into flats. the concierge was outside on the step, polishing the brass knob of the front door.

'Does your window look out on the street?' he asked her.

'What's that got to do with you?'

'I'm a police officer. I wanted to find out whether you knew the person who keeps his car in the garage opposite, the first one on the right.'

'That's the dentist.'

'You see him now and again?'

'I see him when he comes to fetch his car.'

'Have you seen him this week?'

'Here! That reminds me–what was all that messing about in his garage yesterday night? Was it burglars? I said to my husband . . .'

'It wasn't burglars.'

'Was it you?'

'Never mind. Have you seen him take his car out this week?'

'I believe I did.'

'You don't remember which day? Or what time?'

'It was one night, pretty late. Hang on. I'd got up out of bed. Don't look at me like that. It'll come back to me.'

She seemed to be doing some mental arithmetic.

'I'd just got up out of bed, because my husband had toothache, and I'd given him an aspirin. If he was here he'd tell you straight away what day it was. I noticed Monsieur Serre's car coming out of the garage, and I remember saying what a coincidence.'

'Because your husband had toothache?'

'Yes. And there was a dentist opposite the house at that very moment. It was after midnight. Mademoiselle Germaine had come in. Right, then it was Tuesday, because she only goes out on Tuesday nights, to play cards round at some friends.'

'The car was coming out? It wasn't going in?'

'It was coming out.'

'Which way did it go?'

'Towards the Seine.'

'You didn't hear it stop a little farther on, for instance at Monsieur Serre's house?'

'I didn't take any more notice of it. I'd bare feet and the floor was cold, because we sleep with the window half-open. What's he done?'

What could Maigret have answered? He thanked her and moved away, crossed the little garden and rang. Eugénie opened the door, giving him a black, reproachful look.

'The gentlemen are upstairs,' she told him curtly.

They'd finished with the ground floor. From upstairs noisy footsteps could be heard, the rumble of furniture being dragged across the floorboards.

Maigret went up, found old Madame Serre sitting on a chair in the middle of the landing.

'I no longer know where to go,' she said. 'It's like moving house. What can they be looking for, Monsieur Maigret?'

Guillaume Serre, standing in the centre of a room flooded with sunlight, was lighting a fresh cigar.

'My goodness, why did we let her go!' sighed the old lady. 'If I'd only known. . . .'

She did not state precisely what she would have done had she foreseen the worries that her daughter-in-law's disappearance would bring down upon her.

Chapter Six

It was twenty to four when Maigret made up his mind, twenty-five past four when the questioning began. But the fateful, almost dramatic moment was that when the decision was taken.

Maigret's behaviour had come as a surprise to those working with him in the house at the Rue de la Ferme. Ever since the morning, there'd been something unusual about the way in which the Chief-Inspector was directing operations. It wasn't the first search of this sort in which they'd taken part, but the more this one proceeded, the more it took on a different nature from any other. It was difficult to define. Janvier, because he knew his Chief better than the others, was the first to feel the change.

When he set them to work, there had been a slight, almost fierce flicker of glee in Maigret's eyes; he had loosed them on the house rather as he might have loosed a pack of hounds on a fresh scent, urging them on, not by his voice but by his whole attitude.

Had it become a personal issue between himself and Guillaume Serre? Or more precisely: would events have taken the same course, would Maigret have made the same decision, at the same moment, had the man from the Rue de la Ferme not been heavier than he, physically and morally?

He had seemed, from the start, impatient to get to grips with him.

At other times, one might have attributed different motives to him, wondered if he didn't take a more or less malicious pleasure in turning the house upside-down.

They had seldom been given the chance of working in a home like this, where everything was peaceful and serene, harmonious in a muted minor key, where even the most outdated objects were in no way ludicrous, and where, after hours of exhaustive searching, they hadn't come across even one questionable detail.

When he had made his pronouncement, at twenty to four, they still hadn't found anything. The search party was feeling a certain amount of discomfort, expecting the Chief to withdraw with apologies.

What was it that decided Maigret? Did he know himself? Janvier went so far as to suspect him of having drunk too many *apéritifs* when, about one o'clock, he'd gone to have a bite on the terrace of the café opposite. On his return, it was true, a smell of Pernod could be detected on his breath.

Eugénie hadn't laid the table for her employers. Several times she'd come up to whisper, now in the ear of Madame Serre, now in that of the dentist. At one moment, they'd caught sight of the mother eating, standing up, in the kitchen, as one might during a household removal, and not long after that, Guillaume having refused to come down, the charwoman took him up a sandwich and a cup of coffee.

They were working in the attic by then. This was the most personal part of the house, more personal than the bedrooms and the linen cupboards.

It was enormous, lit by dormer-windows that shed two large luminous rectangles upon the dingy floorboards. Janvier had opened two leather gun-cases, and a ballistics man had examined the weapons.

'These belong to you?'

'They belonged to my father-in-law. I have never done any shooting.'

An hour earlier, in Guillaume's room, they'd found a revolver, which had been examined, and which Maigret had placed on the pile of objects to be taken away for a subsequent check-up.

There was a bit of everything in that pile, including the dentist's professional records and, from an escritoire in the old lady's room, the death certificates of her husband and her first daughter-in-law.

There was also a suit of clothing on which Janvier had noticed a slight tear in the sleeve, and which Guillaume Serre claimed not to have worn for ten days.

They stumbled about among old trunks, packing-cases, pieces of broken-down furniture which had been taken up to the attic because they were no more use. In a corner stood a child's high chair of an old-fashioned type, with coloured knobs on either side of the tray, and also a rocking-horse, minus tail and mane.

They didn't stop working at lunch-time. The men took it in turns to knock off for a bite, and Moers was satisfied with a sandwich brought to him by the photographer.

Towards 2 p.m., they 'phoned through to Maigret, from the office, to tell him that a pretty heavy envelope had just come by air from Holland. He had them open it. Inside were Maria's letters, written in Dutch.

'Get hold of a translator and put him to work.'

'Here?'

'Yes. He's not to leave Headquarters until I come.'

Guillaume Serre's attitude had not altered. He followed them about, didn't miss a single action or gesture on their part, but not even once did he seem agitated.

He had a special way of staring at Maigret, and one could see that, for him, the others didn't count. It was indeed a match between the two. The plain-clothes men were merely lay figures. Even the police force didn't count. This was a more personal combat. And in the dentist's eyes one could see an indefinable expression that might have been one of reproach or of contempt.

In any case, he didn't allow this large-scale operation to intimidate him. He raised no more objections, submitted to this invasion of his home and privacy with lofty resignation, in which not the slightest trace of anxiety was perceptible.

Was he a weakling? A tough customer? The two theories were equally plausible. His torso was that of a wrestler, his behaviour that of a self-assured man, and yet, nevertheless, Maria's description of him as an overgrown schoolboy did not appear incongruous. His skin was pale, sickly-looking. In a drawer, they'd found a mass of doctor's prescriptions, pinned together in separate sheafs, some of them dating from twenty years back; the family's medical history could have been reconstructed with the help of these prescriptions, some of which were yellow with age. There was also, in the upstairs bathroom, a small white-painted cabinet containing phials of patent medicine, boxes of pills both new and old.

In this house nothing was ever thrown away, not even old brooms, which were stacked in a corner of the attic beside down-at-heel cracked leather shoes that would never be any use again.

Each time they left a room to launch an attack upon the next, Janvier gave his Chief a look which meant:

'Another wash-out!'

For Janvier still expected to make some discovery. Did Maigret, on the other hand, rely on their finding nothing? He didn't seem surprised, watched them go ahead, puffing lazily at his pipe, sometimes forgetting, for a whole quarter of an hour, to glance round at the dentist.

They realized his decision by implication, and that made it strike them even more forcibly.

Everybody was coming down from the attic, where Guillaume Serre had closed the dormer windows. His mother had just come out of her room to watch them go. They were standing on the landing, in an uneasy group.

Maigret had turned to Serre and said, as if it were the most natural thing in the world:

'Would you mind putting on a tie and a pair of shoes?'

Throughout the day, so far, the man had been wearing slippers.

Serre had grasped his meaning, had stared at him, undoubtedly surprised, but managing not to let it show. His mother had opened her mouth to speak, either to protest or to demand an explanation, and Guillaume had clasped her arm, led her back into her room.

Janvier had asked under his breath:

'You arresting him?'

Maigret had made no reply. He didn't know. To tell the truth, he'd only just made up his mind, on the spur of the moment, here, on the landing.

'Come, in, Monsieur Serre. Will you take a seat?'

The clock on the mantelpiece said four twenty-five. It was a Saturday. Maigret had only realized that from the bustle in the streets, as they crossed the city in a car.

The Chief-Inspector closed the door. The windows were open, and papers on the desk fluttered under the weights that prevented them from blowing away.

'I asked you to sit down.'

He himself went into the wall cupboard to hang up his hat and coat there and to rinse his hands under the enamel fountain.

For the next ten minutes he didn't say a word to the dentist, being too busy signing the things that were waiting on his desk. He rang for Joseph, gave him the file; then, slowly and deliberately, he filled the half-dozen pipes set out in front of him.

It was seldom that anyone in Serre's position could stand it for long without asking questions, losing his nerve, crossing and uncrossing his legs.

At last there was a knock at the door. It was the photographer who'd worked with them all day and been sent on a mission by Maigret. He handed the Chief-Inspector the still damp print of a document.

'Thank you, Dambois. Stay back there. Don't leave without letting me know.'

He waited until the door closed again, lit one of the pipes:

'Would you bring your chair nearer, Monsieur Serre?'

They were now facing each other, separated by the width of the desk, across which Maigret held out the document in his hand.

He added no comment. The dentist took the print, brought a pair of spectacles out of his pocket, examined it carefully and put it down on the table.

'I'm waiting.'

'I've nothing to say.'

The photograph was that of a page from the ironmonger's ledger, the one recording the sale of the second sheet of glass and the second half-pound of putty.

'You realize what that implies?'

'Am I to understand that I'm charged?'

Maigret hesitated.

'No,' he decided. 'Officially, you're summoned as a witness. If you wish, however, I am ready to charge you, more exactly to ask the Director of Prosecutions to indict you, which would entitle you to have legal advice.'

'I've already told you that I don't want a lawyer.'

These were only the preliminary moves. Two heavy-weights were sizing each other up, taking each other's measure, feeling their way, in the office which had become a sort of ring, and silence reigned in the Duty Room, where Janvier had just put his colleagues in the picture.

'I reckon we're in for a long session!' he told them.

'Think the Chief'll go the limit?'

'He's got that look on his face.'

They all knew what that meant, and Janvier was the first to ring up his wife and tell her not to be surprised if he didn't come home that night.

'Have you a weak heart, Monsieur Serre?'

'An enlarged heart, like yourself, in all probability.'

'Your father died of heart trouble when you were seventeen, didn't he?'

'Seventeen and a half.'

'Your first wife died of heart trouble. Your second wife also had heart trouble.'

'According to statistics, about thirty per cent of people die of heart failure.'

'Your life's insured, Monsieur Serre?'

'Since I was a child.'

'Of course, I saw the policy earlier on. If I remember rightly, your mother is not insured.'

'That's correct.'

'Your father was?'

'I believe so.'

'And your first wife?'

'I saw you take the documents away.'

'Your second wife, as well?'

'It's quite a usual procedure.'

'What is less usual is to keep a sum of several million francs, in gold and currency, in a safe.'

'D'you think so?'

'Can you tell me why you keep this money at home, where it can bring in no interest?'

'I imagine that thousands of people, nowadays, do the same. You forget the financial bills that have resulted several times in a panic, the excessive rate of taxation and the constant devaluations. . . .'

'I understand. You admit that your intention was to conceal your capital and defraud the Treasury?'

Serre was silent.

'Did your wife – I mean your second wife, Maria – know that this money was shut up in your safe?'

'She did.'

'You told her about it?'

'Her own money was in there as well a few days ago.'

He took his time before answering, weighed his words, let them fall one by one while keeping his eyes fixed gravely on the Chief-Inspector.

'I didn't find any marriage-contract among your papers. Am I to conclude that you were married under the joint-possession laws?'

'That is correct.'

'Isn't that odd, considering your ages?'

'I have already given you the reason. A contract would have obliged us to draw up a balance-sheet of our respective goods.'

'The joint-possession, however, had no existence in actual fact?'

'We each continued to retain control of our own affairs.'

And didn't all this seem quite natural?

'Was your wife wealthy?'

'She is wealthy.'

'As wealthy as you are, or wealthier?'

'About the same.'

'Does she have the whole of her money in France?'

'Only part of it. From her father, she inherited shares in a cheese factory in Holland.'

'In what form did she keep her other assets?'

'Mainly in gold.'

'Even before she met you?'

'I see what you're getting at. Nevertheless, I will tell you the truth. It was I who advised her to sell out her securities and to buy gold.'

'This gold was kept, with yours, in your safe?'

'It used to be.'

'Until when?'

'Tuesday. At the beginning of the afternoon, when she'd nearly finished packing, she came downstairs and I gave her what belonged to her.'

'Then this sum, when she left, was in one of the two suit-cases or in the trunk?'

'I suppose so.'

'She didn't go out before dinner?'

'I didn't hear her go out.'

'So, to your knowledge, she didn't go out?'

He nodded in confirmation.

'Did she telephone at all?'

'The only telephone in the house is in my study and she did not make use of it.'

'How am I to know, Monsieur Serre, that the money which I found in the safe is *yours alone*, and not yours *and* your wife's?'

Without emotion, still maintaining an expression of weariness or disdain, the dentist took from his pocket a green note-book which he handed to the Chief-Inspector. Its pages were covered with tiny figures. Those on the left-hand side were headed with the initial O; those on the right with the initial M.

'What does O stand for?'

'Ours. I mean my mother and myself. We've always shared everything, without making any distinction between what is hers and what is mine.'

'The M, I suppose, stands for Maria?'

'You are right.'

'I see a certain figure that occurs at regular intervals.'

'Her share of the household expenses.'

'Every month she paid you the cost of her bed and board?'

'If you like. Actually, she didn't pay me any money, because it was in the safe, but her account was debited with the amount.'

Maigret leafed through the note-book for a few minutes without speaking, got up and went into the room next door where, like schoolboys, the plain-clothes men immediately pretended to be busy.

He gave instructions to Janvier in a low voice, hesitated as to whether he should have beer sent up for himself, swallowed, as if automatically, the dregs of a glass which stood on Vacher's desk.

When he returned, Serre, who had not moved from his chair, had just lit one of his long cigars and murmured not without insolence:

'D'you mind?'

Maigret was loth to say yes, shrugged his shoulders.

'You've thought about this second window-pane, Monsieur Serre?'

'I haven't bothered to do so.'

'You're wrong. It'd be much better if you could find some reasonable explanation.'

'I'm not looking for one. . . .'

'D'you continue to maintain that you have only once replaced the pane in your study window?'

'The day after the thunderstorm.'

'Would you like us to have the weather-bureau confirm that there was no thunderstorm at Neuilly on Tuesday night?'

'It's pointless. Unless it would give you any satisfaction. I'm speaking of last week's thunderstorm.'

'The day after, you went to the ironmonger's in the Rue de Longchamp and you bought a sheet of glass and some putty.'

'I have told you that already.'

'You are prepared to swear that you haven't been back to the shop since then?'

And he pushed across the desk the photograph of the ledger entry.

'Why, in your opinion, should they have troubled to enter these purchases of glass and putty twice in their books?'

'I've no idea.'

'Why should the shopkeeper state that you came in on Wednesday, about eight o'clock in the morning?'

'That's his business.'

'When did you last use your car?'

'Last Sunday.'

'Where did you go?'

'We took a drive for two or three hours, my mother and I, as is our custom every Sunday.'

'In which direction?'

'Towards the forest of Fontainebleau.'

'Did your wife go with you?'

'No. She wasn't feeling well.'

'You'd decided to separate?'

'There was no question of a separation. She was tired, run down. She didn't always get on with my mother. By mutual agreement we decided that she should go back to her own country for a few weeks or a few months.'

'She took her money with her, all the same?'

'Yes.'

'Why?'

'Because there was a possibility that she wouldn't come back. We're no longer children. We're able to look at life calmly. It is a sort of experiment that we are making.'

'Tell me, Monsieur Serre, there are two frontiers to cross before you reach Amsterdam, aren't there? The French customs, on the way out, are fairly strict about the currency regulations. Wasn't your wife afraid that her gold would be discovered and impounded?'

'Am I obliged to answer?'

'I think it's in your own interests.'

'Even if I risk proceedings?'

'They'd probably be less serious than a charge of murder.'

'Very well. One of my wife's suit-cases was provided with a false bottom.'

'Specially for this trip?'

'No.'

'She'd already had occasions to use it?'

'Several times.'

'To cross the frontier?'

'The Belgian frontier and, once, the Swiss frontier. You're aware, I'm sure, that until just recently it was easier and less expensive to procure gold in Belgium and especially in Switzerland.'

'You admit your complicity in these transfers of capital?'

'I do.'

Maigret got up, went back into the Duty Room.

'Mind coming here a moment, Janvier?'

Then, to Serre:

'My assistant will take down this part of our interview. Please repeat to him word for word what you've just told me. See that he signs his statement, Janvier.'

He went out, got Vacher to show him the office that had been assigned to the translator. He was a little man with glasses who was typing his translation straight onto the machine and pausing from time to time to consult the dictionary that he'd brought with him.

There were at least forty letters, most of them comprising several sheets.

'Where have you begun?'

'At the beginning. I'm onto the third letter. All three are dated about two and a half years ago. In the first one, the lady tells her friend that she's getting married, that her future husband is a distinguished man, of imposing appearance, belonging to the highest French professional class, and that his mother looks like I can't remember which painting in the Louvre. I can tell you the name of the painter.'

He turned over the pages.

'A Clouet. Painting is mentioned all the time in these letters. When she's saying what the weather's like, she cites Monet or Renoir.'

'I'd like you to begin at the end, from now on.'

'As you wish. You realize that if I spend all night at it, I won't have finished by tomorrow morning?'

'That's why I'm asking you to begin at the end. What's the date of the last letter?'

'Last Sunday.'

'Can you read it to me quickly?'

'I can give you some idea of it. Wait a moment.'

> 'Gertrude darling,
> 'Paris has never been so resplendent as this morning and I very nearly went with G. and his mother to the forest of Fontainebleau, which must be adorned with all the glories of a Corot or a Courbet. . . .'

'Is there a lot about the glories?'

'Shall I skip?'

'Please.'

The translator ran his eyes down a page and moved his lips silently as if in prayer.

'Here you are:

> 'I wonder what effect returning once again to our Holland and its pastel shades will have upon me and now that the time comes near, I feel I'm being cowardly.
> 'After all that I've written to you about my life here, about G. and my mother-in-law, you must be wondering what has happened to me and why I am no longer happy.
> 'It's perhaps because of the dream I had last night, which has spoilt my day. Do you recall the little picture that hangs in The Hague museum and made us blush? It isn't signed. It's attributed to a painter of the Florentine School whose name I have forgotten, and depicts a faun carrying away over his shoulder a completely naked woman who is resisting. You remember?
> 'The faun, in my dream, had G.'s face, and his expression was so fierce that I awoke trembling and bathed in perspiration.
> 'Not with fear, that was the strangest thing. My memory is confused. There was some fear, certainly, but also another emotion. I'll try to explain it to you on Wednesday, when we'll at last be able to chat as we did so much when you came over on your last trip.
> 'I'm to leave on Tuesday night, it's settled. There's no doubt about it. So there are only two more days to wait. I've heaps of things to do during that time. It'll pass quickly. Nevertheless, it seems to me still far away, almost unreal.
> 'Sometimes I have the feeling, especially after that dream, that something will happen to prevent my departure.
> 'Don't worry. My decision is final. I shall follow your advice. I cannot stand this life here for much longer. But . . .'

'You in here, Chief?'

It was Janvier, with sheets of paper in his hand.

'It's done. He's waiting for you.'

Maigret took the papers, left the translator to his task, crossed the Duty Room deep in thought.

Nobody, at that time, could have foretold how long the questioning would take. Guillaume Serre looked up at the Chief-Inspector, took a pen of his own accord from the desk.

'I suppose I have to sign?'

'Yes, here. Have you read it through?'

'I've read it. Might I trouble you for a glass of water?'

'You wouldn't prefer red wine?'

The dentist looked at him, gave the faintest of smiles, inscrutable, heavy with irony and bitterness.

'That, too?' he said disdainfully.

'That, too, Monsieur Serre. You're so afraid of your mother that you are reduced to drink in hiding.'

'Is that a question? I've got to answer?'

'If you wish to.'

'Allow me to inform you then that my mother's father was a drunkard, that her two brothers, who are now dead, were drunkards as well, and that her sister ended her days in a lunatic asylum. My mother has lived in fear of seeing me take to drink in my turn, for she refuses to believe that this tendency is not hereditary. When I was a student, she waited my return with anxiety, and would even sometimes keep a watch on the cafés in the Boulevard Saint-Michel where I was sitting with my friends. There have never been any spirits in the house and though there's wine in the cellar, she's kept the habit of carrying the key on her.'

'She allows you a glass of wine and water at every meal, doesn't she?'

'I know that she called to see you and spoke to you.'

'Did she tell you what she said to me?'

'Yes.'

'Are you very fond of your mother, Monsieur Serre?'

'The two of us have almost always lived together.'

'Rather like a married couple?'

He coloured slightly.

'I don't know what you mean.'

'Is your mother jealous?'

'I beg your pardon?'

'I'm asking you whether, as often happens with a widow and an only son, your mother shows signs of jealousy towards the people you know. Have you many friends?'

'Has this any connection with the alleged disappearance of my wife?'

'I didn't find in the house a single letter from a friend, or even one of those group photographs that one sees in most homes.'

He didn't speak.

'Nor is there any photograph of your first wife.'

Still silence.

'Another thing that struck me, Monsieur Serre. The portrait hanging over the mantelpiece is surely of your maternal grandfather?'

'Yes.'

'The one who drank?'

A sign of assent.

'In a drawer I came across a certain number of pictures of yourself as a child and as a young man, also pictures of women and men who must have been your grandmother, your aunt and your uncles. Always on your mother's side. Doesn't it seem surprising to you that there isn't a single portrait of your father or of his family?'

'It hadn't struck me.'

'Were they destroyed after your father's death?'

'My mother could answer that question better than I.'

'You don't remember if they were destroyed?'

'I was quite young.'

'You were seventeen. What memory have you of your father, Monsieur Serre?'

'Is this part of your interrogation?'

'Neither my questions nor your answers, as you see, are being recorded. Your father was a solicitor?'

'Yes.'

'Did he take personal charge of his practice?'

'Not often. His chief clerk did most of the work.'

'Did he lead a very social life? Or was he exclusively devoted to the family circle?'

'He went about a great deal.'

'He had mistresses?'

'I couldn't tell you.'

'Did he die in his bed?'

'On the stairs, going up to his room.'

'Were you at home?'

'I'd gone out. When I came back, he'd been dead for nearly two hours.'

'Who attended him?'

'Doctor Dutilleux.'

'Is he still alive?'

'He died at least ten years ago.'

'Were you there when your first wife died?'

He drew his heavy brows together, staring at Maigret fixedly, and his lower lip was thrust out in a kind of disgust.

'Answer me, please.'

'I was in the house.'

'What part of the house?'

'In my study.'

'What time was it?'

'About nine p.m.'

'Did your wife keep to her room?'

'She'd gone up early. She didn't feel very well.'

'Had she felt ill for some time?'

'I don't remember.'

'Was your mother with her?'

'She was upstairs as well.'

'With her?'

'I've no idea.'

'Was it your mother who called you?'

'I think so.'

'When you got to the room, your wife was dead?'

'No.'

'Did she die a long time afterwards?'

'Fifteen or twenty minutes later. The doctor was ringing the door-bell.'

'Which doctor?'

'Dutilleux.'

'He was your family doctor?'

'He attended me when I was a child.'

'A friend of your father's?'

'Of my mother.'

'Did he have children?'

'Two or three.'

'You've lost sight of them?'

'I never knew them personally.'

'Why didn't you inform the police that somebody had tried to break open your safe?'

'I had nothing to inform the police.'

'What did you do with the tools?'

'What tools?'

'The ones the burglar left in the room when he made his getaway.'

'I saw neither tools nor burglar.'

'You didn't make use of your car on Tuesday night or early Wednesday morning?'

'I did not.'

'You were unaware that somebody used it?'

'I've had no reason, since then, to go into the garage.'

'When you garaged your car, last Sunday, were there scratches on the boot and the right mudguard?'

'I didn't notice anything.'

'Did you get out of the car, you and your mother?'

He didn't answer for a moment.

'I asked you a question.'

'I'm trying to remember.'

'It shouldn't be so difficult. You were driving along the road to Fontainebleau. Did you set foot to the ground?'

'Yes. We went for a walk in the country.'

'You mean on a country road?'

'A little path running between the fields on the right-hand side of the road.'

'Could you find this path again?'

'I think so.'

'Was it tarred?'

'I don't believe it was. No. That seems unlikely.'

'Where is your wife, Monsieur Serre?'

And the Chief-Inspector rose, not expecting any answer.

'Because we've got to find her, haven't we?'

Chapter Seven

About five o'clock, already, Maigret had got up for a moment to open the communicating door between his office and the Duty Room and had winked at Janvier. A little later he'd got up again to go and shut the window, despite the heat, because of the noise from outside.

At ten to six he passed through the Duty Room, his jacket over his arm.

'All yours!' he told Janvier.

The latter and his colleagues had grasped the situation a long while ago. From the moment when, at the Rue de la Ferme, the Chief-Inspector had ordered Serre to come along, Janvier was pretty sure that he wouldn't get away from Headquarters very easily. What surprised him was that the Chief had made his decision so abruptly, without waiting to have all the evidence in his hands.

'She's in the waiting-room,' he said under his breath.

'Who?'

'The mother.'

Maigret stationed Marlieux, a young plain-clothes man, who knew shorthand, behind the door.

'Same questions?' asked Janvier.

'The same. And any others that come into your head.'

The idea was to wear down the dentist. The others could take it in turns, go out for a cup of coffee or a pint, make contact with the outside world again, while he would stay as long as need be in the same office, in the same chair.

Maigret began by calling in on the translator, who'd decided to take off his jacket and tie.

'What's she say?'

'I've translated the last four letters. There's a passage in the last but one that might interest you.

> 'I've made up my mind, Gertrude dear. I am still wondering how it came about. Yet I had no dreams last night, or if I had, I have forgotten them.'

'Does she say much about her dreams?'

'Yes. They're always coming into it. And she interprets them.'

'Go on.'

> 'You've often asked me what has gone wrong and I answered that you were imagining things and that I was happy. The truth is that I was trying to persuade myself of it.
>
> 'Honestly, I've done all I could, for two and a half years, to try and believe that this house was my home and that G. was my husband.
>
> 'In my heart, you see, I knew that it wasn't true, that I'd always been a stranger here, more of a stranger than I was in the boarding-house you know,

where we two spent so many happy hours.

'How did I suddenly come to see things as they really are?

'Do you remember, when we were little girls? We used to play at comparing everything we saw—people, streets, animals—with the pictures in our photograph albums. We wanted life to be like them. Then, later on, when we began to visit the museums, it was paintings that we used for comparison.

'I did the same here, but I did it on purpose, without believing in it, and this morning I suddenly saw the house as it really is, I saw my mother-in-law, I saw G. with a fresh vision, without illusions.

'I hadn't had any for some time—I mean illusions. You've got to understand me. I no longer had any, but I stubbornly refused to admit it.

'Now that's over. I made up my mind to leave on the spot. I haven't told anyone yet. The old lady hasn't any inkling. She still behaves the same towards me, meek and smiling, so long as I do everything she wants.

'*She's the most selfish woman I have ever known.*

'Those words are underlined,' the translator remarked. 'Shall I go on?

'As for G., I wonder whether it won't be a relief for him to see me go. He knows that from the beginning we had nothing in common. I could never get used to the feel of his skin, to his smell. Do you understand now why we've never shared the same room, which surprised you so much at the start?

'After two and a half years, it's exactly as though I'd just met him in the street or in the underground, and I have the same feeling of recoil whenever he comes to my room. Luckily it doesn't happen often.

'I even think, between ourselves, that he only comes because he believes it gives me pleasure, or because he feels it's his duty.

'Perhaps it's his mother who tells him to? It's possible. Don't laugh. I don't know how it is with your own husband, but G. has the crest-fallen look of a schoolboy who's just been given a hundred lines. Can you see what I mean?

'I've often wondered if he was the same with his first wife. It's probable. He would be the same, I expect, with anyone. These people, you see, I mean the mother and son, live in a world of their own and have no need of anybody else.

'It seems astonishing that the old lady once had a husband of her own. They never speak about him at home. Besides themselves, there's nobody in the world except the people whose pictures are on the walls, people who are dead, but whom they talk about as if they were more alive than all the living.

'I can't stand it any longer, Gertrude. I'll talk to G. presently. I'll tell him that I feel the need to breathe the air of my own country, and he'll understand. What I'm wondering is, how he'll pluck up the courage to tell his mother. . . .'

'Is there much more?' asked Maigret.

'Seven pages.'

'Go on translating. I'll be back.'

At the door he turned round:

'When you're hungry or thirsty, ring down to the *Brasserie Dauphine*. Get them to send up anything you want.'

'Thank you.'

From the corridor he saw, in the glass-panelled waiting-room, old Madame Serre sitting on one of the green velvet chairs. She was bolt upright, her hands folded in her lap. When she caught sight of Maigret, she made as if to get up, but he passed on without stopping and went down the stairs.

The examination had barely begun and yet it already came as a surprise to see life still going on outside, in broad sunlight, people walking to and fro, taxis, buses with men reading the evening paper on the platform on their way home.

'Rue Gay-Lussac!' he told the driver. 'I'll tell you where to stop.'

The tall trees in the Luxembourg Gardens swayed in the breeze, and all the chairs were taken; there were a lot of bright dresses; some children were still playing along the paths.

'Is Maître Orin at home?' he asked the concierge.

'He hasn't been out for over a month, poor man.'

Maigret had suddenly remembered him. He was probably the oldest solicitor in Paris. The Chief-Inspector had no idea of his age, but he'd always known him as an old man, a semi-invalid, which didn't stop him from always having a smiling face and talking about women with a wicked twinkle in his eye.

He lived, together with a housekeeper almost as old as himself, in a bachelor flat cluttered up with books and prints, which he collected, and most of the prints dealt with bawdy subjects.

Orin was seated in an arm-chair in front of the open window, his knees covered by a rug, despite the weather.

'Well, m'lad? What a pleasant surprise! I'd begun to think everyone had forgotten me or thought that I'd been laid to rest in Père-Lachaise long ago. What's the trouble this time?'

He didn't try to deceive himself, and Maigret coloured slightly, since it was true that he'd seldom called on the lawyer for other than selfish reasons.

'I wondered just now if, by any chance, you would have known a man called Serre who, if I'm not mistaken, died thirty-two or thirty-three years ago.'

'Alain Serre?'

'He was a solicitor.'

'That'd be Alain.'

'What sort of man was he?'

'I suppose I'm not allowed to ask what it's all about?'

'About his son.'

'I never saw the boy. I knew there was a son, but I never met him. You see, Maigret, Alain and I belonged to a gay set, whose life didn't revolve round the family hearth. We were to be found mostly at the club or behind the scenes at variety shows, and we knew all the chorus girls by their Christian names.'

He added, with a ribald grin:

'If you see what I mean!'

'You didn't know his wife?'

'I must have been introduced to her. Didn't she live somewhere in Neuilly? For several years Alain went out of circulation. He wasn't the only one it happened to. There were even a few who looked down on us, once they got married. I didn't expect to see him again. And then, a long time afterwards . . .'

'About how long?'

'I don't know. Some years. Let me see. The club had already moved from the Faubourg Saint-Honoré to the Avenue Hoche. Ten years? Twelve years? Anyway, he came back to us. He behaved oddly at first, as if he thought we bore him a grudge for dropping us.'

'Then?'

'Nothing. He went the pace redoubled. Let's see. He went about for a long time with a little singer with a big mouth they used to call. . . . We had a nickname for her. . . . Something smutty. . . . I can't call it to mind.'

'Did he drink?'

'Not more than anyone else. Two or three bottles of champagne occasionally. . . .'

'What became of him?'

'What becomes of us all in the end. He died.'

'That's all?'

'If you want to know the sequel, m'lad, you'll have to ask aloft. It's St. Peter's business and not mine. What misdeed has his son committed?'

'I don't know yet. His wife has disappeared.'

'A gay dog?'

'No. Quite the reverse.'

'Juliette! Bring us something to drink.'

Maigret had to stay another quarter of an hour with the old man who insisted on trying to find, among his prints, a sketch of the singer.

'I wouldn't swear that it's a good likeness. A very talented chap did it, one night when the whole gang of us were up in his studio.'

The girl was naked and walking on her hands, and her face could not be seen by reason of the fact that her hair was sweeping the floor.

'Come and see me again, Maigret my boy. If you'd had time to share my humble meal. . . .'

A bottle of wine was warming in a corner of the room and a pleasant smell of cooking filled the flat.

The police at Rouen hadn't been able to pick up Sad Freddie any more than those at Le Havre. Perhaps the expert safe-breaker was no longer in that town. Was he on his way back to Paris? Had he read Ernestine's message?

Maigret had sent a plain-clothes man on a mission along the river-bank.

'Where shall I start from?'

'As far upstream as you can.'

He'd also telephoned his wife that he wouldn't be back to dinner.

'D'you think I'll see you tonight?'

'Probably not.'

He wasn't hoping for too much. He, too, knew that he'd assumed a big responsibility by rushing matters and taking Guillaume Serre down to Headquarters before he had the slightest proof.

Now it was too late. He could no longer let him go.

He felt drowsy, glum. He sat down on the terrace of the *Brasserie Dauphine*, but, after reading right through the bill of fare, he ended by ordering a sandwich and a glass of beer, for he wasn't hungry.

He went slowly up the staircase at Headquarters. The lights had just come on, although it was still daylight. As his head reached the first-floor level, he glanced automatically at the waiting-room, and the first thing that caught his eye was a green hat that had begun to get on his nerves.

Ernestine was there, sitting opposite Madame Serre, with her hands in her lap like the old lady, and the same air of patience and resignation. She saw him straight away, and deliberately assumed a fixed stare, giving a slight shake of the head.

He understood that she was asking him not to recognize her. Immediately after, she began talking to the old lady as though the ice had been broken some time before.

He shrugged his shoulders, pushed open the door of the Duty Room. The shorthand writer was at work, a pad of paper on his knee. The weary voice of Janvier could be heard, punctuated by his footsteps as he paced up and down the room next door.

'According to you, Monsieur Serre, your wife fetched a taxi on the corner of the Boulevard Richard-Wallace. How long was she away?'

Before relieving him, he climbed up to Moers' attic, where the latter was busy filing documents.

'Tell me, my boy, apart from the brick dust, there were no traces of anything else in the car?'

'The car had been cleaned out very thoroughly.'

'You're sure?'

'It's only by chance that I found a little powdered brick in a fold of the mat, under the driver's seat.'

'Suppose the car hadn't been cleaned and that the driver had got out on a country road.'

'A tarred road?'

'No. Suppose, I'm saying, that he got out, also the person with him, that they'd both gone for a walk on the path and then climbed back into the car.'

'And that it hadn't been cleaned afterwards?'

'Yes.'

'There'd be marks left. Maybe not many. But I'd have found them.'

'That's all I wanted to know. Don't leave yet.'

'Right you are. By the way, I found two hairs in the room of the woman who's disappeared. She was a natural blonde, but gave herself henna rinses. I can tell you what face-powder she used, too.'

The Chief-Inspector went downstairs again, this time went into his office, throwing off his jacket. He smoked a pipe in there all afternoon. Janvier had smoked cigarettes, and Serre cigars. The air was blue with smoke that drifted in a haze up near the light.

'Aren't you thirsty, Monsieur Serre?'

'The Sergeant gave me a glass of water.'

Janvier went out.

'You wouldn't prefer a glass of beer? Or wine?'

Still the same air of bearing Maigret a personal grudge for these little snares.

'Thank you all the same.'

'A sandwich?'

'D'you expect to keep me here much longer?'

'I don't know. Probably. It'll depend on you.'

He went to the door, called out to the plain-clothes men:

'Could one of you fetch me a road-map of the Fontainebleau district?'

He was taking his time. All this was just talk, it was merely scratching the surface.

'When you go for a meal, get them to send up some sandwiches and beer, Janvier.'

'Right you are, Chief.'

The road-map was brought to him. 'Show me the spot where you pulled up on Sunday.'

Serre searched for a moment, took a pencil from the desk, marked a cross where the main road met a country lane.

'If there's a farm with a red roof on the left, it'll be this lane here.'

'How long did you go on walking?'

'About a quarter of an hour.'

'Were you wearing the same shoes as today?'

He pondered, looked at his shoes, nodded.

'You're sure about that?'

'Certain.'

His shoes had rubber heels, on which concentric circles were stamped around the maker's name.

'Don't you think, Monsieur Serre, that it'd be simpler and less tiring for you to spill the beans? When did you kill your wife?'

'I didn't kill her.'

Maigret sighed, went to give fresh instructions next door. Couldn't be helped! It'd probably take hours more. The dentist's complexion was already slightly muddier than in the morning, and dark circles had begun to show beneath his eyes.

'Why did you marry her?'

'My mother advised me to.'

'For what motive?'

'For fear I'd be left to live alone one day. She thinks that I'm still a child and that I need someone to look after me.'

'And to stop you from drinking?'

Silence.

'I don't suppose that your marriage with Maria Van Aerts was a love match?'

'We were both nearing our fifties.'

'When did you start to quarrel?'

'We never quarrelled.'

'What did you do with your evenings, Monsieur Serre?'

'I?'

'You.'

'I mostly read, in my study.'

'And your wife?'

'Writing, in her room. She used to go to bed early.'

'Did your father lose much money?'

'I don't understand.'

'Have you ever heard that your father used to lead what they called in those days a fast life?'

'He went about a great deal.'

'Did he spend large sums?'

'I believe so.'

'Your mother made scenes?'

'We're not the sort of people who make scenes.'

'How much did your first marriage bring you in?'

'We don't speak the same language.'

'You and your first wife were married under the joint-possession law?'

'Correct.'

'And she had money. So you must have inherited.'

'Is that unusual?'

'So long as your second wife's body isn't found, you can't inherit from her.'

'Why shouldn't she be found alive?'

'You believe that, Serre?'

'I didn't kill her.'

'Why did you take your car out on Tuesday night?'

'I didn't take it out.'

'The concierge in the house opposite saw you. It was round about midnight.'

'You forget that there are three garages, three former stables, whose doors are adjacent. It was at night, you say so yourself. She may have got them confused.'

'The ironmonger, he couldn't have mistaken someone else for you, in broad daylight, when you went in to buy putty and another window-pane.'

'My word's as good as his.'

'Providing you didn't kill your wife. What did you do with the trunk and the suit-cases?'

'That's the third time I've been asked that question. You've forgotten to mention the tools this time.'

'Where were you on Tuesday about midnight?'

'In bed.'

'Are you a light sleeper, Monsieur Serre?'

'No. My mother is.'

'Neither of you heard anything?'

'I seem to remember telling you that already.'

'And on Wednesday morning you found the house as usual?'

'I suppose that, since an enquiry has been opened, you've the right to question me. You've decided, haven't you, to put me through an endurance test? Your detective has already asked me all these questions. Now it's starting all over again. I can see that it's going to go on all night. To save time, I'll tell you once and for all that I didn't kill my wife. I also inform you that I will not answer any questions which have already been put to me. Is my mother here?'

'What makes you think that she is?'

'Does it seem peculiar to you?'

'She's sitting in the waiting-room.'

'D'you mean to let her spend the night there?'

'I shall make no attempt to prevent her. She's quite free.'

This time Guillaume Serre looked at him with hatred.

'I wouldn't like to have your job.'

'I wouldn't like to be in your shoes.'

They stared at each other in silence, each determined not to lower his gaze.

'You killed your wife, Serre. As you probably killed the first one.'

The other didn't move a muscle.

'You'll confess to it.'

A contemptuous smile curled the dentist's lips, and he threw himself back in his chair and crossed his legs.

Next door the waiter from the *Brasserie Dauphine* could be heard putting down plates and glasses on a desk.

'I wouldn't mind something to eat.'

'Perhaps you'd like to take off your coat?'

'No.'

He started to eat a sandwich slowly, while Maigret went to fill a glass with water from the fountain in the wall cupboard.

It was eight o'clock in the evening.

They could see the windows darkening gradually, the view dissolving into specks of light that seemed as far away as the stars.

Maigret had to send out for tobacco. At eleven o'clock, the dentist was smoking his last cigar and the air had got more and more thick. Twice the Chief-Inspector had gone out for a stroll through the building and had seen the two women in the waiting-room. The second time they'd drawn their chairs closer together and were gossiping together as if they'd known each other for years.

'When did you clean your car?'

'It was last cleaned a fortnight ago, in a garage at Neuilly, at the same time as they changed the oil.'

'It hasn't been cleaned again since Sunday?'

'No.'

'You see, Monsieur Serre, we've just performed a decisive experiment. One of my men who, like yourself, is wearing rubber heels, drove out to the crossing which you marked on the Fontainebleau road. As you stated that you did on Sunday with your mother, he got out of the car and went for a walk along the country lane. It hasn't a tarred surface. He got back in the car and returned here.

'The experts from our technical branch, who're supposed to know their job, then examined the mats in the car.

'Here is the dust and gravel that they gathered up.'

He pushed a small paper bag across the desk.

Serre made no move to take it.

'We'd have found the same thing on the mat in your car.'

'That proves I killed my wife?'

'It proves that your car has been cleaned since Sunday.'

'Couldn't someone have got into my garage?'

'It's unlikely.'

'Didn't your men get in?'

'What are you insinuating?'

'Nothing, Chief-Inspector. I'm not accusing anyone. I'm merely pointing out to you that this operation was undertaken without witnesses, therefore without legal warranty.'

'Wouldn't you like to speak to your mother?'

'You'd love to know what I'd have to say to her? Nothing, Monsieur Maigret. I've nothing to say to her, and she has nothing to say to me.'

A thought suddenly crossed his mind.

'Has she had anything to eat?'

'I've no idea. I can only repeat that she's a free agent.'

'She won't leave as long as I'm here.'

'She may be in for a long stay.'

Serre lowered his eyes and his manner changed. After a long hesitation, he muttered, as if slightly ashamed:

'I suppose it would be asking too much to have a sandwich sent in to her?'

'That was done a long time ago.'

'Did she eat it?'

'Yes.'

'How is she?'

'She talks all the time.'

'To whom?'

'To a certain person who happens also to be in the waiting-room. A girl who used to be on the streets.'

And again there was a gleam of hate in the dentist's eyes.

'You arranged that deliberately, didn't you?'

'Not at all.'

'My mother has nothing to tell.'

'All the better for you.'

They passed the next quarter of an hour in silence, then Maigret plodded into the next-door room, glummer than ever, motioned to Janvier who was dozing in a corner.

'Same routine, Chief?'

'Anything you like.'

The stenographer was worn out. The translator still worked on in his cubbyhole.

'Go and fetch Ernestine, the one with the green hat, and bring her to Lucas's office.'

When Lofty came in, she didn't look pleased.

'You oughtn't to have interrupted us. She'll start suspecting something.'

Perhaps because it was late at night, Maigret spoke to her more familiarly than usual, without noticing it.

'What've you been filling her up with?'

'How I didn't know why I'd been made to come here, how my husband's been missing two days and I had no news, how much I hate the police and the tricks they're always trying on.

'"They're just keeping me waiting here to try and shake me!" I told her. "They reckon they can get away with anything."'

'What did she say?'

'She asked me if I'd been here before. I said yes, I'd been put through it for a whole night, a year ago, because my husband had had a scrap in a café and they wanted to make out he'd knifed somebody. To start off with, she looked at me like she was sort of disgusted. Then, bit by bit, she began to ask me questions.'

'What about?'

'Mostly about you. I told here everything bad I could think up. I took good care to add that you always managed to make people talk, however tough you had to get with 'em.'

'What!'

'I know what I'm doing. I told her about the time when you kept somebody stark naked in your office for twenty-four hours, in midwinter, taking care the window was left wide open.'

'There's been so such thing.'

'It shook her. She's less sure of herself than she was when I got here. She spends all her time listening.

'"Does he beat people?" she asked me.

'"It's been known."'

'Would you like me to go back to her?'

'If you want to.'

'Only I'd like to be taken back to the waiting-room by one of the men, and have him be rough with me.'

'Still no news of Alfred.'

'You haven't had any either?'

Maigret had her taken back in the way that she'd asked for and the plain-clothes man returned grinning wryly.

'What happened?'

'Nothing much. When I passed by the old girl, she put up her arm as if she thought I was going to hit her. I'd hardly got out of the room when Lofty burst out crying.'

Madame Maigret rang up to find out if her husband had eaten anything.

'Shall I wait for you?'

'Certainly not.'

He had a headache. He was disgruntled with himself, with everybody else. Perhaps he was a bit uneasy as well. He wondered what would happen if they suddenly received a telephone call from Maria Van Aerts announcing that she'd changed her plans and had quietly settled down in some town or other.

He drank a pint already gone tepid, told them to send up some more before the *brasserie* closed and went back into his office, where Janvier had opened the window. The clamour of the city had subsided. Now and then a taxi crossed the Pont Saint-Michel.

He sat down, his shoulders drooping. Janvier went out. After a long pause, he said musingly:

'Your mother's got it into her head that I'm torturing you.'

He was surprised to see the other raise his head sharply, and for the first time he saw his face look anxious.

'What have they been telling her?'

'I don't know. It's probably the girl who's in there with her. These people like to make up stories so's to seem more interesting.'

'Could I see her?'

'Who?'

'My mother.'

Maigret pretended to hesitate, to weigh up the pros and cons, finally shook his head.

'No,' he said decisively. 'I think I'll question her myself. And I'm wondering if I shouldn't have Eugénie brought down, too.'

'My mother doesn't know anything.'

'Do you?'

'I don't either.'

'Then there's no reason why I shouldn't question her as I've questioned you.'

'Haven't you any pity, Inspector?'

'For whom?'

'An old woman.'

'Maria would have liked to become an old woman, too.'

He walked up and down the office, his hands behind his back, but what he was waiting for didn't come.

'Your turn, Janvier! I'm going to have a crack at the mother.'

Actually he didn't know yet whether he would do so or not. Janvier said later that he'd never known the Chief so tired and so surly as on that night.

It was one in the morning. Everybody at Headquarters had lost confidence, and chagrined glances were exchanged behind the Chief-Inspector's back.

Chapter Eight

Maigret was emerging from the Duty Room on his way to look in on the translator when one of the cleaners, who, half an hour before, had invaded the building, came up to tell him:

'There's a lady asking to speak to you.'

'Where?'

'It's one of the two who were in the waiting-room. Seems she's not feeling well. She came into the office I was sweeping out, white in the face like she'd come over queer, and asked me straight off to fetch you.'

'The old lady?' Maigret asked, frowning.

'No, the girl.'

Most of the doors that gave onto the corridor were open. In an office two doors away, the Chief-Inspector caught sight of Ernestine holding one hand to her breast, and strode quickly forward, scowling, his lips framing a question.

'Shut the door,' she whispered when he was within earshot.

And directly he'd done so:

'Phew! I couldn't stick it any longer and that's the truth, but I'm not sick. I put on an act so's to get away from her for a bit. Not that I'm feeling any too bright, either. You wouldn't have a stiff drink about the place?'

He had to go back to his office to get the bottle of brandy that he always kept in the cupboard. Not having any smaller glasses, he poured the spirit into a tumbler and she swallowed it at a gulp, with a shudder.

'I don't know how you manage to take the son. The mother's got me right down. In the finish, I reckoned I'd go crackers.'

'Did she talk?'

'She's wider than me. That's just what I wanted to tell you. To start off I made sure she'd swallowed all the bull I was stuffing her up with.

'Then, I don't know how it happened, she started to pop in a question here and there, all innocent-like. I've been third-degree'd before now and I reckoned I could hold my own.

'With her, I didn't have an earthly.'

'Did you tell her what you were?'

'Not right out. That woman's very, very clever, Monsieur Maigret. How could she have guessed I'd been on the beat? Tell me, does it still show? Then she says to me:

'"You're no stranger to these kind of people, are you?"

'It was your mob she was referring to.

'In the end, she's asking me what it's like in jail, and I'm telling her.

'If you'd told me, when I sat down there in front of her, that I'd give the game away, I'd have refused to credit it.'

'Did you tell her about Alfred?'

'In a way. Without saying exactly what his racket is. She thinks he's a kite-man. She's not all that interested. For three-quarters of an hour now, at least, she's been asking me about life in jail: what time you get up, what you have to eat, what the wardresses act like. . . . I thought you'd be interested to know and I made out I'd come over queer; I got up saying I was going to ask for a drink, that it wasn't human leaving women to hang about all night. . . .

'Mind if I have another drop?'

She really was worn out. The brandy brought the colour back into her cheeks.

'Her son won't talk?'

'Not yet. Has she said anything about him?'

'She harks to every sound, gets jumpy every time a door opens. Something else she asked me. She wanted to know if I'd met anybody who'd got guillotined. Now I feel better, I'll go back to her. I'll be on my guard this time, don't worry.'

She took the opportunity to put on some powder, looked at the bottle without venturing to ask for a third drink.

'What's the time?'

'Three o'clock.'

'I don't know how she sticks it. She doesn't look tired, and she's sitting up as straight as at the start of the evening.'

Maigret let her out, took a breath of air at a window opening on to the courtyard and swallowed a mouthful of brandy out of the bottle. As he crossed the office where the translator was working, the latter showed him a passage that he'd underlined in one of the letters.

'This dates back a year and a half,' he said.

Maria had written to her friend:

> Yesterday I had a good laugh. G. came to my room, not for what you might think, but to talk to me about a scheme I'd proposed the day before to go and spend a couple of days in Nice.
>
> They're terrified of travelling, these people. Only once in their lives have they ever been out of France. Their one trip abroad goes back to the time when the father was still alive and they all went over to London together. Incidentally, it appears that they were all seasick and had to call in the ship's doctor.
>
> But that's nothing to do with the case.
>
> Whenever I say something that doesn't suit them, they don't answer straight away. They just stop talking, and, as the saying goes, one can hear a pin drop.
>
> Then, later on or next day, G. comes up to my room, looking distressed, beats about the bush, finally confesses what's worrying him. Briefly, it would seem that my notion of going to Nice for the Carnival was ludicrous, almost indecent. He made no bones about telling me that his mother had been shocked by it and pleaded with me to give up the idea.
>
> Well, it so happened that the drawer of my bedside-table was open. He glanced into it by accident and I saw him turn pale.
>
> 'What's that?' he stammered, pointing at the little automatic with a mother-of-pearl butt that I bought during my trip to Egypt.
>
> Do you remember? I wrote to you about it at the time. People had told me that a woman on her own was never safe in places like that.
>
> I don't know why I'd put it in that drawer. I replied coolly:
>
> 'It's a pistol.'
>
> 'Is it loaded?'
>
> 'I don't remember.'
>
> I picked it up. I looked in the magazine. There were no bullets in it.
>
> 'Have you any ammunition?'

'There must be some somewhere.'

Half an hour later, my mother-in-law came up on some excuse, for she never enters my room without giving a reason. She also beat about the bush for a while, then explained to me that it was most unseemly for a woman to carry fire-arms.

'But it's more like a toy,' I retorted. 'I keep it as a souvenir, because the handle's pretty and my initials are engraved on it. I don't think it could harm anybody much, either.'

She gave in, finally. But not before I'd had to give her the box of ammunition that was in the bottom of the drawer.

The funny part is that, no sooner had she gone, than I found in one of my handbags another ammunition-clip that I'd forgotten about. I didn't tell her. . . .

Maigret, who was holding the brandy bottle in his hand, poured some out for the translator, then he went to give some to the typist and the plain-clothes man who, to try to keep awake, was doodling on his blotter.

When he went back into his office, which Janvier vacated automatically, the bell had gone for another round.

'I've been thinking, Serre. I'm beginning to believe that you haven't been lying as much as I supposed.'

He'd dropped the 'Monsieur', as if so many hours alone together had brought a sort of familiarity. The dentist merely regarded him mistrustfully.

'Maria wasn't meant to disappear any more than your first wife. Her disappearance wasn't to your advantage. She'd packed her bags, announced her departure for Holland. She really intended to take the night-train.

'I don't know if she was supposed to die in the house or not until she got outside. What d'you say to that?'

Guillaume Serre made no reply, but his expression betrayed much more concern.

'If you like it better, she was meant to die a natural death, by which I mean a death that would *pass as natural.*

'This didn't take place, since, if it had, you'd have had no motive for disposing of her body or her luggage.

'There's another thing that doesn't add up. You'd said good-bye to each other. She'd no reason then to go back into your study. Yet her dead body was lying there at a certain time that night.

'I'm not asking you to answer me, but to follow my reasoning. I've only just found out that your wife owned a pistol.

'I'm ready to believe that you shot her in self-defence. After that you got in a panic. You left the body where it had fallen, while you went to get your car out of the garage. It was then, round about midnight, that the concierge saw you.

'What I'm trying to find out, is what changed both your plans and hers. You were in your study, weren't you?'

'I don't remember.'

'That's what you stated.'

'Possibly.'

'I'm convinced that your mother, however, was not in her room, but with you.'

'She was in her room.'

'So you remember that?'

'Yes.'

'Then you remember, also, that you were in your study? Your wife hadn't gone out to fetch a taxi yet. If she'd brought a cab back that night, we'd have found the driver. In other words, it was before leaving the house that she changed her mind and went to your study. Why?'

'I've no idea.'

'You admit that she came to see you?'

'No.'

'You're being unwise, Serre. There are very few instances, in criminal records, when a dead body hasn't been found sooner or later. We shall find hers. And I'm certain, now, that a post-mortem will reveal that she was killed by one or several bullet wounds. What I'm wondering is whether it was a shot fired by your gun or a shot fired by hers.

'The seriousness of your case will depend on that. If the bullet came from her pistol, the conclusion will be drawn that, for one reason or another, she took it into her head to go and settle some score with you and threaten you.

'Money perhaps, Serre?'

He shrugged his shoulders.

'You leaped at her, disarmed her and squeezed the trigger without meaning to. Another theory could be that she threatened your mother and not you. A woman's more likely to feel hatred for another woman than for a man.

'A final possibility, again, is that your own revolver was not in your room, where you put it soon after, but in the drawer of your desk.

'Maria comes in. She's armed. She threatens you. You pull the drawer open and shoot first.

'In either case, you're in no danger of execution. There can be no question of premeditation, since it's quite normal to keep a pistol in the desk of one's study.

'You can even plead self-defence.

'What remains to be explained is why your wife, on the point of leaving, should suddenly have rushed in to see you with a gun in her hand.'

He threw himself back and slowly filled a pipe, without taking his eyes off the other.

'What d'you say to that?'

'This can go on for ever,' said Serre in a tone of disgust.

'You still refuse to talk?'

'I'm answering your questions obediently.'

'You haven't told me why you shot her.'

'I didn't shoot her.'

'Then your mother did?'

'My mother didn't shoot her either. She was up in her room.'

'While you were quarrelling with your wife?'

'There was no quarrel.'

'Pity.'

'I'm so sorry.'

'You see, Serre, I've done my best to discover any reason your wife may have had for settling with you and threatening you.'

'She didn't threaten me.'

'Don't be too positive about it, because you may regret your claims later on. It's you who will plead with me or with the jury to believe that your life or your mother's was in danger.'

Serre smiled sardonically. He was tired, slumped in upon himself, his shoulders slightly hunched about his neck, but he hadn't lost any of his self-possession. His beard showed blue through the skin on his cheeks. The sky, beyond the window-panes, was already not quite so dark and the air in the room was becoming cooler.

It was Maigret who felt the cold first and went over to close the window.

'It wasn't to your advantage to have a corpse on your hands. *I mean a corpse that nobody could be allowed to see.* D'you follow me?'

'No.'

'When your first wife died, it was in such a manner that you were able to call in Doctor Dutilleux to make out the death certificate.

'That's how Maria was supposed to die, from apparently natural causes. She had a weak heart too. What had worked once could work again.

'But something went wrong.

'D'you see, now, what I'm getting at?'

'I didn't kill her.'

'And you didn't dispose of her body, together with her luggage and the burglar's tools?'

'There wasn't any burglar.'

'I'll probably confront you with him in a few hours.'

'You've found him?'

His tone was slightly uneasy, all the same.

'We were able to find his fingerprints in your study. You were careful to wipe over the furniture, but there's always some piece that gets forgotten. He happens to be an old offender, an expert in his way, well-known here, Alfred Jussiaume–"Sad Freddie", they call him. He told his wife what he'd seen. She is now out there in the waiting-room with your mother. As for Jussiaume, he's in Rouen and has no further reason to remain in hiding.

'We already have the concierge who saw you take your car out of the garage. We've also got the ironmonger who sold you a second sheet of glass at eight o'clock on Wednesday morning.

'The technical branch will prove that your car has been cleaned since that date.

'That makes quite a lot of evidence, doesn't it?'

'When we have found the body and the luggage, my job will be over.'

'Then perhaps, you'll decide to explain why, instead of a, shall we say, lawful corpse, you found yourself landed with a body that you had to dispose of at once.

'There was some hitch.

'What was it, Serre?'

The man pulled a handkerchief out of his pocket, wiped his lips and forehead, but didn't open his mouth to reply.

'It's half-past three. I'm beginning to get fed up. Are you still determined not to talk?'

'I've nothing to say.'

'Very good,' said Maigret, getting up. 'I don't like having to bully an old woman. But I see that I am forced to question your mother.'

He expected a protest, at any rate some display of feeling. The dentist didn't bat an eyelid, and it seemed to Maigret that he even showed a kind of relief, that his nerves relaxed.

'You take over, Janvier. I'll get busy on the mother.'

It really was his intention; he was unable to put it into practice immediately, for Vacher had just appeared, in great excitement, a parcel in his hand.

'I've got it, Chief! Took me some time, but I think this is it.'

He undid the parcel wrapped in an old newspaper, revealing broken bits of brick, some reddish dust.

'Where?'

'On the Quai de Billancourt, opposite the Île Seguin. If I'd started down-stream instead of starting up-stream, I'd have been here hours ago. I've been all over the wharves where they unload. Billancourt was the only place where a barge unloaded bricks lately.'

'When?'

'Last Monday. She sailed away about noon on Tuesday. The bricks are still there and kids must have been playing around, broken a fair amount of them. There's a red dust covering a good bit of the quay. Shall I take it up to Moers?'

'I'll go myself.'

As he went through the waiting-room, he looked at the two women sitting there in silence. It seemed, from their attitudes, as if there was now a chill between them.

Maigret entered the laboratory, where he felt he'd earned a cup of coffee, which Moers had just made.

'Have you got the sample of brick dust? Like to compare them?'

The colour was the same, the pattern seemed identical. Moers used magnifying slides and an electric projector.

'Does it add up?'

'Very likely. Comes from the same district, anyhow. It'll take me about thirty minutes or an hour to do the analysis.'

It was too late to have the Seine dragged. Nor would the River patrol be able to send a diver down until sunrise. Then, if they found Maria's body, or only the luggage and the tool-box, the circle would be closed.

'Hello! River Patrol? Maigret here.'

He still seemed to be in a bad temper.

'I'd like you to drag the Seine as soon as possible, Quai de Billancourt, at the place where a cargo of bricks was unloaded recently.'

'In an hour from now it'll be dawn.'

What stopped him from waiting? No jury would ask for further proof to find Guillaume Serre guilty even if he persisted in his denials. Without heeding the typist, who was staring at him, Maigret took a long pull at the bottle, wiped his mouth, went out into the passage and threw open purposefully the door of the waiting-room.

Ernestine thought he'd come for her and sprang quickly to her feet. Madame Serre, however, did not move.

It was the latter to whom Maigret spoke.

'D'you mind coming a moment?'

There was a large choice of empty offices. He pushed open a door at random, closed the window.

'Please take a seat.'

And he began to circle round the room, glancing at the old lady sourly from time to time.

'I don't much like to break bad news,' he growled at last. 'Especially to someone your age. Have you ever been ill, Madame Serre?'

'Except when we were seasick, crossing the Channel, I've never had to call in the doctor.'

'So, naturally, you don't suffer from heart trouble?'

'No.'

'Your son does, however?'

'He's always had an enlarged heart.'

'He killed his wife!' he shot out point-blank, raising his head and staring her in the face.

'Did he tell you so himself?'

He hated to use the old trick of a false confession.

'He still denies it, but that won't help. We've got proof.'

'That he's a murderer?'

'That he shot Maria, in his study.'

She had not moved. Her features had stiffened slightly; one had the impression that she'd stopped breathing, but she showed no other sign of emotion.

'What proof have you?'

'We've found the spot where his wife's body was thrown into the river, together with her luggage and the burglar's tools.'

'Ah!'

That was all she said. She was waiting, her hands stiffly folded on her dark dress.

'Your son refuses to plead self-defence. That's a mistake, because I'm convinced that, when his wife entered the study, she was armed and meant to do him harm.'

'Why?'

'That's what I'm asking you.'

'I've no idea.'

'Where were you?'

'In my room, as I told you.'

'You didn't hear anything?'

'Nothing. Only the door closing. Then the sound of a motor engine, in the street.'

'The taxi?'

'I thought it must be a taxi, since my daughter-in-law had said she was going to fetch one.'

'You're not sure? It might have been a private car?'

'I didn't see it.'

'Then it might easily have been your son's car?'

'He swore to me that he didn't go out.'

'You realize the discrepancy between what you're saying now and the statements that you made to me when you called here of your own accord?'

'No.'

'You stated positively that your daughter-in-law went away in a taxi.'

'I still think that she did.'

'But you're no longer certain about it. Are you so certain now that there was no attempted burglary?'

'I saw no sign of any.'

'What time did you come downstairs on Wednesday morning?'

'About half-past six.'

'Did you go into the study?'

'Not immediately. I got the coffee ready.'

'You didn't go and open the shutters?'

'Yes, I believe so.'

'Before your son came down?'

'Probably.'

'You wouldn't swear to it?'

'Put yourself in my place, Monsieur Maigret. For two days I've hardly known where I am. I've been asked all sorts of questions. I've been sitting in your waiting-room for I don't know how many hours. I'm tired. I'm doing my best to hold out.'

'Why did you come here tonight?'

'Isn't it natural for a mother to follow her son in such circumstances? I've always lived with him. He might be in need of me.'

'Would you follow him to prison?'

'I don't understand. I can't believe that . . .'

'Let me put it another way: if I made out a charge against your son, would you be willing to share the responsibility for what he did?'

'But since he hasn't done anything!'

'Are you sure of that?'

'Why should he have killed his wife?'

'You avoid giving me a straight answer. Are you convinced that he didn't kill her?'

'So far as I can tell.'

'Is there any chance that he did so?'

'He had no motive for it.'

'But he did!' he said harshly, staring her in the face.

She sat as if in suspended animation. She breathed:

'Ah!'

Then she opened her bag to take out her handkerchief. Her eyes were dry. She wasn't crying. She merely dabbed at her lips with the handkerchief.

'Might I have a glass of water?'

He had to hunt around for a moment, since he didn't know the office as well as his own.

'As soon as the Director of Prosecutions arrives at the Palais de Justice, your son will be indicted. I can tell you now that he hasn't the slightest chance of getting away with it.'

'You mean that he . . .'

'He'll go to the guillotine.'

She didn't faint, but sat rigid on her chair, staring blankly ahead.

'His first wife's body will be exhumed. I dare say you know that traces of certain poisons can be found in a skeleton.'

'Why should he have killed them both? It isn't possible. It isn't true, Chief-Inspector. I don't know why you're telling me this, but I refuse to believe you. Let me speak to him. Allow me to talk to him in private and I'll find out the truth.'

'Were you in your room the whole of Tuesday evening?'

'Yes.'

'You didn't go downstairs at all?'

'No. Why should I have gone down, when the woman was leaving us at last?'

Maigret went over for a while to cool his forehead against the window-pane, then walked into the office next door, grabbed the bottle and drank from it the equivalent of three or four singles.

When he came back, he had assumed the heavy gait of Guillaume Serre and his obstinate glare.

Chapter Nine

He was sitting in a chair that wasn't his, both elbows on the table, his biggest pipe in his mouth, his eyes fixed upon the old lady whom he'd likened to a Mother Superior.

'Your son, Madame Serre, didn't kill either his first or his second wife,' he said, spacing out the words.

She frowned in surprise, but didn't look any the happier.

'Nor did he kill his father,' he added.

'What do you . . .?'

'Hush! . . . If you don't mind, we'll settle this as quickly as possible. We'll not bother about proof for the time being. That'll come in due course.

'We won't argue about your husband's case, either. What I'm almost certain of is that your first daughter-in-law was poisoned. I'll go further. I'm convinced that it wasn't done by arsenic or any of the strong poisons that are usually used.

'By the way, Madame Serre, I might tell you that, in nine cases out of ten, poison is a woman's weapon.

'Your first daughter-in-law, like the second, suffered from heart trouble. So did your husband.

'Certain drugs, which wouldn't seriously affect people in good health, can be fatal to cardiac cases. I wonder if Maria didn't provide us with the key to the problem in one of her letters to her friend. She speaks of a trip to England which you once took with your husband, and emphasizes that you were all so badly seasick that you had to be seen by the ship's doctor.

'What would be prescribed in such a case?'

'I've no idea.'

'That's very unlikely. They usually give you atropine in some form or other. Now, a fairly strong dose of atropine can be fatal to a person with a weak heart.'

'You mean that my husband . . .'

'We'll go into that another time, even if it's impossible to prove anything. Your husband, during his later days, was leading a disorderly life and throwing his money away. You've always been afraid of poverty, Madame Serre.'

'Not for myself. For my son. Which doesn't mean that I would have . . .'

'Later on, your son got married. Another woman came to live in your house, a woman who, overnight, bore your name and had as much right there as you.'

She compressed her lips.

'This woman, who also had a weak heart, was rich, richer than your son, richer than all the Serres put together.'

'You believe that I poisoned her, having first poisoned my husband?'

'Yes.'

She gave a little strained laugh.

'Doubtless I also poisoned my second daughter-in-law?'

'She was going away, discouraged, after having tried in vain to live in a house where she was treated like a stranger. Very likely she taking her money with her. By a coincidence, she had heart trouble, too.

'You see, I wondered from the start why her body disappeared. If she'd simply been poisoned, you only had to call in a doctor who, given Maria's state of health, would have diagnosed a heart attack. Perhaps the attack itself was intended to come on later, in the taxi, at the station or on the train.'

'You seem very sure of yourself, Monsieur Maigret.'

'I know that something happened which obliged your son to shoot down his wife. Let's suppose that Maria, just as she was going to fetch a taxi or, more likely, as she was on the point of telephoning for one, felt certain symptoms coming on.

'She knew you both, having lived with you for two and a half years. She was a widely read woman, in all sorts of subjects, and it wouldn't surprise me if she had acquired some medical knowledge.

'Realizing that she'd been poisoned, she went into your husband's study while you were in there with him.'

'Why do you say that I was in there?'

'Because, unfortunately for her, she laid the blame on you. If you'd been in your room, she'd have gone upstairs.

'I don't know if she threatened you with her pistol or if she merely reached for the telephone to call the police. . . .

'There was only one way out for you: to shoot her down.'

'And, according to you, it was I who . . .'

'No. I've already told you that it's more likely to have been your son who fired, or, if you'd rather, finished your work for you.'

The drab light of dawn blended with the electric lamps. The lines in their faces were etched more deeply. The telephone bell rang.

'That you, Chief? I've done the test. It's ten to one the brick dust we found in the car came from Billancourt.'

'You can go home to bed, my boy. Your job's through.'

He got up once again, circled the room.

'Your son, Madame Serre, is determined to shoulder all the blame. I don't see any way of stopping him. If he's been able to keep his mouth shut all this time, he's capable of keeping it shut for good. Unless . . .'

'Unless . . .?'

'I don't know. I was thinking aloud. Two years ago I'd a man as tough as he is in my office and after fifteen hours we still hadn't got a word out of him.'

He threw open the window abruptly, in a kind of rage.

'It took twenty-seven and a half hours to break his nerve.'

'Did he confess?'

'He spilled everything in one long stream, as if it were a relief to get rid of it.'

'I didn't poison anybody.'

'The answer doesn't lie with you.'

'But with my son?'

'Yes. He's convinced that you only did it for his sake, partly out of fear that he'd be left penniless, partly out of jealousy.'

He had to restrain himself from raising his hand to her, despite her age, for the old woman's thin lips had just twitched in an involuntary smile.

'Which is a lie!' he said flatly.

Then, coming closer to her, his eyes on hers, his breath on the woman's face, he rapped out:

It's not for his sake that you're afraid of povery, it's for your own! It's not for his sake that you murdered, and if you came here tonight, it's because you were afraid he might talk.'

She tried to shrink away, threw herself back in her chair, for Maigret's face was thrust into hers, hard, menacing.

'Never mind if he does go to prison, or even if he's executed, so long as you can be sure of staying in the clear. You believe that you've still many years to live, in your house, counting your money. . . .'

She was frightened. Her mouth opened as if to call for help. Suddenly, with a violent, unexpected jerk, Maigret wrenched from her withered hands the bag that she was clinging to.

She gave a cry, shot forward to retrieve it.

'Sit down.'

He undid the silver clasp. Right at the bottom, beneath the gloves, the note-case, the handkerchief and the powder-compact, he found a folded paper which contained two white tablets.

A hush like that in a church or a cavern enclosed them. Maigret let his body relax, sat down, pressed a bell-push.

When the door opened, he said slowly, without a glance at the plain-clothes man who'd appeared:

'Tell Janvier to lay off him.'

And, as the detective still stood there, in amazement:

'It's all over. She's confessed.'

'I haven't confessed to anything.'

He waited until the door closed again.

'It comes to the same thing. I could have carried on the experiment to the end, let you have the private talk with your son that you wanted. Don't you think that you've caused enough deaths already for one old woman?'

'You mean that I would have . . .'

He was toying with the tablets.

'You'd have given him his medicine, or rather what he would have thought was his medicine, and there'd have been no danger of his ever talking again.'

The corners of the roof-tops had begun to be crested with sunlight. The telephone rang again.

'Chief-Inspector Maigret? River Patrol here. We're at Billancourt. The diver's just gone down for the first time and he's found a pretty heavy trunk.'

'The rest'll turn up as well!' he said indifferently.

An exhausted and astonished Janvier was framed in the doorway.

'They told me. . . .'

'Take her down to the cells. The man, too, as an accessory. I'll see the prosecutor directly he comes in.'

He'd no longer any business with either the mother or the son.

'You can go off to bed,' he told the translator.

'It's over?'

'For today.'

The dentist was no longer there when he entered his office, but the ashtray was full of very black cigar-butts. He sat down in his chair and was about to doze off, when he remembered Lofty.

He found her in the waiting-room, where she'd gone to sleep, shook her by the shoulder and, instinctively, she put her green hat straight.

'That's the lot. Off you go now.'

'Has he confessed?'

'It was her.'

'What! It was the old girl who . . .'

'Later!' he murmured.

Then, turning round, since he was assailed by a twinge of remorse:

'And thanks! When Alfred comes back, advise him to . . .'

But what was the good? Nothing would cure the Sad Man of his mania for burgling the safes that he had once put in, or wean him from his belief that each would be the last and that this time he was really going to live in the country.

On account of her age, old Madame Serre was not executed and left the Court with the complacent air of one who is at last going to set the women's prison in order.

When her son came out of Fresnes jail, after two years, he made straight for the house in the Rue de la Ferme and, that very evening, took the same stroll round the neighbourhood that he'd been accustomed to take in the days when he had a dog to exercise.

He continued to go and drink red wine in the little café and, before entering, to look uneasily up and down the street.

Shadow Rock Farm
Lakeville, Connecticut
8 May 1951

The Little Man from Archangel

Paris

The Little Man from Archangel

Translated from the French by Nigel Ryan

Chapter One

He made the mistake of telling a lie. He felt it intuitively the moment he opened his mouth to reply to Fernand Le Bouc, and it was actually from timidity, lack of sangfroid, that he did not alter the words which came to his lips.

What he said was:

'She's gone to Bourges.'

Le Bouc asked, as he rinsed a glass behind his counter:

'Is La Loute still there?'

He replied without looking at him:

'I suppose so.'

It was ten o'clock in the morning, and as it was Thursday, the market was in full swing. In Fernand's small bistro, almost entirely enclosed in glass, on the corner of the Impasse des Trois-Rois, five or six men were standing at the bar. At that moment it didn't matter who was there, but this was to become important, and Jonas Milk was later to try to identify each face.

Near him was Gaston Ancel, the red-faced butcher, in his blood-stained apron, who came in three or four times a morning for a quick glass of white wine and who had a particular way of wiping his mouth afterwards. He was constantly cracking jokes in his loud voice and, in his butcher's shop, used to tease the customers, while at the cash desk Madame Ancel apologized for her husband's bad language.

With Ancel, a cup of coffee in his hand, stood Benaiche, the policeman on duty at the market, known to everybody as Julien.

The little old man with the greenish coat and trembling hands must have spent the night outside, as he did most of the time. Nobody knew who he was, nor where he came from, but they had got used to him and he had ended up by becoming part of the surroundings.

Who were the others? An electrician whom Jonas didn't know, with someone whose pocket was stuffed with pencils, a foreman or the boss of some small business.

He never recalled the sixth, but he could have sworn that there was a figure between himself and the window.

At the tables behind the men, three or four women vegetable vendors dressed in black were eating sandwiches.

It was the same atmosphere as on any market morning, that is to say, on Tuesdays, Thursdays and Saturdays. That Thursday a clear and warm June sun beat down full on the fronts of the houses, while under the huge roof of the covered-in market the people were bustling round the hampers and stalls in a bluish half-light.

Jonas had been anxious to avoid any hitch in his routine. As ten o'clock approached, his shop being free of customers, he had walked the five yards of pavement which separated him from Fernand's bistro, and from there, through the windows, he could watch the boxes of second-hand books arrayed against his shop front.

He could quite well not have opened his mouth. Some of them, at Fernand's, used to go up to the bar without a word, for it was known in advance what they were going to have. For him, it was invariably an espresso coffee.

Even so he said, possibly out of humility, or from a need to be precise: 'An espresso coffee.'

Practically everyone knew everyone else, and sometimes they didn't say good morning to each other, thinking they had already met earlier in the day.

Fernand Le Bouc, for example, was on his feet from three o'clock in the morning for the arrival of the lorries, and Ancel, the butcher, who awoke at five, had already been in at least twice to the bar.

The shops were clustered round the slate roof of the market, which had no walls and was bordered by a gutter littered with broken crates and packing-cases, rotting oranges, and trampled wood shavings.

The housewives who trod in this debris had no idea that the square, before their arrival, long before they were awake, had already seen, amidst the noise of heavy lorries and the smell of diesel oil, several hours of feverish existence.

Jonas was watching the coffee falling drop by drop from the tiny chromium tap into the brown cup. He had another habit: before being handed his coffee he would unwrap the transparent paper containing his two pieces of sugar.

'Is Gina all right?' Le Bouc had asked him.

He had at first replied:

'She's all right.'

It was only because of what Fernand said next that he felt obliged to tell a lie.

'I was wondering if she was ill. I haven't seen her this morning.'

The butcher interrupted his conversation with the policeman to remark:

'That's funny! I haven't seen her either.'

Normally Gina did her shopping early, in bedroom slippers, often without combing her hair, sometimes in a sort of flowered dressing-gown affair, before the arrival of the crowds.

Jonas opened his mouth, and it was then that, despite his instinct which told him it was unwise, he could not bring himself to change the words he had prepared:

'She's gone to Bourges.'

From time to time his wife did happen to go to Bourges to see La Loute, as she was called, the daughter of the grain merchant over the way, who had been living there for the past two years. But almost invariably, as everyone must have known, she took the half-past eleven bus.

He was annoyed by his reply, not only because it was a lie and he did not like telling lies, but because something told him it was a mistake. Yet he couldn't reveal the truth, still less so because at any moment Palestri, Gina's father, would be climbing out of his carrier-tricycle to come and have a drink.

It was the butcher who asked, addressing no one in particular:

'Does anybody really know what La Loute does in Bourges?'

And Fernand, indifferently:

'Whoring, probably.'

It was strange that the butcher should have been present just then and taken part in the conversation, because his own daughter Clémence, the eldest, the one who was married, had been more or less mixed up in the affair.

Jonas was drinking his piping hot coffee in little sips, and the steam was misting over his glasses, which made him look different from the way he usually looked.

'See you later,' he said, placing the money on the linoleum of the counter.

Nobody had touched the books in the two boxes. It was rare for him to sell any during the market, and in the morning he hardly ever did more than a few exchanges. Mechanically he straightened the books, glanced at the window display and went into his shop where there was a sweet smell of dust and mildewed paper.

He hadn't dared to visit Clémence, the butcher's daughter, that night, but he had seen her a short time before, doing her shopping while she pushed the baby in its pram. He had gone up to her, deliberately.

'Good morning, Clémence.'

'Good morning, Monsieur Jonas.'

If she called him 'Monsieur', it was because she was twenty-two years old while he was forty. She had been at school with Gina. Both of them were born in the Place du Vieux-Marché. Gina was the daughter of Palestri, the greengrocer who, while his wife kept shop, delivered the orders in his three-wheeler.

'Nice day!' he had called out again, peering at Clémence through his thick lenses.

'Yes. It looks as if it's going to be a hot one.'

He bent over to look at the baby, Poupou, who was enormous.

'He's growing!' he observed gravely.

'I think he's cutting his first tooth. Give my love to Gina!'

All this was at about nine o'clock. As she uttered her last remark, Clémence had glanced into the back of the shop as if she was expecting to catch sight of her friend in the kitchen.

She hadn't seemed embarrassed. Pushing Poupou's pram before her, she had moved off towards Chaigne's, the grocer's, and gone into the shop.

That meant that Gina had lied, and Jonas had been almost sure of it since the evening before. He had shut the shop as usual at seven o'clock, or rather he had closed the door without removing the handle, for as long as he stayed up there was no point in missing a customer, and some of them used to come fairly late, to exchange their books from the lending library department. From the kitchen it was possible to hear the bell which the door operated when it opened. The house was narrow, one of the oldest in the Place du Vieux-Marché, with a coat-of-arms still carved on one of the stones and the date 1596.

'Dinner's ready!' Gina had called out, while at the same time he could hear a sizzling sound from the oven.

'I'm coming.'

She was wearing a tight-fitting red cotton dress. He had never dared say a word to her on that subject. She had large breasts and ample haunches and she always made her dressmaker give her close-fitting dresses, beneath which she wore only a slip and a brassiere, so that when she moved, even the contour of her navel was outlined.

It was fish that she was cooking, and before it there was sorrel soup. They did not lay a tablecloth, but ate on the oil-cloth, and often Gina did not take the trouble to use dishes, merely putting the pans straight on the table.

Outside, with strangers, she was gay, with a naughty sparkle in her eye, a smile at her lips, and she laughed all the more for having dazzling white teeth.

She was the most beautiful girl in the Market, everyone was agreed, even if some of them made certain reservations or put on a disapproving expression when she came into the conversation.

Alone with Jonas her face would darken. Sometimes the transformation was noticeable the moment she crossed the doorway of the shop. Gaily she would throw out some last jest to a passer-by, and in the time it took her to turn round to enter the house, her face would lose all expression, her walk was no longer the same, and if she still swayed her hips it was with a sudden lassitude.

They sometimes ate without uttering a word, as quickly as possible, as if to have done with a chore, and he would still be at table when she began, behind his back, to wash up the dishes at the sink.

Had they spoken that evening? As he hadn't known then what was afoot, he had not noticed, but he could not recall a single remark being said.

The old market-place, so teeming with life in the morning, was becoming very calm as the evening drew on, and there was only the sound of the cars passing in the Rue de Bourges, more than a hundred yards away, a mother calling from time to time from the doorway to her children who had lingered on under the great slate roof.

While she was washing up she had announced:

'I'm going to see Clémence.'

The butcher's eldest daughter had married an employee at the waterworks two years before and it had been a fine wedding at which everyone from the square had been present. She was called Reverdi now and the young family lived in a flat in the Rue des Deux-Ponts.

As he did not press his wife for an explanation she had added, turning her back to him:

'There's a film they want to see.'

On those occasions Gina would sometimes go and sit with the baby, which was only eight months old. She would take a book with her, and the key, and would not be back until midnight, for the Reverdis went to the second house.

The lights hadn't been turned on yet. There was enough daylight from the window and the door into the backyard. The air was bluish, of an extraordinary stillness, as it often is at the end of very long summer days. Some birds were twittering in the lime tree belonging to Chaigne the grocer, the only tree in the whole cluster of houses, in the middle of an enormous yard cluttered with barrels and crates.

Gina had gone upstairs. The staircase rose not from the kitchen, but from the little room separating it from the shop, which Jonas called his office.

When she came down again, she had neither hat nor coat on. Actually she only wore a hat for going to Mass on Sundays. On other days she went about bareheaded, her brown hair all untidy and, when it fell on her cheek, she would flick it back with a toss of her head.

'See you later!'

He had noticed that she was clutching close to her the large rectangular patent-leather bag which he had given her for her last birthday. He had almost called her back to say:

'You're forgetting your book.'

But she was already away down the pavement, walking briskly, almost running in the direction of Rue des Prémontrés. He had remained a little while on the doorstep, following her with his eyes, then just breathing in the still warm air of the evening and watching the lamps which were beginning to light up, to the left, in the Rue de Bourges.

What had he done until midnight? The boxes of books which he used to put on the pavement in the morning had been brought in. He had changed the places of a few volumes for no particular reason except to arrange them by the colour of their covers. He had switched on the light. There were books everywhere, on the shelves up to the ceiling and in piles on the counter, on the floor in the corners. They were second-hand books, nearly all of them worn, dirty, held together with sticking-paper, and he lent out more of them than he sold.

On one side of the room could be seen only old bindings, seventeenth- and eighteenth-century editions, an old La Fontaine published in Belgium, a Latin bible with curious engravings, some Bourdaloue sermons, five copies in different formats of *Télémaque*, then below, more recent collections such as *The History of the Consulate and the Empire* bound in dark green.

Jonas didn't smoke. Apart from coffee, he did not drink either. He only went to the cinema once in a while to please Gina. Did it really please Gina? He wasn't sure. She insisted on it, however, as she insisted on taking a *loge*, which, to her way of thinking, showed that she was a married woman.

He didn't hold it against her. He didn't hold anything against her, even now. By what right could he have expected anything from her?

His little office-room, between the shop and the kitchen, had no window, received no air except through the two doors, and here, too, there were books up to the ceiling. But most important of all, in the desk at which he never sat down without a sigh of satisfaction, were his books on philately and his stamps.

For he wasn't just a second-hand bookseller. He was a stamp dealer. And if his shop, squeezed between the food shops of the Vieux-Marché, was not much to look at, the local shopkeepers would have been surprised to learn that the name of Jonas Milk was known by dealers and collectors the world over.

In a drawer within arm's reach were arranged precision instruments for counting and measuring perforations on stamps, studying the texture of the paper, the water-mark, discovering the defects of an issue or a surcharge, checking on the colours.

Unlike the majority of his colleagues, he bought everything that came to hand, sent abroad for those packets of five hundred, a thousand and ten thousand stamps which are sold to beginners and are theoretically of no value.

These stamps, despite the fact that they had passed through the hands of experienced dealers, he studied one by one, rejecting nothing out of hand, and every now and then he would make a find.

A certain issue, for example, unremarkable in its ordinary form, became a rarity when the vignette was printed from a defective block; another had been printed in the experimental stage in a colour different from the one finally selected, and the specimens of it were great rarities.

Most dealers, like most collectors, confine themselves to one period, one type of stamp.

Jonas Milk had specialized in freaks, in stamps which, for one reason or another, were out of the ordinary.

That night, magnifying glass in hand, he had worked until half-past eleven. At one moment he had made up his mind to shut up the house and go and fetch his wife. Clémence and her husband lived only ten minutes away, in a quiet street leading to the canal.

He would have enjoyed walking slowly back with Gina along the deserted pavements, even if they had found nothing to say to one another.

From fear of displeasing her, he did not carry out his project. She was quite capable of believing that he had gone out to watch over her, to make sure that she really had gone to Clémence's, or that she was coming home alone.

He went into the kitchen and lit the gas to make himself a cup of coffee, for coffee didn't prevent him from sleeping. He took the opportunity to tidy up, as his wife hadn't even put the pans away.

He didn't hold that against her either. Since his marriage the house had been dirtier than when he had lived in it alone and had managed for himself almost entirely. He did not dare tidy up or do any polishing in his wife's presence, for fear that she might take it as a reproach, but when she was not there, he always found something that needed attention.

That day for example, it was the oven, which she had not found time to clean and which smelt of herring.

Midnight sounded from St Cecilia's Church, at the far end of the Market, on the corner of the Rue de Bourges. He calculated, as he had done on other occasions, that the cinema had finished at half-past eleven, that it took the Reverdis barely twenty minutes to reach the Rue des Deux-Ponts, that they would probably stop for a few minutes to chat with Gina.

She would not be home before half-past twelve, and so, leaving one light on downstairs, he went up to the first floor, wondering whether his wife had taken a key with her. He did not remember seeing one in her hand. Usually it was almost a ritual act to slip it into her bag at the last moment.

It would only be a matter of going downstairs to open the door for her, since he wouldn't go to sleep yet. Their room had a low ceiling, with a large white-painted beam in the middle and a walnut bed, a double-fronted wardrobe with mirrors, which he had bought at the sale-room.

Even here the smell of old books came up from below mixed with the smells of the kitchen, that evening the smell of herrings.

He undressed, put on his pyjamas and cleaned his teeth. There were two windows, and from the one giving onto the yard he could see, beyond the Chaignes' yard, the windows of the Palestris, Gina's family. They had gone to bed. Like the rest of the Market people they rose before daybreak and there was no light except in the window of Gina's brother Frédo's room. Had he, perhaps, just returned from the cinema? He was a strange fellow, with his hair growing low over his forehead, his thick eyebrows, his way of looking at Jonas as if he could not forgive him for marrying his sister.

At half-past twelve she hadn't come back and Milk, in bed but still wearing his glasses, was staring at the ceiling with melancholy patience.

He was not anxious yet. He might have been, for it had happened before that she did not come in, and once she had stayed away for three whole days.

On her return she had not given him any explanation. She could not have been very proud of herself, at heart. Her face was drawn, her eyes tired, she had seemed to carry an alien smell about her, but as she passed in front of him she had none the less drawn herself up to toss him a look of defiance.

He had said nothing to her. What was the use? What could he have said? On the contrary, he had been softer, more attentive than usual, and two evenings later it was she who had suggested a walk along the canal, where she had slipped her hand into his arm.

She was not a bad girl. She did not hate him, like her brother Frédo. He was convinced that she was doing her best to be a good wife, and that she was grateful to him for having married her.

Twice or three times he gave a start on hearing noises, but it was the mice downstairs, of which he had given up trying to rid himself. All round the Market, where hung such delicious smells, where so many appetizing victuals were piled, the walls were riddled with warrens forming a secret city for the rodents.

Fortunately both rats and mice found sufficient to eat outside not to be tempted to set on the books, so that Jonas no longer bothered with them. Occasionally the mice ran about the bedroom while he and Gina were in bed, they came right up to the foot of the bed as if curious to see human beings sleeping, and they had lost their fear of the human voice.

A motor-bike belonging to the young Chenu, from the fishmonger's, came to a halt on the far side of the square, then the silence returned and the church clock struck the quarter, then one o'clock, and only then did Jonas get up and go over to the straw-bottomed chair where he had laid his clothes.

The first time it had happened, he had run about the town, ashamed, searching in the dark corners, looking into the window of the only bar still open in the neighbourhood of the factory.

Today there was a possible explanation. Perhaps Poupou, Clémence's baby, was ill and Gina had stayed on to help out?

He dressed, still hoping, went downstairs, glanced into the kitchen which was empty and smelt of cold herring. He picked up his hat on his way through his office, walked out of the house locking the door behind him.

And what if Gina hadn't got a key? If she came back while he was away? If she was returning from Clémence's by another route?

He decided to turn the key in the lock once more, so that she could let herself in again. The sky was clear above the vast slate roof, with a few clouds gleaming in the moonlight. Some way off a couple were walking along the Rue de Bourges and the air was so still that in spite of the distance, he could hear each remark they exchanged.

As far as the Rue des Deux-Ponts he met nobody, saw only one lighted window, possibly someone waiting like him, or an invalid, someone in pain?

He was disturbed by the noise of his shoes on the pavings and it gave him the feeling of an intruder.

He knew the Reverdis' house, the second on the left after the corner, and he could see at once that there was no light on the floor the young couple occupied.

What was the use of ringing, starting a disturbance, giving rise to questions which no one could answer?

Perhaps Gina had gone back home after all. It was more than likely that she had lied, that she had not been to Clémence's, that the young couple had not been to the cinema at all.

He remembered that she had not taken a book with her as she used to do when she went to look after Poupou and it had also struck him that she took her black patent-leather bag.

For no particular reason he stood for a good five minutes on the edge of the pavement, gazing at the windows behind which there were people sleeping, then he moved off almost on tiptoe.

When he reached the Place du Vieux-Marché an enormous lorry from Moulins, the first of the day, was almost blocking the Rue des Prémontrés and the driver was asleep in the cab with his mouth wide open.

In his doorway he called:

'Gina!'

As if to conjure fate, he tried to speak in a natural voice, without betraying anxiety.

'Are you there, Gina?'

He locked the door again and bolted it, hesitated whether to make a fresh cup of coffee, decided against it and went up to his room and got back into bed.

If he slept, he was not conscious of doing so. He had left the light on for no reason and an hour went by before he removed his spectacles, without which he could see only a vague, misty world. He heard some other lorries arriving, the slamming of doors, crates and boxes being stacked on the ground.

He also heard Fernand Le Bouc opening his bar, then the first vans of the retailers.

Gina hadn't come back. Gina wouldn't be coming back.

He must have dropped off to sleep, because he didn't notice the transition from night to day. At one moment there was still a darkness pierced by the lights of the market, then suddenly there had been sunshine in the bedroom and on the bed.

With a hesitant hand he felt the place beside him, and, of course, it was empty. Usually Gina was warm, lying like a gun dog, and she had a strong feminine smell. Sometimes in her sleep she would turn over sharply and, one thigh over Jonas' thigh, press on it hard, breathing more and more heavily as she did so.

He decided not to go down, nor to get up before the right time, to follow the same routine as every other day. He did not go to sleep again and, to keep his mind occupied, he listened to the noises of the market, which he tried to identify with the same meticulousness as he applied to the scrutiny of a postage stamp.

He, too, had practically been born here. Not quite. Not like the others. But they talked to him in the mornings as they talked to one another, with the same familiar friendliness, and he had his place, so to speak, at Le Bouc's counter.

Twice he heard Ancel the butcher's voice on the pavement arguing with a man delivering some quarters of beef, and there was a row about some mutton which was fairly infuriating him. Chaigne's grocery opposite opened later, and the next house belonged to the Palestris where Angèle, Gina's mother, was already at work.

It was she who attended to the business. Louis, her husband, was a pleasant fellow, but he could not stop himself from drinking. So to keep him occupied they had bought him a three-wheeler and he delivered the orders, not only for his own shop, but for the market people who had no means of transport.

It used to humiliate him. He didn't admit it. On the one hand he was content to spend the whole day out of the house, free to drink at his leisure. But on the other hand he was no dupe, and realised that he didn't count, that he was no longer the real head of the family, and this made him drink all the more.

What ought Angèle to have done? Jonas had wondered to himself and had not found the answer.

Gina had no respect for her father. When he came to see her between errands, she would put the bottle of wine and a glass down on the table, with the words:

'There! Is that what you want?'

He would pretend to laugh, to take it as a joke. He knew it was meant seriously and yet he did not resist the need to fill his glass, though he might call out on leaving:

'You're a proper bitch!'

Jonas tried not to be present when that happened. In front of him, Palestri felt even more humiliated, and that was perhaps one of the reasons why he had nearly as big a grudge against him as his son had.

He rose at six, went down to make his coffee. He was always the first one down and in summer his first action was to open the door into the yard. Often Gina wasn't to be seen downstairs until about half-past seven or eight when the shop was already open.

She liked to hang about in dressing-gown and slippers, her face glistening after her night's sleep, and it did not disturb her to be seen thus by strangers; she would go and stand on the doorstep, walk past the Chaignes' on her way to say good-morning to her mother, return with vegetables or fruit.

' 'Morning, Gina!'

' 'Morning, Pierrot!'

She knew everybody, the wholesalers, the retailers, the heavy-lorry drivers as well as the country women who came to sell the produce from their gardens or their backyards. As a little girl she used to run about with bare behind between the crates and baskets.

She was no longer a little girl now. She was a woman of twenty-four and her friend Clémence had a child, while others had two or three.

She had not come home and Jonas, with careful movements, was setting down his boxes in front of the shop window, rearranging the price tickets and going over to the baker opposite to buy some *croissants*. He always bought five, three for himself, two for his wife, and when they automatically wrapped them up for him in brown tissue paper, he did not protest.

He could easily throw away the two extra *croissants*, and this gave him the idea of saying nothing, which, to him, meant not admitting that Gina had gone off without telling him.

Besides, had she really gone off? When she left in the evening she was only wearing her red cotton dress, only had with her her patent-leather bag.

She might come back in the course of the day, at any moment. Perhaps she was already there?

Once again he tried to conjure the fates.

'Gina!' he called, going inside, a note almost of delight in his voice.

Then he ate alone, on a corner of the kitchen table, washed up his cup, his plate, and swept up the crumbs from the *croissants*. To set his mind at rest he went upstairs to make sure that his wife's suitcase was still in the cupboard. She only possessed that one. The day before, when he was having his coffee at Le Bouc's, for example, she could have taken her case out of the house and left it somewhere.

The postman called and it whiled away a little time reading the post, glancing cursorily over the stamps he had ordered from Cairo.

Then all of a sudden it was ten o'clock and he went round to Fernand Le Bouc's, as he did every other morning.

'How's Gina?'

'She's all right.'

'I was wondering if she was ill. I haven't seen her this morning.'

Why hadn't he answered anything else rather than:

'*She's gone to Bourges.*'

He was angry with himself for this clumsy mistake. She might come back in half an hour, in an hour, and how would his reply be interpreted then?

A girl who sold flowers not far from the shop came rushing in to change her book, as she did every morning, for she read a novel a day.

'Is this a good one?'

He said it was. She always chose the same kind of book whose gaudy covers were a guarantee of the contents.

'Gina not here?'

'Not at the moment.'

'Is she all right?'

'Yes.'

An idea suddenly occurred to him, which made him blush, for he was ashamed of distrusting other people, of what he called evil thoughts about them. As soon as the little florist departed he went up to his room, opened the wardrobe with the mirrors at the back of which, under his and Gina's clothes which were hanging there, he kept a steel strong box bought at Viroulet's.

The safe was in its place and Jonas had to make an effort to go any further, take the key from his pocket and insert it in the lock.

If Gina had returned at that moment he would have fainted for shame.

But Gina did not return and no doubt she would not be returning so soon.

The transparent envelopes containing his rarest stamps, among others the Trinidad five cents blue of 1847, with the picture of the steamer *Lady McLeod*, had vanished.

Chapter Two

He was still standing in front of the wardrobe with the mirrors, with beads of sweat on his upper lip, when he heard footsteps in the shop, then in the little room. It was rare for him to close the outside door in summer, for the house, built in depth, was ill-ventilated. Standing stock still, he waited for the male or female voice of a customer to call:

'Anyone there?'

But the steps went on into the kitchen, where the visitor waited before returning to the foot of the stairway. It was a man's step, heavy, dragging slightly, and Jonas, rooted to the spot, was wondering whether the stranger was going to climb the stairs, when the harsh voice of his father-in-law grated up the staircase:

'You there, Gina?'

Why was he seized with panic, as if he had been caught out? Without shutting the steel box, he pushed the wardrobe doors to, hesitating whether to go down or let it be thought that there was nobody at home. A footstep sounded on the bottom stair. The voice called again:

'Gina!'

Only then did he stammer out:

'I'll be down in a moment.'

Before leaving the room he had time to see in the mirror that his face had reddened.

By that hour, however, Palestri was not yet drunk. Even in the evenings he never reached the point of reeling. Early in the morning his eyes would be slightly red and bleary, and he had a tumbledown look, but after a glass or two of *marc*, or rather *grappa*, its Italian version, he was no longer entirely steady.

He did not only drink *grappa*, which Le Bourc bought especially for him, but everything he was offered or whatever he could find in the other bars where he dropped in.

When Jonas came down, his pupils were beginning to lose their lustre and his face was flushed.

'Where's Gina?' he asked, looking in the direction of the kitchen where he had expected to find her.

It surprised him as well to see his son-in-law coming down from the first floor when there was nobody downstairs, and he seemed to be waiting for some explanation. Jonas had not had the time to reflect. Just as a short while before at Fernand's, he had been caught on the wrong foot. And since he had mentioned Bourges once already, was it not better to continue?

He felt a need to defend himself, even though he had done nothing. Palestri overawed him with his roughness, his great desiccated, gnarled body standing there.

He stammered:

'She's gone to Bourges.'

He realized that he was not convincing, that his eyes, behind the thick lenses, must appear to be avoiding the other's gaze.

'To see La Loute?'

'That's what she said.'

'Did she say good-bye to her mother?'

'I don't know . . .'

Like a coward, he was retreating towards the kitchen, and as Gina used to do, took the bottle of red wine from the cupboard, put it on the wax tablecloth with a glass beside it.

'When did she go?'

Later he was to ask himself why, from that moment onwards, he acted as if he were guilty. He remembered, for example, his wife's suitcase in the cupboard. If she had gone the day before to see her friend, she would have taken the case with her. So she must have left the house that same day.

That is why he replied:

'This morning.'

Louis had stretched out his hand to the glass he had poured himself, but seemed to be hesitating suspiciously before drinking from it.

'By the 7.10 bus?'

There was only that one before the half-past eleven bus, which had not yet gone through. So Jonas was forced to answer yes.

It was stupid. He was becoming caught up in a web of lies, which were bound to lead to others, and from which he would never be able to extricate himself. At seven in the morning the market was almost deserted. It was the time of the lull between the wholesalers and the ordinary customers. Gina's mother would certainly have seen her daughter passing, and in any case the girl would have gone into the shop to say good-morning to her.

Other people would have seen her as well. There are some streets where people stay in their houses as if in water-tight compartments and each scarcely knows his neighbour. The Place du Vieux-Marché was different, it was rather like a barracks where the doors remained open and people knew from hour to hour what was going on in the family next door.

Why did Palestri eye his son-in-law suspiciously? Wasn't it because he looked as if he were lying? At all events he emptied his glass, in a gulp, wiped his mouth with his usual gesture, similar to that of the butcher, but did not go away immediately: he was gazing round him at the kitchen and Jonas thought he understood the reason for the contraction of his eyebrows.

There was something unnatural, that morning, in the atmosphere of the house. It was too tidy. There was nothing lying about, there was no sense of the disarray that Gina always left behind her.

''Bye!' he finally mumbled, heading for the door of the shop.

He added, as if for his own benefit:

'I'll tell her mother she's gone. When's she coming back?'

'I don't know.'

Would it have been better for Jonas to have called him back and confessed the truth, told him that his daughter had gone off, taking his valuable stamps with her?

The ones downstairs, in the drawers of the desk, were only the common or garden stamps he bought by the packet, and the ones he had already sorted, which he was swapping or selling to schoolboys.

The strong-box, on the other hand, contained till the day before a veritable fortune, the rare stamps which he had discovered, by dint of patience and flair, over more than twenty-five years, for he had first taken an interest in stamps while at school.

One specimen alone, the pearl of his collection, a French stamp of 1849 with the head of Ceres on a bright vermilion ground, was worth, at the catalogue valuation, six hundred thousand francs.

The Trinidad stamp, with the steamer *Lady McLeod* was assessed at three hundred thousand francs, and he possessed others of considerable value, such as the Puerto Rican two peseta pink with the overprinted surcharge, for which he was being offered thirty-five thousand francs.

He had never calculated the total value of his collection, but it could not have been much less than ten million francs.

The people of the Old Market had no suspicion of this wealth. He never spoke of it to anyone and he did not mind being thought a crank.

One evening, however, when one of the catalogues was lying about on the desk, Gina had begun idly turning over its pages.

'What does that mean, *double surcharge?*'

He had explained it to her.

'And *sep-ol?*'

'Sepia and olive colour.'

'And 2 *p?*'

'Two pesetas.'

The abbreviations intrigued her.

'It's very complicated!' she had sighed.

She was on the point of shutting the catalogue when she had asked one last question.

'And the figure 4000 in this column?'

'The value of the stamp.'

'You mean that stamp is worth four thousand francs?'

He had smiled.

'Certainly.'

'Do all the figures in this column stand for the value of the stamps?'

'Yes.'

She had turned over the pages of the catalogue with renewed interest.

'Here it says 700,000. Are there really stamps worth seven hundred thousand francs?'

'Yes.'

'Have you got one?'

'I haven't got that one, no.'

'Have you other ones as valuable?'

'Not quite.'

'Some very valuable ones?'

'Some fairly valuable.'

'Is that what you bought a steel safe for?'

This happened the previous winter and he remembered that it was snowing outside, that he could see a white rim round the window panes. The stove was roaring in the little room. It must have been about eight o'clock in the evening.

'Goodness!'

'What?'

'Nothing. I'd never have thought it.'

In the Place du Vieux-Marché he had the reputation of having money and it would have been difficult to trace the origin of this rumour. Perhaps it was due to the fact that he had remained a bachelor for a long time? Ordinary folk naturally imagine that a bachelor puts money to one side. Apart from that, before marrying Gina, he used to eat in the restaurant, at Pepito's, another Italian, in the first house in the Rue Haute, past the Grimoux-Marmion grocery, which stood on the corner of the square.

Probably for these tradespeople who were in and out of his shop all day, he seemed something of an amateur. Could anyone really make a living buying, selling and hiring out old books? Weren't there times when an hour or even two went by without any customer going into his shop?

So, since he was alive, and since, moreover, he had a woman in two hours a day for the whole morning on Saturdays, he must have had money.

Had Gina been disappointed that he didn't change any of his habits after marrying her? Had she been expecting a new existence?

He hadn't asked himself the question, and only now did he realize that he had been living without noticing what was happening around him.

If he looked in the drawer of the till, where he kept the money in a big wallet grey with use, would he find the right amount there? He was almost sure he would not. Gina had sometimes pilfered small amounts, rather in the manner of a child wanting to buy sweets. At first she contented herself with a few hundred franc pieces, which she took from the drawer with the compartments where he kept the change.

Later on she had ventured opening the wallet and he had sometimes noticed that a thousand franc note would be missing.

Yet he gave her plenty of money for housekeeping, never refused her a new dress, underclothes, or shoes.

Perhaps at first she acted merely on a private whim, and he suspected that she had taken money in the same way from her parents' till when she lived with them. Only it must have been more difficult then, for Angèle, despite her jolly, motherly air, had a sharp eye for money. He had never mentioned it to Gina. He had thought a lot about it, and had finally come to the conclusion that it was for her brother that she stole in this way. She was five years older than he and yet people could sense an affinity between them of the kind that is normally only found between twins. There were times when one might have thought Frédo was in love with his sister, and that she reciprocated it.

It was enough for them, wherever they were, to exchange a glance to understand one another, and if Gina frowned her brother became as anxious as a lover.

Was that why he disliked Jonas? At the wedding he had been the only one not to congratulate him, and he had left right in the middle of the reception. Gina had run after him. They had whispered together a long time in the corridor of the Hôtel du Commerce where the banquet had taken place. When she came back, still dressed in white satin, it was obvious that she had been crying, and she had at once poured herself out a glass of champagne.

At the time Frédo was only seventeen. Their marriage had taken place two weeks before Clémence Ancel, their bridesmaid, had hers.

Resigned, he opened the drawer with his key, picked up the wallet and discovered to his surprise that there was not a single note missing.

It was explicable. He hadn't thought. The day before Gina had not left until after dinner and, up till the last moment, he might have had to open the cash drawer. With the stamps it was another matter, as sometimes he went a whole week without touching the steel box.

There were still some details which he did not understand, but they were material details of no great importance. For example, he always carried his keys in his trouser pocket, attached to a silver chain. When had his wife managed to get hold of them without his knowing? Not at night, because he slept more lightly than she did, and besides he was the first down in the morning. Occasionally, it was true, in order not to wake her, he would go downstairs in pyjamas and dressing-gown to make his coffee. It had not happened the day before, but the day before that, and he hadn't touched the safe since then.

'Have you got a book about bee-keeping, please?'

It was a boy about twelve years old, who had just come in, and spoken in an assured voice, his face covered in freckles, his copper-coloured hair streaked with sunlight.

'Are you thinking of keeping bees?'

'I found a swarm in a tree in the vegetable garden and my parents are going to let me make a hive, provided I do it with my own money.'

Jonas had fair ginger hair too, with freckles on the bridge of his nose. But at this child's age he must have already worn glasses as thick as the ones he was wearing now.

He had wondered to himself sometimes whether on account of his short-sightedness he saw things and people differently from others. The question intrigued him. He had read, for example, that the various species of animals do not see us as we really are, but as their eyes show us to them, and that for some we are ten times as tall, which is what makes them so timid when we approach them.

Does the same phenomenon occur with a short-sighted person, even though his sight is more or less corrected by spectacles? Without glasses the world was to him only a more or less luminous cloud in which floated shapes so insubstantial that he could not be sure of being able to touch them.

His spectacles, on the other hand, revealed to him the details of objects and faces as if he had been looking at them through a magnifying glass or as if they had been engraved.

Did this cause him to live in a separate sphere? Were these spectacles, without which he had to grope his way, a barrier between himself and the world outside?

In a shelf of books about animals he finally found one on bees and bee-hives.

'How about that one?'

'Is it expensive?'

He consulted, on the back cover, the pencilled price.

'A hundred francs.'

'Would you let me have it if I paid half next week?'

Jonas didn't know him. He was not from the neighbourhood. He was a country boy whose mother had probably come into the market with vegetables or poultry.

'You can take it.'

'Thank you. I will be in again next Thursday without fail.'

Outside in the sun of the street and the shade of the covered market the clientèle had changed insensibly. Early in the morning there was a preponderance of working-class women doing their shopping after taking their children to school. It was also the time for the vans from the hotels and restaurants.

As early as nine o'clock, and especially around ten o'clock the shoppers were better dressed, and at eleven some of them brought their maids with them to carry the parcels.

The shavings in the gutter, trampled underfoot, were losing their golden hue to turn brown and sticky, and were now becoming mixed with outer leaves of leeks, carrots and fish heads.

Gina had taken no change of clothes with her, no underclothes, not even a coat, though the nights were still cool.

If she had been intending to stay in the town, on the other hand, would she have had the nerve to take his most valuable stamps?

After seven o'clock in the evening, there were no more buses to Bourges, nor for anywhere else, only a train at 8.52 which connected with the Paris train, and, at 9.40, the slow train from Moulins.

The station employees knew her, but he didn't dare go and question them. It was too late. He had twice spoken of Bourges and he was obliged to stick to it.

Why had he behaved in this way? He could not account for it. It was not from fear of ridicule, because everyone, not only in the Place du Vieux-Marché, but throughout the town, knew that Gina had had many lovers before marrying him. It could not have passed unnoticed either, that since her marriage she had had several adventures.

Was it a sort of shame that had prompted him to reply, first to Le Bouc, then to Palestri:

'She has gone to Bourges?'

Shame which was born of shyness? What happened between him and Gina did not concern anybody else, and he believed himself to be the last person to have any right to discuss it.

But for the disappearance of the stamps he would have waited all day, then all night, hoping from one moment to the next to see her return like a dog which has run away.

The room upstairs had not been done, and the strong box had not been closed, so he went up, made his bed as meticulously as when he was a bachelor and the maid was away.

It was as a maid that Gina had come into the house. Before her there had been another, old Léonie, who at the age of seventy still put in her eight or nine hours a day with different employers. In the end her legs had swollen up. Latterly she could hardly manage to climb the stairs, and as her children, who lived in Paris, did not care to look after her, Doctor Joublin had put her in a home.

For a month Jonas had been without anyone, and it didn't worry him unduly. He knew Gina, like everyone else, through having seen her pass by, or from selling her an occasional book. At that time she had behaved in a provocative manner with him as she used to with all men, and he blushed every time she came into his shop, especially in summer, when it seemed to him that she left behind her a trace of the smell of her armpits.

'Haven't you got anyone yet?' Le Bouc had asked him one morning when he was having his coffee in the little bar.

He had never understood why Le Bouc and the others from the Square did not use the familiar '*tu*' with him, for they nearly all used it among themselves, calling one another by their Christian names.

They didn't call him Milk, however, almost as if it were not his name, nor Monsieur Milk, but nearly always, Monsieur Jonas.

And yet at the age of two he was living in the Square, just next door to Ancel's, the butcher's, and it was his father who had converted the fishmonger's, '*A La Marée*', now kept by the Chenus.

It was not because he had not been to the communal school either, like most of them, but to a private school, then to the *lycée*. The proof was that they were already addressing his father before him as Monsieur Constantin.

Fernand had asked him:

'Haven't you got anybody yet?'

He had replied no, and Le Bouc had leant over his counter.

'You ought to have a word or two with Angèle.'

He had been so surprised that he had asked, as if there could have been two Angèles:

'The greengrocer?'

'Yes. She's having trouble with Gina. She can't do anything with her. I think she wouldn't be sorry to see her working outside so that someone else could break her in.'

Up till then Gina had been more or less helping her mother in the shop, and slipping off at every opportunity.

'You wouldn't like to talk to her yourself?' Jonas had suggested.

It seemed to him incongruous, indecent almost, on his part, as a bachelor, although he had no ulterior motives, to go and ask a woman like Angèle to let him have her daughter for three hours a day.

'I'll have a word with her father. No! I'd better see Angèle. I'll give you her reply tomorrow.'

To his great surprise, the reply next day was yes, or as good as yes, and he was almost frightened by it. Angèle had told Le Bouc, to be precise:

'*Tell that Jonas I'll come round and see him.*'

She had come, late one afternoon during a slack period, had insisted on seeing over the house, and had discussed wages.

That meant changing his habits, and it was not without reluctance that he gave up going at half-past twelve and sitting in Pepito's little restaurant, where he had his own pigeon-hole for his table-napkin and his bottle of mineral water.

'After all, if she's going to work at all, it might as well be worth her while. It's high time she got down to some cooking, and we hardly have time in our place at midday to eat more than a piece of sausage or some cheese.'

Didn't Gina resent his having engaged her, at first? Anyone would have thought she was doing everything possible to make herself unbearable so that he would throw her out.

After a week with him she was working from nine o'clock in the morning until one. Then Angèle had decided:

'It's absurd to cook for one person alone. It costs no more to do it for two. She might just as well have lunch with you and do the washing-up before leaving.'

Suddenly his life had changed. He didn't know everything, because he didn't hear the gossip, perhaps also because people didn't speak freely in front of him. He didn't understand, at first, why Gina was always in low spirits and why she would suddenly turn aggressive only, soon afterwards, to burst into tears in the middle of her housework.

It was then three months since Marcel Jenot had been arrested and Jonas hardly ever read the papers. He had heard his name mentioned at Le Bouc's, for it had created quite a sensation. Marcel Jenot, the son of a dressmaker who worked for most of the women of the Market, including the Palestris, was under-cook at the Commercial Hotel, the best and most expensive in town. Jonas must have seen him at some time or other without paying any attention. His photograph, in the papers, showed a young man with a high forehead and a serious expression with, however, a rather disquieting curl to his lip.

At twenty-one he had just finished his military service in Indo-China and was once more living with his mother in the Rue des Belles-Feuilles, the street beyond Pepito's restaurant.

Like most young men of his age he owned a motor-cycle. One evening on the Saint-Amand road, a large car-load of Parisians had been stopped by a motor-cyclist who seemed to be asking for help and then, brandishing an automatic, had demanded money from the occupants, after which he had punctured the four tyres of the car and made off.

The motor-cycle's number plate, at the time of the hold-up, was covered with a layer of black paint. How had the police managed to trace it to Marcel? The papers must have explained it, but Jonas didn't know.

The investigation was under way when Gina had gone into service with him, and a month later the trial had taken place at Montluçon.

It was Le Bouc who had told the bookseller about it.

'How is Gina?'

'She does her best.'

'Not too upset?'

'Why?'

'Marcel is being tried next week.'

'Which Marcel?'

'The one in the hold-up. It's her boy friend.'

She actually had to stay away for a few days and when she came back to resume work, it was a long time before she opened her mouth.

That had been nearly three years ago now. A year after she had joined him as a housemaid Jonas married her, surprised at what was happening to him. He was thirty-eight and she twenty-two. Even when, in the sunlight, her body almost naked under her dress, she used to move to and fro around him and he breathed her smell, he had never made a single ambiguous gesture.

At Le Bouc's they had adopted the habit of asking him, with a smile at the corner of the mouth:

'Well, well! And how's Gina?'

He would reply, naively:

'She's very well.'

Some of them went so far as to give him a wink, which he would pretend not to see, and others seemed to suspect him of keeping something up his sleeve.

By keeping his ears pricked and asking a few questions here and there, he could easily have found out the names of all the lovers Gina had had since she had begun to knock about with men at the age of thirteen. He could also have found out about what had happened between her and Marcel. He was not unaware that she had been questioned several times by the police in the course of the inquiry and that Angèle had been summoned by the magistrate.

What would be the use? It was not in his character. He had always lived alone, without imagining that he would one day be able to live otherwise.

Gina did not keep house as well as old Léonie. Her tablecloths, when she took the trouble to use them, were seldom clean and, if she sometimes sang as she worked, there were days when her face remained set, her mouth truculent.

Often, in the middle of the morning, she would disappear on the pretext of doing some shopping up the road and come back, with no apology, two hours later.

Even so, hadn't her presence in the house become essential to Jonas? Had there been a conspiracy, as some people claimed, to force his hand?

One afternoon Angèle had called in the clothes she always wore during the day in her shop, for she only really dressed up on Sundays.

'Well now, Jonas!'

She was one of the few people not to call him Monsieur Jonas. True, she addressed most of the customers in the most familiar manner.

'Don't touch those pears, love!' she would shout at Doctor Martroux's wife, one of the most prim and proper women in the town. 'When I go to see your husband I don't play with his instruments.'

That day she strode into the kitchen and sat down on a chair.

'I've come to tell you I've had an offer for my daughter.'

Her gaze made an inventory of the room, where nothing can have escaped her attention.

'Some people from Paris who have just settled in the town. The husband, an engineer, has been appointed assistant manager of the factory and they are looking for someone. It's a good post, and Gina would get board and lodging. I promised them a reply the day after tomorrow. You can think it over.'

He had had twenty-four hours of panic and had turned the question over in his mind in all its aspects again and again. . . . As a bachelor he couldn't have a living-in maid. Besides there was only one bedroom in the house. That Angèle knew. So why had she come to offer him a sort of first refusal?

It was difficult enough to keep Gina in the house all day for she would have nothing to do for hours on end.

Had Angèle thought of all this?

During this time Gina seemed to be unaware of what was going on and behaved in her normal way.

They always had lunch together, in the kitchen, opposite one another, she with her back to the oven, from where she reached for the pots as she needed them, without having to get up.

'Gina!'

'Yes.'

'There's something I want to ask you.'

'What?'

'You promise to answer me frankly?'

He could still see her clearly as he pronounced these words, but the next moment she was nothing more than a wraith before his eyes, for his spectacles had suddenly misted over.

'Aren't I always frank?'

'Yes.'

'Usually I get criticized for being too frank.'

'Not by me.'

'What do you want to ask?'

'Do you like the house?'

She looked round her with what seemed to him like indifference.

'I mean,' he persisted, 'would you like to live here altogether?'

'Why do you ask me that?'

'Because I should be happy if you would accept.'

'Accept what?'

'Becoming my wife.'

If there had been a plot, Gina was not in it, for she exclaimed with a nervous laugh:

'Don't be silly!'

'I'm serious.'

'You'd marry me?'

'That's what I am suggesting.'

'*Me?*'

'You.'

'You realize what sort of a girl I am?'

'I think I know you as well as anybody else.'

'In that case you're a brave man.'

'What's your answer?'

'My answer's that you're very kind, but that it's impossible.'

There was a splash of sunlight on the table and it was on this that Jonas fastened his gaze, rather than on the young girl's face.

'Why?'

'Because.'

'You don't want me?'

'I didn't say that, Monsieur Jonas. You are certainly very decent. In fact you're the only man who never tried to take advantage of the situation. Even Ancel himself, though he's the father of one of my friends took me into the shed in his backyard when I was only fifteen. I could name nearly all of them, one by one, and you would be amazed. To start with I wondered when you were going to pluck up courage.'

'Do you think you couldn't be happy here?'

Then she made her frankest reply:

'It would be peaceful, at any rate.'

'Well, that's something, isn't it?'

'Yes, of course. Only supposing we didn't get on together? Better not say any more about it. I'm not the kind of girl to make a man like you happy.'

'It's not me that counts.'

'Who does then?'

'You.'

He was sincere. He was so overcome with tenderness while he was talking about this subject, that he didn't dare move from fear of allowing his emotion to break out.

'Me and happiness . . .' she said bitterly, between her clenched teeth.

'Let's say peace, as you just called it yourself.'

She had glanced at him sharply.

'Was it my mother who suggested it to you? I knew she'd been to see you, but . . .'

'No. She only told me you were being offered a better job.'

'My mother has always wanted to get me out of the way.'

'Won't you think it over?'

'What's the point?'

'Wait at any rate until tomorrow before giving me a definite answer, will you?'

'If you insist!'

That day she had broken a plate while she was doing the washing up, and as had happened now, two years later, she had gone off forgetting to clean the stove.

At about four o'clock in the afternoon, as usual, Jonas had gone for his cup of coffee at Le Bouc's and Fernand had watched him closely.

'Is it true, what they're saying?'

'What are they saying?'

'That you are going to marry Gina.'

'Who told you that?'

'Louis, just now. He had a quarrel with Angèle over it.'

'Why?'

Le Bouc had looked uncomfortable.

'They don't have the same ideas.'

'He's against it?'

'I'll say!'

'Why?'

Louis had certainly given a reason, but Le Bouc did not pass it on.

'You never can tell just what's going on in his head,' he replied evasively.

'Is he angry?'

'He talked about going and knocking your block off. That won't stop him doing what Angèle decides. It makes no difference him protesting, he's got no say in his house.'

'And Gina?'

'You must know what she said to you better than I do. The most difficult of all will be her brother.'

'Why?'

'I don't know. It's just a hunch. He's a strange lad, with ideas all his own.'

'He doesn't like me?'

'Apart from his sister he probably likes nobody. She's the only one who can stop him making a fool of himself. A month ago he wanted to join up in Indo-China.'

'She didn't want him to?'

'He's only a boy. He's never been anywhere. As soon as he got there he would be even more unhappy than he is here.'

A customer was going into the shop, near by, and Jonas made for the door.

'See you soon.'

'Good luck!'

He had slept badly, that night. At eight o'clock Gina had come in to start work without speaking, without looking at him, and he had waited a long quarter of an hour before questioning her.

'Have you got the answer?'

'Do you really mean it?'

'Yes.'

'You won't hold it against me later?'

'I promise.'

She had shrugged her shoulders.

'In that case it's as you wish.'

It was so unexpected that it made him empty of all emotion. He looked at her dumbfounded, without daring to approach, without taking her hand, and even less did it occur to him to kiss her.

Afraid of having misunderstood her, he insisted:

'You are consenting to marry me?'

She was sixteen years younger than he and yet it was she who had looked at him as if he were a child, a protective smile at her lips.

'Yes.'

So as not to betray himself in front of her, he had gone up to his room and, before leaning out of the window, had stood for a long while in a trance in front of one of the wardrobe mirrors. It was in May. A shower had just fallen but the sun was shining again and making great bright patches on the wet tiles of the immense roof. There was a market, like today, and he had gone out to buy strawberries, the first of the season.

A big, strong woman, dressed in black, a blue apron round her middle, was entering his shop in an authoritative manner and casting a great shadow. It was Angèle, whose hands always smelt of leeks.

'Is it true what Louis tells me? What's she gone to Bourges for?'

He was smaller than she was and a great deal less powerful. He stammered:

'I don't know.'

'Did she take the bus this morning?'

'Yes.'

'Without coming to see me?'

She, too, was looking at him suspiciously.

'Was there a quarrel between the two of you?'

'No.'

'Answer me like a man, for God's sake! What's gone wrong?'

'Nothing . . .'

She had begun to address him familiarly the day of the engagement, but Louis had never been willing to follow her example.

'*Nothing! Nothing!* . . .' she mimicked. 'You ought at least to be capable of preventing your wife from running away. When did she promise to come back?'

'She didn't say.'

'That's better than ever!'

She seemed to flatten him with a look, with all her vigorous bulk, and then, turning sharply on her heel to leave, she ground out:

'Little rat!'

Chapter Three

His first impulse had been to go and buy a slice of ham, or some cold meat from Pascal, the butcher on the other side of the market, just at the beginning of the Rue du Canal, or even not to eat at all, or perhaps to make do with the two extra *croissants* he had been given that morning. He ought not to have taken them. That did not fit in with the supposed departure of Gina for Bourges. Strictly he would only have needed to buy three *croissants*.

It was not on his own account that he was so distraught, out of self-respect or fear or what people would say.

It was on her account. Her theft of his stamps, which were all he cared about in the world apart from her, made no difference: he considered it his duty to defend her.

He did not know yet what against. He had been a prey, particularly since that morning, to a vague uneasiness which almost prevented him from thinking about his own distress. In time, every one of his feelings would doubtless detach themselves more clearly and he would be able to single them out. For the moment, stunned, he was dealing with the immediate problems first, in the belief that by acting in this way it was Gina that he was protecting.

On the rare occasions when she had to visit La Loute and had spent the whole day at Bourges, he had returned to his bachelor habits and eaten at Pepito's. This, then, was what he had to do today and when, at noon, the bell announcing the end of the market pealed out into the sunlight, vibrating like a convent bell, he began to bring the boxes of books indoors.

Already the refuse lorry was advancing yard by yard round the square, while five men loaded on to it everything they could shovel up out of the gutter. Many of the market women, especially the ones from the country, had already left, and some, before taking their bus, were eating the snacks they had brought with them, at Le Bouc's or the Trianon Bar.

It went against the grain to leave the house, rather as if he were betraying something, and, against all evidence, he told himself that Gina would perhaps return while he was away.

The Rue Haute was a narrow, gently sloping street, despite its name, and formed the main artery of the most densely populated neighbourhood. The shops in it were more varied than elsewhere. American surplus stores and cheap jewellery were sold in it, and there were at least three junk shops and old clothes stores.

Since the chemical products factory had been installed a kilometre away, it had become a sort of Italian quarter at the far end, which some people actually called Little Italy. As the factory grew in importance, workers had come from elsewhere, first of all Poles, who had installed themselves a little farther up, then at the end, almost outside the factory gates, a few families of Algerians.

Pepito's restaurant with the olive-coloured walls and the crinkled paper cloths, had nevertheless preserved its peaceful character and, at midday, the same habitués were to be found there, who, as Jonas had done for such a long time, took their meals there year in year out.

Marie, the *patron's* wife, did the cooking while her husband ran the bar and their niece waited at table.

'Why, Monsieur Jonas!' the little Italian cried out on catching sight of him. 'What a pleasant surprise to see you!'

Then, afraid suddenly that he had committed a gaffe to appear so pleased: 'Gina's not ill, I trust?'

And he had to repeat his old refrain:

'She's gone to Bourges.'

'Well, we all have to change our routine now and again.There, your old table's free. Julia! Lay a place for Monsieur Jonas.'

It was probably here that Jonas became most aware of the vacuum which had just been created in his life. For years Pepito's restaurant, where nothing had changed, had been a second home for him. Yet, here he was, feeling out of place, seized with panic at the idea that he might have to return every day.

The Widower was in his place, and seemed almost to be on the point of welcoming Jonas with the batting of his eyelids which in the old days had served as a greeting.

They had never spoken to one another. For years, they had occupied two tables opposite one another by the window, and they used to arrive at more or less the same time.

Jonas knew his name, through Pepito. He was Monsieur Métras, chief clerk at the Town Hall, but in his mind he always labelled him The Widower.

He had never seen Madame Métras, who had died fifteen years before. As there were no children in the family, the husband, left to his own devices, had taken to having his meals at Pepito's.

He must have been fifty-five years old, perhaps more. He was a tall man, very broadly built, thick and hard, with iron grey hair, bushy eyebrows and darker hair sprouting from his nostrils and ears. His complexion was greyish as well, and Jonas had never seen him smile. He didn't read the paper as he ate, like most single diners, never joined in a conversation with anybody, and chewed his food carefully, gazing straight to his front.

Many months had passed before they batted eyelids at one another in greeting, and Jonas was the only person to whom The Widower had ever made this concession.

A diminutive, asthmatic dog, fat and almost impotent, used to sit under the table; it could not have been far off twenty years old, for it had once been Madame Métras' dog.

The Widower used to go and fetch if from his flat on coming out of his office, and take it to the restaurant where they gave it its food. Then he led it off again, slowly, waiting while it relieved itself before returning to the Town Hall, and in the evening the performance was repeated.

Why, while Jonas was eating, did The Widower watch him today more closely than before? It wasn't possible that he already knew. Yet anyone would have sworn that he was thinking to himself, restraining a snigger:

'Ah! So, you're back again!'

Rather as if the two of them had been members of the same club, as if Jonas had left it for a time and finally come back, repentant, to the fold.

All this existed only in his imagination, but what was not imagination was his terror at the idea of once again sitting opposite the chief clerk every day.

'What will you have for dessert, Monsieur Jonas? There's éclairs and apple tart.'

He had always liked pudding, particularly apple tart, which he chose, and he felt guilty at yielding to his greed at such a moment.

'What's your news, Monsieur Jonas?'

Pepito was tall like Palestri, dry and lean, but unlike his compatriot, he was always smiling and affable. Anyone would have thought running a restaurant was all a game for him, he did it with such good humour. Maria, his wife, had become enormous as a result of living in a kitchen six yards square, but that did not prevent her remaining young and alluring. She, too, was jolly and would burst into laughter over nothing.

As they had no children, they had adopted a nephew whom they had had sent over from their country and who could be seen doing his homework in the evening at one of the restaurant tables.

'How's Gina?'

'She's all right.'

'The other day my wife met her in the market and, I don't know why, she got the impression that she was expecting a baby. Is that true?'

He said no, almost ashamed, for he was sure it was his fault if Gina was not pregnant.

What had misled Maria was that recently Gina had taken to eating more than usual, with a sort of frenzy, and from being plump as she was before, had become fat to the extent of needing to alter her clothes.

At first he had rejoiced at her appetite, for in the early days of their marriage, she hardly ate at all. He used to encourage her, seeing it as a sign of contentment, thinking that she was acclimatizing herself to their life, and that she might end by actually feeling happy.

He had said so to her and she had replied with a vague, rather protective smile, which she turned on him increasingly often now. She had not her mother's authoritative personality, quite the opposite. She did not concern herself with business, or money, or the decisions that had to be taken in household matters.

Yet, despite the difference in age, it was she who adopted an indulgent manner now and then towards Jonas.

He was her husband and she treated him as such. But in her eyes, perhaps, he was not quite a man, a real male, and she seemed to look on him as a backward child.

Had he been wrong not to have been more severe with her? Ought he to have taken her in hand? Would that have changed matters?

He had no desire to think about it. The Widower, opposite, was hypnotizing him and he finished up his apple tart faster than he would have wished, in order to escape his gaze.

'So soon?' exclaimed Pepito when he asked for the bill. 'Aren't you going to have your coffee?'

He would take it at Le Bouc's, with the possibility in the back of his mind of hearing some news there. In the old days he used to eat as slowly as Monsieur Métras, and the majority of single men who lunched in the restaurant and who, for the most part, chatted with the *patron* afterwards.

'Julia! Monsieur Jonas' bill.'

And, addressing him:

'Shall we be seeing you this evening?'

'Perhaps.'

'She hasn't gone for long?'

'I don't know yet.'

It was starting all over again. He was floundering, no longer knowing what to reply to the questions that were being put to him, realizing that it would be worse tomorrow and worse still in the days to follow.

What would happen, for example, if La Loute came to see her family and disclosed that Gina had not been to Bourges? It was unlikely, but he was envisaging everything. The woman everyone called La Loute was really Louise Hariel, and her parents kept the grain store in the market, just opposite Jonas, on the other side of the great roof.

He had seen her, in the same way as he had seen Gina, running about among the crates when she was not yet ten. At that time, with her round face, her blue eyes with long lashes and her curly hair, she looked like a doll. It was odd, for her father was a thin, plain little man and her mother, in the drab background of the grain store, which faced north and never got the sun, looked like a dried-up old spinster.

The two Hariels, man and wife, wore the same grey smock and, from living together, each behind their own counter, making the same movements, they had ended by resembling one another.

La Loute had been the only one of the girls of the Square to be educated in a convent, which she had not left until the age of seventeen. She was also the best-dressed and her clothes were very lady-like. On Sundays when she went to High Mass with her parents, everyone used to turn round, and the mothers held up her deportment as an example to their daughters.

For about two years she had worked as a secretary to the Privas Press, a business which had been flourishing for three generations, then, all of a sudden, it had been put about that she had found a better job in Bourges.

Her parents didn't mention the subject. The two of them were the most cantankerous shopkeepers in the Old Market and many customers preferred to go all the way to the Rue de la Gare for their purchases.

La Loute and Gina were good friends. With Clémence, the butcher's daughter, they had for long been an inseparable trio.

At first people had said that La Loute was working with an architect in Bourges, then with a bachelor doctor with whom she had lived on marital terms.

Various people had met her there, and there was talk of her expensive tastes, her fur coat. The latest news was that she had a baby Citroen, which had been seen outside her parents' door one evening.

La Loute had not spent the night with them. The neighbours claimed to have heard raised voices, which was strange, for the Hariels hardly ever opened their mouths and someone had actually called them the two fish.

To Jonas, Gina had contented herself with saying, on one of her returns from Bourges:

'She leads her life as best she can and it's not easy for anyone.'

After a moment's reflection she had added:

'Poor girl. She's too kind.'

Why too kind? Jonas had not inquired. He recognized that it was none of his business, that it was women's and even girls' gossip, that friends like Clémence, La Loute and Gina, when they got together, became schoolgirls again and had a right to their own secrets.

Another time, Gina had said:

'It's all plain sailing for some people.'

Was she referring to Clémence, who had a young husband, a good-looking fellow, and who had had the finest wedding in the Old Market?

He himself wasn't young, nor a good-looking fellow, and all he had been able to offer was security. Had Gina really wanted security, *peace*, as he had said the first day?

Where was she at that moment, with the stamps which she imagined she could sell without difficulty? Surely she could have had hardly any money on her, even if, without Jonas' knowledge, she had put some aside for the occasion? Her brother could not have given her anything either, because it was she who slipped him money from time to time.

Because she had seen the prices in the catalogue she had told herself that she had only to call at any stamp dealer, in Paris or anywhere else, to sell them. It was true of certain of them, the ones only comparatively rare, but it was not the case for the valuable ones, like the 1849 Ceres.

Stamp dealers, like diamond merchants, form a sort of confraternity throughout the world, and are more or less known to one another. They know, usually, in whose hands such and such a rare stamp is, and watch for a chance to acquire it for their customers.

At least five of the stamps she had taken were known in this way. If she were to offer them for sale at any reputable dealers there was a good chance that the assistant would detain her on some pretext and telephone the police.

She was in no danger of being put into prison, because she was his wife and theft is not recognized between married people. Even so they would start an inquiry and they would get into touch with him.

Would it be in this way, on account of her ignorance, that her escapade would come to an end?

He was not sure he would wish that. He didn't wish it. It hurt him to think of Gina's shame, her discomfiture, her rage.

Wouldn't it be still worse if she were to entrust the sale to someone else? By now she was no longer alone, on that score he had no illusions. And this time it was not a question of some young male from the town whom she had not been able to resist following for a night or two.

She had set off deliberately and her departure had been premeditated, organized at least twenty-four hours in advance. In other words, he had lived with her for twenty-four hours without realizing that it was probably the last day they would spend together.

He was walking along the street now, with slow steps, and the bare space under the tile roof seemed immense, given over to a few men who were hosing it down and scrubbing the cement flooring with brooms. Most of the shops were shut until two o'clock.

He was shrinking from the moment of going into Le Bouc's to drink his coffee, for he didn't feel like speaking to anybody, least of all to answer any more questions. He was devoid of hatred, or bitterness. What was filling his heart was a sad, anxious, and almost serene tenderness, and he stopped for a good minute watching two puppies, one of them lying on its back in the sun, with its four paws waving in the air, playing at biting each other.

He remembered the smell of herrings, in the kitchen, the oven which Gina in her haste had not washed and to which bits of fish were sticking. He tried to remember what they had found to talk about at that last meal, but could not do so. Then he tried to recall the minute details of the day before, which he had spent like an ordinary day, when it was really the most important one in his life.

One image came back to him: he was behind his counter, serving an old gentleman who didn't know exactly what he wanted when Gina, who had gone up a little earlier than usual to do her face, had come down in her red dress. It was one of last year's dresses, and this was the first time he had seen it this season; because Gina had put on weight it clung more closely than ever to her body.

She had gone over to the doorway and into the triangle of sunlight, and he could never remember having seen her looking so lovely.

He hadn't told her so because, when he paid her a compliment, she would shrug her shoulders irritably and sometimes her face would cloud over.

Once she had countered almost dryly:

'Forget it! I'll be an old woman soon enough, for God's sake!'

He thought he understood. He had no wish to analyse the matter any further. Obviously she meant that she was losing her youth in this old house which smelt of mouldering paper. It was doubtless an ironic way of reassuring him, of letting him know that they would soon be on equal terms and that he would no longer need to be afraid.

'I'm going to go and say good-morning to Mama,' she had told him.

Usually, at that hour, her visits to her mother's shop didn't last for long, for Angèle, harassed with customers, had no time to waste. But Gina had been absent for nearly an hour. When she had come back, she didn't come from the right, but from the left, in other words from the opposite direction to the house of her parents, and yet she was not carrying any parcels.

She never received any letters, it suddenly struck him. Not counting La Loute, she had several married friends who no longer lived in the town. Oughtn't she to have received at least a post-card from them now and again?

The Post Office was in the Rue Haute, five minutes from Pepito's. Did she have her mail sent there poste restante? Or had she been to make a telephone call from the box?

During the two years they had been married she had never mentioned Marcel, who had been sentenced to five years in prison. When she had gone off on her escapades, it was perforce with other men, which had led Jonas to suppose that she had forgotten about Jenot.

It was at least six months since she had gone out in the evening on her own, except to look after Clémence's baby, and each time she had returned punctually. Besides, if she had seen a man, he would have noticed, for she was not a woman on whom love left no mark. He knew the look on her face when she had been with a man, her slack, shifty manner, and even the smell of her body which was not the same.

Madame Hariel, the grain seller, stood behind her shop door with the handle removed, her pale face pressed to the glass panel, watching him as he wandered along the pavement like a man who does not know where he is going, and he finally headed in the direction of Le Bouc's bar. The latter was still at lunch with his wife at the back of the café, and they were finishing their black pudding.

'Don't move,' he said. 'I've plenty of time.'

It was the slack time of the day. Fernand, before having his lunch, had swept up the dirty sawdust and the red floor stones shone brightly, the house smelt of cleanliness.

'Did you have lunch at Pepito's?'

He nodded. Le Bouc had a bony face, and used to wear a blue apron. Except on Sundays and two or three times at the cinema, Jonas had never seen him in a coat.

With his mouth full, he said as he went over to the percolator:

'Louis asked me just now if I had seen Gina go past and I said I hadn't. He was having one of his bad bouts. It's a pity that a fine chap like him can't stop himself from drinking.'

Jonas unwrapped his two lumps of sugar and held them in his hand, while waiting for his cup of coffee. He liked the smell of Le Bouc's bar, even though it was loaded with alcohol, just as he liked the smell of old books which reigned in his own house. He liked the smell of the market as well, especially during the fresh fruit season, and he sometimes stolled about among the stalls to breathe it in, at the same time keeping an eye on his bookshop from afar.

Le Bouc had just said, referring to Louis:

'A fine chap . . .'

And Jonas noticed for the first time that it was an expression he often used. Ancel was a fine chap as well, and Benaiche the police constable, for whom the retailers filled a crate of provisions every morning, which his wife came to fetch at nine o'clock.

Angèle, too, despite her shrewish temperament, was a fine woman.

Everybody, around the Market, except perhaps for the Hariels, who shut themselves up in their own house as if to avoid God knows what contagion, greeted one another each morning with good humour and cordiality. Everybody also worked hard and respected hard work in others.

Of Marcel, when the hold-up affair had come to light, they had said pityingly:

'It's funny. Such a nice lad . . .'

Then they had added:

'It must be Indo-China that did it to him. That's no place for young lads.'

If they spoke of La Loute and the mysterious life she led at Bourges, they didn't hold that against her either.

'Girls today aren't what they used to be. Education's changed too.'

As for Gina, she remained one of the most popular figures in the Market and when she passed by with a sway of her hips, a smile on her lips, her teeth sparkling, their faces would light up. They all followed her latest adventures. She had been seen one evening, when she was hardly seventeen, lying with a lorry driver on the back of a lorry.

'Hullo there, Gina!' they used to call out to her.

And no doubt they envied the good fortune of the men who had slept with her. Many of them had tried. Some had succeeded. Nobody held it against her for being what she was. They were nearer to being grateful, for without her the Vieux-Marché would not have been quite what it was.

'Is it true that she took the morning bus?' asked Le Bouc, returning to his place at the table.

As Jonas made no reply, he took his silence to mean that he was correct, and went on:

'In that case, she will have been with my niece, Gaston's daughter, who's gone to see a new specialist.'

Jonas knew her. She was a young girl with a pretty but anaemic face who had a deformed hip and in order to walk had to thrust the right-hand side of her body forward. She was seventeen years old.

Since the age of twelve, she had been in the hands of specialists, who had made her undergo various courses of treatment. She had been operated on two or three times without any appreciable success and, at about the age of fifteen, she had spent an entire year in plaster.

She remained sweet and cheerful and her mother came several times a week to change books for her, sentimental novels which she chose carefully herself, out of fear that one of the characters might have been crippled as she was.

'Is her mother with her?'

'No. She went by herself. Gina will have kept her company.'

'Is she coming back this evening?'

'On the five o'clock bus.'

So, then, they would know that Gina had not gone to Bourges. What would he say to Louis when he came to demand an explanation?

For the Palestri family would certainly want explanations from him. They had entrusted their daughter to him, and considered him henceforth responsible for her.

Incapable of looking after her, living in fear of a scandal which might at any moment break out, Angèle had thrust her into his arms. It was that, to put it bluntly that she had come to do when she had talked to him about a place for her daughter with the assistant manager of the factory. The story may have been true, but she had taken advantage of it.

Even now he was grateful to her for it, for his life without Gina had had no flavour; it was a little as if he had not lived before.

What intrigued him was what had happened in the Palestri family during that period. That there had been discussions there was no question. Frédo's attitude was not in any doubt either, and he must have argued with his parents that they were pushing his sister into the arms of an old man.

But Louis? Did he, too, prefer to see his daughter chasing men than married to Jonas?

'It looks as if we're in for a hot summer. That's what the almanack says, anyway. Storms next week.'

He wiped his spectacles which the steam of his coffee had misted over, and stood there for a moment like an owl in the sun, blinking his pink eyelids. It was rare for him to take off his glasses in public; he didn't know exactly why he had done so, for he had never found himself in this position before. It gave him a sense of inferiority, rather as when one dreams that one is stark naked or trouserless in the middle of a crowd.

Gina used to see him like this every day and perhaps that was why she treated him differently from the others. His thick lenses, not rimmed with metal or tortoise-shell, worked both ways. While they enabled him to observe the minutest details of the world outside, they enlarged his pupils for other people and gave them a fixed look, a hardness which in reality they did not possess.

Once, standing in his doorway, he had heard a small boy who was passing say to his mother:

'Hasn't that man got large eyes!'

Actually his eyes weren't large. It was the glasses which gave them a globular appearance.

'See you later,' he sighed, after counting out his coins and putting them on the counter.

'See you later. Good afternoon.'

At around five o'clock Le Bouc would close his bar, for in the afternoon few customers came. If he stayed open it was mainly for the convenience of his neighbours. The day before a market he would go to bed at eight in the evening so as to be up at three next morning.

Tomorrow, Friday, there was no market. Every other day, four days in the week to be precise, the space beneath the tiled roof stood empty and served as a parking place for cars and a playground for children.

For the last two or three weeks, the children were to be seen charging about on roller skates which made a screeching sound for miles around, then, as if they had been given the word, they changed their game and took up skittles, spinning-tops or yo-yos. It followed a rhythm, like the seasons, only more mysterious, for it was impossible to tell where the decision came from and the vendor at the bazaar in the Rue Haute was taken by surprise every time.

'I want a kite, please.'

He would sell ten, twenty, in the space of two days, order others and then only sell one for the rest of the year.

Taking his keys from his pocket reminded Jonas of the steel strong-box and Gina's departure. He encountered the smell of the house again, and the atmosphere was stale, now that the sun no longer fell on its front. He took out the two book-boxes, mounted on legs with castors, then stood in the middle of the shop, not knowing what to do with himself.

Yet he had spent many years like this, alone, and had never suffered from it. Had not even noticed that there was something missing.

What did he do in the old days, at this time? He sometimes would read, behind the counter. He had read a great deal, not only novels, but works on the most varied subjects, sometimes the most unexpected ones, ranging from political economy to the report of an archaeological excavation. Everything interested him. He would pick out at random a book on mechanics, for example, thinking only to glance over a couple of pages, and then read it from cover to cover. He had read in this way, from the first page to the last, *The History of the Consulate and the Empire*, as he had read, before selling them to a lawyer, twenty-one odd volumes of nineteenth-century trials.

He particularly liked works on geography, ones following a region from its geological formation right up to its economic and cultural expansion.

His stamps acted as reference marks. The names of countries, sovereigns and dictators, did not evoke in his mind a brightly coloured map or photographs, but a delicate vignette enclosed in a transparent packet.

It was in this way, rather than through literature, that he came to know Russia, where he had been born forty years before.

His parents were living in Archangel at the time, right at the top of the map, on the White Sea, where five sisters and a brother had been born before him.

Of the entire family he was the only one not to know Russia, which he had left at the age of one. Maybe this was why at school he had begun to collect stamps. He must have been thirteen when one of his classmates had shown him his album.

'Look!' he had said to him. 'There's a picture of your country.'

It was, he could remember, all the better now that he possessed the stamp along with many other Russian ones, a 1905 blue and pink with a picture of the Kremlin.

'I've got some other ones, you know, but they're portraits.'

The stamps, issued in 1913 for the third centenary of the Romanovs, depicted Peter I, Alexander II, Alexis Michaelovitch, Paul I.

Later he was to make a complete collection of them, including the Winter Palace and the wooden palace of the Boyar Romanovs.

His elder sister Alyosha, who was sixteen when he was born, would now be fifty-six—if she were still alive. Nastasia would be fifty-four and Daniel, his only brother, who died in infancy, would have been just fifty.

The other three sisters, Stéphanie, Sonia and Doussia, were forty-eight, forty-five and forty-two and, because he was the nearest to her in age, also because of her name, it was of Doussia that he thought most often.

He had never seen their faces. He didn't know anything about them, whether they were dead or alive, if they had rallied to the party or been massacred.

The manner of his departure from Russia had been typical of his mother, Natalie, typical of the Oudonovs, as his father would say, for the Oudonovs had always passed as eccentrics.

When he was born in their house at Archangel, where there had been eight servants, his father, who owned an important fishing fleet, had just left as an administrative officer for the army, and was somewhere behind the front line.

In order to be nearer him his mother–a regular carrier-pigeon, as his father kept saying–had left with all her family in the train for Moscow and they had descended on Aunt Zina.

Her real name was Zinaida Oudonova, but he had always heard her called Aunt Zina.

She lived, according to his parents, in a house so big that you could lose yourself in the corridors, and she was very rich. It was in her house that Jonas fell ill at the age of six months. He had contracted an infectious form of pneumonia which he did not seem to be able to throw off, and the doctors had recommended the gentler climate of the South.

They had some friends in the Crimea, at Yalta, the Shepilovs, and without a word of warning, his mother had decided one morning to go to them with the baby.

'I leave the girls in your care, Zina,' she had said to the aunt. 'We shall be back in a few weeks, as soon as we've got the colour back into this lad's cheeks.'

It was not easy, in the middle of a war, to travel across Russia, but nothing was impossible for an Oudonov. Fortunately his mother had found the Shepilovs at Yalta. She had lingered, as was to be expected with her, and it was there that the Revolution had taken her by surprise.

There was no further news of the father. The daughters were still with Zina in Moscow, and Natalie talked about leaving the baby at Yalta to go and fetch them.

The Shepilovs had dissuaded her. Shepilov was a pessimist. The exodus was starting. Lenin and Trotsky were taking over power. The Wrangel army was being formed.

Why not go to Constantinople to let the storm pass, and return in a few months?

The Shepilovs had taken his mother and they had become part of the Russian colony which invaded the hotels of Turkey, some of them with money, others in search of any sort of employment to keep themselves alive.

The Shepilovs had managed to bring out some gold and jewellery. Natalie had a few diamonds with her.

Why had they gone on to Paris from Constantinople? And how, from Paris, had they finished up in a little town in the Berry?

It was not altogether a mystery. Shepilov, before the war, used to entertain lavishly on his estates in the Ukraine and thus he had entertained a certain number of French people, in particular, for several weeks at a time, the Comte de Coubert whose château and farms were some eight miles from Louvant.

They had met after the exodus, which they still thought of as purely temporary, and Coubert had suggested to Shepilov that he should instal himself in his château. Natalie had followed, and with her Jonas, who had still no comprehensive grasp of the world across which he was being dragged in this way.

During this time Constantin Milk, who had been taken prisoner by the Germans, had been released at Aix-la-Chapelle following on the armistice. He was given neither provisions nor money, nor any means of transport, and there was no question of returning under these circumstances to the distant soil of Russia.

Stage by stage, begging his way with others like himself, Milk had reached Paris and one day the Comte de Coubert had seen his name in a list of Russian prisoners recently arrived.

Nothing was known of Aunt Zina, nor the girls, who probably had not had time to cross the frontier.

Constantin Milk wore thick spectacles, as his son was soon to do, and, being short in the leg, had the build of a Siberian bear. He had quickly tired of the life of inaction in the château and, one evening, had announced that he had bought a fishmongery in the town with Natalie's jewels.

'It may be a little hard for an Oudonov,' he had said with his enigmatic smile, 'but she'll jolly well have to get down to it.'

From his door Jonas could see the shop '*A la Marée*', with its two white marble counters and its big copper scales. He had lived for years on the first floor, in the room with the sky-light now occupied by Chenu's daughter.

Until the time he went to school he had spoken hardly anything but Russian and then had almost completely forgotten it.

Russia was for him a mysterious and bloody country where his five sisters, including Doussia, had very probably been massacred with Aunt Zina, like the Imperial family.

His father like the Oudonovs whom he used to taunt, had also been a man of sudden decisions, or at any rate, if they matured slowly he never mentioned them to anyone.

In 1930, when Jonas was fourteen years old and going to the local *lycée*, Constantin Milk had announced that he was leaving for Moscow. As Natalie insisted that they should all go together, he had looked at his son and declared:

'*Better make sure that at least one of us is left!*'

Nobody knew what fate was in store for him out there. He had promised to send news somehow or other, but at the end of a year they had still heard nothing.

The Shepilovs had set up house in Paris where they had opened a bookshop in the Rue Jacob, and Natalie had written to ask them whether they would look after Jonas, whom she had sent to a *lycée* in Paris, while she in her turn would undertake the journey to Russia.

That was how he came to enter Condorcet.

In the meantime another war had broken out, in which his eyesight had prevented him from taking part, whole populations had been disturbed once more, there had been new exoduses, new waves of refugees.

Jonas had applied to all the authorities imaginable, Russian as well as French, without obtaining any news of his family.

Could he hope that his father, at eighty-two years old, and his mother, at seventy-six, were still alive?

What had happened to Aunt Zina, in whose house people lost themselves, and his sisters, whose faces were unknown to him?

Did Doussia even know that she had a brother somewhere in the world?

All around him the walls were covered with old books. In his little room was a large stove which he kept roaring hot in winter as a luxury, and today he would have sworn that the smell of herrings still hung in the air in the kitchen.

The huge roof of the market was streaked with sunlight opposite his window and all around there were shops hardly larger than his own, except on the side of the Rue de Bourges where St Cecilia's Church stood.

He could put a name to every face, recognize everyone's voice and, when people saw him in his doorway or when he went into Le Bouc's, they used to call out:

'Hullo, Monsieur Jonas!'

It was a world in which he had shut himself up, and Gina had walked in one fine day with a sway of her hips, bringing a warm smell of armpits with her into this world of his.

She had just walked out again, and he was overcome with a fit of giddiness.

Chapter Four

It was not that day that the complications were to begin, but he still had the feeling of a person who is incubating an illness.

In the afternoon, fortunately, the customers were fairly numerous in the shop and he received, among others, a visit from Monsieur Legendre, a retired railway guard, who used to read a book a day, sometimes two, changed them by the half-dozen and always sat down in a chair for a chat. He used to smoke a meerschaum pipe which made a spluttering noise each time he sucked at it, and as he had a habit of pressing down the burning tobacco, the entire top joint of his index finger was a golden brown colour.

He was not a widower nor a bachelor. His wife, small and thin, used to shop at the market, a black hat on her head, three times a week, and stop in front of all the stalls, disputing the price before buying a bunch of leeks.

Monsieur Legendre stayed for nearly an hour. The door was open. In the shadow of the covered market the cement, after being washed down, was drying slowly, leaving damp patches and, as it was Thursday, a crowd of children had taken possession of it and this time were playing at cowboys.

Two or three customers had interrupted the ex-railwayman's discourse and he waited, quite used to it, for the bookseller to finish serving them before carrying on the conversation at the exact point where he had left off.

'As I was saying . . .'

At seven o'clock, Jonas hesitated whether to lock up and go and have dinner at Pepito's as it seemed to him he ought to do, but finally he hadn't the heart. Instead he decided to walk across the Square and buy some eggs at Coutelle's, the dairy, where, as he expected, Madame Coutelle asked him:

'Isn't Gina there?'

It was without conviction, this time, that he replied:

'She's gone to Bourges.'

He made himself an omelette. It was good for him to keep himself occupied. His movements were meticulous. Just before pouring the whipped-up eggs into the pan he yielded once more to gluttony, as he had done at midday with the apple tart, and went into the yard to pick a few chives which were growing in a box.

Oughtn't he to have been indifferent to what he ate, seeing that Gina had gone? He arranged the butter, bread and coffee on the table, unfolded his napkin and ate his meal slowly, to all appearances thinking of nothing.

He had read in some book or other, probably war memoirs, that a certain time nearly always elapses before the most seriously wounded feel any pain, that sometimes they do not even realize at once that they have been hit.

In his case it was a little different. He felt no violent pain, nor despair. It was more that a void had been created inside him. He was no longer in a state of equilibrium. The kitchen, which had not changed, seemed to him not so much strange as lifeless, without any definite shape, as if he had been looking at it without his glasses.

He did not weep, did not sigh, that evening, any more than the day before. After eating a banana which had been bought by Gina, he did the washing up, swept out the kitchen, then went over to the doorway to watch the sun setting.

He did not stay where he was because the Chaignes, the grocers from next door, had brought their chairs out onto the pavement and were chatting in low voices with the butcher, who had come to keep them company.

If he no longer had his valuable stamps at least he still had his collection of Russian ones, for this, which was purely of sentimental value, he had stuck into an album rather in the way that in other houses family portraits are pasted in.

Yet he did not feel himself to be particularly Russian, witness the fact that he only felt at home in the Vieux-Marché.

The shopkeepers had been friendly when the Milks had set themselves up there, and although to start with Milk's father did not speak one word of French, he had soon made great headway. It sometimes provoked his great laugh, devoid of bitterness, to be selling fish by the pound when, a few years earlier, he owned the most important fishing fleet in Archangel, and his boats went as far as Spitzbergen and Novaya Zembla. A little while before the war he had even equipped his ships as whalers, and it was perhaps a sort of sense of humour all his own that prompted him to call his son Jonas.

Natalie was slower to adapt herself to their new life and her husband used to tease her in Russian in front of the customers, who did not understand a word.

'Come on, Ignatievna Oudonova, dip your pretty little hands into that tub and serve this fat lady with half a dozen whiting.'

Jonas knew practically nothing about the Oudonovs, his mother's family, except that they were merchants who provisioned boats. While Constantin Milk, whose grandfather was a shipowner before him, had kept some of his rough plebeian habits, the Oudonovs liked good manners and mixed in high society.

When he was in a good mood, Milk did not call his wife Natalie, but Ignatievna Oudonova, or simply Oudonova, and she would pout as if it were a reproach.

Her chief despair was that there were no synagogues in the town, for the Milks, like the Oudonovs, were Jews. There were other Jews in the district, especially among the second-hand shops and small stores in the Rue Haute, but because the Milks were red-haired, with fair skin and blue eyes, the local people did not seem to be aware of their race.

To the world at large they were Russians, and in a sense it was true.

At school, at first, when he had hardly been able to speak French and often used comical expressions, Jonas had been the butt of many gibes, but it had not lasted long.

'They are very nice,' he would say to his parents when they asked him how his schoolmates treated him.

It was perfectly true. Everybody was nice to them. After his father's departure, nobody went into the shop without asking Natalie:

'Still no news?'

Jonas was rather proud at heart that his mother had abandoned him to go and join her husband. It had upset him more to leave the Old Market to go to Condorcet, and above all to meet the Shepilovs again.

Serge Sergeevitch Shepilov was an intellectual, and it could be seen in the attitudes he struck, in his way of speaking, of looking at the person he was talking to with a certain air of condescension. After eleven years of living in France he still regarded himself as an exile and went to all the White Russian meetings, worked for their newspaper and their reviews.

When Jonas used to go and see them on holidays, in the bookshop in the Rue Jacob, at the back of which they lived in a minute studio, Shepilov liked to address him in Russian then, stopping short, would remark bitterly:

'Ah, but then you've forgotten the language of your country!'

Shepilov was still alive. So, too, was his wife, Nina Ignatievna. Both old now, they had eventually installed themselves in Nice where the odd article which Shepilov sold to a newspaper from time to time enabled them to vegetate. Around the samovar they spent their declining years in the cult of the past and the denigration of the present.

'If your father hasn't been shot or sent to Siberia, then it's because he's rallied to the party cause, in which case I prefer never to see him again.'

Jonas hated nobody, not even the Bolsheviks, whose rise had scattered his family. If he ever thought of Doussia, it was less as a real person than as a sort of fairy. In his imagination Doussia resembled nobody he knew; she had become the symbol of fragile, tender femininity which brought tears to his eyes every time he thought of it.

So as not to be left with nothing to do for the whole evening, he turned over the pages of Russian stamps, and in the little room where he had turned on the light, the history of his country unfolded itself before his eyes.

This collection, almost complete, had taken him a long time to build up, and it had required a great deal of patience, letters and exchanges with hundreds of philatelists, even though the entire album was worth less commercially than four or five of the stamps Gina had taken away.

The first stamp, which was also the first issued in Russia, dating from 1857, depicted an eagle in relief, and although Jonas possessed the ten and twenty kopeks, he had never managed to get hold of the thirty kopeks.

For years, the same symbol had been used with minor variations until the tercentenary in 1905, which the school friend from Condorcet had shown him.

Then with the 1914 war there came the charity stamps with the portrait of Murometz and the Cossack of the Don. He particularly liked, for its style and engraving, a St George and the Dragon which, however, was only catalogued at forty francs.

He thought to himself as he fondled them:

'When this stamp was issued my father was twenty years old. . . . He was twenty-five. . . . He was meeting my mother. . . . That one dates from Alyosha's birth. . . .'

In 1917 it was the Phrygian cap of the Democratic Republic, with the two crossed sabres, then the stamps of Kerensky, on which a powerful hand was breaking a chain.

1921, 1922 saw the advent of illustrations with harder, coarser lines, and from 1923 onwards the commemorations started once again, no longer of the Romanovs, but of the fourth anniversary of the October Revolution, the fifth anniversary of the Soviet Republic.

Some more charity stamps at the time of the famine, then, with the U.S.S.R. pictures of workers, ploughmen, soldiers, the portrait of Lenin, in red and black for the first time in 1924.

He did not soften or feel touched with nostalgia. It was more curiosity which had impelled him to assemble this collection of pictures of a far-off world and place them side by side.

A Samoyed village, or a group of Tajiks beside a cornfield plunged him into the same dreamland as a child with a book of holy pictures.

The idea of going back there had never occurred to him, and it was not due to fear of the fate which might await him, nor, as with Shepilov, hatred for the Party.

From the moment he had come of age, on the contrary, two years before the war, he had renounced his *Nansen* passport and become a naturalized Frenchman.

France itself was too big for him. After school he had worked for several months in a bookshop in the Boulevard Saint-Michel and the Shepilovs had been unable to believe their ears when he had told them that he preferred to return to the Berry.

He had gone back alone, had taken a furnished room with old Mademoiselle Buttereau, who had died during the war, and had gone to work as a clerk in Duret's bookshop, in the Rue de Bourges.

It was still in existence. Old Duret had retired, almost gaga, but the two sons continued the business. It was the chief newsagent-bookshop in town and one of its windows was devoted to devotional objects.

He had not yet taken to eating at Pepito's at that time, because it was too expensive. When the bookseller's shop, where he now lived, had become vacant, he had moved in there as if the Rue de Bourges, only a stone's throw away, had been too far.

He was back once again in the heart of the Old Market of his childhood and everyone had recognized him.

Gina's departure had suddenly destroyed this equilibrium, acquired by perseverance, with the same brutality as the Revolution, earlier on, had scattered his own family.

He did not peruse the album to the end. He made himself a cup of coffee, went and removed the handle from the door, turned the key in the lock, shot the bolt, and a little while later went up to his room.

It was, as always when there was no market, a quiet night, without any noise except for the occasional distant motor horn, and the even more distant rumble of a goods train.

Alone in his bed, without the spectacles which made him look like a man, he huddled up like a frightened child and finally went to sleep, with a sad twist to his lips, one hand in the place where Gina ought to have been.

When the sun woke him, coming into his room, the air was still as calm as ever and the bells of St Cecilia's were sounding out the first Mass. All of a sudden he felt the void of his loneliness again, and he almost dressed without washing as sometimes happened before Gina's day. But he was intent at all costs on following the same routine as every other day, so that he even hesitated when he was being served his *croissants* at the baker's opposite.

'Only three,' he finally murmured regretfully.

'Isn't Gina there?'

These people didn't know yet. True, they were almost new to the Square, where they had bought the business only five years before.

'No. She's not there.'

He was surprised not to be pressed, that the news was received with indifference.

It was half-past seven. He hadn't closed the door to go across the Square. He never did. When he came back he had a shock, for a man rose before him and as he was walking with his eyes cast down, plunged in thought, he had not recognized him immediately.

'Where is my sister?' Frédo's hard voice was demanding.

He stood in the middle of the shop, in a leather jerkin, his black hair still damp, showing the track of his comb.

Since the day before, Jonas had been expecting something to happen, but he was taken by surprise, and still holding his *croissants* in their brown tissue paper wrappings, he stammered:

'She hasn't come back.'

Frédo was as big as, and broader in the shoulders than his father, and when he became angry, his nostrils would palpitate, alternately dilating and closing together.

'Where has she gone?' he went on, without taking his suspicious gaze off Jonas.

'I . . . but . . . to Bourges.'

He added, and perhaps it was a mistake, especially addressed to Frédo:

'At any rate she said she was going to Bourges.'

'When did she say that?'

'Yesterday morning.'

'What time?'

'I don't remember. Before the bus left.'

'Did she take the 7.10 bus yesterday morning?'

'She must have done.'

Why was he trembling in front of a mere boy of nineteen, who was taking liberties in demanding an explanation from him? He wasn't the only one in the neighbourhood to be afraid of Frédo. Since his earliest childhood the Palestri boy had had a sullen character, some even said sinister.

True, he didn't seem to like anybody, except his sister. With his father, when the latter had had too much to drink, he behaved intolerably and the neighbours had overheard some highly unsavoury rows. It was said that once Frédo had hit Palestri, and that his mother had gone for him, locked him up in his room like a ten-year-old.

He had climbed out through the window over the roofs, had stayed away for a week, during which time he had looked in vain for work at Montluçon.

He had not passed his certificate at school and had refused to learn any proper trade. He had worked with a few shopkeepers as errand boy, delivery-man, later as a salesman. Nowhere had he remained for more than a few months or a few weeks.

He was not lazy. As one of his ex-employers said:

'That lad rebels against any form of discipline. He wants to be a general before being a plain soldier.'

As much as Jonas liked the Old Market, Frédo appeared to hate it, just as he despised and hated, in the mass, its inhabitants, as, no doubt, he would have hated anywhere he had happened to be.

Angèle alone liked to treat him as if he were still a child, but it was by no means certain that she wasn't a little afraid as well. When he was fifteen she had found a long clasp-knife in his pocket, which he spent hours fondly sharpening. She had taken it away from him. He had said, unconcerned:

'I'll buy another.'

'I forbid you to do any such thing!'

'By what right?'

'Because I'm your mother!'

'As if you'd become it on purpose! I bet my father was drunk!'

He didn't drink himself, didn't go dancing, used to frequent a small bar in the Italian quarter, in the shady part of the Rue Haute where Poles and Arabs mixed and where there were always to be seen groups of men holding disquieting conferences in the back of the room. The place was called the Luxor Bar. Following Marcel's hold-up the police had taken an interest in it, for Marcel, before Frédo, had been a regular customer.

All they had found had been a retired boxer on probation, whose papers were not in order. Ever since they had nevertheless kept their eye on the Luxor Bar.

Jonas was not afraid in the real sense of the word. Even if Frédo had hit him in a moment of fury, it would not have mattered to him. He was not brave, but he knew that physical pain does not last indefinitely.

It was Gina whom he felt he was defending at this moment, and he had the impression that he was making a mess of it, he could have sworn that his face had reddened to the roots of his hair.

'Did she say she would not be coming back to sleep?'

'I . . .'

He thought very rapidly. Once already when the question of Bourges had arisen, he had spoken without thinking. This time he must take care.

'I don't remember.'

The young man sneered derisively.

'So you can't remember whether you were to expect her or not?'

'She didn't know herself.'

'Well then, did she take her travelling-case?'

Think fast, all the time, and not get caught out, not contradict himself. He couldn't help glancing at the staircase.

'I don't think so.'

'She didn't take it,' Frédo stated.

His voice grew hard, became accusing.

'Her case is in the cupboard, and her coat.'

He was waiting for an explanation. What could Jonas reply? Was this the moment to admit the truth? Was it to Gina's brother that he was to make his confession?

He stiffened, managed to say curtly:

'Possibly.'

'She didn't take the bus to Bourges.'

He feigned astonishment.

'I had a friend in the bus and he didn't see her.'

'Perhaps she took the train.'

'To go to see La Loute?'

'I imagine so.'

'Gina didn't go to see La Loute either. I rang her up this morning before coming here.'

Jonas did not know that La Loute had a telephone, or that Frédo was on speaking terms with her. If he knew her number perhaps he had already been to call on her there himself?

'Where is my sister?'

'I don't know.'

'When did she leave?'

'Yesterday morning.'

He almost added:

'I swear!'

He almost believed it, by sheer force of repetition. What difference did it make if Gina had left on Wednesday evening or Thursday morning?

'Nobody saw her.'

'People are so used to seeing her passing that no one takes any notice now.'

Frédo, who was a whole head taller than he was, seemed to be hesitating whether to seize him by the shoulders and shake him, and Jonas, resigned, didn't move. His eyes didn't flinch until the moment that his visitor turned away to walk over to the door, without touching him.

'We'll soon see. . . .' Frédo growled heavily.

Never had a morning been so bright and so calm. The Square had scarcely come to life and the sound of the grocer lowering his orange blind could be heard, with the handle squeaking out in the silence.

Standing in the doorway, Frédo was a huge and menacing shadow.

As he turned his back, he opened his mouth, no doubt for some insult, thought better of it, walked across the pavement and started up his motor-bike.

Jonas was still standing motionless in the middle of the shop, forgetting his *croissants*, forgetting that it was breakfast time. He was trying to understand. Already the day before he had had a premonition of danger hanging over him, and now he had just been threatened under his own roof.

What for? Why?

He had done nothing except to take a wife into his house, whom Angèle had given to him, and for two years he had done his best to give her peace.

'*She's gone to Bourges . . .*'

He had said it without thinking, to stave off questions, and now it was bringing new ones in its wake. While he was at the baker's, Frédo had not only come into his house, but had gone upstairs, opened the cupboard, searched the wardrobe, since he knew that his sister had not taken her suitcase or coat.

Was it possible that *they* might be thinking what had suddenly come into his mind?

From red, he turned suddenly pale, so absurd and terrible was the notion. Did they really believe it? Had it really occurred to anybody, whether Frédo or not, that he had disposed of Gina?

Didn't they all know, everybody in the Old Market, and in the town as well, that it was not his wife's first escapade, that she had had them before marrying him, when she still lived with her parents, and that this was the reason they had given her to him?

He had no illusions about that. Nobody else would have married her. And Gina did not have the calm, the sangfroid of La Loute, who more or less got away with it in Bourges.

She was a female who could not control herself, that they all knew, including her father.

Why in Heaven's name would he have . . . ?

Even in his mind he hesitated to formulate the word, or to think of it. But wasn't it better to face the reality?

Why would he have killed her?

It was that, he was sure, that Frédo suspected. And perhaps, the day before, the same idea had already come, in a vaguer form, into Palestri's mind.

Otherwise why were they pestering him so?

If he was jealous, if he suffered every time Gina went off after a man, every time he detected an alien smell about her, he had never let anybody see it, not even her. He had never reproached her. On the contrary! When she returned, he was more gentle than ever, to help her forget, to prevent her from feeling uncomfortable in his presence.

He needed her as well. He wanted to keep her. He did not consider that he had the right to shut her up, as Angèle had once shut up her son.

Were they really thinking that?

He was on the point of running round to the Palestris' at once to tell Angèle the truth, but he realized that he was too late. He would no longer be believed. He had too often repeated that she had gone to Bourges, had given too many details.

Perhaps she would come back, in spite of everything? The fact that she had not taken her coat perplexed him. For if she had hidden in some part of the town why should she have taken the stamps, which she would not have been able to sell?

Mechanically he had gone into the kitchen, and once again, with mechanical gestures, he was making coffee, sitting down to drink it and eat his *croissants*. The Chaignes' lime tree was full of birds and he opened the door into the yard to throw them crumbs as usual.

If only it had been possible for him to question the clerk at the station, he would know, but it was too late for that, too.

Was somebody waiting for Gina with a car? That would have explained her going off without her coat. He could still present himself to the police and tell them everything, ask them to make inquiries for him. Who could tell? Tomorrow they would very likely reprimand him for not having done so, and see in that a proof against him!

Still unthinking, he went up to the bedroom where the door of the cupboard and the two doors of the wardrobe stood wide open. There was even a pair of his trousers on the floor. He put them back in their place, made the bed, cleaned out the bathroom and changed his dirty towel. It was laundry day and he thought about getting the dirty washing ready, as Gina was not there to do it. In the basket, which he emptied, there were some petticoats and brassieres; he had begun to list the various items, when he was interrupted by steps downstairs.

It was Madame Lallemand, the mother of the little invalid girl who had been to Bourges the day before. She had come in to change some books for her daughter.

'What did the doctor say?' he remembered to ask.

'It seems there's a specialist in Vienna who might be able to cure her. It isn't certain and there'd be the business of the journey, and staying there several months in a foreign country without being able to speak the language. It all costs a lot of money. My daughter says she would rather stay as she is, but all the same I'm going to write to her uncle, who has a good business in Paris and may be able to help us.'

While he was choosing the books, the woman seemed to notice the silence in the house where, at that time Gina would normally have been heard moving about.

'Isn't your wife in?'

He confined himself to a shake of the head.

'Yesterday somebody asked my daughter if she'd been with her on the bus.'

'You don't know who?'

'I didn't ask. I have so little time for other people, you see . . .'

He did not react. From now on he was prepared for everything. His principal feeling was not even fear, but disappointment, and yet he had never expected anything from other people, had been content to live in his own corner, as humbly as possible.

'I think she would enjoy these two.'

'There's nothing about sick people in them?'

'No. I've read them.'

It was true that he sometimes read novels meant for young girls and actually enjoyed them. On these occasions he would think of Doussia, whom he would picture as each of the heroines in turn.

After that the gas bill was brought and he opened the till, paid, intended to go upstairs to finish off the laundry, when a young man brought in some school books to sell to him. Jonas was sure that he would come in a week or two to buy them back, that he was selling them only because he was short of pocket money. But as other peoples' affairs were no concern of his, he made an offer.

'Is that all?'

He was still a businessman.

'If they were not in such bad condition . . .'

There were three shelves of them, all school books, and it was these that brought in the most money, because the editions seldom changed, and the same books would pass through his hands a great many times in a few years. There were some he recognized, by a stain on the cover, for example, before he so much as touched them.

In the end he was able to go upstairs, finish off his list, tie up the dirty washing in a pillow case which he hid under the counter to await the arrival of the laundry man. It did not seem odd to him to send Gina's washing to the laundry. In his mind she was still, always would be, part of the household.

At ten o'clock he went over to Le Bouc's bar, where there was only a lorry driver whom he didn't know. He heard the usual:

''Morning, Monsieur Jonas.'

And he gave the ritual response:

''Morning, Fernand. An espresso coffee, please.'

'There you are.'

He picked up his two bits of sugar and began to unwrap them. The driver held his glass of white wine in his hand and said nothing, all the time keeping an eye on his lorry through the window. Contrary to his usual habit, Le Bouc worked the percolator in silence, and Jonas thought he seemed uncomfortable.

He had been expecting one question, and as it did not come, he volunteered:

'Gina hasn't come back.'

Fernand murmured, placing the steaming cup on the counter:

'So they tell me.'

So they had been talking about it here too. Not Frédo, surely, who did not frequent the bars of the Vieux-Marché. Was it Louis? But how would Louis have known, since his son, when he left, had gone off in the direction of the town?

They had certainly questioned the young cripple as she stepped out of the bus!

He couldn't understand it any longer. There was something entirely beyond him in this undercurrent of distrust. The time that Gina had been away for three days there had been no talk and, at most, a few people had given her a lewd glance.

Only the butcher had commented:

'How's your wife?'

He had replied:

'Very well, thank you.'

And Ancel had exclaimed, with a conspiratorial look at the assembled company:

'Heavens above!'

Why were they making a tragedy out of what had amused them only six months earlier? If he had been alone with Le Bouc, he would have been tempted to ask him. He probably would not have done so when all was said and done, from pure shame, but he would have felt like it.

And why did he need to explain himself, as though he felt guilty? Even now, he could not prevent himself from saying, with ill-affected indifference:

'She must have been held up.'

Le Bouc contented himself with a sigh, and avoided his gaze:

'No doubt.'

What had he done to them? Yesterday morning, when Gina had already departed, he still felt he was on good terms with them.

They were letting him drop all of a sudden, without a word of explanation, without letting him show his defence.

He had done nothing, nothing!

Was he going to be forced to shout it out aloud to them?

He was so upset that he inquired, as if he had not always known, the price of his coffee:

'How much is that?'

'The usual: thirty francs.'

They must be talking about him all over the Square. There were rumours of which he knew nothing. Somewhere there must have been a misunderstanding which a few words would suffice to clear up.

'I'm beginning to be anxious,' he went on, with a forced smile.

The observation fell flat. Le Bouc stood before him like a wall.

Jonas was making a mistake. He was talking too much. He gave the impression of defending himself before he had been accused. And nobody would ever dare to accuse him of getting rid of Gina.

Frédo, perhaps. But everyone knew him to be hot-headed.

Once again he was not guilty of anything. He had nothing to hide. If he had mentioned Bourges, it was out of tact on Gina's behalf. He had not opened the strong-box then, and he envisaged an affair lasting a night or a couple of days. Would he have done better to reply to the people asking him for news of his wife:

'She's in bed with some man or other?'

They must believe him if he affirmed that it was not from vanity or self-respect that he had spoken about Bourges. If he had been vain, he would not have married Gina, whom nobody wanted, and it had given rise to enough laughter in the neighbourhood to see her married in white. Angèle herself had tried to oppose it.

'All my friends were married in white,' she had answered.

'Your friends aren't you.'

'I don't know one who was a virgin when she married, if that's what you mean, and you weren't one either when you married Papa.'

What she said of her friends and her mother was probably quite true. Anyhow, Angèle had made no reply. Only the others had not advertised themselves as much as she had.

If he had been ridiculous, as well, in his get-up, he had none the less looked around him proudly as he left the church with her arm in his.

He was not vain. He was not ashamed of what she was.

And yet he had just tried to lie to himself, by convincing himself that it was for her sake, and not for his own, that he had invented the trip to Bourges.

From what would he have wanted to shield her, since she had never made any secret of her escapades? As for the others, they must have enjoyed seeing her deceive him and been grateful to him for the fun they derived from it.

All the same he had answered:

'*She's gone to Bourges.*'

After that he had stuck to it doggedly.

As he made for his shop, where a stranger was browsing among the books in the cases outside, he was trying to find the answer, or rather to accept it, since it gave him no satisfaction to do so.

If he had felt the need to protect Gina, wasn't it ultimately because he felt guilty towards her?

He didn't want to think about it any more. It was quite enough to have gone as far as he had. If he went on in this vein God knows where he would end in his discovery of things better left undiscovered.

Besides, nobody knew about all that. It was not what they were going to accuse him of. He had not killed her. He had not got rid of her. He was not guilty in their sense of the word.

Why, from that moment on, did they all, even Le Bouc, whom he liked best of the lot, to whose bar he went more as a friend than for love of coffee, why did they all look on him with suspicion?

'How much is this?' the customer asked him, holding out a book on underwater fishing.

'The price is marked on the back. A hundred and twenty francs.'

'A hundred francs,' the other suggested.

He repeated:

'A hundred and twenty.'

He must have spoken in an unusual tone of voice, for the man hastily dug into his pocket for the money, looking at him in astonishment.

Chapter Five

They left him alone until the Monday, too much alone in fact, for he was beginning to believe they were creating a vacuum around him. Perhaps he was becoming too susceptible and prone to read non-existent motives into people's actions?

After badgering him for two whole days for news of Gina with as much insistence as if they were dunning him they no longer mentioned it to him, and he was beginning to suspect them, Le Bouc, Ancel, and the others, of deliberately avoiding all reference to his wife.

Why did they abruptly cease taking any interest in her? And if they knew where she was, what reason had they for keeping it from him?

He was on the watch for the slightest nuance. For example, when he had lunched at Pepito's on the Friday, the Widower had then distinctly batted his eyelids at him just as he used to in the old days, whereas yesterday they had scarcely flickered. Was the chief clerk under the impression that Jonas had returned for good and would be once again having his meals opposite him every day?

Pepito was not surprised to see him back, but he hadn't asked for news of Gina.

'There is creamed cod today,' he had announced, knowing that Jonas liked it.

It could not have been said that his manner was exactly cold, but he was certainly more reserved than usual.

'Will you be dining here this evening?' he had asked as Jonas rose to leave.

'I don't think so.'

Logically, Pepito ought to have remarked:

'Is Gina coming back this afternoon?'

For Pepito did not know the reason why Jonas, although he was alone, preferred to have dinner at home. In actual fact it was in order not to resume, all at once, his bachelor's existence, in order not to sever all the links with the other life he had known, and also because getting his meal and washing up afterwards kept him occupied.

The afternoon had been gloomy. The sultry air had penetrated through the open doorway. Jonas had settled down to sorting and marking one of the batches of books he brought down from the stock in the loft, where there were all kinds, the majority of them school prizes, which still bore in faded ink the names of their winners, long since deceased.

There had been few customers. Louis had passed by on his three-wheeler, slowing up, but had not stopped until reaching Fernand's bar.

At four o'clock, by which time he had departed, Jonas had gone for his coffee and Le Bouc had shown the same reserve as he had in the morning. Next he had repaired to Ancel's to buy a cutlet for his dinner. Ancel was not there. His assistant served him and Madame Ancel appeared from the back of the shop to take the money without asking any questions.

He had dinner, tidied up, continued working fairly late on his inventory of the attic stock, which stood in a large pile in a corner, and patching the torn volumes with adhesive paper.

He worked in the shop where there was a light, but he had removed the door handle. The rest of the house was in darkness. Somebody walked past and back again around nine o'clock; he only half saw the figure in the darkness and he would have sworn it was Angèle.

They were spying on him. Without asking him anything, they were coming to see if Gina was back.

He went to bed at ten o'clock, fell asleep and soon the sounds of an eve-of-market night began. Saturday's market was the most important one and, at certain hours of the day, the cars had to mount the pavement to find a parking space. It was hotter than the day before. The sun, a light yellow hue, no longer had the same airiness, and towards eleven o'clock it was as if a storm were going to break, and the market women could be seen peering anxiously at the sky. It broke somewhere in the country, for there was a rumbling in the distance, after which the clouds became luminous once more and finally disappeared, leaving nothing but an untrammelled blue.

He ate at Pepito's again and the Widower was there with his dog. It was Jonas who this time, as if seeking some sort of sympathy, of support, however vague, was the first to flutter his eyelids, and Monsieur Métras returned the salute, with a face devoid of expression.

Pepito's was closed on Sundays and Jonas made the round of the shops to buy his provisions, carrying Gina's straw shopping basket. He did not buy his vegetables at Angèle's but at a shop in the Rue Haute. At the butcher's, Ancel served him in person this time, without the remotest suggestion of a friendly jest. He also had to buy some bread, some coffee and some more salt, which had run out, and, for Sunday evening, he took home some spaghetti. It was a tradition from Gina's day, because it was quick to make.

The floor of the Old Market was washed down with hoses, a few cars came and parked in it and then in the evening, like the day before, he spent his time patching up books and marking the prices in pencil on the back. He had looked through the newspaper. He was not expecting to find news of his wife, nor indeed hoping for it, for that would have meant bad news, but he was nevertheless disappointed.

It was the fourth night that he had slept alone, and as he had gone to bed early, he heard some of the neighbours returning from the cinema; the following morning, before he got up, he heard others, women for the most part, making for St Cecilia's Church.

Ever since he had married Gina, he had accompanied her to Mass on Sundays, always the ten o'clock High Mass, and for this occasion she dressed up in her best clothes, in summer wore a blue suit with a hat and white gloves.

When the question of the wedding had arisen, he had realized that for the Palestri family it would have to take place in church.

Up till then he had never been inside it except for a few funerals, had never observed the rites of any religion, except, up to his mother's departure, the Jewish ones.

He had not said he was a Jew, nor hidden the fact. Immediately after the decision had been taken, he had gone to find the parish priest of St Cecilia's, Abbé Grimault, and had asked to be baptized.

For a period of three weeks he had taken catechism lessons at the priest's house almost every evening, in a little parlour with a round table covered with a crimson velvet cloth with tassels. The air was pervaded with a smell, at once stale and strong, which Jonas had never come across before, and which he was never to find again, anywhere else.

While he was reciting his lessons like a schoolboy, the Abbé Grimault, who was born on a farm in the Charolais, would puff at his cigar and gaze into space, which did not prevent him, however, from correcting his pupil the moment he went wrong.

Jonas had asked that he should not be treated too strictly and the priest had understood. Even so, a godfather and godmother had to be found. Justine, the Abbé's servant, and old Joseph, the sacristan, an engraver by trade, filled these rôles, and Jonas gave them each a handsome present. He gave another to the church. He had written to tell Shepilov that he was getting married, but had not dared mention the christening, nor the religious ceremony.

It had given him pleasure to become a Christian, not only because of the marriage, but because it brought him nearer to the inhabitants of the Old Market, nearly all of whom went to church. At first he stood a little stiffly and made his genuflections and signs of the cross out of time, but then he had picked up the habit and Gina and he kept to the same places every Sunday, at the end of a row.

He went to Mass that Sunday as on every other Sunday, and it was the first time he had gone alone. They seemed to be watching him as he went to his place, and to nudge one another as he passed.

He did not pray, because he had never really prayed, but he wanted to, and as he watched the dancing light of the candles and breathed the smell of the incense, he thought of Gina and also of his sister Doussia, though he never knew what she looked like.

After the service, groups formed outside the church and for a quarter of an hour the Square was full of life. The Sunday clothes lent a gay note, then, little by little, the pavements emptied and for the rest of the day there was virtually nobody to be seen there.

At noon Ancel, who worked on Sunday mornings, drew his blinds. All the other blinds in the Square were already lowered, except those of the bakery and cake shop which closed at half-past twelve.

For Jonas and his wife, it was the day for the backyard. This meant that in good weather they would base themselves in the yard, as long as they were not going out. It was in fact almost impossible to stay in the shop in the summer with the door shut, because of the lack of air, and if the door was left open the passers-by would think they were not observing their Sabbath rest.

Not only did they spend the afternoon in the courtyard but they lunched there as well, under the lime-tree branch which stretched over the Chaignes' garden wall and gave them some shade.

The whole length of the wall was covered by a vine, old and twisted, its leaves marked with rust, but it none the less produced each year a few bunches of acid grapes.

They had tried keeping a cat. They had had several. All of them, for some reason or other, had gone to seek a home elsewhere.

Gina didn't like dogs. Actually she didn't like any animals, and when they went for a walk in the country, she would eye the cows uneasily from a safe distance.

She didn't like the country either, nor taking walks. She had never wanted to learn to swim. She was only in her element when her extremely high heels came in contact with the hard smooth surface of a pavement, and she had in addition a horror of quiet streets like the one in which Clémence lived; she needed animation, noise, the many-coloured display of shop windows.

When they went to have a drink, she did not choose the spacious cafés of the Place de l'Hôtel de Ville, or the Place du Théâtre, but the bars with juke boxes.

He had bought her a wireless set and on Sundays she would take it out into the yard, using an extension to plug it into the kitchen.

She hardly ever sewed, was content to keep her clothes and linen more or less in disrepair, and her blouses were often missing a button, while a good half of her petticoats had holes in them.

She used to read, listening to the music and smoking cigarettes, and sometimes in the middle of the afternoon she would go up to her bedroom, remove her dress and stretch out on top of the cover.

He read on this Sunday, too, in one of the two iron chairs which he had bought second-hand for use in the yard. He went back into the shop twice to change his book and in the end became interested in a work on the life of spiders. There was one in the corner, which he had known for a long time, and now and then he raised his eyes to observe it with renewed interest, like a man who has just made a discovery.

The post had brought him no news of Gina the day before or on Friday. He had been hoping, without believing it, that she would perhaps send him a word, and now he was beginning to realize that the idea was ridiculous.

From time to time, without interrupting his reading, his thoughts superimposed themselves on the printed text, without his losing the place. True they were not clear cut, consecutive thoughts. Various images came to his mind, such as that of Angèle, then, straightaway afterwards, for no reason, he pictured Gina lying naked on an iron bed, in a hotel bedroom.

Why an iron bed? And why, all round her, whitewashed walls, like those in the country?

It was unlikely that she had taken refuge in the country, which she detested. She was certainly not alone. Since Wednesday evening when she had left she must have bought herself some underclothes, unless she had been content to wash her petticoat and brassiere at night and put them on again in the morning unironed.

Clémence, her husband and Poupou must have been with the Ancels, where the whole family used to gather and the youngest of the daughters, Martine, played the piano. They had a very large yard with, at the back, the shed Gina had talked about. She had not told him whether she had allowed the butcher to have her. Probably she had, but it was also probable that Ancel had not dared to go the whole way.

Twice during the afternoon he thought he heard the piano, the sound of which reached his back yard when the wind was in the right direction.

The Chaigne family had a car and were not at home on Sundays. Angèle used to sleep the entire afternoon while Louis, dressed in a navy blue suit, went to play skittles and did not return until he had made a tour of the town's cafés.

How did a young man like Frédo spend his time? Jonas had no idea. He was the only one in the family not to go to Mass and he was not to be seen all day.

At five o'clock a few old women passed by on their way to benediction and the bells rang out for a moment. Le Bouc's bar was closed. Jonas had made himself some coffee and, feeling slightly hungry, he nibbled a piece of cheese.

Nothing else happened. He had dined, after which, not having the heart to work, he had finished his book on spiders. It was only nine o'clock and he had gone for a stroll, closing the door behind him, had headed in the direction of the narrow canal where a lock-gate stood out black against the moonlit sky. Two narrow barges, of the Berry type, were moored to the quay and he could see rings forming around them on the surface of the water.

He passed Clémence's, in the Rue des Deux-Ponts, and this time there was a light on the first floor. Did Clémence know something about Gina? Even if she did, she wouldn't tell him anything. He did not stop, as he was tempted to do, but passed quickly by, for the window was open and Reverdi, in shirt sleeves, was moving about the room talking.

The nearer he got to his home, the more the closed shutters in the streets, the deserted pavements, the silence, filled him with a sort of uneasiness, and he caught himself increasing his pace as if to flee from some indefinable menace.

Was it because others, like Gina, felt the same fear that they hurried into the garishly lighted bars, to seek the company of shouts and music?

He could see some of those bars in the distance, in the second part of the Rue Haute, on the same side as the Luxor, and he could just make out the couples along the walls.

He slept badly, still with the feeling of a threat, which had pursued him even into his bedroom. He had removed his spectacles and switched off the light when a memory had jangled in his brain, not exactly a personal memory, for the passage of time had confused the fragments of what he had seen and heard with what he had subsequently been told.

He was not six years old when the drama had occurred, and since then there had been no further sensational events in the town until the Marcel hold-up.

He was born in 1916, so it had taken place in 1922, and he was just starting to go to school. It must have been November. The Maison Bleue was already in existence, so called because the outside was painted in sky-blue from top to bottom.

It had not changed since then. It stood surmounted by a very steep roof, at the corner of the Rue des Prémontrés and the Square, just beside Ancel's butcher's shop, two houses from the fishmonger's where Jonas lived at the time.

The sign had not changed either. In letters of a darker blue than the façade was written: '*La Maison Bleue*'. Then, in smaller letters: '*Children's clothing. Baby garments a speciality.*'

The woman now known as the widow Lentin still had her husband at the time, a fair-haired man who wore long moustaches and who, since his wife ran the business, worked at odd jobs outside.

At certain periods, he could be seen sitting all day long on a chair in front of the house, and Jonas remembered a phrase he had heard frequently repeated:

'*Lentin's having one of his bouts.*'

Gustave Lentin had fought in the Tonkin campaign, a name which Jonas had heard for the first time when people were talking of him, and which to Jonas seemed a terrible word. He had caught the fevers there, as the people of the Vieux-Marché put it. For weeks he was like any other man, with a rather dark, at times stormy look in his eyes, and he would embark on some job or other. Then it would get around that he was in bed, 'covered with an icy sweat and trembling in his limbs, his teeth clenched like a dead man's'.

Jonas had not invented this description. He did not know where he had heard it, but it had remained engraved on his memory. Doctor Lourel, since dead, who had worn a beard, came to see him twice a day, striding rapidly, his worn leather bag in his hand, and Jonas, from the pavement opposite, used to glue his eyes to the windows, wondering if Lentin was dying.

A few days later he would reappear, emaciated, his eyes sad and empty, and his wife would help him out onto his chair beside the doorway, would move him during the day, as the sun followed its course.

The shop did not belong to Lentin but to his parents-in-law, the Arnauds, who lived in the house with the couple. Madame Arnaud remained in Jonas' mind as a woman almost entirely round, with white hair gathered in a bun at the back of her head and so sparse that the pink of her skull showed through it.

He could not remember her husband.

But he had seen the crowd, one morning, as he was about to leave for school. There was a wind blowing that day. It was a market day. An ambulance and two other black cars were standing in front of the Maison Bleue and the crowd was shoving so much that one might have thought it was a riot, if it had not been for the oppressive silence which reigned.

Although his mother had dragged him away and assured him afterwards that he could not have seen anything, he was convinced, to this day, that he had seen on a stretcher carried by two male nurses in white smocks, a man with his throat cut. A woman was screaming, he was sure, in the house, in the way that mad women scream.

'You imagine you actually saw what you heard told afterwards.'

It was possible, but it was difficult to admit that that image had not really appeared before his eyes as a child.

Lentin, it was afterwards learnt, suffered from the feeling of being a useless passenger in the house of his in-laws. Several times he was said to have let it be known that things would not go on as they were, and they had imagined suicide. They used to watch him. His wife sometimes followed in the street at a discreet distance.

That night he had not woken her up, even though he was racked with fever. She had been the first down, as usual, imagining him still sleeping and then, silently, a razor in his hand, he had gone into the bedroom of his father and mother-in-law and had cut their throats one after the other as he had seen done by the Tonkinese soldiers, and as, out there, he had perhaps done himself.

Only old Madame Arnaud had had the time to cry out. Her daughter had rushed up the stairs, but when she reached the open door her husband had finished his work and, standing in the middle of the room and fixing her with a 'mad look', he had in turn severed his own carotid artery.

Madame Lentin was quite white now, diminutive, her hair as thin as her mother's, and she went on selling children's clothing and baby garments.

Why had Jonas thought of this drama just as he was dropping off to sleep? Because he had passed in front of the Maison Bleue a short while ago and had had a glimpse of a shadow behind the curtain?

It disturbed him. He forced himself to think of something else. As he was still not able to sleep after half an hour he got up to take a tablet of gardenal. In fact he took two, and the effect was almost immediate. Only towards four o'clock he awoke in the silence of the dawn and lay with his eyes open until it was time to get up.

He was stiff and uncomfortable. He almost decided against going to the baker for his *croissants*, as he was not hungry, but it was a form of discipline he had imposed on himself and he crossed the deserted Square, saw Angèle laying her baskets out on the pavement. Did she see him? Did she pretend not to see him?

'Three?' the baker's wife asked him from force of habit.

It annoyed him. He had the impression he was being spied on, and above all that the others knew things he did not. Ancel, without taking the cigarette from his lips, was unloading some sides of beef, which did not even cause him to stoop, and yet he must have been five or six years older than Jonas.

He ate, took out his boxes of books, decided to finish off the stock from the attic before going up to do his room, and at half-past nine he was still working, looking in a bibliography to see whether a dilapidated Maupassant which he had just found in the pile was a first edition.

Somebody came in and he did not immediately raise his eyes. He knew, by the silhouette, that it was a man, and the latter, without pressing him, was examining the books on a shelf.

When he finally looked up, Jonas recognized Police Inspector Basquin, to whom he had on many occasions sold books.

'Excuse me,' he stammered. 'I was busy with . . .'

'How are you, Monsieur Jonas?'

'All right. I'm all right.'

He could have sworn that Basquin had not come that morning to buy a book from him, more especially as he had one in his hand.

'And Gina?'

He reddened. It was unavoidable. The more he tried not to the more he reddened, and he felt his ears burning.

'I trust she's all right, too.'

Basquin was three or four years younger than he and had been born the far side of the canal, in a group of five or six houses surrounding the brickworks. He was fairly often to be seen at the market, and if ever one of the shopkeepers was robbed, it was nearly always he who took charge of it.

'Isn't she here?'

He hesitated, first said no, then, like a man plunging into the water, said all in one breath:

'She left on Wednesday evening telling me that she was going to look after the baby for Ancel's daughter, Clémence. Since then she hasn't come back and I've heard no news.'

It was a relief finally to let out the truth, to dispose once and for all of this fairy tale about the visit to Bourges, which was haunting him. Basquin looked a decent sort of fellow. Jonas had heard tell that he had five children, a very blonde wife with a sickly appearance, who in reality was more hardy than some women who appear outwardly strong.

In this way, often, in the Old Market, one learns the history of people one has never seen, by odds and ends of conversations picked up here and there. Jonas did not know Madame Basquin, who lived in a small new house on the edge of the town, but it was possible that he had seen her when she was doing her shopping, without realizing who she was.

The Inspector did not have a crafty look, as though he wanted to catch Jonas out. He was relaxed, familiar, as he stood by the counter, book in hand, like a customer talking about the rain or the fine weather.

'Did she take any luggage with her?'

'No. Her case is upstairs.'

'And her dresses, her clothes?'

'She was only wearing her red dress.'

'No coat?'

Didn't that prove that Basquin knew more than he wanted to show? Why, otherwise, would he have thought of the coat? Frédo had thought of it, certainly, but only after searching in the bedroom.

Did that mean that Frédo had warned the police?

'Her two coats are in the cupboard as well.'

'Had she any money on her?'

'If she had, it wasn't much.'

His heart was thumping against his constricted chest and he had difficulty in speaking naturally.

'You have no idea where she might have gone?'

'None, Monsieur Basquin. At half-past twelve on Wednesday night, I was so worried that I went round to Clémence's.'

'What did she tell you?'

'I didn't go in. There wasn't any light. I thought that they were all in bed and I didn't want to disturb them. I hoped that Gina might have come back another way.'

'You didn't meet anyone?'

That was the question which frightened him most of all, for he realized that what he was being asked for was an alibi. He searched desperately in his memory, then confessed, abashed:

'No. I don't think so.'

A recollection occurred to him.

'I heard a couple talking in the Rue de Bourges, but I didn't see them.'

'You didn't pass anyone, either going or coming back?'

'I don't remember. I was thinking about my wife. I wasn't paying any attention.'

'Try to remember.'

'I am trying.'

'Someone, at a window, might have seen you passing.'

He was triumphant.

'There was a lighted window at the corner of the Rue des Prémontrés and the Rue des Deux-Ponts.'

'Whose house?'

'I don't know, but I could show it to you.'

'Was the window open?'

'No, I don't think so. The blind was lowered. I actually thought of an invalid . . .'

'Why an invalid?'

'No particular reason. It was all so quiet . . .'

Basquin was watching him gravely, without severity, without antipathy. On his side, Jonas found it natural that he should be doing his duty and preferred it to be him than anyone else. The Inspector was sure to understand sooner or later.

'It has happened before that Gina . . .' he began, shamefacedly.

'I know. But she's never been away four days before, has she? And there was always someone who knew where she was.'

What did he mean by that? That when she went on a spree Gina kept some people informed, her brother, for example, or one of her friends, like Clémence? Basquin had not just spoken idly. He knew what he was talking about, seemed to know more about it than even Jonas himself.

'Did you have a quarrel on Wednesday?'

'We never quarrelled, I promise you.'

Madame Lallemand, the mother of the young cripple, came in to exchange her two books and the conversation was left in suspense. Had she heard any rumours? She appeared to know the Inspector, at any rate to know who he was, for she looked embarrassed and said:

'Give me anything of the same kind.'

Had she realized that it was an actual interrogation that the bookseller was undergoing? She left hurriedly like someone who realizes they are not wanted and in the meantime Basquin, having replaced his book on the shelf, had lit a cigarette.

'Not even,' he resumed, 'when she had spent the night out?'

Jonas said forcefully:

'Not even then. I never even reproached her.'

He saw the policeman frown and realized that it was hard to believe. Yet he was speaking the truth.

'You are asking me to believe that it made no difference to you?'

'It did hurt me.'

'And you avoided showing it?'

It was genuine curiosity which had perhaps nothing professional about it, that he read in Basquin's eyes, and he would have liked to make him understand exactly how he felt. His face was covered with sweat and his spectacles were beginning to mist over.

'I didn't need to show it to her. She knew it already. In actual fact she was ashamed, but she wouldn't have let it be seen for anything in this world.'

'Gina was ashamed?'

Raising his head he almost cried out, he was so sure that he was right:

'Yes! And it would have been cruel to add to her shame. It wouldn't have been any good. Don't you understand? She couldn't help it. It was in her nature . . .'

Stupefied, the Inspector was watching him speak, and for a moment Jonas hoped he had convinced him.

'I had no right to reproach her.'

'You are her husband.'

He sighed wearily:

'Of course . . .'

He realized that his hopes had been premature.

'How many times did it happen in the past two years? For it was two years ago that you got married, wasn't it?'

'Two years ago last month. I haven't counted the number of times.'

It wasn't entirely true. He could have remembered it in a few moments, but it was not important and the question reminded him of the ones the priest asks in the confessional.

'The last time?'

'Six months ago.'

'Did you know who it was with?'

He raised his voice again.

'No! No! Why should I want to know?'

How could it have helped him, to know the man Gina had slept with? To have even more vivid pictures in his mind and suffer all the more?

'You love her?'

He replied almost in a whisper:

'Yes.'

It made him wince to talk about it, because it concerned no one but himself.

'In short, you love her but you're not jealous.'

It wasn't a question. It was a conclusion, and he did not take it up. He was discouraged. It was no longer the more or less marked coldness of the market people that he was up against, but the reasoning of a man who, on account of his profession, ought to have been capable at least of understanding.

'You're sure Gina left the house on Wednesday evening?'

'Yes.'

'At what time?'

'Directly after dinner. She washed up, but forgot to clean the stove, and told me she was going round to the Reverdis.'

'Did she go up to her room?'

'I think so. Yes.'

'You aren't sure?'

'Yes, I am. I remember now.'

'Did she stay there long?'

'Not very long.'

'Did you see her to the door?'

'Yes.'

'So you saw which way she went?'

'Towards the Rue des Prémontrés.'

He pictured in his mind's eye the red of her dress in the grey light of the street.

'You're sure your wife didn't spend the night of Wednesday to Thursday here?'

He reddened again as he said:

'Certain.'

And he was about to open his mouth to explain, for he was intelligent enough to know what was coming next. Basquin was too quick for him.

'Yet you told her father that she had taken the bus to Bourges, at 7.10 on Thursday morning.'

'I know. It was wrong.'

'You were lying?'

'It wasn't exactly a lie.'

'You repeated it to different people and you gave details.'

'I was just going to explain . . .'

'Answer my question first. Had you any reason for hiding from Palestri the fact that his daughter had gone off on Wednesday evening?'

'No.'

He hadn't had any particular reason for hiding it from Louis, and besides, that was not how it had all started. If only he could have a chance to tell the story the way it had happened, there would be some hope of being understood.

'You admit that Palestri knew all about his daughter's conduct?'

'I think so. . . . Yes. . . .'

'Angèle as well. . . . She certainly didn't make any secret of it . . .'

He could have wept at his own impotence.

'It's no use pretending that Gina was ashamed, she never tried to hide it herself, quite the opposite.'

'That's not the same thing. It isn't that sort of shame.'

'What sort is it?'

He was tempted to give up, from weariness. They were two intelligent men face to face, but they didn't speak the same language and they were on completely different planes.

'It was all the same to her what people said. It was . . .'

He wanted to explain that it was in regard to herself that she was ashamed, but he was not being given the chance.

'And to you, was it all the same to you?'

'Of course it was!'

The words had been faster than his thoughts. It was true and yet untrue. He realized that that was going to contradict what he had still to explain.

'So you had no reason to hide the fact that she had gone?'

'I didn't hide it.'

His throat was dry, his eyes smarted.

'What difference,' went on Basquin without giving him a chance to go back on what he had said, 'would it make whether she left on Wednesday evening or Thursday morning?'

'Exactly.'

'Exactly what?'

'It doesn't make any difference. That proves that I wasn't really lying.'

'When you said that your wife had taken the bus at 7.10 to go and see La Loute at Bourges? And in repeating it to at least six people, including your mother-in-law?'

'Listen, Monsieur Basquin . . .'

'I am only too anxious to listen.'

It was true. He was trying to understand, but even so there was in Jonas'

manner something which was beginning to irritate him. Jonas noticed it, and
that made him lose his bearings even more. As at Le Bouc's during the last
few days, there was a wall between himself and the other man, and he was
beginning to wonder if he was like other men.

'I was hoping that Gina would come back on Thursday in the morning.'

'Why?'

'Because, most times, she only used to go away for the night.'

It hurt him to say it, but he was ready to suffer more than that for the sake
of being left in peace.

'When I saw that she didn't come, I told myself that she would be back
during the day and I carried on as if nothing had happened.'

'Why?'

'Because it wasn't worth the bother of . . .'

Would someone else have behaved differently in his place? He had to take
advantage of the fact that he was being allowed to get a few words in.

'I went into Le Bouc's around ten o'clock, as I do every day.'

'And you announced that your wife had left for Bourges by the morning
bus to go and see her friend.'

Jonas lost his temper, stamped his foot, shouted:

'No!'

'You didn't say so in the presence of five or six witnesses?'

'Not like that. It's not the same thing. Le Bouc asked me how Gina was
and I replied that she was all right. Ancel, who was near me, can confirm it. I
think it was also Fernand who remarked that he hadn't seen her at the market
that morning.'

'What difference does that make?'

'Wait!' he begged. 'It was then that I said she had gone to Bourges.'

'Why?'

'To explain her absence and give her time to come back without there
being any fuss.'

'You said just now that it was all the same to her.'

He shrugged his shoulders. He had said so, certainly.

'And that it was all the same to you as well . . .'

'Let's say I was caught off my guard. I was in a bar, surrounded by
acquaintances, and they were asking me where my wife was.'

'They asked you *where* she was?'

'They mentioned that they had not seen her. I replied that she had gone to
Bourges.'

'Why Bourges?'

'Because she used occasionally to go there.'

'And why mention the 7.10 bus?'

'Because I remembered that there wasn't a bus to Bourges in the evening.'

'You thought of everything.'

'I thought of that by chance.'

'And La Loute?'

'I don't even think I was the first to mention her. If I remember rightly,
Le Bouc said:

'"Has she gone to see La Loute?"'

'Because everyone knows that La Loute is at Bourges and that Gina and
she are friends.'

'Strange!' murmured Basquin, looking at him more closely than ever.

'It's all quite simple,' answered Jonas, forcing a smile.

'Perhaps it isn't as simple as all that!'

And the Inspector pronounced these words in a grave tone, with an expression of annoyance on his face.

Chapter Six

Was Basquin hoping that Jonas would change his mind and make a confession? Or was he simply anxious again to underline the unofficial character of his visit? Whatever the case, he behaved before leaving as he had done on his entry, like a customer who has dropped in, glancing through a few books with his back turned to the bookseller.

Finally he looked at his watch, sighed, picked up his hat from the chair.

'It's time I was getting along. No doubt we shall have another opportunity to talk all this over again.'

He did not say it as a threat, but as if the two of them had a problem to solve.

Jonas followed him to the door, which had been open all the time, and with a reflex action common to all shopkeepers, glanced up and down the street. He was still shaken. The sun shone full upon him when he turned to the right and he could not make out the faces around Angèle. What he was sure of was that there was a group on the pavement, round the greengrocer's wife, most of them women, and that everybody was looking in his direction.

Turning to the left, he caught sight of another group, in Le Bouc's doorway with, as a focal point, Ancel's working overalls with their narrow blue and white stripes and his bloodstained apron.

So they had known what was going on ahead of him and had been keeping an eye open for the Inspector's visit. Through the wide open door of the shop they must have caught fragments of conversation, when Jonas had raised his voice. Perhaps some of them had even approached softly without being noticed?

He was even more shocked than he was frightened by the thought. They were not behaving decently to him and he did not deserve it. He was ashamed of giving the impression of running away or retreating abruptly into his shop, but there and then, without warning, he was in no fit state to face their hostile curiosity.

For that their silence was hostile there could be no doubt. He would have preferred whistles and insults.

Well, this was the silence that he was going to have to endure for the next few days, during which he lived as if in a universe detached from the rest of the world.

He made himself go on with his work, without realizing precisely what he was doing, and, a few minutes before four o'clock, instinct made him look at his watch. It was time for his cup of coffee at Le Bouc's. Was he going to change his routine? He was tempted to do so. That was the simplest solution. But in spite of everything that Basquin might think, it was from loyalty to

Gina, it was for Gina's sake that he was so anxious for life to continue as before.

When he came out of the door, there was no longer anybody spying on him, and the Chaignes' red-haired dog, which had been sleeping in the sun, struggled lazily to its feet and came over to sniff his heels and offer its head to be patted.

In Le Bouc's bar he found only a stranger, and the old beggar-woman who was eating a hunk of bread and a piece of sausage in a corner.

''Afternoon, Fernand. An espresso coffee, please,' he said, carefully noting the inflexions of his own voice.

He was striving to remain natural. Without a word, Fernand placed a cup under the chromium tap and let the steam escape, avoiding his eyes, ill at ease, as if he were not convinced that they weren't all behaving rather cruelly.

He couldn't act differently from the others. Jonas understood that. All the Old Market, at the moment, was forming a bloc against him, including, in all likelihood, people who didn't know anything about the affair.

He didn't deserve it, not only because he was innocent of everything they might accuse him of, but because he had always tried, discreetly, quietly, to live like them, with them, and to be like them.

He believed, only a few days before, that he had succeeded by dint of patience and humility. For he had been humble as well. He did not lose sight of the fact that he was a foreigner, a member of another race, born in far-off Archangel, whom the fortunes of wars and revolutions had transplanted to a small town in the Berry.

Shepilov, for instance, did not possess this humility. Having fled to France, he did not think twice before taking it on himself to criticize the country and its customs, even its politics, and Constantine Milk himself, when he had his fishmonger's shop, did not hesitate to talk to Natalie in Russian in front of the customers.

No one had resented it, in his case. Was it because he had asked nothing and did not worry about what his neighbours thought? The ones who had known him talked of him still with affection, as of a strong and colourful personality.

Jonas, perhaps because his first conscious memories had been of the Vieux-Marché, had always tried to become integrated. He did not ask the people to recognize him as one of themselves. He felt that that was impossible. He behaved with the discretion of a guest, and it was as a guest that he saw himself.

They had let him be, let him open his shop. In the morning they called out their ritual:

''Morning, Monsieur Jonas!'

There had been about thirty of them at his wedding reception, and outside the church the whole of the market had ranged themselves in two rows on the steps.

Why were they suddenly changing their attitude?

He would have sworn that things would not have turned out the same if what had happened to him had happened to one of themselves. He had become a foreigner again over-night, a man from another clan, from another world, come to eat their bread and take one of their daughters.

It did not anger him, nor embitter him, but it caused him pain, and like

Basquin, he, too, repeated insistently:

'Why?'

It was hard to be there, at Fernand's bar, which was like a second home to him, and to see the latter silent, distant, to be obliged to remain silent himself.

He didn't ask what he owed, as he had done last time, but put the money down on the linoleum of the counter.

'Good-night, Fernand.'

'Good-night.'

Not the usual:

'*Good-night, Monsieur Jonas.*'

Only a vague and cold:

'*Good-night.*'

It was Monday, and this was to go on for four days, until the Friday. Gina sent no word of herself. There was nothing about her in any of the papers. At one moment he thought that Marcel might have escaped and that she had rejoined him, but an escape would probably have attracted a certain amount of publicity.

During those four days he managed, by sheer will-power, to remain the same, rose every morning at the usual time, went across to the other side of the Square for his three *croissants*, made his coffee, then, a little later in the morning, went up to do his room.

At ten o'clock he would go into Le Bouc's, and when Louis was there one time, on the Wednesday, he had the strength of mind not to retreat. He was expecting to be harangued by Palestri, who had already had a few drinks. On the contrary, he was greeted by an absolute silence; on seeing him everyone stopped talking, except for a stranger who was talking to Le Bouc and who uttered another remark or two, looking round him in surprise, only to end up in an embarrassed silence.

Each day at noon he went round to Pepito's, and neither he nor his niece once engaged him in conversation. The Widower went on blinking his eyelids, but then hadn't he, too, been living in a world of his own for a long time?

Customers still came to his shop, fewer than usual, and he did not see Madame Lallemand, whose daughter ought to have finished her last two books.

Often two whole hours would pass without anyone coming in through the doorway, and to keep himself occupied, he undertook the cleaning of his shelves, one by one, dusting book after book, so that he came across various works which had been there for years and which he had forgotten about.

He spent hours thus occupied on his bamboo steps, seeing the Square outside now deserted, now enlivened with the colourful bustle of the market.

He hadn't spoken to Basquin about the missing stamps. Was that going to recoil upon him too? The Inspector had only asked him whether Gina had any money, and he had replied that she could not have had much, which was true.

He, too, was beginning to be afraid that some accident had befallen Gina. Once at least, he was sure, she had spent the night in a squalid furnished room in the Rue Haute, with a North African. Mightn't she have fallen this time on a sadist or a madman, or one of those desperadoes who kill for a few hundred francs?

It comforted him to think that she had taken the stamps for it enabled him almost for sure to dismiss this theory.

He felt so alone, so helpless, that he was tempted to go and seek the advice of the Abbé Grimault, in the tranquillity of his parlour, where the smell and the semi-obscurity were so soothing. What could the priest have said to him? Why should he understand any better than Basquin, who at least had a wife himself?

In the evening he made his supper, did the washing up. He did not again touch the album of Russian stamps, which reminded him that he was of another race. He was feeling almost guilty, by now, for having amassed this collection, as if it were an act of treason towards the people amongst whom he lived.

However, it was not from patriotism or nostalgia for a country which he did not know, that he had gathered all these stamps together. He could not have said exactly what impulse he had obeyed. Perhaps it was because of Doussia? He had talked about her to Gina, one Sunday afternoon, in the backyard, and Gina had asked:

'Is she older than you?'

'She was two when I was born. She would be forty-two now.'

'Why do you say *would be*?'

'Because she may be dead.'

'Did they kill children so young?'

'I don't know. It's possible that she's still alive.'

She had looked at him wonderingly.

'How strange!' she had murmured finally.

'What?'

'Everything. You. Your family. Your sisters. All these people who are perhaps living quietly over there without your knowing it and may very well be wondering what's happened to you. Haven't you ever wanted to go and see them?'

'No.'

'Why not?'

'I don't know.'

She hadn't understood and she must have thought that he had disowned his family. It wasn't true.

'Do you think they shot your father?'

'They may have sent him to Siberia. Perhaps again they've let him go back to Archangel.'

How ironical if all the family had been reunited out there in their town, in their own house—who could say? All except him!

On one occasion he found himself next to Constable Benaiche at Le Bouc's bar and Benaiche pretended not to see him. Now though he went three times a week to the market on duty, he was not part of the market and he must know what they thought of Jonas at the police station.

Basquin had given him to understand that they would be meeting again, and Jonas was hourly expecting his arrival. He had forced himself to prepare answers to the questions he anticipated. He had even summarized, on a scrap of paper, his movements on the Thursday, the day he had talked so much about the visit to Bourges, with a list of people he had spoken to.

Four days of living as though in a glass frame, like certain animals on which experiments are being made in laboratories and which are observed hour by hour. There was a violent storm on the Thursday morning, when the market was at its height, which caused a stampede, for the rain fell in huge drops mixed with hailstones, and two women he didn't know took refuge in his shop. The downpour lasted nearly an hour and activities outside were almost suspended; he was himself unable to go to Le Bouc's at ten o'clock and it was about half-past eleven before he went to have his coffee in the bar, which smelt of damp wool.

He was still compelling himself to say, as usual, as if nothing had happened:

''Morning, Fernand.'

And he ordered his coffee, while unwrapping his two pieces of sugar.

That afternoon, towards five o'clock, a policeman on a bicycle stopped outside the shop and came in, leaving his machine propped up at the edge of the pavement.

'You are Jonas Milk?'

He said yes, and the man handed him a yellow envelope, then a notebook like the ones postmen use for registered packages.

'Sign here.'

He signed, waited until he was alone again before opening the envelope, which contained an official letter printed on coarse paper, summoning him to the police station for the following day, Friday, at ten o'clock in the morning.

They were not going to continue to question him with an air of casually passing by. They were summoning him. On the dotted line followed the word: 'Reason' there was written in indelible pencil:

'*Personal Matters.*'

He felt a desire, that evening, to put in writing all that had happened since the Wednesday evening, and in particular, during the whole of Thursday, with a sincere explanation of every one of his actions, every one of his words, but it was in vain that he sat at his desk and tried to decide where to start.

They had not yet accused him of anything. They had not said they suspected him of anything whatsoever. They had merely asked him insidious questions and created a vacuum around him.

Perhaps it would be better after all for him at last to have an opportunity to explain everything from beginning to end. He did not know who, over there, would see him. The summons was signed by the superintendent, whom he knew by sight. He was called Devaux and, if only from the hair in his nostrils and ears, he looked like Monsieur Métras. He was a widower, too, lived with his daughter who had married a young doctor from Saint-Amand, with a house in the Rue Gambetta.

He slept badly, woke up almost every hour, had confused nightmares, and dreamed, among other things, of the canal and the lock-gate, which had been raised to allow a barge to pass and which would not go down again. Why was he to blame? It was a mystery, but everybody was accusing him and he had been given a ridiculously short time to make the bridge work; he was bathed in sweat, gripping the operating handle with his hands, while Ancel, who was carrying a quarter of beef on his shoulder, was sneering at him.

They were treating him like a convict. That is what emerged clearly from his dream. There was also some talk of Siberia.

'You who come from Siberia . . .'

He endeavoured to explain that Archangel is not in Siberia, but they knew

better than he did. Siberia, God knows why, had something to do with the
fact that he was the person who had to turn the handle, and Madame Lentin
came into it too, he could not recall how, perhaps because he remembered
her pale face behind her lace window curtains.

He was almost afraid to go back to sleep, so much did these nightmares
exhaust him, and at five o'clock in the morning, he preferred to get up and go
out in the street for some air.

In this way he reached the Square outside the station, where there was a
bar open, and he had a cup of coffee and ate some *croissants* which had just
arrived and were still warm. Would the baker's wife be surprised when he
did not come for his three *croissants* as on other days? He passed by the bus
station, too, where two large green coaches, one of them for Bourges, were
waiting for the time to go, without anyone in them.

At eight o'clock he opened his shop, carried out the two boxes, took them
in again at half-past nine and then, with his hat on his head, his summons in
his pocket, he went out and locked his shop.

It was not quite time to go to Le Bouc's, but since he would be at the police
station at ten o'clock, he went in and drank his coffee.

They must have noticed his hat. They must have seen, too, that he locked
his door. However, they did not ask him any questions, but ignored him as
they had ignored for the past four days. Nevertheless he said:

'See you later.'

He took the Rue Haute. About five hundred yards up on the left there was
a square, in the middle of which stood the grey building of the Town Hall.

Here also there was a market less important than the one opposite his
shop, a few barrows of vegetables and fruit, two or three stalls, a woman
selling baskets and bootlaces.

To reach the police station one did not go in by the main entrance but by a
small door in the side street, and he went into the first room which smelled
like a barracks and was divided in two by a sort of black wooden counter.

Five or six people were waiting on a bench and, out of humility or
timidity, he was going to sit in the queue, when a police sergeant called to
him:

'What do you want?'

He stammered:

'I've had a summons.'

'Let's see.'

He glanced at it, disappeared through a door, and said on returning a little
later:

'Wait a minute.'

Jonas remained standing to start off with, and the hands of the clock, on
the rough white wall, pointed to ten past ten, a quarter past ten, twenty past
ten. Then he sat down, fiddling with his hat, wondering whether, as at the
doctor's, all the people ahead of him had to go in first.

It was not the case, for when they called a name, a woman rose and was led
in the opposite direction to the one the sergeant had taken a short time
before. Then they said another name and told an elderly man who was going
towards the desk:

'Sign here. . . . Now here. . . . You've got four hundred and twenty-two
francs?'

He held the money in his hand and, in exchange, was given a pink piece of paper which he folded carefully and put in his wallet before leaving.

'Next!'

It was an old woman, who leaned towards the sergeant and spoke to him in a low voice, and Jonas was unconsciously straining his ears to hear, when a bell rang.

'One moment!' the man in uniform interrupted her. 'Monsieur Milk! This way please.'

He went down a corridor onto which there opened a number of offices, until he came to the one where the superintendent, sitting in front of a piece of mahogany furniture, had his back to the window.

'Sit down,' he said, without looking up.

He wore spectacles for reading and writing, which Jonas did not know, only having seen him in the street, and he took them off each time he looked at him.

'Your name is Jonas Milk, born at Archangel on the 21st of September, 1916, naturalized a Frenchman on the 17th of May, 1938?'

'Yes, Superintendent.'

The man had in front of him some closely written sheets of paper which he appeared to be perusing in order to refresh his memory.

'Two years ago you married Eugénie Louise Joséphine Palestri.'

He nodded his head and the superintendent leaned back in his chair, played with his spectacles for a moment, before asking him:

'Where is your wife, Monsieur Milk?'

To hear himself addressed by that name, to which he had become unaccustomed, was enough to discompose him.

'I don't know, Superintendent.'

'I see here'–and he tapped the papers in front of him with his horn-rimmed spectacles, which he had folded up–'that you have provided at least two different accounts of her departure.'

'Let me explain.'

'One moment. On the one hand, to several of your neighbours you declared spontaneously and in the presence of witnesses, on Thursday morning, then on Thursday afternoon and on Friday, that your wife had left the town by the 7.10 bus.'

'That is correct.'

'She did take the bus?'

'No. It is correct that I said so.'

It was starting all over again. The huge sheets of official paper contained the report from Inspector Basquin, who must have, back in his office, reconstructed their conversation from memory.

'On the other hand, when you were questioned afterwards by one of my colleagues, you changed your wife's departure to Wednesday evening.'

As he was opening his mouth, a sharp rap of the glasses on the dossier interrupted him.

'One moment, Monsieur Milk, I am bound to warn you first that we have been requested to start a search for her as a missing person.'

Was it Louis who had come and asked for this? Or Angèle? Or Frédo? He didn't dare enquire, although he was burning to know.

'These affairs are always delicate, especially when it concerns a woman, and even more so, a married woman. I summoned you to ask you a certain number of questions and I shall be obliged to go into somewhat intimate details. It is understood that I am not accusing you of anything and you have the right not to reply.'

'I only ask to . . .'

'Please let me do the talking. I shall first of all outline the position as briefly as possible.'

He put on his spectacles, looked for another piece of paper on which he had apparently jotted down a few notes.

'You are forty years old and your wife, better known under the name of Gina, is twenty-four. If I understand rightly, she did not pass for a model of virtue before she met you and, as a neighbour, you were aware of her conduct. Is that correct?'

'That is correct.'

Life, described thus, in official language, how odious it became!

'Nevertheless you married her, in the full knowledge of the facts and, in order that the wedding should take place in church, a condition without which the Palestris would not have given their consent, you became converted to Catholicism and were baptized.'

This was another shock, for it revealed that an intensive enquiry had been going on about him during the empty days he had just passed. Had they been to question the Abbé Grimault, and others as well, whose names were perhaps yet to emerge?

'By the way, Monsieur Milk, I should like to ask you a question which has nothing to do with this matter. You are a Jew, I believe?'

For the first time he replied as if he were ashamed of it:

'Yes.'

'You were here during the occupation?'

'Yes.'

'So you remember that at one time the German authorities made it compulsory for your co-religionists to wear a yellow star on their clothes?'

'Yes.'

'How is it that you never wore this star and yet did not get into trouble?'

In order to remain calm he had to dig his nails into the palms of his hands.

What could he reply? Was he to renounce his own people? He had never felt himself to be a Jew. He had never believed himself to be different from the people who surrounded him at the Old Market and they, just because of his fair hair and blue eyes, had never thought that he was of another race.

It was not in order to deceive them that he had not worn the yellow star, at the risk of being sent to a concentration camp or condemned to death. He had taken the risk, naturally, because he wanted to remain like the others.

The superintendent, who did not know him, had not found all this out on his own. Nor was it Basquin, who at the time was a prisoner-of-war in Germany.

It had come from somebody else, from somebody at the market, one of the people who used to give him a friendly greeting every morning.

'Did your wife know that you were a Jew?'

'I never talked about it to her.'

'Do you think that would have affected her decision?'

'I don't think so.'

As he said it, he thought bitterly of the Arab with whom she had once spent the night.

'And her parents?'

'It never occurred to me to wonder.'

'Let's leave that on one side. Do you speak German?'

'No.'

'Russian, of course?'

'I used to speak it once, with my parents, but I have forgotten it and I could hardly even understand it now.'

What has this to do with the disappearance of Gina? Was he finally going to discover what they had against him?

'Your father came to France as an emigré, at the time of the revolution.'

'He was a prisoner in Germany and when the armistice was signed, in 1918 . . .'

'Let's call him an emigré, since at that time he did not return to Russia. I suppose he formed part of some White Russian group?'

He seemed to remember that at first Shepilov had made him a member of some political society, but Constantin Milk had never been an active member and had dedicated himself entirely to his fishmonger's business.

Without waiting for his answer, Superintendent Devaux went on:

'Yet in 1930 he did not hesitate to go back to his country. Why?'

'To find out what had become of my five sisters.'

'Did you hear any news of him?'

'Never.'

'Not a letter, or by word of mouth, nor through friends?'

'In no way at all.'

'How is it, in that case, that your mother went off in her turn?'

'Because she could not live without her husband.'

'Have you ever indulged in political activities?'

'Never.'

'You don't belong to any group, or party?'

'No.'

Devaux put on his spectacles to consult his notes once again. He looked put out. One would have said that it was only with a certain reluctance that he was asking certain questions.

'You carry on a considerable correspondence with foreign countries, Monsieur Milk.'

Had they questioned the postman as well? Who else?

'I am a philatelist.'

'Does that call for such an extensive foreign correspondence?'

'Given my method of work, yes.'

He felt the desire to explain the mechanics of his operations, the research work among the raw material which he had sent to him from the four corners of the earth, for stamps with peculiarities which had escaped his colleagues.

'We'll leave that on one side,' the superintendent said once again, apparently in a hurry to get to the end of the interview.

Nevertheless he added:

'How are your relations with your neighbours?'

'Good. Very good. I mean up to the last few days.'

'What has happened in the last few days?'

'They have been avoiding me.'

'You received, I believe, a visit from your brother-in-law, Alfred Palestri, known as Frédo?'

'Yes.'

'What do you think of him?'

He said nothing.

'Are you on bad terms?'

'I don't think he likes me.'

'For what reason?'

'Perhaps he wasn't pleased that I married his sister.'

'And your father-in-law?'

'I don't know.'

After a glance at his notes, the superintendent resumed:

'It would appear that both of them were opposed to your marriage. Gina, at the time, was in your service, if I am not mistaken?'

'She was working in my house as my servant.'

'Did she sleep in the house?'

'No.'

'Did you have intimate relations with her?'

'Not before we were married.'

'The idea of starting a family never came to you before?'

'No.'

It was true. It never occurred to him.

'I am going, for my own guidance, to ask you another indiscreet question and you are perfectly entitled to refuse to answer. How did you manage?'

He did not understand at once. The superintendent had to elucidate:

'A man has his needs . . .'

Before the war there was a house, not far from the Town Hall, in the Rue du Pot-de-Fer to be precise, which Jonas visited regularly. The new laws had upset his arrangements for a time, then he had discovered a street corner, near the station, where four or five women walked their beat of an evening in front of a private hotel.

He admitted to it, since he was in any case being forced to strip his soul bare.

'According to what you said, you were not jealous of your wife?'

'I didn't say that. I said I did not let her see it.'

'I understand. So you were jealous?'

'Yes.'

'What would you have done if you had caught her in the arms of another man?'

'Nothing.'

'You wouldn't have been furious?'

'I should have suffered.'

'But you wouldn't have used violence, either against her or against her partner?'

'Certainly not.'

'Did she know that?'

'She must have known it.'

'Did she take advantage of the fact?'

He felt like replying:

'It's all written down in front of you!'

But if he had already been overawed once when Inspector Basquin had interrogated him in his shop, which he had entered with the casual air of a customer, he was very much more so in this formal office where, on top of everything else, they had just touched on sensitive points, and left him as if he had been flayed alive.

There were words, sentences, which went on resounding in his head and he had to make an effort to understand what was being said to him.

'You never threatened her?'

He started.

'What with?'

'I don't know. You never uttered any threat against her?'

'Never in my life. It would never have occurred to me to do so!'

'Not even during a quarrel at home, for example, or perhaps after a few drinks?'

'We never had any quarrels and you must have been told that I only drink coffee.'

The superintendent slowly lit his pipe, which he had been filling, and leant back in his armchair, his spectacles in his hand.

'In that case, how can you explain that your wife is frightened of you?'

He thought he had misheard him.

'What did you say?'

'I said "that she is frightened of you".'

'Gina?'

'Your wife, yes.'

He started to his feet, overawed though he was by his surroundings. It was with some difficulty that he was able to pronounce clearly the words that came, in a confused torrent, to his lips.

'But, Superintendent, she was never frightened of me. . . . Frightened of what? . . . When she came back, on the contrary, I . . .'

'Sit down.'

He was twisting his hands together. It was meaningless, as if he was living one of his nightmares of the night before.

'Afraid of me!' he repeated. 'Of me!'

Whoever could be afraid of him? Not even the stray dogs of the market, or the cats. He was the most inoffensive being on the face of the earth.

The superintendent, meanwhile, who had put his spectacles on again, ran his eyes over a report while his fingers underlined a passage.

'On several occasions, your wife declared that you would end up by killing her.'

'When? Who to? It's not possible.'

'I am not at liberty, at present, to disclose the name of the person to whom she made these confidences, but I can assure you that she made them, and not just to one person.'

Jonas was capitulating. It was too much. They had just gone too far. That the neighbours had turned against him he could endure, by gritting his teeth.

But that Gina . . .

'Listen, Superintendent . . .'

He stretched out his hands in supplication, in a final outburst of energy.

'If she was afraid of me, why . . .'

What was the use? In any case, the words failed him. He had forgotten what he was going to say. It no longer mattered.

Afraid of him!

'Keep calm. Once again I am not accusing you of anything. An inquiry has been opened as a result of your wife's disappearance and it is my duty not to neglect anything, to listen to all the evidence.'

Without realizing, he nodded his approval.

'The fact is that for some mysterious reason, ever since the morning when your wife's disappearance was noted, you have been lying.'

He did not protest, as he had done with Inspector Basquin.

'Afraid of me!' he kept repeating to himself with bitter obstinacy.

'This has inevitably given rise to certain rumours.'

His head went on nodding affirmatively.

'All I am asking is to clear the matter up with your help.'

The face and outline of the superintendent suddenly danced in front of his eyes and he felt himself being overcome by a weakness which he had never known before.

'You . . . you haven't a glass of water?' he had time to stammer.

It was the first time in his life that he had fainted. It was very hot in the room. The superintendent rushed to the door and Jonas had time to hear water flowing from a tap.

He could not have been unconscious for more than a few seconds, for when he opened his eyes, the glass was clinking against his teeth and the cold water was trickling down his chin.

He looked without resentment, his eyes half-closed, at the man who had just caused him so much pain, who now stood bending over him.

'Do you feel better?'

He blinked his eyelids, as he did to greet the Widower, who was rather like the superintendent to look at. Perhaps after all the superintendent was a decent fellow and was sorry for him?

'Have another drink.'

He shook his head. He was embarrassed. A nervous reaction made him suddenly feel like crying. He mastered himself, but it was a good minute before he was able to speak. Then it was to stammer:

'I am sorry.'

'Relax and keep quiet.'

The superintendent opened the window, suddenly letting in the noises from the street, went and sat down in his place again, not knowing what to do or say.

Chapter Seven

'I don't think, Monsieur Milk,' the superintendent was saying, 'that you have quite grasped the point. Once again, for some reason or other, your wife has disappeared, and we have been asked to investigate. We have had no choice but to collect statements and check certain rumours which were circulating.'

Jonas was calm again now, too calm, and the smile on his face looked as if an india-rubber could have wiped it away. He was looking at the other politely, his mind elsewhere; in actual fact he was listening to the crowing of a cock, which had just broken, strident and proud, into the noises from the street. At first it had surprised him so much that he had a feeling of unreality, of floating, until he recalled that just opposite the police station there was a man who dealt in birds and farmyard animals.

By rising from his chair he could have seen the cages piled on top of one another on the pavement, hens, cocks, and pedigree ducks underneath, then on top, parakeets, canaries and other birds, some bright red, others blue, whose names he did not know. To the right of the door, a parrot stood on its perch and passers-by were constantly amazed that it was not attached.

In the Square a woman with a shrill voice, a costermonger, was calling on the world at large to buy her fine salads and the intervals in her monotonous cry were roughly regular, so that he ended up by waiting for it.

'I went about it a bit brutally, perhaps, and I am sorry . . .'

Jonas shook his head as if to say that all was well.

Gina was frightened of him. The rest did not matter. He could stand up to anything now, and the superintendent had no need to approach the question in a roundabout way.

'I will not conceal from you that there is another somewhat disturbing piece of evidence. On Wednesday, shortly before midnight, a woman was leaning out of her window, in the Rue du Canal, a quarter of a mile from where you live. She was waiting for her husband who, for reasons that need not concern us, had not returned home at the usual time. Anyway, she saw a rather small man, about your size, who was carrying a large sack on his shoulder, heading towards the lock and keeping close to the wall.'

'Did she recognize me?'

He was not angry, or indignant.

'I did not say that, but clearly it is a coincidence.'

'Do you think, Superintendent, that I would have had the strength to carry my wife from the Place du Vieux-Marché to the canal?'

If Gina was very little bigger than he was, she was heavier and he was not a strong man.

Monsieur Devaux bit his lips. Since Jonas had fainted, he was less at his ease and was minding how he went, without realizing that it was no longer necessary. Isn't there a moment when the intensity of pain brings on insensitivity? Jonas had passed that crisis and, while he listened to what was being said, he was concentrating on the noises from the street.

It wasn't the same sound as in his quarter. The cars were more frequent, the pedestrians in more of a hurry. The light itself was different, and yet it was not ten minutes' walk from here to the Vieux-Marché.

The cupboards, behind the superintendent, were made of mahogany like the desk, with green baize cloth stretched behind gold-coloured lattice work, and above, in a wooden frame, could be seen a photograph of the President of the Republic.

'I thought of that objection, Monsieur Milk. But you are not unaware, if you read the papers, that this problem has often, alas, been overcome.'

He did not understand straight away.

'You cannot have failed to read or hear stories of dismembered bodies being found in rivers or waste land. Once again, I am not accusing you.'

He was not being accused of cutting Gina into pieces and carrying them into the canal!

'What we have to do now, unless your wife reappears or we find her, is to exculpate you from the affair, and therefore to study all the possibilities calmly.'

He was replacing his spectacles in order to cast an eye over his notes.

'Why, after her disappearance, were you in such a hurry to take your washing and hers to the laundry?'

They knew his slightest acts, as if he had been living in a glass cage.

'Because it was laundry day.'

'Was it you who normally counted the washing and made up the parcel?'

'No.'

No and yes. Which proved how difficult it is to express an absolute truth. It was among Gina's duties, as in other households, and Gina usually attended to it. Only she never knew which day of the week it was and sometimes Jonas reminded her, while she was doing their room:

'Don't forget the laundry.'

It was also a habit of theirs to put the pillow-case with it under the counter, so as not to hold up the van driver, who was always in a hurry.

Gina lived in disorder. Indeed, had she not forgotten, before leaving, to wash the pan in which she had cooked the herrings? Jonas, who had lived alone a long time and had not always had a maid, had kept up the habit of thinking of everything and often, when Gina was away, of doing the chores she ought to have taken on.

'Your wife has just disappeared, Monsieur Milk. You told me a short while ago that you were in love with her. Yet you took the trouble to devote yourself to a job which men do not normally do.'

He could only repeat:

'It was laundry day.'

He felt that the other was examining him curiously. Basquin, too, had looked at him like that at certain moments, as a man who is trying to understand, but without success.

'You were not trying to hide compromising traces?'

'Traces of what?'

'On the Friday or the Saturday, you also turned out your kitchen.'

How often this had happened before Gina's day, when the maid was ill, and even after his marriage!

'These are details of no significance individually, I agree, but which added together are nothing if not disturbing.'

He nodded in agreement, a submissive schoolboy.

'You have no idea what liaisons your wife may have formed of late?'

'None.'

'Has she been away more often than usual?'

'No.'

As always, in the morning, she would roam about the market, preferably in dressing-gown and slippers. In the afternoon she would probably dress, powder her face, put on scent and go and do her shopping in the town, or see one of her girl friends.

'Hasn't she received any letters either?'

'She never has had any letters at the house.'

'Do you think she received them somewhere else, at the poste restante, for example?'

'I don't know.'

'What you must admit is curious, seeing that you are an intelligent man, is that she should have gone off without taking any clothes, not even a coat and, according to your own statement, almost without any money. She didn't take a bus, nor the train, we have confirmed that.'

In the end he felt it better to mention the stamps. He was tired, he was in a hurry to get outside this office, and not have to listen to any more of these questions which had so little relation to reality.

'My wife,' he said, smarting at being finally driven to it, and with a sense of betrayal, 'had premeditated her departure.'

'How do you know, and why didn't you say so to Inspector Basquin?'

'In the wardrobe with the looking-glass in our bedroom there is a box which used to contain my rarest stamps.'

'Did she know about it?'

'Yes.'

'Are these stamps of any great value?'

'Several million francs.'

He wondered if he had been wise to speak, for the superintendent's reaction was not what he had expected. He was being looked at, not with incredulity, but with a hint of suspicion.

'You mean that you possessed several million francs' worth of stamps?'

'Yes. I began collecting them at school, when I was about thirteen, and I have never given it up.'

'Who, apart from your wife, has seen these stamps you possess?'

'Nobody.'

'So that you cannot prove that they were in the cupboard?'

He had become calm, patient, detached almost, as if it were no longer anything to do with Gina and himself, and that was perhaps because he was on professional ground.

'I can prove, as far as most of them are concerned, that I acquired them at a particular moment, either by purchase or by exchange, some of them fifteen years ago, some two or three years ago. Philatelists form a fairly small circle. It is nearly always known where the rarer specimens are to be found.'

'Excuse my interrupting you, Monsieur Milk. I know nothing about philately. I am trying, at present, to put myself in the position of a jury. You are saying that while still living in a manner which I would, with all due respect, describe as very modest, and I hope I don't offend you, you say that you had several millions' worth of stamps and that your wife has taken them away with her. You go on to say that as far as most of them are concerned, you are able to establish that they came into your possession a number of years ago. Is that correct?'

He nodded his head, listening to the cock which was crowing once more, and the superintendent, exasperated, got up to close the window.

'Do you mind?'

'As you wish.'

'The first question that will arise is whether, last Wednesday, these stamps were still in your possession, for there was nothing to stop you from reselling them a long time ago. Is it possible for you to prove this was not so?'

'No.'

'And can you prove that you have not still got them?'

'They are no longer in the box.'

'We are still in the realms of theory, aren't we? What was there to prevent you from having put them somewhere else?'

'Why should I?'

In order to incriminate Gina, that is what the superintendent was thinking. To make it seem that she had gone off taking his fortune with her.

'Do you see now how difficult and delicate my task is? The inhabitants of your neighbourhood, for some reason unknown to me, seem to have a grudge against you.'

'Up to these last few days, they have been very nice to me.'

The superintendent was studying him closely and Jonas found the explanation in his eyes. He did not understand either. Human beings of all sorts had been in and out of his office and he was accustomed to the most unusual kinds of confidences. But Jonas baffled him, and he could see him pass from sympathy to irritation, amounting at times to aversion, only to start again and try to find a fresh point of contact.

Had it not been the same with Basquin? Didn't that go to prove that he was not like other men? Would it have been different in the country where he was born, at Archangel, among the people of his own race?

All his life he had sensed it, intuitively. Even at school he made himself inconspicuous, as if in order to be forgotten, and he had been uncomfortable when, against his will, he came top in his class.

Hadn't they encouraged him to consider himself at home in the Vieux-Marché? Hadn't they suggested, at one moment, that he should join a shopkeepers' defence committee, and even become the treasurer? He had refused, feeling that it was not his place.

It was not without good reason that he had shown such humility. He could only assume that he had not shown enough, since they were turning against him.

'When did these stamps disappear, according to your story?'

'Normally I keep the key to the box in my pocket, with the key to the front door and the one for the till.'

He displayed the silver chain.

'On Wednesday morning I dressed as soon as I got up, but the day before I went down in my pyjamas.'

'So that your wife would have taken the stamps on the Tuesday morning?'

'I presume so.'

'Are they easy to sell?'

'No.'

'Well?'

'She doesn't know it. As I told you, dealers know one another. When a rare specimen is brought to them, they usually make enquiries about its origin.'

'Have you alerted your colleagues?'

'No.'

'For what reason?'

He shrugged his shoulders. He was beginning to sweat, and missed the noises from the street.

'So your wife went off without a coat, without luggage, but with a fortune she will not be able to realize. Is that right?'

He nodded.

'She left the Old Market on Wednesday evening, over a week ago now, and no one saw her go, no one saw her in the town, she didn't take the bus, nor the train: in short, she melted into thin air without leaving the slightest trace. Where, in your opinion, would she have the best chance of selling the stamps?'

'In Paris, obviously, or in a big city like Lyons, Bordeaux, Marseilles. Abroad, too.'

'Can you furnish me with a list of the stamp dealers in France?'

'The principal ones, yes.'

'I will send them a circular letter warning them. Now, Monsieur Milk . . .'

The superintendent rose to his feet, hesitated, as if he had not yet discharged the most disagreeable part of his task.

'It remains to me to ask your permission to instruct two of my men to accompany you and pay a visit to your house. I could obtain a search warrant but, at this stage of the affair, I prefer to keep matters on a less official footing.'

Jonas had also risen to his feet. He had no reason for refusing since he had nothing to hide and since, in any case, he was not the stronger of the two.

'Now?'

'I should prefer it that way, yes.'

To prevent him from covering up traces?

It was at once laughable and tragic. All this had started with an innocent little remark:

'*She has gone to Bourges.*'

It was Le Bouc who, innocently too, had asked:

'On the bus?'

From there, little by little, there had grown ripples, then waves, which had invaded the market and finally reached as far as the police station, in the centre of the town.

He was no longer Monsieur Jonas, the bookseller in the Square whom everybody greeted cheerfully. For the superintendent, and in the reports, he was Jonas Milk, born at Archangel, Russia, on the 21st of September, 1916, naturalized French on the 17th of May, 1938, exempted from military service, of Jewish origin, converted to Catholicism in 1954.

There remained one more facet of the affair to be revealed, which he was far from expecting. They were standing up. The conversation, or rather the interrogation, seemed to be at an end. Monsieur Devaux was playing with his spectacles, which now and then caught a ray from the sun.

'Anyway, Monsieur Milk, you have a simple way of establishing that these stamps were in your possession.'

He looked at him uncomprehendingly.

'They amount, you said, to a capital value of several million francs. They were bought from your income, and consequently, it must be possible to find, in your income tax returns, a record of the sum you invested. Naturally this does not concern me personally, and it falls in the province of the Direct Taxation authorities.'

They would corner him there, too, he knew in advance. He wouldn't be able to get them to accept a perfectly simple truth. He had never bought a stamp for fifty thousand francs, or a hundred thousand, or three hundred thousand, even though he had possessed stamps of that value. He had discovered some by examining them with his magnifying glass, stamps whose rarity other people had failed to spot, and some of the others he had acquired by a series of exchanges.

As the superintendent had said, he lived very modestly.

What was the use of worrying about it, in the state he was already in? Only one thing counted. *Gina was afraid of him.* And, in the doorway of the office, he in his turn timidly asked a question.

'She really said I would kill her one day?'

'That is what emerges from the evidence.'

'To several people?'

'I can assure you so.'

'She didn't say why?'

Monsieur Devaux hesitated, reclosed the door, which he had just opened.

'Do you insist on my replying?'

'Yes.'

'You will note that I made no allusion to it during the course of the conversation. Twice, at least, when talking about you, she declared:

'*He's vicious.*'

He turned scarlet. This was the last word he had been expecting.

'Think about it, Monsieur Milk, and we will resume the discussion another day. For the present, Inspector Basquin will accompany you with one of his men.'

The superintendent's statement did not shock him, and he finally felt he was beginning to understand. Often Gina had watched him stealthily when he was busy, and when he raised his head, she had seemed confused. The look on her face was similar then to certain of Basquin's and the superintendent's looks.

All the same she lived with him. She saw him in all his behaviour, day and night.

Despite this, she had not grown used to it, and he remained an enigma to her.

She must have wondered, when she was still working with him as a maid, why he did not treat her as other men used to treat her, including Ancel. She was never overdressed and there was a wanton freedom in her movements which might have been taken as a provocation.

Had she thought him impotent, at that time, or did she attribute special tastes to him? Had she been the only one during the years, to think so?

He could picture her, serious-faced, preoccupied, when he had spoken of marrying her. He could picture her undressing the first evening and calling to him as, fully dressed, he was pacing about the room without daring to look at her.

'Aren't you going to undress?'

It was almost as if she was expecting to discover something abnormal about him. The truth was that he was ashamed of his over-pink, plump body.

She had turned down the bed, lain down with her knees apart, and watching him undress, as he was approaching awkwardly, she had exclaimed with a laugh, which in reality was perhaps just uneasiness:

'Are you going to keep your glasses on?'

He had taken them off. All the time he had lain upon her, he had felt that she was watching him, and she had not taken part, nor made any pretence at taking part in his pleasure.

'*You see!*' she had said.

What exactly did that mean? That, in spite of everything, he had got what he wanted? That, despite appearances, he was almost a normal man?

'Shall we go to sleep?'

'If you like.'

'Good-night.'

She had not kissed him and he had not dared to do so either. The superintendent forced him to reflect that in two years they had never kissed. He had tried twice or three times and she had turned her head away, not abruptly, with no apparent revulsion.

Although they slept in the same bed, he approached her as seldom as possible, because she did not participate, and when, towards morning, he would hear her panting near to him, finally subsiding in the depths of the bed with a sigh that almost rent her in two, he used to keep his eyes closed and pretend to be asleep.

As the superintendent had just told him, they had not yet questioned him about that, but it would come.

What was it that frightened Gina?

Was it his calm, his gentleness, his abashed tenderness when she came back from one of her escapades? One would sometimes have said that she was defying him to beat her.

Would she then have been less afraid of him? Would she have stopped thinking of him as vicious?

'Basquin!' called the superintendent, who had moved towards the corridor.

In an office, Jonas saw the inspector at work in his shirt-sleeves.

'Take somebody with you and accompany Monsieur Milk.'

'Right, Superintendent.'

He must have know what he had to do, for he did not ask for instructions.

'Dambois!' he called out in his turn, addressing someone out of sight in another office.

Neither of them were in uniform but everyone, in the Old Market as in the town centre, knew them.

'Think it over, Monsieur Milk,' Monsieur Devaux was saying again by way of good-bye.

What he was thinking over was not what the superintendent imagined. He was no longer trying to defend himself, to reply to the more or less grotesque charges which they had levelled against him.

It was an inner debate which occupied his mind, a debate infinitely more tragic than their tale about a woman being cut up into pieces.

In a curious way they were right, but not in the way they imagined, and Jonas suddenly felt himself really guilty.

He had not effected Gina's disappearance or thrown her body into the canal.

He was not vicious either, in the sense they understood him to be, and he knew of no peculiarity in himself, no sexual abnormality.

He hadn't yet registered the point, for the revelation had been too recent, it had come at the moment he least expected it, in the neutral atmosphere of an official building.

'Do you mind waiting for me a moment, Monsieur Jonas?'

Basquin went on giving the name he was used to, but it did not even please him any longer.

That stage was past. He had reached the office divided by a dark wooden counter where some new visitors were waiting on the bench, and he pretended, to keep up appearances, to be reading an official notice advertising the sale of some horses and oxen in the main square.

Wasn't it to her brother, to start with, that Gina had confided that she was frightened of him? Very probably. That explained Frédo's fierce opposition to the marriage.

Who else had she spoken to? Clémence? La Loute?

He tried to remember the words the superintendent had repeated to him: *'That man will kill me one of these days . . .'*

Why? Because he did not react as she had expected when she ran after other men? Because he was too soft, too patient?

Did she think to herself that he was acting and that one day he would give free reign to his real instincts? He had told her, when he had talked to her about marriage:

'I can at least offer you *peace and quiet.'*

Those words or something like them. He had not talked to her of love, or happiness, but of peace and quiet, because he was too humble to imagine that he could give her anything else.

She was beautiful, full of vitality, and he was sixteen years older, a dusty, lonely little bookseller whose only passion in life was collecting stamps.

That was not entirely true. That was how it seemed, what people must think. The truth is that he lived intensely, in his inner self, a rich and varied life, the life of the entire Old Market, the entire neighbourhood, of which he knew the minutest movements.

Behind the shelter of his thick spectacles, which seemed to isolate him and gave him an inoffensive air, was it not rather as if he had stolen the lives of the others, without their noticing it?

Was that what Gina had discovered on entering his house? Was that why she had spoken of vice and been afraid?

Did she hold it against him that he had bought her?

For he had bought her, he knew it and she knew it. Angèle knew it better than anyone, for she had sold her, and Louis as well, who had not dared to say anything for fear of his wife, and Frédo, who had revolted against it.

They had not sold her for money, but for peace and quiet. He was so well aware of it that he had been the first to use the words as a bait, a temptation.

With him, Gina would have a front of respectability and her escapades would be covered up. Her material needs would be assured and Angèle would tremble no more at the thought of seeing her end up on the streets.

Had the neighbours who had been at the wedding thought of it? Their smiles, their congratulations, their contentment, especially at the end of the feast, were they sincere?

Weren't they, too, a little ashamed of the bargain which, in a sense, they had just countersigned?

The Abbé Grimault had not openly tried to dissuade him from his designs. Doubtless he, too, preferred to see Gina married. Nevertheless even Jonas' conversion had evoked little enthusiasm in him.

'I daren't ask you whether you have faith, since I would not wish to induce you to tell a lie.'

So he knew that Jonas didn't believe in it. Did he also guess that it had not been simply to marry Gina that he had become a Catholic and that he had sometimes thought about it long before he met her?

'I hope that you will be happy with her, and bring her happiness.'

The good wish was genuine, but it could be seen that he placed little confidence in it. He did his duty as a priest in joining them together as he had done in receiving the little man from Archangel into the bosom of the Roman Catholic church.

How was it that during the two years it had never once occurred to Jonas that Gina could be afraid of him?

Now the scales had fallen from his eyes and details he had taken no notice of were coming back to him.

He was realizing, at last, that he was a foreigner, a Jew, a solitary, a man from the other end of the world who had come like a parasite to embed himself in the flesh of the Old Market.

'If you will come this way . . .'

The two men were ready with their hats on, and with Jonas between them, half a head smaller than either, they set off for the Rue Haute in the hot, sun-soaked air.

'Did it go off all right?' asked Basquin, who had obviously been to have a word with his chief.

'I suppose so. I'm not sure.'

'The superintendent is a man of remarkable intelligence, who would have had an important post in Paris a long time ago if he didn't insist on living with his daughter. He was called to the bar at the age of twenty-three and started off his career with the prefecture. It was sheer accident that he joined the police.'

From time to time Basquin returned the greeting of a passer-by and people turned to stare at Jonas, who was walking between the two policemen.

'During the last four days, since the day I came to see you, we have been circulating your wife's description everywhere.'

The inspector was surprised at Jonas' lack of reaction and kept shooting him little glances out of the corner of his eye.

'True, there are plenty of pretty dark girls in red dresses. Quite apart from the fact that she may have bought herself a new dress.'

As he passed the restaurant, Jonas saw the top of Pepito's head above the curtains, and Pepito was looking at him. Would he be lunching there? Would they give him the chance? It was already half-past eleven. They were probably going to search the house from top to bottom and the corners were full of odd bits and pieces, for Jonas never threw anything away.

Who could say, at this stage, that they were not going to arrest him?

It remained for him to pass Le Bouc's, and he decided to turn his head away, not from shame, but to spare them embarrassment.

For despite everything they must have been embarrassed. They must have egged one another on. Any one of them, on their own, with the exception of Frédo, would not have dared to turn against him so brutally.

'*If you'll say it, then I'll say so too . . .*'

Why not, since he had taken them in? He took the keys from his pocket and opened the door, under which he found a yellow cinema programme.

'Come in, gentlemen.'

The shop, which had had the sun all the morning and in which the air was stagnating, was like a furnace. Two great black flies were flying clumsily about.

'Presumably you would rather I left the door open?'

The smell of books was stronger than usual and, in order to create a draught, he went and opened the door into the yard, where a blackbird was hopping about. He knew it. The blackbird came every morning and was not afraid of Jonas.

'Call me if you need me.'

It was Basquin who took the lead.

'I'd like to visit the bedroom first. I suppose it's this way?'

'Go on up! I'll follow.'

He wanted a cup of coffee, but didn't dare ask for permission to go and make himself one, still less to go and have one at Le Bouc's.

The bedroom was tidy, the counterpane carefully spread on the bed, and the dressing-table immaculate. As he went in Jonas' eye fell immediately upon Gina's comb which was dirty, with one or two hairs caught in it. He was so used to seeing it in the same place that he had not noticed it during the past few days, nor washed it.

'Is this the only bedroom in the house?'

'Yes.'

'So that this is the bed you both slept in?'

'Yes.'

Through the open window Jonas thought he could hear stealthy footsteps on the pavement, muffled whispers.

'Where does this door lead to?'

'The lavatory and bathroom.'

'And that one?'

He pushed it open. It had once been a bedroom looking out onto the yard, but it was so tiny that there was only just room for a bed. Jonas used it as a loft and box-room for his shop. It contained broken chairs, an old chest with the lock torn off, dating from their flight from Russia, a dress-maker's model, which he had bought for Gina and which she had never used, cracked crockery, piles of books, the ones which he had no hope of ever selling, and even a chamber pot. No one ever dusted this room. The skylight was not opened more than once a year and the air was musty, everything was covered with a layer of grey powder.

The two policemen exchanged glances. Presumably it meant that nobody could have gone in there recently without leaving traces. They had kept their hats on and Basquin was finishing a cigarette, the stub of which he went and threw down the lavatory.

'Are these the clothes?' he asked, pointing to the wardrobe with the looking-glass.

Jonas opened its two doors and the inspector ran his hand over the dresses, the coats, then over Jonas' two suits and overcoat.

'She didn't have another coat?'

'No.'

In the bottom of the wardrobe stood three pairs of Gina's shoes, a pair of slippers and a pair of his own shoes. That was their entire wardrobe.

'Is that the famous strong-box?'

He was thus admitting that the superintendent had spoken to him while Jonas was waiting in the front office.

'Do you mind opening it?'

He took out his keys again, put the strong-box onto the bed and raised the lid.

'I thought it was empty!' exclaimed Basquin.

'I never said that.'

There were in fact still about fifty transparent packets each containing a stamp or a stamped card.

'Well, what did she take?'

'About a quarter of the stamps which were in here. The whole lot, with the packets, wouldn't have fitted into her bag.'

'The rarest ones?'

'Yes.'

'How could she have recognized them?'

'I had shown them to her. And also because they were on top of the others, as I had just been looking at them.'

The two men exchanged glances behind his back, and they must have been thinking he was a lunatic.

'You don't have any weapons in the house?'

'No.'

'You have never possessed a revolver?'

'Never.'

The detective with Basquin was examining the floor, the woven carpet of blue and red flowers, the blue curtains, as if in search of traces of blood. He made an even more careful study around the dressing-table and went off to pursue his investigations in the bathroom.

Basquin stepped onto the straw-bottomed chair to look on top of the wardrobe, then he pulled open the drawers of the chest one by one.

The top one was Gina's drawer, and everything was in chaos, her three nightdresses, petticoats, brassieres, combinations which she scarcely ever wore, stockings, an old bag, a powder case, two boxes of aspirin and a small rubber object.

In the bag the inspector found a handkerchief stained with lipstick, some coins, a propelling-pencil and a receipt for two hundred and twenty-seven francs for a purchase she had made at Prisunic.

Jonas' drawer was in better order, with the shirts on one side, the pyjamas on the other, the socks, underpants, handkerchiefs and vests in the middle. There was also a brand new wallet which Gina had given him for his birthday and he never used because he considered it too smart. It still smelled of new leather and was empty.

Lastly, the bottom drawer contained, thrown in anyhow, everything that had not found a home elsewhere, medicines, the two winter blankets, a silver-mounted hat brush given to them as a wedding present, some hairpins and two advertisement ashtrays which they didn't use.

Basquin did not forget the drawer of the bedside table, where he found a pair of broken glasses, some gardenal, a razor and finally a photograph of Gina naked.

It was not Jonas who had taken it, nor he who had put it there. It dated back to well before their marriage, for Gina could not have been more than twenty at the time and, if her bosom was already well-developed, her waist was narrower, her hips less powerful.

'Look,' she had said to him one day when, by a miracle, she was tidying up her things. 'Do you recognize me?'

The features were not very clearly defined. True, the photograph was blurred. Gina was standing at the foot of a bed, in a hotel bedroom probably, and it was obvious that she did not know what to do with her hands.

'Don't you think I was better looking than I am now?'

He had said no.

'It amuses me to keep it, because I can compare myself. The day will come when people will no longer believe it's me.'

She looked at herself in the glass, displaying her bosom, feeling her hips.

'I didn't take that photograph,' he told Basquin hurriedly. 'She was much younger then.'

The inspector glanced at it again, curiously.

'So I see,' he said.

Then, after a look at his colleague:

'Let's take a look at the ground floor.'

It was rather like a public sale, when the most personal furniture and objects of a family are piled up in the street for inquisitive passers-by to come and finger them.

What did it matter now that they should turn his home inside out, after what had already been done to him?

Not only was he no longer at home in his own house, but he was no longer at home in his own skin.

Chapter Eight

As they passed through the little room on their way from the bedroom to the kitchen, Jonas glanced automatically in the direction of the shop and saw some faces pressed to the window; he even caught a glimpse of one urchin who must have ventured into the house, hurriedly beating a retreat and causing a burst of laughter.

The detectives examined everything, the cupboard where the groceries, the scales and the coffee-grinder were kept, the brooms hanging from its doors, the contents of the other cupboards, the table drawer, and they studied with particular attention the meat axe and the carving knives as if in search of tell-tale signs.

They went into the yard as well, where Basquin pointed to the windows of the Palestris' house.

'Isn't that Gina's home?'

'Yes.'

One of the windows actually belonged to the bedroom, now Frédo's, which she occupied as a young girl.

The little room took longer. The drawers were full of papers of all sorts, envelopes crammed with stamps, marked with signs which the inspector had to have explained, and for a long time he turned over the pages of the Russian album, with a series of sidelong glances at Jonas.

'You haven't done the same for the other countries, have you?'

He could only reply that he hadn't. He knew what they would deduce from that.

'I see you have the entire Soviet series. It's the first time I've had a chance of seeing them. How did you get hold of them?'

'You can pick them up everywhere in the trade.'

'Ah!'

The inquisitive eavesdroppers did not disappear until the two men set to work on the shop, where they ran their hands behind the rows of books.

'Have you dusted here recently?'

Was it also going to count against him that in order to keep himself occupied, he had undertaken a spring-cleaning of the shelves? It was all the same to him. He was no longer trying to defend himself.

At a particular moment during the morning, he could not have said precisely which moment, and in any case it did not matter, something had snapped. It was as if someone had cut a wire, or better still, perhaps, as if he had suddenly become independent of the law of gravity.

He could see the two of them, the inspector and Dambois, who were carrying out their duty conscientiously, but their comings and goings, their actions, the words they spoke, no longer had any connection with himself. A little knot of people outside continued to watch the house, and he did not even glance up to see whom it was composed of; for him they were nothing more than a patch of life in the sunlight.

He was beyond everything. He had passed to the other side. He was waiting, patiently, for his companions to finish, and when they finally made up their minds to depart, he removed the door handle and locked the door behind them. It was no longer his own house. Furniture and objects were still in the same place. He could still have placed his hand on each thing with his eyes closed, but all real contact had ceased to exist.

He was hungry. The idea of going to eat at Pepito's did not occur to him. In the kitchen he found the remains of some cheese from the day before and a hunk of bread, and he began to eat, standing in front of the door into the backyard.

At that particular moment he had decided nothing, at least not consciously, and it was when his gaze alighted on a clothes line stretched between the house and the Chaignes' wall that his thoughts took a definite shape.

He had come by a long road, from Archangel to here, by way of Moscow, Yalta and Constantinople to finish up in an old house in the Market Place. His father had gone back again. Then his mother.

'*I insist on this one at least remaining!*' Constantin Milk had said, pointing to Jonas at the moment of setting out on his adventure.

Now it was his turn. His decision was taken, but he still finished his cheese and bread with his eye first on the clothes line, which was made of twisted steel wire, then on the branch of the lime tree which projected from the grocer's garden next door. One of the two iron chairs stood, by chance, directly beneath the branch.

It was true, as he had told the inspector, that he had never possessed a weapon and had a horror of all violence, so much so that the noise of children's pistols in the Square made him jump each time he heard it.

He was reflecting, wondering whether he had anything still to do upstairs, or in the shop or the little room.

He had nothing left to do anywhere. They hadn't understood him, or else he hadn't understood the others, and this latest misunderstanding was now beyond all hope of being cleared up.

He had a momentary impulse to explain everything in a letter, but it was a last vanity of which he was ashamed, and he rejected the idea.

He had some difficulty in undoing the knots by which the metal cord was attached and he had to fetch the pliers from the kitchen drawer. He was not sad, nor bitter. He felt, on the contrary, a serenity which he had never known before.

He was thinking of Gina, and now it was no longer Gina as other people saw her and as she saw herself, it was a disembodied Gina, confused in his mind with the image he had created of his sister Doussia, a woman such as probably does not exist: Woman.

Would she find out that he had died because of her? He was trying to lie to himself again, and it made him blush. It was not on her account that he was departing, it was on his own account, perhaps in fact it was because he had been forced, in his own eyes, to stoop too far.

Could he go on living after what he had discovered about himself and about the others?

He climbed onto the iron chair to attach the cord to the branch of the tree and grazed his finger-tip on a loose strand of wire; it bled, and he sucked it, as he used to do when he was a little boy.

Although you could see the kitchen door from the Palestris' window, from the bedroom that used to be Gina's, the Chaignes' party wall blocked the view from where he was standing. All he had to do now was to make a slip knot and he used the pliers so as to be sure that it would hold.

A hot nausea suddenly rose to his head at the sight of the loop which hung suspended, and he wiped his brow and upper lip, had difficulty in swallowing his saliva.

He felt ridiculous standing on the iron chair, hesitating, trembling, seized with panic at the thought of the physical pain which he was going to feel, and worse still, of the slow choking, of the struggle which his body, hanging in mid-air, would instinctively make against suffocation.

What was preventing him from living, after all? The sun would continue to shine, the rain to fall, the Square to be filled with the sounds and smells of market day. He was still capable of making himself coffee, alone in the kitchen, listening to the songs of the birds.

The blackbird, just then, his blackbird, came and perched on the box where the chives were growing, beside a tuft of thyme, and as he watched it hopping about, Jonas' eyes filled with tears.

There was no need for him to die. Nobody was forcing him. With patience and an extra effort of humility, he could still come to terms with himself.

He stepped down from the iron chair and suddenly ran into the house in order to flee from the temptation, to be sure of not turning back. He struck a match over the gas ring, poured some water into the kettle to make himself some coffee.

He would find good reasons for acting as he was. Who could tell? Perhaps Gina would come back one day and would need him. Even the people from the market would understand, in the end. Hadn't Fernand Le Bouc already shown signs of embarrassment?

In the semi-darkness of the cupboard, he ground the coffee-mill, which was fixed to the wall. It was a china mill, with a Dutch landscape in blue on a white background, and a picture of a windmill. He had never been to Holland. He, who as a baby had covered such immense distances, had never travelled since, as though he had been afraid of losing his place in the Old Market.

He would be patient. The superintendent, Basquin had told him, was an intelligent man.

Already the smell of coffee was doing him good, while the steam misted over his glasses. He mused to himself, whether he would have kept his glasses on to hang himself, then he thought of Doussia again, telling himself that perhaps it was thanks to her that he had not taken the final step.

He did not yet dare to return to the yard to undo the knot. The alarm-clock, on the mantelpiece, pointed to ten to two and it comforted him to hear its familiar tick.

He would come to terms with himself, avoid thinking about certain subjects. He felt an urge to see his Russian stamps again, as though to cling onto something, and taking his cup with him, he went and sat at his desk in the little room.

Was he a coward? Would he regret not having done today what he had decided to do? If life became too burdensome later on, would he still have the courage to do it?

There was nobody in sight outside. The Square was empty. The clock of St Cecilia's struck two and according to the rites, he ought to have replaced the handle in the door.

It no longer had the same importance as it had before, and he had plenty of time to return to his old habits bit by bit. He opened the drawer and took out the album, on the first page of which he had gummed a photograph of his father and mother outside their fishmongery. He had taken it with a cheap camera which he had been given for Christmas at the age of eleven. He was just going to turn over the page when a shadow outlined itself against the shop-window. A woman he did not know was knocking at the door, trying to see inside, surprised to find the shop shut.

He thought it was a customer and almost did not open the door. It was a working-class woman about forty years old, and she must have borne several children and worked hard all her life, for one could see in her the deformities, the lassitude of women of that type, grown old before their time.

Shielding her eyes with her hand, she was peering into the obscurity of the shop, and in the end he rose to his feet, almost out of charity.

'I was afraid there was nobody at home,' she said, looking at him curiously.

He said quietly:

'I was working.'

'You are Gina's husband?'

'Yes.'

'Is it true they mean to arrest you?'

'I don't know.'

'They told me so this morning, and I wondered if I would be too late.'

'Won't you sit down?' he said, pointing to a chair.

'I haven't time. I must get back to the hotel. They don't know I've come out yet, as I took the back door. The management's new in the business and seem to think they've got to be strict.'

He listened without understanding.

'I work as a chambermaid at the Commercial Hotel. Do you know it?'

It was there that he had attended the wedding reception of Ancel's daughter. The walls were painted in imitation marble and the hall was bedecked with green plants.

'Before my husband went to the factory I used to live in this area, at the corner of the Rue Gambetta and the Rue des Saules. I knew Gina well when she must have been about fifteen years old. That's why I recognized her at once when she came to the hotel.'

'When has she been to the hotel?'

'Several times. Each time the traveller from Paris comes here, that's to say nearly every two weeks. It's been going on for months now. He's called Thierry, Jacques Thierry. I looked up his name in the register, and he's in chemical products. Seems he's an engineer, though he's still young. I'd bet he's not yet thirty. He's married and has two lovely children, I know because to start with he always put a photo of his family on the bedside table. His wife's a blonde. His eldest, a boy, is five or six, like my youngest.

'I don't know where he met Gina but one afternoon I saw him in the corridor with her and she went into his bedroom.

'Since then, everytime he's come, she stops in to see him at the hotel for an hour or two, all according, and I'm the last one to be in the dark about what goes on, since it's me that has to remake the bed. Begging your pardon for telling you, but they say you've been in trouble and I thought it might be better for you to know.

'Gina was like that at fifteen, if that's any consolation, and I should add something that you perhaps don't know but I'm told by people who ought to know, and that is that her mother was the same before her.'

'Did she go to the hotel on Wednesday last week?'

'Yes. Around half-past two. When they told me the story, this morning, I wasn't sure of the day and went and looked at the register. He arrived early on Tuesday and left again on Wednesday evening.'

'By train?'

'No. He always comes by car. I gather he has other factories to visit on his way.'

'Were they together a long time, on Wednesday?'

'Same as usual,' she replied, with a shrug.

'What dress was she wearing?'

'A red dress. You couldn't help noticing.'

He had wanted to be sure.

'Now I would rather not get mixed in the affair because as I told you before, the management's got its own ideas. But if they really mean to put you in prison and there isn't any other way, I will repeat what I've told you.'

'You haven't got the address of this man in Paris?'

'I copied it down on a piece of paper and brought it with me.'

She seemed surprised to see him so unmoved and so gloomy, when she must have expected him to feel relieved.

'It's number 27, Rue Championnet. I don't suppose he'll have taken her home. When I think of his wife, who looks so delicate, and his children ...'

'I am most grateful to you.'

'My name is Berthe Lenoir, in case you need me. I would rather no one came to the hotel. We live in the housing estate opposite the factory, the second block on the right, the one with blue shutters.'

He thanked her again and, when he was left alone, felt more disconcerted than ever, rather like a prisoner who, recovering his freedom after many long years, does not know what to do with it.

He could furnish them with proof now that he had not disposed of Gina and that he had not thrown her body into the canal. What surprised him most was what he had been told about the man she had gone off with, for he did not correspond to the type she usually chose.

Their affair had been going on for about six months and during the whole of that time she had not run away once.

Was she in love with him? And he, was he going to break up his household? Given her situation, why had Gina taken the stamps?

Mechanically he had put on his hat and was heading for the door, in order to go to the police station. This seemed to him to be the only logical thing to do. It could do no harm to Gina who, the moment the complaint was withdrawn, had nothing to answer the police for. He would not claim back his stamps. They had nothing against her lover either.

It was a curious sensation to find himself on the pavement once more, in the sun, which was even hotter than in the morning, and to pass Le Bouc's, telling himself that he would be going back there again.

For there was nothing to stop him going back. The people of the market would soon find out what had happened and instead of holding it against him, would be sorry for him. They would be a bit ashamed at first, for having deserted him so quickly, but it only needed a few days for everything to be once again as it had been in the past, and for them to call out cheerfully:

'Good-morning, Monsieur Jonas!'

Would Angèle be cross with him for not having kept a better watch on her daughter? Had she been able to do so herself, before Gina's marriage?

Only Frédo would not change his attitude, but there was a very small chance of Frédo becoming reconciled with the human race. He would sooner or later go off, God knows where, far away from the Vieux-Marché which he hated, and would be just as unhappy somewhere else.

He very nearly went into Fernand's there and then, as if it were all forgotten already, then he told himself that it was too soon, and set off up the Rue Haute.

He was convinced that Gina would come back, as she had always done before, only more marked this time, and that then she would need him.

Hadn't everything become easy? He would go into the police station, walk over to the black wooden counter dividing the first room in two.

'I want to speak to Superintendent Devaux, please.'

'What name?'

Unless it was the same sergeant as that morning, who would be sure to recognize him.

'Jonas Milk.'

For here they called him Milk. It hardly mattered, this time, if they kept him waiting. The superintendent would be surprised. His first thought would be that he had resolved to make a clean breast of everything.

'I know where my wife is,' Jonas would announce.

He would provide him with the name and address of the chambermaid and advise him not to go and see her at the hotel; he would also hand over the piece of paper with the address of the traveller in chemical goods.

'You can check up, but I must insist on their not being troubled. Madame Thierry may very well know nothing, and there's no point in telling her the truth.'

Would they understand him this time? Were they going to look on him again as a man from another planet? Or would they at last condescend to consider him as a human being, like other human beings?

The Rue Haute, at that hour, was almost deserted. In the Place de l'Hôtel de Ville the costermongers' carts had disappeared and a few pigeons were still foraging among the cobblestones.

He saw the bird-cages in the distance, opposite the police station, but he could not hear the cock crowing.

That morning in the superintendent's office he had fainted for the first time in his life and it had not been an unpleasant sensation; it had even seemed to him at one moment that his body no longer weighed anything, as if he were in the process of becoming disembodied. At the moment of losing consciousness he had thought of Doussia.

He was slowing his pace without realizing. He had only another twenty yards to cover and he could see distinctly the round eyes of the parrot on its perch. A policeman came out of the station and mounted a bicycle, possibly on his way to deliver a summons on coarse paper like the one he had received the day before.

Was it really the day before? It seemed such a long way off! Hadn't he lived since then, almost as much as during the rest of his existence?

He had stopped ten paces from the door with the blue lantern above it and, with his eyes wide open, stood staring at nothing. A boy of about fifteen who was running by collided with him, almost knocked him down, and he just caught hold of his glasses in time. What would have happened if they had broken on the pavement?

The bird-seller, wearing a dark grey smock like an ironmonger's, was watching him, wondering perhaps if he had been taken ill, and Jonas turned about, once again crossed the Square with the small cobblestones and went down the Rue Haute.

Pepito, who was sweeping out his restaurant with his door open, saw him pass. So did Le Bouc. There was only a little girl with very fair hair, who was playing dolls all by herself beneath the slate roofs of the Old Market, to watch him as he removed the handle from his door.

Chapter Nine

It was a dull grey day. A small lorry was parking, two of its wheels on the pavement, opposite the bookseller's shop. The baker's wife hadn't noticed that he had not appeared that morning to buy his three *croissants*. The boy who had taken a book on bees the week before and was bringing in his fifty francs, tried to open the door and looked inside without seeing anything.

At a quarter past ten, in Le Bouc's, Ancel remarked:

'Odd! Jonas hasn't been in this morning.'

He had added, but without malice:

'Little bastard!'

Le Bouc had said nothing.

It was only at eleven o'clock that, in Angèle's shop, a woman who had tried to go in the shop to buy a book had asked:

'Is your son-in-law ill?'

Angèle had retorted, leaning over a basket of spinach, with her great behind in the air:

'If he is, I hope he croaks!'

Which had not prevented her from asking:

'Why do you say that?'

'His shop's shut.'

'Can they have arrested him already?'

A little while later, when she was free of customers, she went to have a look for herself, pressed her face to the window, but everything appeared to be in order within the house except for Jonas' hat, which stood on a straw-bottomed chair.

'Have you seen Jonas, Mélanie?' she asked, on her way past the Chaignes'.

'Not this morning.'

When Louis came back, and parked his three-wheeler, she told him:

'It seems Jonas has been arrested.'

'So much the better.'

'The handle isn't in the door and I couldn't see anything going on inside.'

Louis went for a drink at Le Bouc's.

'They've arrested Jonas.'

Constable Benaiche was there, having a glass of white wine.

'Who?'

'The police, I presume.'

Benaiche frowned, shrugged his shoulders, said:

'Strange.'

Then he emptied his glass.

'I didn't hear anything up at the station.'

The only one to seem uneasy was Le Bouc. He said nothing, but after a few minutes' thought, he retired to the back room where there was a telephone on the wall by the lavatory door.

'Get me the police station, please.'

'The number's ringing now.'

'Police here.'

He recognized the sergeant's voice.

'That you, Jouve?'

'Who's that?'

'Le Bouc. I say, is it true that you've arrested Jonas?'

'The bookseller?'

'Yes.'

'I haven't heard anything about him this morning. But it doesn't concern me. Wait a second.'

His voice came back, a little while later:

'No one here knows anything about it. The superintendent's out to lunch, but Basquin, who's here, would have heard.'

'His door's closed.'

'So what?'

'I don't know. No one's seen him this morning.'

'I'd better put you on to the inspector. Hang on.'

Another pause, and it was Basquin's voice:

'Jouve tells me Jonas hasn't been seen today?'

'Yes. His shop's shut. There's nothing going on inside.'

'Do you think he would have gone?'

That was not what Fernand had in mind, but he preferred not to volunteer any opinion.

'I don't know. It seems odd to me. He's a queer chap.'

'I'll be right round.'

When he arrived ten minutes later, several people emerged from the bar and walked over to Jonas' shop.

The inspector knocked at the door, normally at first, then louder and louder, finally called out, looking up towards the open window on the first floor:

'Monsieur Jonas!'

Angèle, who had come up, had lost her habitual caustic wit. At Fernand's, Louis, who was gulping down two glasses of *grappa* one after the other, growled:

'I'll bet he's gone to earth in some corner, like a rat.'

He didn't believe it. He was blustering, uneasiness reflected in his red-rimmed eyes.

'Is there a locksmith nearby?' asked Basquin, who had tried shaking the door in vain.

'Old Deltour. He lives in . . .'

Madame Chaigne interrupted the woman who was speaking.

'It's not worth the trouble of forcing the door. You only have to get over the wall of the yard by climbing on a chair. Follow me, Inspector.'

She led him through her shop, then through the kitchen where a stew was simmering, as far as the yard, which was littered with barrels and crates.

'It's Jonas!' she called out as she passed her husband, who was hard of hearing.

Then:

'Look! A barrel will do even better than a chair.'

She remained standing, in her white apron, her hands on her hips, watching the inspector hoisting himself onto the wall.

'Can you get down the other side?'

He did not reply at once, for he had just found the little man from Archangel hanging from the branch which grew out over the yard. The kitchen door was open with, on the wax tablecloth, a cup containing the remains of some coffee, and a blackbird crossed the doorstep, coming from inside the house, and flew off to the top of the lime tree where it had its nest.

'Golden Gate'
Cannes
29 April 1956

Maigret and
the Minister

Maigret and the Minister
Translated from the French by Moura Budberg

Chapter One

Every evening when he came home Maigret stopped at the same spot on the pavement, just after the gas-lamp, and raised his eyes to the lighted windows of his flat. It was an automatic movement. Probably if he had been asked point-blank whether there was a light there or not he would have hesitated before replying. In the same way, almost as if it were a superstition with him, he began unbuttoning his coat between the second and third floors and searching for the key in the pocket of his trousers, though invariably the door opened as soon as he stepped on the doormat.

These were rites that had taken years to become established and on which he depended more than he would have cared to admit. It was not raining tonight, so it did not apply, but his wife, for instance, had a special way of taking his wet umbrella from his hand at the same time as she bent to kiss him on the cheek.

He brought out the traditional question:

'No telephone calls?'

She replied, closing the door:

'Yes, there was one. I'm afraid it's hardly worth while taking off your coat.'

The day had been grey, neither hot nor cold, with a sudden shower towards two o'clock in the afternoon. At the Quai des Orfèvres, Maigret had attended only to routine business.

'Did you have a good dinner?'

The light in their flat was warmer, more intimate than at the office. He could see the newspapers and his slippers waiting for him beside his armchair.

'I dined with the Chief, Lucas and Janvier at the Brasserie Dauphine.'

Afterwards the four of them had gone to a meeting of the Police Provident Fund of which, for three years running and much against his will, Maigret had been elected vice-president.

'You've got time for a cup of coffee. Take your coat off for a minute. I said you wouldn't be back before eleven.'

It was half past ten. The meeting had not lasted long. There had been time for some of them to have a half pint in a bar and Maigret had come home on the métro.

'Who was it that telephoned?'

'A minister.'

Standing in the middle of the sitting-room, he frowned at her.

'What Minister?'

'The Minister of Public Works. Point, I think he said.'

'That's right, Auguste Point. He telephoned here? In person?'

'Yes.'

'You didn't tell him to ring the Quai des Orfèvres?'

'He wanted to speak to you personally. He has to see you very urgently. When I said you weren't in, he wanted to know if I was the servant. He sounded upset. I told him I was Madame Maigret. He apologised, wanted to know where you were and when you would be back. He gave me the impression of being a timid man.'

'That's not his reputation.'

'He even wanted to know if I was alone or not. And then he explained that his call was to be kept secret, that he wasn't calling from the Ministry but from a public booth and that it was important for him to be in touch with you as quickly as possible.'

While she was speaking, Maigret watched her, still frowning, with a look that proclaimed his distrust of politics. It had happened several times in the course of his career that he had been approached by a statesman, a deputy or senator or some high official, but it had always been through the proper channels. He would be summoned to the Chief's office and the conversation would always begin: 'I'm sorry, my dear Maigret, to put you in charge of a business you won't like.'

And indeed they invariably turned out to be pretty unsavoury affairs.

He was not personally acquainted with Auguste Point; had never seen him in the flesh. He was not the kind of man to be often quoted in. the newspapers.

'Why didn't he ring up the Quai?'

He was really talking to himself. But Madame Maigret replied even so:

'How do I know? I'm only repeating what he said to me. First of all, that he was speaking from a public box . . .'

This detail had particularly impressed Madame Maigret to whom a Minister of the Republic was an individual of some importance, not to be imagined creeping in the dark into a public telephone box at the corner of some street.

'. . . Then he said that you were not to go to the Ministry, but to his private apartment which he keeps . . .'

She consulted a scrap of paper on which she had made some notes:

'. . . at 27 Boulevard Pasteur. You don't need to wake the concierge, it's on the fourth floor, on the left.'

'He's waiting there for me?'

'He'll wait as long as he can. He has to be back at the Ministry before midnight.'

Then, in a different tone, she asked:

'Do you think it's a hoax?'

He shook his head. It was certainly unusual, bizarre, but it didn't sound like a hoax.

'Will you have some coffee?'

'No thanks, not after the beer.'

Still standing, he poured himself a drop of sloe gin, took a fresh pipe from the mantelpiece and moved towards the door.

'See you soon.'

Back in the Boulevard Richard-Lenoir, the humidity that had hung in the air all day had changed to a dust-like fog that threw a halo round the street lamps. He did not take a taxi, for it was as quick to reach the Boulevard Pasteur by métro; besides, he did not feel he was on official business.

All the way, as he stared mechanically at the moustachioed gentleman reading the newspaper opposite him, he was wondering what it could possibly be that Auguste Point wanted of him and why he had arranged for them to meet so urgently and so mysteriously.

All he knew of Auguste Point was that he was a lawyer from the Vendée, as far as he could remember from La Roche-sur-Yon, and that he had come into politics late in life. He was one of those deputies elected after the war for their personal qualities and their conduct during the occupation.

What that conduct had been exactly Maigret did not know. Yet, while others of his colleagues had come and gone and left no trace behind them, Auguste Point had been re-elected time after time, and three months ago, when the last Cabinet was formed, he had been given the Public Works portfolio.

The superintendent had heard no scandal about him of the kind that circulate around most politicians. Nor was there any gossip about his wife or his children, if he had any.

By the time he left the métro at the Pasteur station, the fog had grown thick and yellow and Maigret could taste its dusty flavour on his lips. He saw no one in the boulevard; heard only some steps in the distance, towards Montparnasse, and in the same direction a train that whistled as it left the station.

A few windows were still lit and gave an impression of peace and security in the fog. These houses, neither rich nor poor, neither old nor new and divided into flats all very similar to one another, were inhabited mainly by people of the middle class, teachers, civil servants, employees who took the métro or the bus to work at the same time every morning.

He pressed the street button and, when the door opened, muttered an indistinct name at the concierge as he moved towards the lift. It was a very narrow lift, designed for two. Smoothly and noiselessly, it began its slow ascent past a dimly lit staircase. The doors on all floors were of an identical dark brown; even the doormats were alike.

He rang the bell on the left, and the door opened immediately as if someone had been waiting inside with a hand on the knob.

Auguste Point stepped outside and sent the lift down again; Maigret had not thought of doing that.

'I'm sorry to disturb you at such a late hour,' he murmured. 'Will you come in, please?'

Madame Maigret would have been disappointed, for he resembled as little as possible her idea of a Minister. He was about the same build and height as the superintendent, though squarer and tougher looking, one might say more of true peasant stock. His roughly chiselled features, the large nose and mouth, put one in mind of a bust carved out of horse-chestnut.

He wore a plain grey suit with a ready-made tie. Two things about him were striking–the bushy eyebrows, as wide and thick as a moustache, and the almost as long hairs that covered his hands.

He was studying Maigret, without attempting to conceal it, without even a polite smile.

'Sit down, Superintendent.'

The flat, smaller than the one in the Boulevard Richard-Lenoir, probably consisted of only two, perhaps three rooms and the tiniest of kitchens. They had moved from the hall, where some clothes were hanging, to the study that was typical of a bachelor's lodgings. A few pipes were standing in a rack on the wall, ten or twelve of them, some of clay, one a beauty of a meerschaum. An old-fashioned desk, like the one Maigret's father had had long ago, was covered with papers and tobacco ash; it had a set of pigeonholes and small drawers. He did not yet dare examine the photographs on the wall of Auguste Point's father and mother in the same black and gold frames which he might have found in any farm in the Vendée.

Sitting in his swivel chair, again so similar to that of Maigret's father, Auguste Point was playing with a box of cigars.

'I wonder would you care . . .' he began.

The superintendent murmured, smiling:

'I prefer my pipe.'

'Some of this?'

The Minister offered him an open packet of grey tobacco and lit his own pipe which he had allowed to go out.

'You must have been surprised, when your wife told you . . .'

He was trying to open the conversation but was not pleased with his attempt. Something curious was taking place.

They sat there in the warm, peaceful study, both of the same build and of about the same age, unashamedly studying one another. It was as if they had discovered the resemblance and were intrigued by it but were not quite ready yet to admit its existence.

'Look, Maigret, between men like us, there's no point in the usual formalities. I only know you from the newspapers and from what I've heard about you.'

'As with me, Your Excellency.'

With a slight gesture, Auguste Point gave Maigret to understand that at this moment the use of the title was inappropriate.

'I'm in terrible trouble. Nobody knows it yet, nobody even suspects it, neither the President of the Council nor even my wife and she normally knows my every movement. You're the only one I've turned to.'

For a moment he looked away and pulled at his pipe, as if embarrassed by what could be mistaken for vulgar calculated flattery.

'I didn't want to do the conventional thing and go straight to the police. What I'm doing is irregular. You were under no obligation to come here, just as you are under no obligation to help me.' He rose, sighing.

'Will you have a drink?'

And with what could be taken as a smile:

'Don't worry. I'm not trying to bribe you. It's just that tonight I really need something to drink.'

He went into the next room and came back with a half-finished bottle and two thick glasses of the kind used in country inns.

'It's only some home-made spirits that my father distills every autumn. This one is about twenty years old.'

They looked at each other, each holding a glass.

'Your health!'

'And yours, Your Excellency.'

This time Auguste Point seemed not to hear the last words.

'If I don't know how to begin, it isn't because I'm embarrassed, but because the story is difficult to tell with any degree of clarity. You read the newspapers?'

'I do, on the evenings when the world of crime allows me some peace.'

'You follow political events?'

'Not much.'

'You know that I'm not what is called a politician?'

Maigret nodded.

'Very well. You're probably aware of the Clairfond disaster?'

This time Maigret could not help giving a start and a certain anxiety, a certain caution must have shown in his expression, because the other man bent his head and added in a low voice:

'Unhappily this is what it's all about!'

A short time ago in the métro, Maigret had tried to puzzle out why the Minister had arranged to meet him in secret. The Clairfond affair had never entered his mind, though recently all the newspapers had been full of it.

The Sanatorium of Clairfond, in Haute Savoie, between Ugines and Mégève, at a height of more than fourteen hundred metres, was one of the most spectacular post-war achievements. It was some years ago now and Maigret had no idea whose was the original idea of establishing a home for abandoned children comparable to the modern privately owned sanatoria. At the time it had been much in the news. Some people had seen in it a purely political enterprise and there had been violent debates in the Chamber of Deputies. A commission had been selected to study the project and eventually, after much discussion, it had materialised.

A month later came the disaster, one of the most distressing in history. Snow had begun to melt at a time when it hadn't happened in human memory. The mountain streams had swelled, as did a subterranean river, the Lize, so unimportant, that it is not even marked on the map. It had undermined the foundations of a whole wing at Clairfond.

The inquest, opened on the day after the disaster, had not yet been completed. The experts could not come to an agreement. Neither could the newspapers which, according to their political persuasion, propounded different theories.

One hundred and twenty-eight children had died when one of the buildings collapsed; the others were urgently evacuated.

After a moment of silence Maigret murmured:

'You were not in the Cabinet at the time of the construction, were you?'

'No. I wasn't even a member of the parliamentary commission that allocated the funds. To tell you the truth, up to a day or so ago I only knew what everyone knows of the business from the newspapers.'

He paused.

'Have you heard anything about the Calame report, Superintendent?'

Maigret looked at him, in surprise, and shook his head.

'You will be hearing about it soon. I'm afraid you'll be hearing too much about it. I suppose you don't read the weekly papers, the *Rumeur*, for instance?'

'Never.'

'Do you know Henri Tabard?'

'By name and reputation only. My colleagues of the Rue des Saussaies would know him better than I do.'

He was referring to the Department of Security which came under the Ministry of the Interior, and was often asked to deal with cases connected in some way with politics.

Tabard was a carping journalist whose gossip-filled weekly had the reputation of a cheap blackmailing rag.

'Read this—it appeared six days after the disaster.'

It was short, and sinister.

'"Will someone one day decide under pressure of public opinion to reveal the contents of the Calame Report?" Is that all?' The superintendent was surprised.

'"Contrary to popular belief, it won't be because of foreign policy, nor because of events in North Africa that the present government will fall at the end of the spring, but because of the Calame report. Who is keeping back the Calame report?"'

There was an almost comic sound to the words and Maigret smiled as he asked:

'Who is Calame?'

But Auguste Point was not smiling. He was emptying his pipe into a large copper ashtray while he explained:

'He was a professor in the National School of Civil Engineering. He died two years ago of cancer, I believe. His name is not widely known, but it is famous in the world of engineering, and public works. Calame was called in as consultant for large undertakings in countries as different as Japan and South America and he was an indisputable authority on everything concerning the resistance of material, particularly concrete. He wrote a book, which neither you nor I have read, but which every architect knows, called *The Diseases of Concrete*.'

'Was Calame involved in the building of Clairfond?'

'Only indirectly. Let me tell you the story in a different way, more from my own standpoint. At the time of the disaster, as I told you, I knew nothing of the sanatorium, that was not in the newspapers. I couldn't even remember if I had voted for or against the project five years ago. I had to look up the records to find out that I had voted for it. Like you, I don't read the *Rumeur*. It was only after the second paragraph appeared that the President of the Council called me in and asked me:

'"You know the Calame report?"

'I replied candidly that I did not. He seemed surprised and I'm not sure that he didn't glance at me with a certain suspicion.'

'It should be among your archives,' he said to me.

'It was then that he told me the whole story. During the debate on the subject of Clairfond, five years ago, as the parliamentary commission was divided, one of the deputies, I don't know who, had suggested consulting the opinion of an engineer of unquestioned standing. He put forward the name of Professor Julien Calame, of the National School of Civil Engineering, and the latter spent some time studying the project, and even went to the site in Haute Savoie. He then made a report which normally should have been sent to the commission.'

Maigret began to understand.

'This report was an unfavourable one?'

'Wait a moment. When the President talked to me about it, he had already ordered a search in the archives of the Chamber of Deputies. The report should have been found in the files of the commission. It turned out that not only was it not there, but that part of the accounts had also disappeared. You see what it all means?'

'That there were people interested in keeping the report unpublished?'

'Read this.'

It was another paragraph from the *Rumeur*, again short, but no less menacing.

'Is M. Arthur Nicoud powerful enough to prevent the Calame report from seeing the light of day?'

Maigret knew that name as he knew hundreds of others. He had heard of the firm Nicoud and Sauvegrain because it was mentioned almost everywhere where there were public works, whether roads, bridges or locks.

'It was the firm Nicoud and Sauvegrain who built Clairfond.'

Maigret was beginning to regret that he had come. Though he felt drawn to Auguste Point, what he had heard made him as uneasy as when an unsavoury story was told in the presence of a woman.

He could not help wondering what part Auguste Point could have played in the tragedy that had cost the lives of one hundred and twenty-eight children. He was almost on the brink of asking straight out:

'And where do you come into all this?'

He could imagine that some people had taken bribes, politicians, perhaps persons in high office.

'I'll try to finish quickly. The President asked me to have a thorough search made in the archives of my Ministry. The National School of Civil Engineering comes under the Ministry of Public Works, so that, logically, we should have had somewhere in our files, at least a copy of the Calame report.

The words 'Calame report' recurred.

'You found nothing?'

'Nothing. We searched through tons of dusty paper in the attic and we found nothing.'

Maigret was beginning to feel restless, uneasy in his chair and the other man noticed it.

'You don't like politics?'

'I confess I don't.'

'Neither do I. Strange as it may seem it was to fight against politics that twelve years ago I agreed to stand at the election. And when, three months ago, I was asked to join the Cabinet, it was again with the idea of bringing a little cleanliness into public affairs that I allowed myself to be persuaded. My wife and I are simple people. You can see the sort of flat we occupy in Paris, during the parliamentary sessions, since I became a deputy. It is more like a bachelor's rooms. My wife could have remained in La Roche-sur-Yon where we have a house, but we are not in the habit of living apart.'

He was speaking quite naturally, without any hint of sentimentality in his voice.

'Since I have been a Minister, we live officially in the Ministry, Boulevard Saint-Germain, but we come to seek refuge here as often as we can, particularly on Sundays. But all that's beside the point. If I rang you from a public box, as your wife no doubt told you—for if I'm not mistaken you have the same kind of wife as I have—if I did that, it's because I'm suspicious of being overheard. I'm convinced, rightly or wrongly, that all my calls from the Ministry, maybe even from here are recorded somewhere, I prefer not to know where. I might add, to my shame, that this evening I walked in one door of a cinema on the boulevard and out of the other and twice changed taxis. I can't even be sure this house is not being watched.'

'I saw no one as I arrived.'

Maigret was feeling a sort of compassion for Auguste Point. Up to now Point had tried to talk in a detached fashion. But when he came to the essential point of their meeting, he became evasive and went round in circles, as though he feared that Maigret would get a wrong impression of him.

'The Ministry's archives have been turned upside down and God alone knows how many papers there are there which no human being can remember. During this time, I had telephone calls from the President at least twice a day and I'm not at all sure that he trusts me. Searches have been made also in the School of Civil Engineering without any result until yesterday morning.'

Maigret couldn't help asking, as one does at the end of a novel:

'The Calame report has been found?'

'Something, anyway, that appears to be the Calame report.'

'Where?'

'In the attic of the school.'

'A professor?'

'A supervisor. Yesterday morning I was given a note from a certain Piquemal, of whom I'd never heard. On it someone had written in pencil: "With reference to the Calame report". I asked him in at once. I took care to send my secretary, Mlle Blanche, from the room, though I've had her with me for twenty years as she comes from La Roche-sur-Yon and worked in my chambers there. You'll see that this is important. My parliamentary private secretary was not in the room either. I was left alone with a man of middle age who stood staring at me, saying nothing, with a grey paper parcel under his arm.

'"M. Piquemal?" I asked, a little anxiously, since for a moment, I thought that I was facing a maniac.

'He nodded.

'"Sit down."

'"It's not worth while."

'I had the impression that his eyes weren't friendly. He asked me, almost impertinently:

'"Are you the Minister?"

'"Yes."

'"I'm a supervisor at the School of Civil Engineering."

'He stepped forward, handed me the parcel and uttered in the same tone:

'"Open it and give me a receipt."

'The parcel contained a document of about forty pages, obviously a carbon copy:

'"Report concerning the construction of a sanatorium at Clairfond in Haute Savoie." The document was not signed by hand but the name of Julien Calame with his qualifications, was typed on the last page, as well as the date.

'Still standing, Piquemal repeated:

'"I want a receipt."

'I wrote one out for him. He folded it, slipped it into a worn brief-case and moved to the door. I called him back.

'"Where did you find these papers?"

'"In the attic."

'"You will probably be called upon to make a written declaration."

'"You know where to find me."

'"Have you shown this document to anyone?"

'He looked me straight in the eye, contemptuously.

'"No one."

'"Were there no other copies?"

'"Not so far as I know."

'"Thank you."'

Auguste Point looked at Maigret in embarrassment.

'That's where I made a mistake,' he went on. 'I think it was because of Piquemal's bizarre behaviour, for he looked like an anarchist about to throw his bomb.'

'How old was he?' asked Maigret.

'Forty-five perhaps. Neither smartly nor badly dressed. His eyes were the eyes of a fanatic or a madman.'

'Did you gather any information about him?'

'Not straight away. It was five o'clock. There were still four or five people in my waiting-room and I had to preside at an engineers' dinner in the evening. When my visitor left, my secretary came in and I slipped the Calame report into my personal brief-case. I should have telephoned the President of the Council. If I didn't do so, I swear to you that it was again because I was wondering if Piquemal was mad. There was nothing to prove that the document wasn't a false one. Almost every day we are visited by some lunatic or other.'

'So are we.'

'In that case you can understand me. My appointments lasted until seven o'clock. I just had time to go to my flat and change.'

'Did you talk to your wife about it?'

'No. I took my brief-case with me. I told her I'd come to the Boulevard Pasteur after dinner. This kind of thing often happens. We come here together on Sunday for a little meal that she cooks up, and I also come here alone when I have something important to do and want peace and quiet.'

'Where was the banquet?'

'At the Palais d'Orsay.'

'You took your brief-case with you?'

'It remained locked in the care of my driver, whom I trust absolutely.'

'You came back here directly after?'

'About half past ten. Ministers have the privilege of not having to stay after the speeches.'

'You were in evening dress?'

'I took it off before I settled down at this desk.'

'You read the report?'

'Yes.'

'Did it seem authentic to you?'

The Minister nodded.

'It would cause an explosion if it were published?'

'Without any doubt.'

'Why?'

'Because Professor Calame practically prophesied the disaster. Though I'm in charge of Public Works I'm incapable of giving you chapter and verse of all his arguments and particularly of the technical details he provides to support his opinion. At any rate, he quite clearly pronounced himself against the entire project and said it was the duty of every person who read the report to vote against the construction of Clairfond as it was planned or at least to demand a further enquiry. Do you understand?'

'I begin to.'

'How the *Rumeur* got wind of this document I don't know. Have they got another copy? Again I don't know. As far as one can judge the only person in possession of a copy of the Calame report last night was myself.'

'What happened then?'

'Towards midnight, I telephoned the President of the Council, but I was told that he was at a political meeting in Rouen. I almost called him there.'

'You didn't do so?'

'No. Because I was afraid of the lines being tapped. I felt that I was in possession of a case of dynamite which might not only overthrow the government, but also ruin the reputations of a number of my colleagues. It is unbelievable that those who had read the report should have been capable of allowing . . .'

Maigret thought he could guess the rest.

'You left the report here in this flat?'

'Yes.'

'In your desk?'

'Yes, it has a lock. I considered that it was safer here than in the Ministry where there are people coming and going all the time.'

'Your driver remained at the door all the time while you studied the file?'

'I sent him away and took a taxi at the corner of the boulevard.'

'Did you talk to your wife when you got home?'

'Not about the report. I didn't mention it to anybody until the next day, at one o'clock in the afternoon, when I met the President in the Chamber of Deputies. I put him in the picture; we were standing by the window.'

'Was he upset?'

'I think so. Any head of government would have been upset in his place. He asked me to fetch the report and to bring it personally to his study.'

'The report was no longer in your desk?'

'No.'

'And the lock had been tampered with?'

'I don't think so.'

'Did you see the President again?'

'No. I felt quite ill. I drove to the Boulevard Saint-Germain and cancelled all my appointments. My wife telephoned to the President and said that I was unwell, that I had collapsed and would go and see him tomorrow morning.'

'Does your wife know?'

'For the first time in my life I lied to her. I can't remember what I said to her exactly and several times I must have broken off.'

'Does she know you are here?'

'She believes I am at a meeting. I wonder if you quite understand my situation: I find myself suddenly alone, with the feeling that as soon as I open my mouth, I'll be attacked. Nobody would believe my story. I held the Calame report in my hands. I am the only one, beside Piquemal, to have had it. *And at least three times in the course of the last years I have been invited by*

Arthur Nicoud, the builder in question, to his place in Samois.'

Suddenly he slumped. His shoulders seemed narrower, his chin softer. He seemed to be saying:

'Do whatever you like. I have nothing more to say.'

Maigret, without asking permission, poured himself some spirits and only after drinking himself remembered to fill the Minister's glass.

Chapter Two

Probably, at some stage in his own career, Maigret had had a similar experience, but never, he thought, of such intensity. The smallness of the room, its warmth and intimacy, heightened the atmosphere of drama which the smell of the rustic alcohol, the desk like his father's, the enlarged photographs of the old people on the walls made Maigret feel like a doctor who has been summoned with great urgency and into whose hands the patient has placed his life.

The most surprising thing of all was that the man who was sitting opposite him, as if waiting for the diagnosis, resembled him if not exactly like a brother, certainly like a cousin. And not only physically. A glance at the family portraits told the superintendent that his and Auguste Point's origins were very close. Both were born in the country of enlightened peasant stock. Probably the Minister's parents had had the ambition ever since he was born for him to become a doctor or a lawyer, just as Maigret's had done.

Auguste Point had gone beyond their wildest dreams. Were they still alive to know it?

He didn't dare to ask these questions yet. The man opposite him had gone to pieces and he knew it wasn't because of weakness of character. Looking at him, Maigret was overcome by a complex mixture of emotions; he was angry and disgusted and profoundly discouraged. There had been a time in his own life when he had found himself in a similar situation, though less dramatic one, and that, too, had had a political background. He wasn't to blame. He had acted as it was his duty to act, had behaved, not only as an honest man, but strictly according to his obligations as an official. Nevertheless, in the eyes of almost everyone he had done wrong. He had had to go before a disciplinary council and as everything was against him, had been blamed. It was at this time that he had momentarily left the P.J.* and become an exile in the Mobile Brigade of Luçon, in the Vendée, the very department that Auguste Point represented in the Chamber of Deputies. His wife and his friends had told him over and over again that his own conscience was what mattered but often he seemed to behave, without realising it, like a guilty man. On those last days at the P.J. for instance, while his case was being discussed in high places, he didn't dare to give any orders to his subordinates, not even to Lucas or to Janvier and when he came down the main staircase, he had kept close to the wall.

---

* Police Judiciaire, something equivalent to the C.I.D., with a seat in the Quai des Orfèvres, whereas Security Police has its seat in the Rue des Saussaies.

Auguste Point too was no longer capable of thinking with any lucidity about his own case. He had just said all that he had to say. During the last hours he had acted as a man who is drowning and who only hopes for a miracle to save him. Wasn't it strange that he had appealed to Maigret, a man whom he did not know, whom he had never seen?

Without realising it, Maigret had taken on the case and his questions were those of the doctor who tries to establish a diagnosis.

'Have you enquired into the identity of Piquemal?'

'I asked my secretary to telephone the School of Civil Engineering and she was told that Jules Piquemal had been working there for fifteen years as a supervisor.'

'Isn't it peculiar that he didn't hand the document to the School Director but brought it to you himself?'

'I don't know. I didn't think about it.'

'It seems to indicate that he realised its importance, doesn't it?'

'I think so. Yes.'

'In fact, since the Calame report has been rediscovered, Piquemal is the only person, besides yourself, who has had the opportunity of reading it?'

'Not counting the people or person in whose hands it is now.'

'We can leave that at the moment. If I'm not mistaken, only one person, beside Piquemal, has known since Tuesday at one o'clock, that you were in possession of the document?'

'You mean the President of the Council?'

Auguste Point looked at Maigret in dismay. The present head of the government, Oscar Malterre, was a man of sixty-five who, since he was forty, had in one capacity or another, been a member of successive Cabinets. His father had been a mayor, one of his brothers was a deputy and the other a Colonial governor.

'I hope that you are not suggesting . . .'

'I suggest nothing, Your Excellency. I'm trying to understand. The Calame report was in this desk last night. This afternoon, it was no longer there. Are you certain that the door hadn't been forced?'

'You can see for yourself. There is no mark on the wood or on the metal of the keyhole. Could they have used a master key?'

'And the lock of your desk?'

'Have a look. It is not a complicated one. I have often forgotten my key and opened it with a piece of wire.'

'Excuse me, if I ask you all the usual routine questions, just to clear the air. Who besides yourself has the key to the flat?'

'My wife, of course.'

'You told me that she knows nothing of the Calame affair.'

'I didn't talk to her about it. She doesn't even know that I've been here yesterday and today.'

'Does she follow politics at all closely?'

'She reads the papers, keeps enough in touch to enable us to talk together about my work. When it was suggested that I should put myself forward as a deputy, she tried to dissuade me. She didn't want me to become a Cabinet Minister, either. She has no ambition.'

'Does she come from La Roche-sur-Yon?'

'Her father was a solicitor there.'

'Let's come back to the keys. Who else has them?'

'My secretary, Mlle Blanche.'

'Blanche, who?'

Maigret was making notes in his black note-book.

'Blanche Lamotte. She must be . . . wait a moment . . . forty-one . . . no, forty-two years old.'

'You have known her for a long time?'

'She started to work for me as a typist when she was barely seventeen, just out of the Pigier school. She has been with me ever since.'

'Also from La Roche?'

'From a neighbouring village. Her father was a butcher.'

'Pretty?'

Auguste Point seemed to ponder over this as though he had never asked himself the question.

'No. I don't think you could say that.'

'In love with you?'

Maigret smiled to see the Minister blush.

'How did you know that? Let us say that she's in love in her own way. I don't think there's been a man in her life.'

'Jealous of your wife?'

'Not in the usual sense of the word. You might say she's possessive of what she considers to be her field.'

'That means that in the office it is she who is the boss.'

Auguste Point, who was no child, seemed surprised at Maigret discovering such a simple truth.

'She was in your office, you told me, when Piquemal was announced, and you asked her to leave the room. When you called her back, did you still have the report in your hand?'

'I think so . . . But I can assure you . . .'

'Your Excellency, please try to understand, I'm blaming nobody, suspecting nobody. Like yourself, I'm trying to find my way. Has anyone else got keys to the flat?'

'My daughter has one.'

'What age is she?'

'Anne-Marie? Twenty-four.'

'Married?'

'Well, she was going to get married next month. With all this storm ahead, I simply don't know. Do you know the Courmont family?'

'Only by name.'

If the Malterres were famous in politics, the Courmonts were equally so in diplomacy and had been, for at least three generations. Robert Courmont who had a house in the Rue de la Faisanderie and was one of the last Frenchmen to wear a monocle, had been an ambassador for more than thirty years, in Tokyo and in London, and was a member of the Institute.

'His son?'

'Yes, Alain Courmont. He's thirty-two years old and he has already been attached to three or four embassies and now he's head of an important department in the Foreign Office. He has been appointed to Buenos Aires; he was to go there three weeks after his marriage. So you can see that the situation is even more tragic than it seems at first glance. A scandal of these dimensions . . . awaiting me at any moment . . .'

'Did your daughter often come here?'

'Not since we took up residence in the Ministry.'

'You mean she's never been here since then?'

'I would prefer to tell you everything, Superintendent. If I don't, it would be pointless to have turned to you. Anne-Marie has graduated in philosophy and literature. She's not a blue stocking, but neither is she like the usual run of young girls today. One day, about a month ago, I found some cigarette ash here. Mlle Blanche doesn't smoke, neither does my wife. I asked Anne-Marie and she admitted that occasionally she came to the flat with Alain. I didn't try to find out any more. I remember what she said to me, without blushing, looking me straight in the eye: "One must be realistic, father. I'm twenty-four and Alain's thirty-two." Have you any children, Maigret?'

The superintendent shook his head.

'I suppose there was no cigarette ash anywhere today?'

'No.'

Now that he had only to answer questions Auguste Point was beginning to look less depressed, like a patient who answers a doctor, knowing that the doctor will provide him with some relief in the end. Could Maigret be lingering on this question of the keys on purpose?

'Nobody else?'

'My parliamentary private secretary.'

'Who is he?'

'Jacques Fleury.'

'You've known him for a long time?'

'I was at the Lycée with him, then at the University.'

'Also from the Vendée?'

'No, he comes from Niort. It isn't far away. He's about my age.'

'Lawyer?'

'He never read for the bar.'

'Why?'

'He's an odd character. His parents were rich. When he was young, he never wanted regular work. He had a passion for something new every six months. For example, once he took it into his head to run a fishery and he had a few boats. He was also involved in some colonial enterprise that failed. I lost sight of him. When I was elected as deputy, I used to see him now and then in Paris.'

'Ruined?'

'Completely. He always kept up appearances. He never ceased to do so, nor to be extremely amiable. He is the typical amiable failure.'

'Did he ever ask you any favours?'

'I suppose so but nothing important. A short time before I became Cabinet Minister, it just happened that I bumped into him more often and when I found myself in need of a private secretary he was there, at my disposal.'

Auguste Point frowned.

'Since we are on the subject, there is something I'd better explain. You probably cannot imagine what it is like to become a Cabinet Minister from one moment to the next. Take my case. I'm a lawyer, a small provincial lawyer, of course, but this doesn't minimise my knowledge of the Law. Then I was appointed Minister of Public Works. I became, overnight and without any apprenticeship, the head of a Ministry, that was full of competent executives, even such illustrious men as Calame. I did what the others do. I

assumed an air of confidence. I behaved as if I knew it all. This didn't stop
me feeling a certain irony and hostility around me and I was also conscious of
a number of intrigues of which I understood nothing. Even at the head of the
Ministry, I'm an outsider, for even there, I'm among people who are aware
and have been aware for a long time of what goes on behind the scenes. To
have beside me a man like Fleury, with whom I can relax . . .'

'I can understand. When you chose him as your assistant, was he already
in touch with the political world?'

'Only through casual encounters in bars and restaurants.'

'Married?'

'He has been married. He must still be, for I don't think he ever divorced
and he had two children by his wife. They don't live together any longer. He
has at least one other entanglement in Paris, maybe two, for he has the gift of
complicating his existence.'

'You're sure he didn't know you were in possession of the Calame report?'

'He didn't even see Piquemal in the Ministry. I didn't mention anything
to him.'

'What is the relationship between Fleury and Mlle Blanche?'

'Outwardly cordial. Deep in her heart, Mlle Blanche cannot stand him,
because she is a bourgeoise through and through and Fleury's sentimental
life exasperates and upsets her . . . You see—we are getting nowhere.'

'You are quite certain that your wife doesn't suspect that you are here?'

'She noticed, this evening, that I was worried. She wanted to profit from
the fact that for once I had no important engagement in the evening and put
me to bed. I talked to her about a meeting . . .'

'Did she believe you?'

'I don't know.'

'Are you in the habit of lying to her?'

'No.'

It was almost midnight. This time it was the Minister who filled the little
stemless glasses and moved, sighing, to the rack to choose a curved pipe with
a silver ring.

As if confirming Maigret's intuition, the telephone rang. Auguste Point
glanced at the superintendent, wondering if he should answer.

'It's probably your wife. When you get home, you'll be forced to tell her
the whole story.'

The Minister lifted the receiver.

'Hallo! Yes, it's me.'

He looked guilty.

'No. I've got someone with me . . . We had to discuss a very important
matter . . . I'll tell you all about it when I see you. I don't know . . . It won't be
very long . . . Very well . . . I assure you I'm perfectly well . . . What? . . . From
the President? . . . He wants me to what? . . . Very well . . . Yes, I'll do it
straight away . . . see you soon.'

With beads of sweat on his forehead he turned again to Maigret like a man
who does not know to which saint to pray.

'The President's house has rung three times . . . The President has asked
me to ring him at any time . . .'

He wiped his brow. He even forgot to light his pipe.

'What do I do now?'

'I suggest you telephone him. In any case you'll have to admit to him tomorrow morning that you no longer have the report. And there's not a chance that we lay our hands on it overnight.'

Point's next remark was almost comical, it showed his confusion and the instinctive confidence some people have in the power of the police. For he said, almost mechanically:

'You think so?'

Then, sinking heavily into his chair, he dialled a number that he knew by heart.

'Hallo! This is the Minister of Public Works. I'd like to speak to the President . . . Forgive me, Madame . . . It's Auguste Point speaking . . . I believe your husband is expecting . . . Yes . . . I'll wait . . .'

He gulped down his glass of spirits, his eyes fixed on Maigret's waistcoat buttons.

'Yes, my dear President . . . Please forgive me for not calling you earlier . . . I'm better . . . Yes . . . It was nothing . . . Perhaps I was a little tired, yes . . . Also . . . I was going to tell you . . .'

Maigret could hear a voice at the other end of the line that was in no way reassuring. Auguste Point looked like a child who is being scolded and who tries vainly to justify himself.

'Yes, I know . . . Believe me . . .'

At last, he was allowed to speak and was searching for the right words.

'You see, something, well, something quite extraordinary has happened . . . I beg your pardon? . . . It's about the report, yes . . . I took it yesterday to my private flat . . . Yes, in the Boulevard Pasteur . . .'

If only he could have been allowed to tell the story as he wanted to tell it. But he was continually interrupted. He was becoming confused.

'Well, yes . . . I often come here to work when . . . I can't hear you. Yes, I'm here at the moment . . . No, no, my wife did not know I was here, or she would have passed on your message . . . No! I've no longer got the Calame report . . . This is what I've been trying to tell you all the time. I left it here, believing it would be much safer than in the Ministry and when I came to collect it this afternoon, after our conversation . . .'

Maigret turned his head away when he saw tears of humiliation or perhaps irritation drop from the heavy eyelids. 'I spent some time searching for it. No, certainly not, I didn't do that!'

With his hand on the receiver, he whispered to Maigret:

'He is asking whether I alerted the police . . .'

He was listening again—resigned, occasionally muttering a word or two.

'Yes, yes . . . I understand . . .'

His face was bathed in sweat and Maigret was tempted to go and open the window.

'You have my word, my dear President . . .'

The top light was not lit. The two men and the corner of the study were lit only by a lamp with a green shade which left the rest of the room in darkness. From time to time a taxi was heard hooting in the fog on the Boulevard Pasteur and more rarely a train whistled in the distance.

The father's photograph on the wall was that of a man in his middle sixties, taken probably about ten years earlier, judging by Auguste Point's age. The mother's photograph, on the other hand, was of a woman of barely thirty, wearing a dress and hair style dating back to the beginning of the century and Maigret surmised from this that Madame Point, like his own mother, had died when her son was quite small.

There were possibilities which he hadn't mentioned yet to the Minister and which he was beginning to turn over automatically in his mind. Because of the telephone call, of which he had been the accidental witness, he was thinking of Malterre, the President of the Council, who was also Minister of the Interior and, it followed, had the National Security Department in the palm of his hand.

What if Malterre had got wind of Piquemal's visit to the Boulevard Saint-Germain and had had Auguste Point followed . . . Or even if after his conversation with Point . . . Anything might be possible–he might have wanted to get hold of the document to destroy it at the same time keeping it as his trump card.

The journalistic slang in this case was to the point, the Calame report was a bomb which brought its possessor unbelievable power.

'Yes my dear President . . . Not the police, I swear to you . . .'

The other man was probably badgering him with questions that pushed him farther and farther out of his depth. His eyes called for Maigret's help, but there was no help forthcoming. He was already giving in . . .

'The person who is in my study is not here in the capacity of . . .'

After all, he was a strong man, both physically and morally. Maigret, too, knew his own strength and he, too, in the past, had given in when he had been caught in a much less powerful trap. What had crushed him–he remembered it and would remember it all his life–was the impression of being up against an anonymous force, without name or face, impossible to get hold of. And this force had been no ordinary force, it had been the Law.

Auguste Point was dropping the receiver.

'It's Superintendent Maigret . . . I asked him to come and see me privately, I'm certain that he . . .'

He was interrupted. The receiver seemed to vibrate.

'No trail, no. Nobody . . . No, my wife knows nothing, either . . . Nor my secretary. I swear to you, Your Excellency.'

He forgot about the traditional 'dear President' and became humble.

'Yes . . . At 9 a.m. . . . I promise. You want to speak to him? . . . One moment . . .' Humiliated, he glanced at Maigret.

'The President wishes to . . .'

The superintendent seized the instrument.

'I'm here, Your Excellency.'

'I hear that my colleague of Public Works has told you of the incident?'

'Yes, Your Excellency.'

'I needn't underline that the matter must remain rigorously secret. There is no question of holding a regular enquiry. Nor will National Security be informed.'

'I understand, Your Excellency.'

'It is obvious that if you, personally, without any official involvement, without appearing to be interested, should discover anything concerning the Calame report, you'll let me . . .'

He hesitated. He didn't want to be personally implicated.

'. . . You'll let my colleague Point know about it?'

'Yes, Your Excellency.'

'That's all.'

Maigret wanted to hand the receiver over to the Minister but the line had gone dead.

'I'm sorry, Maigret. He forced me to give your name. It's said that he was a famous assize lawyer before entering politics and I can well believe it . . . I apologise for putting you into such a position . . .'

'You're seeing him tomorrow morning?'

'At 9 a.m. He doesn't want the other members of the Cabinet to be informed. What distresses him most is whether Piquemal has talked, or will talk, as he is the only one, beside the three of us, who knows that the document has been discovered.'

'I'll try to find out what kind of a man he is.'

'Without disclosing your identity?'

'In all fairness I must warn you that I am bound to talk about it to my chief. I needn't go into any details, by which I mean I needn't mention the Calame report. But it is necessary that he should know that I'm working for you. If it only concerned myself I could tackle the business outside my work. But no doubt I shall need some of my colleagues . . .'

'Would they have to know everything?'

'They'll know nothing about the report, I promise you.'

'I was ready to offer him my resignation but he took the words out of my mouth. He said that he was not even in a position to dissociate me from the Cabinet because that might, if not reveal the truth, at least arouse suspicions in those who had followed the last political events. From now on I'm the black sheep and my colleagues . . .'

'Are you quite certain that the report you had in your hands was in fact a copy of the Calame report?'

Auguste Point raised his head in surprise.

'Do you suggest that it might not have been genuine?'

'I'm suggesting nothing. I am only considering all the hypotheses. If you are presented with the Calame report, genuine or not, and it disappears immediately afterwards, you are automatically discredited (and in fact so is the whole government) because you'll be accused of having suppressed it.'

'In that case, everyone will be talking about it tomorrow.'

'Not necessarily so soon. I would like to know where and in what circumstances it was found.'

'Do you think you can do that without anyone knowing?'

'I'll try. I presume, Your Excellency, that you have concealed nothing from me? If I go so far as to ask the question, it is because, in present circumstances, it is essential that . . .'

'I know. There is one detail that I haven't mentioned before. I spoke to you, at the beginning, of Arthur Nicoud. When I first met him, I don't remember at what dinner, I was a simple deputy and the idea never crossed my mind that I would find myself one day at the head of Public Works. I knew he was a member of the firm Nicoud and Sauvegrain, the contractors of the Avenue de la Republique. Arthur Nicoud doesn't live the life of a business man, but of a man of the world. Contrary to what one may think you couldn't call him a nouveau riche, nor is he a typical tycoon. He is well-educated. He knows how to live. He goes to the best restaurants in Paris, always surrounded by pretty women, mostly actresses or cinema stars.

'I believe that everybody of any importance in the world of letters, arts, politics has been invited at least once to his Sundays in Samois. I have met many of my colleagues from the Chamber, some press barons and scientists, people whose integrity I'd swear to. Nicoud himself, in his country mansion gives the impression of a man whose main concern is to offer his guests the finest food in an elegant background. My wife has never liked him. We have been there about half a dozen times, never alone, never on an intimate footing. On some Sundays there were about thirty of us lunching at little tables and then we forgathered in the library afterwards or round the swimming-pool.

'What I didn't tell you was that once, I think it was two years ago, yes, two years ago, at Christmas time my daughter received a tiny gold fountain pen with her initials on it, accompanied by Arthur Nicoud's card. I almost made her send the present back. I don't remember now to whom I spoke about it, to one of my colleagues, I think, and I was rather angry. He told me that Nicoud's gesture had no significance, that it was a mania of his, at the end of every year, to send little presents to the daughters or wives of his guests. That year it was fountain pens which he must have ordered by the dozen. Another year it had been compacts, always in gold, because apparently he has a passion for gold. My daughter kept the fountain pen. I believe she still uses it.

'If the story of the Calame report hits the headlines tomorrow and they print that Auguste Point's daughter had received and accepted . . .'

Maigret nodded slowly. He did not minimise the importance of such a detail.

'Nothing else? He never lent you money?'

Auguste Point blushed to the roots of his hair. Maigret could well understand why. It was not because he had something to reproach himself with, but because from now on, anyone might put the question to him.

'Never! I swear to you . . .'

'I believe you. You haven't any shares in the company?'

The Minister said no, with a bitter smile.

'I'll do everything I can, starting from tomorrow morning,' Maigret promised. 'You realise that I know less than you do and that I'm completely unfamiliar with the political world. I also doubt if we would be able to discover the report before the man who has it now makes use of it. You yourself—would you have suppressed it to save your colleagues if it compromised them?'

'Certainly not.'

'What if the head of your Party had asked you to?'

'Not even if the President of the Council himself had put it to me.'

'I was more or less certain that that is what you would say. I'm sorry to have asked the question. I'll be going now, Your Excellency.'

The two men rose and Auguste Point stretched out his large, hairy hand.

'I apologise for involving you in all this. I was so discouraged and confused.'

Now that his fate was in another man's hands, his heart was lighter. He spoke in his normal voice, switched on the top light and opened the door.

'You can't come to see me at the Ministry without arousing curiosity, because you're too well known. And you can't telephone because, as I told you before, I suspect my line is tapped. This flat is known to everybody. How are we going to keep in touch?'

'I will find some way of communicating with you as soon as it's necessary.

You can always telephone me in the evening from a public box as you did today and if I'm not there, leave a message with my wife.'

They both thought of the same thing, at the same moment, and could not help smiling. Standing by the door they looked so like conspirators!

'Good-night, Your Excellency.'

'Thank you, Maigret. Good-night.'

The superintendent did not bother to take the lift. He walked down the four flights, rang for the night door to be opened and found himself back in the street fog that had become thicker and colder. To find a taxi he had to walk to the Boulevard Montparnasse. He turned to the right, his pipe between his teeth, his hands in his pockets and after walking about sixty feet two large lights appeared in front of him and he could hear the engine of a car being started. The fog prevented him from judging the distance. For a moment, Maigret got the impression that the car was coming straight at him, but it only passed by, enveloping him for a few seconds in a yellow glow. He did not have time to raise his hand to hide his face. Besides, he felt sure it would have been useless. No doubt somebody was interested in the person who had paid such a long visit that evening to the Minister's flat, whose windows above, were still lit up.

With a shrug Maigret went on his way and met only a couple walking slowly, arm in arm, mouth to mouth, who just missed bumping into him.

Eventually he found a taxi. There was still a light in his flat on Boulevard Richard-Lenoir. He pulled out his key, as always, and as always his wife opened the door before he had time to find the lock. She was in her nightdress, and bare-footed; her eyes were swollen with sleep and she returned at once to the hollow she had made in the bed.

'What is the time?' she asked in a distant voice.

'Ten minutes past one.'

He smiled as he thought that in another, more sumptuous but anonymous flat another couple was going through the same motions. Auguste Point and his wife were not in their own home. It was not their own home, nor their own bed. They were strangers in the large official building they lived in which must have seemed to them full of traps.

'What did he want you for?'

'To tell the truth, I don't quite know.'

She was only half-awake and trying to come to her senses while he was undressing.

'You don't know why he wanted to see you?'

'I should say to seek my advice.'

He did not want to use the word consolation, which would have been more precise. It was funny. It seemed to him that if he were to utter the words 'Calame report' here, in the familiar, almost tangible intimacy of his own flat—he would have burst into laughter. At the Boulevard Pasteur half an hour ago, the words had been charged with meaning. A Cabinet Minister, with his back to the wall, had spoken them with something like awe. The President of the Council had talked of the Report as of a State matter of the utmost importance. It was a question of some thirty pages that had lain about for years apparently in an attic without anyone bothering about them until a school supervisor had discovered them perhaps by accident.

'What are you thinking about?'

'About a certain Piquemal.'

'Who is that?'

'I don't really know.'

It was true that he was thinking of Piquemal, or rather repeating the three syllables of his name and finding them comical.

'Sleep well.'

'You too. Oh, and please wake me at 7 a.m.'

'Why so early?'

'I have to telephone someone.'

Madame Maigret's hand was already on the switch to put out the light which was on her side of the bed.

Chapter Three

A hand gently touched his shoulder and a voice whispered in his ear:

'Maigret! It's seven o'clock.'

The smell of the coffee in the cup that his wife was handing to him rose to his nostrils. His senses and his brain were beginning to function rather in the same way as an orchestra when the musicians try out their instruments in the pit. As yet there was no co-ordination. Seven o'clock; therefore it was a different day from the others, for usually he got up at eight. Without raising his eyelids he discovered that the day was sunny, whereas the day before had been cloudy. Even before the idea of fog reminded him of the Boulevard Pasteur, he felt a bad taste in his mouth, which had not happened to him for a long time on waking up. He wondered if he was going to have a hangover and thought of the little stemless glasses and the rustic alcohol from the Minister's village.

Gloomy, he opened his eyes and sat up in bed, reassured to find he had no headache. He had not realised, last night, that they had both of them drunk a considerable amount.

'Tired?' his wife asked him.

'No. I'll be all right.'

His eyes swollen, he sipped his coffee, looking around and muttering in a voice still full of sleep.

'It's a fine day.'

'Yes. There's some hoar-frost.'

The sun had the acidity and freshness of a rustic white wine. Paris life was starting in the Boulevard Richard-Lenoir, with certain familiar noises.

'Must you go out so early?'

'No. But I have to telephone Chabot and after eight I risk not finding him at home. If it's market-day at Fontenay-Le-Comte, he may have been out since half past seven.'

Julien Chabot who had become magistrate at Fontenay-Le-Comte where he lived with his mother in the large house where he was born, had been one of his friends from his student days at Nantes and two years ago, coming back from a congress in Bordeaux, he had dropped in to see him. Old Madame Chabot attended the first Mass, at six in the morning, at seven the house was already humming with life, and at eight, Julien went out, not to the Palace of Justice, where he was by no means burdened with work, but to stroll in the streets of the town or along the Vendée.

'Please, may I have another cup?'

He drew the telephone to his side and dialled the operator. At the moment when the operator was repeating the number he suddenly thought that if one of his hypotheses of the night before were correct his telephone must already be tapped. This irritated him. He suddenly experienced once again the distaste that had overcome him when much against his will he had himself become involved in a political intrigue. And alongside this feeling came a sense of grievance against Auguste Point, whom he did not know from Adam, whom he had not previously met and who had found it necessary to appeal to Maigret to get him out of a mess.

'Madame Chabot? . . . Hallo! . . . Is it Madame Chabot speaking? . . . It's Maigret here . . . No! Maigret . . .'

She was somewhat deaf. He had to repeat his name five or six times and explain:

'Jules Maigret, in the Police . . .'

Then she exclaimed:

'You're in Fontenay?'

'No, I'm calling from Paris. Is your son there?'

She spoke too loud, too close to the instrument. He didn't hear what she was saying. More than a minute passed before he recognised his friend's voice.

'Julien?'

'Yes.'

'You can hear me?'

'As clearly as if you were speaking from the station. How are you?'

'Very well. Listen to me. I'm disturbing you because I need some information. Were you having your breakfast?'

'Yes. But it doesn't matter.'

'You know Auguste Point?'

'You mean the Cabinet Minister?'

'Yes.'

'I used to see him often when he was a lawyer at La Roche-sur-Yon.'

'What do you think of him?'

'He is a remarkable man.'

'Give me some details. Anything that comes into your mind.'

'His father, Evariste Point, owns a well-known hotel at Sainte-Hermine, Clemenceau's town; famous not for its rooms, but for its good cuisine. Real lovers of good food came from all over the place to eat there. He must be almost ninety. Several years ago he made over the business to his son-in-law and to his daughter, but he still keeps an eye on it. Auguste Point, his only son graduated at about the same time as we did, but at Poitiers, and then at Paris. Are you still there?'

'Yes.'

'Shall I go on? He was a prodigious worker, a swotter. He opened a solicitor's office, in Town Hall Square, at La Roche-sur-Yon. You know the town. He was there for years, mostly doing litigation work between farmers and landowners. He married the daughter of a solicitor, Arthur Beloin, who died two or three years ago and whose widow still lives at La Roche. I think, if there hadn't been a war, Auguste Point would have continued peacefully to practise as a solicitor in the Vendée and in Poitiers. During the years of occupation one heard very little about him; his life went on as if nothing unusual was happening. Everybody was surprised when a few weeks before they retreated, the Germans arrested him and took him to Niort, and then to somewhere in Alsace. They caught three or four other people at the same time, one of them a surgeon from Bressuires and it was then that we learnt that throughout the war, Auguste Point had hidden British agents and pilots escaped from German camps in the farm he owns near La Roche.

'He came back, thin and a sick man, a few days after the liberation. He did not try to push himself, or worm his way on to committees, nor did he march in any procession. You remember the chaos there was at the time. Politics got mixed up in it, too. Nobody could tell the saints from the sinners. And it was to him they finally turned when they were no longer certain of anything. He did some good work and always with no fuss, without getting a swollen head and we sent him to Paris as deputy. That's more or less the entire story. The Points have kept their house in the town. They live in Paris when the Chamber is in session, then come back as soon as possible and Auguste has retained many of his clients. I believe that his wife helps him a lot. They have a daughter.'

'I know.'

'Well, then you know as much as I do.'

'Do you know his secretary?'

'Mlle Blanche? I often saw her in his office. We call her the Dragon because of the ferocity with which she protects her employer.'

'Nothing more about her?'

'I presume she's in love with him, in the manner of ageing spinsters.'

'She worked for him before she was an ageing spinster.'

'I know. But that's another matter and I can't help you there. What's up?'

'Nothing yet. Do you know a man called Jacques Fleury?'

'Slightly. I met him two or three times but it must be twenty years ago, at least. He must be living in Paris. I don't know what he is doing.'

'Thank you and forgive me again for taking you away from your breakfast.'

'My mother's keeping it warm.'

Not knowing what more to say, Maigret added: 'Is the weather fine, with you?'

'There's some sun, but there's frost on the roofs.'

'It's cold here, too. See you soon, old chap. Give my regards to your mother.'

For Julien Chabot, this telephone call was an event and he was going to ponder over it on his stroll in the streets of the town, wondering why Maigret was so interested in the comings and goings of the Minister of Public Works.

The superintendent's breakfast was accompanied by a lingering after-taste of alcohol and when he went out, he decided to walk, and stopped at a bar in the Place de la République in order to clean out his stomach with a glass of white wine.

He bought all the morning papers, which he was not in the habit of doing, and arrived at the Quai des Orfèvres just in time for the daily report. While his colleagues were gathered in the boss's office, he said nothing, did not really listen, but idly contemplated the Seine and the passers-by on the Pont

Saint Michel. He alone remained behind when the others left. The boss knew what that meant.

'What is it, Maigret?'

'Trouble.'

'In the Department?'

'No. Paris has never been so calm as it's been these last five days. But last night, I was summoned in person by a Cabinet Minister and he's asked me to take on an affair I don't like. There was nothing I could do but accept. I warned him I would talk to you about it, but without giving you any details.'

The Director of the P.J. frowned.

'It stinks?'

'Yes, very much so.'

'Connected with the Clairfond disaster?'

'Yes.'

'And a Cabinet Minister has personally entrusted you . . .'

'The President of the Council has been informed.'

'I don't want to know any more. Get on with it, old chap, if you have to. Be careful.'

'I'll try to.'

'Do you need any men?'

'Yes, definitely, three or four. They won't know precisely what it is about.'

'Why didn't he get in touch with Security?'

'You don't understand?'

'I do. That's why I'm not happy about you. Well . . .'

Maigret went to his office and opened the door leading into the inspectors' room.

'Will you come in for a moment, Janvier?'

Then seeing Lapointe on the point of leaving the room:

'Have you got anything important on?'

'No, sir. Just routine jobs.'

'Pass them on to someone else and wait for me. You, too, Lucas.'

Back in his office with Janvier, he closed the door.

'I'm going to give you a hell of a difficult assignment, old boy. There won't be any written report to edit, nor any account to give to any one but myself. If you make a blunder it may cost you quite a bit.'

Janvier smiled, pleased to be put in charge of a delicate matter.

'The Minister of Public Works has a secretary called Blanche Lamotte, aged about forty-three.'

He had pulled his black note-book out of his pocket.

'I don't know where she lives or what her working hours are. I want to know all about her, the kind of life she leads outside the Ministry and the people she meets. Neither she, nor anyone else, must suspect that the P.J. is interested in her. Perhaps if you watch the staff leaving the building, at noon, you'll be able to discover where she lunches. See what you can do. If she notices you're taking an interest, you'll have to play up to her, if necessary.'

Janvier, who was married and had just had his fourth child, pulled a face.

'Very well, sir. I'll do my best. There's nothing specific that you want me to find out?'

'I want everything you can find and then I'll see what I can make use of.'

'Is it urgent?'

'Very urgent. You won't mention it to anyone, not even to Lapointe or Lucas. Understood?'

He went to the communicating door and opened it again.

'Lapointe! Come here.'

Little Lapointe, as everyone called him because he was the last to join the staff and looked more like a student than a policeman, had already gathered that this was to be a confidential mission and was clearly excited about it.

'You know the School of Civil Engineering?'

'Yes, Rue des Saints-Pères. I used to lunch in a small restaurant almost opposite for a long time.'

'Very well. There is a supervisor there, called Piquemal. His first name is Jules, like mine. I don't know whether he lives in the school or not. I know nothing about him, and I want to know as much as possible.'

He repeated more or less the same as he had said to Janvier.

'For some reason, from the description I've had of him, he gives me the impression of being unmarried. Perhaps he lives in a small hotel. In that case, take a room in the hotel and pretend you're a student.'

Then it was Lucas' turn and there were similar instructions, except that Lucas was assigned to Jacques Fleury, the Minister's parliamentary secretary.

The three inspectors rarely had their photographs in the paper. The general public did not know them, or more precisely, of the three, it knew Lucas and him only by name.

Of course if National Security had had a hand in the business, they would be immediately recognised but that was inevitable. Besides, in that case, as Maigret had already decided that morning, his telephone conversations, whether from his home or from the Quai des Orfèvres, were being listened to by the Rue des Saussaies.

Somebody, the night before, had deliberately shone their lights on him, as much as was possible in such a fog, and if this someone knew Auguste Point's refuge, knew that he was there that night and had a visitor, he was also bound to be able to recognise Maigret at first sight.

Alone in his office he opened the window as if being involved in this business had given him a longing for a breath of fresh air. The papers were on the table. He was on the point of looking at them, then decided to deal first with current affairs, sign reports and summonses.

This almost made him feel a tenderness for the petty thieves, the maniacs, the swindlers, the felons of every variety with whom he usually had to deal.

He made several calls, went back to the inspectors' room to give instructions which had no connection with Point or the wretched Calame report.

By now, Auguste Point must have already gone to the President. Had he told his wife the whole story before he went, as the superintendent had advised him to do?

It was cooler than he had expected and he had to shut the window. He installed himself in his chair and opened the first newspaper in the pile. They were all still full of the Clairfond disaster and all, whatever party they belonged to, were forced, because of public opinion, to clamour for an enquiry.

The majority blamed Arthur Nicoud. One of the articles had the title:

'THE MONOPOLY NICOUD-SAUVEGRAIN.'

It published the list of works entrusted to the firm in the Avenue de la République over recent years by the government and by certain municipalities. The cost of the works was given in columns on the opposite page and the total reached several billions.

Then in conclusion:

'It would be interesting to establish the list of officials, ministers, deputies, senators, municipal counsellors of the city of Paris and others who have been Arthur Nicoud's guests in his luxurious property in Samois.'

'Perhaps a careful study of the counterfoils of M. Nicoud's cheque book would be revealing.'

One paper, the *Globe*, of which the deputy Mascoulin was, if not the owner, certainly the inspiration, had a headline in the style of Zola's famous 'J'accuse'.

'IS IT TRUE THAT . . . ?'

And a number of questions followed, in larger print than usual, in a lay-out that emphasised the text.

'Is it true that the idea of the Clairfond Sanatorium was not born in the minds of legislators desperately concerned with children's health, but in the mind of a dealer in concrete?

'Is it true that this idea had been introduced five years previously to a number of high-placed officials over luxurious lunches given by that dealer in concrete at his property in Samois?

'Is it true that not only did they find there excellent food and wine, but that the guests emerged from their host's private study with fat cheques in their pockets?

'Is it true that when the project took shape, all those who knew the site chosen for the miraculous sanatorium realised the folly and the danger of the enterprise?

'Is it true that the parliamentary commission entrusted with recommendations to the Chamber and presided over by the brother of the present President of the Council found itself obliged to appeal to the experienced opinion of an expert of untarnished reputation?

'Is it true that that specialist, Julien Calame, professor of applied mechanics and civil architecture at the National School of Civil Engineering went to spend three weeks on the spot with the plans . . . and that on his return he handed over to the proper quarter a report catastrophic for the supporters of the project . . . that nevertheless the funds were allocated and the construction of Clairfond started a few weeks later?

'Is it true that up to his death, two years ago, Julien Calame, according to all who saw him, gave the impression of a man with a load on his conscience?

'Is it true that in his report he foresaw the Clairfond disaster almost exactly as it happened?

'Is it true that the Calame report, which must have existed in a number of copies, has disappeared from the archives of the Chamber of Deputies as well as from those of several interested ministries?

'Is it true that at least thirty government employees have lived in terror since the disaster lest a copy of the report should be found?

'Is it true that in spite of all precautions, it has been found at a very recent date?

'. . . and that this resurrected copy has been handed over to the proper quarters.'

Then, in a further headline across the page:

'WE WANT TO KNOW'

'Is the Calame report still in the hands of the person to whom it was given? Or has it been destroyed to save the gang of compromised politicians? If it is not so—where is it at the moment of writing and why has it not yet been published, when public opinion justifiably demands the punishment of those guilty of a disaster that has cost the lives of one hundred and twenty-eight young Frenchmen?'

And at the end of the page, in the same print as the two preceding titles:

'WHERE IS THE CALAME REPORT?'

Maigret found himself wiping his forehead. It was not difficult to imagine Auguste Point's reaction on reading the article.

The *Globe* did not have a large circulation. It was an independent paper. Nor did it represent any of the big parties; only a small fraction, of which Joseph Mascoulin was the leader.

But the other papers would certainly set in motion their own independent enquiries, to discover the truth. And this truth Maigret, too, wished to discover, provided it was discovered in its entirety.

He had, however, the impression that it was not what they were searching for. If Mascoulin, for instance, was the man in whose hands the report was at the moment, why did he not publish it in letters as large as his article? He would have immediately provoked a ministerial crisis, a radical sweep of the parliamentarian ranks and he would have appeared to the public as the defender of the people's interests and of political morality.

For a man who had always worked in the background this was a unique opportunity to achieve great prominence and probably play a tremendous part in the years to come. If he was in possession of the document, why did he not publish it?

It was Maigret's turn to put the questions.

If Mascoulin did not have it, how did he know that the report had been found?

How had he learnt that Piquemal had handed it over to an official person?

And why did he suspect that Auguste Point had not transmitted it higher up?

Maigret had no desire to penetrate or to have knowledge of the shady side of politics. But he did not have to know much about the intrigues that simmer behind the scenes to be aware:

1. That it was in a dubious if not blackmailing paper like the *Rumeur* owned by Hector Tabard that the Calame report had been mentioned three times after the Clairfond disaster.

2. That the discovery of this report had followed this publication in

rather strange circumstances.

3. That Piquemal, a simple supervisor at the National School of Engineering had gone direct to the Minister instead of following the old established rule, in this case, of approaching the director of the school.

4. That Joseph Mascoulin had become aware of this operation.

5. That he seemed equally aware of the disappearance of the report.

Were Mascoulin and Tabard playing the same game? Were they playing it together or each on his own account?

Maigret went to open the window again and stood for a long time looking at the Seine, smoking his pipe. Never had he had to deal with such a complicated case, with so little evidence at his disposal.

When the crime was a burglary or a murder he was at once on familiar ground. Here, on the contrary, it was a question of people whose names and reputations he knew only vaguely from the newspapers. He knew, for instance, that Mascoulin lunched every day at the same table in a restaurant in the Place de le Victoire called 'Filet de Sole' where a constant stream of people came to shake his hand and whisper him some information, Mascoulin was believed to know all there was to know about the private life of all the politicians. His interpellations were rare, his name appeared in the papers only on the eve of an important issue. Then one might read:

'The deputy Mascoulin foretells that the project will be adopted by three hundred and forty-two votes.'

Professionals took these prognostications as they would the Bible, for Mascoulin was rarely mistaken, and then never by more than two or three votes.

He did not take part in any commissions, did not preside over any committee, nevertheless he was more feared than the leader of a big party.

Maigret decided he would go at noon to the 'Filet de Sole' and lunch there, if only to see at closer quarters the man of whom he had only had a glimpse on official occasions.

Mascoulin was a bachelor, though he was over forty. No mistresses were connected with his name. He was never seen at receptions, theatres or night clubs. He had a long, bony head and already at noon, he seemed to need a shave. He dressed badly, that is to say, he paid no attention to his clothes; they were never pressed and gave an impression of doubtful cleanliness.

Why was it that from the description that Auguste Point had given him of Piquemal, Maigret formed the opinion that this man was rather of the same type?

He suspected solitary men, people without an acknowledged passion.

Finally he decided against lunching at the 'Filet de Sole', because that would have seemed a declaration of war, and instead made his way to the Brasserie Dauphine. He found there two colleagues with whom for an hour he succeeded in talking of things other than the Calame report.

One of the afternoon papers had taken up the theme of the *Globe* in a much more prudent manner, with veiled insinuations, demanding only the truth on the subject of the Calame report. One of the editors had tried to interview the President of the Council himself on the subject but did not succeed in approaching him. Auguste Point was not mentioned, for the building of the sanatorium was in fact the business of the Ministry of Public Health.

At three o'clock there was a knock on Maigret's door. He growled and immediately it was opened, and Lapointe came in, with a worried expression on his face.

'You've got news?'

'Nothing definite, sir. Up to now, everything has been a matter of chance.'

'Give me all the details.'

'I tried to follow your instructions. You'll tell me if I made mistakes. First I telephoned the National School of Civil Engineering pretending that I was a cousin of Piquemal's and that I had just arrived in Paris and wanted to see him but didn't have his address.'

'Did they give it to you?'

'Without the slightest hesitation. He lives at the Hotel du Berry, Rue Jacob. It's a modest hotel, with about thirty rooms and the owner herself does most of the cleaning, while her husband does the accounts. I went back home to fetch a suitcase and presented myself at the Rue Jacob as a student, as you suggested. I was lucky, there was a free room and I took it for a week. It was about half past ten when I came down and stopped at the office to have a chat with the proprietor.'

'Did you mention Piquemal?'

'Yes, I told him that I had seen him in the holidays and remembered that he lived here.'

'What did he tell you?'

'That he was out. He leaves the hotel every morning at eight o'clock and goes to a small bar to have his coffee and croissants. He has to be in the school at half past eight.'

'Does he return to the hotel during the day?'

'No. He comes back regularly round about half past seven, goes to his room and goes out again only a couple of times a week. It seems he is the most regular man in the world, never entertains anyone, sees no women, doesn't smoke or drink and spends his evenings and sometimes part of the night reading.'

Maigret sensed that Lapointe had more to say and waited patiently.

'Perhaps I did wrong? But I thought I was doing the right thing. When I discovered that his room was on the same floor as mine and got the number, I thought you would like to know what was inside it. During the day the hotel is almost always empty. There was only someone playing the saxophone on the third floor, probably a musician practising, and I could hear the servant on the floor above me. I tried my key. They are simple keys, an old-fashioned type. It didn't work at first, but I fiddled about a bit and managed to open the door.'

'I hope Piquemal didn't happen to be at home?'

'No. If they search for my fingerprints they'll find them everywhere, because I didn't wear gloves. I opened the drawers, the cupboard, and an unlocked suitcase as well, hidden in a corner. Piquemal has only one extra suit, dark grey, and a pair of black shoes. His comb has got half its teeth missing and his toothbrush is ancient. He doesn't use cream to shave himself, only a brush. The proprietor is right when he says that he spends his evenings reading. There are books all over the place, particularly books on philosophy, political economy and history. Most of them have been bought second-hand on the quais. Three or four of them come from public libraries. I copied a few of the authors' names. Engels, Spinoza, Kirkegaard, St Augustin, Karl Marx, Father Sertillange, St Simon . . . Does it make any sense to you?'

'It does. Go on.'

'There was a cardboard box in one of the drawers containing membership cards, old and new, some from twenty years back, some only three. The oldest is the Association of the Cross of Fire. There is another one dated 1937, belonging to the Action Française. Immediately after the war, Piquemal joined a branch of the Communist party. The card was renewed for three years.'

Lapointe was consulting his notes.

'He has also belonged to the International League of Theosophy, based in Switzerland. You've heard of it?'

'Yes.'

'I forgot to tell you two of the books were about Yoga and there was a practical text-book of Judo as well.'

Judging by all this Piquemal had tried all manner of philosophical and social theories. All extremist parties have men like him who march behind the banners staring fixedly ahead.

'That's all?'

'So far as his room is concerned, yes. No letters. When I came down, I asked the proprietor whether he ever got any mail and he replied that he'd never seen anything except prospectuses and circulars. I went to the bistro at the corner. Unfortunately, it was the aperitif hour. The counter was crowded. I had to wait for a long time and have two drinks before I could speak to the owner without appearing to be leading an enquiry, I told him the same story: that I came from the provinces and was anxious to see Piquemal.

'"The professor?" he asked.'

Which seemed to indicate that in certain circles Piquemal assumed the rank of a professor.

'"If you had come at eight o'clock . . . By now he must be busy teaching . . . I don't know where he lunches."

'"Did he come this morning?"

'"I saw him picking out his croissants, as usual. He always eats three. But today somebody I don't know, and who had arrived before him, came up to him and engaged him in conversation. Generally speaking Piquemal is not forthcoming. He must have too many things on his mind to waste his time in idle talk. He's polite, but cold—you know the kind—'Good morning. How much is that? Goodbye.' It doesn't bother me because I have other clients like him, people who work with their minds and I can imagine how it is with them. But what surprised me was to see M. Piquemal leave with the stranger and instead of going to the left, as he usually does, they turned right."'

'What was the other man like, did they describe him?'

'Not very well. A man about forty, looking like a minor official or a commercial traveller. He walked in without saying anything, a little before eight, went to the counter and ordered a coffee with milk. No beard or moustache. On the corpulent side.'

Maigret could not help thinking that this could be the description of some dozen inspectors from the Rue des Saussaies.

'That's all you know?'

'Yes. After lunch I rang up the National School of Civil Engineering again and asked for Piquemal. This time I didn't tell them who I was and they didn't ask me. But they replied that he hadn't been seen all day.'

'Is he on holiday?'

'No. He just didn't turn up. What is more astonishing is that he didn't telephone to say he would be absent. It's the first time it's ever happened. I went back to my room in the Hotel du Berry. Then I went and knocked at Piquemal's door. I opened it. There was nobody there. Nothing had been moved since my first visit. You've asked me for all the details. I went to the school, and pretended to be the friend from the provinces. I learnt where he lunches—about a hundred yards away, Rue des Saints-Pères, in a Norman restaurant. I went there. Piquemal hadn't lunched today. I saw his napkin with a numbered ring on it and a half-finished bottle of mineral water on his usual table. That's all, sir. Did I do anything wrong?'

What prompted him to ask the last question, in some anxiety, was that Maigret's forehead had a frown on it and his face was troubled. Was this affair going to end like the other political affair with which Maigret had had to deal and which had disgraced him at Luçon? That other time, too, it had all come about because of a certain rivalry between the Rue des Saussaies and the Quai des Orfèvres, each of the police departments receiving different directives, each defending opposing interests whether they liked it or not because of a struggle in high places.

At midnight, the President of the Council had learnt that Auguste Point had approached Maigret.

At 8 a.m. Piquemal, the man who had discovered the Calame report, had been approached by a stranger in the little bar where he was peacefully drinking his coffee and he had followed the man without hesitation, without argument.

'You've done good work, my boy.'

'No spelling mistakes?'

'I don't think so.'

'And now?'

'I don't know. Perhaps you'd better stay on in the Hotel du Berry in case Piquemal returns.'

'In that case, I'll telephone you.'

'Yes, here or at home.'

One of the men who had read the Calame report had disappeared.

Auguste Point who had also read it was still there, but he was a Cabinet Minister and therefore more difficult to conjure away.

At the very thought of it, Maigret seemed to taste again the drink he'd had the night before and all he wanted was a glass of beer somewhere cheek by jowl with ordinary people with ordinary little problems.

Chapter Four

Maigret was on his way back from the 'Brasserie Dauphine' where he had gone to have a pint of beer, when he saw Janvier proceeding rapidly towards Police Headquarters.

It was almost hot, in the middle of the afternoon. The sun had lost its dimness and for the first time this year, Maigret had left his coat in the office. He called 'Hey!' two or three times. Janvier stopped, saw him and walked back to him.

'Do you want a drink?'

Without any particular reason the superintendent was reluctant to go straight back to the Quai des Orfèvres. The spring, probably, had something to do with it, adding to the atmosphere of tension which had surrounded him since the day before.

Janvier had a comic look on his face, the look of a man who is not quite sure whether he is going to get a scolding or be patted on the back. Instead of staying by the counter, they went to the back room, which at this time of day was empty.

'A beer?'

'If I may . . .'

They stayed silent, waiting to be served.

'We aren't the only ones trailing the little lady, boss,' Janvier murmured. 'I get the impression that there are quite a few of us interested in her movements.'

'Tell me the whole thing.'

'I made it my first business, this morning, to go and have a look round near the Ministry, in the Boulevard Saint-Germain. I got to about twenty feet of it when I saw Rougier standing on the opposite pavement, and apparently taking a keen interest in the sparrows.'

Both men knew Gaston Rougier, an inspector from the Rue des Saussaies with whom they were, as a matter of fact, on the best of terms. He was a decent sort, who lived in the suburbs and always had his pockets full of photographs of his seven or eight children.

'Did he see you?'

'Yes.'

'Did he speak to you?'

'The street was almost empty. I couldn't possibly avoid him. When I got up to him, he asked me:

'"You, too?"

'I acted the fool and asked:

'"Me, too, what?"

'Then he winked at me.

'"Nothing. I'm not asking you to let the cat out of the bag. I'm surprised to see so many familiar faces about, this morning, that's all. It's just bad luck that there's not even a bistro opposite this blasted Ministry."

'From where we were standing, we could see into the inner yard and I recognised Ramire of General Information, who seemed to be getting on like a house on fire with the concierge.

'I kept up the acting and went on my way. I didn't stop till I got to a café in the Rue Solferino and tried my luck with the telephone directory. I found Blanche Lamotte's name and her address, 63 Rue Vaneau. It was only a stone's throw away.'

'And there again you bumped into Security?'

'Not quite. You know the Rue Vaneau. It's quiet, almost provincial, even has a few trees in the gardens. No. 63 is an unpretentious block of flats, but quite comfortable. The concierge was in her room, peeling potatoes.

'"Is Mlle Lamotte at home?" I asked.

'I could tell at once she was looking at me somewhat ironically. However, I ignored this.

'"I'm an inspector from an insurance company," I said.

"'Mlle Lamotte has applied for a life insurance and I'm just making the usual enquiries." She didn't actually burst out laughing, but very nearly. And then she asked me:

"'How many different branches of the Police are there in Paris?"

"'I don't know what you mean."

"'As far as you're concerned, I've seen you before with a fat superintendent, whose name I've forgotten, when the little lady in 57 took an overdose of sleeping pills two years ago. This time all your colleagues have been at it."

"'How many of them have been here, then?" I asked.

"'There was one yesterday morning."

"'Did he show you his badge?"

"'I didn't ask him for it. I'm not asking for yours, either. I'm quite capable of recognising a policeman when I see one."

"'Did he ask you a lot of questions?"

"'Four or five: if she lived alone, if she was visited sometimes by a man about fifty, on the fat side . . . I said no."

"'Is that the truth?"

"'It is. Also if she often had a brief-case when she came home. I told him she did sometimes, that she also has a type-writer upstairs in her flat and that she often brings work back in the evening. I suppose that you know as well as I do that she's a Cabinet Minister's secretary."

"'I'm aware of it, yes."

"'He also wanted to know if she had had her brief-case with her last night. I had to admit that I hadn't noticed. Then he pretended to be going away. I went up to the first floor where I go every day, to oblige an old lady. I heard him on the stairs a little later on, but I didn't let on I was there. But I do know that he stopped at the third floor, where Mlle Blanche lives and that he got into her flat."

"'You allowed him to do that?"

"'I've been a concierge long enough to have learnt not to be on bad terms with the police."

"'Did he stay there for a long time?"

"'About ten minutes."

"'Did you see him again?"

"'Not that one."

"'Did you speak to the lady about it?'"

Maigret was listening, staring hard at his glass, trying to fit the incident in with the events that he already knew. Janvier went on:

'She hesitated. She felt she was blushing and decided to tell me the truth.

"'I told her that someone had been here asking questions about her and had gone up to her floor. I didn't mention the police."

"'Did she seem surprised?"

"'At first–yes. Then she murmured: 'I think I know what it's about.'

"'As for the ones that came this morning, a few moments after she had gone to work–there were two of them. They told me as well that they were from the police. The smaller went to show.me his badge but I didn't look at it."

"'Did they go up too?"

"'No. They asked me the same questions and some others as well."

"'What others?"

'"Whether she goes out a lot, who with, who her friends are, male and female, whether she does a lot of telephoning, whether . . ."'

Maigret interrupted the inspector:

'What did she tell you about her?'

'She gave me the names of her friends, of a certain Lucile Cristin who lives in the neighbourhood, who most likely works in an office and has a squint. Mlle Blanche lunches in the Boulevard Saint-Germain, in a restaurant called "The Three Ministries". In the evening she cooks her own dinner. This Lucile Cristin often comes to eat with her. I've not been able to find her address. The concierge also told me about another friend, who doesn't often come to the Rue Vaneau, but whom Mlle Blanche goes to dine with every Sunday. She's married to an agent in the Halles called Hariel and lives in the Rue de Courcelles. The concierge believes she comes from La Roche-sur-Yon, like Mlle Blanche.'

'Did you go to the Rue de Courcelles?'

'I gathered from you I was to leave no stone unturned. As I don't even know what it is all about . . .'

'Go on.'

'Her information was correct. I went to Mme Hariel's flat; she leads a comfortable life, has three children; the youngest is eight. I put on the insurance agent act again. She was perfectly calm and I took it from that that I was the first to come and see her. She knew Blanche Lamotte in La Roche, where they went to school together. They had lost sight of one another and met accidentally in Paris three years ago. Mme Hariel invited her friend to her home and she got the habit of coming to dine every Sunday. Nothing of any interest besides that. Blanche Lamotte leads a regular life, entirely devoted to her work and talks enthusiastically about her boss for whom she would gladly die.'

'That's all?'

'No. About a year ago, Blanche asked Hariel if she knew of any vacant job for a friend of hers, who was in difficulties. It was Fleury. Hariel, who seems to be a kind-hearted man, gave him some work in his office. Fleury had to go there every day at 6 a.m.'

'What happened?'

'He worked for three days, and after that they never saw him again and he never even apologised. Mlle Blanche was very embarrassed by the whole thing and apologised profusely for him. I went back to the Boulevard Saint-Germain with the idea of calling at "The Three Ministries". I could see, long before I got there, not only Gaston Rougier on the old spot but one of his colleagues as well, I've forgotten his name.'

Maigret was trying hard to put all this information into some kind of order. On Monday evening Auguste Point had gone to his flat in the Boulevard Pasteur and had left the Calame report there, believing it to be safer there than elsewhere.

On Tuesday morning, someone who pretended to be from the police, had presented himself at the Rue Vaneau, the residence of Mlle Blanche, and after asking the concierge some questions of no importance had managed to get himself into her flat. Was he really from the police? If he was, the whole business had an even more unpleasant twist to it than the superintendent imagined. However, he had a feeling that this first visit had nothing to do with the Rue des Saussaies. Was it the same man who, finding nothing in the secretary's flat, had gone on to the Boulevard Pasteur and taken the document from there?

'She didn't describe him to you?'

'Only vaguely. An ordinary party–neither young nor old, rather stout, with enough experience in questioning for her to take him for a policeman.'

This was almost the same description that the owner of the bar in the Rue Jacob had given of the man who had approached Piquemal and had left with him. As for this morning's little lot–the ones who had not gone to the secretary's flat–it seemed likely they would be from the Security Department.

'What am I to do now?'

'I don't know.'

'Oh, I forgot, as I recrossed the Boulevard Saint-Germain I thought I caught a glimpse of Lucas in a bar.'

'It could have been him . . .'

'Is he on the same case?'

'More or less.'

'Am I to go on taking an interest in the lady?'

'We'll see after I've talked to Lucas. Wait here for a moment.'

Maigret went to the telephone and called the P.J.

'Is Lucas back?'

'Not yet.'

'Is it you, Torrence? As soon as he turns up, please send him to the Brasserie Dauphine.'

A boy was passing in the street with the latest edition of the afternoon papers bearing large headlines and Maigret walked to the door searching for some change in his pocket. When he came back and sat down beside Janvier he spread out the paper. The headline running across the entire page said:

'HAS ARTHUR NICOUD ESCAPED?'

The news was sensational enough for the paper to have altered its front page.

'The Clairfond case has reopened in an unexpected manner, though there are those who ought to have foreseen it. It is known that the day after the disaster public opinion was greatly upset and demanded a thorough examination of the people responsible. The Nicoud and Sauvegrain enterprise, which five years ago built the now all too famous sanatorium should have been, according to those in the know, made the object of a strict and immediate enquiry. Why has nothing been done? This is what we hope will be explained to us in the next few days. However, Arthur Nicoud, afraid of appearing in public, has considered it safer to seek refuge in a hunting lodge he owns in Sologne. The police were apparently aware of it. We have even been assured that it was, in fact, the police who suggested to the contractor that he should disappear for a time from circulation, in order to avoid trouble. Only this morning, four weeks after the disaster, has it been decided in high places to summon Arthur Nicoud and question him on matters that are of burning interest to everyone. Early this morning two inspectors from the Security Department went to the lodge where they found no one but the game-keeper. He told the officers that his master had left the night before for an unknown destination. But it did not remain unknown for long. Two hours ago, in fact, our special correspondent in Brussels telephoned to say that Arthur Nicoud had arrived in the town later this morning and occupies a luxurious suite in the Hotel Metropole. Our correspondent succeeded in approaching him and put to him the following questions which we reproduce verbatim together with the replies.

'"Is it true that you left your lodge in Sologne so abruptly because you were warned that the police were coming to visit you?"

'"It is completely untrue. I knew and know nothing about the police's intentions; for the last month they have known perfectly well where to find me."

'"Did you leave France, because you could foresee fresh developments?"

'"I came to Brussels because I have some building plans here that necessitated my presence."

'"What building plans?"

'"The construction of an aerodrome for which I have put in a tender."

'"Do you intend to go back to France and place yourself at the disposal of the authorities?"

'"I have no intention of altering anything in my plans."

'"Do you mean to say that you will remain in Brussels until the Clairfond case is forgotten?"

'"I repeat that I'm staying here as long as my business keeps me."

'"Even if an order were issued for you to return?"

'"The police had a whole month in which to question me. It isn't my fault if they haven't done so!"

'"You have heard about the Calame report?"

'"I don't know what you are talking about."

'At this point Arthur Nicoud put an end to the conversation, which our correspondent immediately telephoned to us. It seems–though we were unable to get a confirmation–that an elegant, fair-haired young woman arrived an hour after Nicoud and was shown immediately to his apartment where she probably is at the moment. In the Rue des Saussaies, it has been confirmed that two inspectors went to Sologne to question the contractor on several matters. When we mentioned an order to return, we were told that there could be no question of that for the moment.'

'Is that the case we're working on?' Janvier muttered with a wry expression.

'It is.'

He opened his mouth, probably to ask how it had happened that Maigret had agreed to have anything to do with such an unsavoury political case. But he said nothing. Lucas could be seen crossing the square, slightly dragging his left leg as usual. He did not stop at the bar, but came and sat opposite the two men, wiping the sweat from his face and looking gloomy.

Pointing to the paper, he uttered in a reproachful voice which he never used in Maigret's presence:

'I've just read it.'

And the superintendent felt a little guilty as he faced his colleagues. Lapointe had probably also discovered by now what it was all about.

'A pint?' offered Maigret.

'No. A pernod.'

And this, too, was not characteristic of Lucas. They waited to be served before they began to talk in an undertone.

'I suppose you bumped into the man from the Big House everywhere you went?' It was their way of describing Security.

'You might have warned me to be discreet,' grumbled Lucas. 'If it is a question of getting ahead of them, I can tell you straight away they're way up in front.'

'Tell us.'

'Tell you what?'

'What you've been up to.'

'I started to stroll up and down in the Boulevard Saint-Germain, having got there a few minutes after Janvier.'

'And Rougier?' asked the latter, unable to keep from smiling at the comical side of it.

'He was standing in the middle of the pavement and saw me arrive. I pretended to be going somewhere in a hurry. He laughed at me and greeted me with: "You searching for Janvier? He has just turned the corner of the Rue Solferino." It is always a pleasure to be made to feel a fool by someone from the Rue des Saussaies. As it was impossible to get any information on Jacques Fleury in the neighbourhood of the Ministry, I . . .'

'You looked for a telephone directory?' asked Janvier.

'I didn't think of it. I knew that he frequented the bars in the Champs-Elysées, so I went to Fouquet's.'

'I bet he's in the directory.'

'Possibly. Will you let me say what I've got to say.'

Janvier, by this time, was in a light-headed teasing mood like someone who has just had a good scolding and watches someone else being scolded in his turn.

In fact, all three of them, Maigret included, felt on foreign ground, each as clumsy as the other and each could imagine their colleagues at Security enjoying the joke behind their backs.

'I had a chat with the barman. Fleury is notorious in a way. Most of the time he lives on credit as long as he can and when he owes too much they don't allow him to be served any more. Then he disappears for a few days, until he has exhausted his credit in all the other bars and restaurants.'

'Does he pay in the end?'

'He turns up eventually, full of the joys of spring and settles his account.'

'And then it starts all over again?'

'Yes. It's been going on for years.'

'Even since he's been in the Ministry?'

'With the difference that now he is Private Secretary and people think he has some influence, more of them supply him with food and drink. Before that he used to disappear for months on end. One day he was seen working in the Halles, counting the cabbages coming off a lorry.'

Janvier darted a significant glance at Maigret.

'He has a wife and two children, somewhere in the direction of Vanves. He is supposed to be supporting them. Luckily his wife has a job, something like housekeeping for an elderly gentleman. The children work, too.'

'Who does he go to the bars with?'

'For a long time it was with a woman of about forty, a stout woman with dark hair, they tell me, known as Marcelle; he seemed to be in love with her. Some say that he took her away from the cashier's desk of a Brasserie at the Porte Saint Martin. Nobody knows what became of her. For more than a year, he has been seen with a Jacqueline Page and lives with her in a flat in the Rue Washington, above an Italian grocer's. Jacqueline Page is twenty-three years old and sometimes works as an extra in films. She cultivates all the producers, directors and actors who come to Fouquet's and is as accommodating as they could wish.'

'Is Fleury in love with her?'

'Apparently.'

'Is he jealous?'

'So they say. But he doesn't dare protest and pretends not to notice anything.'

'Have you seen her?'

'I thought I ought to go to the Rue Washington.'

'What sort of a story did you tell her?'

'There was no need of a story. As soon as she opened her door, she exclaimed: "What, another of you?"'

Janvier and Maigret could not help exchanging a smile.

'Another what?' asked Maigret, knowing perfectly well what the reply would be.

'Another policeman, you know what I mean. Two of them had been there before me.'

'Separately?'

'No, together.'

'Did they question her about Fleury?'

'They asked her if he worked in the evenings and brought documents home from the Ministry.'

'What did she tell them?'

'That they had other things to do with their evenings. That girl doesn't mince her words. Curiously enough her mother looks after the pews in the church at Picpus.'

'Did they search the flat?'

'No, they just looked round the rooms. It isn't really a flat. It's more a sort of camping site. The kitchen is just large enough to prepare breakfast in. The other rooms, a living-room, a bedroom and what could be called a dining-room were in complete chaos, with shoes and a woman's underclothes all over the place and records and coloured magazines, paperbacks, not counting the bottles and glasses.'

'Does he come home to lunch?'

'Rarely. Usually she keeps to her bed until the middle of the afternoon. Now and then he rings her up in the morning suggesting she should meet him in a restaurant.'

'Have they got many friends?'

'Just people who go to the same dives as they do.'

'Is that all?'

For the first time, Lucas' voice rang with an almost pathetic reproach as he answered:

'No, it isn't! Your instructions were to provide you with as much information as possible. In the first place I have here a list of about a dozen of Jacqueline's former lovers, including some that she still goes on seeing.'

With an expression of disgust, he threw a paper with pencilled names on it on the table.

'You'll see that it contains the names of two politicians. Another thing: I almost found the girl Marcelle again.'

'How did you do that?'

'On my two legs. I toured the bars of the main boulevards, beginning with the one by the Opéra. As usual it was the last one I came to, in the Place de la République, that was the right one.'

'Marcelle has gone back to being a cashier?'

'No, but they remember her and have seen her in the neighbourhood. The owner of the bar believes that she lives nearby, in the direction of the Rue Blondel. He has met her often in the Rue de Croissant, so he gathers that she works in a newspaper office or a printers.'

'Did you check?'

'Not yet. Must I?'

The tone was such that Maigret murmured:

'Angry?'

Lucas forced himself to smile.

'No. But you must admit it's a rum sort of job. Especially when one learns afterwards from the paper that it's this miserable business we're on to! If I must go on, I'll go on. But I can tell you frankly . . .'

'Don't you think I'm not as fed up as you are?'

'No. I know you are.'

'The Rue de Croissant is not as long as all that. Everyone knows everyone else in that part of the world.'

'And I suppose I'll get there just after the boys of the Rue des Saussaies, like last time!'

'It's very probable.'

'All right, I'll go. May I have another?' He was pointing to his glass which he had just emptied. Maigret gave a sign to the waiter to repeat the order and at the last moment ordered himself a pernod instead of a beer.

Inspectors from other departments had forgathered to have a drink at the bar at the end of the day and waved their hands in greeting. Maigret was frowning, thinking of Auguste Point who must have read the article and must be expecting to see his own name in equally large letters in the papers any minute now. His wife, whom he must have informed of the whole business was probably as anxious as he was. Had he spoken to Mlle Blanche? Did they realise, the three of them, just how much activity was going on around them?

'What am I to do now?' asked Janvier in the tone of one repelled by his assignment, but resigned to seeing it through.

'Are you brave enough to keep watch in the Rue Vaneau?'

'For the whole night?'

'No. I'll send Torrence to relieve you about eleven, let's say.'

'You think something will happen there?'

Maigret admitted:

'No.'

He had not the vaguest idea. Or rather he had so many and such muddled ideas that he could not make head or tail of them. One had to come back to the simpler facts, those one could check. It was certain that on Monday afternoon, the man Piquemal had come to see the Minister of Public Works. He must have approached the porter, filled in a form. Maigret had not seen it, but it must have been put on record and Auguste Point would not have invented such a visit.

At least two persons from the adjoining offices were likely to have heard the conversation: Mlle Blanche and Jacques Fleury.

Security had thought of that, too, as they had made enquiries at their lodgings.

Had Piquemal really handed the Calame report to Auguste Point? It seemed improbable to Maigret that the latter should have conjured up all this comedy which, then, would seem to make no sense at all.

Auguste Point had gone to his private house, on the Boulevard Pasteur. He had left the document in his desk again. The superintendent believed that this was true. Therefore, the person who had come to see Mlle Blanche the next morning and searched her flat, was not certain exactly where the report was to be found.

And in the afternoon the document had disappeared.

Wednesday morning Piquemal also disappeared.

On the same day Joseph Mascoulin's paper first mentioned the Calame report and demanded publicly to know where the document was hidden.

Maigret's lips were moving, he spoke in a low voice, as though to himself.

'It's either one thing or the other–they may have stolen the report to destroy it, or stolen it to use it. Up to now it seems that no one has used it.'

Lucas and Janvier listened without interrupting him.

'Unless . . .'

He slowly drank half his glass, and wiped his mouth.

'It seems complicated, but when it is a question of politics, things are rarely simple. Only one or two people involved in the Clairfond case have any reason to destroy the document. If we learn that it has disappeared after having surfaced for a few hours, suspicion will automatically fall on them.'

'I think I begin to understand,' murmured Janvier.

'In this case, about thirty politicians at least, without counting Nicoud himself, are faced with a scandal and worse. If one succeeds in throwing suspicion on one individual, and if one can produce evidence against him, and this individual is vulnerable–one has the ideal scapegoat. Auguste Point's position is indefensible.'

His two colleagues glanced at him in surprise. Maigret had forgotten that they knew only a part of the case. The point when it was possible to keep things secret from them had been passed.

'He is on the list of Nicoud's guests at Samois,' he told them. 'The contractor made his daughter a present of a gold fountain pen.'

'You saw it?'

He nodded.

'And it was he who . . . ?'

Lucas did not finish his question. Maigret had understood it. The inspector had wanted to say:

'It was he who asked you to help him?'

This at last dissipated the embarrassment that had weighed on the three men.

'Yes, it was. By now, I would be surprised if others didn't know it, too.'

'We needn't be secretive any more?'

'Certainly not as far as Security is concerned.'

They lingered over their glasses another quarter of an hour. Maigret was the first to rise, to wish them good-night and go to his office in case he was wanted. There was no message for him. Point had not telephoned nor had anyone connected with the Clairfond case.

At dinner, Mme Maigret saw by his face that he had better not be questioned. He spent the evening reading an international police magazine and went to bed at ten.

'You have a lot of work on your plate?'

They were on the point of going to sleep. She had kept the question for a long time on the tip of her tongue.

'Not much, but what there is is nasty.'

Twice, before falling asleep, he was tempted to ring up Auguste Point. He did not know what he would have said to him, but he would have liked to establish contact.

At eight o'clock he was up. Behind the curtains, a light mist clung to the window-panes and seemed to have hushed the noise of the street. He walked to the corner of the Boulevard Richard-Lenoir to take the bus and stopped to buy the newspapers.

The bomb had exploded. The papers asked no more questions, but announced in headlines:

'THE CLAIRFOND CASE'

Disappearance of Jules Piquemal, who found
the Calame Report

The report which was handed in at a very high level
is understood to have also disappeared.

His newspapers under his arm, he got into the bus and did not read any more before arriving at the Quai des Orfèvres.

As he walked down the passage he heard the telephone ringing in his office, and hurried to lift the receiver.

'Superintendent Maigret?' the telephonist asked. 'It's the third time in a quarter of an hour that you have been called from the Ministry of Public Works. I'm putting you through now.'

He still had his hat on his head and was still wearing his coat, slightly damp from the morning fog.

Chapter Five

The voice was that of a man who had not slept the night before, nor on the preceding nights either and who made no effort to choose his words because he had passed the stage of worrying what he sounded like. It was that flat, lifeless disheartened tone that indicates in a man rather the same symptom as when a woman weeps in a particular dreary way, her mouth wide open, and looks ugly without minding it.

'Can you come and see me at once, Maigret? Unless it embarrasses you personally, there is no reason now to avoid the Boulevard Saint-Germain. I warn you that the waiting-room is full of journalists and the telephone never stops. I have promised them a press conference at 11 a.m.'

Maigret glanced at his watch.

'I'll come straight away.'

There was a knock at the door. Little Lapointe walked in as Maigret was still holding the receiver, frowning deeply.

'You've got something to tell me?'

'Yes, some fresh news.'

'Important?'

'I think so.'

'Put on your hat and come with me. We can talk on the way.'

He stopped for a moment at the door to ask the doorman to warn the chief that he would not be at the morning briefing. In the car park he went to one of the small black cars of the P.J.

'You drive.'

And as they were driving along the embankment:

'What have you got to tell me?'

'I spent the night at the Hotel du Berry in the room I rented.'

'Piquemal hasn't reappeared?'

'No. A man from Security kept watch all night in the street.'

Maigret was prepared for this. It was not disturbing.

'I didn't want to go to Piquemal's room while it was dark, for I'd have had to switch on the light and it would have been seen from the street. I waited till it was light and then gave it a more thorough search than I did the first time. I went through all the books one after the other and searched between the pages. In a treatise on political economy I found this letter, which had been slipped in as a book-mark.'

Driving with one hand, he pulled his wallet out of his pocket with the other and passed it to Maigret.

'On the left side. The letter that's headed the Chamber of Deputies.'

It was a small note, like those the deputies use for short memoranda. It was dated the previous Thursday. The writing was small, uneven, with letters climbing one on top of the other and the ends of the words almost indecipherable.

> Dear Sir,
> I thank you for your communication. I am greatly interested in what you tell me and will be glad to see you tomorrow, towards 8 p.m. at the Brasserie du Croissant, Rue Montmartre. I beg you not to mention the matter in question to anybody until then.
>
> Yours

There was no real signature, simply a scrawl that might have meant anything.

'I expect it's Joseph Mascoulin,' growled the superintendent.

'Yes, it's him. I went earlier to a friend who is a stenographer in the Chamber and knows most of the deputies' handwriting. I had only to show him the first line and the scrawl at the end.'

They were already in the Boulevard Saint-Germain, opposite the Ministry of Public Works. Maigret could recognise several cars belonging to the Press. He glanced at the opposite pavement, but saw no one from the Rue des Saussaies. Now that the bomb had actually exploded, had they called off the watch?

'Do I wait for you?'

'Yes, it would be better that way.'

He crossed the yard, went up the main stairs and found himself in a waiting-room with a dark-red carpet and yellow pillars. He recognised a few faces here and there. Two or three journalists were on the point of approaching him but an usher forestalled them.

'Will you come this way, Superintendent. The Minister is expecting you.'

Auguste Point was standing in the huge dark study, with all its lamps lit, and seemed to him stouter and more massive than the Boulevard Pasteur flat. He shook Maigret's hand, held it for an instant in his own, with the pressure of one who has just sustained a great shock and is grateful for the slightest display of sympathy.

'Thank you for coming, Maigret. I cannot help reproaching myself now for involving you in all this. You can see that I was right to be anxious!'

He turned to a middle-aged woman who had been telephoning and had put down the receiver.

'May I introduce Mlle Blanche, my secretary, whom I mentioned to you.'

Mlle Blanche glanced suspiciously at Maigret, very much on the defensive. She did not stretch out her hand, but merely nodded in his direction.

Her face was insignificant, not attractive, but under her simple black dress, brightened only by a narrow strip of white lace at the neck, Maigret was aware with surprise of a body still young and rounded and very desirable.

'If you don't mind, we'll go to my flat. I've never been able to get used to this office; I never feel at ease in it. You'll take all the calls, Blanche, won't you?'

'Yes, Your Excellency.'

Auguste Point opened the door at the back and murmured, in the same flat voice:

'I'll go first. It's rather complicated getting there.'

He was not quite familiar himself with the surroundings and seemed lost in the deserted corridors, hesitating before several doors.

They came to a narrow staircase, went up and walked through two large empty rooms. The sight of a servant in a white apron, carrying a broom, indicated that they had reached the private apartments.

'I meant to introduce Fleury to you. He was in the office next door. At the last moment I forgot about it.'

Now they could hear the sound of a woman's voice. Point pushed open another door and they found themselves in a small sitting-room where a woman was sitting by the window with a young girl beside her.

'My wife and daughter. I thought it best to talk in their presence.'

Madame Point could have been any little middle-aged bourgeoise whom one meets shopping in the street. Her face too looked tense, her eyes a little vacant.

'I must tell you straight away how grateful I am to you, Superintendent. My husband has told me everything and I know how much the conversation you had with him has helped him.'

Newspapers, with sensational headlines, were spread out on the table.

At first Maigret paid slight attention to the young girl who seemed calmer, more controlled than either of her parents.

'Would you like a cup of coffee?'

It all reminded him a little of a house where someone has just died, the daily routine suddenly interrupted, people coming and going and bustling about without knowing where to settle or what to do. He still wore his overcoat. Anne-Marie asked him to take it off and hung it over an arm-chair.

'Have you read this morning's papers?' the Minister asked at last, still standing.

'I only had the time to see the headlines.'

'They don't mention my name yet, but everyone in the Press knows about it. They must have got their information in the middle of the night. I was told so by a typesetter in the Rue du Croissant. I immediately telephoned the President.'

'What was his reaction?'

'I don't know whether he was surprised or not. I've lost my capacity of judging people's reactions. Obviously I was interrupting his sleep. It seemed to me that he showed some astonishment, but I found as I talked to him on the telephone that he was less disturbed than I had expected him to be.'

He seemed to be talking in a forced manner, without any conviction, as though words had no longer any importance.

'Sit down, Maigret. I apologise for standing all the time, but I haven't been able to make myself sit down since this morning. It's driving me mad. I've got to keep standing and walking up and down. Before you came in I had been pacing my office for an hour while my secretary was answering the telephone. Where was I? Ah, yes. The President said something like: "Well, my friend, we'll have to face the music!" I believe those were his exact words. I asked him if it was his men who were detaining Piquemal. Instead of answering me directly he muttered something like: "What makes you think that?" Then he explained to me that he couldn't swear to what was going on in his departments any more than I or any other Minister could. He gave me a lecture on the subject: "We are made responsible for everything"—he was saying—"though, in fact, we're only passing through and the people we give orders to know perfectly well they had a different boss yesterday and may well have a different one tomorrow!" I suggested that the best I could do was to offer him my resignation the next morning.

'"You're too hasty, Point," he said. "You're taking me unawares. In politics things don't happen as they're expected to happen. I'll think your suggestion over and ring you up shortly."'

'I suppose that he telephoned some of our colleagues. Perhaps they met to discuss the matter. I don't know. At the moment they have no reason to keep me informed.

'I spent the rest of the night pacing up and down my room while my wife tried to reason with me.'

Point's wife looked at Maigret as if to say: 'Help me! You see what a state he is in!'

It was true. That earlier evening, in the Boulevard Pasteur, Point had seemed to Maigret like a man staggering under a sudden blow and incapable of dealing with it but prepared to put up a good fight. Now he spoke as though he was no longer concerned with events, as though he had given up, knowing his destiny had been taken out of his hands.

'Did he call you back?' asked Maigret.

'At about half past five. As you see there were quite a number of us awake last night. He said that my resignation would serve no useful purpose, that it would only be considered an admission of guilt and that all I had to do was to tell the truth.'

'Including the contents of the Calame report?' asked the superintendent. Point managed a smile.

'No. Not exactly. Just when I believed the conversation had come to an end he added: "I daresay you'll be asked whether you had read the report." I replied: "I *have* read it."

'"That's what I had understood. It's a very lengthy report, filled, I presume, with technical details on a subject not necessarily familiar to a legal mind. It might be more exact to say that you had skimmed through it. You haven't got it to hand at the moment to refresh your memory. The reason I am saying this, my friend, is to help you avoid more serious difficulties than those you will have to face already. If you speak of the contents of the report and implicate anyone—whoever it may be—it doesn't concern me and I don't care one way or the other—but you'll be accused of making charges which you are unable to support. Do you understand me?"'

For at least the third time since the beginning of the conversation, Point lit his pipe and his wife turned to Maigret.

'Please smoke, if you wish. I'm used to it.'

'From seven o'clock onwards the telephone never stopped ringing— mainly journalists wanting to question me. At first I told them that I had no announcement to make. Then they almost seemed to be threatening me. Two newspaper editors rang me personally. In the end I asked everybody to come to my office at eleven o'clock today, for a press conference. I had to see you beforehand. I suppose that . . .'

He had had the courage, perhaps through tact, or fear or even superstition, to wait until now to put the question.

'I suppose you haven't discovered anything?'

Perhaps it was on purpose, to make the gesture more significant and thus inspire confidence in the Minister, but when he pulled the letter from his pocket and handed it to Auguste Point he did it in complete silence. There was something theatrical about it, that was out of character.

Madame Point did not move from the sofa where she was sitting, but Anne-Marie came up to her father and read over his shoulder.

'Who is it from?' she asked.

Maigret in his turn was asking Point:

'Do you recognise the handwriting?'

'It means something to me, but I can't quite place it.'

'This letter was sent last Thursday by Joseph Mascoulin.'

'To whom?'

'To Julien Piquemal.'

There was a silence. Point, without a word, handed the note to his wife. Each of them was trying to assess the importance of this discovery.

When Maigret began to speak again it was, as at the Boulevard Pasteur, in the form of an interrogation.

'What sort of terms are you on with Mascoulin?'

'No terms at all.'

'Have you quarrelled?'

'No.'

Point looked grave, anxious. Maigret although he never meddled in politics, was not quite ignorant of parliamentary custom. In a general way, the deputies, even though belonging to different parties, and even though attacking one another ferociously on the political platform, could still maintain friendly relations with one another, reminiscent, in their familiarity, of relations in schools and barracks.

'You are not on speaking terms?' Maigret insisted.

Point drew his hand across his forehead.

'All this goes back a few years, to my first days in the Chamber. A bright new Chamber, as you probably remember, and we all swore we would keep out anyone whose hands weren't clean. It was immediately after the war and the country was swept by a wave of idealism, a thirst for decency. The majority of my colleagues, at any rate a large number of them, were as new to politics as I was.'

'Not Mascoulin.'

'No. There were a few left from the old Chamber, but everyone was convinced that the newcomers would create the right atmosphere. After a few months, I was not quite so confident. After two years, I was discouraged. You remember, Henriette?'

He turned to his wife.

'It got to the point,' she said, 'where he had decided not to stand for Parliament again.'

'I had to speak at a dinner and I expressed my misgivings in so many words, and the press was there to put it all on record. I should be very surprised, if they don't remind me of some parts of my speech any day now. The subject of it was, dirty hands. I tried to explain that basically it was not our political machine that was deficient, but the climate in which politicians have to live, whether they like it or not. I needn't repeat it all now. You remember the famous slogan: "The Republic of Comrades". We meet every day. We shake hands like old friends. After a few weeks everybody is on familiar terms and each man tries to help the next. As the days go by, you shake more and more hands and if these are not quite clean, you shrug your shoulders tolerantly, and say: "Oh, well, he's not a bad chap," or "He has to do it to keep his votes." You follow me? I had stated publicly that if each of us refused once and for all to shake dirty hands, the hands of any individual not quite straight, the political atmosphere would be purified immediately.'

He added bitterly, after a few moments:

'I practised what I preached. I avoided certain journalists and certain unsavoury business men who haunt the corridors of the Palais Bourbon. I refused certain services which I believed I ought to refuse to some influential electors. And one day in the Hall of Lost Steps Mascoulin came up to me, his hand outstretched. I pretended not to see him and turned very ostentatiously towards another colleague. I know he went scarlet in the face and has never forgiven me. He is the type of man who doesn't forgive.'

'You did something similar with Hector Tabard, the editor of *Rumeur*?'

'I refused to see him a couple of times and he didn't insist.'

He glanced at his watch.

'I have one hour left at my disposal, Maigret. At eleven o'clock, I'll have to face the journalists and answer their questions. I had thought of presenting them with a statement, but it wouldn't satisfy them. I've got to tell them that Piquemal came to me with the Calame report and that I went to my flat in the Boulevard Pasteur to read it.'

'And that you didn't do so?'

'I will try to be less explicit. The most difficult, the most impossible part will be to get them to accept that I left the famous report in a flat without any supervision and that when the next day I wanted to pick it up to take it to the President of the Council–it had disappeared. Nobody will believe me. Piquemal's disappearance doesn't simplify anything, on the contrary. They will say that it was one way of shutting up an embarrassing witness. The only thing that could have saved me would have been to present them with the thief.'

He added, as though apologising for his resentment:

'I couldn't have expected that in forty-eight hours, even from you. What do you think I should do?'

Mme Point interrupted with determination.

'Hand in your resignation and we'll go back to La Roche-sur-Yon. The people who know you will know you're not guilty. You don't have to worry about the others. Your conscience is clear, isn't it?'

Maigret's eyes turned to Anne-Marie and he saw her draw her lips together. He saw that the young woman did not share her mother's views and that as far as she was concerned such a retreat on her father's part would mean that she would have to give up all her hopes.

'What is your opinion?' Point murmured, hesitantly.

This was a responsibility the superintendent could not accept.

'And what is yours?'

'I feel I ought to hold out. At least, if there's even the slightest hope of finding the thief.'

It was once again an indirect question.

'I keep on hoping, right to the last minute,' muttered Maigret, 'otherwise I would never take on a case in the first place. Because I'm on foreign ground with politics, I wasted time in activities which may appear useless. But I'm not at all sure that they are as useless as they seem.'

Maigret had to instill some assurance in Point, if not a certain confidence, before he met the journalists, so he began to go over the situation, clarifying it.

'Don't you see, Your Excellency, we have arrived at a point where I feel more at home. Until now I've had to work by stealth as it were, though in fact we've bumped into the men from the Rue des Saussaies all the way along the line. No matter where we went, the men from Security were always there–at the door of your Ministry, at your secretary's lodgings, at Piquemal's or at your Parliamentary Private Secretary's place. At one moment I wondered what they were looking for, and whether the two departments weren't perhaps pursuing parallel enquiries. Now I am inclined to believe that all they wanted was to see what we discovered. It wasn't you, or your secretary, nor Piquemal or Fleury that was being watched, it was me and my men. Once Piquemal's disappearance and the disappearance of the documents became official, then Security could call off their watch as it automatically became the P.J.'s business anyway, being on Paris territory. A man doesn't disappear without leaving a trace. And a thief is always caught in the end.'

'Some time or other . . .' murmured Point with a sad smile.

And Maigret, rising and looking him straight in the eyes:

'It's your job to hold out until then.'

'It doesn't only depend on me.'

'It depends mostly on you.'

'If Mascoulin is behind this manoeuvre he will challenge the government quite soon.'

'Unless he prefers to profit from what he knows to increase his influence.'

Point glanced at him with surprise.

'You know so much? I thought you knew very little of politics.'

'This kind of thing doesn't only happen in politics; there are Mascoulins in every walk of life. I believe—tell me if I'm wrong—that he has one passion only, a passion for power, but he is a cold-blooded animal who knows how to bide his time. Every now and then he opens fire in the Chamber or in the Press by uncovering some kind of scandal or misuse of authority.'

Point was listening with renewed interest.

'Little by little, in this way, he has created a reputation for himself of a merciless crusader. So that all the embittered and the rebels of Piquemal's type go to him as soon as they think they have uncovered something dubious. I expect he receives the same sort of letters as we do when some mysterious crime is committed. We get letters from madmen, cranks and maniacs, and people who snatch the opportunity of satisfying their hatred for a relative, or some old friend or neighbour. Among them there are always some that provide us with real evidence, without which a good number of murderers would still be scouring the streets. Piquemal—the Hermit, the searcher after truth in all extremist parties, in religion, in philosophy—he's precisely the type of man who, when he found the Calame report would never for a moment have considered handing it over to his immediate supervisors, whom he doesn't trust. He turned to the professional crusader, convinced that by doing so, the report would escape God knows what secret conspiracy.'

'If Mascoulin has the report in his hands, why hasn't he used it yet?'

'For the reason I have just given you. He must, periodically, launch a scandal in order to keep up his reputation. But the blackmailing newspapers like *Rumeur* don't publish all the information they get either. On the contrary it's the things they keep silent about which are the most profitable. The Calame report is too precious a morsel to throw as food to the common herd. If Mascoulin has it in his possession, how many top people do you reckon he has at his mercy, including Arthur Nicoud?'

'Quite a number. Several dozen.'

'We don't know how many Calame reports he holds, which he can use at any moment and which will allow him to do his worst, when he feels in a strong enough position.'

'I had thought of that,' Point admitted. 'And it's that that frightens me. If it's Mascoulin who is keeping the report back, it's in perfect safety and I would be surprised if we ever found it. And if we don't produce it or if we have no actual proof that a certain person has destroyed it, I will be disgraced, because it is I who will be accused of its disappearance.'

Maigret saw Mme Point turn her head away because a tear was running down her cheek. Point saw it, too, and for a moment, was almost overcome himself, while Anne-Marie was saying:

'Maman!'

Mme Point shook her head as if to indicate that it was nothing and left the room abruptly.

'You see!' her husband said, as if there were no need for further comment.

Did Maigret do wrong, when he allowed himself to be impressed by the dramatic atmosphere that surrounded him and declared with complete assurance:

'I can't promise you to find the report, but I'll be damned if I don't put my hand on the man or woman who got into your flat and stole it. That at least is my profession.'

'You think you can?'

'I'm certain.'

He had risen from his chair. Point murmured:

'I'm coming down with you.'

And turning to his daughter:

'Run and tell your mother what the superintendent has just said to me. It will do her good.'

They went back the same way as they had come through the corridors of the Ministry and found themselves once again in Point's office where a tall, slender individual, with grey hair, was opening the mail, while Mlle Blanche answered the telephone.

'I would like to introduce Jacques Fleury, my Parliamentary Private Secretary . . . Superintendent Maigret.'

The latter had the impression that he had seen the man somewhere before, probably in a bar or a restaurant. He carried himself well, was dressed with a certain elegance in direct contrast to the careless attire of the Minister. He was the type one frequently meets in the bars of the Champs-Elysées in the company of pretty women.

His hand was dry, his handshake firm. He looked younger, more energetic, from a distance; close to, one saw the weary pouches under the eyes, the slight droop of the lips which he concealed by a nervous smile.

'How many are there in there?' Point asked him, pointing to the waiting-room.

'A good thirty. There are some correspondents from foreign papers as well. I don't know how many camera men, they're still coming in.'

Maigret and the Minister exchanged glances. Maigret seemed to be saying with an encouraging wink:

'Keep your chin up!'

Point asked him:

'Will you go out through the waiting-room?'

'As you will be telling them that I'm in charge of the enquiry, it no longer matters. On the contrary.'

He was aware all the time of the suspicious eyes of Mlle Blanche on him; he had not had time to win her over. She seemed to be still hesitating about the opinion she should be forming of him. Maybe the composure of her employer convinced her, however, that Maigret's intervention was a good thing.

When the superintendent crossed the room the photographers were the first to rush towards him and he did nothing to avoid them. The reporters, too, showered him with questions.

'Are you in charge of the Calame report?'

He waved them away with a smile.

'In a few minutes, the Minister himself will answer your questions.'

'You're not denying that you are connected with it?'

'I deny nothing.'

Some of them followed him to the marble staircase, hoping to force a declaration out of him.

'Ask the Minister,' he repeated. One of them asked:

'D'you believe that Piquemal has been murdered?'

It was the first time that this hypothesis had been clearly stated.

'You know my favourite answer,' he replied, 'I believe nothing.'

A few moments later, after some more camera clicks he got into the car of the P.J. where Lapointe had been spending his time reading the newspapers.

'Where are we going? To the Quai?'

'No. Boulevard Pasteur. What are the papers saying?'

'They are chiefly concerned with Piquemal's disappearance. One of them, I don't remember which, went to interview Mme Calame, who is still in the flat where she lived with her husband, Boulevard Raspail. She appears to be an energetic little woman who doesn't mince her words and didn't try to avoid questions. She hadn't read the report, but remembers well that her husband went to spend a few weeks in the Haute Savoie, about five years ago. On his return, he was very busy and it often happened that he worked till late at night.

'"Never before had he had so many telephone calls," she said. "Crowds of people whom we didn't know from Adam came to see him. He was anxious and worried. When I asked him what was bothering him, he told me it was his work and responsibilities. He often spoke of responsibilities at that time. I had the impression that something was gnawing at him. I knew he was ill. Over a year before the doctor had told me that he was suffering from cancer. I remember that once he sighed: 'Heavens, how difficult it is for a man to know where his duty lies!'"'

They were driving down the Rue Vaugirard and a bus was making them slow down.

'There's a whole column about it,' added Lapointe.

'What did she do with her husband's papers?'

'She left them all as they were in his study which she cleans regularly, just as she did when he was alive.'

'Had anybody come to see her recently?'

'Two people,' replied Lapointe, with an admiring glance at his boss.

'Piquemal?'

'Yes. That was the first visit, about a week ago.'

'Did she know him?'

'Fairly well. While Calame was alive, he often came to get advice from him. She thinks he was studying mathematics. He explained that he wanted to find one of his papers he had once given to his teacher.'

'Did he find it?'

'He had a brief-case with him. She left him in the study, where he remained about an hour. When he came out, she asked him if he had found what he wanted and he said no, that unfortunately his papers must have been lost. She didn't look in his brief-case. She had no suspicion. It was only two days after . . .'

'Who was the second visitor?'

'It was a man about forty, who pretended to be a former pupil of Calame and asked her if she had kept his files. He, too, talked of some work which they had done together.'

'Did she allow him into the study?'

'No. She thought the coincidence was too strange and replied that all her husband's papers had been left in the School of Engineering.'

'Did she describe her second visitor?'

'The paper doesn't mention it. If she did the reporter is keeping it to himself and is probably pursuing his own little enquiry.'

'Park here, by this pavement. It's here.'

By day the boulevard was as peaceful as by night with its own particular reassuring character of middle-class life.

'Do I wait for you?'

'You come with me. We'll probably have some work to do.'

The concierge's glass door was on the left of the hall. She was an elderly, rather dignified woman, who looked tired.

'What is it?' she asked the two men, without getting out of her arm-chair, while a marmalade cat jumped from her lap and came to rub itself against Maigret's legs. He gave his name, and was careful to take off his hat and adopt a respectful tone.

'M. Point has asked me to make enquiries about a robbery of which he was a victim two days ago.'

'A robbery? In the house? He never said anything to me about it!'

'He will confirm it to you, when he sees you and if you have any doubts about it, all you have to do is to telephone him.'

'That's all right. If you're the superintendent, I've got to believe what you say, haven't I? But how could it have happened? This is a quiet house. The police haven't had to set foot in it for the thirty-five years I've been here.'

'I would like you to try and remember what happened on Tuesday, particularly in the morning.'

'Tuesday . . . Wait a moment . . . That was the day before yesterday.'

'Yes. The Minister came to his flat that evening.'

'Did he tell you that?'

'He not only told me, but I met him there. You opened the door for me a little after ten o'clock.'

'I believe I remember, yes.'

'He must have left a short time after me.'

'Yes.'

'Did you open the door to anyone that night?'

'Certainly not. The tenants seldom come home later than midnight. They are all quiet people. I would have remembered if I had.'

'When do you open the door in the morning?'

'At half past six, sometimes seven.'

'After that you remain in the lodge?'

It consisted of one room, with a gas cooker, a round table, a sink, and behind the curtain, a bed with a dark red cover.

'Except when I sweep the stairs.'

'What time is that?'

'Not before nine. After I've taken round the post that comes at half past eight.'

'The lift has glass windows, so I suppose that you can see who goes up and down?'

'Yes. I always watch it, it's a habit.'

'That morning did you see someone going up to the fourth floor?'

'I'm certain I didn't.'

'Nobody asked you if the Minister was at home that morning or even early in the afternoon?'

'Nobody. There was only a telephone call.'

'To you?'

'No, to the flat.'

'How do you happen to know?'

'Because I was on the stairs between the fourth and the fifth floors.'

'What time was it?'

'Perhaps ten o'clock. Perhaps a little earlier. My feet don't allow me to work quickly any more. I heard the telephone behind the door. It rang for a long time. Then, a quarter of an hour later, when I'd finished cleaning and came down there was the telephone again, and I remember I said to myself: "You can ring as long as you like."'

'And then?'

'Nothing.'

'You went back to the lodge?'

'To tidy myself up a bit.'

'You didn't leave the house?'

'For about a quarter of an hour or twenty minutes, as I do every morning, just for my shopping. The grocer is next door, the butcher's at the corner. From the grocers I can see who comes and goes. I always keep an eye on the house.'

'And from the butcher's?'

'I can't see, but I'm never there long. I live alone with my cat and buy the same thing almost every day. At my age, you don't have much of an appetite.'

'You don't know exactly what time it was when you were at the butchers?'

'Not precisely. There is one of those great big clocks over the cashier's desk, but I never look at it.'

'When you got back, you saw no one leave that you hadn't seen come in?'

'I don't remember. No. I'm more concerned with the ones that come in, than with the ones that go out, apart from the tenants that is, because with them I have to be able to answer whether they're in or not. There are always the tradesmen, the gas-men, and the vacuum cleaner salesmen.'

He knew that he would get nothing more from her and that if, later on, she remembered some detail, she would be sure to let him know.

'The inspector and I are going to question your tenants,' said Maigret.

'Go ahead. You'll see they're all good people, except perhaps the old woman on the third, who . . .'

Maigret felt much more himself now he was back on a routine job again.

'We'll come to see you before we leave,' he promised.

And he took care to stroke the cat before he left.

'You take the flats on the left,' he said to Lapointe, 'and I'll tackle the ones on the right. You understand what I'm looking for?'

And he added, familiarly:

'Go to it, old chap!'

Chapter Six

Before ringing at the first door Maigret hesitated, turned to Lapointe who on his side was about to ring the bell.

'You're not thirsty?'

'No, boss.'

'You start. I'll be back in a moment.'

At a pinch he might have made the telephone call he had suddenly thought of from the concierge's lodge. But apart from the fact that he preferred to talk without witnesses, he felt it would be good to have a drink, a glass of white wine, for instance. He had to walk about a hundred yards before he found a small bar where there was not a soul besides the owner.

'A glass of white,' he ordered.

He changed his mind.

'No, I'll have a pernod.'

It was more in harmony with his mood and with the time of day, also with this tidy little bar that seemed permanently empty. He waited to be served and had drunk half of his glass before he went to the telephone.

When the newspapers report the story of an enquiry, one gets the impression that the police follow a straight line, that they know where they are going from the start. Events follow one another logically, like the entries and exits of characters in a well-directed play.

Unnecessary comings and goings are rarely mentioned; neither are the tedious searches in various directions that come to nothing and the haphazard soundings to right and left.

Maigret could not have mentioned a single enquiry during which at one moment or the other, he had not floundered. This morning he had not had the time, at the P.J., to enquire after Lucas, Janvier and Torrence who had all been given instructions the day before, all of which this morning seemed of no importance.

'The P.J.? Will you call Lucas, please. If he isn't there, get me Janvier.'

He heard Lucas' voice at the other end.

'Is that you, boss?'

'It is. First of all will you make a note of something very urgent. I want you to get hold of a photograph of Piquemal, the chap from the School of Engineering. It's useless to look for one in his hotel room. He hasn't one there. I'd be surprised if they haven't one of those group-photos at the school, the kind they take usually at the end of the year. The men at the Identity Department may be able to make some use of it. I want them to get on to it as quickly as possible. There's still time to get the photo into the afternoon papers. It is to be transmitted to all police-stations too. To be sure to miss nothing, I want enquiries made at the Legal Medical Institute.'

'O.K., boss.'

'Any news?'

'I've found the woman called Marcelle; her name is Marcelle Luquet.'

In his own mind, Maigret had already abandoned this line of enquiry, but he did not want to make Lucas feel he had worked for nothing.

'And? . . .'

'She works as a proof-reader at the "Imprimerie du Croissant"; she's a member of the night-team there. It isn't where they print the *Rumeur* or the *Globe*. She's heard Tabard mentioned, but doesn't know him personally. She has never met Mascoulin.'

'Did you talk to her?'

'I gave her a cup of coffee and cream at the Rue Montmartre. She's a nice woman. She lived alone until she met Fleury and fell in love with him. She still loves him. She bears him no grudge for leaving her and if he'd have her back tomorrow, she'd go back to him like a shot. According to her he's just a great child who needs understanding and affection. She insists that though he may be capable of childish manoeuvring, he is incapable of real dishonesty.

'Is Janvier with you?'

'Yes.'

'Put him on, will you?'

Janvier had nothing to say. He had walked the street in front of the block in the Rue Vaneau, until Torrence came to relieve him.

'Blanche Lamotte came home on foot, alone, about 11 p.m. and went up to her room, where the light was on for about half an hour.'

'There was no one about from the Rue des Saussaies?'

'No one. I was able to count the people in the street, coming back from the cinema or the theatre.'

Torrence had had an even less eventful time. He had only seen seven people in the Rue Vaneau the whole night.

'The light went on at 6 a.m. I suppose she gets up early to do her chores. She went out at ten minutes past eight and walked in the direction of the Boulevard Saint-Germain.'

Maigret went back and finished his pernod at the counter and as it was a small one, he ordered another, while he was filling his pipe.

When he came back to the block in the Boulevard Pasteur, he found that Lapointe was busy at his third flat and he began patiently to do his own stint. Questioning people can be a long drawn out affair. At this hour both men found only women at their chores. Their first reaction was to close the door on them thinking they were peddling some kind of domestic gadget or were insurance agents. At the word police, they all gave a start in exactly the same way. While the men talked to them, their minds were elsewhere, on what was boiling at the time on the stove, or what the baby was up to on the floor, or on the vacuum cleaner they had left running. Some of them were embarrassed at being caught in their working clothes and automatically tried to straighten their hair.

'Please try to remember what you did on Tuesday morning . . .'

'Tuesday, yes . . .'

'Did you happen, for instance, to open your door between ten and midday?'

The first woman whom Maigret questioned was not at home at the time but in the hospital where her sister was having an operation. The second, quite a young woman, was holding a child on her arm, supporting it on her hip and was constantly confusing Tuesday and Wednesday.

'I was here, yes. I'm always here in the morning. I do my shopping at the end of the afternoon, after my husband comes back.'

'Did you happen to open your door?'

With infinite patience they had to be gradually led back to the atmosphere of Tuesday morning. Had they been asked point blank: Did you see, in the lift or on the stairs, a stranger to the block going up to the fourth floor . . . ? they would have replied confidently 'no' without giving themselves time to think.

At the third floor Maigret caught up with Lapointe, because he had found no one on the left-hand side of the second floor.

The tenants, who resembled the house, lived quiet uneventful domestic lives behind their doors. The smells varied from one floor to the other, as did the colours of the wallpaper, but it all belonged to the same honest, laborious class of people, that class which is always slightly intimidated by the police. Maigret was struggling with a deaf old woman, who did not ask him in and made him repeat every question. He could hear Lapointe talking behind the door opposite.

'Why do you want me to open my door?' cried the deaf woman. 'Has that cat of a concierge accused me of spying on the tenants?'

'Certainly not, Madame. You aren't being accused of anything.'

'Then why do the police come and question me?'

'We're trying to establish whether a man . . .'

'What man?'

'A man whom we don't know, but whom we're searching for.'

'What are you searching for?'

'A man.'

'What has he done?'

He was still trying to make her understand when the door opposite opened. Lapointe was signalling to Maigret that he had discovered something and the superintendent abruptly left the irate old woman.

'This is Mme Gaudry, boss. Her husband works in a bank on the Boulevard des Italiens. She has a little boy of five.'

Maigret could see the boy hiding behind his mother, clutching at her skirt.

'She sometimes sends the boy to shop in the neighbourhood in the morning, only if the shop is on this side of the boulevard.'

'I don't allow him to cross the road. And I always keep the door half-open when he is out. That is how on Tuesday . . .'

'You heard someone go up?'

'Yes. I was waiting for Bob. At one moment I thought it was him. Most people take the lift, but I don't allow him to do that yet.'

'I can easily work the lift!' the boy said. 'I've done it already.'

'And you got punished for it! What happened was, I just looked out at the very moment a man was crossing the landing and going up to the fourth floor.'

'What time was it?'

'About half past ten. I had just put my stew into the oven.'

'Did the man speak to you?'

'No. At first I only saw him from the back. He was wearing a light beige

overcoat, perhaps it was a raincoat, I didn't look too close, and he had broad
shoulders and a thick neck.'

She glanced at Maigret's neck.

'Rather like mine?'

She hesitated, blushing.

'Not quite. He was younger than you are. In the forties, I would say. I
could see his face when he got to the turn of the stairs and he looked back at
me and seemed upset to find me there.'

'He stopped at the fourth floor?'

'Yes.'

'Did he ring the bell?'

'No. He went into M. Point's flat; it took him quite a time to open the
door.'

'As though he were trying several keys?'

'I couldn't swear to that, but it was as if he wasn't familiar with the lock.'

'Did you see him leave?'

'I didn't see him because coming down he took the lift.'

'Was he there for a long time?'

'Less than ten minutes.'

'Did you stay on the landing all that time?'

'No. But Bob wasn't back yet and I left the door half-open. I heard the lift
go up, stop at the fourth floor and go down again.'

'Could you describe him, apart from his stoutness?'

'It's not easy. He had a red complexion like a man who likes his food.'

'Spectacles?'

'I don't think so. In fact, I'm certain he hadn't any.'

'Was he smoking a pipe? A cigarette?'

'No . . . Wait a moment . . . I'm almost certain he was smoking a cigar . . . It
struck me because my brother-in-law . . .'

It all corresponded, the cigar included, to the description supplied by the
bar owner in the Rue Jacob of the man who had approached Piquemal. It
could also have corresponded to the description of the stranger who had
visited Mlle Blanche in the Rue Vaneau.

A few moments later Maigret and Lapointe met on the pavement.

'Where are we going?'

'Take me to the Embankment. After that, you'll go to the Rue Vaneau and
Rue Jacob to find out if, by any chance, the man was smoking a cigar.'

When Maigret got to his office he found that Lucas had already obtained a
photograph in which Piquemal appeared, though unfortunately only in the
background; it was however clear enough for the specialists of the Identity
Department to work with.

He sent in his name to the Director of the P.J. and spent about half an hour
there putting him in the picture.

'Well, at least we've got something to go on!' sighed the chief when
Maigret had finished.

'Yes, I agree.'

'I shall be even happier when we learn—if we ever do learn—who this man
is.'

They both had the same suspicion and preferred not to speak of it. It was
not impossible that the individual whose tracks they had discovered three
times now, was someone belonging to the other Department, to the Rue des

Saussaies. Maigret had good friends there, especially a man called Catroux, to whose son he had been godfather. He hesitated to approach him for if Catroux knew anything, he risked putting him in a false position.

Piquemal's photograph would appear in the afternoon papers. It would be an irony of fate if the man the P.J. were looking for was all the time in the hands of the Security Department. The latter may have withdrawn him temporarily from circulation because he knew too much. Perhaps they had taken him to the Rue des Saussaies to pump him? The papers were going to announce that the P.J. and Maigret in particular were in charge of the case. It would be fair play for Security to let him loose in the country, then a few hours later to announce that they had caught Piquemal.

'You do believe, of course,' insisted the chief, 'that Point is an honest man and is not concealing anything from you?'

'I could swear to it.'

'And the people round him?'

'I think so. I've made enquiries about each one of them. I don't know everything about their lives, of course, but what I do know makes me think that we must look elsewhere. The letter I showed you . . .'

'Mascoulin?'

'He's certainly mixed up in this business. The letter proves it.'

'What are you going to do?'

'Maybe it won't get me very far, but for some reason I'd like to have a closer look at him. All I have to do is go and lunch at the "Filet de Sole", in the Place de le Victoire where he is supposed to hold his meetings.'

'Be careful.'

'I know.'

He went through the inspectors' office to give some instructions. Lapointe had just come back.

'What about the cigars?'

'It's curious that it should have been a woman who noticed this detail. The owner of the bistro can't say whether the man smoked a pipe, a cigar or a cigarette, though he stayed at his bar for more than a quarter of an hour. Mlle Blanche's concierge is quite definite.'

'He smoked a cigar?'

'No–a cigarette. He threw the butt on the stairs and put it out with his foot.'

It was one o'clock when Maigret walked into the famous restaurant in the Place de la Victoire, feeling apprehensive, for as a humble official it was hardly prudent to measure oneself against a Mascoulin. He had nothing specific against him except a brief note which the deputy could explain in hundreds of different ways. Here, Mascoulin, was on his own ground. Maigret was clearly the intruder and the head waiter watched him come in without rushing to welcome him.

'You have a table?'

'For how many?'

'I'm alone.'

Most of the tables were occupied and there was a continuous hum of conversation, accompanied by the noise of knives and forks and the clinking of glasses. The head waiter looked around and moved towards a table smaller than the others, tucked in behind the door. Finally, in response to a sign, the cloak-room attendant came to take Maigret's coat and hat.

Three other tables were free, but if the superintendent had mentioned them, he would probably have been told that they were reserved, which was quite possible. He had to wait for a long time before his order was taken and had every opportunity of observing everyone in the room.

The restaurant was popular among top people, and at luncheon, they were mostly men, financiers, well known lawyers, journalists and politicians, all belonging more or less to the same circle and making signs of recognition to one another. Some had recognised the superintendent and he was probably talked of in hushed tones at several tables.

Joseph Mascoulin was sitting in the right-hand corner, on a seat against the wall, in the company of Maitre Pinard, a lawyer almost as famous as the deputy for the ferocity of his speeches. A third companion had his back to Maigret; he was a middle-aged man with narrow shoulders and sparse grey hair swept over the bald skull. It was only when he turned sideways that the superintendent recognised him to be Sauvegrain, the brother-in-law and associate of Nicoud whose photograph he had seen in the papers.

Mascoulin who was eating a steak, had already spotted Maigret and stared at him as if there was no one else of any interest in the room. At first his eyes lit up with curiosity which was followed by a faint gleam of irony and now he seemed to be waiting with amusement for the superintendent's next move. The latter had at last given his order, added to it half a bottle of Pouilly and gone on smoking his pipe in little puffs, returning the deputy's stare with unconcern. The difference between them was that, as always in such cases, Maigret's eyes appeared vacant. One had the impression that the object he was staring at was as neutral, as uninteresting as a blank wall and that he was thinking of nothing beyond the Sole Dieppoise which he had just ordered.

He was far from knowing the complete history of Nicoud and his enterprise. Popular belief claimed that Sauvegrain, the brother-in-law, who until he married Nicoud's sister about ten years ago, was only an obscure contractor, participated in the business only in name. He had an office in the Avenue de la République, not far from Nicoud. It was a vast, luxurious office, but Sauvegrain spent his days in it waiting for visitors of little importance who were sent to him to pass the time.

Mascoulin must have had his reasons for accepting him openly at his table. Was Maitre Pinard there because he looked after Sauvegrain's interests?

A newspaper editor stopped at Maigret's table on his way out and shook his hand.

'On the job?' he asked. And as the superintendent pretended not to understand:

'I don't think I've ever seen you here before.'

His eyes turned in Mascoulin's direction.

'I didn't know that the P.J. took on that kind of case. Have you found Piquemal?'

'Not yet.'

'Still searching for the Calame report?'

This was said in a bantering tone, as though the Calame report had existed only in the imagination of certain people or as though if it did exist, Maigret would never be able to find it.

'We're searching'—was Maigret's evasive reply.

The journalist opened his mouth, didn't say what was on the tip of his tongue, and walked out with a cordial wave of the hand. In the doorway he just avoided bumping into a newcomer whom Maigret probably would not have seen if his eyes hadn't been on the newspaper man.

Just as he was about to push open the second door, the man saw the superintendent through the glass pane and his face expressed alarm. Normally, he would have acknowledged Maigret, whom he had known for many years. He almost did so, then threw a hesitant glance in Mascoulin's direction and hoping perhaps that Maigret hadn't had time to recognise him, made an abrupt about turn and vanished.

Mascoulin, from his corner, had missed nothing of the scene, but his poker face registered nothing.

What was Maurice Labat doing at the 'Filet de Sole' and why had he beaten a retreat when he saw Maigret in the restaurant?

For about ten years he had been working in a department in the Rue des Saussaies and there had even been a time, true, a very brief one, during which he was believed to have had an influence on the Minister.

Suddenly it was learnt that he had handed in his resignation, then that he had not done so at his own will, but to avoid some more serious unpleasantness. Since then he had continued to be seen on the fringe of circles who frequented places like the 'Filet de Sole'. He had not, as had many others, in the same situation, opened a private investigation agency. No one knew what his profession was, nor what his resources were. Besides having a wife and children he had a mistress in a flat in the Rue de Ponthieu, who was twenty years younger than he and must have cost him a pretty penny.

Maigret was neglecting his Sole Dieppoise and not paying it the attention it deserved, for the Labat incident had given him plenty to think about.

Was it not natural to presume that the person whom the former policeman had come to see at the 'Filet de Sole' was none other than Mascoulin? Labat was that man in a thousand whom one could entrust with the slightly shady jobs and he must have kept some friends in the Rue des Saussaies. Did he hope in beating a hasty retreat that Maigret had not had time to recognise him? Had Mascoulin, whom the superintendent was not able to observe at that moment, given him a sign not to come in? If Labat had been about forty, stout and smoking a cigar, the superintendent would have been certain that he had discovered the man who had gone to the Boulevard Pasteur and the Rue Vaneau and the one who had spirited Piquemal away.

But Labat was barely thirty-six. He was a Corsican and looked like one. Small and slender he wore high heeled shoes in order to appear taller and had a brown moustache like two commas. Last but not least he smoked cigarettes from morning till night and his fingers were yellow with nicotine. But his appearance nevertheless gave Maigret food for thought, and he reproached himself for being so hypnotised by the Rue des Saussaies. Labat had been one of them, but was no longer and there must have been dozens like him in Paris, whom Security had got rid of for more or less similar reasons. Maigret made a mental note to get hold of a list of these men. He was on the point of telephoning straight away to Lucas to ask him to provide one. The reason why he did not do so, strange as it may seem, was that he hesitated to cross the room under Mascoulin's mocking eyes. The latter, who had not ordered any dessert, was already at the coffee stage. Maigret did not order any dessert either, only some coffee and brandy, and began to fill his pipe, going over faces that he had known in the Rue des Saussaies. He felt like a man searching for a name that is on the tip of his tongue but which keeps eluding him.

From the moment the stout man had been mentioned and particularly since a cigar had been brought into the picture, something had been stirring in his memory. He was so wrapped up in his own thoughts that he hardly noticed that Mascoulin had risen and was wiping his lips with his napkin and exchanging a few words with his companions. More precisely he watched him rise, push the table to make way for himself and finally move quietly across the room towards him, but it was as though all this did not concern him at all.

'May I, Superintendent?' Mascoulin was saying, holding the back of the chair facing Maigret.

His face was serious, with a slight, ironical quiver in the corner of his mouth which might have been only a nervous tic.

For a moment, Maigret was taken aback. He had not expected this. He had never heard Mascoulin's voice, which was grave and had a pleasant quality to it. It was said that it was because of his voice that some women, in spite of his unappealing Grand Inquisitor's face, fought for places in the Chamber when he was expected to speak.

'What a curious coincidence that you should have come here today. I was going to telephone you.'

Maigret remained impassive for he was determined to make Mascoulin's task as difficult as possible, but the deputy did not seem to be at all put out of countenance by his silence.

'I've only learnt just now that you are working on Piquemal and the Calame report.' He spoke in an undertone, because of the other people in the room; they were being watched from several tables.

'I've not only got important information to pass on to you, but I believe I ought to make an official announcement. Perhaps you would like to send one of your inspectors to the Chamber a little later, to put it on record? Anyone will tell him where to find me.'

Maigret remained unperturbed.

'It's about this Piquemal with whom it happens I was in contact last week.'

Maigret had Mascoulin's letter in his pocket and began to understand why the man felt it necessary to speak to him.

'I don't remember which day it was, my secretary handed me one of the many letters which I receive every week and which he has to answer. It was signed "Piquemal" and had an address of an hotel in the Rue Jacob, the name of which I have forgotten—the name of some provincial town, I think.'

Without taking his eyes off Mascoulin's face Maigret sipped his coffee and went on puffing at his pipe.

'Every day, as you can imagine, I receive hundreds of letters from every type of person: cranks, semi-lunatics, honest men who point out some violation of rights or other, and it is my secretary's job to separate the sheep from the goats. He's a worthy young man in whom I have full confidence.'

Why did it cross Maigret's mind, as he was studying the other man's face, that Mascoulin was a homosexual? There had never been the slightest hint of anything like that. If he was, he concealed it carefully. It occurred to the superintendent that it might explain certain traits in his character.

'The Piquemal letter seemed sincere to me and I'm certain you will have the same impression, if I can find it again, for I shall consider it my duty to send it to you. In it he told me that he was the only man in Paris who knew the whereabouts of the Calame report and could lay hands on it. He added that he addressed himself to me rather than to an official body because he knew that too many people were interested in hushing up the story and that I was the only one who inspired him with confidence. I apologise for repeating these words. I sent him a note on the off chance, giving him an appointment.'

Very calmly, Maigret pulled his note-book out of his pocket and took out the letter with the Chamber of Deputies heading, which he merely showed, without handing it across the table in spite of Mascoulin's movement to snatch it.

'Is it this note?'

'I believe so. I seem to recognise my own handwriting.'

He did not ask how it had come to be in Maigret's possession, avoided showing any surprise and said:

'I see you know all about it. I met him at the Brasserie de Croissant which is not far from the printers and where I keep some of my appointments in the evening. He seemed to me a little too excited, too cranky for my taste. I let him speak.'

'He told you he was in possession of the report?'

'Not exactly. Men like him never behave as simply as that. They need an atmosphere of conspiracy. He told me he was working in the School of Engineering, that he had been Professor Calame's assistant and that he believed he knew where to find the report Calame had written on the subject of the Clairfond sanatorium. The conversation didn't last more than ten minutes, as I had some proofs to read.'

'After that Piquemal brought you the report?'

'I never saw him again. He suggested bringing it to me on Monday or Tuesday, at the latest on Wednesday. I replied that I didn't want to touch it—you can understand my reasons. That report is sheer dynamite, as we have seen today.'

'To whom did you advise him to hand it?'

'To his chief.'

'You mean the Director of the School of Engineering?'

'I don't think I was so precise. I may have mentioned the Ministry which naturally came to mind.'

'Did he try to telephone you?'

'Not that I know of.'

'Nor to see you?'

'If he did, he didn't succeed for as I told you before, I had no news of him except from the papers. It seems that he followed my advice, exaggerating it slightly, for he went straight to the Minister. As soon as I heard about his disappearance I told myself I must let you know about the incident. Now it's done. Considering the possible repercussions it might have, I prefer to make a statement and have it properly recorded. So, this afternoon . . . if . . .'

There was nothing else for it. Maigret would have to send someone to him to take his statement. The inspector would find Mascoulin surrounded by his colleagues and journalists. Was it not an excellent way of accusing Auguste Point?

'Thank you,' was all he said. 'I'll give the necessary instructions.'

Mascoulin seemed taken aback, as though he had expected something different. Had he imagined that the superintendent would put embarrassing questions to him or would show in some way that he disbelieved him?

'I'm only doing my duty. If I'd known how things were going to turn out I'd have told you about it before . . .'

He seemed to be playing a part all the time, almost, one would have sworn, without attempting to conceal it. He appeared to be saying: 'I've been smarter than you. Try to find an answer to that one!' Was Maigret wrong? Certainly, from one point of view, because he had nothing to win—on the contrary, he had everything to lose, in measuring himself against a man as powerful and as crafty as Mascoulin.

The latter stood up and stretched out his hand. The superintendent was suddenly reminded of Point and his story about dirty hands. Without weighing up the pros and cons he picked up his cup of coffee which was empty and carried it to his lips, thus ignoring the hand that was offered to him.

A shadow seemed to flicker in the deputy's eyes. The quiver in the corner of his mouth, far from disappearing, became more accentuated.

But he only murmured:

'Goodbye, Monsieur Maigret.'

Did he intentionally stress the 'Monsieur'? It seemed to Maigret he did. If so it was a barely disguised threat, for it meant that Maigret was not to be allowed to enjoy his title of superintendent for very long.

He followed him with his eyes as he went back to his table and bent over his companions, then called in an absent-minded way:

'Waiter, the bill, please!'

At least a dozen persons who, in one capacity or another, played an important part in the life of the country, had their eyes fixed on him.

Maigret must have drunk his brandy without noticing it; as he went out, he was surprised to find the flavour of it still in his mouth.

Chapter Seven

It was not the first time he had made this kind of entrance, more as a friend than as a boss. He opened the door of the inspectors' office and pushing his hat to the back of his head, went and sat on a corner of a table. He emptied his pipe on the floor by knocking it against his heel and then filled another one. He was watching them as they busied themselves about their different jobs, with the expression of a paterfamilias who comes back home in the evening, pleased to be among his brood and summing them up.

Some time elapsed before he growled:

'Lapointe, my boy, I reckon you're going to have your picture in the papers.'

Lapointe raised his head, trying not to blush, his eyes expressing incredulity. In fact, all of them, with the exception of Maigret, who was much too used to it, were secretly delighted when newspapers published their photographs. But every time it happened, they never failed to protest.

'With such publicity, it'll be easy now to work under cover and not be noticed!'

The others were listening too. If Maigret had come to speak to Lapointe in the general common office, it meant that what he had to say to him was addressed to them all.

'You're going to provide yourself with a shorthand note-book and go to the Chamber. You won't have any trouble finding the deputy Mascoulin, I'm sure, and I'll be surprised if you don't find him surrounded by people. He will make a statement to you, which you will carefully take down. Then you'll come here and type it and leave it on my desk.'

The afternoon papers were sticking out of his pocket, with the photograph of Auguste Point and his own on the front page. He had hardly looked at them. He knew almost exactly what was being said.

'Is that all?' asked Lapointe who had gone to fetch his overcoat and hat from the cupboard.

'For the moment.'

Maigret remained where he was, smoking dreamily.

'Listen, my children . . .'

The inspectors raised their heads.

'I want you to think of some of the Rue des Saussaies men, who were either dismissed or obliged to resign . . .'

'You mean recently?' asked Lucas.

'It doesn't matter when. Let's say during the last ten years.'

Torrence exclaimed:

'There must be a whole list of them!'

'Well, give me some names then.'

'Baudelin. The one who is enquiry agent for an insurance company now.'

Maigret tried to recall Baudelin, a tall, pale young man who probably left Security not for dishonesty or indiscreet behaviour, but because he brought more energy and skill to pretending to be ill, than doing his job.

'Anyone else?'

'Falconet.'

This one was over fifty; he had been asked to advance the age of retirement because he had started to drink and had become unreliable.

'Anyone else?'

'Little Valencourt.'

'Too small.'

Contrary to what they had expected at the beginning, they could only think of a few names and each time, after conjuring up the man's appearance, Maigret shook his head.

'It doesn't really fit. I'm looking for a stoutish man, someone like myself.'

'Fischer.'

There was a general burst of laughter, because the man weighed at least eighteen stone.

'Thanks!' growled Maigret.

He stayed a while with them and finally sighed and got to his feet.

'Lucas! Would you please telephone the Rue des Saussaies and ask for Catroux?'

Now that he was only interested in inspectors who had left Security, he no longer felt that he was asking his friend to betray his colleagues. Catroux, who had worked for twenty years in the Rue des Saussaies would be better placed than the P.J. men to answer his question. There was a feeling in the air that the superintendent was on to something, that he was working on an idea; it was still vague, perhaps not quite clear to him yet. His sham gruffness, his eyes that stared at people without seeing them, were a sign that he knew now in which direction to search.

He kept trying to remember a name which he had on the tip of his tongue a moment ago. Lucas was telephoning, talking in a warm, familiar way to the man on the other end of the line who must have been a friend.

'Catroux is not there, boss.'

'You're not going to tell me that he's on some mission at the other end of France?'

'No, he's ill.'

'In hospital?'

'No, at home.'

'Did you ask for his address?'

'No, I thought you had it.'

It is true, they were good friends, Catroux and he. Nevertheless they had never been in each other's homes. Maigret could only remember leaving his colleague one day at his door, at the far end of the Boulevard des Batignolles, on the left, and he remembered a restaurant to the right of the door.

'Has Piquemal's photo appeared in the papers?'

'Yes, on the second page.'

'No one has telephoned about it?'

'Not yet.'

He went to his office, opened a few letters, brought Torrence some papers that concerned him and finally went down to the yard where he hesitated to use one of the P.J. cars. Finally he took a taxi. Though his visit to Catroux was quite innocent, he considered it more prudent not to keep a car from the Quai des Orfèvres waiting at the door.

At first he mistook the house, for there were now two restaurants at fifty yards distance from one another. He asked the concierge:

'M. Catroux?'

'On the second floor, to the right. The lift is being mended.'

He rang the bell. He did not remember Mme Catroux who opened the door to him and recognised him at once.

'Come in, M. Maigret.'

'Is your husband in bed?'

'No, he's in an arm-chair. It's only a bad touch of 'flu. Usually he has one at the beginning of every winter. This time it caught up with him at the end.'

On the walls were portraits of two children, a boy and a girl, at every age. Not only were both now married, but photographs of grandchildren were beginning to increase the collection.

'Maigret?' Catroux's delighted voice called out before the superintendent had reached the door of the room where he was sitting.

It was not a sitting-room, but a large room where one felt the greater part of the life of the house was lived. Catroux, wrapped up in a thick dressing-gown, was sitting near the window, newspapers in his lap, more of them on a chair nearby, a bowl of tisane on a small table. He held a cigarette in his hand.

'You're allowed to smoke?'

'Sh . . . sh . . . Don't side with my wife. Only a few puffs now and again, to take away the taste.'

He was hoarse and his eyes were feverish.

'Take off your overcoat. It must be very hot in here. My wife insists that I've got to sweat. Do sit down.'

'Can I give you a drink, M. Maigret?' the wife asked.

She looked like an old woman and the superintendent was surprised by that. He and Catroux were about the same age. It seemed to Maigret that his own wife looked much younger.

'Of course, Isabelle. Whatever he says go and bring the bottle of old calvados.'

There was an embarrassed silence between the two men. Catroux obviously knew that his colleague from the P.J. had not come to enquire about his health and he perhaps expected even more embarrassing questions than Maigret had in mind.

'Don't worry, old chap. I have no desire to get you into any trouble.'

At this point, the other man glanced at the front page of the newspaper as though saying: 'This is what it's about, isn't it?'

Maigret waited for his glass of calvados.

'And what about me?' his friend protested.

'You're not supposed to have any.'

'The doctor said nothing about that.'

'I don't need a doctor to tell me what to do.'

'Just a drop, to kid myself!'

She gave him a drop and disappeared discreetly, as Mme Maigret would have done.

'I have an idea at the back of my mind,' admitted Maigret. 'A moment or two ago my inspectors and I tried to draw up a list of people who have worked with you and been chucked out.'

Catroux was looking at the paper, trying to link what Maigret was saying with what he had just read.

'Chucked out, why?'

'Never mind why. You know what I mean. It happens with us too but less often because there are fewer of us.'

Catroux gave a teasing smile.

'Is that why you think?'

'Perhaps also because we are not involved with so many things. Let's put it this way, the temptation is less strong. We racked our brains just now, but we could only think of a few names.'

'Which names?'

'Baudelin, Falconet, Valencourt, Fischer . . .'

'Is that all?'

'More or less. I thought it would be better to come and see you. They are not what I'm looking for. I want the men who have gone to the bad.'

'Someone like Labat?'

Was it not strange that Catroux should have mentioned this particular name? He could almost have been doing it on purpose as a way of slipping Maigret some information.

'I did think of him. He's probably mixed up in it all right. But he's not the one I'm looking for.'

'You've got a definite name in mind?'

'A name and a face. I started off with a description, and from the beginning it reminded me of someone. Since then . . .'

'What is the description? We'll get on quicker than if I give you a whole list. Particularly as I haven't got all the names in my head either.'

'First of all people took him to be a policeman straight away.'

'This could apply to plenty of people.'

'Middle-aged. Somewhat stouter than average but not as stout as I am.'

Catroux seemed to be estimating his friend's size.

'Either I'm greatly mistaken, or he is making enquiries on his own behalf or for someone else.'

'A private investigator?'

'Perhaps. He needn't necessarily have put his name on an office door, or advertised in the papers.'

'There are plenty of them, including lots of old, honourable men, who have reached the age limit and then opened an agency. Louis Canange, for example. And Cadet, who was my boss.'

'We have some of those, too. I mean the other kind.'

'What else is in your description?'

'He smokes cigars.'

Immediately Maigret realised that his friend had thought of a name. His forehead wrinkled. A disturbed expression crossed his face.

'It means something to you?'

'Yes.'

'Who?'

'A bad one.'

'That's what I'm looking for.'

'A bad one in a small way, but dangerous.'

'Why?'

'Firstly, that kind of person is always dangerous. Furthermore, he's believed to do some politicians' dirty work.'

'It fits perfectly.'

'You think he's mixed up in this business?'

'If he answers to the description I've given you, if he smokes cigars and meddles in politics there's every chance he's my man. You don't want to . . .'

Suddenly Maigret could see a face before him, a rather large face with bags under the eyes, thick lips, deformed by cigar smoking.

'Wait . . . It's coming back to me. It's . . .'

But he still could not get the name.

'Benoit,' prompted Catroux, 'Eugene Benoit. He's opened a small private office in the Boulevard Saint-Martin, on the ground floor over a watch-makers. His name is on the window-pane. I think the door is more often closed than open; the whole staff of the agency consists of himself.'

It was the man whom the superintendent had been trying to remember for the past twenty-four hours.

'I don't suppose it would be very easy to get his photo?'

Catroux thought a moment before replying.

'It depends on the exact date when he left the service. It was . . .'

He made some calculations under his breath and then called out:

'Isabelle!'

Isabelle was not far away and came running.

'Look in the lower shelf of the bookcase for a register of the Security

Office. There's only one, dating back several years. It contains two or three hundred photos.'

His wife found it at once and he turned the pages, pointed his finger to his own portrait, and found what he was searching for at the back of the book.

'There you are! There he is. He's a few years younger there, but he hasn't changed much. He's always been stout, as far as I can remember.'

Maigret also recognised him, for he had in fact met him in the past.

'Do you mind if I cut out the photo?'

'Of course not. Isabelle, bring some scissors.'

Maigret slipped the bit of shiny paper into his pocket and got to his feet.

'You're in a hurry?'

'Yes, I am rather. And I'm sure you'd rather I didn't tell you too much.'

The other man understood what he meant. Until Maigret knew exactly what Security were doing it was healthier for Catroux that his colleague should tell him as little as possible about it.

'You aren't afraid?'

'Not really.'

'And you believe that Point . . . ?'

'I'm convinced that they are trying to make a scapegoat of him.'

'Another drink.'

'No thank you. Get well soon.'

Mme Catroux saw him to the door and when he got out of the house he took another taxi and told him to go to the Rue Vaneau. He was just trying out his luck. He knocked at the concierge's lodge. She recognised him.

'Forgive me for bothering you again. I would like you to look carefully at a photograph and tell me if this was the man who went up to Mlle Blanche's flat. Take your time.'

It was not necessary. With a moment's hesitation, she shook her head.

'Definitely not.'

'You're certain?'

'Quite certain.'

'Even if the photo dates back a few years and the man has changed?'

'Even if he was wearing a false beard, I'd swear that's not the man.'

He looked at her out of the corner of his eye. For a moment the idea occurred to him that this was something she had been told to say. But no, she looked perfectly sincere!

'Thank you,' he sighed, slipping the photograph back into his pocket.

It was a blow. He had been almost certain that he was on the right track and it had come to nothing at the first testing.

His taxi was waiting and because it was close by he told him to go to the Rue Jacob and walked into the bistro where Piquemal had always had his breakfast. There was hardly anyone there at this time of day.

'Would you care to have a look at this photo?' he asked the owner.

He almost avoided looking at him, for fear of what the reply would be.

'It's certainly the man. Only he seemed to me a little older than that.'

'That's the man who came up to Piquemal and left your place with him?'

'That's him.'

'You are quite certain?'

'Quite.'

'Thank you.'

'You won't have a drink?'

'Not now, thanks. I'll be coming back.'

This changed everything. Until now Maigret had presumed that the same man had visited different places: Mlle Blanche's flat, Piquemal's little bar, the Hotel du Berry, the professor's widow and the Boulevard Pasteur. Suddenly it turned out that there were at least two men.

His next visit was to Mme Calame, whom he found reading the papers.

'I hope you'll find my husband's report. I can understand now why he was so worried in the last years. I've always had such a horror of these filthy politics.'

She studied him with suspicion, thinking perhaps to herself that it was for the sake of these 'filthy politics' that he had come to see her.

'What is it you want, today?'

He handed her the photograph. She examined it carefully, then raised her head in surprise.

'Ought I to be able to recognise him?'

'Not necessarily. I was wondering if he was the man who visited you two or three days after Piquemal.'

'I've never seen him.'

'You couldn't be mistaken about that?'

'No. It could be the same type of person, but I'm certain it's not the man who came here.'

'Thank you.'

'What happened to Piquemal? Do you think they killed him?'

'Why?'

'I don't know. If they are desperate to hush up the report my husband wrote, then they've got to get rid of everyone who knows about it.'

'They didn't get rid of your husband.'

This reply clearly put her out. She felt herself obliged to protect her husband's memory.

'My husband knew nothing about politics. He was a scientist. He was doing his duty when he wrote the report and when he passed it on to the proper quarters.'

'I'm quite sure that he was doing his duty.'

He decided to go before she started discussing the matter in greater depth. The taxi-driver looked enquiringly at him.

'Where now?'

'To the Hotel du Berry.'

He found a couple of journalists there looking for information on Piquemal. They rushed up to Maigret, but he shook his head.

'I've nothing to tell you, boys. Just a routine check. I promise you that . . .'

'D'you hope to find Piquemal alive?'

So they were thinking it too?

He left them in the passage while he was showing the photograph to the hotel proprietor.

'What am I supposed to do with this?'

'Tell me if he's the man who came to talk to you about Piquemal.'

'Which one?'

'Not my inspector, who hired a room, but the other one.'

'No.'

He was quite definite. So far, Benoit was the man who had left the bar with Piquemal, but he had not been seen anywhere else.

'Thank you.'

He jumped into the taxi.

'Drive on . . .'

Only when they had started and he had got rid of the journalists, did he give the address of the Boulevard Pasteur. He did not stop at the lodge, but went straight up to the third floor. No one answered the bell, so he had to go down again.

'Mme Gaudry is not at home?'

'She went out half an hour ago with her son.'

'You don't know when she'll be back?'

'She didn't have her hat on. She must be shopping in the neighbourhood. I don't think she'll be long.'

Rather than wait on the pavement he went to the bar where he had been in the morning, and telephoned the P.J. on the off chance. Lucas answered from the inspector's office.

'Anything fresh?'

'Two telephone calls about Piquemal. The first from a taxi-driver who believes he drove him yesterday to the Gare du Nord. The other from a cinema cashier who thinks she sold him a ticket yesterday evening. I'm going to check.'

'Is Lapointe back?'

'A few minutes ago. He hasn't started to type yet.'

'Put him on, will you?'

And to Lapointe:

'Well. Any photographers?'

'Yes, they were there, boss, clicking away the whole time while Mascoulin was speaking.'

'Where did he see you?'

'In the Pillar room. It was just like Saint-Lazare station! The ushers had to hold the crowd back to give us room to breathe!'

'Was his private secretary there?'

'I don't know. I wouldn't recognise him. We never met.'

'Is it long?'

'It'll make about three typed pages. Some of the reporters took shorthand notes the same time as I did.'

So Mascoulin's statement would be in the last edition of the evening papers.

'He insisted I was to bring it to him to sign.'

'What did you say?'

'That it wasn't my affair. That I would wait for your orders.'

'Do you know if there is a night session at the Chamber?'

'I don't think so. I heard them say that it would be over by 5 p.m.'

'Type it out and wait for me.'

Little Mme Gaudry was not back yet. He walked up and down the pavement for a while and saw her arrive, carrying a shopping bag of provisions, her son trotting at her side. She recognised him.

'Is it me you want to see?'

'Just for a moment.'

'Come upstairs. I've just been doing my shopping.'

'Maybe it isn't worth while coming up.'

The boy was pulling at her sleeve, asking:

'Who is it? Why does he want to talk to you?'

'Be quiet. He just wants some information from me.'

'What information?'

Maigret had pulled the photograph out of his pocket.

'Do you recognise him?'

She managed to free herself, bent over the piece of shiny paper and answered quite spontaneously.

'Yes, that's him.'

It established that Eugene Benoit, the man with the cigar, had been in two places: first in the Boulevard Pasteur where he had probably taken possession of the Calame report, then in the Rue Jacob bar, where he had gone up to Piquemal and with whom he was seen leaving in the opposite direction to the School of Engineering.

'Haven't you found him?' asked Mme Gaudry.

'Not yet. It won't take us long, though.'

He hailed another taxi to take him to the Boulevard Saint-Martin, regretting that he had not taken a P.J. car, for it meant having to discuss his expenses with the accountant.

The house was an old one. The lower part of the window-panes, on the ground floor, was grimy, and on it, in black letters, were the words:

THE BENOIT AGENCY
INVESTIGATIONS OF ALL KINDS

On both sides of the doorway name-plates announced an artificial flowers business, a Swedish masseuse and other professions, some of them of the more unexpected kind. The stairs on the left, were dark and dirty. The name of Benoit appeared again on an enamel plate attached to a door. He knocked, knowing beforehand that there would be no reply, for there was a heap of handbills pushed under the door. After waiting for a moment, to ease his conscience, he went down and finally found the lodge at the bottom of the yard. There was no concierge in it, only a shoemaker who used it as a workshop.

'Is it long since you saw M. Benoit?'

'I haven't seen him today, if that's what you want to know.'

'And yesterday?'

'I don't know. I don't think so. I didn't notice.'

'And the day before?'

'Nor that day either.'

He had a mocking air about him and Maigret pushed his badge under the man's nose.

'I've told you all I know. I don't mean any harm. The tenants' business doesn't concern me.'

'D'you know his private address?'

'It would be in the ledger.'

He rose reluctantly and went to fetch a filthy register from a dresser in the kitchen, and turned the pages with fingers, black with wax.

'The last I have is the Hotel Beaumarchais in the Boulevard Beaumarchais.'

It was not far away and Maigret walked there.

'He moved three weeks ago,' they told him. 'He only stayed here for two months.'

This time he was directed to a rather shady pension in the Rue Saint-Denis, in front of which stood a huge girl who opened her mouth to say something, then recognised him at the last moment and shrugged her shoulders.

'He has room 19. He's not at home.'

'Did he spend the night here?'

'Emma! Did you do M. Benoit's room this morning?'

A head came over the banisters of the first floor.

'Who's asking for him?'

'Never mind who it is. Tell me.'

'No. He didn't spend the night here.'

'And the night before?'

'No.'

Maigret asked for the key of the room. The girl who had answered from the first floor followed him to the third, on the pretext that she was showing him the way. As the doors were numbered, he had no need of her at all. But he asked her a few questions.

'Does he live alone?'

'Are you asking me if he sleeps alone?'

'Yes.'

'Quite often,'

'Has he got a regular girl-friend?'

'He has plenty of them.'

'What kind?'

'The kind that is willing to come here.'

'Are they often the same ones?'

'I have seen the same face two or three times.'

'Does he pick them up in the street?'

'I'm not there to see.'

'He's not been here for two days?'

'Two or three days. I'm not quite sure.'

'Do men sometimes come and see him?'

'If you mean what I think you mean, he's not that type, and the hotel isn't, either. There's one of those kind of places farther down the street.'

The room revealed little to Maigret. It was a typical room for a place of that sort, with a brass bed, an old chest of drawers, a dilapidated arm-chair and hot and cold running water. The drawers contained some underclothes, an unfinished box of cigars, a broken watch, fish-hooks of different sizes in a cellophane bag, but no papers of interest. In a suitcase with expanding sides he found only shoes and dirty shirts.

'Does he often stay away at night?'

'More often than not. And every Saturday he goes to the country until Monday.'

This time Maigret drove back to the Quai des Orfèvres where Lapointe had long since finished typing Mascoulin's statement.

'Get me the Chamber on the phone and find out if the deputies are still there.'

'Am I to say you want to speak to him?'

'No. Don't mention either me or the P.J.'

When he turned to Lucas, the latter shook his head.

'There was one other call after the first two. They've been checked.

Torrence is still on it. There was nothing there.'

'Nothing to do with Piquemal?'

'No. The taxi-driver was quite certain it was, but his client was traced back to his own house and it wasn't Piquemal.'

There would be new leads, especially in tomorrow's post.

'The session in the Chamber finished half an hour ago,' Lapointe announced. 'It was just a vote on . . .'

'I don't care what the vote was on.'

He knew Mascoulin lived in the Rue d'Antin, two steps away from the Opéra.

'Are you busy at the moment?'

'No, nothing important.'

'In that case come with me and bring the statement with you.'

Maigret never took the wheel. He had tried several times, after the P.J. had been provided with a number of small black cars and he had forgotten he was driving, he was so deep in thought. Two or three times, he had remembered his brakes only at the last moment and now he had no wish to repeat the experience.

'Do we take a car?'

'Yes.'

It was as if to apologise to the accountant for all his taxis that afternoon.

'Do you know the number in the Rue d'Antin?'

'No. It's the oldest house.'

The house looked respectable, old, but well maintained.

Maigret and his companion stopped in front of the lodge which was like the sitting-room of a petty bourgeois family and smelt of floor polish and velvet.

'M. Mascoulin.'

'You have an appointment?'

Maigret took a chance and said yes. At the same time the woman in black looked at him, then glanced at the front page of the paper and back at him again.

'I suppose I have to let you go up, M. Maigret. It's on the first floor on the left.'

'Has he been living here long?'

'It'll be eleven years in December.'

'Does his secretary live with him?'

She gave a little laugh.

'Certainly not.'

He got the impression that she had guessed what he was driving at.

'They work late at night?'

'Often. Almost always. I think M. Mascoulin must be the busiest man in Paris, to go by all the post he gets here and at the Chamber.'

Maigret was tempted to show her Benoit's photograph and ask if she had seen him before, but she would probably talk about it to her tenant and Maigret was not prepared to show his hand just yet.

'Are you connected with him by private telephone?'

'How do you know that?'

It was not difficult to guess because beside the ordinary instrument there was another, lighter one, attached to the wall. Mascoulin took no chances. And she would warn him of Maigret's arrival as soon as he and Lapointe were on the stairs. It was not important. He could have prevented it by leaving Lapointe in the lodge.

To begin with, no one answered the bell but a little later Mascoulin himself opened the door, without even bothering to show that he was surprised.

'I thought that you would come in person and that you would choose to come here. Come in.'

The floor was littered with newspapers, periodicals, parliamentary debates, reports. There were more of them in a room that served as a sitting-room and that was about as attractive as a dentist's waiting-room. Obviously Mascoulin was interested in neither luxury nor comfort.

'I expect you would like to see my study?'

There was something insulting in his irony, in his manner of pretending to guess his visitors' intentions, but the superintendent retained his composure.

'I'm not one of your fans coming to ask for your autograph,' was all he replied.

'Will you come this way?'

They went through a padded double door and found themselves in a spacious study, both windows of which looked out on to the street. Green filing-cabinets covered two of the walls. There were law-books that one finds in every lawyer's room everywhere and finally here too the floor was littered with newspapers and files as many as in any Ministry.

'May I introduce Rene Falk, my secretary?'

Rene Falk was not more than twenty-five, blond, frail, with a strangely childish, petulant expression.

'Pleased to meet you,' he murmured, looking at Maigret in much the same manner as Mlle Blanche had looked at him the first time she met him. Like Mlle Blanche too, he was no doubt fanatically devoted to his employer and regarded every stranger as an enemy.

'You've brought the statement? With several copies, I presume?'

'I've brought three copies; two of them are for you to sign, as you wished, and the third for your files or for whatever purpose you choose.'

Mascoulin took the documents, passed one to Rene Falk, who began to read it at the same time as his boss.

Sitting at his desk, he took a pen, added a comma here and there, deleted a word and then murmured, turning to Lapointe:

'I hope this doesn't offend you at all?'

When he came to the last line, he signed, carried over the corrections to the second copy which he also signed.

Maigret stretched out his hand, but Mascoulin did not give him the pages. Neither did he carry over the corrections to the third copy.

'Correct?' he asked his secretary.

'Yes, I think so.'

'Put them through the machine.'

He looked maliciously in Maigret's direction.

'A man who has as many enemies as I have cannot afford to be careless,' he said. 'Particularly when there are so many people determined to keep a certain document from the public eye.'

Falk opened a door and left it open behind him so that a small room was visible, no doubt previously a kitchen or bathroom. A photostatic machine was standing on a white wood table. The secretary pressed some buttons. The machine gave a buzzing sound as he pushed in the pages one after the other, at the same time as other sheets of special paper. Maigret, who knew the system, but who had rarely seen a machine of this kind in a private house, followed the operation with apparent indifference.

'Marvellous invention, isn't it?' Mascoulin said, his lips curving in the same ugly smile. 'A carbon copy can be disputed. But you can't argue with a photostat.'

A faint smile flickered across Maigret's face and the deputy noticed it.

'What's in your mind?'

'I was just wondering if, out of all the people who have had the Calame report in their possession recently, one of them had had the idea of having it photostated.'

It was not inadvertently that Mascoulin had let him see the machine. Falk could easily have disappeared with the documents for a moment, without the superintendent knowing what he was going to do in the next room.

The pages came out through a slot and the secretary spread them out, still damp, on the table.

'It would be a nasty trick to play on anyone interested in hushing the affair up, wouldn't it?' Mascoulin said with a leer. Maigret looked at him in silence, his expression perfectly neutral, and at the same time at its most ominous.

'Yes, a nasty trick,' he repeated. And an imperceptible cold shudder ran down his spine.

Chapter Eight

It was half past six when the two men reached the Boulevard Saint-Germain and the yard of the Ministry was empty. As Maigret and Lapointe crossed it in the direction of the stairs leading to the Minister, a voice sounded behind them.

'Hi! You two, over there! Where are you going?'

The guard had not seen them come in. They stood still, turning to him in the middle of the yard and he limped up to them, glanced at the badge Maigret showed him, then looked at his face.

'I beg your pardon. I saw your picture in the paper a moment ago.'

'Good for you! Now you are here, can you tell me . . .' It had become a habit, this taking the photograph out of his brief-case. 'Have you seen this face before?'

The man, anxious not to blunder a second time, examined it carefully, after putting on steel-framed spectacles with thick lenses. He was not saying yes or no. Before committing himself he would have liked to ask what it was all about, but did not dare.

'He's a little older now, isn't he?'

'Yes, a few years older.'

'He has a black two-seater, an old model?'

'It's possible.'

'Then it's probably the chap I pinched for parking in the yard in the space reserved for the Ministry cars.'

'When was that?'

'Can't remember the day. At the beginning of the week.'

'Did he give his name?'

'He just shrugged his shoulders and went and parked his car at the other end.'

'Did he go up the big staircase?'

'Yes.'

'Try and remember the day, while we are upstairs.'

In the waiting-room on the first floor, the usher was still at his post reading the newspapers. Maigret showed him the photograph, too.

'When might he have been here?' the man asked.

'Around the beginning of the week.'

'I wasn't here. My wife died and I had to take four days off. We'll have to ask Joseph. He'll be here next week. Am I to announce you to His Excellency?'

A moment later Auguste Point himself opened the door of his study. He seemed tired but calm. He let Maigret and Lapointe in without asking any questions. His secretary, Mlle Blanche, and his private parliamentary secretary were both in the study. The Ministry did not as yet supply its servants with radios and the one on the table, a small portable, no doubt belonged to Point–the three people in the study had probably been listening to it when the usher interrupted them.

'. . . The session was a brief one, devoted exclusively to current affairs, but the lobbies were at fever pitch all the afternoon. All kinds of conflicting rumours have been circulating. A sensational announcement is expected on Monday, but it is still not known . . .'

'Switch it off!' said Point to his secretary.

Fleury made as if to move towards one of the doors but Maigret held him back.

'You needn't go, M. Fleury. Nor you, Mademoiselle.'

Point was watching him anxiously, for it was difficult to guess what the superintendent had come for. On the other hand he looked like a man who has an idea and is so obsessed by it that he forgets everything else.

He appeared to be mentally drawing a plan of the study. He studied the walls, the doors.

'Will you allow me, Your Excellency, to put two or three questions to your colleagues?'

He turned first to Fleury.

'I imagine you were in your study during Piquemal's visit?'

'I knew nothing of . . .'

'I don't doubt it. But *now* you know. Where were you at that time?'

He pointed to a folding door that was half-open.

'Is that your study?'

'Yes.'

The superintendent went and had a look at it.

'Were you alone?'

'I couldn't really tell you that. I'm not often alone for any length of time. Visitors come and go the whole day. The Minister sees some of them, the more important ones, and I see the rest, myself.'

Maigret opened a door that led directly from the parliamentary secretary's office to the waiting-room.

'Do they come in this way?'

'Usually, yes. Except those the Minister sees first and then brings to me for one reason or another.'

The telephone rang. Point and Mlle Blanche exchanged glances. Mlle Blanche lifted the receiver.

'No. His Excellency is not here . . .'

She listened, a fixed expression in her eyes. She, too, looked exhausted.

'The same thing?' asked Point, when she put down the receiver.

She nodded, keeping her eyes down.

'He said his son was . . .'

'Please . . .'

He turned to Maigret.

'The telephone has never stopped since midday. I've taken several of the calls myself. Most of them say the same thing: "If you try to hush up the Clairfond affair, we'll break you!" There are different versions of it, some more polite than others. Some even give their names, often the parents of the children who died in the disaster. One woman was terribly distressed, and yelled at me down the phone "You're not going to cover up for the murderers, are you! If you haven't destroyed the report, show it, so that the whole of France can know . . ."'

He had dark shadows under his eyes, from lack of sleep, his face was grey.

'The President of my electoral committee in La Roche, a man who was my father's friend and knew me when I was in short trousers, rang me a moment ago, almost directly after my statement went on the air. He didn't accuse me, but I could feel he had his doubts. He said sadly "They don't understand out here, son. They knew your parents and they believe they know you. Even if you have to sink the lot of them, you've got to tell everything you know."'

'You'll be telling it soon,' replied Maigret.

Point lifted his head abruptly, not sure if he'd heard aright, and asked, hesitantly:

'You really think so?'

'I'm quite certain now.'

Fleury was leaning against a chest at the other side of the office. Maigret gave the Minister Benoit's photograph; he looked at it, puzzled.

'Who is this?'

'You don't know him?'

'His face doesn't remind me of anyone.'

'He hasn't been to see you, recently?'

'If he'd been to see me, his name would be in the register in the waiting-room.'

'Would you show me your office, Mlle Blanche?'

Fleury was unable from a distance to see the photograph and Maigret noticed that he was biting his nails, as if it was a lifelong habit.

The door of Mlle Blanche's office, adjoining that of the parliamentary secretary, was small and narrow.

'This is where you came when Piquemal arrived and your employer asked you to leave him alone with him?'

Very tense, she nodded her head in affirmation.

'You closed the door behind you?'

She nodded again.

'You can hear what is being said in the next room?'

'If I put my ear to the door and if the conversation was loud enough, I probably would.'

'You didn't do that?'

'No.'

'Does it ever happen that you do?'

She preferred not to answer. Perhaps she might listen, for example, if Point were visited by a woman she considered attractive or dangerous?

'Do you know this man?'

She was waiting for this, for she had glanced at the photograph when the Minister was looking at it.

'Yes.'

'Where did you see him?'

She spoke in a low voice, so that the others should not hear her.

'In the office near mine.'

She pointed with her finger to the wall that separated them from Fleury's office.

'When?'

'On the day of Piquemal's visit.'

'After it?'

'No. Before.'

'Was he sitting or standing?'

'He was sitting, with his hat on, and a cigar in his mouth. I didn't like the way he was looking at me.'

'Did you see him again?'

'Yes. Afterwards.'

'Are you saying that he was still there when Piquemal left, and that he stayed in that office all the time the visit lasted?'

'I think so. He was there, before and after. You believe that . . . ?'

She probably wanted to talk to him about Fleury, but all he said was:

'Sh . . . Come.'

When he returned to the large office, Point looked at him with reproach, as though upset that Maigret should have been badgering his secretary.

'Will you need your parliamentary secretary this evening, Your Excellency?'

'No. Why?'

'Because I would like to have a talk with him.'

'Here?'

'Preferably in my office. Will it be convenient for you to come with us, M. Fleury?'

'I have a dinner engagement, but if it's a matter of urgency.'

'Will you telephone and say you'll be busy.'

Fleury did so. Leaving the door of his office open he telephoned 'Fouquet's'.

'Bob? It's Fleury speaking. Has Jacqueline arrived . . . ? Not yet . . . ? You're certain . . . ? When she comes ask her to start without me . . . Yes . . . I'll probably not come to dinner . . . Later, yes . . . I'll be seeing you . . .'

Lapointe was watching him out of the corner of his eye. Point, perplexed, was looking at Maigret, obviously longing to ask for an explanation. But the superintendent appeared not to notice.

'Are you busy tonight, Your Excellency?'

'I was to preside at a banquet, but I cried off before the others could do it first.'

'I may possibly telephone to give you some news, probably rather late.'

'Even if it's in the middle of the night . . .'

Fleury had reappeared, carrying his coat and hat, looking like a man who is only standing up through sheer force of habit.

'Ready? Ready, Lapointe?'

They went down the great staircase in silence, moved towards the car which they had left by the pavement.

'Get in . . . To the Quai, Lapointe.'

They did not exchange a word on the way. Fleury opened his mouth twice to speak, but thought better of it and bit his nails continuously.

On the dusty stairs Maigret made him go in front and walk first into his office, where he went to close the window.

'You can take off your coat. Make yourself comfortable.'

He made a sign to Lapointe, who joined him in the passage.

'You'll stay with him until I come back. I'll be some time. It's possible that you'll have to be on duty for a part of the night.'

Lapointe flushed red.

'You have an appointment?'

'It doesn't matter.'

'You can telephone?'

'Yes.'

'If she wants to come and keep you company . . .'

Lapointe shook his head, meaning it wouldn't do.

'Ask for sandwiches and coffee to be sent over from the brasserie. Don't take your eyes off Fleury. Don't let him telephone anybody. If he asks questions—you know nothing. I want him to stew in his own juice for a while.'

It was the classic treatment. Lapointe had taken part in most of the enquiry, but now he was at sea.

'Go and keep him company. Don't forget the sandwiches.'

He went into the inspectors' room and found Janvier, not yet gone for the night.

'Have you anything special on tonight?'

'No. My wife . . .'

'She's waiting for you? Can you telephone her?'

He sat down on one of the tables and lifting the receiver off another instrument dialled Catroux's number.

'It's Maigret speaking . . . Forgive me for bothering you again . . . Something came back to me a moment ago because of some fish hooks I found. Once when I met Benoit, on a Saturday, at the Gare de Lyon, he was going fishing. What did you say? He's a rabid fisherman? Do you know where he usually goes to fish?'

Maigret now, was quite confident of what he was doing; he knew he was on the right track and it seemed that nothing was going to stop him.

'. . . What? He has a hut somewhere? Are you in a position to find out where? . . . Yes . . . Now . . . I'll be waiting near the phone . . .'

Janvier was still talking to his wife, asking how all the children were and they all came in turn to wish him good-night.

'Good-night, Pierrot . . . Sleep well . . . Yes, I'll be there when you wake up. Is that you, Monique? Has your little brother been a good boy? . . .'

Maigret waited, with a sigh. When Janvier hung up he murmured:

'We could have quite an exciting night. Perhaps I'd better ring my wife too.'

'Shall I get you the number?'

'I have to wait for an important message first.'

Catroux had promised to telephone a colleague, another fisherman, who had gone with Benoit to the river on some occasions.

It was all a matter of luck now. It was possible that the colleague would not be at home. He could be on some mission outside Paris. Silence reigned in the office for about ten minutes and finally Maigret sighed:

'I want a drink!'

At the same moment the telephone rang.

'Catroux?'

'Yes. Do you know Seineport?'

'A little higher than Corbeil, near a floodgate.' Maigret was remembering an enquiry, long ago . . .

'That's it, it's a small village on the bank of the Seine, a favourite place with rod fishermen. Benoit owns a hut near the village. It used to be a water bailiff's hut, very dilapidated; he bought it for a song about ten years ago.

'I'll find it.'

'Good luck!'

He did not forget to call his wife, but alas he had no children to come and wish him good-night on the telephone.

'Ready?'

As he passed the half-open door of his office Lapointe had lit the lamp with the green shade and was sitting in Maigret's own chair, his legs crossed, his expression tense, his eyes half-closed.

'See you soon, boy.'

The parliamentary secretary started, got up to ask something, but the superintendent had already closed the door.

'We take the car?'

'Yes. We're going to Seineport, about ten miles away.'

'I've been there before with you.'

'That's right. Are you hungry?'

'If we have to stay long . . .'

'We'll stop at the Brasserie Dauphine.'

The waiter was surprised to see them.

'So I needn't take the sandwiches and beer to your office that M. Lapointe ordered?'

'Yes, do please. But first of all, give us something to drink. What will you have, Janvier?'

'I don't know . . .'

'A pernod?'

Maigret needed one. Janvier could see it and he had one, too.

'Will you prepare us a couple of sandwiches each.'

'With what?'

'It doesn't matter. With some paté, if you have it.'

Maigret seemed to be the calmest man in the world.

'We are too accustomed to criminal cases,' he muttered to himself, his glass in his hand.

No reply was needed. He was mentally making one himself.

In a criminal case, there is usually one guilty man or a group of guilty men acting together. In politics it's quite different and the proof is that there are so many parties in the Chamber.

This idea appeared to amuse him.

'A great number of people have an interest in the Calame report, and from different points of view. It's not only the politicians who would be in a mess if the report were published. Nor only Arthur Nicoud. There are some for whom possession of the report would provide hard cash, those for whom it would mean power.'

There were few customers there that night. The lamps were lit, the atmosphere was heavy as before a storm.

They ate their sandwiches at Maigret's usual table and Maigret was reminded of Mascoulin's table at the 'Filet de Sole'. They both had their table in different places, and in even more different surroundings.

'Some coffee?'

'Yes, please.'

'A brandy?'

'No. I'm driving.'

Maigret took none either and a little later they left Paris by the Porte d'Italie and drove along the road to Fontainebleau.

'It's funny to think that if Benoit had smoked a pipe instead of those stinking cigars, our job would have been infinitely more difficult.'

They were crossing the suburbs. Soon they had only large trees on both sides of the road and cars with their lights on, going in both directions. Many of them overtook the small black car.

'You don't want me to put on any speed?'

'It isn't necessary. Either they are there, or . . .'

He knew men of Benoit's type well enough to be able to put himself in their place. Benoit did not have much imagination. He was just a small-time trickster and his little intrigues had not brought him much luck.

He needed women, never mind what kind of women, a loose bohemian life, in places where he could behave rather ostentatiously and pretend to be a hefty lad, with, at the end of the week, a day or two's fishing.

'As far as I remember, there's a little café in the square at Seineport. Stop there and we'll make some enquiries.'

They crossed the Seine at Corbeil, followed a road along the river with forests on the other side. Four or five times, Janvier had to brake sharply to avoid the rabbits and every time he growled:

'Get out of the way, you little idiot!'

From time to time a light showed through the darkness, then there was a knot of street lamps, and the car stopped in front of a café where some men were playing cards.

'Am I to come in, too?'

'If you'd like a drink.'

'Not now.'

Maigret went in and had a quick drink at the counter.

'D'you know Benoit?'

'The one from the police?'

At Seineport Benoit had not considered it necessary, after so many years, to disclose that he was no longer in Security.

'D'you know where he lives?'

'Did you come from Corbeil?'

'Yes.'

'You must have passed him. Did you see a quarry about a mile from here?'

'No.'

'At night you can miss it. His house is just opposite, on the other side of the road. If he's there, you'll see a light.'

'Thank you.'

One of the card-players lifted his head.

'He *is* there.'

'How d'you know?'

'Because yesterday, I sold him a side of lamb.'

'A whole side for him alone?'

'He doesn't stint himself, it seems to me.'

A few minutes later, Janvier driving very slowly, pointed to a spot of light in the wood.

'This must be the quarry.'

Maigret looked on the other side of the road and about a hundred yards away, on the river bank, saw a light in a window.

'You can leave the car here. Let's go.'

There was no moon, but they soon found a thickly overgrown path.

Chapter Nine

They walked silently, unheard by whoever was in the cottage, one after the other. That part of the river bank must once have belonged to a large estate and the cottage would doubtless have been the gamekeeper's lodge.

The grounds were neglected now. A broken-down fence surrounded what used to be a vegetable garden. Through the lighted window Maigret and Janvier could see the beams of the ceiling, white-washed walls, and a table at which two men were playing cards.

In the dark Janvier looked at Maigret as though asking him what they were going to do.

'Stay here,' whispered the superintendent. He himself, however, moved towards the door. It was locked and he knocked on it.

'Who is it?' a voice came from inside.

'Open up, Benoit.'

There was a silence, the sound of steps. From his place at the window Janvier could see the former policeman standing by the table. He was hesitating as to what he should do, then pushed his companion into the next room.

'Who is it?' repeated Benoit from the other side of the door.

'Maigret.'

Another silence. The bolt was pushed back, the door opened. Benoit looked at Maigret's silhouette, a bewildered expression in his eyes.

'What do you want with me?'

'Just a little chat. Come, Janvier.'

The cards were still on the table.

'All alone?'

Benoit did not answer at once, suspecting that Janvier had been watching at the window.

'You were perhaps playing patience?'

Janvier said, pointing to the door:

'The other one's in there, boss.'

'I thought so. Bring him in.'

Piquemal would have found it difficult to run away because the door led into a sink-hole without any communication with the outside world.

'What do you want with me? Have you got a warrant?' Benoit blurted out trying to regain his composure.

'No.'

'In that case . . .'

'In that case—nothing! Sit down. And you, Piquemal. I hate talking to men who are standing up.'

He fiddled with some cards on the table.

'Were you trying to teach him the Belote for two players?'

It was probably true. Piquemal had probably never played a game of cards in his life before.

'Are you going to sit down. Benoit?'

'I have nothing to say.'

'Very well. In that case, I'll just have to do the talking, won't I?'

There was a bottle of wine on the table and only one glass. Piquemal, who did not play cards, did not drink either, nor did he smoke. Had he ever been to bed with a woman? Probably not. He was looking at Maigret savagely, like an animal at bay.

'Have you been working for Mascoulin for a long time?'

In fact, in this setting, Benoit made a better impression than in Paris, perhaps because he was in his natural element. He had remained the peasant who must have been the braggart of his village and he had been wrong to leave it to try his luck in Paris. His tricks, his shady practices were those of a peasant at a fair.

To give himself courage, he poured himself some wine and added mischievously:

'I needn't offer you any?'

'Thanks. Mascoulin needs people like you, if only to check on the information that comes in to him.'

'Go on talking.'

'When he received the letter from Piquemal, he realised that it was the opportunity of a lifetime and that he had every chance, if he played his cards well, of holding a large number of political figures at his mercy.'

'As you say.'

'As I say!'

Maigret was still standing. His hands clasped behind his back, his pipe between his teeth, he paced up and down from the door to the fireplace, stopping from time to time in front of one of the men, while Janvier, sitting on the corner of the table, listened attentively.

'What surprised me most was that having seen Piquemal and having actually laid hands on the report, he should have sent him to the Minister of Public Works.'

Benoit smiled knowingly.

'I only understood it just now, when I saw the photostat at Mascoulin's place. Shall we take events in their chronological order, Benoit? You can always stop me if I'm wrong.'

'Mascoulin receives Piquemal's letter. Being a cautious man, he calls you and tells you to make enquiries. You realise that it is a serious, genuine document, that the chap is indeed well placed to get hold of the Calame report. At this stage you tell Mascoulin that you know someone quite important in Public Works – the parliamentary private secretary. Where did you meet him?'

'It doesn't concern you.'

'It's unimportant anyway. He's waiting in my office and we'll be able to settle details like that shortly. Fleury is a poor creature, always short of funds. But he has the advantage of being accepted in circles where scum like you find the door shut in their faces. I dare say he's given you the odd tip before on some of his friends, in return for a few notes.'

'Do go on.'

'Now perhaps you'd like to go along with me. If Mascoulin himself takes the report from Piquemal he is practically forced to make it public and to explode the whole scandalous business, for Piquemal is an honest man in his way, a fanatic, whom you would have to kill to silence him. To take the report to the Chamber would of course put Mascoulin in the limelight for a time. But it would be more interesting to hold on to it, and keep all the people the report compromises in suspense. It took me quite a long time to work that one out. I'm not vicious enough to put myself in his shoes. So Piquemal goes to Mme Calame where he knows, because he's seen it before, that there is a copy of the report. He slips it into his brief-case and rushes to Mascoulin, Rue d'Antin. Knowing that he is there, there is no reason for you to follow him, as you know what's going to happen and so you dash to the Ministry of Public Works, where Fleury brings you to his office. Under some pretext or other Mascoulin keeps Piquemal with him while his smooth secretary photographs the report. With all the appearance of an honest man, he then despatches his visitor to the person it concerns, that is to say, to the Minister. I think that's correct, so far?'

Piquemal was looking intensely at Maigret, deep in his own thoughts, in the grip of a violent emotion.

'You are there, in Fleury's office, when Piquemal hands over the papers. All that you have to do now, is to find out, through Fleury, where and when you can get hold of them. In this way, thanks to the honest Mascoulin, the Calame report will be placed at the disposal of the public. But, thanks to you, Auguste Point, the Minister in question, will be unable to present it to the Chamber. So there will be a hero in the story – Mascoulin. There will be a villain, accused of having destroyed the document to save his face, as well as the face of all his colleagues who are compromised – a certain Auguste Point, who has the misfortune of being an honest man and of having refused to shake dirty hands. Quite clever, isn't it?'

Benoit poured himself another glass, which he began to drink slowly, glancing uncertainly at Maigret. He seemed to be asking himself what card it would be in his best interest to play, as he had done at the belote.

'That's almost the whole story. Fleury told you that his boss had taken the Calame report to the Boulevard Pasteur. You didn't dare to go there at night, because of the concierge, but the next morning you waited until she had gone to do her shopping. Did Mascoulin burn the report?'

'It's not my business.'

'Whether he burnt it or not, it doesn't matter, because he had the photostat. That was quite enough to keep quite a number of people at his mercy.'

It was a mistake, Maigret realised afterwards, to insist on Mascoulin's power. If he hadn't—would Benoit have acted differently? Probably not, but it was a risk to take.

'The bomb exploded, as foreseen. Other people were searching for the document for different reasons, among others a certain Tabard, who had been the first to remember Calame's part in the affair and to allude to it in his paper. You know that wretched Tabard, don't you? It wouldn't have been power he would have got from the report, but hard cash. Labat, who worked for him, probably knocked his heels around Mme Calame's place. Did he see Piquemal leave her house? I don't know and it's possible that we'll never know. But it has no importance. Anyhow Labat sent one of his men to the widow, then another to the Minister's secretary . . . You remind me, all of you, of a lot of crabs crawling and scratching about in a basket. Others, too, more officially, asked themselves what exactly had happened and tried to find out.'

He was referring to the Rue des Saussaies. Once the President of the Council had been informed it was natural that a more or less discreet enquiry should be made by the Security Department. From then on the situation became almost comical. Three different groups had chased the report, each for quite specific reasons.

'The weak spot was Piquemal because it was difficult to tell if he might not talk under interrogation. Was it you, I wonder, who had the bright idea of bringing him here, or was it Mascoulin? You're not prepared to say. Well, it doesn't matter. Anyway the point was to withdraw him from circulation for a while. I don't know how you went about it or what story you had to tell him. He'll talk when he sees fit to do so, when he realises that he's been nothing but a pawn in the hands of two blackguards, a big one and a small one.'

Piquemal gave a start, but remained silent.

'Well, that's about it, this time. We're outside the Seine department, as you will no doubt point out to me, and I'm acting in excess of my duty.'

He waited for a moment, then murmured:

'Put the handcuffs on him, Janvier.'

Benoit's first reaction was to resist and he was twice as strong as Janvier. Then, after a moment's reflection, he stretched out his wrists, and chuckled to himself.

'It'll cost you something, the two of you. You realise I haven't said a word.'

'Not a word. Will you come with us, too, Piquemal, please? You're perfectly free, but I don't suppose you want to stay here?'

As they went out Maigret turned back to switch off the light.

'You've got the key?' he asked. 'It would be better to lock the door, for it'll be some time before you're fishing here again.'

They climbed into the small car and drove in silence.

At the Quai des Orfèvres they found Fleury still sitting in his chair. He jumped when he saw the former inspector of the Rue des Saussaies in the doorway.

'I needn't introduce you . . .' growled Maigret.

It was half past eleven. The P.J. building was deserted, with lights only in two of the offices.

'Get me the Ministry.'

Lapointe dialled a number.

'I'm putting you on to Superintendent Maigret.'

'Forgive me for disturbing you, Your Excellency. You weren't in bed, I hope? You're with your wife and daughter? . . . I've got news, yes . . . It's important . . . Tomorrow you'll be able to give the Chamber the name of the man who burgled you in the Boulevard Pasteur and took away the Calame report . . . Not at once, no . . . In an hour . . . perhaps . . . or may be two . . . Yes, wait for me if you prefer . . . I can't guarantee it won't be the morning.'

It lasted three hours. For Maigret and his men it was an old, familiar routine. They all stayed together for a long time in the superintendent's office, Maigret doing the talking and stopping now and then in front of one man or the other.

'Just as you please, boys. I've all the time in the world, you know. You take one of them Janvier . . . This one, I think . . .'

He pointed to Piquemal who so far had not opened his mouth.

'And you can get busy with M. Fleury, Lapointe.'

Thus, in each office, there were two men, one questioning, the other trying to keep silent. It was a test of endurance. Sometimes Lapointe or Janvier would appear in the doorway, make a sign to the superintendent and then they would both walk out into the passage, and talk in undertones.

'I have at least three witnesses to confirm my story,' Maigret said to Benoit. 'Among them, and this is the most important one, a tenant from the Boulevard Pasteur who saw you enter Point's flat. You still refuse to talk?'

In the end Benoit made a statement that was characteristic of him:

'What would you do in my place?'

'If I were as much of a blackguard as to be in your place, I'd make a clean breast of it.'

'No.'

'Why?'

'You know very well why.'

He couldn't move against Mascoulin! Benoit knew well that Mascoulin would always manage to wriggle out of the mess somehow and God alone knows what would happen to his accomplice.

'Don't forget that he's the one that has the report.'

'So?'

'So nothing. I'm keeping my mouth shut. They'll charge me with burgling the flat in the Boulevard Pasteur. How long will I get for that?'

'About two years.'

'As for Piquemal, he came with me of his own accord. I never threatened him. So I didn't kidnap him.'

Maigret realised he would get nothing further from him.

'You admit you went to the Boulevard Pasteur?'

'I'll admit it if I can't do anything else. That's all.'

And a few minutes later it became impossible for him to do anything else. Fleury had collapsed and Lapointe came to tell his chief.

'He knew nothing about Mascoulin, had no idea until tonight, who Benoit was working for. He couldn't refuse to help Benoit because of certain transactions between them in the past.'

'Did you get him to sign a statement?'

'I'm doing it now.'

If Piquemal was an idealist, he was an idealist who had gone wrong. He continued in fact to keep silent. Was he relying on the possibility that this would bring him something from Mascoulin?

At half past three Maigret, leaving Janvier and Lapointe with the three men, drove in a taxi to the Boulevard Saint-Germain where there was a light in a second floor window. Point had given orders that Maigret should be taken immediately to his flat.

Maigret found the family in the small sitting-room where he had been received before.

'You have the document?'

'No. But the man who stole it from the Boulevard Pasteur is in my office and has confessed.'

'Who is it?'

'An old Security man who went crooked and works for anyone who will pay him.'

'Who was he working for this time?'

'For Mascoulin.'

'In that case . . .' began Point, his expression darkening again.

'Mascoulin will say nothing, he'll be quite content to wait, and then when the need arises, he can put pressure on anyone who is compromised. He'll let Benoit take the blame. As for Fleury . . .'

'Fleury?'

Maigret nodded.

'He's a miserable creature. He found himself in such a position that he couldn't refuse . . .'

'I told you so,' interrupted Mme Point.

'I know. I didn't believe it.'

'You're not made for political life. When all this is over I hope you . . .'

'The essential thing,' Maigret was saying, 'is to establish that you didn't destroy the Calame report and that it was stolen from you as you said.'

'Will they believe me?'

'Benoit will confess.'

'Will he say who he did it for?'

'No.'

'Neither will Fleury?'

'Fleury didn't know.'

'So that in the end . . .'

A burden had been lifted from his heart but there was nothing to celebrate in it. Maigret had undoubtedly saved his reputation, but Point had lost the game. Unless at the last moment, and it was very unlikely, Benoit decided to tell the whole truth, the real winner was Mascoulin. Mascoulin himself was so confident of his victory that even before Maigret had come to the end of his enquiry he had purposely shown him the photostatic machine. It had been a warning. It simply meant–To whom it may concern–take care!

Anyone who had something to fear from the publication of the report, whether it was Arthur Nicoud, still in Brussels, a politician or anyone else, each one knew now that Mascoulin had only to lift a finger, and they would be finished, their careers ruined.

There was a long silence in the room; Maigret was not feeling very proud of himself.

'In a few months, when all this is forgotten, I'll hand in my resignation and go back to La Roche-sur-Yon,' murmured Point, staring at the carpet.

'Is that a promise?' his wife pleaded.

'It is.'

She had no reservations about her happiness, because her husband meant more to her than anything else in the world.

'Can I call Alain?' Anne-Marie asked.

'At this hour?'

'Don't you think it's worth waking him up for?'

'If you wish . . .'

She, too, did not quite realise what the situation meant.

'Will you have something to drink?' murmured Point, looking almost timidly at Maigret. Their eyes met. Once again the superintendent had the impression that the man beside him resembled him like a brother. Both had the same heavy, sad expression in their eyes, the same hunched shoulders.

The drink was merely a pretext to sit down together for a moment. The young woman was telephoning.

'Yes . . . It's all finished . . . We mustn't talk about it yet . . . We must let Papa surprise them all, when he goes up to the tribune in the Chamber.'

What were the two men to say to one another?

'Your health!'

'Yours, Your Excellency!'

Mme Point had left the room and Anne-Marie soon followed her.

'I'm going to bed,' murmured Maigret, as he stood up. 'You need it even more than I do.'

Point stretched out his hand, clumsily, as if it were not an everyday gesture, but the expression of a feeling that he was too shy to admit.

'Thanks, Maigret.'

'I did what I could.'

'Yes . . .'

They walked to the door.

'In fact, I too refused to shake his hand . . .'

And on the landing, before turning his back on his host:

'He'll get what's coming to him, one of these fine days.'

Striptease

Striptease

Translated from the French by Robert Brain

Chapter One

Célita was the first to see the new girl.

As usual, at three o'clock in the afternoon, she had heard the alarm-clock go off on the little table between the two beds, and curling up in the sheets she had left Marie-Lou to stop the bell ringing, and next to get up and open the shutters, bring in the nylons and brassières which were drying on the window ledge, and then light the small kitchen gas-stove to make coffee.

Marie-Lou liked to sleep naked and always spent a long time wandering around the three small rooms of the flat, even when the windows were open, without dreaming of putting on any clothes. There was no sun today: the sky was overcast, the light glaucous, which meant it would rain.

'Aren't you ever going to get up?'

When, for reasons of economy, they had first decided to share the flat, they planned to take it in turns getting the breakfast, but, confronted with Célita's complete inertia, Marie-Lou had resigned herself to doing it almost every day.

In the mornings her skin had an oily look, and it was perhaps because of that that she looked somehow fatter, cruder, particularly as the light exaggerated her skin's irregularities, the bluish patch under her arms where she shaved and a brown wart just below her left breast. Like many fat people, she felt no embarrassment as she traipsed from the bedroom to the dining-room and the narrow kitchen, indifferent to the fact that her heavy nakedness could be seen from the windows opposite.

That day Célita could only be bothered to have a quick shower, and with her hair tied in a pony tail she hurriedly pulled on her clothes which had been scattered on the chairs and over the floor.

'Going out?'

'I've got to sew up my red dress. Some dolt ripped it again last night, trying to grab hold of me as I went past him.'

This meant that Marie-Lou would be left to do the housework all on her own again, just as she had been left to get the breakfast. All Célita did was to fetch the milk and bread from outside the door.

The fat girl hardly ever complained, and Célita, instead of showing any gratitude, rather despised her for it; once she said to Natasha:

'She's still nothing but a chambermaid at heart!'

Marie-Lou had indeed been a housemaid for more than three years.

Célita walked briskly through the Cannes streets where people had already begun the second half of their day; she wore a thin pair of ballerina shoes, a green coat thrown across her shoulders.

She made a detour to buy a piece of red silk, and in the small triangular square in front of the church of Notre-Dame she was held up by a crowd of curious onlookers drawn up in two ranks for a wedding group to pass between. She watched with the rest, even raised herself on tiptoe to do so.

The bride was wearing a white dress with a train and a veil, and the groom, in a morning suit, held a top hat in his hand, just as in the photographs you see in magazines.

From within the half-darkness of the church the rumbling of the organ could be heard, and suddenly some girls ran forward to fling handfuls of rice at the couple who were being kept on the steps by the photographers, and all the time the women outside were dabbing at their eyes with handkerchiefs.

Did she suddenly feel outside all this, or was it only a moment of depression that affected her? Her eyelids felt hot and began to smart, and just when everything and everyone about her was becoming blurred, she recognised, in the row of faces opposite her, the man with grey hair whom she had noticed two or three times at the Monico, although he had never spoken to her. She didn't even know whether he lived in the town or if he was a tourist; all he had done was to sit on a bar-stool and stare at her.

Nevertheless she was certain he had just recognised her, even with her hair untidy and no make-up on, and furthermore that he had seen signs of an emotion of which she now felt ashamed.

She hated him looking at her like that, so kindly, almost pitying her, and she felt like poking her tongue out at him, then walked away from the line of people, crossly, shoving aside those next to her, so that they followed her with their eyes.

The Monico was only a couple of hundred yards away, not far from the harbour, in a narrow street crowded with cars which were parked there all day. The door was open and when Célita pulled the door curtain aside, she found the two charwomen, Madame Blanc and old Madame Touzelli, sweeping up the paper streamers and little coloured balls, the atmosphere still saturated with champagne and whisky.

Above the garnet-red benches, the window, which was always hidden in the evenings by heavy curtains, was now wide open and the cabaret stage in daylight looked as incongruous as Marie-Lou's nakedness when she made the coffee in their flat.

Célita had been surprised that the *patron*, Monsieur Léon, wasn't there when she came in, since most of his afternoons were spent at the Monico; when she pushed open the door leading to the cloakroom at the end of the bar, she saw the trap-door open and realised he was busy in the cellar.

She climbed the spiral staircase, which she had climbed up and down countless times in the last few months, and reached the empty, low-ceilinged room which the girls used as their dressing-room.

She rarely went there during the day and it was strange to see the yard below where a man from the brewery was stacking barrels. Dresses hung from a rod, in different colours and different styles; she unhooked hers, a red Spanish dancer's one, and throwing her coat off her shoulders, she sat down on a stool and started sewing.

After a while, she thought of Natasha and of the box of American face-powder a naval officer had brought her. The expensive-looking box stood on the long dressing-table where all the girls kept their personal things, and Célita opened the window, emptied her powder-box out into the yard, then filled it to the brim with Natasha's powder.

She didn't stop to ask herself if it was unhappiness or sheer bad temper, yet her face, now that she was sewing again, was as clouded as the sky. She knew that it made her features even more pointed, her eyes more cunning, that she looked like an animal, frightened by a storm, ready to scratch. She hated sewing, just as she hated housework. In fact there were quite a number of things she hated doing! . . .

She heard a noise downstairs, and through an odd kind of fanlight which had been fitted flush with the floor she saw the *patron* and Emile in the cloakroom, climbing up from the cellar, each of them carrying bottles of whisky.

'Stack them in the cupboard . . .' Monsieur Léon said.

He put his down on the table, pushed open the bar door, while Emile, noticing Célita looking through the pane of glass, gave a smile of happy surprise and winked at her.

Célita was aware what went on in the basement: they had both been filling empty whisky bottles with contraband whisky. It was none of her business, but she would not be very upset if the *patron* were caught, for she loathed cheats. If she cheated a bit herself, it was because she had to and she loathed herself for it.

There was no point in thinking about it. She finished her work and bit off the thread with her teeth. The skirt, which she had worn every evening for the past three years, was becoming threadbare and would not last much longer. Its red colour looked faded in the daylight. Emile was signing to her from below, but she couldn't make out what he wanted and she half-opened the door to ask him:

'What is it?'

He put his finger to his lips, beckoned her to come down quietly.

He was seventeen, but short and puny, so that he looked fifteen and everybody treated him like a little boy. It was he who helped Monsieur Léon in the afternoons, ran errands and finished up darting from car to car, slipping behind the wind-screen wipers brochures extolling the Monico's floor-show.

In the evenings, and up till four o'clock in the morning, he would wait on the pavement outside the night club, opening car doors, ushering in customers, floating in a uniform which was much too big for him.

At present he was standing in front of a small window let into the door like a peep-hole, through which one might see what was going on in the main room.

Célita had missed the beginning, but not much of it, to judge from the conversation she overheard. The two charwomen were still cleaning. In the centre of the stage, bright with the daylight from outside, stood a young girl, intimidated, not the sort of girl one expected to find here so much as, for instance, amongst the people who had been watching the wedding a while ago.

Monsieur Léon was leaning on the bar, his jacket off and his shirt sleeves rolled up above his hairy wrists, and he was appraising the new girl with a slow, heavy look.

'Who sent you here?'

'Nobody did, sir. I just came on my own.'

Emile gave Célita a nudge with his elbow; he had moved aside to make room for her at the peep-hole and was obviously pleased to feel her so close to him.

'You come from Bergerac, you say?'

'Yes, monsieur.'

'And you heard about the Monico in Bergerac?'

'No. I haven't come straight from there.'

She wore a very simple black dress, a red hat, and she had put on a pair of white string gloves, as if she was going to Mass.

'Tell me.'

'Tell you what?'

'Where you've been before you landed up here.'

'I went to Toulouse first; there's a cabaret there called the Moulin Bleu.'

'I know the one. Did you work there?'

'No.'

'Why not?'

She hesitated, blushed, fiddled nervously with her black patent-leather handbag, which looked new and strangely incongruous compared to her other things.

'They didn't want me.'

'You really are nineteen?'

'I can show you my identity card.'

Her fingers fumbling through nervousness, she opened her bag as if she was not yet used to it, and held the identity card out to the *patron*, who read, half-aloud:

'Maud Leroy, born May 13th . . .'

'You see! . . .'

'I see. And after Toulouse?'

'I went to Marseilles by train and worked as a waitress in a bar for a week.'

'Which one?'

'Freddy's Bar.'

'Have you been to bed with Freddy?'

Emile gave another nudge with his elbow; Monsieur Léon seemed more than ever like an enormous cat playing with a mouse.

'Who told you that?'

'Freddy's a friend of mine. And before that?'

'What do you mean?'

'How many men had you slept with?'

She was obviously telling the truth when she answered:

'Two.'

Célita realised that her breast was crushing into Emile's shoulder, but she didn't move.

'Did Freddy tell you about me?'

'No. It was a customer. And as I left Bergerac because I wanted to become a striptease dancer . . .'

'Why?'

Disconcerted by the question, she could not think of an answer.

'Do you think it's an easy thing to do?'

'I think I could do it.'

'When did you arrive in Cannes?'

'I came this morning on the night train. I called here once before, at eleven, but the door was locked. I've taken a room at the Hôtel de la Poste.'

'Take your dress off.'

'Now?'

He answered with a shrug of his shoulders and the new girl looked anxiously at the two charwomen, who were apparently taking no notice of her.

'What are you waiting for?'

'Nothing . . .'

At last she made up her mind, and first put her handbag down on the table. She managed to force a smile onto her lips, and slowly, keeping her eyes glued to Monsieur Léon, she began to take off her black dress, over her head, just as she would have done in her bedroom.

'Never over your head. The other way. A woman with her arms in the air and her head inside a dress looks plain awkward.'

'I didn't know.'

'You'll learn.'

'Do I have to take my petticoat off too?'

Emile took advantage of this to press even harder against Célita, as if he wanted to see better, and she pretended not to notice.

The young girl's petticoat had fallen around her feet, and now she only wore brassière and pants; her bare skin was an almost chalky white against the night club's sombre red walls; Célita began to resent the clandestine nature of this undressing in broad daylight, with the street noises coming through the windows.

'You don't shave your armpits?'

'Do I have to?'

'Of course you have to! Let's have a look at your breasts.'

Her nipples were still smooth and bright pink. Leaning heavily on the bar, Monsieur Léon looked like a horse-dealer than a *voyeur*, yet Célita couldn't help muttering:

'Filthy bastard!'

At the same moment she shifted a little away from Emile, who, in embarrassment, stopped looking through the peep-hole with quite the same concentration.

'You can put your clothes on now.'

'Wasn't I any good?'

'I told you to put your clothes on. Have you read the notice by the door?'

As she adjusted the straps of her petticoat, she nodded her head.

'Every Friday, in addition to our usual show, we have a striptease competition for amateurs. Come along here a bit before ten o'clock, and sit down at this table . . .'

He pointed to a table at the front, near the band.

'Behave as if you were a customer and when the compère invites you, stand up as if you were hesitating. Do you get it?'

'And afterwards?'

'Don't worry about that. That's up to me. If it comes off, you're hired.'

When she had her clothes on again, she looked more than ever like any innocent young girl and it was hard to believe that she had just stripped, without a murmur.

'Thank you.'

'That's all right. Ten o'clock at the latest.'

'Yes.'

'Without fail.'

'Without fail.'

Just as she pulled the velvet curtain aside to go out, he called her back roughly:

'Have you got any money for supper?'

She turned around, blushed again.

'I don't need anything.'

'How much money have you got left?'

'Two hundred francs.'

'You'd better take this on account.'

He held out a five-hundred-franc note which she slipped into her handbag.

Emile had already moved away on tiptoe. Célita went back up the iron staircase to fetch her handbag, and when she passed through the main room, the *patron* was listening to the racing results on a small wireless hidden behind the counter.

'Where have you been?'

'Upstairs. I came in to sew up my Spanish skirt.'

He studied her suspiciously; they knew each other well and he was used to her lying.

'There'll be a new girl in tonight,' he announced, as if to test her.

'So much the better: it was getting a bit dull. Dancer?'

'Striptease.'

'Has Madame Florence engaged her?'

It was a low trick, reminding him that it was his wife, whom everybody called Madame Florence, who was the real boss.

He didn't answer, but if the bar had not been between them, he might easily have slapped her. It had happened before, and yet he was incapable of doing without her. And would Célita, for her part, have been glad to do without him?

At that moment she despised and hated him, because she was scared, as she was each time a new girl appeared, as scared as Madame Florence was also.

She went out without saying goodbye and retraced her steps to the Place du Commandant-Maria, where she lived with Marie-Lou. Marie-Lou had finished tidying up the flat and was now stretched out on the sofa, filing her nails.

'There's going to be a new girl tonight.'

'Who?'

'Nobody. Just a kid who turned up here by train this morning.'

'She'll be like the rest of them.'

She wasn't the first, and no doubt she wouldn't be the last, to be tried out this way. Some of them only stayed for a single evening, and there had even been one who had panicked at the last moment before walking onto the floor, and had run and locked herself in the lavatory.

Most of them wanted to go even further than the professionals and were so clumsy and crude about it that it became obscene and made the clients feel uneasy. Two or three had kept it up for a few days. One, a little Italian girl, had got herself installed in a suite at the Carlton by the end of the week.

'Did you see her?'

'Yes.'

After a silence during which Marie-Lou went on filing her nails, the fat girl murmured:

'Is that all?'

'What are you getting at?'

'I'm just surprised you've got nothing to say about her.'

'Thanks.'

'It's a pleasure.'

These two understood each other, as well.

At half-past eight, wearing the dresses they always wore for dancing with clients of the club between numbers, they were mingling with the crowds in front of brightly-lit shop-windows, walking precariously on their high heels. For most of the passers-by the day was over. A few couples, one or two families, were going into the cinema.

They found Natasha and Ketty already sitting down to supper at Justin's bar-restaurant in the Place du Marché; they also shared a flat, for the same reasons of economy.

'Spaghetti, Justin!' Célita called out as she walked past the zinc counter.

They ate here almost every evening and were well known to the other customers, mostly shop-keepers from the neighbourhood and, during the night, lorry-drivers, butchers, peasants who brought their vegetables to market in small trucks.

It was Marie-Lou's turn to announce the news this time:

'It seems there's a new girl.'

Oddly enough they looked at Célita, as if she would inevitably know all about it.

'What's she like?' asked Natasha.

And Célita, pursing her lips:

'Just the sort to send one of us packing. We'll soon see who.'

It was drizzling now, and as the pavement was not very wide, they walked two by two, like schoolgirls, along the wet road, their heads lowered, not talking. When they turned the street corner it was half-past nine, and the Monico's sign was still not alight. Nevertheless there was a middle-aged man standing there with his face pressed up against the glass of the display box, staring at the photographs by the gleam of the street-lamp.

The four women were about thirty yards away from him when the sign and the box containing the photos were suddenly illuminated. The man, revealed by the light, jumped back, surprised, ashamed, and strode hurriedly away.

'Did you see that?' Marie-Lou enquired.

'What of it?'

'Nothing.'

Emile burst out of the door, wearing a uniform with epaulettes and braid on it, and stationed himself on the kerb. Inside, Madame Florence was already at the cash-desk, while Ludo the barman was arranging his bottles on the shelves.

'Good evening, Madame Florence.'

'Good evening.'

'Good evening, Madame Florence . . .'

'Good evening . . .'

They filed past her, as if past the Mother Superior at a convent, and they felt the same schoolgirl fears. The musicians were tuning their instruments.

'Marie-Lou!'

'Yes, madame.'

'Your nails? . . .'

Triumphantly, Marie-Lou held out her newly manicured hands; the day before, Madame Florence had remarked on her dirty nails.

'And your hair?'

It was visibly greasy, and, on looking closer, you could see little white specks of dandruff.

'I couldn't get an appointment at the hairdresser's today. I'll go tomorrow.'

'Without fail, then.'

Natasha and Ketty were going through the cloakroom, and Célita was about to follow them when she was also called back.

'Célita!'

'Yes, Madame Florence.'

'It seems you were here this afternoon?'

Emile would never have told her; Emile worshipped Célita with a schoolboy's ardour. When he had called her down to look through the window with him that afternoon, it was more through a desire to feel her close to him than to let her share in the fun.

And considering their relationship, it would not have been in Léon's interest to say anything either.

Had Madame Florence called in at the Monico before the two cleaning-women had gone home? She often did, and somehow or other nothing escaped her.

'I forgot to take my skirt home with me yesterday. A customer grabbed hold of it and tore it. I came in to sew it up again.'

Unlike Marie-Lou, Célita did not look down at the floor, but straight at Madame Florence, with even a slightly mocking twist at the corner of her lips.

'See that it doesn't happen again.'

'Very well, Madame Florence.'

The irony was obvious. It was a kind of game they had been playing for months. But it was still difficult to pick the eventual winner. The only positive thing at present was that one of them was the *patronne*, Monsieur Léon's legal wife, and the other was not.

'Well, why are you standing there?'

'I didn't know you had finished.'

Madame Florence could not fail to know of her husband's visits to the Place du Commandant-Maria, on the afternoons when Marie-Lou was out shopping. Léon, certainly, had done the same with others, with nearly all of them, in fact, but this time it had lasted longer, it was somehow different.

He took no notice of Célita at the Monico, or if he did, it was almost always to nag her. Yet he didn't do so to put Madame Florence on the wrong scent, but probably because he often found himself hating the dancer.

Outside in the street, Emile rushed forward, a red umbrella in his hand, towards a motor-car which had stopped and he was on the point of opening the door when the driver, who was only lighting a cigarette, drove off again. Disappointed, he went back to his post by the entrance, whence he could hear the music from the band. It was rather like fishing. Some days were good, some bad. And every time a car came round the corner of the street, Emile felt the same little tug at his heart as a fisherman feels when his float sinks.

'The show will be starting right away, ladies and gentlemen . . .'

'When does that mean?'

He never dared lie too openly. The show itself rarely started before midnight, sometimes later if there were not enough people.

Some of them pulled aside the red curtain, and when they saw the empty room, turned away, in spite of the fact that the band would strike up, as if at a signal.

'We'll come back later . . .'

'You'd better book a table . . .'

On the other hand, a miracle sometimes happened and in the space of a few minutes the place was so full that clients were jammed around the bar.

In their dressing-room upstairs the four women were putting on their make-up; Natasha, almost at once, turned to Célita and asked:

'Was it you who pinched my powder?'

Célita didn't answer. The others paid hardly any attention to them.

'If you'd only asked me I'd have given you some. But . . .'

She grabbed hold of Célita's handbag, took out her powder-case and threw the contents in the waste-paper basket, on top of a pile of soiled pieces of cotton-wool.

Her action provoked no protest from Célita, who simply gave her a hard, penetrating look as she went on brushing her hair.

Somebody was hurrying along outside, along the dark street, the rhythmic sound of her high heels disturbing the silence of the night. Emile looked at his watch, and when the woman passed him, he murmured with a touch of anxiety in his voice:

'Hurry up, Mademoiselle Francine!'

She was a pretty girl, plump and fresh, with curly hair. She went no further than the bar and was aware that everybody was staring at her: Ludo, the musicians, Jules the waiter, who was placing champagne buckets on the tables.

'I'm terribly sorry, Madame Florence. I'm a bit late . . .'

'Eleven minutes.'

Without waiting, the *patronne* had taken a notebook from the drawer, with a list of names of all the employees, some of them with crosses after them.

'It's because the woman next door, the one who keeps an eye on my little boy in the evenings, hadn't come home and I couldn't leave Pierrot . . .'

'I'm sorry, Francine.'

A cross was added to three others already there, each of which meant five hundred francs off Francine's wages.

'I ran as quickly as I could . . .'

It was true. She was still panting.

'Go and take your coat off.'

Francine was not a singer or a dancer, performed no part in the show. She was a dance-hostess and, on top of that, was in charge of the cloakroom, hanging up customers' coats and hats in the recess.

Monsieur Léon arrived at five to ten and sat on a stool at the bar, looking around to make sure that everything was in order.

'Are the hats ready?' he asked Jules the waiter.

Every evening they handed out party hats made of paper and cardboard, sometimes cowboy hats, sometimes sailors' berets or top-hats in all sorts of colours.

'Do you think she'll come?' his wife asked; he had told her about the new girl.

'I'm certain she will.'

Eventually Emile led in two clients, who were going to sit at the bar, when Francine rushed up to show them to a table. Once there, they were practically caught.

Almost immediately afterwards, Maud Leroy, the girl who had come that afternoon, pushed her way through the double thickness of red velvet and stood there a moment, confused, finding some difficulty recognising the room.

Madame Florence was also a little taken aback, for the new girl was not the sort they were used to at the Monico. With a frown, she glanced at her husband out of the corner of her eye, as if she were trying to puzzle something out.

It was Ludo, the barman, who called out:

'There's a good table in the front, mademoiselle.'

Another client appeared, a regular, who sat down on the stool at the end of the bar, his back to the wall.

'A scotch, Ludo.'

'Coming up, doctor.'

He called almost all of them 'doctor', and some were flattered by it.

Madame Florence half-opened the door of the cloak-room, just next to the cash-desk, and called up the iron staircase:

'Are you ready there?'

Instantly there was a sound of activity. Natasha and Ketty came down first. As she started down the stairs, Marie-Lou asked:

'Did you really pinch her powder?'

Célita looked at her expressionlessly, and merely shrugged her shoulders.

Downstairs the new girl was sitting bolt upright at her table, in front of a glass of yellowish liquid which had automatically been brought for her. Ketty, who was almost as fat as Marie-Lou, though more aggressive, more sensually coarse, walked over to the two men.

'Isn't anybody going to ask me to dance?'

Natasha standing near the bar, waited to follow her.

Célita and Marie-Lou came in next, and all that now remained to be done was to 'get in tune', to create the right atmosphere.

Emile, triumphant, suddenly flung aside the curtain and let in, not one couple, but three couples at once, a party of Dutch people, terribly sunburnt in spite of the dull weather of the last few days.

Five minutes later, Gianini, the band-leader, was barking out the words of the tunes' refrains through his megaphone, and everybody was dancing on the tiny floor, colliding with each other.

At half-past eleven, three-quarters of the tables were occupied, and Madame Florence called out in a low voice, giving the signal:

'Ketty! Marie-Lou!'

It was time for them to go and dress for their numbers, while downstairs the other two, plus Francine, carried on as dancing partners right up to the last moment.

Only the new girl had not danced, and none of the clients had yet dared to address a word to her.

The girls had been able to examine her at their leisure as they danced or drank at the bar; so had the musicians, and Ludo, the barman, who had sent drinks across to her three times. She had drunk them mechanically, for the sake of appearances, and although she still sat as stiffly on her chair as during a sermon in church, her face was not quite so pale.

Madame Florence, without missing a thing that happened in the room, had looked across at Léon more often than usual.

She would soon be forty and the struggle was becoming too much for her.

Chapter Two

She was curled up in bed like a gun-dog, the sheet twisted around her body to such an extent that all that could be seen of her was a mass of tawny hair, one temple, one eye staring at the strips of light through the shutters. Occasionally her glance, turning without a sound or a move on her part, shifted to the next bed, or to the alarm-clock, although its dial faced the other way.

Célita did not know what time it was, but she was sure that the bell would soon start ringing, and when at last it did and the legs of the alarm-clock began to vibrate on the marble-topped table, she shut her eyes at once and at the same time her face assumed an exaggerated expression of innocent, yet sulky sleep, while Marie-Lou's heavy warm body slowly came to life and her arm reached out in semi-darkness.

Without looking, Célita knew her friend was sitting on the edge of her bed, her feet fumbling around on the floor for her slippers, and then, rubbing her breasts and waist, wandering out of the bedroom to the kitchen to light the gas-stove which made its usual little pop.

When Marie-Lou had opened the windows and the shutters in the dining-room, sunshine invaded the flat and the noises from the Place du Commandant-Maria became more distinct.

Between her barely parted eyelashes Célita watched the fat girl, who returned to the room after leaning out of the window, grabbed a gaudy dressing-gown which she wrapped around her before setting off again, raised her head and called out:

'Is Pierrot better?'

She was speaking to Francine, who lived in the house opposite, on the second floor; her boy had been away from school with a cold.

'What did you say?' Marie-Lou called again, after a silence; the din made by a lorry had drowned the reply.

Francine repeated herself, adding:

'He's at school. I was waiting for you to get up to ask you to do me a favour.'

There was a dairy at the corner and any customers there would be noticing, through the bead curtain, these two women who were just getting up at three o'clock in the afternoon.

'What kind of favour?'

'Could you look after him for me between four and six?'

Francine's five-year-old son quite often came and spent the afternoon at Marie-Lou and Célita's flat, or else one of them took him on the beach.

He was big for his age, with red cheeks and yellow hair; he would have looked pudding-faced or sleepy but for the sparkle which could be seen through the narrow slits of his eyelids.

'I'm sorry,' Marie-Lou answered. 'I can't today. I've got an appointment at the hairdresser's.'

'What about Célita?' the distant voice asked.

Through the open door between the two rooms, Marie-Lou glanced at the bed and saw the dishevelled head on the pillow. She lowered her voice and, with a gesture of her hand which must have meant something, replied:

'Better not . . . You understand? . . .'

Francine must indeed have understood, since she didn't press the matter. 'I've got to go inside now . . . The water's boiling . . .'

Célita continued to pretend she was sleeping and soon smelt the coffee being made. She heard the door open, the crack of a thin length of bread being broken, a cup clink against a saucer.

Marie-Lou was taking care not to wake her, and Célita, for her part, was not going to make the first move; so she remained in bed, quite still.

She had a guilty conscience, but, instead of owning up, she was feeling bitter towards her friend for what she considered to have been a betrayal. The night before, or rather that morning, as they came home from the Monico together, Marie-Lou hadn't once opened her mouth, and she had undressed straightaway and gone to bed without saying goodnight.

It was going to be worse with the others, Célita was expecting it. Anyway, they hated her already. A little more or less, what did it matter? . . .

And was the celebrated Maud, the new girl, also waking up at this moment in her bedroom at the Hôtel de la Poste? Had Monsieur Léon already been to knock at her door?

Madame Florence was the only one who had not reacted like the rest, and for a brief moment, as Célita's eyes chanced to meet hers, a look of understanding, tinged with complicity, had passed between them.

Although their positions were dissimilar, they would both defend themselves, and in either case it was over the same man.

Nothing had been premeditated. Célita had only done it on the spur of the moment, although she was admittedly aware that she was playing a dirty trick. She was not drunk. She had had three or four glasses of whisky at the most, and, God knows, the ones Ludo poured were short measure, particularly when he served the hostesses.

A few minutes before midnight, having peered through the peep-hole to make sure Ketty was ready in the cloakroom, Madame Florence had given Gianini the signal. When the dance ended, there was a drum-roll followed by a crash on the cymbals and then he made his usual speech:

'Ladies and gentlemen, the management of the Monico has the greatest pleasure in presenting to you their striptease review, the most daring, the most artistic show in all the Riviera. To begin with, here is Mademoiselle Ketty, the incomparable cover-girl, in her original number . . .'

At that moment Célita was sitting at the bar with a young Englishman who had bought her a drink, but would not dance.

As usual, the place had been plunged into absolute darkness for Ketty's number. The first flash of the photographer's flare revealed her swathed in black silk, like a girl posing for a magazine cover, a long cigarette-holder in her hand.

Darkness. Flash. Darkness. . . . Each time, Ketty was sitting in the same place, slightly more undressed, until she finally appeared completely naked except for the regulation g-string.

The Englishman only bothered to give her a quick look and went on talking in laboured French about night clubs in London where you couldn't buy a drink after eleven o'clock in the evening.

'And now, ladies and gentlemen . . .'

Marie-Lou's turn: her number was cruder and more ordinary. She was also dressed in black. Her dress, her corset, her underclothes were all fastened by zips, which she invited the customers to undo.

'You're next, Célita . . .'

She excused herself to the Englishman, walked through the small cloakroom, climbed the iron staircase. Natasha was already busily completing the last stages of a flashy get-up, in the style of the early 1900's, topped by a hat trimmed with ostrich feathers.

They could hear snatches of the music and the applause.

Célita went down first in her Spanish costume and, as they each did in turn, watched the end of the previous act through the peep-hole; Marie-Lou was also now naked, wearing only a g-string like Ketty, except that hers was covered with spangles, and she was walking across the floor for the last time before taking her leave and collecting her clothes.

When she pushed open the door, breathless, her body was hot, shining with sweat.

'Your go . . .'

'And now, ladies and gentlemen, I have the pleasure . . .'

She had heard those phrases so many times before that she now failed to distinguish the individual words, and like the horses at the circus, she waited for the first bars of music before going onto the floor.

As she danced a flamenco, at the end of which she would lose her bodice and red skirt, Célita noticed that the Englishman had disappeared, then, a little later, that the new girl, in her corner, was staring fixedly into space.

Célita was the only trained dancer; her mother had enrolled her at a dancing school in Paris when she was eight, and she had been a member of several corps de ballet. She was also the only one not to expose her breasts, even though hers were firmer and higher than Marie-Lou's, for example. Nor did she have the g-string clinging to the skin of her abdomen, but, both for the Spanish dances and for the can-can, she wore linen pants with flounces.

The club was full for a Friday and already there was a blanket of smoke hovering overhead, and the comic hats had been distributed. During the show Monsieur Léon was in his usual position near the door, where he encouraged the applause.

Had Célita won her struggle with him? He was beginning to think so; she fervently hoped so.

Their eyes met for an instant, but she couldn't read anything in his look, apart from a certain impatience, and she was convinced it was on account of Maud.

Like Marie-Lou, a little earlier, she hurried off towards the cloakroom, brushing past Natasha, who was waiting for her cue, holding a very long-handled mauve parasol.

Marie-Lou was already downstairs, sitting at the table with the two men who had arrived first; they had offered her a drink at last. In the dressing-room, Ketty was also getting ready to go down and she merely said:

'Quite a crowd!'

If there were enough people left at two o'clock, they would have to put on a second show and the whole thing would start again, with Gianini making the same announcements, the girls going up and down the same iron staircase, getting dressed and undressed all over again, excuses to be made as they parted from clients who might or might not be there on their return.

She put on her hostess's dress, which was getting worn too, went down, watched, from the cloakroom, the end of Natasha's number, the most intricate and sophisticated of them all. Natasha had a beautiful body, but she was so tall that she looked more like a statue in a square than a woman you would take to bed. Célita hadn't thought that one up. It was a remark made by an Italian client who came to Cannes once a month to gamble at the Casino and only appeared in the Monico when he had lost money up to a self-imposed limit earlier in the evening.

Another drum roll, a crash on the cymbals, followed by an almost solemn silence, during which Célita slipped into the room and remained standing near the door.

'This is Friday night, ladies and gentlemen, and every Friday we have our amateur striptease competition . . . The management of the Monico is convinced that among our charming spectators there are hidden talents, women and young girls who are burning with the desire to start a career of . . .'

Each week the same old words, the same winks, the same pauses which Gianini had perfected once and for all. The lights were put out and replaced by a spotlight which searched the room while the compère poured out his patter; it stopped from time to time at certain tables, emphatically or merely glancing, revealing now a face, now a bosom, sometimes legs interlinked.

'Let's see which girl or young lady is going to win the bottle of champagne the management has kindly presented . . . You, madame?'

He knew he would get a good laugh if he chose one of the lobster-faced Dutch women, who giggled like a child, while her husband teased her, pretending to push her forward.

Célita didn't take her eyes off Maud during all this, Maud who sat completely still, her lips drained of all colour, her nostrils pinched, seeming to have stopped breathing.

Célita was aware that she wasn't the only one watching her in this way; Madame Florence at the cash-desk, and the *patron* at the door, were no less attentive, although for different reasons.

At one moment the young girl put her hand out to her bag as if she were going to seize it and rush into the street. Jules, working the spotlight, must have noticed this movement and suspected the danger, because the light was suddenly swung onto her.

Gianini saw that the time had come.

'You, mademoiselle? . . .'

Like a hunted animal, she remained perfectly still.

'Will you tell me your christian name?'

Her lips moved, but there was not the slightest sound.

'What did you say? . . . Hortense? . . . Ursule? . . . Pélagie? . . .'

This time the people at the next table heard her murmur something and one of them repeated in a loud voice:

'Maud.'

'What a pretty name, Maud! . . . Well now, Mademoiselle Maud . . . You aren't married, I suppose . . .'

Did she know what was happening to her? She shook her head mechanically.

'Will you oblige the ladies and gentlemen by standing up? Then we can all see just how nice you are.'

She got to her feet, with an abrupt jerk.

'That's fine! Perfect! You see, you're getting used to it already. Don't be scared. The rest will come quite naturally. How old are you, Maud?'

'Nineteen.'

'Nineteen! How marvellous! I want all the other nineteen-year-olds in the audience to raise their little fingers! . . . Nobody? . . . What, sir? . . . Ninety? . . . That's not quite the same you know . . . You see, Maud, you're already in a class of your own . . . Are you engaged?'

'No.'

'Louder.'

'No!'

'Unfortunate for him, but fortunate for the rest of us, eh? Come closer, Maud . . . Don't be nervous . . . You've just been admiring our pretty girls doing their acts, and now you're going to show us that you needn't have done it for years to be good at it . . .'

In spite of his glibness and his teasing, he was following all the girl's reactions carefully and he sensed in time her mounting panic. He made a sign to the band and they understood. After a crash from the bass drum, heavy, rhythmic music accompanied him as he went on talking, insistently, like a hypnotist:

'Come just another two steps closer, Maud . . . Two steps . . . I said two steps . . . Of course you can! . . . You see? . . . Very good . . . Ladies and gentlemen, Mademoiselle Maud is now going to perform for you her first striptease act . . .'

He conducted the band with both hands now, and they played with a strong beat, haunting chords, while the spotlight, turning red, enveloped Maud in a suggestive glow.

The first time, the newcomer, with her eyes glued to Gianini, lifted her hands to her shoulders to slip off her dress, but her arms fell down again, weakly, standing out white beside her body.

He smiled at her, urging her on, still beating time with his hands as if he were carving strange shapes in the air.

Suddenly she glanced fearfully across at the door where, through a fog of smoke, she saw the *patron's* gaze fixed on her.

The whole thing was becoming painful and somebody at a table opened his mouth to call out:

'That's enough! . . .'

At that moment Célita was feeling as embarrassed as the rest, waiting for something that just wasn't happening. Weren't they all conscious of taking part in some cruel game?

Her hands were rising again, pink and pale, her fingers stretched the straps of her black dress so that they parted to reveal, first, the polished nakedness of her round shoulders, then the hollows of her armpits, her still thin arms.

Her body remained motionless, stiff, while the dress slowly slipped down till, having passed her hips, it fell suddenly around her feet.

One person alone started applauding from a corner. Another hissed: 'Ssssh! . . .'

Perhaps the music, like a sort of voodoo incantation, was having a soothing effect on the audience's taut nerves, for no one spoke or touched his glass; everybody's eyes, without an exception, converged on that still unmoving silhouette in the purple spotlight.

Slowly the girl bent down and extricated her legs and then, probably unconsciously, she did something which was almost inspired. Her hands gradually moved back up her body, caressing lovingly the silk of her stockings; then, as she took off her petticoat, she revealed her body little by little, a body which somehow looked more intimate than that of any of the other girls who had just preceded her.

Even Gianini was holding his breath now, careful not to break the spell she was casting, trying to match the girl's gestures with his music, encouraging, even provoking them.

Célita hurt herself as her pointed teeth bit into her lips. Twice, three times, she thought, she hoped, that Maud would panic at the last minute, that she would suddenly break off, see the faces watching her, and run away.

Nothing like that happened. Ignoring Monsieur Léon's instructions, the girl took off her petticoat over her head; it was like a sudden deliverance: the feeling of her near-nakedness was like a slap in her face; you could see the blood rush to her cheeks, as she now took her eyes off the band-leader and dared, at last, to search the darkened room.

There were sighs of relief, particularly when she allowed a smile to flit across her face, a smile which was directed only at herself, at her own secret thoughts.

Gianini grasped the situation and accelerated the beat until the music throbbed savagely like a jungle tom-tom.

Then she began to dance. Not a trained dance. It was hardly a dance at all, strictly speaking, but the movements, still hesitant, of a being who was slowly coming to life.

Throughout, everybody could feel that the whole thing was suspended on a thread, that the slightest thing, a cough, a laugh, a jolt, would be enough to break the spell.

The hardest part still remained to be done: Célita knew that better than anybody, she who had never consented to reveal her breasts in public.

A deep, long breath. A frightened, anxious look into the dark space around her, and Maud slipped one hand behind her back to unfasten her brassière.

At that instant Célita bit her lip so hard that she felt a drop of blood; she realised the new girl had just won a victory, that neither she nor any of the other girls had ever been able to hold an audience in such breathless suspense.

After another crash on the cymbals, Gianini, with beads of sweat on his forehead, abruptly changed the beat again; the instruments made the music seem to pant, hesitatingly at first, plaintively, then bit by bit almost triumphantly.

Was this what the girl from Bergerac had imagined when she left home determined to become a striptease artist? Were those looks, caressing her body, sending her into a kind of trance?

Unlike Marie-Lou, she did not merely mime the stages of love-making. She was living them, defying the people who were watching her. They could see the tremors run across her skin, and both men and women alike forgot her breasts, her stomach, her buttocks, to stare into the wild light in her eyes.

When she fell to her knees, everybody stood up, a few applauding; they were quickly silenced, for, with her eyelids half-closed, her body was sustaining a mysterious struggle until, at last, she fell down backwards, drained of all strength.

Célita had been as fascinated as the rest of them, but it only made her doubly furious, particularly when the oppressive silence was followed by an ovation which made the glasses jump on the tables; they clapped hands, stamped their feet, called out, stood on tiptoe to peer over other people's shoulders at the girl's body, now so still, as if it had been emptied of all substance.

'Ladies and gentlemen . . .'

Gianini's voice was lost in the din. Anxiously, Monsieur Léon was pushing his way through the crowd, no longer able to see anything from the door.

'Well done, my dear!'

He was so overcome that Célita and Madame Florence glanced at each other.

The *patron* was holding out his hand to Maud, helping her to get up, picked up her clothes and led her away to the door with the peep-hole.

They were still applauding and Gianini struck up a samba which attracted some couples onto the floor where the lights had been turned on again.

Florence had left the till. She must have gone to join her husband and the girl in the passage. Natasha muttered, as she walked past:

'So you were right after all, darling . . .'

Célita remembered that she had told them at Justin's a while ago that the new girl might take the place of one of them. She had said it to tease them, not really believing it.

Maud Leroy threatened to take not merely the place of one of them, but Célita's own particular place. Madame Florence had realised this too. It was all very well to hate each other, to fight over the same man, but nonetheless, in a case like this, they might join forces.

After the first show there was always a certain upheaval. Clients would ask for the bill and Jules wouldn't know which way to turn, while Francine hurried to and fro, laden with overcoats and furs.

Nobody was paying any attention to a black patent leather handbag which was lying beside an empty glass, on the table where Maud had sat. This bag, which was so new, fascinated Célita, and she had already noticed that afternoon how it contrasted with the tired-looking clothes the girl wore.

But it was not an intuition: simply curiosity. Nothing prevented her from going and sitting at the next table; it was unoccupied and it was a place where one or other of the girls often sat. Marie-Lou was busy with her two clients. Natasha was standing at the bar trying to persuade an American to buy her a drink; he had just come in and must at first have thought everything was over.

'Bring me a scotch, Jules.'

'In a minute, Mademoiselle Célita. When I've given them their change.'

She put the bag on her lap, as if it were her own, and began searching around inside, found an enamelled-copper powder-case, a handkerchief, two letters, a tube of aspirins, some cotton-wool and an almost empty packet of cigarettes.

What made her take one of the three cigarettes left and light it? Sheer defiance? To pay back the new girl for the wrong she was unwittingly doing her?

She slid her fingers down the small pockets sewn into the sides of the bag and drew out a small rectangular card. Printed on it were the words: *Galeries Nouvelles.* And below, stamped in violet ink, the sum: *4450 francs.*

When Jules returned, the bag was back in its right place on the table and Célita was no longer there. She was slipping towards the exit. Emile, who was much occupied with departing clients, noticed her, but had no time to say anything.

A narrow street, too narrow for motor-cars, old houses, without a single light still shining, on either side, ran off to the right towards the Place du Marché.

A few lorries had already arrived and were beginning to be unloaded. Two men in overalls and leather caps were eating sandwiches and drinking coffee at Justin's bar.

She asked him for a *jeton* for the telephone.

He noticed she looked drawn, that her eyes were feverish, but he thought nothing of it as he watched her walk to the box.

'Hello! . . . Is that the police? . . . A handbag priced at four thousand, four hundred and fifty francs was stolen from the Galeries Nouvelles in the Rue Foch this morning . . . The thief is now at the Monico where she's just done a striptease act . . . Her name is Maud Leroy . . .'

'Who is that speaking?' a voice answered, unimpressed.

She hung up, left the box, forgetting to shut the door.

'I'll pay you later, Justin . . .'

'Have you got a crowd there?'

When she returned to the Monico, things had calmed down again and Emile, back on sentry duty, opened his mouth to ask her a question. But she slipped between the velvet curtains before he had time to speak.

Florence, at the cash-desk, frowned. The grey-haired man, whom she had noticed that afternoon watching the wedding procession, was sitting at the bar, and she went straight to work:

'Will you buy me a drink?'

'If you want me to.'

She jerked herself up onto the stool next to his.

'Thanks, A scotch, Ludo.'

'Cigarette?' her companion offered.

She took one and lit it.

'Been out for some fresh air?'

For a moment she wondered whether he was making fun of her, he was smiling at her so oddly. She had already noticed that smile of his the two or three times he had been there before; it was only a sketch of a smile and it had been enough to stop her talking to him. He was too pleased with himself; he studied people with a curiosity that seemed too compassionate.

She remembered saying to Marie-Lou:

'That one thinks he's God the Father!'

Marie-Lou had added, bantering:

'God the Father watching the girls strip!'

He was soberly dressed, in a tweed suit, and suggested a doctor or a lawyer, perhaps a professor?

Neither Monsieur Léon nor the new girl was in the room. A little later they both appeared together, and the *patron* led the girl to her table, where she found her bag; then he left her on her own and went to have a word, first with his wife, then with Gianini, who listened to him, going on quietly playing his accordion.

The amateur's trick could not be repeated at the second show because too many of the clients had stayed on who had seen it earlier.

Since Maud had not left, but had been given something to drink, it meant that she would appear with the others, although she would presumably be announced as the sensational newcomer.

Provided that . . .

Célita turned and looked towards the door, wondering whether the police had taken her telephone call seriously and if they would send a detective around.

'Had a bad day?' her companion with the grey hair asked her, in a light tone.

'Why do you think that?'

'You were a bundle of nerves this afternoon. You don't much like watching others getting married, is that it?'

She went on drinking, not answering him. At the same moment Emile came in, tried to attract the *patron*'s attention, but succeeded only when it was too late and Detective-Inspector Moselli, who occasionally called to keep an eye on the Monico, was walking up to the cash-desk.

'Nothing!' Célita spat at him. 'Nothing's the matter with me, do you hear! Just what are you trying to insinuate? . . .'

She realised too late that she had behaved unwisely. Everything was happening very rapidly now. At the end of the counter the inspector was speaking to Madame Florence in a low voice, and her husband had joined them. The policeman had not entered unnoticed, and people were looking in his direction, Marie-Lou, Natasha, and Francine, sitting alone at a table.

After a moment Monsieur Léon went over to Maud, who mechanically picked up her bag from the table and followed the *patron* into the small cloakroom; the inspector went in after them.

Célita expected the glance, or rather series of glances, that Madame Florence duly gave her; the first furtive, hesitant, as if the *patronne* were not yet sure what was going on. The second revealed a certain surprise as if she were thinking:

'Well, my girl, I never thought you'd be capable of going as far as that!'

An admiring glance? A little, perhaps. Are there not times when we admire, despite ourselves, people who have the courage to do harm?

She probably had an inkling that Célita was actually working for both of them. Yet Célita realised, from the resigned look on the *patronne*'s face, that her attempt would hang fire.

Natasha, always more curious than the others, was making her way to the cloakroom, pretending to be going to the lavatory.

'What's making you so scared?

She was beginning to hate this insidious voice, the way the man in the tweed suit looked at her, sarcastically and yet indulgently.

'Not you, at all events!' she answered drily.

And she got down from her stool to go and sit with Francine.

'Did you see that?' the latter asked.

'See what?'

'The detective. He's come for the new one. I wonder what they're up to at the back.'

They were all to find out a little later. The policeman in due course came back into the room together with the *patron* and they both had a drink at the bar. Not until the inspector had gone did Maud come and sit down at her former table, holding her bag in her hand, her eyes moist and her cheeks flushed.

Natasha moved eagerly from one to another of the girls, whispering in their ears and indicating Célita with her glance.

Monsieur Léon must have handed over the money for the handbag, thus making sure they would hear no more of the matter. Had the shop even noticed the theft? It was unlikely. The strangest thing of all was that Célita, even at the moment of discovering the price-ticket, had realised the girl was not wholly guilty. She probably only had an old bag of her own, hardly presentable enough for the day she was going to take such an important step . . . She only had two hundred francs left . . . It was double or quits . . .

For the rest of the evening, Monsieur Léon just looked right through Célita. When she went upstairs to change for the second show, Natasha ignored her, and later, outside in the street, Marie-Lou was to be equally disdainful and silent.

She knew what it meant; she was being put in quarantine, just as she had been at school.

Now Marie-Lou had finished her bath; she came into the bedroom, her body dripping, and without bothering to find out if Célita were awake or not, gathered up her underwear and clothes.

Célita preferred to keep still, her eyes shut, hoping only that her friend would not notice the two tears which were squeezing between her eyelids.

She wasn't even to be allowed to mind Pierrot!

She would be by herself until the evening, because Marie-Lou had put on the blue frock which she wore to go to the Monico and was obviously planning not to come home first.

The door had opened and shut, the footsteps faded away along the pavement. Célita had jumped out of bed, tempted to run and call her friend back.

She had never felt quite so lonely in the three-roomed flat, where flies were now buzzing in the sunshine and all the noises from outside seemed hostile.

She almost felt she had been caught in a trap.

She lifted the telephone receiver, dialled a number, heard it ringing at the other end of the line, then finally a hesitant voice, the voice of somebody who wasn't used to speaking on the telephone.

'Yes . . .'

'Is that the Monico?'

'This is the Monico, yes . . .'

She thought she recognised Madame Touzelli's mumbling voice.

'Has Monsieur Léon arrived?'

'No, madame.'

'Madame Florence is not there either?'

'There's nobody here.'

Angrily she hung up, poured herself a cup of cold coffee, had nothing to eat and ran herself a bath; she must get some clothes on as quickly as possible and go out somewhere, along the Rue d'Antibes or on the Croisette, anywhere, so long as she could escape from this loneliness in the flat.

Chapter Three

She had hesitated a moment between her tight trousers, toreador-style, which she wore with a blouse when she went on the beach, and a dress with red spots which she had bought a week ago, at the Galeries Nouvelles, the same shop where Maud had stolen the patent-leather handbag. She had finally chosen the dress. She had made herself look pretty and smart, done her hair nicely, and set off to window-shop in the Rue d'Antibes.

Cannes had been nothing but an ordinary, small provincial town during the past days, when the sky had been overcast and it had been cold. No sooner had the sun begun to shine again that it was impossible not to feel that you were on the Riviera; the tourists were invading the streets, speaking every possible language, men in shorts, like scoutmasters, revealing hairy calves, and women dressed that way as well, some of them enormously fat, others who even wandered about the pavements and into the shops in bathing-costumes, smelling of sun-tan lotion, which was almost becoming the town's distinctive smell.

Once, when Célita and Marie-Lou were out for a walk, more respectably dressed than most of the other women in the streets, two housewives had nonetheless turned round to look at them, guessing what sort of women they were and passing uncomplimentary remarks in voices loud enough for them to hear. It had spoiled Célita's afternoon, but Marie-Lou had only murmured, philosophically:

'Don't take any notice, darling! I don't know why we bother how we dress, they always know what we do to earn our living.'

It was true. The very day before, when the married couple were coming out of church, the other people had realised that she belonged to a different kind of world, though the only one to recognise her as the dancer from the Monico had been the man with grey hair.

She turned down a side street to go to the Croisette, perhaps because somebody was eyeing her too inquisitively. From a distance she recognised

Francine, in her blue costume, on the other side of the street, walking along with a middle-aged man.

Célita knew beforehand that they would go into a boarding-house, halfway along the street, where you could hire rooms by the night, or even by the hour. Francine went in first, then the man, with his head slightly bowed; when she passed the house she looked inside, saw the gloomy corridor, the door with its frosted glass, with all of which she was too familiar.

She didn't go there very often, almost always towards the end of the month, when she hadn't enough money to pay the rent, or as last week, when she wanted a new dress.

She had never asked Léon for a thing, and he would probably never have given her anything. Yet he knew very well how she set about procuring the necessary cash, since he was more often than not the middleman when the customers wanted to proposition any of the hostesses.

Could he ever become jealous? He hadn't been so with Florence, in the days when they had both been living at Pigalle, he as a barman in a low sort of club, while she, much younger then, had unashamedly been on the game and continued doing so during his eighteen months in prison.

Nobody here really knew the story behind his conviction. It was mentioned as seldom as possible at the Monico, and then only in whispers. One of the musicians maintained that two rival gangs had had a brawl in the bar where Léon was working, with one man killed and another left seriously injured in the street, and that Léon had copped it with the rest of them. Ludo didn't hold with this story; he knew a lot about those Corsican and Marseilles gangs. Ludo claimed that the present owner of the Monico had always operated on his own, a lone wolf, whom both the gangs suspected of being in league with the police.

Whichever it was, Léon had married Florence when he came out of prison, and afterwards they had set up in business together, with both the Monico and their flat in the Boulevard Carnot in his wife's name, as nearly always happened in such cases.

It was now some years since Madame Florence had been on the job. She was thirty-nine, almost forty. She had become middle-class and respectable, and for some time she had been looking unhealthily fat.

Célita, at thirty-two, felt she herself was already old.

Until yesterday the struggle had been between these two women, and Célita had been confident of victory. She remembered that day, during her first week at the Monico, when the *patron* had called to see her in her hotel bedroom, at the Hôtel de la Poste, as he had done with Maud. To begin with, he had seemed to think he was only getting his due, as if it were just a matter of routine.

'I suppose I have to put up with it?' she had said to him calmly, as he took off his coat and tie.

'Does it surprise you?'

He had been intrigued and taken aback by her tone of voice.

'I'm not surprised at anything any more.'

'What did you expect then?'

'Nothing.'

She had drawn the curtains and climbed into bed. The whole time she had stared at the ceiling, her body inert, her face indifferent.

'Are you doing this on purpose?'

'Perhaps.'

'Are you always so mild?'

She realised that he was put out, not so pleased with himself.

'What else would you like?'

Later as he got dressed, he had mumbled:

'You think you've been real smart, I bet.'

She had had to hide her little smile of satisfaction, because she knew now that she had chosen the right line, that he was intrigued, humiliated, and that he would come again, determined to bring her to heel.

That evening, all the others, except Natasha, who had not yet arrived in Cannes, heard about the visit she had been paid.

'Well, did he get what he wanted?'

Marie-Lou, like a good friend, had warned her.

'Whatever happens, don't get ideas and imagine that this is it! It's just a craze of his. He's got to feel himself the boss, show he's a real man, you see? He'll probably go and see you a couple of times, just casually, but it's such a trifling affair his wife's not even jealous . . .'

It was true. To judge by her attitude, Madame Florence practically went out of her way to show Célita, who was the new girl then, that she knew all about it and took no offence.

'We'll see!' Célita had replied to Marie-Lou, out of sheer bravado.

'See what?'

'Nothing.'

Had she thought up her plan even then? She couldn't say herself. More likely it had just come to her bit by bit. At first, it had been a kind of game. For her he wasn't Monsieur Léon, or even plain Léon. He was the man. And, beside him, there was Madame Florence, the woman to be ousted.

Célita had not been deaf to the mutterings that went on behind her back, and Marie-Lou, ever incapable of holding her tongue, had been less able to conceal from her that she was thinking just the same.

'You're envious, Célita. If something nice happens to other people it makes you mad, and you'd do almost anything to stop them being happy.'

This was not quite true. Once, soon after Natasha's arrival, when they were both still friends, they had had a long talk on the subject. Natasha was more intelligent than Marie-Lou or Ketty, or the other girls who had passed some time at the Monico. She used to read a lot and was the only one never to go to bed with any clients. Nobody was quite sure if she'd even let the *patron* have her.

She was married to a commercial traveller and had a child, a little girl of three. She had left her husband, and the divorce she had asked for was now being heard. She claimed custody of her daughter and any day now she expected the court's decision.

'They say I'm envious because I'm different from them.'

'Other people hate one to be different from them.'

'It's not envy with me, it's just that I loathe injustice . . .'

Natasha had seemed to be sympathetic at that time, and they had nearly shared a flat together in the Rue Pasteur.

'Some people get all the luck, and they're always the ones who deserve it least. Look at Marie-Lou for example; she's as stupid as the backside of a cow and everyone's nice to her . . .'

Why had Natasha tired of her? A few days later she had turned cold and deliberately avoided Célita, who had asked her openly:

'Have I done anything wrong?'

'What do you mean wrong?'

'I don't know. I just wondered why you've changed towards me.'

'You tire me.'

After a silence, she added, searching for the right words:

'You're too complicated. You try to dramatise yourself the whole time . . .'

Was it her fault if drama seemed to cling to her? Hadn't she always tried to do her best, intensely, passionately?

Natasha should have understood, she knew the story of her past.

'When I was four I had to sleep with the woman next door—just like Pierrot—in the Rue Caulaincourt, while my mother was dancing in night clubs, and when I was eight she sent me to a ballet school where I suffered absolute hell, dancing on my toes and dislocating every part of my body. And all that time I had a brother and sister in Hollywood, being spoiled by their wealthy parents. Do you know who my father is?'

She had told her: José Delgado, the famous singer and film star, whose photo was often in the papers.

'I was born too soon, when he was a nobody, sharing a room in Montmartre with my mother. He never married her, and left for the United States when I was two. Over there he got married three times, had other children; they say he's getting divorced again, and there'll be yet another wedding . . .'

'What difference does it make to you?' Natasha had retorted.

She didn't understand, and yet she could not have led a very happy life herself, having left her husband and her daughter. As for Marie-Lou, provided she no longer had to work as a maid-of-all-work and get up at six o'clock in the morning, all her problems were solved. Now and again she fell in love, which might last for three weeks or a month. The latest was a croupier from the casino who looked like an undertaker's mute.

At the age of sixteen Célita had been in the chorus of various operettas touring smaller towns and second-rate casinos, having her meals more often in trains and station snack-bars than in proper restaurants.

Nevertheless she had once had her own man, when she was twenty-two, a man with whom she lived, admittedly in a hotel room, in the Boulevard Saint-Martin, making plans for their future together. When she found out she was pregnant, she had imagined he would have shared her joy. In her third month, she was still dancing at the Châtelet.

Her friend worked in a shipping firm and she was happy to think she would soon be able to escape from the theatre. They would have a little house in the suburbs, more children, a car later on.

Everything seemed settled when a woman, a sly-looking, small brunette, who wasn't even pretty, took him from her.

'They're married now, Natasha. They're happy. They've got three children going to school . . .'

'And yours?'

'Mine died. It was a little girl. Since her father had left me she was all I had.'

She paused, wanting some sympathy, at least some sign of approbation.

'Can you imagine what it was like?'

'What happened?'

'I didn't want to board her in the country. I needed to have her near me. In the evenings, like Francine, I let a woman on the same floor look after her for me. Nothing's happened to Francine's little boy. Nothing will happen to him. Nothing awful ever happens to other people. When my baby was thirteen months old she was suffocated by the woman who was looking after her; she had taken her into her own bed because she was crying. She was drunk that evening, I know, because she stank of alcohol the next morning, and she hadn't noticed anything.'

'You haven't had much luck, you poor thing.'

And Célita flung back:

'It's not a matter of luck, it's a matter of justice!'

She had decided to fend for herself, to fight, if need be. Operettas were almost a thing of the past. The theatres were turning dancers away, or they wanted them young.

'I'm thirty-two. It'll soon be too late . . .'

She didn't like talking about her experiences of the last ten years.

'Before long they won't even take me as a shop-assistant at Prisunic!'

Did Marie-Lou ever worry about the future? Or Ketty? Or Natasha? Were they still hoping to find a husband, at the Monico or elsewhere?

'Nobody's ever bothered their head over me. I'm damned if I'm going to bother about other people!'

Poor Madame Florence, if Célita should succeed!

It was a three-sided struggle, because the first one to deal with was Léon himself. He wanted people to think of him as a real man, and he believed he had had a lot of experience. As far as he was concerned, the girls who came and went at the Monico were worth a visit, sometimes two, after which he couldn't care less. He did it rather as if he were a stockman branding his herd.

But, after six months, he had still not been able to leave off Célita, and he could not have explained how she managed it. She was sometimes convinced that he had guessed where her ambitions lay.

'You know, sweetheart,' he had told her the second week, 'it's no use your getting any big ideas. There's nothing doing. Maybe we do go to bed together now and then, but it ends there. There are plenty of others, smarter girls than you at that, who've tried to get their clutches on me. Just ask my wife . . .'

A month later, staring into her eyes, he was questioning her, furious:

'What have you been planning inside your little head?'

She forced a laugh.

'You're the nastiest, most vicious bitch I've ever come across.'

He hated not to understand something and felt humiliated when somebody stood up to him.

'Can you ever have actually been in love with anyone?'

'It would be funny if I was just beginning to learn now . . .'

Between Madame Florence and Célita, the war was at once pettier and more cruel, made up of slight annoyances and smiling treacheries. Some months Célita had collected so many five-hundred-franc fines that at the end she got nothing, and even in front of the clients, the *patronne* never hesitated to insult her.

Yet Célita remained and it was Florence who was frightened; only two days ago Léon had spent a couple of hours at the Place du Commandant-

Maria, and for the first time he had said afterward, just as he was going:
'It would be more convenient if you got rid of Marie-Lou and had the place to yourself . . .'

Was she imagining things or was he beginning to need her?

But now there was Maud . . .

And Maud was there, on the beach, lying in the sun near a blue parasol. Célita was making her way along the Croisette, which, almost overnight, had assumed its summer look. Here, everybody was on holiday, climbing out of motor-cars, walking about taking photos, or relaxing on the sandy beach, stretched out in their bathing-costumes.

Did these holiday-makers in their brightly coloured clothes, their bodies sunburnt to a greater or less degree, also have their worries?

At any rate there was one consolation: Maud was not with Léon in her hotel bedroom, as Célita had feared.

One of them had gone to fetch her, Ketty or Natasha. They had enrolled her in their little group straightaway, and she was lying, near the parasol, in the spot usually reserved for Célita.

While his mother was at the boarding-house, Pierrot, his hair gleaming in the sun, was playing under the watchful eyes of the three young women in bikinis, as they chatted among themselves.

Ketty saw Célita first, glancing up, and pointed her out to the others. They must have been talking about her because Ketty said:
'Careful! There she is . . .'

They didn't wave to her, pretended not to have noticed her. Like them, Célita was wearing dark glasses, which made her features look hard; she walked more slowly, seemed to hesitate whether to go down on the sand, then casually sat in one of the deck-chairs near the railing, just opposite them.

Pierrot had seen her and rushed up to tell Natasha:
'Do you know Célita's up there?'

Natasha must have replied:
'Leave her alone! Don't look her way! We've got nothing to do with her.'
'Why not?'
'It doesn't matter. Don't worry your head over it.'
'Has she been naughty?'

Maud's skin was whiter than the others', and instead of a bikini she was wearing a respectable lastex bathing-costume. Pierrot was obviously not satisfied with the replies he had been given, and after staring at Célita for quite a while, screwing up his eyes because of the sun, he turned away regretfully and went to paddle in the water.

The three women, knowing they were being watched, played a little game of pretending to whisper secrets to each other with great glee.

Célita had not spent much time at school, but the same sort of thing went on at kindergarten and, later on, before and after dancing-lessons, except that the mothers also joined in then, even nastier than their daughters.

A young married couple were holding hands on a bench close by, watching the sea; perhaps they were seeing it for the first time. Meanwhile, a little further along, an old man could not take his eyes off a plump woman lying face down on the sand, who had unfastened the top part of her bikini.

The second show, the night before, had been less of a triumph for Maud than the first. She had made practically the same gestures, in the same order, but it seemed, this time, as if she didn't have her heart in it, as if she was repeating a lesson she had learnt, and just as she was about to uncover her breasts, she had stood there for a moment, lost, as if she had forgotten what was to come next, or as if she had suddenly become aware of the incongruousness of her behaviour.

Yet they had applauded her. She had not waited for the *patron* to come to her, but picked up her clothes and hurried through the door with the peep-hole. A little later, Monsieur Léon had gone up to her in the dressing-room, probably to tell her not to lose heart.

He would go and see her, as he had gone to see the rest. It would be interesting to know if she could keep him returning for more than a week.

Léon must be very angry with Célita for having called the police. He had steered clear of her all evening and not said goodnight to her. Perhaps she had been wrong to leave the flat, where he might have gone to see her this afternoon, to reproach her for it?

The other three were keeping up their play-acting, though with less enthusiasm. Natasha called to Pierrot and gave him a bun which she had just bought from a beach vendor.

'Hello, Mademoiselle Célita.'

She jumped, even though she recognised Emile's voice. He was wearing blue jeans, a green cotton shirt, and was carrying a bundle of brochures.

'Are you by yourself?'

Before she could answer he saw the others on the beach.

'I knew it,' he said.

'Knew what?'

'That they'd do this to you. They decided last night never to speak to you again and treat you as if you didn't exist.'

He remained standing, one hand resting on the arm of an unoccupied chair.

'Sit down for a moment.'

'No thanks. I don't want to disturb you and I'm not looking very smart. Marie-Lou tried to stick up for you.'

'Are you sure she did?'

'Yes. I heard her say: "It's not really her fault! She gets so unhappy . . ."'

'Isn't the *patron* at the Monico?'

'Was it you who rang up just before four? I thought it might have been, but Madame Touzelli had already hung up. He's taken Madame Florence to Nice, to see a doctor.'

'Is she ill?'

'I don't know. He rang up a doctor I've never heard of and made an appointment . . . You won't be angry, Mademoiselle Célita, will you, if I tell you . . .'

He hesitated, abashed, turned towards the sea and went on:

'. . . If I tell you that I'm on your side?'

'You don't think I played a dirty trick?'

'That's not for me to say, is it? I know that as far as you're concerned I don't count, I'm just a kid, and what I think isn't important . . .'

'What do you think?'

Down on the beach they were nudging each other, staring at the odd couple, Emile and Célita.

'You needn't be frightened! Tell me!' she went on.

'I don't think you were getting what you're after, with the boss, that is.'
'What am I after?'
'Madame Florence's place. Everybody knows that. She too.'
'Has she said anything to you about it?'
'I've heard her mention it to her husband.'
'What did she say to him?'
'You want me to tell you?'
'Yes.'
'. . . *"If you suppose I'll ever let that whore take my place at the desk . . ."*'
'Did you believe her?'
He blushed without answering and there was a slightly awkward silence.
But after a while he sighed, then murmured, still hesitating:
'If you ever need me for anything, I'll be there.'
'Do you think I ever will?'
'I know the boss. I was fifteen when I came to the club. He thinks he's a
tough nut. He doesn't stick his neck out with Ludo though, because Ludo
probably knows a bit too much about him. As for Madame Florence, she
knows him better than anybody else; she gives him a bit of rope, but she
realises he'll always come back to her in the end. Can I ask you one question
that's been on my mind?'
'Go ahead.'
'Do you love him?'
She looked at him, her eyes hard.
'Tell me you don't love him,' he went on, 'that he sometimes disgusts
you.'
'All men disgust me.'
'Me too?'
'You're only a child.'
'You think that too. I know you do, and you don't see that I'm the only
person who loves you. You sleep with the boss. You sleep with other men
too. I'm not saying that to make you angry. Some of them have even told me
details about it afterwards . . .'
He spoke ardently, in a low voice.
'Why do you keep on treating me like a kid? Listen! Don't look at me like
that. What's stopping you doing with me what you do with other people?'
She could only shrug her shoulders, amazed and angered at the same time.
'Is it such a big thing to ask you? And you see how happy it'd make me!'
'Who else have you been asking this sort of thing?'
He smiled, flattered, in spite of himself, and acknowledged:
'Some people don't have to be asked.'
'Who?'
'You'd be surprised if you knew.'
'Who?' she repeated.
'One of them's pretty near here.'
'Ketty?'
'I don't count Ketty, she does it with everybody.'
'Natasha?'
He nodded his head and Célita sat still, musing. It was quite possible after
all. And thinking about it she even seemed to understand Natasha's reasons
for wanting to seduce Emile.
'I swear it's different with you, Mademoiselle Célita. I only told you about

that to prove I wasn't still a kid. I love you . . .'

She had to smile.

'It's true, honest it is; and if I had a proper job and didn't have military service still to do, I'd marry you like a shot . . .'

'Thank you.'

'Why do you say it like that?'

'No reason, Emile. I really meant thank you.'

'Then, is it yes?'

'It's no.'

'But why?'

'There's no why about it. Now please leave me alone.'

Thereupon, disconcerted, but unable to give up hope, he stuttered:

'Not even for five minutes?'

'What do you mean?'

'Just for us to be alone somewhere for five minutes . . .'

He couldn't understand why she suddenly got up and walked away without saying a word. She was abandoning thus her sole ally, leaving him bewildered in the middle of the Croisette, a batch of pink leaflets in his hand.

He had naively asked her for five minutes!

She was prepared for what would happen, yet she determined nonetheless to go to Justin's for supper that evening as usual, merely planning her entry a little late so she could be the last to arrive. Francine always had her meals with her little boy, but the four others were there, at the table at the back, and Maud was sitting in the place usually kept for Célita.

When she came in, Justin looked embarrassed.

'They said you weren't coming.'

'It doesn't matter, Justin. I'll eat here.'

It was Natasha who was directing operations, she felt sure of it, and Maud was obviously uncomfortable that Célita was sitting by herself at a table near the door.

No move was made towards her. To rile her, the four women were endeavouring to carry on an animated conversation, but it was proving difficult, there were many silences, and they looked like amateur actors putting on a play in the village hall.

'So I told the old boy what I thought of him . . .'

'The one with the little beard?'

'No, the other one, who comes with that woman with all the new dresses and always pretends to go to the toilet in the hope of catching me in the cloakroom . . .'

Ketty interrupted her:

'He tried it on me as well. He wanted to make a date with me.'

'I told him I was an artiste, and for the sort of thing he was after I could give him a good address . . .'

Did she look round at Célita on purpose? Was the glance meant to insinuate things?

'Whose address did you give him?'

'He didn't want it. In any case he didn't have time to listen to any more. He'd just seen his wife, through the peep-hole, coming across the floor, and he dashed off to the lavatory . . .'

'Justin! Is there any strawberry tart?'

'It's all gone, Mademoiselle Natasha. But there's still some *mille-feuilles.*'

It was hard to eat without looking at them, hard too to look at them blankly enough, and the meal seemed to last an eternity to Célita. Finally, she kept her mind occupied by counting cigarette butts in the sawdust on the floor below the bar, then the bottles on the shelves.

It was essential to stick it out, not only here, but later at the Monico where it would probably be worse. That afternoon on the beach they had had plenty of time to work each other up and plan all manner of spiteful things.

'Justin! Some Brie and a coffee, please!'

'Coming, mademoiselle.'

A newsvendor came in and she got through the rest of the meal by burying her head in a paper. She left last as she intended, which entailed her being three minutes late, and from the doorway she saw Madame Florence taking the black notebook from the drawer.

'Good evening, Madame Florence.'

The *patronne* pointed to the alarm-clock on the shelf; Célita didn't give her time to speak.

'Yes, I know, five hundred francs.'

Ludo, overhearing this, opened his eyes wide; it was the first time he had ever heard anyone speak so cheekily to the *patronne*. Madame Florence was about to retort and call Célita back as she pushed open the door into the cloakroom, but in the end she simply marked a cross against her name, then, after a moment's hesitation, added another.

It was Saturday and the people were different; younger on the whole, they turned up earlier. Until half-past ten nothing much happened, although they all continued to ignore Célita and exchanged knowing looks as if something were being hatched between them.

At half-past ten the place was three-quarters full and almost everybody was dancing. Célita had been cornered by a dentist from Lille who had come to the Riviera to enjoy himself and was determined to enjoy himself at any cost. To be ready for the cabaret, about which he asked incessant questions, he had chosen a table on the very edge of the floor and in twenty minutes he had already finished his first bottle of champagne.

Unfortunately he was a keen dancer, and although he had obviously never been taught, he was convinced that his improvisations were irresistible. Every five minutes he went up to Gianini confidentially, and asked him to play one of his favourite tunes.

'One thing about you, you do let me do the leading,' he told Célita happily, as he made her perform the most fantastic steps. 'I hate women who think it's their job to show a man how to dance . . .'

He didn't care if he jostled other couples or trod on his partner's toes, or that he almost fell over several times. On the contrary, the more violent the bumps the gayer he seemed, like somebody driving a dodgem car at a fair.

He felt down Célita's thighs and remarked:

'Funny to think I'll soon be seeing you without any clothes on, here on this very floor! How does it make you feel! Do you get excited?'

Still, every so often he had to sit down for a rest and, above all, a drink, and this gave Célita some respite.

It was while she was enjoying one of these respites that certain looks, smiles, attitudes made her feel that something was going to happen any moment now, but she found it in vain to imagine where the blow would fall.

They were all there, almost all of them with a man, except Natasha and the new girl who were dancing together.

'Let's have another,' the dentist said, wiping his lips.

Since Madame Florence was watching her, Célita didn't dare refuse, and she was back on the floor again in the grip of her dishevelled partner. Had someone told the band to quicken the rumba rhythm? Gianini had been watching the dentist and probably thought he'd have a bit of fun.

Célita was following him as well as she could, bumped from left to right, and then all at once her leg twisted, for no apparent reason. She was on her knees before she realised that Natasha had danced past with the new girl and had deliberately hooked one of her high heels in such a way as to jerk off Célita's shoe.

Instinctively she tried to retrieve it, but she could not go on squatting between the dancers' legs and the shoe had already been kicked far away from her.

The dentist, who had no idea what was happening, asked her:

'Have you twisted your ankle?'

'No. It's my shoe . . .'

Unable to dance with only one slipper, she attempted to leave the floor but had little success in pushing her way through the throng.

Three times, four times, she bend down to pick up her black suede shoe, already smudged with dust, whenever it came near her, and each time somebody sent it flying out of reach. It had developed into a game, a sort of football match everybody eventually joins in.

'Excuse me, please.'

She shoved several couples aside, made her way, limping, to her table, as people burst out laughing. Can one ever feel sorry for a woman who looks ridiculous?

'How did it happen?' her partner asked her, resignedly following her off the floor.

'It doesn't matter! Don't bother about me.'

Maud, who was still dancing with Natasha, was not laughing, nor did she try to kick the suede shoe, which had already lost a heel in the scrum. And Marie-Lou was the first to drop the game and take her partner over to the bar.

The music stopped. The floor emptied. Amongst the streamers in the middle lay the pathetic shoe, stared at by everyone until Jules decided to go and pick it up.

'Is this yours, Mademoiselle Célita?'

The question must have been ironical, when she was sitting there with one foot bare.

'I'll try and find the heel for you. It must be under one of the tables.'

'Don't worry, thanks, Jules.'

And her idiot dentist asked:

'I hope you've got another pair?'

'Upstairs, yes.'

It was better not to try and cross the room until the customers had started dancing again.

'Will you pour me a drink?'

She bravely managed to smile at him over her glass.

'Skin off your nose!'

Chapter Four

Alone in the dressing-room, she collapsed onto a stool in front of the mirror and stared at herself, severely, without pity; probably, at that moment, she hated herself as much as the others hated her.

The grotesque incident of the shoe had shaken her more than if it had been something more serious, and if she had had even five thousand francs to her name she would have left the place that very minute.

She had no idea where she would have gone. She was too old for the Paris clubs. There was indeed a cabaret in Geneva which was a kind of Mecca for striptease artistes, where she had already been for two spells, but it was like a factory belt, fifteen girls every night, sometimes more, following one after another in a series of arranged items. Try Nice? Marseilles?

Still, what was the point of thinking about it when she didn't even have the train fare? She had never had any money, here less than ever, since as soon as she had her hands on a few notes she went and staked them at the Casino, not even at roulette or chemin de fer, for she had no ticket for the gaming-room, but at lotto in the big hall.

She would go back there the following week, however much she lost, as if to try to force her own fate into such a position that it would eventually have to play fair and make her win.

And while she was waiting for this to happen one day, she was more or less trapped in Cannes, with no chance of escaping; nor was it for the first time: she had been in a similar predicament in the past, in Ankara, an odd sort of place, a capital city built out of nothing, right in the middle of the Asia Minor desert.

She had blessed her good luck when she had been sent out there by a Porte Saint-Martin agency with a six-months contract, and never dreamt that the six months would turn out to be two years.

The cabaret had been a shabby affair, and right round the room there were private boxes which could be curtained off. In all her life she had never fought off so many hands. Each day she swore she would put some money aside for the journey back, whatever the cost, but after two years she was still there, towards the end almost resigned to the fact that she would be there for ever, which might have happened had it not been for a Belgian diplomat who was returning to Europe with his family and offered her the job of accompanying his children as their governess.

'You mustn't tell my wife where I met you. I'll pretend that you're a schoolmistress who wants to go home.'

During the journey he made the most of her, suggested keeping her with them at their home in Brussels, not very enthusiastically it is true, because although it was convenient for him, he was nonetheless terrified his wife would find out about their relationship.

She had those marvellous green eyes which change colour according to the weather, like the sea, and her hair was naturally dark auburn, she never had to tint it; and everybody told her with sickening repetition that her chin and her pointed nose reminded them of the young Colette, the Colette of *Claudine à Paris*.

Everybody considered her sexy. Just now, hadn't the dentist on the spree asked her about her act, which he had not yet seen:

'Doesn't it make you excited when you come out in front of everybody naked?'

He didn't know that she never appeared naked. And besides, if he'd had the opportunity to question them all, one after the other, he would have got a shock to learn that the girls from the Monico were less sexy than those on the beach, for example, where Célita often watched women, young girls even, brazenly revealing themselves to all eyes, lying out flat on the warm, flesh-like sand, bringing themselves to a climax of excitement.

Maybe Maud was like that though; unless, as Célita suspected, she was simply putting it on last night.

As far as the others were concerned, men hardly aroused them at all. Marie-Lou, for example, sometimes got struck on somebody, but more like a teenager, almost like a little girl, and it was usually because, as she naively put it, 'he's such a sweet person'.

Natasha found she could sleep alone for weeks and months on end since she left her husband, and what had happened with Emile was something apart, a strange, unexpected pleasure she had allowed herself in passing, rather as one might treat oneself to some untried delicacy when travelling.

Francine lived for Pierrot and nobody else; she would have liked more children provided the father passed out of her life as soon as possible.

Ketty was the exception. She alone was aggressively and crudely sex-conscious, so that she spoke about making love in the dirtiest way, like some of the clients they tried to avoid, but Célita suspected that she exaggerated it all to hide the fact she was frigid.

For Célita, Madame Florence and probably millions of other women as well, a man didn't mean sex, nor was it, at any rate not entirely, a question of security.

That afternoon Emile had asked her a question which kept running through Célita's head:

'*Do you love him?*'

He had added, naively, like the kid he was:

'*Doesn't he sometimes disgust you?*'

Well, no, he didn't. And perhaps, in her own way, Célita was in love with Léon. Because she had chosen to conquer him. Because she had selected him as her adversary.

He was a match for her in fact, and since he was continually slipping out of her range, he made the contest difficult, and all the more exciting.

Madame Florence had been through it all too, probably, for she had remained faithful to him, working for him while he was in prison, and also now helped him day after day, showing him she was intelligent enough to ignore his weaknesses.

Célita had decided to take him from her, and it was neither dastardly nor treasonable on her part. It was honest warfare.

Was she going to give up the struggle because of a shoe kicked off her foot, because of a ridiculous girls' conspiracy like a boarding-school conspiracy?'

It was not true that she had a spare pair of shoes here, as she had told the dentist. The only shoes she kept at the Monico were some red satin ones, with rhinestones sewn on them, which she wore for her Spanish dances.

Downstairs they probably thought she was sulking, or crying, or getting her things together to leave. She trembled when she heard steps on the iron staircase, but did not glance through the glass pane down by the floor to see who was coming.

When the door opened she saw Léon's reflection in the mirror. He held a hammer in one hand, the retrieved heel in the other, and without saying anything he looked about for the shoe, picked it up, walked across to the window ledge.

He loved doing odd jobs, particularly difficult ones, and he turned the black suede shoe round and round in his big fingers for a long time before taking some nails from his pocket and setting to work.

The window ledge was unsuitable for what he wanted to do, so he looked about him again, finally noticed the stool Célita was sitting on.

Wasn't he paying her this visit to hold out the olive branch? He was absorbed in his task, frowning, biting his tongue, and he turned the stool upside down to mend the shoe on one of its legs, using it like a cobbler's last.

'Hold the toe.'

He had several goes before he was satisfied with the solidity of his handiwork.

'That'll hold for now, but you'd better not dance on it.'

She took the shoe from his hands.

'Thanks.'

'That's all right.'

At the door he spoke again, without turning round:

'You must admit you asked for it!'

When she came downstairs, shortly after him, Natasha had taken her place at the dentist's table, and he looked at Célita in embarrassment but didn't invite her back. It would not be long before Marie-Lou and Ketty went up to change into their costumes, and as she walked towards the bar and hoisted herself onto a stool, Célita realised that Marie-Lou would not be sleeping at the Place du Commandant-Maria that night.

The last Saturday in every month, the 'Man from Switzerland', as they called him, not knowing his real name, would sit in a corner by himself, indifferent to what was going on about him: one evening, quite naturally, without realising how odd his behaviour seemed, he had taken a newspaper from his pocket and started reading.

He was a bank manager from Geneva and each month he came to Cannes to see a rich customer who was ending his days in one of the most beautiful villas on the Riviera, which he never left except in a car, accompanied by his chauffeur and his nurse.

On his first visit to the Monico, the Swiss had watched them one by one and stayed till closing time. He had danced only once, solely to have the opportunity of speaking to Marie-Lou, who, with her innocent ways, inspired more confidence in him than did the others.

'I shan't be coming back with you tonight,' Marie-Lou had announced to Célita as they were getting dressed to go. 'That chap's waiting for me at the corner.'

They had been seen walking off towards the Croisette. Marie-Lou came home at seven o'clock the next morning, and, since she hadn't got her key, had knocked on the door for ages before she could wake Célita.

'I'm sorry, darling. Do you know what he did? He put his alarm on for six o'clock without telling me that I'd got to go and take care not to let the servants see me. He's staying at the Carlton, in a suite with an enormous drawing-room, number 301, I remember. We didn't even go inside together. He was scared of the porter and told me:

'"Go up to number 301 in ten minutes and don't speak to anybody."

'He expected I'd be walking up and down the Croisette while I waited. Of course I went and had a chat with Louis, the night-porter . . .'

Since then the same performance happened every month and the Swiss had never thought of changing his partner. He was satisfied with Marie-Lou, and as she herself said, he hated anything unexpected, anything that makes life complicated, insisted that everything should conform, once and for all, to established rites.

Because he was there this evening Célita almost changed her plans once again, for the idea of going home alone, particularly tonight, made her depressed. She couldn't leave Cannes without money, but nothing obliged her to stick to Léon, nothing prevented her from going for another man.

The person in the grey tweed suit, the one she had called 'God the Father', was here again, sitting in the same place as the night before, with his irritating smiling equanimity, and she was convinced it was to see her that he came. She obviously fascinated him. Had he witnessed the scene over the shoe?

Why shouldn't she join the battle all over again, with him, starting from scratch?

She leant over to Ludo who had just poured her a whisky:

'Do you know who that is?'

He looked in the direction indicated, shook his head.

'I was wondering too. He doesn't come from Cannes, but he's French and drives a big convertible. Last week, when I was doing some extra work at the Yacht Club, he was there, with all the nobs.'

The man had guessed they were talking about him, and even what they were saying, because, joining in the game, he took a visiting-card from his gold-monogrammed wallet, called the barman and required him to give it to Célita:

She read:

Comte Henri de DESPIERRES

There were two addresses, one on the left, the other on the right: on one side, 'Château de Despierres, par Périgueux'; on the other, '23, rue François-Ier, Paris'.

She walked over and gave him back his card, saying very coldly:

'Thank you.'

'May I buy you a drink?'

'Not now. I've just had a scotch, and I'd been drinking champagne before that. I'll have to go and get ready soon in any case.'

'I know the time-table.'

She saw Léon, near the door, watching them, and once again she was tempted to drop everything and start afresh.

'Are you staying on the Riviera long?'

'Until my wife decides she's had enough.'

She had already noticed the ring he wore on the third finger of his right hand, as well as the signet ring, on which she now realised his coat-of-arms was engraved.

'Disappointed?' he asked.

'Why?'

'You might have had ideas about me. If things start going wrong one way, it's only natural to try another.'

'What do you mean?'

He merely looked in the *patron*'s direction.

'Who told you about that?' she insisted.

'Nobody. I've got eyes. You're a strange girl, Célita.'

He had seen her name on the photos, in the front, but she was nonetheless disconcerted.

'Your friends are upstairs already. I thought you had to go and change. What are you doing tonight? The can-can?'

The whole time he seemed to be laughing at her, pleasantly, teasing her as an elder brother might, and that made her angry; she pursed her lips, left him without saying a word, and went up to the dressing-room.

The show was starting. Ketty was going onto the floor. Marie-Lou was finishing pulling on her black mesh tights and after hesitating a moment, because she had promised not to speak to Célita, she said quietly:

'This evening, I'm . . .'

'I know, I saw him . . .'

Marie-Lou was not one for complications and now, as she was alone in the dressing-room with Célita, she found herself in a more difficult position than the rest of them.

'You know it wasn't me who . . .'

'Don't upset yourself about me!'

'Maud didn't want to either. Even so . . .'

'Ah!'

'I promise you. She felt lost here, in a new place, so she clung to Natasha, or rather Natasha got her claws into her, and the kid doesn't dare . . .'

Madame Florence's voice called, from below:

'Marie-Lou!'

'Coming, madame!'

She pulled at her black satin dress, looked at herself one last time in the mirror and hurried downstairs. Célita, in her lawn knickers and brassière, was putting on her stockings when Maud and Natasha arrived in their turn. In the fanlight she watched them come through the cloakroom and saw Natasha's gesture as she pushed the new girl, who hesitated, towards the staircase.

They both knew she was alone upstairs. Did Maud suppose that Célita would make a scene or tear her eyes out like a cat? But quite the opposite was going to happen, for Célita had made up her mind.

She was going to stay. She refused to alter her objectives. Count What's-his-name downstairs didn't interest her in the slightest, in spite of his tweed suits, his two houses and the signet ring with his coat-of-arms.

Natasha was undressing completely, whereas Maud was only bothering to re-do her face and change her knickers beneath her tucked-up skirt.

Célita, now ready to go down, looked from one to the other of them, and faced the new girl.

'I'm sorry,' she said, in a clear voice which did not tremble, nor ask for favours. 'I know when I'm in the wrong and I realise I played a mean trick. I've been made to pay for it. I don't bear a grudge against anybody.'

Nobody could tell what was going on underneath this. Abashed, Maud Leroy sought for an answer and, after glancing at Natasha, she mumbled:

'I don't bear you any grudge either, mademoiselle.'

She hadn't got used yet to their customary informality.

'You may as well shake hands now,' Natasha interposed. 'There's no point in going on hurting each other.'

Maud's hand was soft, the tips of her fingers rough, like the hands of women who do a lot of sewing.

Natasha went on, still naked, holding her g-string in her hand:

'It was I who found the heel of your shoe and gave it to the *patron*. As for the dentist downstairs, nothing would please me better if you'd have him back. In any case he'll be so tight after the show they'll probably have to cart him out to a taxi.'

As Célita was going downstairs, Natasha called her back:

'Aren't you going to shake hands with me as well?'

'If you want to . . .'

It was not peace, but an armistice. Or rather, to Célita's way of thinking, it was indisputedly war, this time. Léon had put himself out to come and mend her shoe, seeming to attach no importance to it, precisely because it was important.

She had sized up the new girl. He would go back to Maud once, twice, perhaps more often. She had youth on her side. But might not her mere nineteen years prevent her understanding what he wanted?

Florence understood, so did Célita. Because both of them were real women. Like all males, Léon had the urge to dominate, to convince himself that he was carrying off a victory, that he was reducing a female to mercy.

That was what he was looking for when he made love in such a brutal, almost vicious way, a cruel flame shining in his eyes.

Célita was ready to struggle with him, a kind of endless struggle, in which she was never absolutely vanquished and the man continually had to prove his prowess.

'You're a little bitch!' he often told her, at the very moment when he should have been most satisfied with her.

He would ask her questions, staring into her eyes, their teeth almost touching.

'You do it on purpose, don't you? Tell me you do it on purpose!'

She said yes, to goad him.

'Do you hate me?' he asked.

'I'm not sure.'

This was true, since she had joined in the game herself in the end. He was the male. He was the enemy. Whatever happened she had to win.

It was no longer a matter of security as far as she was concerned, and she wasn't holding on to him simply because she was scared of the Prisunic or the pavement which might lie in wait for her.

Life had done its best to drown her; each time that she had got her head above water, at the price of a terrible effort, somebody or something had been there to push her under again.

It was for her own sake, for the image she had formed of herself, that it was absolutely necessary to win this particular game.

She hadn't enough time left to take part in many more. On each occasion the odds grew longer against her. She had been putting all she had into this one for six months, all her ardour, all her determination.

Florence was also playing her last card, even more desperately, since she was forty years old and was falling ill.

Each was defending what she considered her own property. Neither was asking for any pity.

The position was clear, was it not?

A while ago Célita had almost given in, just over a shoe, because she had felt humiliated. She wouldn't have left, since that was impossible, but she had envisaged throwing herself at that lousy 'God the Father', who was a Count into the bargain.

She felt angry with herself now for having been able to think of it, even for a moment.

Maud had shaken her by the hand. Her skin was pale, there were needle-pricks at the tips of her fingers, and one felt something about her body to be unfinished or not quite healthy. In a few minutes she would be walking out onto the floor again, white with fear, glueing her eyes on Gianini, who supported her with his music as effectively as if he were holding her by the shoulders.

Perhaps she was not quite so innocent as she appeared? She had been able to make her decision all by herself, at Bergerac, and she had set off into the unknown with hardly enough to live on for a week. She had paid the price at Marseilles, sleeping with a barkeeper whom even Léon seemed to consider a brute. She had not hesitated to steal a handbag and later, for the detective's benefit, she had known how to burst into tears in the most touching way.

As for the striptease part of it, which kept everybody breathless, Célita was becoming more and more convinced that it was a fake.

In any case she had made a mistake to get involved in the fight, to climb into the ring as it were, to come between Célita and Madame Florence.

She was the wrong weight.

'And now, ladies and gentlemen, we have pleasure in introducing to you Mademoiselle Célita, the famous Spanish dancer who has been acclaimed in the leading cabarets of Europe . . .'

Her face at the peep-hole, she smiled sarcastically. Marie-Lou brushed past her, hurried towards the stair-case, leaving behind her a strong smell of sweat.

In five minutes everyone would know that Célita had sued for peace.

That evening there was another skirmish, but one of a different sort. Just before, as if to prove Natasha's point, the dentist, who had been giving a solo performance on the dance-floor, wearing a cardboard cowboy's hat, had suddenly collapsed while hanging onto a table, which had thereupon overturned, together with the bucket, the bottle of champagne, and the glasses.

The *patron* had helped Ludo to get rid of him, Jules had tidied up the mess and the band had struck up a rumba, while Maud, who had received as much applause as on the night before, went and sat by herself in the corner, still the same shy little girl.

Célita had deliberately not rejoined the Count; she saw him pay for his drinks, then, instead of collecting his things from the cloakroom, walk over and sit down beside the new girl.

Maud was obviously still observing the rules of the game, or at least pretending to observe them, because, knowing Célita had previously been with her new escort, she turned towards her with a questioning look, as if asking her permission.

'Go ahead, girl!'

At least that was the meaning behind Célita's dumb show. Strange to say, it was the *patron* who seemed displeased, or worried. Was he afraid Maud might be taken from him even before he had had time to make the most of her?

Marie-Lou, who had just learnt of the reconciliation, passed close to Célita, and whispered to her, touching her shoulder:

'You did the right thing!'

'Thanks!'

She probably thought her advice had borne fruit. Poor fat fool!

Somebody asked her to dance just as a considerable party entered, four couples in a group, probably straight from the gala night at the Casino, since they were in evening dress, and tables were pushed closer together to make room for them.

The Count was not dancing. Leaning towards Maud he was talking to her seriously, as if he were proffering her the advice of an older and more experienced man of the world. Had he shown her his visiting-card yet?

During a break between dances, as Célita was having a drink at the bar, Ludo said to her:

'I saw the name on the card. I know him now. I'd heard about him but I didn't know this was the one. He married an American twenty years older than him, and she makes his life a misery . . .'

It was now Célita's turn to put on a 'God the Father' smile as she looked over at Maud's companion.

'You prostitute!' she couldn't help muttering to herself.

To think that she had almost taken him on!

She looked around for Léon, found him in conversation with a regular visitor, a shopkeeper from the Rue d'Antibes who only came to the Monico when his wife was staying with her mother, at Grenoble. The *patron* gave Célita a wink across the crowded room, as if to say to her:

'Well done, my girl!'

He had heard that she had made her apology, but he was far from suspecting the reasons that had prompted her to do so.

It was a long evening, an exhausting one, mainly on account of the party in evening dress, who, as well as champagne, had ordered caviare; all the girls except Maud, who only had one possible number, were obliged to dance twice instead of once.

The party looked as though they would never get tired, and even at four o'clock there was no telling when they would go.

Léon still kept his eye on Maud and the Count. At one stage, when the latter went off to the lavatory, the *patron* made a point of being in the cloakroom in order to waylay him.

Naturally enough he didn't make a scene. Célita could see him through the peep-hole, jovial, but embarrassed.

She could almost swear he would be saying something of this kind: 'That girl's not like the rest, you know . . . I'd be careful if I were you . . .'

He was keen to stake his claim to her before anyone else stole a march on him. Who knows but he might not presently send his wife off home by herself while he saw Maud back to the Hôtel de la Poste?

'Idiot!'

He reminded her of Emile who, trembling, begged her for five minutes as if his life depended on it.

The 'man from Switzerland' was getting impatient. Marie-Lou had asked Madame Florence if she might leave before closing-time, but to no avail. Upstairs there was a typewritten notice, next to the mirror, giving the 'House Rules', which dealt with every possible contingency, particularly that the artistes were required to stay until 4 a.m. at least, and in any case never to leave until the last customer had gone. It also covered things like fines, personal hygiene, and the prohibiting of 'throwing cotton-wool, etc. down the W.C.'.

Two hours ago Célita had considered the idea of escaping from this tiny world in which chance had deposited her.

She was finding herself more deeply involved than ever, but she was going to face it with defiance.

She could no longer risk defeat.

They did not always bother to change in the morning before they returned home. Especially when it was very late, they often went off in the dresses they wore between shows, and carried, over their arms, the clothes in which they had come.

Closing-time was like the end of classes at school. The musicians could be seen putting their instruments away in their cases, Jules and the barman went round collecting glasses and empty bottles, while Madame Florence made up little bundles of banknotes and slipped them into a big yellow envelope which she took away in a handbag almost as big as a cabinet minister's portfolio.

Léon saw to the lights, sniffing in the corners, treading on cigarette ends, for he was haunted by fear of a fire, and he was always the last to leave, locking the door before joining his wife in their car.

They said goodbye more or less all round, as the opportunity arose. Everyone had, as it were, to fend for himself.

'Are you going to Justin's?'

'No. I'm not hungry.'

'I could do with some spaghetti . . .'

Marie-Lou met her 'man from Switzerland' at the street corner and they went off arm-in-arm towards the Carlton like a regular couple. They could hear the sound of the sea, saw it becoming paler with approaching day. In the harbour some fishermen were starting the motor on their boat, and at the Forville market the farmers' wives were setting out their baskets and crates, while Justin busily served coffee and white wine.

Célita had not seen the Count leaving. Maud had remained until the end and there was just a chance that the *patron* might have accompanied her back.

She was walking alone, careful not to twist the heel which had been mended, and just as she was taking the short cut, by the footbridge over the railway, she heard steps behind her.

She was always frightened at night-time, and although the sky had begun to turn pale, it was still dark. Without turning round she walked more quickly, her ears alert, sensing that the unknown person behind her had also quickened his pace.

She was almost about to break into a run, her key already in her hand, so that she could get inside the door as quickly as possible, when a voice called:

'Célita!'

She stopped still, murmuring:

'Idiot!'

For it was Emile's voice. He had stayed to change in the cloakroom and was wearing his blue jeans and a sports shirt, and must have been shivering in them.

He ran the few yards still separating them while she waited for him.

'What is it?'

'Nothing. . . . I saw Marie-Lou with her man from Switzerland, and I thought you'd be going home alone . . .'

They walked along side by side and Emile skipped now and then as he did when he was nipping from car to car to put his leaflets behind the windscreen-wipers.

'I thought you were going back to Le Cannet on your bike . . .'

His father had been killed during the war and he lived at Le Cannet with his mother, who was a charwoman.

'I don't have to . . .' he said, without further explanation.

One didn't have to be very smart, after his avowals that afternoon, to guess what he was hoping for, and Célita wondered what she was going to do. She wasn't the maternal type, like Marie-Lou, for example, who, though only twenty-five, treated all men, including her pompous bank-manager, like over-grown babies.

Nor was she curious for experience like Natasha, for whom the boy had been a sort of delicacy one enjoys between meals.

She found herself in an awkward situation, since she didn't want to hurt Emile's feelings and at the same time felt a little scared of him. At the Monico, although he was right on the bottom rung of the ladder, for that very reason people were careless when he was about; he noticed everything, heard everything, and was even the only one to go to Florence and Léon's flat sometimes.

Was he already convinced he would attain his object? At any rate he wasn't talking about it.

'I hear you've been very nice, Mademoiselle Célita.'

'Who told you that?'

'Everyone. I was glad, and I knew you would from the start. I even had a bet with Ludo.'

'You bet him I'd apologise?'

'I bet him you wouldn't have things in for them. You're different from the rest. Natasha planned the whole thing. You'd better watch her. The others aren't intelligent enough to be nasty. By the way, I found out about the doctor at Nice. It's Madame Florence who's ill.'

'How do you know?'

'Because he's a specialist in women's diseases.'

'A gynaecologist?'

'That's the word, yes. I saw it in the telephone book but I couldn't remember it.

They came in sight of the square, where the greengrocer was taking down the shutters of her shop, and an Arab was sitting on a bench, asleep, his head resting on his bent arms. Francine's light was on.

'You left the window open when you came out,' Emile remarked.

He was right. When she had left the flat Célita had not been in the mood to think about shutting windows.

'You shouldn't do that, not on the ground floor. You never know who might have climbed in . . .'

She looked at him, trying hard not to laugh, for she saw through his little game.

'You're afraid for me, I suppose?'

'What if that bloke on the bench had decided to have a sleep inside, or to burgle the place . . .'

'But he didn't, did he?'

'He's not the only one.'

'And you think you'd better come in and make sure?'

A moment before, he was smiling too, as if enjoying juggling with his little speeches. But now she had her foot on the doorstep Emile's face suddenly clouded over, he was so upset that he looked as if he would burst into sobs.

'Please, Mademoiselle Célita. I implore you . . .'

She wanted to say no, and she could not bring herself to do so. Not long ago Léon had looked at Maud with almost the same imploring expression and now she would have sworn that he had not had the patience to wait until the next day, that he had gone to the Hôtel de la Poste even if it did mean a row with Madame Florence.

She stayed there, hesitating, her hand holding the key she had already inserted in the lock.

'I'll leave as soon as you say . . . And if . . .'

He was loth to make this promise, but finally decided it was better than nothing at all.

'. . . And if you don't want me to, I won't touch you . . .'

She opened the door, pushed the light button, leaving the door open behind her. He closed it and she turned right in the passage, feeling him trembling all over behind her back.

With the second key she opened the door of the flat, remembering how untidy she had left it, with the beds unmade.

She realised bitterly, that it was too late to go back on her decision.

'Poor Emile,' she said, turning on the lights. 'I think you'll be disappointed; you see how women live when they're left to themselves.'

A kind of fury stirred in her breast, and she shoved open the bathroom door to reveal the unemptied bath, the towels lying on the floor.

'Look . . .'

She switched on the light in the dining-room; the breakfast things had not been cleared from the table and the cups had dregs of coffee settled at the bottom.

'And here . . .'

The two unmade beds, the rumpled sheets, the greyish pillows at one end

with traces of lipstick on them, and knickers soaking in the washbasin . . .
'You still want to stay?'

She threw her coat over a chair, kicked off her shoes and, as she stroked her bruised foot, the poor booby declared, as if he were reciting the Hail Mary:
'I love you!'

Chapter Five

At the beginning of the evening they were all misled into thinking things were well again, including Célita, except perhaps that Célita did not dare to be hopeful too soon, being used to fate going against her. She had been to Justin's with Marie-Lou, and they had found Natasha and Ketty already sitting down to eat; as there were only two empty places at the table, Célita had paused for a moment, imagining that one of the two places was for Maud.

'I don't think she'll be coming,' Natasha had said to her. 'That's why I told them only to set four places.'

Something had happened, you could see from the excited look on their faces. Natasha continued:

'I rang up her hotel twice and both times they told me she was out. I called there on my way here. The proprietress told me that Maud had gone out at lunch-time without leaving a message, or having any breakfast, and she hasn't been back.'

At half-past nine the four of them trooped into the Monico, like a line of schoolgirls almost, and each of them said good-evening to Madame Florence; Célita thought she was looking drawn. At twenty-five to ten, as they sat in the dressing-room getting ready, Marie-Lou looked at her watch and murmured:

'Five hundred francs!'

A little later they were downstairs, at separate tables; they were told to do this in order to make the room seem 'furnished'. Madame Florence's eyes had dark rings under them and she had that anxious look of people who appear to be expecting an agonising pain at any moment, so that Célita remembered her visit to the gynaecologist at Nice.

For a moment she had imagined that the *patronne* might perhaps be pregnant, but it was unlikely to happen now, at forty years old, for the first time.

It must be some disease of the womb since she had consulted a specialist. Half the women Célita had met had had some kind of operation, usually the removal of one ovary, sometimes of both, and it frightened her; the word 'womb' conjured up something mysterious to her, something almost sinister, and the thing she feared most in all the world was to see herself, one day, with a violet scar on her stomach.

Monsieur Léon, standing at the door, must have been aware of Maud's absence. He must also have noticed the looks the women were exchanging from each corner of the room, and twice he went through the curtain to stand with Emile on the pavement outside.

A quarter to ten . . . Ten to ten . . . Across the room Marie-Lou mouthed the words:

'A thousand francs!'

Célita had noticed that the *patron* had shaved with more care than usual, that there was still some talcum powder near his ear and that he was wearing a loud tie she had not seen before. Had he not looked worried, and if Maud had been there, she would have known for certain that he had gone to see her and got what he was after.

She was way off the mark, as she wasn't long in realising. A couple had just come in, regular customers who always chose a place near the band. They were a husband and wife who, although both only in their middle fifties, had nonetheless been nicknamed Philemon and Baucis, since throughout the evening they would be holding hands, smiling at the show, smiling at each other, saying only a few words from time to time, like a very old married couple who knew they always thought the same thoughts.

Gianini was playing an old-fashioned waltz for them, popular thirty years ago, which they had requested the first time they had come and which must have brought happy memories back to them.

Léon went up to the till, leant over to whisper something to his wife. His face was more flushed than usual, as if he had caught a touch of the sun. Madame Florence shrugged her shoulders, with a resigned air, and he hurried outside like a man with a mission to accomplish.

Indeed he did have one. Célita would get all the details later, bit by bit, from Emile, or from Ludo, who could hear from his place what they were saying at the cash-desk.

The Hôtel de la Poste was a few yards away, in the same street, and that was where Léon was running.

When he came back a quarter of an hour later he was alone, but his face was lit up and he was obviously finding it difficult not to look triumphant as he told his wife what had happened.

Maud had not arrived on time because she had gone to sleep after coming back from the islands, at seven that evening, and there had been nobody to wake her.

'Poor child!' Célita had sneered, when she heard the whole story from Emile, having gone out for a moment, against the rules.

As for the *patron*, he was behaving so like a love-sick swain that it was becoming embarrassing. It was out of character for him to lose control of himself like this and everyone had noticed his loud tie and the boyish, almost frisky manner he was unintentionally adopting.

Did he realise he was making a fool of himself? He imagined he had set his 'mark' on the new girl, as he would put it, when in fact it was she who had set her mark so oddly on him.

He stood there, waiting for her impatiently, moved by the fact that he had found her asleep, unaware of the time, just like a child! Had she too caught a touch of the sun?

The business had not taken place in the drab hotel bedroom, for that would not have been romantic enough. He had gone with her by boat to the Iles de Lérins, like the honeymoon couples, and no doubt Maud had romantically let her hand trail in the water flowing by the side of the boat.

Had they climbed the uneven steps to the fortress, hand in hand, and visited the cell of the Man in the Iron Mask? Had they been to see the monks at Saint-Honorat afterwards?

Célita and Florence, both probably occupied with the same thoughts, did not dare look at each other now, they were so ashamed for him. It was not a touching sight, since he was long past Emile's age, but just ridiculous.

The silly ass was looking at his watch every couple of minutes, unsuspecting that even the members of the band were exchanging winks.

Ketty was dealing with four new clients, Natasha and Marie-Lou were dancing together, when the new girl finally appeared, in the same little black dress she had worn the previous evenings, and half-opened the curtains with the hesitating, timid look of a mouse.

She went straight up to Madame Florence. Célita could not hear what she was saying, but she saw the *patronne*'s cold, resigned face as she dryly accepted the explanation–there was little else she could do–and directed her to her place at the front of the room.

Célita had under-estimated the girl from Bergerac; she realised that now. Maud Leroy had chosen the fragile approach: the 'poor little thing who is scared of life and needs a man's support'.

Léon, despite his experience of all sorts, had fallen for it! Even his walk had changed, had become lighter, more elastic. So youthful did he now imagine himself again that it seemed he might at any moment start jumping over the chairs, like people leaving the cinema who fancy themselves as the hero of the film.

He avoided catching Célita's eye, or his wife's. Had the latter already been warned of his new idea, which he was about to see realised? A reporter from the *Nice-Matin*, Julien Bia, who sometimes called at the Monico for a drink, came in, and this evening he had his camera with him. It was obvious that it had been arranged for him to come, that Léon had either called to see him or telephoned to him.

Sure enough, the *patron* rushed up to him, led him off to Maud's table, called Jules to order a bottle of champagne and three glasses.

He was determined to launch the kid, to make her into a star, and the journalist who had interviewed most of the visiting celebrities along the Riviera, nonetheless gravely took a pen and pad from his pocket and dutifully prepared to take notes.

He asked her questions as if she were somebody really important, jotted down her answers, and the little slut played her role so well that Célita had a furious desire to walk over and slap her face.

Her sweet-little-girl look was too good to be true, shy and sulky at the same time. Trust Léon, the former pimp, not to make the mistake of buying her a new dress and giving her a hair-do and a manicure!

She was quite capable of having thought of that for herself. She still managed to appear the sort of kid one might meet in the street or behind a counter, or, better still, the young girl who has just stepped off an all-night train, slightly rumpled, tired-looking, holding a cheap suitcase, and you don't know where she's come from, nor where she's going.

Nor would she have changed her underclothes, nor her stockings; she was too clever for that. Her cheap little pants, like those worn by typists and skivvies, stimulated men's imagination and gave them a greater impression of feminine mystery than the mesh tights, black wasp-waists and spangled g-strings the professional girls wore.

What could she be telling the reporter in her artless way, as if her adventure was the most ordinary thing in the world, as if all the small-town girls of France were leaving home to start taking their clothes off in night clubs the very next day?

It would be in the paper tomorrow. Not everything, since more than fifteen minutes had gone by, enough time for the reporter to fill two columns with her story, before he put away his pen and paper in his pocket.

He got up, stepped backwards to take the photographs while Léon modestly moved a little apart from her along the bench and Madame Florence turned her head away.

Julien Bia was not leaving yet. He waited until Maud's number was over, because he also had to have some shots of the girl in action. He even took one of her, almost naked as she leaned over backwards on the floor, in a sort of spasm, but this one would certainly never appear in the newspaper. It was for Léon!

Gianini had changed his compère's patter, and it was obviously not he who had composed the new formula.

'And now, ladies and gentlemen, the management of the Monico have the honour and the pleasure of presenting to you the great discovery of the year, the artist who will be tomorrow's unrivalled queen of striptease, Mademoiselle Maud Le Roy, nineteen years old, who has astounded, and will continue to astound, everyone who has seen her . . .'

The management had the *honour* . . .

The name Le Roy they had split into two words and it would appear as such in the paper the next morning, not only in the account of the interview, but in the large advertisements which would announce Maud to the public in letters four times the size of those of the other dancers.

And besides this, outside the club and on the walls of the town, a band was to be pasted across the old notices until new ones should be ready:

Mademoiselle Maud Le Roy
The year's most exciting sensation

Célita and Florence were not the only ones to have realised all this and to be acting accordingly. As the evening wore on, the others also became glummer, as if the new girl had just taken something away from them.

The atmosphere was different. Granted, whenever a new artiste had arrived, there had always been a certain tense curiosity, and in a way they formed common cause against the stranger as they waited to see whether she would last, and whether she would prove a good sort or not.

Nor was it the first time the *patron* had taken a personal interest in a dancer, but at least he had remained himself, and more often than not it had been the girl who won sympathy.

This time a new element had entered into the Monico and Célita had been alone in sensing the danger right from the first day.

'It's time, Marie-Lou . . . Tell Kitty . . .'

'Yes, madame.'

Madame Florence was not so bad-tempered, not so much the *patronne*, and all at once they wanted to be nice to her.

Occasionally Léon had to sit with some of the clients, or buy a detective or a journalist a drink or a bottle of wine. He had never been known to remain sitting there like this, for two hours, indifferent to the thousand details on which he normally kept an eye.

Contrary to what one might have expected, they hardly mentioned it when they were upstairs changing, or when they passed each other on the iron staircase or in the cloakroom. Nor did they exchange the facile little jokes which the situation might have provoked.

It was rather like an illness weighing upon them all, perhaps because they realised that the situation was out of their control, and there was also a degree of embarrassment in addition to their natural uneasiness.

Would one of them be kicked out now there was another permanent number in the show? Ketty was the least successful performer, who was usually sent on first when people had not quite settled into their seats. But Ketty had been there the longest. As a hostess, she had more go than the others. And lastly—but it was never mentioned—she was ready to follow any client back to his hotel, after the show, or arrange to meet him the next day.

Was Marie-Lou perhaps in a more dangerous position since it was impossible to get her to wash herself properly and send her clothes to be cleaned, in spite of fines and Madame Florence's continued admonitions?

Her good temper stood her in favour; she was the only one who never had her bad days, and she coped equally well with rowdy drunks and the kind of client who wanted to tell his life story.

Natasha's sculptural nakedness was the photo in the glass show-case which attracted the most people. And up till now Célita's had been the 'prestige' number. She was a real dancer, the only one. In other words, the Monico was not a vulgar dive where one went to watch girls undressing, it was an artistic cabaret.

'I'll be the one!' she announced to Marie-Lou whom she found deep in thought by the cloakroom door.

They were obviously all preoccupied by the same subject, for Marie-Lou simply replied:

'More likely me!'

They had been sharing a secret all day. Marie-Lou had come home early, because her Swiss friend, scared of the servants as usual, had made her get up at six o'clock. She had spent a good ten minutes in the bathroom before going back to bed, for she had had three abortions and the last had almost finished her off, so that now she took double precautions.

Célita had vaguely heard her getting into bed; then, later, the alarm had sounded, Marie-Lou had gone to make the coffee, and when she had set the table and there was a resemblance of order in the dining-room, she had come and pulled off the sheet Célita had twisted around her.

'Get up, lazybones!' she had called, good-humouredly, although normally she would never open her mouth before she had drunk her coffee.

Célita had finally opened her eyes and had then realised. Marie-Lou, with her floral wrap open, revealing her big breasts and the black triangle below her stomach, was wearing Emile's cap on her head.

'Well, my little slut! . . .'

What could Célita say? She didn't regret what she had done. In all her life she had never seen a person's face show such happiness as Emile's had done last night, and on leaving he had awkwardly kissed her two hands and mumbled:

'Thank you! I'm sorry . . .'

'Sorry about what?'

Then he said something she had not expected, which she was to recall many times afterwards:

'For only being me!'

He was a good boy! That evening when she had come into the Monico with the others, he had had the tact, so uncommon among men, not to stare at her in any special way, but to act as if nothing had happened between them.

Marie-Lou had been nice about it too, in the end. She had not teased her too much. And almost immediately she had become serious and promised:

'Don't worry. I won't breathe a word.'

She had told her how she had lain with the boy one afternoon, almost by accident, when she had been to the Monico to fetch her dress, and the *patron* had been out. They had done it in the cloakroom among the bottles and party hats, while the two old women were sweeping up the paper streamers on the other side of the peep-hole.

Marie-Lou realised that it meant more to Célita than it had to her. There was at least one quality one was bound to grant her: humility. She placed herself on the bottommost rung of the ladder, seeing herself as a household drudge who had preferred to earn her living by taking off her clothes in public than by drying dishes and washing floors.

Natasha impressed her because she read serious books, and because you could tell she'd had some education. In her eyes, Célita was even better. She not only had a famous father, but she was a real dancer, who had appeared in the big theatres in Paris.

Ketty came of peasant stock too and had spent her youth in a poverty-stricken village in Savoy. But as she was so fond of asserting, she was egalitarian and no one could impress her, neither the rich nor the well-educated, although she did have an unconscious passion for doctors, perhaps because she contrasted them with the priests, for whom her Catholic childhood had left her with nothing but hatred.

It was half-past twelve when the journalist left, escorted right to the door by the *patron*, who stayed a few minutes longer with him on the pavement outside. When Léon came back, he went straight over to the till, a little humiliated to have to go and explain things to his wife, and he had hardly begun talking to her before he was frowning at the sight of an American officer in mufti sitting down at Maud's table and engaging her in conversation.

Through Ludo, Célita later learnt what Léon had said to Madame Florence:

'Julien Bia is of my opinion. He thinks she's terrific and says I should sign her up, with a long contract.'

Madame Florence had replied:

'Most of them are terrific the first few days.'

That was true. More precisely, it was either all or nothing. They were either flops, overcome by panic, or their very shyness, the excitement they felt as they faced the public, communicated itself to the audience, won the day for them.

It wasn't till later when they tried to perfect a proper number that difficulties began, and so few of them were able to surmount them that cabaret proprietors were always at a loss how to reinvigorate their programmes.

But how could Léon be anything but optimistic after his excursion to the islands?

'She's caught on. She's a much more intelligent girl than I thought. Her nervousness is deceptive. You know what she said to Bia?

'"You've got to try and make the spectators feel they're surprising a woman in her bedroom, not watching an artiste do an act . . ."

'She added:

'"Since I'm no artiste and haven't had any experience, it won't be difficult for me."

'"Unless you find you can't help getting experienced," our friend Bia retorted, the wise guy.

'And she said:

'"I'll take care to stay just as I am, not to change my way of life or my ideas."'

It was half-past one when Ludo had reported this conversation to Célita, and the *patronne*, who had been feeling, or pretending to feel, unwell all evening, had gone home to bed, a rare thing for her, and left the cabaret in her husband's care.

Célita had wondered whether this was a strategic withdrawal, a rather naive way of making an impression on Léon, yet it was true that Madame Florence had not been in good health for some time, and she had been to consult a gynaecologist.

The Maud affair had gone further than they could have foreseen, and it was impossible, as yet, to say which of them, she herself or Léon, had had the idea that showed near-genius.

This too emerged from the conversation between Léon and his wife immediately after the departure of the journalist. For Maud had said to the latter:

'I'll take care to stay just as I am, not to change my way of life or ideas.'

Whereupon Julien Bia had objected, looking around him rather ironically:

'You'll have a hard job if you spend all your evenings here.'

And, raising his glass:

'And if you start drinking champagne and whisky with the clients!'

Was it not a stroke of genius on Maud's part to have answered:

'That's exactly why I'm going to ask Madame Florence not to let that happen to me. It's in her interest as well as mine. Sitting here at a table or at the bar I'm no use. I'm not a hostess. And if the clients see me here doing that sort of job, they'll stop believing in my act. Don't you see! I must stay looking like the girl next door.'

She must have slid the *patron* a conspiratorial glance, as she said this. Either he had thought up this idea, or it was she, and, if so, she was formidable.

How could the fool's conceit of himself as a potent male fail to be flattered by her wanting to keep out of other men's touch? What exactly had passed between them on the island? Célita was tempted to believe nothing had happened at all. Maud had probably pretended to be the poor little girl whose two experiences of sex—no, three, since there was the Marseilles episode—had left her wounded, feeling unclean, needing time to forget, needing patience, tenderness.

'Smart work!' Célita couldn't help saying to Ludo.

'You smelt a rat from the start! I'm beginning to wonder if it mightn't have been better for all concerned if Inspector Moselli had hauled her off without further ado.'

'What did Madame Florence reply?'

'They've made no decision yet. The *patronne* did her bit. Besides, that's when she mentioned the pains in her stomach and announced that she didn't think she'd be able to last out until closing time.'

That was quite smart work too, since there are occasions when one should know how to beat a retreat. That evening she was an obstacle, sitting there at the cask-desk, and her husband couldn't help feeling that she was spying on him—and hating her for it. Don't men need to imagine that they are free?

Her indisposition, whatever it was, came just in time, and after the second show Maud did not return to sit at her table. She descended the iron staircase wearing her hat, carrying a handbag, like a visitor, and Léon escorted her to the door, and then out onto the pavement.

He did not, however, go into her hotel but returned straight away looking worried, and went behind the bar, where he unhooked the telephone receiver to call his flat.

'Is that you? . . . he asked in a low voice. 'How are you feeling? . . . Have you switched on the electric pad? . . . Nothing special here, no . . . Wait a sec . . . there are still . . .'

His eyes swept the room.

'Still about twenty clients. We'll be shutting early . . .'

She asked no questions about Maud, and in the end it was he who felt it necessary to add, as if reassuring her:

'I've sent the little one home to bed. She could hardly stand upright.'

'A double scotch, Ludo,' Célita called out loudly.

'Do you think you should, mademoiselle?'

She nodded her head. She felt miserable. It was not so much sadness as discouragement, sickness at heart. It made her furious to watch a man like Léon, who thought himself a real male, whom she had taken for a real male, in such a state over a little go-getter.

Once again, she felt she was not being treated fairly.

For the way Léon was behaving today was the way she would have wanted him to behave, though a little differently, with more dignity, *over her*.

She knew she was a real woman, a real female to match him, and he would never have made such a fool of himself by falling in love with her, as he had now, almost to the point of losing all perspective and dignity.

It was part of the game. It was to be expected. They would have made—they had already begun to make—a fine couple, passionate, tearing away from each other only to come together more completely, shattering one another's pride, humbling each other.

He had understood her so well that he had occasionally felt frightened of her, frightened of being dragged down into the abyss where she was making him want to remain engulfed with her.

Had Célita's hatred of Madame Florence become less bitter? She knew this was not so. She was sure of herself. She had only needed a little more time to detach him from a tiresome and ageing woman.

What could be wrong in that? They were the wild beasts, the three of them, and wild beasts make their own laws.

'Let the best one win!' is the sporting phrase.

She was convinced she was the best.

He had never looked such a numbskull as he did that evening, with his air of sudden rejuvenation and embarrassment at his happiness. He didn't know what to do with himself, where to look. Deep down, he already missed his wife, or rather her reassuring presence at the cash-desk.

He couldn't fail to notice that everyone at the Monico, the entire staff, was glancing at him furtively, then exchanging woebegone looks with each other, even including Jules, the bald waiter, with the watery eyes of a spaniel.

'I'm fed up, Ludo!' she declared, emptying her glass.

'Take a sleeping tablet as soon as you get home, and you'll feel better tomorrow.'

She looked the *patron* up and down, and said sarcastically:

'Tomorrow? You think so?'

Léon heard her order another double scotch, knowing very well that she had just finished one and had had several drinks with clients. Would he say something to her, to stop her drinking, or would he tell Ludo not to serve her any more?

She looked straight at him, on purpose, trying to provoke some sort of reaction, even to the extent of having a public showdown, here and now, right away: she was feeling ready to explode.

He preferred to pretend he had noticed nothing, to push open the door to the cloakroom and come back with some paper hats which it was unusual to distribute at so late an hour, since the customers no longer needed them.

'See that?'

'You'd better be careful, Mademoiselle Célita. When I was a lad I had a job in the Vincennes Zoo and at certain times of the year we weren't allowed to go in the cages of the male animals, even to clean them. It didn't stop them, a fortnight or three weeks later, being as quiet as lambs, quieter than ever, as if they were trying to make up for the way they had behaved.'

It didn't make her laugh. Natasha, whose partner had just left, came up to her and glanced at her watch.

'A whole hour to go! God, how my feet hurt!'

'It's not my feet,' Célita answered, 'it's my nerves, and I've decided to get tight.'

'You think that'll help?'

'Have you heard the latest?'

'What latest? So much seems to be happening these days!'

The night before, they would willingly have jumped at each other's throats, and now they found themselves on the same side, albeit with different reactions. With a trace of resentment in her voice, Célita began:

'Your protégée . . .'

She stopped.

'I'm sorry.'

'Carry on. It's been a long time since I had a protégée. We have enough to do looking out for ourselves. Do you mean Maud?'

'She'll be hitting the headlines tomorrow.'

'So I've heard.'

'That's not all: she's only going to come down here for her number.'

Incredulous, Natasha turned to Ludo, who nodded in confirmation.

'That beats the lot.'

'You feel the same?'

'It won't affect me much. If they decide to sack me, I've always got a job to go to in Geneva. As for you, you'd better keep off the drink, or you'll make a fool of yourself in a minute.'

She didn't need to watch her long to see that. It was true. Célita's nerves were so tense that she needed something to make her relax, a scene, a fight, anything violent which could serve as an outlet for her pent-up fury, which was choking her.

'Why don't you report sick too and go home to bed? Take a couple of gardenal tablets . . .'

Ludo's advice again!

Célita was sorry the Count wasn't there; she could easily have picked a quarrel with him. He irritated her enough to be a good pressure valve.

After distributing a few hats, Léon went and smoked a cigarette in the street with Emile, a thing he often did towards the end of the evening.

Célita was still bent on making some sort of scandal and she went so far as to look around for a suitable victim among the clients, but there were only two couples left in the room and they were engrossed in each other.

She felt like going out into the street, without her coat, walking past the *patron*, along to the Hôtel de la Poste, and knocking on Maud's door.

'Open up, you little bitch!'

She would be forced to get out of bed and open the door, or Célita would make a terrible din on the landing.

'Now go back inside. Shut the door. Let's get it over with . . .'

Would Maud dare to put on her 'poor little thing' act and flutter her eyelashes over her falsely innocent eyes?

Célita wanted to use her hands, her nails on the soft, over-white skin. She needed to hurt, to make her cry out, make her beg for pardon.

'Now have you got it into your head that he's not for you? Answer me, girl! Answer me, you pathetic whore! Answer me, I tell you!'

She put her hand to her brow, looked across at Ludo, who shook his head, thinking she wanted another drink.

'Do you know her address at Bergerac?'

'I only know that her mother's a postwoman there.'

'Is her name really Leroy?'

She was forgetting the scene she had witnessed through the peep-hole, when the new girl had held out her identity card to Léon and he had read out her surname, half-aloud. If she couldn't go and fight it out with her in the Hôtel de la Poste, there was still another way of getting even.

When she left with Marie-Lou, half an hour later, Marie-Lou exclaimed: 'Where are we going?'

'To the post office.'

One of the counters was open all night. On a form she wrote out, with a scratchy pen:

'Madame Leroy, Post Office, Bergerac, Dordogne.'

Then, after pondering a moment, beneath the address:

'Your daughter Maud performing in striptease show at Monico in Cannes.'

'Signature?' the counter-clerk asked, after reading it without any reaction.

She added the first name that came into her head: 'Caroline Dubois', and there were no further questions.

Marie-Lou had been waiting discreetly at the door.

'You're sure you've not gone and done something silly?'

She laughed:

'It doesn't matter a hoot what I do at this stage! . . . You don't feel like getting tight?'

'No. If you're going drinking, I'm going home.'

It was not really drink Célita wanted: she just wanted something to happen; it was more like some vague, unsatisfied need.

She undressed without talking, in the bedroom which seemed gloomier than ever, more impersonal, plainly utilitarian in a way that wasn't even aggressively ugly.

Contrary to habit she went to bed naked, without cleaning her teeth, and it was Marie-Lou who got into bed last and turned off the light.

'Goodnight.'

'Goodnight.'

Minutes went past and by now Célita was aware what it was for which she had this almost painful longing: for a man, any kind of man as long as he would knock her down, hurt her, and shatter her nerves.

Perhaps it was because she had drunk too much and a kind of dislodgement was taking place in her mind, which was numbed between sleeping and waking, but she suddenly felt she had to get up, put on her coat, nothing else, and go and look for the first man she met in the street and ask him to relieve her need.

The night before, when she hadn't wanted it, Emile had been there.

Below, through the half-open window and the closed shutters, she could hear steps, bicycles passing, men going home from night-work or starting out for their day's jobs.

Her eyes open in the darkness, her body taut, her nipples hurting, she clenched her teeth, grinding their enamel, and a long time afterwards Marie-Lou's sleepy voice enquired from the next bed:

'What's wrong?'

In answer, shouting:

'Nothing! Do you hear? There's nothing wrong with me! I'm . . .'

And suddenly relaxed, empty, she burst into loud sobs.

Chapter Six

Each of her own accord, the three of them had chosen from their wardrobes their simplest, least conspicuous dress, and they had put on hardly any make-up; there in the garden, conscious of being observed, they seemed to be imitating the gestures and attitudes of girls on their way out from High Mass.

Natasha, having arrived first, had waited for the others in the steep, narrow street where Monsieur Léon's old Pontiac was parked behind a long, low-slung sports-car, bright red, which belonged to the surgeon.

When her friends looked questioningly at her, Natasha had said:

'It began a quarter of an hour ago. Apparently we can wait in the garden, and anyhow, unless something goes wrong, we shan't find out much this morning.'

They were at the Estérel Clinic, in a quiet, old part of the town, where only cats and dogs were wandering along the streets, sectioned into blocks of shade and sunlight, and the people from a wineshop opposite were washing out bottles.

The garden, with its pale gravel paths, was shaded by trees, the foliage of each a different green, and near the wall at the back some hens were clucking behind a trellis fence.

It was unusual for them to be out of doors at such an early hour, all together too, for it was little more than half-way through the morning and they had had hardly any sleep. Most of the windows in the clinic were wide open and the patients, men and women wearing cotton dressing-gowns with thin blue stripes, came and stared at them one after the other.

Of the three, Célita was the palest and the most anguished. During the ten days Madame Florence had spent under observation, undergoing repeated examinations, X-rays, analyses, she had come almost every afternoon at visiting hours, and the place was now familiar to her.

She knew that the ground floor was reserved for maternity cases, and she had been in the corridor two days ago just when the woman in Ward 6 was being brought back, accompanied by a nurse with a blood-stained apron, who was carrying a baby.

The curtain at the window occasionally swelled out with the breeze, and, when it blew to one side, revealed the bed, the mother, motionless and relaxed, some white carnations on the bedside table and further inside, the child's enamelled cradle.

Directly above Ward 6, the window-panes were of frosted glass, and behind those windows they were operating on the *patronne*.

Natasha was also feeling a little queasy.

'Apparently, at the last moment, when they came to take her away on the stretcher, she sat up in bed screaming that she wouldn't go through with it, she'd changed her mind, she'd sooner die in peace, and she made such a struggle that they had to give her two injections.'

The sky was blue, the air warm and still; birds were chirping in the trees, and a blackbird, completely unafraid, was hopping about the lawn, spying with a mischievous eye on the three girls.

'Where is he?' Célita asked.

'I think there's a waiting-room for relatives upstairs, next door to the operating theatre. I didn't see him. His car was already here when I arrived.'

They heard footsteps on the gravel, then saw Francine, who had walked up quickly, wearing her blue suit, a white hat on her blonde hair.

'It's Thursday,' she explained, 'and I couldn't find anybody to look after Pierrot, as he isn't going to school. I couldn't bring him along here either.'

'What did you do about it?'

'He's playing in the street; there aren't many cars about, and the woman in the dairy said she'd keep an eye on him through the shop-window.'

She, in turn, looked up at the window with the frosted panes.

'Well?'

She realised nobody had any news, that they would just have to wait. After a while she asked Natasha:

'Have you heard from Ketty?'

'No. But someone saw her in Nice. That's the third person who's told me that, so it must be true . . .'

Ketty, to everybody's surprise, had been Maud's first victim: it happened before Madame Florence entered the clinic, while she still sat behind the till at the Monico, for part of the night at least. Hadn't the *patronne*, even then, given up hope? She was obviously seriously ill, and it had been all the more upsetting in that it had happened so suddenly and had coincided with the business of Maud.

Célita, for one, was aware that the suddenness had only been apparent; Florence had admitted as much to her, from her hospital bed.

'I've been expecting something to happen for a long time,' she had confided in a gloomy voice. 'That's why I used to refuse to see the doctor. I've practically always had something the matter with me inside, and I haven't been able to bear having any relations with Léon for months, it hurts me so much.'

In less than two weeks she had become not only a sick woman, but exhausted, aged, pitiable, her skin loose, her eyes grown too large and feverish, staring at you as if they sought the answer to some terrifying question.

'They won't tell me what's wrong with me, but with all the tests they've been taking I know it's a cancer and I'll never get out of this bed again . . . Poor Léon!'

She was sorry for him. She bore him no ill will, only regretted that she wouldn't be there to protect him.

'That girl would have to turn up at a time like this! . . . He doesn't know what to do now . . . He's ashamed . . . He hardly dares look me in the eyes any longer, and still he hasn't got the guts to get rid of her . . .'

There were long silences, during which she stared up at the ceiling.

'Deep down, he's a weakling . . .'

A little later she added:

'Like all men! . . . If something does happen to me he'll be desperately unhappy, because he'll be haunted all his life by the fear that it was his fault . . .'

As far as the future was concerned this was probably the truth, but for the present Célita was convinced that Léon would not be too upset if his wife were to disappear from the scene. He would never admit it to himself. He would be bound to repulse such a thought if it ever entered his head. It would nonetheless sort things out.

He was struggling with the many complications, and, contrary to what one might have supposed, all his worries were bringing him closer to Maud instead of drawing them apart. Who knows? Perhaps he was thinking of her at this very moment, as he waited upstairs for the result of the operation?

Maud had not come, of course. He had left her while she was still asleep; for he spent his nights with her now, at the Louxor, formerly a luxury hotel on the Croisette, which had been converted into furnished apartments a few years ago.

In the afternoons, the girl could be seen sunbathing on her balcony, sipping fruit juice and playing the gramophone.

She had three rooms, bright and gay, with a view of the sea and the beach, and she only came down, wrapped in a gown, when it was time for a bathe.

Was Ketty responsible for what had happened the evening after the article in the *Nice-Matin* appeared, when the club was bursting with people? She had been sitting at a table in the front row with a middle-aged man, who looked, and acted, like a cattle-dealer or a large-scale farmer, and who had already drunk quite a lot.

Wasn't it Ketty's job to make the clients drink? It was time for the second show, and between the two shows Maud had stayed upstairs reading in a wicker chair they had installed in the dressing-room for her.

It was one of those evenings which, for no apparent reason, have a more electric atmosphere than usual, and glasses had been broken at the bar, loud remarks had greeted the flashes which went with Ketty's number.

Ketty had just come downstairs again and was back sitting in the same place, and her companion's large hand, with its prominent veins, was digging into her thigh.

That evening Maud was evidently finding it hard to go into her trance, as they were calling it now that the journalist had used the word in his article, and this was precisely the trouble with her number: it was liable to fall flat if people didn't sense her quivering all over.

She had just knelt down, the upper part of her body naked, and leaning backwards, clasping her breasts in both hands, she began swaying in time with the music, her face looking agonised, her mouth twisted with the effort.

Most of the spectators were taken in, holding their breath, but that evening there were some on whom the charm failed to work, and Maud felt it, as did Gianini, who was making signs at his musicians.

In a minute, half a minute, it would probably all have been successfully over, when Ketty's companion, standing up for a better look, just as he would have done at the local fair, had called out in a croaking voice:

'Want any help, sweetheart?'

Immediately, the spell was broken, and the whole room, torn from the magic, had burst out laughing, while Maud, completely thrown off balance, tried to get up and instead fell awkwardly over on her side.

Léon, red with fury, had rushed forward. He stayed a long time in the dressing-room, where Maud could be heard crying, talking to her the while in a low voice, almost pleading with her. When he came down again, he looked bad-tempered, and, against all the traditions of the house, he had called out in a loud voice:

'Ketty!'

Except for the cattle-dealer, who still sat in his place waiting for her to return, everybody had understood. When Ketty came downstairs again she was wearing her coat, carrying her clothes over her arm, her shoes in her hand, and Madame Florence, to whom her husband had hurriedly whispered something, handed her an envelope already prepared.

'Cheerio, girls!' she allowed herself the luxury of calling out as she left.

That night she had still slept in the rooms she shared with Natasha and the next morning she was gone, avowedly to Geneva, where she claimed they were eagerly expecting her.

From what had been heard since, she had not even attempted to go there; for she had been seen several times on the pavements of Nice around the Place de la Victoire.

How had Léon managed to remain so calm and collected during all this while, and still find time to devote to his new girl-friend? Everything had happened at once. The very next day Madame Florence entered the clinic and an hour later Léon received a letter asking him to present himself at the police station.

Once again Célita's inspiration had been a bad one, for her telegram had no more produced the desired effect than her telephone call to the police. When Léon went to see him, the superintendent had a long letter in front of him from Maud's mother, insisting on her daughter's return.

What had gone on behind the scenes they had only been able to glean in fragments. The fact remained that it was only once, on the evening after Léon's visit to the police station, that Maud had not appeared in the cabaret, and that the next morning somebody had seen the *patron* entering a lawyer's office.

Ludo, who should know about this sort of thing, had stated:

'As soon as she's eighteen, they can't touch her or the *patron*.'

Two days later Madame Leroy arrived at Cannes and at three o'clock that same afternoon, as she didn't know her daughter's address, she appeared at the Monico, just when the cleaning-women were raising clouds of dust. Emile had spoken to her, and described her to Célita:

'A rather fat little body, dressed in black as if she was in mourning, with a moustache.'

She had just spent quite a while staring at the photograph of Maud in the window and was still boiling with indignation.

'So it's true! She's doing that! My daughter, whom I brought up as a . . . as a . . .'

She was so comical that it was hard to feel sorry for her, especially since she later asked Emile:

'How much does she get paid, for doing that?'

Emile had telephoned the *patron*'s home to warn him and, getting no answer, next called the clinic, finally the Hôtel de la Poste, where Maud was still living at that time.

'Monsieur Léon? There's a lady here who insists on seeing you . . .'

'Let me speak, I'll teach him!' little Madame Leroy burst in, trying to grab the receiver from Emile.

'No, madame . . . He's coming round . . . It's her mother, *patron* . . . I keep telling her you'll be coming, but . . .'

Léon was anxious in case Emile had given her Maud's address and within a few minutes he came running up, his tie crooked, though not before he had taken the trouble to ring his solicitor, who duly arrived soon afterwards. Since it was impossible to talk in peace in the club, with the two old women still busy working, the three of them had gone off to the solicitor's home in the Square Mérimée, opposite the Casino.

Nobody knew what passed between them, except that after about an hour Maud had been summoned by telephone and had joined them. What kind of scene had been played there? What bargain had they concluded? Whatever the case Madame Leroy was never seen again at the Monico, and she had taken the train back the same evening.

If the *patron* had any idea who had sent the telegram, he had given no sign of it, and in any case, even without the telegram, Madame Leroy would have heard about it sooner or later, since a Paris weekly published in its next

number not one but five photos of Maud, including her 'ecstasy' one, as the
paper called it, together with a gossip-story on the 'girl who had found her
vocation as a striptease dancer'.

Ketty's departure already left a gap. Madame Florence's absence from the
cash-desk caused genuine distress, and they found themselves to their
surprise, talking in whispers, walking around on tiptoe.

The final blow, which seemed to destroy all hope of returning to normal
life, was Maud's move to the Louxor and the kind of ceremonial which, from
then on, accompanied her arrival and departure. She never turned up now
before the stroke of midnight, a few minutes before she was due to go on.
The *patron* left the Monico in his car just in time to go and fetch her. From a
branch of a famous Paris shop he had bought her a white coat, which, as
befitted her new status, she would take off at the door and hand to Francine.

What irritated Célita most was the shy, almost humble manner Maud
adopted in the club, both towards the clients and with the other girls and the
staff. To everyone she addressed a formal little 'Good evening', as if to
apologise for being there at all, then sat down at her table waiting her turn,
since she didn't have to change, and never failed to applaud Célita's number,
which preceded hers.

'And now, ladies and gentlemen, the management of the Monico have the
pleasure and the honour . . .'

She did not always remain in the dressing-room between the two shows;
sometimes she went off to the Casino, alone or with the *patron*.

Monsieur Léon, aware that, even looking on the bright side, his wife
would be incapacitated for many weeks, if not months, had sent for a sister of
his, whom nobody had ever heard of before, a pretty enough woman, a little
too fat, a little past her best, but still appetising, and not unlike him to look at.

She and her husband ran a café at Le Havre, near the docks, and it was
noticeable in the way she sat at the till. But from her raucous voice, with its
common undertones, and other significant details which didn't escape
women like the ones at the Monico, they had guessed that once upon a time
she had earned her living by other means.

Unlike Florence, she was never heard to say:

'Now, ladies . . .'

She called out, with false chumminess:

'Come along, girls . . .'

She was on familiar terms with them from the start.

'You, Ginger, it's time you got a move on . . .'

'Ginger' meant Célita, while Natasha had become 'Lanky' and Marie-
Lou 'Fatty'.

She had one child, a little boy about the same age as Pierrot, and she got on
well with Francine; whenever they had a moment to spare, they would be
talking about measles and worm powders.

Célita had still not left, had not created a scandal, as Natasha, in
particular, had expected and as Ludo feared. She fretted a good deal,
certainly, but she was careful to attack neither Léon nor the new favourite,
though this didn't mean that she had given in.

Between her and Florence a kind of trust had been established, even a sort
of intimacy. Yet during her almost daily visits to the clinic, the two women
hardly spoke, probably because they had no need of long phrases to
understand each other.

Léon, moreover, was not hiding much from his wife. He even told her more than Célita imagined, and for that reason Florence was the first to bring up the subject of the Louxor apartment.

'I think he was right. He couldn't leave her at the Hôtel de la Poste. Do you realise how unhappy he is?'

Was Florence deluding herself? Was her illness depriving her of her intuition, her woman's instinct, to that extent?

'You don't believe me, but it's the truth. At a certain age men are completely defenceless, even the ones who think they're so well protected; in fact, especially those. It can happen to women too . . .'

She interrupted herself, to scold Célita gently.

'Why did you bring flowers again? He sends me so many the nurse doesn't know where to put them now. It's salving his conscience, you see? I know he loves me. But it's too strong for him . . .'

After quite a long silence she added:

'You, too, you very nearly succeeded . . . And with you I'd have been more frightened . . .'

Hearing the *patronne* talk like that, in the muted monotonous voice of a nun. Célita felt disheartened; she was left to carry on the fight alone.

Another day Florence had said:

'He can tell you're all against him, and that hurts him, particularly in your case . . .'

'He said that? He mentioned me?'

Florence gave no details and Célita suspected her of lying, even guessing the motives which prompted the *patronne* to say that to her.

Even had she been in good health, the idea might have occurred to her of their making common front against the enemy, leaving them free to resume the battle against each other, mercilessly, later.

Wasn't that what Célita had imagined she could read in Florence's eyes, the night of Maud's arrival?

Now that she was out of the game, temporarily or permanently, she didn't want Célita to give up.

If anyone was to take Léon from her, whether it was while she was alive or after her death, at all costs it must not be Maud.

'It's tragic, you see for a man like him to be in a position like this, and so he's miserable. Yesterday he sat there, where you are now, and started crying, holding my hand and asking me to forgive him . . .'

Célita pressed her nails into the palms of her hands to stop herself crying out in fury.

Now, as she waited in the garden with her companions, thinking of the body cut open, up there on the operating-table, she heard again Florence's last words the day before, just as the bell was ringing for the end of visiting hours.

'Off you go! I may never see you again. Don't be too hard on him. One day, you'll see . . .'

It was only to her that Florence had spoken like this; didn't it constitute a sort of will? With Marie-Lou, Natasha or Francine she merely asked questions which showed she still took an interest in the cabaret, enquiring how many clients there had been, when they had closed: and presumably Léon's sister, who was called Alice, told her the figure for the takings each day.

Natasha had had a talk with the chief nursing sister who lived in the same building as she did. She had insisted on discovering the result of the tests, especially to learn whether it was a case of cancer of the uterus, and, without giving a direct answer, the sister had made a vague gesture and uttered a sigh . . .

'What a long time!' Marie-Lou was getting impatient. 'Do you think that's a good sign?'

'Some operations last two or three hours, and even longer,' Natasha replied; she knew a little about everything. 'It depends on what they find . . .'

A little wizened old man, his skull brown with the sun, was leaning on a window-sill on the second floor, wearing the patient's blue-striped dressing-gown, and he had waved at them two or three times.

'Do you know who he is?' asked Célita.

'I feel I've met him somewhere,' Marie-Lou answered.

'I daren't look up to see for sure. Let's walk along to the end of the path and I can have a good look on my way back . . .'

Then she too had given a little wave towards the second-floor window.

'Who is it?'

'You've never seen him; it was before your time. He owns a wholesale grocery business in the Rue d'Antibes, with his two sons; both of them are married and have got children. He loves me. I used to call him grandfather and he lapped it up.

'Only a year ago he was still coming twice a week; he had his fixed days for it. He only drank mineral water because he was on a diet, but he always bought us a bottle of champagne, Lulu and me.

'You never knew Lulu either. She went and got married in Morocco to somebody she met through an advertisement.

'One evening the poor old boy saw one of his sons come in and he rushed off to the cloakroom, where he stayed hiding for nearly two hours. He always left at midnight, whether the show was over or not, because that was the time the café shut, where he was supposed to be playing cards.'

In this way they tried to keep their minds off what was happening behind the frosted-glass windows and each time they passed they paused a moment in front of Ward 6, where the young mother was now giving her baby the breast.

'If Florence died . . .' Marie-Lou began.

'Touch wood!' Francine exclaimed.

And Célita also touched the little twig the other woman had picked up.

'You're right. Let's not think about it . . .'

But all at once they started thinking about it, not only out of pity for Florence, but because their means of livelihood was at stake. Once Léon was free to do what he pleased, would he carry on with the Monico, and even if he did so, the way he was behaving now, wasn't it likely that he would soon be forced to shut down?

Célita suspected Ludo of following the course of events with special interest and of having his eye on the night club. It might be his opportunity to step into the *patron*'s shoes. He was divorced, his son was grown up and doing his military service. If Célita, in whom he showed a marked interest, were to manoeuvre skilfully . . .

She rejected the thought as soon as it entered her head, not only because now wasn't the time for it, when Florence was lying there with her stomach cut open, but because she knew it would never work.

It was not so much security she was looking for. Security was only of secondary importance. The important thing was that she no longer had any wish to live without a man, that she had decided this man was Léon and that she refused to give up.

There was one person who had seen through her better than her friends, better even than Madame Florence, and, strange as it may seem, this person had never had a proper conversation with her and hardly knew her.

This was the Comte de Despierres, who had been in a lot during the last few days, invariably sitting at the bar, watching the people coming and going with his irritating smile. Célita had got it into her head that he came to see her, since she was always the one he bought drinks for. He asked few questions, and when he did, they were brief and cynical. Was it Ludo, with whom she sometimes saw him gossiping across the counter, who kept him informed?

Once, for example, he had simply asked:

'Not dead yet?'

'Are you speaking of the *patronne*?' she had replied severely.

'That'll still be one of them out of your way, won't it?'

She hated him, and nonetheless she could not help going over to join him as soon as he beckoned her.

'How are the lovers getting on? No jewels yet?'

'She's too smart for that.'

'Yet, you see, her heart's not set on having that place at the cash-desk.'

'How do you know?'

'I can see through her as well as I can through you. That's all I want.'

'Because you're so intelligent, I suppose? So very superior and intelligent . . .'

'I'm not sure about that, but I know women. As far as that girl's concerned, she's just using the *patron* of the Monico as a stepping-stone. He can help her over the first step, which is the most difficult. She knows very well she's got to smooth away her rough edges, and before she aims higher, she'll need a halo.'

The notion of the halo made her laugh.

'Let's say, if you like, a past which is more or less spicy, a good wardrobe, some jewels, her entrée into the casino and probably a car into the bargain . . .'

Célita gazed at him with wide staring eyes, struck by the truth of his remarks, and he went on in a careless tone, like a conjuror condescending to do a few card tricks:

'At thirty-two'—and he pointed his cigarette towards the cash-desk—'you might fancy that seat over there. Not at nineteen. At nineteen that would be considered sheer burial alive; they imagine they're going to go much further.'

He stubbed out the cigarette in the trade-marked ash-tray.

'And she will go further!'

She wondered whether Léon, who was watching them from across the room and frowning, realised that he was the indirect subject of the conversation. Rather than let the Count see that he had impressed her she preferred to murmur nonchalantly:

'I didn't know you went in for fortune-telling.'

She only really understood two days later, when she had to undergo, in her heart of hearts, a humiliating experience.

Curiously enough, the state of nervous excitement in which she had been living since Maud's arrival had been accompanied with a parallel sexual excitement, and one afternoon, when Marie-Lou was on the beach, she had not sent Emile away when he hoisted himself up onto the window-sill from the street.

Emile now had more free time than before, since the *patron* did not call in so regularly at the Monico during the afternoons and was sometimes even seen in a pair of bathing-trunks, lying stretched out next to Maud on the Louxor beach.

Célita suspected that Emile, to save time, got rid of many of his leaflets by throwing them down drains.

He always returned with a piece of news for her; he was the only one who ever went to the Louxor apartment to do errands, and he had found Léon there reading the paper, in his pyjamas, in an armchair on the balcony.

'He didn't seem to mind me seeing him like that, making himself at home, and he even showed me the bedroom and said:

'"Cosy, isn't it?"'

Emile was no longer so deeply moved when Célita complied with his wishes, but he showed his satisfaction with exuberance.

'Gee, you're a nice sort of a girl! And your skin's so soft!'

Célita, more and more often, aspired to something better. Why didn't the Count, who intrigued and repelled her at the same time, make some move? The idea of making love with him, even though she despised him, did not displease her.

She had many times considered it, telling herself that, since he came back so often and never took any notice of the others, he must have considered it as well.

One evening, to try out the ground, she had murmured, as she lightly pressed her breast against the man's arm, almost inadvertently:

'You're always talking about women and you know such a lot about them. Yet you don't seem to do much about it . . .'

At once, from the smile which lit up the man's face, from a sense of relief which she detected in him, she had a presentiment of the truth.

'That's just it!' he said, wrinkling his eyelids. 'I have an infinite appreciation for women, and they can be exquisite friends. All my life I've regretted not having a sister. Why, nothing would give me greater pleasure than your coming one afternoon and having a cup of tea with me on the Croisette . . .'

And then, since she was still at a loss as to what he was implying:

'When did you guess that I was an invert?'

He didn't say homosexual, but used a term which was more elegant somehow, and scientific at the same time.

'You look disappointed?'

'Why should I be disappointed?'

'I could be an excellent friend for you, because you're as complicated a creature as one could wish for, and what fascinates me most about you is that you have all the vices. I once had a friend who . . .'

'Thank you.'

'It was meant as a compliment.'

He had realised something had gone wrong, that the spell, if there had been a spell, was broken.

'I'm very sorry. I was mistaken.'

His last words were:

'It's a great pity.'

He did not return to the Monico and Célita preferred not to think about him any more.

'Couldn't we go and ask if it's over yet?' Marie-Lou enquired, anxious to get back to bed.

It was eleven o'clock. Florence had been on the operating-table for nearly two hours. Maud was probably still asleep, or at least reclining in her swing-chair on the balcony, watching the multi-coloured specks of the bathers on the sand and the sails gliding across the bay.

What none of them could guess was that, at that moment, Léon had come out into the corridor, on the first floor, and stopped a nurse as she went by.

'Do you know where I can find a telephone?'

'Try the office on the ground floor.'

There he timidly asked permission to use the telephone, gave the Louxor number, which he knew by heart, and was obliged to speak in the presence of the secretary.

'Is that you? . . . Yes . . . No, it's not over yet . . . No! Nobody can tell me a thing . . . The door's shut . . .'

His voice became softer, almost a whisper, as he added:

'I shan't be long . . .'

It was said so tenderly that he might just as well have said 'darling'.

'Are you waiting for number seventeen?'

'Yes.'

'Didn't anyone tell you it'll be another hour? If there's anything you've got to do . . .'

He was tempted, but resisted. As he walked past the front door, at the foot of the stairs, he noticed the four women waiting in the garden, and, sulkily, he muttered some unkind words at them as if the only reason for their coming was to make him feel guilty.

As he didn't dare to smoke inside, he had been intending to have a cigarette on the steps of the entrance; now he preferred to go without.

It did not take quite an hour, but forty minutes, and the four women were so tired of standing, their feet were so sore, that they had finally sat down on a bench, as if they were in a public garden.

It had never entered their heads that there was another entrance to the clinic, and it was Natasha who heard the surgeon's red car starting up, and Léon's almost immediately afterwards.

'Why don't you go in?'

They sent Célita off to reconnoitre and she made her way to the office, forcing herself not to look into the wards, whose doors were all ajar.

'Are you for number seventeen?'

'Yes, madame.'

'She can't be seen today, and it's not certain yet whether the doctor will allow any visitors tomorrow. I should warn you that it's highly unlikely.'

'The operation?'

The woman in the office, whose job it was to record, in a number of columns, all the births, illnesses and deaths, looked at Célita as if she had asked something ridiculous.

'It's over, naturally.'

'But . . .'

'She's still under the effects of the anaesthetic and she'll sleep till this evening.'

'Is the doctor at all hopeful?'

Again this word did not seem to have the same meaning for the secretary as it does for ordinary mortals; perhaps it meant absolutely nothing to her, for she simply looked at Célita, her eyes quite expressionless.

'I suppose we oughtn't to send any flowers?'

'Until further notice, certainly not.'

'Couldn't I just see her, even through the crack in the door?'

'Impossible.'

'Thank you.'

She rejoined the others in the garden and the four of them moved off towards the iron gates, where Marie-Lou remembered to wave her hand at the little old man on the second floor.

'Well?'

'Nothing, except that she's alive. They say she'll sleep till this evening.'

'And then?'

Célita merely shrugged her shoulders and Marie-Lou declared:

'As far as I'm concerned, I need a drink before I go and do the same; I'll treat you all.'

In a nearby street they discovered a little bar, where people came in the evenings to play bowls, but which was empty at this time of day.

The owner, in his shirt-sleeves, had been reading the paper in an easy chair, where the cat had taken his place now that he had been interrupted; he looked in some bewilderment at these unwonted women customers, who all chose vermouth, since he hadn't got their regular drinks.

Marie-Lou, again, had the last word:

'She'll pull through all right, trust me. And before a month's out you'll see her doling me out the fines because the polish on my toe-nails is chipping off or I've been eating garlic. Let's have the same again, Arthur!'

Chapter Seven

For a long time now, one might say ever since Maud's arrival at the Monico, Célita had been trying to make some sort of contact with Léon but, whether deliberately or not, he was continually slipping away from her. When she arrived in the evening, if he was already there, he nodded to her in the same way as he did to the others, seeming preoccupied, and if, during the course of the night, he had anything to say to her concerning her work, it was brief and to the point.

One afternoon, before Florence had her operation, he had arrived at the clinic while Célita was sitting at her bedside and, after kissing his wife on the forehead, he had gone over to stand in front of the window; he did not move from there for the rest of her visit.

Day after day, she would watch carefully for a chance to get him to herself at last. She had nothing particular to say to him. She was not at present hoping for anything from him, but she could not bear to live with this hostile vacuum between them.

A dozen times she had been on the point of making a scene at the height of the evening's entertainment, and this might have been a relief. She purposely infringed all the sacrosanct rules of the house, under his very eyes, as if to defy him: going out during the show to have a breath of fresh air on the pavement, or again, when she knew she was being watched, refusing to dance with a good client, on the excuse that her feet were hurting her.

She never managed to be alone with him and it would scarcely have helped to go to the Monico one afternoon, since she would have to be very lucky to choose one of the rare days on which he now went there, and, in any case, the cleaning-women would have been there, or the tradesmen.

Natasha had left and her absence changed the atmosphere once again. Probably everybody, Léon included, had rather the feeling that it was the beginning of the end.

Performers had come and gone, of course, replacing each other in more or less rapid succession during the last few years, but that had been due to the normal necessity for a different programme; whereas, this time, it was more like the rats leaving the sinking ship.

For Natasha the whole thing had happened within two evenings, in the most unexpected way. They had all noticed a young man at the bar, very dark, Asiatic-looking, who only knew a few words of French, but, according to Natasha, spoke very good English without the trace of an accent.

She had kept him company until closing time, and after having a snack at Justin's, she had let herself be taken out for a run in a motor-boat with him, just as day was breaking.

The next evening he was there again when they opened, correct and shy, and Natasha had shown the others his photograph, which had recently appeared in the *Nice-Matin*. He was a Persian prince, a genuine one, a cousin of the Shah, who had studied at Cambridge and was now spending a few weeks in France. He had been photographed with the Prefect, who had welcomed him off his plane.

As she was getting ready for the first show Natasha had announced:

'Guess what he wants me to do? First he asked if I knew Paris well: the Louvre and the museums and all; then he offered me a hundred thousand francs, and all expenses paid, if I would be his guide and interpreter for a month. What would you do, if you were me?'

The Persian had waited for her answer until the second show, smiling, courteous, getting up to offer Natasha a stool each time she went over to join him.

Eventually she informed the others:

'I've said yes, dears. If things were different here, I might have hesitated, but the way the club's going now . . .'

'When are you leaving?'

'Tomorrow, by car. He's brought an Italian racing motor and he's already reserved an apartment at the Plaza . . .'

'Have you told the boss the news?'

'Not yet. I'll tell him when I go.'

Would Célita have tried to seize an opportunity like that, if she had known

English? Probably. In one go, Natasha was escaping from their world, and they caught themselves looking at her with something like respect.

Immediately after her departure, Léon called Francine as she too was getting ready to go home.

'From tomorrow you'll have to do your number again, for a few days . . .'

Célita and Marie-Lou were already on their way to the Place du Commandant-Maria. They were almost ready for bed when they heard somebody tapping on the shutters. It was poor Francine, very upset, wanting to tell them her news.

She had twice tried to do a striptease number several months before, and Madame Florence had told her, bluntly:

'You'd better stick to the cloakroom, my poor Francine. You make yourself look like a dirty picture.'

It was true. When fully dressed, Francine made the best impression, and without any effort she could pass for a pleasant, attractive little housewife. Once naked, she looked like one of those buxom nudes you see in paintings in art galleries, her pink flesh forming plump curves, by no means uncomely.

Unfortunately, there was the business of transformation: in other words, the act of taking her clothes off, when, although she did her best to follow the rhythm of the music, everything would go wrong; she became absurd, not to say indecent, and the g-string, whether it was of pink or black satin, appeared erotic and shocking on her rounded belly.

'I couldn't say I wouldn't do it. He seemed so upset. He said that everyone was letting him down and that I was the only one he could depend on . . .'

And to Célita:

'Will you mind if I come round tomorrow, so you can tell me what to do?'

So they had rehearsed a number there, between the uncleared table and the Henri II sideboard. To replace Francine in the cloakroom, while he waited for a Paris agency to send him a new performer, Léon had hired an old woman with a thin, lugubrious face, who normally sold national lottery tickets round the cafés.

The musicians had taken advantage of the situation to ask for a rise in wages, to which the *patron* had finally agreed, after a violent angry outburst.

And Célita continued to wait her turn to accost him, watching out for a favourable moment.

On Sunday, returning from driving Maud back to the Louxor in his car, he stepped onto the pavement and found himself face to face with Célita, who had ostensibly come out to smoke a cigarette.

'What do you think you're doing here, eh?'

Emile had discreetly moved a few paces away from them.

'I was waiting for you, Monsieur Léon.'

She called him MonsieurLéon as if they were still in the club, not standing outside in the street. Had he any idea that she wanted to make a scene? At all events, he made as if to go straight inside the door, and when she barred his way, there was a resigned look on his face.

'I suppose you want a rise, too?' he muttered a little bitterly.

'No. I simply want your permission to go and see Madame Florence.'

Madame Florence had spent another week in the clinic after the operation and had then been taken home by ambulance, three days before this. Since then, Célita had not dared go to see her, because she would have been no longer on neutral ground, but in Florence's own home, and Emile was the only one ever to have been inside the flat in the Boulevard Carnot.

Léon looked her sternly in the eyes. He had hesitated, realising perhaps that he would do better to keep quiet, but his rancour got the better of him, probably because his own conscience was not clear, and he said:

'If you're counting on taking her place, you're wasting your time.'

Then, without waiting to think, without knowing what she was doing, her features hardened and she had slapped him, standing stiff on her high heels and he had seized her wrist and twisted it, as she spat in his face:

'Have you no shame? Tell me, aren't you ashamed of yourself?'

It was as if she had regained her real personality, her real temperament.

'And you, you little bitch, weren't you ashamed of yourself when you were doing your level best to try and take her place?'

He spoke low, aware that they were only separated from the customers by a velvet curtain, and still holding her wrist so that he hurt her, he went on, speaking close to her, so that their breaths mixed, a look of hatred in his face:

'Do you want me to remind you of all the things you've done, all the things you've said?'

At that moment she still regarded him as an equal, but he then uttered a sentence, just one, which forced Célita to close her eyes and give up the struggle:

'*Do you want me to remind you about the gardenal? Do you, you whore?*'

He saw that she was finished and brusquely let go of her, not without giving her a push which almost threw her against the wall.

'Go and see Florence as often as you like, but get any idea out of your head that you'll one day take her place at the desk!'

She didn't burst into tears. Avoiding Emile, who longed for a sign from her so that he could comfort her, she started walking alone towards the end of the street, beside the line of parked cars.

The gardenal business had been a mistake and she had realised as much almost at once, but she had never imagined Léon would have dared throw that in her face, because there were even more unpleasant truths she could fling back at him.

In any case, it was a dirty trick to play and he wouldn't be feeling proud of the way he had just extricated himself. Didn't that prove what a mess he had made of his life since Maud had got him in her clutches?

It had happened the previous Christmas. At the Monico the party had gone on until half-past five in the morning and everybody had had a lot to drink, including Célita, and even Léon, who usually remained sober.

Léon had done something which was quite out of character, since, at any rate at the club, he took his role as *patron* very seriously.

Had Célita looked more desirable than other evenings, or was it the alcohol that made him behave that way? At all events, at four o'clock, at a time when she had no business in the dressing-room, since the shows were finished, he had whispered to her:

'Go upstairs and wait till I come . . .'

He had in due course gone up to join her there among the costumes lying around untidily, and she had seen an expression on his face that she was more used to seeing on the faces of his clients.

'Our own little Christmas . . .' he had whispered in her ear, before he took her, the whole time watching the cloakroom below through the fanlight at floor-level.

Had Florence guessed what had been going on when she saw them coming back one after the other? A little later on, she had simply said:

'You'd better fasten your dress properly, Célita.'

The next morning Célita only vaguely remembered how she had got home. A client had driven her off, together with Marie-Lou and another man, and for a long time they had stayed in the car, which he had parked at the end of the jetty, nobody saying a word, the darkness outside blurred by a fine rain.

The way the night had ended had disgusted her, that and now the fact that Marie-Lou, at eleven o'clock, was already up, almost fresh-looking, putting on some scent before going out to lunch, at the Napoule, with a woman friend of hers who was married with children.

She could not get back to sleep, caught in the grip of a depression such as she had rarely known before. She had never felt so dirty, physically and morally, and though she could not remember anything about it, she knew that if she opened her handbag she would find a crumpled ten-thousand-franc note in it, which she had almost begged from her last partner.

Outside, people were returning home from Mass, families with children, walking in front holding each other by the hand, and inside the houses there would be a warm smell of turkey or black pudding.

Marie-Lou, when she left, had forgotten to close the shutters of the dining-room, and through the connecting door, which was ajar, Célita could see from her bed a greyish rectangle of falling rain.

She tried to go back to sleep. Her head ached, her whole body ached; she was ashamed of herself, frightened of the future, seeing no reason why it should be any better than the past or the present.

She twisted and turned in the sheets, and the pillow was clammy. When she had got out of bed to drink a glass of water, she had noticed, on the ledge in the bathroom, the gardenal which she sometimes used.

She took two pills, hoping they would make her sleep at last and stop her thinking, but instead of putting her right out as usual, the drug had plunged her into a state of half-dazedness.

In vain she struggled to sink more deeply into unconsciousness. Each time she returned, not to the surface, but to middle water, water as glaucous and dispiriting as the rectangle of grey rain.

Her thoughts were out of joint, however, though they did not become fantastic as they do in dreams, and they even seemed rational.

Since she loathed herself, since life wasn't offering her, nor ever would offer her, anything clean and pleasant, why not simply end it?

At the Monico, Léon had taken her as he might a whore, and what she had done subsequently was to act like a whore again. Was that what she was to become, at thirty-two, now that she no longer had any chance to rise, but every chance of slipping still lower, right to the gutter?

If, instead of two gardenal tablets, she had taken four, or six, or eight . . .

She would feel no pain. She would fall asleep, and that evening Léon would realise, too late, what he had lost.

She imagined Marie-Lou's return home, her screams, the demented landlady bursting in, people ringing the police and the doctor, Léon hurrying round in his turn, Florence having pangs of remorse (?) and, later, at the club, the mournful whisperings.

Then there would be the funeral, with the whole staff walking behind the hearse, even the musicians.

The passers-by would stop and say:

'It's that girl who used to dance at the Monico . . .'

Subsequently she had preferred to suppress the memory of that afternoon.

If it hadn't been Christmas, if it hadn't been raining, if she had not got drunk the night before, and if there had not been that episode in the car at the end of the jetty, probably nothing would have happened.

Why, to crown everything, did Marie-Lou have to go out to lunch with a proper family?

Célita was alone in the world, huddled in a not very clean bed, staring at the window, unable to go peacefully to sleep, when she suddenly got an idea into her head, which would have appeared preposterous to anybody in their right senses.

She had taken only two pills, but she might have taken more; nobody could know. When she had thought of dying, hadn't she chiefly wanted to make Léon feel sorry?

It was not so clear as that, but that was still the sense of her reasoning.

If Léon should hear that she were dying, wouldn't she achieve the same result, with the difference that she would be there to profit from it?

It was simple, as long as she planned the details and the setting suitably, and she pondered over it for nearly an hour.

Eventually with her face haggard, seeming to totter, which demanded no great effort, she had gone to knock on the door of the old landlady who lived alone at the other end of the corridor, and when it opened, she stood propped against the doorpost, in a theatrical pose, speaking with difficulty:

'Please ring Monsieur Tourmaire at once and tell him I'm feeling very ill, that I'm scared I'm going to die . . .'

At the Monico they practically always used christian names, but Léon did possess a surname.

'Do you know his number?'

'It's in the book. He lives at 57 Boulevard Carnot . . .'

She swayed when she let go her hold on the doorpost and the old lady had to support her as she helped her back to bed.

'Is there anything I could do?'

Yet the landlady had never liked either her or Marie-Lou, because of the underclothes they would hang outside the window, which had been the cause of innumerable squabbles.

'Hello! . . . Monsieur Tourmaire? . . . This is Mademoiselle Perrin's landlady . . . What? . . .'

Célita's surname was equally unfamiliar to him, although he must have read it on her papers. It was better known to Madame Florence, because she had to fill it in every month on the national insurance forms.

'Mademoiselle Célita then . . . She says she's feeling very ill, that she's going to die, and she wants you to come straightaway . . .'

That wasn't exactly it. The landlady was talking too much and Célita was beginning to regret her play-acting.

'He's coming. Where is it you feel ill?'

'Everywhere . . . Here specially . . .'

She pointed to her stomach, her abdomen.

'I'll get you a hot-water bottle . . .'

Léon took scarcely a quarter of an hour to get there and was very alarmed.
'What's happened?'

Indicating the old lady, she murmured in a weak voice:

'Tell her to get out!'

Whereupon, pretending to suffer a spasm, then another, she pointed at the
bottle of gardenal pills which she had placed in full view on the bedside
table.

He became still more anxious, but in a different way, as if he were
suddenly realising his responsibilities and the consequences this business
might have in store for him.

'I'll call a doctor . . .'

It was plain that he wasn't keen to do so.

'No . . . not the doctor . . .' she begged.

She was clinging to the man's large hand as if he alone could prevent her
dying.

'I didn't want to fetch you . . . In the end I didn't have the courage to go
without seeing you again . . .'

'Have you vomited?'

'No.'

'You must vomit. Get out of bed.'

'I can't . . .'

He went and fetched a bowl from the kitchen, made Célita sit on the edge
of the bed.

'Stick your finger down your throat . . . Right down . . . Once more . . .'

She obeyed, crimson, her eyes moist.

'Go on . . . You've got to be sick . . . If you can't manage it, I'll take you
along to the hospital . . .'

She vomited, bitter liquid for the most part, and he handed her a tumbler
of water.

'Drink this and do it again. It'll wash out your stomach . . .'

Three times he made her drink and throw up the liquid . . .

'I saw them do this once before, in a similar case, one evening in
Montmartre; one of the girls had . . .'

This memory that now came back to him was to spoil everything. He
looked at her more intently, took her pulse, stared at her eyes and lifted her
eyelids as he had seen the doctor do.

She had forgotten that a man who had spent much of his life in and out of
Montmartre would have seen almost everything.

'How many tablets did you take?'

'I can't remember . . .'

She was still striving to win.

'Six perhaps . . . Or it may have been only five . . .'

'Or was it just one? Come on, admit it!'

She shook her head furiously.

'Two?'

What could she do but change her tactics and burst into sobs? Since he
wasn't going to believe her tale she had better tell him the truth and make it
sound pathetic.

'Ever since this morning when Marie-Lou woke me up as she was getting
dressed, I've been thinking of you, picturing you at home with another
woman, your wife because she was the one who had the luck to meet you

when you were still free, while I . . .'

He had listened to her right to the end and she had said a great deal more, her breast heaving, carried away by her own game, not really knowing any more when she was being melodramatic and when sincere.

'Every night when I leave you, I watch you going off with her . . .'

She sensed he was weakening, then hardening himself again, only to weaken once more, and it was then that she staked her all.

'I know I'm a bitch. I hate your wife and I shan't be happy till the day she's gone. You want the whole truth? Well, if I could murder her and be sure of not getting caught, I'd do it without turning a hair. I hate myself for it, but I want you and I'd do anything to get you . . . Last night, when you had me in your arms, I almost called out to her to come and see us, to show her that you were mine as well as hers, to shout at her that I'm the one you love . . . That's what you said, didn't you? . . . Answer me!'

Between his teeth, he snarled:

'Little slut!'

And he had slapped her, then flung himself on her, viciously.

That day she had not been sure whether she had won or lost. When he was dressed again he was visibly disturbed, and though he had often returned in the course of time, he never referred to what had happened that day.

Had he at last given her the answer just now when he had spat at her:

'*Do you want me to remind you about the gardenal? Do you, you whore?*'

She must calm herself. She would not leave. She would only leave if she was thrown out by brute force, and then it would be the gardenal for good and all, because then she'd have nothing more to lose.

All these cars, some of them worth thousands of pounds, belonged to men, even to married couples, who had paid to see four women take their clothes off, and especially to see Maud perform her dirty little act for them, in which she herself thrilled as she threw men into excitement at the sight of her body.

'What I could do to that bitch!' she muttered under her breath, alone in the middle of the pavement.

One day, she was sure of this, she had to feel sure of it, she would have a chance to get her own back, and till then it was essential to keep calm, to preserve complete calm.

'Calm down, Célita, calm down!' she repeated to herself like an incantation.

And in fact her features did gradually resume their normal expression, she was even able to force a smile for Emile's benefit, when he looked at her, a little frightened:

'Well, did you hear me slap his face?'

Léon did not give her the sack there and then, which meant that he would not do so at all, and consequently that all was not lost.

The very next morning she rang the bell of the Tourmaires' flat, in a prosperous-looking, yellowish-stuccoed house of the type that was built in Cannes fifty years ago. There was a marble staircase, the doors were of a dark wood, fitted with copper handles.

A young girl, not more than sixteen, with untidy hair and a dirty face, opened the door to her.

'I want to see Madame Florence, please. Tell her it's Célita . . .'

'I'll ask the nurse. If you'll wait in here . . .'

She showed her into a drawing-room with polished furniture of no particular style, which, with its rugs and ornaments, the lithographs and portraits on its walls, its andirons and copper guard in front of the fireplace, might have been the drawing-room of some retired couple with ample means.

Léon and Florence, who had spent most of their lives in the chaos of Montmartre and still lived on the fringe of decent society, were obviously doing their best to establish more reassuring surroundings at home. Heavy drapes framed the windows and through the short muslin curtains one could make out the motionless foliage of the plane trees in the sun.

A strong-looking woman with masculine features, wearing a white blouse, appeared in the doorway.

'You may go in and see Madame Tourmaire, but please do not stay more than ten minutes, and don't let her talk more than is absolutely necessary, because the slightest effort tires her . . .'

'How is she?'

The nurse put a finger to her lips, pointed to the half-open door, and said in a louder voice, which the sick woman would hear:

'The convalescence is taking its usual course and the doctor is quite satisfied with her progress so far. Now, as always after these operations, it's simply a question of time, patience and will-power . . .'

They had started lying to the invalid, and it was a bad sign; Célita sensed this and her heart grew heavy. Yet it was true that a few months earlier she had longed for her death, and would have been capable of carrying out what she had told Léon.

With illness it was another matter, and Célita could not help thinking that one day she might be in her place.

Florence's eyes, in her colourless face, were even larger and more pathetic than at the clinic, and Célita felt a sort of repulsion as she held the hot moist hand which emerged from beneath the sheets to take hers. Most of all she noticed the smell in the room, which was not the smell of medicines, but a human smell which came from the bed and oppressed her to such an extent that she dared not breathe deeply.

'Monsieur Léon gave me permission to come, otherwise I would not have thought of disturbing you.'

'Sit down.'

The voice was from far away. The eyes indicated a cane-seated chair and Célita noticed a crucifix above the bed, which was of walnut wood, in the same style as the wardrobe with two mirrors that stood between the windows.

'I gather you mustn't talk too much and I really only came to tell you that everything's fine at the Monico. Dear old Francine is not doing so badly, some of the clients seem to like her. Yesterday I told her to do a really comic number, but she doesn't dare. We're expecting a new dancer from Paris . . .'

She was talking for the sake of talking, because Madame Florence's fixed stare disconcerted her. Besides, the nurse was still there in an armchair by the window.

'It's getting hot already, the season's begun, and the Croisette is swarming with tourists, the cars have to just creep along . . .'

Why did Florence look as though she were laughing at her? It was barely noticeable: the slightest curve of her pale lips.

'You'll be up and about by the height of the summer, when we'll need you more than ever . . .'

She went on, saying anything that came into her head:

'It's amazing how well Madame Alice gets on . . .'

Perhaps that was a blunder, since Alice, who was only her sister-in-law, had taken the *patronne*'s place at the desk.

'Though of course it's not the same without you. All the regulars ask after you. You must get well soon . . .'

She was losing heart. Her thoughts tumbled over each other. Perhaps she was being affected by the idea that this was the room where Léon and Florence slept together.

Suddenly she was feeling further from her ambition than ever, the whole atmosphere was so weird. Emile had said to her:

'They've got a marvellous flat, with carpets everywhere . . .'

She had not imagined it like this. It was as if she had discovered a different Florence, another Léon.

At the Monico they belonged, although on a higher level, to the same sort of group as she did, the same world. With the *patron* in the club or standing at the entrance, and Florence at the cash-desk, the ties which one felt linked them were ties which could be broken.

Here, in spite of the absence of children, they were not only a married couple but a family, and in the black-and-gold oval frames there were two portraits, of an old man and an old lady in clothes of around 1900.

'Is that your mother?' she asked, foolishly.

The woman with the grey hair, done in a tight bun on the top of her head was wearing a whaleboned bodice and a cameo brooch pinned on her bosom, and had the angular and stubborn features of a peasant.

Florence shook her head and murmured:

'Léon's grandmother; she brought him up, his sister too . . .'

She looked towards the mantelpiece and Célita walked over to it to find a rather blurred photograph of a chubby little boy, holding a hoop in his hand.

'When he was six . . .' Florence whispered.

The nurse stood up, indicating that it was time to leave.

'If my visits don't upset you, I'll come and see you again . . .'

She felt Florence wanted to say something to her, but didn't dare, perhaps through modesty, perhaps because of the presence of the nurse.

'Till then . . .'

She was accompanied out onto the landing and she was still reluctant to leave; it seemed to her that something had been left undone, she didn't know what, but she felt vaguely uneasy about it.

'May I really come again?' she asked the nurse.

'You had better telephone before you do. We're giving her injections to make her sleep as much as possible.'

In a hardly audible voice she asked again:

'Is there any hope?'

The answer was neither yes nor no. Just a vague shrug of the shoulders.

That night the new girl arrived from Paris, a blonde, with regular features and a body which was more perfect, though less statuesque, than Natasha's. She appeared with a suitcase full of make-up articles and showed her surprise and disappointment when she saw the lack of amenities in the communal dressing-room.

'Aren't there any wardrobes where we can put our things?'

'You've got to hang them on the rod behind the curtain.'

'What about our underclothes?'

Célita showed her the fibre boxes balanced on a plank.

'It looks pretty miserable to me.'

'It is miserable,' Célita agreed.

The new girl called herself Gilda, but her real name was Emma Willenstein, and she had appeared in two or three classy cabarets in Paris; she showed them the programmes.

'Who's the star performer advertised outside? Isn't she here?'

'She only turns up when it's time for her act, and she leaves straightaway afterwards.'

Gilda must have lived in France or Belgium for a long time since she spoke French fluently, with an accent which was hard to recognise at first, because, although she had been born in Cologne, her mother was a Czech.

'They told me I could rent the rooms of the girl who has left . . . But I don't reckon I'll stay around in this mouldy spot for more than a week or two; I've got an engagement for July and August, at Ostend . . .'

That evening everybody's eyes were on her, from the barman to the band, in the way one always watches a newcomer. Célita didn't object when she was told her number would come before Gilda's, which meant a step downwards in the hierarchy for her.

The German girl's dress, of thick white silk, with a skirt as wide as a crinoline, must have cost a lot of money, and her act was studied, a new one for Cannes, because, instead of the traditional g-string, she finished up completely naked, hiding the vital parts with a feather fan which she mimed her readiness to close if the audience demanded it.

Maud applauded, as she had always applauded Célita, and Léon looked across as if to ask her permission to go and congratulate the new recruit in the cloakroom. Anyway, he only stayed there a few seconds, and was soon back leaning against the door as Gianini finished announcing Maud Le Roy, and she, accompanied by a clash of cymbals, advanced onto the floor.

A little later Gilda came downstairs into the room, looked about for Célita, then went and sat at her table. It was rather as if she had just made her choice. For, just as everybody will stare at a newcomer, wondering whether they will like her, the newcomer, for her part, is always a little lost and needs help in getting acclimatised to the club.

'I watched her number through the little window.'

She meant what they called the peep-hole.

'I suppose she sleeps with the boss.'

'Ssh! She's his official mistress . . .'

'And at the desk, is that his wife?'

'His sister. His wife's ill; she's just had an operation.'

'Funny sort of joint! What's he done all his life?'

'He was a barman in Montmartre for ages.'

'And the fat girl, who looks as though she needs a wash?'

Two or three times during the course of the evening she repeated:

'Funny sort of joint!'

Finally Célita grew so irritated by it that she kept out of her way. In a sense this joint had come to be almost her home and up till quite lately they had really considered themselves members of a family, with a family's loves, hates, jealousies.

Célita knew better than anybody how everything had changed, but it did not make it any less disagreeable to have a stranger taking it upon herself to tell her, looking round the place in her sarcastic, disdainful way.

Anyway, it was plain that she must have come from a funny sort of joint herself, for at about three o'clock in the morning she left the American with the crew-cut and the white linen suit, with whom she had been sitting, and went across to the bar to whisper something in Ludo's ear. Ludo shook his head, sent her over to Monsieur Léon, who was standing near the door, and he also said no to her.

Célita could guess what had happened without having to listen to Gilda, who, with an angry look, had just told her boy-friend.

The new girl had supposed she would be allowed to leave before closing time to accompany the American to his hotel.

The American obviously did not want to sit there drinking champagne while he waited for her, because she wrote something down for him on a piece of paper, which he slipped into his pocket before he left, giving Léon a sulky look as he went by.

Now that the summer holidays had begun, the clients were different, had become noisier and more vulgar; less champagne was consumed and every night there was some customer or other who complained at being charged a thousand francs for a bottle of beer they could buy for a hundred francs in a café.

'Don't forget there's a floor show,' Jules would start explaining each time, and some of them would take their revenge on him by not giving him a tip.

Francine was talking of taking a month off to go with her little boy to the mountains.

The club was slowly emptying. It was half-past three. Célita sat alone at a table, thinking of nothing in particular, vaguely watching Marie-Lou yawning while a white-haired man chattered to her, at the same time busily kneading her fat thigh with his hand.

At one moment the light seemed to fade, a thing which often happened when there was a storm in the mountains.

A few minutes later the telephone rang on the cash-desk and Alice lifted the receiver. At first it seemed that she could not hear because of the music, then she glanced over towards the door. Nor could what she was saying be heard either, certainly not by Célita, who was sitting near the band; but she saw Alice hesitate, then got up and pass behind Ludo, to whom she whispered a few words.

Ludo, frowning, looked from the *patron* to Célita, while Alice leaned over the counter at the end of the bar, to speak to her brother, whom she had beckoned over with her hand.

Célita did not move, held her breath, not missing anything that was happening, and when she saw the *patron* rush outside without his hat, without a word to anybody, she felt her hands turn icy cold.

Her eyes must have been eloquent; through the crowd, the noise, the streamers hanging from the ceiling, Ludo understood her unspoken question, answered her with a movement of his eyelids as he took hold of a bottle of brandy and poured himself a full glass.

Madame Florence was dead.

Chapter Eight

There had been a violent storm the previous night and the air was clean and transparent, so that in the far distance every detail of the mountains was visible, the little white houses standing out in relief as in stereoscopic views; at a very early hour some of the residents of La Californie and Le Cannet had been able to see Corsica, whose peaks made a jagged line in the merging turquoise blue of sea and sky.

At a quarter to ten it was already hot and hazy, and women in shorts were coming down the Boulevard Carnot, towards the market, glancing curiously at the little groups of people standing under the plane trees, aware that something was going to happen; but not until they reached No. 57 did they discover the black drapes with the fringes and silver drops. Some of the women crossed themselves.

The people waiting were mainly men, proprietors of cabarets or bars from Juan-les-Pins, Nice and also from the other side of the Estérel: Saint-Raphael, Saint-Tropez, Toulon and Marseilles; most of them looked lost at being up and about so early, and some of the faces seemed familiar, as they had appeared in the papers, in odd items of local news.

Célita arrived with Marie-Lou and Francine and they joined Ludo, Jules and Gianini on the pavement.

'Have you been upstairs?'

Ludo nodded and they in turn went into the house, as each of the others had done before going out to wait in the street; they climbed the staircase, stopping on the second landing, a little out of breath. The door was shut. Célita felt her bag heavy in her hand, a rectangular bag as big as Madame Florence's, which was a kind of sign of her profession; for whenever she did not go home to the Place du Commandant-Maria for the night, it could hold all her toilet articles and even a nightdress.

Since she was hesitating, Marie-Lou gave her a little shove and they went through into the passage, where a dim electric light was burning and there was a smell of hot wax and flowers.

The bedroom, where the curtains had been drawn across the windows, was hung in black. The bed and the wardrobe with the mirrors had been removed; there was nothing left but a stand of some sort, covered with a cloth—perhaps the Henri II table from the dining room?—supporting the oak coffin with its heavy silver ornamentation.

Each of the two women dipped a twig of box in the holy water and made the sign of the cross in the air, then stood there motionless, as if praying, their lips moving, not daring to look around too much.

Several dark figures were disclosed in the dancing light of the candles: Monsieur Léon, his sister Alice, a man who was presumably her husband, two women they didn't know and a little, shrunken old lady, who looked like a church chair-attendant.

It was Florence's mother, who had never been mentioned at the Monico, but had now come down from her village in Berry where she made cheese from the milk of her goats.

They could not see Maud there. Nobody knew whether she would be at the funeral. As they went out, they touched Léon's hand, mumbling some unintelligible syllables meant for condolences, and they were almost surprised to find the sun shining outside and the noises of the street.

Marie-Lou and Francine, who suspected nothing, were left wondering when Célita said to them:

'I'll be back in a minute.'

They watched her almost run to the corner of the street and disappear into a bar.

'What's bitten her?'

'I don't know,' Marie-Lou replied. 'The last two days she's been up and down the whole time, crying one minute, laughing out loud the next, and then not saying a single word, as if she were hiding something.'

And Francine sighed:

'She's always been so melodramatic.'

They would surely have been still more anxious had they seen Célita hurriedly swallow two glasses of cognac, while keeping an eye on the street.

The day after Madame Florence's death the telephone had rung about four o'clock in the afternoon, and Célita had answered it while Marie-Lou went on eating; they had just sat down to lunch.

'Yes, speaking . . .' she said, with surprise.

At the other end of the line a voice she had not recognised had mysteriously announced:

'This is Mademoiselle Motta. Do you remember me?'

'No.'

'You saw me yesterday. I was the nurse who was looking after Madame Tourmaire. Are you alone?'

Célita had hesitated, then answered: 'Yes.'

'I've been asked to give you a message and I wanted to do it without saying a word to anybody else. A few minutes before she died Madame Tourmaire muttered:

'"Tell Célita that I'm depending on her . . ."'

'When I asked what she meant, she added:

'"Just tell her that, she'll understand."'

'That was all. I've given you the message. It was my duty, I suppose.'

She had hung up and Célita had told Marie-Lou nothing when she looked at her enquiringly. Ten minutes later, however, as if a thought had been pursuing her the whole time, she had exclaimed:

'It's fantastic!'

'What is?'

'Nothing. You wouldn't understand, and anyhow it's too late!'

'Too late for what?'

'Nothing, Marie-Lou, you fool. Forget it!'

From that time on she had become strange. At times she would stare in front of her as if she were seeing things nobody else could see, and she wore the appearance of a sleep-walker.

Francine was right: Célita had always been melodramatic, not only with other people, but with herself, and it was probably true that she needed to play certain roles, or exaggerate her own, because she could not put up with life as it really was.

Nobody could have any inkling of her decision, or know that all that was happening now at 57 Boulevard Carnot, and the ceremony of prayers of intercession for the deceased which would shortly take place, with the organ and incense, in the dimly lit church, followed by the funeral procession across the town, was but the prologue to a final scene which Célita, and she alone, had planned, since it was the only one, in her eyes, that was possible.

Had Madame Florence had any idea that her message would arrive too late? Célita had held out as long as possible; the situation could still have been saved when she had slapped Léon in the street, with Emile looking on. But not now.

There were certain things he should never have said. He had not thrown her out, but even that was a sign of his contempt, and all the more unbearable in that it meant he was simply not bothering to do so, because he was convinced that she would end up by walking out of her own accord. Who knows? Perhaps, by waiting, he had grown angry that she was still there, as a kind of witness?

Maybe he would get tired of Maud, as Florence had apparently believed, or else, as Ludo had predicted, Maud would be the one to leave, to climb one further rung of the ladder, as soon as she had the opportunity. In any case that would take weeks, even months, and whatever the final outcome, Léon would only loathe Célita all the more.

He was the one she hated, because she had humbled herself in vain to get him in her clutches, because he despised her for doing so, never realising that Maud's game was even more disgusting.

Yet it would have to be on Maud that Célita would have her revenge, convinced as she was that this was the best means to hurt him, to make him suffer for a long time, to force him to remember her for the rest of his life.

She knew that if she had spoken to anybody of what she was about to do, nobody would have believed her capable of it, not even Marie-Lou, who lived with her.

For three days she had been growing more excited, on her own, almost cold-bloodedly, one might say, and things were not necessarily all so gloomy, in the future she was planning for herself; she was still capable of calculations, even of fairly cynical calculations.

Once Maud Le Roy was dead, Célita would be put in prison, of course, and it would be an enormous relief for her to find peace at last between four walls and not to have to think any more. Whilst she foresaw, in this way, the consequences of her action, she was concerned about its external repercussions, the reports in the newspapers, how the people at the Monico would be dumbfounded, and above all, the way Léon would react.

Wouldn't he realise, at last, that the episode the previous Christmas had not just been a poor piece of play-acting?

They would not condemn her to death, for this would be a *crime passionnel* if ever there was one. If she weren't acquitted—and she had not much hope of that—she would get away with a not very long term, five years perhaps, and the chances were that Léon would come and visit her while she was in prison.

Célita allowed herself a smile now and then, at the thought that she was after all going to carry out the *patronne*'s dying wishes, though in a way Madame Florence had not foreseen.

The material preparations had taken two days. She knew that it would be impossible, without formalities which were out of the question for her, to buy a revolver at a gunsmith's, and she could not think of anyone to borrow one from. But she knew where to find one, at the Monico, of all places, in one of the drawers of the cash-desk, where Léon had put it last autumn after there had been armed robberies at two establishments on the Riviera.

The club was closed. The show-case with the photographs of the naked girls had been taken away temporarily and a black-edged notice announced: 'Closed owing to bereavement.'

She had telephoned several times. Now that the *patron* had stopped going to the club regularly every afternoon, Emile had been given a key, so that he could open it for the charwomen and the delivery men.

For a day and a half, the telephone had kept ringing with no reply, and she didn't know Emile's address at Le Cannet. Nor did she see him on the Croisette, where she looked for him, because he had given up distributing the leaflets.

The second day, about six in the afternoon, after having already telephoned in vain at four, she pushed the door on the off-chance, and it had opened, almost knocking over Emile, who had been squatting down to pick up the letters the postman had pushed through the slit in the door.

'It's you!' he said, surprised, as he stood up.

'I've come to collect one or two things I need.'

'It's lucky for you the boss just sent me over to collect the letters. I hardly got here a minute ago . . .'

The shutters were closed and it was dark, which was lucky too, for Célita was not sure how best to play her role.

'I'm going upstairs for a moment . . .'

Then, just as she was pushing open the door with the peep-hole:

'You wouldn't go and buy me a packet of cigarettes, would you?'

She could not think of any other ruse to be rid of him and she sighed with relief when, not suspecting a thing, Emile went off whistling.

She had brought a screw-driver in case the drawer was locked, as it probably would be. The tobacconist's was not far and Emile always walked quickly.

The lock gave way immediately; nobody had thought of removing the short-barrelled revolver which she hurriedly hid in her bag.

She had not had time, however, to leave the bar, and as Emile came in, she picked up a bottle of whisky.

'Any objection?'

'Of course not.'

'Do you want some?'

'You know spirits burn my stomach, even wine does.'

He watched her climb the stairs to the dressing-room, and then return with a frock over her arm.

'Mademoiselle Célita . . .'

'I'm in a hurry, Emile . . .'

'It's not what you think . . .'

'I know . . . I'll see you tomorrow . . .'

And she did see him, as he greeted them but did not dare to join their group. The motor hearse drew in front of the house, the undertaker's men climbed the stairs and reappeared carrying the coffin on their shoulders.

'Do you think she'll come?'

Célita, suddenly furious, looked at Marie-Lou, who of course could not understand how her entire plan was based on Maud's presence at the funeral.

Léon came out through the door, dressed in black, with a stiff, very white collar, and a black tie which gave him the air of a head waiter and revealed for the first time—God knows why—that his nose was slightly crooked and one eye was higher than the other.

Beside him trotted the little old lady with the wrinkled face, then, together, came Alice, her husband, and Maud, also in black, even to a black hat and gloves, looking like a member of the family.

They waited a little longer, out in the sunshine, while people in the street stopped to watch them form up into a procession. Ludo, Gianini and the musicians took their places, Emile, without losing sight of Célita, sidled in beside old Jules, and then, haphazardly, came Léon's colleagues, who all knew each other, some tradesmen, equally acquainted, amongst them, and a few strangers.

The parish church was at the top of the boulevard, but Léon had insisted that the service take place at Notre-Dame, near the Monico, probably because it was the town's fashionable church. The hearse was laden with wreaths and one of them, for which a subscription list had been sent round, bore a card with the words:

To our dearly departed employer
THE STAFF

It had been Ludo's suggestion; he knew the way things were done.

Léon, hat in hand, walked with his head lowered, and Célita noticed that his hair was already getting thin. Maud was just behind him, and like Alice's, her eyes were red and from time to time she dabbed at her face with a handkerchief, while the little old lady, for all that she was the dead woman's mother, looked about inquisitively at this town she had not seen before, which she was unlikely to have the opportunity to revisit.

Célita was calm, a little tense, but calm. She had been thinking very hard. Now that she had made her decision and had predicted the slightest detail which might occur, it was almost as if she were no longer concerned with the business at all, as if she had set going a mechanism that would now work without her, and like Florence's mother, she found herself staring at things in the street, then at the church as they entered it, the same church from which, not so long ago, she had watched a bride leaving.

The two charwomen, Madame Blanc and Madame Touzelli, were already there, kneeling in the pew second from the back, and you could see they were used to it. Marie-Lou also knew when to cross herself, genuflect, stand up or sit down, have her collection money ready, and Célita watched her, in order to follow her example.

There was no Mass, only a service of intercession, and the church was more than half full; when they left, people pressed forward on both sides of the porch, almost as inquisitive as at a wedding.

Célita found it all rather unreal, like a painting, or more like a film when the sound-track suddenly fails. She could hardly recognise Léon in his mourning clothes, a suit he had bought ready-made, which was too tight across the shoulders. He was starting to get a pot-belly. He had cut himself shaving and there was still a little red mark on his cheek.

She preferred not to look at Maud, whom the people walking in front of her concealed most of the time, for she wasn't tall. The hearse drove very slowly and the cortège made its way towards the Carnot bridge, blocking the traffic for a while, then went along the Rue de Grasse, climbing slowly towards Les Broussailles, where the cemetery was situated, not far from the new hospital.

There were fewer people than there had been on the way to the church, and two men left the procession to rush off to a bistro for a quick drink, and then returned to their places, wiping their mouths.

'Do you believe in heaven and hell?' Marie-Lou asked out of the blue, impressed by the intercession service.

Célita did not answer the question, but found it had a slightly disturbing effect. She preferred not to think about it, particularly now.

She was past going back. Her pride in herself was at stake. She had envisaged every possible outcome and there was no time to go over it again.

'I often wonder . . .'

'Shut up, will you?'

She had said it so harshly that Marie-Lou and Francine looked at her with astonishment. They should have learnt to expect almost anything from her.

They were approaching too fast, now, along streets which became more and more empty, with the splash of colour made by a local shop only appearing at rare intervals.

She refused to ask herself why she had taken her decision. She had just *had* to, and that was that! She would do it whatever happened. She could feel the weight of the revolver in her handbag and nothing else mattered to her any more.

She glimpsed Maud's face as she turned round to look at the procession and for an instant their eyes met. Strangely enough Maud was the first to look away, embarrassed. Had she persuaded Léon to give Célita the sack? If that were achieved, she would no longer have any enemies left at the Monico, since Marie-Lou and Francine hardly counted. They were soft stuff. In any case Francine had just told them that it was fixed, she was going away for a month, with Pierrot, to the mountains, and she wasn't sure whether she would return to the Monico. A business-man from Grasse, who came to see her once or twice a week, and whom Pierrot already called 'uncle', was eager to set her up and keep her permanently.

The women's heels twisted on the uneven cobblestones of the rising street; they passed in front of old villas, large mansions which had known their heyday when Cannes was still a winter resort and were now converted into flats. The cross, carried by a choir-boy, wavered above their heads and they were now approaching the cemetery, were passing in front of brand new tombstones, stacked along the pavement.

The priest began to chant his prayers again.

'What's the matter?'

'Nothing. I nearly fell.'

It was true. Her head was going round as if she were on a swing at the fair, everything she saw was becoming blurred in the sun.

They followed some well-trodden paths, then more recent ones, and the procession stopped not far from a wall, the cross silhouetted against the sky at the end of its long black wooden pole, and in the midst of the dark figures there appeared a rectangular hole in the yellowish earth.

She had to do it, that was all!

She had thought things over beforehand. Later she would perhaps think things over again. For the moment she had ceased to exist.

She only knew that she must slip between two men who were standing in the front row, since she had decided to do her deed at the very moment when the coffin had been lowered and Léon was throwing in the first shovelful of soil.

'Sorry . . .' murmured one of the men she was pushing, as he stepped back to make room for her.

Maud was in full view, opposite her. She had taken her place next to Léon, as if to be ready to comfort him with a squeeze of his hand.

The grave-diggers had begun work, their faces sweating, and the coffin was being lowered, supported by ropes, stopped for a moment as if it had met an obstacle, then started falling again.

Célita opened her bag with her right hand; it disappeared inside, feeling the revolver, seizing the grip.

Nobody was taking any notice of her. She would have time to take aim. Barely three yards separated her from Maud and there was no obstacle between them.

'*Libera me, Domine* . . .'

The liturgical phrases became but a murmur as they were drowned by the noise of a concrete-mixer somewhere outside the cemetery.

Célita's clammy hand still clasped the grip of the revolver in her bag, her index finger probed, searched for the trigger, found it.

She stared at Maud, suddenly bewildered, as if she were no longer conscious of where she was or what she was doing. Did she even still know who the young girl was who was looking down into the hole and why she was going to kill her?

Somebody handed Léon a shovel, with a little earth on it, and he bent down awkwardly, while Célita, noticed by nobody, took the revolver from her bag.

But now it was not Maud at whom she aimed. She raised the gun slowly, the muzzle turned towards herself; panic had overcome her, there was no other solution but to kill herself.

All she had to do was to raise her arm slightly, turn her wrist. Then it would be over. There would be no more problems, no more unpleasantness nor humiliation, no more Célita, nothing any more.

Léon was straightening up again, his face crimson, looking about him, wondering if there was anything else he had to do, and his eyes rested on Célita, on the gun she was holding in her hand.

Then, without thinking, without realising how theatrical her action would seem, she threw the revolver into the grave and, pushing through the crowd, began running down the paths, convinced she was being chased, searching for the way out; when she found it, she started off down the steep road leading to the town, her eyes mad.

Chapter Nine

Marie-Lou was the only one of the old lot left; Francine had gone the day after the funeral and they had had one new girl from Marseilles, then another, an Italian whose name could not be announced on the bills because she hadn't yet got her work permit.

Alice, the *patron*'s sister, had returned to Le Havre because her husband needed her, and a former cashier from the Café des Allées had been engaged.

Léon continued to fetch Maud and take her back after her performance: he was living altogether at the Louxor now, going only occasionally to the Boulevard Carnot to collect his belongings.

It was Ludo who got indirect news of Célita and passed it on to Marie-Lou. The fat girl had taken the Italian to share the flat in the Place du Commandant-Maria, because it was too expensive for her alone.

'She's been seen at Nice,' he told her one evening. 'Apparently she was in a small bar, with Ketty . . .'

Marie-Lou was too upset to say anything, because for her, and for Ludo as well, those words could mean only one thing.

A few days later a regular client was also to mention her: he had seen her standing in a doorway, near a hotel.

The season was in full swing. The motor-cars were almost bumper to bumper, taking an hour to drive along the Croisette, and women even appeared in the Rue d'Antibes in bikinis; Marie-Lou had met a woman who was at least sixty, wearing one in the chemist's.

The end came, as they learned from the newspaper, a few days before August 15th.

The body of an entirely naked woman, covered with bruises 'which might have been due to its being repeatedly buffeted against the rocks', had been recovered from the sea between Nice and Villefranche.

Two days later, the *Nice-Matin* announced that the corpse had been identified as that of 'one Céline Perrin, single, aged thirty-two, born in Paris, Rue Caulaincourt, cabaret dancer, who had been summoned twice by the police during the last few days, for soliciting on the streets'.

Finally:

'Investigations are being carried out in certain special areas of the town, particularly amongst North Africans, because the dead woman's handbag and clothes have not been found, and three days before the discovery of the body Céline Perrin had been seen in the company of an Arab whose description is in the hands of the police.'

'Do you think she'd do that, Ludo?'

The barman looked at Marie-Lou without replying, sighed, took a bottle of cognac from the shelves and poured himself a full glass, exactly as he had done for Madame Florence.

'Give me some too.'

Then she began to say:

'If she did that, I think she . . .'

But what was the use of talking?

She emptied her glass in one gulp, because the *patron* was making signs to her to go and change for her number.

The Premier

The Premier

Translated from the French by
Daphne Woodward

All characters in this book are fictitious and are not
intended to represent any actual persons living or dead

Chapter One

For more than an hour he had been sitting motionless in the old Louis-Philippe armchair, with its almost upright back and shabby black leather upholstery, that he had lugged round with him from one Ministry to another for forty years, till it had become a legend.

They always thought he was asleep when he sat like that with eyelids lowered, raising just one of them, from time to time, to reveal a slit of gleaming eyeball. Not only was he not asleep, but he knew exactly what he looked like, his body rather stiff in a black coat that hung loosely on him, something like a frock-coat, and his chin resting on the tall, stiff collar that was seen in all his photographs and which he wore like a uniform from the moment he emerged from his bedroom in the morning.

As the years went by his skin had grown thinner and smoother, with white blotches that gave it the appearance of marble, and by now it clung to the prominent cheekbones and sheathed his skeleton so closely that his features, as they became more strongly marked, seemed to be gradually fining down. In the village once he had heard one little boy call out to another:

'Look at that old death's-head!'

He sat without stirring, scarcely a yard away from the log fire, whose flames crackled now and then in a sudden down-draught, his hands folded on his stomach in the position in which they would be placed when his dead body was laid out. Would anybody have the nerve, then, to slip a rosary between his fingers, as someone had done to one of his colleagues, who'd also been several times Prime Minister and a leading Freemason?

He had got more and more into the habit of withdrawing like this into immobility and silence, at all times of the day, but most often at dusk, when Mademoiselle Milleran, his secretary, had come in noiselessly, without stirring the air, to switch on his parchment-shaded desk lamp, and gone away again into the next room; and it was as though he'd erected a wall around himself, or rather as though he had huddled up tightly into a blanket, retiring from everything except the sense of his individual existence.

Did he sometimes fall into a doze? If so he wouldn't admit it, convinced that his mind was ceaselessly alert; and to prove this to himself and to those around him, he would sometimes amuse himself by describing their comings and goings.

This afternoon, for instance, Mademoiselle Milleran—her name was the same, but for one letter, as that of a former colleague who had been President of the Republic, though not, it was true, for long—this afternoon, Mademoiselle Milleran had come in twice on tiptoe and the second time, after making sure that he wasn't dead, that his chest was still rising and falling as he breathed, she had pushed back a log that threatened to roll out on to the carpet.

He had chosen for himself, as his own corner, the room nearest to his bedroom, and the massive, unstained, unpolished wooden table was as plain as a butcher's chopping-block.

This was his famous study, so often photographed that it, too, now belonged to the legend, like every nook and corner of Les Ebergues. The whole world knew that his bedroom was like a monk's cell, that the walls were whitewashed and that the Premier slept on an iron bedstead.

The public was familiar with every angle of the four low-ceilinged rooms, converted stables or cowsheds, whose interior doors had been removed and whose walls were entirely lined with pitch-pine shelves packed with books.

What was Milleran doing, while he kept his eyes shut? He hadn't dictated anything to her. She had no letters to answer. She didn't knit, didn't sew. And the morning was her time for looking through the newspapers and marking with red pencil any articles that might interest him.

He was convinced that she made notes, rather in the way certain animals heap up in their lair anything and everything they come across, and that once he was dead she'd write her memoirs. He had often tried to catch her at it, but never succeeded. He'd been no more successful when he tried to tease an admission out of her.

One would have sworn that in the next room she was keeping as still as he and that they were spying on each other.

Would she remember the five o'clock news?

Ever since morning a gale had been blowing, threatening to carry away the slates on the roof and the west wall, rattling the windows so that you would have thought someone was continually knocking on them. The Newhaven–Dieppe steamer, after a difficult crossing that had been mentioned on the wireless, had had to make three shots at getting into Dieppe harbour, after being almost forced to turn back.

The Premier had insisted on going out, all the same, about eleven o'clock, muffled in his ancient astrakhan coat that had been through so many international conferences, from London to Warsaw, from the Kremlin to Ottawa.

'You surely don't mean to go out?' Madame Blanche, his nurse, had protested on finding him dressed up like that.

She knew that if he wanted to she wouldn't be able to stop him, but she put up a fight in the forlorn hope.

'Dr Gaffé told you again only yesterday evening . . .'

'Is it the doctor's life or mine that comes into this?'

'Listen, sir . . . At least let me ring up the doctor and ask him . . .'

He had merely looked at her with his light-grey eyes, his steely eyes as the newspapers called them. She always began by trying to stare him out, and at such moments anybody would have felt certain they hated each other.

Perhaps, after putting up with her for twelve years, he really had come to hate her? He'd sometimes asked himself. He wasn't sure of the answer. Wasn't she, perhaps, the only person who wasn't awed by his fame? Or who pretended not to be?

In the old days he'd have settled the question without hesitation, confident of his judgment, but as he grew older he was becoming more cautious.

In any case, this woman, who was neither young nor attractive, had ended by absorbing more of his attention than he gave to so-called serious problems. Twice, in a moment of anger, he had thrown her out of Les Ebergues and forbidden her to come back. As it was he wouldn't let her sleep there, although there was a spare room; he made her take lodgings in a house in the village.

Both times she had turned up next morning, in time for his injection, her hard, commonplace, fifty-year-old face entirely devoid of expression.

He hadn't even chosen her. The last time he had been Prime Minister, ten years ago, he'd found her at his side one night when, after speaking for three hours in the Chambre des Députés in the teeth of relentless opposition, he'd fainted away.

He could still remember his astonishment at finding himself lying on a dusty floor and seeing the white-overalled woman with a hypodermic syringe in her hand, the only serene, comforting face amid the general anxiety.

For some time after that she had come every day to give him treatment at the Hôtel Matignon; and later, when the Government fell, to his bachelor flat on the Quai Malaquais.

Les Ebergues had then been still just a country hide-out, bought at haphazard as a place for brief holidays. When he had decided to retire and live there permanently, she had announced, without consulting him:

'I shall come with you.'

'And suppose I don't need a nurse?'

'They won't let you go away there without someone to look after you.'

'Who are *they*?'

'Professor Fumet, to begin with . . .'

He had been his doctor and friend for more than thirty years.

'*Those gentlemen* . . .'

He had understood, and the expression had amused him. He still used it to refer to the few dozen people–were there as many as that?–who really ran the country.

'Those gentlemen' didn't mean only the Prime Minister and the Cabinet, the Council of State, the Bench, the Bank of France and a few senior permanent civil servants, but also applied to the Sûreté Générale, in the Rue des Saussaies, which was concerned that no ill should befall the famous statesman.

Had not two detectives been sent to Bénouville, the village nearest to Les Ebergues, where they had taken up residence at the inn so as to mount guard over him, while a third, who lived at Le Havre with his wife and family, came on his motorcycle at intervals to take his turn of duty?

At this very moment, despite the squalls and rain-bursts that seemed to come from sea and sky at the same time, one of the three would be standing leaning against the wet trunk of the tree by the side-gate, with eyes fixed on the lighted window.

Madame Blanche had come to Bénouville. For a long time he had supposed she was a widow, or that, although a spinster, she, like many old maids in jobs, had herself addressed as 'Madame' to enhance her dignity.

It was three years before he discovered that she had a husband in Paris, a certain Louis Blain, who kept a bookshop near Saint-Sulpice, specialising in religious works. She had never mentioned it to him, she simply went up to Paris once a month.

One day when he was in a bad temper he had growled, while she was attending to him with her usual calm face:

'You must admit you're a stiff-necked woman! I might almost say a depraved woman, in one sense of the word. There you are, fresh as if you'd just got up, not a hair out of place, mind and body alert, and you come into the bedroom of an old man who's gradually rotting away. Incidentally, does my room stink in the morning?'

'It smells like any other bedroom.'

'Before I grew old myself I used to be sickened by the smell of old men. But you, you pretend not to notice. You have the satisfaction of saying to yourself:

'"The man I see every morning, ugly and naked, half-dead already, is the same one whose name is in all the history books, and who any day now will have his statue, or at least his avenue, in most of the towns of France . . ." Like Gambetta! . . . Like poor Jaurès, whom I knew so well . . .'

She had merely enquired:

'Are you keen on your name being given to avenues?'

Perhaps it was precisely because she saw him naked, a weak old man, that he resented her?

And yet he didn't resent Emile, his chauffeur and valet, who was equally familiar with his sordid, unadorned privacy.

Was that because Emile was a man?

Anyhow, Madame Blanche and Emile had gone out with him, into the north wind that forced them to bend double, Madame Blanche with her cape, which flapped like a loose sail, Emile in his strict, black uniform with the tight-fitting leather gaiters.

There were no trippers to photograph them that morning, and no journalists, nobody except Soulas, the swarthiest of the three detectives, smoking a damp cigarette beneath his tree and beating his arms across his chest now and then to warm himself.

The house, which had no upper storey except for three little attics above the kitchen, consisted of two buildings that had been connected together, and stood all alone, or rather crouched on the cliff-top, about a quarter of a mile from the village of Bénouville, between Etretat and Fécamp.

As usual, Emile walked on the Premier's left, ready to prop him up if his leg gave way, and Madame Blanche, obeying the orders he had given her once and for all, followed a few paces behind.

This daily walk had also been publicised by the Press, and in summer a tourist-agency at Fécamp would bring bus-loads of trippers to watch from a distance.

A narrow lane, starting from behind the house, wound through the fields till it joined the coastguard path, at the very edge of the cliff. The land belonged to a local farmer who turned his cows out to graze there, and from time to time the ground would crumble beneath the hooves of one of the beasts, which would be found three hundred feet below, on the rocks of the shore.

He knew he was wrong to go out in bad weather. All his life he had known when he was wrong, but all his life he had persisted, as though challenging fate. Had he done so badly, after all?

The drifting sky was low. One saw it moving in from the open sea, bringing dark clouds that broke into tatters, and the air tasted of salt and seaweed; the same wind that was whipping up evil-looking white horses on the surface of the water was storming the cliffs to fling itself savagely on the countryside.

Through the roar he heard Madame Blanche's voice, coming faintly from behind:

'Sir . . .'

No! He had made up his mind to go to the edge, to watch the wild sea, before going back to be an invalid in the Louis-Philippe armchair.

He was being careful about his leg. He knew it well, better than Gaffé, the young doctor from Le Havre who came every day to see him, better than Lalinde, the former staff doctor, who paid a 'friendly visit' from Rouen once a week, better even than Professor Fumet, who was only sent for on serious occasions.

It might happen any moment. Since the attack three years ago, that had kept him in bed for nine weeks, and then on a chaise-longue, his way of walking had never been quite natural. His left leg seemed to float, as it were. It seemed to take its time about obeying, and whenever it moved forward there was a slight sideways motion, at each step, that he couldn't prevent.

'I waddle like a duck!' he had said jokingly at the time.

Nobody had laughed. He'd been the only one who'd made light of the business. And yet he followed, with almost impassioned interest, everything that went on inside him.

It had begun one morning when he was out for his walk, just like today except that in those days he used to go further, as far as the dip in the cliffs which was known as the Valleuse du Curé.

He'd never had a moment's anxiety except about his heart, which had played him a few tricks, and he'd been advised to take care of it. It had never occurred to him that his legs, let alone his hands, might let him down as well.

That day–it was in March; the weather was bright and cold; the white cliffs of England had been visible in the distance–he had felt in his left leg, beginning at the thigh and creeping slowly downwards, a skin-deep warmth accompanied by the prickly sensation that one feels, for instance, after sitting for a long time beside a stove or in front of a log fire.

With no uneasiness, curious as to what was happening to him, he had gone on walking, his faithful stick in his hand (his pilgrim's staff, as the papers called it) until, without thinking, he had rubbed his thigh with his hand. To his stupefaction, it had been rather like touching another person's body. There was no contact. He was touching his own flesh, pinching it, and he felt it no more than if his flesh had been cardboard.

Had that scared him? He had turned round to tell Madame Blanche about it, when, all of a sudden, his leg had given way, slipped from under him, and he had found himself huddled up at the side of the path.

He felt no pain, had no sense of any danger, simply conscious of his ridiculous posture and the rotten trick his leg had so unexpectedly played him.

'Help me up, Emile!' he had said, stretching out his hand.

In the Chamber of Deputies, where everyone, or almost everyone, uses '*tu*' and effects Christian-name terms with everyone else, he had never addressed anyone in that way; nor did he even use '*tu*' to his cook-housekeeper, Gabrielle, who had been with him for more than forty years. He called his secretary by her surname, Milleran, as if she were a man without ever using '*tu*', and Madame Blanche was always Madame Blanche as far as he was concerned.

'You didn't hurt yourself?'

He had noticed that the nurse, bending over him, had turned pale, for the first time in his acquaintance with her, but he hadn't attributed any importance to it.

'Don't get up for a moment,' she had advised. 'Tell me first of all whether . . .'

He was struggling to stand up, with Emile's help, and then his eyes had, despite himself, become a little set, his voice had been slightly less assured than usual, as he observed:

'Funny thing . . . It won't take my weight any more . . .'

He had lost his left leg. It wasn't his, any longer. It refused to obey him!

'Help him to sit down, Emile. You'll have to go and fetch . . .'

She must have known, just as the others knew later on. Fumet, who understood his character, had offered to tell him frankly what had happened. He'd said no. He refused to be ill. He didn't want to know his illness, and not for a moment had he been tempted to open one of his medical books.

'Can you carry me, Emile?'

'Certainly, sir.'

Madame Blanche protested. He didn't give in. It was impossible to bring the car along that narrow path. They'd have to fetch a stretcher, probably from the priest, who doubtless kept one in reserve for burials.

He preferred to cling with his arms round the neck of Emile, who was strongly built and had firm muscles.

'If you get tired, put me down in the grass for a bit . . .'

'It'll be all right!'

Gabrielle watched them coming, standing in the door of her kitchen. This was before he'd taken on young Marie to help her.

Less than half an hour later, Dr Gaffé, who must have driven like a lunatic, was by his bedside, and almost at once he rang up Dr Lalinde at Rouen.

It wasn't till about four o'clock that, glancing at his hand, the Premier noticed it looked funny. He moved his fingers playfully, like a child, and these fingers didn't take their usual positions.

'Look at this, doctor!'

It hadn't surprised Gaffé, who had not gone home to Le Havre for lunch, nor Lalinde, who had arrived about two o'clock and had afterwards made a long telephone call to Paris.

Later on, he learnt that for several days one of his eyes had been fixed, his mouth twisted.

'A stroke, I suppose?'

He could hardly speak. They hadn't answered him, one way or the other, but the professor had arrived that same evening, followed by an ambulance which, a little later, took the lot of them off to Rouen.

'I give you my word, my dear Premier,' Fumet said, 'that you won't be kept in the clinic against your will. It's not a matter of getting you into hospital, only of taking X-rays and making tests that aren't possible here . . .'

Contrary to his expectation, it wasn't an unpleasant memory. He remained very detached. He watched them all: Gaffé, who hadn't begun to breathe more freely until Lalinde had arrived to share his responsibility; Lalinde himself, sandy-haired, rosy-cheeked, blue-eyed, with bushy eyebrows, trying to give an impression of self-confidence; then Fumet, the big man, used to distinguished patients and to the little court of admiring disciples that followed him from bed to bed as he made his rounds.

When they felt obliged to withdraw into corners to talk in low tones, he was amusing himself in studying the characters of the three men, and the idea of death didn't even occur to him.

He'd been seventy-eight years old at that time. The first question he had asked at Rouen, while he was being undressed and the X-ray apparatus was got ready, was:

'Did the inspectors come along behind?'

Nobody had paid attention, but they were surely there, or one of them at least, and the alarm had certainly been given to the Ministry of the Interior.

There had been some unpleasant moments, particularly when he'd been given a lumbar puncture and again when they'd taken an encephalogram. But he had never stopped joking, and at about four in the morning, when they were busy in the laboratory, he asked whether someone could get him a quarter bottle of champagne.

The funny thing was that they'd found him one, in a rather shady Rouen night-club that was still open, and probably it was one of the policemen, one of his watchdogs, as he sometimes called them, who had been sent on the errand.

That was a long time ago, now. It was no more than a story to tell. For two months the village of Bénouville had been invaded by French and foreign journalists determined to be in at his death. In the newspaper offices the obituary notices had been written, blocks made of photographs with some claim to be historic, and the printers stood by ready to set it all up.

Wouldn't the same articles be used sooner or later, with a change of date and a few details, for he had taken no part in politics since then?

He'd never fallen again, like a tripped hare, but now and then, though less acutely, he'd had the feeling that his leg was taking its time to obey him. It sometimes came over him at night, too, in bed, a sort of cramp, or rather, a numbness that didn't hurt at all. When it happened out walking, Emile would notice almost at the same time as himself. A kind of signal passed between them. Emile would come closer and the Premier would clutch his shoulder, stand still, though without taking his eyes off the landscape. Madame Blanche would come up then, and hand him a pink tablet, which he would swallow without a word.

The three of them would wait in silence. It had happened once in the middle of the village, when people were just coming out of mass, and the peasants had wondered why they stood riveted to the ground like that, for the Premier didn't appear to be in pain, or out of breath, and he made it a point of vanity to keep smiling vaguely all the time.

He hated it to happen on days when Madame Blanche had urged him not to go out, and so this morning he'd paid more attention than usual to the behaviour of his leg. For fear of putting the nurse in the right, he had not stayed out long; all the same, he had sneezed twice.

When they got back he had flung at her triumphantly:

'You see!'

'Wait till tomorrow to find out if you've not caught a cold.'

That was her way. One had to take her as she was. Whereas Milleran, the secretary, never resisted him, was so unobtrusive that he hardly noticed her presence in the house. She was pale, with soft, blurred features, and anybody who had only seen her two or three times would probably not have recognised her again. All the same she was efficient, and at this moment, for example, he felt sure she had her eye on the little clock in her office, waiting to come in on the dot and turn on his wireless.

The ministerial crisis had lasted a week, and as usual the Republic was said to be in danger. Cournot, the French President, had sent for about a dozen political leaders in succession, and didn't know where to turn next.

He'd known Cournot as a very young man, fresh from Montauban, where his father sold bicycles. He was a militant Socialist, one of those who sit in gloomy offices, dealing with tiresome secretarial work, and are seldom heard of except at annual conferences. He hardly ever spoke in the Chamber, and when he did it was usually at night sittings, to almost empty benches.

Had Cournot realised, when he chose that self-effacing line, that it would lead him one day to the Elysée, where his two daughters, with their husbands and children, had moved in at the same time as he did?

One eyelid slightly raised, his hands still folded on his stomach, sitting stiff-backed in the Louis-Philippe armchair, he was watching the clock, like his secretary next door; but his clock, presented to him by the President of the United States during a state visit to Washington, was a historic piece, which would end up in some museum.

Unless Les Ebergues were itself to become a museum, as some people were already suggesting, and everything should stay in its place, with Emile as custodian.

He felt sure Emile had been thinking about it for several years, the way another man might think of his pension. Wasn't time beginning to drag for him, as he looked forward to the little speech he would make to visitors, to the tips they would slip into his hand on leaving, and the souvenir postcards he might perhaps sell?

At two minutes to five, fearing Milleran might be the first to move, he put out his hand noiselessly, furtively, and turned the knob on the wireless set. The dial lit up, but for a few seconds no sound came. In the next room, for there was no door between it and the Premier's study, the secretary got to her feet and at the very moment when she came tiptoeing in, music blared out, a jazz tune in which the trumpets seemed to be challenging the noise of the storm.

'I'm sorry . . .' she murmured.

'You see, I wasn't asleep!'

'I know.'

Madame Blanche, in such circumstances, would have smiled, sarcastically or disbelievingly. Milleran simply vanished as though she had melted into thin air.

'*At the third pip it will be precisely . . .*'

It was too early yet for the proper news bulletin, which would be broadcast at a quarter past seven, but there was a short summary of the latest headlines, between two musical programmes:

'*This is Paris-Inter calling . . . After devoting last night and this morning to consultations, Monsieur François Bourdieu, Leader of the Socialist Group, was received by the President of the Republic at three o'clock this afternoon and informed him that he was giving up his attempt to form a Cabinet . . .*'

The Premier's face betrayed no sign of his feelings, as he still sat motionless in his armchair, but his fingers were clenched now and the tips had gone whiter.

The announcer had a cold and coughed twice over the microphone. There came a rustle of papers, then:

'According to unconfirmed rumours circulating in the corridors of the Chamber, Monsieur Cournot is said to have requested Monsieur Philippe Chalamont, Leader of the Left Independent Group, to visit him late this afternoon, and to be intending to ask him to form a coalition government . . . Argentine . . . The general strike which was called yesterday at Buenos-Aires, and which has brought out about seventy per cent of workers . . .'

The voice broke off without warning in the middle of a sentence; at the same time the lights in the study and the neighbouring rooms went out, and now there was nothing except the sound of the wind, the dancing firelight.

He didn't move. Milleran, next door, struck a match, opened the drawer where she kept a supply of candles, for it was not the first time this had happened.

There was a brief flash as the lights seemed to be coming on again, the bulbs gave out a cloudy glow, like those of certain night trains, then they faded slowly and it was complete darkness.

'I'll bring you a candle at once . . .'

Before she had had time to stick it upright on a china ashtray, a light appeared, moving along a passage that connected the former cowsheds with the kitchen and the rest of the house. This passage, which had not existed in the old days and which the Premier had had built, was known as the tunnel.

It was Gabrielle, the old cook, who was coming through the tunnel now, brandishing a big oil lamp with pink flowers painted on its globe.

'The young doctor has just arrived, sir,' announced Gabrielle; she always referred thus to Dr Gaffé, who was just thirty-two, to distinguish him from Dr Lalinde.

'Where is he?'

'In the kitchen, with Madame Blanche.'

This made him suddenly angry, perhaps because of the name that had been mentioned on the wireless and the news that had been broadcast.

'Why did he come in by the kitchen?'

'Well now, I never asked him!'

'What are they doing?'

'They're having a chat, while the doctor warms his hands at my stove. After all, he can't touch you with icy-cold hands.'

He loathed not being informed of comings and goings in the house.

'I've told you a hundred times . . .'

'I know, I know! It's not me you ought to tell. It's the people that come; I can't shut the door of my kitchen in their faces.'

There was a front door by which Milleran was supposed to let in visitors. It was perfectly visible, being lit by a lantern. But more often than not people would persist in coming in through the kitchen, whence a murmur of unknown voices would suddenly become audible.

'Tell the doctor I'm waiting . . .'

Then he called:

'Milleran!'

'Yes, sir.'

'Is the telephone working?'

She tried it.

'Yes, I can hear the click.'

'Ask the electric company how long it will take them to repair . . .'

'Very good, sir . . .'

He received Dr Gaffé in a cold, unsmiling silence which made the doctor, who was shy by nature, feel more awkward than ever.

'Madame Blanche tells me you went for a walk this morning?'

The young doctor made this remark in a casual tone while opening his bag, and he received no answer.

'In weather like this,' the doctor went on, embarrassed, 'it was perhaps a little unwise . . .'

Madame Blanche came forward to help the Premier out of his coat. He stopped her with a glance, took it off himself, rolled up his shirt-sleeve. Milleran's voice could he heard on the telephone, then she came in to announce:

'They don't know yet. There's been a general breakdown. They think it's the cable that . . .'

'Leave us.'

Dr Gaffé came to see him every day at the same time, and nearly every day he solemnly took his blood-pressure.

The Premier had asked him once:

'You think it's necessary?'

'It's an excellent precaution.'

'You make a point of it?'

Gaffé had got flustered. At his age he still blushed. He was so much in awe of his patient that once when he had to give him an injection he had fumbled so badly that Madame Blanche had been obliged to take the hypodermic away from him.

'You make a point of it?' the Premier had insisted.

'Well, the thing is . . .'

'Is what?'

'I think Professor Fumet makes a point of it . . .'

'It's he who gives you instructions?'

'Of course.'

'And he alone?'

What was the use of forcing the doctor to tell a lie? Fumet himself must have had orders from higher quarters. Because the Premier, while still alive, had become a historical personage, he wasn't allowed to take care of his health just as he thought fit. They pretended to obey him, the whole pack of them, but who gave them their real orders? And to whom, God knows when, God knows how, did they report?

Was it also by order that visitors went to the kitchen instead of ringing at the front door?

Gabrielle had told the truth: Gaffé's hands were still cold and the Premier thought he looked ridiculous, squeezing the little rubber bulb and staring very solemnly at the needle on the round dial.

Because he was cross, he deliberately refrained from asking, as he usually did, out of politeness as it were:

'How much?'

None the less, Gaffé murmured, his satisfaction no less absurd than his solemnity:

'Seventeen . . .'

The same as the day before, the day before that, every day for months and months past!

'Any pain, any discomfort during the night?'

'Nothing.'

'And your leg?'

He was feeling his pulse and the Premier couldn't restrain himself from glaring resentfully at him.

'No respiratory difficulty?'

'No respiratory difficulty,' he replied curtly, 'and I may as well tell you at once that I made water in the usual way.'

For he knew that would be the next question.

'I wonder if this electric failure . . .' muttered Gaffé.

Without listening to him, the Premier was putting on his coat, with the same sour expression, taking care to avoid Madame Blanche's eye, for he did not want to lose his temper.

Probably because of the electric failure, the consequent silence of the wireless which was his only contact with the outside world, he felt like a prisoner in this cottage flattened on the cliff-top, between the black hole of the sea and the black countryside which was not even dotted any longer with the little twinkling lights that indicated the presence of life.

The oil lamp in his study, the candle in Milleran's office, its flame wavering with each draught, reminded him of the stickiest evenings in his childhood, when the houses didn't yet have electric light and gas had not been brought to Evreux.

Hadn't Gaffé said something just now about respiratory difficulties? He might have answered that he suddenly felt as though he were being physically and morally smothered.

He had been shut up at Les Ebergues and the few human beings who surrounded him had become his gaolers, whether they wanted to or not.

He was forgetting that it was he who had left Paris, swearing dramatically that he would never set foot there again, in a sulky mood, because . . . But that was another story. His reasons were his own business, and everybody, papers and politicians alike, had misinterpreted his retirement.

Was it he who insisted that this young doctor, a nice young fellow, but a silly greenhorn, should come every day from Le Havre to take his blood-pressure and ask him some footling questions, always the same ones? Was it he who was forcing two poor devils of police inspectors to live at the inn at Bénouville, and a third to settle at Le Havre with his wife and children, so as to mount guard under the elm beside the gate?

All right, so he was in a bad temper. These fits of anger had come over him all his life, just as some people feel the blood running to their heads, or some women grow suddenly depressed. For forty years his rages had been the terror not only of his own staff but of many people in high places, including generals, leading magistrates, statesmen.

The effect on him was the same as that produced on other people by alcohol, which doesn't always cloud the intelligence but sometimes stimulates it, and his bouts of ill-temper didn't throw him off his course. Far from it!

The electric failure was going to last, he knew it was. He didn't go so far as to suggest that they had engineered it on purpose, though that would have been perfectly possible.

'I'll be here tomorrow at the same time, Premier . . .' faltered the doctor, whom Madame Blanche was about to escort through the tunnel again.

'Not that way!' he protested. 'By the proper door,`please.'

'I beg your pardon . . .'

'Not at all.'

It was he who went to the tunnel, and called out:

'Emile!'

'Yes, sir.'

'Bring the car under the window and fix it like last time. You can manage it?'

'Certainly.'

'Get it going by seven o'clock, if the lights haven't come on again.'

'I'll see to it at once.'

At that moment the telephone rang. Milleran's flat voice could be heard saying:

'Les Ebergues, yes . . . Who is speaking? . . . A call from the Elysée? . . . Just a moment, please . . . Hold on . . .'

He suspected nothing, let himself be caught, as on previous occasions.

'Hello?'

As soon as he heard the voice he understood, but all the same he listened to the end.

'That you, Augustin?'

A pause, as usual.

'Xavier here . . . You'd better hurry, old chap . . . Don't forget I've promised to be at your funeral, and here I am in hospital again . . .'

A whinnying laugh. Silence. At last, a click.

Milleran had understood.

'I beg your pardon,' she stuttered, taking the blame on herself and fading into the semi-darkness of her office.

Chapter Two

He had a book on his knees, the *Mémoires de Sully*, but he was not turning the pages, and Milleran, her ear cocked in the next room, was about to come in and make sure the oil lamp was giving him enough light, when he spoke to her. He would sometimes keep silent for two hours and then give her an order or ask her a question as though she'd been sitting in front of him, and he felt so sure of her that he would not have forgiven any lapse in her attention.

'Ask the Post Office where that call came from?'

'I'll do it at once, sir.'

Still staring at the page of his book, he heard her at the telephone, and she soon informed him, without leaving her chair:

'Evreux.'

'Thank you.'

He had suspected as much. Yet Xavier Malate's last call, two months.

earlier, had come from Strasbourg; the previous one, much further back, from the Hôpital Cochin in Paris.

In the whole course of his life the Premier had avoided forming an attachment to anybody, not so much from principle, or from hard-heartedness, as to safeguard his independence, which he prized above all else. The only woman he ever married came into his life for a brief three years, long enough to bear him one daughter, and that daughter, now a woman of forty-five, married, with a son in his first year of Law School, had always been a stranger to him.

He was eighty-two years old. All he wanted now was peace, and that he thought he had attained. Strangely enough, the only human being who still clung to him and had the power, at a distance, to disturb him so much that he couldn't read, was a man for whom he cared nothing, now or at any other time.

Was this Malate's importance due to the fact that of all the members of his own generation with whom he had had any degree of intimacy, he was the sole survivor?

Malate used to declare confidently, as though announcing a certainty:

'I'll be at your funeral.'

He himself had been in hospital a dozen times, in Paris and elsewhere. A dozen times the doctors had given him only a few weeks to live. Each time he'd bounced up again, returned to the surface, and he was still there, with his obsession about outliving his old schoolfellow.

A long time ago somebody had said:

'He's a harmless imbecile.'

The speaker, whoever he was, had been astonished by the reaction of the Premier, whose cordiality had suddenly vanished as he answered curtly, as though touched on the raw:

'There is no such thing as a harmless imbecile.'

After a pause he had added, as though he had been wondering whether to speak his mind to the full:

'There is no such thing as an imbecile.'

He had proferred no further explanation. It was difficult to put into words. Underlying a certain kind of stupidity, he suspected something Machiavellian that frightened him. He refused to believe it could be unconscious.

By what right had Xavier Malate irrupted into his life and stubbornly kept his place there? What feelings or thought-processes prompted him to the tricks, never twice the same, that brought his boyhood friend to the telephone to listen to the mean message he delivered in his harsh voice?

The Premier knew the hospital, in the Rue Saint-Louis at Evreux, from which this latest call had been made. It was only a few yards from the house where Malate's father had had his printing works, at the corner of the next street, to be precise.

He and Xavier had been at the town *lycée*, in the same form; and it must have been in the third form, when they were both a little over thirteen years old, that the thing had happened.

Later on, Malate had claimed that it was the future Cabinet Minister and Prime Minister who had had the original idea. That was possible, but by no means certain, for the Premier himself could not remember making the suggestion, which didn't seem like him.

All the same, he had joined in the conspiracy. At that time they had an English master whose name he had now forgotten, like those of at least half his schoolmates, in spite of the important part the man had played in his life for four years.

He could still see him pretty clearly, however, short, badly dressed, always wearing a black jacket too big for him and shiny with age, his hair hanging in grey elf-locks under his bowler hat. He reminded one of a priest, especially as he was a bachelor and was perpetually reading a black-bound volume of Shakespeare that looked like a breviary.

He seemed very old to the boys, but he could not have been more than fifty-five to sixty, and his mother was still alive; he used to visit her at Rouen from Saturday evening to Monday morning.

People called him an imbecile too, because he took lessons without appearing to see his pupils, for whom he seemed to feel a lofty contempt, if not a measure of disgust, and his only reaction was, if one of them grew restless, to give him two hundred lines.

It was too late to find out what he had really been like, what he used to think.

The practical joke had taken some time to prepare, for success depended on the most careful planning. With the help of an old workman employed by his father, Xavier Malate had undertaken the hardest part, the setting up and printing of about fifty invitations to the teacher's funeral, on paper with a deep black border.

These had been posted one Saturday evening, for delivery on the Sunday morning, for in those days letters were still delivered on Sundays. They had made quite sure that the English master had set out by train for Rouen, whence he would return at seven minutes past eight on the Monday morning, in time to drop his bag at home before his first lesson at nine o'clock.

He lived in a humble street, on the first floor, above one of those local grocer's shops whose windows display jars of sweets, tinned foods, a few vegetables, and whose door rings a bell as it opens.

The funeral invitations had said that the coffin would be fetched at half past eight, and they had managed, heaven knows how, to get the hearse used for paupers' burials in front of the house on the minute.

Some ingenuity had been displayed in selecting the people to whom the invitations were sent: several town councillors, other local authorities, some shopkeepers who supplied the *lycée*, and even the parents of a few younger boys, who were not in the secret.

The conspirators had not been there, since they had a class at eight o'clock. What exactly had happened? The Premier, though he remembered the preparations in some detail, had entirely forgotten what occurred afterwards and could only depend on what Malate had told him, years later.

In any case there had been no English lesson that morning. The master had stayed away for over a week, ill, so they said. The headmaster had opened an enquiry. Malate's guilt had been easily proved, and for several days there had been speculations as to whether he would give away his accomplices.

He had held his tongue, thus becoming a kind of hero. A hero never seen at the *lycée* again, by the way, for in spite of wire-pulling by his father, who was the printer of the little local paper, he had been expelled and sent to boarding school at Chartres.

Was it true that he had run away from there, been found by the police at Le Havre, where he was trying to stow away on board a ship, sent as an apprentice to an uncle who had an import business at Marseilles?

It was perfectly possible, and of no real importance. For the next thirty years, as far as the Premier was concerned, Malate had ceased to exist, like the English master and so many of his other schoolfellows.

He had met him again when he was forty-two years old, a Cabinet Minister for the first time, at the Ministry of Public Works in the Boulevard Saint-Germain.

Every day for a week, at about ten in the morning, the office messenger had brought him a slip bearing the name X. Malate, with the space left for the purpose of visit filled in by the words 'Strictly personal', underlined twice.

In his memory the name was vaguely associated with a face, hair that needed cutting, and thin legs, but that was all.

Seven times running he had told the messenger:

'Say I'm at a meeting.'

The eighth time he had given way. As a Deputy, he had learnt by experience that the only hope of getting rid of a certain type of pest is by seeing them. He remembered an old lady, always dressed in black, with a wheezy dog tucked under her arm, who had haunted various government offices day after day for two years, trying to get her brother into the Académie Française.

Malate had come into the rather austere-looking office, and the thin, knobbly-kneed lad had grown to be a tall, fat man with the unhealthy red face of a heavy drinker and bulging eyes. Very much at ease, he held out his hand as though they had seen each other only the day before.

'How are you, Augustin, old boy?'

'Sit down.'

'Don't you recognise me?'

'I do.'

'Well then?'

His eyes had a slightly aggressive glint, which meant, of course:

'So now you're a Minister you cut your old pals?'

At ten o'clock in the morning he already smelt of drink, and though his suit was well tailored it showed traces of the kind of bohemian negligence that the Premier detested.

'Don't be frightened, Augustin. I'm not going to waste your time. I know it's valuable, and I've not got much to ask you . . .'

'It's true I'm extremely busy.'

'Heavens! I realise that all right. Since we left Evreux, I first, you'll remember, a lot of time has gone by and we've grown from kids into men. You've done well, and I congratulate you. I've not done so badly either. I'm married, I have two kids, and if I can get just the slightest bit of help, everything will be grand . . .'

In cases like this the Premier turned to ice, not so much from hardness of heart as from clear-sightedness. He had realised that, whatever one did for him, Xavier Malate would all his life be in need of just a bit more help.

'A contract for enlarging the harbour at Algiers is to be given out next month, and it just so happens that I work in a big engineering concern in which my brother-in-law is a partner . . .'

A surreptitious touch on the bell warned the messenger, who promptly opened the door.

'Take Monsieur Malate to see Monsieur Beurant.'

Malate must have got the wrong idea, for he broke into effusive gratitude: 'Thank you, old man. I knew I could count on you. You realise, don't you, that if it hadn't been for me you'd have been expelled from school too, and then you'd probably not be here now? Ah, well! Honesty is the best policy, whatever they may say. I suppose it's practically in the bag?'

'No.'

'What d'you mean?'

'That you must put your case before the head of the contracts department.'

'But you'll explain to him that . . .'

'I'm going to ring through and ask him to give you ten minutes. That's all.'

He had eventually used '*tu*' to him, after all, and he regretted it as a weakness, almost a piece of cowardice.

Later on he had received nauseating letters in which Malate talked about his wife, who had twice attempted suicide, and so he daren't leave her alone any more, his children who hadn't enough to eat and couldn't go to school because they had no decent clothes.

He had stopped asking for a Government contract, but was pleading for help of any kind, for a job, however humble, even as a lock-keeper or as watchman on road-works.

Malate had no suspicion that his former Evreux schoolfellow had asked for his police record from the Rue des Saussaies, and he persisted, his letters growing steadily longer and more tedious, or more harrowing.

He had been inditing such letters, which were nearly all on café notepaper, for over twenty years, sometimes changing his victim, occasionally achieving his aim, and though he had married and was a father, he had deserted his wife and children ten years ago.

'He's here again, sir,' the messenger would announce from time to time.

Malate altered his tactics, taking to hanging round the ministerial building, looking seedy and unshaven, in the hope that his one-time schoolmate would take pity on him.

One morning his former friend had walked straight up to him and declared curtly:

'The next time I see you anywhere near here, I'll have you arrested.'

In the course of his career he had disappointed other hopes, had shown himself unrelenting to quite a number of people.

Malate was the only one who had taken a kind of revenge, and the years had not softened his hatred.

He had succeeded up to a point, for on several occasions the Premier had approached the Rue des Saussaies to find out where he was.

'*I'm in hospital at Dakar with a stiff bout of malaria. But you needn't gloat. I shan't peg out this time, because I've sworn I'll be at your funeral.*'

He really was at Dakar. Then in prison at Bordeaux, where he'd been given twelve months for writing dud cheques. From there he had written, on a sheet of prison paper:

'*Life's a funny thing. One man becomes a Cabinet Minister, another becomes a convict.*'

The word convict was exaggerated, but dramatic.

'*All the same, I'll be at your funeral.*'

The office of Prime Minister didn't intimidate him, and in fact it was to the Hôtel Matignon that he first began to telephone, giving the name of some politician or celebrity.

'Xavier here . . . Well? How does it feel to be Premier? . . . All the same, you know, I'll still be at your . . .'

The electric lights had not come on again, and Milleran, too, had an oil lamp now. The treacly-looking circles of light in the dusky rooms recalled his old home at Evreux. The Premier even remembered, all of a sudden, the peculiar smell his father's clothes used to have when he got home, for, being the local doctor, an odour of camphor and phenol used to trail around with him. Of red wine, too.

'Ring up and find out what's happening about the electricity.'

She tried, announced before long:

'The telephone's cut off as well now.'

Gabrielle appeared, to announce:

'Dinner is ready, sir.'

'I'm coming at once . . .'

He didn't feel he was to blame about Malate, and he was only annoyed with himself for allowing his former friend's threat to get on his nerves. He, who believed in nothing except a certain human dignity he could hardly have put into words, in freedom too, at any rate in a measure of freedom of thought, was beginning to suspect Xavier Malate of having baleful powers.

Logically, considering the unhealthy life he had been leading for forty years and more now, the printer's son should have been dead. Not a year went by without his paying a visit, long or short, to some hospital or other. He had even been found to have tuberculosis and sent to a mountain sanatorium where patients died every week, and from which he had emerged cured.

He had had three or four operations, the last two for cancer of the throat, and now, going round and round in imperceptibly diminishing circles, he was back at his starting-point, Evreux, as though he had decided to die in his native town.

'Milleran!'

'Yes, sir?'

'Ring up the hospital at Evreux tomorrow and ask them to read you the record of a man called Xavier Malate.'

It was not the first time she had dealt with the matter, and she asked no questions. Through the window Emile could be heard, bringing the Rolls alongside the house. The black limousine, with its old-fashioned wheels, was more than twenty years old, but like so many other things in this place it belonged, as it were, to the Premier's personality. It had been presented to him by the Lord Mayor of London, on behalf of the citizens of the English capital, when he had been given the Freedom of the City.

Walking slowly, with his hands behind his back, he went along the tunnel to the dining-room, with its blackened beams, where a solitary place was laid on a long, narrow table that came from some former convent or monastery.

Here too the walls were whitewashed, as they are in the poorest villager's cottage, and there was not a single picture or ornament; the floor was paved with the same grey, worn flagstones as the kitchen.

An oil lamp stood in the middle of the table, and it was not Gabrielle who served, but young Marie, taken on two years ago when she was only sixteen.

The first day he had heard her asking Gabrielle:

'What time's the old boy have his dinner?'

He would never be anything more to her than 'the old boy'. She had heavy breasts, her dress was too tight, and on her weekly day off she made herself up like a tart. Looking out of his window one evening the Premier had seen her under the elm, her skirts hitched up to her waist, her hands behind her clutching the trunk of the tree, placidly satisfying the needs of one of the policemen. He was doubtless not the only one, and in the overheated rooms she gave off a strong feminine odour.

'Do you think it's proper, sir, for you to have a girl like that here?'

His only answer to Gabrielle's question had been a rather melancholy:

'Why not?'

After all, in earlier days hadn't he occasionally come across Gabrielle in intimate converse with a delivery man, and once with a policeman in uniform?

'I can't understand you. You let her do whatever she likes. She's the only person in the house who's never scolded.'

Perhaps that was because he didn't expect her to be faithful or devoted, only to do the heavy work for which he had engaged her. Perhaps, too, because she was eighteen years old, healthy, sturdy and common, and the last person of that type that he was likely to have about him?

She represented a generation about which he knew nothing, to which he was and would remain just the old boy.

His dinner was always the same, having been prescribed once and for all by Professor Fumet, and Marie had found that astounding, too: a poached egg on dry toast, a glass of milk, a piece of cottage cheese and some fresh fruit.

He had ceased long ago to feel this as a privation. He even felt surprised, almost disgusted, at the thought that intelligent men, with serious problems to solve every day of their lives, could bother about food and, in the company of pretty women, so much enjoy talking about it.

One day when he had been walking with Emile down a street at Rouen, he had stopped short outside a food shop and gazed for a long time at the trussed fowls, a pheasant *en gelée* still decked with its many-coloured tail, a ewe-lamb lying on a bed of fresh, costly greenstuff.

'What do you think of that?'

'They say it's the best shop in Rouen.'

He had spoken for his own benefit, not for Emile's:

'Man is the only animal who finds it necessary to decorate the corpses of his victims in order to whet his appetite. Look at those neat rounds of truffle slipped under the skin of the capons to make a symmetrical pattern, that cooked pheasant with his beak and tail so artistically put back in place . . .'

It was twenty-five years since he had last smoked a cigarette, and only rarely was he allowed a glass of champagne.

He didn't rebel, felt no bitterness. He obeyed his doctors, though not for fear of dying, for death had long ceased to frighten him. He lived with it in an intimate relationship which, if not cheerful, was at least resigned.

He had been mistaken just now in thinking that he and Xavier Malate were the only survivors of their generation. Unless Eveline had died since his last birthday. She was a sort of counterbalance to the printer's son. His recollection of her was rather vague, although he'd been in love with her when he was about twelve years old.

Her father had kept the ironmonger's shop in the Rue Saint-Louis, nearly opposite the *lycée*, and she'd been two or three years older than himself, so she would be about eighty-five now.

Had he ever spoken to her? Two or three times, perhaps? He wasn't even sure, at that, that he wasn't mixing her up with her sister or some other little girl in the district. On the other hand, he was positive that she'd had red hair, fiery red, was thin and lanky, with two pigtails hanging down her back, and wore a pinafore with small red checks.

She had waited before writing to him, not only till he became a Minister but until he was Prime Minister, on the eve of an international conference where the destiny of France was at stake, or so people believed, as they always do. Didn't he believe so himself at the time?

Eveline didn't ask him for anything, but sent him an envelope containing a little medal from Lourdes, with a note saying:

> I shall pray that you may succeed in your task. This will help you to save the country.
> The little girl from the Rue Saint-Louis–
> Eveline ARCHAMBAULT

She had never married, presumably, for Archambault was the name he could see in his mind's eye, in big black letters above the ironmongery. When she sent him this little token she was well over fifty, and the address on the back of the envelope showed that she still lived in the same street, the same house.

She was there to this day. He sometimes imagined her, a little old woman dressed in black, trotting along, close to the house-walls, on her way to early mass on some grey morning.

Since that first medal she had formed the habit of sending him birthday wishes every year, and the envelope always contained some pious object, a rosary, a religious picture, an *agnus dei*.

He had made enquiries through the Prefecture, learnt that she was quite well provided for, and had sent her a signed photograph.

The glass panel in the door between the dining-room and the kitchen was covered with a red-checked curtain, in the style of a village inn. He could see Gabrielle's shadow moving to and fro on the other side. Madame Blanche had already left, for it was Emile who helped the Premier to get to bed. The telephone had been installed in the house where she lodged, at the near end of the village, and she took her meals at Bignon's inn, known nowadays as the Hôtel Bignon, where the policemen put up.

He heard Emile's footsteps, then caught sight of his shadow against the curtain, as he came into the kitchen from out of doors, announcing:

'All right now! It's working.'

'What's working?' Gabrielle mumbled.

'The wireless.'

The old cook wasn't interested in the wireless; she went on grilling herrings for the servants' supper, while Emile slumped down on the bench and poured himself a glass of cider.

Since five o'clock the Premier had been deliberately avoiding the thought of Chalamont, who had been mentioned in the Paris-Inter broadcast, and the telephone call had come like a dispensation of providence to take his mind off the subject. In any case he had trained himself to accomplish that feat easily: to turn his thoughts in a given direction and prevent them from straying in any other.

It was too soon to think about Philippe Chalamont, for there were only rumours so far, and even if the President of the Republic asked him to form a Cabinet, Chalamont would not necessarily agree.

Young Marie stood behind him, vacant-eyed, watching him eat; she could hardly have looked sloppier, and it was obvious she would never learn, but would end up sooner or later in her right place, as a barmaid in some harbourside café at Fécamp or Le Havre.

'Will Monsieur take a *tisane*?'

'I *always* take a *tisane*.'

He went off, with hunched shoulder, not knowing what to do with his arms, which, now that his body had shrunk, had become too long. He used to say to himself:

'If man is descended from the apes I must be returning to my origin, for I look more and more like a gorilla.'

Emile had put the loud-speaker on the table, with the flex going out through the window-frame and connected up with the car wireless. When the time came for the news, he would only have to switch on. Emile had thought of this himself, during their first year at Les Ebergues. With a storm just like tonight's blowing, the electricity had failed in the middle of an unusually violent debate in the U.N.

The Premier, furious, was prowling round his office, lit, as now, by an oil lamp, except that they hadn't yet found a globe for it, when Emile had knocked on the door.

'If you will allow me, sir, I would like to make a suggestion. Have you thought of the wireless in the car, sir?'

On that occasion he had gone out in the dark, swathed in a rug made of wildcat skins—it was a present from the Canadians—and sat in the back of the Rolls, with the dial of the wireless as his only light, until the midnight news.

Since then Emile, who enjoyed playing the handyman, had improved the system, bought a second loud-speaker which only needed connecting with the wireless set.

There was no electric failure in Paris, and they probably didn't realise that in Normandy the storm was bringing down trees, telegraph poles and chimneys. Journalists and photographers were mounting guard in the courtyard of the Elysée, where it was raining, and in the corridors and bar of the Chamber little knots of over-excited Deputies were forming in the window-nooks.

An anxious calm would be reigning in the Ministries, where every crisis improved or endangered the prospects of promotion of hundreds of civil servants, and the Prefects, each in his own fief, would be waiting with equal anxiety for the seven-fifteen news.

For forty years, on such occasions, it had invariably been his name that had been put forward in the last resort. He had usually remained secluded in his flat on the Quai Malaquais, the one he had moved into when first called to the Bar.

Milleran had not been his secretary in those days. She was still a little girl, and in her place, waiting silently in the room with him, ready to jump on the telephone, there had been an ungainly young man with a pointed nose, whose name was Chalamont.

There was a difference of twenty years in their ages, and it had been curious to see how the secretary took on the gait, voice, posture and even the mannerisms of his chief. Over the telephone it was so marked that most people were taken in and addressed him as 'Minister'. Wasn't it even stranger, perhaps, to note that the face of this lad of twenty-five was as impassive as that of a middle-aged man who had had many years to harden him?

Was it because of this mimicry, because one could feel that his admiration was intensely sincere, that the Premier had kept him on, carrying him along from one Ministry to the next, first as attaché, then as secretary, finally as Principal Private Secretary?

Chalamont was now Deputy for the sixteenth arrondissement, and lived with his wife, who had brought him a large fortune, in a flat overlooking the Bois de Boulogne. He didn't need to make a living out of politics, but he stuck to the political world from choice, some people said as a vice, for he was a savage fighter.

And yet, though he was the leader of quite a large group, he had only once been in the Cabinet, and then only for three days.

Wasn't it characteristic of him that on that occasion he had chosen to be Minister of the Interior, and thus have the police records at his disposal?

What the public, and a good many political men, did not know was that during those three days there had been an almost uninterrupted series of telephone calls between Les Ebergues and Paris, and that Bénouville had noticed an unusual number of cars whose number-plates indicated that they came from the Seine Department, all making for the house on the cliff.

On the morning when the new government had presented itself in the Chamber there had been no electric failure, and the old man of Les Ebergues had been listening, with a gleam of ever-increasing satisfaction in his eyes, to the course of the debate.

The proceedings had lasted just three hours, and the new-born government had been defeated before Chalamont had even had time to move into his office in the Place Beauvau.

Was the Premier still as powerful as that today? Hadn't people rather forgotten the statesman who had retired haughtily to the Normandy coast and whom children, learning about him at school, imagined to have died long ago?

'May I go to dinner, sir?'

'By all means, Milleran. Tell Emile to turn on the wireless at ten past seven.'

'Will you need me?'

'Not this evening. Goodnight.'

She had a room between Gabrielle's and Emile's, above the kitchen, and young Marie slept in a small ground-floor room, once a store-room, which had had a window put in its outside wall.

Alone in the book-lined rooms, only two of which had any light this evening, the Premier moved slowly from one to another, scrutinising certain shelves, certain bindings, now and then running his finger along the top of a volume. One day young Marie had caught him at this kind of suspicious inspection, and she had asked:

'Have I left some dust?'

He had turned slowly towards her, had given her a long stare before replying briefly:

'No.'

It might be she, it might be Milleran, or even Emile, and he wouldn't allow himself to suspect one of them rather than another. He had known about it for months, and felt sure there must be at least two of them hunting, one inside the house and one outside, possibly one of the detectives?

He had been neither surprised nor annoyed, and at first it had rather amused him.

For a man who had nothing left to do except die in a manner worthy of the legend that had grown up around him, this was an unhoped-for diversion.

Who? Not only, *who* was ferreting among his books and papers, looking for something, but *who* had set them to it?

He, too, had been Minister in the Place Beauvau, not for three days but, on several occasions, for months, once for two whole years. So he knew the methods of the Rue des Saussaies as well as he knew the records that were such a temptation to fellows like Chalamont.

Nearly every evening since making his discovery, he had distributed through the four rooms a number of reference marks, 'witnesses', as he privately termed them, which were sometimes no more than a thread of cotton, a hair, a scarcely visible scrap of paper, sometimes a volume just slightly out of alignment.

In the mornings he made his round, like a fisherman going to pick up his lobster-pots, for he had always forbidden anybody to go into those rooms before he did. The housework was left until he was up, and then done not with a vacuum cleaner, which he hated the noise of, but with broom and feather-duster.

Why had they thought first of all of the Memoirs of Saint-Simon? One morning he had found that one of the volumes, which he had pushed in by a quarter of an inch the previous evening, was back in line with the rest. The detectives living at the Bénouville inn could not have guessed that Saint-Simon had been among his favourite bedside books all his life.

A calf-bound folio of Ovid, whose size would have made it an ideal hiding-place, had been handled next, then, a few weeks later, an entire row of illustrated books on art, most of which were bound in boards.

It had all begun about the time when he had told a foreign journalist that. he was writing his memoirs.

'But you have already published them, Premier, and they were even printed in the biggest magazine in my country.'

He was in a good humour that day. He liked the journalist. It amused him to give the fellow a scoop, if only to annoy certain other journalists whom he couldn't stand.

'My official memoirs have been published,' he retorted.

'So you didn't tell the whole truth in them?'

'Perhaps not the *whole* truth.'

'And you're going to tell it this time? Really the whole of it?'

His mind was not made up then. It had all been in the nature of a joke. He had indeed begun, for his own amusement, to write a commentary on the events he had been mixed up with, giving little sidelights that no one else knew about.

It had become a kind of secret game, and now he was still wondering, with amusement, who would find those notes in the end, and how.

They were already looking. So far, nobody had looked in the right place.

Naturally the entire Press had printed the information about his 'secret notebooks', as they were called, and the reporters had come to Les Ebergues in greater numbers than ever before, all asking the same questions:

'Are you going to publish during your lifetime? . . . Will you have them held back until some years after your death, like the Goncourts did? . . . Are you revealing the shady side of twentieth-century politics, foreign as well as domestic? . . . Are you bringing in other world statesmen you've known? . . .'

He had given evasive replies. The journalists had not been alone in the interest they took in those memoirs, and several important personages, including two generals, whom he hadn't seen for a number of years, had visited the Normandy coast that summer, as though by chance, and felt impelled to pay their respects to him.

They were no sooner seated in his study than he began to wonder when the question would come. They'd all taken the same tone, casual, joking.

'Is it true you've written something about me in your private papers?'

All he would say was:

'The Press reports were very exaggerated. I've only just begun to jot down notes, and I don't know yet whether anything will come of it . . .'

'I know some people who are trembling at the idea . . .'

He would reply innocently:

'Ah!'

He knew what was being said on the quiet, what two newspapers had had the temerity to say in print: that, piqued at being left in silence, forgotten, he was revenging himself by suspending this undefined threat over the heads of the Establishment.

For a few days he had even wondered whether there might not be a grain of truth in this, and his conscience had been uneasy.

But if it had been like that he wouldn't have gone on, and he would in fairness have destroyed the pages he had already written.

He had reached an age at which a man can no longer fool himself.

It was actually because of Chalamont, his former secretary, whose name would be mentioned over the wireless in a few minutes, that he had decided against drawing back; not that Chalamont was important, but his case was typical.

As had been more or less announced just now, would not the President of the Republic probably be going to give him the job of forming a government?

Chalamont would undoubtedly remember that once when his old chief was asked about his prospects of receiving a portfolio, he had replied curtly:

'He'll never be Prime Minister as long as I'm alive.'

After pausing as he always did when he wanted to stress the importance of his pronouncements, he had added:

'Nor when I'm dead, either.'

At this very moment, when the storm outside was wrenching at the roof-tiles and a shutter was banging, Chalamont would be at the Elysée and the journalists would be in the rain-swept courtyard, waiting for his answer.

The door of the Rolls opened and closed again. Almost at once, the loud-speaker, standing on the oak table, began to crackle faintly, and the Premier sat down in his Louis-Philippe armchair, folded his hands, closed his eyes, and waited too.

Chapter Three

First of all came the news agencies' reports, terse and impersonal:

'*Paris . . . Latest developments in the political situation . . . At five o'clock this afternoon the President of the Republic received Monsieur Philippe Chalamont, Leader of the Left Independent Group, at the Elysée and asked him to form a coalition Cabinet. The Deputy for the sixteenth arrondissement postponed his reply until tomorrow morning. At the end of this news bulletin we shall broadcast a short interview with Monsieur Chalamont by our representative, Bertrand Picon . . .*

'*Saint-Etienne . . . The fire that broke out last night in an electrical equipment factory . . .*'

The Premier sat motionless, no longer listening, keeping an eye on a log which was threatening to roll on to the floor. Two or three gusts of wind made it shake and crackle, and finally he got up, squatted down by the hearth, cautiously, for he was not forgetting his leg, took the tongs and tidied up the fire.

He would have half an hour to wait. The French radio correspondents were speaking, one after another, from London, New York, Budapest, Moscow, Beirut, Calcutta. Before settling into his armchair again he took several slow turns round the table and regulated the wick of the oil lamp.

'*And now we come to today's sport . . .*'

Another five minutes and it would be Chalamont's turn.

When the moment arrived there was a brief interruption while they switched from the live broadcast to the tape, for the interview was a recorded one. That was perceptible from the sound, which had changed, and from the voices, which had a different timbre, so that one could tell that the two speakers had been out of doors.

'*Ladies and gentlemen, it is a quarter to six and we are in the courtyard of the Elysée, I and a number of newspaper reporters . . . This wet, windy day is the eighth that has gone by since the Government fell, and as usual Paris has been full of gossip.*

'*At the present moment the question is: are we to have a Chalamont government?*

'*Just over half an hour ago, Monsieur Philippe Chalamont, summoned by Monsieur Cournot, arrived in his car and strode rapidly past us and up the steps, with no more than a wave of his hand to indicate that he had nothing to say to us yet.*

'*The Leader of the Left Independent Group and Deputy for the sixteenth arrondissement, whose photograph has often appeared in the papers, is a vigorous man who looks younger than his sixty years. He is very tall, with a bald forehead, and rather stout . . .*

'*As I said before, it is raining. There is not room for all of us under the porch of the main entrance, where the doorkeepers are indulgently turning a blind eye to our presence, and a charming lady among our number has valiantly opened a red umbrella . . .*

'*Outside the gate, in the Faubourg Saint-Honoré, the Municipal Guards are keeping a discreet watch over the small crowd that gathers in little knots and disperses again . . . Hello! . . . I believe . . . Yes . . . Is that him, Danet? . . . Thanks, old man . . .*

'*Excuse me . . . I'm told that at this very moment Monsieur Chalamont is crossing the immense hall of the Elysée, which is dazzling with light . . . Yes, as I bend down I can see him myself . . . He's just put on his overcoat . . . He's taking his gloves and hat from the attendant . . . Close to us, his chauffeur has opened the door of the car . . . So in an instant we shall know whether he has taken on the job of forming a Cabinet . . .*'

There was the sound of a bus going past, then some confused noises and a kind of scuffle, with voices in the background:

'*Don't push . . .*'

'*Let me through, old man . . .*'

'*Monsieur Chalamont . . .*'

Then again the well-pitched, faintly conceited tones of Bertrand Picon.

'*Minister, I would like you, sir, to tell our listeners . . .*'

Although Chalamont had only been a Cabinet Minister for three days and, indeed, had spent only a few hours in the office in the Place Beauvau, ushers, journalists and all habitués of the Palis-Bourbon would address him for the rest of his life as 'Minister', just as others, simply because they had once presided over some vague Parliamentary Committee, were known as 'President'.

'*. . . first of all, for what reason Monsieur Cournot sent for you this afternoon . . . I am correct, am I not, in thinking that it was in order to ask you to form a coalition Cabinet? . . .*'

The old man's fingers whitened as he sat still in his armchair. He heard an embarrassed cough, and then, at last, the voice:

'*—As a matter of fact the President of the Republic has done me the honour . . .*'

A car hooted, emerging from the confused background noises. What gave the old man at Les Ebergues the impression that Chalamont was peering around, in the wet, gloomy courtyard of the Elysée, as though looking for a ghost? There was a strange note of anxiety in his voice. For the first time, after a lifetime of effort, he had been asked to lead his country's government, and he knew that someone, somewhere, was listening, he couldn't possibly fail to think of it, someone who was silently bidding him to refuse.

Another voice, not Picon's, probably that of a journalist, broke in:

'*May we tell our readers that you have agreed and that you will begin your interviews this evening?*'

Even over the radio, especially over the radio, which is merciless, one could sense a blank, a hesitation; then came laughter, inexplicable at such a moment, and whispers of mirth.

'*Ladies and gentlemen, you can hear the Press representatives laughing, but I assure you their amusement has no connection with what has been said on either side. A moment ago Monsieur Chalamont suddenly flapped his hand, as though something had touched it unexpectedly, and we noticed that the umbrella of the lady journalist I told you about was dripping on to it . . . Excuse that aside,*

*Minister, but our listeners wouldn't have understood . . . Would you please speak
into the microphone . . . You were asked whether . . .'*

'I thanked the President for the honour he had done me, which I very much
appreciate . . . and . . . er . . . I asked him' (a car hooted very close by, in the
Faubourg Saint-Honoré) '. . . to allow me . . . to allow me to think things over
and give him my reply in the morning . . .'*

'*But your group met at three o'clock this afternoon, and it is rumoured that
you were given a free hand . . .*'

'*That is the case . . .*'

It seemed as though he were trying to get away, to dive into his car, whose
door the chauffeur was still holding open.

The speaker had felt impelled to mention that he was rather stout because
that was what struck one at the first glance; he had the portly appearance
characteristic of men who were thin for a good deal of their lives and don't
know how to carry off the fat that has accrued to them. His double chin and
low-slung belly looked like padding, whereas his nose, for instance, was still
sharp and his lips so thin as to be almost non-existent.

'*Minister, sir . . .*'

'*With your permission, gentlemen . . .*'

'*One last question. Can you tell us who are the chief people you intend to
consult?*'

Another blank. They might have cut out these pauses when they edited
the tape. Had they refrained because they, too, realised that there was
something unusual and pathetic about such hesitancy? The photographers
on the steps must be sending up a barrage of flashlights during the interview,
lighting up the driving rain and bringing Chalamont's face out of the
darkness for a second to emphasise its pallor and anxiety.

'*I can't answer that question yet.*'

'*Will you be seeing anyone this evening?*'

'*Gentlemen . . .*'

He was almost suppliant, as he struggled to escape from the cluster of
people who were cutting him off from his car.

Suddenly there came a sharp, piercing voice which might have been that
of a little boy, but the Premier recognised it as belonging to a highly
esteemed reporter, as it snapped:

'*Aren't you intending to spend the night on the road?*'

An unintelligible stutter.

'*Gentlemen, I have nothing more to say . . . Excuse me . . .*'

Another pause. The slam of a car door, the sound of an engine, the crunch
of gravel, and finally, silence; then Bertrand Picon again, speaking in more
measured tones from a different setting, the studio:

'*You have been listening to the interview with Monsieur Philippe Chalamont
which was recorded as he left the Elysée. Refusing to make any further comment,
the Deputy for the sixteenth arrondissement drove back to his home on the
Boulevard Suchet where a group of journalists, undismayed by the bad weather,
is mounting guard outside the door. We shall know tomorrow whether France
has any immediate prospect of emerging from the deadlock which has now existed
for over a week, and whether we are soon to have a government.*

'*Paris-Inter calling . . . That is the end of the news . . .*'   Music. The door of
the Rolls opened and there came a tap at the window, outside which Emile's
face could be seen as a pale blur. A sign told him that he could turn off the

wireless, and the noise of the storm grew stronger.

In the soft light of the oil lamp the old man's face looked haggard, and his immobility was so striking that when, shortly afterwards Emile came into the study, bringing with him a little of the cold and damp from outside, he stopped with a frown.

The Premier kept his eyes closed, and Emile, standing at the entrance of the tunnel, gave a cough.

'What is it?'

'I came to ask you whether I'm to leave the Rolls outside until the final news?'

'You can put it in the garage.'

'You're sure you don't want . . . ?'

'Quite sure. Is Milleran at table?'

'She's having dinner.'

'And so are Gabrielle and young Marie?'

'Yes, sir.'

'Had your supper?'

'Not yet . . .'

'Then go and get it.'

'Thank you, sir.'

Just as the man was going away, he called him back:

'Who's on duty tonight?'

'Justin, sir.'

Inspector Justin Aillevard was a fat, melancholy little man. It was no use sending him word to go to bed, or even suggesting that he might come in out of the rain, for he took his orders from the Rue des Saussaies and it was to the Rue des Saussaies that he was responsible. The most that Gabrielle could manage now and again was to invite the policeman on duty to come into the kitchen for a moment and give him a glass of cider or calvados, according to the weather, and perhaps a slice of cake still warm from the oven.

As the Premier did not say he could go, Emile still waited, and he had to wait a long time before hearing the hesitant words:

'We may perhaps have a visitor tonight . . .'

'Do you want me to stay up?'

The chauffeur realised that for some mysterious reason his reactions were being closely watched, and that those eyes, open now, were studying his face more keenly than usual.

'I don't know yet . . .'

'I'm quite ready to stay up . . . You know it doesn't bother me . . .'

In the end he was dismissed, with a touch of impatience:

'Get along and eat.'

'Very good, sir.'

This time he really did go, and a moment later he was straddling the bench to sit down at the kitchen table.

Could Loubat—the name had just come back to him—the sharp-voiced journalist who'd questioned Chalamont, have information that the Premier didn't possess? Or had he merely spoken on the off-chance, on the strength of thirty years spent behind the scenes in the Chamber of Deputies and the various Ministries?

It was twelve years since the two politicians had last come face to face. During the Premier's last period in Paris they had occasionally been at the same sitting at the Palais-Bourbon, but one was on the Government bench and the other with his Parliamentary group, and they had taken care not to meet.

Their quarrel, as some people called it, or, as others put it, the hatred between them, was well known, but a variety of theories existed as to its origin.

An explanation favoured by young parliamentarians, those of the new generation, was that the Premier accused his former colleague of having been the mainspring of the plot that had kept him out of the Elysée.

In the first place, that credited Chalamont with an influence he was far from possessing; in the second place it revealed ignorance of the fact that for certain definite reasons it would have been political suicide for Chalamont to have taken such an attitude.

The Premier preferred not to dwell on that episode of his life, even though his motives had been very different from the ones attributed to him.

He had been at the apex of his glory in those days. His energy, his uncompromising spirit and the measures he had relentlessly adopted had saved the country from the very brink of the abyss. His photograph, surmounted by a tricolour cockade or ribbon, was enshrined in the shop-windows of every town in France, and allied nations were inviting him to triumphant receptions.

When the Head of the State died, he had been on the point of retiring from political life, in which he had spent long enough, and it was neither vanity nor ambition that had made him change his plans.

He had talked about it to Fumet one day later on, when he was dining with the Professor in his flat in the Avenue Friedland. He'd been in a good temper that evening, though still with the slightly crabby undertone that characterised his personality.

'You see, my dear Doctor, there is a fact which is overlooked not only by the public, but by those who shape public opinion, and it always bothers me when I read the life of a famous statesman. People talk about the leaders' interests, their pride or their ambition. What they forget, or refuse to see, is that beyond a certain stage, a certain level of success, a statesman is no longer himself, he becomes the prisoner of public events. Those aren't quite the right words . . .'

Fumet, who had a nimble mind and who was the doctor, and in most cases the personal friend, of everybody who was anybody in the country, was watching him through a cloud of cigar smoke.

'Let's put it this way, that there comes a moment, a rung of the ladder, at which a man's personal interests and ambitions become merged with those of his country.'

'Which is tantamount to saying that at a certain level treason, for example, becomes unthinkable?'

He had sat for a moment in silence. He would have liked to give a definite, clear-cut reply, and he followed up his thought as far as he could:

'Sheer treason, yes.'

'On condition, I take it, that the man is worthy of his office?'

At that moment he had thought of Chalamont, and answered:

'Yes.'

'And that isn't always the case?'

'It always would be, if it were not for certain forms of cowardice which are to some extent collective, and above all, for certain kinds of indulgence.'

It was in this spirit that he had felt it his duty to stand for the Presidency of the Republic. Contrary to the rumours that had been spread, he had had no intention of changing the Constitution, or of reducing the prerogatives of the executive.

He was perhaps said to have brought a rather sterner spirit into politics, and those who knew him best had spoken of his secular Jansenism.

He hadn't gone to Versailles himself. He had stayed in his flat on the Quai Malaquais, along with Milleran, Chalamont's successor.

At the luncheon that followed the opening meeting his chances were already being discounted, and with a few words over the telephone he had withdrawn from the contest.

Three weeks afterwards he left Paris, a voluntary exile, and though he kept his bachelor flat he hadn't set foot in it since.

Had his departure made Chalamont think he could get forgiveness more easily, and that the road was at last open? The Deputy for the XVIth had put out feelers, and his way of doing it had been typical of the man. He hadn't written, or come to Les Ebergues. The frontal attack was never in his line, and his schemes were usually very long-term affairs.

One morning the Premier had been surprised to see his son-in-law, François Maurelle, arrive at Les Ebergues, by himself. He was a nonentity, colourless but conceited, who had been working as a surveyor somewhere outside Paris when Constance first met him.

Why had she chosen him? She wasn't pretty, a bit on the masculine side, and her father had always regarded her with a curiosity in which there was more surprise than affection.

Maurelle's own intentions had been clear; less than a year after the marriage he had informed his father-in-law that he intended to stand for Parliament.

He had been defeated twice: the first time in the Bouches-du-Rhône, where he had been ill-advised to stand at all; next time at Aurillac, where at a second attempt he had finally worn down the voters' resistance.

The couple lived in the Boulevard Pasteur, in Paris, and spent their summer holidays in the Cantal.

He was a big, flabby chap, always dressed up to the nines, always with his hand held out and his lips ready to smile, the kind of fellow who won't express his views even on the most harmless subject without first peering at you to try and guess what yours may be.

The Premier had done nothing to help him, merely staring at him as malevolently as if he'd been a slug in the salad.

'I was at Le Havre, after driving a friend to the boat, and I thought I'd just like to drop in on you . . .'

'No.'

That was an unpopular trick of his. His 'no' was celebrated, for he brought it out frequently, without anger or any other inflexion. It wasn't even a contradiction: it simply took note of an almost mathematical fact.

'I assure you, my dear Premier . . .'

The old man waited with a far-away gaze.

'As a matter of fact . . . Though in any case I'd have come specially . . . It just so happens that the day before yesterday I was talking about my trip to a bunch in the Chamber . . .'

'To whom?'

'Give me a little time . . . And please don't think I'm trying to influence you . . .'

'That would be impossible.'

'I know . . .'

He smiled, and if one had slapped his face one's fingers would perhaps have got stuck in those plump, flaccid cheeks.

'I suppose I ought not to have done it—I hope you don't mind . . . I only promised to give you the message . . . It's from somebody who used to work with you and who's very much upset about a situation . . .'

The Premier had picked up a book from the table and seemed to be absorbed in it, paying no further attention to his visitor.

'As you'll have guessed, it's Chalamont . . . He doesn't bear you any grudge, he realises that you acted for the best, but to quote his own words he thinks he has perhaps been sufficiently punished . . . He's not a young man now . . . He could aim very high if you . . .'

The book snapped shut.

'Did he tell you about the luncheon at Melun?' asked the Premier as he rose to his feet.

'No. I know nothing about the business. I suppose he did something he shouldn't, but it's twenty years ago now . . .'

'Sixteen.'

'Excuse me. It was before I was in the Chamber. Do you think I may tell him . . .'

'That the answer is no. Good evening.'

With that, leaving his son-in-law stranded, he had gone into his bedroom and shut the door.

This time Chalamont wouldn't rest content with sending him a fellow like Maurelle. This was not a question of some secondary post in a Cabinet. The stake now was the ambition he'd been pursuing all his life, the part he'd been rehearsing since he was twenty years old, and which he'd at last been invited to play.

The years he had spent as the Premier's secretary, or rather as his fervent disciple, his marriage to a rich woman, the humdrum work he had done for various committees, the elocution lessons he had taken, at the age of forty, with a teacher from the Conservatoire, and the three languages he had mastered, his tremendous erudition, his foreign travels, his entire life, private and social, all of this had been undertaken solely with a view to the high office to which he would one day accede.

And now, as he stood in the courtyard of the Elysée, under the rain that was making its cobbles glisten, someone had asked him an innocent yet terrible question:

'Aren't you intending to spend the night on the road?'

The man who put that question had known that it would fling Chalamont into confusion.

At this moment the arbiter of his fate was an old man, cut off from the outside world even more completely than usual owing to an electric failure and a telephone break-down, who sat in a Louis-Philippe armchair, with the sea beating against the cliff hard by and squalls of wind threatening, at ever-diminishing intervals, to carry away the roof of his house.

Twice, three times, the Premier muttered to himself:

'He won't send anybody . . .'

Then, hesitantly:

'He'll come . . .'

At once he would have liked to take back his words, for he was not so sure. At forty years old, or at fifty, he had still believed himself to be a good judge of men, and would pronounce his verdicts without hesitation or remorse. At the age of sixty he had already been less sure of himself, and now he did no more than grope in the dark for momentary truths.

The definite fact was that Chalamont had not refused the Head of State's invitation. He had got himself a breathing-space. But that couldn't mean that he intended to defy the taboo laid on him by his former chief.

So he hadn't lost hope . . .

A cracking sound from outside the house—a branch being maltreated by the wind—roused a doubt, a suspicion, in his mind, and although he had already made his daily inspection he got up and walked through Milleran's office, where the lamp threw a dim light into the two rooms beyond. He went to the fourth room, the furthest from his bedroom; here were the books he never opened, but kept because they were presentation copies with inscriptions, or because they were rare editions.

He was no bibliophile and had never bought a book for the sake of its binding or its rarity. He had never indulged in any passion, craze or hobby, as the English call it, holding aloof from fishing, shooting and all other sports, sailing and climbing, novels, paintings and the theatre, and he had wanted to reserve his whole energy for his duties as a statesman, a little as Chalamont, his pupil, had tried to do.

He had not even wanted to be a father, his married life having lasted hardly three years, and though he had had mistresses he had only looked to them for relaxation, an interval of charm and elegance usually, with just a touch of affection, and had never repaid them with anything more than brief, condescending attention.

In this respect, too, legend was far from the truth, especially on the subject of Marthe de Creveaux, the Countess as she was called at the time, and as her faithful admirers continued to call her after her death.

Would he go on to the end of his notes, his genuine memoirs, which in a way were corrections, or would he leave behind him, uncaring, the image that had grown up by slow degrees and had so completely ousted the real person?

Before bending down to the lowest shelf he crossed the room and drew the curtain, for he never allowed the shutters to be closed until he was getting into bed. Once they were closed he felt as though he were shut up in a box, already removed from the world, and the irregular throbbing of his heart would sometimes seem to his ears like an alien sound. Once, in fact, he had listened more attentively, convinced that it had stopped beating.

The *Roi Pausole* was in its place, a very handsome edition illustrated by distinctly licentious drawings; the artist had sent him this inscribed copy when he was Prime Minister. It was printed on hand-made Japanese paper, in unbound sections, each followed by its set of loose-leaf illustrations, and protected by a grey cardboard case.

Would it occur to anyone, when he died, to leaf through his books, one by one, before sending them to the Salle Droust to be scattered by auction?

His daughter, from what he knew of her, wouldn't open them. Nor would her husband. They might perhaps keep a few as souvenirs, but certainly not this one, for the illustrations would shock them.

It was amusing to imagine the fate of documents of the greatest importance, carried by the chances of an auction into the hands of people who hadn't even known they existed.

Not long ago he had moved Chalamont's confession, written in a feverish hand on paper with the heading of the Prime Minister's office, and had put it into this book by Pierre Louys. He had chosen that particular book because he had suddenly noted a resemblance between his one-time secretary, now that he'd put on flesh, and the King of Boeotia as depicted by the illustrator.

Several of his hiding-places had been selected owing to equally unexpected comparisions, many of them humorous. As for the celebrated memoirs, they were not in the form of a connected manuscript, as everyone imagined; they were simply notes, explanations and corrections, in tiny writing, in the margins of the three volumes of his official autobiography. Only instead of the French edition he had used the American one, which stood on the shelf side by side with the Japanese edition and some twenty other translations.

The paper he was looking for was in its place, in the second section, between pages 40 and 41, and the ink had had time to fade a bit.

'*I, the undersigned, Philippe Chalamont* . . .'

Hearing a sound, he started and put the book back in place, as furtively as a child surprised in a prank. It was only Emile, turning down his bed for the night, and Emile could not see him from the bedroom.

Had the man been surprised at not finding him in his study, and had he glanced into Milleran's office? If so, was he wondering what the Premier could possibly be up to in the semi-darkness of the fourth room?

Had Chalamont tried to telephone from Paris? Had he set out, with his chauffeur? In that case, even with the bad weather, it would hardly take him more than three hours.

'Young Marie asks can she go to the village?'

He replied indifferently:

'Let her go.'

'She says her mother's going to have a baby in the night.'

Young Marie already had six or seven brothers and sisters, he wasn't quite sure how many, and it didn't matter anyhow. But an idea did occur to him.

'How will they let the doctor know?'

The nearest doctor was at Etretat, and it would not be possible to telephone to him.

'It's not the doctor who's delivering her, it's old Babette . . .'

He didn't ask who Babette was. He'd only meant to offer the car. But if they didn't need it . . .

'Will you be going to bed as usual?'

'Yes, at ten o'clock.' He had no reason for making any change in the pattern of his life. He invariably went to bed at ten o'clock, whether tired or not, and invariably got up, winter and summer alike, at half past five in the morning.

The only member of the household who'd protested against this timetable had been young Marie, although before coming to work for him she'd been a farm-hand and used to get up at four to milk the cows.

'Shall I make up the fire?'

The Premier was edgy, impatient, and this made him angry with himself, for he considered it humiliating to be affected, however slightly, by other people's actions or opinions.

If at the age of eighty-two he still was not secure from outside influences, what hope was there that he ever would be?

This reminded him, for a second, of the death of one of his friends, also an ex-Premier, the most ferocious anti-clerical of the Third Republic, who to everyone's astonishment had sent for a priest at the last moment . . .

He sat down in his usual place and opened Sully's *Memoirs*, while Emile went back to the kitchen, whence he would return in due course to put him to bed.

He didn't read, however. He felt obliged to run over the Chalamont business again, as though searching his own conscience. He always thought of that chapter as entitled 'the luncheon at Melun', and there were at least three people, apart from himself, for whom those words had the same sinister ring.

It had happened in June. The weather was bright and hot. Cars were rushing out of Paris, three abreast, towards the Forest of Fontainebleau. The Parisians were off for a day in the country, all unaware of the drama in progress, or else telling themselves, out of habit or from laziness, that those whom they had elected for the purpose would bring it safely to an end.

The financial crisis was probably the blackest the country had been through since the *assignats* of the Revolution. Every expedient had been attempted and they had gone almost hat in hand to beg the help of foreign governments. Every day the country was being drained of its substance, like a body bleeding to death, as the newspapers put it, and the outlook could hardly have been gloomier.

Three weeks earlier the Chamber had granted full powers to the government, after a stormy and inglorious night sitting. Every morning since then the papers had been asking:

'How are they going to use them?'

The Governor of the Bank of France was sending hourly messages, each more alarming than the last. Ascain, the Finance Minister, who had known, when he accepted that office, that it would bring him nothing but unpopularity and might mean the end of his political career, was conferring every morning with the Premier.

After the disastrous experiments made by previous governments, which had lived from day to day, robbing Peter to pay Paul, the only solution was a large-scale devaluation. And even that, if it were to be effective, must happen at the right moment, abruptly and unexpectedly enough to prevent speculation.

There were journalists on guard day and night outside the Hôtel Matignon in the Rue de Varennes, others in front of the Ministry of Finance in the Rue de Rivoli, and others, again, in the Rue de Valois, where the

Governor of the Bank of France lived.

The three men with whom the decision rested were spied upon continually, their words, their mood, their slightest frown interpreted in one way or another.

But little by little the details of the operation had been settled, and all that remained was to fix the new exchange-rate and the date of the devaluation.

Nerves were so strained in the Bourse and the foreign Stock Exchanges that the three men responsible ended by being afraid to be seen together for fear it might be taken for a signal.

So they decided to meet for luncheon, one Sunday, at a country house belonging to Ascain, just outside Melun. The appointment had been kept so secret that even their wives did not know about it, and Madame Ascain had not been there to receive her guests.

When he had arrived with Chalamont, who was then his Principal Private Secretary, the Premier had caught a frown on the face of Lauzet-Duché, the Governor of the Bank, but he had not felt called upon to give any reason for bringing the younger man.

Had not Chalamont become almost his shadow? Besides, even before his time, hadn't the Premier felt the need of a silent presence by his side?

The house was built of golden-yellow stone; it looked on to a sloping street and was surrounded on three sides by a lovely garden, enclosed by iron railings and walls. It had belonged to Ascain's father, who was a solicitor, and the mark left by the brass plate could still be seen, to the left of the gate.

They had talked of nothing in particular during luncheon, in front of the servants; then they had taken coffee under a lime-tree at the far end of the garden. As they were more secure from inquisitive ears in that spot than anywhere else, they had sat on in their wicker armchairs, round a small table loaded with liqueurs that nobody touched, to decide the rate of devaluation and fix the zero hour, which, for technical reasons had to be Monday, just before the Stock Exchange closed.

Reaching their decision after weeks of nervous strain, they had felt so relieved at the idea that matters were now out of their hands, that Ascain, who was short and plump, had suddenly pointed to a corner of the garden which was screened by a row of plane-trees and suggested:

'We ought to have a game of skittles.'

It was so unexpected, immediately after their serious conversation, that they had all burst out laughing, including Ascain, who had thrown out his proposal as a joke.

'There's a proper skittle-alley over there, behind the plane-trees,' he explained. 'My father had a passion for the game and I still keep the place in order. Like to have a look?'

Lauzet-Duché, a former Inspector of Finance, seldom relaxed his grave manner, which was enhanced by a square-cut pepper-and-salt beard.

Still not knowing what they were going to do, the four men walked across the lawn to the plane-trees and there, indeed, was the skittle-alley, with its cindered track and a big flat stone on which the Finance Minister, bending down, began to arrange the skittles that were lying about.

'Shall we have a go?'

The newspapers had never got hold of that story. For more than an hour the four men who had just determined the fate of the franc and the fortunes of millions of people, had played skittles, at first condescendingly and then with growing enthusiasm.

The next day, fifteen minutes after the opening of the Bourse, the telephone in the Prime Minister's office rang, and Chalamont picked it up, listened in silence, and then said:

'Just a moment, please.'

And, turning to his chief:

'Lauzet-Duché wants to speak to you personally . . .'

'Hello?'

'Is that you, Prime Minister?'

Right away he had sensed trouble.

'Forgive me for asking, but I suppose you have told nobody about the decision we took yesterday? And you haven't mentioned it in talking by telephone to Ascain, by any chance?'

'No. Why?'

'I don't know anything definite yet. It's only an impression so far. I'm told that when the Stock Exchange opened there were some rather disturbing dealings . . .'

'By which bank?'

'It's too soon to say. I'm to have a report every fifteen minutes . . . May I ring you back?'

'I shan't budge from my office . . .'

By half past two over thirty thousand million francs' worth of government stock had been thrown on to the market. By three o'clock the Bank of France was beginning to buy back on the quiet, to prevent a collapse.

Lauzet-Duché, the Rue de Rivoli and the Prime Minister were in constant touch by telephone, and things reached a point where they wondered if the devaluation would not have to be postponed. This unexpected, unforeseeable speculation had already robbed it of much of its effect.

On the other hand, to draw back now might start a panic.

The Premier was livid when he finally gave the signal, in much the same spirit as a general launching a battle half-lost in advance.

This would no longer be a blood-letting operation, affecting the whole of France to a more or less equal extent. Those in the know had already escaped, and what was more they had made huge profits at the expense of the medium and small investors.

During all these discussions Chalamont, as white-faced as his chief, had remained in the office, lighting one cigarette after another and throwing each one away after a few tense puffs.

He was not fat in those days. The caricaturists usually depicted him as a raven.

In a few minutes the news-vendors would be out on the boulevards with special editions. The telephone switchboards at the Prime Minister's house, the Ministry of Finance and the Bank of France were overwhelmed with calls.

In the spacious office with its carved panelling the Premier sat tapping his blotter with the end of his pencil, his eyes fixed on some detail of a tapestry that hung on the opposite wall.

When at last he stood up, he moved like an automaton.

'Sit down, Chalamont.'

His voice was clear, firm, with no more warmth than a machine.

'No. Not there. At my desk, please.'

He began to walk up and down, hands behind his back.

'Take a pen and a sheet of paper . . .'

And then he dictated, still walking up and down, with head lowered and hands clasped behind his back, pausing now and then for the right word:

'I, the undersigned, Philippe Chalamont . . .'

There was the sound of the pen moving over the paper, the sound of heavy breathing, and, about half-way through the dictation, a sound that resembled a sob.

'I can't . . .'

But the voice cut him short:

'Go on!'

The dictation went on till the bitter end.

Chapter Four

'Do you really think anybody will come and call in this weather?' muttered Emile sceptically.

It was five minutes to ten. At about half past nine the electric bulbs had lit up feebly, as though trying to come back to life, but after blinking two or three times they had gone out again. A little later, Emile had come in and asked:

'How are you going to manage for the night, sir?'

Seeing that the old man had not immediately realised what he meant, he explained:

'About the light . . . I went to the ironmonger's and bought the smallest oil lamp I could find, but I'm afraid even that will be too strong . . .'

For several months the old man had given up sleeping in the dark; he had a tiny electric light, a special type that had been ordered from Paris. This decision had been taken on his doctors' insistence, after a distressing incident that had deeply humiliated him.

For a long time the doctors, Gaffé and Lalinde, had been urging him not merely to let the nurse stay at Les Ebergues instead of going off to sleep in the village, but to have her all night within call, on a camp-bed in his study, for instance, or in the tunnel.

He had flatly, obstinately refused, and Fumet, to whom they had finally appealed to persuade him, had advised that, on the contrary, he should not be harassed about it.

He understood that for a man who in the whole of his life had never relied on anybody, prizing his independence above everything, the nurse's presence would be tantamount to surrender.

The fact that his chauffeur now turned into a valet, morning and evening, to help him to dress or to get to bed, was quite distressing enough for a man who had always jealously guarded his privacy.

'If I need help I can always ring for it,' he had said, indicating the pear-shaped bell-cord that hung above the bed.

'Or if not,' he had added, 'I shall be too far gone for anyone's help.'

As a precaution, a very loud bell, shrill as would have befitted a school or a factory, had been placed, not in Emile's room because he might happen to be away, but on the first-floor landing, above the kitchen, so that there were three people to hear it.

But one night that had proved inadequate. In the middle of a nightmare he couldn't entirely shake off, though he was unable to recall it later, he had sat up in bed, in pitch darkness, oppressed, his body bathed in cold sweat, with a sensation of horror that he had never experienced before. He knew there was something he ought to do, that it was agreed on, that *they* had insisted he must do it, but he couldn't quite remember what it was, he was groping in the dark.

It was like a night he had been through at about eight years old, when he had mumps and had seen the ceiling coming slowly down on top of him, while his eiderdown floated up to meet it.

He struggled with his torpor, wanting to do as they had advised, for he was not hostile to them, whatever they might think, and feeling around in the emptiness, his hand touched a smooth, cold surface. Without realising it, he had been trying to find the switch of the lamp on his bedside table, and all at once there was a crash on the floor; the tray, the bottle of mineral water and the glass had been knocked over.

He still couldn't find the flex of the lamp, or the switch. They must have pulled the bedside table further away; that was a little mystery he would try to clear up later. Meanwhile he felt an urgent, imperative need of action.

Then, leaning forward, he had tipped over and fallen heavily to the floor, all of a piece, landing in a position as ridiculous as on the cliff path, the day his left leg had played him that dirty trick.

He could feel splinters of glass all round him, and felt sure that blood was running over his hand, though he didn't know where it came from. He tried to get up, but in vain, there was no strength in his legs, and in the last resort the instinct of the baby in its cot returned to him and he began to shout.

There had been no storm that night. And yet, incredible as it might seem, of the three whose bedrooms were above the kitchen, not so far off, not one had heard him; it was young Marie, so difficult to wake in the morning, who had arrived in her nightdress, smelling of bed. She had turned on the light and stood there for quite a while, as though on her guard, hesitant, suspicious.

Had she believed him to be dead or dying? In the end she, too, had uttered a cry and, instead of giving him a hand, had rushed off upstairs to call the others. When they had come hurrying she had lagged behind, still half-frightened.

His wrist had been bleeding, but it wasn't a deep cut. Gaffé had been unable to decide exactly what had been wrong with the Premier.

'It happens to everybody, at any age. Probably a nightmare, brought on by cramp or by a momentary disturbance of the circulation. That would explain why you couldn't get up . . .'

He had talked again about having Madame Blanche there on a camp-bed.

The Premier's only concession had been to sleep from then on with a faint light in his room. They'd found him this lamp, hardly bigger than the bulb in a pocket torch, and he had grown accustomed to the nightlight, which had gradually come to form part of his world.

Emile had remembered it this evening, and, without saying anything, had gone down to the village and bought the little oil lamp. As luck would have it, at the very moment when he mentioned it, the electric current made a spasmodic return, died away again, then revived, and at last one could feel, from the brightness of the light, that this time it had come back for good.

'I'll fix up the oil lamp all the same, just in case . . .'

Morning and evening, for his valeting duties, Emile wore a white linen jacket, and it was probably the way in which the white of the jacket emphasised his black hair and rugged, irregular features that had prompted someone to remark:

'Your man looks more like a footpad than a servant . . .'

He'd been born at Ingrannes, in the depths of the Forest of Orleans, in a family whose men had been gamekeepers, from father to son, for longer than anyone could remember, and he and his brothers had been brought up with the dogs. But he made one think of a poacher rather than a gamekeeper. In spite of his sturdy frame and bulging muscles he moved about the house more softly than the ethereal Milleran, and a disturbing glint sometimes came into his mocking yet guileless eyes.

The Premier had taken him over the year he had become Foreign Minister. He had found Emile, just released from military service, among the chauffeurs at the Quai d'Orsay, where he had been accepted through the influence of his local 'Squire', and he contrasted so strongly with the well-schooled chauffeurs of the Quai that he had found him amusing to watch.

It hadn't been easy to tame him, for at the least approach Emile's face would close up and one would be confronted with an expressionless, irritating wooden mask.

That particular Cabinet had survived for three years, and when it had been finally defeated Emile had muttered hesitantly, hanging his head and fidgeting awkwardly with his cap:

'I suppose there's no chance I could go along with you?'

He had gone along with him for twenty-two years, hanging around him like a dog at his master's heels, and had never spoken of getting married. Presumably he felt no need to do so, but the moment a passable unmarried woman, thin or fat, young or middle-aged, came into his field of vision he would cover her as a cock or a rabbit might, without hesitation but nonchalantly, as though it were part of his natural functions.

The Premier had more than once amused himself by watching his goings-on, for he felt that in his dealings with women his chauffeur revealed the same instinct as a poacher dealing with game. When a new victim came along, Emile scarcely appeared to notice her, except that his small black eyes became more set and his movements slower and more silent than usual. He melted into his surroundings at such times, just as a poacher in a forest becomes a tree or a rock, and waited patiently for an hour, a day or a week, till the propitious moment arrived. Whereupon, with an unerring instinct, he pounced.

Young Marie had certainly had her turn in the first week, if not on the first night, and the Premier would not have been surprised to learn that from time to time Milleran submitted, passively but not unwillingly, to the attentions of the only active male in the household.

Once in Paris he had been almost an eye-witness of one of these forthright conquests, which were an aspect of natural history and had a touch of its rough poetry. It was at the Ministry of Justice, when he was Keeper of the Seals. There had just been some changes in the staff, and on the morning of a big luncheon party a housemaid had arrived from the country, young and dewy, with the 'bloom' still on her.

The great house had been the scene of feverish activity and things had been a bit confused. About nine o'clock in the morning, the Keeper of the Seals had happened to be in a room that was being turned out, just in time to witness the meeting between Emile and the new maid.

He had sensed what was happening. Some people maintain that cock and hen birds communicate with each other by a kind of telepathy, and if so, Emile must have possessed the same faculty of emitting and receiving waves, for on merely catching sight of the girl from behind he made a dead set and his brown pupils contracted.

Later on, as the Premier came out of his own suite, where he had gone to put on his morning-coat, he had seen Emile come into the corridor, emerging from the linen-room and closing the door noiselessly behind him; his face was flushed and wore a satisfied expression, and he paused to tidy himself up.

The two men's eyes met, and Emile simply gave an imperceptible wink, as much as to say:

'That's that!'

As though he had just snared a rabbit at the expected spot.

Girls would pester him, claiming that they were pregnant by him. Their fathers would join in now and then, and some of them wrote to the Premier, who still remembered one typical phrase:

'. . . *and I rely on you, Minister, to see that the skunk puts matters to rights by marrying my daughter* . . .'

To which Emile would reply, unabashed:

'If a fellow had to marry every girl he put in the family way! . . .'

What kind of stories would Emile relate, in future years, to sightseers who came to Les Ebergues? And what did he really think about the old man he served?

'If you've no objection I'll stay in the kitchen and make myself some coffee. Like that, if the gentlemen were to come . . .'

Was it he who had hunted through the volumes of Saint-Simon and various other books?

Milleran was equally devoted, and would be much more afflicted by his death. She would find it difficult, at forty-seven, to submit to a new kind of discipline and get used to another employer. Would she yield to the insistence of the publishers who would try to persuade her to write about his private life, so far as she knew it?

Those idiots were unaware that he'd never had any private life, and that at the age of eighty-two his entire store of human relations—he would not venture upon the words 'friendship' or 'affection'—consisted of the few people who lived at Les Ebergues.

Gabrielle, whose surname was Mitaine and who came from the Nièvre, had been married. Widowed at forty, left with one little boy, she had come into his service, and even now she went once a month to Villeneuve-Saint-Georges, to see her son, who was now a man of forty-nine, married, with three children, and worked as head steward in a restaurant-car on the Paris–Ventimiglia line.

Gabrielle was just turned seventy-two. Didn't the thought of death probably haunt her far more than it did her master?

As for young Marie, she would hardly remember the years she had spent working for the 'old boy'.

Perhaps it would be Madame Blanche who'd remember him longest, although he was more often gruff with her than with any of the others?

In point of fact there were just two people with whom he was on close terms, to whom he really mattered, two who were poles apart and offset each other, so to speak: Xavier Malate, who pursued him with a hatred as tenacious as unrequited love, and was clinging to life so as not to leave it before he did; Eveline, the sandy-haired girl in the Rue Saint-Louis, who, after losing sight of him for sixty years and more, was now sending him consecrated medals every year.

His daughter, his son-in-law and his grandson didn't count, they had never been part of his existence. They were outsiders, almost strangers.

As for Chalamont . . .

Was he really driving towards Le Havre at this moment? Was the Premier right to be going to bed, when he might perhaps have to get up again at any moment?

'If they come, what room shall I show them into?'

He hesitated for a second. He didn't want to leave Chalamont alone in the studies. This house was not a Ministry, there were no ushers and no waiting-room. When a visitor arrived, Milleran left him to wait in one of the book-lined rooms.

At least one visitor came almost every day. Usually only one was allowed, on Professor Fumet's advice, for despite his apparent coldness he exerted himself too much for his guests.

Milleran would say warningly to the newcomer, the moment she let him in:

'Don't keep the Premier for more than half an hour. The doctors say he mustn't tire himself.'

Those who arrived like this, or at least, those who gained admission, were statesmen from almost every country in the world, historians, university professors, students.

They all had questions to ask. Some of them, those who were writing a book about him, or a thesis, brought along imposing lists of specific questions.

Almost invariably he began the conversation grudgingly, finding it irksome, and seemed to withdraw into his shell.

Then, after a few minutes, he grew lively, and not every visitor noticed that he was now asking the questions instead of submitting to them.

Some people, when the half-hour was up, would conscientiously prepare to take their leave. Or Milleran would appear, silently, in the doorless opening between the two studies.

'We shan't be a minute . . .'

The minute would stretch out, the half-hour would become an hour, two hours, and sometimes one of these passing visitors, much to his surprise, would be asked to stay to lunch.

This exhausted the Premier, but it cheered him up, and when he was alone again with Milleran he would rub his hands gleefully.

'He came here to pick my brains, and I've been picking his!'

At other times he would enquire jokingly, before an appointment:

'Who am I to put on my act for today?'

There was some truth in the jest.

'I have to take care of my statue!' he had declared once, in a gay mood.

Without admitting it even to himself, he did take an interest in the impression he was to leave behind him, and there were occasions when the surly retorts for which he was celebrated were not entirely sincere, but formed part of his act. At such times he wouldn't have Milleran around, for he felt rather ashamed of himself in front of her, just as in front of Madame Blanche he felt ashamed of his weakened body.

'Do you need anything else, sir?'

The old man glanced round him. The bottle of water and the glass were in the usual place, so was the sleeping-tablet he took every night. The tiny, flat light was switched on. The oil lamp was ready to replace it if need be.

'Goodnight, sir. I hope I shan't have to disturb you before morning . . .'

The central light went out, Emile's footsteps drew further away, the kitchen door opened and closed again, and the room was left to silence and solitude, rendered almost tangible by contrast with the storm outside.

Since he had grown old, he scarcely felt the need of sleep, and for years he had lain in bed like this, for two or three hours every evening, quite still, his eyes shut, in a state of suspended animation.

It was not exactly insomnia. He felt neither annoyance nor impatience and it was by no means disagreeable. Far from it! During the day he sometimes thought with pleasure of the moment when he would thus be left to his own company.

Now he had taken to the little glowing disc it was still more pleasant, for its pinkish light helped, even through his closed eyelids, to create an atmosphere of secret, inner life.

At such times everything softened and mingled, the walls, the furniture, every gleam on which was known to him, the familiar objects he saw without looking at them, whose weight and substance even seemed palpable, the wind, the rain, the cry of the night bird or the sound of the waves at the cliff-foot, the creak of a shutter, the movements of somebody undressing in one of the bedrooms, everything, even to the stars twinkling in the silent sky, played its part in a symphony of which he, as he lay apparently inert, was the centre and to which his heart beat time.

Was this how death would come, taking him unawares on some not far-distant night? He knew that everybody in the household was expecting to find him, one morning, cold and stiff in his bed. He knew, too, that old people often did die in their sleep, unawares.

He sensed that Milleran's fear was rather that it would happen at nightfall, while he sat, dozing as it seemed, in his armchair, hands folded on his stomach.

In bed, too, he took that position, the attitude of a dead man prepared for his last journey, and he didn't do it on purpose, but because his body had gradually come to find it comfortable and natural.

Was that a portent?

He didn't believe in portents. He refused to believe in anything, even in the value of his life-work. At least ten times in the course of his life he had felt bound to make a superhuman effort, believing it to be indispensable, and for weeks, months, years he had led a hectic existence, pursuing his objective in the teeth of universal opposition.

On those occasions his energy, his vigorous metabolism, which used to amaze Professor Fumet, would spread not only to his immediate collaborators and to the Chamber, but to the whole country, to the invisible nation, which, after a period of mistrust and uncertainty, would be surprised to find itself following him blindly.

Because of this almost biological faculty, it was always at difficult, desperate moments that he was called in.

How often he had heard the same words uttered by a Head of State driven to the last ditch: 'Save France . . .' or: 'Save the Republic . . .' or perhaps: 'Save freedom . . .'

Every crisis had found him with faith unimpaired, for without that he could have done nothing, a faith so firm that he could sacrifice everything for it, not only himself but others, which had often been harder.

Cold sweat broke out on him even now, he still felt physically unwell, when he recalled his first action as Minister of the Interior; he saw himself, in a black, relentless setting of coal-mines and blast furnaces, holding a final parley, all alone between men on strike, whose leaders had turned them into rioters with hate-filled hearts, and the soldiers he had called in.

All the time he was trying to make himself heard, his voice had been drowned by jeering. Then, when he had stopped, a sombre and probably grotesque figure, his arms falling helplessly to his sides, there had been a long, vibrant silence, betraying irresolution, hesitation.

The two camps were watching each other closely, defying each other, and suddenly, as though at a signal—it was proved afterwards that there actually was a signal—bricks, cobblestones and scraps of cast-iron came flying through the air, while the soldiers' horses began to whinny and paw the ground.

He knew he would be blamed for his decision to the end of his life, that tomorrow, and for many a long day, most of his countrymen would curse him.

He knew, too, that it was necessary.

'Colonel, give the order to charge.'

A week later there were posters on the walls showing him with a hideous grin and with blood dripping from his hands, and the Government was overthrown.

But order had been preserved.

. Ten times, twenty times, he had withdrawn from the limelight in this way, having completed his task, and had sat, grumpy and silent, on the opposition benches, until he was needed again.

On one occasion some man or other, a nonentity, a kind of Xavier Malate, had come to ask him for a job to which he had no right, and on being refused, had put a bullet through his head in the waiting-room, as he left his office.

For some time now, on the advice of his doctors–his Three Musketeers–he had been taking a light sedative at bedtime, which didn't send him off to sleep at once, but brought on a gradual, delicious drowsiness to which he had grown accustomed.

Sometimes he didn't swallow it immediately, but gave himself the pleasure of prolonging, for half an hour or more, his clear-headed wakefulness, his conversation with himself. He had begun to hoard his life. He felt he had a whole lot of problems left to solve, not only with calm and composure, but in the completely dispassionate mood that he could achieve only at night, in bed.

This was the most secret of all his tasks, concerning no one except himself; he would have liked to finish it before taking his departure, leaving nothing obscure, looking everything straight in the face. Was it not to help himself in this that he had begun to read so many volumes of memoirs, confessions, private diaries?

Coming to the end of one of these books he was invariably disappointed, irritated, feeling the author had cheated. He wanted pure truth, truth in the raw, as he was trying to find it in his own case, even if it turned out to be sickening or repugnant.

But all the writers he had come across had *arranged* their material, he was far enough on in life to know that. All of them held, believed they held or pretended to hold, a truth, and he, despite his grim search for truth, had not found it.

Just now, hearing Chalamont's voice over the radio, he had been compelled to brace himself. Had he felt any doubt about being in the right when, in his office in the Hôtel Matignon, he had dictated that letter of infamy which his assistant, bathed in sweat so that the whole room stank of it, had taken down, to the last word, and signed?

If he had needed further proof than that submissiveness, he received more than enough in the next few days, when discreet investigation by the Ministry of Finance revealed the fact that Vollard's Bank had been behind the last-minute speculation which had cost the country thousands of millions of francs.

Vollard's Bank, in the Rue Vivienne, little known to the general public, was a private firm, working in close co-operation with one of the biggest financial concerns in Wall Street, and Etienne Vollard, its Chairman, was Chalamont's father-in-law.

Didn't the Prime Minister, aware of this family connection, bear a heavy responsibility for taking his assistant to the luncheon-party at Melun and insisting that he should be present?

Not for an instant had it occurred to him that Chalamont might betray him. In Ascain's garden, whether before the skittle game or afterwards, he had felt as sure of his assistant as of himself.

Looking at it more closely, his confidence had been in the mission rather than the individual. It all tied up with what he had said to Fumet, in the Avenue Friedland. He had felt certain that Chalamont had once and for all crossed the invisible frontier beyond which the individual man ceases to count, all that matters being the task he has set himself.

That day, the day of the dictation, the Premier's world had tottered and almost collapsed.

He remembered how, the letter written, his secretary had made for the door and clutched the handle. The idea that he might commit suicide, as the unsuccessful petitioner had done, had not occurred to him and would anyhow not have influenced him.

'Stay here!'

Chalamont still had his back turned, would not wheel round and face him, but he did stop where he was.

'It is impossible for me at present, and will be for some time, to accept your resignation or to kick you out.'

He spoke rapidly, in an undertone, jerking out the syllables.

'Imperative reasons make it impossible, unfortunately, for me to bring you into the courts, with your father-in-law and his accomplices.'

It was true that legal proceedings, with the resultant scandal, at such a moment, would have destroyed public confidence and led to even greater tragedy.

That, much more than the personal disappointment he had suffered, was the reason for his resentment against Chalamont. The latter knew that whatever might happen, they would have to shelter him, keep quiet, smother up the matter. Vollard's Bank had been gambling on a certainty, and Etienne Vollard, with his pearl-grey top-hat, would be seen tomorrow in the owners' stand at Longchamp or Auteuil, where he had horses running. If he won the President of the Republic's Stakes the week after next, the Head of the State could hardly avoid shaking hands with him and congratulating him!

'Until further notice you will carry out your duties as usual, and in public there will be no change in our relationship.'

This strain had gone on for a fortnight, though the Premier had been so busy that he could give little thought to his assistant.

When they were alone he avoided speaking to him, and if forced to do so, gave him his instructions in an impersonal tone.

On several occasions Chalamont had opened his mouth as though tormented by the need to say something, and at such times he would gaze pathetically at his chief.

He was no longer a boy, a young man, or even what is known as a budding politician. He was a mature man, his face already lined, and this made his humility disgusting rather than tragic.

How was he behaving in the evening, at dinner with his wife? What had he said to his father-in-law and his partners? What thoughts were revolving in his head when he got into his car and told the chauffeur, seated in front of him, to drive to the Hôtel Matignon?

One morning the Premier found on his desk a letter addressed in his principal secretary's writing, and as Chalamont was not there, he left it untouched until the man came in; then he picked up the unopened envelope, holding it between finger and thumb, and tore it into small pieces which he dropped into the waste-paper basket.

Now they were to have their last conversation. It was brief. Without deigning to glance at the other man, as he stood at the far side of the desk, he said:

'From now on you are relieved of your duties with me.'

Chalamont did not move, and his chief, picking up a file, added:

'I was forgetting . . . You can consider our acquaintance at an end . . . You may go now.'

He had opened the file and picked up the red pencil he used for making notes on documents.

'I said, you may go now!'

'You absolutely refuse to listen to me?'

'*Absolutely*. Leave the room, please.'

Lying in bed, he started, for he heard a noise outside. Straining his ears, he recognised the footsteps of one of the policemen, who was stamping his feet to warm them.

During the last week poor Cournot had appealed to all the political leaders in succession. Some had refused outright. Others had opened negotiations which had dragged on for a day or two. On those occasions arrangements had taken shape, names had been mentioned, lists of probable Ministers had even been put forward, but then each time the structure collapsed at the last moment and the party leaders again began to file through the Elysée.

But where others had failed, Chalamont had a chance of success. His group was a small one, but influential because of its position, half-way between the centre and the left, and it had the further advantage of not being committed to any hard-and-fast policy. Moreover, at a time when the different parties held divergent views about economic questions and about wages, the public found something reassuring about the Left Independents.

Among Chalamont's other trump cards were his adaptability, his skill in trimming his sails, and the fact that at the age of sixty he was beginning to count as one of the old guard at the Palais-Bourbon, where he could rely on long-standing friendships and on a network of connections built up by services rendered and minor compromises.

What would the Premier say now, then and there, if they came and asked him:

'Do you think Chalamont can find a way out of the crisis?'

Would he venture to keep silent, or would he frankly say what he thought:

'Yes.'

'Do you think that his coming to power would prevent the general strike that is threatening the country?'

There again, the answer was undoubtedly:

'Yes.'

When Chalamont had been his right hand he had twenty times helped him to settle disputes with the unions, and although he was the son-in-law of a banker, lived on the edge of the Bois and sat in the Chamber for the wealthiest arrondissement in Paris, he could handle the workers' representatives as no one else could do.

The Premier tried to halt his argument, which was making him feel uncomfortable, but he wanted to play fair.

'Is Chalamont cut out to be a statesman?'

He hesitated and refused to answer that question, but then it led to another:

'Which of today's politicians would make a better Prime Minister?'

Oh, very well! He could think of nobody! Perhaps he was the victim of old age, which ends by distorting even the soundest judgment? If so the newspapers seemed to have grown old with him, which was true to some extent, for many of them still had as their editors, or on their board of directors, men whom the Premier had known in those positions thirty or forty years ago.

However that might be, every time a government fell they, too, would allude to 'the great team', lamenting the dearth of men of the former mould, not merely in France but among the leaders of her allies.

Had the world really experienced an age of genuinely great men, of whom the Premier was the sole survivor except for Count Cornelio, the Italian, who was ending his days in a mental home outside Rome?

Again he listened, and this time it was Emile, in the kitchen, who had joggled the bench as he got up. He nearly rang for him, to tell him to go to bed. His thoughts had taken a disagreeable turn, and he was tempted to swallow the pill that lay beside the glass of water.

Outside, the Antifer light, off Etretat, and the lighthouse of Notre-Dame-du-Salut, above Fécamp, must be sweeping the lowering sky with their beams, which would meet almost directly over Les Ebergues.

There would be boats out at sea, with men, stiff in their oilskins, wearing sou'westers and rubber boots, standing on slippery decks and hauling at wet, cold tackle. In the village there would be at least one lighted window, that of the room where young Marie's mother was having her baby.

He hadn't had the curiosity, before getting into bed, to find out whether the telephone was working again. Most likely not. Telephone breakdowns always lasted longer than electricity failures.

It was eleven o'clock. Suppose Chalamont's car had broken down, too, somewhere by the side of the deserted road?

Had he really, during the last few years, been attempting to get back the confession he had signed in such dramatic circumstances?

Save for that paper, already yellowing, there was no evidence against him except the bare word of an old man whom many people now thought of as disappointed, embittered, with a lasting grudge against the world for not allowing him to end his career as President of the Republic.

Ascain had died in his fine house at Melun, to which he had retired after being heavily defeated at the polls, and where he had presumably spent his last years in playing skittles. He had left no memoirs. He had left no money either, and his two sons, one a vet and the other a traveller in patent medicines, had sold the property that had come down to them from their grandfather, the solicitor.

Ascain would bring no charge now. As for Lauzet-Duché, he had been the first to go, carried away by a stroke while making a speech at the end of a banquet in Brussels.

The others didn't know. In any case, how many still survived, even of the civil servants who had been merely on the outskirts of the affair, each knowing only one small part of it?

All that remained was a scrap of paper.

Was that what someone had been seeking at Les Ebergues for several months past? Up and down the house, in other books besides *Le Roi Pausole*, there were a hundred documents as dangerous to various people as that one was to Chalamont. Anyone who spends a great part of his life, particularly a life as long as his own, not only in the political arena but in the wings as well, is bound to witness any number of cowardly and disreputable actions.

And if someone were to ask him now:

'Do you know one single politician who in the entire course of his career has never . . .'

He cut his thought off short, as he used to cut off other people's words.

'No!'

He wasn't going to play that game. He'd been about to fall into his own trap, and with a brusque movement he propped himself on one elbow, seized the pill and swallowed it with a mouthful of water.

He needed sleep and wanted to get to sleep quickly, without thinking any longer.

The last picture to drift more or less coherently through his mind was that of a man, whose features he could not distinguish, lying in a hospital bed. This was supposed to be Xavier Malate, and while a nun was changing him, handling him like a baby, he was tittering and explaining that they wouldn't get him to die out of turn.

'Augustin first!' he said with a wink.

Chapter Five

Without needing to open his eyes he knew it was still night, and that the little flat lamp was shedding a faint light in one corner of the room, like a tiny moon. He also knew that something unusual was happening, though he couldn't have said what, something missing, a *lack*, rather than something too much, and when he had roused up sufficiently he realised that what had disturbed him was the silence surrounding the house after the storm that had been raging for days, as though, all at once, the universe had ceased to vibrate.

There was a ray of light under the door into the study, he could see it through the tiny slit between his eyelids. To see the time by his alarm-clock he would have had to turn his head, and he didn't feel like moving.

He listened. There was someone moving in the next room, without excessive caution, not furtively, and he recognised the sound of logs being dumped on the hearth and the familiar crackle of the kindling. When the smell of the burning wood began to reach his nostrils, not before, he called out:

'Emile!'

The chauffeur opened the door; he had not yet shaved or put on his white jacket, and the sleepless night had clouded his eyes.

'Did you call, sir?'

'What time is it?'

'A few minutes past five. It suddenly turned cold, late in the night, and now it feels like frost. So I'm starting the fire. Did I wake you?'

'No.'

After a short silence, Emile remarked:

'So you see, nobody came, after all.'

The old man repeated:

'Nobody came, you're right.'

'Would you like your tea straight away?'

From his bed he could watch the flames leaping in the study fireplace.

'Yes, please.'

Then, as Emile reached the door, he called him back:

'Open the shutters first, if you don't mind.'

Just as, in the evening, he liked to cloak himself in solitude, in the morning he was eager to resume contact with life, eager in an anxious, almost frightened way.

Day was still far off, there was no sign of dawn, and yet the night was not black but white, and a light, pale-coloured vapour, which was actually fog, had time to float into the room while Emile leant out to push back the shutters.

'The cold's as sharp as mid-winter, and later on, with this damp rising as though the ground were a sponge, we shan't be able to see as far as the garden gate.'

During this brief contact with the outer world they had heard the foghorn wailing, muted, in the distance. At some point during the night the wind had fallen to a flat calm, but ordinary life, in abeyance during the tempest of the last few days, had not yet got under way again and the countryside still lay, as it were, in limbo.

'I'll bring your tea in five minutes.'

Coffee had been forbidden, and now he was only allowed weak tea. Of all the privations he had to endure, this was the only one he found painful, and he sometimes went into the kitchen while Gabrielle was getting breakfast for the staff, just for a whiff of the coffee they were to drink.

Chalamont hadn't come, but it was too soon to think about that, nothing definite being known as yet. But not to have received the visit he had regarded as almost certain was a disappointment, though still vague and unacknowledged. He felt ill at ease, anxious, as though he, too, suddenly lacked something, as though there were something missing in life.

Sitting up in bed, he drank his tea, while Emile prepared his linen and his suit, for he was always fully dressed first thing in the morning, and very few people could boast of having seen him with his toilet incomplete. Even a dressing-gown, he considered, belonged to the privacy of the bedroom, and he never wore one in his study.

On his way to take a shower—he had had to give up baths—he glanced out of the window and saw the glowing tip of a cigarette close to the house.

'Is that still Aillevard?'

'No. Rougé took over from him just before two o'clock, about the time when the weather changed, and I gave him a cup of coffee a while ago.'

The house was starting to stir again. There was a light in Gabrielle's room—she'd be coming down to start her fire—and in Milleran's as well. Water was running through a pipe. A cow mooed in the nearest byre and another answered it from further off, more faintly. While the storm lasted not a cow had been heard.

He took his shower, tepid and very short, as he had been advised; after which Emile helped him to dry himself and get into his clothes. Emile smelt strongly of cold cigarette, especially in the early morning. It made the Premier feel queasy, but he didn't like to ask the man to stop smoking.

'If you don't need me I'll go up quickly to change and shave.'

Usually this, too, was an hour he enjoyed. In summer it was already light and he could see children taking cattle to pasture in the fields along the cliff-top. Closer to him the house would be gradually waking up and he would stroll about idly, without impatience, in the four low-ceilinged rooms, going from one shelf to another, pausing, moving on, halting on the threshold to sniff the smell of damp soil and grass which, only quite recently, had gone back to being the same as in his childhood.

In autumn and winter he watched the slow dawn breaking, and there was nearly always a thin mist rising from the ground, in a sheet of unequal density, pierced with holes through which one sometimes glimpsed the church belfry.

Today the dawn was colourless, sketched with white gouache and charcoal, and only the whiter glow of the thickening fog showed that the light was strengthening.

The others were in the kitchen, eating. The tree near the front door was growing visible in misty outline, with its trunk that leaned eastward because of the sea-wind and its leafless branches which all stretched eastward too; then the dim, ghostly figure of the policeman on guard came into view beside it. He seemed very far away, in another world, and even his footsteps were inaudible, as though the fog was muffling sounds as well as blurring forms.

Now and again the Premier looked at the time, then at the little white wireless set on his desk. Before the moment had come to switch it on, he saw young Marie advancing through the fog, growing gradually taller and clearer, her red jersey striking the only note of colour in the landscape.

Tiny drops of moisture must be clinging to her untidy hair, as it did to every blade of grass she walked over. When she noisily opened the kitchen door, exclamations could be heard, laughter from Emile. Her mother must have had the baby, but he didn't call her to make sure.

He was counting the minutes now, and he turned on the wireless too soon, had to put up with a stupid popular song followed by the whole of the weather report, to which he paid no attention. Thursday, November 4th. Feast of St Charles. Paris market prices. Fruit and vegetables . . .

'And here is our first news bulletin. Home news. Paris. As we anticipated yesterday evening, there was considerable activity all night in the Boulevard Suchet, where Monsieur Philippe Chalamont, entrusted by the President of the Republic with the task of forming a Cabinet on a multi-party basis, was visited by a number of prominent politicians belonging to various parties. Leaving the Deputy for the sixteenth arrondissement's flat at about four o'clock this morning, Monsieur Ernest Grouchard, Leader of the Radical Party, whose visit had immediately succeeded that of the Leader of the Socialist Group, declared his satisfaction at the way the negotiations were proceeding. It is thought that Monsieur Chalamont will go to the Elysée fairly early in the morning, to give the Head of the State his definite reply, as promised. Marseilles. The Mélina, a liner belonging to the Messageries Maritimes, on board which . . .'

He switched off, without noticing that Milleran had come into the study. His reaction was a gloomy amazement, a sensation of emptiness not unlike what he had felt earlier when the noise of the storm had suddenly given out.

He had been waiting for Chalamont, almost certain he would come. Had he been secretly hoping for the visit? He didn't know. He didn't want to know, especially not just now.

While he had been imagining his former subordinate driving through the rain and wind, and had even gone so far as to think he might have had a breakdown on the way, Chalamont had been in his flat in the Boulevard Suchet, coldly playing the game, receiving the political leaders, one by one.

It was so unexpected, so monstrous, that he could not shake off his stupefaction, and at one moment he put the tip of his first finger to the corner of his eye, which was slightly moist.

Realising that his secretary was standing in front of him, he asked her, as though collecting his thoughts from a great distance and resentful of her intrusion:

'What is it?'

'I wanted to ask whether I should ring up Evreux right away.'

He took a little time to remember, while Milleran went on:

'A hospital is open night and day, so perhaps there's no need to wait till nine o'clock?'

He still sat sluggishly in his armchair, and his set, vacant stare began to worry Milleran, though she knew from experience that she must pretend not to notice it. Simply to break the silence, she announced:

'Young Marie has a little sister. That's the fifth girl in the family.'

'Leave me alone for a while, if you don't mind.'

'May I go into my office?'

'No. Somewhere else. Wherever you like.'

There remained one explanation, on which he pinned his hopes: that Chalamont's confession had vanished. To check this theory, he was sending Milleran away, and as soon as she was in the kitchen he went to the furthest bookcase and, with a feverish hand, pulled out *Le Roi Pausole* in its heavy cardboard case.

At that moment he was hoping . . .

But the second folder opened of its own accord at page 40, and there lay the sheet of paper with the heading of the Prime Minister's office, ironical, looking no more important than an old love-letter or a four-leaved clover forgotten between the pages of a book. And indeed it was of very slight importance, despite its dramatic statement and the care he had taken of it, for it had not prevented anything.

'*I, the undersigned, Philippe Chalamont . . .*'

With a gesture of impatience such as he had rarely indulged in during his life, and of which he was at once ashamed, he hurled the book to the ground, so that he suffered the humiliation of being obliged to get down and pick up the scattered parts, the loose engravings, the original drawings.

Because of his ex-secretary, he was reduced to watching the door, for fear someone might suddenly come in and find him on all fours on the floor. And he'd look even more ridiculous if his leg suddenly played him one of its tricks while he was in this position!

Milleran waited in the kitchen, unaware of what was going on, listening hard, and it was at least ten minutes before the bell recalled her to the study.

The Premier had gone back to the Louis-Philippe armchair. His strained manner had disappeared, replaced by a calm that she found uncomfortable because it was obviously artificial, like his voice, which had an unaccustomed, unnaturally suave note when he said:

'You may telephone now.'

He cared nothing for Malate just then, but it was important for life to go on as usual, for the little everyday events to follow one another in the expected order. That was a kind of moral hygiene and the only way of keeping a cool head.

If the paper had disappeared from the Pierre Louys book he would have understood Chalamont's behaviour, accepted it, perhaps even approved it, and it would not have affected him personally.

With the document still in his hands, things were different. That meant that his former secretary had reached the cynical conclusion that the way lay open, that the obstacle that had delayed him on his way up the political ladder had in his opinion ceased to exist.

The old man was still living, of course, on the top of some cliff in Normandy, but the scrap of paper he had brandished for so long had lost its value as a scarecrow, just as the ink of the writing on it was fading.

Chalamont was behaving as though the Premier were dead.

He had made his decision during the night, with his eyes open, knowing what he was about, weighing the risks, foreseeing every eventuality.

It had not occurred to him to ring up. The breakdown was nothing to do with his silence. He had not set out for Les Ebergues, had sent nobody, this time, to plead his cause or negotiate on his behalf.

'Hello? Is that Evreux hospital?'

Was the Premier really going to bother about that maniac who had been haunting him for so many years? Had he come down to that? He was tempted to rush into the next room, take the telephone away from his secretary and ring off. Everything was annoying him, including the fog, too motionless and stupid, which was pressing against the window and making the outside world look unearthly.

'Yes . . . You say he's . . . I can't quite hear you, mademoiselle . . . Yes . . . Yes . . . That's better . . . You don't know how long he's been there? . . . I understand . . . I shall probably ring you again later . . . Thank you . . .'

'Well, so what?' he snarled, when Milleran came in, looking embarrassed.

'Dr Jaquemont, or Jeaumont, I couldn't get the name clearly, is operating on him now . . . He went into the theatre at a quarter past seven . . . They expect it to take a long time . . . It seems that . . .'

'Why did you say you'd ring back?'

'I don't know . . . I thought you'd want to know . . .'

He grunted:

'You aren't here to think!'

It was all too idiotic. Here he was, worrying about the fate of a man who meant nothing to him, who ought to be shut up in a lunatic asylum, for no earthly reason except that the fellow had been assuring him for forty years:

'I'll be at your funeral.'

Now it was Malate who was on the operating-table, at the age of eighty-three—for he was a year older than his former schoolfellow—with a cancer of the throat that two previous operations had done nothing to cure. Whether he died or whether he didn't, what difference would it make? What did it matter?

'Tell Emile to take the car and go to Etretat for the papers.'

'I think the barber's arriving,' she announced, looking out of the window and seeing a man on a bicycle, distorted by the fog to an apocalyptic monster.

'Let him come in, then.'

The barber, Fernand Bavet, who was also a saddler, came every morning to shave him, for the Premier was among the survivors of a period when men did not shave themselves, and he had always refused to do it, just as he had refused to learn to drive a car.

Bavet was a florid, full-blooded man with a throaty voice.

'Well, sir, what do you think of this pea-souper? One can't see three yards in front of one's nose, and I nearly ran into one of your guardian angels . . .'

Most barbers' hands smell of cigarette smoke, which is unpleasant enough. Bavet's smelt of fresh leather as well, of newly slaughtered animals, and his breath stank of *calvados*.

As the Premier grew older he became more sensitive to smells, and was disgusted by things he never noticed in the old days, as though his body, as it dried up, was being purified by a kind of disincarnation.

'Now tell me, you who're in the know, are we going to have a government, after all?'

Bavet's good humour met with no response and he lapsed into resigned silence, a little vexed, all the same, for he was fond of telling his café cronies:

'The old man? I shave him every day and with me he's just like anybody else, I speak as straight to him as I would to one of you . . .'

Still, everybody has good days and bad ones, haven't they? His job finished, the barber put away his instruments, bowed to his customer and went off to the kitchen, where Gabrielle always gave him a drink. The engine of the car was running; Emile was warming it up before starting out to fetch the papers from Etretat, since the grocer's at Bénouville only took one local daily, printed at Le Havre, and two or three Paris papers which arrived very late.

A three-minute news bulletin was being broadcast every hour, and at nine o'clock the Premier listened again, but only to hear a repetition of what he knew already.

Thereupon, turning to Milleran, who was opening the letters, he enquired, so impatiently that she jumped:

'Well? Aren't you going to ring up Evreux?'

'I'm very sorry . . .'

She hadn't dared, not quite knowing, as things were, what she should do and what she shouldn't.

'Get me Evreux, mademoiselle . . . Yes, the same number as before . . . A priority call, yes . . .'

For each successive government had had the courtesy to leave him the right to priority over the telephone, as though he were still in office. Would that favour continue under a Chalamont government?

Why did the day still seem so empty? It was no different from any other, and yet he felt as though he were going round and round in space, like a fish in a bowl, opening and shutting his mouth soundlessly, just like one.

On other days the hours were never too long. In a few minutes, when she had finished opening the envelopes and setting aside bills, prospectuses and the invitations some people persisted in sending him, Milleran would bring him the letters to read, and in the usual way he enjoyed this; there was an element of surprise that he appreciated, and it didn't bore him to say what answers should be sent, or to dictate a few letters when he thought it worth while.

In the last few days he hadn't cursed the storm, which ought to have annoyed him, but now he was glowering at the foggy scene outside as though suspecting that nature was perfidiously scheming to smother him.

He felt some difficulty in breathing. In a quarter of an hour Madame Blanche would arrive to give him his injection, and because of yesterday's outing, which she had tried to prevent, and his two sneezes, which she hadn't failed to notice, she would watch him distrustfully, suspecting that he was concealing something from her.

He couldn't stand women who looked at one as though one were a child caught telling a fib. Madame Blanche had threatened him with a cold, and she'd be watching for the symptoms of a cold. Wasn't it often from a cold that old people died when they had no other illness?

'Hello? Yes . . . What did you say? . . . No, don't disturb him . . . Thank you, mademoiselle . . .'

'Disturb whom?'

'The surgeon.'

'Why?'

'I was talking to the matron and she thought you might want to hear details . . .'

'Details of what?'

Before she had time to reply, he went on sharply:

'He's dead, isn't that it?'

'Yes . . . During the operation . . .'

With a rudeness in which he seldom indulged, he exclaimed:

'What the hell do you suppose I care about that? Wait! Send a line to the director of the hospital to say they're not to chuck him into a pauper's grave. He's to have a decent funeral, but no more. Ask what it will cost and make out a cheque for me to sign.'

Did he feel relieved that Xavier Malate should have been the first to go, in spite of his bragging? His old schoolfellow had been mistaken. He'd clung to life for no purpose. His last chance now was for their two funerals to take place on the same day, and the Premier was determined that shouldn't happen.

There was only one person left now who had known the Rue Saint-Louis in his time, the little red-headed girl of those days. Was she going to die too, and leave him to be the last?

For quite a long time, on his way to the *lycée*, he used to gaze with an agreeable agitation at the chalky-white sign with its black letters, including an N written backwards, which composed the words: 'Ernest Archambault, Ironmonger'. There was no actual shop. From the front the house looked just like others in the district, with lace-curtained windows and ferns in copper pots. At the end of a dank alley-way one could see the yard and a glass-roofed workshop from which the clang of hammers emerged, audible as far as the *lycée*.

In the classroom Xavier Malate had sat two rows away from him, near the stove, which it was his privilege to stoke up. Between them sat a boy who was taller than the others, better dressed, with a rather affected manner, who lived in a château outside the town and sometimes came to school on horseback, wearing riding boots, carrying a crop, and followed by a servant mounted on a heavier animal. He was a Count, whose name he had forgotten like so many others.

Who was the present occupant of the house where he had been born and lived until he was seventeen? Had it been pulled down? In his time the bricks had been almost black, there had been a green-painted door and a brass plate announcing his father's surgery hours.

He still had, put away somewhere, a box full of old photos he'd always meant to sort out. There was one of his father, who'd had a sandy moustache and a little pointed beard like Henri III, and he could still remember how he had smelt of sour wine.

He had scarcely known his mother, for she had died when he was five and was still, apparently, a chubby little boy as fat as butter. An aunt had arrived from the country to look after him and his elder sister, and later on his sister, still almost a child, with short skirts and pigtails, had run the house with the help of one maid, who for some mysterious reason was always changing.

In actual fact nobody had brought him up. He had brought himself up. He could still recall the names of certain streets which had perhaps influenced his career.

The Rue Dupont-de-l'Eure, for instance. He even remembered the dates, for he had always had a memory for figures, including, later on, for telephone numbers. *1767–1855. Patriot, Politician renowned for his integrity.*

Rue Bayet (1760–1794).

A patriot, too, and a Girondist Deputy during the Revolution. But it was not on the scaffold that he had died at the age of thirty-four. He had committed suicide at Bordeaux, which he had chosen as his exile after being deserted by his party.

Rue Jules-Janin. Writer and critic, Member of the Académie Française . . .

At the age of fifteen, because of Janin, he had dreamt of the Académie Française, and had almost chosen literature as his career.

Rue Gambetta (1838–1882) . . .

Come to think of it, he might have met Gambetta if he'd lived in Paris instead of at Evreux.

Rue Jean-Jaurès (1859–1914) . . .

As a schoolboy he hadn't known that one day he would sit in the Chamber as Jaurès' colleague and would witness his assassination.

He didn't admit it in his memoirs, not even in the secret ones: but right from boyhood he had known he, too, would one day have his street, even his statue in public places.

In those days he had felt nothing more than pitying condescension for his father, who spent his time, day and night, in all weathers, hastening from one patient to another, carrying his heavy, shapeless bag of instruments, or in his surgery, with its frosted glass windows, seeing an endless stream of poor patients who filled the waiting-room to overflowing and were often to be found sitting on the stairs.

He resented, as a piece of humbug, the way his father carried on in practice although he didn't believe in medicine, and it was not until much later, after his father's death, that he began to reflect on something he'd been fond of saying:

'I do my patients as much good as other doctors, who believe in their vocation, and I run less risk of doing them harm.'

So his father had not been the uncouth, slightly bohemian, rather drunken fellow that he had imagined, in whom, as a child, he had refused to take any interest.

At the age of twenty he had returned to Evreux for his sister's marriage to one of the clerks at the Town Hall. Had he seen her three times after that, before she died of peritonitis when she was getting on for seventy? He hadn't gone to her funeral, and he seemed to remember that he'd been on an official visit to South America at the time. He had nephews and nieces with children of their own, but he'd never felt any desire to get to know them.

Why had Milleran rushed off to the kitchen as soon as she had seen Madame Blanche approaching the house? To tell her he didn't seem quite himself, or that Xavier Malate's death had upset him?

In the first place, it wasn't true. And in the second place, as he always said, he loathed the sidelong glances they gave him, as though they were constantly expecting . . .

Expecting what?

When the nurse came in, carrying the little bowl with the syringe, he looked her straight in the eye and forestalled her enquiries by declaring:

'I feel perfectly fit and I haven't a cold. Give me my injection quickly and leave me in peace.'

It cost him an effort every morning, in his bedroom, the door of which he always closed behind her, to let down his trousers in front of her eyes and expose his livid thigh.

'The left side today . . .'

Left and right, on alternate days.

'Have you taken your temperature?'

'I have not, and I don't intend to.'

The telephone rang. Milleran knocked on the door; nothing in the world would have induced her to open it, for she knew the reception she would get.

'What is it?'

'A journalist who insists on speaking to you . . .'

'Tell him I'm busy.'

'He says you'll remember his name . . .'

'What is his name?'

'Loubat.'

It was the squeaky-voiced reporter who had thrown Chalamont off his stride the previous evening, in the courtyard of the Elysée, by asking whether he meant to spend the night on the road.

'What am I to tell him?'

'That I have nothing to say.'

Madame Blanche was asking:

'Did I hurt you?'

'No.'

It was no business of hers. Having pulled up his trousers he opened the door, to hear his secretary saying into the telephone:

'I assure you I did tell him . . . No . . . I can't . . . You don't know him . . . What?'

Feeling his presence behind her, she started.

'What does he want?'

'Just a minute, please . . .' she said again into the telephone.

Then, putting her hand over the mouthpiece, she explained:

'He insists on my asking you a question.'

'What question?'

'Whether it's true that you and Chalamont are reconciled.'

She spoke again into the mouthpiece:

'Just a moment . . . No . . . I asked you to hold on . . .'

The Premier stood motionless, as though wondering what line to take, and all at once he grabbed the receiver and rapped out, before hanging up with a jerk:

'Go and ask him yourself. I wish you good day.'

Then, turning to Milleran, he enquired, in a voice almost as disagreeable as the journalist's:

'Do you know why he rang up this morning?'

'No.'

'To make sure I was still alive.'

She tried to laugh, as though he were joking.

'I mean it!'

'But . . .'

'I know what I am talking about, *Mademoiselle* Milleran.'

It was only on particular occasions that he addressed her in that way, with sarcastic emphasis. He went on, enunciating each syllable separately:

'For him, this morning, I ought logically to be dead. And he has expert knowledge!'

What did it matter whether she understood or not! He was not talking to her but to himself, or perhaps to History, and what he said was the literal truth.

If he were alive, really alive, it would be unthinkable for Chalamont . . .

'Turn on the wireless, please. It's ten o'clock. The President will be beginning his audiences at the Elysée. You'll see!'

She didn't know what she was to see. Bewildered, she was looking anxiously at Madame Blanche, who was going off to the kitchen with her battered bowl.

'*At the fourth pip it will be . . .*'

He had picked up the little clock and was putting it exactly right.

'*And here is the latest news. We have just been informed that Monsieur Philippe Chalamont, who was called to the Elysée yesterday afternoon, has paid a second visit to the President of the Republic. He has officially undertaken to form a Cabinet on a wide coalition basis, whose main lines are already known, and it is hoped, in well-informed circles, that the list of Ministers will be announced before the end of the afternoon . . .*'

She didn't know whether to switch off or not.

'Leave it, for heaven's sake. Don't you understand it's not finished yet?'

He was right. After a pause, a crackling of paper, the announcer began again:

'*A few names have already been mentioned . . .*'

She was watching him as, pale and tense, with angry eyes, he glared at her and at the wireless set, as though ready to burst into rage at any moment.

'*. . . Monsieur Etienne Blanche, Radical Socialist, is expected to be Keeper of the Seals . . .*'

An old hand who'd been in two of the Premier's Cabinets, once at the Board of Trade and once, already, at the Ministry of Justice.

'*. . . Monsieur Jean-Louis Lajoux, Secretary of the Socialist Party, Minister of State . . .*'

He had been starting his career when the Premier left the scene, and though he vaguely remembered him, it was only as a background figure.

'*. . . Ferdinand Jusset, another Socialist . . .*'

Another old hand, about whom there was a note, slipped into a volume of La Bruyère.

'*And then Monsieur Vabre, Monsieur Montois and . . .*'

'That'll do!' he said curtly.

He very nearly added:

'Get me Paris on the telephone . . .'

There were at least ten numbers on the tip of his tongue, he knew them by heart, and he need only ring one of them in order to sink the ministry that was being formed.

He was on the point of doing it, and the effort to contain himself, remain worthy of himself, was so great that he felt an attack coming on. His fingers, his knees began to shake, and as usual at such moments his nerves refused to obey him; the mechanism suddenly began to race at increasing speed.

Without a word he went hastily into his bedroom, hoping Milleran had not noticed anything and wouldn't go and fetch Madame Blanche. With feverish haste he snatched out of a drawer two sedative pills, prescribed for him to take at such moments.

In ten minutes, at most, the drug would take effect and he would relax, gradually becoming languid and a little vague, as though after a sleepless night.

Meanwhile he stood leaning against the wall, near the square window with its small panes, watching young Marie as, in her red jersey, she stood in the fog, more translucent now, but still thick, hanging out washing on a line slung between two apple-trees.

He was tempted to open the window and call to her, say no matter what, for it was too stupid to expect washing to dry in this sodden atmosphere.

But why interfere? It didn't concern him.

Was there anything left that did concern him?

All he had to do was to wait, trying to keep as calm as possible, until the drug took effect.

Even Emile wasn't back from Etretat, where Gabrielle must have given him a whole lot of errands.

'Hush! . . . One . . . two . . . three . . . four . . .'

Standing motionless, he was counting his pulse, as though his life were still of importance.

Chapter Six

The instructions given by Gaffé and Dr Lalinde, with the approval of Professor Fumet, were to take one pill, not two, at a moment of crisis, and another three hours later if need be. He had deliberately doubled the dose, partly because he was in a hurry to calm his panic-stricken nerves, but chiefly as a protest, in defiance.

The result was that before the usual ten minutes were up he began to see black spots before his eyes, flickering so that he felt dizzy, and that once seated in his armchair, in which he had hastily taken refuge, he felt torpor creeping over him.

If he had been an ordinary man he would have surrendered to it with relief, but they wouldn't let him. At the slightest change in his habits or behaviour they would begin by summoning the young doctor from Le Havre, who in his turn would send for the man from Rouen, and once they were together the pair would shift the responsibility to Fumet, by telephone.

Did Fumet, in his turn, report to somebody higher up, while the three police inspectors were informing their own boss of the Premier's off-moments, as though he were a kind of sacred animal?

The idea made him cross, illogically, for a few minutes earlier he had been moping about being forgotten in Paris, almost in a rage because somebody was ignoring his veto.

When Milleran came in with the letters she had sorted, he was looking surly, his small eyes were tired but aggressive, and as she was about to put down the letters on his desk he stopped her with a gesture.

'Read them to me.'

He had not the energy to read them himself, for his eyelids were heavy and his brain dulled.

He began by asking:

'Where's Madame Blanche?'

'In the waiting-room.'

This was the name given to the library furthest from his bedroom, the one that led to the front hall and was, indeed, used as a waiting-room when necessary. If Madame Blanche was settled there, with a book or some magazines, it was because she wasn't pleased with the state she had found him in and expected him to be needing her, unless it was Milleran who had said something to her.

What was the use of bothering about it, mulling over the same old suspicions and resentments? He said again, resignedly:

'Read them to me.'

The public believed that he had a great deal of correspondence, as he used to when he was Prime Minister, but in actual fact the postman usually brought a mere handful of letters every morning, except on the days following the publication of an article about him in some magazine or newspaper with a big circulation.

From time to time somebody would come bothering him for this purpose, from one country or another, invariably asking the same questions and taking the same photos, and he knew so well where they would ask him to stand that he would get into position even before the photographer opened his mouth.

The resulting correspondence was almost identical each time. He would be asked for his autograph, often on cards specially cut to be filed in a collection, or on postcard photographs of himself such as were on sale in stationers' shops.

From Oslo a girl of sixteen, writing poor French in a careful hand, sent him a list of questions, with blank spaces for the answers, explaining that her teacher had asked her to write an essay of not less than six pages on the Premier's career.

The questions began like those on a passport application form:

'*Place of birth:*

'*Date of birth:*

'*Education:*'

She could have found those particulars in any encyclopaedia, even in her own country.

'*What made you choose politics as your career?*

'*Which statesman did you admire most when you began your career?*

'*Did you hold certain theories when you were very young, and have any of them altered as time went on?*

'*If so, why?*

'*What recreations have you gone in for?*

'*Which of them do you still keep up?*

'*Are you satisfied with your life?*'

Milleran had been surprised when he had sent a serious reply to the girl, who in a few years would doubtless have settled down as a wife and mother.

An old couple—younger than he was, though!—ingenuously requested him to help them end their days in the way they had always dreamt of, by making them a present of a cottage in the country, not too far from Bergerac, where the husband had just been pensioned off from his job as a postman.

A lot of people supposed him to be rich. Humble people wouldn't have understood how a man who had led the country so often and for such long periods, living in palatial government houses and surrounded by official pomp, could be left with no private fortune at the age of eighty-two.

Yet so it was, and the Chamber had voted him a pension without his asking for it. The government also paid Madame Blanche's salary and, since he had left Paris, Emile's wages.

Were they afraid it might be said later on that France had left one of her great men to die in poverty?

So even at Les Ebergues, after retiring from public life, he was not completely independent, he remained a kind of civil servant.

'After all, there are funds for preserving historic monuments!' he sometimes said jokingly.

At other times he would point out that owners of premises scheduled as of historic interest were forbidden by law to make the slightest structural alteration in them. Didn't he come under the same heading? Had he any right to reveal himself in a light different from that in which the history books displayed him?

The care taken in this respect was such that three policemen took turns outside his door, and he felt convinced that his telephone was regularly tapped, his correspondence, especially letters from well-known foreigners, opened before being sent on to him. Or did Milleran take it upon herself to report to the authorities about what he wrote and whom he saw?

> Dear Sir,
>   I am at present writing a large-scale work on a man with whom you were well acquainted, and venture . . .

He was not jealous, although there were many letters of that kind. For some twenty years there had been five of them, known as the Grand Old Men, each representing his own country more or less uninterruptedly, and between them they had controlled world policy.

They used to meet periodically, in one continent or another, nearly always in some well-known spa, for conferences to which journalists and photographers would flock in hundreds.

The slightest word uttered by one of them, the faintest frown on emerging from a meeting, would be reported in Press communiqués with banner headlines in all the newspapers.

Sometimes they had quarrels, followed by spectacular reconciliations, often staged merely for their own amusement; some of their talks, whose outcome the world awaited in breathless suspense, had turned only on trivial subjects.

The Englishman, who in private was the most humorous and cynical of the five, would look at his watch on arriving.

'How long are we supposed to argue before agreeing on this communiqué?'

And he would produce from his pocket a ready-drafted announcement.

'If only they were decent enough to leave us some cards, we could have a game of bridge . . .'

They all belonged to the same generation, except the American, who had died young, at sixty-seven, before any of the others. They had summed one another up so precisely that each knew the true worth of all the others, and even their little eccentricities.

'Gentlemen, with my country about to go to the polls, it is imperative for me today to put my foot in it, as our journalist friends will report presently. So we will announce that I banged on the table and that my obstinacy has brought the conference to a deadlock.'

There was nearly always a garden surrounding the luxury hotels that were taken over on these occasions, and as soon as one of the five ventured into it he would be set upon by reporters and photographers.

All five were accustomed to power and fame, and yet the varying shares of publicity they received had now and then caused sulks and sub-acid comments from one to another; these white-haired statesmen, depicted in profile on their countries' stamps, descended on such occasions to behaving like a bunch of actors.

In the margins of his book the Premier had noted some traits of this kind, not all of them, only the most typical, especially those with a certain human quality.

And now, when, except for Cornelio, who had lost his wits, he was the last survivor of the group, he still felt a slight twinge when somebody wrote to ask him for information about one of them, and not about himself!

In London, New York, Berlin, Stockholm, all over the world, people were still writing books about him and about the others, and he sometimes caught himself feeling tempted to make up the whole of each of them!

'I'll answer that tomorrow. Remind me. You may go on reading.'

An unknown man wanted his help in obtaining a post in the prison administration.

> I come from Evreux, like yourself, and when I was young my grandfather often talked to me about you, for you lived in the same street and he knew you well . . .

Milleran was watching him furtively, wondering whether he had dozed off, but his white, smooth-skinned hand, which now had the unquestionable beauty of an inanimate object, signed to her to continue.

> Dear Sir,
>   I have applied everywhere, I have knocked on every door, and you are my last hope. The whole world acknowledges your benevolence and your deep understanding of human nature, and I am confident that you will understand me, you who . . .

A professional sponger.

'Next one!'

'That's all, sir.'

'Didn't I have an appointment for today?'

'Yes, the Spanish general was coming, but he sent a message to say he's ill with influenza at San Sebastian . . .'

Speaking of generals, there was one who seemed likely to outlive them all, and of whom the Premier thought with some envy and a touch of annoyance. He was ninety-three years old, but he turned up every Thursday, alert and inclined to be waggish, at the meetings of the Académie Française, of which he was a member. A month ago there had been an article about him in a weekly paper, including a photo where he appeared in shorts, bare-chested, doing exercises in his garden under the indulgent eye of his wife, who sat on a bench in the background as though watching a child at play.

Was it really worth it?

At Evreux, at this very moment, someone was laying out Xavier Malate, whose worries were at an end. He was through with everything. And he, who had been haunted by the idea of burial, would have nobody to walk behind his hearse, unless some old maid automatically turned up to follow it, as occasionally happens.

For a long time the Premier had paid no attention to the deaths of people in his circle, most of whom were his elders. He considered they had had their day, even those who died at fifty.

Then, when men hardly older than himself began to die as well, he had sometimes felt a certain selfish satisfaction, if not downright pleasure.

Someone else had been taken, and he was spared!

But the ranks of his own generation had gradually thinned, the Five Grand Old Men had begun to drop out, and on each occasion nowadays he caught himself counting, without grief but feeling vaguely apprehensive, as though it began to occur to him that his turn might really come one day.

He had never attended funerals, except on the very rare occasions when he was obliged to represent the government of the day. He had avoided death-chambers, every kind of ceremonial death-watch, not because they depressed him, but because he considered that kind of pomp to be in bad taste.

He would simply send in his card, or have himself represented by a member of his staff, and to his staff, too, he left the task of drawing up letters or telegrams of sympathy.

But Xavier Malate's death today had made a different impression on him, though he couldn't say exactly in what way. The drug had slowed down his mental processes, as though he were half asleep, and his thoughts were at one remove from reality.

For instance, he kept seeing the face of an old woman with thin hair and very long teeth. Heaven knew what had conjured it up, and there was no reason why she should resemble Eveline Archambault, whom he hadn't seen since she was just a little girl.

All the same he felt certain it was she, as she looked nowadays, and her face wore a curiously sweet expression, tinged with silent reproach.

She had doubtless prayed all her life that he might find religion before he died, as though words said to a priest could make any difference to anything. Like him she was seated in an armchair, an old rug over her knees, and a kind of stale smell emanated from her.

In the end he realised that the rug was the one that used to be wrapped round his mother's legs in the last weeks of her life. But what about the rest?

But for the fear of seeming ridiculous, he would have told Milleran to ring up Evreux again, the town hall, for instance, to enquire about Eveline, to find out whether she were still alive, if she were ill, if she had all she wanted.

He felt tired. He knew it was the natural effect of the drug he'd taken, but it gave him a depressingly helpless sensation, and if he'd had the right, he would have gone to bed.

A neighbour's cow, escaped from the byre, was running round the orchard, knocking against the boughs of the apple-trees, pursued by a little boy armed with a stick.

That little boy would still be living long after he himself was dead. All those around him would outlive him, as would most of the earth's present population.

Would Emile tell the truth about Les Ebergues, later on? Perhaps so, for he liked vulgar stories and people would give him bigger tips if he made them laugh.

He had not been the first to use the cliff-top farm as a country house; before him a lawyer from Rouen—dead too now!—used to bring his family there for the holidays. The Premier had only made the additions required for his own convenience, such as the tunnel that now linked what were originally two separate buildings.

Names were of no importance to him, so he had not altered the one the property went by when he bought it.

The local people had told him that the word '*ébergues*' referred to portions of the cod-fish prepared for use as bait, and as Fécamp was a cod-fishers' port and fishing was the mainstay of the whole coast, he had been satisfied with that explanation. Probably the skipper of a fishing-smack or the owner of a small fleet had lived in the house at one time?

But one day when Emile was tearing away the ivy that had crept over the parapet of an old well, he had brought to light an inscription, roughly cut in the stone:

Les Ebernes

1701

The Premier had happened to mention this to the schoolmaster, who was also Secretary of the District Council and sometimes came to borrow books from him. The schoolmaster had had the curiosity to look up the old land-survey maps, and had found the property marked on them by the same name as that on the well.

However, nobody could tell him what '*ébernes*' were, until at last he found the explanation in the big *Littré* dictionary:

'*Eberner:* to wipe excrement off a child.

'*Eberneuses:* women who wipe excrement off children.'

What kind of women had once lived in the house and been given the nickname that had stuck to the place afterwards? And what later and more prudish occupant had given that cunning twist to the spelling of the name?

He had mentioned that, too, in his secret memoirs, but would they ever be published? He was not sure whether he still wanted them to be. When the future of the country was at stake he had always been prompt to take the most fateful decisions, with no fear of committing an error, but, faced with the question of what he should reveal about his own life, he became hesitant and was tormented by scruples.

The picture the world had formed of him was cut and dried, it took no account of the changes wrought by time, it was rudimentary and often downright false, and his legend included one particular chapter he had always tried to correct, but in vain.

It had appeared in the scandal-mongering rags of the day, and later in a national newspaper, under the heading: 'A Gentleman and his Tailor'.

For thirty years his opponents had made the most of it during every election campaign. Only the title had altered from time to time, the variants including 'Tradesman's Entrance' and 'The Countess's Chambermaid'.

The chambermaid and the Countess, for they had been real people, were both dead now, but the 'Gentleman', who was about the same age as the Premier, still survived and could be seen every afternoon at the races, upright as ever, but with creaky joints.

This was the notorious Créveaux case, which had kept the Premier out of several successive Cabinets, just as another man had been barred from office for ten years by a certain letter hidden between the pages of *Le Roi Pausole*.

The difference was that he himself had been innocent, at least of the charge brought against him. He was hardly more than forty, and had just joined a Cabinet for the first time–as Minister of Public Works, in which capacity he was about to be visited by Xavier Malate.

Wasn't it odd the way things linked up through time and space, wreathing together mockingly, as it were? Could it have been on the actual day of Xavier's visit that . . .

Anyway, that didn't matter. In those days Marthe de Créveaux, Marthe de C. . . ., as the spiteful columnists used to call her, held regular receptions in her private mansion in the Rue de la Faisanderie, where it was her ambition to bring together everybody who was anybody in Paris diplomatic and political circles, admitting no one else except a few writers, provided they were members or prospective members of the Académie Française.

At that time the new Minister had never set foot in her house, for he went about very little even in those days, and was regarded as an uncouth, solitary being, so that the caricaturists were beginning to depict him in the guise of a bear.

Was it this reputation that had impelled Marthe de Crévaux to get hold of him, or was it because shrewd observers were beginning to foretell that he would soon be someone to be reckoned with?

The only daughter of a rich Bordeaux merchant, she had acquired a title by marrying the Comte de Créveaux, and thus launched herself in society as well. After that, Créveaux had resumed his bachelor habits, and there were days when Marthe, in her ground-floor dining-room, was entertaining a covey of ministers and ambassadors to luncheon, while her husband, in the second-floor suite he called his bachelor flat, was surrounded by a gay bunch of actresses and dramatists.

The Minister of Public Works had not been more than twice to the house in the Rue de la Faisanderie before it was rumoured that the Countess had taken him in hand, just as she had chosen to play Egeria to two or three political men before him. There was some truth in the rumour. She was familiar with a world of which the future Prime Minister knew very little, and she had decided to polish him up.

Was she beautiful, as the newspapers declared? After hearing her talked about, one was surprised, on seeing her for the first time, to discover that she was a small, helpless-seeming woman, looking much younger than one had expected, with nothing forceful or self-willed in her manner.

Though she spent her whole time launching and protecting men she found interesting, each of them felt he wanted to protect her from the others and from herself.

He wasn't certain he'd ever been fooled. Frankly, he had known what he wanted in those days, and he'd known she could help him to get it. Besides, he was flattered at being selected, when he was no more than a promising beginner, and even the luxurious atmosphere of her house had played its part.

Within a fortnight people were growing accustomed to speaking of them in one breath, and whenever the Comte de Créveaux met the young minister he would hold out his hand with ironical emphasis and exclaim:

'Our very dear friend . . .'

Contrary to what had been supposed, and was still believed by some people who claimed to be in the know, physical attraction had played very little part in their relationship, and though Marthe, whose sexual needs were small, had given it to be understood that they were passionately in love, they had very seldom been in bed together.

Her great idea was to give him lessons in social behaviour, and she had even set about teaching him how to dress.

It was embarrassing to remember all this, at the age of eighty-two, when one was living in a little house on the Normandy coast where death would be one of the next visitors.

Because of this memory and a few others, he would have refused to have his life over again, if it had been offered to him.

For weeks and months had he not studied the attitudes and the manner she taught him, which she declared to be those befitting the perfect statesman?

And he, whose style of dress was correct and restrained, but with no attempt at smartness, had finally yielded to Marthe's insistence and paid a visit to the most fashionable tailor of the day, in the Faubourg Saint-Honoré.

'He's the only possible man, darling, unless you go to London for your clothes. He's my husband's tailor, by the way.'

Nowadays he wondered whether he wouldn't prefer to have some dishonourable action on his conscience, as Chalamont had, rather than such a humiliating memory.

He could see the tailor, patronising and ironical, his own reflection in the mirror, with one coat-sleeve not yet tacked in place . . .

Hadn't he believed it mattered, if only for a short time, and hadn't he gone to the point of changing the shape of his hats, the colour of his ties and gloves?

He'd taken to riding in the Bois, too, very early each morning.

The people who addressed him as 'Minister' had no suspicion that he was behaving like a boy in calf-love. Furthermore, in Marthe de Créveaux's house there was a young woman who was to get very much into the news because of him, and her name was Juliette.

She acted as companion as well as lady's maid, for Marthe couldn't bear to be alone and had to have someone with her even when she went shopping or to have a dress tried on, with the car following her from door to door. It was Juliette, too, who kept the list of her appointments, reminded her about them, answered the telephone, paid for small purchases in shops.

She came of a good middle-class family, dressed in trim navy or black, and looked every inch the convent-educated girl.

Was she a nymphomaniac even in those days? Probably, and he had probably not been the first to discover the fact.

On various occasions she had been alone on the ground floor with the future Prime Minister, while Marthe was getting dressed, and she had played her game so well that one fine day, tried beyond his strength, he had taken her, on a sofa in the drawing-room.

It became a habit, a necessity, and for her there could be no pleasure without danger, which she deliberately carried to the furthest limit, devising the most perilous situations.

The inevitable happened: Marthe de Créveaux caught them, and wounded pride, instead of prompting her to keep the secret, led to a scene of tragi-comic fury that brought all the servants running.

Thrown out of the house together with Juliette, the Premier had had no choice but to take a room for her in a quiet hotel, for he couldn't take her to the Ministry and would not have her in his flat on the Quai Malaquais.

The next day a minor newspaper had given a fairly accurate description of the incident, in a few lines, winding up with what purported to be the Comtesse de Créveaux's comment:

'When I think that I knocked off the man's corners and even bought his clothes for him!'

Had she really said that? It was possible, the words sounded just like her. She had not foreseen that they were to dog him right through his career and add greatly to his difficulties.

For the journalists, delighted with the windfall, had made an investigation, and the result had been the famous 'Gentleman and his Tailor' article.

It asserted that Marthe de C. . . . had sent the young minister to her husband's tailor, whose address was given, and that it was Créveaux who, in due course, had paid the bill.

As white-faced as Chalamont had been when he wrote that letter, the Minister of Public Works had seized the telephone, rung up the tailor. He could recall nothing more agonising than his feelings as he had listened to the voice at the other end of the line.

It was true! The journalist had not made it up. The tailor, his voice polite but unruffled, offered his apologies: he had believed . . . he had thought . . .

'So you took me for a pimp?' he had shouted into the telephone.

'Oh, Minister, I assure you that . . .'

In the ordinary way he waited to pay his tailor, like any other shop-keeper, till the bill was sent in. It was barely three months since he had been to the Faubourg Saint-Honoré, and he had felt no surprise at not hearing from the man. After all, didn't some firms, especially in the luxury trade, send in their accounts only once a year?

Did Marthe de Créveaux pay in this way for the clothes of every man she took under her wing? He had never known because he had never seen her again, though she had written to him 'to get rid of a misunderstanding and make peace' when he had become Prime Minister.

Her end had been sad, for she, who had been so feverishly active, was bedridden with paralysis for five years, and when at last she died she was so wasted that she weighed no more than an eight-year-old girl.

Juliette had not remained on the minister's hands for long, taken over by a journalist who introduced her to the newspaper world, where she soon made good on her own merits.

She had interviewed her ex-lover on several occasions, and had never failed to be astonished because he took no advantage of his renewed opportunity, as most men on whom she made a professional call no doubt did.

Her death had been more sudden than that of her former mistress, but no less sensational, for she was among the passengers on board a plane that crashed in flames in Holland on its way to Stockholm.

As for himself, he had sent the tailor a cheque, of course, but hundreds of thousands of people were still convinced that . . .

And after all, didn't it come to much the same thing?

He didn't like the man he had been in those days. He didn't like himself as a little boy or as an adolescent, for that matter.

And nowadays the play-acting of the Five Grand Old Men, the airs they had put on, seemed to him to have been ridiculous.

Was all his indulgence reserved for the old man he had grown into, who was gradually drying up, like the Countess, until he'd become nothing but parchment stretched over a skeleton, with a brain spinning emptily in his bony skull?

For what did he think about all day long, while people crept like mice about the great man whose slightest sneeze was turned into a drama?

About himself! Himself! Always about himself!

He prowled round and round himself, sometimes with satisfaction, but usually discontented and bitter.

He had already told his story once, his story as the public wanted to have it, and no mere marginal notes scribbled later on would suffice to show him in his true light.

It was all false, because it was all described from a false angle.

The corrective notes were also false, being nothing but a shot at countering the legend.

As for the real man, as he had been and as he now was . . .

He stared uncomprehendingly at Gabrielle, who was standing in front of him, perhaps forgetting that she came every day at this time to tell him the same thing:

'Lunch is ready, sir.'

It was Gabrielle's privilege to make this announcement, and she would not have left young Marie to do it for anything in the world. But surely, at the age of seventy, she should have got beyond such childishness?

The fog pressing against the dining-room windows was so dense that it seemed almost like a snowy landscape beneath a heavy, unbroken, motionless expanse of cloud, such as one sometimes sees in winter, when earth and sky are indivisible.

Young Marie had at last replaced her red jersey by a black dress and a white apron. She had been taught to hold the old man's chair while he bent forward, and then give it a gentle push, and this frightened her; she was always afraid of taking too long and letting him sit down on nothing.

'It seems you have another little sister?'

'Yes, sir.'

'Is your mother pleased?'

'I don't know.'

What was the use? Why utter meaningless words? The menu was almost as monotonous as the evening one. Half a grapefruit, for the vitamins, followed by three ounces of grilled meat, which had to be cut up for him now that his false teeth had got so loose, two potatoes and some boiled greens. Dessert would be an apple, a pear, or a few grapes, of which he wasn't allowed to eat the skins.

Would Chalamont, in Paris, follow tradition by inviting his new colleagues to a fashionable restaurant, where the main lines of his Cabinet's policy would be laid down over dessert?

In his own day the choice had almost always been a private room at Foyot's, near the Senate, or at Lapérouse's.

Men who'd often been in the same team would be there, swapping memories of previous Cabinets, old stagers would invariably be offered the same inglorious posts, and there were nearly always some new-comers, still ignorant of the rites, who would keep an uneasy eye on the old-timers.

Even the voices, the clatter of forks and the tinkle of glasses seemed to have a special resonance at those luncheons, and the head waiters, who knew all the guests, busied around with conspiratorial smiles, playing their part in the distribution of portfolios.

Different, but no less typical, was the noise made by the reporters and Press photographers lunching in the main restaurant on the ground floor, who were just as conscious as the group upstairs of their role in the day's events.

Those two hours, in point of fact, were the most agreeable in the life of a government. Later in the afternoon, after the Ministers had been presented at the Elysée and been photographed on the steps with the President in their midst, his face wearing the inevitable smile, the time came to draft the ministerial statement, and then the difficulties began, with endless wrangling about each word, each comma.

Each of them had family matters and practical problems to consider as well. Were they to move into the various Ministries without waiting for the vote of confidence in the Chamber? Would there be room for the children? What furniture of one's own should one take along, and what dresses would one's wife need for official receptions?

He had been through this experience on twenty-two occasions, his biographers had made the tally for him, and on eight of them he had been the central figure.

Today it was Chalamont's turn, and suddenly something unexpected happened: remembering the bustle in Foyot's dining-rooms, the Premier tried to visualise his one-time subordinate in that setting; but although he had spent more time with that man than with anyone else, been in closer contact with him than with any other, he was surprised to find himself unable to recall his features.

Yet it was only two days since he'd seen his photograph in the papers.

Chalamont had altered in the last ten years, as was to be expected. But his memory didn't even present him with the Chalamont of ten years ago. It conjured up a young man of twenty-five whose expression, though already determined, was anxious, to whom he remembered saying at the time:

'You'll have to learn to control your feelings.'

'I know, chief. I assure you I'm trying hard.'

He had always called him 'Chief', adopting the term by which a great surgeon or doctor is addressed by his juniors. He was no sentimentalist. He was cold and cynical. All the same his cheeks would sometimes flush, all of a sudden, with a bright colour that his usual pallor made all the more remarkable.

Did Chalamont, too, look back over his life now and then, or was he, at sixty, still too young for that? Would he be willing to have his time over again, and if so . . .

The Premier remembered precisely in what circumstances his former secretary could not keep from blushing, despite his self-control. It was whenever he felt, rightly or wrongly, that someone was trying to make him feel small.

He had formed an opinion about his own character which he believed to be accurate, and which may indeed have been so. He clung to this, and at the least threat to his self-confidence the blood would instantly rush to his head.

He never argued, never protested. He made no attempt to retort, but maintained a cautious silence; yet his flaming cheeks alone betrayed his feelings.

In the Prime Minister's office in the Hôtel Matignon the blood had not risen to his cheeks; on the contrary, it had seemed to drain out of his whole body.

'Are you tired?' young Marie enquired suddenly, arriving from worlds away.

He looked at the hand he had just brushed across his face, then he gazed round him, as though awaking from sleep. His plate was hardly touched.

'Perhaps I am,' he confessed in an undertone, so as not to be heard in the kitchen.

He made as if to rise, whereupon young Marie rushed to pull out his chair, and he looked so bent and feeble that she took hold of his arm.

'Thank you . . . I'm not hungry any longer . . .'

She didn't know whether to follow him or not. She watched him as he moved away, shoulders bowed, long arms dangling, while he went with a wavering step into the passage leading to his study. She must have thought he might be going to fall, for she held herself ready to leap after him.

But he didn't even need to lean against the wall, and when at last he disappeared young Marie shrugged her shoulders, turned to clear the table.

When she went back to the kitchen with the dishes and plates, Milleran asked anxiously:

'What's happening?'

'I don't know. I think he's gone to bed. He looks tired.'

But the Premier was not in bed, and when Milleran tiptoed into the study she found him asleep, with half-open mouth, in the Louis-Philippe armchair. His lower lip was slightly pendulous, as though from great weariness, or disgust.

Chapter Seven

This time he really had gone to sleep, for he didn't hear Madame Blanche come when Milleran fetched her, nor was he aware that she was standing beside him, watch in hand, feeling his pulse with a light finger. Neither did he know that she had telephoned to the doctor, in lowered tones, or that while she was about it Milleran sat on a chair facing him, gazing steadily at him with a grave, sad face.

Then the women signed to each other and whispered together. Milleran made way for Madame Blanche and went to her office.

More than half an hour went by like this, in a silence broken only by the regular ticking of the little clock, and at last the sound of a motor was heard, and a car drew up. Emile had said something to somebody, his voice hushed, too.

There was a kind of impromptu ballet going on around him, for now Madame Blanche, in her turn, made way for Dr Gaffé, who, after taking the patient's pulse again, sat down facing him, as erect and formal as in a waiting-room.

At one moment Emile had come in and put a log back into the fire, and the Premier had had no suspicion of all these furtive comings and goings. Yet he would have sworn that he had all along been aware of sitting supine in his armchair, with his lips parted and his breath whistling through them.

Had there really been a temporary separation between his mind and his body, the latter sitting inert while the former, still agile, flew in circles like a bird, sometimes into unknown worlds, sometimes through a universe not far removed from reality?

How could he have known, for instance, that when the effort became too exhausting he knitted his bushy eyebrows, or that he occasionally groaned at his helplessness? Yet later on they confirmed his impression that he had frowned and groaned. So what about it?

His own conviction was that he had got far enough outside himself to return and take a look at the almost inert carcase which was beginning to seem alien to him, and for which he felt more repulsion than pity.

During those two hours he had seen a vast number of faces, and had gone in pursuit of some of them, wondering what they were doing at his bedside. Others were familiar, but all the same he couldn't understand how they got there, the presence of the station-master of a little town in Southern France for example, where he had spent a brief holiday several years in succession.

Why was he here today? The old man knew the station-master had died long ago. But that little girl, whose hair had been arranged in ringlets and tied with a wide tricolour ribbon so that she could present him with a bouquet? Did her being here mean that she was dead too?

That was what had been worrying him most, while Gaffé waited, watching him, not daring to light a cigarette. He was trying to disentangle those among all these people who were still alive and those who were already in the other world, and his impression was that the frontier between life and death was hard to trace, that perhaps, even, there wasn't one?

Was that the great secret? He knew that during those two hours, when he had been intensely alive despite his body's inertia, he had a dozen times been on the point of solving all problems.

What made the job so difficult and disheartening was that he could never remain for long on the same plane. Perhaps his mind was not nimble enough, or lacked balance? Or could it be a question of weight? Or of habit? He was going up and down, sometimes gradually, sometimes by leaps and bounds, coming out into different worlds, some of which were fairly close to what is called reality, fairly familiar, while others were so remote and unlike that neither people nor objects were recognisable.

He had seen Marthe de Créveaux again. But she wasn't at all as he remembered her. It was not only that, as the papers had said when she died, she weighed no more than a little girl, but she looked like one, she had a little girl's innocence, and she was stark naked.

At the same time he blamed himself for remembering her only in order to clear his conscience, not so much from the business of the tailor as from the affair of the Legion of Honour. For it wasn't true that he had never shown partiality. That was a legend he had built up, like the others, the legend of the upright, uncompromising politician, doing his duty without fear or favour.

All the same, he had given the Legion of Honour to one of Marthe's protégés, an obscure country squire whose only title to such distinction was his ownership of a pack of hounds.

And a few days later hadn't he given an official reception to an African potentate who must be propitiated for degrading practical reasons, though his proper place was in prison?

He had never asked pardon of anyone, and he was not going to begin at his time of life. Who but himself had any right to judge him?

He went on struggling. Of the faces that approached, glancing at him as thronging passers-by, in a street, cast a glance at the victim of an accident and go on their way, most were vacant-eyed, and he kept trying to stop one and ask whether this were not a procession of the dead that he was witnessing.

If so he too must be dead. And yet not quite, for they refused to treat him as one of themselves.

What was he, then, following his zigzag flight like some clumsy night-bird?

Very well! If it was because of Chalamont that they were cold-shouldering him, he would leave Chalamont in peace. He had understood. He'd understood long ago, even perhaps at the Hôtel Matignon, but he had refused to show pity then, because he believed he had no right to do so.

He hadn't shown himself any pity, either. Why should he have shown any to his assistant?

'Time to pay, gentlemen!'

A voice shouted the words, like the attendant in a cheap dance-hall who calls out in the intervals:

'Pass along the money, please!'

Had he been indignant when Chalamont had informed him that, after careful consideration, he had decided that his career would benefit if he were to have an *established position*, in other words if he married a woman with enough money to enable him to live in some style?

He'd been so far from indignant that he had attended the wedding as one of the witnesses.

Everything derives from everything. Everything counts. Everything helps. Everything changes. There is no waste. The day the wedding took place, at Saint-Honoré-d'Eylau, the die was cast and the Premier ought to have known it.

The moment had come when Chalamont had been summoned to pay for his situation, to repay his wife and his father-in-law, failing which he would be *displaced* in their esteem . . .

Just as Marthe de Créveaux's lover had had to bestow a decoration on a stag-hunter.

All this was on the lowest level, where he kept returning and getting bogged down. But in the course of the two hours he had made other discoveries, explored regions where he felt so much a stranger that he was not even certain what he had seen there.

He had felt cold, and that, too, was an attested fact, for the doctor was to tell him, later, that he had shivered more than once. Now it was his meeting with his father and Xavier Malate that had made him feel cold. He couldn't remember where he had met them, or what had passed between them, but he had seen them, and what had particularly struck him was that they had seemed to be on such cordial terms.

He had not expected that. It bothered him. It upset all his notions of human values. And why did the two of them, who had nothing in common except the fact of being dead, look at him with one and the same expression? It wasn't pity. That word had been withdrawn from circulation. Neither was it indifference. It was . . . – the expression was inaccurate and bombastic, but he couldn't find a better–it was a *sublime serenity*.

In his father's case that might be all right. He was willing to concede the point. But that Malate should be endowed with sublime serenity, merely because he had died under the surgeon's knife! . . .

He didn't know what would happen next, and wondered whether he was going to wake up in the Louis-Philippe armchair at Les Ebergues. He was not sure whether he wanted to, but all the same he felt a little anxious.

They had caught him unawares, giving him no time to prepare for his departure, and it seemed to him that he had a great many things to do, a lot of questions to settle.

It was a pain in his right arm that proved to him that he was still in the body, and he opened his eyes, to discover, without surprise, that facing him sat Dr Gaffé, who felt called upon to give him an encouraging smile.

'Had a good sleep, sir?'

Night was falling, and the doctor, at last able to move, got up to turn on the light. Milleran stirred in her office next door, walked quietly out to the first room, doubtless to tell Madame Blanche that he was awake now.

'So you see,' said the old man gravely, 'it appears that I'm not dead.'

Why did Gaffé think fit to protest at this, when he was expecting it to happen from one day to the next, and there was no reason why it shouldn't be today?

The Premier had not been joking, he had merely taken note of a fact.

'Did you suddenly feel unwell during luncheon?'

He almost began to put on his usual act, replying in ambiguous or boorish monosyllables. But why bother?

'For no sufficient reason I lost my temper, so I took two sedative pills.'

'Two!' exclaimed the doctor, relieved.

'Two. Now the effect has worn off.'

Except that he was left with a nasty taste in his mouth, stiff limbs.

'Let's see your blood-pressure . . . No! Don't get up . . . Madame Blanche will help me to take your coat off . . .'

He submitted meekly and didn't ask about his blood-pressure, the figure of which, for once, the doctor forgot, or preferred not, to tell him. In addition to this, Gaffé paraded his stethoscope over his chest and back, with the dedicated air he took on at such times.

'Cough, please . . . Again . . . Good . . . A deep breath . . .'

He had never been so biddable, and neither the doctor nor Madame Blanche could guess why—neither could Milleran, pricking up her ears in the next-door room.

The truth was that in his secret heart he had decided that it was all over. He couldn't have said at what precise moment this feeling of detachment had come over him, but it must have been during the strange journey of exploration he had made while his carcase lolled motionless and he was temporarily released from it.

It hadn't been painful, much less agonising: he felt rather like a bubble rising to the surface of the water all of a sudden, for no apparent reason, and bursting, to mingle with the atmosphere. An easy separation, bringing him a relief so great that he could have cried out in delight, like a child watching the ascent of a red balloon:

'Oh!'

He would have liked to joke with them, in gratitude for their attentiveness and all they were doing for him, but they wouldn't understand and would probably have thought he was light-headed.

He had never been light-headed. So he had no standard of comparison, but he felt convinced that never in his life had he been so rational as at present.

'I suppose,' said Gaffé quietly, after a glance at Madame Blanche, 'that if I asked you to go to bed you'd dislike the idea? Simply as a precaution, of course. You yourself admit that you've been under a strain just lately . . .'

He had said nothing of the kind. Milleran must have told the doctor that, while he was supposed to be asleep . . .

'There's frost in the air. It's going to be a very cold night, and there's no doubt that twenty-four hours''rest in bed . . .'

He thought it over, as a straightforward suggestion, and responded with an equally straightforward one:

'Suppose we put it off till this evening?'

In point of fact he was tempted to do as Gaffé wanted, but he had something else to see to first. And both the doctor and Madame Blanche would doubtless have been astonished if they could have read his thoughts.

He was eager to get away from the lot of them, Milleran, Emile, Gabrielle, young Marie. He was tired. He'd done his share and now he was giving up. Had it been possible, he would have asked them to put him into clean pyjamas and lay him down in his bed, close to the shutters against the fog outside, put out the lights, except the tiny moon-like disc of the nightlight.

Then, with the sheets up to his chin, curled upon utter, self-contained silence, in a solitude broken only by his weakening pulse, he would ebb slowly away, a little melancholy but quite without bitterness, and very rapidly, released both from shame and pride, he would settle his last accounts.

'*I beg your pardon . . .*'

Whose? That, as he had discovered, did not matter. There was no need of any name.

'*I did my best, with all the strength of a man and all a man's weaknesses . . .*'

Would he see around him the attentive faces of Xavier Malate, Philippe Chalamont, his father, and others as well, those of Eveline Archambault, Marthe, the station-master and the little girl with the bouquet?

'*I realise it's nothing to be proud of . . .*'

They gave him no encouragement. He didn't need encouragement. He was all alone. The others had been merely witnesses, and he had learnt that witnesses have no right to set up as judges. Neither had he. No one had . . .

'*Forgive me . . .*'

No sound of any kind, except the blood still pumping jerkily through his veins, and a crackling of logs in the next room.

He would keep his eyes open to the very last.

Chapter Eight

'Madame Blanche, would you mind going to the kitchen and waiting until I call? I have things to see to with Milleran. I promise not to take long, and not to get excited.'

Gaffé had granted him his respite and given him an injection to pep him up, saying he would come back about seven o'clock.

'To be quite frank, as you've always asked me to be with you,' he had said, 'there's a slight wheezing sound in your bronchial tubes. But I don't think it's anything to worry about, for your temperature and pulse don't suggest that there's any infection so far.'

They were not accustomed to finding him so meek, and it made them uneasy, but what could he do to avoid worrying them? Whatever line he took it would not stop their exchange of anxious glances. There was no understanding, any longer, between him and them. Or rather, he still understood them, but they couldn't follow him any more.

'Will you come with me, Milleran, so that we can have a grand cleaning-up?'

She followed him, bewildered, into the first office, where he did not bend down straight away to the bottom shelf, but took out Volume III of *Vidal-Lablache,* where there was a document of disastrous import to a man who had been in past Cabinets and would doubtless be in future ones.

Still holding this, he put back the book and went on to another and yet another, plucking out now a letter, now a scrap of paper that had been crumpled, as its creases still showed.

'Why have you turned so pale, Milleran? You look as though you were going to faint.'

Yet he wasn't looking at her. He simply knew. Then, turning at last to the Pierre Louys volume, he went on again in an encouraging tone with no shade of blame or anger:

'You knew all this, didn't you?'

Thereupon, as he straightened up again, adding Chalamont's confession to the other papers in his hand, she burst into tears, took a few steps towards the door as though to run away into the darkness, changed her mind, came back to fling herself at his feet and tried to grab his hand.

'Forgive me, sir . . . I didn't want to, I swear I didn't . . .'

This immediately restored his peremptory, authoritative manner, for he could never abide tears, bursts of emotion, any more than he could tolerate certain kinds of rudeness or silliness. He wouldn't have any woman writhing on the ground, kissing his hand and dropping tears on it.

He commanded her:

'Get up!'

Then, his tone already gentler:

'Steady, Milleran . . . There's nothing to be excited about . . .'

'I assure you, sir, that . . .'

'You did as you were told to do, and quite right too. *By whom?*'

He was in a hurry for her to recover herself, to emerge from this melodramatic atmosphere, and in order to help her he went to the length of patting her shoulder, an unusual gesture with him.

'Who was it?'

'Superintendent Dolomieu.'

'When?'

She hesitated.

'When I was still in Paris?'

'No. About two years ago. I had a day off and went to Etretat, and he was there, waiting for me. He said it was part of his official duty, he was giving me instructions on behalf of the government . . .'

'The government was quite right and I should probably have done the same myself. You were asked to copy the papers?'

She shook her head, and another sob jerked out. There was still a shiny, damp track down one of her cheeks.

'No. Inspector Aillevard has a photostat machine in his room . . .'

'So you used to give him the papers and he returned them to you next day?'

'Sometimes only an hour later. Not one is missing. I took care he gave them all back to me.'

She couldn't understand the Premier's attitude, couldn't manage to believe in it. Instead of being angry or downcast, as she would have expected, he showed a calm she had seldom known him to display, and his face was lit by a smile.

One would have thought he found it a good game, which amused him more than anyone.

'As things are now, it won't matter much if we destroy these papers, will it?'

She was trying to smile too, almost succeeding, for there was something detached and airy about him which was infectious. This was the first time he had ever seemed to regard her as an equal, so that their relationship took on a personal touch.

'Perhaps it would be better, all the same, for the originals to be got rid of . . .'

He showed her the Chalamont letter.

'Did you find that?'

She nodded, not without a shade of price.

'Funny thing! If Chalamont has chosen an inquisitive fellow as his Minister of the Interior, and if the chap happens to send for his chief's file . . .'

He knew Dolomieu, who had been under his orders and was Director of General Information at the Rue des Saussaies. Would he take advantage of Chalamont's access to power to get himself appointed Director of the Sûrete Nationale, or even Prefect of Police?

What did it matter, after all!

'Since you know where these papers are, come and help me . . .'

In the first room she only missed two, whose places of concealment he pointed out to her with childish satisfaction.

'So you hadn't found those?'

In the second room, she had found all his hiding-places; in his study, she had only missed one.

If the policeman on duty was watching them through the window he must have been surprised to see the Premier and his secretary bending over the hearth, throwing in papers that burnt with tall, roaring flames.

'We shall have to burn the books as well.'

'What books?'

So she hadn't thought of the American edition of his memoirs, and she was astounded to see its pages black with notes, probably wondering when he could have written them without her knowledge.

'No point in burning the bindings, they're too thick, and we mustn't put too many pages at a time into the fire.'

It was a long job tearing out the pages a few at a time and stirring them with the tongs to help them burn. While she was squatting down and attending to it, he stood behind her.

'Madame Blanche as well?' he asked, knowing she would understand.

She did understand, gave an affirmative gesture, added, after a moment's reflection:

'She couldn't have done otherwise . . .'

He hesitated to name anyone else.

'Emile?'

'From the very beginning.'

In other words, Emile had already been reporting on his behaviour to the Rue des Saussaies when he was still a Cabinet Minister, then Prime Minister.

Hadn't he always known it at the back of his mind, he who had considered it his duty to have other people spied on?

Or had he been ingenuous? Cunning? Needing to feel that he was an exception, that the rules didn't apply to him?

'And Gabrielle?'

'That's not the same thing. In Paris, when you were away from home, an inspector came now and then to ask her questions . . .'

He had been standing for too long, and he felt the need to sit down, in his place, his armchair, in his usual position. It was as comforting as getting home and slipping on one's old clothes. The tall, dancing flames were roasting him down one side and on one cheek, but it would soon be over. As his elbow knocked against the silent wireless set, where it stood on the desk, unneeded from now on, he said:

'Take this too . . .'

She misunderstood him, or pretended to misunderstand, so as to do her bit to cheer up a situation that was depressing her:

'You want to burn the wireless?'

He gave a faint chuckle.

'Give it to whoever you like.'

'May I keep it myself . . .?'

She stopped herself just in time from adding:

'. . . as a souvenir.'

He had understood, but he didn't scowl. He had never seemed so gentle in all his life, and he was like one of those old men who are to be seen in the country or the suburbs, sitting in sunny doorways, gazing for hours on end at a tree or some drifting clouds.

'I'm sure Gaffé will have telephoned to Dr Lalinde.'

Now he had confided in her, she was ready to reciprocate.

'Yes. He said he was going to.'

'Was he very frightened when he found me asleep?'

'He didn't know you'd taken the medicine.'

'What about you?'

She didn't answer, and he realised he mustn't begin to pester them with questions. They, too, had done what they could, like Xavier, like Chalamont, like that swine Dolomieu.

What did the word 'swine' remind him of?

'*That swine . . .*'

He couldn't recall it, and yet when the word had been spoken it had seemed to be of considerable importance.

There was a name on the tip of his tongue, but why make the effort? Now he'd come full circle, that kind of thing had ceased to concern him.

It was a strange impression, agreeable and a little terrifying, not needing to think any longer.

A few more flames, a few pages writhing and then falling to ashes between the tongs, and all threads would be severed.

Gabrielle could come to announce that the Premier's dinner was waiting for him. The Premier would follow her obediently, would sit down on the chair offered by young Marie, with her perpetual dread of his sitting down on air. He wasn't hungry. He would eat, to please them. He would answer the questions put to him by Gaffé when he came, perhaps accompanied by Lalinde, around seven o'clock, and he'd allow his pulse to be taken yet again, let himself be put to bed as he'd promised.

He wouldn't be sarcastic with any of them, not even ironical with Lalinde, who was always a shade pompous.

He would be unfailingly patient from now on, only taking care not to cry out, not to call for help, when the moment arrived. He meant to see to that by himself, decently, with discretion.

Whether it came tomorrow, in a week or in a year, he would wait, and when his glance fell on Sully's *Memoirs*, he murmured:

'You can put that book away.'

What was the sense of reading other people's recollections any longer? It didn't interest him, neither did any other book, and they could have burnt the whole library for all he cared.

'There we are!'

There had been nothing dramatic about it, when all was said and done, and he was almost pleased with himself. There was even a gleam of mischief in his grey eyes as he thought about his household's reactions.

Seeing him so calm and gentle, wouldn't they shake their heads sadly and whisper behind his back:

'Have you noticed how he's sinking?'

Gabrielle, no doubt, would add:

'Like a lamp dying down . . .'

Merely because he'd ceased to concern himself with their little affairs.

'Are you asleep?' Milleran enquired anxiously, noticing all of a sudden that his eyes were closed.

He shook his head, raised his lids, smiled at her as though she were not only Milleran, but the whole of the human race.

'No, my child.'

He added, after a moment's silence:

'Not yet.'

Noland
14 October 1957

Maigret
in Society

Maigret in Society

Translated from the French by
Robert Eglesfield

Chapter One

It was one of those exceptional months of May which one experiences only two or three times in one's life and which have the brilliance, the taste and the scent of childhood memories. Maigret called it a choral May, for it reminded him both of his first communion and of his first springtime in Paris, when everything seemed new and wonderful.

In the street, in the bus, in his office, he would suddenly come to a halt, struck by a distant sound, by a gust of warm air, by the bright splash of colour of a blouse which took him back twenty or thirty years.

The day before, just as they were setting out to have dinner with the Pardons, his wife had asked him, almost blushing as she spoke:

'You don't think I look too silly, at my age, in a floral dress?'

That evening their friends the Pardons had staged an innovation. Instead of inviting them to their flat, they had taken the Maigrets to a little restaurant on the Boulevard du Montparnasse where the four of them had had dinner on the terrace.

Maigret and his wife, without saying anything, had exchanged conspiratorial glances, for it was on this terrace that, nearly thirty years before, they had had their first meal together.

'Is there stewed mutton?'

The owners of the restaurant had changed, but there were still stewed mutton on the menu, wobbly lamps on the table, evergreens in tubs, and Chavignol in carafes.

All four of them were in high spirits. Over coffee, Pardon had taken a magazine with a white cover out of his pocket.

'You know, Maigret, there's something about you in the *Lancet*.'

The chief-inspector, who knew the famous and austere English medical journal by name, had frowned.

'I mean there's something about your profession. It's in an article by a certain Dr Richard Fox and this is the passage that concerns you:

> 'A skilled psychiatrist, using his scientific knowledge and the experience gained in his consulting-room, is in a fairly good position to understand his fellow human beings. But it is possible, especially if he allows himself to be influenced by theories, that he will understand them less perfectly than a good schoolmaster, a novelist, or a detective.'

They had talked about this for some time, now jokingly, now more seriously. Then the Maigrets had walked part of the way home through the silent streets.

The chief-inspector could not know that this remark by the London doctor was going to come back to him several times during the following days, or that the memories awakened in him by this perfect month of May would appear to him almost in the guise of a premonition.

The next day too, in the bus taking him towards the Châtelet, he found himself looking at people's faces with the same curiosity as when he had been a newcomer to the capital.

Climbing the staircase of Police Headquarters as a divisional chief-inspector, and being greeted respectfully on the way, seemed strange to him. Was it so long since the time when, very much over-awed, he had first entered this service whose chiefs still struck him as legendary beings?

He felt at once gay and melancholy. With his window open, he went through his post, and sent for young Lapointe to give him some instructions.

In twenty-five years the Seine had not changed, neither the boats passing by, nor the anglers sitting in the same places as if they had never budged.

Puffing at his pipe, he was doing his housework, as he put it, clearing his desk of the dossiers piling up on it, and dealing with unimportant business, when the telephone rang.

'Can you come and see me for a moment, Maigret?' asked the Director.

The chief-inspector made his way unhurriedly to the Director's office, where he remained standing by the window.

'I've just had a curious phone call from the Quai d'Orsay. Not from the Foreign Minister in person but from his principal private secretary. He asked me to send over there straight away somebody capable of assuming responsibilities. Those are the words he used.

' "An inspector?" I asked.

' "Somebody of a higher rank would be preferable. It's probably something to do with a crime." '

The two men looked at one another with a hint of malice in their eyes, for neither of them had a high regard for ministries of any sort, least of all a ministry as starchy as the Foreign Office.

'I thought that you would like to go yourself . . .'

'Perhaps it would be best . . .'

The Director picked up a paper from his desk and held it out to Maigret.

'You have to ask for a certain Monsieur Cromières. He is expecting you.'

'Is he the principal private secretary?'

'No. He is the person who is handling the case.'

'Shall I take an inspector along with me?'

'I don't know anything more about the business than what I have just told you. Those people like being mysterious.'

Maigret finally picked on Janvier to accompany him and the two of them took a taxi. At the Quai d'Orsay they were not directed towards the great staircase but towards a narrow, unprepossessing staircase at the back of the courtyard, as if they were being shown in by the side-door or the tradesmen's entrance. They wandered along the corridors for quite a while before finding a waiting-room where an usher wearing a chain, unimpressed by the name of Maigret, made him fill up a form.

At last they were shown into a room where an official, very young and dapper, was standing silent and motionless opposite an old woman as impassive as himself. One had the impression that they had been waiting like that for a long time, probably since the telephone call from the Quai d'Orsay to Police Headquarters.

'Chief-Inspector Maigret?'

The latter introduced Janvier, to whom the young man granted only a distant glance.

'Not knowing what the trouble was, I took the precaution of bringing along one of my inspectors . . .'

'Take a seat.'

Young Cromières was trying hard to look important and there was something very 'Foreign Office' about his condescending manner of speaking.

'If the Quai got in touch straight away with Police Headquarters . . .'

He pronounced the word 'Quai' as if he were talking about some sacrosanct institution.

'. . . it was because, Chief-Inspector, we are faced with a somewhat exceptional situation . . .'

While looking at him, Maigret also kept an eye on the old woman, who was apparently deaf in one ear, for she bent forward to hear better, cocking her head to one side and watching the movements of the men's lips.

'Mademoiselle . . .'

Cromières consulted a form on his desk.

'Mademoiselle Larrieu is the maidservant, or the housekeeper, of one of the most distinguished of our former ambassadors, the Comte de Saint-Hilaire, of whom you must have heard . . .'

Maigret remembered having seen the name in the papers, but that struck him as going back a very long time.

'Since he retired about twelve years ago, the Comte de Saint-Hilaire had been living in Paris, in his flat in the Rue Saint-Dominique. This morning Mademoiselle Larrieu came here at half-past eight and had to wait some time before being shown into the presence of a responsible official.'

Maigret pictured to himself the deserted offices at half-past eight in the morning, and the old woman sitting motionless in the ante-room, her eyes fixed on the door.

'Mademoiselle Larrieu has been in the Comte de Saint-Hilaire's service for over forty years.'

'Forty-two,' she specified.

'Forty-two years. She accompanied him on his various missions and she looked after his house. During the past twelve years, she was the only person living with the ambassador in the Rue Saint-Dominique flat. It was there, this morning, that after finding the bedroom empty when she took in her master's breakfast, she discovered him in his study, dead.'

The old woman looked at each of them in turn, with sharp, searching, suspicious eyes.

'From what she says, Saint-Hilaire would appear to have been hit by one or more bullets.'

'She didn't call the police?'

The fair-haired young man assumed a conceited expression.

'I can understand your surprise. But do not forget that Mademoiselle Larrieu has spent a large part of her life in the diplomatic world. For all that the Comte de Saint-Hilaire was no longer on the active list, she considered that in the Service there are certain rules of discretion . . .'

Maigret winked at Janvier.

'She didn't think of sending for a doctor either?'

'It seems there can be no doubt about the question of death.'

'Who is over there in the Rue Saint-Dominique now?'

'Nobody. Mademoiselle Larrieu came straight here. To avoid any misunderstanding and waste of time, I am authorized to inform you that the Comte de Saint-Hilaire was not in possession of any state secrets and that you must not look for a political reason for his death. However, extreme prudence is nonetheless indispensable. When a well-known man is involved in something of this sort, especially if he has been in the Service, the newspapers are only too apt to give enormous prominence to the affair and to put forward the most improbable hypotheses . . .'

The young man stood up.

'If you will be good enough to come with me, we will go over there now.'

'You too?' Maigret asked with an innocent air.

'Oh, have no fear. I have no intention of interfering with your inquiries. If I accompany you, it is simply to make sure that there is nothing there which might cause us any embarrassment.'

The old woman stood up too. All four went downstairs.

'We had better take a taxi. That would be less conspicuous than one of the Quai limousines . . .'

The journey was ludicrously short. The car drew up in front of an imposing late eighteenth-century building outside which there was no crowd, no inquisitive onlookers. Under the archway, once they had gone through the main entrance, it felt suddenly cool, and in what looked more like a drawing-room than a lodge they could see a uniformed concierge as impressive as the usher at the Ministry.

They went up four steps on the left. The lift was standing motionless in a hall of dark marble. The old woman took a key out of her handbag and opened a walnut door.

'This way . . .'

She led them along a corridor to a room which obviously overlooked the courtyard but where the shutters and the curtains were closed. It was Mademoiselle Larrieu who turned on the electric light, and beside a mahogany desk they saw a body lying on the red carpet.

The three men removed their hats in a single movement, while the old servant looked at them with an almost defiant air.

'What did I tell you?' she seemed to be muttering.

Sure enough, there was no need to bend over the body to see that the Comte de Saint-Hilaire was well and truly dead. One bullet had entered by way of the right eye, blowing open the skull, and judging by the tears in the black velvet dressing-gown and by the bloodstains, other bullets had struck the body in several places.

Monsieur Cromières was the first to go up to the desk.

'You see this? It would appear that he was busy correcting proofs . . .'

'He was writing a book?'

'His memoirs. Two volumes have already appeared. But it would be absurd to look for the reason for his death there, because Saint-Hilaire was the most discreet of men and his memoirs were more literary and picturesque than political in character.'

Cromières was talking in flowery language, listening to himself talk, and Maigret began to feel irritated. There they were, the four of them, in a room with the shutters closed, at ten o'clock in the morning, while the sun was shining outside, looking at an old man's disjointed, blood-spattered body.

'I suppose,' muttered the chief-inspector, not without a certain irony, 'that in spite of everything this is still a matter for the Parquet?'

There was a telephone on the desk, but he preferred not to touch it.

'Janvier, go and phone from the lodge. Get on to the Parquet and the local police inspector . . .'

The old woman kept looking at them, one after another, as if it were her job to watch them. Her eyes were hard, with no sympathy, no human warmth in them.

'What are you doing?' asked Maigret, seeing the man from the Quai d'Orsay opening the doors of a bookcase.

'I am just having a look . . .'

He added, with a self-assurance that was unpleasant in a young fellow of his age:

'It is my duty to make quite sure that there aren't any papers here the divulgation of which would be inopportune . . .'

Was he as young as he looked? To what service did he belong in fact? Without waiting for the chief-inspector's permission, he examined the contents of the bookcase, opening files and putting them back one after another.

In the meantime, Maigret walked up and down, impatient, out of temper.

Cromières started on the other pieces of furniture, rummaging in the drawers, and the old woman remained standing by the door with her hat on and her bag in her hand.

'Will you take me to his bedroom?'

She went in front of the man from the Quai, while Maigret stayed in the study where Janvier soon joined him.

'Where are they?'

'In the bedroom . . .'

'What are we doing?'

'For the moment, nothing. I'm waiting for the young gentleman to be good enough to leave the place to us.'

It was not just Cromières who irritated the chief-inspector. It was also the way in which the case presented itself, and perhaps, above all else, the unfamiliar atmosphere into which he had suddenly been plunged.

'The local inspector will be here in a minute.'

'You've phoned the Criminal Records Office?'

'Moers is on the way with his men.'

'And the Parquet?'

'I've phoned them too.'

The study was roomy and comfortable. Though there was nothing solemn about it, the place had an air of distinction which had struck the chief-inspector as soon as he had come in. Every piece of furniture, every object was beautiful in itself. And the old man on the floor, with his head practically blown off, retained, in this setting, a certain grandeur.

Cromières returned, followed by the old housekeeper.

'I don't think there is anything more for me to do here. Once again, I recommend prudence and discretion to you. It cannot be a case of suicide, seeing that there is no weapon in the room. We are agreed on that point, I presume? As to whether a theft has been committed, I leave that to you to discover. In any case, it would be regrettable if the Press were to give undue prominence to this affair . . .'

Maigret looked at him in silence.

'I shall ring you up, if you don't mind, to find out what news you have,' the young man went on. 'It is possible that you may need certain information, in which case you can always apply to me.'

'Thank you.'

'In a chest of drawers in the bedroom, you will find a number of letters which will probably surprise you. It is an old story which everybody knows at the Quai d'Orsay and which has nothing to do with this affair.'

He retired regretfully.

'I count on you . . .'

The old woman followed him to shut the door behind him, and returned a little later without either hat or handbag. She had not come back to put herself at the chief-inspector's disposal, but rather to keep an eye on the two men.

'Do you sleep in the flat?'

When Maigret spoke to her, she was not looking at him, and she did not seem to have heard him. He repeated his question in a louder voice. This time she cocked her head, turning her good ear towards him.

'Yes. I have a little room behind the kitchen.'

'There aren't any other servants?'

'Not here, no.'

'You do the housework and the cooking here?'

'Yes.'

'How old are you?'

'Seventy.'

'And the Comte de Saint-Hilaire?'

'Seventy-seven.'

'When did you leave him last night?'

'About ten o'clock.'

'He was in his study?'

'Yes.'

'He wasn't expecting anybody?'

'He didn't say so.'

'Did anybody ever come to see him in the evening?'

'His nephew.'

'Where does his nephew live?'

'In the Rue Jacob. He is an antique-dealer.'

'Is he called Saint-Hilaire too?'

'No, he is the son of Monsieur's sister. His name is Mazeron.'

'You've got that, Janvier? . . . This morning, when you found the body . . . Because it *was* this morning you found it, wasn't it?'

'Yes. At eight o'clock.'

'You didn't think of ringing Monsieur Mazeron?'

'No.'

'Why not?'

She did not answer. She had the fixed stare of certain birds and, like certain birds too, she sometimes remained perched on one leg.

'You don't like him?'

'Who?'

'Monsieur Mazeron.'

'That's none of my business.'

Maigret knew now that with her everything was going to be difficult.

'What is none of your business?'

'Family matters.'

'The nephew didn't get on with his uncle?'

'I didn't say that.'

'What did you do, last night, at ten o'clock?'

'I went to bed.'

'When did you get up?'

'At six o'clock, as usual.'

'And you didn't set foot in this room?'

'There was no reason for me to come in here.'

'Was the door shut?'

'If it had been open, I should have noticed straight away that something had happened.'

'Why?'

'Because the lamps were still alight.'

'As they are now?'

'No. The ceiling light was not on. Just the desk lamp and the standard lamp in that corner.'

'What did you do at six o'clock?'

'First of all I washed.'

'And then?'

'I cleaned my kitchen and I went to buy some croissants.'

'The flat remained empty during that time?'

'Like every morning.'

'And then?'

'I made some coffee, I had my breakfast, and finally I went to the bedroom with the tray.'

'Had the bed been slept in?'

'No.'

'Was the room untidy?'

'No.'

'Last night, when you left him, was the Count wearing this black dressing-gown?'

'Yes, as he always did in the evening when he didn't go out.'

'Did he go out often?'

'He liked the cinema.'

'Did he invite friends here?'

'Scarcely ever. Now and then he used to go out to lunch.'

'Do you know the names of the people he met?'

'That is none of my business.'

There was a ring at the door. It was the local inspector with his secretary. He looked at the study in surprise, then at the old woman, and finally at Maigret, with whom he shook hands.

'How is it that you got here before us? Did she phone you?'

'She didn't even do that. She went to the Quai d'Orsay. Do you know the victim?'

'It's the former ambassador, isn't it? I know him by name and by sight. Every morning he used to go for a stroll round here. Who did that to him?'

'We don't know anything yet. I'm waiting for the Parquet.'

'The police doctor should be here any minute now . . .'

Nobody touched the furniture or anything else in the room. There was a strange feeling of uneasiness and it was a relief to see the doctor arrive. He gave a little whistle as he bent over the body.

'I suppose I can't turn him over before the photographers get here?'

'No, don't touch him . . . Have you an approximate idea of the time he died?'

'A good while ago . . . At first sight, I should say ten hours or so . . . It's queer . . .'

'What's queer?'

'He seems to have been hit by at least four bullets . . . One here, another there . . .'

Going down on his knees, he examined the body more closely.

'I don't know what the medical expert will think about it. For my part, I wouldn't be surprised if the first bullet had killed him and in spite of that the murderer had gone on firing. Mind you, that's just a theory . . .'

In less than five minutes the flat filled up with people. First came the Parquet, represented by the deputy public prosecutor Pasquier and by an examining magistrate whom Maigret did not know very well and who was called Urbain de Chézaud.

Doctor Paul's successor, Doctor Tudelle, arrived with them. Almost immediately afterwards the flat was invaded by the experts from the Criminal Records Office and their bulky apparatus.

'Who found the body?'

'The housekeeper.'

Maigret pointed to the old woman who, with no visible emotion, was still watching everybody's movements and gestures.

'Have you questioned her?'

'Not yet. I've just exchanged a few words with her.'

'Does she know anything?'

'If she does, it won't be easy to make her talk.'

He recounted the story of the Foreign Office.

'Has anything been stolen?'

'At first sight, it seems not. I'm waiting for the Criminal Records people to finish their work to make sure.'

'Any relatives?'

'A nephew.'

'Has he been informed?'

'Not yet. I intend to go myself, while my men are at work, to tell him what has happened. He lives just a few streets away, in the Rue Jacob.'

Maigret could have telephoned to the antique-dealer to ask him to come round, but he preferred to meet him in his own setting.

'If you don't need me any more, I'll go over there now. Janvier, you stay here . . .'

It was a relief to come out into the daylight, and the patches of sunshine under the trees on the Boulevard Saint-Germain. The air was warm, the women were wearing light-coloured dresses, and a municipal watering-cart was slowly sprinkling one half of the roadway.

He had no difficulty in finding the Rue Jacob antique-shop, one window of which contained nothing but old weapons, mostly swords. He pushed open the door, making a bell ring inside the shop, and three or four minutes went by before a man emerged from the shadows.

Seeing that the uncle was seventy-seven, Maigret could not expect the nephew to be a youngster. He was nonetheless surprised to find himself face to face with something like an old man.

'What can I do for you?'

He had a long pale face, bushy eyebrows and a practically bald pate, and his baggy clothes made him look thinner than he was.

'You are Monsieur Mazeron?'

'Alain Mazeron, yes.'

There were more weapons littering the shop, muskets, blunderbusses, and, right at the back, two suits of armour.

'Chief-Inspector Maigret, of the Judicial Police.'

The eyebrows came together. Mazeron was trying to understand.

'You are the Comte de Saint-Hilaire's nephew, aren't you?'

'He is my uncle, yes. Why?'

'When did you last see him?'

He answered unhesitatingly:

'The day before yesterday.'

'Have you any other relatives?'

'I am married, with children.'

'When you last saw your uncle, did he seem quite normal?'

'Yes, he was even rather gay. Why do you ask?'

'Because he is dead.'

Maigret saw in Mazeron's eyes the same mistrust that the old housekeeper had shown.

'He has had an accident?'

'In a manner of speaking . . .'

'What do you mean?'

'That he was killed last night in his study by several bullets fired from a revolver or an automatic pistol.'

The antique-dealer's face registered incredulity.

'Did he have any enemies you know of?'

'No . . . Certainly not . . .'

If Mazeron had merely said no, Maigret would have paid no attention. The 'certainly not', which came rather as an afterthought, made him prick up his ears.

'You have no idea who would stand to benefit by your uncle's death?'

'No . . . No idea whatever . . .'

'Was he a rich man?'

'He had a small private fortune . . . He lived mainly on his pension . . .'

'He sometimes came here?'

'Sometimes . . .'

'To have lunch or dinner with you?'

Mazeron seemed absentminded, and replied briefly, as if he were thinking of something else.

'No . . . Usually in the morning, in the course of his walk . . .'

'He dropped in for a chat with you?'

'That's it. He used to come in and sit down for a moment.'

'Did you go to see him at his flat?'

'Now and then . . .'

'With your family?'

'No . . .'

'Did you say you had some children?'

'Two . . . Two girls . . .'

'You live in this building?'

'On the first floor . . . One of my daughters, the elder, is in England . . . The other, Marcelle, lives with her mother . . .'

'You don't live with your wife?'

'Not for some years now . . .'

'You are divorced?'

'No . . . It's rather complicated . . . Don't you think we ought to go over to my uncle's?'

He went to look for his hat in the half-light of the back-shop, hung a notice saying that he was out on the door, locked up, and followed Maigret along the pavement.

'Do you know how it happened?' he asked.

You could tell that he was anxious, worried.

'I know next to nothing.'

'Was anything stolen?'

'I don't think so. There was no sign of disorder in the flat.'

'What does Jaquette say?'

'You are talking about the housekeeper?'

'Yes . . . That's her Christian name . . . I don't know if it's her real name, but she has always been known as Jaquette . . .'

'You don't like her?'

'Why do you ask me that?'

'She doesn't seem to like you.'

'She doesn't like anybody except my uncle. If it had been left to her to decide, nobody would ever have been allowed into that flat.'

'Do you think she would have been capable of killing him?'

Mazeron looked at him in astonishment.

'Killing him—her?'

The idea obviously struck him as utterly ridiculous. And yet, a moment later, he found himself thinking again.

'No! . . . It isn't possible . . .'

'You hesitated.'

'Because of her jealousy . . .'

'You mean to say that she was in love with him?'

'She hasn't always been an old woman . . .'

'You think that they were once . . .'

'It's probable . . . I wouldn't swear to it . . . With a man like my uncle, it's hard to tell . . . You've seen the photographs of Jaquette when she was young?'

'I haven't seen anything yet . . .'

'You'll see . . . It's all very complicated . . . Especially happening just now . . .'

'What do you mean by that?'

Alain Mazeron looked at Maigret with a certain weariness and sighed:

'I see that you don't know anything.'

'What ought I to know?'

'I wonder . . . It's a tiresome story . . . Have you found the letters?'

'I'm just beginning my inquiries.'

'Today is Wednesday, isn't it?'

Maigret nodded.

'Just the day of the funeral . . .'

'Whose funeral?'

'The Prince de V——'s. You'll understand when you have read the letters . . .'

They reached the Rue Saint-Dominique just as the Criminal Records car was leaving, and Moers gave a wave of the hand to Maigret.

Chapter Two

'What are you thinking about, Chief?'

Janvier was surprised at the effect produced by this question which he had asked simply to break a rather lengthy silence. It seemed as though the words had not penetrated straight away to Maigret's brain, that they were just so many sounds which he had to put in order before he could make out what they meant.

The chief-inspector looked at his companion with big vague eyes and an air of embarrassment, as if he had just given away a secret of his.

'About these people,' he murmured.

Clearly he was not talking about those who were lunching all around them in this Rue de Bourgogne restaurant, but about the others, those of whom they had never heard the day before and whose secret lives it was their job to discover today.

Every time he bought a suit, an overcoat or a pair of shoes, Maigret wore them first of all in the evening, to go for a stroll with his wife through the streets of the district or else to go to the cinema.

'I need to get used to them,' he would say to Madame Maigret when she teased him affectionately.

It was the same when he was immersing himself in a new case. Other people did not realize this, on account of his massive silhouette and the calm expression on his face which they took for self-assurance. In fact, he was going through a more or less prolonged period of hesitation, uneasiness, even timidity.

He had to get used to an unfamiliar setting, to a house, to a way of life, to people who had their own particular habits, their own way of thinking and expressing themselves.

With certain categories of human beings it was relatively easy, for instance with his more or less regular customers or with people like them.

With others he had to start from scratch every time, especially as he distrusted rules and ready-made ideas.

In this new case, he was labouring under an additional handicap. He had made contact, that morning, with a world which was not only very exclusive but which for him, on account of his childhood, was situated on a very special level.

He realized that all the time he had been in the Rue Saint-Dominique he had failed to show his usual confidence; he had behaved awkwardly; his questions had been guarded and clumsy. Had Janvier noticed?

If so, it had certainly not occurred to him that this was the effect of a distant period in Maigret's past, the years spent in the shadow of a château of which his father had been the steward and where, for a long time, the Comte and Comtesse de Saint-Fiacre had been, in his eyes, creatures of another species.

For lunch, the two men had picked this restaurant in the Rue de Bourgogne, on account of its terrace, and they had soon noticed that the place was patronized by officials from the nearby ministries, especially from the Premier's department, so it seemed, with a few officers in mufti who belonged to the War Office.

They were not ordinary pen-pushers. All of them had at least the rank of head clerk, and Maigret was astonished to see how young they were. Their self-assurance surprised him too. From the way they talked and behaved, you could tell that they were sure of themselves. Some of them recognizing him and talking about him in low voices, he felt annoyed at their knowing looks and their irony.

Did the people at the Quai des Orfèvres, who were ministry officials too, give the same impression of knowing all the answers?

This was what he had been thinking about when Janvier had roused him from his reverie. About the morning in the Rue Saint-Dominique. About the dead man, that Comte Armand de Saint-Hilaire, an ambassador for so many years, who had just been murdered at the age of seventy-seven. About the strange Jaquette Larrieu and her little staring eyes which penetrated to the very depths of his being while she listened to him, her head cocked to one side, watching every movement of his lips. And finally about the pale and flabby Alain Mazeron, all alone in his Rue Jacob shop, among his swords and his suits of armour, whom Maigret could not manage to class in any known category.

What were the terms used by the English doctor in the article in the *Lancet*? He could not remember. It was something to the effect that a first-class schoolmaster, a novelist and a detective were in a better position than a doctor or a psychiatrist to understand other people.

Why did the detective come last, after the schoolmaster and particularly after the novelist?

That annoyed him slightly. He was in a hurry to feel at home in this new case, as if to give the lie to the author of the article.

They had begun with asparagus and now they had gone on to ray with browned butter sauce. The sky above the street was still as blue as ever and the women passing by were dressed in bright colours.

Before deciding to go and have lunch, Maigret and Janvier had spent an hour and a half in the dead man's flat, which was already more familiar to them.

The body had been taken off to the Morgue, where Doctor Tudelle was engaged in carrying out the post-mortem. The people from the Parquet and the Criminal Records Office had gone. With a sigh of relief, Maigret had opened curtains and shutters, letting the sunlight into the rooms, where it had given back to the furniture and other objects their normal appearance.

It did not embarrass the chief-inspector to have Jaquette and the nephew following him around, watching his gestures and facial expressions, and now and then he would turn towards them and ask a question.

No doubt they had been surprised to see him coming and going for such a long time, without looking at anything in particular, as if he were inspecting a flat to let.

The study, which had seemed so stuffy that morning in artificial light, fascinated him, and he kept coming back to it with a secret pleasure, for it was one of the most delightful rooms he had ever seen.

It was a high-ceilinged room, lit by a French window opening on to a flight of three steps, beyond which one discovered with some surprise a well-kept lawn and a huge linden-tree standing in a world of stone.

'Who has the use of this garden?' he had asked, looking up at the windows of the other flats.

The reply came from Mazeron.

'My uncle.'

'None of the other tenants?'

'No. The building belonged to him. He was born here. His father, who was still quite rich, occupied the ground floor and the first floor. When he died, my uncle, who had already lost his mother, kept this small flat and the garden for himself.'

This little detail was significant. It was surely a rare thing, in Paris, for a man of seventy-seven to be living in the house where he was born.

'And what happened when he was serving as an ambassador abroad?'

'He closed the flat and opened it up again when he came home on leave. Contrary to what you might suppose, the building brought him in hardly anything. Most of the tenants have been here so long that they pay derisory rents, so that some years, what with repairs and taxes, my uncle was out of pocket.'

There were not many rooms in the flat. The study did service as a drawing-room. Next to it was a dining-room, opposite the kitchen, and overlooking the street there was a bedroom and a bathroom.

'Where do you sleep?' Maigret had asked Jaquette.

She made him repeat his question and he began to think that this was an idiosyncrasy of hers.

'Behind the kitchen.'

There in fact he found a sort of box-room in which an iron bedstead, a wardrobe and a washbasin had been installed. A big ebony crucifix hung over a holy-water basin adorned with a sprig of box.

'Was the Comte de Saint-Hilaire a religious man?'

'He never missed Mass on Sunday, even in Russia.'

What struck him most of all was a subtle harmony, a distinction which Maigret would have been hard put to it to define. The various pieces of furniture were of different styles and no attempt had been made to form an ensemble. Every room was none the less beautiful in itself; each had acquired the same patina, the same personality.

The study was almost entirely lined with bound volumes, while other books in white or yellow covers were arranged on shelves in the corridor.

'Was the window shut when you found the body?'

'It was you who opened it. I didn't even touch the curtains.'

'And the bedroom window?'

'That was shut too. Monsieur le Comte was sensitive to the cold.'

'Who had the key to the flat?'

'He and I. Nobody else.'

Janvier had questioned the concierge. The little door cut out of the main door stayed open until midnight. The concierge never went to bed before that time; he sometimes went into his bedroom, behind the lodge, from which he did not necessarily see people coming in and going out.

The day before, he had not noticed anything out of the ordinary. It was a respectable house, he kept repeating insistently. He had been there for thirty years and the police had never had occasion to set foot in the place.

It was too soon to reconstruct what had happened the previous evening or during the night. He had to wait for the medical expert's report, then for the report of Moers and his men.

One thing seemed clear: Saint-Hilaire had not gone to bed. He was wearing dark grey, pin-striped trousers, a lightly starched white shirt and a bow-tie with spots, and, as usual when he stayed at home, he had put on his black velvet dressing-gown.

'Did he often stay up late?'

'It depends what you mean by late.'

'What time did he usually go to bed?'

'I was nearly always in bed before he was.'

It was infuriating. The most commonplace questions came up against the mistrust of the old servant, who only rarely gave a direct answer.

'You didn't hear him leave his study?'

'Go into my bedroom and you'll see that you can't hear anything there except the lift, which is on the other side of the partition.'

'How did he spend his evenings?'

'Reading. Writing. Correcting the proofs of his books.'

'Did he go to bed at midnight, say?'

'Perhaps a little earlier, or a little later, depending on the day.'

'And when he went to bed, he never called you, he never had need of your services?'

'What for?'

'He might have felt like a hot drink before going to bed, or perhaps . . .'

'He never had a hot drink at night. And if he wanted something to drink, he had his liqueur cabinet.'

'What did he drink usually?'

'Claret with his meals. And in the evening, a glass of brandy.'

They had found the glass, empty, on the desk, and the experts from the Criminal Records Office had taken it away to see if there were any fingerprints on it.

If the old man had had a visitor, he did not appear to have offered him a drink, for no other glass had been found in the study.

'Did the Comte de Saint-Hilaire possess any firearms?'

'Some fowling-pieces. They are in the cupboard at the end of the corridor.'

'He was a keen shot?'

'He sometimes did a little shooting when he was invited to a château.'

'He didn't own a pistol or a revolver?'

Once again she fell silent, and, as before, her pupils narrowed like those of a cat and her gaze became immobile, expressionless.

'Did you hear my question?'

'What did you ask me?'

Maigret repeated his query.

'I think he had a revolver.'

'With a cylinder?'

'What do you mean by a cylinder?'

He tried to explain. No, it wasn't a gun with a cylinder. It was a flat weapon, bluish in colour, with a short barrel.

'Where did he keep this automatic of his?'

'I don't know. I haven't seen it for a long time. The last time, it was in the chest of drawers.'

'In his bedroom?'

She showed him the drawer in question, which contained nothing but handkerchiefs, suspenders and braces in various colours. The other drawers were full of neatly folded linen, shirts, pants, handkerchiefs, and, right at the bottom, dress-shirts.

'When did you last see the automatic?'

'Some years ago.'

'How many years ago, roughly?'

'I don't know. Time goes so quickly . . .'

'You never saw it anywhere except in that chest of drawers?'

'No. Perhaps he had put it in one of the drawers in his desk. I never opened those drawers, and in any case they were always locked.'

'Do you know why?'

'Why do people lock pieces of furniture?'

'He distrusted you?'

'Certainly not.'

'Whom then?'

'Don't you ever lock anything, you?'

There was a key, sure enough, a highly ornamental bronze key which opened the drawers of the Empire desk. The contents revealed nothing, except that Saint-Hilaire, like everybody else, accumulated useless little objects, some old empty wallets for instance, two or three gold-rimmed amber cigar-holders which had not been used for a long time, a cigar-cutter, some drawing-pins and paper-clips, and pencils in every conceivable colour.

Another drawer contained writing-paper stamped with a coronet, envelopes, visiting-cards, bits of string carefully rolled up, a pot of paste and a penknife with a broken blade.

The copper tressil-work doors of one bookcase were lined with green cloth. Inside there were no books but instead, on every shelf, bundles of letters neatly tied with string, with a label bearing a date attached to each bundle.

'This is what you were talking about earlier?' Maigret asked Alain Mazeron.

The nephew nodded.

'You know who wrote these letters?'

He nodded again.

'Was it your uncle who told you about them?'

'I don't know if he ever mentioned them to me, but everybody knows about them.'

'What do you mean by everybody?'

'In diplomatic circles, in society . . .'

'Have you ever had occasion to read any of these letters?'

'Never.'

'You can leave us and go and cook your lunch,' Maigret said to Jaquette.

'If you think I'm going to eat on a day like this!'

'Leave us all the same. You can certainly find something to do.'

She was obviously reluctant to leave him alone with the nephew. Several times, he had intercepted glances of something like hatred which she had surreptitiously shot at him.

'You understand?'

'I know that it is none of my business, but . . .'

'But what?'

'A person's letters are sacred . . .'

'Even if they can help in tracking down a murderer?'

'They won't help you to do anything.'

'I shall probably need you soon. In the meantime . . .'

He glanced at the door and Jaquette reluctantly withdrew. How indignant she would have been if she had been able to see Maigret taking the Comte de Saint-Hilaire's place behind the desk on which Janvier was arranging the bundles of letters!

'Sit down,' Maigret said to Mazeron. 'You know whom this correspondence is from?'

'Yes. You will doubtless find that all the letters are signed Isi.'

'Who is Isi?'

'Isabelle de V———. My uncle always called her Isi . . .'

'She was his mistress?'

Why did Maigret think that Mazeron looked like a sacristan, as if sacristans had a particular type of face? Mazeron too, like Jaquette, allowed a certain time to elapse before answering his questions.

'It seems they were never lovers.'

Maigret untied the string round a bundle of yellowed letters dating from 1914, a few days after the outbreak of war.

'How old is the Princess now?'

'Wait a moment while I work it out . . . She is five or six years younger than my uncle . . . So she is between seventy-one and seventy-two . . .'

'Did she come here often?'

'I have never seen her here. I don't think she has ever set foot in the place, or if she has it was before.'

'Before what?'

'Before her marriage to the Prince de V———.'

'Listen, Monsieur Mazeron. I would like you to tell me this story as clearly as you can . . .'

'Isabelle was the daughter of the Duc de S———.'

It was a curious experience for Maigret, coming across names he had learnt at school in lessons on French history.

'Well?'

'My uncle was twenty-six when he met her, about 1910. To be more precise, he had met her when she was a little girl in the Duke's château, where he sometimes spent his holidays. After that he had seen nothing of her for a long time, and it was when they met again that they fell in love with one another.'

'Your uncle had already lost his father?'

'Two years before.'

'Was there anything left of the family fortune?'

'Just this house and a little landed property in Sologne.'

'Why didn't they get married?'

'I don't know. Possibly because my uncle was just starting his career in the Service and he had been sent to Poland as second or third secretary to the Ambassador.'

'Were they engaged?'

'No.'

Maigret felt a certain embarrassment as he looked through the letters spread out in front of him. Contrary to his expectations, they were not love-letters. The girl who had written them recounted, in quite a lively style, the day-to-day happenings of her own life and the life of Parisian society.

She did not use the familiar *tu* form with her correspondent, whom she called her *great friend,* and she signed the letters: *your faithful Isi.*

'What happened next?'

'Before the war–I'm talking about the war of 1914–in 1912, unless I'm mistaken, Isabelle married the Prince de V——.'

'Was she in love with him?'

'By all accounts, no. People even say that she told him so to his face. All I know about it is from hearing my father and mother talking about it when I was a child.'

'Your mother was the Comte de Saint-Hilaire's sister?'

'Yes.'

'She didn't marry into her own class?'

'She married my father, who was a painter who enjoyed a certain vogue at the time. He is almost completely forgotten now, but there is still a canvas of his in the Luxembourg. Later on, in order to earn a living, he became a picture restorer.'

During this part of the morning, Maigret had had the impression that he was having to drag out every scrap of truth almost by force. He could not manage to obtain a clear picture. These poeple seemed unreal to him, as if they had come out of a 1900 novel.

'If I understand correctly, Armand de Saint-Hilaire didn't marry Isobelle because he wasn't rich enough?'

'I suppose so. That's what I was always told and it seems the likeliest explanation.'

'So she married the Prince de V——, whom you say she didn't love, and she was honest enough to tell him so.'

'It was an arrangement between two great families, between two great names.'

Hadn't it been the same in the old days with the Saint-Fiacres, and when it had been a question of finding a wife for her son, hadn't the old Countess turned to her Bishop for help?

'Did the couple have any children?'

'One child, a boy, after they had been married several years.'

'What became of him?'

'Prince Philippe must be forty-five now. He married a Mademoiselle de Marchangy and lives nearly all the year round in his château at Genestoux, near Caen, where he owns a stud and several farms. He has five or six children.'

'For something like fifty years, to judge by this correspondence, Isabelle and your uncle went on writing to each other. Practically every day they sent each other letters several pages long. Did the husband know that this was going on?'

'So they say.'

'Did you know him?'

'Only by sight.'

'What sort of man was he?'

'A man of the world and a collector.'

'A collector of what?'

'Medals, snuffboxes . . .'

'Did he mix very much with other people?'

'He entertained once a week in his Rue de Varenne house, and in autumn at his château at Saint-Sauveur-en-Bourbonnais.'

Maigret had pulled a wry face. On the one hand, he knew that all this was probably true, but at the same time the people concerned struck him as having no material existence.

'The Rue de Varenne,' he pointed out, 'is only five minutes' walk from here.'

'All the same, I'd be ready to swear that for fifty years my uncle and the Princess never met.'

'Although they wrote to each other every day?'

'You've got the letters in front of you.'

'And the husband knew all about it?'

'Isabelle would never have agreed to conduct a correspondence behind his back.'

Maigret felt almost tempted to lose his temper, as if somebody had been poking fun at him. And yet there the letters were, before his very eyes, full of revealing passages.

'*. . . this morning, at eleven o'clock, the Abbé Gauge called to see me and we talked a great deal about you. It is a comfort to me to know that the bonds which join us are of a sort that men are powerless to break . . .*'

'Is the Princess very devout?'

'She has had a chapel consecrated in her house in the Rue de Varenne.'

'And her husband?'

'He was a Catholic too.'

'He had mistresses?'

'So they say.'

Another letter, from a more recent bundle:

'*. . . I shall be grateful to Hubert all my life for having understood . . .*'

'I suppose that Hubert is the Prince de V——?'

'Yes. He was once a staff-officer at the cavalry school of Saumur. Every morning he went riding in the Bois de Boulogne until last week, when he was thrown from his horse.'

'How old was he?'

'Eighty.'

In this case there was nobody but old people, with relations between them which did not seem human.

'You are quite sure about all that you have told me, Monsieur Mazeron?'

'If you have any doubts, ask anybody you like.'

Anybody in a world of which Maigret had only a vague and doubtless inaccurate idea!

'Let's continue,' he sighed wearily. 'This is the Prince who, you told me earlier, has just died?'

'On Sunday morning, yes. It was in all the papers. He died from the effects of his riding accident and the funeral is taking place at this very moment at Sainte-Clotilde.'

'He never had anything to do with your uncle?'

'Not as far as I know.'

'And what happened if they met at some social gathering?'

'I imagine they avoided frequenting the same salons and the same clubs.'

'They hated each other?'

'I don't think so.'

'Did your uncle ever talk to you about the Prince?'

'No. He never mentioned him.'

'And what about Isabelle?'

'He told me, a long time ago, that I was his sole heir and that it was a pity I didn't bear his name. It saddened him too that I had two daughters and no son. If I had had a son, he added, he would have applied for a decree allowing the latter to bear the name Saint-Hilaire.'

'So you are your uncle's sole heir?'

'Yes. But I haven't finished what I was telling you. Indirectly, without mentioning any names, he spoke to me that day of the Princess. He said something to this effect:

' "I still hope to marry one day, heaven knows when, but it will be too late to have any children . . ." '

'If I've understood you correctly, this is the situation. About 1910 your uncle met a girl whom he loved and who loved him, but they didn't get married because the Comte de Saint-Hilaire was practically penniless.'

'That's correct.'

'Two years later, when your uncle was in an embassy in Poland or somewhere else, young Isabelle made a marriage of convenience and became the Princesse de V——. She has a son, so it wasn't an unconsummated marriage. The couple must have lived together as husband and wife, at least at the time.'

'Yes.'

'Unless in the meantime Isabelle and your uncle had seen each other again and given way to their passion.'

'No.'

'How can you be so sure? You think that in that particular world . . .'

'I say no because my uncle spent the whole of the First World War away from France, and when he came back the child, Philippe, was two or three years old.'

'All right. The sweethearts saw each other again . . .'

'No.'

'They never saw each other again?'

'I've already told you so.'

'For fifty years, then, they wrote to each other practically every day, and one day your uncle spoke to you about a marriage which was to take place in a more or less distant future. Which means, I suppose, that he and Isabelle were waiting for the Prince to die in order to get married.'

'I imagine so.'

Maigret mopped his forehead and looked at the linden-tree outside the French window, as if he needed to resume contact with a more humdrum reality.

'Now we come to the epilogue. Ten or twelve days ago—the exact date doesn't matter–the eighty-year-old Prince was thrown from his horse in the Bois de Boulogne. On Sunday morning, he died from his injuries. Yesterday, Tuesday, that is to say two days later, your uncle was killed in his study. The consequence is that the two old people, who for fifty years had been waiting for the time to come when they could finally be joined together, won't be joined together after all. Is that right? Thank you, Monsieur Mazeron. Now will you please give me your wife's address.'

'23, Rue de la Pompe, at Passy.'

'Do you know the name of your uncle's solicitor?'

'His solicitor is Maître Aubonnet, of the Rue de Villersexel.'

Again a few hundred yards away. All these people, with the exception of Madame Mazeron, lived practically next-door to one another, in the district of Paris with which Maigret was least familiar.

'You are free to go now. I suppose I can always find you at your shop?'

'I shan't be there very much this afternoon, because I shall have to make arrangements for the funeral and the announcement of my uncle's death, and first of all I intend to get in touch with Maître Aubonnet.'

Mazeron had left reluctantly and Jaquette, suddenly appearing from her kitchen, had gone to shut the door behind him.

'Do you need me at the moment?'

'Not just now. It's lunchtime. We shall be back this afternoon.'

'Am I obliged to stay here?'

'Where would you go?'

She had looked at him as if she did not understand.

'I asked you where you intended to go.'

'Me? Nowhere. Where would I go, indeed?'

On account of her attitude, Maigret and Janvier had not left straight away. Maigret had telephoned to the Quai des Orfèvres.

'Lucas? Have you got somebody there who could come and spend an hour or two in the Rue Saint-Dominique? Torrence? Fine! Tell him to take a car . . .'

With the result that while the two men were lunching, Torrence, for his part, was dozing in the Comte de Saint-Hilaire's armchair.

As far as they could see, nothing had been stolen from the flat. Nobody had broken in. The murderer had come in through the door, and since Jaquette swore that she had let nobody in, they were forced to conclude that the Comte himself had opened the door to his visitor.

Was he expecting him? Or was he not? He hadn't offered him a drink. They had found only one glass on the desk, next to the bottle of brandy.

Would Saint-Hilaire have stayed in his dressing-gown to receive a woman? Probably not, judging by the little they knew about him.

So it was a man who had come to see him. The Count hadn't been suspicious of him, since he had sat down at his desk, in front of the proofs which he had been correcting a few minutes earlier.

'You didn't notice if there were any cigarette-ends in the ash-tray?'

'I don't think so.'

'No cigar-stubs either?'

'No.'

'I bet you that before tonight we'll have a phone call from young Monsieur Cromières.'

He was another one who had the knack of getting Maigret's back up.

'The Prince's funeral must be over by now.'

'Probably.'

'So Isabelle will be at home now in the Rue de Varenne, together with her son, her daughter-in-law and her grandchildren.'

There was a silence. Maigret frowned as if he could not make up his mind about something.

'Are you going to go and see them?' Janvier asked, with a certain anxiety in his voice.

'No . . . Not with people like that . . . Are you having coffee? . . . Waiter! Two black coffees . . .'

One would have sworn that he had a grudge against everybody today, even including the more or less high-ranking officials who were lunching at the neighbouring tables and eyeing him ironically.

Chapter Three

As soon as he turned the corner of the Rue Saint-Dominique, Maigret saw them and let out a groan. There were a good dozen of them, reporters and photographers, in front of the Comte de Saint-Hilaire's house, and some of them had sat down on the pavement with their backs against the wall, as if in readiness for a long siege.

They for their part had recognized him from a distance, and they rushed up to him.

'This is going to please our dear Monsieur Cromières!' he muttered to Janvier.

It was inevitable. As soon as a case was reported to a local police-station, there was always somebody who told the Press.

The photographers, who had dozens of pictures of him in their files, all took fresh shots of him, as if he looked different from the day before or any other day. The reporters started asking questions. These, fortunately, showed that they knew less about the case than might have been feared.

'Is it suicide, Chief-Inspector?'

'Have any documents disappeared?'

'For the moment, gentlemen, I have nothing to say.'

'Can we assume that it's probably a political affair?'

They walked backwards in front of him, with their notebooks in their hands.

'When will you be able to give us a statement?'

'Perhaps tomorrow, perhaps a week from now.'

He made the mistake of adding:

'Perhaps never.'

He tried to correct the slip he had made.

'I'm joking, of course. Now please help us by letting us work in peace.'

'Is it true that he was writing his memoirs?'

'So true that two volumes have already been published.'

A policeman in uniform was standing outside the door. A few moments later, in response to Maigret's ring at the bell, Torrence, in shirtsleeves, came and opened the door to him.

'I had to send for a policeman, Chief. They had got into the building and were having fun ringing the bell every five minutes.'

'Nothing new? No phone calls?'

'Twenty or thirty. The papers.'

'Where's the old girl?'

'In the kitchen. Every time the phone rings, she rushes to it in the hope of answering before I do. The first time, she tried to snatch the receiver out of my hands.'

'She hasn't made any phone calls herself, has she? You know there's another phone in the bedroom?'

'I left the study door open so that I could hear her coming and going. She hasn't been into the bedroom.'

'She hasn't been out?'

'No. She tried to once, to go and get some new bread, so she told me. As you hadn't left me any instructions on that point, I decided not to let her go. What do I do now?'

'You go back to the Quai.'

For a moment, the chief-inspector had thought of going back there himself, and taking Jaquette, whom he wanted to question at leisure. But he didn't feel prepared for this interrogation. He preferred to stay a little longer in the flat and in the end it would probably be in Saint-Hilaire's study that he would try to get the old servant to talk.

In the meantime, he opened the lofty French window to its full extent and sat down in the chair which the Count had so often occupied. His hand was reaching out towards one of the bundles of letters when the door opened. It was Jaquette Larrieu, more sour-tempered and suspicious than ever.

'You haven't any right to do that.'

'You know who these letters are from?'

'It doesn't matter whether I do or don't. It's a private correspondence.'

'You will do me the favour of going back to the kitchen or your bedroom.'

'Can't I go out?'

'Not yet.'

She hesitated, searching for a cutting reply, which she failed to find, and finally, pale with anger, left the study.

'Janvier, go and fetch me that photograph in a silver frame that I saw this morning in the bedroom.'

Maigret had not paid much attention to it in the morning. Too many things had still been unfamiliar to him. It was a principle with him not to try to form an opinion too quickly, for he distrusted first impressions.

During lunch at the restaurant, he had suddenly remembered a lithograph which he had seen for years in his parent's bedroom. It must have been his mother who had chosen it and hung it up. The frame was white, in the style fashionable at the beginning of the century. The picture showed a young woman on the shore of a lake, wearing a princess dress, with a wide ostrich-feather hat on her head and a sunshade in her hand. The expression on her face was melancholy, like the landscape, and Maigret was sure that his mother considered the picture to be highly poetic. Wasn't that the poetry of the period?

The story of Isabelle and the Comte de Saint-Hilaire had brought back the memory of that picture to him so clearly that he could see even the wallpaper with the pale-blue stripes in his parents' room.

Now inside the silver frame which he had noticed in the morning in the Count's bedroom and which Janvier brought along to him, he discovered the same figure, a dress in the same style, an identical melancholy.

He had no doubt that it was a photograph of Isabelle about 1910, when she was still a young girl and when the future ambassador had met her.

She was not very tall, and she seemed to have a slim waist, possibly because of the corset she was wearing, while her bust, as they used to call it in those days, was rather large. Her features were finely chiselled, her lips thin, her eyes a pale blue or grey.

'What do I do now, Chief?'

'Sit down.'

He needed somebody there, as if to check his impressions. In front of him, the bundles of letters were arranged year by year and he took them one after another, not reading everything of course, for that would have taken him several days, but a passage here and there.

My good friend . . . Dearest friend . . . Sweet friend . . .

Later on, perhaps because she felt in closer harmony with her correspondent, she wrote simply: *Friend.*

Saint-Hilaire had kept the envelopes, which bore stamps of various countries. Isabelle had travelled a great deal. For a long time, for instance, her August letters were written from Baden-Baden or Marienbad, the aristocratic spas of the time.

There were also letters from the Tyrol, and a good many from Switzerland and Portugal. She recounted in a self-satisfied, lively manner the little happenings which filled her day and gave quite witty descriptions of the people she met. Often she referred to them just by their surnames, sometimes by a mere initial.

Maigret took some time to find his bearings. With the help of the stamp on the envelope and the context of the reference, he gradually managed to solve these conundrums.

Marie, for instance, was a queen still reigning at that time, the Queen of Rumania. It was from Bucharest, where she was staying at court with her father, that Isabelle was writing, and a year later she was at court in Italy.

'My cousin H——.'

The name–that of the Prince of Hesse–was given in full in another letter, and there were others, all first or second cousins.

During the First World War, she sent her letters by way of the French Embassy in Madrid.

'My father explained to me yesterday that it is necessary for me to marry the Prince de V—— whom you have met several times at home. I asked him for three days in which to consider the matter, and during this time I have wept a great deal . . .'

Maigret puffed at his pipe, shot an occasional glance at the garden, at the leaves of the linden-tree, and passed the letters one by one to Janiver, studying his reactions.

He felt a mild irritation in the face of these evocations which seemed so unreal to him. As a child, hadn't he looked with the same sort of embarrassment at the woman on the shore of the lake, in his parents' bedroom? In his eyes, she had been an unreal, impossible creature, surrounded by a false poetry.

Yet here, in a world which had evolved further, which had grown much harder, he had found, in a living person, a very similar picture.

'*This afternoon, I had a long conversation with Hubert and I was absolutely frank. He knows that I love you, that we are separated by too many obstacles, and that I am yielding to my father's wishes . . .*'

Only the week before, Maigret had had to deal with a simple, brutal crime of passion, the case of a lover who had stabbed to death the husband of the woman he loved, had then killed the woman, and had finally tried unsuccessfully to cut open his veins. It is true that this took place in the lower-class district of the Faubourg Saint-Antoine.

'*He has agreed that our marriage shall remain unconsummated and I for my part have promised never to see you again. He has a high regard for you and does not question the respect which you have always shown me . . .*'

There were moments when Maigret felt an almost physical sense of revolt.

'Do you believe it, Janvier?'

The inspector was baffled.

'She sounds as if she meant it . . .'

'Read this one!'

It was three years later.

'*I know, friend, that this is going to hurt you, but if it is any consolation to you, it hurts me even more than it does you . . .*'

It was in 1915. She announced that Julien, the Prince de V——'s brother, had just been killed in Argonne at the head of his regiment. Once again, she had had a long conversation with her husband, who had come to Paris on leave.

What she told the man she loved was, to put it briefly, that she was going to have to sleep with the Prince. She did not use those terms of course. Not only was there not a single brutal or shocking word in her letter, but the subject itself was treated in an almost immaterial fashion.

'*As long as Julien was alive, Hubert did not worry, feeling sure that his brother would have an heir and that the name of V—— . . .*'

The brother was no longer there. It was accordingly Hubert's duty to ensure the continuation of the family.

'*I spent the night in prayer and in the morning I went to see my confessor . . .*'

The priest had shared the Prince's opinion. One could not, for a question of love, allow a name to die out which, for the past five centuries, had been found on every page of the history of France.

'*I understood where my duty lay . . .*'

The sacrifice had taken place, since a child, Philippe, had been born. She announced the birth too, and on this subject there was a phrase which gave Maigret pause:

'*Thank God, it is a boy . . .*'

Wasn't that saying, in black and white, that if the child had been a girl, she would have had to start all over again?

And if she had had another girl, and then another . . .

'You've read it?'

'Yes.'

It was as if they had both fallen prey to the same feeling of discomfort. They were both of them accustomed to a somewhat crude reality, and the passions with which they came in contact usually took a dramatic turn seeing that they ended up at the Quai des Orfèvres.

Here, on the other hand, it was as difficult as trying to catch hold of a cloud. And when they attempted to grasp the characters, the latter remained as nebulous and unsubstantial as the lady of the lake.

For two pins Maigret would have stuffed all these letters into the green-curtained bookcase, muttering as he did so:

'A lot of rubbish!'

At the same time, he was filled with a certain respect which bordered on emotion. Not wanting to be taken in, he tried to harden his heart.

'Do you believe it all?'

More dukes, princes and dethroned monarchs met in Portugal. Then a journey to Kenya, in the husband's company. Another journey, to the United States this time, where Isabelle had felt rather at a loss because life there was too coarse for her liking.

'. . . *The bigger he grows, the more Philippe resembles you. Isn't it miraculous? Isn't it as if Heaven wanted to reward us for our sacrifice? Hubert has noticed it too, I can see that from the way he looks at the child . . .*'

Hubert, in any case, was no longer admitted to the marriage bed and he did not fail to look elsewhere for consolation. In the letters, he was not Hubert any more, but H . . .

'*Poor H. has a new folly and I suspect that she is making him suffer. He is growing visibly thinner and becoming more and more irritable . . .*'

Follies of this kind recurred every five or six months. For his part, Armand de Saint-Hilaire, in his letters, obviously made no attempt to convince his correspondent that he was leading a life of chastity.

Isabelle wrote to him, for instance:

'*I hope that the women of Turkey are not as unapproachable as people say and above all that their husbands are not too ferocious . . .*'

She added:

'*Be careful, friend. Every morning, I pray for you . . .*'

When he was French Minister in Cuba, then Ambassador in Buenos Aires, she worried about the women of Spanish blood.

'*They are so beautiful! and I, far away and forgotten, tremble at the idea that one day you may fall in love . . .*'

She showed an interest in his health.

'*Are your boils still giving you trouble? In this heat, they must be . . .*'

She knew Jaquette.

'*I am writing to Jaquette to give her the recipe for the almond tart you like so much . . .*'

'Hadn't she promised her husband never to see Saint-Hilaire again? . . . Listen to this . . . It's from a letter sent to this address:

' "*What an ineffable yet painful joy it was for me yesterday to see you from a distance at the Opera . . . I like your greying temples, and a slight paunch gives you an incomparable air of dignity . . . All evening I was proud of you . . . It was only when I got back to the Rue de Varenne and looked at myself in the mirror that I felt frightened . . . How could I have failed to disappoint you? . . . Women fade quickly and I am now almost an old woman . . .*" '

They had seen each other like that, from a distance, fairly frequently. They even gave each other assignations of a sort.

'*Tomorrow, about three o'clock, I shall go for a walk in the Tuileries Gardens with my son . . .*'

Saint-Hilaire, for his part, passed underneath her windows at times fixed in advance.

When her son was about ten years old, there was a characteristic reference to him which Maigret read out aloud.

'*Philippe, finding me busy writing once more, asked me innocently: "Are you writing to your sweetheart again?"*'

Maigret heaved a sigh, mopped his forehead, and tied the bundles up again one after another.

'Try to get me Doctor Tudelle on the phone.'

He needed to find himself back on solid ground. The letters had been returned to their place in the bookcase and he promised himself not to touch them again.

'He's on the line, Chief . . .'

'Hullo, doctor . . . Yes, Maigret speaking . . . You finished ten minutes ago? . . . No, of course I'm not asking you for all the details . . .'

While he was listening, he scribbled words and meaningless symbols on Saint-Hilaire's pad.

'You're sure of that? . . . You've already sent the bullets to Gastine-Renette? . . . I'll phone him a little later . . . Thank you . . . The best thing to do would be to send your report to the examining magistrate . . . That would please him . . . Thank you again . . .'

He started walking up and down the room with his hands behind his back, stopping now and then to look at the garden where a cheeky blackbird was hopping around in the grass a few feet away from him.

'The first bullet,' he explained to Janvier, 'was fired from the front, practically at point-blank range . . . It's a ·301 bullet in a nickel-plated copper envelope . . . Tudelle isn't as experienced as Doctor Paul yet, but he's pretty certain that it was fired from a Browning automatic . . . He's absolutely definite on one point: that first bullet caused almost instantaneous death. The body fell forward and slipped from the armchair on to the carpet . . .'

'How does he know?'

'Because the other shots were fired from above.'

'How many others?'

'Three. Two in the stomach and one in the shoulder. Seeing that automatics hold six cartridges, or seven if you slip one into the barrel, I wonder why the murderer suddenly stopped firing after the fourth bullet. Unless of course the gun jammed . . .'

He glanced at the carpet, which had been cleaned after a fashion, but where the outline of the bloodstains was still visible.

'Either the killer wanted to make sure that his victim was dead, or else he was in such a state of excitement that he went on firing automatically. Get me Moers, will you?'

He had been too impressed, that morning, by the unusual aspect of the case to attend to the material clues himself, and he had left all that to the experts from the Criminal Records Office.

'Moers? . . . Yes . . . How are you getting on? . . . Yes, of course . . . First of all, did you find the cartridge-cases in the study? . . . No? . . . Not one? . . .'

That was strange and seemed to suggest that the murderer knew that he was not going to be disturbed. After four loud shots—very loud shots if the gun was a ·301 automatic—he had taken the time to search the room for the cartridge-cases which would have been ejected quite a long way.

'The doorhandle?'

'The only prints that are reasonably clear are the servant's.'

'The brandy-glass?'

'The dead man's prints.'

'The desk and the rest of the furniture?'

'Not a thing, Chief. I mean there aren't any foreign prints apart from yours.'

'The lock and the windows?'

'The enlargements of our photos show no signs of a forced entry.'

Isabelle's letters might not resemble those of the lovers Maigret usually had to deal with, but the crime was real enough.

Two details, however, seemed at first sight to contradict one another. The murderer had gone on firing at a dead man, at a man who had stopped moving and who, with his head shattered, presented a horrifying sight. Maigret remembered the white hair, still quite plentiful, sticking to the gaping skull, one eye which had stayed open, and a bone protruding from the torn cheek.

The medical expert stated that after the first shot the corpse was on the floor, in front of the armchair, in the place where it had been found.

This meant that the murderer, who had probably been standing on the other side of the desk, had walked round in order to fire again once, twice, three times, from above, at close quarters, less than two feet away according to Tudelle.

At that distance, there was no need to take aim in order to hit a given spot. In other words, it seemed that he had hit the chest and stomach on purpose.

Didn't that suggest an act of vengeance, or an exceptional degree of hatred?

'You're sure there isn't a gun anywhere in the flat? You hunted everywhere?'

'Even up the chimney,' answered Janvier.

Maigret too had looked for the automatic which the old servant had mentioned, admittedly in rather vague terms.

'Go and ask the policeman on duty at the door if it isn't a ·301 that he's carrying in his holster.'

A good many uniformed policemen were equipped with a gun of that calibre.

'Get him to lend it to you for a minute.'

He too went out of the study, crossed the corridor, and pushed open the door of the kitchen, where Jaquette Larrieu was sitting on a chair, holding herself very stiffly. Her eyes were shut and she looked as if she were asleep. She started at the noise.

'Will you come with me . . .'

'Where?'

'Into the study. I should like to ask you a few questions.'

'I have already told you that I don't know anything.'

Once in the room, she looked all round her as if to make sure that nothing had been disturbed.

'Sit down.'

She hesitated, unaccustomed, no doubt, to sitting down in this room in her employer's presence.

'In that chair, please . . .'

She obeyed reluctantly, looking at the chief-inspector more suspiciously than ever.

Janvier came back with an automatic in his hand.

'Give it to her.'

She shrank from taking it, opened her mouth to say something, then shut it again. Maigret could have sworn that she had been on the point of asking: 'Where did you find it?'

The weapon fascinated her. She found it difficult to take her eyes off it.

'You recognize this gun?'

'How can you expect me to recognize it? I have never examined it closely and I don't imagine it's the only one of its kind.'

'It *is* the type of weapon the Count possessed, though?'

'I suppose so.'

'The same size?'

'I can't say.'

'Hold it in your hand. Is it roughly the same weight?'

She flatly refused to do what they asked.

'It wouldn't be any use, seeing that I have never touched the one that was in the drawer.'

'You can take it back to the policeman, Janvier.'

'You don't need me any more?'

'Stay where you are, please. I suppose you don't know whether your master ever gave or lent his pistol to anybody, to his nephew for instance, or to somebody else?'

'How should I know? All I know is that I haven't seen it for a long time.'

'Was the Comte de Saint-Hilaire afraid of burglars?'

'Certainly not. Neither burglars nor murderers. The proof of that is that in summer he used to sleep with his window open, even though we are on the ground floor and anybody could have got into his bedroom.'

'He didn't keep any valuables in the flat?'

'You and your men know better than I do what there is there.'

'When did you enter his service?'

'Straight after the 1914 war. He had just come back from abroad. His valet had died.'

'Then you were about twenty years old at the time?'

'Twenty-eight.'

'How long had you been in Paris?'

'A few months. Before that, I had lived with my father in Normandy. When my father died, I had to find a job.'

'Had you had any affairs?'

'What did you say?'

'I asked you whether you had had any sweethearts, or a fiancé.'

She looked at him resentfully.

'Nothing like what you are thinking.'

'So you lived alone in this flat with the Comte de Saint-Hilaire?'

'Is there anything wrong in that?'

Maigret was not asking questions in any logical order, for nothing struck him as logical in this case, and he moved from one subject to another as if he were looking for the tender spot. Janvier, who had come back into the room, had sat down near the door. When he lit a cigarette and dropped the match on the floor, the old woman, who did not miss anything, called him to order.

'You might use an ashtray.'

'Incidentally, did your master smoke?'

'He did for a long time.'

'Cigarettes?'

'Cigars.'

'And recently he stopped smoking?'

'Yes. On account of his chronic bronchitis.'

'But he seemed to be in excellent health.'

Doctor Tudelle had told Maigret, over the telephone, that Saint-Hilaire had obviously enjoyed exceptionally good health.

'A sound body, the heart in perfect condition, no sign of sclerosis.'

But certain organs had been too badly damaged by the bullets to allow a complete diagnosis.

'When you entered his service, he was almost a young man.'

'He was seven years older than me.'

'You knew that he was in love?'

'I used to post his letters for him.'

'You weren't jealous?'

'Why should I have been jealous?'

'You never happened to see the person he wrote to every day here in this flat?'

'She has never set foot in the flat.'

'But you have seen her?'

She made no reply.

'Answer my question. When the case goes to the Assizes, you will be asked much more embarrassing questions and you won't be allowed to remain silent.'

'I don't know anything.'

'I asked you whether you had seen this person.'

'Yes. She used to go past in the street. Sometimes too I took letters to her and delivered them to her personally.'

'In secret?'

'No. I asked to see her and I was taken along to her rooms.'

'Did she talk to you?'

'Sometimes she asked me questions.'

'You are talking about forty years ago, I suppose?'

'Then and more recently.'

'What sort of questions did she ask?'

'Mostly about Monsieur le Comte's health.'

'Not about the people who came here?'

'No.'

'You accompanied your master abroad?'

'Everywhere!'

'As Minister, and later as Ambassador, he had to keep up a large establishment. What exactly was your function?'

'I looked after him.'

'You mean to say that you were not on the same footing as the other servants, that you didn't have to bother about the cooking, the cleaning, the receptions?'

'I supervised.'

'What was your title? Housekeeper?'

'I didn't have a title.'

'Have you had any lovers?'

She stiffened, her eyes more contemptuous than ever.

'Were you his mistress?'

Maigret was afraid that she was going to hurl herself at him with all her claws bared.

'I know from his correspondence,' he went on, 'that he had several affairs.'

'He had a right to, hadn't he?'

'Were you jealous?'

'I sometimes had to show certain persons the door, because they weren't suitable for him and because they would have made trouble for him.'

'In other words, you looked after his private life.'

'He was too good-natured. He had remained very naïve.'

'Yet he filled the delicate role of ambassador with considerable distinction.'

'That isn't the same thing.'

'You never left him?'

'Do the letters say I did?'

It was Maigret's turn not to reply, to insist:

'How long were you parted from him?'

'Five months.'

'When was that?'

'When he was Minister in Cuba.'

'Why?'

'Because of a woman who insisted on him getting rid of me.'

'What sort of woman?'

Silence.

'Why couldn't she stand you? Did she live with him?'

'She came to see him every day and often spent the night at the Legation.'

'Where did you go?'

'I took a little room near the Prado.'

'Did your master come to see you there?'

'He didn't dare. He just used to ring me up to ask me to be patient. He knew perfectly well that it wouldn't last. All the same, I bought my ticket to go back to Europe.'

'But you didn't go?'

'He came to fetch me the day before I was due to leave.'

'Do you know Prince Philippe?'

'If you've really read the letters, you don't need to ask me all these questions. It shouldn't be allowed, going through somebody's correspondence after he's dead.'

'You haven't answered my question.'

'I used to see him when he was young.'

'Where?'

'In the Rue de Varenne. He was often with his mother.'

'You didn't think of ringing up the Princess this morning, before going to the Quai d'Orsay?'

She looked at him full in the face, without flinching.

'Why didn't you, seeing that by your account, you had served for a long time as a link between them?'

'Because today was the day of the funeral.'

'And later this morning, while we were out of the house, weren't you tempted to tell her what had happened?'

She stared at the telephone.

'There has always been somebody in the study.'

There was a knock at the door. It was the policeman on duty in the street.

'I don't know if this is of any interest to you. I thought you might like to see the paper.'

It was an early edition of an evening paper which must have come out an hour before. A fairly prominent headline across two columns at the bottom of the front page announced:

MYSTERIOUS DEATH OF AMBASSADOR

The text was brief.

'This morning, at his home in the Rue Saint-Dominique, the body was discovered of the Comte Armand de Saint-Hilaire, who for many years served as French Ambassador in various capitals, including Rome, London and Washington.

'Since his retirement some years ago, Armand de Saint-Hilaire had published two volumes of memoirs, and he was correcting proofs of a third volume when, so it seems, he was murdered.

'The crime was discovered early this morning by an old servant.

'It is not yet known whether some mysterious motive is to be looked for.'

He handed the paper to Jaquette, and looked hesitantly at the telephone. He wondered whether they had read the paper in the Rue de Varenne, or whether somebody had already told Isabelle the news.

In that case, how was she going to react? Would she dare to come here herself? Would she send her son to make inquiries? Or would she just sit and wait in the silence of her house, where, as a sign of mourning, the shutters had doubtless been closed?

Shouldn't Maigret . . .

He stood up, annoyed with himself, annoyed with everything, and went and planted himself in front of the French window, knocking his pipe out on his heel, to Jaquette's indignation.

Chapter Four

The old woman, a small, erect figure on her chair, listened in amazement to the chief-inspector's voice, which had assumed a tone which she had not heard before. Admittedly it was not to her that Maigret was speaking, but to an invisible person at the other end of the line.

'No, Monsieur Cromières, I haven't issued any statements to the Press, and I haven't invited any reporters or photographers along as Ministers are so fond of doing. As for your second question, I haven't anything new to tell you, nor any ideas, as you put it, and if I discover anything I shall report it immediately to the examining magistrate . . .'

Maigret in Society

He intercepted a furtive glance from Jaquette in Janvier's direction. She seemed to be calling the latter to witness the chief-inspector's ill-concealed anger, and there was a faint smile on her lips, rather as if she were saying to the inspector:

'Well, well! Just listen to your chief!'

Maigret took his companion out into the corridor.

'I'm going to nip round to the solicitor's. Go on asking her questions, not pressing her too hard, but gently—you know what I mean. You may appeal to her more than I do.'

It was true. If he had realized, before setting out that morning, that he was going to have to deal with a tough old maid, he would have brought along young Lapointe rather than Janvier, because, of all the inspectors at Police Headquarters, it was Lapointe who had the greatest success with middle-aged women. One had actually said to him, shaking her head sadly:

'I wonder how a well-bred young man like you can carry on this profession!'

She had added:

'I'm sure it must go against the grain!'

The chief-inspector found himself in the street again, where the reporters had left one of their number on duty while they went to have a drink in a nearby pub.

'Nothing new, old chap . . . It isn't worth your while to follow me . . .'

He was not going far. There was never any need to go far in this case. It was as if, for all those who were remotely or closely connected with it, Paris were reduced to a few aristocratic streets.

The solicitor's house, in the Rue de Villersexel, was of the same period and the same style as that in the Rue Saint-Dominique, with a carriage entrance too, a wide staircase with a red carpet, and a lift which probably went up smoothly and noiselessly. He did not need to use it, for the office was on the first floor. The brass handles of the double doors were highly polished, as was the plate asking visitors to go in without ringing.

'If I find myself faced with another old man . . .'

He was pleasantly surprised to see, among the clerks, a good-looking woman of about thirty.

'Maître Aubonnet, please!'

True, the office was a little too quiet, a trifle austere, but he was not kept waiting and was shown almost immediately into a huge room where a man aged forty-five at the most stood up to greet him.

'Chief-Inspector Maigret . . . I have come to see you about one of your clients, the Comte de Saint-Hilaire . . .'

The other man replied with a smile:

'In that case, it isn't a matter for me but for my father. I'll go and see if he's available just now.'

The younger Maître Aubonnet went into another room and stayed there for some time.

'Will you come this way, Monsieur Maigret . . .'

This time, of course, the chief-inspector found himself in the presence of a real old man, who was not even in very good condition. The elder Aubonnet was sitting in a high-backed armchair, blinking his eyes with the bewildered expression of a man who has just been roused from his afternoon nap.

Maître Aubonnet had obviously been very fat at one time. He had retained a certain corpulence, but his body was flabby, with folds everywhere. He was wearing a shoe on one foot and a felt slipper on the other, the ankle of which was swollen.

'I suppose you've come to talk to me about my poor old friend? . . .'

The mouth was slack too, and the syllables which emerged from it formed a sort of paste. On the other hand, there was no need to ask any questions to start him talking.

'Just imagine, Saint-Hilaire and I first met at Stanislas . . . That's how many years ago? . . . Wait a moment . . . I'm seventy-seven . . . So it's sixty years now since we were in the sixth form together . . . He intended to enter the Foreign Service . . . My own dream was to join the Saumur cavalry . . . They still had horses in those days . . . They weren't all motorized . . . You know, I've never had a chance to do any riding in the whole of my life? . . . All because I was an only son and I had to take over my father's office . . .'

Maigret forebore to ask him whether this father of his was already living in the same house at that time.

'Even in his school-days, Saint-Hilaire was a *bon vivant*, but a *bon vivant* of a rather rare type, a person of tremendous distinction . . .'

'I suppose he has left a will with you?'

'His nephew, young Mazeron, asked me the same question just now. I was able to set his mind at rest . . .'

'Does the nephew inherit everything?'

'Not the whole estate, no. I know the will by heart, since it was I who drew it up.'

'A long time ago?'

'The last will dates back ten years or so.'

'Were the previous wills different?'

'Only in minor particulars. I wasn't able to show the nephew the document, seeing that all the interested parties have to be present.'

'Who are they?'

'Broadly speaking, Alain Mazeron inherits the block of flats in the Rue Saint-Dominique and the bulk of the fortune, which in any case isn't very great. Jaquette Larrieu, the housekeeper, receives a pension which will enable her to end her days in comfort. As for the furniture, knick-knacks, pictures, and personal belongings, Saint-Hilaire bequeaths them to an old friend . . .'

'Isabelle de V——.'

'I see you know all about it.'

'Do you know her?'

'Fairly well. I knew her husband better, because he was one of my clients.'

Wasn't it rather surprising to see the two men choosing the same solicitor? 'They weren't afraid of running into each other in your office?'

'That never happened. The idea that it might probably never occurred to them, and I don't know that they would have found it terribly embarrassing. You see, they were made, if not to be friends, at least to have a high regard for each other, for they were both of them men of honour and, what is more, men of taste . . .'

Even the words he used seemed to come from the past. It was a long time, in fact, since Maigret had last heard the expression *man of honour*.

The old solicitor, in his armchair, shook with silent laughter at a fleeting thought.

'Men of taste, yes,' he repeated maliciously, 'and you could add that in one respect they had identical tastes . . . Now they are dead, I don't think I am betraying a professional secret in telling you this, particularly as you too are obliged to be discreet . . . A solicitor is nearly always a confidant . . . Apart from that, Saint-Hilaire was an old friend who used to come and tell me all about his pranks . . . For about a year, the Prince and he had the same mistress, a lovely girl with an opulent bosom who was appearing in some boulevard revue or other . . . They didn't know . . . Each had his own day . . .'

The old man gave Maigret a meaning look.

'Those people knew how to live . . . For several years now, I have had hardly anything to do with the office, where my eldest son has taken my place . . . All the same, I come downstairs to my office every day and I go on helping my old clients . . .'

'Did Saint-Hilaire have many friends?'

'The same was true of his friends as of the clients I mentioned just now. At our age, you see people dying off one after another. I do believe that in the end I was the last person he used to visit. He had kept the full use of his legs, and he still went for a walk every day. He sometimes came up here to see me, sitting where you are sitting now . . .'

'What did you talk about?'

'About the old days, of course, and especially the boys we knew at Stanislas. I could still give you most of the names. It's astonishing, how many of them have had distinguished careers. One of our schoolmates, who wasn't the most intelligent, was Prime Minister I don't know how many times and died only last year. Another is a military member of the Academy . . .'

'Had Saint-Hilaire made any enemies?'

'How could he have made any? On the professional level, he never jostled anybody out of a position, as is so often the case nowadays. He obtained his posts by patiently waiting his turn. And in his memoirs, he didn't pay off any old scores, which explains why few people have read them . . .'

'And what about the V——'s?'

The solicitor looked at him in surprise.

'I've already spoken to you about the Prince. He knew the whole story, of course, and he knew that Saint-Hilaire would keep his word. If it hadn't been for society, I'm convinced that Armand would have been received at the house in the Rue de Varenne and that he might even have had his place at table there.'

'The son knows all about it too?'

'Certainly.'

'What is he like?'

'I don't think he has anything like his father's intelligence. It's true that I don't know him as well as I knew his father. He seems far less communicative, which is probably due to the difficulty, in our day and age, of bearing a name as heavy as his. Social life doesn't interest him. He is very rarely to be seen in Paris. He spends most of the year in Normandy, with his wife and children, looking after his farms and his horses . . .'

'Have you seen him recently?'

'I shall be seeing him tomorrow, as well as his mother, at the reading of the will, so that I shall probably have to deal with both estates on the same day.'

'The Princess hasn't rung you up this afternoon?'

'Not yet. If she reads the papers, or if somebody tells her the news, she will doubtless get in touch with me. I still can't understand why anybody should murder my old friend. If it had happened anywhere except in his own home, I should have sworn that the murderer had killed the wrong person by mistake.'

'I suppose Jaquette Larrieu was his mistress?'

'That isn't the right word. Mind you, Saint-Hilaire never talked to me about her. But I knew him. I knew Jaquette too, when she was young, and she was a very pretty girl. Now, Armand rarely let a pretty girl come within reach without trying his luck. He did that in an aesthetic spirit, if you see what I mean. And it's more than likely that, if the opportunity occurred . . .'

'Jaquette hasn't any relatives?'

'I don't know of any. If she had any brothers and sisters, the odds are that they died a long time ago.'

'Thank you very much . . .'

'I suppose you are in a hurry? In any case, don't forget that I remain entirely at your service. You look a decent fellow too, and I hope you find the scoundrel who's responsible.'

Always this impression of being immersed in a distant past, in a world which had, so to speak, vanished. It was bewildering to find oneself back in the street, in a living Paris, with women in tight-fitting trousers doing their shopping, bars full of nickel-plated furniture, cars throbbing in front of traffic-lights.

He made for the Rue Jacob, but all in vain, for on the door of the shuttered shop he found a card framed in black which announced:

'*Closed on account of death in the family.*'

He pressed the bell several times without getting any reply, and crossed over to the other pavement to look at the windows on the first floor. They were open but there was no sound to be heard. A woman with copper-coloured hair and big, slack breasts, emerged from the darkness of a picture-gallery.

'If it's Monsieur Mazeron you want, he isn't at home. I saw him go off about midday after closing his shutters.'

She didn't know where he had gone.

'He doesn't talk much to other people . . .'

Maigret could go and see Isabelle de V—— of course, but the thought of that particular visit daunted him slightly, and he preferred to put it off until later, trying in the meantime to find out a little more.

He had rarely felt so nonplussed by other human beings. Would a psychiatrist, a schoolmaster or a novelist, to quote the list in the *Lancet*, have been in a better position to understand people from another century?

One thing was certain: the Comte Armand de Saint-Hilaire, a gentle, inoffensive old fellow, a man of honour, to use the solicitor's expression, had been murdered, in his own house, by somebody about whom he had no suspicions.

The possibility that this was an unpremeditated, accidental crime, a stupid, anonymous murder, could be ruled out, first of all because nothing had disappeared, and secondly because the former ambassador had been sitting peacefully at his desk when the first bullet, fired at close quarters, had struck him in the face.

Either he had gone to open the door to his visitor himself, or else the latter had a key to the flat, although Jaquette maintained that there were only two keys in existence, hers and the Count's.

Maigret, still turning over these rather confused thoughts in his head, went into a bar, ordered a glass of beer and shut himself up in the call-box.

'Is that you, Moers? . . . Have you got the inventory in front of you? . . . Will you look and see if there's any mention of a key . . . The key to the flat, yes . . . What's that? . . . Yes? . . . Where did they find it? . . . In his trouser-pocket? . . . Thank you . . . Nothing new? . . . No . . . I shall be coming back to the Quai late in the day . . . If you've anything to tell me, ring Janvier, who has stayed behind in the Rue Saint-Dominique . . .'

They had found one of the two keys in the dead man's trouser-pocket, and Jaquette had hers too, since she had used it to open the door that morning, when Maigret and the man from the Foreign Office had followed her into the ground-floor flat.

People didn't commit murder without a motive. What remained, once theft had been ruled out? A crime of passion, between two old men? A matter of money?

Jaquette Larrieu, according to the solicitor, received a more than adequate pension for the rest of her life.

The nephew, for his part, inherited the block of flats and the bulk of the estate.

As for Isabelle, it was hard to imagine that, almost immediately after her husband's death, the idea should have occurred to her . . .

No, there was no satisfactory explanation, and the Quai d'Orsay for its part categorically ruled out any political motive.

'Rue de la Pompe!' he said to the driver of a yellow taxi.

'Right, Chief-Inspector.'

A long time ago now, he had stopped feeling flattered at being recognized like that. The concierge directed him to the fifth floor, where a pretty little brunette began by opening the door an inch or so before showing Maigret into a flat which was ablaze with sunshine.

'Excuse the mess . . . I was busy making a dress for my daughter . . .'

She was wearing tight-fitting trousers in black silk which showed the shape of her plump buttocks.

'I suppose you've come to see me about the murder, though I don't know what you hope to find out from me.'

'Your children aren't here?'

'My elder daughter is in England to learn the language. She's living with a family, *au pair*, and my younger daughter is working. It's for her that I'm . . .'

She pointed to the table, where there was some light, coloured material out of which she was cutting a dress.

'I suppose you've seen my husband?'

'Yes.'

'How is he taking it?'

'Is it a long time since you last saw him?'

'Nearly three years.'

'And the Comte de Saint-Hilaire?'

'The last time he came up here was just before Christmas. He brought some presents for my daughters. He never failed to remember. Even when he was in some post abroad and they were still little, he didn't forget them at

Christmas and always sent them some small gift. That's how they come to have dolls from all over the world. You can still see them in their room.'

She was not more than forty years old and she had remained extremely attractive.

'Is it true, what the papers say? He was murdered?'

'Tell me about your husband.'

The life promptly went out of her face.

'What do you want me to say?'

'You married for love, didn't you? Unless I'm mistaken, he is much older than you.'

'Only ten years. He has always looked older than he is.'

'You loved him?'

'I don't know. I was living alone with my father, who was sour and embittered. He regarded himself as a great painter who wasn't appreciated at his true value, and it grieved him to earn his living by restoring pictures. I for my part worked in a shop on the Grande Boulevards. I met Alain. Aren't you thirsty?'

'No thank you. I've just had a glass of beer. Go on . . .'

'Perhaps it was the air of mystery about him that attracted me. He wasn't like other men, he talked very little, and what he said was always interesting. We got married and had a daughter straight away . . .'

'You lived in the Rue Jacob?'

'Yes. I liked that street too, and our little first-floor flat. At that time, the Comte de Saint-Hilaire was still an ambassador, in Washington, unless I'm mistaken. During one of his leaves he came to see us, and later he invited us to the Rue Saint-Dominique. I was very impressed by him.'

'How did he get on with your husband?'

'I can't really say. He was a man who was pleasant with everybody. He seemed surprised that I should be his nephew's wife.'

'Why?'

'It was only much later that I thought I understood, and I'm still not sure. He must have known Alain better than I thought, certainly better than I did at the time . . .'

She broke off, as if she were worried about what she had just said.

'I don't want to give you the impression that I'm talking like this out of spite, because my husband and I are separated. Besides, I'm the one who left.'

'And he didn't try to stop you?'

Here the furniture was modern, the walls lightcoloured, and he could see part of a neat white kitchen. Familiar noises rose from the street and nearby was the green expanse of the Bois de Boulogne.

'I trust you don't suspect Alain?'

'To be perfectly frank, I don't suspect anybody yet, but I'm not ruling out any hypothesis *a priori*.'

'You'd be on the wrong track if you did, I'm sure of that. In my opinion, Alain is a poor devil who has never been able to adjust himself to life and never will be able to adjust himself. It's surprising, isn't it, that after leaving my father because he was embittered I should marry a man even more embittered than he was? It was a long time before I really noticed. The fact of the matter is, I've never seen him satisfied with anything, and I wonder now if he has ever smiled in the whole of his life.

'He worries about everything, about his health and his business, about what people think of him, about the way neighbours and customers look at him . . .

'Everybody, he imagines, has a grudge against him.

'It's difficult to explain. You mustn't laugh at what I'm going to say. When I was living with him, I had the impression that I could hear him thinking from morning till night, and it was a sound as nerve-racking as the ticking of an alarm-clock. He used to come and go in silence, looking at me all of a sudden as if his eyes were turned towards the inside where I couldn't tell what was happening. Is he still as pale as ever?'

'He is pale, yes.'

'He was already when I met him, and he stayed that way in the country and at the seaside. It was like an artificial pallor . . .

'And nothing showed outside. It was impossible to make contact with him . . . For years we slept in the same bed and sometimes, when I woke up, I found myself looking at him as if he were a stranger.

'He was cruel . . .'

She tried to take the word back.

'I'm probably exaggerating. He thought that he was fair, and he wanted to be fair at all costs. It was a mania with him. He was scrupulously fair and that's what made me talk about cruelty. I noticed it most of all when we had the children. He regarded them in the same way as he regarded me and other people, with a cold lucidity. If they did something naughty, I tried to defend them.

' "At their age, Alain . . ."

' "*There's no reason why they should get into the habit of cheating.*"

'That was one of his favourite words. Cheating . . . Dirty tricks . . .

'He was just as strict about the little details of everyday life:

' "*Why did you buy fish?*"

'I tried to explain that . . .

' "*I said veal.*"

' "When I went to do my shopping . . ."

'He stubbornly repeated:

' "*I said veal, and you had no business to buy fish.*" '

She broke off again.

'I'm not talking too much, am I? I'm not saying silly things?'

'Go on.'

'I've finished. After a few years, I thought I could understand what the Americans mean by mental cruelty and why it has become grounds for divorce over there. There are schoolteachers, both men and women, who, without raising their voices, can impose a sort of reign of terror on their class.

'With Alain, we felt suffocated, my daughters and I, and we didn't even have the consolation of seeing him go off to the office every morning. He was downstairs, under our feet, from morning till night, coming upstairs ten times a day to watch what we were doing with cold eyes.

'I had to account to him for every franc I spent. When I went out, he insisted on knowing which way I was going to go, and when I got back he questioned me about the people I had spoken to, what I had said to them and what they had replied . . .'

'Were you unfaithful to him?'

She showed no indignation. Indeed, it seemed to Maigret that she was tempted to smile with a certain satisfaction, even a certain pleasure, but that she restrained herself.

'Why do you ask me that? Has somebody told you something about me?'

'No.'

'As long as I was living with him, I didn't do anything he could hold against me.'

'What made you decide to leave him?'

'I was at the end of my tether. I was suffocating, as I told you, and I wanted my daughters to grow up in an atmosphere they could breathe freely.'

'You hadn't a more personal reason for wanting to regain your freedom?'

'Perhaps.'

'Your daughters know about it?'

'I haven't concealed the fact from them that I have a lover, and they back me up.'

'He lives with you?'

'I go and see him in his flat. He's a widower of my age, who hadn't been any happier with his wife than I had with my husband, so that it's rather as if we were sticking the bits together again.'

'Does he live in this district?'

'In this building, two floors down. He's a doctor. You'll see his plate on the door. If, one day, Alain agrees to a divorce, we intend to get married, but I doubt if he will ever do that. He's very Catholic, out of tradition rather than conviction.'

'Does your husband earn a good living?'

'He has his ups and downs. When I left him, it was agreed that he would pay me a modest allowance for the children. He kept his word for a few months. Then there were some delays. And finally he stopped paying completely, on the pretext that they were big enough to earn their living. But that doesn't make him a murderer, does it?'

'Did you know about his uncle's liaison?'

'Are you talking about Isabelle?'

'Had you heard that the Prince de V—— died on Sunday morning and that he was buried today?'

'I read it in the paper.'

'Do you think that if Saint-Hilaire hadn't been killed he would have married the Princess?'

'Probably. All his life he had hoped that they would be united one day. I found it touching to hear him talking about her as if she were a woman in a class apart, an almost supernatural creature, when he was a man who appreciated the realities of life, sometimes even a little too much . . .'

This time she smiled openly.

'One day, a long time ago, when I went to see him about something or other, I forget what, I had a job to escape from his clutches. He was a cool customer, and no mistake. In his eyes, it was perfectly normal . . .'

'Did your husband find out?'

She shrugged her shoulders.

'Of course not.'

'He was jealous?'

'In his fashion. We didn't often have intercourse, and it was always cold, almost mechanical. What he would have condemned wasn't that I should be attracted by another man but that I should be guilty of a misdemeanour, a sin, an act of treachery, something he regarded as unclean. Forgive me if I've talked too much or if I've given the impression of wanting to do him down, because that isn't the case. You've seen that I haven't made myself out to be better than I am. I shan't go on feeling a real woman much longer, and I'm making the most of it while I can . . .'

She had a sensual mouth and sparkling eyes. For several minutes she had kept crossing and uncrossing her legs.

'You are sure you won't have something to drink?'

'No thank you. It's time I was going.'

'I assume all this remains confidential?'

He smiled at her and made for the door, where she gave him a hot, plump hand.

'I must carry on with my daughter's dress,' she said, almost regretfully.

So he had managed, after all, to escape for a moment from the circle of old people. Leaving the flat in the Rue de la Pompe, it was without any feeling of surprise that he found himself back in the street, among all its noises and smells.

He found a taxi straight away and told the driver to take him to the Rue Saint-Dominique. Before going into the block of flats, he decided after all to go and have the glass of beer which he had refused at Madame Mazeron's, and in the bar he rubbed shoulders with chauffeurs from the ministries and great houses.

The reporter was still at his post.

'You can see that I didn't try to follow you. You can't tell me whom you've been to see?'

'The solicitor.'

'Did he tell you anything new?'

'Not a thing.'

'Still no clues?'

'No.'

'And it isn't a political affair?'

'Apparently not.'

The uniformed policeman was there too. Maigret rang the bell, next to the lift-shaft. It was Janvier, in his shirtsleeves, who opened the door to him, and Jaquette was not in the study.

'What have you done with her? Have you let her go out?'

'No. She tried to, after the phone call, saying that there was nothing left to eat in the house.'

'Where is she?'

'In her room. She's resting.'

'What phone call are you talking about?'

'Half-an-hour after you had gone, the phone rang, and I answered it. I heard a woman's voice, a rather quiet voice, at the other end of the line.'

' "Who is that?" she asked.

'Instead of answering, I asked in my turn:

' "Who is calling?"

' "I should like to speak to Mademoiselle Larrieu."

' "Who shall I say?"

'There was a silence, then:

' "The Princess de V——."

'All this time, Jaquette had been looking at me as if she knew what it was all about.

' "Here she is."

'I gave her the receiver and straight away she said:

' "It's me, Madame la Princesse . . . Yes . . . I would have come along, but these gentlemen won't allow me to go out . . . There were lots of them all over the flat, with all sorts of apparatus . . . They spent hours asking me questions and even now there's an inspector listening to me . . ." '

Janvier added:

'She looked as if she were defying me. After that, she listened most of the time.

' "Yes . . . Yes, Madame la Princesse . . . Yes . . . I understand . . . I don't know . . . No . . . Yes . . . I'll try . . . I should like to, as well . . . Thank you, Madame la Princesse . . ." '

'What did she say then?'

'Nothing. She went back to her chair. After a quarter of an hour of silence, she muttered sadly:

' "I suppose you aren't going to let me get out? Even if there's nothing left to eat in the house and I have to go without my dinner?"

' "We'll see about that later on."

' "In that case, I don't see what we are doing sitting face to face like this, and I'd rather go and have a rest. Have I got your permission to do that?"

'Since then she has been in her room. She has locked the door.'

'Nobody has been?'

'No. There have been a few phone calls, from an American news agency and some provincial papers . . .'

'You didn't manage to get anything out of Jaquette?'

'I started asking her the most innocent questions imaginable, in the hope of winning her confidence. All that happened was that she said in a sarcastic voice:

' "Young man, you can't teach your grandmother to suck eggs. If your chief thought I was going to tell you some secrets . . ." '

'The Quai didn't ring at all?'

'No. Just the examining magistrate.'

'Does he want to see me?'

'He asked if you would call him if you had any news. Alain Mazeron has been to see him.'

'And you didn't tell me?'

'I was keeping it till the end. Apparently the nephew went to see him to complain that you had read Saint-Hilaire's private correspondence without his permission. As executor, he asked for seals to be affixed to the flat until the will had been read.'

'What did the magistrate say to him?'

'He told him to come and see you.'

'And Mazeron hasn't been back?'

'No. He may be on the way, because it isn't long since I had that phone call. Do you think he'll come?'

Maigret hesitated, and finally pulled a telephone directory towards him. After finding what he was looking for, standing there with a serious, preoccupied expression on his face, he dialled a number.

'Hullo. Is that the V—— residence? I should like to speak to the Princesse

de V——. This is Chief-Inspector Maigret of the Judicial Police speaking
. . . Yes, I'll hold the line . . .'

There was as it were a different kind of silence in the room, and Janvier
held his breath as he looked at his chief. Several minutes went by.

'Yes, I'll wait . . . Thank you . . . Hullo . . . Yes, Madame, this is Chief-
Inspector Maigret . . .'

It was not his everyday voice, and he felt a certain emotion as when, in his
childhood, he had occasion to speak to the Comtesse de Saint-Fiacre.

'I thought that you might possibly wish me to get in touch with you, if
only to give you a few details . . . Yes . . . Yes . . . When you wish . . . I will
come to the Rue de Varenne then an hour from now . . .'

The two men looked at each other in silence. Finally Maigret heaved a
sigh.

'You had better stay here,' he said in the end. 'Ring up Lucas and ask him
to send you somebody, preferably Lapointe. The old girl can go out
whenever she likes and one of the two of you will follow her.'

He had an hour to wait. To while away the time, he took a bundle of letters
out of the bookcase with the green curtain.

'*Yesterday, at Longchamp, I caught sight of you in a morning coat, and you
know how I like to see you dressed like that. You had a pretty redhead on your
arm who . . .*'

Chapter Five

Maigret did not expect to find a house that still smelt of the funeral, as in
lower-class or even middle-class homes, with the scent of tapers and
chrysanthemums, a red-eyed widow, and relatives from distant parts,
dressed in deep mourning, sitting around eating and drinking. On account
of his country childhood, the smell of alcohol, and especially that of marc-
brandy, remained associated for him with death and funerals.

'Drink this, Catherine,' they used to say to the widow before setting off for
the church and the cemetery. 'You need something to buck you up.'

She would drink up, weeping at the same time. The men used to drink at
the local inn, and when they returned home.

If hangings decorated with silver tears had adorned the main entrance in
the morning, they had been removed a long time ago and the courtyard had
resumed its normal appearance, half in the shade, half in the sun, with a
uniformed chauffeur washing a long black limousine, and three cars,
including a yellow sports car, waiting at the foot of the steps.

It was as huge as the Élysée and Maigret remembered that the house had
often served as the setting for balls and charity bazaars.

At the top of the steps, he pushed open a glass door and found himself all
alone in an entrance-hall paved with marble. Double doors standing open on
his left and right afforded him a glimpse of the state rooms in which various
objects, no doubt the old coins and snuffboxes which had been mentioned to
him, were displayed as in a museum.

Should he make for one of those doors, or go up the double flight of stairs leading to the first floor? He was hesitating when a majordomo, appearing from heaven knows where, came up to him in silence, took his hat out of his hands, and without asking for his name murmured:

'This way.'

Maigret followed his guide up the staircase, across another drawing-room on the first floor, and then through a long room which was obviously a picture-gallery.

He was not kept waiting. The servant opened a door a little way, and announced in a soft voice:

'Chief-Inspector Maigret.'

The boudoir which he entered did not look out on to the courtyard but on to a garden, and the foliage of the trees, full of birds, brushed against the two open windows.

Somebody got up from an armchair and for a moment he failed to realize that it was the woman he had come to see, the Princess Isabelle. His surprise must have been obvious for as she came towards him she said:

'You expected me to look rather different, didn't you?'

He did not dare to say yes. He made no reply, taken aback by her appearance. In the first place, for all that she was dressed in black, she did not give the impression of being in deep mourning, though he would have been hard put to it to say why. She did not appear to be greatly distressed.

She was smaller than in the photographs, but, unlike Jaquette for instance, she was not bent under the weight of the years. He had no time to analyze his impressions. He would do that later. For the moment, he registered mechanically.

What surprised him most of all was finding a plump woman, with full, smooth cheeks and a dumpy body. Her hips, scarcely hinted at by the princess dress in the photograph in Saint-Hilaire's room, had become as broad as those of any farmer's wife.

Was the boudoir in which they were standing the room where she spent most of her life? There were old tapestries on the walls. The floor shone brightly and every piece of furniture was in its place, something which, for no particular reason, reminded Maigret of the convent where, in the past, he had sometimes visited an aunt of his who was a nun.

'Please take a seat.'

She pointed to a gilded armchair to which he preferred an upright chair, even though he was afraid of breaking its delicate legs.

'My first impulse was to go over there,' she confided to him, sitting down in her turn, 'but then I realized that he wouldn't be there any more. The body has been taken to the Morgue, I suppose?'

She was not afraid of words, nor of the pictures which they evoked. Her face was serene, almost joyful, and that too recalled the convent, the peculiar serenity of the good nuns who never really looked as if they belonged to this world.

'I badly want to see him one last time. I shall come back to that later. What I want to know first of all is whether he died in pain.'

'You can set your mind at rest, Madame. The Comte de Saint-Hilaire was killed instantly.'

'He was in his study?'

'Yes.'

'Sitting?'

'Yes. It seems that he was busy correcting proofs.'

She closed her eyes, as if to give the picture time to take shape in her mind, and Maigret made so bold as to ask a question in his turn.

'Have you ever been to the Rue Saint-Dominique?'

'Only once, a long time ago, with Jaquette's connivance. I had chosen a time when I was sure that he wouldn't be there. I wanted to see the setting of his life, so as to be able to visualize him at home, in the various rooms.'

An idea struck her.

'You mean you haven't read the letters?'

He hesitated, then decided to tell the truth.

'I've looked through them. Not all of them though . . .'

'Are they still in the Empire bookcase with the gilt lattice-work?'

He nodded.

'I thought that you would have read them. I don't hold it against you. I realize that it was your duty.'

'How did you hear about his death?'

'From my daughter-in-law. My son Philippe had come from Normandy with his wife and children to attend the funeral. A little while ago, after we had got back from the cemetery, my daughter-in-law happened to glance at one of the newspapers that the servants usually put out on a table in the hall.'

'Your daughter-in-law knows all about it?'

She looked at him with an astonishment which bordered on innocence. If he had not known who she was, he might well have thought that she was playing a part.

'All about what?'

'About your relationship with the Comte de Saint-Hilaire.'

Her smile too was a nun's smile.

'But of course. How could she have failed to know about it? We never made any attempt at concealment. There was nothing wrong about it. Armand was a very dear friend . . .'

'Did your son know him?'

'My son too knew all about it, and when he was a boy I sometimes pointed out Armand to him from a distance. I think the first time was at Auteuil . . .'

'He never went to see him?'

She replied, not without a certain logic, her own logic if nothing else:

'Whatever for?'

The birds went on twittering in the foliage and a pleasantly cool breeze came in from the garden.

'Won't you have a cup of tea?'

Alain Mazeron's wife, in the Rue de la Pompe, had offered him some beer. Here it was tea.

'No thank you.'

'Tell me all that you have discovered, Monsieur Maigret. You see, for fifty years, I have been accustomed to living in imagination with him. I knew what he was doing at every hour of the day. I visited the cities where he was living, when he was still an ambassador, and I arranged things with Jaquette so as to have a look inside all his successive houses. At what time was he killed?'

'As far as we can tell, between eleven o'clock and midnight.'

'Yet he wasn't ready to go to bed.'

'How do you know?'

'Because before going to his room he always wrote me a few words which finished his daily letter. He began it every morning with a ritual phrase:

' *"Good morning, Isi . . ."*

'Just as he would have greeted me if fate had allowed us to live together. He would add a few lines and then, during the day, he would come back to the letter to tell me what he had been doing. At night, his last words were invariably:

' *"Good night, pretty Isi . . ." '*

She gave an embarrassed smile.

'I must apologize for telling you something that probably makes you laugh. For him, I had remained the Isabelle of twenty.'

'He had seen you since.'

'Yes, from a distance. Consequently he knew that I had become an old woman, but for him the present was not as real as the past. Can you understand that? In the same way, he hadn't changed for me. But now tell me what happened. Tell me everything, without trying to spare my feelings. When a woman gets to my age, you know, it means that she is no weakling. Who was the murderer? How did he get in?'

'Somebody got in all right, seeing that no weapon has been found in the room or in the flat. As Jaquette maintained that she locked the door about nine o'clock as she does every night, bolting it and putting the chain on too, we are forced to conclude that the Comte de Saint-Hilaire let in his visitor himself. Do you know if he often received people in the evening?'

'Never. Since his retirement he had become very much a man of habit and he had adopted a daily routine that was practically invariable. I could show you the letters he wrote to me in the last few years . . . You would see that the first sentence is often:

' *"Good morning, Isi . . . I send you my usual morning greeting, since a new day is beginning, while I, for my part, am beginning my monotonous circus routine . . ."*

'That was what he called his carefully planned days, in which there was no room for the unexpected . . .

'Unless I receive a letter by this evening's post . . . But of course not! It was Jaquette who posted them, in the morning, on her way to buy croissants. If she had posted one this morning, she would have told me on the telephone . . .'

'What do you think of her?'

'She was absolutely devoted to us, to Armand and me. When he broke his arm, in Switzerland, it was she who wrote to me at his dictation, and when, later on, he underwent an operation, she sent me a letter every day giving me the latest news.'

'You don't think she was jealous?'

She smiled again and Maigret found it hard to get used to it. This calm and serenity surprised him, for he had been expecting a more or less dramatic interview.

It was as if death, here, did not have the same meaning as it did elsewhere, as if Isabelle were living quite naturally with it, without fear, regarding it as part of the normal course of life.

'She was jealous, but as a dog is jealous of its master.'

He hesitated to ask certain questions, to broach certain subjects, and it was she who introduced them with a disarming simplicity.

'If, in the old days, she sometimes happened to be jealous in another way, as a woman, it was of his mistresses, not of me.'

'Do you think she was his mistress once?'

'There can be no doubt about that.'

'He told you so in a letter?'

'He never concealed anything from me, even the humiliating things which men hesitate to tell their wives. For instance, he wrote to me, not so many years ago:

'*"Jaquette is nervy today. I must remember to pleasure her tonight . . ."*'

She seemed to be amused at Maigret's astonishment.

'Does it surprise you? Yet it's so natural.'

'You weren't jealous either?'

'Not of that. My only fear was that he might meet a woman capable of taking my place in his mind. Go on with what you were telling me, Chief-Inspector. You don't know anything about his visitor?'

'Only that he fired a first shot with a heavy-calibre weapon, probably a ·301 automatic.'

'Where was Armand hit?'

'In the head. The medical expert says that death was instantaneous. The body slipped down on to the carpet, at the foot of the armchair. Then the murderer fired three more shots.'

'Why, since he was dead?'

'We don't know. Did the killer get into a panic? Was he in such a state of fury that he lost his self-control? It's difficult to answer that question as yet. At the Assizes, a murderer who has attacked his victim again and again, stabbing him for instance a good many times, is often accused of cruelty. Well, judging by my experience and that of my colleagues, it is nearly always timid characters—I hesitate to say sensitive types—who behave like that. They are panic-stricken, don't want to see their victims suffer, and lose their heads . . .'

'You think that that is what happened here?'

'Unless it is a case of revenge, of hatred held in check for a long time, something which is much rarer.'

He was beginning to feel at ease with this old woman who could say anything and hear anything.

'What would seem to contradict this theory is that the murderer, afterwards, had the presence of mind to pick up all the cartridge-cases. They must have been scattered all over the room, quite a way from the body. But he didn't miss a single one, nor did he leave any fingerprints. There remains one last question which puzzles me, especially after what you have just told me about your relations with Jaquette. After she had found the body, this morning, she doesn't seem to have thought of ringing you up and instead she went, not to the local police-station, but to the Foreign Office.'

'I think I can give you an explanation of that. Just after my husband's death, the telephone kept ringing nearly all the time. People we hardly knew wanted information about the funeral arrangements, or wanted to express their sympathy to me. My son decided to cut the telephone off.'

'So that Jaquette may have tried to ring you up?'

'Very probably. And if she didn't come herself to give me the news, it must have been because she knew that she would find it difficult to see me on the day of the funeral.'

'You don't know any enemies the Comte de Saint-Hilaire had?'

'Not one.'

'In his letters to you, did he sometimes mention his nephew?'

'Have you seen Alain?'

'This morning.'

'What did he say?'

'Nothing. He has been to see Maître Aubonnet. The will is going to be read tomorrow, and the solicitor will be getting in touch with you as your presence is necessary.'

'I know.'

'You know the terms of the will?'

'Armand insisted on leaving me his furniture, so that, if he happened to die before me, I should still have the impression to some extent of having been his wife.'

'Are you going to accept this bequest?'

'It was his wish, wasn't it? Mine too. If he hadn't died, once I had come out of mourning I should have become the Comtesse de Saint-Hilaire. That had always been agreed between us.'

'Your husband knew about your plans?'

'Of course.'

'Your son and daughter-in-law too?'

'Not only them, but all our friends. We had nothing to hide, as I said before. Now, on account of the name which I still bear, I shall be obliged to go on living in this big house instead of going and settling down, as I had often dreamed of doing, in the Rue Saint-Dominique. Armand's flat will be reconstructed here all the same. No doubt I haven't a very long time to live, but however little time I have left, I shall live in his setting, you understand, as if I were his widow.'

Maigret was experiencing a phenomenon which annoyed him intensely. To begin with he was captivated by this woman who was so different from anything he had known before. Not only by her, but by the legend which she and Saint-Hilaire had created and in which they had lived.

At first sight, it was as absurd as a fairy-story or those edifying tales in religious story-books.

Here, in front of her, he found himself believing in it. He began to adopt their way of seeing and feeling, rather as in his aunt's convent he used to walk on tiptoe and speak in a whisper, full of unctuous piety.

Then, all of a sudden, he looked at the old lady in a different way, with the eyes of a man from the Quai des Orfèvres, and he was filled with revulsion.

Were they making fun of him? Were all these people—Jaquette, Alain Mazeron, his wife in the tight-fitting trousers, Isabelle, and even the solicitor Aubonnet—in a conspiracy to fool him?

There was a dead man, a real corpse, with his skull shattered and his belly gaping open. That implied the existence of a murderer, and it could not have been any common criminal who had been able to gain entrance to the former ambassador's flat and kill him at point-blank range without his becoming suspicious and trying to defend himself.

Maigret had learnt, over the years, that people did not kill without a motive, without a serious motive. And even if, in this case, the killer was a madman or a madwoman, he or she was still a creature of flesh and blood, who lived in the victim's circle.

Was Jaquette, with her aggressive mistrust, mad? Was Mazeron, whom his wife accused of mental cruelty, unbalanced? Or was it Isabelle who was not in her right mind?

Every time he started thinking along these lines, he got ready to change his attitude, to put some cruel questions, if only in order to dispel this infectious blandness.

And every time, a surprised or ingenuous or mischievous glance from the Princess disarmed him, made him feel ashamed of himself.

'In fact, you have no idea who could have benefited by killing Saint-Hilaire?'

'Benefited? Certainly not. You know as well as I do the broad lines of the will.'

'And what if Alain Mazeron needed money badly?'

'His uncle used to give him some whenever that was the case and in any event he would have left him his fortune.'

'Mazeron knew that?'

'I don't doubt it. Once my husband died, Armand and I would have married, it is true, but I would never have allowed my family to inherit his money.'

'And Jaquette?'

'She was aware that provision had been made for her old age.'

'She was also aware that you intended to go and live in the Rue Saint-Dominique?'

'She looked forward to my doing so.'

Something in Maigret protested. This was all false, inhuman.

'And your son?'

Surprised by the question, she waited for him to explain what he meant, and as Maigret remained silent, she asked in her turn:

'What has my son got to do with it?'

'I don't know. I'm just feeling my way. He is the heir to the name.'

'He would have been even if Armand had gone on living.'

Obviously. But might he not have considered it demeaning for his mother to marry Saint-Hilaire?

'Was your son here last night?'

'No. He is staying with his wife and children at a hotel in the Place Vendôme where they are in the habit of residing when they come to Paris.'

Maigret frowned, looking at the walls as if, through them, he were gauging the size of the Rue de Varenne house. Surely it contained a goodly number of empty rooms, of unoccupied suites?

'You mean to say that since his marriage he has never stayed in this house?'

'In the first place, he very rarely comes to Paris, and never for long, because he hates society life.'

'His wife too?'

'Yes. In the first years of their marriage they had a suite of rooms in the house. Then they had a first child, a second, a third . . .'

'How many have they altogether?'

'Six. The eldest is twenty, the youngest seven. What I am going to say may shock you, but I cannot live with children. It's a mistake to think that all women are born to be mothers. I had Philippe because it was my duty to have him. I looked after him as much as I was expected to look after him. But it would have been too much for me to bear, years later, to have children shouting and galloping all over the house. My son knows that. So does his wife.'

'They don't hold it against you?'

'They accept me as I am, with all my faults and vagaries.'

'Were you alone here last night?'

'With the servants and two nuns who were watching in the mortuary chapel. The Abbé Gauge, who is my confessor and also an old friend of mine, stayed until ten o'clock.'

'You said a little while ago that your son and his family were here in the house.'

'They are waiting to say goodbye to me, at least my daughter-in-law and the children are. You must have seen their car in the courtyard. They are going back to Normandy, except for my son who has to accompany me to the solicitor's tomorrow.'

'Will you allow me to have a few words with your son?'

'Why not? I was expecting you to make that request. I even thought that you would like to see the whole family and that is why I asked my daughter-in-law to postpone her departure.'

Was this naïvety on her part? Or was it defiance? To come back to the English doctor's theory, would a schoolmaster have found it easier to discover the truth than Maigret?

He felt more humble and helpless than ever in front of these human beings on whom he was trying to pass judgment.

'Come this way.'

She led him across the gallery, stopping for a moment with her hand on the handle of a door behind which he could hear the sound of voices.

She opened the door and said simply:

'Chief-Inspector Maigret . . .'

And in a huge room, the chief-inspector noticed first of all a child eating a cake, then a girl of about ten who was asking her mother something in a whisper.

The latter was a tall fair-haired woman of about forty. With her florid pink complexion, she reminded him of one of those stout Dutchwomen you see in coloured prints and post-cards.

A boy of thirteen was looking out of the window. The Princess introduced everybody and Maigret registered the pictures one by one, planning to put them together again later like the pieces of a jigsaw puzzle.

'Frederick, the eldest . . .'

A lanky young man, fair-haired like his mother, bowed slightly without holding out his hand.

'He intends to enter the diplomatic service too.'

There was another girl, of fifteen, and a boy of twelve or thirteen.

'Isn't Philippe here?'

'He has gone down to see if the car is ready.'

One had the impression that life had been suspended, as in a station waiting-room.

'Come this way, Monsieur Maigret.'

They went along another corridor at the end of which they met a tall man who watched them coming towards him with a slightly annoyed expression.

'I was looking for you, Philippe. Chief-Inspector Maigret would like to have a few words with you. Where will you see him?'

Philippe held out his hand, looking a little vague perhaps, but fairly curious to see a detective at close quarters.

'Oh, it doesn't matter where. Here will do.'

He pushed open a door leading into a study papered in red with ancestral portraits on the walls.

'I will leave you now, Monsieur Maigret, but please don't leave me without news. As soon as the body is brought back to the Rue Saint-Dominique, be good enough to let me know.'

She disappeared, light and unsubstantial.

'You want to talk to me?'

Whose study was it? Probably nobody's, because there was nothing in it to indicate that anybody had ever worked here. Philippe de V—— pointed to a chair and held out his cigarette-case.

'No thank you.'

'You don't smoke?'

'Just a pipe.'

'So do I, usually. But not in this house. My Mother hates it.'

In his voice there was a sort of irritation, perhaps even impatience.

'I suppose you want to talk to me about Saint-Hilaire?'

'You know that he was murdered last night.'

'My mother told me a little while ago. It's a curious coincidence, you must admit.'

'You mean that his death might be connected with your father's death?'

'I don't know. The paper doesn't say anything about the circumstances of the crime. I suppose that suicide is out of the question?'

'Why do you ask? Had the Count any reason to commit suicide?'

'I can't think of any, but then you never know what's going on in people's heads.'

'Did you know him?'

'My mother pointed him out to me when I was a child. Later on I came across him now and then.'

'Did you speak to him?'

'Never.'

'Did you bear him a grudge?'

'Whatever for?'

He too seemed genuinely surprised at the questions he was asked. He too gave the impression of being a decent fellow who had nothing to hide.

'All her life my mother kept up a sort of mystic love for him of which we had no reason to feel ashamed. Indeed, my father was the first to smile at it with a certain affectionate amusement.'

'When did you arrive from Normandy?'

'On Sunday afternoon. I had come by myself, last week, after my father's accident, but then I had gone back home because he didn't seem to be in danger. I was surprised on Sunday when my mother rang me up to tell me that he had succumbed to an attack of uraemia.'

'You came along with your family?'

'No. My wife and children didn't arrive until Monday. Except for my eldest son, of course, who is a boarder at the École Normale.'

'Did your mother speak to you about Saint-Hilaire?'

'What do you mean?'

'Perhaps this is a stupid question. Did she tell you, at a given moment, that now she would be able to marry the Count?'

'She didn't need to speak to me about that. I had known for a long time that if my father died before her, that marriage would take place.'

'You have never shared in your father's social life?'

Everything seemed to surprise him and he thought carefully before replying.

'I think I can understand your point of view. You have seen photographs of my father and mother in the illustrated magazines, either when they visited some foreign court or when they attended a big wedding or a society engagement-party. I myself attended some of those events, of course, when I was between eighteen and twenty-five. When I say twenty-five, I'm speaking vaguely. After that, I married and went to live in the country. Did they tell you that I had been to the agricultural school at Grignon? My father gave me one of his estates in Normandy and I live there with my family. Is that what you wanted to know?'

'You haven't any suspicions?'

'As to Saint-Hilaire's murderer, you mean?'

It seemed to Maigret that the other man's lower lip had quivered slightly, but he would not have dared to take his oath on it.

'No. You couldn't call it a suspicion.'

'An idea has occurred to you all the same?'

'It's quite preposterous and I'd rather not talk about it.'

'You've thought of somebody whose life was going to be changed by your father's death?'

Philippe de V—— raised his eyes which he had lowered for a moment.

'Let us say that something of the sort entered my head but I didn't dwell on it. I've heard so much about Jaquette and her devoted loyalty . . .'

He seemed displeased at the turn the conversation had taken.

'I don't want to hustle you. But I have to say goodbye to my family and I should like them to get home before dark.'

'Are you staying a few days in Paris?'

'Until tomorrow evening.'

'In the Place Vendôme?'

'My mother told you?'

'Yes. As a matter of form, I must ask you one last question, which I hope you won't take amiss. I have had to put it to your mother too.'

'Where I was last night, I suppose. At what time?'

'Let us say between ten o'clock and midnight.'

'That's quite a long stretch. Wait a moment. I dined here with my mother.'

'Alone with her?'

'Yes. I left at about half-past nine when the Abbé Gauge arrived, because I have no great liking for the man. I went back to the hotel to say goodnight to my wife and the children.'

There was a silence. Philippe de V—— looked straight in front of him, hesitant and embarrassed.

'Then I went for a stroll along the Champs-Élysées . . .'

'Until midnight?'

'No.'

This time, he looked Maigret in the face, with a rather sheepish smile.

'This may strike you as peculiar, in view of my recent bereavement. It happens to be a sort of tradition with me. At Genestoux, I am too well known to be able to indulge in any sort of affair, and the idea has never entered my head. It may have something to do with my youthful memories. In any case, whenever I come to Paris, I am in the habit of spending an hour or two with a pretty woman. As I don't want it to have any consequences or to complicate my life, I content myself with . . .'

He made a vague gesture.

'On the Champs-Élysées?' asked Maigret.

'I wouldn't say this in front of my wife, who wouldn't understand. In her opinion, outside a certain society . . .'

'What is your wife's maiden name?'

'Irène de Marchangy . . . I can give you a few details about my companion yesterday, if they are of any use to you. She's a brunette, not very tall; she was wearing a pale green dress; and she has a beauty-spot under one breast. I think it's the left breast, but I can't be sure.'

'You went to her home?'

'I suppose that she lives in the Rue de Berry hotel where she took me, because there were some clothes in the wardrobe and personal belongings in the bathroom.'

Maigret smiled.

'Forgive my insistence and thank you for being so patient.'

'Your mind's easy as far as I'm concerned? This way . . . I'll leave you to go down by yourself, because I'm in a hurry to . . .'

He looked at his watch, held out his hand.

'The best of luck!'

In the courtyard, a chauffeur was waiting beside a limousine whose engine was running with a gentle hum which was scarcely perceptible.

Five minutes later, Maigret literally plunged into the fuggy atmosphere of a café and ordered a beer.

Chapter Six

He was awakened by the sunshine coming in through the slats of the Venetian shutter, and, with a gesture which, after so many years, had become automatic, he put his hand out towards his wife's place. The sheets were still warm. From the kitchen, at the same time as the smell of freshly ground coffee, there came a gentle whistling sound, that of the water singing in the kettle.

Here too, as in the aristocratic Rue de Varenne, there were birds chirping in the trees, though not so close to the windows, and Maigret had a feeling of physical well-being with which, however, was mingled something unpleasant and still rather vague.

He had had a restless night. He remembered having a number of dreams and even, once at least, waking up with a start.

Hadn't his wife, at one moment, spoken quietly to him and handed him a glass of water?

It was hard to remember. There were several stories tangled up together and he kept losing the thread. They had one thing in common: in all of them he played a humiliating part.

One picture returned to his mind, clearer than the rest, the picture of a place which resembled the V—— house, but which was bigger and less luxurious. It had something about it of a convent or a ministry, with endless corridors and an infinite number of doors.

What he was doing there was not very clear in his mind. He knew only that he had a task to perform and that it was of capital importance. The trouble was that he could find nobody to guide him. Pardon had told him that this would be the case when he had taken leave of him in the street. He could not see Doctor Pardon in his dream, nor the street. He was nonetheless certain that his friend had warned him what to expect.

The fact of the matter was that he was not entitled to ask his way. He had tried, at the beginning, before it had been borne in on him that it was not done. The old people just looked at him, smiling and shaking their heads.

For there were old people everywhere. Perhaps it was an alms-house or a home for the aged, although it did not give him that impression.

He recognized Saint-Hilaire, an erect figure with a pink face beneath his silky white hair. An extremely goodlooking man, who obviously knew it and seemed to be laughing at the chief-inspector. Maître Aubonnet was sitting in a bathchair with rubber wheels and was amusing himself by driving very fast up and down a gallery.

There were many others, including the Prince de V—— who, with one hand on Isabelle's shoulder, was indulgently watching Maigret's efforts.

The chief-inspector was in a delicate situation, because he had not been initiated yet and nobody would tell him what tests he still had to undergo.

He was in the position of a raw recruit in the army, of a new boy at school. The others kept playing tricks on him. For instance, every time he pushed open a door, it closed again by itself, or else, instead of opening into a bedroom or a drawing-room, it led into another corridor.

Only the old Comtesse de Saint-Fiacre was prepared to help him. Not having the right to speak, she tried to make him understand by means of gestures what was wrong. For instance she pointed to his knees and, looking down, Maigret saw that he was wearing short trousers.

Madame Maigret, in the kitchen, was at last pouring the water on to the coffee. Maigret opened his eyes, annoyed at the memory of this stupid dream. The long and short of it was that he had as it were offered himself as a candidate for a club which, in this case, was a club of old people. And if they had refused to take him seriously, it was because they regarded him as a little boy.

Even sitting on the edge of his bed, he was still annoyed, gazing vaguely at his wife who, after putting a cup of coffee on the bedside table, was opening the shutters.

'You shouldn't have eaten those snails last night . . .'

To cheer himself up after a disappointing day, he had taken her out to dinner and he had eaten some snails.

'How do you feel?'

'All right.'

He was not going to let himself be impressed by a dream. He drank his coffee and went into the dining-room, where he glanced at the newspaper while he was having his breakfast.

They gave a few more details than the day before about Armand de Saint-Hilaire's death, and they had found quite a good photograph of him. There was one of Jaquette too, surprised just as she was going into a dairy shop. It had been taken the day before, in the late afternoon, when she had gone to do her shopping with Lapointe on her heels.

'_At the Quai d'Orsay, the theory of a political crime is completely ruled out. On the other hand, in informed circles, the Count's death is being linked with another death, of an accidental nature, which occurred three days ago._'

That meant that in the next edition or so, the story of Saint-Hilaire and Isabelle would be recounted at full length.

Maigret still felt dull and obtuse, and it was at moments such as this that he wished he had chosen a different profession.

He waited for a bus in the Place Voltaire, and he was lucky enough to get one with a platform on which he could smoke his pipe while he watched the streets go by. At the Quai des Orfèvres, he greeted the policeman on duty outside with a wave of the hand and climbed the stairs which a charwoman was sweeping after sprinkling them with water to keep down the dust.

On his desk he found a whole pile of documents, reports and photographs.

The photographs of the dead man were impressive. Some of them showed the whole body, just as it had been found, with one leg of the desk in the foreground and the stains on the carpet. There were others too of the head, the chest and the stomach, taken while the body was still fully clothed.

Other numbered photographs showed the hole made by each bullet on entering the body, and a dark swelling under the skin, on the back, where one of the bullets, after breaking the collar-bone, had come to a stop.

There was a knock at the door and Lucas appeared, looking as fresh as a daisy, close-shaved, with some talcum powder below one ear.

'Dupeu is here, Chief.'

'Send him in.'

Inspector Dupeu, just like Isabelle's son, had a large family, six or seven children, but it was not out of irony that Maigret had given him a certain task to perform the day before. He had simply happened to be available at the time.

'Well?'

'What the Prince told you was true. I went to the Rue de Berry about ten o'clock. As usual, there were four or five of them walking up and down. There was only one little brunette among them, and she told me she hadn't been there the night before because she had been to see her baby in the country. I waited quite a while and then I saw another one come out of a hotel with an American soldier.

' "Why are you asking me that?" she said in a worried way when I put my question to her.

' "Is he wanted by the police?"

' "No. It's just a check-up."

' "A big chap, about fifty years old, and rather stout?" '

Dupeu went on:

'I asked the girl if she had a beauty spot under one breast and she said yes, and that she had another one on the hip. Naturally the man didn't tell her his name, but he was the only one she picked up the night before last, because he paid her three times as much as she usually asks.

' "Yet he didn't even stay half-an-hour . . ." '

' "What time did he accost you?" '

' "At ten to eleven. I remember that because I was coming out of the bar next door where I'd been for a coffee and I looked at the clock behind the counter." '

Maigret remarked:

'If he spent only half-an-hour with her, he must have left her before half-past eleven?'

'That's what she told me.'

Isabelle's son had not been lying. Nobody in this case seemed to be lying. It was true that, leaving the Rue de Berry at half-past eleven, he could quite easily have got to the Rue Saint-Dominique before midnight.

Why should he have gone to see his mother's old sweetheart? And above all, why should he have killed him?

The chief-inspector had had no better luck with the nephew, Alain Mazeron. The day before, when Maigret had gone along the Rue Jacob just before dinner-time, he had found nobody there. He had telephoned later at about eight o'clock without getting a reply.

He had then told Lucas to send somebody to the antique-dealer's early in the morning. It was Bonfils who in his turn came into the office with some equally disappointing information.

'He wasn't in the least upset by my questions.'

'His shop was open?'

'No. I had to ring the bell. He looked out of the first-floor window before coming down in his braces, unshaven. I asked him for an account of his movements yesterday afternoon and evening. He told me that to begin with he had gone to see the solicitor.'

'That's true.'

'I don't doubt it. After that he went to the Rue Drouot, where there was an auction-sale of helmets, uniform buttons and weapons of the Napoleonic period. He says that there's tremendous competition for these relics between certain collectors. He bought one lot, and showed me a pink form with a list of the things which he has to go and collect this morning.'

'After that?'

'He went and had dinner in a restaurant in the Rue de Seine where he nearly always has his meals. I checked up on that.'

Another one who had not been lying! It was a queer profession, thought Maigret, in which you felt disappointed that somebody hadn't committed murder! Yet this was the case here, and the chief-inspector, despite himself, felt a grudge against each of these people in turn for being innocent or appearing so.

For the fact remained that there was a corpse.

He picked up his telephone.

'Will you come downstairs, Moers?'

He didn't believe in the perfect crime. In twenty-five years of detective work, he hadn't come across a single one. True, he could think of a few crimes which had gone unpunished. Often the police knew the identity of the criminal, who had had time to escape abroad. Or else they were crimes of violence or poisoning.

This was not the case here. No ordinary criminal would have entered the Rue Saint-Dominique flat and fired four shots at an old man sitting at his desk only to go away without taking anything.

'Come in, Moers. Sit down.'

'You've read my report?'

'Not yet.'

Maigret did not confess that he had not had the courage to read it, any more than the eighteen-page report from the medical expert. The day before, he had left Moers and his men to look for material clues, and he put his trust in them, knowing that nothing would escape their notice.

'Has Gastine-Renette sent in his conclusions?'

'They are in the file. The weapon involved is a ·301 automatic, either a Browning or one of the many imitations that are to be found on the market.'

'You are sure that not a single cartridge-case was left in the flat?'

'My men searched every square inch.'

'No weapon either?'

'No weapons or ammunition, except for some fowling pieces and the cartridges to go with them.'

'Any fingerprints?'

'Those of the old woman, the Count and the concierge's wife. I had taken their fingerprints on the off-chance before leaving the Rue Saint-Dominique. The concierge's wife came twice a week to help Jaquette Larrieu with the heavy work.'

Moers too seemed perplexed and annoyed.

'I've added an inventory of everything we found in the furniture and the cupboards. But I've spent a good part of the night going through it without spotting anything suspicious or unexpected.'

'Any money?'

'A few thousand francs in a wallet, some change in a drawer in the kitchen, and in the desk some Rothschild's Bank cheque-books.'

'Any stubs?'

'Some cheque-stubs too. The poor old chap had so little idea that he was going to die that he ordered a suit ten days ago from a tailor on the Boulevard Haussmann.'

'No marks on the window-sill?'

'None whatever.'

They looked at one another and understood one another. They had worked together for years and they could scarcely remember a single case in which, going over the scene of the crime with a fine-tooth comb, as the papers say, they had not discovered a few more or less suspicious details, at least at first sight.

Here, it was all too perfect. Everything had a logical explanation except, of course, the old man's death.

By wiping the grip of the pistol and putting it in Saint-Hilaire's hand, the murderer could have given the impression of a case of suicide. Provided, of course, that he had stopped after the first bullet. But why had he fired the other three?

And why couldn't they find the former ambassador's automatic? Old Jaquette admitted having seen it, only a few months before, in the chest of drawers in the bedroom.

The gun was no longer in the flat and, according to the servant's description, it had roughly the same size and weight as a ·301 automatic.

Supposing the former ambassador had let somebody into the flat . . .

Somebody he knew, since he had sat down again at his desk, in his dressing-gown . . .

In front of him, a bottle of brandy and a glass . . . Why hadn't he offered his visitor a drink?

Maigret tried to imagine the scene. This visitor going to the bedroom–along the corridor or by way of the dining-room–taking the pistol, coming back to the study, going up to the Count and firing the first shot at point-blank range . . .

'It doesn't make sense,' he sighed.

What is more, there had to be a motive, a motive strong enough for the person who had done this to run the risk of a death-sentence.

'I suppose you haven't submitted Jaquette to the paraffin test?'

'I wouldn't have dared to without asking you first.'

When a firearm is discharged, especially an automatic, the explosion projects a certain distance characteristic particles which become engrained in the skin of the person who fires the gun, particularly along the edge of the hand, and remain for some time.

Maigret had thought of that, the day before. But had he any right to suspect the old servant more than anybody else?

Admittedly she was the best placed to commit the crime. She knew where to find the gun; she could come and go in the flat while her master was working, without arousing his suspicions, go up to him and fire; and it was quite likely that, with the body lying before her on the carpet, she would have gone on pulling the trigger.

She was sufficiently meticulous to have gone calmly to bed afterwards, a few yards from her victim? Or that, in the morning, on her way to the Quai d'Orsay, she would have stopped somewhere, on the banks of the Seine, for instance, to get rid of the gun and the cartridge-cases?

She had a motive, or an apparent motive. For nearly fifty years, she had lived with Saint-Hilaire, in his shadow. He concealed nothing from her and, in all probability, they had at one time been on intimate terms.

The ambassador did not seem to have attached very much importance to this, nor did Isabelle, who referred to it with a smile.

But what about Jaquette? Wasn't she, to all intents and purposes, the old man's real companion?

She knew about his platonic love for the Princess, she posted his daily letters, and it was she too who had once admitted Isabelle to the flat in her master's absence.

'I wonder if . . .'

The theory was distasteful to Maigret, who considered it too easy. Although he could conceive it, he couldn't *feel* it.

With the Prince de V—— dead and Isabelle free, the old sweethearts were at last entitled to get married. They had only to wait until the end of the period of mourning to go through the marriage ceremony at town hall and church, and after that they would be able to live together in the Rue Sainte-Dominique or the Rue de Varenne.

'Listen, Moers . . . Go over there . . . Be nice to Jaquette . . . Don't frighten her . . . Tell her that it's just a formality . . .'

'You want me to carry out the test?'

'It would relieve me of one worry . . .'

When he was told, a little later, that Monsieur Cromières was on the telephone, he sent word that he was out and that it wasn't known when he would be back.

This morning, the Prince de V——'s will was going to be read. There, facing the old solicitor Aubonnet, there would be Isabelle and her son, and, later in the day, the Princess would return to the same room for the reading of another will.

The two men in her life, the same day . . .

He telephoned to the Rue Saint-Dominique. He had hesitated, the day before, to affix seals on the study door and the bedroom door. He had preferred to wait, so that he could inspect the two rooms again.

Lapointe, whom he had left on duty, had obviously dropped off to sleep in an armchair.

'Is that you, Chief?'

'Nothing new?'

'Not a thing.'

'Where's Jaquette?'

'This morning, at six o'clock, when I was on duty in the study, I heard her dragging a vacuum cleaner along the corridor. I dashed out to ask her what she was going to do and she looked at me in astonishment.

' "Clean the rooms, of course!"

' "Clean what rooms?"

' "First the bedroom, then the dining-room, then . . ." '

Maigret grunted:

'Did you let her?'

'No. She didn't seem to understand why.

' "What shall I do, then?" she asked.'

'What did you reply?'

'I asked her to make me some coffee and she went out to buy me some croissants.'

'She didn't stop anywhere on the way to make a phone call or post a letter?'

'No. I told the policeman on duty at the door to follow her at a distance. She really did just go to the baker's and she only stayed there a minute.'

'Is she furious?'

'It's hard to say. She comes and goes, moving her lips as if she were talking to herself. Just now, she's in the kitchen and I don't know what she's doing.'

'There haven't been any phone calls?'

The French window leading into the garden must have been open, for Maigret could hear the blackbirds singing over the telephone.

'Moers will be with you in a few minutes. He's already on the way. You aren't too tired?'

'I must admit that I've been asleep.'

'I'll send somebody to relieve you a little later.'

An idea occurred to him.

'Don't ring off. Go and ask Jaquette to show you her gloves.'

She was a devout person and he would have sworn that, for Sunday Mass, she wore a pair of gloves.

'I'll hold the line.'

He waited with the receiver in his hand. It took quite a long time.

'Are you there, Chief?'

'Well?'

'She has shown me three pairs.'

'She wasn't surprised?'

'She gave me a nasty look before going to open a drawer in her room. I caught sight of a missal, two or three rosaries, some postcards, medallions, handkerchiefs and gloves. Two pairs are in white cotton.'

Maigret could imagine her in summer, with white gloves and, no doubt, a touch of white in her hat.

'And the other pair?'

'In black kid, rather worn.'

'Good. See you later.'

Maigret's question was connected with Moers's errand. Saint-Hilaire's murderer could have learnt from the newspapers and magazines that a person who fires a revolver has his hands encrusted with powder for some time after the shot. If Jaquette had used the automatic, mightn't she have though of putting on a pair of gloves? In that case, wouldn't she have got rid of them?

To clear this point up, Maigret started searching through the file which was still spread out in front of him. He found the inventory, with the contents of every piece of furniture listed room by room.

Servant's bedroom . . . One iron bedstead . . . One old mahogony table covered with a fringed tablecloth in crimson velvet . . .

His finger followed the lines of typescript:

Eleven handkerchiefs, including six marked with the Initial J . . . Three pairs of gloves . . .

She had shown the three pairs to Lapointe.

He went out, without taking his hat, and made for the door connecting Police Headquarters with the Palais de Justice. He had never been to see the examining magistrate, Urban de Chézaud, who had previously been at Versailles and with whom he had never had occasion to work. He had to go up to the third floor, where the oldest offices were, and he finally found the magistrate's visiting-card on a door.

'Come in, Monsieur Maigret, I'm delighted to see you and I was wondering whether to ring you up.'

He was about forty, with an intelligent air about him. On his desk, Maigret recognized the duplicate of the file which he had received himself and he noticed that certain pages had already been annotated in red pencil.

'We haven't many material clues, have we?' sighed the magistrate as he invited the chief-inspector to sit down. 'I have just had a telephone call from the Quai d'Orsay . . .'

'Young Monsieur Cromières . . .'

'He says that he has tried unsuccessfully to get in touch with you and he wonders where this morning's papers obtained their information.'

The magistrate's clerk, behind Maigret, was busy typing. The windows overlooked the courtyard so that there could never be any sunshine in the room.

'Have you any news?'

Because he liked the magistrate, Maigret made no attempt to conceal his discouragement.

'You've read that,' he sighed, pointing to the file. 'This evening or tomorrow I'll send you a preliminary report. Theft isn't the motive of the crime. It seems to me that it isn't a question of financial interest either, because it would be too obvious. The victim's nephew is the only person who benefits by Saint-Hilaire's death. And then he's gaining only a few months or a few years.'

'Has he any pressing financial obligations?'

'Yes and no. It's difficult to get anything positive out of these people without bluntly accusing them. And I haven't any grounds for an accusation. Mazeron lives apart from his wife and children. He has a secretive, rather unpleasant character, and his wife describes him as a sort of sadist.

'From the look of his antique shop, you would imagine that nobody ever goes into it. Admittedly he specializes in military trophies and there's a small number of enthusiasts who are mad about that sort of thing.

'He has been known to ask his uncle for money. But there is no proof that the latter didn't give it him with good grace.

'Was he afraid that once Saint-Hilaire had married he would lose the inheritance? That's possible. But I don't think so. Families like that have a mentality of their own. Every member regards himself as the trustee of property which it is his duty to hand on, more or less intact, to his direct or indirect descendants.'

He noticed a smile on the magistrate's lips and remembered that the latter was called Urbain de Chézaud, a name with a particle.

'Go on.'

'I have been to see Madame Mazeron, in her flat at Passy, and I can see no earthly reason why she should have gone and killed her husband's uncle. The same goes for their two daughters. One of them, in any case, is in England. The other is working.'

Maigret filled his pipe.

'Do you mind if I smoke?'

'Of course not. I smoke a pipe too.'

It was the first time that he had ever met a pipe-smoking magistrate. It is true that the latter added:

'At home, in the evening, while I'm studying my files.'

'I have been to see the Princesse de V——.'

He glanced at the other man.

'You know about that business, I suppose?'

Maigret could have sworn that Urbain de Chézaud moved in circles where people were interested in Isabelle.

'I have heard about it.'

'Is it true that a lot of people know about her liaison with the Count, if liaison is the right word?'

'In certain circles, yes. Her friends call her Isi.'

'That's what the Count calls her too in his letters.'

'You have read them?'

'Not all of them. And not from beginning to end. There are enough to fill several volumes. It seemed to me, though it's only an impression, that the Princess wasn't as overwhelmed by the news of Saint-Hilaire's death as one might have expected.'

'In my opinion, nothing in her life has ever succeeded in disturbing her composure. I have met her on occasion. I have heard about her from friends. One gets the impression that she has never passed a certain age and that time, for her, has come to a halt. Some say that she has remained as she was at twenty, others that she hasn't changed since her schooldays in the convent.'

'The newspapers are going to publish her story. They've begun making references to it.'

'I've noticed that. It was bound to happen.'

'In the course of the conversation we had together, she didn't say anything that gave me the slightest hint of a line to follow. This morning, she's at the solicitor's, for the reading of her husband's will. She'll be going back there this afternoon for Saint-Hilaire's.'

'He has left her something?'

'Just his furniture and personal belongings.'

'Have you been to see her son?'

'Philippe, his wife, and their children. They were all gathered together in the Rue de Varenne. The son has stayed behind in Paris by himself.'

'What do you think about them?'

Maigret was obliged to reply:

'I don't know.'

Philippe too, strictly speaking, had a motive for killing Saint-Hilaire. He had become the head of the historic V—— family which was related to all the courts of Europe.

His father had tolerated Isabelle's platonic love for the discreet ambassador whom she saw only from a distance and to whom she wrote childish letters.

Once he was dead, the situation was bound to change. In spite of her seventy-two years and her sweetheart's seventy-seven years, the Princess was going to marry Saint-Hilaire, lose her title, change her name.

Was that a sufficient motive for committing a crime and, as Maigret kept reminding himself, for risking a death-sentence? For replacing, in fact, a mild scandal with a scandal of a much more serious nature.

The chief-inspector muttered in embarrassment:

'I've checked his movements on Tuesday evening. He booked in with his family at a hotel in the Place Vendôme, as he was in the habit of doing. When the children had gone to bed, he went out by himself and went up the Champs-Élysées on foot. On the corner of the Rue de Berry he took his pick of the five or six prostitutes who were available and accompanied one of them to her room.'

Maigret had often known murderers, *after* their crime, to go and look for a woman, any woman, as if they felt a need for relaxation.

He could not remember a single one acting in this way *before*. Could it have been to produce an alibi?

In that case, the alibi was incomplete, since Philippe de V—— had left the prostitute about half-past eleven, which had left him enough time to go to the Rue Saint-Dominique.

'That's how things stand at the moment. I shall go on looking for a new trail, without much hope of finding one, perhaps another of the former ambassador's friends nobody has told me about yet. Saint-Hilaire was very regular in his habits, like most old people. Nearly all his friends are dead . . .'

The telephone rang. The clerk got up to answer it.

'Yes . . . He's here . . . Would you like to speak to him?'

And, turning to the chief-inspector:

'It's for you . . . It seems that it's very urgent . . .'

'Do you mind?'

'Go ahead.'

'Hullo . . . Maigret, yes . . . Who's that speaking?'

He did not recognize the voice because Moers, who finally gave his name, was in a state of great excitement.

'I tried to get you at your office. They told me that . . .'

'Yes, yes.'

'I'm coming to the point. It's so extraordinary; I've just finished the test . . .'

'I know. Well?'

'It's positive.'

'You're sure?'

'Absolutely certain. There's no doubt that Jaquette Larrieu fired one or more shots within the last forty-eight hours.'

'She let you carry out the test?'

'She was no trouble at all.'

'How does she explain it?'

'She doesn't. I haven't said anything to her. I had to come back to the laboratory to finish the test.'

'Is Lapointe still with her?'

'He was there when I left the Rue Saint-Dominique.'

'You are certain about what you've just told me?'

'Positive.'

'Thank you.'

He hung up, his face serious, a crease in the middle of his forehead, with the magistrate looking at him inquiringly.

'I was wrong,' Maigret murmured regretfully.

'What do you mean?'

'On the off-chance, without taking it seriously, I must admit, I told the laboratory to try the paraffin test on Jaquette's right hand.'

'And it's positive? That's what I thought they were telling you over the telephone, but I found it hard to believe.'

'So did I.'

He ought to have felt a great load off his mind. After an investigation lasting barely twenty-four hours, the problem which had seemed insoluble a few minutes before had now been solved.

Yet the fact was that he felt no sense of satisfaction.

'While I'm here, will you sign a warrant for me,' he sighed.

'You are going to send your men to arrest her?'

'I shall go myself.'

And, hunching his shoulders, Maigret lit his pipe again, while the magistrate silently filled in the blanks of a printed form.

Chapter Seven

Maigret looked into his office on the way in order to pick up his hat. Just as he was going out again, an idea suddenly struck him and, cursing himself for not having thought of it before, he rushed for the telephone.

To save time, he dialled the Rue Saint-Dominique number himself without going through the switchboard. He was anxious to hear Lapointe's voice, to make sure that nothing had happened over there. Instead of the bell he heard the staccato buzz indicating that the line was engaged.

He did not think, and for a few seconds he panicked.

Whom could Lapointe be ringing up? Moers had left him a little earlier. Lapointe knew that he would be getting in touch with the chief-inspector straight away to give him his report.

If the inspector left behind in Saint-Hilaire's flat was using the telephone, it meant that something unexpected had happened and that he was calling Police Headquarters or a doctor.

Maigret tried again, opened the door of the adjoining office and saw Janvier lighting a cigarette.

'Go down and wait for me in the courtyard at the wheel of a car.'

He had one last try, only to hear the same buzz in reply.

A little later he could be seen running down the stairs, jumping into the little black car and banging the door.

'Rue Saint-Dominique. As fast as you can. Sound the siren.'

Janvier, who did not know about the case's latest developments, glanced at him in surprise, for the chief-inspector loathed the siren and rarely used it.

The car sped towards the Pont Saint-Michel and turned right along the embankment, while the other cars drew in to the kerb and the passers-by stopped to follow it with their eyes.

Possibly Maigret's reaction was ridiculous but he could not get rid of the mental picture of Jaquette dead and Lapointe beside her, hanging on to the telephone. It became so real in his mind that he got to the point of wondering how she had committed suicide. She could not have thrown herself out of the window, since the flat was on the ground floor. There was no weapon available, except for the kitchen knives . . .

The car stopped. The policeman, at his post by the carriage gateway, out in the sun, was obviously surprised at the siren. The bedroom window was ajar.

Maigret rushed across to the archway, climbed the stone steps, pressed the electric bell, and found himself straight away face to face with a Lapointe who was at once calm and astonished.

'What's up, Chief?'

'Where is she?'

'In her room.'

'When did you last hear her moving around?'

'Just now.'

'Whom were you phoning?'

'I was trying to get through to you.'

'What for?'

'She's getting dressed to go out and I wanted to ask you for instructions.'

Maigret felt ridiculous in front of Lapointe and Janvier who had joined them. In contrast with the anxiety of the last few minutes, the flat was quieter than ever. The study was still full of sunshine, the door open on to the garden, the linden-tree noisy with birds.

He went into the kitchen, where everything was in order, and heard some slight noises in the old servant's room.

'Can I see you, Mademoiselle Larrieu?'

He had once called her madame and she had protested:

'Mademoiselle, if you please!'

'Who is it?'

'Chief-Inspector Maigret.'

'Just a minute.'

Lapointe went on in a whisper:

'She has had a bath in her employer's bathroom.'

Maigret had rarely been so displeased with himself and he remembered his dream, the old people who looked at him condescendingly, shaking their heads because he was wearing short trousers and because he was just a little boy in their eyes.

The door of the little room opened, and a whiff of scent reached him, a scent which had been unfashionable for years and which he recognized because his mother had always used it on Sundays to go to High Mass.

It was indeed as if to go to High Mass that old Jaquette was dressed. She was wearing a black silk dress, a black tucker round her neck, a black hat trimmed with white silk, and an immaculate pair of gloves. All that was missing was a missal in one hand.

'I am obliged,' he murmured, 'to take you to the Quai des Orfèvres.'

He was prepared to show her the warrant signed by the magistrate but, contrary to his expectations, she showed neither surprise nor indignation. Without a word, she crossed the kitchen, making sure that the gas was turned off, and went into the study to close the French window.

She asked only one question:

'Is anybody going to stay here?'

And as nobody answered her straight away, she added:

'If not, I had better shut the bedroom window.'

Not only, knowing that she had been found out, had she no intention of committing suicide, but she had never been so dignified, so much in control of her feelings. It was she who went out first. Maigret said to Lapointe:

'You had better stay behind.'

She walked in front, giving a little nod of the head to the concierge looking at her through the glass door.

Wouldn't it have been ridiculous, abominable to put handcuffs on this woman who was seventy years old? Maigret invited her to get into the car and took his place beside her.

'You don't need the siren any more.'

The weather was still magnificent and they passed a big red and white coach full of foreign tourists. Maigret could not think of anything to say, any question to ask.

Hundreds of times, he had returned to the Quai des Orfèvres like this, in the company of a suspect, a man or a woman, whom he was going to have to submit to a merciless examination. This could last for hours, and sometimes the interrogation had ended only at daybreak, when the people of Paris were setting out to go to work.

For Maigret, this phase of an investigation was always unpleasant.

Now, for the first time in his life, he was to carry out the operation on an old woman.

In the courtyard of Police Headquarters, he helped her out of the car, but she pushed his hand away and walked with a dignified bearing towards the staircase as if she were crossing the square in front of a church. He had motioned to Janvier to accompany them. All three went up the main staircase and into the chief-inspector's office where the breeze was puffing out the curtains.

'Sit down, please.'

Although he had pointed to an armchair, she chose an upright chair, while Janvier, who was familiar with the routine, settled down at one end of the desk and took a note-book and pencil.

Maigret cleared his throat, filled a pipe, walked over to the window, and came back to plant himself in front of the old woman who was watching him with her bright, motionless little eyes.

'First of all I have to inform you that the examining magistrate has just signed a warrant for your arrest.'

He showed it to her. She granted it only a polite interest.

'You are charged with having committed the wilful murder of your employer, the Comte Armand de Saint-Hilaire, during the night of Tuesday to Wednesday last. A technician from the Criminal Records Office carried out the paraffin test on your right hand a little while ago. This test consists of collecting the particles of powder and chemical substances which are engrained in a person's skin when that person makes use of a firearm, particularly an automatic pistol.'

He watched her, hoping for some reaction, but it was she who seemed to be studying him, it was she who was the calmer and more self-possessed of the two.

'You don't say anything?'

'I have nothing to say.'

'The test was positive, which means that it established, beyond any possible doubt, that you used a firearm recently.'

Impassive as she was, she might just as well have been in church listening to a sermon.

'What have you done with that weapon? I suppose on Wednesday morning, on your way to the Quai d'Orsay, you threw it into the Seine with the cartridge-cases? I warn you that the necessary steps will be taken to recover the pistol, that divers will go down to the river bed.'

She had decided to keep quiet and keep quiet she did. As for her eyes, they remained so serene that one might have thought that she was not involved in what was going on, that she was there by accident, listening to a conversation which had nothing to do with her.

'I don't know what your motive was, although I can guess. You had lived for nearly fifty years with the Comte de Saint-Hilaire. You had been as intimate with him as two human beings can be.'

An ephemeral smile hovered over Jaquette's lips, a smile in which there was mingled both coquetry and a secret satisfaction.

'You knew that after the Prince's death your employer would put the dream of his youth into effect.'

It was annoying to talk to no purpose, and now and then Maigret had to keep a firm grip on himself to refrain from shaking the old woman by the shoulders.

'If he hadn't been killed he would have got married, isn't that so? Would you have kept your position in the household? And if you had, would that position have been quite the same?'

With his pencil poised in mid-air, Janvier was still waiting for a reply for him to record.

'On Tuesday evening, you went into your employer's study. He was correcting the proofs of his book. Did you have a quarrel with him?'

After another ten minutes of questions without a single reply, Maigret, utterly exasperated, felt the need to go and relax for a moment in the inspectors' room. That reminded him that Lapointe had been in the Rue Saint-Dominique since the previous evening.

'Are you busy, Lucas?'

'Nothing urgent.'

'In that case, go and take over from Lapointe.'

Then, as it was after midday, he added:

'Drop into the Brasserie Dauphine on the way. Tell them to send up a plate of sandwiches and some beer and coffee for us.'

And, thinking of the old woman:

'A bottle of mineral water too.'

In his office, he found Jaquette and Janvier sitting motionless on their chairs as if they were in a picture.

For half an hour he walked up and down the room, puffing at his pipe, stopping in front of the window, and planting himself a few feet from the servant to look her in the face.

It was not an interrogation, for she remained stubbornly silent, but a long, more or less disconnected monologue.

'It's possible – I'm telling you this straight away – that the experts will find that this is a case of diminished responsibility. Your lawyer will certainly argue that it was a crime of passion . . .'

It seemed ridiculous, but it was true.

'Remaining silent won't help you at all. Whereas if you plead guilty you have every chance of moving the jury. Why not start now?'

Children play a game of this sort: you must not open your mouth, whatever your partner may say or do, and above all you must not laugh.

Jaquette neither spoke nor laughed. She followed Maigret with her eyes as he came and went, behaving all the time as if she were not involved, showing no emotion, no reaction of any sort.

'The Count was the only man in your life.'

What was the use? He searched in vain for her Achilles' heel. There was a knock at the door. It was the waiter from the Brasserie Dauphine, who put the tray down on the chief-inspector's desk.

'You had better eat something. At the rate we are going now, we shall probably be a long time yet.'

He offered her a ham sandwich. The waiter had gone. She picked up a corner of the crumby bread and, for a wonder, opened her mouth.

'I haven't eaten any meat for fifteen years. Old people don't need it.'

'Would you prefer cheese?'

'In any case, I'm not hungry.'

He went into the inspectors' room again.

'Somebody ring up the brasserie and tell them to send over some cheese sandwiches.'

He for his part ate as he walked up and down, as if out of revenge, with his pipe in one hand and the sandwich in the other, and now and then he stopped to have a drink of beer. Janvier had put down his useless pencil to have something to eat too.

'Would you prefer to talk to me alone?'

This evoked nothing but a shrug of her shoulders.

'You are entitled as from now to the services of any lawyer you choose. I'm prepared to send for the one you indicate straight away. Do you know a lawyer?'

'No.'

'Do you want me to give you the list of lawyers?'

'It isn't any use.'

'Would you prefer me to choose one for you?'

'There isn't any point.'

They had made some progress, since she was at least talking.

'You admit that you shot your employer?'

'I have nothing to say.'

'In other words, you've sworn to keep quiet, whatever happens?'

Once again there was the same exasperating silence. Pipe smoke was floating about the office, into which the sunlight was falling at an angle. The atmosphere began to smell of ham, beer, coffee.

'Would you like a cup of coffee?'

'I only drink coffee in the morning, with a lot of milk.'

'What would you like to drink?'

'Nothing.'

'Are you planning to go on a hunger strike?'

It had been a mistake to say that, because she suppressed a smile at the idea, which might possibly appeal to her.

He had seen suspects of all sorts here, in similar circumstances, both tough characters and weak characters, some who cried, others who grew paler and paler, and yet others who defied him and laughed at him.

It was the first time that anybody, sitting on that chair, had shown so much indifference and calm obstinacy.

'You still don't want to say anything?'

'Not now.'

'When are you thinking of talking?'

'I don't know.'

'Are you waiting for something?'

Silence.

'Would you like me to ring up the Princesse de V——?'

She shook her head.

'Is there anybody to whom you want to send a message, or anybody you would like to see?'

The cheese sandwiches were brought in and she looked at them apathetically. She shook her head and said again:

'Not now.'

'So you're determined not to say anything, drink anything or eat anything.'

It was a hard chair, and nearly all those who had sat on it had soon begun to feel uncomfortable. At the end of an hour, she was still holding herself as erect as ever, without moving her feet or her arms, and without having changed her position.

'Listen, Jaquette . . .'

She frowned, shocked at this familiarity, and it was the chief-inspector who showed some embarrassment.

'I warn you that we shall stay in this room as long as is necessary. We have material evidence that you have fired one or more shots. All I am asking you to do is to tell me why and in what circumstances. By your stupid silence . . .'

He had used the word unintentionally and he corrected himself.

'By your silence you are running the risk of putting the police on the wrong track and casting suspicion on other people. If, half-an-hour from now, you haven't answered my questions, I shall ask the Princess to come here and I shall put her in your presence. I shall summon her son too, Alain Mezeron, and Mazeron's wife, and we shall see whether that general confrontation . . .'

He called out angrily:

'What is it?'

There was a knock at the door. Old Joseph beckoned him into the corridor and, with his head bent forward, whispered:

'There's a young man who insists . . .'

'What young man?'

Joseph held out a visiting-card bearing the name of Julien de V——, Isabelle's grandson.

'Where is he?'

'In the waiting-room. He says that he's in a hurry because there's an important lecture he mustn't miss.'

'Ask him to wait a moment.'

He went back into the office.

'Isabelle's grandson, Julien, is asking to see me. Do you still insist on remaining silent?'

It was admittedly exasperating, but it was pathetic too. Maigret thought that he could see signs of a conflict taking place in the old woman, and he felt unwilling to hustle her. Even Janvier, who was just a spectator, looked a little conscience-stricken.

'You'll have to talk sooner or later. In that case why . . .'

'Am I entitled to see a priest?'

'You want to make a confession?'

'I'm just asking for permission to talk to a priest for a few minutes. The Abbé Barraud.'

'Where can I get hold of the Abbé Barraud?'

'At the Sainte-Clotilde presbytery.'

'He's your confessor, is he?'

He did not want to miss the slightest chance, and he picked up the telephone.

'Get me the Sainte-Clotilde presbytery . . . Yes . . . I'll hold the line . . . The Abbé Barraud . . . It doesn't matter how you spell it . . .'

He moved the pipes about on his desk, arranging them in Indian file like soldiers.

'Hullo . . . The Abbé Barraud? . . . This is Police Headquarters . . . Maigret, divisional chief-inspector . . . I have one of your parishioners in my office who would like to talk to you . . . Yes . . . It's Mademoiselle Larrieu . . . Can you take a taxi and come round to the Quai des Orfèvres? . . . Thank you . . . Yes . . . She'll wait here for you . . .'

And to Janvier:

'When the priest arrives, show him in here and leave them together . . . There's somebody I've got to see in the meantime . . .'

He made for the glass-sided waiting-room where the only person was the young man in black whom he had glimpsed the day before in the Rue de Varenne in the company of his parents and his brothers and sisters. When he saw Maigret, he stood up and followed the chief-inspector into a little office which was unoccupied.

'Sit down.'

'I haven't got long. I have to go back to the Rue d'Ulm, where I've got a lecture in half-an-hour.'

In the tiny office, he seemed taller and lankier than before. The expression on his face was serious and rather sad.

'Yesterday, when you came to see my grandmother, I nearly spoke to you.'

Why did Maigret feel that he would have liked to have a son like this boy? He had a natural ease of manner at the same time as a sort of innate modesty, and if he was a little withdrawn, one could tell that it was out of tact.

'I don't know whether what I'm going to tell you will be of any use to you. I thought about it a lot last night. On Tuesday afternoon, I went to see my uncle.'

'Your uncle?'

The young man blushed, a slight blush which disappeared straight away and which he replaced with a shy smile.

'That's what I called the Comte de Saint-Hilaire.'

'You used to go and see him?'

'Yes. I didn't talk about it to my parents, but I didn't try to conceal it from them either. I first heard about him when I was a boy.'

'From whom?'

'From my governesses, then, later on, from my schoolmates. My grandmother's love-story is almost legendary.'

'I know.'

'When I was about ten or eleven, I asked her about him, and the two of us got into the habit of talking about Saint-Hilaire. She used to read me certain letters, those, for instance, in which he described diplomatic receptions or gave an account of his conversations with heads of state. Have you read his letters?'

'No.'

'He wrote very well, in a lively style, rather like Cardinal de Retz. It may have been on account of the Count and his stories that I chose the diplomatic career.'

'When did you get to know him personally?'

'Two years ago. I had a friend at Stanislas whose grandfather had also been in the Service. One day, at his home, I met the Comte de Saint-Hilaire and asked to be introduced to him. I thought I could sense his emotion as he looked me up and down, and I was rather moved too. He asked me some questions about my studies and my plans for the future.'

'You went to see him in the Rue Saint-Dominique?'

'He had invited me there, though he had added: "Provided that your parents have no objection." '

'Did you meet him often?'

'No. About once a month. It all depended. For instance, I asked his advice after my baccalaureate, and he encouraged me in my decision to go through the École Normale. He considered, as I did, that even if it didn't help me in my career, it would still provide me with a solid basis.'

'One day, without thinking, I said:

' "I feel rather as if I were talking to an uncle."

' "And I to a nephew," he replied. "Why don't you call me uncle?" '

'That's why I used the word just now.'

'You didn't like your grandfather?'

'I didn't know him very well. For all that they belonged to the same generation, he and the Comte de Saint-Hilaire were two very different men. My grandfather, for me, remained somebody impressive and inaccessible.'

'And your grandmother?'

'We were great friends. We still are.'

'She knew about your visits to the Rue Saint-Dominique?'

'Yes. I used to tell her all about our conversations. She would ask me for details, and sometimes it was she who reminded me that I hadn't been to see our friend for a long time.'

Although he was drawn to the young man, Maigret nonetheless studied him with an astonishment bordering on mistrust. They were not accustomed, at the Quai des Orfèvres, to meeting young men of this kind, and once again he had an impression of an unreal world, of people who came, not out of life, but out of a book of moral uplift.

'So on Tuesday afternoon you went to the Rue Saint-Dominique.'

'Yes.'

'Had you any special reason for this call?'

'In a way. My grandfather had died two days before. I thought that my grandmother would like to know how her friend was reacting.'

'You didn't feel the same curiosity?'

'Perhaps I did. I knew that they had sworn to marry one day if it were possible.'

'The idea appealed to you?'

'It did rather.'

'And to your parents?'

'I never talked about it to my father, but I've every reason to think that he didn't mind the idea. As for my mother . . .?'

Since he did not finish his sentence, Maigret prompted him:

'Your mother . . . ?'

'I'm not being unkind about her if I say that she attaches greater importance to titles and privileges than anybody else in the family.'

Probably because she had not been born a princess but simply Irène de Marchangy.

'What happened in the course of this conversation in the Rue Saint-Dominique?'

'Nothing that I can explain at all clearly. All the same, I thought I ought to tell you about it. Right from the beginning, the Comte de Saint-Hilaire seemed worried and it was suddenly borne in on me that he was very old. Before then, he had never looked his age. You could tell that he was in love with life, that he enjoyed every aspect of it, every moment of it, as a connoisseur. To my mind he was a man of the eighteenth century who had strayed into the twentieth. You understand what I mean?'

Maigret nodded.

'I didn't expect to find him broken up by the death of my grandfather, who was two years older than he was, especially seeing that that death had been accidental and hadn't really been very painful. But on Tuesday afternoon Saint-Hilaire was out of spirits and avoided looking at me as if he had something to hide.

'I said something like this:

' "A year from now, you'll finally be able to marry my grandmother . . ."

'He turned his head away, so I pressed the point:

' "How do you feel about it?"

'I wish I could remember his exact words. It's strange that I can't remember them, seeing that I was so struck by their meaning and all that they implied.

'What he said, in substance, was:

' "I won't be allowed to."

'And when I looked at his face, I thought I could see fear in it.

'As you can see, it's all pretty vague. At the time, I didn't attach much importance to it, imagining that it was the natural reaction of an old man hearing about the death of another old man and telling himself that it would be his turn soon.'

'When I heard that he had been murdered, that scene came back to me.'

'Did you mention it to anybody?'

'No.'

'Not even to your grandmother?'

'I didn't want to bother her. I could swear that the Count felt that he was in danger. He wasn't a man to imagine things. In spite of his age, his mind was still exceptionally clear and his philosophy of life kept him proof against baseless fears.'

'If I understand you correctly, you think he foresaw what has happened to him.'

'He foresaw something unpleasant, yes. I decided to tell you about it because, ever since yesterday, it has been worrying me.'

'He never talked to you about his friends?'

'About his dead friends. He hadn't any friends left who were still alive, but that didn't upset him too much.

' "When you come to think of it," he used to say, "it isn't as unpleasant as all that to be the last to go."

'And he added sadly:

' "It means there's still one memory in which the others can go on living." '

'He didn't talk to you about his enemies?'

'I'm convinced that he never had any. A few envious colleagues, perhaps, at the beginning of his career, which was swift and brilliant. They too are dead and buried.'

'Thank you. You did right to come.'

'You still don't know anything?'

Maigret hesitated, and nearly mentioned Jaquette who, at that very moment, would be shut up in his office with the Abbé Barraud.

At Police Headquarters, they sometimes called the chief-inspector's office the confessional, but this was the first time that it had really served as one.

'Nothing certain, no.'

'I must be getting back to the Rue d'Ulm.'

Maigret accompanied him to the head of the stairs.

'Thank you again.'

He walked along the huge corridor for a while, with his hands behind his back, lit his pipe, and went into the inspectors' room.

'Is the Abbé next door?'

'He's been there quite a while.'

'What's he like?'

And Janvier replied with a somewhat bitter irony:

'He's the oldest of the lot.'

Chapter Eight

'Get me Lucas on the phone.'

'Rue Saint-Dominique?'

'Yes. I sent him to relieve Lapointe.'

He was beginning to lose patience. The conversation was going on in an undertone in the adjoining office, and when he went up to the door, all he could hear was the sort of whispering one heard outside a real confessional.

'Lucas? . . . All quiet over there? . . . Nothing but phone calls from journalists? . . . Go on telling them there's nothing new . . . What? . . . No, she hasn't talked yet . . . Yes, she's in my office, but not with me or anybody else from Headquarters . . . She's with a priest . . .'

The next minute, the examining magistrate was on the line, and Maigret repeated roughly the same words.

'No, don't worry, I'm not hustling her. On the contrary . . .'

He could not remember being so gentle and patient in the whole of his life. Once again the English article Pardon had read him came back to him and evoked an ironic smile.

The contributor to the *Lancet* had been wrong. It wasn't a schoolmaster in the end, nor a novelist, nor even a detective, who was going to solve the problem of Jaquette, but an octogenarian priest.

'How long have they been in there?'

'Twenty-five minutes.'

He hadn't even the consolation of having a glass of beer, for the tray had been left next door. By the time he got to it, the beer would be warm. It was warm already. He was tempted to go down to the Brasserie Dauphine, but hesitated to leave just then.

He felt that the solution was within reach, and tried to guess what it was, not so much in his capacity as a chief-inspector of the Judicial Police whose duty it was to identify a criminal and get a confession out of him, as in his capacity as a human being.

For it was as a human being that he had conducted this case, as if it had been a personal matter, so much so that in spite of himself he had brought childhood memories into it.

Wasn't he involved to some extent? If Saint-Hilaire had been an ambassador for several decades, if his platonic love for Isabelle dated back nearly fifty years, he, Maigret, had twenty-five years' service at Police-Headquarters to his credit, and as recently as the previous day he had felt convinced that every conceivable variety of individual had passed before him.

He didn't regard himself as a superman; he didn't consider himself infallible. On the contrary, it was with a certain humility that he began all his investigations, even the simplest.

He distrusted the evidence, suspected hasty judgments. He patiently tried to understand, never forgetting that the most obvious motives are not always the most important.

If he hadn't a very high opinion of men and their capabilities, he went on believing in man himself.

He looked for his weak points. And when, in the end, he put his finger on them, he didn't crow with joy, but on the contrary felt a certain sadness.

Since the previous day, he had felt out of his depth, for he had found himself unexpectedly faced with people whose very existence he had never suspected. All their attitudes, their remarks, their reactions were unfamiliar to him, and he tried in vain to classify them.

He wanted to like them, even Jaquette, for all that she got his back up.

He discovered, in their way of life, a grace, a harmony, a certain innocence too which appealed to him.

Suddenly, he coldly reminded himself:

'Saint-Hilaire has been killed for all that.'

By one of these people, that was practically certain. By Jaquette, if scientific tests still meant anything.

For a few moments, he felt an intense dislike for them all, including the dead man, and including that young man who had just aroused in him more keenly than ever before the longing for fatherhood.

Why shouldn't these people have been like others? Why shouldn't they have known the same sordid interests and the same passions?

This all too innocent love-story suddenly annoyed him. He stopped believing in it, and started looking for something else, a different explanation, more consistent with his experience.

Don't two women who have loved the same man for so many years inevitably end up by hating each other?

Wouldn't a family allied to most of the royal families of Europe react strongly to the threat of a marriage as ridiculous as that envisaged by the two old people?

None of them made any accusations. None of them had any enemies. All of them lived in apparent harmony, except Mazeron and his wife who had finally separated.

Irritated by the whispering which was still going on, Maigret nearly flung the door open, and possibly what restrained him was the reproachful glance which Janvier shot at him.

He too had been won over!

'I hope you've got somebody watching the corridor?'

He had got to the point of envisaging the possibility of the old priest's vanishing with his penitent.

All the same, he felt sure that he was on the verge of discovering the truth which had eluded him so far. It was all very simple, he knew that. Human dramas are always simple when you consider them afterwards.

Several times since the previous day, and especially since that morning, though he couldn't have said exactly when, he had been on the point of understanding.

A discreet knocking on the communicating door made him jump.

'Shall I come with you?' asked Janvier.

'It would be a good idea if you did.'

The Abbé Barraud, who was indeed a very old man, was standing up, a skeletal figure with long, untidy hair forming a halo round his head. His cassock was shiny with wear, and it was badly darned here and there.

Jaquette did not seem to have left her chair, on which she was sitting as erect as ever. Only the expression on her face had changed. She was no longer tense, no longer in a fighting mood. She no longer showed any sign of defiance, of a fierce determination to remain silent.

If she was not smiling, she was none the less full of serenity.

'I must apologize, Chief-Inspector, for keeping you waiting such a long time. You see, the question Mademoiselle Larrieu asked me was rather delicate and I had to consider it carefully before giving her a reply. I must admit that I nearly asked you for permission to telephone the Archbishop to ask his opinion.'

Janvier, sitting at the end of the table, was taking down the conversation in shorthand. Maigret, as if he felt the need to keep himself in countenance, had installed himself at his desk.

'Sit down, Monsieur l'Abbé.'

'I may stay?'

'I imagine your penitent still has need of your services.'

The priest sat down on a chair, took a little wooden box out of his cassock, and took a pinch of snuff. This gesture, and the grains of snuff on the greyish cassock, brought back old memories to Maigret.

'Mademoiselle Larrieu, as you are aware, is extremely devout, and it is her piety which has led her to adopt an attitude which I have felt it my duty to persuade her to abandon. What was worrying her was the thought that the Comte de Saint-Hilaire might not be given Christian burial, and that is why she had decided to wait until the funeral had taken place before saying anything.'

For Maigret, it was like a child's balloon suddenly bursting in the sunshine, and he blushed at having been so close to the truth without managing to guess it.

'The Comte de Saint-Hilaire committed suicide?'

'I am afraid that that is the truth of the matter. But as I told Mademoiselle Larrieu, we have no proof that he didn't repent what he had done at the last moment. No death is instantaneous in the eyes of the Church. Infinity exists in time as well as in space, and an infinitely small lapse of time, though it may defy measurement by doctors, is sufficient for contrition.

'I don't believe that the Church will refuse its last blessing to the Comte de Saint-Hilaire.'

For the first time, Jaquette's eyes became misty, and she took a handkerchief out of her bag to wipe them, while her lips formed a girlish pout.

'Speak up, Jaquette,' said the priest encouragingly. 'Repeat what you have just told me.'

She swallowed her saliva.

'I was in bed. I was asleep. I heard an explosion and I rushed into the study.'

'You found your master sprawled on the carpet with half his face shot away.'

'Yes.'

'Where was the pistol?'

'On the desk.'

'What did you do?'

'I went to get a mirror from my room to make sure that he had stopped breathing.'

'You made certain that he was dead. After that?'

'My first impulse was to telephone the Princess.'

'Why didn't you?'

'First of all because it was nearly midnight.'

'You weren't afraid that she would disapprove of your plan?'

'I didn't think of it straight away. I told myself that the police were going to come and suddenly I realized that because it was suicide the Count wouldn't be given Christian burial.'

'How long was it from the moment when you knew your employer was dead to the moment when you in your turn fired the gun?'

'I don't know. Ten minutes perhaps? I knelt down beside him and I said a prayer. Then, standing up, I took hold of the pistol and I fired, without looking, and asking the dead man and Heaven to forgive me.'

'You fired three bullets?'

'I don't know. I pulled the trigger until it didn't work any more. Then I noticed some bright dots on the carpet. I don't know anything about guns. I realized that they were cartridge-cases and I picked them up. I didn't sleep a wink all night. Early next morning I went and threw the gun and the cartridge-cases into the Seine, from the Pont de la Concorde. I had to wait quite a while, because there was a policeman on duty in front of the Chamber of Deputies who seemed to be looking at me.'

'Do you know why your employer committed suicide?'

She glanced at the priest, who gave her an encouraging nod.

'For some time he had been worried and upset.'

'Why?'

'A few months ago, the doctor advised him to give up drinking wine and spirits. He was a great wine-lover. He gave it up for a few days, then he started drinking it again. That gave him stomach-ache and he had to get up in the night to take some bicarbonate of soda. In the end I was buying him a packet every week.'

'What's the name of his doctor?'

'Doctor Ourgaud.'

Maigret picked up the receiver.

'Get me Doctor Ourgaud please.'

And, to Jaquette:

'He had been his doctor for a long time?'

'You might almost say he had always been his doctor.'

'How old is Doctor Ourgaud?'

'I don't know exactly. About my age.'

'And he is still in practice?'

'He goes on seeing his old patients. His son has set up just across the landing from him, on the Boulevard Saint-Germain.'

Right to the very end, they remained not only in the same district but among people who might be said to belong to the same species.

'Hullo. Doctor Ourgard? This is Chief-Inspector Maigret.'

The doctor asked him to speak louder and closer to the receiver, apologizing for being rather hard of hearing.

'As you may have guessed, I should like to ask you a few questions about one of your patients. Yes, it's him I'm talking about. Jaquette Larrieu is here in my office and has just told me that the Comte de Saint-Hilaire committed suicide.–What's that? . . . You were expecting me to come and see you? . . . You had guessed it was that? . . . Hullo. I'm speaking as close to the receiver as I can . . . She says that for several months, the Comte de Saint-Hilaire had been suffering from stomach-ache . . . I can hear you perfectly . . . Doctor Tudelle, the medical expert who carried out the post-mortem, says that he was surprised to find an old man's organs in such good condition . . .

'What's that? . . . That's what you kept telling your patient? . . . He didn't believe you? . . .

'Yes . . . Yes . . . I see . . . You couldn't manage to convince him . . . He went to see your colleagues . . .

'Thank you, Doctor . . . I shall probably have to trouble you to take your evidence . . . But no! On the contrary, it's very important . . .'

He hung up. His face was serious and Janvier thought he could distinguish a certain emotion in it.

'The Comte de Saint-Hilaire,' he explained in a rather dull voice, 'had got it into his head that he was suffering from cancer. In spite of his doctor's assurance to the contrary, he started going to different doctors to be examined, deciding every time that the truth was being kept from him.'

Jaquette murmured:

'He had always been so proud of his health! In the old days he often used to say to me that he wasn't afraid of death, that he was prepared for it, but that he would find it hard to put up with being ill. When he had the 'flu, for instance, he used to hide like a sick animal and tried to keep me out of his bedroom as much as possible. He was very touchy about it. One of his friends, several years ago, died of a cancer which kept him in bed for nearly two years. He was given various complicated treatments and the Count used to say impatiently: "Why don't they let him die? If I were in his place, I should ask them to help me to go as soon as possible." '

Isabelle's grandson, Julien, could not remember the exact words Saint-Hilaire had used a few hours before he died. Thinking he would find him happy to see his dream close to fulfilment, he had found himself in the presence of an anxious, worried old man, who seemed to be afraid of something.

At least, that was what the young man had thought. Because he was not yet an old man. Jaquette, for her part, had understood straight away. And Maigret, who was more than half-way along the road, closer to the old people than to the students of the Rue d'Ulm, understood too: Saint-Hilaire expected to be bed-ridden before very long.

And that just as an old love, which nothing had dimmed in fifty years, was on the point of entering real life.

Isabelle, who saw him only from a distance and who had kept ever-present the picture of their youth, would become a sick-nurse at the same time as she became his wife, and she would know only the infirmities of a wornout body.

'Excuse me,' he said suddenly, going towards the door.

He made his way along the corridors of the Palais de Justice, went up to the third floor, and spent half-an-hour closeted with the examining magistrate.

When he came back to his office, the three people were still in the same place and Janvier was chewing his pencil.

'You are free to go,' he told Jaquette. 'A car will take you home. Or rather, I think I ought to have you taken to Maître Aubonnet's, where you have an appointment. As for you, Monsieur l'Abbé, you will be dropped at the presbytery. In the next few days, there will be some formalities to be completed, some documents to be signed.'

And, turning to Janvier:

'Will you take the wheel?'

He spent an hour with the Director of Police Headquarters, and afterwards he was seen in the Brasserie Dauphine, where he drank two big glasses of beer at the bar.

Madame Maigret was expecting him to ring up to tell her that he would not be coming home for dinner, as often happened in the course of an investigation.

She was surprised, at half-past six, to hear him coming up the stairs, and she opened the door at the very moment that he reached the landing.

He was more serious than usual, serious and serene, but she did not dare to ask him any questions when, as he kissed her, he pressed her against him for a long time without saying anything.

She could not know that he had just been immersed in a distant past and a rather less distant future.

'What's for dinner?' he finally asked, looking as if he were pulling himself together.

Noland
21 June 1960

Maigret
Loses his Temper

Maigret Loses his Temper

Translated from the French by
Robert Eglesfield

Chapter One

It was a quarter past twelve when Maigret passed under the perpetually cool archway and through the gate flanked by two uniformed policemen who were standing right up against the wall to obtain a little shade. He gave them a casual wave and stood for a moment motionless and undecided, glancing first towards the courtyard, then towards the Place Dauphine, then back towards the courtyard.

In the corridor upstairs, and then on the dusty staircase, he had stopped two or three times, pretending to be lighting his pipe again, in the hope that one of his colleagues or his inspectors would suddenly appear. It was unusual for the staircase to be deserted at that time, but that year, on June 12, a holiday atmosphere was already reigning at Police Headquarters.

Some people had already left at the beginning of the month to avoid the rush in July and August, and others were getting ready for the annual exodus. That particular morning, after a wet spring, the weather had suddenly turned hot, and Maigret had worked in his shirt-sleeves with the windows open.

Except for his report to the Director and one or two visits to the inspectors' room, he had remained on his own, getting on with the tiresome administrative task he had begun some days before. Files piled up in front of him, and from time to time he raised his head like a schoolboy, glancing towards the motionless foliage of the trees, and listening to the hum of Paris life, which had just taken on the special quality it has on hot summer days.

For the past two weeks, he had not missed a single meal at the Boulevard Richard-Lenoir and he had not been disturbed once during the evening or the night.

Normally he would have had to turn left along the Quai in the direction of the Pont Saint-Michel, to take a bus or a taxi. The courtyard remained empty. Nobody joined him.

So, with a slight shrug of his shoulders, he turned right instead and walked into the Place Dauphine, cutting across it diagonally. He had suddenly felt an urge, on leaving the office, to go to the Brasserie Dauphine and, in spite of the advice of his friend Pardon, the Rue Picpus doctor, at whose home he and Madame Maigret had dined the previous week, to treat himself to an apéritif.

For several weeks now he had behaved himself, contenting himself with a glass of wine at mealtimes, and sometimes, in the evening, when he and his wife went out, a glass of beer.

Never mind! Pardon had recommended him to watch his liver, but he hadn't forbidden him to have an apéritif, just one, after weeks of almost total abstinence.

At the bar he found some familiar faces, at least a dozen men from Police

Headquarters who had scarcely more work than he had, and who had left early. This happened at fairly long intervals: a pause lasting a few days, a dead calm, nothing but routine business, as they put it, then, all of a sudden, cases breaking at an ever increasing rate, leaving nobody any time to draw breath.

The others nodded to him and moved up to make room for him at the bar. Pointing to the glasses filled with an opaline drink, he growled:

'The same thing . . .'

The *patron* had already been there thirty years before, when the chief-inspector had started at the Quai des Orfèvres, but at that time he had been the son of the house. Now, there was a son too, wearing a chef's white hat in the kitchen, and looking like the *patron* when he had been a boy.

'How are things, Chief?'

'All right.'

The smell had not changed. Every little restaurant in Paris has its particular smell, and here for example, against a background of apéritifs and spirits, a connoisseur would have distinguished the rather tart scent of the ordinary wines of the Loire. As for the kitchen, tarragon and chives were the predominant aromas.

Maigret automatically ran his eyes over the menu on the slate: mackerel from Brittany and *foie de veau en papillottes*. At the same moment, in the dining-room with its paper tablecloths, he caught sight of Lucas, who seemed to have taken refuge there, not in order to lunch, for there was nobody at table yet, but to chat in peace with somebody Maigret did not know.

Lucas for his part saw him, hesitated, got up, and came over to him.

'Have you a moment to spare, Chief? I think that this might interest you . . .'

The chief-inspector followed him, with his glass in his hand. Lucas introduced the other man:

'Antonio Farano . . . Do you know him?'

The name meant nothing to the chief-inspector, but it seemed to him that he had already seen the handsome face of this Italian who could have been a film star. No doubt the red sports car outside the door belonged to him. It went with his appearance, with his light-coloured clothes, which were rather too well cut for Maigret's taste, and with the heavy signet ring on his finger.

Lucas went on, while the three men were sitting down:

'He called at the Quai to see me just after I'd left. Lapointe told him that he might find me here . . .'

Maigret noticed that while Lucas was drinking the same apéritif as himself, Farano was just having a fruit juice.

'He's Émile Boulay's brother-in-law . . . He manages one of Boulay's cabarets, the Paris-Strip, in the Rue de Berri . . .'

Lucas winked discreetly at his chief.

'Repeat what you've just told me, Farano . . .'

'Well, my brother-in-law has disappeared . . .'

He had kept his native accent.

'When?' asked Lucas.

'Last night, probably . . . We don't know exactly . . .'

He was overawed by Maigret, and to keep himself in countenance he took a cigarette case out of his pocket.

'Mind if I smoke?'

'Of course not.'

Lucas explained for the chief-inspector's benefit:

'You know Boulay, Chief. He's that little man who arrived from Le Havre four or five years ago . . .'

'Seven years ago,' corrected the Italian.

'All right, seven years ago . . . He bought a night-club in the Rue Pigalle, the Lotus, and now he owns four . . .'

Maigret wondered why Lucas wanted to involve him in this case. Since he had taken over the Crime Squad, he had rarely had anything to do with that milieu, which he had known very well in the old days, but which he had rather lost sight of.

It was at least two years since he had last set foot in a cabaret. As for the criminals of Pigalle, he only knew a few of them now, mainly old hands, for that was a little world of its own which was constantly changing.

'I was wondering,' Lucas broke in again, 'whether this might have some connection with the Mazotti case . . .'

Ah! he was beginning to understand. When was it that Mazotti had been rubbed out while he was coming out of a bar in the Rue Fontaine about three o'clock in the morning? It was about a month ago. It had happened towards the middle of May.

Maigret remembered a report from the police in the 9th *arrondissement* which he had passed to Lucas, saying:

'Probably a settling of old scores . . . Do what you can . . .'

Mazotti had not been an Italian, like Farano, but a Corsican who had started on the Côte d'Azur before coming up to Paris with a little gang of his own.

'My brother-in-law didn't kill Mazotti,' Farano was saying in tones of conviction. 'You know very well, Monsieur Lucas, that that isn't his line . . . Besides you questioned him twice in your office . . .'

'I've never accused him of killing Mazotti . . . I questioned him just as I questioned everybody Mazotti had gone for . . . That's quite a crowd . . .'

And to Maigret he added:

'As a matter of fact I sent him a summons for today at eleven o'clock, and I was surprised not to see him . . .'

'He never sleeps out, does he?' the chief-inspector asked innocently.

'Never! . . . It's easy to see that you don't know him. He isn't like that at all. He loves my sister, home life. He never came home later than four in the morning . . .'

'And last night he didn't come home? That's it, is it?'

'That's it . . .'

'Where were you?'

'At the Paris-Strip . . . We didn't close till five . . . The season is in full swing for us, because Paris is already full of tourists . . . Just as I was counting the takings, Marina phoned me to ask if I'd seen Émile . . . Marina's my sister . . . I hadn't seen my brother-in-law all night . . . He didn't often come down to the Champs-Élysées . . .'

'Where are his other night-clubs?'

'All in Montmartre, a few hundred yards from each other. That was his idea and it paid off. With cabarets more or less next door to each other, you can move your artistes from one place to the next during the night and cut down on your overheads . . .

'The Lotus is right at the top of the Rue Pigalle, the Train Bleu practically next door, in the Rue Victor-Massé, and the Saint-Trop' a little lower down, in the Rue Notre-Dame-de-Lorette . . .

'Émile was doubtful about opening a cabaret in another part of Paris, and it's the only one he didn't look after himself, you might say. He let me run it for him . . .'

'So your sister phoned you shortly after five?'

'Yes. She's so used to being woken up by her husband . . .'

'What did you do?'

'First of all I called the Lotus, where they told me that he had left about eleven. He also looked in at the Train Bleu, but the cashier can't say exactly when. As for the Saint-Trop', it was closed when I tried to get it on the phone.'

'As far as you know, your brother-in-law didn't have an appointment last night?'

'No. As I've already said, he was a quiet man, very regular in his habits. After dinner at home . . .'

'Where does he live?'

'In the Rue Victor-Massé . . .'

'In the same building as the Train Bleu?'

'No. Three houses further on . . . After dinner, he used to go first of all to the Lotus to supervise the preparations. That's the biggest night-club and he looked after it himself . . . Then he went down to the Saint-Trop', where he stayed a little while, after that to the Train Bleu, and then he started his tour all over again. He used to do it two or three times in the course of the night, because he kept an eye on everything . . .'

'Was he wearing a dinner-jacket?'

'No. He wore a dark suit, midnight blue, but never a dinner-jacket . . . He didn't bother much about looking smart . . .'

'You talk about him in the past tense . . .'

'That's because something must have happened to him . . .'

At several tables people had begun eating, and every now and then Maigret found his gaze wandering towards the plates and the carafes of Pouilly. Although his glass was empty, he resisted the temptation to order another.

'What did you do next?'

'I went to bed, after asking my sister to ring me if there was any news.'

'Did she phone you again?'

'About eight o'clock . . .'

'Where do you live?'

'In the Rue de Ponthieu.'

'Are you married?'

'Yes, to an Italian girl. I spent the morning phoning the staff of the three cabarets. I was trying to find out where and when he had last been seen . . . It isn't as simple as you might think . . . For a good part of the night the clubs are packed to capacity and everybody is busy doing his job . . . What's more, Émile didn't stand out in a crowd . . . He's a skinny little man whom none of the customers ever took to be the boss, and sometimes he spent a long time outside with the doorman . . .'

Lucas nodded to indicate that all this was true.

'It seems that nobody saw him after half-past eleven . . .'

'Who was the last to see him?'

'I haven't been able to question everybody . . . Some of the waiters, barmen and musicians aren't on the phone . . . As for the girls, I don't know the addresses of most of them . . . I won't be able to make any serious inquiries before tonight when everybody will be at his post . . .

'So far, the last person to have spoken to him seems to be the doorman of the Lotus, Louis Boubée, a little fellow no bigger or heavier than a jockey, and better known in Montmartre by the nickname of Mickey . . .

'Between eleven o'clock and half-past eleven, Émile came out of the Lotus and stood for a while on the pavement near Mickey, who kept rushing forward to open the door every time a car drew up . . .'

'Did they talk to each other?'

'Émile didn't talk much . . . It seems that he looked at his watch several times before going off towards the bottom of the street . . . Mickey thought that he was making for the Saint-Trop' . . .'

'Has your brother-in-law got a car?'

'No. Not since the accident . . .'

'What accident?'

'It was seven years ago . . . He was still living at Le Havre, where he had a little night-club, the Monaco . . . One day when he was driving to Rouen with his wife . . .'

'He was already married to your sister?'

'No. I'm talking about his first wife, a French girl from the country near Le Havre, Marie Pirouet . . . She was expecting a baby . . . In fact they were going to Rouen to consult a specialist . . . It was raining . . . The car skidded on a bend and ran into a tree . . . Émile's wife was killed on the spot . . .'

'And what about him?'

'He got off with a gash in the cheek that left him with a scar. In Montmartre most people imagine it was made by a knife . . .'

'Did he love his wife?'

'He was crazy about her . . . He had known her since childhood . . .'

'He was born at Le Havre?'

'In a village nearby, I forget which . . . She came from the same village . . . After she died, he never touched a driving wheel again, and as far as possible he avoided getting into a car . . . In Paris, for instance, he hardly ever took a taxi . . . He walked a lot and, when he had to, he used the Métro . . . Besides, he didn't like moving outside the 9th *arrondissement* . . .'

'You think somebody's got rid of him?'

'All I can say is that, if nothing had happened to him, he'd have come home a long time ago . . .'

'Does he live alone with your sister?'

'No. My mother lives with them, and also my other sister, Ada, who works as his secretary . . . Not to mention the two children, a boy of three, Lucien, and a little girl of ten months . . .'

'Have you any suspicions?'

Antonio shook his head.

'You think your brother-in-law's disappearance has some connection with the Mazotti case?'

'What I'm sure about is that Émile didn't kill Mazotti . . .'

Maigret turned towards Lucas, who had been in charge of the inquiry.

'What about you?'

'That's what I think too, Chief . . . I questioned him twice, and I got the impression that he was telling the truth . . . As Antonio says, he's a puny little fellow, almost shy, the sort you wouldn't expect to find running a set of night-clubs . . . And yet, when he had to deal with Mazotti he knew how to tackle him . . .'

'What do you mean?'

'Mazotti and his gang had organized a racket which had nothing original about it but which they'd perfected . . . Under the pretext of offering protection, they demanded more or less considerable sums of money every week from every night-club proprietor . . .

'Most of them, to begin with, refused to pay . . . Then a well-organized little comedy was put on for their benefit . . . When the night-club was full, Mazotti would arrive with one or two of his toughs . . . They would sit down at a table if there was a table free, or at the bar if there wasn't, order some champagne, and then, in the middle of a turn, start a brawl . . . First there'd be some muttering, then voices would be raised . . . The barman or the head-waiter would be bawled out and called a thief. . . .

'The whole thing would end up with glasses being broken and a more-or-less general free-for-all, and of course most of the customers went off swearing that they'd never set foot in the place again . . .

'The next time Mazotti called, the owner usually decided to pay up . . .'

'Émile didn't?'

'No. He didn't call in the local chuckers-out, like some of his colleagues—who weren't any the better for it, because Mazotti ended up by buying them off . . . His idea was to send to Le Havre for a few dockers to settle Mazotti's hash . . .'

'When was the last scrap?'

'The night Mazotti died . . . He'd gone to the Lotus, about one o'clock in the morning, with two of his usual pals . . . Émile Boulay's dockers threw them out . . . A few blows were exchanged . . .'

'Was Émile there?'

'He'd taken refuge behind the bar, because he can't bear the sight of fighting . . . Afterwards Mazotti went to lick his wounds in a bar in the Rue Fontaine, Chez Jo, which is more or less his headquarters. There were about four or five of them drinking at the back of the bar . . . When they came out, at three in the morning, a car went past and Mazotti was hit by five bullets, while one of his pals got one in his shoulder . . . The car was never identified . . . Nobody talked . . . I questioned most of the night-club proprietors . . . I'm still working on the case . . .'

'Where was Boulay when Mazotti was shot?'

'Well, Chief, as you know, it's difficult to find out anything for certain in that milieu. It seems that he was at the Train Bleu, but I don't put much trust in his witnesses . . .'

'Émile didn't kill Mazotti,' repeated the Italian.

'Did he carry a gun?'

'An automatic, yes . . . He had a licence issued by the Prefecture of Police . . . That wasn't the gun that killed Mazotti . . .'

Maigret gave a sigh and signalled to the waitress to fill up the glasses, for he had been dying for another drink for long enough.

Lucas explained:

'I wanted to put you in the picture, Chief, and I thought you'd be interested to hear what Antonio had to say . . .'

'I've told you nothing but the truth . . .'

Lucas went on:

'I summoned Émile to the Quai for this morning . . . I must admit it worries me that he disappeared last night of all nights . . .'

'What did you want to ask him?'

'It was just routine. I was going to ask him the same questions as last time, to check with his first answers and with the other affidavits . . .'

'The two occasions you had him in your office, did he seem frightened?'

'No. Irritated rather . . . Above all else he wanted to keep his name out of the papers . . . He kept saying that it would do tremendous harm to his business, that his cabarets were well conducted, that nothing ever happened in them, and that if his name was mentioned in connection with a settling of scores, he would never get over it . . .'

'That's right,' said Antonio approvingly, making as if to get up.

He added:

'You don't need me any more, do you? I've got to join my sisters and my mother who are in a terrible state . . .'

A few moments later, they heard the roar of the red car shooting off towards the Pont-Neuf. Maigret took a slow sip of his apéritif, darted a sidelong glance at Lucas, and sighed:

'Are you expected anywhere?'

'No . . . I was thinking of . . .'

'Eating here?'

And, as he nodded, Maigret decided:

'In that case, we'll have a meal together . . . I'll give my wife a ring . . . You go ahead and order . . .'

'Would you like some mackerel?'

'Yes, and some *foie de veau en papillottes* . . .'

It was the *foie de veau* which tempted him most of all, together with the atmosphere of the brasserie where he hadn't set foot for weeks.

The case was not terribly important, and so far Lucas had looked after it by himself. Nobody, outside the underworld, was concerned about Mazotti's death. Everybody knew that that sort of settling of scores always found a solution in the end, even if it consisted of another killing.

The best about those cases was that the Public Prosecutor's Department and the examining magistrates were not constantly spurring the police on to find the culprit. As one magistrate put it:

'It means one less to be given board and lodging for years in prison . . .'

The two men chatted together as they ate. Maigret learnt a little more about Émile Boulay and ended up by getting interested in that curious little man.

The son of a Norman fisherman, Émile had signed on at the age of sixteen, as a steward with the Compagnie Transatlantique. That had been before the war. He was in New York as a member of the crew of the *Normandie* when hostilities broke out in France.

How had such a puny little man come to be accepted by the American Marines? He had spent the war with them before going back into service, this time as a deputy chief steward, on the *Ile-de-France*.

'You know, Chief, that nearly all of them dream of setting up on their own account, and after two years of marriage Boulay bought a bar at Le Havre which he turned into a dance-hall before long. Strip-tease was just beginning at the time, and it seems that he had soon made quite a pile . . .

'When the accident happened, and his wife was killed, he was already planning to extend his activities to Paris . . .'

'Did he keep on the cabaret at Le Havre?'

'He put a manager in . . . One of his old pals on the *Ile-de-France* runs it for him . . .

'In Paris he bought the Lotus, which wasn't doing as well as it is now . . . It was a second-rate joint, a tourist trap like dozens of others round the Place Pigalle . . .'

'Where did he meet Antonio's sister?'

'At the Lotus . . . She was working in the cloakroom . . . She was only eighteen . . .'

'What was Antonio doing at that time?'

'He was a worker at Renault's, in the body assembly shop . . . He had been the first to arrive in France . . . Then he had sent for his mother and his two sisters . . . They lived in the Javel district . . .'

'In fact Émile seems to have more or less married the whole family . . . Did you go and see him at home?'

'No . . . I had a look at the Lotus and his other night-clubs, but I didn't think it necessary to go to his flat . . .'

'You're sure he didn't kill Mazotti?'

'Why should he have killed Mazotti? He was winning the game . . .'

'He might have been frightened . . .'

'Nobody in Montmartre thinks he did it . . .'

They drank their coffee in silence and Maigret refused the calvados which the *patron* came to offer him as usual. He had drunk two apéritifs, and after that he had contented himself with a single glass of Pouilly, so that, walking back to Police Headquarters with Lucas, he felt reasonably pleased with himself.

In his office he took off his jacket, loosened his tie, and set to work on the administrative files. It was a question of nothing less than a complete reorganization of all the Police services, on which he'd been asked to prepare a report, and he was applying himself to the task like a good pupil.

In the course of the afternoon his thoughts occasionally went to Émile Boulay, to the little Montmartre empire which the former steward with the Compagnie Transatlantique had built up, to the young Italian with the red car, and to the flat in the Rue Victor-Massé where the three women lived with the children.

During this time Lucas was ringing up the hospitals and the various police-stations. He had also issued a description of Boulay, but by half-past six these inquiries had not produced any results.

The evening was almost as hot as the day had been, and Maigret went for a walk with his wife, spending nearly an hour over a single glass of beer, at a table outside a café in the Place de la République.

They talked mainly about the holidays. A good many of the passers-by were carrying their jackets over one arm, and most of the women were wearing printed cotton dresses.

The next day was a Thursday. Another glorious day. The night reports did not mention Émile Boulay, and Lucas had no news.

There was a violent but short-lived storm about eleven o'clock, after which steam seemed to be rising from the roadway. He went home for lunch, and then came back to his office and the pile of files.

When he left the Quai des Orfèvres, there was still no news of the little man from Le Havre, and Lucas had spent a fruitless afternoon in Montmartre.

'It does seem, Chief, that it's Boubée, the man they call Mickey and who's been the doorman at the Lotus for years, who was the last to see him. . . . He thinks he remembers seeing Émile turn the corner of the Rue Pigalle and the Rue Notre-Dame-de-Lorette as if he was making for the Saint-Trop', but he didn't attach any importance to it . . . I'll go back to Montmartre tonight, when everybody'll be at his post . . .'

Lucas was to discover nothing more. At nine o'clock on Friday morning Maigret had just finished looking through the daily reports when he called Lucas into his office.

'They've found him,' he announced, lighting his pipe.

'Alive?'

'Dead.'

'In Montmartre? In the Seine?'

Maigret held out a report from the 20th *arrondissement*. It stated that a corpse had been found at daybreak in the Rue des Rondeaux, just outside the cemetery of Père Lachaise. The body was lying across the pavement, not far from the railway embankment. It was dressed in a dark blue suit, and in the wallet, which contained a fair amount of money, there was an identity card in the name of Émile Boulay.

Lucas looked up, frowning.

'I wonder . . . ,' he began.

'Go on reading . . .'

The rest was in fact calculated to astonish the inspector even more. The report went on to state that the corpse, which had been taken to the Medico-Legal Institute, was in a state of advanced decomposition.

Admittedly not many people went along that part of the Rue des Rondeaux, which was a dead end. All the same, a corpse could not have remained on the pavement there for two days, or even a few hours, without being found.

'What do you think about it?'

'It's very odd . . .'

'Have you read it all?'

'Not the last few lines . . .'

Émile Boulay had disappeared the night of Tuesday–Wednesday. Given the state of the body, it was probable that he had been killed that night.

Two whole days had gone by, two days of considerable heat.

It was hard to understand what reason the murderer or murderers could have had for keeping the body all that time.

'Stranger still!' exclaimed Lucas, putting the report on the desk.

The strangest thing in fact was that, according to the first examination, the crime had not been committed with a firearm, nor with a knife either.

As far as could be seen pending the post-mortem, Émile Boulay had been strangled.

Now neither Maigret nor Lucas, despite their long years of service in the police, could remember a single crime in the underworld committed by strangulation.

Every district in Paris, every social class, has so to speak its own way of killing, just as it has its own method of committing suicide. There are streets where you throw yourself out of the window, others where you gas yourself, and still others where you take an overdose of barbiturates.

The police know the knifing districts, those where bludgeons are used and those, like Montmartre, where firearms are preferred.

Not only had the little night-club owner been strangled, but, for two days and three nights, the murderer had kept the body.

Maigret was already opening the cupboard to get his jacket and his hat.

'Let's go!' he growled.

At last he had an excuse to leave his administrative imposition.

In fine June weather, cooled by a light breeze, the two men made for the Medico-Legal Institute.

Chapter Two

The pink buildings of the Medico-Legal Institute, on the Quai de la Rapée, look more like a laboratory for pharmaceutical products, say, than the old mortuary under the big clock of the Palais de Justice.

Behind a window, in a well-lighted office, Maigret and Lucas found an employee who recognized them straightaway and said with a polite smile:

'I suppose it's about the fellow from the Rue des Rondeaux?'

The electric clock above his head gave the time as five-past ten, and through the window they could see the barges on the other side of the Seine moored in front of the warehouse docks.

'There's somebody waiting there already,' continued the official, who appeared to want to make conversation. 'It seems he's a relative . . .'

'Did he give his name?'

'I'll ask him for it when he's identified the body and comes here to sign his declaration . . .'

The man's concern with the corpse was purely theoretical, in the form of cards in a card index.

'Where is he?'

'In the waiting-room . . . I'm afraid you'll have to wait too, Monsieur Maigret . . . Doctor Morel is in the middle of his work . . .'

The corridor was white, with a light-coloured floor, and the waiting-room was bright too with its two benches and its chairs in polished wood, and its big table which only lacked a few magazines to make you think you were at the dentist's. The walls, decorated with oil-paint, were bare, and Maigret had often wondered what sort of pictures or engravings they could have hung on them.

Antonio was sitting on one of the chairs, his chin in his hands, and although he still looked handsome, his face was a little puffy, like that of a man who has not had enough sleep, while his cheeks were unshaven.

He stood up as the police officers came in.

'Have you seen him?' he asked.

'Not yet.'

'I haven't either. I've been waiting over half an hour. It's Émile's identity card all right that they showed me . . .'

'Who?'

'An inspector with a queer name . . . Wait a minute . . . Mornique? . . . Bornique? . . .'

'Yes, Bornique . . .'

Maigret and Lucas exchanged glances. This was bound to happen with Bornique of the 20th *arrondissement*. There were a few like him in the district police stations—not only inspectors but chief-inspectors too—who insisted on competing with Police Headquarters and who made it a point of honour to arrive before the men from the Quai des Orfèvres.

Maigret had only learnt about the finding of the body from the daily reports, and since the discovery the men of the 20th *arrondissement* had not been idle. It was precisely to avoid this sort of excessive zeal that Maigret had been working for several weeks on a reorganization of the police force.

'Do you think the doc's going to be much longer? The women are nearly crazy . . .'

'Was it Bornique who went and told them?'

'It was before eight o'clock this morning. They'd just got up and were seeing to the kids.

' "Which of you's called Marina Boulay?" he asked.

'Then he held out an identity card to my sister.

' "That's your husband's card, isn't it? Do you recognize his photograph? When did you last see him?"

'You can imagine the scene. Ada phoned me straightaway. I was asleep. I didn't stop to have breakfast or even make myself a cup of coffee. A few minutes later, I was in the Rue Victor-Massé and the inspector all but treated me as a suspect.

' "Who are you?"

' "The brother-in-law . . ."

' "This lady's?"

' "No. Her husband's . . ." '

Antonio's nerves were still on edge.

'I had to argue for a long time before he agreed to let me come and identify the body instead of my sister. She insisted on coming with me. As I guessed it wouldn't be very pretty, I made her stay at home . . .'

He nervously lit a cigarette.

'The inspector didn't come with you?'

'No. It seems he's got other things to do. He told me that the clerk here would give me a form to fill up and sign . . .'

After a pause he added:

'You see that I was right to feel worried. The day before yesterday you looked as if you didn't believe me. Where is it, the Rue des Rondeaux?'

'It runs alongside the cemetery of Père Lachaise . . .'

'I don't know that part of Paris. What sort of district is it?'

A door opened. Doctor Morel, in a white smock, his cap on his head and a gauze mask hanging under his chin, looked around for the chief-inspector.

'I've just been told you were waiting to see me, Maigret . . . Would you like to come along?'

He led them into a room where the only light came in through frosted glass panes and where the walls were lined with metal cabinets, as in an office, with the difference that the cabinets were of an ususual size. A body, covered with a cloth, was stretched out on a trolley.

'His brother-in-law had better identify him first,' said the chief-inspector.

With the traditional gesture, the sheet was drawn away from the face. The dead man's features had been invaded by a beard a quarter of an inch long, and reddish in colour, like his hair. The skin had a blue tint here and there, and on the left cheek the scar which Antonio had mentioned at the Brasserie Dauphine stood out clearly.

As for the body, it looked slight and thin under the sheet.

'It's him all right?'

'Yes, of course it's him . . .'

Sensing that the Italian was feeling sick, Maigret sent him to the office with Lucas to carry out the formalities.

'Can we put him away?' asked the doctor, motioning to a man in a grey smock who had already opened one of the drawers. 'Will you come with me, Maigret?'

He took him into an office equipped with a wash-basin, and while he was speaking, disinfected his hands and face, took off his white smock, and reassumed the appearance of an ordinary man.

'I suppose you'd like a few details to be getting on with until I send in my report? . . . As usual, we'll have to make some analyses which will take several days . . . What I can tell you straightaway is that the body shows no signs of any wounds . . . The man was strangled or, to be more precise . . .' Morel was searching for words, as if he wasn't too sure of himself.

'This isn't official, you understand . . . I shan't be so dogmatic in my report . . . If I had to reconstruct the murder in the light of the post-mortem, I would say that the victim was attacked from behind, that the murderer put an arm round his neck and pulled so sharply that a cervical vertebra was broken . . .'

'So he was standing up?'

'Standing up, or just possibly seated . . . I personally think that he was standing and that he wasn't expecting this attack . . . There was no real struggle . . . He didn't put up a fight . . . I examined his fingernails carefully, and I didn't find any shreds of wool in them, as there would have been if he had clawed at his attacker's clothes. Nor did I find any blood or hairs, and there weren't any scratches on his hands either. Who is he?'

'A night-club owner. Have you any idea when he was killed?'

'Two full days at least, and three at the most, have elapsed since the man died, and I might add one detail, still off the record: in my opinion the body wasn't exposed to the open air during that period . . . You'll be getting a preliminary report this evening . . .'

Lucas reappeared.

'He's signed the papers . . . What shall I do with him? . . . Shall I let him go back to the Rue Victor-Massé?'

Maigret nodded, because he still had to examine Émile's clothes and the contents of his pockets. Later in the day this task would be done again, more scientifically, in the laboratory.

These things were in another room, piled up on a table. The dark-blue suit was not torn anywhere and there was only a little dust on it. There was no blood. It was scarcely rumpled. As for the black shoes, they were as clean as those of a man who has just left home, with just a couple of recent scratches on the leather.

Maigret would have been willing to bet that the crime had not been committed in the street but in a house, and the murderer had got rid of the body, by leaving it on the pavement of the Rue des Rondeaux, only towards the end of the previous night.

Where had it been brought from? The murderer had almost certainly used a car. The corpse had not been dragged along the pavement.

As for the contents of the pockets, they were rather disappointing. Had Émile Boulay been a smoker? It seemed not. There was no pipe, cigarettes, lighter or matches. Nor any of those shreds of tobacco you always find in the bottom of a smoker's pockets.

A gold watch. In the wallet, five hundred-franc notes and three fifties. The ten-franc notes were loose in one of the pockets, and in the other there was some small change.

A bunch of keys, a pen-knife, a crumpled handkerchief, and another handkerchief, neatly folded, in the breast pocket. A little packet of aspirins and some peppermints.

Lucas, who was emptying the wallet, exclaimed:

'Look! My summons . . .'

A summons which Émile Boulay would have found it difficult to answer . . .

'I thought he was in the habit of carrying an automatic,' growled Maigret.

The firearm was not among the objects spread out on the table, but there was a cheque-book which the chief-inspector looked through. It was practically new. Only three cheques had been drawn. The only large one was a cheque for five thousand francs made out to 'self.'

The stub was dated May 22 and Lucas observed straightaway:

'That's funny! That's the day I summoned him for the second time to the Quai des Orfèvres. I'd seen him there the first time on the 18th, the day after Mazotti's death . . .'

'Will you phone the lab to fetch these things and examine them?'

A few minutes later the two men got back into the car which Lucas drove with prudent slowness.

'Where are we going, Chief?'

'First of all to the Rue des Rondeaux . . . I want to see the place where he was found . . .'

In the sunshine, in spite of the cemetery and the railway, the place did not look sinister. From some way off they could see a few sightseers being kept at bay by a couple of policemen, some housewives at their windows, and some children playing. When the car stopped, Maigret was greeted by Inspector Bornique, who said with an air of false modesty:

'I was expecting you, Chief-Inspector. I thought you'd be coming and I was careful to . . .'

The policemen stood to one side, revealing the silhouette of a body drawn in chalk on the greyish pavement.

'Who found him?'

'An employee of the gas company who goes on duty at five o'clock in the morning and who lives in that house over there . . . That's his wife you can see at the third-floor window . . . I've got his statement, of course. It so happened that I was on night duty . . .'

It was not the moment, with the sightseers there, to rebuke him.

'Tell me, Bornique, did you get the impression that the body had been thrown out of a car or that it had been laid on the pavement?'

'That it had been laid on the pavement . . .'

'On its back?'

'No, face down . . . At first sight, you'd have taken it for a drunk who was sleeping it off . . . Except for the smell . . . Because I must say, the smell . . .'

'I suppose you've questioned the neighbours?'

'All those that are at home . . . Mainly women and old men, because the younger men have gone off to work . . .'

'Nobody saw anything or heard anything?'

'Only an old woman, up there on the fifth floor, who suffers from insomnia, so it seems. It's true that her concierge says that she doesn't know what she's talking about any more . . . She says that about half-past three this morning she heard the brakes of a car . . . They don't get many in this part of the street, which doesn't lead anywhere . . .'

'She didn't hear any voices?'

'No. Just a car door opening, then some footsteps, then the door shutting again . . .'

'She didn't look out of the window?'

'She's practically bed-ridden . . . Her first idea was that there was somebody ill in the house and they'd sent for an ambulance . . . She waited to hear the door open and shut, but the car went off almost immediately, after turning round in the street . . .'

Inspector Bornique added, as a man who knows his job:

'I'll be coming back at midday and this evening, when the men are home from work.'

'Has the Parquet been?'

'Very early. They didn't stay long. It was just a formality . . .'

Watched by the sightseers, Maigret and Lucas got back into the car.

'The Rue Victor-Massé . . .'

Piles of cherries and already some peaches could be seen on the hawkers' barrows with housewives circling around them. Paris was very gay that morning, with more passers-by on the shady pavements than on those exposed to the sun.

In the Rue Notre-Dame-de-Lorette they caught sight of the yellow front of the Saint-Trop', whose entrance was closed by an iron grille, and on the left of the door a frame containing photographs of nudes.

In the Rue Victor-Massé an almost identical frame figured on the longer façade of the Train Bleu, and Lucas drew up a little farther on, outside a middle-class house. It was a greyish building, fairly prosperous-looking, and a couple of brass plates announced the names, one of a doctor, the other of a building society.

'What is it?' asked a rather disagreeable concierge, opening her glass door.

'Madame Boulay . . .'

'Third floor on the left, but . . .'

After looking at the two men, she changed her tone.

'You're from the police, aren't you? . . . In that case you can go up . . . Those poor women must be in an awful state . . .'

There was an almost silent lift, and a red carpet on the staircase which was better lit than most of the old apartment-houses in Paris. On the third floor they could hear voices behind a door. Maigret rang the bell and the voices stopped, footsteps drew near, and Antonio appeared in the doorway. He had taken off his jacket and was holding a sandwich.

'Come in . . . Don't take any notice of the mess . . .'

A baby was crying in a bedroom. A little boy was clinging to the dress of a young woman who was already fairly plump. She had not had time to do her hair, which hung down over her back.

'My sister Marina . . .'

She was red-eyed, as was only to be expected, and looked somewhat distraught.

'Come this way . . .'

She took them into an untidy drawing-room, with a rocking-horse overturned on the carpet, and some dirty cups and glasses on the table.

An old, much fatter woman, wearing a sky-blue dressing-gown, appeared at another door and looked suspiciously at the newcomers.

'My mother,' said Antonio, introducing her . . . 'She speaks hardly any French . . . She'll never get used to it . . .'

The flat was huge and comfortable, equipped with the rustic furniture that you find in the big stores.

'Where's your sister?' asked Maigret, looking around him.

'With the baby . . . She'll be coming soon . . .'

'How do you explain all this, Chief-Inspector?' asked Marina, who had less of an accent than her brother.

She had been eighteen or nineteen when Boulay had met her. That meant she was twenty-five or twenty-six now, and she was still very beautiful, with a mat complexion and dark eyes. Had she kept her pride in her appearance? It was not easy to judge in the circumstances, but the chief-inspector would have been willing to bet that she had stopped taking any trouble over her figure or her clothes, that she'd been living happily with her mother, her sister, her children and her husband, without bothering about the rest of the world.

As soon as he had come in, Maigret had sniffed the air, recognizing the smell of the place which reminded him of that of Italian restaurants.

Antonio had obviously become the head of the family. Hadn't he rather occupied that position in the time of Émile Boulay? Hadn't it been he that the former steward had had to ask for Marina's hand?

Still holding his sandwich, he asked:

'Have you discovered anything?'

'I'd like to know if he had his automatic in his pocket when he went out on Tuesday evening.'

Antonio glanced at his sister, who hesitated for a moment and then rushed into another room. She left the door open, revealing a dining-room which she crossed before going into a bedroom. She opened a drawer and came back with a dark object in her hand.

It was the automatic, which she handled gingerly, like someone who is frightened of firearms.

'It was in its usual place,' she said.

'He didn't always carry it on him?'

'Not always, no . . . Not recently . . .'

Antonio broke in.

'After Mazotti was killed and his gang went back to the South, Émile didn't feel the need to be armed any more . . .'

That was a significant point. It meant that when he had left home on Tuesday evening, Émile Boulay hadn't been expecting a dangerous or delicate encounter.

'At what time did he leave you, Madame?'

'A few minutes before nine, as usual. We had dinner at eight. Then he went to kiss the children goodnight in their beds, as he always did before going out . . .'

'He didn't strike you as being worried?'

She made an effort to remember. She had very beautiful eyes, which, under normal circumstances, must have been gay and caressing.

'No . . . I don't think so. You know, Émile wasn't at all demonstrative, and people who didn't know him must have imagined that he was very reserved . . .'

Tears came to her eyes.

'In reality he was very kind, very attentive . . .'

She turned towards her mother who was listening, her hands folded over her stomach, and said a few words to her in Italian. Her mother nodded in confirmation.

'I know what they think about people who run night-clubs . . . They think they're some kind of gangsters and it's true there are a few like that . . .'

She wiped her eyes, and looked at her brother as if to ask his permission to go on.

'But he was timid if anything . . . Perhaps not in business matters . . . He lived in the midst of dozens of women he could have done what he liked with, but instead of treating them as most of his colleagues do, he regarded them as employees, and if he was strict with them, he was also respectful . . . I know that because I worked for him before becoming his wife . . .'

'You can believe me or not if you like, but he spent weeks circling round me like a young man would have done . . . When he spoke to me during the show, it was to ask me questions: where I was born, where my family lived, whether my mother was in Paris, whether I had any brothers and sisters . . .

'Not once, during all that time, did he touch me. Nor did he ever offer to take me home . . .'

Antonio nodded, with a look which implied that he wouldn't have allowed anything else to happen.

'Of course,' she went on, 'he knew what Italian girls were like, because there are always two or three at the Lotus . . . One evening, he asked me if he could meet my brother . . .'

'He did the right thing,' conceded Antonio.

The mother must have understood a little French, and now and then she opened her mouth as if she was going to break in. But, failing to find the words she wanted, she ended up by keeping quiet.

A girl came in, dressed in black, with her hair already done and her face freshly made up. This was Ada, who was barely twenty-two and obviously looked just as her sister had done at that age. She glanced inquisitively at the visitors and told Marina:

'She's finally gone off to sleep . . .'

Then she said to Maigret and Lucas:

'Won't you sit down?'

'I understand, Mademoiselle, that you were your brother-in-law's secretary?'

She too had the merest hint of an accent: just enough to give her an added charm.

'That's saying a lot . . . Émile looked after all his business himself . . . And it's the sort of business that doesn't require a lot of paper-work . . .'

'Did he have an office?'

'We call it the office anyway . . . Two little rooms on the *entresol*, over the Lotus . . .'

'When did he go there?'

'He usually slept until midday and had lunch with us . . . About three o'clock the two of us went over to the Place Pigalle . . .'

Maigret observed the two sisters one after the other, wondering whether, for instance, Marina might not feel a certain jealousy of her younger sister. He found no trace of any such feeling in her eyes.

Marina, as far as he could judge, had, only three days before, been a woman content with her lot, happy leading a fairly lazy life, with her mother and her children, in the Rue Victor-Massé flat, and probably, if her husband had not been killed, she would have had a large family.

Very different, with a more energetic, clear-cut personality, Ada went on:

'There were always some people waiting—artistes, musicians, the head-waiter or the barman of one night-club or another, not to mention the travellers in wines and champagne . . .'

'What did Émile Boulay attend to on the day he disappeared?'

'Wait a minute . . . it was Tuesday, wasn't it? . . . We went down into the club to audition a Spanish dancer whom he took on . . . Then he saw the representative of an air-conditioning firm . . . He was planning to instal air-conditioning in his four night-clubs . . . At the Lotus in particular they kept having trouble with the ventilation . . .'

Maigret remembered a catalogue he had noticed among the dead man's effects.

'Who looks after his financial affairs?'

'What do you mean?'

'Who paid the bills, the staff?'

'The accountant, of course . . .'

'Did he have an office over the Lotus too?'

'Yes, a little room overlooking the yard . . . He's an old chap who's always grumbling, and whenever there's any money to be spent, it hurts him as if it was his own . . . He's called Raison . . . Monsieur Raison, as everybody says, because if they didn't call him Monsieur . . .'

'Is he at the Place Pigalle now?'

'Sure to be. He's the only one who works in the morning, because he's free in the evening and all night.'

'I suppose that each night-club has its own manager?'

Ada shook her head.

'No. It doesn't work like that. Antonio runs the Paris-Strip because it's in another part of Paris with a different clientele and a different style . . . You understand what I mean? . . . Besides, Antonio is one of the family . . .

'The other three night-clubs are practically next door to one another . . . In the course of the evening, certain artistes go from one to another . . . Émile too circulated between them and kept an eye on everything . . . About three o'clock in the morning we'd sometimes send some crates of champagne from the Lotus to the Train Bleu, say, or some bottles of whisky . . . If one of the clubs was full and short of staff, we'd send reinforcements from another club where there were fewer people . . .'

'In other words Émile Boulay ran the three Montmartre night-clubs in person.'

'More or less . . . Although in each club there was a head-waiter who was in charge . . .'

'And Monsieur Raison looked after the accounts and the paper-work . . .'

'That's about it.'

'And you?'

'I followed my brother-in-law around and took notes . . . A reminder to order this or that . . . to make an appointment with such and such a tradesman or such and such a contractor . . . to ring up an artiste who was working somewhere else to try and book her . . .'

'Did you follow him around in the evening too?'

'Only part of the evening.'

'Till what time usually?'

'Ten or eleven . . . The longest job was getting everything ready about nine o'clock . . . There's always somebody missing, a waiter, a musician or a dancer . . . Or else there's a delivery of champagne or novelties which is late . . .'

Maigret said thoughtfully:

'I'm beginning to get the hang of it . . . Were you with him on Tuesday evening?'

'Yes, like every evening . . .'

He glanced again at Marina and found no trace of jealousy in her face.

'At what time did you leave your brother-in-law?'

'At half-past ten . . .'

'Where were you at the time?'

'At the Lotus . . . It was a sort of headquarters . . . We'd already dropped into the Train Bleu and the Saint-Trop'.'

'You didn't notice anything special?'

'No, nothing . . . Except that I thought it was going to rain . . .'

'Did it rain?'

'A few drops, just as I was leaving the Lotus . . . Mickey offered to lend me an umbrella, but I hung on and five minutes later the rain stopped . . .'

'Did you make a note of Boulay's appointments?'

'I reminded him about them if necessary. It wasn't often necessary, because he thought of everything . . . He was a calm, thoughtful man, who ran his business seriously . . .'

'He didn't have an appointment that particular evening?'

'Not as far as I know . . .'

'Would you have known?'

'I suppose so . . . I don't want to make myself out to have been more important than I was . . . For instance, he never discussed his business or his plans with me . . . But he talked about them in front of me . . . When he saw people I was nearly always there . . . I don't remember him asking me to leave the room once . . . He'd say things to me like:

' "We'll have to change the curtains in the Train bleu . . ."

'I'd make a note of it and remind him about it the following afternoon . . .'

'What was his reaction when he heard that Mazotti had been killed?'

'I wasn't there at the time. He must have heard about it during the night, like the whole of Montmartre, because that sort of news travels fast.'

'And the next day, when he got up?'

'He asked me for the papers straightaway . . . I went to buy them for him at the corner of the street . . .'

'You mean he wasn't in the habit of reading the papers?'

'He just glanced at one morning paper and the evening one.'

'Did he play the horses?'

'Never . . . Neither horses, nor cards, nor any sort of game . . .'

'Did he talk to you about Mazotti's death?'

'He told me that he expected to be summoned by the police and got me to phone the head-waiter at the Lotus to find out if the police had already called there . . .'

Maigret turned towards Lucas who understood his silent query.

'Two inspectors from the 9th *arrondissement* went there,' he said.

'Did Boulay seem worried?'

'He was afraid of getting some unfavourable publicity . . .'

It was Antonio's turn to enter the conversation.

'That was always his big worry . . . He often told me to see that my place was decently run.

' "Just because we earn our living showing naked women," he used to say, "that doesn't mean we're gangsters . . . I'm a respectable business-man and I want people to know it . . ." '

'That's right . . . I've heard him say the same thing . . . But you're not drinking, Chief-Inspector . . .'

Although he had no desire for Chianti at half-past eleven in the morning, he moistened his lips all the same.

'Had he any friends?'

Ada looked round her, as if that in itself were an answer.

'He hadn't any need of friends . . . His life was here . . .'

'Did he speak Italian?'

'Italian, English and a little Spanish . . . He had learnt his languages on board the transatlantic liners, and then in the United States . . .'

'Did he ever talk about his first wife?'

Marina showed no embarrassment while her sister replied:

'He visited her grave every year and her picture is still on the bedroom wall . . .'

'One more question, Mademoiselle Ada . . . When he died, Boulay had a cheque-book in his pocket . . . Did you know about that?'

'Yes. He always had it on him, but didn't use it much . . . The big payments were made by Monsieur Raison . . . Émile always had a wad of banknotes in his pocket too . . . That's necessary in the business . . .'

'Your brother-in-law was summoned to Police Headquarters on May 18 . . .'

'I remember . . .'

'Did you go with him to the Quai des Orfèvres?'

'As far as the door . . . I waited for him on the pavement . . .'

'Did you take a taxi?'

'He didn't like taxis or cars in general . . . We went on the Métro . . .'

'Later he received a summons for May 23 . . .'

'I know . . . It annoyed him . . .'

'Still because of the publicity?'

'Yes.'

'Now on May 22 he drew quite a large sum—five thousand francs—out of the bank . . . Did you know that?'

'No.'

'You didn't look after his cheque-book?'

She shook her head.

'Did he prevent you from seeing it?'

'No . . . It was his personal cheque-book and it never occurred to me to open it . . . He didn't lock it up, and left it lying about on the chest of drawers in his bedroom . . .'

'Did he ever draw large sums out of the bank?'

'I doubt it . . . It wasn't necessary . . . When he needed some money, he took it out of the till at the Lotus or one of the other night-clubs and left a note in its place . . .'

'You've no idea why he should have drawn all that money?'

'None at all.'

'You've no means of finding out?'

'I can try . . . I can ask Monsieur Raison . . . I can look through his correspondence . . .'

'Will you be good enough to do that today and give me a ring if you discover anything . . .'

On the landing, Antonio, looking rather embarrassed, asked a question.

'What do we do about the night-clubs?'

And as Maigret looked at him uncomprehendingly, he made his meaning clearer:

'Do we open them in spite of everything?'

'Personally, I can see no reason for . . . But I imagine that's a matter for your sister to decide, isn't it?'

'If we close them, people are going to wonder . . .'

Maigret and Lucas got into the lift, which had just stopped at that floor, leaving the Italian in perplexity.

Chapter Three

On the pavement, Maigret lit his pipe, blinking his eyes in the sunshine, and he was going to speak to Lucas when a little scene which was typical of Montmartre life unfolded before them. The Train Bleu was not far away, with its neon sign extinguished and its shutters closed. Right opposite the Boulay's house, a young woman rushed out of a little hotel, wearing a black evening dress, with a tulle scarf around her bare shoulders. In the daylight her hair was of two different colours and she had not bothered to renew her make-up.

She was tall and slim, with the build of a music-hall dancer. Running across the street on extremely high heels, she went into a little bar where she was probably going to have a cup of coffee and some croissants.

Another person came out of the hotel practically on her heels, a man between forty-five and fifty of the northern business-man type, who, after glancing right and left, made for the corner of the street and hailed a taxi.

Maigret automatically looked up at the windows of the third floor of the house he had just left, and the flat where three women, together with two children, had constructed a little Italy of their own.

'It's a quarter-past eleven. I've got a good mind to go and see Monsieur Raison in his office. While I'm doing that you might ask a few questions in the district, especially in the shops, at the butcher's, the dairy-shop, and so on.'

'Where shall I meet you again, Chief?'

'Why not Chez Jo?'

The bar where Mazotti had been shot. Maigret wasn't following any definite plan. He had no ideas. He was rather like a pointer running around sniffing all over the place. And to tell the truth, he was not averse to savouring once more that Montmartre air which he had not breathed for years.

He turned the corner of the Rue Pigalle and stopped outside the grille across the Lotus doorway, looking for a bell-push which wasn't there. The door behind the grille was shut. Next to it there was another night-club, smaller and rather shabby in appearance, with its façade painted an aggressive mauve, then the narrow window of a lingerie-shop in which some extraordinary briefs and brassières were displayed.

He went on the off-chance into the corridor of a block of flats and found a shrewish concierge in her lodge.

'The Lotus?' he asked.

'Can't you see that it's closed?'

She looked at him suspiciously, possibly scenting the policeman in him.

'It's the accountant I want to see—Monsieur Raison . . .'

'The staircase on the left in the yard . . .'

A dark, narrow yard, cluttered up with dustbins overlooked by windows which, for the most part, had no curtains. A brown door stood half-open, leading to an even darker old staircase, whose steps creaked under Maigret's weight. On one of the doors, on the *entresol*, there was a zinc plate with some words crudely stamped on it: 'The Full Moon.' This was the name of the club next door to Émile's.

Opposite there was a cardboard notice: 'The Lotus.'

Maigret had the disappointing impression of going into a theatre by the stage-door. The dull, dusty, almost shabby surroundings evoked no idea of evening dresses, nor of naked bodies, nor of champagne and music.

He knocked, heard nothing, knocked again, and finally decided to turn the enamel handle. He found himself in a narrow corridor where the paint was flaking off the walls, with a door in front of him and another on his right. It was on this latter door that he knocked again, and at the same time he heard a scuffling sound. He was kept waiting for quite a while before a voice said:

'Come in . . .'

He found a little sunlight filtering through dirty window-panes, and a fat man of indeterminate age, but fairly old, with a few grey hairs brushed back over his bald head, who was straightening his tie while a young woman in a floral dress was standing there trying to assume a casual look.

'Monsieur Raison?'

'That's me,' replied the man, avoiding his eye.

The chief-inspector had obviously disturbed them.

'Chief-Inspector Maigret.'

The atmosphere in the room was stifling, and there was a heady perfume in the air.

'I'm off, Monsieur Jules. Don't forget what I asked you for . . .'

Looking embarrassed, he opened a drawer and, from a worn wallet stuffed with banknotes, he took two or three notes which he held out to her.

They disappeared in a flash into the girl's handbag, and she went off on her stiletto heels.

'They're all the same,' sighed Monsieur Raison, wiping his face with his handkerchief, possibly for fear that some traces of lipstick had been left on it.

'They're paid on Saturday and as early as Wednesday they come and ask you for an advance . . .'

An odd sort of office and an odd sort of man! You wouldn't have thought you were behind the scenes in a night-club, but rather in a more or less shabby den. There were no photographs of artistes on the walls, as you might have expected, but a calendar, some metal filing-cabinets, and some shelves loaded with files. The furniture could have been bought in a junk-shop, and the chair Monsieur Raison offered the chief-inspector had one leg mended with a piece of string.

'Have you found him?'

The accountant had not quite recovered his composure yet. His hairy hand trembled slightly while he was lighting a cigarette, and Maigret noticed that his fingers were stained with nicotine.

In this office, which overlooked the yard, you could hear hardly anything of the noise of the street, except perhaps a vague hum. You were in another world. Monsieur Raison was in shirt-sleeves, with large patches of sweat under his arms, and his stubbly face was covered with sweat too.

Maigret would have been willing to bet that he was not married, that he had no relatives, and that he lived on his own in some gloomy room in the district, cooking his meals on a spirit-stove.

'Have you found him?' he repeated. 'Is he alive?'

'Dead . . .'

Monsieur Raison sighed and piously lowered his eyelids.

'I guessed as much. What happened to him?'

'Strangled . . .'

He raised his head abruptly, as surprised as the chief-inspector had been at the Quai de la Rapée.

'Does his wife know? . . . And Antonio?'

'I've just come from the Rue Victor-Massé . . . Antonio has identified the body . . . I should like you to answer one or two questions . . .'

'I'll answer them as best I can . . .'

'Do you know if Émile Boulay had any enemies?'

The teeth were yellow and Monsieur Raison must have had bad breath.

'That depends what you mean by enemies . . . Business rivals, yes . . . He was doing too well for some people's liking . . . It's a difficult business, where nobody gives any quarter . . .'

'How do you account for the fact that within a few years Boulay was able to buy four cabarets?'

The accountant was beginning to feel better, and now he was on familiar ground.

'If you want my opinion, it's because Monsieur Émile looked after them like he'd have looked after, say, a chain of grocer's shops . . . He was a serious-minded man . . .'

'You mean that he didn't consume his own wares?' said the chief-inspector, unable to resist the temptation to be sarcastic.

The other man registered the hit.

'If you're thinking of Léa, you're wrong . . . She treats me like her father . . . They nearly all come here to tell me their secrets and their little troubles . . .'

'And ask you for an advance . . . If I've understood it correctly, Boulay's only relations with them were those of an employer with his employees?'

'That's right. He loved his wife and family . . . He didn't put on a tough act, and he didn't have a car or a house in the country, or by the sea . . . He didn't throw his money about or try to impress anybody . . . That's pretty rare in this racket . . . He'd have been a success in any line of business . . .'

'So his rivals were jealous of him?'

'Not to the extent of killing him . . . As for the underworld, Monsieur Émile had succeeded in winning their respect . . .'

'Thanks to his dockers.'

'You mean the Mazotti business? . . . I can assure you that he had nothing to do with the murder . . . He simply refused to pay, and to settle those gentlemen's hash he sent for a few toughs from Le Havre . . . That was enough . . .'

'Where are they now?'

'They went back home a fortnight ago . . . The inspector in charge of the case gave them permission to leave Paris . . .'

He was talking about Lucas.

'Boulay was keen on keeping on the right side of the law . . . You can ask your colleague in the Vice Squad, who's in Montmartre nearly every night and knows what's what . . .'

An idea occurred to Maigret.

'Would you mind if I use the phone?'

He rang the home number of Doctor Morel, whom he had forgotten to ask one question that morning.

'Tell me, Doctor, is it possible, before the result of the analyses comes through, for you to tell me roughly how long after dinner Boulay was killed? . . . What? . . . No, I'm not asking for a precise answer . . . To the nearest hour, yes . . . I know that, judging by the contents of the stomach . . . He had had dinner at eight in the evening . . . What's that you say? . . . between midnight and one o'clock in the morning? Thank you . . .'

That was one small point which had been settled.

'I suppose, Monsieur Raison, that you don't work in the evening?'

The accountant shook his head, almost indignantly.

'I never set foot in a night-club . . . That isn't my job . . .'

'I imagine your boss kept you informed about his business affairs?'

'Theoretically, yes . . .'

'Why theoretically?'

'Because, for instance, he didn't talk to me about his plans. When he bought Paris-Strip, to put his brother-in-law in there, I knew about it only the day before the papers were signed . . . He wasn't a talkative man . . .'

'He didn't say anything to you about any appointment on Tuesday evening?'

'Not a thing . . . I'd better try to explain to you how the place works. I'm here in the morning and afternoon . . . In the morning, I'm nearly always on my own . . . In the afternoon the boss used to come along with Ada, who acted as his secretary . . .'

'Where's his office?'

'I'll show you . . .'

It was at the end of the corridor, and it was hardly any bigger or more luxurious than the office the two men had just left. In one corner there was a desk with a typewriter on it. A few filing-cabinets. On the walls, photographs of Marina and the two children. Another photograph of a woman, a blonde with sad eyes, whom Maigret assumed to be Boulay's first wife.

'He called me only when he needed me . . . I did nothing but place orders and settle bills . . .'

'So it was you who saw to all the payments . . . Including the direct payments, I suppose?'

'What do you mean?'

Although Maigret had never belonged to the Vice Squad, he was familiar with night-life in Paris all the same.

'I imagine that certain payments were made in cash, without any receipt, if only to dodge the Inland Revenue . . .'

'You're wrong about that, Monsieur Maigret, if you'll allow me to contradict you . . . I know that's the idea everybody has about the business, and it sounds easy . . . But where Monsieur Boulay was different from all the rest was that he insisted, as I've already said, on keeping on the right side of the law . . .'

'Did you see to his income tax returns?'

'Yes and no . . . I kept his accounts up to date and I handed them over, when the time came, to his lawyer . . .'

'Let's suppose that at a given moment Boulay needed a fairly large sum, five thousand francs . . .'

'That's easy . . . He'd have taken them out of the till in one of the cabarets and left a note in their place . . .'

'Did that ever happen to him?'

'Not for any sum as large as that . . . A thousand, perhaps . . . Two thousand . . .'

'So he had no need to go and draw money out of the bank?'

This time Monsieur Raison hesitated before answering, intrigued by the question.

'Wait a minute . . . In the morning I'm here, and there's always a tidy sum in the safe . . . It's only about midday that I go to the bank to pay in the previous night's takings . . . Besides, I've practically never seen him in the office in the morning, because he was usually still asleep . . . In the evening, as I've already said, he only had to dip into the till of the Lotus, the Train Bleu or the Saint-Trop' . . . The afternoon was a different matter . . . If he had needed five thousand in the middle of the afternoon, he would probably have dropped into the bank . . .'

'That's what he did on May 22. Does that date mean anything to you?'

'Not a thing . . .'

'You've no trace of a payment made that day or the following day?'

They had returned to Monsieur Raison's office, and the accountant was consulting a register bound in black cloth.

'Nothing,' he said.

'You're sure your boss didn't have a liaison?'

'In my opinion that's quite out of the question . . .'

'Nobody was blackmailing him? Can you check from his bank statements whether Boulay drew any other cheques in the same way?'

The accountant went to take a file out of one of the cabinets and ran his pencil down the columns.

'Nothing in April . . . Nor in March . . . Nor in February . . . Nothing in January either . . .'

'That will do . . .'

So on one occasion only in the course of the last few months, Émile Boulay had drawn some money in person out of the bank. That cheque continued to bother the chief-inspector. He sensed that something was escaping him, something that was probably important, and his thoughts went round and round.

He came back to a question he had already asked.

'You're sure your boss didn't make any direct payments?'

'I can't see what he'd have paid for that way . . . I know it's hard to believe, but you can ask Maître Gaillard . . . On that point Monsieur Émile was almost a maniac . . . He maintained that it's precisely when you're in a rather dubious business that you've got to be most straightforward . . .

'Don't forget that everybody's suspicious of us, that we've got the police on our tracks all the time, not just the Vice Squad, but the Fraud Squad too . . .

'Talking about the Fraud Squad, I remember a story . . . Two years ago, at the Saint-Trop', an inspector found some fancy whisky in branded bottles . . .

'I don't need to tell you that that sort of thing goes on in a good many places . . . Naturally the excise people started proceedings . . . Monsieur Émile swore he didn't know anything about it . . . His lawyer looked into it . . . They were able to prove that it was the barman who was working the switch for his own profit . . .

'The boss fixed things up all the same, but I don't need to tell you that the barman was sacked . . .

'Another time I saw him in an even greater fury . . . He'd noticed some suspicious characters among the clientele of the Train Bleu . . . When you're used to the clientele, you can spot straightaway the people who aren't there for the same reasons as the others, you understand?

'On that occasion the police didn't have to intervene . . . Monsieur Émile found out before they did that a musician he'd recently taken on was trafficking in drugs, on a small scale incidentally . . .'

'And he sacked him?'

'That very night . . .'

'How long ago was that?'

'It was before the case of the barman, about three years ago . . .'

'What became of the musician?'

'He left France a few weeks later and he's working in Italy . . .'

Nothing in all this explained the five thousand francs, still less the death of Boulay, whom somebody had kept for two days and three nights, heaven knows where, before leaving him in an empty street alongside the wall of Père Lachaise.

'Do these offices communicate with the night-club?'

'This way . . .'

He opened a door which Maigret had taken for that of a cupboard. He had to switch on a light, for it was almost completely dark, and Maigret saw a steep spiral staircase in front of him.

'Do you want to go downstairs?'

'Why not?'

He followed Monsieur Raison down the staircase, which came out in a room where women's clothes, some of them covered with sequins or imitation pearls, were hung along the walls. There was a dressing-table painted grey and littered with jars of cream, paints and pencils. An insipid, slightly sickening smell hung in the air.

It was here that the artistes changed out of their everyday clothes into their professional trappings, before displaying themselves under the glare of the spot-lights, where men bought champagne at five or six times its price for the privilege of admiring them.

But first they had to cross, as Monsieur Raison and Maigret did now, a sort of kitchen separating the dressing-room from the club.

Two or three thin rays of light were filtering through the shutters. The walls were mauve, the floor covered with paper streamers and multi-coloured cotton balls. The smell of champagne and tobacco remained, and there was still a broken glass in one corner, near the orchestra's instruments which were wrapped in their covers.

'The cleaners don't come until the afternoon. They are the same women who do the cleaning at the Train Bleu. At five o'clock they go to the Rue Notre-Dame-de-Lorette, so that by nine o'clock everything's ready to welcome the customers . . .'

It was as depressing as, say, a seaside resort in winter, with its villas and its casino closed. Maigret looked around him, as if the setting were going to give him an idea, a starting-point.

'Can I get straight out from here?'

'The key of the grille is upstairs, but if you insist . . .'

'No, don't bother . . .'

He climbed the staircase again, only to go down the one into the little yard a little later, after shaking Monsieur Raison by his moist hand.

It was a pleasure, after that, to be bumped into by a boy running along the pavement, and to breathe in the good, healthy smell of a vegetable stall.

He was familiar with the bar run by Jo, whom everybody called Jo-the-Wrestler. He had known it for at least twenty years, if not longer, and the bar had had a great many owners. Perhaps this was because of its strategic position a stone's throw from Pigalle, the Place Blanche and the pavements which a crowd of women paced tirelessly up and down all night.

Closed down a score of times by the police, the bar had nonetheless always become a meeting-place for the local criminals again. And, before Mazotti, some of them had been killed there.

Yet the place looked peaceful enough, at this time of day at least. It presented the traditional appearance of all Paris bistros, with its bar, its mirrors on the wall, its benches, and, in one corner, four card-players, while two plasterers in smocks, their faces stained with white, were drinking wine at the counter.

Lucas was already there, and the *patron*, a colossus with his shirtsleeves rolled up, told him as he saw the chief-inspector come in:

'Here's your boss! . . . What can I serve you, Monsieur Maigret?'

He kept his sarcastic expression throughout the most delicate interrogations, and he had undergone a fair number in his career, which incidentally included no convictions.

'A glass of white wine . . .'

Lucas's face told him that the inspector had discovered nothing important. Maigret was not disappointed. He was still in the period when, as he used to say, he was putting himself in the picture.

The four card-players shot a glance at him now and then, in which there was more irony than fear. There was also a certain irony in Jo's voice when he asked:

'So you've found him?'

'Who?'

'Come, come, Chief-Inspector . . . You're forgetting you're in Montmartre, where news travels fast . . . If Émile disappeared three days ago and we see you prowling around the district . . .'

'What do you know about Émile?'

'Me?'

Jo-the-Wrestler liked playing the fool.

'What could I know? Is a gentleman like him, a virtuous business-man, likely to set foot in my establishment?'

This produced smiles in the card-players' corner, but the chief-inspector drew on his pipe and drank his wine without getting annoyed. Then he announced in a serious voice:

'He's been found . . .'

'In the Seine?'

'No, as it happens, not in the Seine . . . I could almost say he was found in the cemetery . . .'

'He wanted to save himself the cost of a funeral . . . That wouldn't surprise me with him . . . But joking apart, Émile's dead?'

'Yes. Dead three days . . .'

This time, Jo frowned just as Maigret had done that morning.

'You mean to say he died three days ago and he wasn't found until this morning?'

'Stretched out on the pavement in the Rue des Rondeaux . . .'

'Where's that?'

'I've already told you . . . A dead end, running alongside Père Lachaise . . .'

The card-players pricked up their ears, and he could tell that they were as surprised as the *patron*.

'But he can't have been there three days?'

'He was put there last night . . .'

'Then if you want my opinion, I'd say there's something fishy about that . . . It's fairly hot just now, isn't it? . . . And there's no joy in keeping a stiff around the place in this sort of weather . . . Not to mention the fact that that's a queer district to leave that sort of parcel . . . Unless it's a nut who's done the job . . .'

'Tell me, Jo, can you talk seriously for a moment?'

'Dead serious, Monsieur Maigret.'

'Mazotti was killed coming out of your bar . . .'

'Just my luck! . . . I'm beginning to wonder whether he didn't do it on purpose to get my licence taken away . . .'

'You'll have noticed that we haven't bothered you . . .'

'Except that I've spent three mornings with your inspector,' retorted Jo, jerking his head towards Lucas.

'I'm not going to ask you if you know who did it . . .'

'I didn't see a thing . . . I'd gone down to the cellar to get some bottles.'

'I don't care whether that's true or not . . . In your opinion could Émile Boulay have done the killing?'

Jo had turned serious, and, to give himself time to think, he poured himself a glass of wine, taking the opportunity to fill those of Maigret and Lucas. He also darted a glance towards the card-players' table, as if he wanted to ask their advice or to get them to understand his position.

'Why ask *me* that question?'

'Because you are one of the men who knows most about what goes on in Montmartre . . .'

'That's just what people say . . .'

He was flattered all the same.

'Émile was an amáteur,' he murmured in the end, almost regretfully.

'You didn't like him?'

'That's another matter . . . Personally I'd got nothing against him . . .'

'And the others?'

'What others?'

'His rivals . . . I've heard that he was planning to buy some more night-clubs . . .'

'And what of it?'

Maigret returned to his starting-point.

'Would Boulay have been capable of killing Mazotti?'

'I've told you he was an amateur. The Mazotti business wasn't an amateur job, you know that as well as I do. His dockers wouldn't have tackled it that way either . . .'

'Second question . . .'

'How many are there?'

'This may be the last.'

The plasterers were listening, exchanging winks.

'Fire away! I'll see if I can answer.'

'You've just admitted that Émile's success didn't please everybody . . .'

'A fellow's success never pleases other people . . .'

'Only this is a world where they play a cautious game and where the seats are dear . . .'

'Granted. What next?'

'Do you think Émile was killed by a colleague?'

'I've already answered that one too.'

'When?'

'Didn't I say that there was no joy in having a corpse on your hands for two or three days, especially in this sort of weather . . . Let's suppose the people you're talking about are sensitive . . . Or else that they're so closely watched that they daren't take any risks . . . How was he killed?'

In any case the story would be in the afternoon papers.

'Strangled.'

'Then the answer is even more definite, and you know why . . . Mazotti's killing was a clean job . . . If the people round here had wanted to get rid of

Émile, they'd have done it in the same way . . . Have you found the people who killed Mazotti? . . . No! . . . And in spite of all your informers, you won't get them . . . Whereas this story of yours about a man who's strangled, who's kept indoors for three days and who's dumped by a cemetery wall—well, it smells, that's all I can say . . . So much for your second question . . .'

'Thank you . . .'

'Don't mention it. Will you have another?'

He held the bottle inquiringly over the glass.

'Not this morning . . .'

'Don't tell me you're thinking of coming back . . . I've got nothing against you personally, but in this business we prefer not to see too much of you . . .'

'How much do I owe you?'

'The second round is on me . . . The day he spent three hours questioning me, your inspector treated me to a glass of beer and a sandwich . . .'

Outside Maigret and Lucas said nothing for a long time. At one moment Maigret raised his arm to stop a taxi and the inspector had to remind him that they'd come in a car from Police Headquarters. They found it again and got in.

'My home,' growled Maigret.

He had no serious reason for lunching out. To tell the truth, he had no idea yet how to tackle the case. Jo-the-Wrestler had only confirmed what he'd been thinking ever since that morning, and he knew that Jo had been sincere.

It was true that Émile Boulay was an amateur who had paradoxically dug himself in right in the middle of Montmartre.

And, oddly enough, it seemed that he had been killed by another amateur.

'What about you?' he asked Lucas.

The inspector understood what he meant.

'The three women are well-known to all the local shopkeepers. They call them the Italian women. They make fun a bit of the old woman and her broken French. They don't know Ada so well, because she doesn't often go shopping, but they used to see her passing with her brother-in-law.

'The people I've been questioning don't know the news yet . . . The family seems to like eating well . . . According to the butcher, it's amazing what they can put away, and they always insist on the best cuts of meat . . . Every afternoon, Marina goes for a walk round the Square d'Anvers, pushing the pram with one hand and holding the little boy with the other . . .'

'They haven't got a maid?'

'Just a charwoman three times a week . . .'

'Have you got her name and address?'

Lucas blushed.

'I can get them this afternoon.'

'What else do they say?'

'The fishmonger's wife said to me:

' "He's as artful as they come . . ."

'She was talking about Émile, of course.

' "He married the eldest when she was nineteen . . . When he saw that she was beginning to put on weight, he sent for her young sister . . . I bet he'll find another sister or a cousin in Italy when Ada gets fat in her turn . . ." '

That had occurred to Maigret too . . . It wasn't the first time he had seen a husband in love with his sister-in-law.

'Try to find out some more about Ada . . . What I'd particularly like to know is whether she has a boy-friend or a lover . . .'

'Is that what you think Chief?'

'No. But we mustn't neglect anything . . . I'd like to know some more about Antonio too . . . It might be a good idea if you went round to the Rue Ponthieu this afternoon . . .'

'All right . . .'

Lucas stopped the car in front of the block of flats where Maigret lived, and, looking up, the chief-inspector saw his wife leaning on the balcony rail. She gave him a little wave. He waved back and went into the building.

Chapter Four

When the telephone rang, Maigret, who had his mouth full, motioned to his wife to answer it.

'Hallo . . . Who's that speaking? . . . Yes, he's having lunch . . . I'll call him . . .'

He looked at her, frowning and bad-tempered.

'It's Lecoin . . .'

He got up, still chewing, and taking his napkin with him to wipe his mouth. For the last five minutes, as it happened, he had been thinking about his colleague Lecoin, the chief of the Vice Squad, whom he had decided to call on during the afternoon. Maigret's contacts with the underworld of Montmartre, and of Pigalle in particular, went rather a long way back, whereas Lecoin was up to date.

'Hallo . . . Yes, I'm listening . . . No, of course not . . . That doesn't matter . . . I was thinking of coming to see you this afternoon . . .'

The chief of the Vice Squad, who was about ten years younger than Maigret, lived quite close to the Boulevard Richard-Lenoir, on the Boulevard Voltaire, in a flat which was always noisy, for he had six or seven children.

'I've got somebody here that you are sure to know,' he explained. 'He's been one of my informers for a long time now . . . He prefers not to show his face at the Quai, and when he has something to tell me, he comes to see me at home . . . Now it happens that today his tip concerns you rather than me . . . Of course, I don't know what it's worth . . . As for the fellow himself, apart from the frills he likes to add, because he's an artist in his way, you can trust him . . .'

'Who is it?'

'Louis Boubée, *alias* Mickey, the doorman at a night-club in Montmartre . . .'

'Send him over straightaway . . .'

'You're sure you don't mind him coming over to your place?'

Maigret finished his lunch quickly and, when the doorbell rang, his wife had just poured out his coffee, which he took with him into the drawing-room.

He had not seen the man nicknamed Mickey for several years, but he recognized him straightaway. He could scarcely have failed to do so, for

Boubée was a rather extraordinary creature. How old would he be now? The chief-inspector tried to work it out. He had still been a fairly young inspector when his visitor was already working as a doorman in Montmartre.

Boubée had not grown any taller. He was still the size of a child of twelve or thirteen, and the most extraordinary thing about him was that he still looked like a child too. A skinny little boy, with big projecting ears, a long pointed nose, and a grinning mouth which you might have thought was made of india-rubber.

You had to look closer to see that his face was covered with tiny wrinkles.

'Quite a time since we last met, isn't it?' he said, looking around him, with his cap in his hand. 'You remember the Tripoli and La Tétoune?'

The two men must have been the same age, to within two or three years.

'Those were the good old days, weren't they!'

He was referring to a brasserie which had once existed in the Rue Duperré, a stone's throw from the Lotus, and which, before the war, just like its proprietress, had had its hour of fame.

La Tétoune was a portly Marseillaise who was reputed to do the best southern cooking in Paris and who was in the habit of greeting her customers with smacking kisses and speaking to them familiarly.

It was a tradition when you arrived to go and see her in her kitchen, and you met an unusual clientele in her restaurant.

'You remember Fat Louis, who owned the three brothels in the Rue de Provence? And One-eyed Eugène? And Handsome Fernand, who ended up in the cinema?'

Maigret knew that it was useless asking Mickey to come to the point. It was a matter of honour with him: he was quite prepared to give information to the police, but in his own way, without appearing to do so.

The men he was talking about were the big bosses of the underworld of those days, the owners of brothels which still existed, and they used to meet at La Tétoune's. They rubbed shoulders there with their lawyers, for the most part leading barristers, and, as the place became fashionable, you also met actresses there and even ministers.

'In those days, I used to take bets on boxing matches ...'

Another peculiar thing about Mickey was the absence of eyelashes and eyebrows which made him look strange.

'Since you've become the big chief of the Crime Squad, we scarcely ever see you in Montmartre ... Monsieur Lecoin, of course, comes there now and then ... Sometimes I can do him a good turn, as I used to with you in the old days ... You hear so many things, you know ...'

What he did not add was that it was essential for him that the police should shut their eyes to certain activities of his. The clients of the Lotus who gave him a tip as they came out of the club never suspected that Mickey was also in business on his own account.

He sometimes whispered into the ear of some of them:

'Living pictures, Monsieur?'

He could say that in a dozen languages, with a meaning wink. After which he would slip into the client's hand a card bearing the address of a nearby flat.

It was not really very wicked. What you saw there in great secrecy was roughly the same spectacle, though in dustier, more sordid surroundings, as was offered by any Pigalle night-club. With the difference that the women were no longer twenty, but often at least twice as old.

'Your inspector, the little fat one . . .'

'Lucas . . .'

'Yes . . . He called me in about three weeks ago, after Mazotti was killed, but I didn't know very much . . .'

He was gradually coming to the point, in his own way.

'I told him it definitely wasn't my boss who'd done the job, and I wasn't wrong . . . Now I've got a tip. You've always been pretty understanding with me, so I'll give it to you, for what it's worth, of course . . . I'm not talking to the police, get that straight . . . I'm talking to a man I've known a long time . . . We're just having a little chat . . . By accident we just happen to start talking about Mazotti, who, between ourselves, wasn't up to much . . .

'Then I just repeat what somebody told me . . . It's no use looking in Pigalle for the chap who did the job . . . At Easter . . . When was Easter this year? . . .'

'At the end of March . . .'

'Good . . . Well then, at Easter, Mazotti, who was nothing at all, but who wanted people to think he was a man, went down to Toulon . . . There he met Yolande . . . You know her? . . . She's Mattei's woman . . . Mattei is the boss of the False-Noses of Marseilles, who pulled off about twenty hold-ups before they got copped . . . You're with me so far?

'Mattei was in stir, and Mazotti, who thought he could do what he liked, came back to Paris with Yolande . . . I don't need to say any more, do I? . . . There are still a few of Mattei's men in Marseilles, and two or three of them came up to Paris to settle things . . .'

It was plausible. It explained the way the Rue de Douai affair had happened. A professional job, with no hitches.

'I thought that would interest you, and not knowing your address, I went to see your pals . . .'

Mickey showed no signs of taking his leave, which meant that he had not said all that he wanted to say or that he was expecting to be asked some questions. Sure enough, Maigret asked him with an innocent air:

'Have you heard the news?'

'What news?' Mickey asked with a similar air of innocence.

Then, straightaway, he gave a mischievous smile.

'You mean about Monsieur Émile? I heard he'd been found . . .'

'Have you just been round at Jo's place?'

'We're not great friends, Jo and me, but the news has got around . . .'

'What has happened to Émile Boulay interests me more than the Mazotti business . . .'

'Well, in that case, Chief-Inspector, I've got to admit that I don't know a thing . . . And that's the truth I'm telling you . . .'

'What did you think of him?'

'What I said to Monsieur Lucas . . . What everybody thinks . . .'

'And that is?'

'He ran his business his own way, but he kept on the right side of the law . . .'

'Do you remember Tuesday evening?'

'I've a pretty good memory . . .'

He kept smiling all the time, as if each of his words deserved to be emphasized, and he had a mania for winking.

'Nothing special happened?'

'That depends what you regard as special . . . Monsieur Émile came along about nine o'clock with Mademoiselle Ada, to see if everything was ready, like he did every night . . . You know how it is . . . Then he dropped into the Train Bleu and he went round to the Rue Notre-Dame-de-Lorette too . . .'

'What time did you see him again?'

'Wait a minute . . . The orchestra had started playing . . . That means it must have been after ten . . . The club was practically empty . . . You can make as much noise as you like to attract clients, they don't start coming in until after the cinemas and theatres are closed . . .'

'Did his secretary stay with him? . . .'

'No . . . She went off home . . .'

'Did you see her going into the block of flats?'

'I think I followed her with my eyes, because she's a pretty kid and I always give her a bit of the soft talk, but I couldn't swear to it . . .'

'And what about Boulay?'

'He went into the Lotus to make a phone call.'

'How do you know he made a phone call?'

'Germaine, the cloakroom girl, told me so . . . the phone is near the cloakroom . . . The box has got a glass door . . . He dialled a number and got no reply, and when he came out he looked annoyed . . .'

'Why did that strike the cloakroom girl?'

'Because usually, when he made a phone call in the evening, it was to one of his night-clubs, or to his brother-in-law, and he always got a reply . . . Besides, a quarter of an hour later, he tried again . . .'

'Still without success?'

'Yes . . . So he was calling somebody who wasn't at home, and that seemed to irritate him. Between the calls, he went and prowled round the club . . . He had a word with a dancer whose dress was dirty and he tore a strip off the barman . . .

'After a third or fourth try, he came out on to the pavement for a breath of fresh air . . .'

'Did he speak to you?'

'He wasn't a talkative man, you know . . . He just planted himself like that in front of the door . . . He looked at the sky and the traffic and he might say whether we'd have a full house or not . . .'

'Did he finally get an answer?'

'Yes, about eleven o'clock . . .'

'And he went off?'

'Not straightaway . . . He came back on to the pavement . . . That was one of his habits . . . Two or three times, I saw him take his watch out of his pocket . . . Finally, after twenty minutes or so, he started walking down the Rue Pigalle . . .'

'In other words he had an appointment . . .'

'I see we've got the same idea . . .'

'It seems he scarcely ever took a taxi . . .'

'That's right . . . After his accident, he didn't like cars . . . He preferred the Métro . . .'

'You're sure he went down the Rue Pigalle? Not up?'

'Certain!'

'If he'd been going to take the Métro, he would have gone up the street . . .'

'That's what he did when he went to have a look at the Rue de Berri . . .'

'So that in all probability his appointment was in the district . . .'

'First of all I thought he was going to the Saint-Trop', in the Rue Notre-Dame-de-Lorette, but nobody saw him there . . .'

'Do you think he had a mistress?'

'I'm sure he didn't.'

And with another wink the wizened little boy added:

'After all, I know something about it . . . I'm in the business, in a manner of speaking, aren't I?'

'Where does Monsieur Raison live?'

The question surprised Mickey.

'The accountant? He has lived for thirty years at least in the same block of flats, on the Boulevard Rochechouart.'

'Alone?'

'Of course! . . . He hasn't a mistress either, believe me . . . It isn't that he doesn't like women, but his income doesn't match his tastes, and he just messes about with the girls who come to his office to ask for an advance . . .'

'You know what he does in the evening?'

'He plays billiards, always in the same café, on the corner of the Square d'Anvers . . . There aren't many billiard-tables left in the district. He's practically a champion . . .'

Another line of inquiry which seemed to have come to a dead end. Maigret went on asking questions all the same, not wanting to leave anything to chance.

'Where does this Monsieur Raison come from?'

'From a bank . . . He was a cashier, for I don't know how many years, at the branch where the boss had his account, in the Rue Blanche . . . I suppose he gave him a few tips . . . Monsieur Émile needed somebody reliable to do the book-keeping, because in that business there's plenty of waste . . . I don't know how much he pays him, but it must be quite a lot, seeing that Monsieur Raison left the bank . . .'

Maigret kept coming back to the Tuesday evening. It was becoming an obsession. By now he could see before him little Monsieur Émile standing under the neon sign of the Lotus, looking at his watch now and then and finally walking off in a determined way down the Rue Pigalle.

He was not going far, otherwise he would have taken the Métro which was only a hundred yards away. If he had needed a taxi, in spite of his dislike for cars, there were always plenty driving past his night-club.

A sort of map began to take shape in Maigret's mind, the map of a small part of Paris to which everything kept bringing him back. The former steward's three night-clubs were close to one another, and only the Paris-Strip, which was run by Antonio, was an exception.

Boulay and his three Italian women lived in the Rue Victor-Massé. Jo-the-Wrestler's bar, outside which Mazotti had been shot, could almost be seen from the entrance of the Lotus.

The bank where Émile had his account was scarcely any further away, and finally the accountant too lived in the district.

It was rather like a village, which Émile Boulay left only rarely, as if regretfully.

'You've no idea who the person might be he had an appointment with?'

'No, honest I haven't . . .'

After a pause Mickey admitted:

'I've thought about it too, just out of curiosity . . . I'd like to understand . . . In my business, it's essential to understand, isn't it?'

Maigret got up with a sigh. He could think of no other questions he ought to ask. The doorman had told him a certain number of details of which he had been ignorant, and of which he might have remained ignorant for a long time, but these details still did not explain Boulay's death, still less the almost incredible fact that somebody had kept his body for three nights and two whole days before leaving it next to Père Lachaise.

'Thank you, Boubée . . .'

Just as he was going out, the little man said:

'You're still not interested in boxing, are you?'

'Why?'

'Because I've got a tip about a fight tomorrow, if you like to . . .'

'No, thanks . . .'

He did not give him any money. It was not for money that Mickey sold his services, but in exchange for a certain indulgence.

'If I hear anything, I'll give you a ring . . .'

Three quarters of an hour later, in his office at Police Headquarters, Maigret scribbled on a sheet of paper, rang the bell in the inspectors' room, and sent for Lapointe.

The latter did not need to look twice at the chief to know how far he'd got. Nowhere! He had the dull, obstinate look he always had at the worst period of an investigation, when he did not know how to tackle it and struck out, without much confidence, in all directions.

'Go to the Boulevard Rochechouart and check up on a certain Monsieur Raison . . . He's the accountant at the Lotus and the other night-clubs belonging to Émile Boulay . . . It seems that he plays billiards every evening in a café in the Square d'Anvers. I don't know which, but you'll find it . . . Try to find out as much as you can about him and his habits . . . Above all I'd like to know whether he was at the café on Tuesday evening, what time he left, and what time he reached home . . .'

'I'm on my way, Chief . . .'

Lucas, in the meantime, was checking up on Ada and also Antonio. Maigret, to calm his impatience, plunged into his administrative files. About half-past four, he had had enough of them, and, putting on his jacket again, he went out to have a beer by himself at the Brasserie Dauphine. He nearly ordered a second, not because he was thirsty, but to defy his friend Pardon who had recommended him to abstain.

He hated not understanding. It was becoming a personal matter for him. He kept coming back to the same pictures; Émile Boulay, in a blue suit, standing outside the Lotus, going back into the night-club, telephoning, getting no reply, walking round and round, and telephoning again and yet again under the impassive gaze of the cloakroom girl.

Ada had gone home. Antonio was attending to the first customers in the Rue de Berri. In the four night-clubs, the barmen were arranging their glasses and bottles, the musicians were tuning their instruments, and the girls were getting ready in sordid dressing-rooms before taking their places in front of the little tables.

Finally Boulay obtained his number, but he did not go off straightaway. So the appointment was not immediate. He'd been given a particular time.

He stood waiting outside the club again, took his watch out of his pocket several times, and then, all of a sudden, walked away down the Rue Pigalle . . .

He had had dinner at eight o'clock. According to the police doctor, he had been killed four or five hours later, in other words between midnight and one o'clock in the morning.

When he had left the Lotus, it had been half-past eleven.

He had had between half an hour and an hour and a half to live.

Now he had had nothing to do with Mazotti's death. The remaining members of the Corsican's gang were well aware of this and had no reason to kill him.

Finally, nobody in the underworld would have done the job as Émile's murderer had, strangling him, keeping his body for two days, and then running the risk of taking it to the Rue des Rondeaux . . .

Ada was not aware of any appointment her employer had had. Nor was Monsieur Raison. Antonio maintained that he knew nothing more. Even Mickey, who had good reasons for finding out about everything that was going on, was in the dark on this point.

Maigret was pacing up and down his office, feeling irritable, the stem of his pipe clenched between his teeth, when Lucas knocked on the door. The inspector was not wearing the triumphant expression of somebody who had just made a discovery.

Maigret just looked at him and said nothing.

'I don't know much more than I did this morning, Chief . . . Except that Antonio didn't leave his night-club on Tuesday evening, nor at any time during the night . . .'

Of course not! That would have been too easy.

'I've seen his wife, an Italian woman who's expecting a baby . . . They live in a smart little flat in the Rue de Ponthieu . . .'

The chief-inspector's vacant gaze made Lucas feel uneasy.

'It isn't my fault . . . Everybody likes them . . . I spoke to the concierge, the tradesmen, and the night-club's neighbours . . . Then I went back to the Rue Victor-Massé . . . I found the accountant in his office and asked him for the addresses of the artistes who work at the Lotus and do their turns in the other clubs . . . Two of them were still asleep in the same hotel . . .'

He felt as if he were talking to a wall and now and then Maigret turned his back on him to watch the Seine flowing by.

'Another girl, who lives in the Rue Lepic, has a baby and . . .'

The chief-inspector looked so irritable that Lucas got flustered.

'I can only tell you what I know. They are all more or less jealous of Ada of course . . . They've got the impression that sooner or later she'd have become the boss's mistress, but that it hadn't happened yet . . . Not to mention the fact that Antonio, so it seems, would have raised objections . . .'

'Is that all?'

Lucas spread his hands out in a gesture of discouragement.

'What shall I do now?'

'Whatever you like.'

Maigret went home early, after spending a little longer irritably studying that tedious business of the reorganization of the police services, which he felt sure would not be carried out along the lines he was suggesting.

Reports, always reports! They asked his advice. They begged him to draw up a detailed plan. Then it all came to a halt somewhere in the administrative hierarchy and nothing more was heard about it. Unless, of course, they made arrangements contrary to those he had proposed.

'I'm going out tonight,' he told his wife in a grumpy voice.

She knew that it was better not to ask him any questions. He sat down to table and watched the television, growling now and then:

'It's idiotic!'

Then he went into the bedroom to change his shirt and tie.

'I don't know when I'll be back . . . I'm going to Montmartre to visit a few night-clubs . . .'

You would have thought that he was trying to make her jealous, and that he was annoyed to see her smile.

'You ought to take your umbrella . . . the radio says there are going to be some storms . . .'

To tell the truth, if he was in a bad temper, it was because he had the impression that it was his fault that he was in the dark. He was sure that at a certain moment in the day, he could not have said precisely when, he had been on the point of getting on the right track.

Somebody had said something significant to him. But who? He had seen so many people!

It was nine o'clock when he took a taxi, and twenty-past nine when he arrived outside the Lotus, where Mickey greeted him with a conspiratorial wink and opened the red velvet door for him.

The musicians in their white dinner-jackets were not yet in their places, and were chatting in a corner. The barman was wiping glasses on his shelf. A lovely red-head with a very low-cut dress was filing her nails at one end of the room.

Nobody asked him what he had come for, as if they all knew all about it. They just kept darting inquisitive glances at him.

The waiters were putting ice buckets on the tables. Ada, in a dark costume, came out of the room at the back, holding a pencil and notebook, caught sight of Maigret and, after hesitating for a moment, came towards him.

'My brother advised me to open the clubs,' she explained with a certain embarrassment. 'The fact is, none of us knows what we ought to do . . . It seems that it isn't usual to close when there is a death in the family . . .'

Glancing at the notebook and pencil, he asked her:

'What were you doing?'

'What my brother-in-law used to do every evening at this time . . . Checking the stocks of champagne and whisky with the barmen and head-waiters . . . Then organizing the moves of the artistes from one night-club to another . . . They're never all there . . . Every day you have to make some last minute changes . . . I've been round to the Train Bleu . . .'

'How is your sister?'

'She's very cut up . . . Luckily Antonio spent the afternoon with us . . . The undertaker's men came along . . . They're due to bring the body back home tomorrow morning . . . The telephone never stopped ringing . . . And then we had to see about the invitations to the funeral . . .'

She remained very calm, and, while talking to Maigret, she kept an eye on the preparations, just as Boulay would have done. She even broke off to say to a young waiter:

'No, Germain . . . No ice in the buckets yet . . .'

A new man, probably . . .

Maigret asked at random:

'Did he leave a will?'

'We don't know, and that complicates matters, because we don't know what arrangements to make . . .'

'Did he have a solicitor?'

'Not as far as I know . . . Almost certainly not . . . I rang his lawyer, Maître Jean-Charles Gaillard, but he isn't at home . . . He left early this morning for Poitiers, where he has a case, and he won't be back until late tonight.'

Who was it, who had already mentioned a lawyer? Maigret hunted about in his memory, and found the rather unappetizing picture of Monsieur Raison in his little *entresol* office. What had they been talking about at that moment? Maigret had asked if certain payments were not made direct in order to avoid taxation.

He remembered now how the conversation had gone on. The accountant had maintained that Monsieur Émile had not been a man to cheat the Inland Revenue and risk trouble, that he had insisted on everything being above-board and that his income tax returns had been made by his lawyer . . .

'You think it's to him that your brother-in-law would have gone about his will?'

'He asked his advice about everything . . . Don't forget that, when he started, he knew nothing about business . . . When he opened the Train Bleu, some neighbours sued him, I can't remember why, probably because the music prevented them from sleeping . . .'

'Where does he live?'

'Maître Gaillard? In the Rue La Bruyère, in a little private house about the middle of the street . . .'

The Rue La Bruyère! Barely five hundred yards from the Lotus. To get there, you simply had to go down the Rue Pigalle, cross the Rue Notre-Dame-de-Lorette, and, a little further down, turn to the left.

'Did your brother-in-law see him often?'

'Once or twice a month . . .'

'In the evening?'

'No. During the afternoon. Generally after six o'clock, when Maître Gaillard came back from the Palais de Justice . . .'

'Did you use to go with him?'

She shook her head.

Perhaps it was ridiculous, but the chief-inspector had lost his bad-tempered expression.

'Can I use the telephone?'

'Would you prefer to go up to the office or to use the call-box?'

'I'll use the call-box . . .'

As Émile Boulay had done, with the difference that Boulay had started dialling a number only about ten o'clock in the evening. Through the glass he could see Germaine, the cloakroom girl, who was arranging pink tickets in an old cigar-box.

'Hallo . . . Is that Maître Gaillard's house?'

'No, Monsieur . . . This is Lecot's the chemists . . .'

'Sorry . . .'

He must have got one figure wrong. He dialled again, more carefully, and heard a bell ringing in the distance. One minute, two minutes went by, and nobody replied.

Three times he dialled the same number again, without any more success. When he came out of the box, he looked round for Ada, and finally found her in the dressing-room where two women were undressing. They took no notice of him and made no attempt to conceal their bare breasts.

'Is Maître Gaillard a bachelor?'

'I don't know. I've never heard anybody mention his wife. Perhaps he has one all the same. I haven't had occasion to go to his house.'

A little later, out on the pavement, Maigret started questioning Mickey.

'Do you know Jean-Charles Gaillard?'

'The lawyer? I know him by name. It was him that defended Big Lucien, three years ago, and got him acquitted.'

'He was also your boss's lawyer.'

'That doesn't surprise me . . . They say he's very good . . .'

'Do you know if he's married?'

'I'm sorry, Monsieur Maigret, but people like that aren't in my line, and with the best will in the world I can't tell you anything about them . . .'

The chief-inspector went back into the call-box and dialled the same number, but without getting through.

Then, on the spur of the moment, he rang up a barrister he had known for a good many years, Chavanon, and was lucky enough to find him at home.

'Maigret speaking . . . No, I haven't got a client for you in my office . . . I'm not speaking from the Quai des Orfèvres for that matter . . . I'd like some information . . . Do you know Maître Jean-Charles Gaillard?'

'Slightly . . . I see him at the Palais and once I had occasion to lunch with him . . . But he's much too important a person for a humble worker like myself . . .'

'Married?'

'I think so, yes . . . Wait a minute . . . Yes, I'm certain he is . . . Just after the war he married a singer or dancer from the Casino de Paris . . . At least, that's what I've been told . . .'

'You've never seen her? You haven't been to his house?'

'They've never invited me there . . .'

'They aren't divorced? They live together?'

'As far as I know . . .'

'I suppose you don't know if she accompanies him when he has a case in the provinces?'

'It isn't usual . . .'

'Thank you . . .'

He rang the Rue La Bruyère number again, in vain, and the cloakroom girl stared at him with growing curiosity.

Finally he decided to leave the Lotus and, after a little wave to Mickey, went slowly down the Rue Pigalle. In the Rue La Bruyère he soon singled out a building which, in fact, looked like an ordinary middle-class house such as you see everywhere in the provinces and you can still find here and there in certain districts in Paris. There were no lights in any of the windows. A brass plate bore the lawyer's name. He pushed a button just above the plate and a bell rang inside the house.

Nothing moved. He rang twice, three times, but with no more success than when he had telephoned.

For no particular reason he crossed the street to look at the house as a whole.

Just as he raised his head, a curtain moved, behind a window on the first floor which was unlighted, and he could have sworn that for a moment he caught sight of a face.

Chapter Five

Anyone would have thought that Maigret was playing at being a night-club proprietor and that, in spite of the difference in weight and build, he was doing his best to imitate Émile Boulay. Without hurrying, he strolled through the few streets which constituted the former steward's world, and, as the hours went by, these changed in appearance.

First there were the neon signs which became more numerous, and then there were the uniformed commissionaires who appeared outside the doors. Not only did the jazz, coming out through the night-clubs' doors, give a different vibration to the air, but the passers-by were different and the night taxis began to spill out their passengers, while a new fauna moved backwards and forwards between the light and shade.

Women called out to him. He walked along with his hands behind his back. Had Monsieur Émile walked with his hands behind his back? In any case he hadn't smoked like the chief-inspector. He had sucked peppermints.

Maigret walked down the Rue Notre-Dame-de-Lorette as far as the Saint-Trop'. He had known the night-club under another name, at a time when most of its clients had been ladies in dinner-jackets.

Had Montmartre changed so much? The rhythm of the orchestras was no longer the same. There was more neon lighting, but the people looked like those he had known before; some of them had simply changed their jobs, like the doorman at the Saint-Trop', who greeted the chief-inspector familiarly.

He was a colossus with a white beard, a Russian refugee who for years, in another night-club in the district, had sung old ballads of his country, in a fine bass voice, accompanying himself on a balalaika.

'Do you remember last Tuesday evening?'

'I remember all the evenings God has allowed me to live,' replied the former general grandiloquently.

'Did your employer come here that evening?'

'About half-past nine, with a pretty young lady.'

'You mean Ada? He didn't come back alone later on?'

'No, I swear by St George that he didn't.'

Why by St George? Maigret went in, glancing at the bar, and at the tables around which the first customers were sitting, bathed in an orange light. The staff must have been told that he was there, for waiters, musicians and hostesses watched him with a curiosity mingled with a certain anxiety.

Had Boulay been in the habit of staying longer? Maigret went off again, nodded to Mickey outside the Lotus and to the cloakroom girl inside, and asked her for a *jeton* for the telephone.

In the glass call-box he dialled the Rue La Bruyère number yet again, but in vain.

Then he went into the Train Bleu, which was decorated to look like a Pullman carriage. The orchestra was playing so loud that he beat a retreat, plunged into the quiet and darkness of the other part of the Rue Victor-Massé, and came to the Square d'Anvers, where only two cafés were open.

One, the Chope d'Anvers, looked like an old-fashioned brasserie in the provinces. Near the windows, customers were playing cards, and at the back there was a billiard-table, around which two men were slowly circling with almost solemn movements.

One of the two was Monsieur Raison, in his shirt-sleeves. His partner, a man with a huge belly and a cigar between his teeth, was wearing green braces.

Maigret did not go in but stood there for a moment, as if fascinated by the sight, though in fact he was thinking of something else. He started when a voice near him said:

'Good evening, Chief.'

It was Lapointe, whom he had told to check up on the accountant, and who explained:

'I was just going home . . . I've found out how he spent Tuesday evening . . . He left the café at a quarter-past eleven . . . He never stays after half-past eleven . . . Less than ten minutes later he was at home . . .

'The concierge is absolutely definite . . . She hadn't gone to bed because that evening her husband and her daughter had gone to the cinema and she waited up for them . . .

'She saw Monsieur Raison come in and she's certain that he didn't go out again . . .'

Young Lapointe was puzzled, for Maigret didn't seem to be listening to him.

'Have you found anything new?' he ventured. 'Do you want me to stay with you?'

'No. Go to bed . . .'

He preferred to be alone to start his round again. It was not long before he returned to the Train Bleu, or to be more precise opened the curtain and glanced inside, like certain customers who make sure, before going in, that they have found what they are looking for.

Then the Lotus again. Another wink from Mickey, who was engaged in a mysterious conversation with two Americans, to whom he was obviously promising extraordinary amusements.

Maigret did not need to ask for a *jeton* for the telephone, and the bell rang yet again in the house whose façade he now knew and where he was convinced that a curtain had moved.

He gave a start when a man's voice said:

'Hallo . . .'

He was no longer expecting a reply.

'Maître Jean-Charles Gaillard?'

'Speaking . . . Who's that?'

'Chief-Inspector Maigret of Police Headquarters.'

A pause. Then the voice, rather impatiently, said:

'Yes, all right, go on.'

'I must apologize for bothering you at this time of night . . .'

'It's a miracle that you found me . . . I've just come back from Poitiers by car and I was glancing through my post before going to bed . . .'

'Could I come and see you for a few minutes?'

'Are you telephoning from the Quai des Orfèvres?'

'No . . . I'm practically next door . . .'

'Right . . . I'll be expecting you . . .'

Mickey still outside the door, the street getting noisier and noisier, and a woman who emerged from a corner and put her hand on the chief-inspector's arm, drawing back suddenly when she recognized him.

'No offence meant,' she stammered.

He returned, as to an oasis, to the peaceful atmosphere of the Rue La Bruyère, where, outside the lawyer's house, a big pastel-blue American car was standing. There was a light above the door. Maigret went up the three steps from the pavement and, before he could press the electric bell, the door opened into a hall paved with white tiles.

Jean-Charles Gaillard was as tall and broad-shouldered as the Russian doorman at the Saint-Trop'. He was a man of about forty-five, with a florid complexion and a rugby player's build, who must have been all muscle at one time, and who was only just beginning to put on flesh.

'Come in, Chief-Inspector . . .'

He closed the door, and led his guest to the end of the corridor, where he showed him into his study. The room, which was fairly big and comfortably furnished, but without ostentatious luxury, was lit only by a lamp with a green shade standing on a desk partly covered with letters which had just been opened.

'Please sit down . . . I've had a tiring day, and on the way back I ran into a heavy storm which held me up . . .'

Maigret was fascinated by the lawyer's left hand, from which four fingers were missing. Only the thumb was left.

'I should like to ask you two or three questions about one of your clients . . .'

Was the lawyer uneasy? Or just curious? It was hard to say. He had blue eyes, and fair hair cropped short.

'If professional secrecy allows me to reply . . .' he murmured with a smile.

He had finally sat down opposite the chief-inspector, and his right hand was toying with an ivory paper-knife.

'Boulay's body was found this morning . . .'

'Boulay?' echoed the other man, as if he were searching his memory.

'The proprietor of the Lotus and three other night-clubs . . .'

'Ah, yes . . . I see . . .'

'He came to see you recently, didn't he?'

'That depends on what you mean by recently . . .'

'Tuesday, for example . . .'

'Tuesday this week?'

'Yes.'

Jean-Charles Gaillard shook his head.

'If he came I didn't see him . . . He may have called while I was at the Palais . . . I shall have to ask my secretary tomorrow . . .'

Looking Maigret in the eye, he asked a question in his turn.

'You say that his body has been found . . . The fact that you are here suggests that the police are looking into the matter . . . Am I to understand that it was not a case of natural death?'

'He was strangled . . .'

'That's odd . . .'

'Why?'

'Because, in spite of his profession, he was a decent fellow and I didn't think he had any enemies . . . It's true that he was just one of many clients . . .'

'When was the last time you saw him?'

'I should be able to give you a definite reply to that . . . Just a moment . . .'

He got up, and went into the adjoining office, where he turned on the lamps and rummaged around in a drawer, coming back with a red notebook.

'My secretary keeps a note of all my appointments . . . Wait a moment . . .'

He turned the pages, starting at the back, and silently murmuring names. He went through about twenty pages like that.

'Here we are! . . . May 22 at five o'clock . . . There's a mention of another call on May·18 at eleven o'clock in the morning . . .'

'You haven't seen him since May 22?'

'Not as far as I can remember . . .'

'And he hasn't telephoned you?'

'If he rang my office, he would have had my secretary on the line and she will be able to answer your question. She'll be here tomorrow at nine o'clock . . .'

'Did you look after all Boulay's affairs?'

'That depends on what you mean by all his affairs . . .'

He added with a smile:

'That's a dangerous question you've just asked me . . . I don't necessarily know about all his activities . . .'

'I gather it was you who made out his income tax return . . .'

'I can see no harm in replying to that question . . . That's correct . . . Boulay had very little education and would have been incapable of dealing with it himself . . .'

Another pause, after which he went on:

'I must add that he never asked me to cheat . . . Naturally, like everybody else, he wanted to pay as few taxes as possible, but keeping on the right side of the law . . . Otherwise I would not have taken on his affairs . . .'

'You mentioned a call he paid you on May 18 . . . The previous night, a certain Mazotti had been killed not far from the Lotus . . .'

Very calm, Gaillard lit a cigarette, held out the silver box to Maigret, and took it back when he noticed that he was smoking his pipe.

'I can see no harm in telling you why he came. Mazotti had tried the protection trick on him, and, to get rid of him, Boulay had provided himself with the assistance of three or four toughs from his native town of Le Havre . . .'

'I know . . .'

'When he heard about Mazotti's death, he guessed that the police would want to question him . . . He had nothing to hide, but he was afraid of seeing his name in the papers . . .'

'He asked your advice?'

'Precisely. I told him to reply frankly . . . I believe incidentally that that advice stood him in good stead . . . Unless I'm mistaken, he was summoned a second time to the Quai des Orfèvres on the 22nd or the 23rd, and he came to see me again before that interview . . . I don't suppose he was ever suspected?

. . . In my opinion, that would have been a mistake . . .'

'You are sure that he didn't come back this week? On Tuesday, for example?'

'Not only am I sure that he didn't, but, once again, the appointment, if there had been an appointment, would be recorded in this notebook . . . See for yourself . . .'

He held it out to the chief-inspector, who did not touch it.

'Were you at home on Tuesday evening?'

This time the lawyer frowned.

'This is beginning to resemble an interrogation,' he observed, 'and I must admit that I should like to know what you have in mind . . .'

All the same, he ended up by shrugging his shoulders and smiling.

'If I search my memory, I shall probably be able to tell you how I spent my time . . . I pass most of my evenings in this study, because it is the only time I can work in peace . . . In the morning, I have a continuous stream of clients . . . In the afternoon I am usually at the Palais . . .'

'You didn't dine out?'

'I scarcely ever dine out . . . You see, I'm not a society lawyer . . .'

'On Tuesday evening then?'

'Today is Friday, isn't it? . . . Saturday in fact, since it is after midnight . . . This morning I left very early for Poitiers . . .'

'By yourself?'

The question seemed to surprise him.

'By myself of course, seeing that I was going there for a case . . . Yesterday, I didn't leave my office all evening . . . Tell me, is it an alibi you want?'

His voice was still amused and ironical.

'What intrigues me is that this alibi has to be for Tuesday evening, whereas my client's death, if I have understood you correctly, is quite recent . . . Still . . . I am like poor Boulay . . . I like to keep on the right side of the law . . . On Thursday, I didn't go out . . . On Wednesday evening . . . let's see . . . on Wednesday I worked until ten o'clock, and then, as I had a slight headache, I went for a walk in the district . . . As for Tuesday . . . I was in court during the afternoon. A complicated case, which has been dragging on for three years and which is far from being over . . . I came home for dinner . . .'

'You had dinner with your wife?'

Gaillard's gaze rested on the chief-inspector and he said:

'With my wife, yes . . .'

'She is here?'

'She is upstairs . . .'

'Did she go out this evening?'

'She hardly ever goes out, because of her health . . . My wife has been ill for several years and suffers a great deal . . .'

'I'm sorry . . .'

'Don't mention it . . . As I was saying, we had dinner . . . I came downstairs to this study, as usual . . . Ah! . . . Now I remember . . . I felt tired after my afternoon at the Palais . . . I took my car with the idea of driving for an hour or two to relax, as I sometimes do . . . I used to play games a great deal and I miss the fresh air . . . As I was driving along the Champs-Élysées, I saw that they were showing a Russian film I had heard people speak well of . . .'

'In short, you went to the cinema . . .'

'Precisely . . . As you can see, there was no mystery about it . . . Afterwards I dropped into Fouquet's for a drink before coming home . . .'

'Nobody was waiting for you?'

'Nobody.'

'You didn't receive a telephone call?'

He seemed to search his memory again.

'I don't think so, no . . . I must have smoked a cigarette before going up to bed, for I find it difficult to drop off to sleep . . . And now allow me to say that I'm rather surprised . . .'

It was Maigret's turn to play the innocent.

'Why?'

'I was expecting you to question me about my client . . . But you've asked me about myself and about the way I spent my time . . . I could easily take offence at that . . .'

'The fact is, I'm trying to reconstruct Émile Boulay's movements . . .'

'I don't understand . . .'

'He wasn't killed last night, but Tuesday night . . .'

'But you told me . . .'

'I told you that he was found this morning . . .'

'You mean that, since Tuesday, his body . . .'

Maigret nodded. He had taken on a good-natured expression and seemed ready to impart secrets.

'It has been practically established that on Tuesday evening Boulay had an appointment . . . Probably an appointment in this district . . .'

'And you thought that he came here?'

The chief-inspector laughed.

'I'm not accusing you of having strangled your client . . .'

'He was strangled?'

'According to the post-mortem . . . It would take too long to tell you what clues we have collected . . . He was in the habit of coming to ask your advice . . .'

'I wouldn't have received him at midnight.'

'He might have found himself in a delicate situation . . . If, say, someone had tried to blackmail him . . .'

Gaillard lit another cigarette and slowly blew the smoke out in front of him.

'His cheque-book shows that, not long ago, he drew a fairly large sum out of the bank . . .'

'May I ask you how much?'

'Five thousand francs . . . That wasn't something he normally did . . . Usually he took the ready cash he needed out of the till of one of his night-clubs . . .'

'Did that happen only once?'

'Only once, as far as we know . . . I shall know for certain tomorrow, when I check on his account . . .'

'I still can't see where I come into this case . . .'

'I'm coming to that . . .

'Let's suppose that he had given in the first time and that the blackmailer had returned to the attack, making an appointment with him for Tuesday night . . . The idea might have occurred to him to ask your advice. He would have dialled your number several times during the evening, while you were at the cinema . . . Who answers the telephone in the evening, when you are out?'

'Nobody . . .'

And, as Maigret looked surprised, he went on:

'My wife, as I have already said, is ill . . . It all began with a nervous breakdown which has steadily got worse . . . What's more, she suffers from a polyneuritis which the doctors can't manage to cure . . . She scarcely ever leaves the first floor and there is always a maid with her who is really a nurse . . . My wife doesn't know that . . . I have cut off the telephone upstairs . . .'

'And what about the servants?'

'There are two of them and they sleep on the second floor . . . To return to your question, which I understand better now, I don't know of any attempt to blackmail my client . . . I must add that the existence of any blackmail of that sort would surprise me, for, knowing his affairs, I can't see any grounds on which he could have been blackmailed . . . So he didn't come to ask my advice on Tuesday evening . . . And, *a priori*, I don't know how he spent the night . . .

'The fact that he had been killed didn't surprise me very much when you told me, because you don't reach the situation he occupied in that world without making yourself some serious enemies . . . The fact that he had been strangled I find more disturbing, and even more so the fact that his body wasn't found until this morning . . .

'As a matter of interest where was it found? . . . I suppose it was fished out of the Seine?'

'It was stretched out on the pavement, alongside the cemetery of Père Lachaise . . .'

'How did his wife take the news?'

'You know her?'

'I have seen her once . . . Boulay was mad about her . . . He insisted on showing me her and his children. He invited me to dinner in the Rue Victor-Massé and that's how I met the whole family . . .'

'Including Antonio?'

'Including the brother-in-law and his wife . . . A real family gathering . . . At bottom Boulay was very much a bourgeois, and seeing him at home, you would never have suspected that he lived by undressing women . . .'

'Do you know his night-clubs?'

'I went to the Lotus two or three times, over a year ago . . . I also attended the opening of the cabaret in the Rue de Berri . . .'

Maigret was asking himself a lot of questions, without venturing to put them aloud. Living with a sick wife, didn't the lawyer look elsewhere for the pleasures he no longer found at home?

'Have you met Ada?'

'The young sister? Oh, yes! She was at the dinner-party. She's a delightful girl, just as pretty as Marina, but with more of a head on her shoulders.'

'Do you think she was her brother-in-law's mistress?'

'I am putting myself in your place, Chief-Inspector. I realize that you have to look in all directions . . . All the same, some of your theories are absolutely fantastic . . . If you had known Boulay, you wouldn't ask me that question . . . He hated complications . . . An affair with Ada would have made an enemy of Antonio, who, as a good Italian, has a highly developed sense of family . . . Forgive my yawning, but I got up before dawn to arrive in time for my case . . .'

'Are you in the habit of leaving your car in front of the house?'

'Generally speaking, I don't bother to take it to the garage . . . There's nearly always room . . .'

'Forgive me for having bothered you like this . . . One last question . . . Did Boulay leave a will?'

'Not to my knowledge . . . And I can't see why he should have made one . . . He has two children . . . What's more, he married under the joint estate system . . . The inheritance presents no problems at all . . .'

'Thank you . . .'

'Tomorrow morning I shall go to express my sympathy to his widow and place myself at her disposal . . . The poor woman! . . .'

There were so many other questions that Maigret would have liked to ask him . . . For example, how he had come to lose four fingers of his left hand. And also at what time he had left the Rue La Bruyère that morning . . . Finally, on account of something Mickey had said, he would have been interested to consult the list of the lawyer's clients.

A few minutes later, he took a taxi in the Place Saint-Georges and went home to bed. All the same, he got up at eight o'clock in the morning, and at half-past nine he was leaving the office of the Director of Police Headquarters, where he had sat through the morning conference without opening his mouth.

The first thing he did after opening the window and taking off his jacket was to ring up Maître Chavanon, to whom he had telephoned the day before.

'It's me again . . . Maigret . . . Am I disturbing you?'

'I've got somebody with me . . .'

'Just a piece of information . . . Do you know a colleague of yours who is on fairly friendly terms with Jean-Charles Gaillard?'

'Again! Anybody would think you had a grudge against him . . .'

'No, I haven't got a grudge against him, but I'd like to know a few things which concern him . . .'

'Why not ask the man himself? Go and see him . . .'

'I have seen him.'

'Well, then? Was he unco-operative?'

'On the contrary. The fact remains that there are certain questions which are too delicate to ask straight out . . .'

Chavanon was anything but enthusiastic. Maigret had expected this. In almost all professions there exists an *esprit de corps*. You can speak freely about one another among yourselves, but you don't appreciate any form of intrusion. Least of all by the Police!

'Listen . . . I've told you all I know . . . I don't know who his friends are at the moment, but a few years ago he was very friendly with Ramuel . . .'

'The fellow who defended the butcher in the Rue Caulaincourt?'

'That's the man. I'd be grateful, if you go to see him, if you wouldn't bring me into it. All the more so in that he's just obtained two or three acquittals one after the other and it's rather gone to his head . . . Good luck!'

Maître Ramuel lived in the Rue du Bac, and the next moment Maigret had his secretary on the line.

'It's practically impossible . . . His whole morning is taken . . . Wait a moment . . . If you come about ten to eleven and he has finished quickly with the client he's seeing at half-past ten . . .'

They obviously trooped in and out of his rooms like the patients at a local dentist's. Next, please!

Maigret went along to the Rue du Bac all the same, and, as he was early, he dropped into the café for a glass of white wine. The walls of the waiting-room at Maître Ramuel's were covered with pictures dedicated by the artists. Three people were waiting there, including an old woman who must have been a rich farmer's wife from the country.

Nonetheless, at five to eleven the secretary opened the door and discreetly motioned to the chief-inspector to follow her.

Though still young and baby-faced, Maître Ramuel was already bald. He came forward, holding his hand out in a cordial welcome.

'To what do I owe this honour?'

The room was huge, the walls panelled, the furniture Renaissance pieces, and the floor covered with genuine Oriental carpets.

'Sit down . . . A cigar? . . . Oh, of course not . . . Do smoke your pipe, please . . .'

You could tell that he was full of his own importance and he sat down at his desk like an attorney-general in the ministerial seat.

'I can't see that any of the cases I have in hand . . .'

'I haven't come about one of your clients, Maître . . . What's more, I feel rather embarrassed. I should like you to regard my call as a private visit . . .'

Ramuel was so used to Assize Court trials that in his private life he went on behaving as if he were in court, with the same gestures and the same arm-movements, from which nothing was lacking but the full sleeves of a black gown.

He began by opening his eyes wide in a comical look, and then spread his hands out to express surprise.

'Come now, Chief-Inspector, you aren't going to tell me you're in trouble? . . . The idea of acting as counsel for Chief-Inspector Maigret . . .'

'I just need a little information about somebody . . .'

'One of my clients?'

He assumed an indignant expression.

'I don't need to remind you . . .'

'Have no fear. I'm not asking you to break your oath of professional secrecy . . . For reasons which it would take too long to explain, I need to know something about one of your colleagues . . .'

The brows furrowed, again in an exaggerated way, as if the lawyer were acting his usual comedy before a jury.

'I'm not asking you to betray a friendship either . . .'

'Go on. I make no promises, you understand . . .'

It was annoying, but the chief-inspector had no choice.

'I believe you know your colleague Jean-Charles Gaillard quite well . . .'

An air of false embarrassment.

'We used to see a lot of each other . . .'

'You have quarrelled?'

'Let us say that we meet less frequently than before . . .'

'Do you know his wife?'

'Jeanine? I met her for the first time when she was still dancing at the Casino de Paris . . . That was just after the war . . . A delightful girl at that time . . . And beautiful! . . . They called her the beautiful Lara and people used to turn round to look at her in the street . . .'

'Was that her name?'

'No . . . Her real name was Dupin, but as a dancer she used the name of Jeanine de Lara . . . She would probably have had a brilliant career . . .'

'She gave it up for Gaillard?'

'When he married her, he promised that he wouldn't ask her to leave the stage . . .'

'And he didn't keep his word?'

What followed now was the comedy of discretion. Ramuel seemed to weigh the pros and cons, and heaved a sigh, as if he were being torn by contrary feelings.

'After all, everybody in Paris society knows all about it . . . Gaillard had just come back from the war, covered with medals . . .'

'It was in the war that he lost four fingers?'

'Yes . . . He was at Dunkirk . . . In England he joined the Free French forces . . . He went through the African campaign, and then, unless I'm mistaken, found himself in Syria . . . He was a lieutenant in the Commandos . . . He never talks about it, I must admit . . . He isn't the sort that like talking about their wartime exploits . . . One night when he was supposed to be taking an enemy patrol by surprise, it was he who was surprised, and he only saved his life by grabbing hold of the knife which was being plunged into his chest . . . He's a tough character . . .

'He fell madly in love with Jeanine and decided to marry her . . . At that time he was a probationer advocate under Maître Jouane, the common lawyer, and wasn't earning much . . .

'He was a jealous man, and spent his evenings in the wings of the Casino de Paris . . .

'You can guess the rest . . . Little by little he persuaded his wife to give up dancing . . . He started working extremely hard to keep the pot boiling . . . I often sent him clients . . .'

'He's always stuck to common law?'

This time Ramuel assumed the embarrassed expression of a man wondering whether his interlocutor will be capable of understanding him.

'It's rather complicated . . . There are some lawyers you rarely see at the Palais but who have an important clientele all the same . . . They are the ones who earn the most money . . . They are legal advisers to big companies . . . They know company law backwards, and its subtlest points . . .'

'Is that the case with Gaillard?'

'Yes and no . . . Mind you, I haven't seen him for several years . . . He doesn't often appear in court . . . As for his clientele, I should find it hard to describe . . . Unlike his former chief, he doesn't number big banks and industrial firms among his clients . . .'

Maigret listened patiently, trying to guess at what lay behind the words.

'With the present fiscal laws, a lot of people need professional advice . . . Some people, because of the nature of their work, need to make sure that they are keeping on the right side of the law . . .'

'The proprietor of a chain of night-clubs, for instance?'

Ramuel made a show of surprise and confusion.

'I didn't know I had been so explicit . . . Mind you, I don't know who you're talking about.'

Maigret remembered his conversation the previous day with Louis

Boubeé, *alias* Mickey. Both of them had recalled the days of the Tivoli and La Tétoune, at whose restaurant you used to meet, not only the big bosses of the underworld, but their lawyers and a certain number of politicians.

'Boulay has been killed,' he said abruptly.

'Boulay?'

'Monsieur Émile . . . The owner of the Lotus, the Train Bleu, and two other night-clubs . . .'

'I haven't had time to read the paper this morning . . . Was he a client of Gaillard's?'

He was disarming in his naïvety.

'Obviously that's one of the categories I was talking about . . . It isn't easy, in certain professions, to avoid trouble . . . What happened to this man Boulay?'

'He has been strangled . . .'

'How horrible!'

'You were talking just now about Madame Gaillard . . .'

'It seems that her condition has deteriorated since I lost sight of her. . . . It began, at the time when I was still friendly with them, with nervous breakdowns which became increasingly frequent . . . I suppose that she couldn't get used to middle-class life . . . Let's see . . . How old is she now? . . . In her forties, unless I'm mistaken . . . She must be four or five years younger than he is . . . But she has gone to pieces . . . She has aged very quickly.

'Without being a doctor, Chief-Inspector, I've seen quite a few women, especially among the most beautiful ones, take that bend rather badly . . .

'I've heard people say that she is practically insane, that she sometimes spends weeks at a time in a darkened room . . .

'I'm sorry for Gaillard . . . He's an intelligent fellow, one of the most intelligent I know . . . He worked like a black to get ahead in the world . . . He tried to give Jeanine a brilliant social life . . . Because for a while they lived very well indeed . . .

'But all that wasn't enough . . . And now . . .'

If his face expressed compassion, there nonetheless remained a gleeful, ironical flame in his little eyes.

'What was it that you wanted to know? . . . Mind you, I haven't told you anything confidential . . . You could have questioned anybody in the corridors of the Palais . . .'

'I suppose Jean-Charles Gaillard has never had any trouble with the Bar Council?'

This time Ramuel spread out his arms and looked shocked.

'Come, come! What are you suggesting?'

He stood up and glanced at the clock on the mantelpiece.

'I'm sorry, but you probably saw that a certain number of clients are waiting for me . . . I've got a case at two . . . I presume that nobody knows about your visit and that what we have said remains between ourselves?'

And, going towards the door with a skipping step, he sighed theatrically:

'Poor Jeanine!'

Chapter Six

Before going home for lunch, Maigret had dropped in at the Quai des Orfèvres, and had said to Lapointe, almost absent-mindedly:

'I should like you to go and scout around the Rue La Bruyère and the surrounding area as soon as possible. It seems that a pale-blue American car is usually parked, day and night, outside Maître Jean-Charles Gaillard's private house . . .'

He handed him a piece of paper on which he had scribbled the car's registration number.

'I should like to know at what time the car was there on Tuesday evening, and also at what time it left yesterday morning or during the night . . .'

He had the wide-eyed, vacant look, the bent shoulders, and the heavy, lazy walk that he had at certain times.

At those times, people who saw him, and his colleagues more than anyone else, imagined that he was concentrating. In fact, nothing could have been further from the truth. But however often he told them this, they refused to believe him.

What he was doing in reality was rather ridiculous, not to say childish. He took an idea, a phrase, and repeated it to himself like a schoolboy trying to memorize a lesson. Sometimes he would even start moving his lips and talking under his breath, alone in the middle of his office, in the street, anywhere.

The words did not necessarily mean anything. Sometimes they sounded like a joke.

'There have been cases of a lawyer being killed by his client, but I've never heard of a client being killed by his lawyer . . .'

That did not mean that he was accusing Jean-Charles Gaillard of having strangled the puny proprietor of the Lotus and the other night-clubs. His wife would have surprised him if, while he was eating, she had suddenly asked him:

'What are you thinking about?'

He would probably have replied in good faith that he was not thinking about anything. There were also pictures which he kept passing through his head as if through a magic lantern.

Émile Boulay, in the evening, standing on the pavement outside the Lotus . . . That was a habit of his practically every evening . . . The little man looked at the sky, at the crowd which flowed by, changing in rhythm and almost in nature as the evening wore on, and worked out the takings in his four night-clubs . . .

The second picture was not an everyday one. Boulay went into the call-box, under the eyes of the cloakroom girl, and dialled a number which did not reply . . .

Three times . . . Four times . . . Between calls he went for a little walk, either inside the club or out in the street . . . And it was only at the fifth or sixth attempt that he finally succeeded in getting an answer . . .

But he did not leave straightaway . . . Standing beside Mickey, on the pavement, he took his watch out of his pocket every now and then . . .

'He didn't go home to get his automatic,' Maigret nearly said aloud.

Émile had a licence. He was entitled to be armed. At the time when Mazotti and his gang had been bothering him, he had always been armed.

If he was not armed this particular evening, that was because he had no suspicion of danger.

Finally, without saying anything to the doorman, who looked like a wizened little boy, he started walking unhurriedly down the Rue Pigalle.

That was the last picture. Or at least the last picture of Émile alive.

'Have you any plans for tomorrow?'

He raised his head from his plate and looked at his wife, as if he were surprised to see her opposite him, near the open window.

'Tomorrow?' he echoed, in a voice so neutral that she burst out laughing.

'You were far away! Forgive me for . . .'

'What is there tomorrow?'

'It's Sunday . . . Do you think you'll have some work to do?'

He hesitated before replying. He did not know. He had not thought about Sunday. He hated interrupting an investigation, maintaining that one of the principal chances of success lay in speed. The more days went by, the more difficult it was to obtain clear evidence from witnesses. He himself felt the need to keep going, to stay with the little society into which he had been plunged.

And now here was a Sunday, in other words a hole. And the afternoon too was going to be practically wasted, because for most people Saturday had become a sort of Sunday.

'I don't know yet . . . I'll phone you during the afternoon . . .'

Spreading his arms out in the theatrical manner of Maître Ramuel, he added:

'I'm sorry . . . It isn't my fault . . .'

Naturally, the life of Police Headquarters had already begun slowing down. There were offices that were empty, chief-inspectors and inspectors who had gone off into the country.

'Lapointe isn't back, is he?'

'Not yet, Chief.'

He had just caught sight of fat Torrence, in the inspectors' room, who was showing his colleagues a reel for a fishing-rod. He could not expect everybody to be hypnotized by Émile Boulay like himself.

He did not know what to do while he was waiting for Lapointe, and he had not the courage, on a Saturday afternoon, to plunge back into his administrative plans.

He ended up by dropping in on Lecoin, his colleague of the Vice Squad, who was reading the paper. Lecoin looked more like a gangster than a detective.

'Am I disturbing you?'

'No . . .'

Maigret went and sat down on the window-sill, without knowing very well why he had come.

'Did you know the proprietor of the Lotus?'

'As I know them all . . .'

The conversation, a lazy conversation without either head or tail, lasted almost an hour without producing any results. According to Lecoin, the former steward was a decent chap who did not belong to the underworld and whom some people in Montmartre contemptuously called the Grocer.

At four o'clock Sunday had almost begun, and the chief-inspector once again pushed open the door of the inspectors' room.

'Lapointe?'

'Not back yet, Chief . . .'

He knew that it would not help but nonetheless he opened the door leading into the Palais de Justice and ambled into the adjoining building. That morning he had decided to go to the registry and obtain a list of the clients whom Jean-Charles Gaillard had represented in court.

The Palais de Justice was practically empty, with draughts blowing along the vast corridors, and when he pushed open the door of the registry, he found nobody there. It was curious. Anybody could have gone in and rummaged about in the green filing-cabinets which lined the walls up to the ceiling. Anybody, too, could have taken a gown from the barristers' cloakroom, and even sat in a judge's chair.

'The Zoo is better guarded than this,' he growled.

At last he found Lapointe in his office.

'I've come back empty-handed, Chief . . . But I've questioned nearly all the people who live in that street . . . At any rate those who haven't gone off for the weekend.

'The blue American car is familiar to them all. Some of them know who it belongs to . . . Others notice it every morning, when they set off for their work, without bothering their heads about it . . . When I mentioned Tuesday night to them, most of them shrugged their shoulders hopelessly . . .

'For them it's a long time ago . . . Some had already gone to bed at ten o'clock in the evening . . . Others came back from the cinema about half-past eleven without paying any attention to the cars which, at that time of night, are parked all along the street . . .

'The most common reply was:

' "It's always there . . ."

'They are used to seeing it in its place, you understand, so that even if it isn't there, they think it is . . .

'I went round all the local garages. There's only one of them where they remember the car and a big red-faced fellow who sometimes has it filled up there . . . But he isn't a regular customer . . .

'There are two garages left where I wasn't able to question anybody, for the very good reason that they are closed until Monday morning . . .'

Maigret spread his arms out again like Maître Ramuel. What could he do about it?

'Go back there on Monday,' he sighed.

The telephone rang. He recognized Antonio's voice, and hoped for a moment that the Italian had something new to tell him.

'Is that you, Monsieur Maigret? . . . I've got the undertaker's man with me . . . He suggests arranging the funeral for ten o'clock on Monday morning . . . I don't want to give him an answer without your permission . . .'

What did that matter to Maigret?

'All right . . .'

'You will be receiving an invitation . . . The Requiem Mass will be at the church of Notre-Dame-de-Lorette . . .'

He replaced the receiver and gazed vacantly at Lapointe, who was standing there waiting for instructions.

'You can go now. Have a good Sunday . . . If Lucas is next door, send him in to me . . .'

Lucas was there.

'Anything new, Chief?'

'Not a thing . . . I should like you to go to the court registry first thing on Monday morning, and get hold of the list of cases in which Jean-Charles Gaillard has appeared. No need to go back to the year dot . . . Just the last two or three years . . .'

'Are you going back to Montmartre tonight?'

He shrugged his shoulders. What was the use? He repeated to Lucas what he had already said to Lapointe:

'Have a good Sunday . . .'

And he picked up the receiver.

'Get me my home number . . . Hallo . . . Is that you? . . .'

As if he didn't know that it couldn't be anyone else and as if he didn't recognize her voice!

'Do you remember the times of the trains to Morsang . . . Today, yes. Before dinner if possible . . . 5.52? . . . Would you like to spend tonight and tomorrow there? . . . Good! . . . Get the little suitcase ready . . . No . . . I'll phone them myself . . .'

It was on the banks of the Seine, a few miles upstream from Corbeil. There was an old inn there, the Vieux Garçon, where, for over twenty years, the Maigrets had sometimes gone to spend Sunday.

Maigret had discovered it in the course of an investigation, standing all by itself on the river-bank, and mainly frequented by anglers.

By now the two of them were well-known there. They were nearly always given the same room, and the same table, for dinner and lunch, under the trees on the terrace.

'Hallo . . . Get me the Vieux Garçon at Morsang . . . Near Corbeil . . . The Vieux Garçon, yes . . . It's an inn . . .'

Looking through some old books, he had discovered that the place had been frequented in the past by Balzac and Alexandre Dumas, and then that, later on, literary luncheon-parties had brought together there the Goncourt brothers, Flaubert, Zola, Alphonse Daudet and a few others.

'Hallo . . . Maigret speaking . . . What's that? . . . Yes, it's a lovely day . . .'

He knew that as well as the *patronne*.

'Our room is taken? . . . You've got another, but it doesn't look out on the Seine? . . . That doesn't matter . . . We'll arrive in time for dinner . . .'

So, after all, in spite of Émile Boulay, they went and spent a quiet Sunday by the river. The clientele of the Vieux Garçon had changed over the years. The anglers Maigret had met in the old days had nearly all disappeared. Either they were dead, or they had grown too old to move around.

New anglers had taken their places. They were just as fanatical as their predecessors, and some of them baited their hooks several days in advance.

They used to hear some who got up at four o'clock in the morning to go and moor their boat in the current between a couple of stakes.

There was a new, younger clientele, mainly consisting of couples who owned a small sailing-boat, and these people danced on the terrace to music from a record-player, until one o'clock in the morning.

Maigret slept all the same, heard some cocks crowing, the footsteps of the anglers going fishing, and finally got up at nine o'clock in the morning.

About ten o'clock, as they were finishing their breakfast under the trees and watching the sails going by, Madame Maigret asked:

'Aren't you going to do any fishing?'

He had neither his fishing-rods nor his tackle with him, having left them in their little house at Meung-sur-Loire, but he could always borrow some from the *patronne*.

Why should a lawyer kill his client? You sometimes heard of a patient killing his doctor, out of a conviction that he had been given the wrong treatment. The opposite was extremely rare. The only case he could remember was that of Bougrat . . .

Émile Boulay was not the aggressive type . . . He could not claim that his lawyer had let him down since he had never been convicted and his record was clean . . .

'Pick any rod you like . . . The lines are in the cupboard, and you'll find some maggots in the usual place . . .'

They followed the bank one behind the other, and picked a shady spot near a dead tree. Fate willed it that after half an hour Maigret had already caught a dozen roach. If he had provided himself with a spoon-net, he would probably have also landed the chub weighing over a pound which broke his line.

It is true that after that he did not get another bite. His wife read a magazine, breaking off every now and then to look at him with an amused smile.

They lunched in their corner, with, as usual, people turning to look at them and starting to whisper. Isn't a Chief of the Crime Squad entitled to spend a Sunday in the country like anybody else and go fishing if he feels like it?

He returned to the river-bank, but caught nothing more, and at six o'clock in the evening he and his wife were in the crowded train travelling to Paris.

They ate some cold meat, looking at the darkness falling, the streets which were still practically empty, and the houses across the way where a few lights were beginning to go on.

Boulay did not use to spend his Sundays in the country. His night-clubs were open seven days a week, and he was not the man to leave them without supervision. As for his three women, they probably felt no desire to leave their little Italy in the Rue Victor-Massé.

At nine o'clock on Monday morning Maigret looked in at the Quai des Orfèvres to make sure that there was nothing new, and at a quarter to ten a taxi deposited him in the Rue Pigalle. A funeral notice with a black border was fastened to the grille of the Lotus. In the Rue Victor-Massé, there was another on the door of the Train Bleu.

The pavement opposite what had been Boulay's home was swarming with people. Every now and then, somebody or some small group broke away to go into the house, whose door was hung with black draperies.

He did like the others, waiting his turn in front of the lift, where you could already smell the flowers and tapers. The drawing-room had been transformed into a mortuary chapel, and around the coffin some dark figures were standing—Antonio, Monsieur Raison, and an old head-waiter who was regarded as one of the family—while a woman could be heard sobbing in a nearby room.

He shook hands, went downstairs again, and waited with the others. He recognized faces he had glimpsed in the dead man's night-clubs. All his staff must have been there, and the women in fantastically high heels had tired faces, eyes which looked surprised to see the morning sun.

'Quite a crowd, eh?'

It was the doorman, Louis Boubée, *alias* Mickey, dressed in black, who had tugged the chief-inspector by the sleeve and seemed proud of the success the funeral was having.

'They're all here . . .'

He meant the proprietors of all the night-clubs in Paris, including those on the Champs-Élysées and in Montparnasse, the musicians, the barmen, the waiters . . .

'Have you seen Jo?'

He pointed to Jo-the-Wrestler, who waved to the chief-inspector and who was also dressed in black for the occasion.

'There are all sorts here, aren't there?'

Loud suits, light-coloured hats, big signet-rings, and shoes in suede or crocodile . . . Everybody had come along . . . Boulay might not have belonged to the underworld and might have deserved the nickname of the Grocer, but he still formed part of the night life of Montmartre.

'You still don't know who did it?'

At that moment the lawyer came out of the house, which the chief-inspector had not seen him enter, but the hearse, which had just drawn up alongside the pavement, hid him from Maigret almost immediately.

There were so many flowers and wreaths that they had to fill two whole cars with them. Behind the hearse, Antonio walked by himself, followed by the staff and the dancers. Then came all the other mourners, forming a procession over a hundred yards long.

The shopkeepers, on the way, came out to watch, the housewives stopped on the kerb, and people leaned out of the windows. Finally, running alongside the dark line of people, there were photographers taking shots of the procession.

The organ boomed out just as six men crossed the threshold of the church carrying the coffin. The women followed, wearing thick veils. For a moment, Jean-Charles Gaillard's eyes met those of the chief-inspector, then the two men were separated by the crowd.

Maigret stayed at the back of the church, into which a ray of sunshine penetrated every time the door opened. And he went on passing the same pictures through his head, like a pack of cards.

Boulay taking his watch out of his pocket . . . Boulay waiting for a few minutes before walking down the Rue Pigalle . . .

Antonio had done things handsomely. There was not just a funeral service but a sung Mass.

The congregation took a long time coming out. Four or five cars were waiting for the family and the dead man's closest colleagues, for there was no room left in the Montmartre cemetery and Boulay's body was destined for Ivry.

Antonio found time to make his way through the crowd to reach the chief-inspector.

'Would you like a place in one of the cars?'

Maigret shook his head. He was watching the lawyer walking away and he elbowed his way after him.

'A fine funeral,' he observed, rather as Mickey had said in the Rue Victor-Massé. 'You're not going to the cemetery?'

'I've got some work waiting for me . . . Besides, I wasn't invited . . .'

'The whole of Montmartre was there . . .'

Some of the crowd was still drifting away when the hearse and the other cars drove off.

'You must have recognized quite a few of your clients . . .'

'So would any other lawyer . . .'

Changing the subject, as if he found that one distasteful, Gaillard asked:

'Have you got a line on the murderer?'

'Let's call it the beginning of a line . . .'

'What do you mean?'

'I still haven't got the main thing, namely the motive . . .'

'You've got all the rest?'

'I haven't any proof yet, I'm afraid . . . Did you go into the country yesterday?'

The lawyer looked at him in surprise.

'Why do you ask that?'

They, like many other people, were walking up the Rue Notre-Dame-de-Lorette, which had rarely been so crowded at that hour of the day, and passing the Saint-Trop', where the frame containing the photographs of naked women had been removed, and the funeral notice put in its place.

'No reason in particular,' replied Maigret. 'Because I went there with my wife . . . Because most Parisians, on Sunday, go into the country or to the seaside . . .'

'My wife hasn't been able to go away for a long time now . . .'

'So that you spend Sunday by yourself in the Rue La Bruyère?'

'I take the opportunity to study my files . . .'

Was Jean-Charles Gaillard wondering why the chief-inspector was staying with him? Normally Maigret would have gone down towards the centre of the city. But he continued to keep in step with the lawyer, and soon they found themselves in the Rue La Bruyère, where the blue car was in its place in front of the house.

There was a moment of embarrassment. Maigret showed no sign of going away. The lawyer was holding his key.

'I won't ask you in, because I know how busy you are . . .'

'As it happens, I was just going to ask you if I might use your telephone . . .'

The door opened.

'Come into my study . . .'

The door leading into the adjoining office was open and a secretary about thirty years old stood up. Without taking any notice of Maigret, she spoke to her employer.

'There have been two calls, one of them from Cannes . . .'

'I'll see about them later, Lucette . . .'

Gaillard seemed preoccupied.

'Is it a local call you want to make? . . . The telephone is in front of you . . .'

'Thank you . . .'

Through the window he could see a paved courtyard in the middle of which there was a rather fine linden tree.

Still standing, Maigret dialled his number.

'Hallo . . . Has Inspector Lapointe got back? . . . Put me through to him, will you? . . . Thank you . . . Yes . . . Hallo . . . Lapointe? . . . Did you find what you were looking for?'

He listened for a long time, while the lawyer, without sitting down at his desk, moved some files around.

'Yes . . . Yes . . . I see . . . You're sure about the dates . . . You got him to sign a statement? . . . No, I'm in the Rue La Bruyère . . . Is Lucas back? . . . Not yet? . . .'

While he was talking, he looked at the courtyard, at a couple of blackbirds hopping about on the paving-stones, at the shadow of the lawyer as he walked up and down in front of the window.

'Yes, wait for me . . . I shan't be long and there may be something new . . .'

He too was entitled to play his little comedy. After replacing the receiver, he mimed embarrassment, scratching his head with a perplexed expression.

The two of them were still standing, and the lawyer was looking at him inquisitively. Maigret prolonged the silence on purpose. When he spoke, it was to say, with a hint of reproach in his voice:

'You haven't a very good memory, Monsieur Gaillard . . .'

'What are you insinuating?'

'Or else, for some reason I can't quite fathom, you haven't been telling me the truth . . .'

'What about?'

'Don't you know?'

'I swear I . . .'

He was a tall, strong man, who only a few moments before had been quite sure of himself. But now his face looked like that of a little boy caught red-handed and insisting on protesting his innocence.

'I honestly don't know what you mean . . .'

'Do you mind if I smoke?'

'Or course not.'

Maigret slowly filled his pipe, scowling like a man who has an unpleasant task to perform.

The other man said:

'Won't you sit down?'

'I won't be a moment . . . When I came to see you on Friday, I spoke to you about your car . . .'

'That's possible . . . We had a rather disjointed conversation and I was too struck by what I had just learnt to register any details . . .'

'You told me that your car was usually parked in front of your house and that you left it there for the night . . .'

'That's correct . . . It spent last night there, for instance, and the night before that . . . You may have seen it as you came in . . .'

'But recently there were a few days when it wasn't there . . .'

He acted as if he were searching his memory.

'Wait a moment . . .'

He had suddenly gone very red, and Maigret almost felt sorry for him. It was obvious that it was only thanks to a tremendous effort that he retained an air of self-assurance.

'I can't remember whether it was last week or the week before that the car needed some repairs . . . I can ask my secretary . . . It was she who telephoned to the garage to fetch it . . .'

All the same, he made no move towards the communicating door.

'Call her in . . .'

He finally pushed open the door.

'Will you come in here for a moment . . . The chief-inspector has a question he wants to ask you . . .'

'Don't be alarmed, Mademoiselle . . . It's a very innocent question . . . I should like to know what day you telephoned to the garage in the Rue Ballu to come and fetch the car . . .'

She looked at her employer as if to ask his permission to reply.

'Monday afternoon,' she said at last.

'You mean last Monday?'

'Yes . . .'

She was pretty and pleasant, and her white nylon dress revealed an appetizing body. Was there something between her and Gaillard? . . . That was none of Maigret's business for the moment.

'Was it a big repair job?'

'I can show you the bill from the garage . . . I received it this morning . . . they had to change the silencer . . . They had thought they would be able to bring the car back on Wednesday morning . . .'

'And they didn't?'

'They rang up to apologize . . . It's an American car . . . Contrary to their expectations, there wasn't a spare silencer available in Paris and they had to telephone to their depot at Le Havre . . .'

Jean-Charles Gaillard was pretending to have no interest in the conversation and, seated at last at his desk, was looking through a file.

'When was the car delivered?'

'Thursday or Friday . . . Will you excuse me? I've a note of it in my diary . . .'

She went into her office and came back a moment later.

'Thursday evening . . . They had the silencer delivered by express post and worked all day . . .'

'You didn't come back after dinner?'

Another glance at the lawyer.

'No . . . That rarely happens . . . Only when there is some urgent work to be done . . .'

'That didn't happen last week?'

She shook her head unhesitatingly.

'I haven't worked in the evening for at least a fortnight . . .'

'Thank you, Mademoiselle . . .'

She went out, closing the door behind her, and Maigret stood there, his pipe in his mouth, in the middle of the study.

'Well, that's that,' he muttered in the end.

'What's what?'

'Nothing . . . A little fact which may be important, just as it may not. You know enough about our work to know that we've no right to neglect anything . . .'

'I don't see what my car . . .'

'If you were in my place, you would see . . . Thank you for letting me use your telephone . . . It's time that I went back to the office . . .'

The lawyer stood up.

'You have nothing else to ask me?'

'What would I have to ask you? I put all the questions to you on Friday that I wanted to put to you. I presume you answered me truthfully? . . .'

'I have no reason to . . .'

'Quite. All the same, with regard to your car . . .'

'I admit that I had forgotten all about it . . . This was the third or fourth time in the last few months that that car needed repairs, and that's why I'm thinking of selling it . . .'

'You used taxis for three days?'

'That's correct . . . I sometimes take taxis even when the car is outside my house . . . You don't have to look for a place to park . . .'

'I see. Have you got a case this afternoon?'

'No . . . I've already told you that I don't often appear in court . . . I am more a legal adviser . . .'

'So you will be at home all afternoon?'

'Unless I have an appointment somewhere else . . . Just a moment . . .'

He opened the door of the adjoining office again.

'Lucette! . . . Will you look and see if I have to go out this afternoon?'

Maigret had the impression that the young woman had been crying. Neither eyes nor nose were red, but her eyes were troubled and uneasy.

'I don't think so . . . All your appointments are here . . .'

All the same, she consulted the red diary.

'No . . .'

'There's your answer,' concluded the lawyer.

'Thank you.'

'Do you think you'll need me?'

'I've nothing definite in mind, but one never knows . . . Goodbye, Mademoiselle . . .'

She nodded to him, without looking at him. As for Jean-Charles Gaillard, he led the chief-inspector into the corridor. The door of a waiting-room was half-open, and as they passed they caught sight of the legs of a man who was waiting.

'Thank you again for letting me use the telephone . . .'

'Don't mention it . . .'

'And forgive me for bothering you . . .'

When, after walking about fifty yards along the pavement, Maigret turned round, Gaillard was still standing at the door and following him with his eyes.

Chapter Seven

It had happened several times, indeed quite often, but never in such a clear, characteristic way. You work in a given direction, all the more stubbornly in that you are less sure of yourself and have less data in hand.

You tell yourself that you remain free, when the time comes, to turn round and search in another direction.

You send inspectors right and left. You think you are marking time, and then you discover a new clue and you start moving cautiously forward.

And all of a sudden, just when you least expect it, the case slips out of your grasp. You cease to be in control of it. It is events which are in command and which force you to take measures which you had not foreseen, and for which you were not prepared.

In these cases there are a few uncomfortable hours to get through. You rack your brains. You ask yourself whether you did not set off in the wrong direction from the start, and whether you are not going to find yourself faced with a blank wall, or, worse still, with a reality different from what you had imagined.

What, in fact, had been Maigret's sole starting-point? A simple conviction, backed up, admittedly, by experience: *Members of the underworld do not strangle.* They use a revolver, and sometimes a knife, but in all the records at Police Headquarters there was no trace of a single crime by strangulation which could be laid at their door.

A second accepted idea was that they leave their victim where he lies. Again, there was not a single case in the archives of a criminal having kept a corpse at home for several days before dumping it on a pavement.

Thus the chief-inspector had been hypnotized by Émile Boulay's last evening, by his telephone calls, by his wait on the pavement, beside the uniformed Mickey, until the moment when the former steward had walked slowly away down the Rue Pigalle.

The whole edifice of Maigret's thought was built on these foundations and on the story of the five thousand francs withdrawn from the bank on May 22.

It presumed that there was no passionate drama in the little Italy in the Rue Victor-Massé, that the three women got along together as well as they appeared to do, that Boulay had no mistress elsewhere, and finally that Antonio was an honest individual.

If a single one of these hypotheses—or rather of these convictions—was incorrect, the whole of his case fell to the ground.

Perhaps that was why he kept his bad-tempered look and moved ahead only with a certain repugnance.

It was a hot afternoon; the sun was beating down on the window, so that the chief-inspector had lowered the blind. He and Lucas had taken off their jackets, and, behind closed doors, were engaged in a task which would probably have made an examining magistrate shrug his shoulders.

It is true that the magistrate in charge of the case was leaving them in peace, convinced that it was a matter of an unimportant underworld vendetta, and the Press was showing no greater interest.

'A lawyer doesn't kill his clients . . .'

This was becoming a refrain which Maigret could not get rid of any more than he could get rid of a song heard again and again on the radio or the television.

'A lawyer . . .'

Yet he had gone that morning, after the funeral, to the house of Maître Jean-Charles Gaillard, though admittedly he had been as cautious as possible. As if by accident, coming out of the church, he had accompanied him as far as the Rue La Bruyère, and, if he had asked a few questions he had taken care not to press him too hard.

'A lawyer doesn't kill . . .'

That was no more certain, and no more logical either, than the other statement he had taken as his starting-point.

'Criminals don't strangle . . .'

Only you can't summon a well-known lawyer to the Quai des Orfèvres and submit him to an interrogation lasting several hours without risking having the Bar, if not the whole machinery of the Law, after your skin.

Some professions are more sensitive than others. He had noticed this when he had telephoned to his friend Chavanon, and then when he had called on the ineffable Maître Ramuel.

'A lawyer doesn't kill his clients . . .'

Now it was Jean-Charles Gaillard's clients that the two men were considering, in the golden atmosphere of Maigret's office. Lucas had come back from the registry with a list which a clerk had helped him to compile.

And Lucas, too, was beginning to have an idea. It was still very vague. He could not manage to express what he was thinking.

'The clerk said something odd to me . . .'

'What?'

'First of all, when I mentioned the name of Jean-Charles Gaillard, he gave a peculiar smile . . . Then I asked him for the list of cases Gaillard had taken on during the last two years and his eyes got even more malicious . . .

' "You won't find many," he told me.

' "Because he hasn't got a big clientele?"

' "On the contrary! From all I hear, he has a huge clientele and people say he earns more than certain leading barristers who appear every week at the Assizes . . ." '

Lucas, intrigued, went on:

'I tried to get him to talk, but for a while he rummaged about in his files in silence. Every now and then, noting a name and a date on a piece of paper, he muttered:

' "An acquittal . . ."

'Then a little later:

' "Another acquittal . . ."

'And all the time he had that knowing look of his which infuriated me.

' "Well, well! A conviction . . . With a stay of execution, of course . . ."

'This went on for quite a while. The list got longer. Acquittal followed acquittal, with an occasional stay of execution or a light sentence . . .

'I finally insinuated:

' "He must be very good . . ."

'Then he looked at me as if he were quietly laughing at me and said:

' "Above all else, he knows how to pick his cases . . ." '

It was that phrase which intrigued Lucas and on which Maigret's brain had started working.

Obviously it was more pleasant, not only for the accused, but for his counsel, to win a case than to lose it. His reputation grew all the time and his clientele increased with each new success.

'To pick his cases . . .'

For the moment, the two men were going through the list Lucas had brought. They had carried out a preliminary classification. On one sheet of paper, the inspector had noted down the common law cases. As neither of them was familiar with that domain, they decided to leave it aside for the moment.

The other cases turned out to be few in number: thirty or so in two years. Which enabled Jean-Charles Gaillard to state:

'I don't often appear in court . . .'

Lucas took the names one by one.

'Hippolyte Tessier . . . Forgery . . . Acquitted on September 1 . . .'

Both of them would search their memories. If they found nothing, Maigret would go and open the door of the inspectors' room.

'Tessier . . . Forgery . . . Does that mean anything to you?'

'Isn't he a former manager of a casino somewhere in Brittany who tried to start a secret gaming-club in Paris?'

They went on to the next case.

'Julien Vendre . . . Housebreaking . . . Acquitted . . .'

Maigret remembered this man. He was a quiet fellow, who looked like a sad little clerk, and who had made a speciality of stealing transistors. He had not been caught red-handed and there was no definite proof against him. The chief-inspector had advised the magistrate not to press the charge but to wait for the man to incriminate himself further . . .

'Put him down on the third sheet . . .'

In the meantime, fat Torrence was installed in the shade of a café opposite the lawyer's house; and a police car, with no distinguishing marks, was waiting a few yards along the street, not far from the blue American car.

If Torrence had to spend the whole afternoon at his table, watching the door across the street, how many glasses would he drink?

'Urban Potier . . . Receiving . . . One year in prison with a stay of execution . . .'

It was Lucas who had been in charge of the investigation a few months before, and the man had come several times to the Quai des Orfèvres—a fat individual as unprepossessing as Monsieur Raison, the accountant, with tufts of black hair coming out of his nostrils.

He kept a junk-shop on the Boulevard de la Chapelle. You could find anything there, old oil-lamps as well as refrigerators and threadbare clothes.

'I'm an honest shopkeeper . . . Humble, but honest . . . When that fellow came and sold me those lead pipes, I didn't know he'd stolen them . . . I took him for . . .'

At every name Maigret hesitated. A dozen times the door of the inspectors' room was opened.

'Put it down . . .'

'Gaston Mauran . . . Stealing cars . . .'

'A little red-haired fellow.'

'It doesn't say so on my paper . . .'

'Last spring?'

'Yes . . . In April . . . He belonged to a gang that disguised cars and sent them into the provinces to be resold . . .'

'Call Dupeu . . .'

Inspector Dupeu had been in charge of that case, and, by a stroke of luck, happened to be in the next room.

'It was a little red-haired fellow, wasn't it, who spun us that story about his old sick mother?'

'Yes, Chief . . . As a matter of fact, he did have an old sick mother . . . He was only nineteen at the time . . . He was the least important member of the gang . . . He just kept watch while Mad Justin stole the cars . . .'

Two cases of procuring; some more burglaries. Nothing world-shaking. Nothing which hit the front page of the newspapers.

In contrast, all the lawyer's other clients were more or less professionals.

'Go on,' sighed Maigret.

'That's the lot . . . You told me not to go further back than two years ago . . .'

There was not enough there to occupy the time of a lawyer who had his own town house in Paris, even if it was really only a very ordinary house.

Of course you had to count the cases which had not got as far as the court and which probably formed the majority.

Then there was another class of clients, those for whom Jean-Charles Gaillard made income tax returns, as he did for Boulay.

Maigret felt ill. He was hot. He was thirsty. It seemed to him that he was getting nowhere and he was tempted to start again from scratch.

'Get me the Inspector of Taxes for the 9th *arrondissement* . . .'

This was like a shot in the dark, but, at the point where he was, he had no right to neglect anything.

'What's that? . . . Monsieur Jubelin? . . . All right, put me through to Monsieur Jubelin . . . From Chief-Inspector Maigret . . . Yes, of Police Headquarters . . . Hallo . . . No, the chief-inspector wants to speak to Monsieur Jubelin in person . . .'

The inspector must have been a busy man, or else very conscious of his own importance, for it took nearly five minutes to get through to him.

'Hallo . . . I'm putting you through to the chief-inspector . . .'

Maigret grabbed the receiver with a sigh.

'I'm terribly sorry to bother you, Monsieur Jubelin . . . I just want to ask you for a piece of information . . . What's that? . . . Yes, it's indirectly connected with Émile Boulay . . . You've read the papers . . . I see . . . No, it isn't his income tax returns I'm interested in . . . I might be later, but in that case I promise you that I shall go through the usual administrative channels . . . Yes, of course, I understand your scruples . . .

'My question is rather different . . . Did Boulay have any difficulties with you? . . . Yes, that's what I mean . . . Did you ever have occasion, for example, to threaten him with prosecution . . . No? . . . That's what I thought . . . All his accounts perfectly in order . . . I see . . . I see . . .'

He listened, nodding his head and scribbling on his blotting-pad. Monsieur Jubelin's voice was so loud that Lucas could hear practically everything he was saying.

'In short, he had a good adviser . . . A lawyer, I know . . . Jean-Charles Gaillard. As it happens, it was about him that I wanted to ask you . . . I suppose he looked after the affairs of several tax-payers of yours? . . . What's that you say? . . . Of far too many?'

Maigret winked at Lucas and summoned up his reserves of patience, for the inspector had suddenly become extremely voluble.

'Yes . . . Yes . . . Very clever, obviously . . . What? . . . Irreproachable returns . . . You tried to contest them? . . . Without success . . . I see . . . May I ask you one more question? . . . To what class did most of Gaillard's clients belong? . . . A bit of everything, I see . . . Yes . . . Yes . . . A lot of people from his district . . . Proprietors of hotels, restaurants and night-clubs . . . Yes, obviously, it's difficult . . .'

This lasted another ten minutes or so, but soon the chief-inspector was listening with only half an ear, for his interlocutor, so reticent to begin with, had begun describing in great detail his fight against tax-evaders.

'Whew!' he sighed as he replaced the receiver. 'You heard that?'

'Not all of it . . .'

'As I had expected, Émile Boulay's returns were irreproachable . . . Jubelin repeated that word heaven knows how many times with a sort of nostalgia . . . For years he had been trying to catch him out . . . Only last year, he went through all his accounts with a fine-tooth comb without being able to find a single flaw in them . . .'

'And the others?'

'Quite! The same is true of all Jean-Charles Gaillard's clients.'

Maigret looked thoughtfully at the list drawn up by the inspector. He remembered the clerk's remark:

'He knows how to pick his cases . . .'

Now, in the fiscal domain too, the lawyer knew how to pick his clients: hoteliers in Montmartre and elsewhere who let their rooms, not only by the night, but by the hour, bar-keepers like Jo-the-Wrestler, night-club proprietors and racehorse owners . . .

As Jubelin had said a little earlier over the telephone:

'With people like that, it's difficult to furnish proof of takings and overheads . . .'

Standing at his desk, Maigret looked down the list once again. He had to choose and possibly the rest of the investigation depended on the choice he made.

'Get me Dupeu . . .'

The inspector came back into the office.

'Do you know what has become of Gaston Mauran, the man you were talking to us about just now?'

'A month or two ago I caught sight of him at the petrol pump of a garage in the Avenue d'Italie . . . Quite by accident . . . I was driving my wife and kids into the country and I was wondering where I was going to fill up with petrol . . .'

'Go and phone the garage proprietor to check whether Mauran is still working there . . . But he isn't to say anything to him . . . I don't want him to take fright and slip through our fingers . . .'

If it did not work with this man, he would pick another, then another, and so on until he had found what he was looking for.

Now, what he was looking for was not very clear. In all the lawyer's cases there was a certain characteristic, a common feature which he would have been hard put to it to define.

'A lawyer doesn't kill his clients . . .'

'Do you need me any longer, Chief?'

'Yes, stay here . . .'

He spoke as if he were talking to himself, not displeased at having an audience.

'When you come to think of it, they all had good reason to be grateful to him . . . Either they appeared in court and were acquitted . . . Or else the Inspector of Taxes was obliged to accept their returns . . . I don't know if you

see what I'm getting at . . . A lawyer, in the ordinary run of things, is bound
to have a few dissatisfied clients . . . If he loses a case, if his client is stung by
the Inspector of Taxes . . .'

'I see, Chief . . .'

'Well, it isn't easy to make a choice . . .'

Dupeu came back.

'He's still working at the same garage . . . He's there now . . .'

'Go and take a car from the yard and bring him here as quickly as you
can . . . Don't scare him . . . Tell him it's just a question of checking up on
a few details . . . But I don't want him to feel too confident either . . .'

It was half-past four and the heat was not abating, on the contrary. The air
was stagnant. Maigret's shirt was beginning to stick to his body.

'How about going for a drink?'

A brief interval, while they were waiting for Gaston Mauran, at the
Brasserie Dauphine.

Just as the two men were on the point of leaving the office, the telephone
rang. The chief-inspector hesitated before turning back, but finally, to
satisfy his conscience, he picked up the receiver.

'Is that you, Chief? Torrence speaking . . .'

'I can recognize your voice. Well?'

'I'm speaking to you from the Avenue de la Grande-Armée.'

'What are you doing there?'

'About twenty minutes ago, Gaillard came out of his house and got into
his car. Luckily a traffic jam at the corner of the Rue Blanche gave me time to
jump into mine and catch up with him.'

'He didn't notice that he was being followed?'

'No, definitely not . . . You'll see in a moment why I'm so sure . . . He
headed straightaway for the Étoile, taking the shortest route . . . The traffic
didn't allow him to drive fast, and in the Avenue de la Grande-Armée he
slowed down even more . . . I drove behind him past several garages. He
seemed to be hesitating . . . Finally he drove the car into the Garage
Moderne, near the Porte Maillot . . . I waited outside . . . It was only when
I saw him come out on foot and walk in the direction of the Bois that I went
in . . .'

This was precisely the little unexpected element which was going to rob
Maigret of his freedom of action, or, to be more exact, force him to act at a
certain moment, in a certain way which he had not foreseen.

His face, while he was listening to Torrence, became increasingly serious,
and he seemed to have forgotten the glass of beer he had promised himself.

'It's a big place, with an automatic system for washing cars . . . I had to
show my badge to the foreman . . . Jean-Charles Gaillard isn't a regular
customer . . . They don't remember seeing him before at the garage . . . He
had asked if they could wash his car in an hour at the outside . . . He said he'd
call back about half-past five . . .'

'Have they begun the job?'

'They were going to, but I asked them to wait . . .'

He had to make a decision straightaway.

'What shall I do?'

'Stay there and prevent them touching the car . . . I'll send somebody over
to bring it here . . . Don't worry . . . He'll have the necessary papers . . .'

'And when Gaillard comes back?'

'You'll have an inspector with you . . . I don't know yet who it will be . . . I would rather there were two of you . . . You'll be very polite, but you'll make sure all the same that he accompanies you here . . .'

He suddenly remembered the young car-thief he was expecting.

'Don't bring him straight into my office . . . Keep him waiting . . . He'll probably get on his high horse . . . Don't take any notice . . . Above all, don't let him get near a telephone . . .'

Torrence sighed unenthusiastically:

'All right, Chief . . . But hurry up . . . In this heat I should be surprised if he spent a long time walking about the Bois . . .'

Maigret wondered for a moment whether to go straight to the examining magistrate to get sanction for what he was doing. But he was practically certain that the magistrate would prevent him from acting according to his instinct.

In the adjoining office he looked at the inspectors one after the other.

'Vacher . . .'

'Yes, Chief . . .'

'Have you ever driven an American car?'

'Once or twice . . .'

'Go over to the Garage Moderne, in the Avenue de la Grande-Armée. It's right at the bottom, near the Porte Maillot . . . You'll find Torrence there, and he'll show you a blue car . . . Bring it here and leave it in the yard, touching it as little as possible . . .'

'I get you . . .'

'You, Janin, you'll go with him, but you'll stay at the garage with Torrence . . . I've given him instructions . . .'

He looked at his watch. It was only a quarter of an hour since Dupeu had left for the Avenue d'Italie. He turned to Lucas.

'Come along . . .'

Provided they did not take long, they were still entitled to their beer.

Chapter Eight

Before having the mechanic brought in, Maigret had questioned Dupeu.

'How did it go?'

'At first he seemed surprised and asked me if I worked with you. He struck me as more intrigued than worried. Twice he said:

' "You're sure it's Chief-Inspector Maigret who wants to see me?"

'Then he went to wash his hands with petrol and took off his overalls. On the way he asked me only one question:

' "Have they any right to re-open a case which has been tried?" '

'What did you reply?'

'That I didn't know, but I supposed not. All the way here, he remained puzzled.'

'Bring him in and leave us alone . . .'

Mauran would have been very surprised, when he was being shown into the office, if he had known that the famous chief-inspector was more nervous than he was. He looked at him coming into the room, a gawky young man with tousled red hair, china-blue eyes, and freckles round his nose.

'The other times,' he began, as if he wanted to get the first blow in, 'you left it to your inspectors to question me . . .'

There was a certain craftiness in him and at the same time a certain innocence.

'I'd better tell you straightaway that I've done nothing . . .'

He was not afraid. True, it impressed him to find himself face to face with the big chief, but he was not afraid.

'You're pretty sure of yourself . . .'

'Why shouldn't I be? . . . The court found me not guilty, didn't it? . . . Anyway, practically not guilty . . . And I played the game, you know that more than anybody . . .'

'You mean you gave the names of your accomplices?'

'They had taken advantage of my innocence, the lawyer proved that . . . He explained that I'd had a difficult childhood, that I had to support my mother, that she was ill . . .'

While he was talking, Maigret had a curious impression. The mechanic was expressing himself with a certain affectation, exaggerating his Parisian accent; at the same time there was an amused sparkle in his eyes, as if he were pleased with the part he was playing.

'I don't suppose you've sent for me about that business? Since then, I've been on my best behaviour, and I'd like to see the fellow who could say any different . . . Well, then? . . .'

He sat down without being invited to do so, which was a rare occurrence, and even took a packet of Gauloises out of his pocket.

'Can I smoke?'

And Maigret, watching him all the time, nodded.

'And what if, for some reason or other, we re-opened the case?'

Mauran gave a start, uneasy all of a sudden.

'That isn't possible . . .'

'Suppose there are a few points I want to clear up . . .'

The telephone on Maigret's desk suddenly rang and Torrence's voice said:

'He's here . . .'

'Did he protest?'

'Not very much. He says he's in a hurry and wants to see you straight-away . . .'

'Tell him I'll see him as soon as I'm free . . .'

Gaston listened, frowning, as if wondering what sort of trick was being played on him.

'It's all an act, isn't it?' he said when the chief-inspector had replaced the receiver.

'What's an act?'

'Bringing me here . . . Trying to frighten me . . . You know perfectly well that everything's fixed up . . .'

'What's fixed up?'

'I'm speaking clearly, aren't I . . . Nobody messes me about any more . . .'

At that moment, not without a certain awkwardness, he gave a wink which puzzled Maigret more than all the rest.

'Listen, Mauran, it was Inspector Dupeu who was in charge of your case . . .'

'The chap who's just brought me along, yes . . . I'd forgotten his name . . . He was all right . . .'

'What do you mean, all right?'

'He was all right, that's all . . .'

'In what way?'

'Don't you get me?'

'You mean that he didn't set any traps for you and that he questioned you gently?'

'I reckon he questioned me like he was supposed to question me . . .'

Behind the words, in the young man's attitude, there was something ambiguous which the chief-inspector tried to pin down.

'He had to, hadn't he?'

'Because you were innocent?'

Mauran, for his part, seemed to be becoming uneasy, as if he did not understand any more, and as if Maigret's words were baffling him as much as his were baffling the detective.

'Look . . .' he said hesitantly, after drawing on his cigarette.

'What?'

'Nothing . . .'

'What were you going to say?'

'I've forgotten . . . Why did you send for me?'

'What were you going to say?'

'It seems to me there's something wrong here . . .'

'I don't understand . . .'

'You're sure? In that case I'd better keep my trap shut . . .'

'It's a bit late to do that . . . What were you going to say?'

Maigret was not threatening but firm. Standing against the light, he formed a solid mass which Gaston Mauran was beginning to consider with a sort of panic.

'I want to go,' he stammered, suddenly standing up.

'Not before you've talked.'

'So this is a trap, is it? . . . What's gone wrong! . . . Is there somebody in the racket who hasn't kept the bargain?'

'What bargain?'

'First of all tell me what you know . . .'

'I ask the questions here . . . What bargain?'

'You'll go on repeating that to me till tomorrow if need be, won't you? . . . I was told that, but I didn't believe it . . .'

'What else were you told?'

'That they'd let me off lightly . . .'

'Who told you that?'

The young man turned his head away, determined to say nothing, but sensing that he would end up by giving way.

'This isn't fair,' he finally muttered between his teeth.

'What isn't?'

Then Mauran suddenly lost his temper, and, getting on his high horse, looked the chief-inspector in the eyes.

'You know very well, don't you . . . And what about the thousand francs?'

He was so taken aback by Maigret's face that his arms fell to his sides. He saw the imposing mass advancing towards him, and two powerful hands which stretched out, seized him by the shoulders, and started shaking him.

Maigret had never been so pale in his life. His face, which was completely expressionless, looked like a block of stone.

His voice, neutral and impressive, issued an order.

'Say that again!'

'The . . . the . . . You're hurting me . . .'

'Say that again!'

'The thousand francs . . .'

'What thousand francs?'

'Let go of me . . . I'll tell you everything . . .'

Maigret released his hold on him, but he remained deathly pale, and at one moment he put his hand on his chest where his heart was pounding wildly.

'I suppose I've been had . . .'

'Gaillard?'

Mauran nodded.

'He promised you that we'd let you off lightly?'

'Yes . . . He didn't use those words . . . He said you'd be understanding . . .'

'And that you'd be acquitted?'

'That at the worst I'd be put on probation . . .'

'He made you pay a thousand francs to defend you?'

'Not to defend me . . . It was extra . . .'

'To pass on to somebody else?'

The young mechanic was so over-awed that tears came into his eyes.

'To you . . .'

Maigret stood motionless for two full minutes, his fists clenched, and finally a little colour gradually returned to his face.

Suddenly he turned his back on his caller, and, although the blind was drawn, he stood a little longer in front of the window.

When he turned round, he had practically regained his usual expression, but Mauran would have sworn that he had aged, that he was suddenly very tired.

He went and sat down at his desk, motioned towards a chair, and automatically started filling a pipe.

'Smoke . . .'

He said that as an order, as if to exorcize heaven knows what demons.

Softly, in a quiet, subdued voice, he went on:

'I suppose you're telling the truth . . .'

'I swear on my mother's head that I am . . .'

'Who sent you to Jean-Charles Gaillard?'

'An old man who lives on the Boulevard de la Chapelle . . .'

'Don't be frightened . . . Your case won't be re-opened . . . You're talking about a certain Potier, who runs a junk shop . . .'

'Yes . . .'

'You did a bit of stealing and passed the stolen goods to him . . .'

'It didn't happen often . . .'

'What did he say to you?'

'To go and see that lawyer . . .'

'Why him rather than another?'

'Because he was in league with the police . . . I can see now that that isn't true . . . He swindled me out of a thousand francs . . .'

Maigret reflected.

'Listen. In a moment somebody will be brought into this office. You won't speak to him. You will simply look at him and then accompany the inspector into the next room . . .'

'I'm sorry, you know . . . I'd been given to believe that it always happened like that . . .'

Maigret managed to smile at him.

'Hallo . . . Torrence? . . . Will you bring him over? . . . I've got somebody in my office I'd like you to keep over there in case I need him again . . . Yes, straightaway . . .'

He drew on his pipe, apparently completely calm, but there was a sort of lump in his throat. He fixed his eyes on the door which was going to open, and which did open; he saw the lawyer, a smart figure in a light-grey suit, take two or three quick steps, looking irritable, open his mouth to speak, to protest, and then suddenly catch sight of Gaston Mauran.

Torrence could understand nothing of this silent scene. Jean-Charles Gaillard had stopped short. His face had changed expression. The young man, very ill-at-ease, rose from his chair and, without looking at the newcomer, walked towards the door.

The two men were left alone, face to face. Maigret, both hands lying flat on the desk, was struggling not to get up, not to walk deliberately towards his visitor, and, although the latter was taller and heavier than himself, not to slap him across both cheeks.

Instead, he said in a curiously weak voice:

'Sit down . . .'

He must have been even more awe-inspiring than he had been when he had seized the young mechanic by the shoulders for the lawyer obeyed automatically, forgetting to protest at the removal of his car and at the fact that two inspectors had brought him without a warrant to the Quai des Orfèvres, where they had kept him waiting like any common suspect.

'I suppose,' Maigret began wearily, as if, for him, the case was closed, 'you have understood the situation . . .'

And as the lawyer tried to reply, he went on:

'Let me do the talking . . . I shall be as brief as possible, because I find it unpleasant remaining alone with you . . .'

'I don't know what that boy . . .'

'I told you to keep quiet . . . I didn't have you brought here to question you . . . I'm not going to ask you for any explanations . . . If I had obeyed my first impulse, I should have sent you to the Depot without seeing you, and you would have waited there for the results of the investigation . . .'

He pulled towards him List No. 3, that of Gaillard's clients who had appeared in court and had been acquitted or given light sentences.

He read out the names in a monotonous voice, as if he were reciting a litany. Then, raising his head, he added:

'I need hardly say that these people will be questioned . . . Some of them will keep quiet . . . Or rather they will begin by keeping quiet . . . When they learn that the sums they paid over for a definite purpose never reached their destination . . .'

Gaillard's expression had changed too. All the same, he tried to put up a fight, and started a sentence:

'I don't know what that young scoundrel . . .'

Then Maigret struck the table a blow which made all the objects on it jump into the air.

'Shut up!' he roared. 'I forbid you to open your mouth until I ask you to speak . . .'

They had heard the sound of the blow in the inspectors' room, and they all looked at one another.

'I don't need to explain to you how you worked it . . . And I understand now why you picked your clients carefully . . . Knowing that they would be acquitted, or given a light sentence, it was easy for you to make them believe that in return for a fee . . .'

No! He could not talk about that any more.

'I have every reason to believe that my name wasn't the only one you used . . . You looked after people's income tax returns . . . Just now I got in touch with Monsieur Jubelin and I shall be having a long talk with him . . .'

His hand was still trembling slightly when he lit his pipe.

'It will be a long, delicate investigation. What I can tell you now is that it will be carried out with exemplary care . . .'

Gaillard had stopped glaring at him defiantly and lowered his head, his hands on his knees, with a gap where the four fingers of the left hand were missing.

The chief-inspector's gaze fell on that hand and he hesitated for a moment.

'When the case goes to the Assizes, your counsel will refer to your conduct during the war, and probably also to your marriage to a woman accustomed to a brilliant life, and the illness which to all intents and purposes cut her off from society . . .'

He leaned back in his armchair and closed his eyes.

'Extenuating circumstances will be put forward . . . Why did you need so much money when your wife no longer went out and you apparently led a lonely life, devoted to work? . . . I don't know and I'm not asking you . . .

'Other people will ask you all these questions, and perhaps you understand why . . . This is the first time, Monsieur Gaillard, that . . .'

His voice failed once more and, without any false shame, he went over to the cupboard and took the bottle of brandy and a glass. This bottle was not there for him but for those who, in the course of a long and dramatic interrogation, needed it.

He drained the glass at one draught, returned to his seat, and lit his pipe which had gone out.

He was a little calmer and spoke now in a casual tone, as if the case no longer concerned him.

'At this very moment, experts are going over your car with a fine-tooth comb . . . I am not telling you anything new when I say that if it has been used to carry a corpse, there is a good chance that that corpse has left traces behind . . . You are so well aware of that that after my call this morning you felt the need to have it washed . . .

'Don't say anything! For the last time I order you to keep quiet, otherwise you'll be taken straightaway to a cell in the Depot . . .

'I must also tell you that a team of specialists are on their way to the Rue La Bruyère . . .'

Gaillard gave a start and stammered:

'My wife . . .'

'They aren't going there to bother your wife . . . This morning, looking out of the window, I noticed a sort of shed in the yard . . . It will be examined inch by inch . . . The cellar too . . . And the rest of the house, all the way up to the attic if need be . . . This evening I shall question your two servants . . . I said don't talk!

'The counsel you choose will have no difficulty in showing that there was no premeditation . . . The fact that your car happened to be out of action, and that you had no other means of transport to get rid of the body, proves that . . . You had to wait to get the car back and it can't have been very pleasant spending two days and three nights with a corpse in the house . . .'

He ended up by talking to himself, without so much as a glance at the other man. All the little details he had collected during the last few days came back to him and put themselves in their places. All the questions he had asked himself found an answer . . .

'Mazotti was killed on May 17 and we questioned all the people who had recently been victims of his racket . . . At least one of your clients, Émile Boulay, received a preliminary summons . . .

'Probably he got in touch with you straightaway, since you looked after his financial affairs and had intervened in two other rather unimportant matters . . .

'He accordingly came here on May 18, and he was asked the usual questions.

'After that he was summoned a second time for the 22nd or 23rd, I don't know why, probably because Inspector Lucas wanted to ask him for some further details . . .

'Now it was on the 22nd, in the afternoon, that Boulay went to the bank to draw five thousand francs . . . He needed some ready money straightaway . . . He couldn't wait until the evening to take it out of the till in one of his night-clubs . . .

'And we have found no sign of that sum anywhere . . .

'I'm not asking if it was you who received it . . . I know it was . . .'

He said these last words with a contempt such as he had never shown any human being before.

'On the 8th or 9th of June, Boulay received a third summons for Wednesday the 12th . . . He took fright, because he was terrified of scandal . . . In spite of his profession, or perhaps precisely because of his profession, he clung above all else to his respectability . . .

'On the evening of June 11, the day before he was due to come here, he was worried, and furious too, for he had paid five thousand francs as the price of his peace of mind . . .

'At ten o'clock that night he started calling your house, but without success. He rang again several times, and, when you finally replied, you agreed to see him a quarter of an hour or half an hour later . . .

'It is easy to imagine what he said to you, in the privacy of your study. He had paid so as not to get mixed up in the Mazotti case, so as to keep his name out of the papers . . .

'Instead of leaving him alone, as he had every right to expect, the police were insisting on questioning him again, and, in the corridors at Police Headquarters, he risked meeting journalists and photographers.

'He felt that he had been deceived. He was as indignant as Gaston Mauran was just now . . . He told you that he was going to speak his mind and remind the police of the bargain he had made with them . . .

'That's all . . .

'If he left your house alive, if he came here the next morning and poured out his grievances . . .

'The rest doesn't concern me, Monsieur Gaillard. I have no desire to hear your confession.'

He picked up the receiver.

'Torrence? . . . You can let him go . . . Don't forget to get his address, because the examining magistrate will need to see him. Then come and fetch the individual in my office . . .'

He waited, standing up, impatient to be rid of the lawyer's presence.

Then the latter, his head bowed, murmured in a barely audible voice:

'Have you never had a passion, Monsieur Maigret?'

He pretended not to have heard.

'I have had two . . .'

The chief-inspector preferred to turn his back on him, quite determined not to allow himself to be moved.

'First my wife, whom I tried to make happy in every possible way . . .'

His voice was bitter. A silence followed.

'Then, when she was confined to her room and I felt the need to amuse myself in spite of everything, I found gambling . . .'

Footsteps sounded in the corridor. There was a gentle knock on the door.

'Come in!'

Torrence stood in the doorway.

'Take him to the office at the back until I get back from the Palais . . .'

He did not watch Gaillard going out. When he picked up the receiver, it was to ask the examining magistrate if he could receive him straightaway.

A little later, he went through the little glass door which separates the domain of the police from that of the magistrates.

He was away from Police Headquarters for an hour. When he came back, he was holding an official paper in his hand. He opened the door of the inspectors' room and found Lucas impatient for news.

Without any explanation, he handed him the warrant made out in the name of Jean-Charles Gaillard.

'He's in the office at the back, with Torrence . . . The two of you will take him to the Depot . . .'

'Shall we handcuff him?'

That was the regulation procedure, to which there were a few exceptions. Maigret did not want to appear to be taking his revenge. The lawyer's last words were beginning to disturb him.

'No . . .'

'What shall I tell the warder? . . . To take away his tie, his belt, his shoelaces?'

More regulations, and more exceptions!

Maigret hesitated, shook his head and remained alone in his office.

When he came home to dinner that evening, somewhat later than usual, Madame Maigret noticed that his eyes were shining and rather fixed, and that his breath smelt of alcohol.

He scarcely opened his mouth during the meal and he got up to switch off the television which was annoying him.

'Are you going out?'

'No.'

'Is your case over?'

He made no reply.

He had a restless night, got up feeling bad-tempered, and decided to walk to the Quai des Orfèvres, as he sometimes did.

He had scarcely entered his office before the door of the inspectors' room opened. Lucas, with a grave, mysterious expression, closed it behind him.

'I've got some news for you, Chief . . .'

Did he guess what the inspector was going to say? Lucas always asked himself this question and never knew the answer.

'Jean-Charles Gaillard has hanged himself in his cell . . .'

Maigret did not flinch, did not open his mouth, but just stood there looking at the open window, the rustling foliage of the trees, the boats gliding along the Seine, and the passers-by swarming like ants across the Pont Saint-Michel.

'I haven't any details yet . . . Do you think that . . .?'

'Do I think what?' asked Maigret, suddenly aggressive.

And Lucas, beating a retreat, said:

'I was wondering . . .'

He shut the door hard and it was only an hour later that a relaxed Maigret appeared, apparently preoccupied with routine matters.

Noland
19 June 1962